THE

CONAN DOYLE STORIES

THE

CONAN DOYLE STORIES

THE RING AND THE CAMP
PIRATES AND BLUE WATER
TERROR AND MYSTERY
TWILIGHT AND THE UNSEEN
ADVENTURE AND MEDICAL LIFE
TALES OF LONG AGO

BY ARTHUR CONAN DOYLE

Blitz Editions

Published in this edition by Blitz Editions, an imprint of
Bookmart Limited, Registered No. 2372865 England.
Trading as Bookmart Limited, 60 Charles Street,
Leicester LE1 1FB.

ISBN 1 85605 050 5

Production services by
Book Production Consultants, Cambridge, England.

Printed and bound in Norway by Norbok International.

PREFACE

THESE stories have already been published in six separate volumes, which subdivided them roughly into those which dealt with the sea, with sport and war, with the preternatural, with medicine and with history. I am occasionally asked which of these very varied subjects and styles represents my own particular choice. The answer is that I am interested in many aspects of life, and try to write only of that which really attracts me, but that if it were needful to discriminate, and if all my work were to be destroyed save only that one single section which I might elect to preserve, my choice would certainly be those short historical pictures which come under the heading of "Tales of Long Ago."

April 26, 1929. ARTHUR CONAN DOYLE.

CONTENTS

Tales of the Ring

PAGE

1 THE CROXLEY MASTER 3
2 THE LORD OF FALCONBRIDGE 51
3. THE FALL OF LORD BARRYMORE 77
4. THE CRIME OF THE BRIGADIER 92
5. THE KING OF THE FOXES 107
6. THE BULLY OF BROCAS COURT 122

Tales of the Camp

7. A STRAGGLER OF '15 139
8. THE POT OF CAVIARE 155
9. THE GREEN FLAG 170
10. THE THREE CORRESPONDENTS 188
11. THE MARRIAGE OF THE BRIGADIER 212
12. THE LORD OF CHÂTEAU NOIR 222

Tales of Pirates

13. CAPTAIN SHARKEY: HOW THE GOVERNOR OF SAINT KITT'S CAME HOME. 239
14. THE DEALINGS OF CAPTAIN SHARKEY WITH STEPHEN CRADDOCK 252
15. THE BLIGHTING OF SHARKEY 267
16. HOW COPLEY BANKS SLEW CAPTAIN SHARKEY . 280
17. THE "SLAPPING SAL" 293
18. A PIRATE OF THE LAND (ONE CROWDED HOUR) . 303

CONTENTS

Tales of Blue Water

PAGE

19. THE STRIPED CHEST 321
20. THE CAPTAIN OF THE "POLESTAR" 336
21. THE FIEND OF THE COOPERAGE 363
22. JELLAND'S VOYAGE 378
23. J. HABAKUK JEPHSON'S STATEMENT . . . 386
24. THAT LITTLE SQUARE BOX 422

Tales of Terror

25. THE HORROR OF THE HEIGHTS 447
26. THE LEATHER FUNNEL 465
27. THE NEW CATACOMB 479
28. THE CASE OF LADY SANNOX 495
29. THE TERROR OF BLUE JOHN GAP 506
30. THE BRAZILIAN CAT 526

Tales of Mystery

31. THE LOST SPECIAL 551
32. THE BEETLE-HUNTER 571
33. THE MAN WITH THE WATCHES 590
34. THE JAPANNED BOX 609
35. THE BLACK DOCTOR 623
36. THE JEW'S BREASTPLATE 643
37. THE NIGHTMARE ROOM 665

Tales of Twilight and the Unseen

38. THE BROWN HAND 677
39. THE USHER OF LEA HOUSE SCHOOL 694
40. B. 24 711
41. THE GREAT KEINPLATZ EXPERIMENT 728
42. A LITERARY MOSAIC 746
43. PLAYING WITH FIRE 767
44. THE RING OF THOTH 782
45. THE LOS AMIGOS FIASCO 802
46. HOW IT HAPPENED 811
47. LOT NO. 249 815

CONTENTS

PAGE
48. "De Profundis" 853
49. The Lift 864

Tales of Adventure

50. The Début of Bimbashi Joyce 879
51. The Surgeon of Gaster Fell 889
52. Borrowed Scenes 912
53. The Man from Archangel 924
54. The Great Brown-Pericord Motor 950
55. The Sealed Room 959

Tales of Medical Life

56. A Physiologist's Wife 977
57. Behind the Times 999
58. His First Operation 1004
59. The Third Generation 1011
60. The Curse of Eve 1022
61. A Medical Document 1035
62. The Surgeon Talks 1047
63. The Doctors of Hoyland 1055
64. Crabbe's Practice 1068

Tales of Long Ago

65. The Last of the Legions 1085
66. The Last Galley 1092
67. Through the Veil 1100
68. The Coming of the Huns 1106
69. The Contest 1118
70. The First Cargo 1126
71. An Iconoclast 1135
72. Giant Maximin 1143
73. The Red Star 1160
74. The Silver Mirror 1169
75. The Home-Coming 1180
76. A Point of Contact 1195

INDEX TO STORIES

	PAGE
B. 24	711
Beetle-Hunter, The	571
Behind the Times	999
Black Doctor, The	623
Blighting of Sharkey, The	267
Borrowed Scenes	912
Brazilian Cat, The	526
Brown Hand, The	677
Bully of Brocas Court, The	122
Captain of the "Polestar," The	336
Captain Sharkey: How the Governor of Saint Kitt's came Home	239
Case of Lady Sannox, The	495
Coming of the Huns, The	1106
Contest, The	1118
Crabbe's Practice	1068
Crime of the Brigadier, The	92
Croxley Master, The	3
Curse of Eve, The	1022
Dealings of Captain Sharkey with Stephen Craddock	252
Début of Bimbashi Joyce, The	879
"De Profundis"	853
Doctors of Hoyland, The	1055
Fall of Lord Barrymore, The	77

INDEX TO STORIES

PAGE

Fiend of the Cooperage, The 363
First Cargo, The 1126

Giant Maximin 1143
Great Brown-Pericord Motor, The 950
Great Keinplatz Experiment, The 728
Green Flag, The 170

His First Operation 1004
Home-Coming, The 1180
Horror of the Heights, The 447
How Copley Banks slew Captain Sharkey . . 280
How It Happened 811

Iconoclast, An 1135

Japanned Box, The 609
Jelland's Voyage 378
Jew's Breastplate, The 643
J. Habakuk Jephson's Statement 386

King of the Foxes, The 107

Last Galley, The 1092
Last of the Legions, The 1085
Leather Funnel, The 465
Lift, The 864
Literary Mosaic, A 746
Lord of Château Noir, The 222
Lord of Falconbridge, The 51
Los Amigos Fiasco, The 802
Lost Special, The 551
Lot No. 249 815

Man from Archangel, The 924
Man with the Watches, The 590

INDEX TO STORIES

	PAGE
Marriage of the Brigadier, The	212
Medical Document, A	1035
New Catacomb, The	479
Nightmare Room, The	665
One Crowded Hour (A Pirate of the Land)	303
Physiologist's Wife, A	977
Pirate of the Land, A (One Crowded Hour)	303
Playing with Fire	767
Point of Contact, A	1195
Pot of Caviare, The	155
Red Star, The	1160
Ring of Thoth, The	782
Sealed Room, The	959
Silver Mirror, The	1169
"Slapping Sal," The	293
Straggler of '15, A	139
Striped Chest, The	321
Surgeon of Gaster Fell, The	889
Surgeon Talks, The	1047
Terror of Blue John Gap, The	506
That Little Square Box	422
Third Generation, The	1011
Three Correspondents, The	188
Through the Veil	1100
Usher of Lea House School, The	694

TALES OF THE RING

1. *The Croxley Master*

I

MR. ROBERT MONTGOMERY was seated at his desk, his head upon his hands, in a state of the blackest despondency. Before him was the open ledger with the long columns of Dr. Oldacre's prescriptions. At his elbow lay the wooden tray with the labels in various partitions, the cork box, the lumps of twisted sealing-wax, while in front a rank of empty bottles waited to be filled. But his spirits were too low for work. He sat in silence, with his fine shoulders bowed and his head upon his hands.

Outside, through the grimy surgery window over a foreground of blackened brick and slate, a line of enormous chimneys like Cyclopean pillars upheld the lowering, dun-coloured cloud-bank. For six days in the week they spouted smoke, but to-day the furnace fires were banked, for it was Sunday. Sordid and polluting gloom hung over a district blighted and blasted by the greed of man. There was nothing in the surroundings to cheer a desponding soul, but it was more than his dismal environment which weighed upon the medical assistant.

His trouble was deeper and more personal. The winter session was approaching. He should be back again at the University completing the last year which would give him his medical degree; but, alas! he had not the money with which to pay his class fees, nor could he imagine how he could procure it. Sixty pounds were wanted to make his career, and it might have been as many thousands for any chance there seemed to be of his obtaining it.

He was roused from his black meditation by the entrance of Dr. Oldacre himself, a large, clean-shaven, respectable man, with a prim manner and an austere face. He had prospered exceedingly by the support of the local Church interest, and the rule of his life was never by word or action to run a risk of offending the sentiment which had made him. His standard of respectability and of dignity was exceedingly high, and he expected the same from his assistants. His appearance and words were always vaguely benevolent. A sudden impulse came over the despondent student. He would test the reality of this philanthropy.

"I beg your pardon, Dr. Oldacre," said he, rising from his chair; "I have a great favour to ask of you."

The doctor's appearance was not encouraging. His mouth suddenly tightened, and his eyes fell.

"Yes, Mr. Montgomery?"

"You are aware, sir, that I need only one more session to complete my course."

"So you have told me."

"It is very important to me, sir."

"Naturally."

"The fees, Dr. Oldacre, would amount to about sixty pounds."

"I am afraid that my duties call me elsewhere, Mr. Montgomery."

"One moment, sir! I had hoped, sir, that perhaps, if I signed a paper promising you interest upon your money, you would advance this sum to me. I will pay you back, sir, I really will. Or, if you like, I will work it off after I am qualified."

The doctor's lips had thinned into a narrow line. His eyes were raised again, and sparkled indignantly.

"Your request is unreasonable, Mr. Montgomery. I am surprised that you should have made it. Consider, sir, how many thousands of medical students there are in this country. No doubt there are many of them who have a difficulty in finding their fees. Am I to provide for them all? Or why should I make an exception in your favour? I am grieved and disappointed, Mr. Montgomery, that you should have put me into the painful position of having to refuse you." He turned upon his heel, and walked with offended dignity out of the surgery.

The student smiled bitterly, and turned to his work of making up the morning prescriptions. It was poor and unworthy work—work which any weakling might have done as well, and this was a man of exceptional nerve and sinew. But, such as it was, it brought him his board and £1 a week, enough to help him during the summer months and let him save a few pounds towards his winter keep. But those class fees! Where were they to come from? He could not save them out of his scanty wage. Dr. Oldacre would not advance them. He saw no way of earning them. His brains were fairly good, but brains of that quality were a drug in the market. He only excelled in his strength; and where was he to find a customer for that? But the ways of Fate are strange, and his customer was at hand.

"Look y'ere!" said a voice at the door.

Montgomery looked up, for the voice was a loud and rasping one. A young man stood at the entrance—a stocky, bull-necked young miner, in tweed Sunday clothes and an aggressive necktie. He was a sinister-looking figure, with dark, insolent eyes, and the jaw and throat of a bulldog.

"Look y'ere!" said he again. "Why hast thou not sent t' medicine oop as thy master ordered?"

Montgomery had become accustomed to the brutal frankness of the Northern worker. At first it had enraged him, but after a time he had grown callous to it, and accepted it as it was meant. But this was something different. It was insolence—brutal, overbearing insolence, with physical menace behind it.

" What name ? " he asked coldly.

" Barton. Happen I may give thee cause to mind that name, yoong man. Mak' oop t' wife's medicine this very moment, look ye, or it will be the worse for thee."

Montgomery smiled. A pleasant sense of relief thrilled softly through him. What blessed safety-valve was this through which his jangled nerves might find some outlet. The provocation was so gross, the insult so unprovoked, that he could have none of those qualms which take the edge off a man's mettle. He finished sealing the bottle upon which he was occupied, and he ad ressed it and placed it carefully in the rack.

" Look here ! " said he, turning round to the miner, " your medicine will be made up in its turn and sent down to you. I don't allow folk in the surgery. Wait outside in the waiting-room, if you wish to wait at all."

" Yoong man," said the miner, " thou's got to mak' t' wife's medicine here, and now, and quick, while I wait and watch thee, or else happen thou might need some medicine thysel' before all is over."

" I shouldn't advise you to fasten a quarrel upon me." Montgomery was speaking in the hard, staccato voice of a man who is holding himself in with difficulty. " You'll save trouble if you'll go quietly. If you don't you'll be hurt. Ah, you would ? Take it, then ! "

The blows were almost simultaneous—a savage swing which whistled past Montgomery's ear and a straight drive which took the workman on the chin. Luck was with the assistant. That single whizzing uppercut, and the way in which it was delivered, warned him that he had a formidable man to deal with. But if he had underrated his antagonist, his antagonist had also underrated him, and had laid himself open to a fatal blow.

The miner's head had come with a crash against the corner of the surgery shelves, and he had dropped heavily on to the ground. There he lay with his bandy legs drawn up and his hands thrown abroad, the blood trickling over the surgery tiles.

"Had enough ?" asked the assistant, breathing fiercely through his nose.

But no answer came. The man was insensible. And then the danger of his position came upon Montgomery, and he turned as white as his antagonist. A Sunday, the immaculate Dr. Oldacre with his pious connection, a savage brawl with a patient ; he would irretrievably lose his situation if the facts came out. It was not much of a situation, but he could not get another without a reference, and Oldacre might refuse him one. Without money for his classes, and without a situation—what was to become of him ? It was absolute ruin.

But perhaps he could escape exposure after all. He seized his insensible adversary, dragged him out into the centre of the room, loosened his collar, and squeezed the surgery sponge over his face. He sat up at last with a gasp and a scowl.

"Domn thee, thou's spoilt my necktie," said he, mopping up the water from his breast.

"I'm sorry I hit you so hard," said Montgomery, apologetically.

"Thou hit me hard ! I could stan' such fly-flappin' all day. 'Twas this here press that cracked my pate for me, and thou art a looky man to be able to boast as thou hast outed me. And now I'd be obliged to thee if thou wilt give me t' wife's medicine."

Montgomery gladly made it up and handed it to the miner.

"You are weak still," said he. "Won't you stay awhile and rest ?"

"T' wife wants her medicine," said the man, and lurched out at the door.

The assistant, looking after him, saw him rolling with an uncertain step down the street, until a friend met him, and they walked on arm-in-arm. The man seemed in his rough Northern fashion to bear no grudge, and so

Montgomery's fears left him. There was no reason why the doctor should know anything about it. He wiped the blood from the floor, put the surgery in order, and went on with his interrupted task, hoping that he had come scathless out of a very dangerous business.

Yet all day he was aware of a sense of vague uneasiness which sharpened into dismay when, late in the afternoon, he was informed that three gentlemen had called and were waiting for him in the surgery. A coroner's inquest, a descent of detectives, an invasion of angry relatives—all sorts of possibilities rose to scare him. With tense nerves and a rigid face he went to meet his visitors.

They were a very singular trio. Each was known to him by sight; but what on earth the three could be doing together, and, above all, what they could expect from *him*, was a most inexplicable problem.

The first was Sorley Wilson, the son of the owner of the Nonpareil Coalpit. He was a young blood of twenty, heir to a fortune, a keen sportsman, and down for the Easter Vacation from Magdalene College. He sat now upon the edge of the surgery table, looking in thoughtful silence at Montgomery, and twisting the ends of his small, black, waxed moustache.

The second was Purvis, the publican, owner of the chief beershop, and well known as the local bookmaker. He was a coarse, clean-shaven man, whose fiery face made a singular contrast with his ivory-white bald head. He had shrewd, light-blue eyes with foxy lashes, and he also leaned forward in silence from his chair, a fat, red hand upon either knee, and stared critically at the young assistant.

So did the third visitor, Fawcett, the horse-breaker, who leaned back, his long, thin legs, with their box-cloth riding-gaiters, thrust out in front of him, tapping his protruding teeth with his riding-whip, with anxious thought in every line of his rugged, bony face. Publican, exquisite, and horsebreaker were all three equally silent, equally earnest, and equally critical. Montgomery, seated in the midst of them, looked from one to the other.

"Well, gentlemen?" he observed, but no answer came. The position was embarrassing.

"No," said the horsebreaker, at last. "No. It's off. It's nowt."

"Stand oop, lad; let's see thee standin'." It was the publican who spoke.

Montgomery obeyed. He would learn all about it, no doubt, if he were patient. He stood up and turned slowly round, as if in front of his tailor.

"It's off! It's off!" cried the horsebreaker. "Why, mon, the Master would break him over his knee."

"Oh, that be hanged for a yarn!" said the young Cantab. "You can drop out if you like, Fawcett, but I'll see this thing through, if I have to do it alone. I don't hedge a penny. I like the cut of him a great deal better than I liked Ted Barton."

"Look at Barton's shoulders, Mr. Wilson."

"Lumpiness isn't always strength. Give me nerve and fire and breed. That's what wins."

"Ay, sir, you have it theer—you have it theer!" said the fat, red-faced publican, in a thick, suety voice. "It's the same wi' poops. Get 'em clean-bred an' fine, an' they'll yark the thick 'uns—yark 'em out o' their skins."

"He's ten good pund on the light side," growled the horsebreaker.

"He's a welter weight, anyhow."

"A hundred and thirty."

"A hundred and fifty, if he's an ounce."

"Well, the Master doesn't scale much more than that."

"A hundred and seventy-five."

"That was when he was hog-fat and living high. Work the grease out of him, and I lay there's no great difference between them. Have you been weighed lately, Mr. Montgomery?"

It was the first direct question which had been asked

him. He had stood in the midst of them, like a horse at a fair, and he was just beginning to wonder whether he was more angry or amused.

"I am just eleven stone," said he.

"I said that he was a welter weight."

"But suppose you was trained?" said the publican. "Wot then?"

"I am always in training."

"In a manner of speakin,' no doubt, he *is* always in trainin'," remarked the horsebreaker. "But trainin' for everyday work ain't the same as trainin' with a trainer; and I dare bet, with all respec' to your opinion, Mr. Wilson, that there's half a stone of tallow on him at this minute."

The young Cantab put his fingers on the assistant's upper arm. Then with his other hand on his wrist he bent the forearm sharply, and felt the biceps, as round and hard as a cricket-ball, spring up under his fingers.

"Feel that!" said he.

The publican and horsebreaker felt it with an air of reverence.

"Good lad! He'll do yet!" cried Purvis.

"Gentlemen," said Montgomery, "I think that you will acknowledge that I have been very patient with you. I have listened to all that you have to say about my personal appearance, and now I must really beg that you will have the goodness to tell me what is the matter."

They all sat down in their serious, business-like way.

"That's easy done, Mr. Montgomery," said the fat-voiced publican. "But before sayin' anything we had to wait and see whether, in a way of speakin', there was any need for us to say anything at all. Mr. Wilson thinks there is. Mr. Fawcett, who has the same right to his opinion, bein' also a backer and one o' the committee, thinks the other way."

"I thought him too light built, and I think so now," said the horsebreaker, still tapping his prominent teeth with the metal head of his riding-whip. "But happen he may pull through ; and he's a fine-made, buirdly young chap, so if you mean to back him, Mr. Wilson——"

"Which I do."

"And you, Purvis ?"

"I ain't one to go back, Fawcett."

"Well, I'll stan' to my share of the purse."

"And well I knew you would," said Purvis, "for it would be somethin' new to find Isaac Fawcett as a spoil-sport. Well, then, we make up the hundred for the stake among us, and the fight stands—always supposin' the young man is willin'."

"Excuse all this rot, Mr. Montgomery," said the University man, in a genial voice. "We've begun at the wrong end, I know, but we'll soon straighten it out, and I hope that you will see your way to falling in with our views. In the first place, you remember the man whom you knocked out this morning ? He is Barton—the famous Ted Barton."

"I'm sure, sir, you may well be proud to have outed him in one round," said the publican. "Why, it took Morris, the ten-stone-six champion, a deal more trouble than that before he put Barton to sleep. You've done a fine performance, sir, and happen you'll do a finer, if you give yourself the chance."

"I never heard of Ted Barton, beyond seeing the name on a medicine label," said the assistant.

"Well, you may take it from me that he's a slaughterer," said the horsebreaker. "You've taught him a lesson that he needed, for it was always a word and a blow with him, and the word alone was worth five shillin' in a public court. He won't be so ready now to shake his nief in the face of every one he meets. However, that's neither here nor there."

Montgomery looked at them in bewilderment.

"For goodness' sake, gentlemen, tell me what it is you want me to do !" he cried.

"We want you to fight Silas Craggs, better known as the Master of Croxley."

"But why?"

"Because Ted Barton was to have fought him next Saturday. He was the champion of the Wilson coal-pits, and the other was the Master of the iron-folk down at the Croxley smelters. We'd matched our man for a purse of a hundred against the Master. But you've queered our man, and he can't face such a battle with a two-inch cut at the back of his head. There's only one thing to be done, sir, and that is for you to take his place. If you can lick Ted Barton you may lick the Master of Croxley; but if you don't we're done, for there's no one else who is in the same street with him in this district. It's twenty rounds, two-ounce gloves, Queensberry rules, and a decision on points if you fight to the finish."

For a moment the absurdity of the thing drove every other thought out of Montgomery's head. But then there came a sudden revulsion. A hundred pounds!—all he wanted to complete his education was lying there ready to his hand if only that hand were strong enough to pick it up. He had thought bitterly that morning that there was no market for his strength, but here was one where his muscle might earn more in an hour than his brains in a year. But a chill of doubt came over him.

"How can I fight for the coal-pits?" said he. "I am not connected with them."

"Eh, lad, but thou art!" cried old Purvis. "We've got it down in writin', and it's clear enough. 'Anyone connected with the coal-pits.' Doct r Oldacre is the coal-pit club doctor; thou art his assistant. What more can they want?"

"Yes, that's right enough," said the Cantab. "It would be a very sporting thing of you, Mr. Montgomery, if you would come to our help when we are in such a hole. Of course, you might not like to take the hundred pounds; but I have no doubt that, in the case of your winning, we could arrange that it should take the form of a watch or piece of plate, or any other shape which might suggest itself to you. You see, you are responsible for our having lost our champion, so we really feel that we have a claim upon you."

"Give me a moment, gentlemen. It is very unexpected. I am afraid the doctor would never consent to my going—in fact, I am sure that he would not."

"But he need never know—not before the fight, at any rate. We are not bound to give the name of our man. So long as he is within the weight limits on the day of the fight, that is all that concerns any one."

The adventure and the profit would either of them have attracted Montgomery. The two combined were irresistible.

"Gentlemen," said he, "I'll do it!"

The three sprang from their seats. The publican had seized his right hand, the horse-dealer his left, and the Cantab slapped him on the back.

"Good lad! good lad!" croaked the publican. "Eh, mon, but if thou yark him, thou'll rise in one day from being just a common doctor to the best-known mon 'twixt here and Bradford. Thou are a witherin' tyke, thou art, and no mistake; and if thou beat the Master of Croxley, thou'll find all the beer thou want for the rest of thy life waiting for thee at the Four Sacks."

"It is the most sporting thing I ever heard of in my life," said young Wilson. "By George, sir, if you pull it off, you've got the constituency in your pocket, if you care to stand. You know the outhouse in my garden?"

"Next the road?"

"Exactly. I turned it into a gymnasium for Ted Barton. You'll find all you want there: clubs, punching-ball, bars, dumb-bells, everything. Then you'll want a sparring partner. Ogilvy has been acting for Barton, but we don't think that he is class enough. Barton bears you no grudge. He's a good-hearted fellow, though cross-grained with strangers. He looked upon you as a stranger this morning, but he says he knows you now. He is quite ready to spar with you for practice, and he will come at any hour you will name."

"Thank you; I will let you know the hour," said Montgomery; and so the committee departed jubilant upon their way.

The medical assistant sat for a little time in the surgery turning it over in his mind. He had been trained originally at the University by the man who had been middleweight champion in his day. It was true that his teacher was long past his prime, slow upon his feet and stiff in his joints, but even so he was still a tough antagonist; but Montgomery had found at last that he could more than hold his own with him. He had won the University medal, and his teacher, who had trained so many students, was emphatic in his opinion that he had never had one who was in the same class with him. He had been exhorted to go in for the Amateur Championships, but he had no particular ambition in that direction. Once he had put on the gloves with Hammer Tunstall in a booth at a fair, and had fought three rattling rounds, in which he had the worst of it, but had made the prizefighter stretch himself to the uttermost. There was his whole record, and was it enough to encourage him to stand up to the Master of Croxley? He had never heard of the Master before, but then he had lost touch of the ring during the last few years of hard work. After all, what did it matter? If he won, there was the money, which meant so much to him. If he lost, it would only mean a thrashing. He could take punishment without flinching, of that he was certain. If there were only one chance in a hundred of pulling it off, then it was worth his while to attempt it.

Dr. Oldacre, new come from church, with an ostentatious prayer-book in his kid-gloved hand, broke in upon his meditation.

"You don't go to service, I observe, Mr. Montgomery," said he, coldly.

"No, sir; I have had some business to detain me."

"It is very near to my heart that my household

should set a good example. There are so few educated people in this district that a great responsibility devolves upon us. If we do not live up to the highest, how can we expect these poor workers to do so? It is a dreadful thing to reflect that the parish takes a great deal more interest in an approaching glove-fight than in their religious duties."

"A glove-fight, sir?" said Montgomery, guiltily.

"I believe that to be the correct term. One of my patients tells me that it is the talk of the district. A local ruffian, a patient of ours, by the way, is matched against a pugilist over at Croxley. I cannot understand why the law does not step in and stop so degrading an exhibition. It is really a prize-fight."

"A glove-fight, you said."

"I am informed that a two-ounce glove is an evasion by which they dodge the law, and make it difficult for the police to interfere. They contend for a sum of money. It seems dreadful and almost incredible—does it not?—to think that such scenes can be enacted within a few miles of our peaceful home. But you will realize, Mr. Montgomery, that while there are such influences for us to counteract, it is very necessary that we should live up to our highest."

The doctor's sermon would have had more effect if the assistant had not once or twice had occasion to test his highest and come upon it at unexpectedly humble elevations. It is always so particularly easy to "compound for sins we're most inclined to by damning those we have no mind to." In any case, Montgomery felt that of all the men concerned in such a fight—promoters, backers, spectators—it is the actual fighter who holds the strongest and most honourable position. His conscience gave him no concern upon the subject. Endurance and courage are virtues, not vices, and brutality is, at least, better than effeminacy.

There was a little tobacco-shop at the corner of the street, where Montgomery got his bird's-eye and also his local information, for the shopman was a garrulous soul, who knew everything about the affairs of the district. The assistant strolled down there after tea and asked, in a casual way, whether the tobacconist had ever heard of the Master of Croxley.

"Heard of him! Heard of him!" the little man could hardly articulate in his astonishment. "Why, sir, he's the first mon o' the district, an' his name's as well known in the West Riding as the winner o' t' Derby. But Lor', sir"—here he stopped and rummaged among a heap of papers. "They are makin' a fuss about him on account o' his fight wi' Ted Barton, and so the *Croxley Herald* has his life an' record, an' here it is, an' thou canst read it for thysel'."

The sheet of the paper which he held up was a lake of print around an islet of illustration. The latter was a coarse wood-cut of a pugilist's head and neck set in a cross-barred jersey. It was a sinister but powerful face, the face of a debauched hero, clean-shaven, strongly eye-browed, keen-eyed, with a huge, aggressive jaw, and an animal dewlap beneath it. The long, obstinate cheeks ran flush up to the narrow, sinister eyes. The mighty neck came down square from the ears and curved outwards into shoulders, which had lost nothing at the hands of the local artist. Above was written "Silas Craggs," and beneath, "The Master of Croxley."

"Thou'll find all about him there, sir," said the tobacconist. "He's a witherin' tyke, he is, and w're proud to have him in the county. If he hadn't broke his leg he'd have been champion of England."

"Broke his leg, has he?"

"Yes, and it set badly. They ca' him owd K behind his bock, for thot is how his two legs look. But his arms—well, if they was both stropped to a bench, as the sayin' is, I wonder where the champion of England would be then."

"I'll take this with me," said Montgomery; and putting the paper into his pocket he returned home.

It was not a cheering record which he read there. The whole history of the Croxley Master was given in full, his many victories, his few defeats.

"Born in 1857," said the provincial biographer, "Silas Craggs, better known in sporting circles as The Master of Croxley, is now in his fortieth year."

"Hang it, I'm only twenty-three," said Montgomery to himself, and read on more cheerfully.

"Having in his youth shown a surprising aptitude for the game, he fought his way up among his comrades, until he became the recognized champion of the district and won the proud title which he still holds. Ambitious of a more than local fame, he secured a patron, and fought his first fight against Jack Barton, of Birmingham, in May, 1880, at the old Loiterers' Club. Craggs, who fought at ten-stone-two at the time, had the better of fifteen rattling rounds, and gained an award on points against the Midlander. Having disposed of James Dunn, of Rotherhithe, Cameron, of Glasgow, and a youth named Fernie, he was thought so highly of by the fancy that he was matched against Ernest Willox, at that time middle-weight champion of the North of England, and defeated him in a hard-fought battle, knocking him out in the tenth round after a punishing contest. At this period it looked as if the very highest honours of the ring were within the reach of the young Yorkshireman, but he was laid upon the shelf by a most unfortunate accident. The kick of a horse broke his thigh, and for a year he was compelled to rest himself. When he returned to his work the fracture had set badly, and his activity was much impaired. It was owing to this that he was defeated in seven rounds by Willox, the man whom he had previously beaten, and afterwards by James Shaw, of London, though the latter acknowledged that he had found the toughest customer of his career. Undismayed by his reverses, the Master adapted the style of his fighting to his physical disabilities, and resumed his career of victory—defeating Norton (the black), Bobby Wilson, and Levi Cohen, the latter a heavy-weight. Conceding two stone, he fought a draw with the famous Billy McQuire, and afterwards, for a purse of fifty pounds, he defeated Sam Hare at the Pelican Club, London. In 1891 a decision was given against him upon a foul when fighting a winning fight against Jim Taylor, the Australian middle-weight, and so mortified was he by the decision, that he withdrew from the ring. Since then he has hardly fought at all save to accommodate any local aspirant who may wish to learn the difference between a bar-room scramble and a scientific contest. The latest of these ambitious souls comes from the Wilson coal-pits, which have undertaken to put up a stake of £100 and back their local champion. There are various rumours afloat as to who their representative is to be, the name of Ted Barton being freely mentioned; but the betting, which is seven to one on the Master against any untried man, is a fair reflection of the feeling of the community."

Montgomery read it over twice, and it left him with a very serious face. No light matter this, which he had undertaken; no battle with a rough-and-tumble fighter who presumed upon a local reputation. The man's record showed that he was first class—or nearly so. There were a few points in his favour, and he must make the most of them. There was age—twenty-three against forty. There was an old ring proverb that "Youth will be served," but the annals of the ring offer a great number of exceptions. A hard veteran, full of cool valour and ring-craft, could give ten or fifteen years and a beating to most striplings. He could not rely too much upon his advantage in age. But then there was the lameness; that must surely count for a great deal. And, lastly, there was the chance that the Master might underrate his opponent, that he might be remiss in his training, and refuse to abandon his usual way of life, if he thought that he had an easy task before him. In a man of his age and habits this seemed very possible. Montgomery prayed that it might be so. Meanwhile, if his opponent were the best man who ever jumped the ropes into a ring, his own duty was clear. He must prepare himself carefully, throw away no chance, and do the very best that he could. But he knew enough to appreciate the difference which exists in boxing, as in every sport, between the amateur and the professional. The coolness, the power of hitting, above all the capability of taking punishment, count for so much. Those specially developed, gutta-percha-like abdominal muscles of the hardened pugilist will take without flinching a blow which would leave another man writhing on the ground. Such things are not to be acquired in a week, but all that could be done in a week should be done.

The medical assistant had a good basis to start from. He was 5 feet 11 inches—tall enough for anything on two legs, as the old ring men used to say—lithe and spare, with the activity of a panther, and a strength which had hardly yet ever found its limitations. His muscular development was finely hard, but his power came rather from that higher nerve-energy which counts for nothing upon a measuring tape. He had the well-curved nose and the widely opened eye which never yet were seen upon the face of a craven, and behind everything he had the driving force, which came from the knowledge that his whole career was at stake upon the contest. The three backers rubbed their hands when they saw him at work punching the ball in the gymnasium next morning; and Fawcett, the horsebreaker, who had written to Leeds to hedge his bets, sent a wire to cancel the letter, and to lay another fifty at the market price of seven to one.

Montgomery's chief difficulty was to find time for his training without any interference from the doctor. His work took him a large part of the day, but as the visiting was done on foot, and considerable distances had to be traversed, it was a training in itself. For the rest, he punched the swinging ball and worked with the dumb-bells for an hour every morning and evening, and boxed twice a day with Ted Barton in the gymnasium, gaining as much profit as could be got from a rushing, two-handed slogger. Barton was full of admiration for his cleverness and quickness, but doubtful about his strength. Hard hitting was the feature of his own style, and he exacted it from others.

"Lord, sir, that's a turble poor poonch for an eleven-stone man!" he would cry. "Thou wilt have to hit harder than that afore t' Master will know that thou art theer. Ah, thot's better, mon, thot's fine!" he would add, as his opponent lifted him across the room on the end of a right counter. "Thot's how I likes to feel 'em. Happen thou'lt pull through yet." He chuckled with joy when Montgomery knocked him into a corner. "Eh, mon, thou art comin' along grand. Thou hast fair yarked me off my legs. Do it again, lad, do it again!"

The only part of Montgomery's training which came within the doctor's observation was his diet, and that puzzled him considerably.

"You will excuse my remarking, Mr. Montgomery, that you are becoming rather particular in your tastes. Such fads are not to be encouraged in one's youth. Why do you eat toast with every meal?"

"I find that it suits me better than bread, sir."

"It entails unnecessary work upon the cook. I observe, also, that you have turned against potatoes."

"Yes, sir; I think that I am better without them."

"And you no longer drink your beer?"

"No, sir."

"These causeless whims and fancies are very much to be deprecated, Mr. Montgomery. Consider how many there are to whom these very potatoes and this very beer would be most acceptable."

"No doubt, sir. But at present I prefer to do without them."

They were sitting alone at lunch, and the assistant

thought that it would be a good opportunity of asking leave for the day of the fight.

"I should be glad if you could let me have leave for Saturday, Doctor Oldacre."

"It is very inconvenient upon so busy a day."

"I should do a double day's work on Friday so as to leave everything in order. I should hope to be back in the evening."

"I am afraid I cannot spare you, Mr. Montgomery."

This was a facer. If he could not get leave he would go without it.

"You will remember, Doctor Oldacre, that when I came to you it was understood that I should have a clear day every month. I have never claimed one. But now there are reasons why I wish to have a holiday upon Saturday."

Doctor Oldacre gave in with a very bad grace.

"Of course, if you insist upon your formal rights, there is no more to be said, Mr. Montgomery, though I feel that it shows a certain indifference to my comfort and the welfare of the practice. Do you still insist?"

"Yes, sir."

"Very good. Have your way."

The doctor was boiling over with anger, but Montgomery was a valuable assistant—steady, capable, and hard working—and he could not afford to lose him. Even if he had been prompted to advance those class fees, for which his assistant had appealed, it would have been against his interests to do so, for he did not wish him to qualify, and he desired him to remain in his subordinate position, in which he worked so hard for so small a wage. There was something in the cool insistence of the young man, a quiet resolution in his voice as he claimed his Saturday, which aroused his curiosity.

"I have no desire to interfere unduly with your affairs, Mr. Montgomery, but were you thinking of having a day in Leeds upon Saturday?"

"No, sir."

"In the country?"

"Yes, sir."

"You are very wise. You will find a quiet day among the wild flowers a very valuable restorative. Had you thought of any particular direction?"

"I am going over Croxley way."

"Well, there is no prettier country when once you are past the iron-works. What could be more delightful than to lie upon the Fells, basking in the sunshine, with perhaps some instructive and elevating book as your companion? I should recommend a visit to the ruins of St. Bridget's Church, a very interesting relic of the early Norman era. By the way, there is one objection which I see to your going to Croxley on Saturday. It is upon that date, as I am informed, that that ruffianly glove-fight takes place. You may find yourself molested by the blackguards whom it will attract."

"I will take my chance of that, sir," said the assistant

On the Friday night, which was the last before the fight, Montgomery's three backers assembled in the gymnasium and inspected their man as he went through some light exercises to keep his muscles supple. He was certainly in splendid condition, his skin shining with health, and his eyes with energy and confidence. The three walked round him and exulted.

"He's simply ripping!" said the undergraduate. "By Gad, you've come out of it splendidly. You're as hard as a pebble, and fit to fight for your life."

"Happen he's a trifle on the fine side," said the publican. "Runs a bit light at the loins, to my way of thinkin'."

"What weight to-day?"

"Ten-stone eleven," the assistant answered.

"That's only three pund off in a week's trainin'," said the horsebreaker. "He said right when he said that he was in condition. Well, it's fine stuff all there is of it, but I'm none so sure as there is enough." He kept poking his finger into Montgomery, as if he were one of his horses. "I hear that the Master will scale a hundred and sixty odd at the ring-side."

"But there's some of that which he'd like well to pull off and leave behind wi' his shirt," said Purvis. "I hear they've had a rare job to get him to drop his beer, and if it had not been for that great red-headed wench of his they'd never ha' done it. She fair scratted the face off a potman that had brought him a gallon from t' Chequers. They say the hussy is his sparrin' partner, as well as his sweetheart, and that his poor wife is just breakin' her heart over it. Hullo, young 'un, what do you want?"

The door of the gymnasium had opened, and a lad about sixteen, grimy and black with soot and iron, stepped into the yellow glare of the oil-lamp. Ted Barton seized him by the collar.

"See here, thou yoong whelp, this is private, and we want noan o' thy spyin'!"

"But I maun speak to Mr. Wilson."

The young Cantab stepped forward.

"Well, my lad, what is it?"

"It's aboot t' fight, Mr. Wilson, sir. I wanted to tell your mon somethin' aboot t' Maister."

"We've no time to listen to gossip, my boy. We know all about the Master."

"But thou doant, sir. Nobody knows but me and mother, and we thought as we'd like thy mon to know, sir, for we want him to fair bray him."

"Oh, you want the Master fair brayed, do you? So do we. Well, what have you to say?"

"Is this your mon, sir?"

"Well, suppose it is?"

"Then it's him I want to tell aboot it. T' Maister is blind o' the left eye."

"Nonsense!"

"It's true, sir. Not stone blind, but rarely fogged. He keeps it secret, but mother knows, and so do I. If thou slip him on the left side he can't cop thee. Thou'll find it right as I tell thee. And mark him when he sinks his right. 'Tis his best blow, his right upper-cut. T' Maister's finisher, they ca' it at t' works. It's a turble blow, when it do come home."

"Thank you, my boy. This is information worth having about his sight," said Wilson. "How came you to know so much? Who are you?"

"I'm his son, sir."

Wilson whistled.

"And who sent you to us?"

"My mother. I maun get back to her again."

"Take this half-crown."

"No, sir, I don't seek money in comin' here. I do it——"

"For love?" suggested the publican.

"For hate!" said the boy, and darted off into the darkness.

"Seems to me t' red-headed wench may do him more harm than good, after all," remarked the publican. "And now, Mr. Montgomery, sir, you've done enough for this evenin', and a nine-hours' sleep is the best trainin' before a battle. Happen this time to-morrow night you'll be safe back again with your one hundred pounds in your pocket."

II

Work was struck at one o'clock at the coal-pits and the iron-works, and the fight was arranged for three. From the Croxley Furnaces, from Wilson's Coal-pits, from the Heartsease Mine, from the Dodd Mills, from the Leverworth Smelters the workmen came trooping, each with his fox-terrier or his lurcher at his heels. Warped with labour and twisted by toil, bent double by week-long work in the cramped coal galleries, or half-blinded with years spent in front of white-hot fluid metal, these men still gilded their harsh and hopeless lives by their devotion to sport. It was their one relief, the only thing which could distract their minds from sordid surroundings, and give them an interest beyond the blackened circle which inclosed them. Literature, art, science, all these things were beyond their horizon; but the race, the football match, the cricket, the fight, these were things which they could understand, which they could speculate upon in advance and comment upon afterwards. Sometimes brutal, sometimes grotesque, the love of sport is still one of the great agencies which make for the happiness of our people. It lies very deeply in the springs of our nature, and when it has been educated out, a higher, more refined nature may be left, but it will not be of that robust British type which has left its mark so deeply on the world. Every one of these ruddled workers, slouching with his dog at his heels to see something of the fight, was a true unit of his race.

It was a squally May day, with bright sunbursts and driving showers. Montgomery worked all morning in the surgery getting his medicine made up.

"The weather seems so very unsettled, Mr. Montgomery," remarked the doctor, "that I am inclined to think that you had better postpone your little country excursion until a later date."

"I am afraid that I must go to-day, sir."

"I have just had an intimation that Mrs. Potter, at the other side of Angleton, wishes to see me. It is probable that I shall be there all day. It will be extremely inconvenient to leave the house empty so long."

"I am very sorry, sir, but I must go," said the assistant, doggedly.

The doctor saw that it would be useless to argue, and departed in the worst of bad tempers upon his mission. Montgomery felt easier now that he was gone. He went up to his room, and packed his running-shoes, his fighting-drawers, and his cricket-sash into a handbag. When he came down Mr. Wilson was waiting for him in the surgery.

"I hear the doctor has gone."

"Yes; he is likely to be away all day."

"I don't see that it matters much. It's bound to come to his ears by to-night."

"Yes; it's serious with me, Mr. Wilson. If I win, it's all right. I don't mind telling you that the hundred pounds will make all the difference to me. But if I lose, I shall lose my situation, for, as you say, I can't keep it secret."

"Never mind. We'll see you through among us. I only wonder the doctor has not heard, for it's all over the country that you are to fight the Croxley Champion. We've had Armitage up about it already. He's the Master's backer, you know. He wasn't sure that you were eligible. The Master said he wanted you whether you were eligible or not. Armitage has money on, and would have made trouble if he could. But I showed him that you came within the conditions of the challenge, and he agreed that it was all right. They think they have a soft thing on."

"Well, I can only do my best," said Montgomery.

They lunched together; a silent and rather nervous repast, for Montgomery's mind was full of what was before him, and Wilson had himself more money at stake than he cared to lose.

Wilson's carriage and pair were at the door, the horses with blue-and-white rosettes at their ears, which were the colours of the Wilson Coal pits, well known on many a football field. At the avenue gate a crowd of some hundred pitmen and their wives gave a cheer as the carriage passed. To the assistant it all seemed dream like and extraordinary—the strangest experience of his life, but with a thrill of human action and interest in it which made it passionately absorbing. He lay back in the open carriage and saw the fluttering handkerchiefs from the doors and windows of the miners' cottages. Wilson had pinned a blue-and-white rosette upon his coat, and every one knew him as their champion.

"Good luck, sir! good luck to thee!" they shouted from the roadside. He felt that it was like some unromantic knight riding down to sordid lists, but there was something of chivalry in it all the same. He fought for others as well as for himself. He might fail from want of skill or strength, but deep in his sombre soul he vowed that it should never be for want of heart.

Mr. Fawcett was just mounting into his high-wheeled, spidery dogcart, with his little bit of blood between the shafts. He waved his whip and fell in behind the carriage. They overtook Purvis, the tomato-faced publican, upon the road, with his wife in her Sunday bonnet. They also dropped into the procession, and then, as they traversed the seven miles of the high road to Croxley, their two-horsed, rosetted carriage became gradually the nucleus of a comet with a loosely radiating tail. From every side-road came the miners' carts, the humble, ramshackle traps, black and bulging, with their loads of noisy, foul-tongued, open-hearted partisans. They trailed for a long quarter of a mile behind them—cracking, whipping, shouting, galloping, swearing. Horsemen and runners were mixed with the vehicles. And then suddenly a squad of the Sheffield Yeomanry, who were having their annual training in those parts, clattered and jingled out of a field, and rode as an escort to the carriage. Through the dust-clouds round him Montgomery saw the gleaming brass helmets, the bright coats, and the tossing heads of the chargers, the delighted brown faces of the troopers. It was more dream-like than ever.

And then, as they approached the monstrous uncouth line of bottle-shaped buildings which marked the smelting-works of Croxley, their long, writhing snake of dust was headed off by another but longer one which wound across their path. The main road into which their own opened was filled by the rushing current of traps. The Wilson contingent halted until the others should get past. The iron-men cheered and groaned, according to their humour, as they whirled past their antagonist. Rough chaff flew back and forwards like iron nuts and splinters of coal. " Brought him up, then ! " " Got t' hearse for to fetch him back ? " " Where's t' owd K-legs ? " " Mon, mon, have thy photograph took—'twill mind thee of what thou used to look ! " " He fight ?—he's now't but a half-baked doctor ! " " Happen he'll doctor thy Croxley Champion afore he's through wi't."

So they flashed at each other as the one side waited and the other passed. Then there came a rolling murmur swelling into a shout, and a great break with four horses came clattering along, all streaming with salmon-pink ribbons. The driver wore a white hat with pink rosette, and beside him, on the high seat, were a man and a woman—she with her arm round his waist. Montgomery had one glimpse of them as they flashed past: he with a furry cap drawn low over his brow, a great frieze coat, and a pink comforter round his throat; she brazen, red-headed, bright-coloured, laughing excitedly. The Master, for it was he, turned as he passed, gazed hard at Montgomery, and gave him a menacing, gap-toothed grin. It was a hard, wicked face, blue-jowled and craggy, with long, obstinate cheeks and inexorable eyes. The break behind was full of patrons of the sport—flushed iron-foremen, heads of departments, managers. One was drinking from a metal flask, and raised it to Montgomery as he passed; and then the crowd thinned, and the Wilson cortège with their dragoons swept in at the rear of the others.

The road led away from Croxley, between curving green hills, gashed and polluted by the searchers for coal and iron. The whole country had been gutted, and vast piles of refuse and mountains of slag suggested the mighty chambers which the labour of man had burrowed beneath. On the left the road curved up to where a huge building, roofless and dismantled, stood crumbling and forlorn, with the light shining through the windowless squares.

"That's the old Arrowsmith's factory. That's where the fight is to be," said Wilson. "How are you feeling now?"

"Thank you. I was never better in my life," Montgomery answered.

"By Gad, I like your nerve!" said Wilson, who was himself flushed and uneasy. "You'll give us a fight for our money, come what may. That place on the right is the office, and that has been set aside as the dressing- and weighing-room."

The carriage drove up to it amidst the shouts of the folk upon the hill-side. Lines of empty carriages and traps curved down upon the winding road, and a black crowd surged round the door of the ruined factory. The seats, as a huge placard announced, were five shillings, three shillings, and a shilling, with half-price for dogs. The takings, deducting expenses, were to go to the winner, and it was already evident that a larger stake than a hundred pounds was in question. A babel of voices rose from the door. The workers wished to bring their dogs in free. The men scuffled. The dogs barked. The crowd was a whirling, eddying pool surging with a roar up to the narrow cleft which was its only outlet.

The break, with its salmon-coloured streamers and four reeking horses, stood empty before the door of the office; Wilson, Purvis, Fawcett, and Montgomery passed in.

There was a large, bare room inside with square, clean patches upon the grimy walls, where pictures and almanacs had once hung. Worn linoleum covered the floor, but there was no furniture save some benches and a deal table with a ewer and a basin upon it. Two of the corners were curtained off. In the middle of the room was a weighing-chair. A hugely fat man, with a salmon tie and a blue waistcoat with birds'-eye spots, came bustling up to them. It was Armitage, the butcher and grazier, well known for miles round as a warm man, and the most liberal patron of sport in the Riding.

" Well, well," he grunted, in a thick, fussy, wheezy voice, " you have come, then. Got your man? Got your man?"

" Here he is, fit and well. Mr. Montgomery, let me present you to Mr. Armitage."

" Glad to meet you, sir. Happy to make your acquaintance. I make bold to say, sir, that we of Croxley admire your courage, Mr. Montgomery, and that our only hope is a fair fight and no favour and the best man win. That's our sentiment at Croxley."

" And it is my sentiment also," said the assistant.

" Well, you can't say fairer than that, Mr. Montgomery. You've taken a large contrac' in hand, but a large contrac' may be carried through, sir, as anyone that knows my dealings could testify. The Master is ready to weigh in!"

" So am I."

" You must weigh in the buff."

Montgomery looked askance at the tall, red-headed woman who was standing gazing out of the window.

" That's all right," said Wilson. " Get behind the curtain and put on your fighting-kit."

He did so, and came out the picture of an athlete, in white, loose drawers, canvas shoes, and the sash of a well-known cricket club round his waist. He was trained to a hair, his skin gleaming like silk, and every muscle rippling down his broad shoulders and along his beautiful arms as he moved them. They bunched into ivory knobs, or slid into long, sinuous curves, as he raised or lowered his hands.

" What thinkest thou o' that?" asked Ted Barton, his second, of the woman in the window.

She glanced contemptuously at the young athlete.

" It's but a poor kindness thou dost him to put a thread-paper yoong gentleman like yon against a mon as is a mon. Why, my Jock would throttle him wi' one hond lashed behind him."

"Happen he may—happen not," said Barton. "I have but twa pund in the world, but it's on him, every penny, and no hedgin'. But here's t' Maister, and rarely fine he do look."

The prize-fighter had come out from his curtain, a squat, formidable figure, monstrous in chest and arms, limping slightly on his distorted leg. His skin had none of the freshness and clearness of Montgomery's, but was dusky and mottled, with one huge mole amid the mat of tangled black hair which thatched his mighty breast. His weight bore no relation to his strength, for those huge shoulders and great arms, with brown, sledge-hammer fists, would have fitted the heaviest man that ever threw his cap into a ring. But his loins and legs were slight in proportion. Montgomery, on the other hand, was as symmetrical as a Greek statue. It would be an encounter between a man who was specially fitted for one sport, and one who was equally capable of any. The two looked curiously at each other: a bulldog, and a high-bred, clean-limbed terrier, each full of spirit.

"How do you do?"

"How do?" The Master grinned again, and his three jagged front teeth gleamed for an instant. The rest had been beaten out of him in twenty years of battle. He spat upon the floor. "We have a rare fine day for't."

"Capital," said Montgomery.

"That's the good feelin' I like," wheezed the fat butcher. "Good lads, both of them!—prime lads!—hard meat an' good bone. There's no ill-feelin'."

"If he downs me, Gawd bless him!" said the Master.

"An' if we down him, Gawd help him!" interrupted the woman.

"Haud thy tongue, wench!" said the Master, impatiently. "Who art thou to put in thy word? Happen I might draw my hand across thy face."

The woman did not take the threat amiss.

"Wilt have enough for thy hand to do, Jock," said she. "Get quit o' this gradely man afore thou turn on me."

The lovers' quarrel was interrupted by the entrance of a new-comer, a gentleman with a fur-collared overcoat and a very shiny top-hat—a top-hat of a degree of glossiness which is seldom seen five miles from Hyde Park. This hat he wore at the extreme back of his head, so that the lower surface of the brim made a kind of frame for his high, bald forehead, his keen eyes, his rugged and yet kindly face. He bustled in with the quiet air of possession with which the ring-master enters the circus.

"It's Mr. Stapleton, the referee from London," said Wilson. "How do you do, Mr. Stapleton? I was introduced to you at the big fight at the Corinthian Club, in Piccadilly."

"Ah, I dare say," said the other, shaking hands. "Fact is, I'm introduced to so many that I can't undertake to carry their names. Wilson, is it? Well, Mr. Wilson, glad to see you. Couldn't get a fly at the station, and that's why I'm late."

"I'm sure, sir," said Armitage, "we should be proud that anyone so well known in the boxing world should come down to our little exhibition."

"Not at all. Not at all. Anything in the interest of boxin'. All ready? Men weighed?"

"Weighing now, sir."

"Ah, just as well I should see it done. Seen you before, Craggs. Saw you fight your second battle against Willox. You had beaten him once, but he came back on you. What does the indicator say?—one hundred and sixty-three pounds—two off for the kit—one hundred and sixty-one. Now, my lad, you jump. My goodness, what colours are you wearing?"

"The Anonymi Cricket Club."

"What right have you to wear them? I belong to the club myself."

"So do I."

"You an amateur?"

"Yes, sir."

"And you are fighting for a money prize?"

"Yes."

"I suppose you know what you are doing. You realize that you're a professional pug from this onwards, and that if ever you fight again——"

"I'll never fight again."

"Happen you won't," said the woman, and the Master turned a terrible eye upon her.

"Well, I suppose you know your own business best. Up you jump. One hundred and fifty-one, minus two, one hundred and forty-nine—twelve pounds' difference. but youth and condition on the other scale. Well, the sooner we get to work the better, for I wish to catch the seven-o'clock express at Hellifield. Twenty three-minute rounds, with one minute intervals, and Queensberry rules. Those are the conditions, are they not?"

"Yes, sir."

"Very good, then, we may go across."

The two combatants had overcoats thrown over their shoulders, and the whole party, backers, fighters, seconds, and the referee, filed out of the room. A police inspector was waiting for them in the road. He had a notebook in his hand—that terrible weapon which awes even the London cabman.

"I must take your names, gentlemen, in case it should be necessary to proceed for breach of peace.'

"You don't mean to stop the fight?" cried Armitage, in a passion of indignation. "I'm Mr. Armitage, of Croxley, and this is Mr. Wilson, and we'll be responsible that all is fair and as it should be."

"I'll take the names in case it should be necessary to proceed," said the inspector, impassively.

"But you know me well."

"If you was a dook or even a judge it would be all the same," said the inspector. "It's the law, and there's an end. I'll not take upon myself to stop the fight, seeing that gloves are to be used, but I'll take the names of all concerned. Silas Craggs, Robert Montgomery, Edward Barton, James Stapleton of London. Who seconds Silas Craggs ? "

" I do," said the woman. " Yes, you can stare, but it's my job, and no one else's. Anastasia's the name—four a's."

" Craggs ? "

" Johnson. Anastasia Johnson. If you jug him, you can jug me."

" Who talked of juggin', ye fool ? " growled the Master. " Coom on, Mr. Armitage, for I'm fair sick o' this loiterin'."

The inspector fell in with the procession, and proceeded, as they walked up the hill, to bargain in his official capacity for a front seat, where he could safeguard the interests of the law, and in his private capacity to lay out thirty shillings at seven to one with Mr. Armitage.

Through the door they passed, down a narrow lane walled with a dense bank of humanity, up a wooden ladder to a platform, over a rope which was slung waist-high from four corner stakes, and then Montgomery realized that he was in that ring in which his immediate destiny was to be worked out. On the stake at one corner there hung a blue-and-white streamer. Barton led him across, the overcoat dangling loosely from his shoulders, and he sat down on a wooden stool. Barton and another man, both wearing white sweaters, stood beside him. The so-called ring was a square, twenty feet each way. At the opposite angle was the sinister figure of the Master, with his red-headed woman and a rough-faced friend to look after him. At each corner were metal basins, pitchers of water, and sponges.

During the hubbub and uproar of the entrance Montgomery was too bewildered to take things in. But now there was a few minutes' delay, for the referee had lingered behind, and so he looked quietly about him. It was a sight to haunt him for a lifetime. Wooden seats had been built in, sloping upwards to the tops of the walls. Above, instead of a ceiling, a great flight of crows passed slowly across a square of grey cloud. Right up to the topmost benches the folk were banked—broadcloth in front, corduroys and fustian behind; faces turned everywhere upon him. The grey reek of the pipes filled the building, and the air was pungent with the acrid smell of cheap, strong tobacco. Everywhere among the human faces were to be seen the heads of the dogs. They growled and yapped from the back benches. In that dense mass of humanity one could hardly pick out individuals, but Montgomery's eyes caught the brazen gleam of the helmets held upon the knees of the ten yeomen of his escort. At the very edge of the platform sat the reporters, five of them: three locals, and two all the way from London. But where was the all-important referee? There was no sign of him, unless he were in the centre of that angry swirl of men near the door.

Mr. Stapleton had stopped to examine the gloves which were to be used, and entered the building after the combatants. He had started to come down that narrow lane with the human walls which led to the ring. But already it had gone abroad that the Wilson champion was a gentleman, and that another gentleman had been appointed as referee. A wave of suspicion passed through the Croxley folk. They would have one of their own people for a referee. They would not have a stranger. His path was stopped as he made for the ring. Excited men flung themselves in front of him; they waved their fists in his face and cursed him. A woman howled vile names in his ear. Somebody struck at him with an umbrella. "Go thou back to Lunnon. We want noan o' thee. Go thou back!" they yelled.

Stapleton with his shiny hat cocked backwards, and his large, bulging forehead swelling from under it, looked round him from beneath his bushy brows. He was in the centre of a savage and dangerous mob. Then he drew his watch from his pocket and held it dial upwards in his palm.

"In three minutes," said he, "I will declare the fight off."

They raged round him. His cool face and that aggressive top-hat irritated them. Grimy hands were raised. But it was difficult, somehow, to strike a man who was so absolutely indifferent.

"In two minutes I declare the fight off."

They exploded into blasphemy. The breath of angry men smoked into his placid face. A gnarled, grimy fist vibrated at the end of his nose. "We tell thee we want noan o' thee. Get thou back where thou com'st from."

"In one minute I declare the fight off."

Then the calm persistence of the man conquered the swaying, mutable, passionate crowd.

"Let him through, mon. Happen there'll be no fight after a'."

"Let him through."

"Bill, thou loomp, let him pass. Dost want the fight declared off ?"

"Make room for the referee !—room for the Lunnon referee !"

And half pushed, half carried, he was swept up to the ring. There were two chairs by the side of it, one for him and one for the time-keeper. He sat down, his hands on his knees, his hat at a more wonderful angle than ever, impassive but solemn, with the aspect of one who appreciates his responsibilities.

Mr. Armitage, the portly butcher, made his way into the ring and held up two fat hands, sparkling with rings, as a signal for silence.

"Gentlemen !" he yelled. And then in a crescendo shriek, "Gentlemen !"

"And ladies !" cried somebody, for indeed there was a fair sprinkling of women among the crowd.

"Speak up, owd man!" shouted another. "What price pork chops?" cried somebody at the back. Everybody laughed, and the dogs began to bark. Armitage waved his hands amidst the uproar as if he were conducting an orchestra. At last the babel thinned into silence.

"Gentlemen," he yelled, "the match is between Silas Craggs, whom we call the Master of Croxley, and Robert Montgomery, of the Wilson Coal-pits. The match was to be under eleven eight. When they were weighed just now Craggs weighed eleven seven, and Montgomery ten nine. The conditions of the contest are—the best of twenty three-minute rounds with two-ounce gloves. Should the fight run to its full length it will, of course, be decided upon points. Mr. Stapleton, the well-known London referee, has kindly consented to see fair play. I wish to say that Mr. Wilson and I, the chief backers of the two men, have every confidence in Mr. Stapleton, and that we beg that you accept his rulings without dispute."

He then turned from one combatant to the other, with a wave of his hand.

III

"Montgomery—Craggs!" said he.

A great hush fell over the huge assembly. Even the dogs stopped yapping; one might have thought that the monstrous room was empty. The two men had stood up, the small white gloves over their hands. They advanced from their corners and shook hands: Montgomery gravely, Craggs with a smile. Then they fell into position. The crowd gave a long sigh—the intake of a thousand excited breaths. The referee tilted his chair on to its back legs, and looked moodily critical from the one to the other.

It was strength against activity—that was evident from the first. The Master stood stolidly upon his K-leg. It gave him a tremendous pedestal; one could hardly imagine his being knocked down. And he could pivot round upon it with extraordinary quickness ; but his advance or retreat was ungainly. His frame, however, was so much larger and broader than that of the student, and his brown, massive face looked so resolute and menacing, that the hearts of the Wilson party sank within them. There was one heart, however, which had not done so. It was that of Robert Montgomery.

Any nervousness which he may have had completely passed away now that he had his work before him. Here was something definite—this hard-faced, deformed Hercules to beat, with a career as the price of beating him. He glowed with the joy of action ; it thrilled through his nerves. He faced his man with little in-and-out steps, breaking to the left, breaking to the right, feeling his way, while Craggs, with a dull, malignant eye, pivoted slowly upon his weak leg, his left arm half extended, his right sunk low across the mark. Montgomery led with his left, and then led again, getting lightly home each time. He tried again, but the Master had his counter ready, and Montgomery reeled back from a harder blow than he had given. Anastasia, the woman, gave a shrill cry of encouragement, and her man let fly his right. Montgomery ducked under it, and in an instant the two were in each other's arms.

" Break away ! Break away ! " said the referee.

The Master struck upwards on the break, and shook Montgomery with the blow. Then it was " time." It had been a spirited opening round. The people buzzed into comment and applause. Montgomery was quite fresh, but the hairy chest of the Master was rising and falling. The man passed a sponge over his head, while Anastasia flapped the towel before him. " Good lass ! Good lass ! " cried the crowd, and cheered her.

The men were up again, the Master grimly watchful, Montgomery as alert as a kitten. The Master tried a sudden rush, squattering along with his awkward gait, but coming faster than one would think. The student slipped aside and avoided him. The Master stopped, grinned, and shook his head. Then he motioned with his hand as an invitation to Montgomery to come to him. The student did so and led with his left, but got a swinging right counter in the ribs in exchange. The heavy blow staggered him, and the Master came scrambling in to complete his advantage; but Montgomery, with his greater activity, kept out of danger until the call of "time." A tame round, and the advantage with the Master.

"T' Maister's too strong for him," said a smelter to his neighbour.

"Ay; but t'other's a likely lad. Happen we'll see some sport yet. He can joomp rarely."

"But t' Maister can stop and hit rarely. Happen he'll mak' him joomp when he gets his neif upon him."

They were up again, the water glistening upon their faces. Montgomery led instantly and got his right home with a sounding smack upon the Master's forehead. There was a shout from the colliers, and "Silence! Order!" from the referee. Montgomery avoided the counter and scored with his left. Fresh applause, and the referee upon his feet in indignation. "No comments gentlemen, if *you* please, during the rounds."

"Just bide a bit!" growled the Master.

"Don't talk—fight!" said the referee, angrily.

Montgomery rubbed in the point by a flush hit upon the mouth, and the Master shambled back to his corner like an angry bear, having had all the worst of the round.

"Where's that seven to one?" shouted Purvis, the publican. "I'll take six to one!"

There were no answers.

"Five to one!" There were givers at that. Purvis booked them in a tattered notebook.

Montgomery began to feel happy. He lay back with his legs outstretched, his back against the corner-post and one gloved hand upon each rope. What a delicious minute it was between each round. If he could only keep out of harm's way, he must surely wear this man out before the end of twenty rounds. He was so slow that all his strength went for nothing. "You're fightin' a winnin' fight—a winnin' fight," Ted Barton whispered in his ear. "Go canny; tak' no chances; you have him proper."

But the Master was crafty. He had fought so many battles with his maimed limb that he knew how to make the best of it. Warily and slowly he manœuvred round Montgomery, stepping forward and yet again forward until he had imperceptibly backed him into his corner. The student suddenly saw a flash of triumph upon the grim face, and a gleam in the dull, malignant eyes. The Master was upon him. He sprang aside and was on the ropes. The Master smashed in one of his terrible upper-cuts, and Montgomery half broke it with his guard. The student sprang the other way and was against the other converging rope. He was trapped in the angle. The Master sent in another, with a hoggish grunt which spoke of the energy behind it. Montgomery ducked, but got a jab from the left upon the mark. He closed with his man. "Break away! Break away!" cried the referee. Montgomery disengaged and got a swinging blow on the ear as he did so. It had been a damaging round for him, and the Croxley people were shouting their delight.

"Gentlemen, I will *not* have this noise!" Stapleton roared. "I have been accustomed to preside at a well-conducted club, and not at a bear-garden." This little man, with the tilted hat and the bulging forehead, dominated the whole assembly. He was like a head-master among his boys. He glared round him, and nobody cared to meet his eye.

Anastasia had kissed the Master when he resumed his seat. "Good lass. Do't again!" cried the laughing crowd, and the angry Master shook his glove at her, as she flapped her towel in front of him. Montgomery was weary and a little sore, but not depressed. He had learned something He would not again be tempted into danger.

For three rounds the honours were fairly equal. The student's hitting was the quicker, the Master's the harder. Profiting by his lesson, Montgomery kept himself in the open, and refused to be herded into a corner. Sometimes the Master succeeded in rushing him to the side-ropes, but the younger man slipped away, or closed, and then disengaged. The monotonous "Break away! Break away!" of the referee broke in upon the quick, low patter of rubber-soled shoes, the dull thud of the blows, and the sharp, hissing breath of two tired men.

The ninth round found both of them in fairly good condition. Montgomery's head was still singing from the blow that he had in the corner, and one of his thumbs pained him acutely and seemed to be dislocated. The Master showed no sign of a touch, but his breathing was the more laboured, and a long line of ticks upon the referee's paper showed that the student had a good show of points. But one of this iron-man's blows was worth three of his, and he knew that without the gloves he could not have stood for three rounds against him. All the amateur work that he had done was the merest tapping and flapping when compared to those frightful blows, from arms toughened by the shovel and the crowbar.

It was the tenth round, and the fight was half over. The betting was now only three to one, for the Wilson champion had held his own much better than had been expected. But those who knew the ring-craft as well as the staying-power of the old prize-fighter knew that the odds were still a long way in his favour.

"Have a care of him!" whispered Barton, as he sent his man up to the scratch. "Have a care! He'll play thee a trick, if he can."

But Montgomery saw, or imagined he saw, that his antagonist was tiring. He looked jaded and listless, and his hands drooped a little from their position. His own youth and condition were beginning to tell. He sprang in and brought off a fine left-handed lead. The Master's return lacked his usual fire. Again Montgomery led, and again he got home. Then he tried his right upon the mark, and the Master guarded it downwards.

"Too low! Too low! A foul! A foul!" yelled a thousand voices.

The referee rolled his sardonic eyes slowly round. "Seems to me this buildin' is chock-full of referees," said he.

The people laughed and applauded, but their favour was as immaterial to him as their anger.

"No applause, please! This is not a theatre!" he yelled.

Montgomery was very pleased with himself. His adversary was evidently in a bad way. He was piling on his points and establishing a lead. He might as well make hay while the sun shone. The Master was looking all abroad. Montgomery popped one upon his blue jowl and got away without a return. And then the Master suddenly dropped both his hands and began rubbing his thigh. Ah! that was it, was it! He had muscular cramp.

"Go in! Go in!" cried Teddy Barton.

Montgomery sprang wildly forward, and the next instant was lying half senseless, with his neck nearly broken, in the middle of the ring.

The whole round had been a long conspiracy to tempt him within reach of one of those terrible right-hand upper-cuts for which the Master was famous. For this the listless, weary bearing, for this the cramp in the thigh. When Montgomery had sprang in so hotly he had exposed himself to such a blow as neither flesh nor blood could stand. Whizzing up from below with a rigid arm, which put the Master's eleven stone into its force, it struck him under the jaw: he whirled half round, and fell a helpless and half-paralysed mass.

A vague groan and murmur, inarticulate, too excited for words, rose from the great audience. With open mouths and staring eyes they gazed at the twitching and quivering figure.

"Stand back! Stand right back!" shrieked the referee, for the Master was standing over his man ready to give him the *coup-de-grâce* as he rose.

"Stand back, Craggs, this instant!" Stapleton repeated.

The Master sank his hands sulkily and walked backwards to the rope with his ferocious eyes fixed upon his fallen antagonist. The timekeeper called the seconds. If ten of them passed before Montgomery rose to his feet, the fight was ended. Ted Barton wrung his hands and danced about in an agony in his corner.

As if in a dream—a terrible nightmare—the student could hear the voice of the timekeeper—three—four—five—he got up on his hand—six—seven—he was on his knee, sick, swimming, faint, but resolute to rise. Eight—he was up, and the Master was on him like a tiger, lashing savagely at him with both hands. Folk held their breath as they watched those terrible blows, and anticipated the pitiful end—so much more pitiful where a game but helpless man refuses to accept defeat.

Strangely automatic is the human brain. Without volition, without effort, there shot into the memory of this bewildered, staggering, half-stupefied man the one thing which could have saved him—that blind eye of which the Master's son had spoken. It was the same as the other to look at, but Montgomery remembered that he had said that it was the left. He reeled to the left side, half felled by a drive which lit upon his shoulder. The Master pivoted round upon his leg and was at him in an instant.

"Yark him, lad! yark him!" screamed the woman.

"Hold your tongue!" said the referee.

Montgomery slipped on the left again and yet again; but the Master was too quick and clever for him. He struck round and got him full on the face as he tried once more to break away. Montgomery's knees weakened under him, and he fell with a groan on the floor. This time he knew that he was done. With bitter agony he realized, as he groped blindly with his hands, that he could not possibly raise himself. Far away and muffled he heard, amid the murmurs of the multitude, the fateful voice of the timekeeper counting off the seconds.

"One—two—three—four—five—six——"

"Time!" said the referee.

Then the pent-up passion of the great assembly broke loose. Croxley gave a deep groan of disappointment. The Wilsons were on their feet, yelling with delight. There was still a chance for them. In four more seconds their man would have been solemnly counted out. But now he had a minute in which to recover. The referee looked round with relaxed features and laughing eyes, He loved this rough game, this school for humble heroes. and it was pleasant to him to intervene as a *deus ex machina* at so dramatic a moment. His chair and his hat were both tilted at an extreme angle; he and the timekeeper smiled at each other. Ted Barton and the other second had rushed out and thrust an arm each under Montgomery's knee, the other behind his loins, and so carried him back to his stool. His head lolled upon his shoulder, but a douche of cold water sent a shiver through him, and he started and looked round him.

"He's a' right!" cried the people round. "He's a rare brave lad. Good lad! Good lad!" Barton poured some brandy into his mouth. The mists cleared a little, and he realized where he was and what he had to do. But he was still very weak, and he hardly dared to hope that he could survive another round.

"Seconds out of the ring!" cried the referee. "Time!"

The Croxley Master sprang eagerly off his stool.

"Keep clear of him! Go easy for a bit," said Barton; and Montgomery walked out to meet his man once more.

He had had two lessons—the one when the Master got him into his corner, the other when he had been lured into mixing it up with so powerful an antagonist. Now he would be wary. Another blow would finish him; he could afford to run no risks. The Master was determined to follow up his advantage, and rushed at him, slogging furiously right and left. But Montgomery was too young and active to be caught. He was strong upon his legs once more, and his wits had all come back to him. It was a gallant sight—the line-of-battleship trying to pour its overwhelming broadside into the frigate, and the frigate manœuvring always so as to avoid it. The Master tried all his ring-craft. He coaxed the student up by pretended inactivity; he rushed at him with furious rushes towards the ropes. For three rounds he exhausted every wile in trying to get at him. Montgomery during all this time was conscious that his strength was minute by minute coming back to him. The spinal jar from an upper-cut is overwhelming, but evanescent. He was losing all sense of it beyond a great stiffness of the neck. For the first round after his downfall he had been content to be entirely on the defensive, only too happy if he could stall off the furious attacks of the Master. In the second he occasionally ventured upon a light counter. In the third he was smacking back merrily where he saw an opening. His people yelled their approval of him at the end of every round. Even the iron-workers cheered him with that fine unselfishness which true sport engenders. To most of them, unspiritual and unimaginative, the sight of this clean-limbed young Apollo, rising above disaster and holding on while consciousness was in him to his appointed task, was the greatest thing their experience had ever known.

But the Master's naturally morose temper became more and more murderous at this postponement of his hopes. Three rounds ago the battle had been in his hands; now it was all to do over again. Round by round his man was recovering his strength. By the fifteenth he was strong again in wind and limb. But the vigilant Anastasia saw something which encouraged her.

"That bash in t' ribs is telling on him, Jock," she whispered. "Why else should he be gulping t' brandy? Go in, lad, and thou hast him yet."

Montgomery had suddenly taken the flask from Barton's hand, and had a deep pull at the contents. Then, with his face a little flushed, and with a curious look of purpose, which made the referee stare hard at him, in his eyes, he rose for the sixteenth round.

"Game as a pairtridge!" cried the publican, as he looked at the hard-set face.

"Mix it oop, lad; mix it oop!" cried the iron-men to their Master.

And then a hum of exultation ran through their ranks as they realized that their tougher, harder, stronger man held the vantage, after all.

Neither of the men showed much sign of punishment. Small gloves crush and numb, but they do not cut. One of the Master's eyes was even more flush with his cheek than Nature had made it. Montgomery had two or three livid marks upon his body, and his face was haggard, save for that pink spot which the brandy had brought into either cheek. He rocked a little as he stood opposite his man, and his hands drooped as if he felt the gloves to be an unutterable weight. It was evident that he was spent and desperately weary. If he received one other blow it must surely be fatal to him. If he brought one home, what power could there be behind it, and what chance was there of its harming the colossus in front of him? It was the crisis of the fight. This round must decide it. "Mix it oop, lad; mix it oop!" the iron-men whooped. Even the savage eyes of the referee were unable to restrain the excited crowd.

Now, at last, the chance had come for Montgomery. He had learned a lesson from his more experienced rival. Why should he not play his own game upon him? He was spent, but not nearly so spent as he pretended. That brandy was to call up his reserves, to let him have strength to take full advantage of the opening when it came. It was thrilling and tingling through his veins, at the very moment when he was lurching and rocking like a beaten man. He acted his part admirably. The Master felt that there was an easy task before him, and rushed in with ungainly activity to finish it once for all. He slap-banged away left and right, boring Montgomery up against the ropes, swinging in his ferocious blows with those animal grunts which told of the vicious energy behind them.

But Montgomery was too cool to fall a victim to any of those murderous upper-cuts. He kept out of harm's way with a rigid guard, an active foot, and a head which was swift to duck. And yet he contrived to present the same appearance of a man who is hopelessly done. The Master, weary from his own shower of blows, and fearing nothing from so weak a man, dropped his hand for an instant, and at that instant Montgomery's right came home.

It was a magnificent blow, straight, clean, crisp, with the force of the loins and the back behind it. And it landed where he had meant it to—upon the exact point of that blue-grained chin. Flesh and blood could not stand such a blow in such a place. Neither valour nor hardihood can save the man to whom it comes. The Master fell backwards, flat, prostrate, striking the ground with so simultaneous a clap that it was like a shutter falling from a wall. A yell which no referee could control broke from the crowded benches as the giant went down. He lay upon his back, his knees a little drawn up, his huge chest panting. He twitched and shook, but could not move. His feet pawed convulsively once or twice. It was no use. He was done. "Eight—nine—ten!" said the timekeeper, and the roar of a thousand voices, with a deafening clap like the broadside of a ship, told that the Master of Croxley was the Master no more.

Montgomery stood half dazed, looking down at the huge, prostrate figure. He could hardly realize that it was indeed all over. He saw the referee motion towards him with his hand. He heard his name bellowed in triumph from every side. And then he was aware of some one rushing towards him ; he caught a glimpse of a flushed face and an aureole of flying red hair, a gloveless fist struck him between the eyes, and he was on his back in the ring beside his antagonist, while a dozen of his supporters were endeavouring to secure the frantic Anastasia. He heard the angry shouting of the referee, the screaming of the furious woman, and the cries of the mob. Then something seemed to break like an overstretched banjo-string, and he sank into the deep, deep, mist-girt abyss of unconsciousness.

The dressing was like a thing in a dream, and so was a vision of the Master with the grin of a bulldog upon his face, and his three teeth amiably protruded. He shook Montgomery heartily by the hand.

" I would have been rare pleased to shake thee by the throttle, lad, a short while syne," said he. " But I bear no ill-feelin' again' thee. It was a rare poonch that brought me down—I have not had a better since my second fight wi' Billy Edwards in '89. Happen thou might think o' goin' further wi' this business. If thou dost, and want a trainer, there's not much inside t' ropes as I don't know. Or happen thou might like to try it wi' me old style and bare knuckles. Thou hast but to write to t' ironworks to find me."

But Montgomery disclaimed any such ambition. A canvas bag with his share—one hundred and ninety sovereigns—was handed to him, of which he gave ten to the Master, who also received some share of the gate-money. Then, with young Wilson escorting him on one side, Purvis on the other, and Fawcett carrying his bag behind, he went in triumph to his carriage, and drove amid a long roar, which lined the highway like a hedge for the seven miles, back to his starting-point.

"It's the greatest thing I ever saw in my life. By George, it's ripping!" cried Wilson, who had been left in a kind of ecstasy by the events of the day. "There's a chap over Barnsley way who fancies himself a bit. Let us spring you on him, and let him see what he can make of you. We'll put up a purse--won't we, Purvis? You shall never want a backer."

"At his weight," said the publican, "I'm behind him, I am, for twenty rounds, and no age, country, or colour barred."

"So am I!" cried Fawcett; "middle-weight champion of the world, that's what he is—here, in the same carriage with us."

But Montgomery was not to be beguiled.

"No; I have my own work to do now."

"And what may that be?"

"I'll use this money to get my medical degree."

"Well, we've plenty of doctors, but you're the only man in the Riding that could smack the Croxley Master off his legs. However, I suppose you know your own business best. When you're a doctor, you'd best come down into these parts, and you'll always find a job waiting for you at the Wilson Coal-pits."

Montgomery had returned by devious ways to the surgery. The horses were smoking at the door and the doctor was just back from his long journey. Several patients had called in his absence, and he was in the worst of tempers.

"I suppose I should be glad that you have come back at all, Mr. Montgomery!" he snarled. "When next you elect to take a holiday, I trust it will not be at so busy a time."

"I am sorry, sir, that you should have been inconvenienced."

"Yes, sir, I have been exceedingly inconvenienced." Here, for the first time, he looked hard at the assistant. "Good heavens, Mr. Montgomery, what have you been doing with your left eye?"

It was where Anastasia had lodged her protest.

Montgomery laughed. "It is nothing, sir," said he.

"And you have a livid mark under your jaw. It is, indeed, terrible that my representative should be going about in so disreputable a condition. How did you receive these injuries?"

"Well, sir, as you know, there was a little glove-fight to-day over at Croxley."

"And you got mixed up with that brutal crowd?"

"I *was* rather mixed up with them."

"And who assaulted you?"

"One of the fighters."

"Which of them?"

"The Master of Croxley."

"Good heavens! Perhaps you interfered with him?"

"Well, to tell the truth, I did a little."

"Mr. Montgomery, in such a practice as mine, intimately associated as it is with the highest and most progressive elements of our small community, it is impossible——"

But just then the tentative bray of a cornet-player searching for his keynote jarred upon their ears, and an instant later the Wilson Colliery brass band was in full cry with "See the Conquering Hero Comes," outside the surgery window. There was a banner waving, and a shouting crowd of miners.

"What is it? What does it mean?" cried the angry doctor.

"It means, sir, that I have, in the only way which was open to me, earned the money which is necessary for my education. It is my duty, Doctor Oldacre, to warn you that I am about to return to the University, and that you should lose no time in appointing my successor."

2. *The Lord of Falconbridge*

A Legend of the Ring

TOM CRIBB, Champion of England, having finished his active career by his two famous battles with the terrible Molineux, had settled down into the public-house which was known as the Union Arms, at the corner of Panton Street in the Haymarket. Behind the bar of this hostelry there was a green baize door which opened into a large, red-papered parlour, adorned by many sporting prints and by the numerous cups and belts which were the treasured trophies of the famous prize-fighter's victorious career. In this snuggery it was the custom of the Corinthians of the day to assemble in order to discuss, over Tom Cribb's excellent wines, the matches of the past, to await the news of the present, and to arrange new ones for the future. Hither also came his brother pugilists, especially such as were in poverty or distress, for the Champion's generosity was proverbial, and no man of his own trade was ever turned from his door if cheering words or a full meal could mend his condition.

On the morning in question—August 25, 1818—there were but two men in this famous snuggery. One was Cribb himself—all run to flesh since the time seven years before, when, training for his last fight, he had done his forty miles a day with Captain Barclay over the Highland roads. Broad and deep, as well as tall, he was a little short of twenty stone in weight, but his heavy, strong face and lion eyes showed that the spirit of the prize-fighter was not yet altogether overgrown by the fat of the publican. Though it was not eleven o'clock, a great tankard of bitter ale stood upon the table before him, and he was busy cutting up a plug of black tobacco and rubbing the slices into powder between his horny fingers. For all his record of desperate battles, he looked what he was—a good-hearted, respectable householder, law-abiding and kindly, a happy and prosperous man.

His companion, however, was by no means in the same easy circumstances, and his countenance wore a very different expression. He was a tall and well-formed man, some fifteen years younger than the Champion, and recalling in the masterful pose of his face and in the fine spread of his shoulders something of the manly beauty which had distinguished Cribb at his prime. No one looking at his countenance could fail to see that he was a fighting man by profession, and any judge of the fancy, considering his six feet in height, his thirteen stone of solid muscle, and his beautifully graceful build, would admit that he had started his career with advantages which, if they were only backed by the driving-power of a stout heart, must carry him far. Tom Winter, or Spring—as he chose to call himself—had indeed come up from his Herefordshire home with a fine country record of local successes, which had been enhanced by two victories gained over formidable London heavy-weights. Three weeks before, however, he had been defeated by the famous Painter, and the set-back weighed heavily upon the young man's spirits.

"Cheer up, lad," said the Champion, glancing across from under his tufted eyebrows at the disconsolate face of his companion. "Indeed, Tom, you take it over-hard."

The young man groaned, but made no reply.

"Others have been beat before you and lived to be Champions of England. Here I sit with that very title. Was I not beat down Broadwater way by George Nicholls in 1805? What then? I fought on, and here I am. When the big Black came from America it was not George Nicholls they sent for. I say to you—fight on, and by George, I'll see you in my own shoes yet!"

Tom Spring shook his head. "Never, if I have to fight you to get there, Daddy."

"I can't keep it for ever, Tom. It's beyond all reason. I'm going to lay it down before all London at the Fives Courts next year, and it's to you that I want to hand it. I couldn't train down to it now, lad. My day's done."

"Well, Dad, I'll never bid for it till you choose to stand aside. After that, it is as it may be."

"Well, have a rest, Tom; wait for your chance, and, meantime, there's always a bed and crust for you here."

Spring struck his clenched fist on his knee. "I know, Daddy! Ever since I came up from Fownthorpe, you've been as good as a father to me."

"I've an eye for a winner."

"A pretty winner! Beat in forty rounds by Ned Painter."

"You had beat him first."

"And by the Lord, I will again!"

"So you will, lad. George Nicholls would never give me another shy. Knew too much, he did. Bought a butcher's shop in Bristol with the money, and there he is to this day."

"Yes, I'll come back on Painter, but I haven't a shilling left. My backers have lost faith in me. If it wasn't for you, Daddy, I'd be in the kennel."

"Have you nothing left, Tom?"

"Not the price of a meal. I left every penny I had, and my good name as well, in the ring at Kingston. I'm hard put to it to live unless I can get another fight, and who's going to back me now!"

"Tut, man! the knowing ones will back you. You're the top of the list, for all Ned Painter. But there are other ways a man may earn a bit. There was a lady in here this morning—nothing flash, boy, a real tip-top out-and-outer with a coronet on her coach—asking after you."

"Asking after me! A lady!" The young pugilist stood up with surprise and a certain horror rising in his eyes. "You don't mean, Daddy——"

"I mean nothing but what is honest, my lad. You can lay to that!"

"You said I could earn a bit!"

"So, perhaps, you can. Enough, anyhow, to tide you over your bad time. There's something in the wind there. It's to do with fightin'. She asked questions about your height, weight, and my opinion of your prospect. You can lay that my answers did you no harm."

"She ain't making a match, surely?"

"Well, she seemed to know a tidy bit about it. She asked about George Cooper, and Richmond the Black, and Tom Oliver, always comin' back to you, and wantin' to know if you were not the pick of the bunch. *And* trustworthy. That was the other point. Could she trust you? Lord, Tom, if you was a fightin' archangel you could hardly live up to the character that I've given you."

A drawer looked in from the bar. "If you please, Mr. Cribb, the lady's carriage is back again."

The Champion laid down his long clay pipe. "This way, lad," said he, plucking his young friend by the sleeve towards the side window. "Look there, now! Saw you ever a more slap-up carriage? See, too, the pair of bays—two hundred guineas apiece. Coachman, too, and footman—you'd find 'em hard to beat. There she is now, stepping out of it. Wait here, lad, till I do the honours of my house."

Tom Cribb slipped off, and young Spring remained by the window, tapping the glass nervously with his fingers, for he was a simple-minded country lad with no knowledge of women, and many fears of the traps which await the unwary in a great city. Many stories were afloat of pugilists who had been taken up and cast aside again by wealthy ladies, even as the gladiators were in decadent Rome. It was with some suspicion therefore, and considerable inward trepidation, that he faced round as a tall veiled figure swept into the room. He was much consoled, however, to observe the bulky form of Tom Cribb immediately behind her as a proof that the interview was not to be a private one. When the door was closed, the lady very deliberately removed her gloves. Then with fingers which glittered with diamonds she slowly rolled up and adjusted her heavy veil. Finally, she turned her face upon Spring.

" Is this the man ? " said she.

They stood looking at each other with mutual interest, which warmed in both their faces into mutual admiration. What she saw was as fine a figure of a young man as England could show, none the less attractive for the restrained shyness of his manner and the blush which flushed his cheeks. What he saw was a woman of thirty, tall, dark, queen-like, and imperious, with a lovely face, every line and feature of which told of pride and breed, a woman born to Courts, with the instinct of command strong within her, and yet with all the softer woman's graces to temper and conceal the firmness of her soul. Tom Spring felt as he looked at her that he had never seen nor ever dreamed of anyone so beautiful, and yet he could not shake off the instinct which warned him to be upon his guard. Yes, it was beautiful, this face—beautiful beyond belief. But was it good, was it kind, was it true ? There was some strange subconscious repulsion which mingled with his admiration for her loveliness. As to the lady's thoughts, she had already put away all idea of the young pugilist as a man, and regarded him now with critical eyes as a machine designed for a definite purpose.

" I am glad to meet you, Mr.—Mr. Spring," said she, looking him over with as much deliberation as a dealer who is purchasing a horse. " He is hardly as tall as I was given to understand, Mr. Cribb. You said six feet, I believe ? "

" So he is, ma'am, but he carries it so easy. It's only the beanstalk that looks tall. See here, I'm six foot myself, and our heads are level, except I've lost my fluff."

" What is the chest measurement ? "

" Forty-three inches, ma'am."

" You certainly seem to be a very strong young man. And a game one, too, I hope ? "

Young Spring shrugged his shoulders.

" It's not for me to say, ma'am."

" I can speak for that, ma'am," said Cribb. " You read the *Sporting Chronicle* for three weeks ago, ma'am. You'll see how he stood up to Ned Painter until his senses were beat out of him. I waited on him, ma'am, and I know. I could show you my waistcoat now—that would let you guess what punishment he can take."

The lady waved aside the illustration.

" But he was beat," said she coldly. " The man who beat him must be the better man."

" Saving your presence, ma'am, I think not, and outside Gentleman Jackson my judgment would stand against any in the ring. My lad here has beat Painter once, and will again, if your ladyship could see your way to find the battle-money."

The lady started and looked angrily at the Champion

" Why do you call me that ? "

" I beg pardon. It was just my way of speaking."

" I order you not to do it again."

" Very good, ma'am."

" I am here incognita. I bind you both upon your honours to make no inquiry as to who I am. If I do not get your firm promise, the matter ends here."

" Very good, ma'am. I'll promise for my own part, and so, I am sure, will Spring. But if I may be so bold, I can't help my drawers and potmen talking with your servants."

" The coachman and footman know just as much about me as you do. But my time is limited, so I must get to business. I think, Mr. Spring, that you are in want of something to do at present ? "

" That is so, ma'am."

"I understand from Mr. Cribb that you are prepared to fight anyone at any weight?"

"Anything on two legs," cried the Champion.

"Who did you wish me to fight?" asked the young pugilist.

"That cannot concern you. If you are really ready to fight anyone, then the particular name can be of no importance. I have my reasons for withholding it."

"Very good, ma'am."

"You have been only a few weeks out of training. How long would it take you to get back to your best?"

"Three weeks or a month."

"Well, then, I will pay your training expenses and two pounds a week over. Here are five pounds as a guarantee. You will fight when I consider that you are ready, and that the circumstances are favourable. If you win your fight, you shall have fifty pounds. Are you satisfied with the terms?"

"Very handsome, ma'am, I'm sure."

"And remember, Mr. Spring, I choose you, not because you are the best man—for there are two opinions about that—but because I am given to understand that you are a decent man whom I can trust. The terms of this match are to be secret."

"I understand that. I'll say nothing."

"It is a private match. Nothing more. You will begin your training to-morrow."

"Very good, ma'am."

"I will ask Mr. Cribb to train you."

"I'll do that, ma'am, with pleasure. But, by your leave, does he have anything if he loses?"

A spasm of emotion passed over the woman's face and her hands clenched white with passion.

"If he loses, not a penny, not a penny!" she cried. "He must not, shall not lose!"

"Well, ma'am," said Spring, "I've never heard of any such match. But it's true that I am down at heel, and beggars can't be choosers. I'll do just what you say.

I'll train till you give the word, and then I'll fight where you tell me. I hope you'll make it a large ring."

"Yes," said she; "it will be a large ring."

"And how far from London?"

"Within a hundred miles. Have you anything else to say? My time is up."

"I'd like to ask, ma'am," said the Champion, earnestly, "whether I can act as the lad's second when the time comes. I've waited on him the last two fights. Can I give him a knee?"

"No," said the woman, sharply. Without another word she turned and was gone, shutting the door behind her. A few moments later the trim carriage flashed past the window, turned down the crowded Haymarket, and was engulfed in the traffic.

The two men looked at each other in silence.

"Well, blow my dickey, if this don't beat cock-fightin'!" cried Tom Cribb at last. "Anyhow, there's the fiver, lad. But it's a rum go, and no mistake about it."

After due consultation, it was agreed that Tom Spring should go into training at the Castle Inn on Hampstead Heath, so that Cribb could drive over and watch him. Thither Spring went on the day after the interview with his patroness, and he set to work at once with drugs, dumb-bells, and breathers on the common to get himself into condition. It was hard, however, to take the matter seriously, and his good-natured trainer found the same difficulty.

"It's the baccy I miss, Daddy," said the young pugilist, as they sat together on the afternoon of the third day. "Surely there can't be any harm in my havin' a pipe?"

"Well, well, lad, it's against my conscience, but here's my box and there's a yard o' clay," said the Champion. "My word, I don't know what Captain Barclay of Ury would have said if he had seen a man smoke when he was in trainin'! He was the man to work you! He had me down from sixteen to thirteen the second time I fought the Black."

Spring had lit his pipe and was leaning back amid a haze of blue smoke.

"It was easy for you, Daddy, to keep strict trainin' when you knew what was before you. You had your date and your place and your man. You knew that in a month you would jump the ropes with ten thousand folk around you, and carrying maybe a hundred thousand in bets. You knew also the man you had to meet, and you wouldn't give him the better of you. But it's all different with me. For all I know this is just a woman's whim, and will end in nothing. If I was sure it was serious, I'd break this pipe before I would smoke it."

Tom Cribb scratched his head in puzzlement.

"I can make nothing of it, lad, 'cept that her money is good. Come to think of it, how many men on the list could stand up to you for half an hour? It can't be Stringer, 'cause you've beat him. Then there's Cooper; but he's up Newcastle way. It can't be him. There's Richmond; but you wouldn't need to take your coat off to beat him. There's the Gasman; but he's not twelve stone. And there's Bill Neat of Bristol. That's it, lad. The lady has taken into her head to put you up against either the Gasman or Bill Neat."

"But why not say so? I'd train hard for the Gasman and harder for Bill Neat, but I'm blowed if I can train with any heart when I'm fightin' nobody in particular and everybody in general, same as now."

There was a sudden interruption to the speculations of the two prize-fighters. The door opened and the lady entered. As her eyes fell upon the two men her dark, handsome face flushed with anger, and she gazed at them silently with an expression of contempt which brought them both to their feet with hangdog faces. There they stood, their long, reeking pipes in their hands, shuffling and downcast, like two great rough mastiffs before an angry mistress.

"So!" said she, stamping her foot furiously. "And this is training!"

"I'm sure we're very sorry, ma'am," said the abashed Champion. "I didn't think—I never for one moment supposed——"

"That I would come myself to see if you were taking my money on false pretences? No, I dare say not. You fool!" she blazed, turning suddenly upon Tom Spring. "You'll be beat. That will be the end of it."

The young man looked up with an angry face.

"I'll trouble you not to call me names, ma'am. I've my self-respect, the same as you. I'll allow that I shouldn't have smoked when I was in trainin'. But I was saying to Tom Cribb here, just before you came in, that if you would give over treatin' us as if we were children, and if you would tell us just who it is you want me to fight, and when, and where, it would be a deal easier for me to take myself in hand."

"It's true, ma'am," said the Champion. "I know it must be either the Gasman or Bill Neat. There's no one else. So give me the office, and I'll promise to have him as fit as a trout on the day."

The lady laughed contemptuously.

"Do you think," said she, "that no one can fight save those who make a living by it?"

"By George, it's an amateur!" cried Cribb, in amazement. "But you don't surely ask Tom Spring to train for three weeks to meet a Corinthian?"

"I will sav nothing more of who it is. It is no business of yours," the lady answered fiercely. "All I *do* say is, that if you do not train I will cast you aside and take some one who will. Do not think you can fool me because I am a woman. I have learned the points of the game as well as any man."

"I saw that the very first word you spoke," said Cribb.

"Then don't forget it. I will not warn you again. If I have occasion to find fault I shall choose another man."

"And you won't tell me who I am to fight?"

"Not a word. But you can take it from me that at your very best it will take you, or any man in England, all your time to master him. Now get back this instant to your work, and never let me find you shirking it again." With imperious eyes she looked the two strong men down, and then, turning on her heel, she swept out of the room.

The Champion whistled as the door closed behind her, and mopped his brow with his red bandanna handkerchief as he looked across at his abashed companion. "My word, lad," said he, "it's earnest from this day on."

"Yes," said Tom Spring, solemnly, "it's earnest from this day on."

In the course of the next fortnight the lady made several surprise visits to see that her champion was being properly prepared for the contest which lay before him. At the most unexpected moments she would burst into the training quarters, but never again had she to complain of any slackness upon his part or that of his trainer. With long bouts of the gloves, with thirty-mile walks, with mile runs at the back of a mailcart with a bit of blood between the shafts, with interminable series of jumps with a skipping-rope, he was sweated down until his trainer was able to proudly proclaim that "the last ounce of tallow is off him, and he is ready to fight for his life." Only once was the lady accompanied by anyone upon these visits of inspection. Upon this occasion a tall young man was her companion. He was graceful in figure, aristocratic in his bearing, and would have been strikingly handsome had it not been for some accident which had shattered his nose and broken all the symmetry of his features. He stood in silence with moody eyes and folded arms, looking at the splendid torso of the prize-fighter as, stripped to the waist, he worked with his dumb-bells.

"Don't you think he will do?" said the lady.

The young swell shrugged his shoulders. " I don't like it, *cara mia*. I can't pretend that I like it."

" You must like it, George. I have set my very heart on it."

" It is not English, you know. Lucrezia Borgia and Mediæval Italy. Woman's love and woman's hatred are always the same, but this particular manifestation of it seems to me out of place in nineteenth-century London."

" Is not a lesson needed ? "

" Yes, yes ; but one would think there were other ways."

" You tried another way. What did you get out of that ? "

The young man smiled rather grimly, as he turned up his cuff and looked at a puckered hole in his wrist.

" Not much, certainly," said he.

" You've tried and failed."

" Yes, I must admit it."

" What else is there ? The law ? "

" Good gracious, no ! "

" Then it is my turn, George, and I won't be balked."

" I don't think anyone is capable of balking you, *cara mia*. Certainly I, for one, should never dream of trying. But I don't feel as if I could co-operate."

" I never asked you to."

" No, you certainly never did. You are perfectly capable of doing it alone. I think, with your leave, if you have quite done with your prize-fighter, we will drive back to London. I would not for the world miss Goldoni in the Opera."

So they drifted away ; he, frivolous and dilettante, she with her face as set as Fate, leaving the fighting men to their business.

And now the day came when Cribb was able to announce to his employer that his man was as fit as science could make him.

" I can do no more, ma'am. He's fit to fight for a kingdom. Another week would see him stale."

The lady looked Spring over with the eye of a connoisseur.

" I think he does you credit," she said at last. " To-day is Tuesday. He will fight the day after to-morrow."

" Very good, ma'am. Where shall he go ? "

" I will tell you exactly, and you will please take careful note of all that I say. You, Mr. Cribb, will take your man down to the Golden Cross Inn at Charing Cross by nine o'clock on Wednesday morning. He will take the Brighton coach as far as Tunbridge Wells, where he will alight at the Royal Oak Arms. There he will take such refreshment as you advise before a fight. He will wait at the Royal Oak Arms until he receives a message by word, or by letter, brought him by a groom in a mulberry livery. This message will give him his final instructions."

" And I am not to come ? "

" No," said the lady.

" But surely, ma'am," he pleaded, " I may come as far as Tunbridge Wells ? It's hard on a man to train a cove for a fight and then to leave him."

" It can't be helped. You are too well known. Your arrival would spread all over the town, and my plans might suffer. It is quite out of the question that you should come."

" Well, I'll do what you tell me, but it's main hard."

" I suppose," said Spring, " you would have me bring my fightin' shorts and my spiked shoes ? "

" No ; you will kindly bring nothing whatever which may point to your trade. I would have you wear just those clothes in which I saw you first, such clothes as any mechanic or artisan might be expected to wear."

Tom Cribb's blank face had assumed an expression of absolute despair.

" No second, no clothes, no shoes—it don't seem regular. I give you my word, ma'am, I feel ashamed to be mixed up in such a fight. I don't know as you can call the thing a fight where there is no second. It's just a scramble—nothing more. I've gone too far to wash my hands of it now, but I wish I had never touched it."

In spite of all professional misgivings on the part of the Champion and his pupil, the imperious will of the woman prevailed, and everything was carried out exactly as she had directed. At nine o'clock Tom Spring found himself upon the box-seat of the Brighton coach, and waved his hand in good-bye to burly Tom Cribb, who stood, the admired of a ring of waiters and ostlers, upon the doorstep of the Golden Cross. It was in the pleasant season when summer is mellowing into autumn, and the first golden patches are seen amid the beeches and the ferns. The young country-bred lad breathed more freely when he had left the weary streets of Southwark and Lewisham behind him, and he watched with delight the glorious prospect as the coach, whirled along by six dapple greys, passed by the classic grounds of Knowle, or after crossing Riverside Hill skirted the vast expanse of the Weald of Kent. Past Tonbridge School went the coach, and on through Southborough, until it wound down a steep, curving road with strange outcrops of sandstone beside it, and halted before a great hostelry, bearing the name which had been given him in his directions. He descended, entered the coffee-room, and ordered the underdone steak which his trainer had recommended. Hardly had he finished it when a servant with a mulberry coat and a peculiarly expressionless face entered the apartment.

"Beg your pardon, sir, are you Mr. Spring—Mr. Thomas Spring, of London?"

"That is my name, young man."

"Then the instructions which I had to give you are that you wait for one hour after your meal. After that time you will find me in a phaeton at the door, and I will drive you in the right direction."

The young pugilist had never been daunted by any experience which had befallen him in the ring. The rough encouragement of his backers, the surge and shouting of the multitude, and the sight of his opponent had always cheered his stout heart and excited him to prove himself worthy of being the centre of such a scene. But this loneliness and uncertainty were deadly. He flung himself down on the horsehair couch and tried to doze, but his mind was too restless and excited. Finally he rose, and paced up and down the empty room. Suddenly he was aware of a great rubicund face which surveyed him from round the angle of the door. Its owner, seeing that he was observed, pushed forward into the room.

"I beg pardon, sir," said he, "but surely I have the honour of talking to Mr. Thomas Spring?"

"At your service," said the young man.

"Bless me! I am vastly honoured to have you under my roof! Cordery is my name, sir, landlord of this old-fashioned inn. I thought that my eyes could not deceive me. I am a patron of the ring, sir, in my own humble way, and was present at Mousley in September last, when you beat Jack Stringer of Rawcliffe. A very fine fight, sir, and very handsomely fought, if I may make bold to say so. I have a right to an opinion, sir, for there's never been a fight for many a year in Kent or Sussex that you wouldn't find Joe Cordery at the ring-side. Ask Mr. Gregson at the Chop-house in Holborn, and he'll tell you about old Joe Cordery. By the way, Mr. Spring, I suppose it is not business that has brought you down into these parts? Anyone can see with half an eye that you are trained to a hair. I'd take it very kindly if you would give me the office."

It crossed Spring's mind that if he were frank with the landlord it was more than likely that he would receive more information than he could give. He was a man of his word, however, and he remembered his promise to his employer.

"Just a quiet day in the country, Mr. Cordery. That's all."

"Dear me! I had hoped there was a mill in the wind. I've a nose for these things, Mr. Spring, and I thought I had a whiff of it. But, of course, you should know best. Perhaps you will drive round with me this afternoon and view the hop-gardens—just the right time of year, sir."

Tom Spring was not very skilled in deception, and his stammering excuses may not have been very convincing to the landlord, or finally persuaded him that his original supposition was wrong. In the midst of the conversation, however, the waiter entered with the news that a phaeton was waiting at the door. The innkeeper's eyes shone with suspicion and eagerness.

"I thought you said you knew no one in these parts, Mr. Spring?"

"Just one kind friend, Mr. Cordery, and he has sent his gig for me. It's likely that I will take the night coach to town. But I'll look in after an hour or two and have a dish of tea with you."

Outside the mulberry servant was sitting behind a fine black horse in a phaeton, which had two seats in front and two behind. Tom Spring was about to climb up beside him, when the servant whispered that his directions were that he should sit behind. Then the phaeton whirled away, while the excited landlord, more convinced than ever that there was something in the wind, rushed into his stable-yard with shrieks to his ostlers, and in a very few minutes was in hot pursuit, waiting at every cross-road until he could hear tidings of a black horse and a mulberry livery.

The phaeton meanwhile drove in the direction of Crowborough. Some miles out it turned from the high road into a narrow lane spanned by a tawny arch of beech trees. Through this golden tunnel a lady was walking, tall and graceful, her back to the phaeton. As it came abreast of her she stood aside and looked up, while the coachman pulled up the horse.

"I trust that you are at your best," said she, looking very earnestly at the prize-fighter. "How do you feel?"

"Pretty tidy, ma'am, I thank you."

"I will get up beside you, Johnson. We have some way to go. You will drive through the Lower Warren, and then take the lane which skirts the Gravel Hanger. I will tell you where to stop. Go slowly, for we are not due for twenty minutes."

Feeling as if the whole business was some extraordinary dream, the young pugilist passed through a network of secluded lanes, until the phaeton drew up at a wicket gate which led into a plantation of firs, choked with a thick undergrowth. Here the lady descended and beckoned Spring to alight.

"Wait down the lane," said she to the coachman. "We shall be some little time. Now, Mr. Spring, will you kindly follow me? I have written a letter which makes an appointment."

She passed swiftly through the plantation by a tortuous path, then over a stile, and past another wood, loud with the deep chuckling of pheasants. At the farther side was a fine rolling park, studded with oak trees, and stretching away to a splendid Elizabethan mansion, with balustraded terraces athwart its front. Across the park, and making for the wood, a solitary figure was walking.

The lady gripped the prize-fighter by the wrist. "That is your man," said she.

They were standing under the shadow of the trees, so that he was very visible to them, while they were out of his sight. Tom Spring looked hard at the man, who was still some hundreds of yards away. He was a tall, powerful fellow, clad in a blue coat with gilt buttons, which gleamed in the sun. He had white corded breeches and riding-boots. He walked with a vigorous step, and with every few strides he struck his leg with a dog-whip which hung from his wrist. There was a great suggestion of purpose and of energy in the man's appearance and bearing.

"Why, he's a gentleman!" said Spring. "Look 'ere, ma'am, this is all a bit out of my line. I've nothing against the man, and he can mean me no harm. What am I to do with him ? "

" Fight him ! Smash him ! That is what you are here for."

Tom Spring turned on his heel with disgust. " I'm here to fight, ma'am, but not to smash a man who has no thought of fighting. It's off."

" You don't like the look of him," hissed the woman. " You have met your master."

" That is as may be. It is no job for me."

The woman's face was white with vexation and anger. " You fool ! " she cried. " Is all to go wrong at the last minute ? There are fifty pounds—here they are in this paper—would you refuse them ? "

" It's a cowardly business. I won't do it."

" Cowardly ? You are giving the man two stone, and he can beat any amateur in England."

The young pugilist felt relieved. After all, if he could fairly earn that fifty pounds, a good deal depended upon his winning it. If he could only be sure that this was a worthy and willing antagonist !

" How do you know he is so good ? " he asked.

" I ought to know. I am his wife."

As she spoke she turned, and was gone like a flash among the bushes. The man was quite close now, and Tom Spring's scruples weakened as he looked at him. He was a powerful, broad-chested fellow, about thirty, with a heavy, brutal face, great thatched eyebrows, and a hard-set mouth. He could not be less than fifteen stone in weight, and he carried himself like a trained athlete. As he swung along he suddenly caught a glimpse of Spring among the trees, and he at once quickened his pace and sprang over the stile which separated them.

" Halloa ! " said he, halting a few yards from him, and staring him up and down. " Who the devil are you, and where the devil did you come from, and what the devil are you doing on my property ? "

His manner was even more offensive than his words. It brought a flush of anger to Spring's cheeks.

" See here, mister," said he, " civil words is cheap. You've no call to speak to me like that."

" You infernal rascal ! " cried the other. " I'll show you the way out of that plantation with the toe of my boot. Do you dare to stand there on my land and talk back at me ? " He advanced with a menacing face and his dog-whip half raised. " Well, are you going ? " he cried, as he swung it into the air.

Tom Spring jumped back to avoid the threatened blow.

" Go slow, mister," said he. " It's only fair that you should know where you are. I'm Spring, the prize-fighter. Maybe you have heard my name."

" I thought you were a rascal of that breed," said the man. " I've had the handling of one or two of you gentry before, and I never found one that could stand up to me for five minutes. Maybe you would like to try ? "

" If you hit me with that dog-whip, mister——"

" There, then ! " He gave the young man a vicious cut across the shoulder. " Will that help you to fight ? "

" I came here to fight," said Tom Spring, licking his dry lips. " You can drop that whip, mister, for I *will* fight. I'm a trained man and ready. But you would have it. Don't blame me."

The man was stripping the blue coat from his broad shoulders. There was a sprigged satin vest beneath it, and they were hung together on an alder branch.

" Trained, are you ? " he muttered. " By the Lord, I'll train you before I am through ! "

Any fears that Tom Spring may have had lest he should be taking some unfair advantage were set at rest by the man's assured manner and by the splendid physique, which became more apparent as he discarded a black satin tie, with a great ruby glowing in its centre, and threw aside the white collar which cramped his thick muscular neck. He then, very deliberately, undid a pair of gold sleeve-links, and, rolling up his shirt-sleeves, disclosed two hairy and muscular arms, which would have served as a model for a sculptor.

"Come nearer the stile," said he, when he had finished. "There is more room."

The prize-fighter had kept pace with the preparations of his formidable antagonist. His own hat, coat, and vest hung suspended upon a bush. He advanced now into the open space which the other had indicated.

"Ruffianing or fighting?" asked the amateur, coolly.

"Fighting."

"Very good," said the other. "Put up your hands, Spring. Try it out."

They were standing facing one another in a grassy ring intersected by the path at the outlet of the wood. The insolent and overbearing look had passed away from the amateur's face, but a grim half-smile was on his lips and his eyes shone fiercely from under his tufted brows. From the way in which he stood it was very clear that he was a past-master at the game. Tom Spring, as he paced lightly to right and left, looking for an opening, became suddenly aware that neither with Stringer nor with the redoubtable Painter himself had he ever faced a more business-like opponent. The amateur's left was well forward, his guard low, his body leaning back from the haunches, and his head well out of danger. Spring tried a light lead at the mark, and another at the face, but in an instant his adversary was on to him with a shower of sledge-hammer blows which it took him all his time to avoid. He sprang back, but there was no getting away from that whirlwind of muscle and bone. A heavy blow beat down his guard, a second landed on his shoulder, and over went the prize-fighter with the other on the top of him. Both sprang to their feet, glared at each other, and fell into position once more.

There could be no doubt that the amateur was not only heavier, but also the harder and stronger man. Twice again he rushed Spring down, once by the weight of his blows, and once by closing and hurling him on to his back. Such falls might have shaken the fight out of a less game man, but to Tom Spring they were but incidents in his daily trade. Though bruised and winded he was always up again in an instant. Blood was trickling from his mouth, but his steadfast blue eyes told of the unshaken spirit within.

He was accustomed now to his opponent's rushing tactics, and he was ready for them. The fourth round was the same as to attack, but it was very different in defence. Up to now the young man had given way and been fought down. This time he stood his ground. As his opponent rushed in he met him with a tremendous straight hit from his left hand, delivered with the full force of his body, and doubled in effect by the momentum of the charge. So stunning was the concussion that the pugilist himself recoiled from it across the grassy ring. The amateur staggered back and leaned his shoulder on a tree-trunk, his hand up to his face.

"You'd best drop it," said Spring. "You'll get pepper if you don't."

The other gave an inarticulate curse, and spat out a mouthful of blood.

"Come on!" said he.

Even now the pugilist found that he had no light task before him. Warned by his misadventure, the heavier man no longer tried to win the battle at a rush, nor to beat down an accomplished boxer as he would a country hawbuck at a village fair. He fought with his head and his feet as well as with his hands. Spring had to admit in his heart that, trained to the ring, this man must have been a match for the best. His guard was strong, his counter was like lightning, he took punishment like a man of iron, and when he could safely close he always brought his lighter antagonist to the ground with a shattering fall. But the one stunning blow which he had courted before he was taught respect for his adversary weighed heavily on him all the time. His senses had lost something of their quickness and his blows of their sting.

He was fighting, too, against a man who, of all the boxers who have made their names great, was the safest, the coolest, the least likely to give anything away, or lose an advantage gained. Slowly, gradually, round by round, he was worn down by his cool, quick-stepping, sharp-hitting antagonist. At last he stood exhausted, breathing hoarsely, his face, what could be seen of it, purple with his exertions. He had reached the limit of human endurance. His opponent stood waiting for him, bruised and beaten, but as cool, as ready, as dangerous as ever.

"You'd best drop it, I tell you," said he. "You're done."

But the other's manhood would not have it so. With a snarl of fury he cast his science to the winds, and rushed madly to slogging with both hands. For a moment Spring was overborne. Then he side-stepped swiftly; there was the crash of his blow, and the amateur tossed up his arms and fell all asprawl, his great limbs outstretched, his disfigured face to the sky.

For a moment Tom Spring stood looking down at his unconscious opponent. The next he felt a soft, warm hand upon his bare arm. The woman was at his elbow.

"Now is your time!" she cried, her dark eyes aflame. "Go in! Smash him!"

Spring shook her off with a cry of disgust, but she was back in an instant.

"I'll make it seventy-five pounds——"

"The fight's over, ma'am. I can't touch him."

"A hundred pounds—a clear hundred! I have it here in my bodice. Would you refuse a hundred?"

He turned on his heel. She darted past him, and tried to kick at the face of the prostrate man. Spring dragged her roughly away, before she could do him a mischief.

"Stand clear!" he cried, giving her a shake. "You should take shame to hit a fallen man."

With a groan the injured man turned on his side. Then he slowly sat up and passed his wet hand over his face. Finally, he staggered to his feet.

"Well," he said, shrugging his broad shoulders, "it was a fair fight. I've no complaint to make. I was Jackson's favourite pupil, but I give you best." Suddenly his eyes lit upon the furious face of the woman. "Halloa, Betty!" he cried. "So I have you to thank. I might have guessed it when I had your letter."

"Yes, my lord," said she, with a mock curtsy. "You have me to thank. Your little wife managed it all. I lay behind those bushes, and I saw you beaten like a hound. You haven't had all that I had planned for you, but I think it will be some little time before any woman loves you for the sake of your appearance. Do you remember the words, my lord? Do you remember the words?"

He stood stunned for a moment. Then he snatched his whip from the ground, and looked at her from under his heavy brows.

"I believe you're the devil!" he cried.

"I wonder what the governess will think?" said she.

He flared into furious rage and rushed at her with his whip. Tom Spring threw himself before him with his arms out.

"It won't do, sir; I can't stand by."

The man glared at his wife over the prize-fighter's shoulder.

"So it's for dear George's sake!" he said, with a bitter laugh. "But poor, broken-nosed George seems to have gone to the wall. Taken up with a prize-fighter, eh? Found a fancy man for yourself!"

"You liar!" she gasped.

"Ha, my lady, that stings your pride, does it? Well, you shall stand together in the dock for trespass and assault. What a picture—great Lord, what a picture!"

"You wouldn't, John!"

"Wouldn't I, by——! You stay there three minutes and see if I wouldn't." He seized his clothes from the bush, and staggered off as swiftly as he could across the field, blowing a whistle as he ran.

"Quick! quick," cried the woman. "There's not an instant to lose." Her face was livid, and she was shivering and panting with apprehension. "He'll raise the country. It would be awful—awful!"

She ran swiftly down the tortuous path, Spring following after her and dressing as he went. In a field to the right a gamekeeper, his gun in his hand, was hurrying towards the whistling. Two labourers, loading hay, had stopped their work and were looking about them, their pitchforks in their hands. But the path was empty, and the phaeton awaited them, the horse cropping the grass by the lane-side, the driver half asleep on his perch. The woman sprang swiftly in and motioned Spring to stand by the wheel.

"There is your fifty pounds," she said, handing him a paper. "You were a fool not to turn it into a hundred when you had the chance. I've done with you now."

"But where am I to go?" asked the prize-fighter, gazing around him at the winding lanes.

"To the devil!" said she. "Drive on, Johnson!"

The phaeton whirled down the road and vanished round a curve. Tom Spring was alone.

Everywhere over the countryside he heard shoutings and whistlings. It was clear that so long as she escaped the indignity of sharing his fate his employer was perfectly indifferent as to whether he got into trouble or not. Tom Spring began to feel indifferent himself. He was weary to death, his head was aching from the blows and falls which he had received, and his feelings were raw from the treatment which he had undergone. He walked slowly some few yards down the lane, but had no idea which way to turn to reach Tunbridge Wells. In the distance he heard the baying of dogs, and he guessed that they were being set upon his track. In that case he could not hope to escape them, and might just as well await them where he was. He picked out a heavy stake from the hedge, and he sat down moodily waiting, in a very dangerous temper, for what might befall him.

But it was a friend and not a foe who came first into sight. Round the corner of the lane flew a small dog-cart, with a fast-trotting chestnut cob between the shafts. In it was seated the rubicund landlord of the Royal Oak, his whip going, his face continually flying round to glance behind him.

"Jump in, Mr. Spring, jump in!" he cried, as he reined up. "They're all coming, dogs and men! Come on! Now, hud up, Ginger!" Not another word did he say until two miles of lanes had been left behind them at racing speed and they were back in safety upon the Brighton road. Then he let the reins hang loose on the pony's back, and he slapped Tom Spring with his fat hand upon the shoulder.

"Splendid!" he cried, his great red face shining with ecstasy. "Oh, Lord! but it was beautiful!"

"What!" cried Spring. "You saw the fight?"

"Every round of it! By George! to think that I should have lived to have had such a fight all to myself! Oh, but it was grand," he cried, in a frenzy of delight, "to see his lordship go down like a pithed ox and her ladyship clapping her hands behind the bush! I guessed there was something in the wind, and I followed you all the way. When you stopped, I tethered little Ginger in a grove, and I crept after you through the wood. It's as well I did, for the whole parish was up!"

But Tom Spring was sitting gazing at him in blank amazement.

"His lordship!" he gasped.

"No less, my boy. Lord Falconbridge, Chairman of the Bench, Deputy Lieutenant of the County, Peer of the Realm—that's your man."

"Good Lord!"

"And you didn't know? It's as well, for maybe you wouldn't have whacked it in as hard if you had; and, mind you, if you hadn't, he'd have beat you. There's not a man in this county could stand up to him. He takes the poachers and gipsies two and three at a time. He's the terror of the place. But you did him —did him fair. Oh man, it was fine!"

Tom Spring was too much dazed by what he heard to do more than sit and wonder. It was not until he had got back to the comforts of the inn, and after a bath had partaken of a solid meal, that he sent for Mr. Cordery the landlord. To him he confided the whole train of events which had led up to his remarkable experience, and he begged him to throw such light as he could upon it. Cordery listened with keen interest and many chuckles to the story. Finally he left the room and returned with a frayed newspaper in his hand, which he smoothed out upon his knee.

"It's the *Pantiles Gazette*, Mr. Spring, as gossiping a rag as ever was printed. I expect there will be a fine column in it if ever it gets its prying nose into this day's doings. However, we are mum and her ladyship is mum, and, my word! his lordship is mum, though he did, in his passion, raise the hue and cry on you. Here it is, Mr. Spring, and I'll read it to you while you smoke your pipe. It's dated July of last year, and it goes like this:—

"'FRACAS IN HIGH LIFE.—It is an open secret that the differences which have for some years been known to exist between Lord F—— and his beautiful wife have come to a head during the last few days. His lordship's devotion to sport, and also, as it is whispered, some attentions which he has shown to a humbler member of his household, have, it is said, long alienated Lady F——'s affection. Of late she has sought consolation and friendship with a gentleman whom we will designate as Sir George W——n. Sir George, who is a famous lady-killer, and as well-proportioned a man as any in England, took kindly to the task of consoling the disconsolate fair. The upshot, however, was vastly unfortunate, both for the lady's feelings and for the gentleman's beauty. The two friends were surprised in a rendezvous near the house by Lord F—— himself at the head of a party of his servants. Lord F—— then and there, in spite of the shrieks of the lady, availed himself of his strength and skill to administer such punishment to the unfortunate Lothario as would, in his own parting words, prevent any woman from loving him again for the sake of his appearance. Lady F—— has left his lordship and betaken herself to London, where, no doubt, she is now engaged in nursing the damaged Apollo. It is confidently expected that a duel will result from the affair, but no particulars have reached us up to the hour of going to press.' "

The landlord laid down the paper. "You've been moving in high life, Mr. Thomas Spring," said he.

The pugilist passed his hand over his battered face. "Well, Mr. Cordery," said he, " low life is good enough for me."

3. *The Fall of Lord Barrymore*

THERE are few social historians of those days who have not told of the long and fierce struggle between those two famous bucks, Sir Charles Tregellis and Lord Barrymore, for the Lordship of the Kingdom of St. James, a struggle which divided the whole of fashionable London into two opposing camps. It has been chronicled also how the peer retired suddenly and the commoner resumed his great career without a rival. Only here, however, one can read the real and remarkable reason for this sudden eclipse of a star.

It was one morning in the days of this famous struggle that Sir Charles Tregellis was performing his very complicated toilet, and Ambrose, his valet, was helping him to attain that pitch of perfection which had long gained him the reputation of being the best-dressed man in town. Suddenly Sir Charles paused, his *coup d'archet* half-executed, the final beauty of his neck-cloth half-achieved, while he listened with surprise and indignation upon his large, comely, fresh-complexioned face. Below, the decorous hum of Jermyn Street had been broken by the sharp, staccato, metallic beating of a door-knocker.

"I begin to think that this uproar must be at our door," said Sir Charles, as one who thinks aloud. "For five minutes it has come and gone; yet Perkins has his orders."

At a gesture from his master Ambrose stepped out upon the balcony and craned his discreet head over it. From the street below came a voice, drawling but clear.

"You would oblige me vastly, fellow, if you would do me the favour to open this door," said the voice.

"Who is it? What is it?" asked the scandalized Sir Charles, with his arrested elbow still pointing upwards.

Ambrose had returned with as much surprise upon his dark face as the etiquette of his position would allow him to show.

"It is a young gentleman, Sir Charles."

"A young gentleman? There is no one in London who is not aware that I do not show before midday. Do you know the person? Have you seen him before?"

"I have not seen him, sir, but he is very like someone I could name."

"Like someone? Like whom?"

"With all respect, Sir Charles, I could for a moment have believed that it was yourself when I looked down. A smaller man, sir, and a youth; but the voice, the face, the bearing——"

"It must be that young cub Vereker, my brother's ne'er-do-weel," muttered Sir Charles, continuing his toilet. "I have heard that there are points in which he resembles me. He wrote from Oxford that he would come, and I answered that I would not see him. Yet he ventures to insist. The fellow needs a lesson! Ambrose, ring for Perkins."

A large footman entered with an outraged expression upon his face.

"I cannot have this uproar at the door, Perkins!"

"If you please, the young gentleman won't go away, sir."

"Won't go away? It is your duty to see that he goes away. Have you not your orders? Didn't you tell him that I am not seen before midday?"

"I said so, sir. He would have pushed his way in, for all I could say, so I slammed the door in his face."

"Very right, Perkins."

"But now, sir, he is making such a din that all the folk are at the windows. There is a crowd gathering in the street, sir."

From below came the crack-crack-crack of the knocker, ever rising in insistence, with a chorus of laughter and encouraging comments from the spectators. Sir Charles flushed with anger. There must be some limit to such impertinence.

"My clouded amber cane is in the corner," said he. "Take it with you, Perkins. I give you a free hand. A stripe or two may bring the young rascal to reason."

The large Perkins smiled and departed. The door was heard to open below and the knocker was at rest. A few moments later there followed a prolonged howl and a noise as of a beaten carpet. Sir Charles listened with a smile which gradually faded from his good-humoured face.

"The fellow must not overdo it," he muttered. "I would not do the lad an injury, whatever his deserts may be. Ambrose, run out on the balcony and call him off. This has gone far enough."

But before the valet could move there came a swift patter of agile feet upon the stairs, and a handsome youth, dressed in the height of fashion, was standing framed in the open doorway. The pose, the face, above all the curious, mischievous dancing light in the large blue eyes, all spoke of the famous Tregellis blood. Even such was

Sir Charles when, twenty years before, he had by virtue of his spirit and audacity, in one short season taken a place in London from which Brummell himself had afterwards vainly struggled to depose him. The youth faced the angry features of his uncle with an air of debonair amusement, and he held towards him, upon his outstretched palms, the broken fragments of an amber cane.

"I much fear, sir," said he, "that in correcting your fellow I have had the misfortune to injure what can only have been your property. I am vastly concerned that it should have occurred."

Sir Charles stared with intolerant eyes at this impertinent apparition. The other looked back in a laughable parody of his senior's manner. As Ambrose had remarked after his inspection from the balcony, the two were very alike, save that the younger was smaller, finer cut, and the more nervously alive of the two.

"You are my nephew, Vereker Tregellis?" asked Sir Charles.

"Yours to command, sir."

"I hear bad reports of you from Oxford."

"Yes, sir, I understand that the reports *are* bad."

"Nothing could be worse."

"So I have been told."

"Why are you here, sir?"

"That I might see my famous uncle."

"So you made a tumult in his street, forced his door, and beat his footman?"

"Yes, sir."

"You had my letter?"

"Yes, sir."

"You were told that I was not receiving?"

"Yes, sir."

"I can remember no such exhibition of impertinence."

The young man smiled and rubbed his hands in satisfaction.

"There is an impertinence which is redeemed by

wit," said Sir Charles, severely. "There is another which is the mere boorishness of the clodhopper. As you grow older and wiser you may discern the difference."

"You are very right, sir," said the young man, warmly. "The finer shades of impertinence are infinitely subtle, and only experience and the society of one who is a recognized master "—here he bowed to his uncle—" can enable one to excel."

Sir Charles was notoriously touchy in temper for the first hour after his morning chocolate. He allowed himself to show it.

"I cannot congratulate my brother upon his son," said he. "I had hoped for something more worthy of our traditions."

"Perhaps, sir, upon a longer acquaintance——"

"The chance is too small to justify the very irksome experience. I must ask you, sir, to bring to a close a visit which never should have been made."

The young man smiled affably, but gave no sign of departure.

"May I ask, sir," said he, in an easy conversational fashion, "whether you can recall Principal Munro, of my college?"

"No, sir, I cannot," his uncle answered, sharply.

"Naturally you would not burden your memory to such an extent, but he still remembers you. In some conversation with him yesterday he did me the honour to say that I brought you back to his recollection by what he was pleased to call the mingled levity and obstinacy of my character. The levity seems to have already impressed you. I am now reduced to showing you the obstinacy." He sat down in a chair near the door and folded his arms, still beaming pleasantly at his uncle.

"Oh, you won't go?" asked Sir Charles, grimly.

"No, sir; I will stay."

"Ambrose, step down and call a couple of chairmen."

"I should not advise it, sir. They will be hurt."

"I will put you out with my own hands."

"That, sir, you can always do. As my uncle, I could scarce resist you. But, short of throwing me down the stair, I do not see how you can avoid giving me half an hour of your attention."

Sir Charles smiled. He could not help it. There was so much that was reminiscent of his own arrogant and eventful youth in the bearing of this youngster. He was mollified, too, by the defiance of menials and quick submission to himself. He turned to the glass and signed to Ambrose to continue his duties.

"I must ask you to await the conclusion of my toilet," said he. "Then we shall see how far you can justify such an intrusion."

When the valet had at last left the room Sir Charles turned his attention once more to his scapegrace nephew, who had viewed the details of the famous buck's toilet with the face of an acolyte assisting at a mystery.

"Now, sir," said the older man, "speak, and speak to the point, for I can assure you that I have many more important matters which claim my attention. The Prince is waiting for me at the present instant at Carlton House. Be as brief as you can. What is it that you want?"

"A thousand pounds."

"Really! Nothing more?" Sir Charles had turned acid again.

"Yes, sir; an introduction to Mr. Brinsley Sheridan, whom I know to be your friend."

"And why to him?"

"Because I am told that he controls Drury Lane Theatre, and I have a fancy to be an actor. My friends assure me that I have a pretty talent that way."

"I can see you clearly, sir, in Charles Surface, or any other part where a foppish insolence is the essential. The less you acted, the better you would be. But it is absurd to suppose that I could help you to such a career. I could not justify it to your father. Return to Oxford at once, and continue your studies."

" Impossible ! "

" And pray, sir, what is the impediment ? "

" I think I may have mentioned to you that I had an interview yesterday with the Principal. He ended it by remarking that the authorities of the University could tolerate me no more."

" Sent down ? "

" Yes, sir."

" And this is the fruit, no doubt, of a long series of rascalities."

" Something of the sort, sir, I admit."

In spite of himself, Sir Charles began once more to relax in his severity towards this handsome young scapegrace. His absolute frankness disarmed criticism. It was in a more gracious voice that the older man continued the conversation.

" Why do you want this large sum of money ? " he asked.

" To pay my college debts before I go, sir."

" Your father is not a rich man."

" No, sir. I could not apply to him for that reason."

" So you come to me, who am a stranger ! "

" No, sir, no ! You are my uncle, and, if I may say so, my ideal and my model."

" You flatter me, my good Vereker. But if you think you can flatter me out of a thousand pounds, you mistake your man. I will give you no money."

" Of course, sir, if you can't——"

" I did not say I can't. I say I won't."

" If you can, sir, I think you will."

Sir Charles smiled, and flicked his sleeve with his lace handkerchief.

" I find you vastly entertaining," said he. " Pray continue your conversation. Why do you think that I will give you so large a sum of money ? "

" The reason that I think so," continued the younger man, " is that I can do you a service which will seem to you worth a thousand pounds."

Sir Charles raised his eyebrows in surprise.

"Is this blackmail?" he inquired.

Vereker Tregellis flushed.

"Sir," said he, with a pleasing sternness, "you surprise me. You should know the blood of which I come too well to suppose that I would attempt such a thing."

"I am relieved to hear that there are limits to what you consider to be justifiable. I must confess that I had seen none in your conduct up to now. But you say that you can do me a service which will be worth a thousand pounds to me?"

"Yes, sir."

"And pray, sir, what may this service be?"

"To make Lord Barrymore the laughing-stock of the town."

Sir Charles, in spite of himself, lost for an instant the absolute serenity of his self-control. He started, and his face expressed his surprise. By what devilish instinct did this raw undergraduate find the one chink in his armour? Deep in his heart, unacknowledged to anyone, there was the will to pay many a thousand pounds to the man who would bring ridicule upon this his most dangerous rival, who was challenging his supremacy in fashionable London.

"Did you come from Oxford with this precious project?" he asked, after a pause.

"No, sir. I chanced to see the man himself last night, and I conceived an ill-will to him, and would do him a mischief."

"Where did you see him?"

"I spent the evening, sir, at the Vauxhall Gardens."

"No doubt you would," interpolated his uncle.

"My Lord Barrymore was there. He was attended by one who was dressed as a clergyman, but who was, as I am told, none other than Hooper the Tinman, who acts as his bully and thrashes all who may offend him. Together they passed down the central path, insulting the women and browbeating the men. They actually hustled me. I was offended, sir—so much so that I nearly took the matter in hand then and there."

"It is as well that you did not. The prize-fighter would have beaten you."

"Perhaps so, sir—and also, perhaps not."

"Ah, you add pugilism to your elegant accomplishments?"

The young man laughed pleasantly.

"William Ball is the only professor of my Alma Mater who has ever had occasion to compliment me, sir. He is better known as the Oxford Pet. I think, with all modesty, that I could hold him for a dozen rounds. But last night I suffered the annoyance without protest, for since it is said that the same scene is enacted every evening, there is always time to act."

"And how would you act, may I ask?"

"That, sir, I should prefer to keep to myself; but my aim, as I say, would be to make Lord Barrymore a laughing-stock to all London."

Sir Charles cogitated for a moment.

"Pray, sir," said he, "why did you imagine that any humiliation to Lord Barrymore would be pleasing to me?"

"Even in the provinces we know something of what passes in polite circles. Your antagonism to this man is to be found in every column of fashionable gossip. The town is divided between you. It is impossible that any public slight upon him should be unpleasing to you."

Sir Charles smiled.

"You are a shrewd reasoner," said he. "We will suppose for the instant that you are right. Can you give me no hint what means you would adopt to attain this very desirable end?"

"I would merely make the remark, sir, that many women have been wronged by this fellow. That is a matter of common knowledge. If one of these damsels were to upbraid him in public in such a fashion that the sympathy of the bystanders should be with her, then I can imagine, if she were sufficiently persistent, that his lordship's position might become an unenviable one."

"And you know such a woman?"

"I think, sir, that I do."

"Well, my good Vereker, if any such attempt is in your mind, I see no reason why I should stand between Lord Barrymore and the angry fair. As to whether the result is worth a thousand pounds, I can make no promise."

"You shall yourself be the judge, sir."

"I will be an exacting judge, nephew."

"Very good, sir; I should not desire otherwise. If things go as I hope, his lordship will not show face in St. James's Street for a year to come. I will now, if I may, give you your instructions."

"My instructions! What do you mean? I have nothing to do with the matter."

"You are the judge, sir, and therefore must be present."

"I can play no part."

"No, sir. I would not ask you to do more than be a witness."

"What, then, are my instructions, as you are pleased to call them?"

"You will come to the Gardens to-night, uncle, at nine o'clock precisely. You will walk down the centre path, and you will seat yourself upon one of the rustic seats which are beside the statue of Aphrodite. You will wait and you will observe."

"Very good; I will do so. I begin to perceive, nephew, that the breed of Tregellis has not yet lost some of the points which have made it famous."

It was at the stroke of nine that night when Sir Charles, throwing his reins to the groom, descended from his high yellow phaeton, which forthwith turned to take its place in the long line of fashionable carriages waiting for their owners. As he entered the gate of the Gardens, the centre at that time of the dissipation and revelry of London, he turned up the collar of his driving-cape and drew his hat over his eyes, for he had no desire to be personally associated with what might well prove to be a public scandal. In spite of his attempted disguise, however, there was that in his walk and his carriage which caused many an eye to be turned after him as he passed and many a hand to be raised in salute. Sir Charles walked on, and, seating himself upon the rustic bench in front of the famous statue, which was in the very middle of the Gardens, he waited in amused suspense to see the next act in this comedy.

From the pavilion, whence the paths radiated, there came the strains of the band of the Foot Guards, and by the many-coloured lamps twinkling from every tree Sir Charles could see the confused whirl of the dancers. Suddenly the music stopped. The quadrilles were at an end.

An instant afterwards the central path by which he sat was thronged by the revellers. In a many-coloured crowd, stocked and cravated with all the bravery of buff and plum-colour and blue, the bucks of the town passed and repassed with their high-waisted, straight-skirted, be-bonneted ladies upon their arms.

It was not a decorous assembly. Many of the men, flushed and noisy, had come straight from their potations. The women, too, were loud and aggressive. Now and then, with a rush and a swirl, amid a chorus of screams from the girls and good-humoured laughter from their escorts, some band of high-blooded, noisy youths would break their way across the moving throng. It was no place for the prim or demure, and there was a spirit of good-nature and merriment among the crowd which condoned the wildest liberty.

And yet there were some limits to what could be tolerated even by so Bohemian an assembly. A murmur of anger followed in the wake of two roisterers who were making their way down the path. It would, perhaps, be fairer to say one roisterer ; for of the two it was only the first who carried himself with such insolence, although it was the second who ensured that he could do it with impunity.

The leader was a very tall, hatchet-faced man, dressed in the very height of fashion, whose evil, handsome features were flushed with wine and arrogance. He shouldered his way roughly through the crowd, peering with an abominable smile into the faces of the women, and occasionally, where the weakness of the escort invited an insult, stretching out his hand and caressing the cheek or neck of some passing girl, laughing loudly as she winced away from his touch.

Close at his heels walked his hired attendant, whom, out of insolent caprice and with a desire to show his contempt for the prejudices of others, he had dressed as a rough country clergyman. This fellow slouched along with frowning brows and surly, challenging eyes, like some faithful, hideous human bulldog, his knotted hands protruding from his rusty cassock, his great underhung jaw turning slowly from right to left as he menaced the crowd with his sinister gaze. Already a close observer might have marked upon his face a heaviness and looseness of feature, the first signs of that physical decay which in a very few years was to stretch him, a helpless wreck, too weak to utter his own name, upon the causeway of the London streets. At present, however, he was still an unbeaten man, the terror of the Ring, and as his ill-omened face was seen behind his infamous master many a half-raised cane was lowered and many a hot word was checked, while the whisper of " Hooper ! 'Ware Bully Hooper ! " warned all who were aggrieved that it might be best to pocket their injuries lest some even worse thing should befall them. Many a maimed and disfigured man had carried away from Vauxhall the handiwork of the Tinman and his patron.

Moving in insolent slowness through the crowd, the

bully and his master had just come opposite to the bench upon which sat Sir Charles Tregellis. At this place the path opened up into a circular space, brilliantly illuminated and surrounded by rustic seats. From one of these an elderly, ringleted woman, deeply veiled, rose suddenly and barred the path of the swaggering nobleman. Her voice sounded clear and strident above the babel of tongues, which hushed suddenly that their owners might hear it.

"Marry her, my lord! I entreat you to marry her! Oh, surely you will marry my poor Amelia!" said the voice.

Lord Barrymore stood aghast. From all sides folk were closing in and heads were peering over shoulders. He tried to push on, but the lady barred his way and two palms pressed upon his beruffled front.

"Surely, surely you would not desert her! Take the advice of that good, kind clergyman behind you!" wailed the voice. "Oh, be a man of honour and marry her!"

The elderly lady thrust out her hand and drew forward a lumpish-looking young woman, who sobbed and mopped her eyes with her handkerchief.

"The plague take you!" roared his lordship, in a fury. "Who is the wench? I vow that I never clapped eyes on either of you in my life!"

"It is my niece Amelia," cried the lady, "your own loving Amelia! Oh, my lord, can you pretend that you have forgotten poor, trusting Amelia, of Woodbine Cottage at Lichfield?"

"I never set foot in Lichfield in my life!" cried the peer. "You are two impostors who should be whipped at the cart's tail."

"Oh, wicked! Oh, Amelia!" screamed the lady, in a voice that resounded through the Gardens. "Oh, my darling, try to soften his hard heart; pray him that he make an honest woman of you at last."

With a lurch the stout young woman fell forward and

embraced Lord Barrymore with the hug of a bear. He would have raised his cane, but his arms were pinned to his sides.

"Hooper! Hooper!" screamed the furious peer, craning his neck in horror, for the girl seemed to be trying to kiss him.

But the bruiser, as he ran forward, found himself entangled with the old lady.

"Out o' the way, marm," he cried. "Out o' the way, I say!" and pushed her violently aside.

"Oh, you rude, rude man!" she shrieked, springing back in front of him. "He hustled me, good people; you saw him hustle me! A clergyman, but no gentleman! What! you would treat a lady so—you would do it again? Oh, I could slap, slap, slap you!"

And with each repetition of the word, with extraordinary swiftness, her open palm rang upon the prize-fighter's cheek.

The crowd buzzed with amazement and delight.

"Hooper! Hooper!" cried Lord Barrymore once more, for he was still struggling in the ever-closer embrace of the unwieldy and amorous Amelia.

The bully again pushed forward to the aid of his patron, but again the elderly lady confronted him, her head back, her left arm extended, her whole attitude, to his amazement, that of an expert boxer.

The prize-fighter's brutal nature was roused. Woman or no woman, he would show the murmuring crowd what it meant to cross the path of the Tinman. She had struck him. She must take the consequence. No one should square up to him with impunity. He swung his right with a curse. The bonnet instantly ducked under his arm, and a line of razor-like knuckles left an open cut under his eye.

Amid wild cries of delight and encouragement from the dense circle of spectators, the lady danced round the sham clergyman, dodging his ponderous blows, slipping under his arms, and smacking back at him most successfully. Once she tripped and fell over her own skirt, but was up and at him again in an instant.

"You vulgar fellow!" she shrieked. "Would you strike a helpless woman! Take that! Oh, you rude and ill-bred man!"

Bully Hooper was cowed for the first time in his life by the extraordinary thing that he was fighting. The creature was as elusive as a shadow, and yet the blood was dripping down his chin from the effects of the blows. He shrank back with an amazed face from so uncanny an antagonist. And in the moment that he did so his spell was for ever broken. Only success could hold it. A check was fatal. In all the crowd there was scarce one who was not nursing some grievance against master or man, and waiting for that moment of weakness in which to revenge it.

With a growl of rage the circle closed in. There was an eddy of furious, struggling men, with Lord Barrymore's thin, flushed face and Hooper's bulldog jaw in the centre of it. A moment after they were both upon the ground, and a dozen sticks were rising and falling above them.

"Let me up! You're killing me! For God's sake let me up!" cried a crackling voice.

Hooper fought mute, like the bulldog he was, till his senses were beaten out of him.

Bruised, kicked, and mauled, never did their worst victim come so badly from the Gardens as the bully and his patron that night. But worse than the ache of wounds for Lord Barrymore was the smart of the mind as he thought how every club and drawing-room in London would laugh for a week to come at the tale of his Amelia and her aunt.

Sir Charles had stood, rocking with laughter, upon the bench which overlooked the scene. When at last he made his way back through the crowds to his yellow phaeton, he was not entirely surprised to find that the back seat was already occupied by two giggling females, who were exchanging most unladylike repartees with the attendant grooms.

"You young rascals!" he remarked, over his shoulder, as he gathered up his reins.

The two females tittered loudly.

"Uncle Charles!" cried the elder, "may I present Mr. Jack Jarvis, of Brasenose College? I think, uncle, you should take us somewhere to sup, for it has been a vastly fatiguing performance. To-morrow I will do myself the honour to call, at your convenience, and will venture to bring with me the receipt for one thousand pounds."

4. *The Crime of the Brigadier*

IN all the great hosts of France there was only one officer towards whom the English of Wellington's Army retained a deep, steady, and unchangeable hatred. There were plunderers among the French, and men of violence, gamblers, duellists, and *roués*. All these could be forgiven, for others of their kidney were to be found among the ranks of the English. But one officer of Massena's force had committed a crime which was unspeakable, unheard of, abominable; only to be alluded to with curses late in the evening, when a second bottle had loosened the tongues of men. The news of it was carried back to England, and country gentlemen who knew little of the details of the war grew crimson with passion when they heard of it, and yeomen of the shires raised freckled fists to Heaven and swore. And yet who should be the doer of this dreadful deed but our friend the Brigadier, Etienne Gerard, of the Hussars of Conflans, gay-riding, plume-tossing, débonnaire, the darling of the ladies and of the six brigades of light cavalry.

But the strange part of it is that this gallant gentleman did this hateful thing, and made himself the most unpopular man in the Peninsula, without ever knowing that he had done a crime for which there is hardly a name amid all the resources of our language. He died of old age, and never once in that imperturbable self-confidence which adorned or disfigured his character knew that so many thousand Englishmen would gladly have hanged him with their own hands. On the contrary, he numbered this adventure among those other exploits which he has given to the world, and many a time he chuckled and hugged himself as he narrated it to the eager circle who gathered round him in that humble café where, between his dinner and his dominoes, he would tell, amid tears and laughter, of that inconceivable Napoleonic past when France, like an angel of wrath, rose up, splendid and terrible, before a cowering continent. Let us listen to him as he tells the story in his own way and from his own point of view.

You must know, my friends, said he, that it was towards the end of the year eighteen hundred and ten that I and Massena and the others pushed Wellington backwards until we had hoped to drive him and his army into the Tagus. But when we were still twenty-five miles from Lisbon we found that we were betrayed, for what had this Englishman done but build an enormous line of works and forts at a place called Torres Vedras, so that even we were unable to get through them! They lay across the whole Peninsula, and our army was so far from home that we did not dare to risk a reverse, and we had already learned at Busaco that it was no ch ld's play to fight against these people. What could we do, then, but sit down in front of these lines and blockade them to the best of our power? There we remained for six months, amid such anxieties that Massena said afterwards that he had not one hair which was not white upon his body. For my own part, I did not worry much about our situation, but I looked after our horses, who were in great need of rest and green fodder. For the rest, we drank the wine of the country and passed the time as best we might. There was a lady at Santarem—but my lips are sealed. It is the part of a gallant man to say nothing, though he may indicate that he could say a great deal.

One day Massena sent for me, and I found him in his tent with a great plan pinned upon the table. He looked at me in silence with that single piercing eye of his, and I felt by his expression that the matter was serious. He was nervous and ill at ease, but my bearing seemed to reassure him. It is good to be in contact with brave men.

"Colonel Etienne Gerard," said he, "I have always heard that you are a very gallant and enterprising officer."

It was not for me to confirm such a report, and yet it would be folly to deny it, so I clinked my spurs together and saluted.

"You are also an excellent rider."

I admitted it.

"And the best swordsman in the six brigades of light cavalry."

Massena was famous for the accuracy of his information.

"Now," said he, "if you will look at this plan you will have no difficulty in understanding what it is that I wish you to do. These are the lines of Torres Vedras. You will perceive that they cover a vast space, and you will realize that the English can only hold a position here and there. Once through the lines you have twenty-five miles of open country which lie between them and Lisbon. It is very important to me to learn how Wellington's troops are distributed throughout that space, and it is my wish that you should go and ascertain."

His words turned me cold.

"Sir," said I, "it is impossible that a colonel of light cavalry should condescend to act as a spy."

He laughed and clapped me on the shoulder.

"You would not be a Hussar if you were not a hothead," said he. "If you will listen you will understand that I have not asked you to act as a spy. What do you think of that horse?"

He had conducted me to the opening of his tent, and there was a Chasseur who led up and down a most admirable creature. He was a dapple grey, not very tall—a little over fifteen hands perhaps—but with the short head and splendid arch of the neck which comes with the Arab blood. His shoulders and haunches were so muscular, and yet his legs so fine, that it thrilled me with joy just to gaze upon him. A fine horse or a beautiful woman, I cannot look at them unmoved, even now when seventy winters have chilled my blood. You can think how it was in the year '10.

"This," said Massena, "is Voltigeur, the swiftest horse in our army. What I desire is that you should start to-night, ride round the lines upon the flank, make your way across the enemy's rear, and return upon the other flank, bringing me news of his dispositions. You will wear a uniform, and will, therefore, if captured, be safe from the death of a spy. It is probable that you will get through the lines unchallenged, for the posts are very scattered. Once through, in daylight you can outride anything which you meet, and if you keep off the roads you may escape entirely unnoticed. If you have not reported yourself by to-morrow night, I will understand that you are taken, and I will offer them Colonel Petrie in exchange."

Ah, how my heart swelled with pride and joy as I sprang into the saddle and galloped this grand horse up and down to show the Marshal the mastery which I had of him! He was magnificent—we were both magnificent, for Massena clapped his hands and cried out in his delight. It was not I, but he, who said that a gallant beast deserves a gallant rider. Then, when for the third time, with my panache flying and my dolman streaming behind me, I thundered past him, I saw upon his hard old face that he had no longer any doubt that he had chosen the man for his purpose. I drew my sabre, raised the hilt to my lips in salute, and galloped on to my own quarters. Already the news had spread that I had been chosen for a mission, and my little rascals came swarming out of their tents to cheer me. Ah ! it brings the tears to my old eyes when I think how proud they were of their Colonel. And I was proud of them also. They deserved a dashing leader.

The night promised to be a stormy one, which was very much to my liking. It was my desire to keep my departure most secret, for it was evident that if the English heard that I had been detached from the army they would naturally conclude that something important was about to happen. My horse was taken, therefore, beyond the picket line, as if for watering, and I followed and mounted him there. I had a map, a compass, and a paper of instructions from the Marshal, and with these in the bosom of my tunic and my sabre at my side, I set out upon my adventure.

A thin rain was falling and there was no moon, so you may imagine that it was not very cheerful. But my heart was light at the thought of the honour which had been done me and the glory which awaited me. This exploit should be one more in that brilliant series which was to change my sabre into a bâton. Ah, how we dreamed, we foolish fellows, young, and drunk with success ! Could I have foreseen that night as I rode, the chosen man of sixty thousand, that I should spend my life planting cabbages on a hundred francs a month ! Oh, my youth, my hopes, my comrades ! But the wheel turns and never stops. Forgive me, my friends, for an old man has his weakness.

My route, then, lay across the face of the high ground of Torres Vedras, then over a streamlet, past a farmhouse which had been burned down and was now only a landmark, then through a forest of young cork oaks, and so to the monastery of San Antonio, which marked the left of the English position. Here I turned south and rode quietly over the downs, for it was at this point that Massena thought that it would be most easy for me to find my way unobserved through the position. I went very slowly, for it was so dark that I could not see my hand in front of me. In such cases I leave my bridle loose and let my horse pick its own way. Voltigeur went confidently forward, and I was very content to sit upon his back and to peer about me, avoiding every light. For three hours we advanced in this cautious way, until it seemed to me that I must have left all danger behind me. I then pushed on more briskly, for I wished to be in the rear of the whole army by daybreak. There are many vineyards in these parts which in winter become open plains, and a horseman finds few difficulties in his way.

But Massena had underrated the cunning of these English, for it appears that there was not one line of defence, but three, and it was the third, which was the most formidable, through which I was at that instant passing. As I rode, elated at my own success, a lantern flashed suddenly before me, and I saw the glint of polished gun-barrels and the gleam of a red coat.

"Who goes there?" cried a voice—such a voice! I swerved to the right and rode like a madman, but a dozen squirts of fire came out of the darkness, and the bullets whizzed all round my ears. That was no new sound to me, my friends, though I will not talk like a foolish conscript and say that I have ever liked it. But at least it had never kept me from thinking clearly, and so I knew that there was nothing for it but to gallop hard, and try my luck elsewhere. I rode round the English picket, and then, as I heard nothing more of them, I concluded rightly that I had at last come through their defences. For five miles I rode south, striking a tinder from time to time to look at my pocket compass. And then in an instant—I feel the pang once more as my memory brings back the moment—my horse, without a sob or stagger, fell stone dead beneath me!

I had not known it, but one of the bullets from that infernal picket had passed through his body. The gallant creature had never winced nor weakened, but had gone while life was in him. One instant I was secure on the swiftest, most graceful horse in Massena's army. The next he lay upon his side, worth only the price of his hide, and I stood there that most helpless, most ungainly of creatures, a dismounted Hussar. What could I do with my boots, my spurs, my trailing sabre? I was far inside the enemy's lines. How could I hope to get back again? I am not ashamed to say that I, Etienne Gerard, sat upon my dead horse and sank my face in my hands in my despair. Already the first streaks were whitening the east. In half an hour it would be light. That I should have won my way past every obstacle and then at this last instant be left at the mercy of my enemies, my mission ruined, and myself a prisoner—was it not enough to break a soldier's heart?

But courage, my friends! We have these moments of weakness, the bravest of us; but I have a spirit like a slip of steel, for the more you bend it the higher it springs. One spasm of despair, and then a brain of ice and a heart of fire. All was not yet lost. I who had come through so many hazards would come through this one also. I rose from my horse and considered what had best be done.

And first of all it was certain that I could not get back. Long before I could pass the lines it would be broad daylight. I must hide myself for the day, and then devote the next night to my escape. I took the saddle, holsters, and bridle from poor Voltigeur, and I concealed them among some bushes, so that no one finding him could know that he was a French horse. Then, leaving him lying there, I wandered on in search of some place where I might be safe for the day. In every direction I could see camp-fires upon the sides of the hills, and already figures had begun to move around them. I must hide quickly, or I was lost.

But where was I to hide? It was a vineyard in which I found myself, the poles of the vines still standing, but the plants gone. There was no cover there. Besides, I should want some food and water before another night had come. I hurried wildly onwards through the waning darkness, trusting that chance would be my friend. And I was not disappointed. Chance is a woman, my friends, and she has her eye always upon a gallant Hussar.

Well, then, as I stumbled through the vineyard, something loomed in front of me, and I came upon a great square house with another long, low building upon one side of it. Three roads met there, and it was easy to see that this was the posada, or wine-shop. There was no light in the windows, and everything was dark and silent, but, of course, I knew that such comfortable quarters were certainly occupied, and probably by someone of importance. I have learned, however, that the nearer the danger may really be the safer the place, and so I was by no means inclined to trust myself away from this shelter. The low building was evidently the stable, and into this I crept, for the door was unlatched. The place was full of bullocks and sheep, gathered there, no doubt, to be out of the clutches of marauders. A ladder led to a loft, and up this I climbed, and concealed myself very snugly among some bales of hay upon the top. This loft had a small open window, and I was able to look down upon the front of the inn and also upon the road. There I crouched and waited to see what would happen.

It was soon evident that I had not been mistaken when I had thought that this might be the quarters of some person of importance. Shortly after daybreak an English light dragoon arrived with a despatch, and from then onwards the place was in a turmoil, officers continually riding up and away. Always the same name was upon their lips: "Sir Stapleton—Sir Stapleton." It was hard for me to lie there with a dry moustache and watch the great flagons which were brought out by the landlord to these English officers. But it amused me to look at their fresh-coloured, clean-shaven, careless faces, and to wonder what they would think if they knew that so celebrated a person was lying so near to them. And then, as I lay and watched, I saw a sight which filled me with surprise.

It is incredible the insolence of these English! What do you suppose Milord Wellington had done when he found that Massena had blockaded him and that he could not move his army? I might give you many guesses. You might say that he had raged, that he had despaired, that he had brought his troops together and spoken to them about glory and the fatherland before leading them to one last battle. No, Milord did none of these things. But he sent a fleet ship to England to bring him a number of fox-dogs, and he with his officers settled himself down to chase the fox. It is true what I tell you. Behind the lines of Torres Vedras these mad Englishmen made the fox-chase three days in the week. We had heard of it in the camp, and now I was myself to see that it was true.

For, along the road which I have described, there came these very dogs, thirty or forty of them, white and brown, each with its tail at the same angle, like the bayonets of the Old Guard. My faith, but it was a pretty sight! And behind and amidst them there rode three men with peaked caps and red coats, whom I understood to be the hunters. After them came many horsemen with uniforms of various kinds, stringing along the roads in twos and threes, talking together and laughing. They did not seem to be going above a trot, and it appeared to me that it must indeed be a slow fox which they hoped to catch. However, it was their affair, not mine, and soon they had all passed my window and were out of sight. I waited and I watched, ready for any chance which might offer.

Presently an officer, in a blue uniform not unlike that of our flying artillery, came cantering down the road—an elderly, stout man he was, with grey side-whiskers. He stopped and began to talk with an orderly officer of dragoons, who waited outside the inn, and it was then that I learned the advantage of the English which had been taught me. I could hear and understand all that was said.

"Where is the meet?" said the officer, and I thought that he was hungering for his bifstek. But the other answered him that it was near Altara, so I saw that it was a place of which he spoke.

"You are late, Sir George," said the orderly.

"Yes, I had a court-martial. Has Sir Stapleton Cotton gone?"

At this moment a window opened, and a handsome young man in a very splendid uniform looked out of it.

"Holloa, Murray!" said he. "These cursed papers keep me, but I will be at your heels."

"Very good, Cotton. I am late already, so I will ride on."

"You might order my groom to bring round my horse," said the young general at the window to the orderly below, while the other went on down the road.

The orderly rode away to some outlying stable, and then in a few minutes there came a smart English groom with a cockade in his hat, leading by the bridle a horse—and, oh, my friends, you have never known the perfection to which a horse can attain until you have seen a first-class English hunter. He was superb: tall, broad, strong, and yet as graceful and agile as a deer. Coal black he was in colour, and his neck, and his shoulder, and his quarters, and his fetlocks—how can I describe him all to you? The sun shone upon him as on polished ebony, and he raised his hoofs in a little, playful dance so lightly and prettily, while he tossed his mane and whinnied with impatience. Never have I seen such a mixture of strength and beauty and grace. I had often wondered how the English Hussars had managed to ride over the Chasseurs of the Guards in the affair at Astorga, but I wondered no longer when I saw the English horses.

There was a ring for fastening bridles at the door of the inn, and the groom tied the horse there while he entered the house. In an instant I had seen the chance which Fate had brought to me. Were I in that saddle I should be better off than when I started. Even Voltigeur could not compare with this magnificent creature. To think is to act with me. In one instant I was down the ladder and at the door of the stable. The next I was out and the bridle was in my hand. I bounded into the saddle. Somebody, the master or the man, shouted wildly behind me. What cared I for his shouts! I touched the horse with my spurs, and he bounded forward with such a spring that only a rider like myself could have sat him. I gave him his head and let him go—it did not matter to me where, so long as we left this inn far behind us. He thundered away across the vineyards, and in a very few minutes I had placed miles between myself and my pursuers. They could no longer tell, in that wild country, in which direction I had gone. I knew that I was safe, and so, riding to the top of a small hill, I drew my pencil and note-book from my pocket and proceeded to make plans of those camps which I could see, and to draw the outline of the country.

He was a dear creature upon whom I sat, but it was not easy to draw upon his back, for every now and then his two ears would cock, and he would start and quiver with impatience. At first I could not understand this trick of his, but soon I observed that he only did it when a peculiar noise—"yoy, yoy, yoy"—came from somewhere among the oak woods beneath us. And then suddenly this strange cry changed into a most terrible screaming, with the frantic blowing of a horn. Instantly he went mad—this horse. His eyes blazed. His mane bristled. He bounded from the earth and bounded again, twisting and turning in a frenzy. My pencil flew one way and my note-book another. And then, as I looked down into the valley, an extraordinary sight met my eyes. The hunt was streaming down it. The fox I could not see, but the dogs were in full cry, their noses down, their tails up, so close together that they might have been one great yellow and white moving carpet. And behind them rode the horsemen—my faith, what a sight ! Consider every type which a great army could show : some in hunting dress, but the most in uniforms ; blue dragoons, red dragoons, red-trousered hussars, green riflemen, artillery men, gold-slashed lancers, and most of all red, red, red, for the infantry officers ride as hard as the cavalry. Such a crowd, some well mounted, some ill, but all flying along as best they might, the subaltern as good as the general, jostling and pushing, spurring and driving, with every thought thrown to the winds save that they should have the blood of this absurd fox ! Truly, they are an extraordinary people, the English !

But I had little time to watch the hunt or to marvel at these islanders, for of all the mad creatures the very horse upon which I sat was the maddest. You understand that he was himself a hunter, and that the crying of these dogs was to him what the call of a cavalry trumpet in the street yonder would be to me. It thrilled him. It drove him wild. Again and again he bounded into the air, and then, seizing the bit between his teeth, he plunged down the slope and galloped after the dogs. I swore and tugged, and pulled, but I was powerless. This English General rode his horse with a snaffle only, and the beast had a mouth of iron. It was useless to pull him back. One might as well try to keep a Grenadier from a wine bottle. I gave it up in despair, and, settling down in the saddle, I prepared for the worst which could befall.

What a creature he was ! Never have I felt such a horse between my knees. His great haunches gathered under him with every stride, and he shot forward ever faster and faster, stretched like a greyhound, while the wind beat in my face and whistled past my ears. I was wearing our undress jacket, a uniform simple and dark in itself—though some figures give distinction to any uniform—and I had taken the precaution to remove the long panache from my busby. The result was that, amidst the mixture of costumes in the hunt, there was no reason why mine should attract attention, or why these men, whose thoughts were all with the chase, should give any heed to me. The idea that a French officer might be riding with them was too absurd to enter their minds. I laughed as I rode, for, indeed, amid all the danger, there was something of comic in the situation.

I have said that the hunters were very unequally mounted, and so, at the end of a few miles, instead of being one body of men, like a charging regiment, they were scattered over a considerable space, the better riders well up to the dogs and the others trailing away behind. Now, I was as good a rider as any, and my horse was the best of them all, and so you can imagine that it was not long before he carried me to the front. And when I saw the dogs streaming over the open, and the red-coated huntsman behind them, and only seven or eight horsemen between us, then it was that the strangest thing of all happened, for I, too, went mad—I, Etienne Gerard! In a moment it came upon me, this spirit of sport, this desire to excel, this hatred of the fox. Accursed animal, should he then defy us? Vile robber, his hour was come! Ah, it is a great feeling, this feeling of sport, my friends, this desire to trample the fox under the hoofs of your horse. I have made the fox-chase with the English. I have also, as I may tell you some day, fought the box-fight with the Bustler, of Bristol. And I say to you that this sport is a wonderful thing—full of interest as well as madness.

The farther we went the faster galloped my horse, and soon there were but three men as near the dogs as I was. All thought of fear of discovery had vanished.

My brain throbbed, my blood ran hot—only one thing upon earth seemed worth living for, and that was to overtake this infernal fox. I passed one of the horsemen—a Hussar like myself. There were only two in front of me now: the one in a black coat, the other the blue artilleryman whom I had seen at the inn. His grey whiskers streamed in the wind, but he rode magnificently. For a mile or more we kept in this order, and then, as we galloped up a steep slope, my lighter weight brought me to the front. I passed them both, and when I reached the crown I was riding level with the little, hard-faced English huntsman. In front of us were the dogs, and then, a hundred paces beyond them, was a brown wisp of a thing, the fox itself, stretched to the uttermost. The sight of him fired my blood. "Aha, we have you, then, assassin!" I cried, and shouted my encouragement to the huntsman. I waved my hand to show him that there was one upon whom he could rely.

And now there were only dogs between me and my prey. These dogs, whose duty it is to point out the game, were now rather a hindrance than a help to us, for it was hard to know how to pass them. The huntsman felt the difficulty as much as I, for he rode behind them, and could make no progress towards the fox. He was a swift rider, but wanting in enterprise. For my part, I felt that it would be unworthy of the Hussars of Conflans if I could not overcome such a difficulty as this. Was Etienne Gerard to be stopped by a herd of fox-dogs? It was absurd. I gave a shout and spurred my horse.

"Hold hard, sir! Hold hard!" cried the huntsman.

He was uneasy for me, this good old man, but I reassured him by a wave and a smile. The dogs opened in front of me. One or two may have been hurt, but what would you have? The egg must be broken for the omelette. I could hear the huntsman shouting his congratulations behind me. One more effort, and the dogs were all behind me. Only the fox was in front.

Ah, the joy and pride of that moment. To know that I had beaten the English at their own sport. Here were three hundred all thirsting for the life of this animal, and yet it was I who was about to take it. I thought of my comrades of the light cavalry brigade, of my mother, of the Emperor, of France. I had brought honour to each and all. Every instant brought me nearer to the fox. The moment for action had arrived, so I unsheathed my sabre. I waved it in the air, and the brave English all shouted behind me.

Only then did I understand how difficult is this fox-chase, for one may cut again and again at the creature and never strike him once. He is small, and turns quickly from a blow. At every cut I heard those shouts of encouragement from behind me, and they spurred me to yet another effort. And then, at last the supreme moment of my triumph arrived. In the very act of turning I caught him fair with such another back-handed cut as that with which I killed the aide-de-camp of the Emperor of Russia. He flew into two pieces, his head one way and his tail another. I looked back and waved the blood-stained sabre in the air. For the moment I was exalted—superb!

Ah! how I should have loved to have waited to have received the congratulations of these generous enemies. There were fifty of them in sight, and not one who was not waving his hand and shouting. They are not really such a phlegmatic race, the English. A gallant deed in war or in sport will always warm their hearts. As to the old huntsman, he was the nearest to me, and I could see with my own eyes how overcome he was by what he had seen. He was like a man paralysed—his mouth open, his hand, with outspread fingers, raised in the air. For a moment my inclination was to return and to embrace him. But already the call of duty was sounding in my ears, and these English, in spite of all the fraternity which exists among sportsmen, would certainly have made me prisoner. There was no hope for my mission now, and I had done all that I could do. I could see the lines of Massena's camp no very great distance off, for, by a lucky chance, the chase had taken us in that direction. I turned from the dead fox, saluted with my sabre, and galloped away.

But they would not leave me so easily, these gallant huntsmen. I was the fox now, and the chase swept bravely over the plain. It was only at the moment when I started for the camp that they could have known that I was a Frenchman, and now the whole swarm of them were at my heels. We were within gunshot of our pickets before they would halt, and then they stood in knots and would not go away, but shouted and waved their hands at me. No, I will not think that it was in enmity. Rather would I fancy that a glow of admiration filled their breasts, and that their one desire was to embrace the stranger who had carried himself so gallantly and well.

5. *The King of the Foxes*

IT was after a hunting dinner, and there were as many scarlet coats as black ones round the table. The conversation over the cigars had turned, therefore, in the direction of horses and horsemen, with reminiscences of phenomenal runs where foxes had led the pack from end to end of a county, and been overtaken at last by two or three limping hounds and a huntsman on foot, while every rider in the field had been pounded. As the port circulated the runs became longer and more apocryphal, until we had the whips inquiring their way and failing to understand the dialect of the people who answered them. The foxes, too, became more eccentric, and we had foxes up pollard willows, foxes which were dragged by the tail out of horses' mangers, and foxes which had raced through an open front door and gone to ground in a lady's bonnet-box. The master had told one or two tall reminiscences, and when he cleared his throat for another we were all curious, for he was a bit of an artist in his way and produced his effects in a *crescendo* fashion. His face wore the earnest, practical, severely accurate expression which heralded some of his finest efforts.

"It was before I was master," said he. "Sir Charles Adair had the hounds at that time, and then afterwards they passed to old Lathom, and then to me. It may possibly have been just after Lathom took them over, but my strong impression is that it was in Adair's time. That would be early in the seventies—about seventy-two, I should say.

"The man I mean has moved to another part of the country, but I dare say that some of you can remember him. Danbury was the name—Walter Danbury, or Wat Danbury, as the people used to call him. He was the son of old Joe Danbury, of High Ascombe, and when his father died he came into a very good thing, for his only brother was drowned when the *Magna Charta* foundered, so he inherited the whole estate. It was but a few hundred acres, but it was good arable land, and those were the great days of farming. Besides, it was freehold, and a yeoman farmer without a mortgage was a warmish man before the great fall in wheat came. Foreign wheat and barbed wire—those are the two curses of this country, for the one spoils the farmer's work and the other spoils his play.

"This young Wat Danbury was a very fine fellow, a keen rider, and thorough sportsman, but his head was a little turned at having come, when so young, into a comfortable fortune, and he went the pace for a year or two. The lad had no vice in him, but there was a hard-drinking set in the neighbourhood at that time, and Danbury got drawn in among them; and, being an amiable fellow who liked to do what his friends were doing, he very soon took to drinking a great deal more than was good for him. As a rule, a man who takes his exercise may drink as much as he likes in the evening, and do himself no very great harm, if he will leave it alone during the day. Danbury had too many friends for that, however, and it really looked as if the poor chap was going to the bad, when a very curious thing happened which pulled him up with such a sudden jerk that he never put his hand upon the neck of a whisky bottle again.

" He had a peculiarity which I have noticed in a good many other men, that though he was always playing tricks with his own health, he was none the less very anxious about it, and was extremely fidgety if ever he had any trivial symptom. Being a tough, open-air fellow, who was always as hard as a nail, it was seldom that there was anything amiss with him ; but at last the drink began to tell, and he woke one morning with his hands shaking and all his nerves tingling like over-stretched fiddle-strings. He had been dining at some very wet house the night before, and the wine had, perhaps, been more plentiful than choice ; at any rate, there he was, with a tongue like a bath-towel and a head that ticked like an eight-day clock. He was very alarmed at his own condition, and he sent for Doctor Middleton, of Ascombe, the father of the man who practises there now.

" Middleton had been a great friend of old Danbury's, and he was very sorry to see his son going to the devil ; so he improved the occasion by taking his case very seriously, and lecturing him upon the danger of his ways. He shook his head and talked about the possibility of *delirium tremens*, or even of mania, if he continued to lead such a life. Wat Danbury was horribly frightened.

" ' Do you think I am going to get anything of the sort ? ' he wailed.

" ' Well, really, I don't know,' said the doctor, gravely. ' I cannot undertake to say that you are out of danger. Your system is very much out of order. At any time during the day you might have those grave symptoms of which I warn you.'

"'You think I shall be safe by evening?'

"'If you drink nothing during the day, and have no nervous symptoms before evening, I think you may consider yourself safe,' the doctor answered. A little fright would, he thought, do his patient good, so he made the most of the matter.

"'What symptoms may I expect?' asked Danbury.

"'It generally takes the form of optical delusions.'

"'I see specks floating all about.'

"'That is mere biliousness,' said the doctor soothingly, for he saw that the lad was highly strung and he did not wish to overdo it. 'I dare say that you will have no symptoms of the kind, but when they do come they usually take the shape of insects, or reptiles, or curious animals.'

"'And if I see anything of the kind?'

"'If you do, you will at once send for me;' and so, with a promise of medicine, the doctor departed.

"Young Wat Danbury rose and dressed and moped about the room feeling very miserable and unstrung, with a vision of the County Asylum for ever in his mind. He had the doctor's word for it that if he could get through to evening in safety he would be all right; but it is not very exhilarating to be waiting for symptoms, and to keep on glancing at your bootjack to see whether it is still a bootjack or whether it has begun to develop antennæ and legs. At last he could stand it no longer, and an overpowering longing for the fresh air and the green grass came over him. Why should he stay indoors when the Ascombe Hunt was meeting within half a mile of him? If he was going to have these delusions which the doctor talked of, he would not have them the sooner nor the worse because he was on horseback in the open. He was sure, too, it would ease his aching head. And so it came about that in ten minutes he was in his hunting-kit, and in ten more he was riding out of his stable-yard with his roan mare Matilda between his knees. He was a little unsteady in his saddle just at first, but the farther he went the better he felt, until by the time he reached the meet his head was almost clear, and there was nothing troubling him except those haunting words of the doctor's about the possibility of delusions any time before nightfall.

" But soon he forgot that also, for as he came up the hounds were thrown off, and they drew the Gravel Hanger and afterwards the Hickory Copse. It was just the morning for a scent—no wind to blow it away, no water to wash it out, and just damp enough to make it cling. There was a field of forty, all keen men and good riders, so when they came to the Black Hanger they knew that there would be some sport, for that's a cover which never draws blank. The woods were thicker in those days than now, and the foxes were thicker also, and that great dark oak-grove was swarming with them. The only difficulty was to make them break, for it is, as you know, a very close country, and you must coax them out into the open before you can hope for a run.

" When they came to the Black Hanger the field took their positions along the cover-side wherever they thought that they were most likely to get a good start. Some went in with the hounds, some clustered at the ends of the drives, and some kept outside in the hope of the fox breaking in that direction. Young Wat Danbury knew the country like the palm of his hand, so he made for a place where several drives intersected, and there he waited. He had a feeling that the faster and the farther he galloped the better he should be, and so he was chafing to be off. His mare, too, was in the height of fettle and one of the fastest goers in the county. Wat was a splendid light-weight rider—under ten stone with his saddle—and the mare was a powerful creature, all quarters and shoulders, fit to carry a lifeguardsman; and so it was no wonder that there was hardly a man in the field who could hope to stay with him. There he waited and listened to the shouting of the huntsman and the whips, catching a glimpse now and then in the darkness of the wood of a whisking tail, or the gleam of a white-and-tan side amongst the underwood. It was a well-trained pack, and there was not so much as a whine to tell you that forty hounds were working all round you.

"And then suddenly there came one long-drawn yell from one of them, and it was taken up by another, and another, until within a few seconds the whole pack was giving tongue together and running on a hot scent. Danbury saw them stream across one of the drives and disappear upon the other side, and an instant later the three red coats of the hunt-servants flashed after them upon the same line. He might have made a shorter cut down one of the other drives, but he was afraid of heading the fox, so he followed the lead of the huntsman. Right through the wood they went in a bee-line, galloping with their faces brushed by their horses' manes as they stooped under the branches. It's ugly going, as you know, with the roots all wriggling about in the darkness, but you can take a risk when you catch an occasional glimpse of the pack running with a breast-high scent; so in and out they dodged, until the wood began to thin at the edges, and they found themselves in the long bottom where the river runs. It is clear going there upon grassland, and the hounds were running very strong about two hundred yards ahead, keeping parallel with the stream. The field, who had come round the wood instead of going through, were coming hard over the fields upon the left; but Danbury, with the hunt-servants, had a clear lead, and they never lost it. Two of the field got on terms with them: Parson Geddes on a big seventeen-hand bay which he used to ride in those days, and Squire Foley, who rode as a featherweight, and made his hunters out of cast thoroughbreds from the Newmarket sales; but the others never had a look-in from start to finish, for there was no check and no pulling, and it was clear cross-country racing from start to finish. If you had drawn a line right across the map with a pencil you couldn't go straighter than that fox ran, heading for the South Downs and the sea ; and the hounds ran as surely as if they were running to view, and yet from the beginning no one ever saw the fox, and there was never a hallo forrard to tell them that he had been spied. This, however, is not so surprising, for if you've been over that line of country you will know that there are not very many people about.

" There were six of them then in the front row : Parson Geddes, Squire Foley, the huntsman, two whips, and Wat Danbury, who had forgotten all about his head and the doctor by this time, and had not a thought for anything but the run. All six were galloping just as hard as they could lay hoofs to the ground. One of the whips dropped back, however, as some of the hounds were tailing off, and that brought them down to five. Then Foley's thoroughbred strained herself, as these slim-legged, dainty-fetlocked thoroughbreds will do when the going is rough, and he had to take a back seat. But the other four were still going strong, and they did four or five miles down the river flat at a rasping pace. It had been a wet winter, and the waters had been out a little time before, so there was a deal of sliding and splashing ; but by the time they came to the bridge the whole field was out of sight, and these four had the hunt to themselves.

" The fox had crossed the bridge—for foxes do not care to swim a chilly river any more than humans do—and from that point he had streaked away southward as hard as he could tear. It is broken country, rolling heaths, down one slope and up another, and it's hard to say whether the up or down is the more trying for the horses. This sort of switchback work is all right for a cobby, short-backed, short-legged little horse, but it is killing work for a big, long-striding hunter such as one wants in the Midlands. Anyhow, it was too much for Parson Geddes' seventeen-hand bay, and, though he tried the Irish trick—for he was a rare keen sportsman

—of running up the hills by his horse's head, it was all to no use, and he had to give it up. So then there was only the huntsman, the whip, and Wat Danbury—all going strong.

"But the country got worse and worse, and the hills were steeper and more thickly covered in heather and bracken. The horses were over their hocks all the time, and the place was pitted with rabbit-holes; but the hounds were still streaming along, and the riders could not afford to pick their steps. As they raced down one slope, the hounds were always flowing up the opposite one, until it looked like that game where the one figure in falling makes the other one rise. But never a glimpse did they get of the fox, although they knew very well that he must be only a very short way ahead for the scent to lie so strong. And then Wat Danbury heard a crash and a thud at his elbow, and looking round he saw a pair of white cords and top-boots kicking out of a tussock of brambles. The whip's horse had stumbled, and the whip was out of the running. Danbury and the huntsman eased down for an instant; and then, seeing the man staggering to his feet all right, they turned and settled into their saddles once more.

"Joe Clarke, the huntsman, was a famous old rider, known for five counties round; but he reckoned upon his second horse, and the second horses had all been left many miles behind. However, the one he was riding was good enough for anything with such a horseman upon his back, and he was going as well as when he started. As to Wat Danbury, he was going better. With every stride his own feelings improved, and the mind of the rider has its influence upon the mind of the horse. The stout little roan was gathering its muscular limbs under it and stretching to the gallop as if it were steel and whalebone instead of flesh and blood. Wat had never come to the end of its powers yet, and to-day he had such a chance of testing them as he had never had before.

"There was a pasture country beyond the heather

slopes, and for several miles the two riders were either losing ground as they fumbled with their crop-handles at the bars of gates, or gaining it again as they galloped over the fields. Those were the days before this accursed wire came into the country, and you could generally break a hedge where you could not fly it, so they did not trouble the gates more than they could help. Then they were down in a hard lane, where they had to slacken their pace, and through a farm where a man came shouting excitedly after them ; but they had no time to stop and listen to him, for the hounds were on some ploughland, only two fields ahead. It was sloping upwards, that ploughland, and the horses were over their fetlocks in the red, soft soil. When they reached the top they were blowing badly, but a grand valley sloped before them, leading up to the open country of the South Downs. Between, there lay a belt of pinewoods, into which the hounds were streaming, running now in a long straggling line and shedding one here and one there as they ran. You could see the white-and-tan dots here and there where the limpers were tailing away. But half the pack were still going well, though the pace and distance had both been tremendous—two clear hours now without a check.

" There was a drive through the pinewood—one of those green, slightly-rutted drives where a horse can get the last yard out of itself, for the ground is hard enough to give him clean going and yet springy enough to help him. Wat Danbury got alongside of the huntsman and they galloped together with their stirrup-irons touching, and the hounds within a hundred yards of them.

" ' We have it all to ourselves,' said he.

" ' Yes, sir, we've shook off the lot of 'em this time,' said old Joe Clarke. ' If we get this fox it's worth while 'aving 'im skinned an' stuffed, for 'e's a curiosity, 'e is.'

" ' It's the fastest run I ever had in my life ! ' cried Danbury.

" 'And the fastest that ever I 'ad, an' that means more,' said the old huntsman. 'But what licks me is that we've never 'ad a look at the beast. 'E must leave an amazin' scent be'ind 'im when these 'ounds can follow 'm like this, and yet none of us have seen 'im when we've 'ad a clear 'alf-mile view in front of us.'

" 'I expect we'll have a view of him presently,' said Danbury; and in his mind he added, 'at least, I shall,' for the huntsman's horse was gasping as it ran, and the white foam was pouring down it like the side of a washing-tub.

"They had followed the hounds on to one of the side tracks which led out of the main drive, and that divided into a smaller track still, where the branches switched across their faces as they went and there was barely room for one horse at a time. Wat Danbury took the lead, and he heard the huntsman's horse clumping along heavily behind him, while his own mare was going with less spring than when she had started. She answered to a touch of his crop or spur, however, and he felt that there was something still left to draw upon. And then he looked up, and there was a heavy wooden stile at the end of the narrow track, with a lane of stiff young saplings leading down to it, which was far too thick to break through. The hounds were running clear upon the grassland on the other side, and you were bound either to get over that stile or lose sight of them, for the pace was too hot to let you go round.

"Well, Wat Danbury was not the lad to flinch, and at it he went full split, like a man who means what he is doing. She rose gallantly to it, rapped it hard with her front hoof, shook him on to her withers, recovered herself, and was over. Wat had hardly got back into his saddle when there was a clatter behind him like the fall of a woodstack, and there was the top bar in splinters, the horse on its belly, and the huntsman on hands and knees half a dozen yards in front of him. Wat pulled up for an instant, for the fall was a smasher; but he saw old Joe spring to his feet and get to his horse's bridle. The horse staggered up, but the moment it put one foot in front of the other Wat saw that it was hopelessly lame —a slipped shoulder and a six weeks' job. There was nothing he could do, and Joe was shouting to him not to lose the hounds, so off he went again, the one solitary survivor of the whole hunt. When a man finds himself there, he can retire from fox-hunting, for he has tasted the highest which it has to offer. I remember once when I was out with the Royal Surrey—but I'll tell you that story afterwards.

"The pack, or what was left of them, had got a bit ahead during this time ; but he had a clear view of them on the downland, and the mare seemed full of pride at being the only one left, for she was stepping out rarely and tossing her head as she went. There were two miles over the green shoulder of a hill, a rattle down a stony, deep-rutted country lane, where the mare stumbled and nearly came down, a jump over a five-foot brook, a cut through a hazel copse, another dose of heavy plough-land, a couple of gates to open, and then the green, unbroken Downs beyond. 'Well,' said Wat Danbury to himself, 'I'll see this fox run into or I shall see it drowned, for it's all clear going now between this and the chalk cliffs which line the sea.'

"But he was wrong in that, as he speedily discovered. In all the little hollows of the Downs at that part there are plantations of fir-woods, some of which have grown to a good size. You do not see them until you come upon the edge of the valleys in which they lie. Danbury was galloping hard over the short-springy turf when he came over the lip of one of these depressions, and there was the dark clump of wood lying in front of and beneath him. There were only a dozen hounds still running, and they were just disappearing among the trees. The sunlight was shining straight upon the long, olive-green slopes which curved down towards this wood, and Danbury, who had the eyes of a hawk, swept them over this great expanse ; but there was nothing moving upon it. A few sheep were grazing far up on the right, but there was no othersight of any living creature. He was certain then that he was very near to the end, for either the fox must have gone to ground in the wood or the hounds' noses must be at his very brush. The mare seemed to know also what that great empty sweep of countryside meant, for she quickened her stride, and a few minutes afterwards Danbury was galloping into the fir-wood.

"He had come from bright sunshine, but the wood was very closely planted, and so dim that he could hardly see to right or to left out of the narrow path down which he was riding. You know what a solemn, churchyardy sort of place a fir-wood is. I suppose it is the absence of any undergrowth, and the fact that the trees never move at all. At any rate a kind of chill suddenly struck Wat Danbury, and it flashed through his mind that there had been some very singular points about this run—its length and its straightness, and the fact that from the first find no one had ever caught a glimpse of the creature. Some silly talk which had been going round the country about the king of the foxes—a sort of demon fox, so fast that it could outrun any pack, and so fierce that they could do nothing with it if they overtook it—suddenly came back into his mind, and it did not seem so laughable now in the dim fir-wood as it had done when the story had been told over the wine and cigars. The nervousness wnich had been on him in the morning, and which he had hoped that he had shaken off, swept over him again in an overpowering wave. He had been so proud of being alone, and yet he would have given ten pounds now to have had Joe Clarke's homely face beside him. And then, just at that moment, there broke out from the thickest part of the wood the most frantic hullaballoo that ever he had heard in his life. The hounds had run into their fox.

"Well, you know, or you ought to know, what your duty is in such a case. You have to be whip, huntsman, and everything else if you are the first man up. You get in among the hounds, lash them off, and keep the brush and pads from being destroyed. Of course, Wat Danbury knew all about that, and he tried to force his mare through the trees to the place where all this hideous screaming and howling came from, but the wood was so thick that it was impossible to ride it. He sprang off, therefore, left the mare standing, and broke his way through as best he could with his hunting-lash ready over his shoulder. But as he ran forward he felt his flesh go cold and creepy all over. He had heard hounds run into foxes many times before, but he had never heard such sounds as these. They were not the cries of triumph, but of fear. Every now and then came a shrill yelp of mortal agony. Holding his breath, he ran on until he broke through the interlacing branches and found himself in a little clearing with the hounds all crowding round a patch of tangled bramble at the farther end.

"When he first caught sight of them the hounds were standing in a half-circle round this bramble-patch with their backs bristling and their jaws gaping. In front of the brambles lay one of them with his throat torn out, all crimson and white-and-tan. Wat came running out into the clearing, and at the sight of him the hounds took heart again, and one of them sprang with a growl into the bushes. At the same instant a creature the size of a donkey jumped on to its feet, a huge grey head, with monstrous glistening fangs, and tapering fox jaws, shot out from among the branches, and the hound was thrown several feet into the air, and fell howling among the cover. Then there was a clashing snap like a rat-trap closing, and the howls sharpened into a scream and then were still.

"Danbury had been on the look-out for symptoms all day, and now he had found them. He looked once more at the thicket, saw a pair of savage red eyes fixed upon him, and fairly took to his heels. It might only be a passing delusion, or it might be a permanent mania of which the doctor had spoken, but, anyhow, the thing to do was to get back to bed and to quiet, and to hope for the best. He forgot the hounds, the hunt, and everything else in his desperate fears for his own reason. He sprang upon his mare, galloped her madly over the downs, and only stopped when he found himself at a country station. There he left his mare at the inn, and made back for home as quickly as steam would take him. It was evening before he got there, shivering with apprehension and seeing those red eyes and savage teeth at every turn. He went straight to bed and sent for Dr. Middleton.

"'I've got 'em, doctor,' said he. 'It came about exactly as you said—strange creatures, optical delusions, and everything. All I ask you now is to save my reason.'

"The doctor listened to his story and was shocked as he heard it.

"'It appears to be a very clear case,' said he. 'This must be a lesson to you for life.'

"'Never a drop again if I only come safely through this,' cried Wat Danbury.

"'Well, my dear boy, if you will stick to that it may prove a blessing in disguise. But the difficulty in this case is to know where fact ends and fancy begins. You see, it is not as if there was only one delusion. There have been several. The dead dogs, for example, must have been one as well as the creature in the bush.'

"'I saw it all as clearly as I see you.'

"'One of the characteristics of this form of delirium is that what you see is even clearer than reality. I was wondering whether the whole run was not a delusion also.'

"Wat Danbury pointed to his hunting-boots still lying upon the floor, flecked with the splashings of two counties.

"'Hum! that looks very real, certainly. No doubt, in your weak state, you over-exerted yourself and so brought this attack upon yourself. Well, whatever the cause, our treatment is clear. You will take the soothing mixture which I will send to you, and we shall put two leeches upon your temples to-night to relieve any congestion of the brain.'

"So Wat Danbury spent the night in tossing about and reflecting what a sensitive thing this machinery of ours is, and how very foolish it is to play tricks with what is so easily put out of gear and so difficult to mend. And so he repeated and repeated his oath that this first lesson should be his last, and that from that time forward he would be a sober, hard-working yeoman as his father had been before him. So he lay, tossing and still repentant, when his door flew open in the morning and in rushed the doctor with a newspaper crumpled up in his hand.

"'My dear boy,' he cried. 'I owe you a thousand apologies. You're the most ill-used lad and I the greatest numskull in the county. Listen to this!' And he sat down upon the side of the bed, flattened out his paper upon his knee, and began to read.

"The paragraph was headed, 'Disaster to the Ascombe Hounds,' and it went on to say that four of the hounds, shockingly torn and mangled, had been found in Winton Fir Wood upon the South Downs. The run had been so severe that half the pack were lamed; but the four found in the wood were actually dead, although the cause of their extraordinary injuries was still unknown. 'So you see,' said the doctor, looking up, 'that I was wrong when I put the dead hounds among the delusions.'

"'But the cause?' cried Wat.

"'Well, I think we may guess the cause from an item which has been inserted just as the paper went to press. "Late last night, Mr. Brown, of Smither's Farm, to the east of Hastings, perceived what he imagined to be an enormous dog worrying one of his sheep. He shot the creature, which proves to be a grey Siberian wolf of the variety known as *Lupus Giganticus*. It is supposed to have escaped from some travelling menagerie."

"That's the story, gentlemen, and Wat Danbury stuck to his good resolutions, for the fright which he had cured him of all wish to run such a risk again; and he never touches anything stronger than lime-juice—at least, he hadn't before he left this part of the country, five years ago next Lady Day."

6. *The Bully of Brocas Court*

THAT year—it was in 1878—the South Midland Yeomanry were out near Luton, and the real question which appealed to every man in the great camp was not how to prepare for a possible European war, but the far more vital one how to get a man who could stand up for ten rounds to Farrier-Sergeant Burton. Slogger Burton was a fine upstanding fourteen stone of bone and brawn, with a smack in either hand which would leave any ordinary mortal senseless. A match must be found for him somewhere or his head would outgrow his dragoon helmet. Therefore Sir Fred. Milburn, better known as Mumbles, was dispatched to London to find if among the fancy there was no one who would make a journey in order to take down the number of the bold dragoon.

They were bad days, those, in the prize-ring. The old knuckle-fighting had died out in scandal and disgrace, smothered by the pestilent crowd of betting men and ruffians of all sorts who hung upon the edge of the movement and brought disgrace and ruin upon the decent fighting men, who were often humble heroes whose gallantry has never been surpassed. An honest sportsman who desired to see a fight was usually set upon by villains, against whom he had no redress, since he was himself engaged on what was technically an illegal action. He was stripped in the open street, his purse taken, and his head split open if he ventured to resist. The ringside could only be reached by men who were prepared to fight their way there with cudgels and hunting-crops. No wonder that the classic sport was attended now by those only who had nothing to lose.

On the other hand, the era of the reserved building and the legal glove-fight had not yet arisen, and the cult was in a strange intermediate condition. It was impossible to regulate it, and equally impossible to abolish it, since nothing appeals more directly and powerfully to the average Briton. Therefore there were scrambling contests in stableyards and barns, hurried visits to France, secret meetings at dawn in wild parts of the country, and all manner of evasions and experiments. The men themselves became as unsatisfactory as their surroundings. There could be no honest open contest, and the loudest bragger talked his way to the top of the list. Only across the Atlantic had the huge figure of John Lawrence Sullivan appeared, who was destined to be the last of the earlier system and the first of the later one.

Things being in this condition, the sporting Yeomanry Captain found it no easy matter among the boxing saloons and sporting pubs of London to find a man who could be relied upon to give a good account of the huge Farrier-Sergeant. Heavy-weights were at a premium. Finally his choice fell upon Alf Stevens of Kentish Town, an excellent rising middle-weight who had never yet known defeat and had indeed some claims to the championship. His professional experience and craft would surely make up for the three stone of weight which separated him from the formidable dragoon. It was in this hope that Sir Fred. Milburn engaged him, and proceeded to convey him in his dog-cart behind a pair of spanking greys to the camp of the Yeomen. They were to start one evening, drive up the Great North Road, sleep at St. Albans, and finish their journey next day.

The prize-fighter met the sporting Baronet at the Golden Cross, where Bates, the little groom, was standing at the head of the spirited horses. Stevens, a pale-faced, clean-cut young fellow, mounted beside his employer and waved his hand to a little knot of fighting men, rough, collarless, reefer-coated fellows who had gathered to bid their comrade good-bye. " Good luck, Alf ! " came in a hoarse chorus as the boy released the horses' heads and sprang in behind, while the high dog-cart swung swiftly round the curve into Trafalgar Square.

Sir Frederick was so busy steering among the traffic in Oxford Street and the Edgware Road that he had little thought for anything else, but when he got into the edges of the country near Hendon, and the hedges had at last taken the place of that endless panorama of brick dwellings, he let his horses go easy with a loose rein while he turned his attention to the young man at his side. He had found him by correspondence and recommendation, so that he had some curiosity now in looking him over. Twilight was already falling and the light dim, but what the Baronet saw pleased him well. The man was a fighter every inch, clean-cut, deep-chested, with the long straight cheek and deep-set eye which goes with an obstinate courage. Above all, he was a man who had never yet met his master and was still upheld by the deep sustaining confidence which is never quite the same after a single defeat. The Baronet chuckled as he realized what a surprise packet was being carried north for the Farrier-Sergeant.

" I suppose you are in some sort of training, Stevens ? " he remarked, turning to his companion.

" Yes, sir ; I am fit to fight for my life."

" So I should judge by the look of you."

" I live regular all the time, sir, but I was matched against Mike Connor for this last week-end and scaled down to eleven four. Then he paid forfeit, and here I am at the top of my form."

" That's lucky. You'll need it all against a man who has a pull of three stone and four inches."

The young man smiled.

"I have given greater odds than that, sir."

"I dare say. But he's a game man as well."

"Well, sir, one can but do one's best."

The Baronet liked the modest but assured tone of the young pugilist. Suddenly an amusing thought struck him, and he burst out laughing.

"By Jove!" he cried. "What a lark if the Bully is out to-night!"

Alf Stevens pricked up his ears.

"Who might he be, sir?"

"Well, that's what the folk are asking. Some say they've seen him, and some say he's a fairy-tale, but there's good evidence that he is a real man with a pair of rare good fists that leave their marks behind him."

"And where might he live?"

"On this very road. It's between Finchley and Elstree, as I've heard. There are two chaps, and they come out on nights when the moon is at full and challenge the passers-by to fight in the old style. One fights and the other picks up. By George! the fellow *can* fight, too, by all accounts. Chaps have been found in the morning with their faces all cut to ribbons to show that the Bully had been at work upon them."

Alf Stevens was full of interest.

"I've always wanted to try an old-style battle, sir, but it never chanced to come my way. I believe it would suit me better than the gloves."

"Then you won't refuse the Bully?"

"Refuse him! I'd go ten mile to meet him."

"By George! it would be great!" cried the Baronet. "Well, the moon is at the full, and the place should be about here."

"If he's as good as you say," Stevens remarked, "he should be known in the ring, unless he is just an amateur who amuses himself like that."

"Some think he's an ostler, or maybe a racing man from the training stables over yonder. Where there are horses there is boxing. If you can believe the accounts.

there is something a bit queer and outlandish about the fellow. Hi ! Look out, damn you, look out ! "

The Baronet's voice had risen to a sudden screech of surprise and of anger. At this point the road dips down into a hollow, heavily shaded by trees, so that at night it arches across like the mouth of a tunnel. At the foot of the slope there stand two great stone pillars, which, as viewed by daylight, are lichen-stained and weathered, with heraldic devices on each which are so mutilated by time that they are mere protuberances of stone. An iron gate of elegant design, hanging loosely upon rusted hinges, proclaims both the past glories and the present decay of Brocas Old Hall, which lies at the end of the weed-encumbered avenue. It was from the shadow of this ancient gateway that an active figure had sprung suddenly into the centre of the road and had, with great dexterity, held up the horses, who ramped and pawed as they were forced back upon their haunches.

" Here, Rowe, you 'old the tits, will ye ? " cried a high strident voice. " I've a little word to say to this 'ere slap-up Corinthian before 'e goes any farther."

A second man had emerged from the shadows and without a word took hold of the horses' heads. He was a short, thick fellow, dressed in a curious brown many-caped overcoat, which came to his knees, with gaiters and boots beneath it. He wore no hat, and those in the dog-cart had a view, as he came in front of the side-lamps, of a surly red face with an ill-fitting lower lip clean shaven, and a high black cravat swathed tightly under the chin. As he gripped the leathers his more active comrade sprang forward and rested a bony hand upon the side of the splashboard while he looked keenly up with a pair of fierce blue eyes at the faces of the two travellers, the light beating full upon his own features. He wore a hat low upon his brow, but in spite of its shadow both the Baronet and the pugilist could see enough to shrink from him, for it was an evil face, evil but very formidable, stern, craggy, high-nosed, and fierce, with an inexorable mouth which bespoke a nature which would neither ask for mercy nor grant it. As to his age, one could only say for certain that a man with such a face was young enough to have all his virility and old enough to have experienced all the wickedness of life. The cold, savage eyes took a deliberate survey, first of the Baronet and then of the young man beside him.

"Aye, Rowe, it's a slap-up Corinthian, same as I said," he remarked over his shoulder to his companion. "But this other is a likely chap. If 'e isn't a millin' cove 'e ought to be. Any'ow, we'll try 'im out."

"Look here," said the Baronet, "I don't know who you are, except that you are a damned impertinent fellow. I'd put the lash of my whip across your face for two pins!"

"Stow that gammon, gov'nor! It ain't safe to speak to me like that."

"I've heard of you and your ways!" cried the angry soldier. "I'll teach you to stop my horses on the Queen's high road! You've got the wrong men this time, my fine fellow, as you will soon learn."

"That's as it may be," said the stranger. "May'ap, master, we may all learn something before we part. One or other of you 'as got to get down and put up your 'ands before you get any farther."

Stevens had instantly sprung down into the road.

"If you want a fight you've come to the right shop," said he; "it's my trade, so don't say I took you unawares."

The stranger gave a cry of satisfaction.

"Blow my dickey!" he shouted. "It *is* a millin' cove, Joe, same as I said. No more chaw-bacons for us, but the real thing. Well, young man, you've met your master to-night. Happen you never 'eard what Lord Longmore said o' me? 'A man must be made special to beat you,' says 'e. That's wot Lord Longmore said."

"That was before the Bull came along," growled the man in front, speaking for the first time.

"Stow your chaffing, Joe! A little more about the Bull and you and me will quarrel. 'E bested me once, but it's all betters and no takers that I glut 'im if ever we meet again. Well, young man, what d'ye think of me?"

"I think you've got your share of cheek."

"Cheek. Wot's that?"

"Impudence, bluff—gas, if you like."

The last word had a surprising effect upon the stranger. He smote his leg with his hand and broke out into a high neighing laugh, in which he was joined by his gruff companion.

"You've said the right word, my beauty," cried the latter, "'Gas' is the word and no error. Well, there's a good moon, but the clouds are comin' up. We had best use the light while we can."

Whilst this conversation had been going on the Baronet had been looking with an ever-growing amazement at the attire of the stranger. A good deal of it confirmed his belief that he was connected with some stables, though making every allowance for this his appearance was very eccentric and old-fashioned. Upon his head he wore a yellowish-white top-hat of long-haired beaver, such as is still affected by some drivers of four-in-hands, with a bell crown and a curling brim. His dress consisted of a short-waisted swallow-tail coat, snuff-coloured, with steel buttons. It opened in front to show a vest of striped silk, while his legs were encased in buff knee-breeches with blue stockings and low shoes. The figure was angular and hard, with a great suggestion of wiry activity. This Bully of Brocas was clearly a very great character, and the young dragoon officer chuckled as he thought what a glorious story he would carry back to the mess of this queer old-world figure and the thrashing which he was about to receive from the famous London boxer.

Billy, the little groom, had taken charge of the horses, who were shivering and sweating.

"This way!" said the stout man, turning towards

the gate. It was a sinister place, black and weird, with the crumbling pillars and the heavy arching trees. Neither the Baronet nor the pugilist liked the look of it.

"Where are you going, then?"

"This is no place for a fight," said the stout man. "We've got as pretty a place as ever you saw inside the gate here. You couldn't beat it on Molesey Hurst."

"The road is good enough for me," said Stevens.

"The road is good enough for two Johnny Raws," said the man with the beaver hat. "It ain't good enough for two slap-up millin' coves like you an' me. You ain't afeard, are you?"

"Not of you or ten like you," said Stevens, stoutly.

"Well, then, come with me and do it as it ought to be done."

Sir Frederic and Stevens exchanged glances.

"I'm game," said the pugilist.

"Come on, then."

The little party of four passed through the gateway. Behind them in the darkness the horses stamped and reared, while the voice of the boy could be heard as he vainly tried to soothe them. After walking fifty yards up the grass-grown drive the guide turned to the right through a thick belt of trees, and they came out upon a circular plot of grass, white and clear in the moonlight. It had a raised bank, and on the farther side was one of those little pillared stone summer-houses beloved by the early Georgians.

"What did I tell you?" cried the stout man, triumphantly. "Could you do better than this within twenty mile of town? It was made for it. Now, Tom, get to work upon him, and show us what you can do."

It had all become like an extraordinary dream. The strange men, their odd dress, their queer speech, the moonlit circle of grass, and the pillared summer-house all wove themselves into one fantastic whole. It was only the sight of Alf Stevens's ill-fitting tweed suit, and his homely English face surmounting it, which brought the Baronet back to the workaday world. The thin stranger had taken off his beaver hat, his swallow-tailed coat, his silk waistcoat, and finally his shirt had been drawn over his head by his second. Stevens in a cool and leisurely fashion kept pace with the preparations of his antagonist. Then the two fighting men turned upon each other.

But as they did so Stevens gave an exclamation of surprise and horror. The removal of the beaver hat had disclosed a horrible mutilation of the head of his antagonist. The whole upper forehead had fallen in, and there seemed to be a broad red weal between his close-cropped hair and his heavy brows.

" Good Lord," cried the young pugilist. " What's amiss with the man ? "

The question seemed to rouse a cold fury in his antagonist.

" You look out for your own head, master," said he. " You'll find enough to do, I'm thinkin', without talkin' about mine."

This retort drew a shout of hoarse laughter from his second. " Well said, my Tommy ! " he cried. " It's Lombard Street to a China orange on the one and only."

The man whom he called Tom was standing with his hands up in the centre of the natural ring. He looked a big man in his clothes, but he seemed bigger in the buff, and his barrel chest, sloping shoulders, and loosely-slung muscular arms were all ideal for the game. His grim eyes gleamed fiercely beneath his misshapen brows, and his lips were set in a fixed hard smile, more menacing than a scowl. The pugilist confessed, as he approached him, that he had never seen a more formidable figure. But his bold heart rose to the fact that he had never yet found the man who could master him, and that it was hardly credible that he would appear as an old-fashioned stranger on a country road. Therefore, with an answering smile, he took up his position and raised his hands.

But what followed was entirely beyond his experience.

The stranger feinted quickly with his left, and sent in a swinging hit with his right, so quick and hard that Stevens had barely time to avoid it and to counter with a short jab as his opponent rushed in upon him. Next instant the man's bony arms were round him, and the pugilist was hurled into the air in a whirling cross-buttock, coming down with a heavy thud upon the grass. The stranger stood back and folded his arms while Stevens scrambled to his feet with a red flush of anger upon his cheeks.

"Look here," he cried. "What sort of game is this?"

"We claim foul!" the Baronet shouted.

"Foul be damned! As clean a throw as ever I saw!" said the stout man. "What rules do you fight under?"

"Queensberry, of course."

"I never heard of it. It's London prize-ring with us."

"Come on, then!" cried Stevens, furiously. "I can wrestle as well as another. You won't get me napping again."

Nor did he. The next time that the stranger rushed in Stevens caught him in as strong a grip, and after swinging and swaying they came down together in a dog-fall. Three times this occurred, and each time the stranger walked across to his friend and seated himself upon the grassy bank before he recommenced.

"What d'ye make of him?" the Baronet asked, in one of these pauses.

Stevens was bleeding from the ear, but otherwise showed no sign of damage.

"He knows a lot," said the pugilist. "I don't know where he learned it, but he's had a deal of practice somewhere. He's as strong as a lion and as hard as a board, for all his queer face."

"Keep him at out-fighting. I think you are his master there."

"I'm not so sure that I'm his master anywhere, but I'll try my best."

It was a desperate fight, and as round followed round it became clear, even to the amazed Baronet, that the middle-weight champion had met his match. The stranger had a clever draw and a rush which, with his springing hits, made him a most dangerous foe. His head and body seemed insensible to blows, and the horribly malignant smile never for one instant flickered from his lips. He hit very hard with fists like flints, and his blows whizzed up from every angle. He had one particularly deadly lead, an uppercut at the jaw, which again and again nearly came home, until at last it did actually fly past the guard and brought Stevens to the ground. The stout man gave a whoop of triumph. "The whisker hit, by George! It's a horse to a hen on my Tommy! Another like that, lad, and you have him beat."

"I say, Stevens, this is going too far," said the Baronet, as he supported his weary man. "What will the regiment say if I bring you up all knocked to pieces in a bye-battle! Shake hands with this fellow and give him best, or you'll not be fit for your job."

"Give him best? Not I!" cried Stevens, angrily. "I'll knock that damned smile off his ugly mug before I've done."

"What about the Sergeant?"

"I'd rather go back to London and never see the Sergeant than have my number taken down by this chap."

"Well, 'ad enough?" his opponent asked, in a sneering voice, as he moved from his seat on the bank.

For answer young Stevens sprang forward and rushed at his man with all the strength that was left to him. By the fury of his onset he drove him back, and for a long minute had all the better of the exchanges. But this iron fighter seemed never to tire. His step was as quick and his blow as hard as ever when this long rally had ended. Stevens had eased up from pure exhaustion. But his opponent did not ease up. He came back on him with a shower of furious blows which beat down the weary guard of the pugilist. Alf Stevens was at the end of his strength and would in another instant have sunk to the ground but for a singular intervention.

It has been said that in their approach to the ring the party had passed through a grove of trees. Out of these there came a peculiar shrill cry, a cry of agony, which might be from a child or from some small woodland creature in distress. It was inarticulate, high-pitched, and inexpressibly melancholy. At the sound the stranger, who had knocked Stevens on to his knees, staggered back and looked round him with an expression of helpless horror upon his face. The smile had left his lips and there only remained the loose-lipped weakness of a man in the last extremity of terror.

"It's after me again, mate!" he cried.

"Stick it out, Tom! You have him nearly beat! It can't hurt you."

"It can 'urt me! It will 'urt me!" screamed the fighting man. "My God! I can't face it! Ah, I see it! I see it!"

With a scream of fear he turned and bounded off into the brushwood. His companion, swearing loudly, picked up the pile of clothes and darted after him, the dark shadows swallowing up their flying figures.

Stevens, half-senselessly, had staggered back and lay upon the grassy bank, his head pillowed upon the chest of the young Baronet, who was holding his flask of brandy to his lips. As they sat there they were both aware that the cries had become louder and shriller. Then from among the bushes there ran a small white terrier, nosing about as if following a trail and yelping most piteously. It squattered across the grassy sward, taking no notice of the two young men. Then it also vanished into the shadows. As it did so the two spectators sprang to their feet and ran as hard as they could tear for the gateway and the trap. Terror had seized them—a panic terror far above reason or control. Shivering and shaking, they threw themselves into the dog-cart, and it was not until the willing horses had put two good miles between that ill-omened hollow and themselves that they at last ventured to speak.

"Did you ever see such a dog?" asked the Baronet.

"No," cried Stevens. "And, please God, I never may again."

Late that night the two travellers broke their journey at the Swan Inn, near Harpenden Common. The landlord was an old acquaintance of the Baronet's, and gladly joined him in a glass of port after supper. A famous old sport was Mr. Joe Horner, of the Swan, and he would talk by the hour of the legends of the ring, whether new or old. The name of Alf Stevens was well known to him, and he looked at him with the deepest interest.

"Why, sir, you have surely been fighting," said he. "I hadn't read of any engagement in the papers."

"Enough said of that," Stevens answered, in a surly voice.

"Well, no offence! I suppose"—his smiling face became suddenly very serious—"I suppose you didn't, by chance, see anything of him they call the Bully of Brocas as you came north?"

"Well, what if we did?'

The landlord was tense with excitement.

"It was him that nearly killed Bob Meadows. It was at the very gate of Brocas Old Hall that he stopped him. Another man was with him. Bob was game to the marrow, but he was found hit to pieces on the lawn inside the gate where the summer-house stands."

The Baronet nodded.

"Ah, you've been there!" cried the landlord.

"Well, we may as well make a clean breast of it," said the Baronet, looking at Stevens. "We have been there, and we met the man you speak of—an ugly customer he is, too!"

"Tell me!" said the landlord, in a voice that sank

to a whisper. "Is it true what Bob Meadows says, that the men are dressed like our grandfathers, and that the fighting man has his head all caved in?"

"Well, he was old-fashioned, certainly, and his head was the queerest ever I saw."

"God in Heaven!" cried the landlord. "Do you know, sir, that Tom Hickman, the famous prize-fighter, together with his pal, Joe Rowe, a silversmith of the City, met his death at that very point in the year 1822, when he was drunk, and tried to drive on the wrong side of a wagon? Both were killed and the wheel of the wagon crushed in Hickman's forehead."

"Hickman! Hickman!" said the Baronet. "Not the gasman?"

"Yes, sir, they called him Gas. He won his fights with what they called the 'whisker hit,' and no one could stand against him until Neate—him that they called the Bristol Bull—brought him down."

Stevens had risen from the table as white as cheese. "Let's get out of this, sir. I want fresh air. Let us get on our way."

The landlord clapped him on the back.

"Cheer up, lad! You've held him off, anyhow, and that's more than anyone else has ever done. Sit down and have another glass of wine, for if a man in England has earned it this night it is you. There's many a debt you would pay if you gave the Gasman a welting, whether dead or alive. Do you know what he did in this very room?"

The two travellers looked round with startled eyes at the lofty room, stone-flagged and oak-panelled, with great open grate at the farther end.

"Yes, in this very room. I had it from old Squire Scotter, who was here that very night. It was the day when Shelton beat Josh Hudson out St. Albans way, and Gas had won a pocketful of money on the fight. He and his pal Rowe came in here upon their way, and he was mad-raging drunk. The folk fairly shrunk into the corners and under the tables, for he was stalkin' round with the great kitchen poker in his hand, and there was murder behind the smile upon his face. He was like that when the drink was in him—cruel, reckless, and a terror to the world. Well, what think you that he did at last with the poker? There was a little dog, a terrier as I've heard, coiled up before the fire, for it was a bitter December night. The Gasman broke its back with one blow of the poker. Then he burst out laughin', flung a curse or two at the folk that shrunk away from him, and so out to his high gig that was waiting outside. The next we heard was that he was carried down to Finchley with his head ground to a jelly by the wagon wheel. Yes, they do say the little dog with its bleeding skin and its broken back has been seen since then, crawlin' and yelpin' about Brocas Corner, as if it were lookin' for the swine that killed it. So you see, Mr. Stevens, you were fightin' for more than yourself when you put it across the Gasman."

"Maybe so," said the young prize-fighter, "but I want no more fights like that. The Farrier-Sergeant is good enough for me, sir, and if it is the same to you, we'll take a railway train back to town."

TALES OF THE CAMP

7. *A Straggler of '15*

IT was a dull October morning, and heavy, rolling fog-wreaths lay low over the wet, grey roofs of the Woolwich houses. Down in the long, brick-lined streets all was sodden and greasy and cheerless. From the high buildings of the Arsenal came the whir of many wheels, the thudding of weights, and the buzz and babel of human toil. Beyond, the dwellings cf the working-men, smoke-stained and unlovely, radiated away in a lessening perspective of narrowing road and dwindling wall.

There were few folk in the streets, for the toilers had all been absorbed since break of day by the huge, smoke-spouting monster, which sucked in the manhood of the town, to belch it forth, weary and work-stained, every night. Stout women, with thick red arms, and dirty aprons, stood upon the whitened doorsteps, leaning upon their brooms, and shrieking their morning greetings across the road. One had gathered a small knot of cronies around her, and was talking energetically, with little shrill titters from her audience to punctuate her remarks.

"Old enough to know better!" she cried, in answer to an exclamation from one of the listeners. "Why, 'ow old is he at all? Blessed if I could ever make out."

"Well, it ain't so hard to reckon," said a sharp-featured, pale-faced woman, with watery-blue eyes. "He's been at the battle o' Waterloo, and has the pension and medal to prove it."

"That were a ter'ble long time agone," remarked a third. "It were afore I were born."

"It were fifteen year after the beginnin' of the century," cried a younger woman, who had stood leaning against the wall, with a smile of superior knowledge upon her face. "My Bill was a-saying so last Sabbath, when I spoke to him o' old Daddy Brewster, here."

"And suppose he spoke truth, Missus Simpson, 'ow long agone do that make it?"

"It's eighty-one now," said the original speaker, checking off the years upon her coarse, red fingers, "and that were fifteen. Ten, and ten, and ten, and ten, and ten—why, it's only sixty and six year, so he ain't so old after all."

"But he weren't a new-born babe at the battle, silly," cried the young woman, with a chuckle. "S'pose he were only twenty, then he couldn't be less than six-and-eighty now, at the lowest."

"Ay, he's that—every day of it," cried several.

"I've had 'bout enough of it," remarked the large woman, gloomily. "Unless his young niece, or grand-niece, or whatever she is, come to-day, I'm off; and he can find someone else to do his work. Your own 'ome first, says I."

"Ain't he quiet, then, Missus Simpson?" asked the youngest of the group.

"Listen to him now," she answered, with her hand half raised, and her head turned slantwise towards the open door. From the upper floor came a shuffling, sliding sound, with a sharp tapping of a stick. "There he go back and forrards doing what he call his sentry-go. 'Arf the night through he's at that game, the silly old juggins. At six o'clock this very mornin' there he was beatin' with a stick at my door. 'Turn out guard,' he cried, and a lot more jargon that I could make nothing of. Then what with his coughin' and 'awkin' and spittin', there ain't no gettin' a wink o' sleep. Hark to him now!"

"Missus Simpson! Missus Simpson!" cried a cracked and querulous voice from above.

"That's him," she cried, nodding her head with an air of triumph. "He do go on somethin' scandalous. Yes, Mister Brewster, sir."

"I want my morning ration, Missus Simpson."

"It's just ready, Mister Brewster, sir."

"Blessed if he ain't like a baby cryin' for its pap," said the young woman.

"I feel as if I could shake his old bones up sometimes," cried Mrs. Simpson, viciously. "But who's for a 'arf of fourpenny?"

The whole company were about to shuffle off to the public-house, when a young girl stepped across the road and touched the housekeeper timidly upon the arm. "I think that is No. 56 Arsenal View," she said. "Can you tell me if Mr. Brewster lives here?"

The housekeeper looked critically at the newcomer. She was a girl of about twenty, broad-faced and comely, with a turned-up nose, and large, honest, grey eyes. Her print dress, her straw hat with its bunch of glaring poppies, and the bundle which she carried had all a smack of the country.

"You're Norah Brewster, I s'pose," said Mrs. Simpson, eyeing her up and down with no friendly gaze.

"Yes; I've come to look after my grand-uncle Gregory."

"And a good job, too," cried the housekeeper, with a toss of her head. "It's about time that some of his own folk took a turn at it, for I've had enough of it. There you are, young woman! in you go, and make yourself at home. There's tea in the caddy and bacon on the dresser, and the old man will be about you if you don't fetch him his breakfast. I'll send for my things in the evenin'."

With a nod she strolled off with her attendant gossips in the direction of the public-house.

Thus left to her own devices, the country girl walked

into the front room and took off her hat and jacket. It was a low-roofed apartment with a sputtering fire, upon which a small brass kettle was singing cheerily. A stained cloth lay over half the table, with an empty brown teapot, a loaf of bread, and some coarse crockery. Norah Brewster looked rapidly about her, and in an instant took over her new duties. Ere five minutes had passed the tea was made, two slices of bacon were frizzling on the pan, the table was re-arranged, the antimacassars straightened over the sombre brown furniture, and the whole room had taken a new air of comfort and neatness. This done, she looked round curiously at the prints upon the walls. Over the fireplace, in a small, square case, a brown medal caught her eye, hanging from a strip of purple ribbon. Beneath was a slip of newspaper cutting. She stood on her tiptoes, with her fingers on the edge of the mantelpiece, and craned her neck up to see it, glancing down from time to time at the bacon which simmered and hissed beneath her. The cutting was yellow with age, and ran in this way:

"On Tuesday an interesting ceremony was performed at the barracks of the third regiment of guards, when, in the presence of the Prince Regent, Lord Hill, Lord Saltoun, and an assemblage which comprised beauty as well as valour, a special medal was presented to Corporal Gregory Brewster, of Captain Haldane's flank company, in recognition of his gallantry in the recent great battle in the Lowlands. It appears that on the ever-memorable 18th of June, four companies of the third guards and of the Coldstreams, under the command of Colonels Maitland and Byng, held the important farmhouse of Hougoumont at the right of the British position. At a critical point of the action these troops found themselves short of powder. Seeing that Generals Foy and Jerome Buonaparte were again massing their infantry for an attack on the position, Colonel Byng dispatched Corporal Brewster to the rear to hasten up the reserve ammunition. Brewster came upon two powder tumbrils of the Nassau division, and succeeded, after menacing the drivers with his musket, in inducing them to convey their powder to Hougoumont. In his absence, however, the hedges surrounding the position had been set on fire by a howitzer battery of the French, and the passage of the carts full of powder became a most hazardous matter. The first tumbril exploded, blowing the driver to fragments. Daunted by the fate of his comrade, the second driver turned his horses, but Corporal Brewster, springing upon his seat, hurled the man down, and urging the powder cart through the flames, succeeded in forcing a way to his companions. To this gallant deed may be directly attributed the success of the British arms, for without powder it would have been impossible to have held Hougoumont, and the Duke of Wellington had repeatedly declared that had Hougoumont fallen, as well as La Haye Sainte, he would have found it impossible to have held his ground. Long may the heroic Brewster live to treasure the medal which he has so bravely won, and to look back with pride to the day when in the presence of his comrades he received this tribute to his valour from the august hands of the first gentleman of the realm."

The reading of this old cutting increased in the girl's mind the veneration which she had always had for her warrior kinsman. From her infancy he had been her hero, and she remembered how her father used to speak of his courage and his strength, how he could strike down a bullock with a blow of his fist, and carry a fat sheep under either arm. True that she had never seen him, but a rude painting at home, which depicted a square-faced, clean-shaven, stalwart man with a great bearskin cap, rose ever before her memory when she thought of him.

She was still gazing at the brown medal and wondering what the "*dulce et decorum est*" might mean, which was inscribed upon the edge, when there came a sudden tapping and shuffling upon the stair, and there at the door was standing the very man who had been so often in her thoughts.

But could this indeed be he? Where was the martial air, the flashing eye, the warrior face which she had pictured. There, framed in the doorway, was a huge, twisted old man, gaunt and puckered, with twitching hands, and shuffling, purposeless feet. A cloud of fluffy white hair, a red-veined nose, two thick tufts of eyebrow and a pair of dimly-questioning, watery-blue eyes—these were what met her gaze. He leaned forward upon a stick, while his shoulders rose and fell with his crackling, rasping breathing.

"I want my morning rations," he crooned, as he stumped forward to his chair. "The cold nips me without 'em. See to my fingers!"

He held out his distorted hands, all blue at the tips, wrinkled and gnarled, with huge, projecting knuckles.

"It's nigh ready," answered the girl, gazing at him with wonder in her eyes. "Don't you know who I am, grand-uncle? I am Norah Brewster from Witham."

"Rum is warm," mumbled the old man, rocking to and fro in his chair, "and schnapps is warm, and there's 'eat in soup, but it's a dish o' tea for me. What did you say your name was?"

"Norah Brewster."

"You can speak out, lass. Seems to me folk's voices isn't as loud as they used."

"I'm Norah Brewster, uncle. I'm your grand-niece come from down Essex way to live with you."

"You'll be brother Jarge's girl! Lor', to think o' little Jarge having a girl."

He chuckled hoarsely to himself, and the long, stringy sinews of his throat jerked and quivered.

"I am the daughter of your brother George's son," said she as she turned the bacon.

"Lor', but little Jarge was a rare 'un," he continued.

"Eh, by Jimini, there was no chousing Jarge. He's got a bull pup o' mine, that I gave him when I took the bounty. You've heard him speak of it, likely."

"Why, grandpa George has been dead this twenty years," said she, pouring out the tea.

"Well, it was a bootiful pup—ay, a well-bred un, by Jimini! I'm cold for lack of my rations. Rum is good, and so is schnapps, but I'd as lief have tea as either."

He breathed heavily while he devoured his food.

"It's a middlin' goodish way you've come," said he at last. "Likely the stage left yesternight."

"The what, uncle?"

"The coach that brought you."

"Nay, I came by the mornin' train."

"Lor, now, think o' that! You ain't afeared of those new-fangled things! To think of you coming by railroad like that! What's the world a-comin' to?"

There was silence for some minutes while Norah sat stirring her tea and glancing sideways at the bluish lips and champing jaws of her companion.

"You must have seen a deal of life, uncle," said she. "It must seem a long, long time to you!"

"Not so very long, neither. I'm ninety come Candlemas, but it don't seem long since I took the bounty. And that battle, it might have been yesterday. I've got the smell of the burned powder in my nose yet. Eh, but I get a power o' good from my rations!"

He did indeed look less worn and colourless than when she first saw him. His face was flushed and his back more erect.

"Have you read that?" he asked, jerking his head towards the cutting.

"Yes, uncle, and I am sure you must be proud of it."

"Ah, it was a great day for me! A great day! The Regent was there, and a fine body of a man, too! 'The ridgment is proud of you,' says he. 'And I'm proud of the ridgment,' say I. 'A damned good answer, too!'

says he to Lord Hill, and they both bust out a-laughing. But what be you a-peepin' out o' the window for ? "

" Oh, uncle, here's a regiment of soldiers coming down the street, with the band playing in front of them."

" A ridgment, eh ? Where be my glasses ? Lor', but I can hear the band, as plain as plain. Here's the pioneers an' the drum-major ! What be their number, lass ? "

His eyes were shining, and his bony, yellow fingers, like the claws of some fierce old bird, dug into her shoulder.

" They don't seem to have no number, uncle. They've something wrote on their shoulders. Oxfordshire, I think it be."

" Ah, yes," he growled. " I heard as they'd dropped the numbers and given them new-fangled names. There they go, by Jimini ! They're young mostly, but they hain't forgot how to march. They have the swing—ay, I'll say that for them. They've got the swing."

He gazed after them until the last files had turned the corner, and the measured tramp of their marching had died away in the distance.

He had just regained his chair when the door opened and a gentleman stepped in.

" Ah, Mr. Brewster ! Better to-day ? " he asked.

" Come in, doctor ! Yes, I'm better. But there's a deal o' bubbling in my chest. It's all them toobes. If I could but cut the phlegm I'd be right. Can't ye give me something to cut the phlegm ? "

The doctor, a grave-faced young man, put his fingers to the furrowed, blue-corded wrist.

" You must be careful," he said ; " you must take no liberties."

The thin tide of life seemed to thrill rather than to throb under his finger.

The old man chuckled.

" I've got brother Jarge's girl to look after me now. She'll see I don't break barracks or do what I hadn't ought to ; why, darn my skin, I knew something was amiss ! "

" With what ? "

" Why, with them soldiers. You saw them pass, doctor—eh ? They'd forgot their stocks. Not one on 'em had his stock on." He croaked and chuckled for a long time over his discovery. " It wouldn't ha' done for the Dook ! " he muttered. " No, by Jimini ! the Dook would ha' had word there."

The doctor smiled.

" Well, you are doing very well," said he. " I'll look in once a week or so and see how you are ! " As Norah followed him to the door he beckoned her outside. " He is very weak," he whispered. " If you find him failing you must send for me."

" What ails him, doctor ? "

" Ninety years ail him. His arteries are pipes of lime. His heart is shrunken and flabby. The man is worn out."

Norah stood watching the brisk figure of the young doctor and pondering over these new responsibilities which had come upon her. When she turned, a tall, brown-faced artillery man, with the three gold chevrons of sergeant upon his arm, was standing, carbine in hand, at her elbow.

" Good morning, miss ! " said he, raising one thick finger to his jaunty, yellow-banded cap. " I b'lieve there's an old gentleman lives here of the name of Brewster, who was engaged in the battle o' Waterloo ? "

" It's my grand-uncle, sir," said Norah, casting down her eyes before the keen, critical gaze of the young soldier. " He is in the front parlour."

" Could I have a word with him, miss ? I'll call again if it don't chance to be convenient."

" I am sure that he would be very glad to see you, sir. He's in here, if you'll step in. Uncle, here's a gentleman who wants to speak with you."

" Proud to see you, sir—proud and glad, sir ! " cried the sergeant, taking three steps forward into the room, and grounding his carbine while he raised his hand palm forwards, in a salute.

Norah stood by the door, with her mouth and eyes open, wondering whether her grand-uncle had ever, in his prime, looked like this magnificent creature; and whether he, in his turn, would ever come to resemble her grand-uncle.

The old man blinked up at his visitor, and shook his head slowly.

" Sit ye down, sergeant," said he, pointing with his stick to a chair. " You're full young for the stripes. Lordy, it's easier to get three now than one in my day. Gunners were old soldiers, then, and the grey hairs came quicker than the three stripes."

" I am eight years' service, sir," cried the sergeant. " Macdonald is my name—Sergeant Macdonald, of H Battery, Southern Artillery Division. I have called as the spokesman of my mates at the gunners' barracks to say that we are proud to have you in the town, sir."

Old Brewster chuckled and rubbed his bony hands.

" That were what the Regent said," he cried. " ' The ridgment is proud of ye,' says he. ' And I am proud of the ridgment,' says I. ' And a damned good answer, too,' says he, and he and Lord Hill bust out—a-laughin'."

" The non-commissioned mess would be proud and honoured to see you, sir," said Sergeant Macdonald. " And if you could step as far you'll always find a pipe o' baccy and a glass of grog awaitin' you."

The old man laughed until he coughed.

" Like to see me, would they? The dogs!" said he. " Well, well, when the warm weather comes again I'll maybe drop in. It's likely that I'll drop in. Too grand for a canteen, eh? Got your mess just the same as the orficers. What's the world a-comin' to at all!"

" You was in the line, sir, was you not?" asked the sergeant, respectfully.

" The line?" cried the old man with shrill scorn. " Never wore a shako in my life. I am a guardsman,

I am. Served in the third guards—the same they call now the Scots Guards. Lordy, but they have all marched away, every man of them, from old Colonel Byng down to the drummer boys, and here am I a straggler—that's what I am, sergeant, a straggler! I'm here when I ought to be there. But it ain't my fault neither, for I'm ready to fall in when the word comes."

"We've all got to muster there," answered the sergeant. "Won't you try my baccy, sir?" handing over a sealskin pouch.

Old Brewster drew a blackened clay pipe from his pocket, and began to stuff the tobacco into the bowl. In an instant it slipped through his fingers, and was broken to pieces on the floor. His lip quivered, his nose puckered up, and he began crying with the long, helpless sobs of a child.

"I've broke my pipe," he cried.

"Don't, uncle, oh, don't," cried Norah, bending over him and patting his white head as one soothes a baby. "It don't matter. We can easy get another."

"Don't you fret yourself, sir," said the sergeant. "'Ere's a wooden pipe with an amber mouth, if you'll do me the honour to accept it from me. I'd be real glad if you will take it."

"Jimini!" cried he, his smiles breaking in an instant through his tears. "It's a fine pipe. See to my new pipe, Norah. I lay that Jarge never had a pipe like that. You've got your firelock there, sergeant."

"Yes, sir, I was on my way back from the butts when I looked in."

"Let me have the feel of it. Lordy, but it seems like old times to have one's hand on a musket. What's the manual, sergeant, eh? Cock your firelock—look to your priming—present your firelock—eh, sergeant? Oh, Jimini! I've broke your musket in halves!"

"That's all right, sir," cried the gunner, laughing, "you pressed on the lever and opened the breech-piece. That's where we load 'em, you know."

"Load 'em at the wrong end! Well, well, to think o' that. And no ramrod, neither! I've heered tell of it, but I never believed it afore. Ah, it won't come up to Brown Bess. When there's work to be done you mark my word and see if they don't come back to Brown Bess."

"By the Lord, sir," cried the sergeant, hotly. "They need some change out in South Africa now. I see by this mornin's paper that the Government has knuckled under to these Boers. They're hot about it, at the non-com. mess, I can tell you, sir."

"Eh, eh," croaked old Brewster. "By Gosh! it wouldn't ha' done for the Dook; the Dook would ha' had a word to say over that!"

"Ah, that he would, sir," cried the sergeant; "and God send us another like him. But I've wearied you enough for one sitting. I'll look in again, and I'll bring a comrade or two with me if I may, for there isn't one but would be proud to have speech with you."

So, with another salute to the veteran, and a gleam of white teeth at Norah, the big gunner withdrew, leaving a memory of blue cloth, and of gold braid behind him. Many days had not passed, however, before he was back again, and during all the long winter he was a frequent visitor at Arsenal View. He brought others with him, and soon through all the lines a pilgrimage to Daddy Brewster's came to be looked upon as the proper thing to do. Gunners and sappers, linesmen and dragoons, came bowing and bobbing into the little parlour, with clatter of side arms, and clink of spurs, stretching their long legs across the patchwork rug, and hunting in the front of their tunics for the screw of tobacco, or paper of snuff, which they had brought as a sign of their esteem.

It was a deadly cold winter, with six weeks on end of snow on the ground, and Norah had a hard task to keep the life in that time-worn body. There were times when his mind would leave him, and when, save an animal outcry when the hour of his meals came round, no word would fall from him. As the warm weather came once more, however, and the green buds peeped forth again upon the trees, the blood thawed in his veins, and he would even drag himself as far as the door to bask in the life-giving sunshine.

"It do hearten me up so," he said one morning, as he glowed in a hot May sun. "It's a job to keep back the flies, though! They get owdacious in this weather and they do plague me cruel."

"I'll keep them off you, uncle," said Norah.

"Eh, but it's fine! This sunshine makes me think o' the glory to come. You might read me a bit o' the Bible, lass. I find it wonderful soothing."

"What part would you like, uncle?"

"Oh, them wars."

"The wars?"

"Ay, keep to the wars! Give me the Old Testament for ch'ice. There's more taste to it, to my mind! When parson comes he wants to get off to something else, but it's Joshua or nothing with me. Them Israelites was good soldiers—good growed soldiers, all of 'em."

"But, uncle," pleaded Norah, "it's all peace in the next world."

"No, it ain't, gal."

"Oh yes, uncle, surely."

The old corporal knocked his stick irritably upon the ground.

"I tell ye it ain't, gal. I asked parson."

"Well, what did he say?"

"He said there was to be a last fight. He even gave it a name, he did. The battle of Arm—Arm——"

"Armageddon."

"Ah, that's the name parson said. I 'specs the third guards'll be there. And the Dook—the Dook'll have a word to say."

An elderly, grey-whiskered gentleman had been walking down the street, glancing up at the numbers of the houses. Now, as his eyes fell upon the old man, he came straight for him.

"Hullo," said he, "perhaps you are Gregory Brewster?"

"My name, sir," answered the veteran.

"You are the same Brewster, as I understand, who is on the roll of the Scots Guards as having been present at the battle of Waterloo?"

"I am that man, sir, though we called it the third guards in those days. It was a fine ridgment, and they only need me to make up a full muster."

"Tut, tut, they'll have to wait years for that," said the gentleman heartily; "but I am the colonel of the Scots Guards, and I thought I would like to have a word with you."

Old Gregory Brewster was up in an instant with his hand to his rabbit-skin cap.

"God bless me!" he cried, "to think of it; to think of it."

"Hadn't the gentleman better come in?" suggested the practical Norah from behind the door.

"Surely, sir, surely; walk in, sir, if I may be so bold."

In his excitement he had forgotten his stick, and as he led the way into the parlour, his knees tottered, and he threw out his hands. In an instant the colonel had caught him on one side and Norah on the other.

"Easy and steady," said the colonel as he led him to his arm-chair.

"Thank ye, sir; I was near gone that time. But Lordy, why, I can scarce believe it. To think of me, the corporal of the flank company, and you the colonel of the battalion. Jimini! how things come round, to be sure."

"Why, we are very proud of you in London," said the colonel. "And so you are actually one of the men who held Hougoumont?" He looked at the bony, trembling hands with their huge, knotted knuckles, the stringy throat, and the heaving, rounded shoulders.

Could this, indeed, be the last of that band of heroes? Then he glanced at the half-filled phials, the blue liniment bottles, the long-spouted kettle, and the sordid details of the sick-room. "Better, surely, had he died under the blazing rafters of the Belgian farm-house," thought the colonel.

"I hope that you are pretty comfortable and happy," he remarked after a pause.

"Thank ye, sir. I have a good deal of trouble with my toobes—a deal of trouble. You wouldn't think the job it is to cut the phlegm. And I need my rations. I gets cold without 'em. And the flies! I ain't strong enough to fight against them."

"How's the memory?" asked the colonel.

"Oh, there ain't nothing amiss there. Why, sir, I could give you the name of every man in Captain Haldane's flank company."

"And the battle—you remember it?"

"Why, I sees it all afore me every time I shuts my eyes. Lordy, sir, you wouldn't hardly believe how clear it is to me. There's our line from the paregoric bottle right along to the snuffbox. D'ye see? Well, then, the pill-box is for Hougoumont on the right, where we was; and Norah's thimble for La Haye Sainte. There it is all right, sir, and here were our guns, and here, behind, the reserves and the Belgians. Ach, them Belgians!" He spat furiously into the fire. "Then here's the French where my pipe lies, and over here, where I put my baccy pouch, was the Proosians a-comin' up on our left flank. Jimini! but it was a glad sight to see the smoke of their guns."

"And what was it that struck you most, now, in connection with the whole affair?" asked the colonel.

"I lost three half-crowns over it, I did," crooned old Brewster. "I shouldn't wonder if I was never to get that money now. I lent 'em to Jabez Smith, my rear rank man, in Brussels. 'Only till pay-day, Grig,' says he. By Gosh! he was stuck by a lancer at Quarter

Brass, and me with not so much as a slip o' paper to prove the debt! Them three half-crowns is as good as lost to me."

The colonel rose from his chair, laughing.

"The officers of the Guards want you to buy yourself some little trifle which may add to your comfort," he said. "It is not from me, so you need not thank me."

He took up the old man's tobacco pouch and slipped a crisp bank-note inside it.

"Thank ye, kindly, sir. But there's one favour that I would like to ask you, colonel."

"Yes, my man?"

"If I'm called, colonel, you won't grudge me a flag and a firing party?"

"All right, my man, I'll see to it," said the colonel. "Good-bye; I hope to have nothing but good news from you."

"A kind gentleman, Norah," croaked old Brewster, as they saw him walk past the window; "but Lordy, he ain't fit to hold the stirrup o' my Colonel Byng."

It was on the very next day that the corporal took a sudden change for the worse. Even the golden sunlight streaming through the window seemed unable to warm that withered frame. The doctor came and shook his head in silence. All day the man lay with only his puffing blue lips and the twitching of his scraggy neck to show that he still held the breath of life. Norah and Sergeant Macdonald had sat by him in the afternoon, but he had shown no consciousness of their presence. He lay peacefully, his eyes half-closed, his hands under his cheek, as one who is very weary.

They had left him for an instant, and were sitting in the front room where Norah was preparing the tea, when of a sudden they heard a shout that rang through the house. Loud and clear and swelling, it pealed in their ears, a voice full of strength and energy and fiery passion.

"The guards need powder," it cried and yet again, "the guards need powder."

The sergeant sprang from his chair and rushed in, followed by the trembling Norah. There was the old man standing up, his blue eyes sparkling, his white hair bristling, his whole figure towering and expanding, with eagle head and glance of fire.

"The guards need powder," he thundered once again, "and by God they shall have it!"

He threw up his long arms and sank back with a groan into his chair. The sergeant stooped over him, and his face darkened.

"Oh, Archie, Archie," sobbed the frightened girl, "what do you think of him?"

The sergeant turned away.

"I think," said he, "that the third guards have a full muster now."

8. *The Pot of Caviare*

IT was the fourth day of the siege. Ammunition and provisions were both nearing an end. When the Boxer insurrection had suddenly flamed up, and roared, like a fire in dry grass, across Northern China, the few scattered Europeans in the outlying provinces had huddled together at the nearest defensible post and had held on for dear life until rescue came—or until it did not. In the latter case, the less said about their fate the better. In the former, they came back into the world of men with that upon their faces which told that they had looked very closely upon such an end as would ever haunt their dreams.

Ichau was only fifty miles from the coast, and there was a European squadron in the Gulf of Liantong. Therefore the absurd little garrison, consisting of native Christians and railway men, with a German officer to command them and five civilian Europeans to support him, held on bravely with the conviction that help must soon come sweeping down to them from the low hills to eastward. The sea was visible from those hills, and on the sea were their armed countrymen. Surely, then, they could not feel deserted. With brave hearts they manned the loopholes in the crumbling brick walls outlining the tiny European quarter, and they fired away briskly, if ineffectively, at the rapidly advancing sangars of the Boxers. It was certain that in another day or so they would be at the end of their resources, but then it was equally certain that in another day or so they must be relieved. It might be a little sooner or it might be a little later, but there was no one who ever ventured to hint that the relief would not arrive in time to pluck them out of the fire. Up to Tuesday night there was no word of discouragement.

It was true that on the Wednesday their robust faith in what was going forward behind those eastern hills had weakened a little. The grey slopes lay bare and unresponsive while the deadly sangars pushed ever nearer, so near that the dreadful faces which shrieked imprecations at them from time to time over the top could be seen in every hideous feature. There was not so much of that now since young Ainslie, of the Diplomatic service, with his neat little ·303 sporting rifle, had settled down in the squat church tower, and had devoted his days to abating the nuisance. But a silent sangar is an even more impressive thing than a clamorous one, and steadily, irresistibly, inevitably, the lines of brick and rubble drew closer. Soon they would be so near that one rush would assuredly carry the frantic swordsmen over the frail entrenchment. It all seemed very black upon the Wednesday evening. Colonel Dresler, the German ex-infantry soldier, went about with an imperturbable face, but a heart of lead. Ralston, of the railway, was up half the night writing farewell letters. Professor Mercer, the old entomologist, was even more silent and grimly thoughtful than ever. Ainslie had lost some of his flippancy. On the whole, the ladies—Miss Sinclair, the nurse of the Scotch Mission, Mrs. Patterson, and her pretty daughter Jessie—were the most composed of the party. Father Pierre, of the French Mission, was also unaffected, as was natural to one who regarded martyrdom as a glorious crown. The Boxers yelling for his blood beyond the walls disturbed him less than his forced association with the sturdy Scotch Presbyterian presence of Mr. Patterson, with whom for ten years he had wrangled over the souls of the natives. They passed each other now in the corridors as dog passes cat, and each kept a watchful eye upon the other lest even in the trenches he might filch some sheep from the rival fold, whispering heresy in his ear.

But the Wednesday night passed without a crisis, and on the Thursday all was bright once more. It was Ainslie up in the clock tower who had first heard the distant thud of a gun. Then Dresler heard it, and within half an hour it was audible to all—that strong iron voice, calling to them from afar and bidding them to be of good cheer, since help was coming. It was clear that the landing party from the squadron was well on its way. It would not arrive an hour too soon. The cartridges were nearly finished. Their half-rations of food would soon dwindle to an even more pitiful supply. But what need to worry about that now that relief was assured? There would be no attack that day, as most of the Boxers could be seen streaming off in the direction of the distant firing, and the long lines of sangars were silent and deserted. They were all able, therefore, to assemble at the lunch-table, a merry, talkative party, full of that joy of living which sparkles most brightly under the imminent shadow of death.

"The pot of caviare!" cried Ainslie. "Come, Professor, out with the pot of caviare!"

"Potz-tausend! yes," grunted old Dresler. "It is certainly time that we had that famous pot."

The ladies joined in, and from all parts of the

long, ill-furnished table there came the demand for caviare.

It was a strange time to ask for such a delicacy, but the reason is soon told. Professor Mercer, the old Californian entomologist, had received a jar of caviare in a hamper of goods from San Francisco, arriving a day or two before the outbreak. In the general pooling and distribution of provisions this one dainty and three bottles of Lachryma Christi from the same hamper had been excepted and set aside. By common consent they were to be reserved for the final joyous meal when the end of their peril should be in sight. Even as they sat the thud-thud of the relieving guns came to their ears—more luxurious music to their lunch than the most sybaritic restaurant of London could have supplied. Before evening the relief would certainly be there. Why, then, should their stale bread not be glorified by the treasured caviare?

But the Professor shook his gnarled old head and smiled his inscrutable smile.

"Better wait," said he.

"Wait! Why wait?" cried the company.

"They have still far to come," he answered.

"They will be here for supper at the latest," said Ralston, of the railway—a keen, bird-like man, with bright eyes and long, projecting nose. "They cannot be more than ten miles from us now. If they only did two miles an hour it would make them due at seven."

"There is a battle on the way," remarked the Colonel. "You will grant two hours or three hours for the battle."

"Not half an hour," cried Ainslie. "They will walk through them as if they were not there. What can these rascals with their matchlocks and swords do against modern weapons?"

"It depends on who leads the column of relief," said Dresler. "If they are fortunate enough to have a German officer——"

"An Englishman for my money!" cried Ralston.

"The French commodore is said to be an excellent strategist," remarked Father Pierre.

"I don't see that it matters a toss," cried the exuberant Ainslie. "Mr. Mauser and Mr. Maxim are the two men who will see us through, and with them on our side no leader can go wrong. I tell you they will just brush them aside and walk through them. So now, Professor, come on with that pot of caviare!"

But the old scientist was unconvinced.

"We shall reserve it for supper," said he.

"After all," said Mr. Patterson, in his slow, precise Scottish intonation, "it will be a courtesy to our guests—the officers of the relief—if we have some palatable food to lay before them. I'm in agreement with the Professor that we reserve the caviare for supper."

The argument appealed to their sense of hospitality. There was something pleasantly chivalrous, too, in the idea of keeping their one little delicacy to give a savour to the meal of their preservers. There was no more talk of the caviare.

"By the way, Professor," said Mr. Patterson, "I've only heard to-day that this is the second time that you have been besieged in this way. I'm sure we should all be very interested to hear some details of your previous experience."

The old man's face set very grimly.

"I was in Sung-tong, in South China, in 'eighty-nine," said he.

"It's a very extraordinary coincidence that you should twice have been in such a perilous situation," said the missionary. "Tell us how you were relieved at Sung-tong."

The shadow deepened upon the weary face.

"We were not relieved," said he.

"What! the place fell?"

"Yes, it fell."

"And you came through alive."

"I am a doctor as well as an entomologist. They had many wounded; they spared me."

"And the rest?"

"Assez! assez!" cried the little French priest, raising his hand in protest. He had been twenty years in China. The professor had said nothing, but there was something, some lurking horror, in his dull, grey eyes which had turned the ladies pale.

"I am sorry," said the missionary. "I can see that it is a painful subject. I should not have asked."

"No," the Professor answered, slowly. "It is wiser not to ask. It is better not to speak about such things at all. But surely those guns are very much nearer?"

There could be no doubt of it. After a silence the thud-thud had recommenced with a lively ripple of rifle-fire playing all round that deep bass master-note. It must be just at the farther side of the nearest hill. They pushed back their chairs and ran out to the ramparts. The silent-footed native servants came in and cleared the scanty remains from the table. But after they had left, the old Professor sat on there, his massive, grey-crowned head leaning upon his hands and the same pensive look of horror in his eyes. Some ghosts may be laid for years, but when they do rise it is not so easy to drive them back to their slumbers. The guns had ceased outside, but he had not observed it, lost as he was in the one supreme and terrible memory of his life.

His thoughts were interrupted at last by the entrance of the Commandant. There was a complacent smile upon his broad German face.

"The Kaiser will be pleased," said he, rubbing his hands. "Yes, certainly it should mean a decoration. 'Defence of Ichau against the Boxers by Colonel Dresler, late Major of the 114th Hanoverian Infantry. Splendid resistance of small garrison against overwhelming odds.' It will certainly appear in the Berlin papers."

"Then you think we are saved?" said the old man, with neither emotion nor exultation in his voice.

The Colonel smiled.

"Why, Professor," said he, "I have seen you more excited on the morning when you brought back *Lepidus Mercerensis* in your collecting box."

"The fly was safe in my collecting-box first," the entomologist answered. "I have seen so many strange turns of Fate in my long life that I do not grieve nor do I rejoice until I know that I have cause. But tell me the news."

"Well," said the Colonel, lighting his long pipe, and stretching his gaitered legs in the bamboo chair, "I'll stake my military reputation that all is well. They are advancing swiftly, the firing has died down to show that resistance is at an end, and within an hour we'll see them over the brow. Ainslie is to fire his gun three times from the church tower as a signal, and then we shall make a little sally on our own account."

"And you are waiting for this signal?"

"Yes, we are waiting for Ainslie's shots. I thought I would spend the time with you, for I had something to ask you."

"What was it?"

"Well, you remember your talk about the other siege—the siege of Sung-tong. It interests me very much from a professional point of view. Now that the ladies and civilians are gone you will have no objection to discussing it."

"It is not a pleasant subject."

"No, I dare say not. Mein Gott! it was indeed a tragedy. But you have seen how I have conducted the defence here. Was it wise? Was it good? Was it worthy of the traditions of the German army?"

"I think you could have done no more."

"Thank you. But this other place, was it as ably defended? To me a comparison of this sort is very interesting. Could it have been saved?"

"No; everything possible was done—save only one thing."

"Ah! there was one omission. What was it?"

"No one—above all, no woman—should have been allowed to fall alive into the hands of the Chinese."

The Colonel held out his broad red hand and enfolded the long, white, nervous fingers of the Professor.

"You are right—a thousand times right. But do not think that this has escaped my thoughts. For myself I would die fighting, so would Ralston, so would Ainslie. I have talked to them, and it is settled. But the others, I have spoken with them, but what are you to do? There are the priest, and the missionary, and the women?"

"Would they wish to be taken alive?"

"They would not promise to take steps to prevent it. They would not lay hands on their own lives. Their consciences would not permit it. Of course, it is all over now, and we need not speak of such dreadful things. But what would you have done in my place?"

"Kill them."

"Mein Gott! You would murder them?"

"In mercy I would kill them. Man, I have been through it. I have seen the death of the hot eggs; I have seen the death of the boiling kettle; I have seen the women—my God! I wonder that I have ever slept sound again." His usually impassive face was working and quivering with the agony of the remembrance. "I was strapped to a stake with thorns in my eyelids to keep them open, and my grief at their torture was a less thing than my self-reproach when I thought that I could with one tube of tasteless tablets have snatched them at the last instant from the hands of their tormentors. Murder! I am ready to stand at the Divine bar and answer for a thousand murders such as that! Sin! Why, it is such an act as might well cleanse the stain of real sin from the soul. But if, knowing what I do, I should have failed this second time to do it, then, by Heaven! there is no hell deep enough or hot enough to receive my guilty craven spirit."

The Colonel rose, and again his hand clasped that of the Professor.

"You speak sense," said he. "You are a brave, strong man, who know your own mind. Yes, by the Lord! you would have been my great help had things gone the other way. I have often thought and wondered in the dark, early hours of the morning, but I did not know how to do it. But we should have heard Ainslie's shots before now; I will go and see."

Again the old scientist sat alone with his thoughts. Finally, as neither the guns of the relieving force nor yet the signal of their approach sounded upon his ears, he rose, and was about to go himself upon the ramparts to make inquiry when the door flew open, and Colonel Dresler staggered into the room. His face was of a ghastly yellow-white, and his chest heaved like that of a man exhausted with running. There was brandy on the side-table, and he gulped down a glassful. Then he dropped heavily into a chair.

"Well," said the Professor, coldly, "they are not coming?"

"No, they cannot come."

There was silence for a minute or more, the two men staring blankly at each other.

"Do they all know?"

"No one knows but me."

"How did you learn?"

"I was at the wall near the postern gate—the little wooden gate that opens on the rose garden. I saw something crawling among the bushes. There was a knocking at the door. I opened it. It was a Christian Tartar, badly cut about with swords. He had come from the battle. Commodore Wyndham, the Englishman, had sent him. The relieving force had been checked. They had shot away most of their ammunition. They had entrenched themselves and sent back to the ships for more. Three days must pass before they could come. That was all. Mein Gott! it was enough."

The Professor bent his shaggy grey brows.

"Where is the man?" he asked.

"He is dead. He died of loss of blood. His body lies at the postern gate."

"And no one saw him?"

"Not to speak to."

"Oh! they did see him, then?"

"Ainslie must have seen him from the church tower. He must know that I have had tidings. He will want to know what they are. If I tell him they must all know."

"How long can we hold out?"

"An hour or two at the most."

"Is that absolutely certain?"

"I pledge my credit as a soldier upon it."

"Then we must fall?"

"Yes, we must fall."

"There is no hope for us?"

"None."

The door flew open and young Ainslie rushed in. Behind him crowded Ralston, Patterson, and a crowd of white men and of native Christians.

"You've had news, Colonel?"

Professor Mercer pushed to the front.

"Colonel Dresler has just been telling me. It is all right. They have halted, but will be here in the early morning. There is no longer any danger."

A cheer broke from the group in the doorway. Everyone was laughing and shaking hands.

"But suppose they rush us before to-morrow morning?" cried Ralston, in a petulant voice. "What infernal fools these fellows are not to push on! Lazy devils, they should be court-martialled, every man of them."

"It's all safe," said Ainslie. "These fellows have had a bad knock. We can see their wounded being carried by the hundred over the hill. They must have lost heavily. They won't attack before morning."

"No, no," said the Colonel; "it is certain that they won't attack before morning. None the less, get back to your posts. We must give no point away." He left the room with the rest, but as he did so he looked back, and his eyes for an instant met those of the old Professor. " I leave it in your hands," was the message which he flashed.

A stern set smile was his answer.

The afternoon wore away without the Boxers making their last attack. To Colonel Dresler it was clear that the unwonted stillness meant only that they were re-assembling their forces from their fight with the relief column, and were gathering themselves for the inevitable and final rush. To all the others it appeared that the siege was indeed over, and that the assailants had been crippled by the losses which they had already sustained. It was a joyous and noisy party, therefore, which met at the supper-table, when the three bottles of Lachryma Christi were uncorked and the famous pot of caviare was finally opened. It was a large jar, and, though each had a tablespoonful of the delicacy, it was by no means exhausted. Ralston, who was an epicure, had a double allowance. He pecked away at it like a hungry bird. Ainslie, too, had a second helping. The Professor took a large spoonful himself, and Colonel Dreslet, watching him narrowly, did the same. The ladies ate freely, save only pretty Miss Patterson, who disliked the salty, pungent taste. In spite of the hospitable entreaties of the Professor, her portion lay hardly touched at the side of her plate.

" You don't like my little delicacy. It is a disappointment to me when I had kept it for your pleasure," said the old man. " I beg that you will eat the caviare."

" I have never tasted it before. No doubt I should like it in time."

" Well, you must make a beginning. Why not start to educate your taste now ? Do, please ! "

Pretty Jessie Patterson's bright face shone with her sunny, boyish smile.

" Why, how earnest you are ! " she laughed. " I had no idea you were so polite, Professor Mercer. Even if I do not eat it I am just as grateful."

"You are foolish not to eat it," said the Professor, with such intensity that the smile died from her face and her eyes reflected the earnestness of his own. "I tell you it is foolish not to eat caviare to-night."

"But why—why?" she asked.

"Because you have it on your plate. Because it is sinful to waste it."

"There! there!" said stout Mrs. Patterson, leaning across. "Don't trouble her any more. I can see that she does not like it. But it shall not be wasted." She passed the blade of her knife under it, and scraped it from Jessie's plate on to her own. "Now it won't be wasted. Your mind will be at ease, Professor."

But it did not seem at ease. On the contrary his face was agitated like that of a man who encounters an unexpected and formidable obstacle. He was lost in thought.

The conversation buzzed cheerily. Everyone was full of his future plans.

"No, no, there is no holiday for me," said Father Pierre. "We priests don't get holidays. Now that the mission and school are formed I am to leave it to Father Amiel, and to push westwards to found another."

"You are leaving?" said Mr. Patterson. "You don't mean that you are going away from Ichau?"

Father Pierre shook his venerable head in waggish reproof. "You must not look so pleased, Mr. Patterson."

"Well, well, our views are very different," said the Presbyterian, "but there is no personal feeling towards you, Father Pierre. At the same time, how any reasonable educated man at this time of the world's history can teach these poor benighted heathen that——"

A general buzz of remonstrance silenced the theology.

"What will you do yourself, Mr. Patterson?" asked someone.

"Well, I'll take three months in Edinburgh to attend the annual meeting. You'll be glad to do some shopping in Princes Street, I'm thinking, Mary. And you, Jessie, you'll see some folk your own age. Then we can come back in the fall, when your nerves have had a rest."

"Indeed, we shall all need it," said Miss Sinclair, the mission nurse. "You know, this long strain takes me in the strangest way. At the present moment I can hear such a buzzing in my ears."

"Well, that's funny, for it's just the same with me," cried Ainslie. "An absurd up-and-down buzzing, as if a drunken bluebottle were trying experiments on his register. As you say, it must be due to nervous strain. For my part I am going back to Peking, and I hope I may get some promotion over this affair. I can get good polo here, and that's as fine a change of thought as I know. How about you, Ralston?"

"Oh, I don't know. I've hardly had time to think. I want to have a real good sunny, bright holiday and forget it all. It was funny to see all the letters in my room. It looked so black on Wednesday night that I had settled up my affairs and written to all my friends. I don't quite know how they were to be delivered, but I trusted to luck. I think I will keep those papers as a souvenir. They will always remind me of how close a shave we have had."

"Yes, I would keep them," said Dresler.

His voice was so deep and solemn that every eye was turned upon him.

"What is it, Colonel? You seem in the blues to-night." It was Ainslie who spoke.

"No, no; I am very contented."

"Well, so you should be when you see success in sight. I am sure we are all indebted to you for your science and skill. I don't think we could have held the place without you. Ladies and gentlemen, I ask you to drink to the health of Colonel Dresler, of the Imperial German army. Er soll leben—hoch!"

They all stood up and raised their glasses to the soldier, with smiles and bows.

His pale face flushed with professional pride.

"I have always kept my books with me. I have forgotten nothing," said he. "I do not think that more could be done. If things had gone wrong with us and the place had fallen you would, I am sure, have freed me from any blame or responsibility." He looked wistfully round him.

"I'm voicing the sentiments of this company, Colonel Dresler," said the Scotch minister, "when I say—— but, Lord save us! what's amiss with Mr. Raltson?"

He had dropped his face upon his folded arms and was placidly sleeping.

"Don't mind him," said the Professor, hurriedly. "We are all in a stage of reaction now. I have no doubt that we are all liable to collapse. It is only to-night that we shall feel what we have gone through."

"I'm sure I can fully sympathize with him," said Mrs. Patterson. "I don't know when I have been more sleepy. I can hardly hold my own head up." She cuddled back in her chair and shut her eyes.

"Well, I've never known Mary do that before," cried her husband, laughing heartily. "Gone to sleep over her supper! Whatever will she think when we tell her of it afterwards? But the air does seem hot and heavy. I can certainly excuse anyone who falls asleep to-night. I think that I shall turn in early myself."

Ainslie was in a talkative, excited mood. He was on his feet once more with his glass in his hand.

"I think that we ought to have one drink all together, and then sing 'Auld Lang Syne,'" said he, smiling round at the company. "For a week we have all pulled in the same boat, and we've got to know each other as people never do in the quiet days of peace. We've learned to appreciate each other, and we've learned to appreciate each other's nations. There's the Colonel here stands for Germany. And Father Pierre is for France. Then there's the Professor for America. Ralston and I are Britishers. Then there's the ladies, God bless 'em! They have been angels of mercy and compassion all through the siege. I think we should drink the health of the ladies. Wonderful thing—the quiet courage, the patience, the—what shall I say?—the fortitude, the—the—by George, look at the Colonel! He's gone to sleep, too—most infernal sleepy weather." His glass crashed down upon the table, and he sank back, mumbling and muttering, into his seat. Miss Sinclair, the pale mission nurse, had dropped off also. She lay like a broken lily across the arm of her chair. Mr. Patterson looked round him and sprang to his feet. He passed his hand over his flushed forehead.

"This isn't natural, Jessie," he cried. "Why are they all asleep? There's Father Pierre—he's off too. Jessie, Jessie, your mother is cold. Is it sleep? Is it death? Open the windows! Help! help! help!" He staggered to his feet and rushed to the windows, but midway his head spun round, his knees sank under him, and he pitched forward upon his face.

The young girl had also sprung to her feet. She looked round her with horror-stricken eyes at her prostrate father and the silent ring of figures.

"Professor Mercer! What is it? What is it?" she cried. "Oh, my God, they are dying! They are dead!"

The old man had raised himself by a supreme effort of his will, though the darkness was already gathering thickly round him.

"My dear young lady," he said, stuttering and stumbling over the words, "we would have spared you this. It would have been painless to mind and body. It was cyanide. I had it in the caviare. But you would not have it."

"Great Heaven!" She shrank away from him with dilated eyes. "Oh, you monster! You monster! You have poisoned them!"

"No! no! I saved them. You don't know the Chinese. They are horrible. In another hour we should all have been in their hands. Take it now, child." Even as he spoke a burst of firing broke out under the very windows of the room. "Hark! There they are! Quick, dear, quick, you may cheat them yet!" But his words fell upon deaf ears, for the girl had sunk back senseless in her chair. The old man stood listening for an instant to the firing outside. But what was that? Merciful Father, what was that? Was he going mad? Was it the effect of the drug? Surely it was a European cheer? Yes, there were sharp orders in English. There was the shouting of sailors. He could no longer doubt it. By some miracle the relief had come after all. He threw his long arms upwards in his despair. "What have I done? Oh, good Lord, what *have* I done?" he cried.

It was Commodore Wyndham himself who was the first, after his desperate and successful night attack, to burst into that terrible supper-room. Round the table sat the white and silent company. Only in the young girl who moaned and faintly stirred was any sign of life to be seen. And yet there was one in the circle who had the energy for a last supreme duty. The Commodore, standing stupefied at the door, saw a grey head slowly lifted from the table, and the tall form of the Professor staggered for an instant to its feet.

"Take care of the caviare! For God's sake don't touch the caviare!" he croaked.

Then he sank back once more and the circle of death was complete.

9. *The Green Flag*

WHEN Jack Conolly, of the Irish Shot-gun Brigade, the Rory of the Hills Inner Circle, and the extreme left wing of the Land League, was incontinently shot by Sergeant Murdoch of the constabulary, in a little moonlight frolic near Kanturk, his twin-brother Dennis joined the British Army. The countryside had become too hot for him; and, as the seventy-five shillings were wanting which might have carried him to America, he took the only way handy of getting himself out of the way. Seldom has Her Majesty had a less promising recruit, for his hot Celtic blood seethed with hatred against Britain and all things British. The Sergeant, however, smiling complacently over his six feet of brawn and his forty-four-inch chest, whisked him off with a dozen other of the boys to the depôt at Fermoy, whence in a few weeks they were sent on, with the spade-work kinks taken out of their backs, to the first battalion of the Royal Mallows, at the top of the roster for foreign service.

The Royal Mallows, at about that date, were as strange a lot of men as ever were paid by a great empire to fight its battles. It was the darkest hour of the land struggle, when the one side came out with crowbar and battering-ram by day, and the other with mask and with shot-gun by night. Men driven from their homes and potato-patches found their way even into the service of the Government, to which it seemed to them they owed their troubles, and now and then they did wild things before they came. There were recruits in the Irish regiments who would forget to answer to their own names, so short had been their acquaintance with them. Of these the Royal Mallows had their full share; and, while they still retained their fame as being one of the smartest corps in the Army, no one knew better than their officers that they were dry-rotted with treason and with bitter hatred of the flag under which they served.

And the centre of all the disaffection was C Company, in which Dennis Conolly found himself enrolled. They were Celts, Catholics, and men of the tenant class to a man; and their whole experience of the British Government had been an inexorable landlord, and a constabulary who seemed to them to be always on the side of the rent-collector. Dennis was not the only moonlighter in the ranks, nor was he alone in having an intolerable family blood-feud to harden his heart. Savagery had begotten savagery in that veiled civil war. A landlord with an iron mortgage weighing down upon him had small bowels for his tenantry. He did but take what the law allowed; and yet, with men like Jim Holan, or Patrick McQuire, or Peter Flynn, who had seen the roofs torn from their cottages and their folk huddled among their pitiable furniture upon the roadside, it was ill to argue about abstract law. What matter that in that long and bitter struggle there was many another outrage on the part of the tenant, and many another grievance on the side of the landowner! A stricken man can only feel his own wound, and the rank and file of the C Company of the Royal Mallows were sore and savage to the soul. There were low whisperings in barrack-rooms and canteens, stealthy meetings in public-house parlours, bandying of passwords from mouth to mouth, and many other signs which made their officers right glad when the order came which sent them to foreign, and better still to active, service.

For Irish regiments have before now been disaffected, and have at a distance looked upon the foe as though he might, in truth, be the friend; but when they have been put face on to him, and when their officers have dashed to the front with a wave and halloo, those rebel hearts have softened and their gallant Celtic blood has boiled with the mad joy of the fight, until the slower Britons have marvelled that they ever could have doubted the loyalty of their Irish comrades. So it would be again, according to the officers, and so it would not be if Dennis Conolly and a few others could have their way.

It was a March morning upon the eastern fringe

of the Nubian desert. The sun had not yet risen; but a tinge of pink flushed up as far as the cloudless zenith, and the long strip of sea lay like a rosy ribbon across the horizon. From the coast inland stretched dreary sand-plains, dotted over with thick clumps of mimosa scrub and mottled patches of thorny bush. No tree broke the monotony of that vast desert. The dull, dusty hue of the thickets and the yellow glare of the sand were the only colours, save at one point where, from a distance, it seemed that a landslip of snow-white stones had shot itself across a low foot-hill. But as the traveller approached he saw, with a thrill, that these were no stones, but the bleaching bones of a slaughtered army. With its dull tints, its gnarled viprous bushes, its arid, barren soil, and this death streak trailed across it, it was indeed a nightmare country.

Some eight or ten miles inland the rolling plain curved upwards with a steeper slope until it ran into a line of red basaltic rock which zigzagged from north to south, heaping itself up at one point into a fantastic knoll. On the summit of this there stood upon that March morning three Arab chieftains—the Sheik Kadra of the Hadendowas, Moussa Wad Aburhegel, who led the Berber dervishes, and Hamid Wad Hussein, who had come northward with his fighting men from the land of the Baggaras. They had all three just risen from their praying-carpets, and were peering out, with fierce, high-nosed faces thrust forwards, at the stretch of country revealed by the spreading dawn.

The red rim of the sun was pushing itself now above the distant sea, and the whole coast-line stood out brilliantly yellow against the rich deep blue beyond. At one spot lay a huddle of white-walled houses, a mere splotch in the distance; while four tiny cock-boats, which lay beyond, marked the position of three of Her Majesty's ten-thousand-ton troopers and the Admiral's flagship. But it was not upon the distant town, nor upon the great vessels, nor yet upon the sinister white litter which gleamed in the plain beneath them, that the Arab chieftains gazed. Two miles from where they stood, amid the sandhills and the mimosa scrub, a great parallelogram had been marked by piled-up bushes. From the inside of this dozens of tiny blue smoke-reeks curled up into the still morning air; while there rose from it a confused deep murmur, the voices of men and the gruntings of camels blended into the same insect buzz.

"The unbelievers have cooked their morning food," said the Baggara chief, shading his eyes with his tawny, sinewy hand. "Truly their sleep has been but scanty; for Hamid and a hundred of his men have fired upon them since the rising of the moon."

"So it was with these others," answered the Sheik Kadra, pointing with his sheathed sword towards the old battlefield. "They also had a day of little water and a night of little rest, and the heart was gone out of them ere ever the sons of the Prophet had looked them in the eyes. This blade drank deep that day, and will again before the sun has travelled from the sea to the hill."

"And yet these are other men," remarked the Berber dervish. "Well, I know that Allah has placed them in the clutch of our fingers, yet it may be that they with the big hats will stand firmer than the cursed men of Egypt."

"Pray Allah that it may be so," cried the fierce Baggara, with a flash of his black eyes. "It was not to chase women that I brought seven hundred men from the river to the coast. See, my brother, already they are forming their array."

A fanfare of bugle-calls burst from the distant camp. At the same time the bank of bushes at one side had been thrown or trampled down, and the little army within began to move slowly out on to the plain. Once clear of the camp they halted, and the slant rays of the sun struck flashes from bayonet and from gun-barrel as the ranks closed up until the big pith helmets joined into a single long white ribbon. Two streaks of scarlet glowed on either side of the square, but elsewhere the fringe of fighting-men was of the dull yellow khaki tint which hardly shows against the desert sand. Inside their array was a dense mass of camels and mules bearing stores and ambulance needs. Outside a twinkling clump of cavalry was drawn up on each flank, and in front a thin scattered line of mounted infantry was already slowly advancing over the bush-strewn plain, halting on every eminence, and peering warily round as men might who have to pick their steps among the bones of those who have preceded them.

The three chieftains still lingered upon the knoll, looking down with hungry eyes and compressed lips at the dark steel-tipped patch.

"They are slower to start than the men of Egypt," the Sheik of the Hadendowas growled in his beard.

"Slower also to go back, perchance, my brother" murmured the dervish. "And yet they are not many—three thousand at the most."

"And we ten thousand, with the Prophet's grip upon our spear-hafts and his words upon our banner. See to their chieftain, how he rides upon the right and looks up at us with the glass that sees from afar! It may be that he sees this also." The Arab shook his sword at the small clump of horsemen who had spurred out from the square.

"Lo! he beckons," cried the dervish; "and see those others at the corner, how they bend and heave. Ha! by the Prophet, I had thought it."

As he spoke a little woolly puff of smoke spurted up at the corner of the square, and a seven-pound shell burst with a hard metallic smack just over their heads. The splinters knocked chips from the red rocks around them.

"Bismillah!" cried the Hadendowa; "if the gun can carry thus far, then ours can answer to it. Ride to the left, Moussa, and tell Ben Ali to cut the skin from the Egyptians if they cannot hit yonder mark. And you, Hamid, to the right, and see that three thousand men lie close in the wady that we have chosen. Let the others beat the drum and show the banner of the Prophet; for by the black stone their spears will have drunk deep ere they look upon the stars again."

A long, straggling, boulder-strewn plateau lay on the summit of the red hills, sloping very precipitously to the plain, save at one point, where a winding gully curved downwards, its mouth choked with sand-mounds and olive-hued scrub. Along the edge of this position lay the Arab host, a motley crew of shock-headed desert clansmen, fierce predatory slave-dealers of the interior, and wild dervishes from the Upper Nile, all blent together by their common fearlessness and fanaticism. Two races were there, as wide as the poles apart, the thin-lipped, straight-haired Arab, and the thick-lipped, curly negro; yet the faith of Islam had bound them closer than a blood tie. Squatting among the rocks, or lying thickly in the shadow, they peered out at the slow-moving square beneath them, while women with water-skins and bags of dhoora fluttered from group to group, calling out to each other those fighting texts from the Koran which in the hour of battle are maddening as wine to the true believer. A score of banners waved over the ragged, valiant crew, and among them, upon desert horses and white Bishareen camels, were the Emirs and Sheiks who were to lead them against the infidels.

As the Sheik Kadra sprang into his saddle and drew his sword there was a wild whoop and a clatter of waving spears, while the one-ended war-drums burst into a dull crash like a wave upon shingle. For a moment ten thousand men were up on the rocks with brandished arms and leaping figures; the next they were under cover, again waiting sternly and silently for their chieftain's orders. The square was less than half a mile from the ridge now, and shell after shell from the seven-pound guns was pitching over it. A deep roar on the right, and then a second one showed that the Egyptian Krupps were in action. Sheik Kadra's hawk eyes saw that the shells burst far beyond the mark, and he spurred his horse along to where a knot of mounted chiefs were gathered round the two guns, which were served by their captured crews.

"How is this, Ben Ali?" he cried. "It was not thus that the dogs fired when it was their own brothers in faith at whom they aimed!"

A chieftain reined his horse back, and thrust a blood-smeared sword into its sheath. Beside him two Egyptian artillerymen with their throats cut were sobbing out their lives upon the ground.

"Who lays the gun this time?" asked the fierce chief, glaring at the frightened gunners. "Here, thou black-browed child of Shaitan, aim, and aim for thy life."

It may have been chance, or it may have been skill, but the third and fourth shells burst over the square. Sheik Kadra smiled grimly and galloped back to the left, where his spearmen were streaming down into the gully. As he joined them a deep growling rose from the plain beneath, like the snarling of a sullen wild beast, and a little knot of tribesmen fell in a struggling heap, caught in the blast of lead from a Gardner. Their comrades pressed on over them, and sprang down into the ravine. From all along the crest burst the hard sharp crackle of Remington fire.

The square had slowly advanced, rippling over the low sandhills, and halting every few minutes to re-arrange its formation. Now, having made sure that there was no force of the enemy in the scrub, it changed its direction, and began to take a line parallel to the Arab position. It was too steep to assail from the front, and if they moved far enough to the right the General hoped that he might turn it. On the top of those ruddy hills lay a baronetcy for him, and a few extra hundreds in his pension, and he meant having them both that day. The Remington fire was annoying, and so were those two Krupp guns: already there were more cacolets full than he cared to see. But on the whole he thought it better to hold his fire until he had more to aim at than a few hundred of fuzzy heads peeping over a razor-back ridge. He was a bulky, red-faced man, a fine whist-player, and a soldier who knew his work. His men believed in him, and he had good reason to believe in them, for he had excellent stuff under him that day. Being an ardent champion of the short-service system, he took particular care to work with veteran first battalions, and his little force was the compressed essence of an army corps.

The left front of the square was formed by four companies of the Royal Wessex, and the right by four of the Royal Mallows. On either side the other halves of the same regiments marched in quarter column of companies. Behind them, on the right, was a battalion of Guards, and on the left one of Marines, while the rear was closed in by a Rifle battalion. Two Royal Artillery seven-pound screw-guns kept pace with the square, and a dozen white-bloused sailors, under their blue-coated, tight-waisted officers, trailed their Gardner in front, turning every now and then to spit up at the draggled banners which waved over the cragged ridge. Hussars and Lancers scouted in the scrub at each side, and within moved the clump of camels, with humorous eyes and supercilious lips, their comic faces a contrast to the blood-stained men who already lay huddled in the cacolets on either side.

The square was now moving slowly on a line parallel with the rocks, stopping every few minutes to pick up wounded, and to allow the screw-guns and Gardner to make themselves felt. The men looked serious, for that spring on to the rocks of the Arab army had given them a vague glimpse of the number and ferocity of their foes; but their faces were set like stone, for they knew to a man that they must win or they must die—and die, too, in a particularly unlovely fashion. But most serious of all was the General, for he had seen that which brought a flush to his cheeks and a frown to his brow.

"I say, Stephen," said he to his galloper, "those Mallows seem a trifle jumpy. The right flank company bulged a bit when the niggers showed on the hill."

"Youngest troops in the square, sir," murmured the aide, looking at them critically through his eyeglass.

"Tell Colonel Flanagan to see to it, Stephen," said the General; and the galloper sped upon his way. The Colonel, a fine old Celtic warrior, was over at C Company in an instant.

"How are the men, Captain Foley?"

"Never better, sir," answered the senior captain, in the spirit that makes a Madras officer look murder if you suggest recruiting his regiment from the Punjaub.

"Stiffen them up!" cried the Colonel. As he rode away a colour-sergeant seemed to trip, and fell forward into a mimosa bush.

He made no effort to rise, but lay in a heap among the thorns.

"Sergeant O'Rooke's gone, sorr," cried a voice.

"Never mind, lads," said Captain Foley. "He's died like a soldier, fighting for his Queen."

"To hell with the Queen!" shouted a hoarse voice from the ranks.

But the roar of the Gardner and the typewriter-like clicking of the hopper burst in at the tail of the words. Captain Foley heard them, and Subalterns Grice and Murphy heard them; but there are times when a deaf ear is a gift from the gods.

"Steady, Mallows!" cried the Captain, in a pause

of the grunting machine-gun. "We have the honour of Ireland to guard this day."

"And well we know how to guard it, Captin!" cried the same ominous voice; and there was a buzz from the length of the company.

The Captain and the two subs. came together behind the marching line.

"They seem a bit out of hand," murmured the Captain.

"Bedad," said the Galway boy, "they mean to scoot like redshanks."

"They nearly broke when the blacks showed on the hill," said Grice.

"The first man that turns, my sword is through him," cried Foley, loud enough to be heard by five files on either side of him. Then, in a lower voice, "It's a bitter drop to swallow, but it's my duty to report what you think to the Chief and have a company of Jollies put behind us." He turned away with the safety of the square upon his mind, and before he had reached his goal the square had ceased to exist.

In their march in front of what looked like a face of cliff, they had come opposite to the mouth of the gully, in which, screened by scrub and boulders, three thousand chosen dervishes, under Hamid Wad Hussein of the Baggaras, were crouching. Tat, tat, tat, went the rifles of three mounted infantrymen in front of the left shoulder of the square, and an instant later they were spurring it for their lives, crouching over the manes of their horses, and pelting over the sandhills with thirty or forty galloping chieftains at their heels. Rocks and scrub and mimosa swarmed suddenly into life. Rushing black figures came and went in the gaps of the bushes. A howl that drowned the shouts of the officers, a long quavering yell, burst from the ambuscade. Two rolling volleys from the Royal Wessex, one crash from the screw-gun firing shrapnel, and then before a second cartridge could be rammed in, a living, glistening black wave tipped with steel, had rolled over the gun, the Royal Wessex had been dashed back among the camels, and a thousand fanatics were hewing and hacking in the heart of what had been the square.

The camels and mules in the centre jammed more and more together as their leaders flinched from the rush of the tribesmen, shut out the view of the other three faces, who could only tell that the Arabs had got in by the yells upon Allah, which rose ever nearer and nearer amid the clouds of sand-dust, the struggling animals, and the dense mass of swaying, cursing men. Some of the Wessex fired back at the Arabs who had passed them, as excited Tommies will, and it is whispered among doctors that it was not always a Remington bullet which was cut from a wound that day. Some rallied in little knots, stabbing furiously with their bayonets at the rushing spearsmen. Others turned at bay with their backs against the camels, and others round the General and his staff, who, revolver in hand, had flung themselves into the heart of it. But the whole square was sidling slowly away from the gorge, pushed back by the pressure at the shattered corner.

The officers and men at the other faces were glancing nervously to their rear, uncertain what was going on, and unable to take help to their comrades without breaking the formation.

"By Jove, they've got through the Wessex!" cried Grice of the Mallows.

"The divils have hurrooshed us, Ted," said his brother subaltern, cocking his revolver.

The ranks were breaking and crowding towards Private Conolly, all talking together as the officers peered back through the veil of dust. The sailors had run their Gardner out, and she was squirting death out of her five barrels into the flank of the rushing stream of savages.

"Oh, this bloody gun!" shouted a voice. "She's jammed again." The fierce metallic grunting had ceased, and her crew were straining and hauling at the breech.

"This damned vertical feed!" cried an officer. "The spanner, Wilson, the spanner! Stand to your cutlasses, boys, or they're into us."

His voice rose into a shriek as he ended, for a shovel-headed spear had been buried in his chest A second wave of dervishes lapped over the hillocks, and burst upon the machine-gun and the right front of the line. The sailors were overborne in an instant, but the Mallows, with their fighting blood aflame, met the yell of the Moslem with an even wilder, fiercer cry, and dropped two hundred of them with a single point-blank volley. The howling, leaping crew swerved away to the right and dashed on into the gap which had already been made for them.

But C Company had drawn no trigger to stop that fiery rush. The men leaned moodily upon their Martinis. Some had even thrown them upon the ground. Conolly was talking fiercely to those about him. Captain Foley, thrusting his way through the press, rushed up to him with a revolver in his hand.

"This is your doing, you villain!" he cried.

"If you raise your pistol, Captin, your brains will be over your coat," said a low voice at his side.

He saw that several rifles were turned on him. The two subs. had pressed forward, and were by his side.

"What is it, then?" he cried, looking round from one fierce mutinous face to another. "Are you Irishmen? Are you soldiers? What are you here for but to fight for your country?"

"England is no country of ours," cried several.

"You are not fighting for England. You are fighting for Ireland, and for the Empire of which it is part."

"A black curse on the Impire!" shouted Private McQuire, throwing down his rifle. "'Twas the Impire that backed the man that druv me on to the roadside. May me hand stiffen before I draw thrigger for it."

"What's the Impire to us, Captain Foley, and what's the Widdy to us ayther?" cried a voice.

"Let the constabulary foight for her."

"Ay, be God, they'd be better imployed than pullin' a poor man's thatch about his ears."

"Or shootin' his brother, as they did mine."

"It was the Impire laid my groanin' mother by the wayside. Her son will rot before he upholds it, and ye can put that in the charge-sheet in the next coort-martial."

In vain the three officers begged, menaced, persuaded. The square was still moving, ever moving, with the same bloody fight raging in its entrails. Even while they had been speaking they had been shuffling backwards, and the useless Gardner, with her slaughtered crew, was already a good hundred yards from them. And the pace was accelerating. The mass of men, tormented and writhing, was trying, by a common instinct, to reach some clearer ground where they could re-form. Three faces were still intact, but the fourth had been caved in and badly mauled, without its comrades being able to help it. The Guards had met a fresh rush of the Hadendowas, and had blown back the tribesmen with a volley, and the Cavalry had ridden over another stream of them, as they welled out of the gully. A litter of hamstrung horses, and haggled men behind them, showed that a spearman on his face among the bushes can show some sport to the man who charges him. But, in spite of all, the square was still reeling swiftly backwards, trying to shake itself clear of this torment which clung to its heart. Would it break, or would it re-form? The lives of five regiments and the honour of the flag hung upon the answer.

Some, at least, were breaking. The C Company of the Mallows had lost all military order, and was pushing back in spite of the haggard officers, who cursed and shoved and prayed in the vain attempt to hold them. Their Captain and the subs. were elbowed and jostled, while the men crowded towards Private Conolly for their orders. The confusion had not spread, for the other companies, in the dust and smoke and turmoil, had lost touch with their mutinous comrades. Captain Foley saw that even now there might be time to avert a disaster.

"Think what you are doing, man," he yelled, rushing towards the ringleader. "There are a thousand Irish in the square, and they are dead men if we break."

The words alone might have had little effect on the old moonlighter. It is possible that, in his scheming brain, he had already planned how he was to club his Irish together and lead them to the sea. But at that moment the Arabs broke through the screen of camels which had fended them off.. There was a struggle, a screaming, a mule rolled over, a wounded man sprang up in a cacolet with a spear through him, and then through the narrow gap surged a stream of naked savages, mad with battle, drunk with slaughter, spotted and splashed with blood—blood dripping from their spears, their arms, their faces. Their yells, their bounds, their crouching, darting figures, the horrid energy of their spear-thrusts, made them look like a blast of fiends from the pit. And were these the Allies of Ireland? Were these the men who were to strike for her against her enemies? Conolly's soul rose up in loathing at the thought.

He was a man of firm purpose, and yet at the first sight of those howling fiends that purpose faltered, and at the second it was blown to the winds. He saw a huge coal-black negro seize a shrieking camel-driver and saw at his throat with a knife. He saw a shock-headed tribesman plunge his great spear through the back of their own little bugler from Millstreet. He saw a dozen deeds of blood—the murder of the wounded, the hacking of the unarmed—and caught, too, in a glance, the good wholesome faces of the faced-about rear rank of the Marines. The Mallows, too, had faced about, and in an instant Conolly had thrown himself into the heart of C Company, striving with the officers to form the men up with their comrades.

But the mischief had gone too far. The rank and file had no heart in their work. They had broken before, and this last rush of murderous savages was a hard thing for broken men to stand against. They flinched from the furious faces and dripping forearms. Why should they throw away their lives for a flag for which they cared nothing? Why should their leader urge them to break, and now shriek to them to re-form? They would not re-form. They wanted to get to the sea and to safety. He flung himself among them with outstretched arms, with words of reason, with shouts, with gaspings. It was useless; the tide was beyond his control. They were shredding out into the desert with their faces set for the coast.

"Bhoys, will ye stand for this?" screamed a voice. It was so ringing, so strenuous, that the breaking Mallows glanced backwards. They were held by what they saw. Private Conolly had planted his rifle-stock downwards in a mimosa bush. From the fixed bayonet there fluttered a little green flag with the crownless harp. God knows for what black mutiny, for what signal of revolt, that flag had been treasured up within Conolly's tunic! Now its green wisp stood amid the rush, while three proud regimental colours were reeling slowly backwards.

"What for the flag?" yelled the private.

"My heart's blood for it! and mine! and mine!" cried a score of voices. "God bless it! The flag, boys—the flag!"

C Company were rallying upon it. The stragglers clutched at each other, and pointed. "Here, McQuire, Flynn, O'Hara," ran the shoutings. "Close on the flag! Back to the flag!" The three standards reeled backwards, and the seething square strove for a clearer space where they could form their shattered ranks; but C Company, grim and powder-stained, choked with enemies and falling fast, still closed in on the little rebel ensign that flapped from the mimosa bush.

It was a good half-hour before the square, having disentangled itself from its difficulties and dressed its ranks, began to slowly move forwards over the ground, across which in its labour and anguish it had been driven. The long trail of Wessex men and Arabs showed but too clearly the path they had come.

"How many got into us Stephen?" asked the General, tapping his snuff-box.

"I should put them down at a thousand or twelve hundred, sir."

"I did not see any get out again. What the devil were the Wessex thinking about? The Guards stood well, though; so did the Mallows."

"Colonel Flanagan reports that his front flank company was cut off, sir."

"Why, that's the Company that was out of hand when we advanced!"

"Colonel Flanagan reports, sir, that the Company took the whole brunt of the attack, and gave the square time to re-form."

"Tell the Hussars to ride forward, Stephen," said the General, "and try if they can see anything of them. There's no firing, and I fear that the Mallows will want to do some recruiting. Let the square take ground by the right, and then advance!"

But the Sheik Kadra of the Hadendowas saw from his knoll that the men with the big hats had rallied, and that they were coming back in the quiet business fashion of men whose work was before them. He took counsel with Moussa the Dervish and Hussein the Baggara, and a woestruck man was he when he learned that the third of his men were safe in the Moslem Paradise. So, having still some signs of victory to show, he gave the word, and the desert warriors flitted off unseen and unheard, even as they had come.

A red rock plateau, a few hundred spears and Remingtons, and a plain which for the second time was strewn with slaughtered men, was all that his day's fighting gave to the English General.

It was a squadron of Hussars which came first to the spot where the rebel flag had waved. A dense litter of Arab dead marked the place. Within the flag waved no longer, but the rifle still stood in the mimosa bush, and round it, with their wounds in front, lay the Fenian private and the silent ranks of his Irishry. Sentiment is not an English failing, but the Hussar Captain raised his hilt in a salute as he rode past the blood-soaked ring.

The British General sent home dispatches to his Government, and so did the Chief of the Hadendowas to his, though the style and manner differed somewhat in each. "The Sheik Kadra of the Hadendowa people to Mohammed Ahmed, the chosen of Allah, homage and greeting," began the latter. "Know by this that on the fourth day of this moon we gave battle to the Kaffirs who call themselves Inglees, having with us the chief Hussein with ten thousand of the faithful. By the blessing of Allah we have broken them, and chased them for a mile, though indeed these infidels are different from the dogs of Egypt, and have slain very many of our men. Yet we hope to smite them again ere the new moon be come, to which end I trust that thou wilt send us a thousand Dervishes from Omdurman. In token of our victory I send you by this messenger a flag which we have taken. By the colour it might well seem to have belonged to those of the true faith, but the Kaffirs gave their blood freely to save it, and so we think that, though small, it is very dear to them."

10. *The Three Correspondents*

THERE was only the one little feathery clump of dôm palms in all that great wilderness of black rocks and orange sand. It stood high on the bank, and below it the brown Nile swirled swiftly towards the Ambigole Cataract, fitting a little frill of foam round each of the boulders which studded its surface. Above, out of a naked blue sky, the sun was beating down upon the sand, and up again from the sand under the brims of the pith-hats of the horsemen with the scorching glare of a blast-furnace. It had risen so high that the shadows of the horses were no larger than themselves.

"Whew!" cried Mortimer, mopping his forehead, "you'd pay five shillings for this at the hummums."

"Precisely," said Scott. "But you are not asked to ride twenty miles in a Turkish bath with a field-glass and a revolver, and a water-bottle and a whole Christmas-treeful of things dangling from you. The hot-house at Kew is excellent as a conservatory, but not adapted for exhibitions upon the horizontal bar. I vote for a camp in the palm-grove and a halt until evening."

Mortimer rose on his stirrups and looked hard to the southward. Everywhere were the same black burned rocks and deep orange sand. At one spot only an intermittent line appeared to have been cut through the rugged spurs which ran down to the river. It was the bed of the old railway, long destroyed by the Arabs, but now in process of reconstruction by the advancing Egyptians. There was no other sign of man's handiwork in all that desolate scene.

"It's palm trees or nothing," said Scott.

"Well, I suppose we must; and yet I grudge every hour until we catch the force up. What *would* our editors say if we were late for the action?"

"My dear chap, an old bird like you doesn't need to be told that no sane modern general would ever attack until the Press is up."

"You don't mean that?" said young Anerley. "I thought we were looked upon as an unmitigated nuisance."

"'Newspaper correspondents and travelling gentlemen, and all that tribe of useless drones'—being an extract from Lord Wolseley's *Soldier's Pocket-Book*," cried Scott. "We know all about *that*, Anerley;" and he winked behind his blue spectacles. "If there was going to be a battle we should very soon have an escort of cavalry to hurry us up. I've been in fifteen, and I never saw one where they had not arranged for a reporter's table."

"That's very well; but the enemy may be less considerate," said Mortimer.

"They are not strong enough to force a battle."

"A skirmish, then?"

"Much more likely to be a raid upon the rear. In that case we are just where we should be."

"So we are! What a score over Reuter's man up with the advance! Well, we'll outspan and have our tiffin under the palms."

There were three of them, and they stood for three great London dailies. Reuter's was thirty miles ahead; two evening pennies upon camels were twenty miles behind. And among them they represented the eyes and ears of the public—the great silent millions and millions who had paid for everything, and who waited so patiently to know the result of their outlay.

They were remarkable men, these body-servants of the Press; two of them already veterans in camps, the other setting out upon his first campaign, and full of deference for his famous comrades.

This first one, who had just dismounted from his bay polo-pony, was Mortimer, of the *Intelligence*—tall, straight, and hawk-faced, with khaki tunic and riding-breeches, drab putties, a scarlet cummerbund, and a skin tanned to the red of a Scotch fir by sun and wind, and mottled by the mosquito and the sand-fly. The other—small, quick, mercurial, with blue-black, curling beard and hair, a fly-switch for ever flicking in his left hand—was Scott, of the *Courier*, who had come through more dangers and brought off more brilliant *coups* than any man in the profession, save the eminent Chandler, now no longer in a condition to take the field. They were a singular contrast, Mortimer and Scott, and it was in their differences that the secret of their close friendship lay. Each dovetailed into the other. The strength of each was in the other's weakness. Together they formed a perfect unit. Mortimer was Saxon—slow, conscientious, and deliberate; Scott was Celtic—quick, happy-go-lucky, and brilliant. Mortimer was the more solid, Scott the more attractive. Mortimer was the deeper thinker, Scott the brighter talker. By a curious coincidence, though each had seen much of warfare, their campaigns had never coincided. Together they covered all recent military history. Scott had done Plevna, the Shipka, the Zulus, Egypt, Suakim; Mortimer had seen the Boer War, the Chilian, the Bulgarian and Servian, the Gordon relief, the Indian frontier, Brazilian rebellion, and Madagascar. This intimate personal knowledge gave a peculiar flavour to their talk. There was none of the second-hand surmise and conjecture which form so much of our conversation; it was all concrete and final. The speaker had been there, had seen it, and there was an end of it.

In spite of their friendship there was the keenest professional rivalry between the two men. Either would have sacrificed himself to help his companion, but either would also have sacrificed his companion to help his paper. Never did a jockey yearn for a winning mount as keenly as each of them longed to have a full column in a morning edition whilst every other daily was blank. They were perfectly frank about the matter. Each professed himself ready to steal a march on his neighbour, and each recognized that the other's duty to his employer was far higher than any personal consideration.

The third man was Anerley, of the *Gazette*—young, inexperienced, and rather simple-looking. He had a droop of the lip which some of his more intimate friends regarded as a libel upon his character, and his eyes were so slow and so sleepy that they suggested an affectation. A leaning toward soldiering had sent him twice to autumn manœuvres, and a touch of colour in his descriptions had induced the proprietors of the *Gazette* to give him a trial as a war-special. There was a pleasing diffidence about his bearing which recommended him to his experienced companions, and if they had a smile sometimes at his guileless ways, it was soothing to them to have a comrade from whom nothing was to be feared. From the day that they left the telegraph-wire behind them at Sarras, the man who was mounted upon a fifteen-guinea thirteen-four Syrian was delivered over into the hands of the owners of the two fastest polo-ponies that ever shot down the Ghezireh ground.

The three had dismounted and led their beasts under the welcome shade. In the brassy, yellow glare every branch above threw so black and solid a shadow that the men involuntarily raised their feet to step over them.

"The palm makes an excellent hat-rack," said Scott, slinging his revolver and his water-bottle over the little upward-pointing pegs which bristles from the trunk. "As a shade-tree, however, it isn't an unqualified success. Curious that in the universal adaptation of means to ends something a little less flimsy could not have been devised for the tropics."

"Like the banyan in India."

"Or the fine hardwood trees in Ashantee, where a whole regiment could picnic under the shade."

"The teak tree isn't bad in Burmah, either. By

Jove, the baccy has all come loose in the saddle-bag! That long-cut mixture smokes rather hot for this climate. How about the baggles, Anerley?"

"They'll be here in five minutes."

Down the winding path which curved among the rocks the little train of baggage-camels was daintily picking its way. They came mincing and undulating along, turning their heads slowly from side to side with the air of a self-conscious woman. In front rode the three Berberee body-servants upon donkeys, and behind walked the Arab camel-boys. They had been travelling for nine long hours, ever since the first rising of the moon, at the weary camel-drag of two and a half miles an hour, but now they brightened, both beasts and men, at the sight of the grove and the riderless horses. In a few minutes the loads were unstrapped, the animals tethered, a fire lighted, fresh water carried up from the river, and each camel provided with his own little heap of tibbin laid in the centre of the tablecloth, without which no well-bred Arabian will condescend to feed. The dazzling light without, the subdued half-tones within, the green palm-fronds outlined against the deep blue sky, the flitting, silent-footed Arab servants, the crackling of sticks, the reek of a lighting fire, the placid supercilious heads of the camels, they all come back in their dreams to those who have known them.

Scott was breaking eggs into a pan and rolling out a love-song in his rich, deep voice. Anerley, with his head and arms buried in a deal packing-case, was working his way through strata of tinned soups, bully beef, potted chicken and sardines to reach the jams which lay beneath. The conscientious Mortimer, with his note-book upon his knee, was jotting down what the railway engineer had told him at the line-end the day before. Suddenly he raised his eyes and saw the man himself on his chestnut pony, dipping and rising over the broken ground.

"Hullo! here's Merryweather!"

"A pretty lather his pony is in! He's had her at that hand-gallop for hours, by the look of her. Hullo, Merryweather, hullo!"

The engineer, a small, compact man with a pointed red beard, had made as though he would ride past their camp without word or halt. Now he swerved, and easing his pony down to a canter, he headed her towards them.

"For God's sake, a drink!" he croaked. "My tongue is stuck to the roof of my mouth."

Mortimer ran with the water-bottle, Scott with the whisky-flask, and Anerley with the tin pannikin. The engineer drank until his breath failed him.

"Well, I must be off," said he, striking the drops from his red moustache.

"Any news?"

"A hitch in the railway construction. I must see the General. It's the devil not having a telegraph."

"Anything we can report?" Out came three note-books.

"I'll tell you after I've seen the General."

"Any dervishes?"

"The usual shaves. Hud-up, Jinny! Good-bye."

With a soft thudding upon the sand and a clatter among the stones the weary pony was off upon her journey once more.

"Nothing serious, I suppose?" said Mortimer, staring after him.

"Deuced serious," cried Scott. "The ham and eggs are burned! No—it's all right—saved, and done to a turn! Pull the box up, Anerley. Come on, Mortimer, stow that note-book! The fork is mightier than the pen just at present. What's the matter with you, Anerley?"

"I was wondering whether what we have just seen was worth a telegram."

"Well, it's for the proprietors to say if it's worth

it. Sordid money considerations are not for us. We must wire about something just to justify our khaki coats and our putties."

"But what is there to say?"

Mortimer's long, austere face broke into a smile over the youngster's innocence. "It's not quite usual in our profession to give each other tips," said he. "However, as my telegram is written, I've no objection to your reading it. You may be sure that I would not show it to you if it were of the slightest importance."

Anerley took up the slip of paper and read—

"Merryweather obstacles stop journey confer General stop nature difficulties later stop rumours dervishes."

"This is very condensed," said Anerley, with wrinkled brows.

"Condensed!" cried Scott. "Why, it's sinfully garrulous. If my old man got a wire like that his language would crack the lamp-shades. I'd cut out half this; for example, I'd have out 'journey,' and 'nature,' and 'rumours.' But my old man would make a ten-line paragraph of it for all that."

"How?"

"Well, I'll do it myself just to show you. Lend me that stylo." He scribbled for a minute in his note-book. "It works out somewhat on these lines—

"'Mr. Charles H. Merryweather, the eminent railway engineer, who is at present engaged in superintending the construction of the line from Sarras to the front, has met with considerable obstacles to the rapid completion of his important task'—of course the old man knows who Merryweather is, and what he is about, so the word 'obstacles' would suggest all that to him. 'He has to-day been compelled to make a journey of forty-miles to the front in order to confer with the General upon the steps which are necessary in order to facilitate the work. Further particulars of the exact nature of the difficulties met with will be made public at a later date. All is quiet upon the line of communications, though the usual persistent rumours of the presence of dervishes in the Eastern desert continue to circulate. *Our own Correspondent.*'

"How's that?" cried Scott, triumphantly, and his white teeth gleamed suddenly through his black beard. "That's the sort of flapdoodle for the dear old public."

"Will it interest them?"

"Oh, everything interests them. They want to know all about it; and they like to think that there is a man who is getting a hundred a month simply in order to tell it to them."

"It's very kind of you to teach me all this."

"Well, it is a little unconventional, for, after all, we are here to score over each other if we can. There are no more eggs, and you must take it out in jam. Of course, as Mortimer says, such a telegram as this is of no importance one way or another, except to prove to the office that we *are* in the Soudan and not at Monte Carlo. But when it comes to serious work it must be every man for himself."

"Is that quite necessary?"

"Why, of course it is."

"I should have thought if three men were to combine and to share their news, they would do better than if they were each to act for himself; and they would have a much pleasanter time of it."

The two older men sat with their bread-and-jam in their hands, and an expression of genuine disgust upon their faces.

"We are not here to have a pleasant time," said Mortimer, with a flash through his glasses. "We are here to do our best for our papers. How can they score over each other if we do not do the same. If we all combine we might as well amalgamate with Reuter at once."

"Why, it would take away the whole glory of the profession!" cried Scott. "At present the smartest man gets his stuff first on the wires. What inducement is there to be smart if we all share and share alike."

"And at present the man with the best equipment has the best chance," remarked Mortimer, glancing across at the shot-silk polo-ponies and the cheap little Syrian grey. "That is the fair reward of foresight and enterprise. Every man for himself, and let the best man win."

"That's the way to find who the best man is. Look at Chandler. He would never have got his chance if he had not played always off his own bat. You've heard how he pretended to break his leg, sent his fellow-correspondent off for the doctor, and so got a fair start for the telegraph-office."

"Do you mean to say that was legitimate?"

"Everything is legitimate. It's your wits against my wits."

"I should call it dishonourable."

"You may call it what you like. Chandler's paper got the battle and the other's didn't. It made Chandler's name."

"Or take Westlake," said Mortimer, cramming the tobacco into his pipe. "Hi, Abdul, you may have the dishes! Westlake brought his stuff down by pretending to be the Government courier, and using the relays of Government horses. Westlake's paper sold half a million."

"Is that legitimate also?" asked Anerley, thoughtfully.

"Why not?"

"Well, it looks a little like horse-stealing and lying."

"Well, *I* think I should do a little horse-stealing and lying if I could have a column to myself in a London daily. What do you say, Scott?"

"Anything short of manslaughter."

"And I'm not sure that I'd trust you there."

"Well, I don't think I should be guilty of newspaper-man-slaughter. That I regard as a distinct breach of professional etiquette. But if any outsider comes between a highly-charged correspondent and an electric wire, he does it at his peril. My dear Anerley, I tell you frankly that if you are going to handicap yourself with scruples you may just as well be in Fleet Street as in the Soudan. Our life is irregular. Our work has never been systematized. No doubt it will be some day, but the time is not yet. Do what you can and how you can, and be first on the wires; that's my advice to you; and also, that when next you come upon a campaign you bring with you the best horse that money can buy. Mortimer may beat me or I may beat Mortimer, but at least we know that between us we have the fastest ponies in the country. We have neglected no chance."

"I am not so certain of that," said Mortimer, slowly. "You are aware, of course, that though a horse beats a camel on twenty miles, a camel beats a horse on thirty."

"What, one of those camels?" cried Anerley in astonishment.

The two seniors burst out laughing.

"No, no, the real high-bred trotter—the kind of beast the dervishes ride when they make their lightning raids."

"Faster than a galloping horse?"

"Well, it tires a horse down. It goes the same gait all the way, and it wants neither halt nor drink, and it takes rough ground much better than a horse. They used to have long distance races at Halfa, and the camel always won at thirty."

"Still, we need not reproach ourselves, Scott, for we are not very likely to have to carry a thirty-mile message. They will have the field telegraph next week."

"Quite so. But at the present moment——"

"I know, my dear chap; but there is no motion of urgency before the house. Load baggles at five o'clock; so you have just three hours clear. Any sign of the evening pennies?"

Mortimer swept the northern horizon with his binoculars.

"Not in sight yet."

"They are quite capable of travelling during the heat of the day. Just the sort of thing evening pennies *would* do. Take care of your match, Anerley. These palm-groves go up like a powder magazine if you set them alight. Bye-bye." The two men crawled under their mosquito-nets and sank instantly into the easy sleep of those whose lives are spent in the open.

Young Anerley stood with his back against a palm tree and his briar between his lips, thinking over the advice which he had received. After all, they were the heads of the profession, these men, and it was not for him, the newcomer, to reform their methods. If they served their papers in this fashion, then he must do the same. They had at least been frank and generous in teaching him the rules of the game. If it was good enough for them it was good enough for him.

It was a broiling afternoon, and those thin frills of foam round the black, glistening necks of the Nile boulders looked delightfully cool and alluring. But it would not be safe to bathe for some hours to come. The air shimmered and vibrated over the baking stretch of sand and rock. There was not a breath of wind, and the droning and piping of the insects inclined one for sleep. Somewhere above a hoopoe was calling. Anerley knocked out his ashes, and was turning towards his couch, when his eye caught something moving in the desert to the south.

It was a horseman riding towards them as swiftly as the broken ground would permit. A messenger from the army, thought Anerley; and then, as he watched, the sun suddenly struck the man on the side of the head, and his chin flamed into gold. There could not be two horsemen with beards of such a colour. It was Merryweather, the engineer, and he was returning. What on earth was he returning for? He had been so keen to see the General, and yet he was coming back with his mission unaccomplished. Was it that his pony was hopelessly foundered? It seemed to be moving well. Anerley picked up Mortimer's binoculars, and a foam-spattered horse and a weary koorbash-cracking man came cantering up the centre of the field. But there was nothing in his appearance to explain the mystery of his return.

Then as he watched them they dipped down into a hollow and disappeared. He could see that it was one of those narrow khors which led to the river, and he waited, glass in hand, for their immediate reappearance. But minute passed after minute and there was no sign of them. That narrow gully appeared to have swallowed them up. And then with a curious gulp and start he saw a little grey cloud wreathe itself slowly from among the rocks and drift in a long, hazy shred over the desert. In an instant he had torn Scott and Mortimer from their slumbers.

"Get up, you chaps!" he cried. "I believe Merryweather has been shot by dervishes."

"And Reuter not here!" cried the two veterans, exultantly clutching at their note-books. "Merryweather shot! Where? When? How?"

In a few words Anerley explained what he had seen.

"You heard nothing?"

"Nothing."

"Well, a shot loses itself very easily among rocks. By George, look at the buzzards!"

Two large brown birds were soaring in the deep blue heaven. As Scott spoke they circled down and dropped into the little khor.

"That's good enough," said Mortimer, with his nose between the leaves of his book. "'Merryweather headed dervishes stop returned stop shot mutilated stop raid communications.' How's that?"

"You think he was headed off?"

"Why else should he return?"

"In that case, if they were out in front of him and others cut him off, there must be several small raiding-parties."

"I should judge so."

"How about the 'mutilated'?"

"I've fought against Arabs before."

"Where are you off to?"

"Sarras."

"I think I'll race you in," said Scott.

Anerley stared in astonishment at the absolutely impersonal way in which these men regarded the situation. In their zeal for news it had apparently never struck them that they, their camp and their servants, were all in the lion's mouth. But even as they talked there came the harsh, importunate rat-tat-tat of an irregular volley from among the rocks, and the high, keening whistle of bullets over their heads. A palm spray fluttered down amongst them. At the same instant the six frightened servants came running wildly in for protection.

It was the cool-headed Mortimer who organized the defence, for Scott's Celtic soul was so aflame at all this "copy" in hand and more to come, that he was too exuberantly boisterous for a commander. The other, with his spectacles and his stern face, soon had the servants in hand.

"*Tali henna! Egri!* What the deuce are you frightened about? Put the camels between the palm trunks. That's right. Now get the knee-tethers on them. *Quies!* Did you never hear bullets before? Now put the donkeys here. Not much—you don't get my polo-pony to make a zareba with. Picket the ponies between the grove and the river out of danger's way. These fellows seem to fire even higher than they did in '85."

"That's got home, anyhow," said Scott, as they heard a soft, splashing thud like a stone in a mud-bank.

"Who's hit, then?"

"The brown camel that's chewing the cud."

As he spoke the creature, its jaw still working, laid its long neck along the ground and closed its large dark eyes.

"That shot cost me fifteen pounds," said Mortimer, ruefully. "How many of them do you make?"

"Four, I think."

"Only four Bezingers, at any rate; there may be some spearmen."

"I think not; it is a little raiding-party of riflemen. By the way, Anerley, you've never been under fire before, have you?"

"Never," said the young pressman, who was conscious of a curious feeling of nervous elation.

"Love and poverty and war, they are all experiences necessary to make a complete life. Pass over those cartridges. This is a very mild baptism that you are undergoing, for behind these camels you are as safe as if you were sitting in the back room of the Authors' Club."

"As safe, but hardly as comfortable," said Scott. "A long glass of hock and seltzer would be exceedingly acceptable. But oh, Mortimer, what a chance! Think of the General's feelings when he hears that the first action of the war has been fought by the Press column. Think of Reuter, who has been stewing at the front for a week! Think of the evening pennies just too late for the fun! By George, that slug brushed a mosquito off me!"

"And one of the donkeys is hit."

"This is sinful. It will end in our having to carry our own kits to Khartoum."

"Never mind, my boy, it all goes to make copy. I can see the headlines—'Raid on Communications': 'Murder of British Engineer': 'Press Column Attacked.' Won't it be ripping?"

"I wonder what the next line will be," said Anerley.

"'Our Special Wounded!'" cried Scott, rolling

over on to his back. "No harm done," he added, gathering himself up again; "only a chip off my knee. This is getting sultry. I confess that the idea of that back room at the Authors' Club begins to grow upon me."

"I have some diachylon."

"Afterwards will do. We're having 'a 'appy day with Fuzzy on the rush.' I wish he *would* rush."

"They're coming nearer."

"This is an excellent revolver of mine if it didn't throw so devilish high. I always aim at a man's toes if I want to stimulate his digestion. O Lord, there's our kettle gone!"

With a boom like a dinner-gong a Remington bullet had passed through the kettle, and a cloud of steam hissed up from the fire. A wild shout came from the rocks above.

"The idiots think that they have blown us up. They'll rush us now, as sure as fate; then it will be our turn to lead. Got your revolver, Anerley?"

"I have this double-barrelled fowling-piece."

"Sensible man! It's the best weapon in the world at this sort of rough-and-tumble work. What cartridges?"

"Swan-shot."

"That will do all right. I carry this big bore double-barrelled pistol loaded with slugs. You might as well try to stop one of these fellows with a peashooter as with a service revolver."

"There are ways and means," said Scott. "The Geneva Convention does not hold south of the first cataract. It's easy to make a bullet mushroom by a little manipulation of the tip of it. When I was in the broken square at Tamai——"

"Wait a bit," cried Mortimer, adjusting his glasses "I think they are coming now."

"The time," said Scott, snapping up his watch, being exactly seventeen minutes past four."

Anerley had been lying behind a camel, staring with an interest which bordered upon fascination at the rocks opposite. Here was a little woolly puff of smoke, and there was another one, but never once had they caught a glimpse of the attackers. To him there was something weird and awesome in these unseen, persistent men who, minute by minute, were drawing closer to them. He had heard them cry out when the kettle was broken, and once, immediately afterwards, an enormously strong voice had roared something which had set Scott shrugging his shoulders.

"They've got to take us first," said he, and Anerley thought his nerve might be better if he did not ask for a translation.

The firing had begun at a distance of some hundred yards, which put it out of the question for them, with their lighter weapons, to make any reply to it. Had their antagonists continued to keep that range the defenders must either have made a hopeless sally or tried to shelter themselves behind their zareba as best they might on the chance that the sound might bring up help. But luckily for them the African had never taken kindly to the rifle, and his primitive instinct to close with his enemy is always too strong for his sense of strategy. They were drawing in, therefore, and now for the first time Anerley caught sight of a face looking at them from over a rock. It was a huge, virile, strong-jawed head of a pure negro type, with silver trinkets gleaming in the ears. The man raised a great arm from behind the rock and shook his Remington at them.

"Shall I fire?" asked Anerley.

"No, no, it is too far; your shot would scatter all over the place."

"It's a picturesque ruffian," said Scott. "Couldn't you kodak him, Mortimer? There's another!"

A fine-featured brown Arab, with a black, pointed beard, was peeping from behind another boulder.

He wore the green turban which proclaimed him hadji, and his face showed the keen, nervous exultation of the religious fanatic.

"They seem a piebald crowd," said Scott.

"That last is one of the real fighting Baggara," remarked Mortimer. "He's a dangerous man."

"He looks pretty vicious. There's another negro!"

"Two more! Dingas, by the look of them. Just the same chaps we get our own black battalions from. As long as they get a fight they don't mind who it's for; but if the idiots had only sense enough to understand, they would know that the Arab is their hereditary enemy, and we their hereditary friends. Look at the silly juggins gnashing his teeth at the very men who put down the slave trade!"

"Couldn't you explain?"

"I'll explain with this pistol when he comes a little nearer. Now sit tight, Anerley. They're off!"

They were indeed. It was the brown man with the green turban who headed the rush. Close at his heels was the negro with the silver earrings—a giant of a man, and the other two were only a little behind. As they sprang over the rocks one after the other, it took Anerley back to the school sports, when he held the tape for the hurdle-race. It was magnificent, the wild spirit and abandon of it, the flutter of the chequered galabeeahs, the gleam of steel, the wave of black arms, the frenzied faces, the quick pitter-patter of the rushing feet. The law-abiding Briton is so imbued with the idea of the sanctity of human life that it was hard for the young pressman to realize that these men had every intention of killing him, and that he was at perfect liberty to do as much for them. He lay staring as if this were a show and he a spectator.

"Now, Anerley, now! Take the Arab!" cried somebody.

He put up the gun and saw the brown fierce face at the other end of the barrel. He tugged at the trigger, but the face grew larger and fiercer with every stride. Again and again he tugged. A revolver-shot rang out at his elbow, then another one, and he saw a red spot spring out on the Arab's brown breast. But he was still coming on.

"Shoot, you ass, shoot!" screamed Scott.

Again he strained unavailingly at the trigger. There were two more pistol-shots, and the big negro had fallen and risen and fallen again.

"Cock it, you fool!" shouted a furious voice; and at the same instant, with a rush and flutter, the Arab bounded over the prostrate camel and came down with his bare feet upon Anerley's chest. In a dream he seemed to be struggling frantically with someone upon the ground, then he was conscious of a tremendous explosion in his very face, and so ended for him the first action of the war.

* * * * *

"Good-bye, old chap. You'll be all right. Give yourself time." It was Mortimer's voice, and he became dimly conscious of a long-spectacled face, and of a heavy hand upon his shoulder.

"Sorry to leave you. We'll be lucky now if we are in time for the morning editions." Scott was tightening his girth as he spoke.

"We'll put in our wire that you have been hurt, so your people will know why they don't hear from you. If Reuter or the evening pennies come up, don't give the thing away. Abbas will look after you, and we'll be back to-morrow afternoon. Bye-bye!"

Anerley heard it all, though he did not feel energy enough to answer. Then, as he watched two sleek brown ponies with their yellow-clad riders dwindling among the rocks, his memory cleared suddenly, and he realized that the first great journalistic chance of his life was slipping away from him. It was a small fight, but it was the first of the war, and the great public at home was all athirst for news. They would have it in the *Courier* ; they would have it in the *Intelligence*, and not a word in the *Gazette*. The thought brought him to his feet, though he had to throw his arm round the stem of the palm tree to steady his swimming head.

There was the big black man lying where he had fallen, his huge chest pocked with bullet-marks, every wound rosetted with its circle of flies. The Arab was stretched out within a few yards of him, with two hands clasped over the dreadful thing which had been his head. Across him was lying Anerley's fowling-piece, one barrel discharged, the other at half cock.

" Scott effendi shoot him your gun," said a voice. It was Abbas, his English-speaking body-servant.

Anerley groaned at the disgrace of it. He had lost his head so completely that he had forgotten to cock his gun ; and yet he knew that it was not fear but interest which had so absorbed him. He put his hand up to his head and felt that a wet handkerchief was bound round his forehead.

" Where are the two other dervishes ? "

" They ran away. One got shot in arm."

" What's happened to me ? "

" Effendi got cut on head. Effendi catch bad man by arms, and Scott effendi shoot him. Face burn very bad."

Anerley became conscious suddenly that there was a pringling about his skin and an overpowering smell of burned hair under his nostrils. He put his hand to his moustache. It was gone. His eyebrows too ? He could not find them. His head, no doubt, was very near to the dervish's when they were rolling upon the ground together, and this was the effect of the explosion of his own gun. Well, he would have time to grow some more hair before he saw Fleet Street again. But the cut, perhaps, was a more serious matter. Was it enough to prevent him from getting to the telegraph-office at Sarras ? The only way was to try and see.

But there was only that poor little Syrian grey of his. There it stood in the evening sunshine, with a sunk head and a bent knee, as if its morning's work was still heavy upon it. What hope was there of being able to do thirty-five miles of heavy going upon that? It would be a strain upon the splendid ponies of his companions—and they were the swiftest and most enduring in the country. The most enduring? There was one creature more enduring, and that was a real trotting camel. If he had had one he might have got to the wires first after all, for Mortimer had said that over thirty miles they have the better of any horse. Yes, if he had only had a real trotting camel! And then like a flash came Mortimer's words, "It is the kind of beast that the dervishes ride when they make their lightning raids."

The beasts the dervishes ride! What had these dead dervishes ridden? In an instant he was clambering up the rocks, with Abbas protesting at his heels. Had the two fugitives carried away all the camels, or had they been content to save themselves? The brass gleam from a litter of empty Remington cases caught his eye, and showed where the enemy had been crouching. And then he could have shouted for joy, for there, in the hollow, some little distance off, rose the high, graceful white neck and the elegant head of such a camel as he had never set eyes upon before—a swan-like, beautiful creature, as far from the rough, clumsy baggles as the cart-horse is from the racer.

The beast was kneeling under the shelter of the rocks with its waterskin and bag of doora slung over its shoulders, and its forelegs tethered Arab fashion with a rope round the knees. Anerley threw his leg over the front pommel while Abbas slipped off the cord. Forward flew Anerley towards the creature's neck, then violently backwards, clawing madly at anything which might save him, and then, with a jerk which nearly snapped his loins, he was thrown forward again. But the camel was on its legs now, and the young pressman was safely seated upon one of the fliers of the desert. It was as gentle as it was swift, and it stood oscillating its long neck and gazing round with its large brown eyes, whilst Anerley coiled his legs round the peg and grasped the curved camel-stick which Abbas had handed up to him. There were two bridle-cords, one from the nostril and one from the neck, but he remembered that Scott had said that it was the servant's and not the house-bell which had to be pulled, so he kept his grasp upon the lower. Then he touched the long, vibrating neck with his stick, and in an instant Abbas' farewells seemed to come from far behind him, and the black rocks and yellow sand were dancing past on either side.

It was his first experience of a trotting camel, and at first the motion, although irregular and abrupt, was not unpleasant. Having no stirrup or fixed point of any kind, he could not rise to it, but he gripped as tightly as he could with his knee, and he tried to sway backwards and forwards as he had seen the Arabs do. It was a large, very concave Makloofa saddle, and he was conscious that he was bouncing about on it with as little power of adhesion as a billiard-ball upon a tea-tray. He gripped the two sides with his hands to hold himself steady. The creature had got into its long, swinging, stealthy trot, its sponge-like feet making no sound upon the hard sand. Anerley leaned back with his two hands gripping hard behind him, and he whooped the creature on.

The sun had already sunk behind the line of black volcanic peaks, which look like huge slag-heaps at the mouth of a mine. The western sky had taken that lovely light-green and pale-pink tint which makes evening beautiful upon the Nile, and the old brown river itself, swirling down amongst the black rocks, caught some shimmer of the colours above. The glare, the heat, and the piping of the insects had all ceased together. In spite of his aching head, Anerley could have cried out for pure physical joy as the swift creature beneath him flew along with him through that cool, invigorating air, with the virile north wind soothing his pringling face.

He had looked at his watch, and now he made a swift calculation of times and distances. It was past six when he had left the camp. Over broken ground it was impossible that he could hope to do more than seven miles an hour—less on bad parts, more on the smooth. His recollection of the track was that there were few smooth and many bad. He would be lucky, then, if he reached Sarras anywhere from twelve to one. Then the messages took a good two hours to go through, for they had to be transcribed at Cairo. At the best he could only hope to have told his story in Fleet Street at two or three in the morning. It was possible that he might manage it, but the chances seemed enormously against him. About three the morning edition would be made up, and his chance gone for ever. The one thing clear was that only the first man at the wires would have any chance at all, and Anerley meant to be first if hard riding could do it. So he tapped away at the bird-like neck, and the creature's long, loose limbs went faster and faster at every tap. Where the rocky spurs ran down to the river, horses would have to go round, while camels might get across, so that Anerley felt that he was always gaining upon his companions.

But there was a price to be paid for the feeling. He had heard of men who had burst when on camel journeys, and he knew that the Arabs swathe their bodies tightly in broad cloth bandages when they prepare for a long march. It had seemed unnecessary and ridiculous when he first began to speed over the level track, but now, when he got on the rocky paths, he understood what it meant. Never for an instant was he at the same angle. Backwards, forwards he swung, with a tingling jar at the end of each sway, until he ached from his neck to his knee. It caught him across the shoulders, it caught him down the spine, it gripped him over the loins, it marked the lower line of his ribs with one heavy, dull throb. He clutched here and there with his hand to try to ease the strain upon his muscles. He drew up his knees, altered his seat, and set his teeth with a grim determination to go through with it should it kill him. His head was splitting, his flayed face smarting, and every joint in his body aching as if it were dislocated. But he forgot all that when, with the rising of the moon, he heard the clinking of horses' hoofs down upon the track by the river, and knew that, unseen by them, he had already got well abreast of his companions. But he was hardly half-way and the time already eleven.

All day the needles had been ticking away without intermission in the little corrugated iron hut which served as a telegraph station at Sarras. With its bare walls and its packing-case seats it was none the less for the moment one of the vital spots upon the earth's surface, and the crisp, importunate ticking might have come from the world-old clock of Destiny. Many august people had been at the other end of those wires, and had communed with the moist-faced military clerk. A French Premier had demanded a pledge, and an English marquis had passed on the request to the General in command, with a question as to how it would affect the situation. Cipher telegrams had nearly driven the clerk out of his wits, for of all crazy occupations the taking of a cipher message, when you are without the key to the cipher, is the worst. Much high diplomacy had been going on all day in the innermost chambers of European chancelleries, and the results of it had been whispered into this little corrugated iron hut. About two in the morning an enormous dispatch had come at last to an end, and the weary operator had opened the door, and was lighting his pipe in the cool, fresh air, when he saw a camel plump down in the dust, and a man, who seemed to be in the last stage of drunkenness, come rolling towards him.

"What's the time?" he cried, in a voice which appeared to be the only sober thing about him.

It was on the clerk's lips to say that it was time that the questioner was in his bed, but it is not safe upon a campaign to be ironical at the expense of khaki-clad men. He contented himself therefore with the bald statement that it was after two.

But no retort that he could have devised could have had a more crushing effect. The voice turned drunken also, and the man caught at the door-post to uphold him.

"Two o'clock! I'm done after all!" said he. His head was tied up in a bloody handkerchief, his face was crimson, and he stood with his legs crooked as if the pith had all gone out of his back. The clerk began to realize that something out of the ordinary was in the wind.

"How long does it take to get a wire to London?"

"About two hours."

"And it's two now. I could not get it there before four."

"Before three."

"Four."

"No, three."

"But you said two hours."

"Yes, but there's more than an hour's difference in longitude."

"By Heaven, I'll do it yet!" cried Anerley, and staggering to a packing-case, he began the dictation of his famous dispatch.

And so it came about that the *Gazette* had a long column, with headlines like an epitaph, when the sheets of the *Intelligence* and the *Courier* were as blank as the faces of their editors. And so, too, it happened that when two weary men, upon two foundered horses, arrived about four in the morning at the Sarras post-office they looked at each other in silence and departed noiselessly, with the conviction that there are some situations with which the English language is not capable of dealing.

II. *The Marriage of the Brigadier*

I AM speaking, my friends, of days which are long gone by, when I had scarcely begun to build up that fame which has made my name so familiar. Among the thirty officers of the Hussars of Conflans there was nothing to indicate that I was superior in any way to the others. I can well imagine how surprised they would all have been had they realized that young Lieutenant Etienne Gerard was destined for so glorious a career, and would live to command a brigade and to receive from the Emperor's own hands that cross which I can show you any time that you do me the honour to visit me in my little cottage. You know, do you not, the little white-washed cottage with the vine in front, in the field beside the Garonne?

People have said of me that I have never known what fear was. No doubt you have heard them say it. For many years, out of a foolish pride, I have let the saying pass. And yet now, in my old age, I can afford to be honest. The brave man dares to be frank. It is only the coward who is afraid to make admissions. So I tell you now that I also am human; that I also have felt my skin grow cold, and my hair rise; that I have even known what it was to run away until my limbs could scarce support me. It shocks you to hear it? Well, some day it may comfort you, when your own courage has reached its limits, to know that even Etienne Gerard has known what it was to be afraid. I will tell you now how this experience befell me, and also how it brought me a wife.

For the moment France was at peace, and we, the Hussars of Conflans, were in camp all that summer a few miles from the town of Les Andelys in Normandy. It is not a very gay place by itself, but we of the Light Cavalry make all places gay which we visit, and so we passed our time very pleasantly. Many years and many scenes have dulled my remembrance, but still the name Les Andelys brings back to me a huge ruined castle, great orchards of apple trees, and above all, a vision of the lovely maidens of Normandy. They were the very finest of their sex, as we may be said to have been of ours, and so we were well met in that sweet sunlit summer. Ah, the youth, the beauty, the valour, and then the dull, dead years that blur them all! There are times when the glorious past weighs on my heart like lead. No, sir, no wine can wash away such thoughts, for they are of the spirit and the soul. It is only the gross body which responds to wine, but if you offer it for that, then I will not refuse it.

Now of all the maidens who dwelt in those parts there was one who was so superior in beauty and in charm that she seemed to be very specially marked out for me. Her name was Marie Ravon, and her people, the Ravons, were of yeoman stock who had farmed their own land in those parts since the days when Duke William went to England. If I close my eyes now, I see her as she then was, her cheeks, dusky like moss roses; her hazel eyes, so gentle and yet so full of spirit; her hair of that deepest black which goes most fitly with poetry and with passion; her figure as supple as a young birch tree in the wind. Ah! how she swayed away from me when first I laid my arm round it, for she was full of fire and pride, ever evading, ever resisting, fighting to the last that her surrender might be the more sweet. Out of a hundred and forty women—— But who can compare where all are so near perfection!

You will wonder why it should be, if this maiden was so beautiful, that I should be left without a rival.

There was a very good reason, my friends, for I so arranged it that my rivals were in the hospital. There was Hippolyte Lesœur, he visited them for two Sundays; but if he lives, I dare swear that he still limps from the bullet which lodges in his knee. Poor Victor also —up to his death at Austerlitz he wore my mark. Soon it was understood that if I could not win Marie, I should at least have a fair field in which to try. It was said in our camp that it was safer to charge a square of unbroken infantry than to be seen too often at the farmhouse of the Ravons.

Now let me be precise for a moment. Did I wish to marry Marie? Ah! my friends, marriage is not for a Hussar. To-day he is in Normandy; to-morrow he is in the hills of Spain or in the bogs of Poland. What shall he do with a wife? Would it be fair to either of them? Can it be right that his courage should be blunted by the thought of the despair which his death would bring, or is it reasonable that she should be left fearing lest every post should bring her the news of irreparable misfortune? A Hussar can but warm himself at the fire, and then hurry onwards, too happy if he can but pass another fire from which some comfort may come. And Marie, did she wish to marry me? She knew well that when our silver trumpets blew the march it would be over the grave of our married life. Better far to hold fast to her own people and her own soil, where she and her husband could dwell for ever amid the rich orchards and within sight of the great Castle of Le Gaillard. Let her remember her Hussar in her dreams, but let her waking days be spent in the world as she finds it. Meanwhile we pushed such thoughts from our mind, and gave ourselves up to a sweet companionship, each day complete in itself with never a thought of the morrow. It is true that there were times when her father, a stout old gentleman with a face like one of his own apples, and her mother, a thin anxious woman of the country, gave me hints that they would wish to be clearer as to my intentions; but in their hearts they each knew well that Etienne Gerard was a man of honour, and that their daughter was very safe as well as very happy in his keeping. So the matter stood until the night of which I speak.

It was the Sunday evening, and I had ridden over from the camp. There were several of our fellows who were visiting the village, and we all left our horses at the inn. Thence I had to walk to the Ravons, which was only separated by a single very large field extending to the very door. I was about to start when the landlord ran after me.

"Excuse me, lieutenant," said he, "it is farther by the road, and yet I should advise you to take it."

"It is a mile or more out of my way."

"I know it. But I think that it would be wiser," and he smiled as he spoke.

"And why?" I asked.

"Because," said he, "the English bull is loose in the field."

If it were not for that odious smile, I might have considered it. But to hold a danger over me and then to smile in such a fashion was more than my proud temper could bear. I indicated by a gesture what I thought of the English bull.

"I will go by the shortest way," said I.

I had no sooner set my foot in the field than I felt that my spirit had betrayed me into rashness. It was a very large square field, and as I came farther out into it I felt like the cockleshell which ventures out from land and sees no port save that from which it has issued. There was wall on every side of the field save that from which I had come. In front of me was the farmhouse of the Ravons, with wall extending to right and left. A back door opened upon the field, and there were several windows, but all were barred, as is usual in the Norman farms. I pushed on rapidly to the door as being the only harbour of safety, walking with dignity as befits the soldier, and yet with such speed as I could summon. From the waist upwards I was unconcerned and even débonnaire. Below, I was swift and alert.

I had nearly reached the middle of the field when I perceived the creature. He was rooting about with his fore feet under a large beech tree which lay upon my right hand. I did not turn my head, nor would the bystander have detected that I took notice of him, but my eye was watching him with anxiety. It may have been that he was in a contented mood, or it may have been that he was arrested by the nonchalance of my bearing, but he made no movement in my direction. Reassured, I fixed my eyes upon the open window of Marie's bed-chamber, which was immediately over the back door, in the hope that those dear, tender, dark eyes were surveying me from behind the curtains. I flourished my little cane, loitered to pick a primrose, and sang one of our devil-may-care choruses in order to insult this English beast, and to show my love how little I cared for danger when it stood between her and me. The creature was abashed by my fearlessness, and so, pushing open the back door, I was able to enter the farmhouse in safety and in honour.

And was it not worth the danger? Had all the bulls of Castile guarded the entrance, would it not still have been worth it? Ah, the hours, the sunny hours, which can never come back, when our youthful feet seemed scarce to touch the ground, and we lived in a sweet dreamland of our own creation! She honoured my courage, and she loved me for it. As she lay with her flushed cheek pillowed against the silk of my dolman, looking up at me with her wondering eyes, shining with love and admiration, she marvelled at the stories in which I gave her some pictures of the true character of her lover.

"Has your heart never failed you? Have you never known the feeling of fear?" she asked.

I laughed at such a thought. What place could fear

have in the mind of a Hussar? Young as I was, I had given my proofs. I told her how I had led my squadron into a square of Hungarian Grenadiers. She shuddered as she embraced me. I told her also how I had swum my horse over the Danube at night with a message for Davoust. To be frank, it was not the Danube, nor was it so deep that I was compelled to swim, but when one is twenty and in love, one tells a story as best one can. Many such stories I told her, while her dear eyes grew more and more amazed.

"Never in my dreams, Etienne," said she, "did I believe that so brave a man existed. Lucky France that has such a soldier, lucky Marie that has such a lover!"

You can think how I flung myself at her feet as I murmured that I was the luckiest of all—I who had found someone who could appreciate and understand.

It was a charming relationship, too infinitely sweet and delicate for the interference of coarser minds. But you can understand that the parents imagined that they also had their duty to do. I played dominoes with the old man, and I wound wool for his wife, and yet they could not be led to believe that it was from love of them that I came thrice a week to their farm. For some time an explanation was inevitable, and that night it came. Marie, in delightful mutiny, was packed off to her room, and I faced the old people in the parlour as they plied me with questions upon my prospects and my intentions.

"One way or the other," they said, in their blunt country fashion. "Let us hear that you are betrothed to Marie, or let us never see your face again."

I spoke of my honour, my hopes, and my future, but they remained immovable upon the present. I pleaded my career, but they in their selfish way would think of nothing but their daughter. It was indeed a difficult position in which I found myself. On the one hand, I could not forsake my Marie; on the other, what would a young Hussar do with marriage? At last, hard pressed, I begged them to leave the matter, if it were only for a day.

"I will see Marie," said I, "I will see her without delay. It is her heart and her happiness which come before all else."

They were not satisfied, these grumbling old people, but they could say no more. They bade me a short good night and I departed, full of perplexity, for the inn. I came out by the same door which I had entered, and I heard them lock and bar it behind me.

I walked across the field lost in thought, with my mind entirely filled with the arguments of the old people and the skilful replies which I had made to them. What should I do? I had promised to see Marie without delay. What should I say to her when I did see her? Would I surrender to her beauty and turn my back upon my profession? If Etienne Gerard's sword were turned to a scythe, then indeed it was a bad day for the Emperor and France. Or should I harden my heart and turn away from Marie? Or was it not possible that all might be reconciled; that I might be a happy husband in Normandy but a brave soldier elsewhere? All these thoughts were buzzing in my head, when a sudden noise made me look up. The moon had come from behind a cloud, and there was the bull before me.

He had seemed a large animal beneath the beech tree, but now he appeared enormous. He was black in colour. His head was held down, and the moon shone upon two menacing and bloodshot eyes. His tail switched swiftly from side to side, and his fore-feet dug into the earth. A more horrible-looking monster was never seen in a nightmare. He was moving slowly and stealthily in my direction.

I glanced behind me, and I found that in my distraction I had come a very long way from the edge of the field. I was more than half-way across it. My nearest refuge was the inn, but the bull was between me and it. Perhaps if the creature understood how little I feared him, he would make way for me. I shrugged my shoulders and made a gesture of contempt. I even whistled. The creature thought I called it, for he approached with alacrity. I kept my face boldly towards him, but I walked swiftly backwards. When one is young and active, one can almost run backwards and yet keep a brave and smiling face to the enemy. As I ran I menaced the animal with my cane. Perhaps it would have been wiser had I restrained my spirit. He regarded it as a challenge—which, indeed, was the last thing in my mind. It was a misunderstanding, but a fatal one. With a snort he raised his tail and charged.

Have you ever seen a bull charge, my friends? It is a strange sight. You think, perhaps, that he trots, or even that he gallops. No, it is worse than this. It is a succession of bounds by which he advances, each more menacing than the last. I have no fear of anything which man can do. When I deal with man, I feel that the nobility of my own attitude, the gallant ease with which I face him, will in itself go far to disarm him. What he can do, I can do, so why should I fear him? But when it is a ton of enraged beef with which you contend, it is another matter. You cannot hope to argue, to soften, to conciliate. There is no resistance possible. My proud assurance was all wasted upon the creature. In an instant my ready wit had weighed every possible course, and had determined that no one, not the Emperor himself, could hold his ground. There was but one course—to fly.

But one may fly in many ways. One may fly with dignity or one may fly in panic. I fled, I trust, like a soldier. My bearing was superb, though my legs moved rapidly. My whole appearance was a protest against the position in which I was placed. I smiled as I ran—the bitter smile of the brave man who mocks his own fate. Had all my comrades surrounded the field, they could not have thought the less of me when they saw the disdain with which I avoided the bull.

But here it is that I must make my confession. When once flight commences, though it be ever so soldierly, panic follows hard upon it. Was it not so with the Guard at Waterloo? So it was that night with Etienne Gerard. After all, there was no one to note my bearing—no one save this accursed bull. If for a minute I forgot my dignity, who would be the wiser? Every moment the thunder of the hoofs and the horrible snorts of the monster drew nearer to my heels. Horror filled me at the thought of so ignoble a death. The brutal rage of the creature sent a chill to my heart. In an instant everything was forgotten. There were in the world but two creatures, the bull and I—he trying to kill me, I striving to escape. I put down my head and I ran—I ran for my life.

It was for the house of the Ravons that I raced. But even as I reached it, it flashed into my mind that there was no refuge for me there. The door was locked. The lower windows were barred. The wall was high upon either side. And the bull was nearer me with every stride. But oh, my friends, it is at that supreme moment of danger that Etienne Gerard has ever risen to his height. There was one path to safety, and in an instant I had chosen it.

I have said that the window of Marie's bedroom was above the door. The curtains were closed, but the folding sides were thrown open, and a lamp burned in the room. Young and active, I felt that I could spring high enough to reach the edge of the window sill and to draw myself out of danger. The monster was within touch of me as I sprang. Had I been unaided, I should have done what I had planned. But even as in a superb effort I rose from the earth he butted me into the air. I shot through the curtains as if I had been fired from a gun, and I dropped upon my hands and knees in the centre of the room.

There was, as it appears, a bed in the window, but I had passed over it in safety. As I staggered to my feet I turned towards it in consternation, but it was empty. My Marie sat in a low chair in the corner of the room, and her flushed cheeks showed that she had been weeping. No doubt her parents had given her some account of what had passed between us. She was too amazed to move, and could only sit looking at me with her mouth open.

" Etienne ! " she gasped. " Etienne ! "

In an instant I was as full of resource as ever. There was but one course for a gentleman, and I took it.

" Marie," I cried, " forgive, oh forgive the abruptness of my return ! Marie, I have seen your parents to-night. I could not return to the camp without asking you whether you will make me for ever happy by promising to be my wife ? "

It was long before she could speak, so great was her amazement. Then every emotion was swept away in the one great flood of her admiration.

" Oh, Etienne ! my wonderful Etienne ! " she cried, her arms round my neck. " Was ever such love ! Was ever such a man ! As you stand there, white and trembling with passion, you seem to me the very hero of my dreams. How hard you breathe, my love, and what a spring it must have been which brought you to my arms ! At the instant that you came, I heard the tramp of your war-horse without."

There was nothing more to explain, and when one is newly betrothed, one finds other uses for one's lips. But there was a scurry in the passage and a pounding at the panels. At the crash of my arrival the old folk had rushed to the cellar to see if the great cider cask had toppled off the trestles, but now they were back and eager for admittance. I flung open the door, and stood with Marie's hand in mine.

" Behold your son ! " I said.

Ah, the joy which I had brought to that humble household ! It warms my heart still when I think of it. It did not seem too strange to them that I should fly in through the window, for who should be a hot headed suitor if it is not a gallant Hussar? And if the door be locked, then what way is there but the window? Once more we assembled all four in the parlour, while the cobwebbed bottle was brought up and the ancient glories of the House of Ravon were unrolled before me. Once more I see the heavy-raftered room, the two old smiling faces, the golden circle of the lamp-light, and she, my Marie, the bride of my youth, won so strangely, and kept for so short a time.

It was late when we parted. The old man came with me into the hall.

"You can go by the front door or the back," said he. "The back way is the shorter."

"I think that I will take the front way," I answered. "It may be a bit longer, but it will give me the more time to think of Marie."

12. *The Lord of Château Noir*

IT was in the days when the German armies had broken their way across France, and when the shattered forces of the young Republic had been swept away to the north of the Aisne and to the south of the Loire. Three broad streams of armed men had rolled slowly but irresistibly from the Rhine, now meandering to the north, now to the south, dividing, coalescing, but all uniting to form one great lake round Paris. And from this lake there welled out smaller streams, one to the north, one southward to Orleans, and a third westward to Normandy. Many a German trooper saw the sea for the first time when he rode his horse girth-deep into the waves at Dieppe.

Black and bitter were the thoughts of Frenchmen when they saw this weal of dishonour slashed across the fair face of their country. They had fought and they had been overborne. That swarming cavalry, those countless footmen, the masterful guns—they had tried and tried to make head against them. In battalions their invaders were not to be beaten ; but man to man, or ten to ten, they were their equals. A brave Frenchman might still make a single German rue the day that he had left his own bank of the Rhine. Thus, unchronicled amid the battles and the sieges, there broke out another war, a war of individuals, with foul murder upon the one side and brutal reprisal on the other.

Colonel von Gramm, of the 24th Posen Infantry, had suffered severely during this new development. He commanded in the little Norman town of Les Andelys, and his outposts stretched amid the hamlets and farmhouses of the district round. No French force was within fifty miles of him, and yet morning after morning he had to listen to a black report of sentries found dead at their posts, or of foraging parties which had never returned. Then the Colonel would go forth in his wrath, and farmsteadings would blaze and villages tremble ; but next morning there was still that same dismal tale to be told. Do what he might, he could not shake off his invisible enemies. And yet, it should not have been so hard, for from certain signs in common, in the plan and in the deed, it was certain that all these outrages came from a single source.

Colonel von Gramm had tried violence and it had failed. Gold might be more successful. He published it abroad over the countryside that five hundred francs would be paid for information. There was no response. Then eight hundred. The peasants were incorruptible. Then, goaded on by a murdered corporal, he rose to a thousand, and so bought the soul of Francois Rejane, farm labourer, whose Norman avarice was a stronger passion than his French hatred.

" You say that you know who did these crimes ? " asked the Prussian Colonel, eyeing with loathing the blue-bloused, rat-faced creature before him.

"Yes, Colonel."

"And it was——?"

"Those thousand francs, Colonel——"

"Not a sou until your story has been tested. Come! Who is it who has murdered my men?"

"It is Count Eustace of Château Noir."

"You lie!" cried the Colonel, angrily. "A gentleman and a nobleman could not have done such crimes."

The peasant shrugged his shoulders.

"It is evident to me that you do not know the Count. It is this way, Colonel. What I tell you is the truth, and I am not afraid that you should test it. The Count of Château Noir is a hard man: even at the best time he was a hard man. But of late he has been terrible. It was his son's death, you know. His son was under Douay, and he was taken, and then in escaping from Germany he met his death. It was the Count's only child, and indeed we all think that it has driven him mad. With his peasants he follows the German armies. I do not know how many he has killed, but it is he who cuts the cross upon the foreheads, for it is the badge of his house."

It was true. The murdered sentries had each had a saltire cross slashed across their brows, as by a hunting-knife. The Colonel bent his stiff back and ran his forefinger over the map which lay upon the table.

"The Château Noir is not more than four leagues," he said.

"Three and a kilometre, Colonel."

"You know the place?"

"I used to work there."

Colonel von Gramm rang the bell.

"Give this man food and detain him," said he to the sergeant.

"Why detain me, Colonel? I can tell you no more."

"We shall need you as guide."

" As guide ! But the Count ? If I were to fall into his hands ? Ah, Colonel——"

The Prussian commander waved him away.

" Send Captain Baumgarten to me at once." said he.

The officer who answered the summons was a man of middle age, heavy-jawed, blue-eyed, with a curving yellow moustache, and a brick-red face which turned to an ivory white where his helmet had sheltered it. He was bald, with a shining, tightly-stretched scalp, at the back of which, as in a mirror, it was a favourite mess-joke of the subalterns to trim their moustaches. As a soldier he was slow, but reliable and brave. The Colonel could trust him where a more dashing officer might be in danger.

" You will proceed to Château Noir to-night, Captain," said he. " A guide has been provided. You will arrest the Count and bring him back. If there is an attempt at rescue, shoot him at once."

" How many men shall I take, Colonel ? "

" Well, we are surrounded by spies, and our only chance is to pounce upon him before he knows that we are on the way. A large force will attract attention. On the other hand, you must not risk being cut off."

" I might march north, Colonel, as if to join General Goeben. Then I could turn down this road which I see upon your map, and get to Château Noir before they could hear of us. In that case, with twenty men——"

" Very good, Captain. I hope to see you with your prisoner to-morrow morning."

It was a cold December night when Captain Baumgarten marched out of Les Andelys with his twenty Poseners, and took the main road to the north-west. Two miles out he turned suddenly down a narrow, deeply-rutted track, and made swiftly for his man. A thin, cold rain was falling, swishing among the tall poplar trees and rustling in the fields on either side. The

Captain walked first with Moser, a veteran sergeant, beside him. The sergeant's wrist was fastened to that of the French peasant, and it had been whispered in his ear that in case of an ambush the first bullet fired would be through his head. Behind them the twenty infantrymen plodded along through the darkness with their faces sunk to the rain, and their boots squeaking in the soft, wet clay. They knew where they were going and why, and the thought upheld them, for they were bitter at the loss of their comrades. It was a cavalry job, they knew, but the cavalry were all on with the advance, and, besides, it was more fitting that the regiment should avenge its own dead men.

It was nearly eight when they left Les Andelys. At half-past eleven their guide stopped at a place where two high pillars, crowned with some heraldic stonework, flanked a huge iron gate. The wall in which it had been the opening had crumbled away, but the great gate still towered above the brambles and weeds which had overgrown its base. The Prussians made their way round it, and advanced stealthily, under the shadow of a tunnel of oak branches, up the long avenue, which was still cumbered by the leaves of last autumn. At the top they halted and reconnoitred.

The black château lay in front of them. The moon had shone out between two rain-clouds, and threw the old house into silver and shadow. It was shaped like an L, with a low arched door in front, and lines of small windows like the open ports of a man-of-war. Above was a dark roof breaking at the corners into little round overhanging turrets, the whole lying silent in the moonshine, with a drift of ragged clouds blackening the heavens behind it. A single light gleamed in one of the lower windows.

The Captain whispered his orders to his men. Some were to creep to the front door, some to the back. Some were to watch the east, and some the west. He and the sergeant stole on tiptoe to the lighted window.

It was a small room into which they looked, very meanly furnished. An elderly man in the dress of a menial was reading a tattered paper by the light of a guttering candle. He leaned back in his wooden chair with his feet upon a box, while a bottle of white wine stood with a half-filled tumbler upon a stool beside him. The sergeant thrust his needle-gun through the glass, and the man sprang to his feet with a shriek.

"Silence, for your life! The house is surrounded and you cannot escape. Come round and open the door, or we will show you no mercy when we come in."

"For God's sake, don't shoot! I will open it! I will open it!" He rushed from the room with his paper still crumpled up in his hand. An instant later, with a groaning of old locks and a rasping of bars, the low door swung open, and the Prussians poured into the stone-flagged passage.

"Where is Count Eustace de Château Noir?"

"My master! He is out, sir."

"Out at this time of night? Your life for a lie!"

"It is true, sir. He is out!"

"Where?"

"I do not know."

"Doing what?"

"I cannot tell. No, it is no use your cocking your pistol, sir. You may kill me, but you cannot make me tell you that which I do not know."

"Is he often out at this hour?"

"Frequently."

"And when does he come home?"

"Before daybreak."

Captain Baumgarten rasped out a German oath. He had had his journey for nothing, then. The man's answers were only too likely to be true. It was what he might have expected. But at least he would search the house and make sure. Leaving a picket at the front door and another at the back, the sergeant and he drove the trembling butler in front of them—his shaking candle sending strange, flickering shadows over the old tapestries and the low, oak-raftered ceilings. They searched the whole house, from the huge, stone-flagged kitchen below to the dining-hall on the second floor with its gallery for musicians, and its panelling black with age, but nowhere was there a living creature. Up above in an attic they found Marie, the elderly wife of the butler; but the owner kept no other servants, and of his own presence there was no trace.

It was long, however, before Captain Baumgarten had satisfied himself upon the point. It was a difficult house to search. Thin stairs, which only one man could ascend at a time, connected lines of tortuous corridors. The walls were so thick that each room was cut off from its neighbour. Huge fireplaces yawned in each, while the windows were six feet deep in the wall. Captain Baumgarten stamped with his feet, and tore down curtains, and struck with the pommel of his sword. If there were secret hiding-places, he was not fortunate enough to find them.

"I have an idea," said he, at last, speaking in German to the sergeant. "You will place a guard over this fellow, and make sure that he communicates with no one."

"Yes, Captain."

"And you will place four men in ambush at the front and at the back. It is likely enough that about daybreak our bird may return to the nest."

"And the others, Captain?"

"Let them have their suppers in the kitchen. This fellow will serve you with meat and wine. It is a wild night, and we shall be better here than on the country road."

"And yourself, Captain?"

"I will take my supper up here in the dining-hall. The logs are laid and we can light the fire. You will call me if there is any alarm. What can you give me for supper—you?"

"Alas, monsieur, there was a time when I might

have answered, 'What you wish!' but now it is all that we can do to find a bottle of new claret and a cold pullet."

"That will do very well. Let a guard go about with him, sergeant, and let him feel the end of a bayonet if he plays us any tricks."

Captain Baumgarten was an old campaigner. In the Eastern provinces, and before that in Bohemia, he had learned the art of quartering himself upon the enemy. While the butler brought his supper he occupied himself in making his preparations for a comfortable night. He lit the candelabrum of ten candles upon the centre table. The fire was already burning up, crackling merrily, and sending spurts of blue, pungent smoke into the room. The Captain walked to the window and looked out. The moon had gone in again, and it was raining heavily. He could hear the deep sough of the wind and see the dark loom of the trees, all swaying in the one direction. It was a sight which gave a zest to his comfortable quarters, and to the cold fowl and the bottle of wine which the butler had brought up for him. He was tired and hungry after his long tramp, so he threw his sword, his helmet, and his revolver-belt down upon a chair, and fell to eagerly upon his supper. Then, with his glass of wine before him and his cigar between his lips, he tilted his chair back and looked about him.

He sat within a small circle of brilliant light which gleamed upon his silver shoulder-straps, and threw out his terra-cotta face, his heavy eyebrows, and his yellow moustache. But outside that circle things were vague and shadowy in the old dining-hall. Two sides were oak-panelled and two were hung with faded tapestry, across which huntsmen and dogs and stags were still dimly streaming. Above the fireplace were rows of heraldic shields with the blazonings of the family and of its alliances, the fatal saltire cross breaking out on each of them.

Four paintings of old seigneurs of Château Noir

faced the fireplace, all men with hawk noses and bold, high features, so like each other that only the dress could distinguish the Crusader from the Cavalier of the Fronde. Captain Baumgarten, heavy with his repast, lay back in his chair looking up at them through the clouds of his tobacco smoke, and pondering over the strange chance which had sent him, a man from the Baltic coast, to eat his supper in the ancestral hall of these proud Norman chieftains. But the fire was hot, and the Captain's eyes were heavy. His chin sank slowly upon his chest, and the ten candles gleamed upon the broad white scalp.

Suddenly a slight noise brought him to his feet. For an instant it seemed to his dazed senses that one of the pictures opposite had walked from its frame. There, beside the table, and almost within arm's length of him, was standing a huge man, silent, motionless, with no sign of life save his fierce, glinting eyes. He was black-haired, olive-skinned, with a pointed tuft of black beard, and a great, fierce nose, towards which all his features seemed to run. His cheeks were wrinkled like a last year's apple, but his sweep of shoulder, and bony, corded hands, told of a strength which was unsapped by age. His arms were folded across his arching chest, and his mouth was set in a fixed smile.

" Pray do not trouble yourself to look for your weapons," he said, as the Prussian cast a swift glance at the empty chair in which they had been laid. " You have been, if you will allow me to say so, a little indiscreet to make yourself so much at home in a house every wall of which is honeycombed with secret passages. You will be amused to hear that forty men were watching you at your supper. Ah ! what then ? "

Captain Baumgarten had taken a step forward with clenched fists. The Frenchman held up the revolver which he grasped in his right hand, while with the left he hurled the German back into his chair.

" Pray keep your seat," said he. " You have no cause to trouble about your men. They have already been provided for. It is astonishing with these stone floors how little one can hear what goes on beneath. You have been relieved of your command, and have now only to think of yourself. May I ask what your name is ?"

"I am Captain Baumgarten, of the 24th Posen Regiment."

"Your French is excellent, though you incline, like most of your countrymen, to turn the 'p' into a 'b.' I have been amused to hear them cry 'avez bitié sur moi!' You know, doubtless, who it is who addresses you."

"The Count of Château Noir."

"Precisely. It would have been a misfortune if you had visited my château and I had been unable to have a word with you. I have had to do with many German soldiers, but never with an officer before. I have much to talk to you about."

Captain Baumgarten sat still in his chair. Brave as he was, there was something in this man's manner which made his skin creep with apprehension. His eyes glanced to right and to left, but his weapons were gone, and in a struggle he saw that he was but a child to this gigantic adversary. The Count had picked up the claret bottle, and held it to the light:

"Tut! tut!" said he. "And was this the best that Pierre could do for you? I am ashamed to look you in the face, Captain Baumgarten. We must improve upon this."

He blew a call upon a whistle, which hung from his shooting-jacket. The old manservant was in the room in an instant.

"Chambertin from bin 15!" he cried, and a minute later a grey bottle streaked with cobwebs was carried in as a nurse bears an infant. The Count filled two glasses to the brim.

"Drink!" said he. "It is the very best in my cellars, and not to be matched between Rouen and Paris. Drink, sir, and be happy! There are cold joints below.

There are two lobsters fresh from Honfleur. Will you not venture upon a second and more savoury supper?"

The German officer shook his head. He drained the glass, however, and his host filled it once more, pressing him to give an order for this or that dainty.

"There is nothing in my house which is not at your disposal. You have but to say the word. Well, then, you will allow me to tell you a story while you drink your wine. I have so longed to tell it to some German officer. It is about my son, my only child, Eustace, who was taken and died in escaping. It is a curious little story, and I think that I can promise you that you will never forget it.

"You must know, then, that my boy was in the artillery, a fine young fellow, Captain Baumgarten, and the pride of his mother. She died within a week of the news of his death reaching us. It was brought by a brother officer who was at his side throughout, and who escaped while my lad died. I want to tell you all that he told me.

"Eustace was taken at Weissenburg on the 4th of August. The prisoners were broken up into parties, and sent back into Germany by different routes. Eustace was taken upon the 5th to a village called Lauterburg, where he met with kindness from the German officer in command. This good Colonel had the hungry lad to supper, offered him the best he had, opened a bottle of good wine, as I have tried to do for you, and gave him a cigar from his own case. Might I entreat you to take one from mine?"

The German again shook his head. His horror of his companion had increased as he sat watching the lips that smiled and the eyes that glared.

"The Colonel, as I say, was good to my boy. But, unluckily, the prisoners were moved next day across the Rhine to Ettlingen. They were not equally fortunate there. The officer who guarded them was a ruffian and a villain, Captain Baumgarten. He took a pleasure in humiliating and ill-treating the brave men who had fallen into his power. That night, upon my son answering fiercely back to some taunt of his, he struck him in the eye, like this!"

The crash of the blow rang through the hall. The German's face fell forward, his hand up, and blood oozing through his fingers. The Count settled down in his chair once more.

"My boy was disfigured by the blow, and this villain made his appearance the object of his jeers. By the way, you look a little comical yourself at the present moment, Captain, and your Colonel would certainly say that you had been getting into mischief. To continue, however, my boy's youth and his destitution—for his pockets were empty—moved the pity of a kind-hearted major, and he advanced him ten Napoleons from his own pocket without security of any kind. Into your hands, Captain Baumgarten, I return these ten gold pieces, since I cannot learn the name of the lender. I am grateful from my heart for this kindness shown to my boy.

"The vile tyrant who commanded the escort accompanied the prisoners to Durlach, and from there to Carlsruhe. He heaped every outrage upon my lad, because the spirit of the Châteaux Noirs would not stoop to turn away his wrath by a feigned submission. Ay, this cowardly villain, whose heart's blood shall yet clot upon this hand, dared to strike my son with his open hand, to kick him, to tear hairs from his moustache—to use him thus—and thus—and thus!"

The German writhed and struggled. He was helpless in the hands of this huge giant whose blows were raining upon him. When at last, blinded and half-senseless, he staggered to his feet, it was only to be hurled back again into the great oaken chair. He sobbed in his impotent anger and shame.

"My boy was frequently moved to tears by the humiliation of his position," continued the Count.

"You will understand me when I say that it is a bitter thing to be helpless in the hands of an insolent and remorseless enemy. On arriving at Carlsruhe, however, his face, which had been wounded by the brutality of his guard, was bound up by a young Bavarian subaltern who was touched by his appearance. I regret to see that your eye is bleeding so. Will you permit me to bind it with my silk handkerchief?"

He leaned forward, but the German dashed his hand aside.

"I am in your power, you monster!" he cried; "I can endure your brutalities, but not your hypocrisy."

The Count shrugged his shoulders. "I am taking things in their order, just as they occurred," said he. "I was under vow to tell it to the first German officer with whom I could talk *tête-à-tête*. Let me see, I had got as far as the young Bavarian at Carlsruhe. I regret extremely that you will not permit me to use such slight skill in surgery as I possess. At Carlsruhe, my lad was shut up in the old caserne, where he remained for a fortnight. The worst pang of his captivity was that some unmannerly curs in the garrison would taunt him with his position as he sat by his window in the evening. That reminds me, Captain, that you are not quite situated upon a bed of roses yourself, are you, now? You came to trap a wolf, my man, and now the beast has you down with his fangs in your throat. A family man, too, I should judge, by that well-filled tunic. Well, a widow the more will make little matter, and they do not usually remain widows long. Get back into the chair, you dog!

"Well, to continue my story—at the end of a fortnight my son and his friend escaped. I need not trouble you with the dangers which they ran, or with the privations which they endured. Suffice it that to disguise themselves they had to take the clothes of two peasants, whom they waylaid in a wood. Hiding by day and travelling by night, they had got as far into France as Remilly, and were within a mile—a single mile, Captain—of crossing the German lines when a patrol of Uhlans came right upon them. Ah! it was hard, was it not, when they had come so far and were so near to safety?"

The Count blew a double call upon his whistle, and three hard-faced peasants entered the room.

"These must represent my Uhlans," said he. "Well, then, the Captain in command, finding that these men were French soldiers in civilian dress within the German lines, proceeded to hang them without trial or ceremony. I think, Jean, that the centre beam is the strongest."

The unfortunate soldier was dragged from his chair to where a noosed rope had been flung over one of the huge oaken rafters which spanned the room. The cord was slipped over his head, and he felt its harsh grip round his throat. The three peasants seized the other end, and looked to the Count for his orders. The officer, pale, but firm, folded his arms and stared defiantly at the man who tortured him.

"You are now face to face with death, and I perceive from your lips that you are praying. My son was also face to face with death, and he prayed, also. It happened that a general officer came up, and he heard the lad praying for his mother, and it moved him so—he being himself a father—that he ordered his Uhlans away, and he remained with his aide-de-camp only, beside the condemned men. And when he heard all the lad had to tell, that he was the only child of an old family, and that his mother was in failing health, he threw off the rope as I throw off this, and he kissed him on either cheek, as I kiss you, and he bade him go, as I bid you go, and may every kind wish of that noble General, though it could not stave off the fever which slew my son, descend now upon your head."

And so it was that Captain Baumgarten, disfigured, blinded, and bleeding, staggered out into the wind and the rain of that wild December dawn.

TALES OF PIRATES

13. *Captain Sharkey: How the Governor of Saint Kitt's came Home*

WHEN the great wars of the Spanish Succession had been brought to an end by the Treaty of Utrecht, the vast number of privateers which had been fitted out by the contending parties found their occupation gone. Some took to the more peaceful but less lucrative ways of ordinary commerce, others were absorbed into the fishing-fleets, and a few of the more reckless hoisted the Jolly Roger at the mizzen and the bloody flag at the main, declaring a private war upon their own account against the whole human race.

With mixed crews, recruited from every nation, they scoured the seas, disappearing occasionally to careen in some lonely inlet, or putting in for a debauch at some outlying port, where they dazzled the inhabitants by their lavishness and horrified them by their brutalities.

On the Coromandel Coast, at Madagascar, in the African waters, and above all in the West Indian and American seas, the pirates were a constant menace. With an insolent luxury they would regulate their depredations by the comfort of the seasons, harrying New England in the summer and dropping south again to the tropical islands in the winter.

They were the more to be dreaded because they had none of that discipline and restraint which made their predecessors, the Buccaneers, both formidable and respectable. These Ishmaels of the sea rendered an account to no man, and treated their prisoners according to the drunken whim of the moment. Flashes of grotesque generosity alternated with longer stretches of inconceivable ferocity, and the skipper who fell into their hands might find himself dismissed with his cargo, after serving as boon companion in some hideous debauch, or might sit at his cabin table with his own nose and his lips served up with pepper and salt in front of him. It took a stout seaman in those days to ply his calling in the Caribbean Gulf.

Such a man was Captain John Scarrow, of the ship *Morning Star*, and yet he breathed a long sigh of relief when he heard the splash of the falling anchor and swung at his moorings within a hundred yards of the guns of the citadel of Basseterre. St. Kitt's was his final port of call, and early next morning his bowsprit would be pointed for Old England. He had had enough of those robber-haunted seas. Ever since he had left Maracaibo upon the Main, with his full lading of sugar and red pepper, he had winced at every topsail which glimmered over the violet edge of the tropical sea. He had coasted up the Windward Islands, touching here and there, and assailed continually by stories of villainy and outrage.

Captain Sharkey, of the 20-gun pirate barque, *Happy Delivery*, had passed down the coast, and had littered it with gutted vessels and with murdered men. Dreadful anecdotes were current of his grim pleasantries and of his inflexible ferocity. From the Bahamas to the Main his coal-black barque, with the ambiguous name, had been freighted with death and many things which are worse than death. So nervous was Captain Scarrow, with his new full-rigged ship and her full and valuable lading, that he struck out to the west as far as Bird's Island to be out of the usual track of commerce. And yet even in those solitary waters he had been unable to shake off sinister traces of Captain Sharkey.

One morning they had raised a single skiff adrift upon the face of the ocean. Its only occupant was a delirious seaman, who yelled hoarsely as they hoisted him aboard, and showed a dried-up tongue like a black and wrinkled fungus at the back of his mouth. Water and nursing soon transformed him into the strongest and smartest sailor on the ship. He was from Marblehead, in New England, it seemed, and was the sole survivor of a schooner which had been scuttled by the dreadful Sharkey.

For a week Hiram Evanson, for that was his name, had been adrift beneath a tropical sun. Sharkey had ordered the mangled remains of his late captain to be thrown into the boat, " as provisions for the voyage," but the seaman had at once committed them to the deep, lest the temptation should be more than he could bear. He had lived upon his own huge frame, until, at the last moment, the *Morning Star* had found him in that madness which is the precursor of such a death. It was no bad find for Captain Scarrow, for, with a short-handed crew, such a seaman as this big New Englander was a prize worth having. He vowed that he was the only man whom Captain Sharkey had ever placed under an obligation.

Now that they lay under the guns of Basseterre, all danger from the pirate was at an end, and yet the thought of him lay heavily upon the seaman's mind as he watched the agent's boat shooting out from the custom-house quay.

" I'll lay you a wager, Morgan," said he to the first mate, " that the agent will speak of Sharkey in the first hundred words that pass his lips."

" Well, captain, I'll have you a silver dollar, and chance it," said the rough old Bristol man beside him.

The negro rowers shot the boat alongside, and the linen-clad steersman sprang up the ladder.

" Welcome, Captain Scarrow ! " he cried. " Have you heard about Sharkey."

The captain grinned at the mate.

" What devilry has he been up to now ? " he asked.

" Devilry ! You've not heard, then ! Why, we've got him safe under lock and key here at Basseterre. He was tried last Wednesday, and he is to be hanged to-morrow morning."

Captain and mate gave a shout of joy, which an instant later was taken up by the crew. Discipline was forgotten as they scrambled up through the break of the poop to hear the news. The New Englander was in the front of them with a radiant face turned up to heaven, for he came of the Puritan stock.

"Sharkey to be hanged!" he cried. "You don't know, Master Agent, if they lack a hangman, do you?"

"Stand back!" cried the mate, whose outraged sense of discipline was even stronger than his interest at the news. "I'll pay that dollar, Captain Scarrow, with the lightest heart that ever I paid a wager yet. How came the villain to be taken?"

"Why, as to that, he became more than his own comrades could abide, and they took such a horror of him that they would not have him on the ship. So they marooned him upon the Little Mangles to the south of the Mysteriosa Bank, and there he was found by a Portobello trader, who brought him in. There was talk of sending him to Jamaica to be tried, but our good little governor, Sir Charles Ewan, would not hear of it. 'He's my meat,' said he, 'and I claim the cooking of it.' If you can stay till to-morrow morning at ten, you'll see the joint swinging."

"I wish I could," said the captain, wistfully, "but I am sadly behind time now. I should start with the evening tide."

"That you can't do," said the agent with decision. "The Governor is going back with you."

"The Governor!"

"Yes. He's had a dispatch from Government to return without delay. The fly-boat that brought it has gone on to Virginia. So Sir Charles has been waiting for you, as I told him you were due before the rains."

"Well, well!" cried the captain, in some perplexity, "I'm a plain seaman, and I don't know much of governors and baronets and their ways. I don't remember that I ever so much as spoke to one. But if it's in King George's service, and he asks a cast in the *Morning Star* as far as London, I'll do what I can for him. There's my own cabin he can have and welcome. As to the cooking, it's lobscouse and salmagundy six days in the week; but he can bring his own cook aboard with him if he thinks our galley too rough for his taste."

"You need not trouble your mind, Captain Scarrow," said the agent. "Sir Charles is in weak health just now, only clear of a quartan ague, and it is likely he will keep his cabin most of the voyage. Dr. Larousse said that he would have sunk had the hanging of Sharkey not put fresh life into him. He has a great spirit in him, though, and you must not blame him if he is somewhat short in his speech."

"He may say what he likes and do what he likes so long as he does not come athwart my hawse when I am working the ship," said the captain. "He is Governor of St. Kitt's, but I am Governor of the *Morning Star*. And, by his leave, I must weigh with the first tide, for I owe a duty to my employer, just as he does to King George."

"He can scarce be ready to-night, for he has many things to set in order before he leaves."

"The early morning tide, then."

"Very good. I shall send his things aboard to-night, and he will follow them to-morrow early if I can prevail upon him to leave St. Kitt's without seeing Sharkey do the rogue's hornpipe. His own orders were instant, so it may be that he will come at once. It is likely that Dr. Larousse may attend him upon the journey."

Left to themselves, the captain and mate made the best preparations which they could for their illustrious passenger. The largest cabin was turned out and adorned in his honour, and orders were given by which barrels of fruit and some cases of wine should be brought off to vary the plain food of an ocean-going trader. In the evening the Governor's baggage began to arrive—great ironbound ant-proof trunks, and official tin packing-cases, with other strange-shaped packages, which suggested the cocked hat or the sword within. And then there came a note, with a heraldic device upon the big red seal, to say that Sir Charles Ewan made his compliments to Captain Scarrow, and that he hoped to be with him in the morning as early as his duties and his infirmities would permit.

He was as good as his word, for the first grey of dawn had hardly begun to deepen into pink when he was brought alongside, and climbed with some difficulty up the ladder. The captain had heard that the Governor was an eccentric, but he was hardly prepared for the curious figure who came limping feebly down his quarter-deck, his steps supported by a thick bamboo cane. He wore a Ramillies wig, all twisted into little tails like a poodle's coat, and cut so low across the brow that the large green glasses which covered his eyes looked as if they were hung from it. A fierce beak of a nose, very long and very thin, cut the air in front of him. His ague had caused him to swathe his throat and chin with a broad linen cravat, and he wore a loose damask powdering-gown secured by a cord round the waist. As he advanced he carried his masterful nose high in the air, but his head turned slowly from side to side in the helpless manner of the purblind, and he called in a high, querulous voice for the captain.

"You have my things?" he asked.

"Yes, Sir Charles."

"Have you wine aboard?"

"I have ordered five cases, sir?"

"And tobacco?"

"There is a keg of Trinidad."

"You play a hand at piquet?"

"Passably well, sir."

"Then up anchor, and to sea!"

There was a fresh westerly wind, so by the time the sun was fairly through the morning haze, the ship was hull down from the islands. The decrepit Governor still limped the deck, with one guiding hand upon the quarter-rail.

"You are on Government service now, captain," said he. "They are counting the days till I come to Westminster, I promise you. Have you all that she will carry?"

"Every inch, Sir Charles?"

"Keep her so if you blow the sails out of her. I fear, Captain Scarrow, that you will find a blind and broken man a poor companion for your voyage."

"I am honoured in enjoying your Excellency's society," said the captain. "But I am sorry that your eyes should be so afflicted."

"Yes, indeed. It is the cursed glare of the sun on the white streets of Basseterre which has gone far to burn them out."

"I had heard also that you had been plagued by a quartan ague."

"Yes; I have had a pyrexy, which has reduced me much."

"We had set aside a cabin for your surgeon."

"Ah, the rascal! There was no budging him, for he has a snug business amongst the merchants. But hark!"

He raised his ring-covered hand in the air. From far astern there came the low deep thunder of cannon.

"It is from the island!" cried the captain in astonishment. "Can it be a signal for us to put back?"

The Governor laughed.

"You have heard that Sharkey, the pirate, is to be hanged this morning. I ordered the batteries to salute when the rascal was kicking his last, so that I might know of it out at sea. There's an end of Sharkey!"

"There's an end of Sharkey!" cried the captain; and the crew took up the cry as they gathered in little knots upon the deck and stared back at the low, purple line of the vanishing land.

It was a cheering omen for their start across the Western Ocean, and the invalid Governor found himself a popular man on board, for it was generally understood that but for his insistence upon an immediate trial and sentence, the villain might have played upon some more venal judge and so escaped. At dinner that day Sir Charles gave many anecdotes of the deceased pirate; and so affable was he, and so skilful in adapting his conversation to men of lower degree, that captain, mate, and Governor smoked their long pipes and drank their claret as three good comrades should.

"And what figure did Sharkey cut in the dock?" asked the captain.

"He is a man of some presence," said the Governor.

"I had always understood that he was an ugly, sneering devil," remarked the mate.

"Well, I dare say he could look ugly upon occasions," said the Governor.

"I have heard a New Bedford whaleman say that he could not forget his eyes," said Captain Scarrow. "They were of the lightest filmy blue, with red-rimmed lids. Was that not so, Sir Charles?"

"Alas, my own eyes will not permit me to know much of those of others! But I remember now that the Adjutant-General said that he had such an eye as you describe, and added that the jury were so foolish as to be visibly discomposed when it was turned upon them. It is well for them that he is dead, for he was a man who would never forget an injury, and if he had laid hands upon any one of them he would have stuffed him with straw and hung him for a figure-head."

The idea seemed to amuse the Governor, for he broke suddenly into a high, neighing laugh, and the two seamen laughed also, but not so heartily, for they remembered that Sharkey was not the last pirate who sailed the western seas, and that as grotesque a fate might come to be their own. Another bottle was broached to drink to a pleasant voyage, and the Governor would drink just one other on the top of it, so that the seamen were glad at last to stagger off—the one to his watch and the other to his bunk. But when after his four hours' spell the mate came down again, he was amazed to see the Governor in his Ramillies wig, his glasses, and his powdering-gown still seated sedately at the lonely table with his reeking pipe and six black bottles by his side.

"I have drunk with the Governor of St. Kitt's when he was sick," said he, "and God forbid that I should ever try to keep pace with him when he is well."

The voyage of the *Morning Star* was a successful one, and in about three weeks she was at the mouth of the British Channel. From the first day the infirm Governor had begun to recover his strength, and before they were half-way across the Atlantic he was, save only for his eyes, as well as any man upon the ship. Those who uphold the nourishing qualities of wine might point to him in triumph, for never a night passed that he did not repeat the performance of his first one. And yet he would be out upon deck in the early morning as fresh and brisk as the best of them, peering about with his weak eyes, and asking questions about the sails and the rigging, for he was anxious to learn the ways of the sea. And he made up for the deficiency of his eyes by obtaining leave from the captain that the New England seaman—he who had been cast away in the boat—should lead him about, and above all that he should sit beside him when he played cards and count the number of the pips, for unaided he could not tell the king from the knave.

It was natural that this Evanson should do the Governor willing service, since the one was the victim of the vile Sharkey, and the other was his avenger. One could see that it was a pleasure to the big American to lend his arm to the invalid, and at night he would stand with all respect behind his chair in the cabin and lay his great stub-nailed forefinger upon the card which he should play. Between them there was little in the pockets either of Captain Scarrow or of Morgan, the first mate, by the time they sighted the Lizard.

And it was not long before they found that all they had heard of the high temper of Sir Charles Ewan fell short of the mark. At a sign of opposition or a word of argument his chin would shoot out from his cravat, his masterful nose would be cocked at a higher and more insolent angle, and his bamboo cane would whistle up over his shoulder. He cracked it once over the head of the carpenter when the man had accidentally jostled him upon the deck. Once, too, when there was some grumbling and talk of a mutiny over the state of the provisions, he was of opinion that they should not wait for the dogs to rise, but that they should march forward and set upon them until they had trounced the devilment out of them. " Give me a knife and a bucket ! " he cried with an oath, and could hardly be withheld from setting forth alone to deal with the spokesman of the seamen.

Captain Scarrow had to remind him that though he might be only answerable to himself at St. Kitt's, killing became murder upon the high seas. In politics he was, as became his official position, a stout prop of the House of Hanover, and he swore in his cups that he had never met a Jacobite without pistolling him where he stood. Yet for all his vapouring and his violence he was so good a companion, with such a stream of strange anecdote and reminiscence, that Scarrow and Morgan had never known a voyage pass so pleasantly.

And then at length came the last day, when, after passing the island, they had struck land again at the high white cliffs at Beachy Head. As evening fell the ship lay rolling in an oily calm, a league off from Winchelsea, with the long dark snout of Dungeness jutting out in front of her. Next morning they would pick up their pilot at the Foreland, and Sir Charles might meet the king's ministers at Westminster before the evening. The boatswain had the watch, and the three friends were met for a last turn of cards in the cabin, the faithful American still serving as eyes to the Governor. There was a good stake upon the table, for the sailors had tried on this last night to win their losses back from their passenger. Suddenly he threw his cards down, and swept all the money into the pocket of his long-flapped silken waistcoat.

"The game's mine!" said he.

"Heh, Sir Charles, not so fast!" cried Captain Scarrow; "you have not played out the hand, and we are not the losers."

"Sink you for a liar!" said the Governor. "I tell you that I *have* played out the hand, and that you *are* a loser." He whipped off his wig and his glasses as he spoke, and there was a high, bald forehead, and a pair of shifty blue eyes with the red rims of a bull terrier.

"Good God!" cried the mate. "It's Sharkey!"

The two sailors sprang from their seats, but the big American castaway had put his huge back against the cabin door, and he held a pistol in each of his hands. The passenger had also laid a pistol upon the scattered cards in front of him, and he burst into his high, neighing laugh.

"Captain Sharkey is the name, gentlemen," said he, "and this is Roaring Ned Galloway, the quartermaster of the *Happy Delivery*. We made it hot, and so they marooned us: me on a dry Tortuga cay, and him in an oarless boat. You dogs—you poor, fond, water-hearted dogs—we hold you at the end of our pistols!"

"You may shoot, or you may not!" cried Scarrow, striking his hand upon the breast of his frieze jacket. "If it's my last breath, Sharkey, I tell you that you are a bloody rogue and miscreant, with a halter and hell-fire in store for you!"

"There's a man of spirit, and one of my own kidney, and he's going to make a very pretty death of it!" cried Sharkey. "There's no one aft save the man at the wheel, so you may keep your breath, for you'll need it soon. Is the dinghy astern, Ned?"

" Ay, ay, captain ! "

" And the other boats scuttled ? "

" I bored them all in three places."

" Then we shall have to leave you, Captain Scarrow. You look as if you hadn't quite got your bearings yet. Is there anything you'd like to ask me ? "

" I believe you're the devil himself ! " cried the captain. " Where is the Governor of St. Kitt's ? "

" When last I saw him his Excellency was in bed with his throat cut. When I broke prison I learnt from my friends—for Captain Sharkey has those who love him in every port—that the Governor was starting for Europe under a master who had never seen him. I climbed his verandah and I paid him the little debt that I owed him. Then I came aboard you with such of his things as I had need of, and a pair of glasses to hide these tell-tale eyes of mine, and I have ruffled it as a governor should. Now, Ned, you can get to work upon them."

" Help ! Help ! Watch ahoy ! " yelled the mate ; but the butt of the pirate's pistol crashed down on to his head, and he dropped like a pithed ox. Scarrow rushed for the door, but the sentinel clapped his hand over his mouth, and threw his other arm round his waist.

" No use, Master Scarrow," said Sharkey. " Let us see you go down on your knees and beg for your life."

" I'll see you——" cried Scarrow, shaking his mouth clear.

" Twist his arm round, Ned. Now will you ? "

" No ; not if you twist it off."

" Put an inch of your knife into him."

" You may put six inches, and then I won't."

" Sink me, but I like his spirit ! " cried Sharkey. " Put your knife in your pocket, Ned. You've saved your skin, Scarrow, and it's a pity so stout a man should not take to the only trade where a pretty fellow can pick up a living. You must be born for no common death, Scarrow, since you have lain at my mercy and lived to tell the story. Tie him up, Ned."

" To the stove, captain ? "

" Tut, tut ! there's a fire in the stove. None of your rover tricks, Ned Galloway, unless they are called for, or I'll let you know which of us two is captain and which is quartermaster. Make him fast to the table."

" Nay, I thought you meant to roast him ! " said the quartermaster. " You surely do not mean to let him go ? "

" If you and I were marooned on a Bahama cay, Ned Galloway, it is still for me to command and for you to obey. Sink you for a villain, do you dare to question my orders ? "

" Nay, nay, Captain Sharkey, not so hot, sir ! " said the quartermaster, and, lifting Scarrow like a child, he laid him on the table. With the quick dexterity of a seaman, he tied his spreadeagled hands and feet with a rope which was passed underneath, and gagged him securely with the long cravat which used to adorn the chin of the Governor of St. Kitt's.

" Now, Captain Scarrow, we must take our leave of you," said the pirate. " If I had half a dozen of my brisk boys at my heels I should have had your cargo and your ship, but Roaring Ned could not find a foremast hand with the spirit of a mouse. I see there are some small craft about, and we shall get one of them. When Captain Sharkey has a boat he can get a smack, when he has a smack he can get a brig, when he has a brig he can get a barque, and when he has a barque he'll soon have a full-rigged ship of his own—so make haste into London town, or I may be coming back, after all, for the *Morning Star*."

Captain Scarrow heard the key turn in the lock as they left the cabin. Then, as he strained at his bonds, he heard their footsteps pass up the companion and along the quarter-deck to where the dinghy hung in the stern. Then, still struggling and writhing, he heard the creak of the falls and the splash of the boat in the water. In a mad fury he tore and dragged at his ropes, until at last, with flayed wrists and ankles, he rolled from the table, sprang over the dead mate, kicked his way through the closed door, and rushed hatless on to the deck.

"Ahoy! Peterson, Armitage, Wilson!" he screamed. "Cutlasses and pistols! Clear away the long-boat! Clear away the gig! Sharkey, the pirate, is in yonder dinghy. Whistle up the larboard watch, bo'sun, and tumble into the boats all hands."

Down splashed the long-boat and down splashed the gig, but in an instant the coxswains and crews were swarming up the falls on to the deck once more.

"The boats are scuttled!" they cried. "They are leaking like a sieve."

The captain gave a bitter curse. He had been beaten and outwitted at every point. Above was a cloudless, starlit sky, with neither wind nor the promise of it. The sails flapped idly in the moonlight. Far away lay a fishing-smack, with the men clustering over their net. Close to them was the little dinghy, dipping and lifting over the shining swell.

"They are dead men!" cried the captain. "A shout all together, boys, to warn them of their danger."

But it was too late.

At that very moment the dinghy shot into the shadow of the fishing-boat. There were two rapid pistol-shots, a scream, and then another pistol-shot, followed by silence. The clustering fishermen had disappeared. And then, suddenly, as the first puffs of a land-breeze came out from the Sussex shore, the boom swung out, the mainsail filled, and the little craft crept out with her nose to the Atlantic.

14. *The Dealings of Captain Sharkey with Stephen Craddock*

CAREENING was a very necessary operation for the old pirate. On his superior speed he depended both for overhauling the trader and escaping the man-of-war. But it was impossible to retain his sailing qualities unless he periodically—once a year, at the least—cleared his vessel's bottom from the long, trailing plants and crusting barnacles which gather so rapidly in the tropical seas.

For this purpose he lightened his vessel, thrust her into some narrow inlet where she would be left high and dry at low water, fastened blocks and tackles to her masts to pull her over on to her bilge, and then scraped her thoroughly from rudder-post to cutwater.

During the weeks which were thus occupied the ship was, of course, defenceless ; but, on the other hand, she was unapproachable by anything heavier than an empty hull, and the place for careening was chosen with an eye to secrecy, so that there was no great danger.

So secure did the captains feel, that it was not uncommon for them, at such times, to leave their ships under a sufficient guard and to start off in the long-boat, either upon a sporting expedition or, more frequently, upon a visit to some outlying town, where they turned the heads of the women by their swaggering gallantry, or broached pipes of wine in the market square, with a threat to pistol all who would not drink with them.

Sometimes they would even appear in cities of the size of Charleston, and walk the streets with their clattering sidearms—an open scandal to the whole law-abiding colony. Such visits were not always paid with impunity. It was one of them, for example, which provoked Lieutenant Maynard to hack off Blackbeard's head, and to spear it upon the end of his bowsprit. But, as a rule, the pirate ruffled and bullied and drabbed without let or hindrance, until it was time for him to go back to his ship once more.

There was one pirate, however, who never crossed even the skirts of civilization, and that was the sinister Sharkey, of the barque *Happy Delivery*. It may have been from his morose and solitary temper, or, as is more probable, that he knew that his name upon the coast was such that outraged humanity would, against all odds, have thrown themselves upon him, but never once did he show his face in a settlement.

When his ship was laid up he would leave her under the charge of Ned Galloway—her New England quartermaster—and would take long voyages in his boat, sometimes, it was said, for the purpose of burying his share of the plunder, and sometimes to shoot the wild oxen of Hispaniola, which, when dressed and barbecued, provided provisions for his next voyage. In the latter case the barque would come round to some prearranged spot to pick him up and take on board what he had shot.

There had always been a hope in the islands that Sharkey might be taken on one of these occasions; and at last there came news to Kingston which seemed to justify an attempt upon him. It was brought by an elderly logwood-cutter who had fallen into the pirate's hands, and in some freak of drunken benevolence had been allowed to get away with nothing worse than a slit nose and a drubbing. His account was recent and definite. The *Happy Delivery* was careening at Torbec on the south-west of Hispaniola. Sharkey, with four men, was buccaneering on the outlying island of La Vache. The blood of a hundred murdered crews was calling out for vengeance, and now at last it seemed as if it might not call in vain.

Sir Edward Compton, the high-nosed, red-faced Governor, sitting in solemn conclave with the commandant and the head of the council, was sorely puzzled in his mind as to how he should use his chance. There was no man-of-war nearer than Jamestown, and she was a clumsy old fly-boat, which could neither overhaul the pirate on the seas, nor reach her in a shallow inlet. There were forts and artillerymen both at Kingston and Port Royal, but no soldiers available for an expedition.

A private venture might be fitted out—and there were many who had a blood-feud with Sharkey—but what could a private venture do? The pirates were numerous and desperate. As to taking Sharkey and his four companions, that, of course, would be easy if they could get at them; but how were they to get at them on a large well-wooded island like La Vache, full of wild hills and impenetrable jungles? A reward was offered to whoever could find a solution, and that brought a man to the front who had a singular plan, and was himself prepared to carry it out.

Stephen Craddock had been that most formidable person, the Puritan gone wrong. Sprung from a decent Salem family, his ill-doing seemed to be a recoil from the austerity of their religion, and he brought to vice all the physical strength and energy with which the virtues of his ancestors had endowed him. He was ingenious, fearless, and exceedingly tenacious of purpose, so that when he was still young his name became notorious upon the American coast.

He was the same Craddock who was tried for his life in Virginia for the slaying of the Seminole Chief, and, though he escaped, it was well known that he had corrupted the witnesses and bribed the judge.

Afterwards, as a slaver, and even, as it was hinted, as a pirate, he had left an evil name behind him in the Bight of Benin. Finally he had returned to Jamaica with a considerable fortune, and had settled down to a life of sombre dissipation. This was the man, gaunt, austere, and dangerous, who now waited upon the Governor with a plan for the extirpation of Sharkey.

Sir Edward received him with little enthusiasm, for in spite of some rumours of conversion and reformation, he had always regarded him as an infected sheep who might taint the whole of his little flock. Craddock saw the Governor's mistrust under his thin veil of formal and restrained courtesy.

"You've no call to fear me, sir," said he; "I'm a changed man from what you've known. I've seen the light again, of late, after losing sight of it for many a black year. It was through the ministration of the Rev. John Simons, of our own people. Sir, if your spirit should be in need of quickening, you would find a very sweet savour in his discourse."

The Governor cocked his Episcopalian nose at him. "You came here to speak of Sharkey, Master Craddock," said he.

"The man Sharkey is a vessel of wrath," said Craddock. "His wicked horn has been exalted over long, and it is borne in upon me that if I can cut him off and utterly destroy him, it will be a goodly deed, and one which may atone for many backslidings in the past. A plan has been given to me whereby I may encompass his destruction."

The Governor was keenly interested, for there was a grim and practical air about the man's freckled face which showed that he was in earnest. After all, he was a seaman and a fighter, and, if it were true that he was eager to atone for his past, no better man could be chosen for the business.

"This will be a dangerous task, Master Craddock," said he.

"If I meet my death at it, it may be that it will cleanse the memory of an ill-spent life. I have much to atone for."

The Governor did not see his way to contradict him. "What was your plan?" he asked.

"You have heard that Sharkey's barque, the *Happy Delivery*, came from this very port of Kingston?"

"It belonged to Mr. Codrington, and it was taken by Sharkey, who scuttled his own sloop and moved into her because she was faster," said Sir Edward.

"Yes; but it may be that you have never heard that Mr. Codrington has a sister ship, the *White Rose*, which lies even now in the harbour, and which is so like the pirate, that, if it were not for a white paint line, none could tell them apart."

"Ah! and what of that?" asked the Governor keenly, with the air of one who is just on the edge of an idea.

" By the help of it this man shall be delivered into our hands."

" And how ? "

" I will paint out the streak upon the *White Rose*, and make it in all things like the *Happy Delivery*. Then I will set sail for the Island of La Vache, where this man is slaying the wild oxen. When he sees me he will surely mistake me for his own vessel which he is awaiting, and he will come on board to his own undoing."

It was a simple plan, and yet it seemed to the Governor that it might be effective. Without hesitation he gave Craddock permission to carry it out, and to take any steps he liked in order to further the object which he had in view. Sir Edward was not very sanguine, for many attempts had been made upon Sharkey, and their results had shown that he was as cunning as he was ruthless. But this gaunt Puritan with the evil record was cunning and ruthless also.

The contest of wits between two such men as Sharkey and Craddock appealed to the Governor's acute sense of sport, and though he was inwardly convinced that the chances were against him, he backed his man with the same loyalty which he would have shown to his horse or his cock.

Haste was, above all things, necessary, for upon any day the careening might be finished, and the pirates out at sea once more. But there was not very much to do, and there were many willing hands to do it, so the second day saw the *White Rose* beating out for the open sea. There were many seamen in the port who knew the lines and rig of the pirate barque, and not one of them could see the slightest difference in this counterfeit. Her white side line had been painted out, her masts and yards were smoked, to give them the dingy appearance of the weather-beaten rover, and a large diamond shaped patch was let into her foretopsail.

Her crew were volunteers, many of them being men who had sailed with Stephen Craddock before—the mate,

Joshua Hird, an old slaver, had been his accomplice in many voyages, and came now at the bidding of his chief.

The avenging barque sped across the Caribbean Sea, and, at the sight of that patched topsail, the little craft which they met flew left and right like frightened trout in a pool. On the fourth evening Point Abacou bore five miles to the north and east of them.

On the fifth they were at anchor in the Bay of Tortoises at the Island of La Vache, where Sharkey and his four men had been hunting. It was a well-wooded place, with the palms and underwood growing down to the thin crescent of silver sand which skirted the shore. They had hoisted the black flag and the red pennant, but no answer came from the shore. Craddock strained his eyes, hoping every instant to see a boat shoot out to them with Sharkey seated in the sheets. But the night passed away, and a day and yet another night, without any sign of the men whom they were endeavouring to trap. It looked as if they were already gone.

On the second morning Craddock went ashore in search of some proof whether Sharkey and his men were still upon the island. What he found reassured him greatly. Close to the shore was a boucan of green wood, such as was used for preserving the meat, and a great store of barbecued strips of ox-flesh was hung upon lines all round it. The pirate ship had not taken off her provisions, and therefore the hunters were still upon the island.

Why had they not shown themselves? Was it that they had detected that this was not their own ship? Or was it that they were hunting in the interior of the island, and were not on the lookout for a ship yet? Craddock was still hesitating between the two alternatives, when a Carib Indian came down with information. The pirates were in the island, he said, and their camp was a day's march from the sea. They had stolen his wife, and the marks of their stripes were still pink upon his brown back. Their enemies were his friends, and he would lead them to where they lay.

Craddock could not have asked for anything better; so early next morning, with a small party armed to the teeth, he set off under the guidance of the Carib. All day they struggled through brushwood and clambered over rocks, pushing their way farther and farther into the desolate heart of the island. Here and there they found traces of the hunters, the bones of a slain ox, or the marks of feet in a morass, and once, towards evening, it seemed to some of them that they heard the distant rattle of guns.

That night they spent under the trees, and pushed on again with the earliest light. About noon they came to the huts of bark, which, the Carib told them, were the camp of the hunters, but they were silent and deserted. No doubt their occupants were away at the hunt and would return in the evening, so Craddock and his men lay in ambush in the brushwood around them. But no one came, and another night was spent in the forest. Nothing more could be done, and it seemed to Craddock that after the two days' absence it was time that he returned to his ship once more.

The return journey was less difficult, as they had already blazed a path for themselves. Before evening they found themselves once more at the Bay of Palms, and saw their ship riding at anchor where they had left her. Their boat and oars had been hauled up among the bushes, so they launched it and pulled out to the barque.

"No luck, then!" cried Joshua Hird, the mate, looking down with a pale face from the poop.

"His camp was empty, but he may come down to us yet," said Craddock, with his hand on the ladder.

Somebody upon deck began to laugh. "I think," said the mate, "that these men had better stay in the boat."

"Why so?"

" If you will come aboard, sir, you will understand it." He spoke in a curious hesitating fashion.

The blood flushed to Craddock's gaunt face.

" How is this, Master Hird ? " he cried, springing up the side. " What mean you by giving orders to my boat's crew ? "

But as he passed over the bulwarks, with one foot upon the deck and one knee upon the rail, a tow-bearded man, whom he had never before observed aboard his vessel, grabbed suddenly at his pistol. Craddock clutched at the fellow's wrist, but at the same instant his mate snatched the cutlass from his side.

What roguery is this ? " shouted Craddock, looking furiously around him. But the crew stood in little knots about the deck, laughing and whispering amongst themselves without showing any desire to go to his assistance. Even in that hurried glance Craddock noticed that they were dressed in the most singular manner, with long riding-coats, full-skirted velvet gowns and coloured ribands at their knees, more like men of fashion than seamen.

As he looked at their grotesque figures he struck his brow with his clenched fist to be sure that he was awake. The deck seemed to be much dirtier than when he had left it, and there were strange, sun-blackened faces turned upon him from every side. Not one of them did he know save only Joshua Hird. Had the ship been captured in his absence ? Were these Sharkey's men who were around him ? At the thought he broke furiously away and tried to climb over to his boat, but a dozen hands were on him in an instant, and he was pushed aft through the open door of his own cabin.

And it was all different from the cabin which he had left. The floor was different, the ceiling was different, the furniture was different. His had been plain and austere. This was sumptuous and yet dirty, hung with rare velvet curtains splashed with wine-stains, and panelled with costly woods which were pocked with pistol-marks.

On the table was a great chart of the Caribbean Sea, and beside it, with compasses in his hand, sat a clean-shaven, pale-faced man with a fur cap and a claret-coloured coat of damask. Craddock turned white under his freckles as he looked upon the long, thin, high-nostrilled nose and the red-rimmed eyes which were turned upon him with the fixed, humorous gaze of the master player who has left his opponent without a move.

"Sharkey?" cried Craddock.

Sharkey's thin lips opened and he broke into his high, sniggering laugh.

"You fool!" he cried, and, leaning over, he stabbed Craddock's shoulder again and again with his compasses. "You poor, dull-witted fool, would you match yourself against me?"

It was not the pain of the wounds, but it was the contempt in Sharkey's voice which turned Craddock into a savage madman. He flew at the pirate, roaring with rage, striking, kicking, writhing, and foaming. It took six men to drag him down on to the floor amidst the splintered remains of the table—and not one of the six who did not bear the prisoner's mark upon him. But Sharkey still surveyed him with the same contemptuous eye. From outside there came the crash of breaking wood and the clamour of startled voices.

"What is that?" asked Sharkey.

"They have stove the boat with cold shot, and the men are in the water."

"Let them stay there," said the pirate. "Now, Craddock, you know where you are. You are aboard my ship the *Happy Delivery*, and you lie at my mercy. I knew you for a stout seaman, you rogue, before you took to this long-shore canting. Your hands then were no cleaner than my own. Will you sign articles, as your mate has done, and join us, or shall I heave you over to follow your ship's company?"

"Where is my ship?" asked Craddock.

"Scuttled in the bay."

" And the hands ? "

" In the bay, too."

" Then, I'm for the bay also."

" Hock him and heave him over." said Sharkey.

Many rough hands had dragged Craddock out upon deck, and Galloway, the quartermaster, had already drawn his hanger to cripple him, when Sharkey came hurrying from his cabin with an eager face.

" We can do better with the hound ! " he cried. " Sink me if it is not a rare plan. Throw him into the sail-room with the irons on, and do you come here, quartermaster, that I may tell you what I have in my mind."

So Craddock, bruised and wounded in soul and body, was thrown into the dark sail-room, so fettered that he could not stir hand or foot, but his northern blood was running strong in his veins, and his grim spirit aspired only to make such an ending as might go some way towards atoning for the evil of his life. All night he lay in the curve of the bilge listening to the rush of the water and the straining of the timbers which told him that the ship was at sea, and driving fast. In the early morning someone came crawling to him in the darkness over the heaps of sails.

" Here's rum and biscuits," said the voice of his late mate. " It's at the risk of my life, Master Craddock, that I bring them to you."

" It was you who trapped me and caught me as in a snare ! " cried Craddock. " How shall you answer for what you have done ? "

" What I did I did with the point of a knife betwixt my blade-bones."

" God forgive you for a coward, Joshua Hird. How came you into their hands ? "

" Why, Master Craddock, the pirate ship came back from its careening upon the very day that you left us. They laid us aboard, and, short-handed as we were, with the best of the men ashore with you, we could offer but a poor defence. Some were cut down, and they were the happiest. The others were killed afterwards. As to me, I saved my life by signing on with them."

"And they scuttled my ship ?"

"They scuttled her, and then Sharkey and his men, who had been watching us from the brushwood, came off to the ship. His mainyard had been cracked and fished last voyage, so he had suspicions of us, seeing that ours was whole. Then he thought of laying the same trap for you which you had set for him."

Craddock groaned.

"How came I not to see that fished mainyard ?" he muttered. "But whither are we bound ?"

"We are running north and west."

"North and west ! Then we are heading back towards Jamaica."

"With an eight-knot wind."

"Have you heard what they mean to do with me ?"

"I have not heard. If you would but sign the articles——"

"Enough, Joshua Hird ! I have risked my soul too often."

"As you wish ! I have done what I could. Farewell !"

All that night and the next day the *Happy Delivery* ran before the easterly trades, and Stephen Craddock lay in the dark of the sail-room working patiently at his wrist-irons. One he had slipped off at the cost of a row of broken and bleeding knuckles, but, do what he would, he could not free the other, and his ankles were securely fastened.

From hour to hour he heard the swish of the water, and knew that the barque must be driving with all set in front of the trade-wind. In that case they must be nearly back again to Jamaica by now. What plan could Sharkey have in his head, and what use did he hope to make of him ? Craddock set his teeth, and vowed that if he had once been a villain from choice he would, at least, never be one by compulsion.

On the second morning Craddock became aware that sail had been reduced in the vessel, and that she was tacking slowly, with a light breeze on her beam. The varying slope of the sail-room and the sounds from the deck told his practised senses exactly what she was doing. The short reaches showed him that she was manœuvring near shore, and making for some definite point. If so, she must have reached Jamaica. But what could she be doing there?

And then suddenly there was a burst of hearty cheering from the deck, and then the crash of a gun above his head, and then the answering booming of guns from far over the water. Craddock sat up and strained his ears. Was the ship in action? Only the one gun had been fired, and though many had answered there were none of the crashings which told of a shot coming home.

Then, if it was not an action, it must be a salute. But who would salute Sharkey, the pirate? It could only be another pirate ship which would do so. So Craddock lay back again with a groan, and continued to work at the manacle which still held his right wrist.

But suddenly there came the shuffling of steps outside, and he had hardly time to wrap the loose links round his free hand, when the door was unbolted and two pirates came in.

"Got your hammer, carpenter?" asked one, whom Craddock recognized as the big quartermaster. "Knock off his leg shackles, then. Better leave the bracelets—he's safer with them on."

With hammer and chisel the carpenter loosened the irons.

"What are you going to do with me?" asked Craddock.

"Come on deck and you'll see."

The sailor seized him by the arm and dragged him roughly to the foot of the companion. Above him was a square of blue sky cut across by the mizzen gaff with the colours flying at the peak. But it was the sight of those colours which struck the breath from Stephen

Craddock's lips. For there were two of them, and the British ensign was flying above the Jolly Roger—the honest flag above that of the rogue.

For an instant Craddock stopped in amazement, but a brutal push from the pirates behind drove him up the companion ladder. As he stepped out upon deck, his eyes turned up to the main, and there again were the British colours flying above the red pennant, and all the shrouds and rigging were garlanded with streamers.

Had the ship been taken, then? But that was impossible, for there were the pirates clustering in swarms along the port bulwarks, and waving their hats joyously in the air. Most prominent of all was the renegade mate, standing on the fo'c'sle head, and gesticulating wildly. Craddock looked over the side to see what they were cheering at, and then in a flash he saw how critical was the moment.

On the port bow, and about a mile off, lay the white houses and forts of Port Royal, with flags breaking out everywhere over their roofs. Right ahead was the opening of the palisades leading to the town of Kingston. Not more than a quarter of a mile off was a small sloop working out against the very slight wind. The British ensign was at her peak, and her rigging was all decorated. On her deck could be seen a dense crowd of people cheering and waving their hats, and the gleam of scarlet told that there were officers of the garrison among them.

In an instant, with the quick perception of a man of action, Craddock saw through it all. Sharkey, with that diabolical cunning and audacity which were among his main characteristics, was simulating the part which Craddock would himself have played, had he come back victorious. It was in *his* honour that the salutes were firing and the flags flying. It was to welcome *him* that this ship with the Governor, the commandant, and the chiefs of the island was approaching. In another ten minutes they would all be under the guns of the *Happy*

Delivery, and Sharkey would have won the greatest stake that ever a pirate played for yet.

"Bring him forward," cried the pirate captain, as Craddock appeared between the carpenter and the quartermaster. "Keep the ports closed, but clear away the port guns, and stand by for a broadside. Another two cable lengths and we have them."

"They are edging away," said the boatswain. "I think they smell us."

"That's soon set right," said Sharkey, turning his filmy eyes upon Craddock. "Stand there, you—right there, where they can recognize you, with your hand on the guy, and wave your hat to them. Quick, or your brains will be over your coat. Put an inch of your knife into him, Ned. Now, will you wave your hat? Try him again, then. Hey, shoot him! stop him!"

But it was too late. Relying upon the manacles, the quartermaster had taken his hands for a moment off Craddock's arm. In that instant he had flung off the carpenter and, amid a spatter of pistol bullets, had sprung the bulwarks and was swimming for his life. He had been hit and hit again, but it takes many pistols to kill a resolute and powerful man who has his mind set upon doing something before he dies. He was a strong swimmer, and, in spite of the red trail which he left in the water behind him, he was rapidly increasing his distance from the pirate.

"Give me a musket!" cried Sharkey, with a savage oath.

He was a famous shot, and his iron nerves never failed him in an emergency. The dark head appearing on the crest of a roller, and then swooping down on the other side, was already half-way to the sloop. Sharkey dwelt long upon his aim before he fired. With the crack of the gun the swimmer reared himself up in the water, waved his hands in a gesture of warning, and roared out in a voice which rang over the bay. Then, as the sloop swung round her head-sails, and the pirate fired an impotent broadside, Stephen Craddock, smiling grimly in his death agony, sank slowly down to that golden couch which glimmered far beneath him.

15. *The Blighting of Sharkey*

SHARKEY, the abominable Sharkey, was out again. After two years of the Coromandel coast, his black barque of death, the *Happy Delivery*, was prowling off the Spanish Main, while trader and fisher flew for dear life at the menace of that patched fore-topsail, rising slowly over the violet rim of the tropical sea.

As the birds cower when the shadow of the hawk falls athwart the field, or as the jungle folk crouch and shiver when the coughing cry of the tiger is heard in the night-time, so through all the busy world of ships, from the whalers of Nantucket to the tobacco ships of Charleston, and from the Spanish supply ships of Cadiz to the sugar merchants of the Main, there spread the rumour of the black curse of the ocean.

Some hugged the shore, ready to make for the nearest port, while others struck far out beyond the known lines of commerce, but none were so stout-hearted that they did not breathe more freely when their passengers and cargoes were safe under the guns of some mothering fort.

Through all the islands there ran tales of charred derelicts at sea, of sudden glares seen afar in the night-time, and of withered bodies stretched upon the sand of waterless Bahama Keys. All the old signs were there to show that Sharkey was at his bloody game once more.

These fair waters and yellow-rimmed palm-nodding islands are the traditional home of the sea rover. First it was the gentleman adventurer, the man of family and honour, who fought as a patriot, though he was ready to take his payment in Spanish plunder.

Then, within a century, his debonair figure had passed to make room for the buccaneers, robbers pure and simple, yet with some organized code of their own, commanded by notable chieftains, and taking in hand great concerted enterprises.

They, too, passed with their fleets and their sacking of cities, to make room for the worst of all, the lonely, outcast pirate, the bloody Ishmael of the seas, at war with the whole human race. This was the vile brood which the early eighteenth century had spawned forth, and of them all there was none who could compare in audacity, wickedness, and evil repute with the unutterable Sharkey.

It was early in May, in the year 1720, that the *Happy Delivery* lay with her fore-yard aback some five leagues west of the Windward Passage, waiting to see what rich, helpless craft the trade-wind might bring down to her.

Three days she had lain there, a sinister black speck, in the centre of the great sapphire circle of the ocean. Far to the south-east the low blue hills of Hispaniola showed up on the skyline.

Hour by hour as he waited without avail, Sharkey's savage temper had risen, for his arrogant spirit chafed against any contradiction, even from Fate itself. To his quartermaster, Ned Galloway, he had said that night, with his odious neighing laugh, that the crew of the next captured vessel should answer to him for having kept him waiting so long.

The cabin of the pirate barque was a good-sized room, hung with much tarnished finery, and presenting a strange medley of luxury and disorder. The panelling of carved and polished sandal-wood was blotched with foul smudges and chipped with bullet-marks fired in some drunken revelry.

Rich velvets and laces were heaped upon the brocaded settees, while metal-work and pictures of great price filled every niche and corner, for anything which caught the pirate's fancy in the sack of a hundred vessels was thrown haphazard into his chamber. A rich, soft carpet covered the floor, but it was mottled with wine-stains and charred with burned tobacco.

Above, a great brass hanging-lamp threw a brilliant yellow light upon this singular apartment, and upon the two men who sat in their shirt-sleeves with the wine between them, and the cards in their hands, deep in a game of piquet. Both were smoking long pipes, and the thin blue reek filled the cabin and floated through the skylight above them, which, half opened, disclosed a slip of deep violet sky spangled with great silver stars.

Ned Galloway, the quartermaster, was a huge New England wastrel, the one rotten branch upon a goodly Puritan family tree. His robust limbs and giant frame were the heritage of a long line of God-fearing ancestors, while his black savage heart was all his own. Bearded to the temples, with fierce blue eyes, a tangled lion's mane of coarse, dark hair, and huge gold rings in his ears, he was the idol of the women in every waterside hell from the Tortugas to Maracaibo on the Main. A red cap, a blue silken shirt, brown velvet breeches with gaudy knee-ribbons, and high sea-boots made up the costume of the rover Hercules.

A very different figure was Captain John Sharkey. His thin, drawn, clean-shaven face was corpse-like in its pallor, and all the suns of the Indies could but turn it to a more deathly parchment tint. He was part bald, with a few lank locks of tow-like hair, and a steep, narrow forehead. His thin nose jutted sharply forth, and near-set on either side of it were those filmy blue eyes, red-rimmed like those of a white bull-terrier, from which strong men winced away in fear and loathing. His bony hands, with long, thin fingers which quivered ceaselessly like the antennæ of an insect, were toying constantly with the cards and the heap of gold moidores which lay before him. His dress was of some sober drab material, but, indeed, the men who looked upon that fearsome face had little thought for the costume of its owner.

The game was brought to a sudden interruption, for the cabin door was swung rudely open, and two rough fellows—Israel Martin, the boatswain, and Red Foley, the gunner—rushed into the cabin. In an instant Sharkey was on his feet with a pistol in either hand and murder in his eyes.

"Sink you for villains!" he cried. "I see well that if I do not shoot one of you from time to time you will forget the man I am. What mean you by entering my cabin as though it were a Wapping alehouse?"

"Nay, Captain Sharkey," said Martin, with a sullen frown upon his brick-red face, "it is even such talk as this which has set us by the ears. We have had enough of it."

"And more than enough," said Red Foley, the gunner. "There be no mates aboard a pirate craft, and so the boatswain, the gunner, and the quartermaster are the officers."

"Did I gainsay it?" asked Sharkey with an oath.

"You have miscalled us and mishandled us before the men, and we scarce know at this moment why we should risk our lives in fighting for the cabin and against the fo'c'sle."

Sharkey saw that something serious was in the wind. He laid down his pistols and leaned back in his chair with a flash of his yellow fangs.

"Nay, this is sad talk," said he, "that two stout fellows who have emptied many a bottle and cut many a throat with me, should now fall out over nothing. I know you to be roaring boys who would go with me against the devil himself if I bid you. Let the steward bring cups and drown all unkindness between us."

"It is no time for drinking, Captain Sharkey," said Martin. "The men are holding council round the mainmast, and may be aft at any minute. They mean mischief, Captain Sharkey, and we have come to warn you."

Sharkey sprang for the brass-handled sword which hung from the wall.

"Sink them for rascals!" he cried. "When I have gutted one or two of them they may hear reason."

But the others barred his frantic way to the door.

"There are forty of them under the lead of Sweetlocks, the master," said Martin, "and on the open deck they would surely cut you to pieces. Here within the cabin it may be that we can hold them off at the points of our pistols."

He had hardly spoken when there came the tread of many heavy feet upon the deck. Then there was a pause with no sound but the gentle lapping of the water against the sides of the pirate vessel. Finally, a crashing blow as from a pistol-butt fell upon the door, and an instant afterwards Sweetlocks himself, a tall, dark man, with a deep red birth-mark blazing upon his cheek, strode into the cabin. His swaggering air sank somewhat as he looked into those pale and filmy eyes.

"Captain Sharkey," said he, "I come as spokesman of the crew."

"So I have heard, Sweetlocks," said the captain, softly. "I may live to rip you the length of your vest for this night's work."

"That is as it may be, Captain Sharkey," the master answered, "but if you will look up you will see that I have those at my back who will not see me mishandled."

"Cursed if we do!" growled a deep voice from above, and glancing upwards the officers in the cabin were aware of a line of fierce, bearded, sun-blackened faces looking down at them through the open skylight.

"Well, what would you have?" asked Sharkey. "Put it in words, man, and let us have an end of it."

"The men think," said Sweetlocks, "that you are the devil himself, and that there will be no luck for them whilst they sail the sea in such company. Time was when we did our two or three craft a day, and every man had women and dollars to his liking, but now for a long week we have not raised a sail, and save for three beggarly sloops, have taken never a vessel since we passed the Bahama Bank. Also, they know that you killed Jack Bartholomew, the carpenter, by beating his head in with a bucket, so that each of us goes in fear of his life. Also, the rum has given out, and we are hard put to it for liquor. Also, you sit in your cabin whilst it is in the articles that you should drink and roar with the crew. For all these reasons it has been this day in general meeting decreed——'"

Sharkey had stealthily cocked a pistol under the table, so it may have been as well for the mutinous master that he never reached the end of his discourse, for even as he came to it there was a swift patter of feet upon the deck, and a ship lad, wild with his tidings, rushed into the room.

"A craft!" he yelled. "A great craft, and close aboard us!"

In a flash the quarrel was forgotten, and the pirates were rushing to quarters. Sure enough, surging slowly down before the gentle trade-wind, a great full-rigged ship, with all sail set, was close beside them.

It was clear that she had come from afar and knew nothing of the ways of the Caribbean Sea, for she made no effort to avoid the low, dark craft which lay so close upon her bow, but blundered on as if her mere size would avail her.

So daring was she, that for an instant the rovers, as they flew to loose the tackles of their guns, and hoisted their battle-lanterns, believed that a man-of-war had caught them napping.

But at the sight of her bulging, portless sides and merchant rig a shout of exultation broke from amongst them, and in an instant they had swung round their fore-yard, and darting alongside they had grappled with her and flung a spray of shrieking, cursing ruffians upon her deck.

Half a dozen seamen of the night-watch were cut down where they stood, the mate was felled by Sharkey and tossed overboard by Ned Galloway, and before the sleepers had time to sit up in their berths, the vessel was in the hands of the pirates.

The prize proved to be the full-rigged ship *Portobello*

—Captain Hardy, master—bound from London to Kingston in Jamaica, with a cargo of cotton goods and hoop-iron.

Having secured their prisoners, all huddled together in a dazed, distracted group, the pirates spread over the vessel in search of plunder, handing all that was found to the giant quartermaster, who in turn passed it over the side of the *Happy Delivery* and laid it under guard at the foot of her mainmast.

The cargo was useless, but there were a thousand guineas in the ship's strong-box, and there were some eight or ten passengers, three of them wealthy Jamaica merchants, all bringing home well-filled boxes from their London visit.

When all the plunder was gathered, the passengers and crew were dragged to the waist, and under the cold smile of Sharkey each in turn was thrown over the side—Sweetlocks standing by the rail and ham-stringing them with his cutlass as they passed over, lest some strong swimmer should rise in judgment against them. A portly, grey-haired woman, the wife of one of the planters, was among the captives, but she also was thrust screaming and clutching over the side.

"Mercy, you hussy!" neighed Sharkey, "you are surely a good twenty years too old for that."

The captain of the *Portobello*, a hale, blue-eyed grey-beard, was the last upon the deck. He stood, a thick-set resolute figure, in the glare of the lanterns, while Sharkey bowed and smirked before him.

"One skipper should show courtesy to another," said he, "and sink me if Captain Sharkey would be behind in good manners! I have held you to the last, as you see, where a brave man should be; so now, my bully, you have seen the end of them, and may step over with an easy mind."

"So I shall, Captain Sharkey," said the old seaman, "for I have done my duty so far as my power lay. But before I go over I would say a word in your ear."

"If it be to soften me, you may save your breath. You have kept us waiting here for three days, and curse me if one of you shall live!"

"Nay, it is to tell you what you should know. You have not yet found what is the true treasure aboard of this ship."

"Not found it? Sink me, but I will slice your liver, Captain Hardy, if you do not make good your words! Where is this treasure you speak of?"

"It is not a treasure of gold, but it is a fair maid, which may be no less welcome."

"Where is she, then? And why was she not with the others?"

"I will tell you why she was not with the others. She is the only daughter of the Count and Countess Ramirez, who are amongst those whom you have murdered. Her name is Inez Ramírez, and she is of the best blood of Spain, her father being Governor of Chagre, to which he was now bound. It chanced that she was found to have formed an attachment, as maids will, to one far beneath her in rank aboard this ship; so her parents, being people of great power, whose word is not to be gainsaid, constrained me to confine her close in a special cabin aft of my own. Here she was held straitly, all food being carried to her, and she allowed to see no one. This I tell you as a last gift, though why I should make it to you I do not know, for indeed you are a most bloody rascal, and it comforts me in dying to think that you will surely be gallow's-meat in this world, and hell's-meat in the next."

At the words he ran to the rail, and vaulted over into the darkness, praying as he sank into the depths of the sea, that the betrayal of this maid might not be counted too heavily against his soul.

The body of Captain Hardy had not yet settled upon the sand forty fathoms deep before the pirates had rushed along the cabin gangway. There, sure enough, at the farther end, was a barred door, overlooked in their previous search. There was no key, but they beat it in with their gunstocks, whilst shriek after shriek came from within. In the light of their outstretched lanterns they saw a young woman, in the very prime and fullness of her youth, crouching in a corner, her unkempt hair hanging to the ground, her dark eyes glaring with fear, her lovely form straining away in horror from this inrush of savage blood-stained men. Rough hands seized her, she was jerked to her feet, and dragged with scream on scream to where John Sharkey awaited her. He held the light long and fondly to her face, then, laughing loudly, he bent forward and left his red handprint upon her cheek.

" 'Tis the Rovers' brand, lass, that he marks his ewes. Take her to the cabin and use her well. Now, hearties, get her under water, and out to our luck once more."

Within an hour the good ship *Portobello* had settled down to her doom, till she lay beside her murdered passengers upon the Caribbean sand, while the pirate barque, her deck littered with plunder, was heading northward in search of another victim.

There was a carouse that night in the cabin of the *Happy Delivery*, at which three men drank deep. They were the captain, the quartermaster, and Baldy Stable, the surgeon, a man who had held the first practice in Charleston, until, misusing a patient, he fled from justice, and took his skill over to the pirates. A bloated fat man he was, with a creased neck and a great shining scalp, which gave him his name. Sharkey had put for the moment all thought of the mutiny out of his head, knowing that no animal is fierce when it is over-fed, and that whilst the plunder of the great ship was new to them he need fear no trouble from his crew. He gave himself up, therefore, to the wine and the riot, shouting and roaring with his boon companions. All three were flushed and mad, ripe for any devilment, when the thought of the woman crossed the pirate's evil mind. He yelled to the negro steward that he should bring her on the instant.

Inez Ramirez had now realized it all—the death of her father and mother, and her own position in the hands of their murderers. Yet calmness had come with the knowledge, and there was no sign of terror in her proud, dark face as she was led into the cabin, but rather a strange, firm set of the mouth and an exultant gleam of the eyes, like one who sees great hopes in the future. She smiled at the pirate captain as he rose and seized her by the waist.

" 'Fore God ! this is a lass of spirit," cried Sharkey ; passing his arm round her. " She was born to be a Rover's bride. Come, my bird, and drink to our better friendship."

" Article Six ! " hiccoughed the doctor. " All *bona robas* in common."

" Aye ! we hold you to that, Captain Sharkey," said Galloway. " It is so writ in Article Six."

" I will cut the man into ounces who comes betwixt us ! " cried Sharkey, as he turned his fish-like eyes from one to the other. " Nay, lass, the man is not born that will take you from John Sharkey. Sit, here upon my knee, and place your arm round me so. Sink me, if she has not learned to love me at sight ! Tell me, my pretty, why you were so mishandled and laid in the bilboes aboard yonder craft ? "

The woman shook her head and smiled. " No Inglese —no Inglese," she lisped. She had drunk off the bumper of wine which Sharkey held to her, and her dark eyes gleamed more brightly than before. Sitting on Sharkey's knee, her arm encircled his neck, and her hand toyed with his hair, his ear, his cheek. Even the strange quartermaster and the hardened surgeon felt a horror as they watched her, but Sharkey laughed in his joy. " Curse me, if she is not a lass of metal ! " he cried, as he pressed her to him and kissed her unresisting lips.

But a strange intent look of interest had come into the surgeon's eyes as he watched her, and his face set rigidly, as if a fearsome thought had entered his mind. There stole a grey pallor over his bull face, mottling all the red of the tropics and the flush of the wine.

"Look at her hand, Captain Sharkey!" he cried. "For the Lord's sake, look at her hand!"

Sharkey stared down at the hand which had fondled him. It was of a strange dead pallor, with a yellow shiny web betwixt the fingers. All over it was a white fluffy dust, like the flour of a new-baked loaf. It lay thick on Sharkey's neck and cheek. With a cry of disgust he flung the woman from his lap; but in an instant, with a wild-cat bound, and a scream of triumphant malice, she had sprung at the surgeon, who vanished yelling under the table. One of her clawing hands grasped Galloway by the beard, but he tore himself away, and snatching a pike, held her off from him as she gibbered and mowed with the blazing eyes of a maniac.

The black steward had run in on the sudden turmoil, and among them they forced the mad creature back into a cabin and turned the key upon her. Then the three sank panting into their chairs and looked with eyes of horror upon each other. The same word was in the mind of each, but Galloway was the first to speak it.

"A leper!" he cried. "She has us all, curse her!"

"Not me," said the surgeon; "she never laid her finger on me."

"For that matter," cried Galloway, "it was but my beard that she touched. I will have every hair of it off before morning."

"Dolts that we were!" the surgeon shouted, beating his head with his hand. "Tainted or no, we shall never know a moment's peace till the year is up and the time of danger past. 'Fore God, that merchant skipper has left his mark on us, and pretty fools we were to think that such a maid would be quarantined for the cause he gave. It is easy to see now that her corruption broke forth in the journey, and that save throwing her over they had no choice but to board her up until they should come to some port with a lazarette."

Sharkey had sat leaning back in his chair with a ghastly face while he listened to the surgeon's words. He mopped himself with his red handkerchief, and wiped away the fatal dust with which he was smeared.

"What of me?" he croaked. "What say you, Baldy Stable? Is there a chance for me? Curse you for a villain! speak out, or I will drub you within an inch of your life, and that inch also! Is there a chance for me, I say!"

But the surgeon shook his head. "Captain Sharkey," said he, "it would be an ill deed to speak you false. The taint is on you. No man on whom the leper scales have rested is ever clean again."

Sharkey's head fell forward on his chest, and he sat motionless, stricken by this great and sudden horror, looking with his smouldering eyes into his fearsome future. Softly the mate and the surgeon rose from their places, and stealing out from the poisoned air of the cabin, came forth into the freshness of the early dawn, with the soft, scent-laden breeze in their faces and the first red feathers of cloud catching the earliest gleam of the rising sun as it shot its golden rays over the palm-clad ridges of distant Hispaniola.

That morning a second council of the Rovers was held at the base of the mainmast, and a deputation chosen to see the captain. They were approaching the after-cabins when Sharkey came forth, the old devil in his eyes, and his bandolier with a pair of pistols over his shoulder.

"Sink you all for villains!" he cried. "Would you dare to cross my hawse? Stand out, Sweetlocks, and I will lay you open! Here, Galloway, Martin, Foley, stand by me and lash the dogs to their kennel!"

But his officers had deserted him, and there was none to come to his aid. There was a rush of the pirates. One was shot through the body, but an instant afterwards Sharkey had been seized and was triced to his own mainmast. His filmy eyes looked round from face to face, and there was none who felt the happier for having met them.

"Captain Sharkey," said Sweetlocks, "you have mishandled many of us, and you have now pistolled John Masters, besides killing Bartholomew, the carpenter, by braining him with a bucket. All this might have been forgiven you, in that you have been our leader for years, and that we have signed articles to serve under you while the voyage lasts. But now we have heard of this *bona roba* on board, and we know that you are poisoned to the marrow, and that while you rot there will be no safety for any of us, but that we shall all be turned into filth and corruption. Therefore, John Sharkey, we Rovers of the *Happy Delivery*, in council assembled, have decreed that while there be yet time, before the plague spreads, you shall be set adrift in a boat to find such a fate as Fortune may be pleased to send you."

John Sharkey said nothing, but slowly circling his head, he cursed them all with his baleful gaze. The ship's dinghy had been lowered, and he, with his hands still tied, was dropped into it on the bight of a rope.

"Cast her off!" cried Sweetlocks.

"Nay, hold hard a moment, Master Sweetlocks!" shouted one of the crew. "What of the wench? Is she to bide aboard and poison us all?"

"Send her off with her mate!" cried another, and the Rovers roared their approval. Driven forth at the end of pikes, the girl was pushed towards the boat. With all the spirit of Spain in her rotting body she flashed triumphant glances at her captors.

"Perros! Perros Ingleses! Lepero, Lepero!" she cried in exultation, as they thrust her over into the boat.

"Good luck, captain! God speed you on your honeymoon!" cried a chorus of mocking voices, as the painter was unloosed, and the *Happy Delivery*, running full before the trade-wind, left the little boat astern, a tiny dot upon the vast expanse of the lonely sea.

* * * * *

Extract from the log of H.M. 50-gun ship *Hecate* in her cruise off the American Main.

"*Jan.* 26, 1721.—This day, the junk having become unfit for food, and five of the crew down with scurvy, I ordered that we send two boats ashore at the nor'western point of Hispaniola, to seek for fresh fruit, and perchance shoot some of the wild oxen with which the island abounds.

"7 *p.m.*—The boats have returned with good store of green stuff and two bullocks. Mr. Woodruff, the master, reports that near the landing-place at the edge of the forest was found the skeleton of a woman, clad in European dress, of such sort as to show that she may have been a person of quality. Her head had been crushed by a great stone which lay beside her. Hard by was a grass hut, and signs that a man had dwelt therein for some time, as was shown by charred wood, bones and other traces. There is a rumour upon the coast that Sharkey, the bloody pirate, was marooned in these parts last year, but whether he has made his way into the interior, or whether he has been picked up by some craft, there is no means of knowing. If he be once again afloat, then I pray that God send him under our guns."

16: *How Copley Banks slew Captain Sharkey*

THE Buccaneers were something higher than a mere band of marauders. They were a floating republic, with laws, usages, and discipline of their own. In their endless and remorseless quarrel with the Spaniards they had some semblance of right upon their side. Their bloody harryings of the cities of the Main were not more barbarous than the inroads of Spain upon the Netherlands—or upon the Caribs in these same American lands.

The chief of the Buccaneers, were he English or French, a Morgan or a Granmont, was still a responsible person, whose country might countenance him, or even praise him, so long as he refrained from any deed which might shock the leathery seventeenth-century conscience too outrageously. Some of them were touched with religion, and it is still remembered how Sawkins threw the dice overboard upon the Sabbath, and Daniel pistolled a man before the altar for irreverence.

But there came a day when the fleets of the Buccaneers no longer mustered at the Tortugas, and the solitary and outlawed pirate took their place. Yet even with him the tradition of restraint and of discipline still lingered; and among the early pirates, the Avorys, the Englands, and the Robertses, there remained some respect for human sentiment. They were more dangerous to the merchant than to the seaman.

But they in turn were replaced by more savage and desperate men, who frankly recognized that they would get no quarter in their war with the human race, and who swore that they would give as little as they got. Of their histories we know little that is trustworthy. They wrote no memoirs and left no trace, save an occasional blackened and bloodstained derelict adrift upon the face of the Atlantic. Their deeds could only be surmised from the long roll of ships which never made their port.

Searching the records of history, it is only here and there in an old-world trial that the veil that shrouds them seems for an instant to be lifted, and we catch a glimpse of some amazing and grotesque brutality behind. Such was the breed of Ned Low, of Gow the Scotchman, and of the infamous Sharkey, whose coal-black barque, the *Happy Delivery*, was known from the Newfoundland Banks to the mouths of the Orinoco as the dark forerunner of misery and of death.

There were many men, both among the islands and on the Main, who had a blood feud with Sharkey, but not one who had suffered more bitterly than Copley

Banks, of Kingston. Banks had been one of the leading sugar merchants of the West Indies. He was a man of position, a member of the Council, the husband of a Percival, and the cousin of the Governor of Virginia. His two sons had been sent to London to be educated, and their mother had gone over to bring them back. On their return voyage the ship, the *Duchess of Cornwall*, fell into the hands of Sharkey, and the whole family met with an infamous death.

Copley Banks said little when he heard the news, but he sank into a morose and enduring melancholy. He neglected his business, avoided his friends, and spent much of his time in the low taverns of the fishermen and seamen. There, amidst riot and devilry, he sat silently puffing at his pipe, with a set face and a smouldering eye. It was generally supposed that his misfortunes had shaken his wits, and his old friends looked at him askance, for the company which he kept was enough to bar him from honest men.

From time to time there came rumours of Sharkey over the sea. Sometimes it was from some schooner which had seen a great flame upon the horizon, and approaching to offer help to the burning ship, had fled away at the sight of the sleek, black barque, lurking like a wolf near a mangled sheep. Sometimes it was a frightened trader, which had come tearing in with her canvas curved like a lady's bodice, because she had seen a patched fore-topsail rising slowly above the violet water-line. Sometimes it was from a Coaster, which had found a waterless Bahama cay littered with sun-dried bodies.

Once there came a man who had been mate of a Guinea-man, and who had escaped from the pirate's hands. He could not speak—for reasons which Sharkey could best supply—but he could write, and he did write, to the very great interest of Copley Banks. For hours they sat together over the map, and the dumb man pointed here and there to outlying reefs and tortuous inlets, while his companion sat smoking in silence, with his unvarying face and his fiery eyes.

One morning, some two years after his misfortune, Mr. Copley Banks strode into his own office with his old air of energy and alertness. The manager stared at him in surprise, for it was months since he had shown any interest in business.

"Good morning, Mr. Banks!" said he.

"Good morning, Freeman. I see that *Ruffling Harry* is in the Bay."

"Yes, sir; she clears for the Windward Islands on Wednesday."

"I have other plans for her, Freeman. I have determined upon a slaving venture to Whydah."

"But her cargo is ready, sir."

"Then it must come out again, Freeman. My mind is made up, and the *Ruffling Harry* must go slaving to Whydah."

All argument and persuasion were vain, so the manager had dolefully to clear the ship once more.

And then Copley Banks began to make preparations for his African voyage. It appeared that he relied upon force rather than barter for the filling of his hold, for he carried none of those showy trinkets which savages love, but the brig was fitted with eight nine-pounder guns and racks full of muskets and cutlasses. The after sail-room next the cabin was transformed into a powder magazine, and she carried as many round shot as a well-found privateer. Water and provisions were shipped for a long voyage.

But the preparation of his ship's company was most surprising. It made Freeman, the manager, realize that there was truth in the rumour that his master had taken leave of his senses. For, under one pretext or another, he began to dismiss the old and tried hands, who had served the firm for years, and in their place he embarked the scum of the port—men whose reputations were so vile that the lowest crimp would have been ashamed to furnish them.

There was Birthmark Sweetlocks, who was known to have been present at the killing of the logwood cutters, so that his hideous scarlet disfigurement was put down by the fanciful as being a red afterglow from that great crime. He was first mate, and under him was Israel Martin, a little sun-wilted fellow who had served with Howell Davies at the taking of Cape Coast Castle.

The crew were chosen from amongst those whom Banks had met and known in their own infamous haunts, and his own table-steward was a haggard-faced man, who gobbled at you when he tried to talk. His beard had been shaved, and it was impossible to recognize him as the same man whom Sharkey had placed under the knife, and who had escaped to tell his experiences to Copley Banks.

These doings were not unnoticed, nor yet uncommented upon in the town of Kingston. The Commandant of the troops—Major Harvey, of the Artillery—made serious representations to the Governor.

"She is not a trader, but a small warship," said he. "I think it would be as well to arrest Copley Banks and to seize the vessel."

"What do you suspect?" asked the Governor, who was a slow-witted man, broken down with fevers and port wine.

"I suspect," said the soldier, "that it is Stede Bonnet over again."

Now, Stede Bonnet was a planter of high reputation and religious character, who, from some sudden and overpowering freshet of wildness in his blood, had given up everything in order to start off pirating in the Caribbean Sea. The example was a recent one, and it had caused the utmost consternation in the islands. Governors had before now been accused of being in league with pirates, and of receiving commissions upon their plunder, so that any want of vigilance was open to a sinister construction.

"Well, Major Harvey," said he, "I am vastly sorry

to do anything which may offend my friend Copley Banks, for many a time have my knees been under his mahogany, but in face of what you say there is no choice for me but to order you to board the vessel and to satisfy yourself as to her character and destination."

So at one in the morning Major Harvey, with a launchful of his soldiers, paid a surprise visit to the *Ruffling Harry*, with the result that they picked up nothing more solid than a hempen cable floating at the moorings. It had been slipped by the brig, whose owner had scented danger. She had already passed the Palisades, and was beating out against the north-east trades on a course for the Windward Passage.

When upon the next morning the brig had left Morant Point a mere haze upon the Southern horizon, the men were called aft, and Copley Banks revealed his plans to them. He had chosen them, he said, as brisk boys and lads of spirit, who would rather run some risk upon the sea than starve for a living upon the shore. King's ships were few and weak, and they could master any trader who might come their way. Others had done well at the business, and with a handy, well-found vessel, there was no reason why they should not turn their tarry jackets into velvet coats. If they were prepared to sail under the black flag, he was ready to command them; but if any wished to withdraw, they might have the gig and row back to Jamaica.

Four men out of six-and-forty asked for their discharge, went over the ship's side into the boat, and rowed away amidst the jeers and howlings of the crew. The rest assembled aft, and drew up the articles of their association. A square of black tarpaulin had the white skull painted upon it, and was hoisted amidst cheering at the main.

Officers were elected, and the limits of their authority fixed. Copley Banks was chosen captain, but, as there are no mates upon a pirate craft, Birthmark Sweetlocks became quartermaster, and Israel Martin the boatswain.

There was no difficulty in knowing what was the custom of the brotherhood, for half the men at least had served upon pirates before. Food should be the same for all, and no man should interfere with another man's drink! The captain should have a cabin, but all hands should be welcome to enter it when they chose.

All should share and share alike, save only the captain, quartermaster, boatswain, carpenter, and master-gunner, who had from a quarter to a whole share extra. He who saw a prize first should have the best weapon taken out of her. He who boarded her first should have the richest suit of clothes aboard of her. Every man might treat his own prisoner, be it man or woman, after his own fashion. If a man flinched from his gun, the quartermaster should pistol him. These were some of the rules which the crew of the *Ruffling Harry* subscribed by putting forty-two crosses at the foot of the paper upon which they had been drawn.

So a new rover was afloat upon the seas, and her name before a year was over became as well known as that of the *Happy Delivery*. From the Bahamas to the Leewards, and from the Leewards to the Windwards, Copley Banks became the rival of Sharkey and the terror of traders. For a long time the barque and the brig never met, which was the more singular, as the *Ruffling Harry* was for ever looking in at Sharkey's resorts; but at last one day, when she was passing down the inlet of Coxon's Hole, at the east end of Cuba, with the intention of careening, there was the *Happy Delivery*, with her blocks and tackle-falls already rigged for the same purpose.

Copley Banks fired a shotted salute and hoisted the green trumpeter ensign, as the custom was among gentlemen of the sea. Then he dropped his boat and went aboard.

Captain Sharkey was not a man of a genial mood, nor had he any kindly sympathy for those who were of the same trade as himself. Copley Banks found him seated astride upon one of the after guns, with his New England quartermaster, Ned Galloway, and a crowd of roaring ruffians standing about him. Yet none of them roared with quite such assurance when Sharkey's pale face and filmy blue eyes were turned upon him.

He was in his shirt-sleeves, with his cambric frills breaking through his open red satin long-flapped vest. The scorching sun seemed to have no power upon his fleshless frame, for he wore a low fur cap, as though it had been winter. A many-coloured band of silk passed across his body and supported a short murderous sword, while his broad, brass-buckled belt was stuffed with pistols.

"Sink you for a poacher!" he cried, as Copley Banks passed over the bulwarks. "I will drub you within an inch of your life, and that inch also! What mean you by fishing in my waters?"

Copley Banks looked at him, and his eyes were like those of a traveller who sees his home at last.

"I am glad that we are of one mind," said he, "for I am myself of opinion that the seas are not large enough for the two of us. But if you will take your sword and pistols and come upon a sand-bank with me, then the world will be rid of a damned villain whichever way it goes."

"Now this is talking!" cried Sharkey, jumping off the gun and holding out his hand. "I have not met many who could look John Sharkey in the eyes and speak with a full breath. May the devil seize me if I do not choose you as a consort! But if you play me false, then I will come aboard of you and gut you upon your own poop."

"And I pledge you the same!" said Copley Banks, and so the two pirates became sworn comrades to each other.

That summer they went north as far as the Newfoundland Banks, and harried the New York traders and the whale-ships from New England. It was Copley Banks who captured the Liverpool ship, *House of Hanover*, but it was Sharkey who fastened her master to the windlass and pelted him to death with empty claret-bottles.

Together they engaged the King's ship *Royal Fortune*, which had been sent in search of them, and beat her off after a night action of five hours, the drunken, raving crews fighting naked in the light of the battle-lanterns, with a bucket of rum and a pannikin laid by the tackles of every gun. They ran to Topsail Inlet in North Carolina to refit, and then in the spring they were at the Grand Caicos, ready for a long cruise down the West Indies.

By this time Sharkey and Copley Banks had become very excellent friends, for Sharkey loved a whole-hearted villain, and he loved a man of metal, and it seemed to him that the two met in the captain of the *Ruffling Harry*. It was long before he gave his confidence to him, for cold suspicion lay deep in his character. Never once would he trust himself outside his own ship and away from his own men.

But Copley Banks came often on board the *Happy Delivery*, and joined Sharkey in many of his morose debauches, so that at last any lingering misgivings of the latter were set at rest. He knew nothing of the evil that he had done to his new boon companion, for of his many victims how could he remember the woman and the two boys whom he had slain with such levity so long ago! When, therefore, he received a challenge to himself and to his quartermaster for a carouse upon the last evening of their stay at the Caicos Bank, he saw no reason to refuse.

A well-found passenger ship had been rifled the week before, so their fare was of the best, and after supper five of them drank deeply together. There were the two captains, Birthmark Sweetlocks, Ned Galloway, and Israel Martin, the old buccaneersman. To wait upon them was the dumb steward, whose head Sharkey split with his glass, because he had been too slow in the filling of it.

The quartermaster had slipped Sharkey's pistols away from him, for it was an old joke with him to fire them cross-handed under the table, and see who was the luckiest man. It was a pleasantry which had cost his boatswain his leg, so now, when the table was cleared, they would coax Sharkey's weapons away from him on the excuse of the heat, and lay them out of his reach.

The captain's cabin of the *Ruffling Harry* was in a deck-house upon the poop, and a stern-chaser gun was mounted at the back of it. Round shot were racked round the wall, and three great hogsheads of powder made a stand for dishes and for bottles. In this grim room the five pirates sang and roared and drank, while the silent steward still filled up their glasses, and passed the box and the candle round for their tobacco-pipes. Hour after hour the talk became fouler, the voices hoarser, the curses and shoutings more incoherent, until three of the five had closed their bloodshot eyes, and dropped their swimming heads upon the table.

Copley Banks and Sharkey were left face to face, the one because he had drunk the least, the other because no amount of liquor would ever shake his iron nerve or warm his sluggish blood. Behind him stood the watchful steward, for ever filling up his waning glass. From without came the low lapping of the tide, and from over the water a sailor's chanty from the barque.

In the windless tropical night the words came clearly to their ears:

"A trader sailed from Stepney Town,
Wake her up! Shake her up! Try her with the mainsail!
A trader sailed from Stepney Town
With a keg full of gold and a velvet gown.
Ho, the bully Rover Jack,
Waiting with his yard aback
Out upon the Lowland Sea."

The two boon companions sat listening in silence. Then Copley Banks glanced at the steward, and the man took a coil of rope from the shot-rack behind him.

"Captain Sharkey," said Copley Banks, "do you remember the *Duchess of Cornwall*, hailing from London, which you took and sank three years ago off the Statira Shoal?"

"Curse me if I can bear their names in mind," said Sharkey. "We did as many as ten ships a week about that time."

"There were a mother and two sons among the passengers. Maybe that will bring it back to your mind."

Captain Sharkey leant back in thought, with his huge thin beak of a nose jutting upwards. Then he burst suddenly into a high treble, neighing laugh. He remembered it, he said, and he added details to prove it.

"But burn me if it had not slipped from my mind!" he cried. "How came you to think of it?"

"It was of interest to me," said Copley Banks, "for the woman was my wife and the lads were my only sons."

Sharkey stared across at his companion, and saw that the smouldering fire which lurked always in his eyes had burned up into a lurid flame. He read their menace, and he clapped his hands to his empty belt. Then he turned to seize a weapon, but the bight of a rope was cast round him, and in an instant his arms were bound to his side. He fought like a wild cat and screamed for help.

"Ned!" he yelled. "Ned! Wake up! Here's damned villainy! Help, Ned, help!"

But the three men were far too deeply sunk in their swinish sleep for any voice to wake them. Round and round went the rope, until Sharkey was swathed like a mummy from ankle to neck. They propped him stiff and helpless against a powder barrel, and they gagged him with a handkerchief, but his filmy, red-rimmed eyes still looked curses at them. The dumb man chattered in his exultation, and Sharkey winced for the first time when he saw the empty mouth before him. He understood that vengeance, slow and patient, had dogged him long, and clutched him at last.

The two captors had their plans all arranged, and they were somewhat elaborate.

First of all they stove the heads of two of the great powder barrels, and they heaped the contents out upon the table and floor. They piled it round and under the three drunken men, until each sprawled in a heap of it. Then they carried Sharkey to the gun and they triced him sitting over the port-hole, with his body about a foot from the muzzle. Wriggle as he would he could not move an inch either to right or left, and the dumb man trussed him up with a sailor's cunning, so that there was no chance that he should work free.

"Now, you bloody devil," said Copley Banks, softly, "you must listen to what I have to say to you, for they are the last words that you will hear. You are my man now, and I have bought you at a price, for I have given all that a man can give here below, and I have given my soul as well.

"To reach you I have had to sink to your level. For two years I strove against it, hoping that some other way might come, but I learnt that there was no other way. I've robbed and I have murdered—worse still, I have laughed and lived with you—and all for the one end. And now my time has come, and you will die as I would have you die, seeing the shadow creeping slowly upon you and the devil waiting for you in the shadow."

Sharkey could hear the hoarse voices of his rovers singing their chanty over the water.

"Where is the trader of Stepney Town?
Wake her up! Shake her up! Every stick a-bending!
Where is the trader of Stepney Town?
His gold's on the capstan, his blood's on his gown.
All for bully Rover Jack,
Reaching on the weather tack
Right across the Lowland Sea."

The words came clear to his ear, and just outside he

could hear two men pacing backwards and forwards upon the deck. And yet he was helpless, staring down the mouth of the nine-pounder, unable to move an inch or to utter so much as a groan. Again there came the burst of voices from the deck of the barque.

> "So it's up and it's over to Stornoway Bay,
> Pack it on! Crack it on! Try her with the stun-sails!
> It's off on a bowline to Stornoway Bay,
> Where the liquor is good and the lasses are gay,
> Waiting for their bully Jack,
> Watching for him sailing back,
> Right across the Lowland Sea."

To the dying pirate the jovial words and rollicking tune made his own fate seem the harsher, but there was no softening in his venomous blue eyes. Copley Banks had brushed away the priming of the gun, and had sprinkled fresh powder over the touch-hole. Then he had taken up the candle and cut it to the length of about an inch. This he placed upon the loose powder at the breach of the gun. Then he scattered powder thickly over the floor beneath, so that when the candle fell at the recoil it must explode the huge pile in which the three drunkards were wallowing.

"You've made others look death in the face, Sharkey," said he; "now it has come to be your own turn. You and these swine here shall go together!" He lit the candle-end as he spoke, and blew out the other lights upon the table. Then he passed out with the dumb man, and locked the cabin door upon the outer side. But before he closed it he took an exultant look backwards and received one last curse from those unconquerable eyes. In the single dim circle of light that ivory-white face, with the gleam of moisture upon the high, bald forehead, was the last that was ever seen of Sharkey.

There was a skiff alongside, and in it Copley Banks and the dumb steward made their way to the beach, and looked back upon the brig riding in the moonlight just outside the shadow of the palm trees. They waited and waited, watching that dim light which shone through the stern port. And then at last there came the dull thud of a gun, and an instant later the shattering crash of the explosion. The long, sleek, black barque, the sweep of white sand, and the fringe of nodding, feathery palm trees sprang into dazzling light and back into darkness again. Voices screamed and called upon the bay.

Then Copley Banks, his heart singing within him, touched his companion upon the shoulder, and they plunged together into the lonely jungle of the Caicos.

17. *The "Slapping Sal"*

IT was in the days when France's power was already broken upon the seas, and when more of her three-deckers lay rotting in the Medway than were to be found in Brest harbour. But her frigates and corvettes still scoured the ocean, closely followed ever by those of her rival. At the uttermost ends of the earth these dainty vessels, with sweet names of girls or of flowers, mangled and shattered each other for the honour of the four yards of bunting which flapped from the end of their gaffs.

It had blown hard in the night, but the wind had dropped with the dawning, and now the rising sun tinted the fringe of the storm-wrack as it dwindled into the west and glinted on the endless crests of the long, green waves. To north and south and west lay a skyline which was unbroken save by the spout of foam when two of the great Atlantic seas dashed each other into spray. To the east was a rocky island, jutting out into craggy points, with a few scattered clumps of palm trees and a pennant of mist streaming out from the bare, conical hill which capped it. A heavy surf beat upon the shore, and, at a safe distance from it, the British 32-gun frigate *Leda*, Captain A. P. Johnson, raised her black, glistening side upon the crest of a wave, or swooped down into an emerald valley, dipping away to the nor'ard under easy sail. On her snow-white quarter-deck stood a stiff little brown-faced man, who swept the horizon with his glass.

"Mr. Wharton!" he cried, with a voice like a rusty hinge.

A thin, knock-kneed officer shambled across the poop to him.

"Yes, sir."

"I've opened the sealed orders, Mr. Wharton."

A glimmer of curiosity shone upon the meagre features of the first lieutenant. The *Leda* had sailed with her consort, the *Dido*, from Antigua the week before, and the admiral's orders had been contained in a sealed envelope.

"We were to open them on reaching the deserted island of Sombriero, lying in north latitude eighteen, thirty-six, west longitude sixty-three, twenty-eight. Sombriero bore four miles to the north-east from our port-bow when the gale cleared, Mr. Wharton."

The lieutenant bowed stiffly. He and the captain had been bosom friends from childhood. They had gone to school together, joined the navy together, fought again and again together, and married into each other's families, but so long as their feet were on the poop the iron discipline of the service struck all that was human out of them and left only the superior and the subordinate. Captain Johnson took from his pocket a blue paper, which crackled as he unfolded it.

"The 32-gun frigates *Leda* and *Dido* (Captains A. P. Johnson and James Munro) are to cruise from the point at which these instructions are read to the mouth of the Caribbean Sea, in the hope of encountering the French frigate *La Gloire* (48), which has recently harassed our merchant ships in that quarter. H.M. frigates are also directed to hunt down the piratical craft known sometimes as the *Slapping Sal* and sometimes as the *Hairy Hudson*, which has plundered the British ships as per margin, inflicting barbarities upon their crews. She is a small brig, carrying ten light guns, with one twenty-four pound carronade forward. She was last seen upon the 23rd ult. to the north-east of the island of Sombriero.

" (Signed) JAMES MONTGOMERY

" (*Rear-Admiral*).

" H.M.S. *Colossus*, Antigua."

" We appear to have lost our consort," said Captain Johnson, folding up his instructions and again sweeping the horizon with his glass. " She drew away after we reefed down. It would be a pity if we met this heavy Frenchman without the *Dido*, Mr. Wharton. Eh ? "

The lieutenant twinkled and smiled.

" She has eighteen-pounders on the main and twelves on the poop, sir," said the captain. " She carries four hundred to our two hundred and thirty-one. Captain de Milon is the smartest man in the French service. Oh, Bobby boy, I'd give my hopes of my flag to rub my side up against her ! " He turned on his heel, ashamed of his momentary lapse. " Mr. Wharton," said he, looking back sternly over his shoulder, " get those square sails shaken out and bear away a point more to the west."

" A brig on the port-bow," came a voice from the forecastle.

" A brig on the port-bow," said the lieutenant.

The captain sprang upon the bulwarks and held on by the mizzen-shrouds, a strange little figure with flying skirts and puckered eyes. The lean lieutenant craned his neck and whispered to Smeaton, the second, while officers and men came popping up from below and clustered along the weather-rail, shading their eyes with their hands—for the tropical sun was already clear of the palm trees. The strange brig lay at anchor in the throat of a curving estuary, and it was already obvious that she could not get out without passing under the guns of the frigate. A long, rocky point to the north of her held her in.

" Keep her as she goes, Mr. Wharton," said the

captain. " Hardly worth while our clearing for action, Mr. Smeaton, but the men can stand by the guns in case she tries to pass us. Cast loose the bow-chasers and send the small-arm men to the forecastle."

A British crew went to its quarters in those days with the quiet serenity of men on their daily routine. In a few minutes, without fuss or sound, the sailors were knotted round their guns, the marines were drawn up and leaning on their muskets, and the frigate's bowsprit pointed straight for her little victim.

" Is it the *Slapping Sal*, sir ? "

" I have no doubt of it, Mr. Wharton."

" They don't seem to like the look of us, sir. They've cut their cable and are clapping on sail."

It was evident that the brig meant struggling for her freedom. One little patch of canvas fluttered out above another, and her people could be seen working like madmen in the rigging. She made no attempt to pass her antagonist, but headed up the estuary. The captain rubbed his hands.

" She's making for shoal water, Mr. Wharton, and we shall have to cut her out, sir. She's a footy little brig, but I should have thought a fore-and-after would have been more handy."

" It was a mutiny, sir."

" Ah, indeed ! "

" Yes, sir, I heard of it at Manilla : a bad business, sir. Captain and two mates murdered. This Hudson, or Hairy Hudson as they call him, led the mutiny. He's a Londoner, sir, and a cruel villain as ever walked."

" His next walk will be to Execution Dock, Mr. Wharton. She seems heavily manned. I wish I could take twenty topmen out of her, but that would be enough to corrupt the crew of the ark, Mr. Wharton."

Both officers were looking through their glasses at the brig. Suddenly the lieutenant showed his teeth in a grin, while the captain flushed a deeper red.

" That's Hairy Hudson on the after-rail, sir."

"The low, impertinent blackguard! He'll play some other antics before we are done with him. Could you reach him with the long eighteen, Mr. Smeaton?"

"Another cable length will do it, sir."

The brig yawed as they spoke, and as she came round a spurt of smoke whiffed out from her quarter. It was a pure piece of bravado, for the gun could scarce carry half-way. Then with a jaunty swing the little ship came into the wind again, and shot round a fresh curve in the winding channel.

"The water's shoaling rapidly, sir," repeated the second lieutenant.

"There's six fathoms by the chart."

"Four by the lead, sir."

"When we clear this point we shall see how we lie. Ha! I thought as much! Lay her to, Mr. Wharton. Now we have got her at our mercy!"

The frigate was quite out of sight of the sea now at the head of this river-like estuary. As she came round the curve the two shores were seen to converge at a point about a mile distant. In the angle, as near shore as she could get, the brig was lying with her broadside towards her pursuer and a wisp of black cloth streaming from her mizzen. The lean lieutenant, who had reappeared upon deck with a cutlass strapped to his side and two pistols rammed into his belt, peered curiously at the ensign.

"Is it the Jolly Roger, sir?" he asked.

But the captain was furious.

"He may hang where his breeches are hanging before I have done with him!" said he. "What boats will you want, Mr. Wharton?"

"We should do it with the launch and the jolly-boat."

"Take four and make a clean job of it. Pipe away the crews at once, and I'll work her in and help you with the long eighteens."

With a rattle of ropes and a creaking of blocks the four

boats splashed into the water. Their crews clustered thickly into them: bare-footed sailors, stolid marines, laughing middies, and in the sheets of each the senior officers with their stern schoolmaster faces. The captain, his elbows on the binnacle, still watched the distant brig. Her crew wêre tricing up the boarding-netting, dragging round the starboard guns, knocking new portholes for them, and making every preparation for a desperate resistance. In the thick of it all a huge man, bearded to the eyes, with a red nightcap upon his head, was straining and stooping and hauling. The captain watched him with a sour smile, and then snapping up his glass he turned upon his heel. For an instant he stood staring.

" Call back the boats!" he cried in his thin, creaking voice. " Clear away for action there! Cast loose those main-deck guns. Brace back the yards, Mr. Smeaton, and stand by to go about when she has weigh enough."

Round the curve of the estuary was coming a huge vessel. Her great yellow bowsprit and white-winged figure-head were jutting out from the cluster of palm trees, while high above them towered three immense masts with the tricolour flag floating superbly from the mizzen. Round she came, the deep-blue water creaming under her fore foot, until her long, curving, black side, her line of shining copper beneath and of snow-white hammocks above, and the thick clusters of men who peered over her bulwarks were all in full view. Her lower yards were slung, her ports triced up, and her guns run out all ready for action. Lying behind one of the promontories of the island, the lookout men of the *Gloire* upon the shore had seen the *cul de sac* into which the British frigate was headed, so that Captain de Milon had served the *Leda* as Captain Johnson had the *Slapping Sal*.

But the splendid discipline of the British service was at its best in such a crisis. The boats flew back; their crews clustered aboard, they were swung up at the davits and the fall-ropes made fast. Hammocks were brought up and stowed, bulkheads sent down, ports and magazines opened, the fires put out in the galley, and the drums beat to quarters. Swarms of men set the head-sails and brought the frigate round, while the gun-crews threw off their jackets and shirts, tightened their belts, and ran out their eighteen-pounders, peering through the open port-holes at the stately Frenchman. The wind was very light. Hardly a ripple showed itself upon the clear blue water, but the sails blew gently out as the breeze came over the wooded banks. The Frenchman had gone about also, and both ships were now heading slowly for the sea under fore-and-aft canvas, the *Gloire* a hundred yards in advance. She luffed up to cross the *Leda's* bows, but the British ship came round also, and the two rippled slowly on in such a silence that the ringing of ramrods as the French marines drove home their charges clanged quite loudly upon the ear.

"Not much sea-room, Mr. Wharton," remarked the captain.

"I have fought actions in less, sir."

"We must keep our distance and trust to our gunnery. She is very heavily manned, and if she got alongside we might find ourselves in trouble."

"I see the shakos of soldiers aboard of her."

"Two companies of light infantry from Martinique. Now we have her! Hard-a-port, and let her have it as we cross her stern!"

The keen eye of the little commander had seen the surface ripple, which told of a passing breeze. He had used it to dart across the big Frenchman and to rake her with every gun as he passed. But, once past her, the *Leda* had to come back into the wind to keep out of shoal water. The manœuvre brought her on to the starboard side of the Frenchman, and the trim little frigate seemed to heel right over under the crashing broadside which burst from the gaping ports. A moment later her topmen were swarming aloft to set her topsails and royals, and she strove to cross the *Gloire's* bows and rake her again. The French captain, however, brought his frigate's head round, and the two rode side by side within easy pistol-shot, pouring broadsides into each other in one of those murderous duels which, could they all be recorded, would mottle our charts with blood.

In that heavy tropical air, with so faint a breeze, the smoke formed a thick bank round the two vessels, from which the topmasts only protruded. Neither could see anything of its enemy save the throbs of fire in the darkness, and the guns were sponged and trained and fired into a dense wall of vapour. On the poop and the forecastle the marines, in two little red lines, were pouring in their volleys, but neither they nor the seamen-gunners could see what effect their fire was having. Nor, indeed, could they tell how far they were suffering themselves, for, standing at a gun, one could but hazily see that upon the right and the left. But above the roar of the cannon came the sharper sound of the piping shot, the crashing of riven planks, and the occasional heavy thud as spar or block came hurtling on to the deck. The lieutenants paced up and down the line of guns, while Captain Johnson fanned the smoke away with his cocked-hat and peered eagerly out.

"This is rare, Bobby!" said he, as the lieutenant joined him. Then, suddenly restraining himself, "What have we lost, Mr. Wharton?"

"Our main topsail yard and our gaff, sir."

"Where's the flag?"

"Gone overboard, sir."

"They'll think we've struck! Lash a boat's ensign on the starboard arm of the mizzen cross-jackyard."

"Yes, sir."

A round-shot dashed the binnacle to pieces between them. A second knocked two marines into a bloody, palpitating mash. For a moment the smoke rose, and the English captain saw that his adversary's heavier metal was producing a horrible effect. The *Leda* was a shattered wreck. Her deck was strewed with corpses. Several of her port-holes were knocked into one, and one of her eighteen-pounder guns had been thrown right back on to her breech, and pointed straight up to the sky. The thin line of marines still loaded and fired, but half the guns were silent, and their crews were piled thickly round them.

"Stand by to repel boarders!" yelled the captain.

"Cutlasses, lads, cutlasses!" roared Wharton.

"Hold your volley till they touch!" cried the captain of marines.

The huge loom of the Frenchman was seen bursting through the smoke. Thick clusters of boarders hung upon her sides and shrouds. A final broadside leapt from her ports, and the mainmast of the *Leda*, snapping short off a few feet above the deck, spun into the air and crashed down upon the port guns, killing ten men and putting the whole battery out of action. An instant later the two ships scraped together, and the starboard bower anchor of the *Gloire* caught the mizzen-chains of the *Leda* upon the port side. With a yell the black swarm of boarders steadied themselves for a spring.

But their feet were never to reach that blood-stained deck. From somewhere there came a well-aimed whiff of grape, and another, and another. The English marines and seamen, waiting with cutlass and musket behind the silent guns, saw with amazement the dark masses thinning and shredding away. At the same time the port broadside of the Frenchman burst into a roar.

"Clear away the wreck!" roared the captain. "What the devil are they firing at?"

"Get the guns clear!" panted the lieutenant. "We'll do them yet, boys!"

The wreckage was torn and hacked and splintered until first one gun and then another roared into action again. The Frenchman's anchor had been cut away, and the *Leda* had worked herself free from that fatal hug. But now, suddenly, there was a scurry up the shrouds of the *Gloire*, and a hundred Englishmen were shouting themselves hoarse: "They're running! They're running! They're running!"

And it was true. The Frenchman had ceased to fire, and was intent only upon clapping on every sail that he could carry. But that shouting hundred could not claim it all as their own. As the smoke cleared it was not difficult to see the reason. The ships had gained the mouth of the estuary during the fight, and there, about four miles out to sea, was the *Leda's* consort bearing down under full sail to the sound of the guns. Captain de Milon had done his part for one day, and presently the *Gloire* was drawing off swiftly to the north, while the *Dido* was bowling along at her skirts, rattling away with her bow-chasers, until a headland hid them both from view.

But the *Leda* lay sorely stricken, with her mainmast gone, her bulwarks shattered, her mizzen-topmast and gaff shot away, her sails like a beggar's rags, and a hundred of her crew dead and wounded. Close beside her a mass of wreckage floated upon the waves. It was the stern-post of a mangled vessel, and across it, in white letters on a black ground, was painted, "*The Slapping Sal.*"

"By the Lord! it was the brig that saved us!" cried Mr. Wharton. "Hudson brought her into action with the Frenchman, and was blown out of the water by a broadside!"

The little captain turned on his heel and paced up and down the deck. Already his crew were plugging the shot-holes, knotting and splicing and mending. When he came back, the lieutenant saw a softening of the stern lines about his eyes and mouth.

"Are they all gone?"

"Every man. They must have sunk with the wreck."

The two officers looked down at the sinister name,

and at the stump of wreckage which floated in the discoloured water. Something black washed to and fro beside a splintered gaff and a tangle of halliards. It was the outrageous ensign, and near it a scarlet cap was floating.

"He was a villain, but he was a Briton!" said the captain, at last. "He lived like a dog, but, by God, he died like a man!"

18. *A Pirate of the Land*

ONE CROWDED HOUR

THE place was the Eastbourne-Tunbridge road, not very far from the Cross in Hand—a lonely stretch, with a heath running upon either side. The time was half-past eleven upon a Sunday night in the late summer. A motor was passing slowly down the road.

It was a long, lean Rolls-Royce, running smoothly with a gentle purring of the engine. Through the two vivid circles cast by the electric head-lights the waving grass fringes and clumps of heather streamed swiftly like some golden cinematograph, leaving a blacker darkness behind and around them. One ruby-red spot shone upon the road, but no number-plate was visible within the dim ruddy halo of the tail-lamp which cast it. The car was open and of a tourist type, but even in that obscure light, for the night was moonless, an observer could hardly fail to have noticed a curious indefiniteness in its lines. As it slid into and across the broad stream of light from an open cottage door the reason could be seen. The body was hung with a singular loose arrangement of brown holland. Even the long black bonnet was banded with some close-drawn drapery.

The solitary man who drove this curious car was broad and burly. He sat hunched up over his steering-wheel, with the brim of a Tyrolean hat drawn down over his eyes. The red end of a cigarette smouldered under the black shadow thrown by the headgear. A dark ulster of some frieze-like material was turned up in the collar until it covered his ears. His neck was pushed forward from his rounded shoulders, and he seemed, as the car now slid noiselessly down the long sloping road, with the clutch disengaged and the engine running free, to be peering ahead of him through the darkness in search of some eagerly-expected object.

The distant toot of a motor-horn came faintly from some point far to the south of him. On such a night, at such a place, all traffic must be from south to north when the current of London week-enders sweeps back from the watering-place to the capital—from pleasure to duty. The man sat straight and listened intently. Yes, there it was again, and certainly to the south of him. His face was over the wheel and his eyes strained through the darkness. Then suddenly he spat out his cigarette and gave a sharp intake of the breath. Far away down the road two little yellow points had rounded a curve. They vanished into a dip, shot upwards once more, and then vanished again. The inert man in the draped car woke suddenly into intense life. From his pocket he pulled a mask of dark cloth, which he fastened securely across his face, adjusting it carefully that his sight might be unimpeded. For an instant he uncovered an acetylene hand-lantern, took a hasty glance at his own preparations, and laid it beside a Mauser pistol upon the seat alongside him. Then, twitching his hat down lower than ever, he released his clutch and slid downward his gear-lever. With a chuckle and shudder the long, black machine sprang forward, and shot with a soft sigh from her powerful engines down the sloping gradient. The driver stooped and switched off his electric head-lights. Only a dim grey swathe cut through the black heath indicated the line of his road. From in front there came presently a confused puffing and rattling and clanging as the oncoming car breasted the slope. It coughed and spluttered on a powerful, old-fashioned low gear, while its engine throbbed like a weary heart. The yellow, glaring lights dipped for the last time into a switchback curve. When they reappeared over the crest the two cars were within thirty yards of each other. The dark one darted across the road and barred the other's passage, while a warning acetylene lamp was waved in the air. With a jarring of brakes the noisy new-comer was brought to a halt.

"I say," cried an aggrieved voice, "'pon my soul, you know, we might have had an accident. Why the devil don't you keep your head-lights on? I never saw you till I nearly burst my radiators on you!"

The acetylene lamp, held forward, discovered a very angry young man, blue-eyed, yellow-moustached, and florid, sitting alone at the wheel of an antiquated twelve-horse Wolseley. Suddenly the aggrieved look upon his flushed face changed to one of absolute bewilderment. The driver in the dark car had sprung out of the seat, a black, long-barrelled, wicked-looking pistol was poked in the traveller's face, and behind the further sights of it was a circle of black cloth with two deadly eyes looking from as many slits.

"Hands up!" said a quick, stern voice. "Hands up! or, by the Lord——"

The young man was as brave as his neighbours, but the hands went up all the same.

"Get down!" said his assailant, curtly.

The young man stepped forth into the road, followed closely by the covering lantern and pistol. Once he made as if he would drop his hands, but a short, stern word jerked them up again.

"I say, look here, this is rather out o' date, ain't it?" said the traveller. "I expect you're joking—what?"

"Your watch," said the man behind the Mauser pistol.

"You can't really mean it!"

"Your watch, I say!"

"Well, take it, if you must. It's only plated, anyhow. You're two centuries out in time, or a few thousand miles longitude. The bush is your mark—or America. You don't seem in the picture on a Sussex road."

"Purse," said the man. There was something very compelling in his voice and methods. The purse was handed over.

"Any rings?"

"Don't wear 'em."

"Stand there! Don't move!"

The highwayman passed his victim and threw open the bonnet of the Wolseley. His hand, with a pair of steel pliers, was thrust deep into the works. There was the snap of a parting wire.

"Hang it all, don't crock my car!" cried the traveller.

He turned, but quick as a flash the pistol was at his head once more. And yet even in that flash, whilst the robber whisked round from the broken circuit, something had caught the young man's eye which made him gasp and start. He opened his mouth as if about to shout some words. Then with an evident effort he restrained himself.

"Get in," said the highwayman.

The traveller climbed back to his seat.

"What is your name?"

"Ronald Barker. What's yours?"

The masked man ignored the impertinence.

"Where do you live?" he asked.

"My cards are in my purse. Take one."

The highwayman sprang into his car, the engine of which had hissed and whispered in gentle accompaniment to the interview. With a clash he threw back his side-brake, flung in his gears, twirled the wheel hard round, and cleared the motionless Wolseley. A minute later he was gliding swiftly, with all his lights gleaming, some half-mile southward on the road, while Mr. Ronald Barker, a side-lamp in his hand, was rummaging furiously among the odds and ends of his repair-box for a strand of wire which would connect up his electricity and set him on his way once more.

When he had placed a safe distance between himself and his victim, the adventurer eased up, took his booty from his pocket, replaced the watch, opened the purse, and counted out the money. Seven shillings constituted the miserable spoil. The poor result of his efforts seemed to amuse rather than annoy him, for he chuckled as he held the two half-crowns and the florin in the glare of his lantern. Then suddenly his manner changed. He thrust the thin purse back into his pocket, released his brake, and shot onwards with the same tense bearing with which he had started upon his adventure. The lights of another car were coming down the road.

On this occasion the methods of the highwayman were less furtive. Experience had clearly given him confidence. With lights still blazing he ran towards the new-comers, and, halting in the middle of the road, summoned them to stop. From the point of view of the astonished travellers the result was sufficiently impressive. They saw in the glare of their own headlights two glowing discs on either side of the long, black-muzzled snout of a high-power car, and above the masked face and menacing figure of its solitary driver. In the golden circle thrown by the rover there stood an elegant, open-topped, twenty-horse Humber, with an under-sized and very astonished chauffeur blinking from under his peaked cap. From behind the wind-screen the veil-bound hats and wondering faces of two very pretty young women protruded, one upon either side, and a little crescendo of frightened squeaks announced the acute emotion of one of them. The other was cooler and more critical.

"Don't give it away, Hilda," she whispered. "Do shut up, and don't be such a silly. It's Bertie or one of the boys playing it on us."

"No, no! It's the real thing, Flossie. It's a robber,

sure enough. Oh, my goodness, whatever shall we do ? "

" What an ' ad.' ! " cried the other. " Oh, what a glorious ' ad.' ! Too late now for the mornings, but they'll have it in every evening paper, sure."

" What's it going to cost ? " groaned the other. " Oh, Flossie, Flossie, I'm sure I'm going to faint ! Don't you think if we both screamed together we could do some good ? Isn't he too awful with that black thing over his face ? Oh, dear, oh, dear ! He's killing poor little Alf ! "

The proceedings of the robber were indeed somewhat alarming. Springing down from his car, he had pulled the chauffeur out of his seat by the scruff of his neck. The sight of the Mauser had cut short all remonstrance, and under its compulsion the little man had pulled open the bonnet and extracted the sparking plugs. Having thus secured the immobility of his capture, the masked man walked forward, lantern in hand, to the side of the car. He had laid aside the gruff sternness with which he had treated Mr. Ronald Barker, and his voice and manner were gentle, though determined. He even raised his hat as a prelude to his address.

" I am sorry to inconvenience you, ladies," said he, and his voice had gone up several notes since the previous interview. " May I ask who you are ? "

Miss Hilda was beyond coherent speech, but Miss Flossie was of a sterner mould.

" This is a pretty business," said she. " What right have you to stop us on the public road, I should like to know ? "

" My time is short," said the robber, in a sterner voice. " I must ask you to answer my question."

" Tell him, Flossie ! For goodness' sake be nice to him ! " cried Hilda.

" Well, we're from the Gaiety Theatre, London, if you want to know," said the young lady. " Perhaps you've heard of Miss Flossie Thornton and Miss Hilda

Mannering? We've been playing a week at the Royal at Eastbourne, and took a Sunday off to ourselves. So now you know!"

"I must ask you for your purses and for your jewellery."

Both ladies set up shrill expostulations, but they found, as Mr. Ronald Barker had done, that there was something quietly compelling in this man's methods. In a very few minutes they had handed over their purses, and a pile of glittering rings, bangles, brooches and chains was lying upon the front seat of the car. The diamonds glowed and shimmered like little electric points in the light of the lantern. He picked up the glittering tangle and weighed it in his hand.

"Anything you particularly value?" he asked the ladies; but Miss Flossie was in no humour for concessions.

"Don't come the Claude Duval over us," said she. "Take the lot or leave the lot. We don't want bits of our own given back to us."

"Except just Billy's necklace!" cried Hilda, and snatched at a little rope of pearls. The robber bowed, and released his hold of it.

"Anything else?"

The valiant Flossie began suddenly to cry. Hilda did the same. The effect upon the robber was surprising. He threw the whole heap of jewellery into the nearest lap.

"There! there! Take it!" he said. "It's trumpery stuff, anyhow. It's worth something to you, and nothing to me."

Tears changed in a moment to smiles.

"You're welcome to the purses. The 'ad.' is worth ten times the money. But what a funny way of getting a living nowadays! Aren't you afraid of being caught? It's all so wonderful, like a scene from a comedy."

"It may be a tragedy," said the robber.

"Oh, I hope not—I'm sure I hope not!" cried the two ladies of the drama.

But the robber was in no mood for further conversation. Far away down the road tiny points of light had appeared. Fresh business was coming to him, and he must not mix his cases. Disengaging his machine, he raised his hat, and slipped off to meet this new arrival, while Miss Flossie and Miss Hilda leaned out of their derelict car, still palpitating from their adventure, and watched the red gleam of the tail-light until it merged into the darkness.

This time there was every sign of a rich prize. Behind its four grand lamps set in a broad frame of glittering brasswork the magnificent sixty-horse Daimler breasted the slope with the low, deep, even snore which proclaimed its enormous latent strength. Like some rich-laden, high-pooped Spanish galleon, she kept her course until the prowling craft ahead of her swept across her bows and brought her to a sudden halt. An angry face, red, blotched, and evil, shot out of the open window of the closed limousine. The robber was aware of a high, bald forehead, gross pendulous cheeks, and two little crafty eyes which gleamed between creases of fat.

"Out of my way, sir! Out of my way this instant!" cried a rasping voice. "Drive over him, Hearn! Get down and pull him off the seat. The fellow's drunk—he's drunk, I say!"

Up to this point the proceedings of the modern highwayman might have passed as gentle. Now they turned in an instant to savagery. The chauffeur, a burly, capable fellow, incited by that raucous voice behind him, sprang from the car and seized the advancing robber by the throat. The latter hit out with the butt-end of his pistol, and the man dropped groaning on the road. Stepping over his prostrate body the adventurer pulled open the door, seized the stout occupant savagely by the ear, and dragged him bellowing on to the highway. Then, very deliberately, he struck him twice across the face with his open hand. The blows rang out like pistol-shots in the silence of the night. The fat traveller turned a ghastly colour and fell back half senseless against the side of the limousine. The robber dragged open his coat, wrenched away the heavy gold watch-chain with all that it held, plucked out the great diamond pin that sparkled in the black satin tie, dragged off four rings—not one of which could have cost less than three figures—and finally tore from his inner pocket a bulky leather note-book. All this property he transferred to his own black overcoat, and added to it the man's pearl cuff-links, and even the golden stud which held his collar. Having made sure that there was nothing else to take, the robber flashed his lantern upon the prostrate chauffeur, and satisfied himself that he was stunned and not dead. Then, returning to the master, he proceeded very deliberately to tear all his clothes from his body with a ferocious energy which set his victim whimpering and writhing in imminent expectation of murder.

Whatever his tormentor's intention may have been, it was very effectually frustrated. A sound made him turn his head, and there, no very great distance off, were the lights of a car coming swiftly from the north. Such a car must have already passed the wreckage which this pirate had left behind him. It was following his track with a deliberate purpose, and might be crammed with every county constable of the district.

The adventurer had no time to lose. He darted from his bedraggled victim, sprang into his own seat, and with his foot on the accelerator shot swiftly off down the road. Some way down there was a narrow side lane, and into this the fugitive turned, cracking on his high speed and leaving a good five miles between him and any pursuer before he ventured to stop. Then, in a quiet corner, he counted over his booty of the evening —the paltry plunder of Mr. Ronald Barker, the rather better-furnished purses of the actresses, which contained four pounds between them, and, finally, the gorgeous jewellery and well-filled note-book of the plutocrat upon the Daimler. Five notes of fifty pounds, four of ten, fifteen sovereigns, and a number of valuable papers made up a most noble haul. It was clearly enough for one night's work. The adventurer replaced all his ill-gotten gains in his pocket, and, lighting a cigarette, set forth upon his way with the air of a man who has no further care upon his mind.

It was on the Monday morning following upon this eventful evening that Sir Henry Hailworthy, of Walcot Old Place, having finished his breakfast in a leisurely fashion, strolled down to his study with the intention of writing a few letters before setting forth to take his place upon the county bench. Sir Henry was a Deputy-Lieutenant of the county ; he was a baronet of ancient blood ; he was a magistrate of ten years' standing ; and he was famous above all as the breeder of many a good horse and the most desperate rider in all the Weald country. A tall, upstanding man, with a strong clean-shaven face, heavy black eyebrows, and a square, resolute jaw, he was one whom it was better to call friend than foe. Though nearly fifty years of age, he bore no sign of having passed his youth, save that Nature, in one of her freakish moods, had planted one little feather of white hair above his right ear, making the rest of his thick black curls the darker by contrast. He was in thoughtful mood this morning, for having lit his pipe he sat at his desk with his blank note-paper in front of him, lost in a deep reverie.

Suddenly his thoughts were brought back to the present. From behind the laurels of the curving drive there came a low, clanking sound, which swelled into the clatter and jingle of an ancient car. Then from round the corner there swung an old-fashioned Wolseley, with a fresh-complexioned, yellow-moustached young man at the wheel. Sir Henry sprang to his feet at the sight, and then sat down once more. He rose again as a minute later the footman announced Mr. Ronald

Barker. It was an early visit, but Barker was Sir Henry's intimate friend. As each was a fine shot, horseman, and billiard-player, there was much in common between the two men, and the younger (and poorer) was in the habit of spending at least two evenings a week at Walcot Old Place. Therefore, Sir Henry advanced cordially with outstretched hand to welcome him.

"You're an early bird this morning," said he. "What's up? If you are going over to Lewes we could motor together."

But the younger man's demeanour was peculiar and ungracious. He disregarded the hand which was held out to him, and he stood pulling at his own long moustache and staring with troubled, questioning eyes at the county magistrate.

"Well, what's the matter?" asked the latter.

Still the young man did not speak. He was clearly on the edge of an interview which he found it most difficult to open. His host grew impatient.

"You don't seem yourself this morning. What on earth is the matter? Anything upset you?"

"Yes," said Ronald Barker, with emphasis.

"What has?"

"*You* have."

Sir Henry smiled. "Sit down, my dear fellow. If you have any grievance against me, let me hear it."

Barker sat down. He seemed to be gathering himself for a reproach. When it did come it was like a bullet from a gun.

"Why did you rob me last night?"

The magistrate was a man of iron nerve. He showed neither surprise nor resentment. Not a muscle twitched upon his calm, set face.

"Why do you say that I robbed you last night?"

"A big, tall fellow in a motor-car stopped me on the Mayfield road. He poked a pistol in my face and took my purse and my watch. Sir Henry, that man was you."

The magistrate smiled.

"Am I the only big, tall man in the district? Am I the only man with a motor-car?"

"Do you think I couldn't tell a Rolls-Royce when I see it—I, who spend half my life on a car and the other half under it? Who has a Rolls-Royce about here except you?"

"My dear Barker, don't you think that such a modern highwayman as you describe would be more likely to operate outside his own district? How many hundred Rolls-Royces are there in the South of England?"

"No, it won't do, Sir Henry—it won't do! Even your voice, though you sunk it a few notes, was familiar enough to me. But hang it, man! What did you do it *for*? That's what gets over me. That you should stick up me, one of your closest friends, a man that worked himself to the bone when you stood for the division—and all for the sake of a Brummagem watch and a few shillings—is simply incredible."

"Simply incredible," repeated the magistrate, with a smile.

"And then those actresses, poor little devils, who have to earn all they get. I followed you down the road, you see. That was a dirty trick, if ever I heard one. The City shark was different. If a chap must go a-robbing, that sort of fellow is fair game. But your friend, and then the girls—well, I say again, I couldn't have believed it."

"Then why believe it?"

"Because it *is* so."

"Well, you seem to have persuaded yourself to that effect. You don't seem to have much evidence to lay before anyone else."

"I could swear to you in a police court. What put the lid on it was that when you were cutting my wire—and an infernal liberty it was!—I saw that white tuft of yours sticking out from behind your mask."

For the first time an acute observer might have

seen some slight sign of emotion upon the face of the baronet.

"You seem to have a fairly vivid imagination," said he.

His visitor flushed with anger.

"See here, Hailworthy," said he, opening his hand and showing a small, jagged triangle of black cloth. "Do you see that? It was on the ground near the car of the young women. You must have ripped it off as you jumped out from your seat. Now send for that heavy black driving-coat of yours. If you don't ring the bell I'll ring it myself, and we shall have it in. I'm going to see this thing through, and don't you make any mistake about that."

The baronet's answer was a surprising one. He rose, passed Barker's chair, and, walking over to the door, he locked it and placed the key in his pocket.

"You *are* going to see it through," said he. "I'll lock you in until you do. Now we must have a straight talk, Barker, as man to man, and whether it ends in tragedy or not depends on you."

He had half-opened one of the drawers in his desk as he spoke. His visitor frowned in anger.

"You won't make matters any better by threatening me, Hailworthy. I am going to do my duty, and you won't bluff me out of it."

"I have no wish to bluff you. When I spoke of a tragedy I did not mean to you. What I meant was that there are some turns which this affair cannot be allowed to take. I have neither kith nor kin, but there is the family honour, and some things are impossible."

"It is late to talk like that."

"Well, perhaps it is, but not too late. And now I have a good deal to say to you. First of all, you are quite right, and it was I who held you up last night on the Mayfield road."

"But why on earth——"

"All right. Let me tell it my own way. First I want you to look at these." He unlocked a drawer and he took out two small packages. "These were to be posted in London to-night. This one is addressed to you, and I may as well hand it over to you at once. It contains your watch and your purse. So, you see, bar your cut wire you would have been none the worse for your adventure. This other packet is addressed to the young ladies of the Gaiety Theatre, and their properties are enclosed. I hope I have convinced you that I had intended full reparation in each case before you came to accuse me?"

"Well?" asked Barker.

"Well, we will now deal with Sir George Wilde, who is, as you may not know, the senior partner of Wilde and Guggendorf, the founders of the Ludgate Bank of infamous memory. His chauffeur is a case apart. You may take it from me, upon my word of honour, that I had plans for the chauffeur. But it is the master that I want to speak of. You know that I am not a rich man myself. I expect all the county knows that. When Black Tulip lost the Derby I was hard hit. And other things as well. Then I had a legacy of a thousand. This infernal bank was paying 7 per cent. on deposits. I knew Wilde. I saw him. I asked him if it was safe. He said it was. I paid it in, and within forty-eight hours the whole thing went to bits. It came out before the Official Receiver that Wilde had known for three months that nothing could save him. And yet he took all my cargo aboard his sinking vessel. He was all right—confound him! He had plenty besides. But I had lost all my money and no law could help me. Yet he had robbed me as clearly as one man could rob another, I saw him and he laughed in my face. Told me to stick to Consols, and that the lesson was cheap at the price. So I just swore that, by hook or by crook, I would get level with him. I knew his habits, for I had made it my business to do so. I knew that he came back from

Eastbourne on Sunday nights. I knew that he carried a good sum with him in his pocket-book. Well, it's *my* pocket-book now. Do you mean to tell me that I'm not morally justified in what I have done? By the Lord, I'd have left the devil as bare as he left many a widow and orphan if I'd had the time!"

"That's all very well. But what about me? What about the girls?"

"Have some common sense, Barker. Do you suppose that I could go and stick up this one personal enemy of mine and escape detection? It was impossible. I was bound to make myself out to be just a common robber who had run up against him by accident. So I turned myself loose on the high road and took my chance. As the devil would have it, the first man I met was yourself. I was a fool not to recognize that old ironmonger's store of yours by the row it made coming up the hill. When I saw you I could hardly speak for laughing. But I was bound to carry it through. The same with the actresses. I'm afraid I gave myself away, for I couldn't take their little fal-lals, but I had to keep up a show. Then came my man himself. There was no bluff about that. I was out to skin him, and I did. Now, Barker, what do you think of it all? I had a pistol at your head last night, and, by George! whether you believe it or not, you have one at mine this morning!"

The young man rose slowly, and with a broad smile he wrung the magistrate by the hand.

"Don't do it again. It's too risky," said he. "The swine would score heavily if you were taken."

"You're a good chap, Barker," said the magistrate. "No, I won't do it again. Who's the fellow who talks of 'one crowded hour of glorious life'? By George! it's too fascinating. I had the time of my life! Talk of fox-hunting! No, I'll never touch it again, for it might get a grip of me."

A telephone rang sharply upon the table, and the

baronet put the receiver to his ear. As he listened, he smiled across at his companion.

"I'm rather late this morning," said he, "and they are waiting for me to try some petty larcenies on the county bench."

TALES OF BLUE WATER

19. *The Striped Chest*

"WHAT do you make of her, Allardyce?" I asked.

My second mate was standing beside me upon the poop, with his short, thick legs astretch, for the gale had left a considerable swell behind it, and our two quarter-boats nearly touched the water with every roll. He steadied his glass against the mizzen-shrouds, and he looked long and hard at this disconsolate stranger every time she came reeling up on to the crest of a roller and hung balanced for a few seconds before swooping down upon the other side. She lay so low in the water that I could only catch an occasional glimpse of a pea-green line of bulwark.

She was a brig, but her mainmast had been snapped short off some ten feet above the deck, and no effort seemed to have been made to cut away the wreckage, which floated, sails and yards, like the broken wing of a wounded gull, upon the water beside her. The foremast was still standing, but the fore-topsail was flying loose, and the headsails were streaming out in long white pennons in front of her. Never have I seen a vessel which appeared to have gone through rougher handling.

But we could not be surprised at that, for there had been times during the last three days when it was a question whether our own barque would ever see land again. For thirty-six hours we had kept her nose to it, and if the *Mary Sinclair* had not been as good a sea-boat as ever left the Clyde, we could not have gone through. And yet here we were at the end of it with the loss only of our gig and of part of the starboard bulwark. It did not astonish us, however, when the smother had cleared away, to find that others had been less lucky, and that this mutilated brig, staggering about upon a blue sea, and under a cloudless sky, had been left, like a blinded man after a lightning flash, to tell of the terror which is past.

Allardyce, who was a slow and methodical Scotchman, stared long and hard at the little craft, while our seamen lined the bulwark or clustered upon the fore shrouds to have a view of the stranger. In latitude 20° and longitude 10°, which were about our bearings, one becomes a little curious as to whom one meets, for one has left the main lines of Atlantic commerce to the north. For ten days we had been sailing over a solitary sea.

" She's derelict, I'm thinking," said the second mate.

I had come to the same conclusion, for I could see no sign of life upon her deck, and there was no answer to the friendly wavings from our seamen. The crew had probably deserted her under the impression that she was about to founder.

" She can't last long," continued Allardyce, in his measured way. " She may put her nose down and her tail up any minute. The water's lipping up to the edge of her rail."

" What's her flag ? " I asked.

" I'm trying to make out. It's got all twisted and tangled with the halyards. Yes, I've got it now, clear enough. It's the Brazilian flag, but it's wrong side up."

She had hoisted a signal of distress, then, before her people had abandoned her. Perhaps they had only just gone. I took the mate's glass and looked round over the tumultuous face of the deep blue Atlantic, still veined and starred with white lines and spoutings of foam. But nowhere could I see anything human beyond ourselves.

"There may be living men aboard," said I.

"There may be salvage," muttered the second mate.

"Then we will run down upon her lee side, and lie to."

We were not more than a hundred yards from her when we swung our foreyard aback, and there we were, the barque and the brig, ducking and bowing like two clowns in a dance.

"Drop one of the quarter-boats," said I. "Take four men, Mr. Allardyce, and see what you can learn of her."

But just at that moment my first officer, Mr. Armstrong, came on deck, for seven bells had struck, and it was but a few minutes off his watch. It would interest me to go myself to this abandoned vessel and to see what there might be aboard of her. So, with a word to Armstrong, I swung myself over the side, slipped down the falls, and took my place in the sheets of the boat.

It was but a little distance, but it took some time to traverse, and so heavy was the roll, that often, when we were in the trough of the sea, we could not see either the barque which we had left or the brig which we were approaching. The sinking sun did not penetrate down there, and it was cold and dark in the hollows of the waves, but each passing billow heaved us up into the warmth and the sunshine once more. At each of these moments, as we hung upon a white-capped ridge between the two dark valleys, I caught a glimpse of the long, pea-green line, and the nodding foremast of the brig, and I steered so as to come round by her stern, so that we might determine which was the best way of boarding her. As we passed her we saw the name *Nossa Sehnora da Vittoria* painted across her dripping counter.

"The weather side, sir," said the second mate. "Stand by with the boathook, carpenter!" An instant later we had jumped over the bulwarks, which were hardly higher than our boat, and found ourselves upon the deck of the abandoned vessel.

Our first thought was to provide for our own safety in case—as seemed very probable—the vessel should settle down beneath our feet. With this object two of our men held on to the painter of the boat, and fended her off from the vessel's side, so that she might be ready in case we had to make a hurried retreat. The carpenter was sent to find out how much water there was, and whether it was still gaining, while the other seaman, Allardyce and myself, made a rapid inspection of the vessel and her cargo.

The deck was littered with wreckage and with hen-coops, in which the dead birds were washing about. The boats were gone, with the exception of one, the bottom of which had been stove, and it was certain that the crew had abandoned the vessel. The cabin was in a deck house, one side of which had been beaten in by a heavy sea. Allardyce and I entered it, and found the captain's table as he had left it, his books and papers—all Spanish or Portuguese—scattered over it, with piles of cigarette ash everywhere. I looked about for the log, but could not find it.

"As likely as not he never kept one," said Allardyce. "Things are pretty slack aboard a South American trader, and they don't do more than they can help. If there was one it must have been taken away with him in the boat."

"I should like to take all these books and papers," said I. "Ask the carpenter how much time we have."

His report was reassuring. The vessel was full of water, but some of the cargo was buoyant, and there was no immediate danger of her sinking. Probably she would never sink, but would drift about as one of those terrible, unmarked reefs which have sent so many stout vessels to the bottom.

"In that case there is no danger in your going below, Mr. Allardyce," said I. "See what you can make of her, and find out how much of her cargo may be saved. I'll look through these papers while you are gone."

The bills of lading, and some notes and letters which lay upon the desk, sufficed to inform me that the Brazilian brig *Nossa Sehnora da Vittoria* had cleared from Bahia a month before. The name of the captain was Texeira, but there was no record as to the number of the crew. She was bound for London, and a glance at the bills of lading was sufficient to show me that we were not likely to profit much in the way of salvage. Her cargo consisted of nuts, ginger, and wood, the latter in the shape of great logs of valuable tropical growths. It was these, no doubt, which had prevented the ill-fated vessel from going to the bottom, but they were of such a size as to make it impossible for us to extract them. Besides these, there were a few fancy goods, such as a number of ornamental birds for millinery purposes, and a hundred cases of preserved fruits. And then, as I turned over the papers, I came upon a short note in English, which arrested my attention.

"It is requested," said the note, "that the various old Spanish and Indian curiosities, which came out of the Santarem collection, and which are consigned to Prontfoot and Neuman, of Oxford Street, London, should be put in some place where there may be no danger of these very valuable and unique articles being injured or tampered with. This applies most particularly to the treasure-chest of Don Ramirez di Leyra, which must on no account be placed where anyone can get at it."

The treasure-chest of Don Ramirez! Unique and valuable articles! Here was a chance of salvage after all! I had risen to my feet with the paper in my hand, when my Scotch mate appeared in the doorway.

"I'm thinking all isn't quite as it should be aboard of this ship, sir," said he. He was a hard-faced man, and yet I could see that he had been startled.

"What's the matter?"

"Murder's the matter, sir. There's a man here with his brains beaten out."

"Killed in the storm?" said I.

"Maybe so, sir. But I'll be surprised if you think so after you have seen him."

"Where is he, then?"

"This way, sir; here in the main-deck house."

There appeared to have been no accommodation below in the brig, for there was the afterhouse for the captain, another by the main hatchway with the cook's galley attached to it, and a third in the forecastle for the men. It was to this middle one that the mate led me. As you entered, the galley, with its litter of tumbled pots and dishes, was upon the right, and upon the left was a small room with two bunks for the officers. Then beyond there was a place about twelve feet square, which was littered with flags and spare canvas. All round the walls were a number of packets done up in coarse cloth and carefully lashed to the woodwork. At the other end was a great box, striped red and white, though the red was so faded and the white so dirty that it was only where the light fell directly upon it that one could see the colouring. The box was, by subsequent measurement, four feet three inches in length, three feet two inches in height, and three feet across—considerably larger than a seaman's chest.

But it was not to the box that my eyes or my thoughts were turned as I entered the store-room. On the floor, lying across the litter of bunting, there was stretched a small, dark man with a short, curling beard. He lay as far as it was possible from the box, with his feet towards it and his head away. A crimson patch was printed upon the white canvas on which his head was resting, and little red ribbons wreathed themselves round his swarthy neck and trailed away on to the floor, but there was no sign of a wound that I could see, and his face was as placid as that of a sleeping child.

It was only when I stooped that I could perceive his

injury, and then I turned away with an exclamation of horror. He had been pole-axed; apparently by some person standing behind him. A frightful blow had smashed in the top of his head and penetrated deeply into his brain. His face might well be placid, for death must have been absolutely instantaneous, and the position of the wound showed that he could never have seen the person who had inflicted it.

"Is that foul play or accident, Captain Barclay?" asked my second mate, demurely.

"You are quite right, Mr. Allardyce. The man has been murdered, struck down from above by a sharp and heavy weapon. But who was he, and why did they murder him?"

"He was a common seaman, sir," said the mate. "You can see that if you look at his fingers." He turned out his pockets as he spoke and brought to light a pack of cards, some tarred string, and a bundle of Brazilian tobacco.

"Hullo, look at this!" said he.

It was a large, open knife with a stiff spring blade which he had picked up from the floor. The steel was shining and bright, so that we could not associate it with the crime, and yet the dead man had apparently held it in his hand when he was struck down, for it still lay within his grasp.

"It looks to me, sir, as if he knew he was in danger, and kept his knife handy," said the mate. "However, we can't help the poor beggar now. I can't make out these things that are lashed to the wall. They seem to be idols and weapons and curios of all sorts done up in old sacking."

"That's right," said I. "They are the only things of value that we are likely to get from the cargo. Hail the barque and tell them to send the other quarter-boat to help us to get the stuff aboard."

While he was away I examined this curious plunder which had come into our possession. The curiosities were so wrapped up that I could only form a general idea as to their nature, but the striped box stood in a good light where I could thoroughly examine it. On the lid, which was clamped and cornered with metal-work, there was engraved a complex coat of arms, and beneath it was a line of Spanish which I was able to decipher as meaning, "The treasure-chest of Don Ramirez di Leyra, Knight of the Order of Saint James, Governor and Captain-General of Terra Firma and of the Province of Veraquas." In one corner was the date 1606, and on the other a large white label, upon which was written in English, "You are earnestly requested, upon no account, to open this box." The same warning was repeated underneath in Spanish. As to the lock, it was a very complex and heavy one of engraved steel, with a Latin motto, which was above a seaman's comprehension.

By the time I had finished this examination of the peculiar box, the other quarter-boat with Mr. Armstrong, the first officer, had come alongside, and we began to carry out and place in her the various curiosities which appeared to be the only objects worth moving from the derelict ship. When she was full I sent her back to the barque, and then Allardyce and I, with a carpenter and one seaman, shifted the striped box, which was the only thing left, to our boat, and lowered it over, balancing it upon the two middle thwarts, for it was so heavy that it would have given the boat a dangerous tilt had we placed it at either end. As to the dead man, we left him where we had found him.

The mate had a theory that, at the moment of the desertion of the ship, this fellow had started plundering, and that the captain in an attempt to preserve discipline, had struck him down with a hatchet or some other heavy weapon. It seemed more probable than any other explanation, and yet it did not entirely satisfy me either. But the ocean is full of mysteries, and we were content to leave the fate of the dead seaman of the Brazilian brig to be added to that long list which every sailor can recall.

The heavy box was slung up by ropes on to the deck of the *Mary Sinclair*, and was carried by four seamen into the cabin, where, between the table and the after-lockers, there was just space for it to stand. There it remained during supper, and after that meal the mates remained with me, and discussed over a glass of grog the event of the day. Mr. Armstrong was a long, thin, vulture-like man, an excellent seaman, but famous for his nearness and cupidity. Our treasure-trove had excited him greatly, and already he had begun with glistening eyes to reckon up how much it might be worth to each of us when the shares of the salvage came to be divided.

"If the paper said that they were unique, Mr. Barclay, then they may be worth anything that you like to name. You wouldn't believe the sums that the rich collectors give. A thousand pounds is nothing to them. We'll have something to show for our voyage, or I am mistaken."

"I don't think that," said I. "As far as I can see they are not very different from any other South American curios."

"Well, sir, I've traded there for fourteen voyages, and I have never seen anything like that chest before. That's worth a pile of money, just as it stands. But it's so heavy, that surely there must be something valuable inside it. Don't you think that we ought to open it and see?"

"If you break it open you will spoil it, as likely as not," said the second mate.

Armstrong squatted down in front of it, with his head on one side, and his long, thin nose within a few inches of the lock.

"The wood is oak," said he, "and it has shrunk a little with age. If I had a chisel or a strong-bladed knife I could force the lock back without doing any damage at all."

The mention of a strong-bladed knife made me think of the dead seaman upon the brig.

"I wonder if he could have been on the job when someone came to interfere with him," said I.

"I don't know about that, sir, but I am perfectly certain that I could open the box. There's a screwdriver here in the locker. Just hold the lamp, Allardyce, and I'll have it done in a brace of shakes."

"Wait a bit," said I, for already, with eyes which gleamed with curiosity and with avarice, he was stooping over the lid. "I don't see that there is any hurry over this matter. You've read that card which warns us not to open it. It may mean anything or it may mean nothing, but somehow I feel inclined to obey it. After all, whatever is in it will keep, and if it is valuable it will be worth as much if it is opened in the owner's offices as in the cabin of the *Mary Sinclair*."

The first officer seemed bitterly disappointed at my decision.

"Surely, sir, you are not superstitious about it," said he, with a slight sneer upon his thin lips. "If it gets out of our own hands, and we don't see for ourselves what is inside it, we may be done out of our rights; besides——"

"That's enough, Mr. Armstrong," said I, abruptly. "You may have every confidence that you will get your rights, but I will not have that box opened to-night."

"Why, the label itself shows that the box has been examined by Europeans," Allardyce added. "Because a box is a treasure-box is no reason that it has treasures inside it now. A good many folk have had a peep into it since the days of the old Governor of Terra Firma."

Armstrong threw the screwdriver down upon the table and shrugged his shoulders.

"Just as you like," said he; but for the rest of the evening, although we spoke upon many subjects, I noticed that his eyes were continually coming round, with the same expression of curiosity and greed, to the old striped box.

And now I come to that portion of my story which fills me even now with a shuddering horror when I think of it. The main cabin had the rooms of the officers round it, but mine was the farthest away from it at the end of the little passage which led to the companion. No regular watch was kept by me, except in cases of emergency, and the three mates divided the watches among them. Armstrong had the middle watch, which ends at four in the morning, and he was relieved by Allardyce. For my part I have always been one of the soundest of sleepers, and it is rare for anything less than a hand upon my shoulder to arouse me.

And yet I was aroused that night, or rather in the early grey of the morning. It was just half-past four by my chronometer when something caused me to sit up in my berth wide awake and with every nerve tingling. It was a sound of some sort, a crash with a human cry at the end of it, which still jarred upon my ears. I sat listening, but all was now silent. And yet it could not have been imagination, that hideous cry, for the echo of it still rang in my head, and it seemed to have come from some place quite close to me. I sprang from my bunk, and, pulling on some clothes, I made my way into the cabin.

At first I saw nothing unusual there. In the cold, grey light I made out the red-clothed table, the six rotating chairs, the walnut lockers, the swinging barometer, and there, at the end, the big striped chest. I was turning away with the intention of going upon deck and asking the second mate if he had heard anything, when my eyes fell suddenly upon something which projected from under the table. It was the leg of a man—a leg with a long sea-boot upon it. I stooped, and there was a figure sprawling upon his face, his arms thrown forward and his body twisted. One glance told me that it was Armstrong, the first officer, and a second that he was a dead man. For a few moments I stood gasping. Then I rushed on to the deck, called Allardyce to my assistance, and came back with him into the cabin.

Together we pulled the unfortunate fellow from under the table, and as we looked at his dripping head we exchanged glances, and I do not know which was the paler of the two.

"The same as the Spanish sailor," said I.

"The very same. God preserve us! It's that infernal chest! Look at Armstrong's hand!"

He held up the mate's right hand, and there was the screwdriver which he had wished to use the night before.

"He's been at the chest, sir. He knew that I was on deck and you asleep. He knelt down in front of it, and he pushed the lock back with that tool. Then something happened to him, and he cried out so that you heard him."

"Allardyce," I whispered, "what *could* have happened to him?"

The second mate put his hand upon my sleeve and drew me into his cabin.

"We can talk here, sir, and we don't know who may be listening to us in there. What do you suppose is in that box, Captain Barclay?"

"I give you my word, Allardyce, that I have no idea."

"Well, I can only find one theory which will fit all the facts. Look at the size of the box. Look at all the carving and metal-work which may conceal any number of holes. Look at the weight of it; it took four men to carry it. On the top of that, remember that two men have tried to open it, and both have come to their end through it. Now, sir, what can it mean except one thing?"

"You mean there is a man in it?"

"Of course there is a man in it. You know how it is in these South American States, sir. A man may be President one week and hunted like a dog the next.

They are for ever flying for their lives. My idea is that there is some fellow in hiding there, who is armed and desperate, and who will fight to the death before he is taken."

"But his food and drink?"

"It's a roomy chest, sir, and he may have some provisions stowed away. As to his drink, he had a friend among the crew upon the brig who saw that he had what he needed."

"You think, then, that the label asking people not to open the box was simply written in his interest?"

"Yes, sir, that is my idea. Have you any other way of explaining the facts?"

I had to confess that I had not.

"The question is what are we to do?" I asked.

"The man's a dangerous ruffian who sticks at nothing. I'm thinking it wouldn't be a bad thing to put a rope round the chest and tow it alongside for half an hour; then we could open it at our ease. Or if we just tied the box up and kept him from getting any water maybe that would do as well. Or the carpenter could put a coat of varnish over it and stop all the blowholes."

"Come, Allardyce," said I, angrily. "You don't seriously mean to say that a whole ship's company are going to be terrorized by a single man in a box. If he's there, I'll engage to fetch him out!" I went to my room and came back with my revolver in my hand. "Now, Allardyce," said I. "Do you open the lock, and I'll stand on guard."

"For God's sake, think what you are doing, sir!" cried the mate. "Two men have lost their lives over it, and the blood of one not yet dry upon the carpet."

"The more reason why we should revenge him."

"Well, sir, at least let me call the carpenter. Three are better than two, and he is a good stout man."

He went off in search of him, and I was left alone with the striped chest in the cabin. I don't think that I'm a nervous man, but I kept the table between me and this solid old relic of the Spanish Main. In the growing light of morning the red and white striping was beginning to appear, and the curious scrolls and wreaths of metal and carving which showed the loving pains which cunning craftsmen had expended upon it. Presently the carpenter and the mate came back together, the former with a hammer in his hand.

"It's a bad business, this, sir," said he, shaking his head, as he looked at the body of the mate. "And you think there's someone hiding in the box?"

"There's no doubt about it," said Allardyce, picking up the screwdriver and setting his jaw like a man who needs to brace his courage. "I'll drive the lock back if you will both stand by. If he rises let him have it on the head with your hammer, carpenter! Shoot at once, sir, if he raises his hand. Now!"

He had knelt down in front of the striped chest, and passed the blade of the tool under the lid. With a sharp snick the lock flew back. "Stand by!" yelled the mate, and with a heave he threw open the massive top of the box. As it swung up, we all three sprang back, I with my pistol levelled, and the carpenter with the hammer above his head. Then, as nothing happened, we each took a step forward and peeped in. The box was empty.

Not quite empty either, for in one corner was lying an old yellow candlestick, elaborately engraved, which appeared to be as old as the box itself. Its rich yellow tone and artistic shape suggested that it was an object of value. For the rest there was nothing more weighty or valuable than dust in the old striped treasure-chest.

"Well, I'm blessed!" cried Allardyce, staring blankly into it. "Where does the weight come in, then?"

"Look at the thickness of the sides and look at the lid. Why, it's five inches through. And see that great metal spring across it."

"That's for holding the lid up," said the mate. "You see, it won't lean back. What's that German printing on the inside?"

"It means that it was made by Johann Rothstein of Augsburg, in 1606."

"And a solid bit of work, too. But it doesn't throw much light on what has passed, does it, Captain Barclay? That candlestick looks like gold. We shall have something for our trouble after all."

He leant forward to grasp it, and from that moment I have never doubted as to the reality of inspiration, for on the instant I caught him by the collar and pulled him straight again. It may have been some story of the Middle Ages which had come back to my mind, or it may have been that my eye had caught some red which was not that of rust upon the upper part of the lock, but to him and to me it will always seem an inspiration, so prompt and sudden was my action.

"There's devilry here," said I. "Give me the crooked stick from the corner."

It was an ordinary walking-cane with a hooked top. I passed it over the candlestick and gave it a pull. With a flash a row of polished steel fangs shot out from below the upper lip, and the great striped chest snapped at us like a wild animal. Clang came the huge lid into its place, and the glasses on the swinging rack sang and tinkled with the shock. The mate sat down on the edge of the table and shivered like a frightened horse.

"You've saved my life, Captain Barclay!" said he.

So this was the secret of the striped treasure-chest of old Don Ramirez di Leyra, and this was how he preserved his ill-gotten gains from the Terra Firma and the Province of Veraquas. Be the thief ever so cunning he could not tell that golden candlestick from the other articles of value, and the instant that he laid hand upon it the terrible spring was unloosed and the murderous steel spikes were driven into his brain, while the shock of the blow sent the victim backwards and enabled the chest to automatically close itself. How many, I wondered, had fallen victims to the ingenuity of the Mechanic of Augsburg. And as I thought of the possible history of that grim striped chest my resolution was very quickly taken.

"Carpenter, bring three men and carry this on deck."

"Going to throw it overboard, sir?"

"Yes, Mr. Allardyce. I'm not superstitious as a rule, but there are some things which are more than a sailor can be called upon to stand."

"No wonder that brig made heavy weather, Captain Barclay, with such a thing on board. The glass is dropping fast, sir, and we are only just in time."

So we did not even wait for the three sailors, but we carried it out, the mate, the carpenter, and I, and we pushed it with our own hands over the bulwarks. There was a white spout of water, and it was gone. There it lies, the striped chest, a thousand fathoms deep, and if, as they say, the sea will some day be dry land, I grieve for the man who finds that old box and tries to penetrate into its secret.

20. *The Captain of the "Polestar"*

[Being an extract from the singular journal of JOHN M'ALISTER RAY, student of medicine.]

SEPTEMBER 11th.—Lat. 81° 40′ N.; long. 2° E. Still lying-to amid enormous ice-fields. The one which stretches away to the north of us, and to which our ice-anchor is attached, cannot be smaller than an English county. To the right and left unbroken sheets extend to the horizon. This morning the mate reported that there were signs of pack ice to the southward. Should this form of sufficient thickness to bar our return, we shall be in a position of danger, as the food, I hear, is already running somewhat short. It is late in the season, and the nights are beginning to reappear. This morning I saw a star twinkling just over the fore-yard, the first since the beginning of May. There is considerable discontent among the crew, many of whom are anxious to get back home to be in time for the herring season, when labour always commands a high price upon the Scotch coast. As yet their displeasure is only signified by sullen countenances and black looks, but I heard from the second mate this afternoon that they contemplated sending a deputation to the captain to explain their grievance. I much doubt how he will receive it, as he is a man of fierce temper, and very sensitive about anything approaching to an infringement of his rights. I shall venture after dinner to say a few words to him upon the subject. I have always found that he will tolerate from me what he would resent from any other member of the crew. Amsterdam Island, at the north-west corner of Spitzbergen, is visible upon our starboard quarter—a rugged line of volcanic rocks, intersected by white seams, which represent glaciers. It is curious to think that at the present moment there is probably no human being nearer to us than the Danish settlements in the south of Greenland—a good nine hundred miles as the crow flies. A captain takes a great responsibility upon himself when he risks his vessel under such circumstances. No whaler has ever remained in these latitudes till so advanced a period of the year.

9 P.M.—I have spoken to Captain Craigie, and though the result has been hardly satisfactory, I am bound to say that he listened to what I had to say very quietly and even deferentially. When I had finished he put on that air of iron determination which I have frequently observed upon his face, and paced rapidly backwards and forwards across the narrow cabin for some minutes. At first I feared that I had seriously offended him, but he dispelled the idea by sitting down again, and putting his hand upon my arm with a gesture which almost amounted to a caress. There was a depth of tenderness too in his wild dark eyes which surprised me considerably "Look here, Doctor," he said, "I'm sorry I ever took you—I am indeed—and I would give fifty pounds this

minute to see you standing safe upon the Dundee quay. It's hit or miss with me this time. There are fish to the north of us. How dare you shake your head, sir, when I tell you I saw them blowing from the mast-head?"—this in a sudden burst of fury, though I was not conscious of having shown any signs of doubt. "Two-and-twenty fish in as many minutes as I am a living man, and not one under ten foot.[1] Now, Doctor, do you think I can leave the country when there is only one infernal strip of ice between me and my fortune? If it came on to blow from the north to-morrow we could fill the ship and be away before the frost could catch us. If it came on to blow from the south—well, I suppose the men are paid for risking their lives, and as for myself it matters but little to me, for I have more to bind me to the other world than to this one. I confess that I am sorry for *you*, though. I wish I had old Angus Tait who was with me last voyage, for he was a man that would never be missed, and you—you said once that you were engaged, did you not?"

"Yes," I answered, snapping the spring of the locket which hung from my watch-chain, and holding up the little vignette of Flora.

"Curse you!" he yelled, springing out of his seat, with his very beard bristling with passion. "What is your happiness to me? What have I to do with her that you must dangle her photograph before my eyes?" I almost thought that he was about to strike me in the frenzy of his rage, but with another imprecation he dashed open the door of the cabin and rushed out upon deck, leaving me considerably astonished at his extraordinary violence. It is the first time that he has ever shown me anything but courtesy and kindness. I can hear him pacing excitedly up and down overhead as I write these lines.

I should like to give a sketch of the character of this

[1] A whale is measured among whalers not by the length of its body, but by the length of its whalebone.

man, but it seems presumptuous to attempt such a thing upon paper, when the idea in my own mind is at best a vague and uncertain one. Several times I have thought that I grasped the clue which might explain it, but only to be disappointed by his presenting himself in some new light which would upset all my conclusions. It may be that no human eye but my own shall ever rest upon these lines, yet as a psychological study I shall attempt to leave some record of Captain Nicholas Craigie.

A man's outer case generally gives some indication of the soul within. The captain is tall and well-formed, with dark, handsome face, and a curious way of twitching his limbs, which may arise from nervousness, or be simply an outcome of his excessive energy. His jaw and whole cast of countenance is manly and resolute, but the eyes are the distinctive feature of his face. They are of the very darkest hazel, bright and eager, with a singular mixture of recklessness in their expression, and of something else which I have sometimes thought was more allied with horror than any other emotion. Generally the former predominated, but on occasions, and more particularly when he was thoughtfully inclined, the look of fear would spread and deepen until it imparted a new character to his whole countenance. It is at these times that he is most subject to tempestuous fits of anger, and he seems to be aware of it, for I have known him lock himself up so that no one might approach him until his dark hour was passed. He sleeps badly, and I have heard him shouting during the night, but his cabin is some little distance from mine, and I could never distinguish the words which he said.

This is one phase of his character, and the most disagreeable one. It is only through my close association with him, thrown together as we are day after day, that I have observed it. Otherwise he is an agreeable companion, well-read and entertaining, and as gallant a seaman as ever trod a deck. I shall not easily forget the way in which he handled the ship when we were caught by a gale among the loose ice at the beginning of April. I have never seen him so cheerful, and even hilarious, as he was that night, as he paced backwards and forwards upon the bridge amid the flashing of the lightning and the howling of the wind. He has told me several times that the thought of death was a pleasant one to him, which is a sad thing for a young man to say; he cannot be much more than thirty, though his hair and moustache are already slightly grizzled. Some great sorrow must have overtaken him and blighted his whole life. Perhaps I should be the same if I lost my Flora—God knows! I think if it were not for her that I should care very little whether the wind blew from the north or the south to-morrow. There, I hear him come down the companion, and he has locked himself up in his room, which shows that he is still in an unamiable mood. And so to bed, as old Pepys would say, for the candle is burning down (we have to use them now since the nights are closing in), and the steward has turned in, so there are no hopes of another one.

September 12th.—Calm, clear day, and still lying in the same position. What wind there is comes from the south-east, but it is very slight. Captain is in a better humour, and apologised to me at breakfast for his rudeness. He still looks somewhat distrait, however, and retains that wild look in his eyes which in a Highlander would mean that he was "fey"—at least so our chief engineer remarked to me, and he has some reputation among the Celtic portion of our crew as a seer and expounder of omens.

It is strange that superstition should have obtained such mastery over this hard-headed and practical race. I could not have believed to what an extent it is carried had I not observed it for myself. We have had a perfect epidemic of it this voyage, until I have felt inclined to serve out rations of sedatives and nerve-tonics with the Saturday allowance of grog. The first symptom of it was that shortly after leaving Shetland the men at the wheel used to complain that they heard plaintive cries and screams in the wake of the ship, as if something were following it and were unable to overtake it. This fiction has been kept up during the whole voyage, and on dark nights at the beginning of the seal-fishing it was only with great difficulty that men could be induced to do their spell. No doubt what they heard was either the creaking of the rudder-chains, or the cry of some passing sea-bird. I have been fetched out of bed several times to listen to it, but I need hardly say that I was never able to distinguish anything unnatural. The men, however, are so absurdly positive upon the subject that it is hopeless to argue with them. I mentioned the matter to the captain once, but to my surprise he took it very gravely, and indeed appeared to be considerably disturbed by what I told him. I should have thought that he at least would have been above such vulgar delusions.

All this disquisition upon superstition leads me up to the fact that Mr. Manson, our second mate, saw a ghost last night—or, at least, says that he did, which of course is the same thing. It is quite refreshing to have some new topic of conversation after the eternal routine of bears and whales which has served us for so many months. Manson swears the ship is haunted, and that he would not stay in her a day if he had any other place to go to. Indeed the fellow is honestly frightened, and I had to give him some chloral and bromide of potassium this morning to steady him down. He seemed quite indignant when I suggested that he had been having an extra glass the night before, and I was obliged to pacify him by keeping as grave a countenance as possible during his story, which he certainly narrated in a very straightforward and matter-of-fact way.

"I was on the bridge," he said, "about four bells in the middle watch, just when the night was at its darkest. There was a bit of a moon, but the clouds were blowing across it so that you couldn't see far from the ship. John M'Leod, the harpooner, came aft from the fo'c'sle-head and reported a strange noise on the starboard bow. I went forrard and we both heard it, sometimes like a bairn crying and sometimes like a wench in pain. I've been seventeen years to the country and I never heard seal, old or young, make a sound like that. As we were standing there on the fo'c'sle-head the moon came out from behind a cloud, and we both saw a sort of white figure moving across the ice-field in the same direction that we had heard the cries. We lost sight of it for a while, but it came back on the port bow, and we could just make it out like a shadow on the ice. I sent a hand aft for the rifles, and M'Leod and I went down on to the pack, thinking that maybe it might be a bear. When we got on the ice I lost sight of M'Leod, but I pushed on in the direction where I could still hear the cries. I followed them for a mile or maybe more, and then running round a hummock I came right on to the top of it standing and waiting for me seemingly. I don't know what it was. It wasn't a bear, anyway. It was tall and white and straight, and if it wasn't a man nor a woman, I'll stake my davy it was something worse. I made for the ship as hard as I could run, and precious glad I was to find myself aboard. I signed articles to do my duty by the ship, and on the ship I'll stay, but you don't catch me on the ice again after sundown."

That is his story, given as far as I can in his own words. I fancy what he saw must, in spite of his denial, have been a young bear erect upon its hind legs, an attitude which they often assume when alarmed. In the uncertain light this would bear a resemblance to a human figure, especially to a man whose nerves were already somewhat shaken. Whatever it may have been, the occurrence is unfortunate, for it has produced a most unpleasant effect upon the crew. Their looks are more sullen than before, and their discontent more open.

The double grievance of being debarred from the herring fishing and of being detained in what they choose to call a haunted vessel, may lead them to do something rash. Even the harpooners, who are the oldest and steadiest among them, are joining in the general agitation.

Apart from this absurd outbreak of superstition, things are looking rather more cheerful. The pack which was forming to the south of us has partly cleared away, and the water is so warm as to lead me to believe that we are lying in one of those branches of the gulf-stream which run up between Greenland and Spitzbergen. There are numerous small Medusæ and sea-lemons about the ship, with abundance of shrimps, so that there is every possibility of " fish " being sighted. Indeed one was seen blowing about dinner-time, but in such a position that it was impossible for the boats to follow it.

September 13th.—Had an interesting conversation with the chief mate, Mr. Milne, upon the bridge. It seems that our captain is as great an enigma to the seamen, and even to the owners of the vessel, as he has been to me. Mr. Milne tells me that when the ship is paid off, upon returning from a voyage, Captain Craigie disappears, and is not seen again until the approach of another season, when he walks quietly into the office of the company, and asks whether his services will be required. He has no friend in Dundee, nor does any-one pretend to be acquainted with his early history. His position depends entirely upon his skill as a seaman, and the name for courage and coolness which he had earned in the capacity of mate, before being entrusted with a separate command. The unanimous opinion seems to be that he is not a Scotchman, and that his name is an assumed one. Mr. Milne thinks that he has devoted himself to whaling simply for the reason that it is the most dangerous occupation which he could select, and that he courts death in every possible manner. He mentioned several instances of this, one of which is rather curious, if true. It seems that on one occasion he did not put in an appearance at the office, and a substitute had to be selected in his place. That was at the time of the last Russian and Turkish War. When he turned up again next spring he had a puckered wound in the side of his neck which he used to endeavour to conceal with his cravat. Whether the mate's inference that he had been engaged in the war is true or not I cannot say. It was certainly a strange coincidence.

The wind is veering round in an easterly direction, but is still very slight. I think the ice is lying closer than it did yesterday. As far as the eye can reach on every side there is one wide expanse of spotless white, only broken by an occasional rift or the dark shadow of a hummock. To the south there is the narrow lane of blue water which is our sole means of escape, and which is closing up every day. The captain is taking a heavy responsibility upon himself. I hear that the tank of potatoes has been finished, and even the biscuits are running short, but he preserves the same impassable countenance, and spends the greater part of the day at the crow's nest, sweeping the horizon with his glass. His manner is very variable, and he seems to avoid my society, but there has been no repetition of the violence which he showed the other night.

7.30 P.M.—My deliberate opinion is that we are commanded by a madman. Nothing else can account for the extraordinary vagaries of Captain Craigie. It is fortunate that I have kept this journal of our voyage, as it will serve to justify us in case we have to put him under any sort of restraint, a step which I should only consent to as a last resource. Curiously enough it was he himself who suggested lunacy and not mere eccentricity as the secret of his strange conduct. He was standing upon the bridge about an hour ago, peering as usual through his glass, while I was walking up and down the quarter-deck. The majority of the men were below at their tea, for the watches have not been regularly kept of late. Tired of walking, I leaned against the bulwarks, and admired the mellow glow cast by the sinking sun upon the great ice-fields which surround us. I was suddenly aroused from the reverie into which I had fallen by a hoarse voice at my elbow, and starting round I found that the captain had descended and was standing by my side. He was staring out over the ice with an expression in which horror, surprise, and something approaching to joy were contending for the mastery. In spite of the cold, great drops of perspiration were coursing down his forehead, and he was evidently fearfully excited. His limbs twitched like those of a man upon the verge of an epileptic fit, and the lines about his mouth were drawn and hard.

"Look!" he gasped, seizing me by the wrist, but still keeping his eyes upon the distant ice, and moving his head slowly in a horizontal direction, as if following some object which was moving across the field of vision. "Look! There, man, there! Between the hummocks! Now coming out from behind the far one! You see her—you *must* see her! There still! Flying from me, by God, flying from me—and gone!"

He uttered the last two words in a whisper of concentrated agony which shall never fade from my remembrance. Clinging to the ratlines he endeavoured to climb up upon the top of the bulwarks as if in the hope of obtaining a last glance at the departing object. His strength was not equal to the attempt, however, and he staggered back against the saloon skylights, where he leaned panting and exhausted. His face was so livid that I expected him to become unconscious, so lost no time in leading him down the companion, and stretching him upon one of the sofas in the cabin. I then poured him out some brandy, which I held to his lips, and which had a wonderful effect upon him, bringing the blood back into his white face and steadying his poor shaking limbs. He raised himself up upon his elbow, and looking round to see that we were alone, he beckoned to me to come and sit beside him.

"You saw it, didn't you?" he asked, still in the same subdued awesome tone so foreign to the nature of the man.

"No, I saw nothing."

His head sank back again upon the cushions. "No, he wouldn't without the glass," he murmured. "He couldn't. It was the glass that showed her to me, and then the eyes of love—the eyes of love. I say, Doc, don't let the steward in! He'll think I'm mad. Just bolt the door, will you!"

I rose and did what he had commanded.

He lay quiet for a while, lost in thought apparently, and then raised himself up upon his elbow again, and asked for some more brandy.

"You don't think I am, do you, Doc?" he asked, as I was putting the bottle back into the after-locker. "Tell me now, as man to man, do you think that I am mad?"

"I think you have something on your mind," I answered, "which is exciting you and doing you a good deal of harm."

"Right there, lad!" he cried, his eyes sparkling from the effects of the brandy. "Plenty on my mind—plenty! But I can work out the latitude and the longitude, and I can handle my sextant and manage my logarithms. You couldn't prove me mad in a court of law, could you, now?" It was curious to hear the man lying back and coolly arguing out the question of his own sanity.

"Perhaps not," I said; "but still I think you would be wise to get home as soon as you can, and settle down to a quiet life for a while."

"Get home, eh?" he muttered, with a sneer upon his face. "One word for me and two for yourself, lad. Settle down with Flora—pretty little Flora. Are bad dreams signs of madness?"

"Sometimes," I answered.

"What else? What would be the first symptoms?"

"Pains in the head, noises in the ears, flashes before the eyes, delusions——"

"Ah! what about them?" he interrupted. "What would you call a delusion?"

"Seeing a thing which is not there is a delusion."

"But she *was* there!" he groaned to himself. "She *was* there!" and rising, he unbolted the door and walked with slow and uncertain steps to his own cabin, where I have no doubt that he will remain until to-morrow morning. His system seems to have received a terrible shock, whatever it may have been that he imagined himself to have seen. The man becomes a greater mystery every day, though I fear that the solution which he has himself suggested is the correct one, and that his reason is affected. I do not think that a guilty conscience has anything to do with his behaviour. The idea is a popular one among the officers, and, I believe, the crew; but I have seen nothing to support it. He has not the air of a guilty man, but of one who has had terrible usage at the hands of fortune, and who should be regarded as a martyr rather than a criminal.

The wind is veering round to the south to-night. God help us if it blocks that narrow pass which is our only road to safety! Situated as we are on the edge of the main Arctic pack, or the "barrier" as it is called by the whalers, any wind from the north has the effect of shredding out the ice around us and allowing our escape, while a wind from the south blows up all the loose ice behind us, and hems us in between two packs. God help us, I say again!

September 14th.—Sunday, and a day of rest. My fears have been confirmed, and the thin strip of blue water has disappeared from the southward. Nothing but the great motionless ice-fields around us, with their weird hummocks and fantastic pinnacles. There is a deathly silence over their wide expanse which is horrible.

No lapping of the waves now, no cries of seagulls or straining of sails, but one deep universal silence in which the murmurs of the seamen, and the creak of their boots upon the white shining deck, seem discordant and out of place. Our only visitor was an Arctic fox, a rare animal upon the pack, though common enough upon the land. He did not come near the ship, however, but after surveying us from a distance fled rapidly across the ice. This was curious conduct, as they generally know nothing of man, and being of an inquisitive nature, become so familiar that they are easily captured. Incredible as it may seem, even this little incident produced a bad effect upon the crew. "Yon puir beastie kens mair, ay, an' sees mair nor you nor me!" was the comment of one of the leading harpooners, and the others nodded their acquiescence. It is vain to attempt to argue against such puerile superstition. They have made up their minds that there is a curse upon the ship, and nothing will ever persuade them to the contrary.

The captain remained in seclusion all day except for about half an hour in the afternoon, when he came out upon the quarter-deck. I observed that he kept his eye fixed upon the spot where the vision of yesterday had appeared, and was quite prepared for another outburst, but none such came. He did not seem to see me, although I was standing close beside him. Divine service was read as usual by the chief engineer. It is a curious thing that in whaling vessels the Church of England Prayer-book is always employed, although there is never a member of that Church among either officers or crew. Our men are all Roman Catholics or Presbyterians, the former predominating. Since a ritual is used which is foreign to both, neither can complain that the other is preferred to them, and they listen with all attention and devotion, so that the system has something to recommend it.

A glorious sunset, which made the great fields of

ice look like a lake of blood. I have never seen a finer and at the same time more weird effect. Wind is veering round. If it will blow twenty-four hours from the north all will yet be well.

September 15th.—To-day is Flora's birthday. Dear lass! it is well that she cannot see her boy, as she used to call me, shut up among the ice-fields with a crazy captain and a few weeks' provisions. No doubt she scans the shipping list in the *Scotsman* every morning to see if we are reported from Shetland. I have to set an example to the men and look cheery and unconcerned; but God knows, my heart is very heavy at times.

The thermometer is at nineteen Fahrenheit to-day. There is but little wind, and what there is comes from an unfavourable quarter. Captain is in an excellent humour; I think he imagines he has seen some other omen or vision, poor fellow, during the night, for he came into my room early in the morning, and stooping down over my bunk, whispered, "It wasn't a delusion, Doc; it's all right!" After breakfast he asked me to find out how much food was left, which the second mate and I proceeded to do. It is even less than we had expected. Forward they have half a tank full of biscuits, three barrels of salt meat, and a very limited supply of coffee beans and sugar. In the after-hold and lockers there are a good many luxuries, such as tinned salmon, soups, haricot mutton, etc., but they will go a very short way among a crew of fifty men. There are two barrels of flour in the store-room, and an unlimited supply of tobacco. Altogether there is about enough to keep the men on half rations for eighteen or twenty days—certainly not more. When we reported the state of things to the captain, he ordered all hands to be piped, and addressed them from the quarter-deck. I never saw him to better advantage. With his tall, well-knit figure, and dark animated face, he seemed a man born to command, and he discussed the situation in a cool sailor-like way which showed that while appreciating the danger he had an eye for every loophole of escape.

"My lads," he said, "no doubt you think I brought you into this fix, if it is a fix, and maybe some of you feel bitter against me on account of it. But you must remember that for many a season no ship that comes to the country has brought in as much oil-money as the old *Polestar*, and every one of you has had his share of it. You can leave your wives behind you in comfort, while other poor fellows come back to find their lassies on the parish. If you have to thank me for the one you have to thank me for the other, and we may call it quits. We've tried a bold venture before this and succeeded, so now that we've tried one and failed we've no cause to cry out about it. If the worst comes to the worse, we can make the land across the ice, and lay in a stock of seals which will keep us alive until the spring. It won't come to that, though, for you'll see the Scotch coast again before three weeks are out. At present every man must go on half rations, share and share alike, and no favour to any. Keep up your hearts and you'll pull through this as you've pulled through many a danger before." These few simple words of his had a wonderful effect upon the crew. His former unpopularity was forgotten, and the old harpooner whom I have already mentioned for his superstition, led off three cheers, which were heartily joined in by all hands.

September 16th.—The wind has veered round to the north during the night, and the ice shows some symptoms of opening out. The men are in a good humour in spite of the short allowance upon which they have been placed. Steam is kept up in the engine-room, that there may be no delay should an opportunity for escape present itself. The captain is in exuberant spirits, though he still retains that wild "fey" expression which I have already remarked upon. This burst of cheerfulness puzzles me more than his former gloom. I cannot understand it. I think I mentioned in an early part of this journal that one of his oddities is that he never permits any person to enter his cabin, but insists upon making his own bed, such as it is, and performing every other office for himself. To my surprise he handed me the key to-day and requested me to go down there and take the time by his chronometer while he measured the altitude of the sun at noon. It is a bare little room, containing a washing-stand and a few books, but little else in the way of luxury, except some pictures upon the walls. The majority of these are small cheap oleographs, but there was one water-colour sketch of the head of a young lady which arrested my attention. It was evidently a portrait, and not one of those fancy types of female beauty which sailors particularly affect. No artist could have evolved from his own mind such a curious mixture of character and weakness. The languid, dreamy eyes, with their drooping lashes, and the broad, low brow, unruffled by thought or care, were in strong contrast with the clean-cut, prominent jaw, and the resolute set of the lower lip. Underneath it in one of the corners was written, "M.B., æt. 19." That anyone in the short space of nineteen years of existence could develop such strength of will as was stamped upon her face seemed to me at the time to be well-nigh incredible. She must have been an extraordinary woman. Her features have thrown such a glamour over me that, though I had but a fleeting glance at them, I could, were I a draughtsman, reproduce them line for line upon this page of the journal. I wonder what part she has played in our captain's life. He has hung her picture at the end of his berth, so that his eyes continually rest upon it. Were he a less reserved man I should make some remark upon the subject. Of the other things in his cabin there was nothing worthy of mention—uniform coats, a camp-stool, small looking-glass, tobacco-box, and numerous pipes, including an oriental hookah—which, by the by, gives some colour to Mr. Milne's story about his participation in the war, though the connection may seem rather a distant one.

11.20 P.M.—Captain just gone to bed after a long and interesting conversation on general topics. When he chooses he can be a most fascinating companion, being remarkably well-read, and having the power of expressing his opinion forcibly without appearing to be dogmatic. I hate to have my intellectual toes trod upon. He spoke about the nature of the soul, and sketched out the views of Aristotle and Plato upon the subject in a masterly manner. He seems to have a leaning for metempsychosis and the doctrines of Pythagoras. In discussing them we touched upon modern spiritualism, and I made some joking allusion to the impostures of Slade, upon which, to my surprise, he warned me most impressively against confusing the innocent with the guilty, and argued that it would be as logical to brand Christianity as an error because Judas, who professed that religion, was a villain. He shortly afterwards bade me good night and retired to his room.

The wind is freshening up, and blows steadily from the north. The nights are as dark now as they are in England. I hope to-morrow may set us free from our frozen fetters.

September 17th.—The Bogie again. Thank Heaven that I have strong nerves! The superstition of these poor fellows, and the circumstantial accounts which they give, with the utmost earnestness and self-conviction, would horrify any man not accustomed to their ways. There are many versions of the matter, but the sum-total of them all is that something uncanny has been flitting round the ship all night, and that Sandie M'Donald of Peterhead and "lang" Peter Williamson of Shetland saw it, as also did Mr. Milne on the bridge—so, having three witnesses, they can make a better case of it than the second mate did. I spoke to Milne after breakfast, and told him that he should be above such nonsense, and that as an officer he ought to set the men a better example. He shook his weather-beaten head ominously, but answered with characteristic caution, "Mebbe, aye, mebbe na, Doctor," he said, "I didna ca' it a ghaist. I canna' say I preen my faith in sea-bogles an' the like, though there's a mony as claims to ha' seen a' that and waur. I'm no easy feared, but maybe your ain bluid would run a bit cauld, mun, if instead o' speerin' aboot it in daylicht ye were wi' me last night, an' seed an awfu' like shape, white an' gruesome, whiles here, whiles there, an' it greetin' and ca'ing in the darkness like a bit lambie that hae lost its mither. Ye would na' be sae ready to put it a' doon to auld wives' clavers then, I'm thinkin'." I saw it was hopeless to reason with him, so contented myself with begging him as a personal favour to call me up the next time the spectre appeared—a request to which he acceded with many ejaculations expressive of his hopes that such an opportunity might never arise.

As I had hoped, the white desert behind us has become broken by many thin streaks of water which intersect it in all directions. Our latitude to-day was 80° 52′ N., which shows that there is a strong southerly drift upon the pack. Should the wind continue favourable it will break up as rapidly as it formed. At present we can do nothing but smoke and wait and hope for the best. I am rapidly becoming a fatalist. When dealing with such uncertain factors as wind and ice a man can be nothing else. Perhaps it was the wind and sand of the Arabian deserts which gave the minds of the original followers of Mahomet their tendency to bow to kismet.

These spectral alarms have a very bad effect upon the captain. I feared that it might excite his sensitive mind, and endeavoured to conceal the absurd story from him, but unfortunately he overheard one of the men making an allusion to it, and insisted upon being informed about it. As I had expected, it brought out all his latent lunacy in an exaggerated form. I can hardly believe that this is the same man who discoursed philosophy last night with the most critical acumen and coolest judgment. He is pacing backwards and forwards upon the quarter-deck like a caged tiger, stopping now and again to throw out his hands with a yearning gesture, and stare impatiently out over the ice. He keeps up a continual mutter to himself, and once he called out, " But a little time, love—but a little time ! " Poor fellow, it is sad to see a gallant seaman and accomplished gentleman reduced to such a pass, and to think that imagination and delusion can cow a mind to which real danger was but the salt of life. Was ever a man in such a position as I, between a demented captain and a ghost-seeing mate ? I sometimes think I am the only really sane man aboard the vessel—except perhaps the second engineer, who is a kind of ruminant, and would care nothing for all the fiends in the Red Sea so long as they would leave him alone and not disarrange his tools.

The ice is still opening rapidly, and there is every probability of our being able to make a start to-morrow morning. They will think I am inventing when I tell them at home all the strange things that have befallen me.

12 P.M.—I have been a good deal startled, though I feel steadier now, thanks to a stiff glass of brandy. I am hardly myself yet, however, as this handwriting will testify. The fact is, that I have gone through a very strange experience, and am beginning to doubt whether I was justified in branding everyone on board as madmen because they professed to have seen things which did not seem reasonable to my understanding. Pshaw ! I am a fool to let such a trifle unnerve me ; and yet, coming as it does after all these alarms, it has an additional significance, for I cannot doubt either Mr. Manson's story or that of the mate, now that I have experienced that which I used formerly to scoff at.

After all it was nothing very alarming—a mere sound, and that was all. I cannot expect that anyone reading this, if anyone ever should read it, will sympathise with my feelings, or realize the effect which it produced upon me at the time. Supper was over, and I had gone on deck to have a quiet pipe before turning in. The night was very dark—so dark that, standing under the quarter-boat, I was unable to see the officer upon the bridge. I think I have already mentioned the extraordinary silence which prevails in these frozen seas. In other parts of the world, be they ever so barren, there is some slight vibration of the air—some faint hum, be it from the distant haunts of men, or from the leaves of the trees, or the wings of the birds, or even the faint rustle of the grass that covers the ground. One may not actively perceive the sound, and yet if it were withdrawn it would be missed. It is only here in these Arctic seas that stark, unfathomable stillness obtrudes itself upon you all in its gruesome reality. You find your tympanum straining to catch some little murmur, and dwelling eagerly upon every accidental sound within the vessel. In this state I was leaning against the bulwarks when there arose from the ice almost directly underneath me a cry, sharp and shrill, upon the silent air of the night, beginning, as it seemed to me, at a note such as prima donna never reached, and mounting from that ever higher and higher until it culminated in a long wail of agony, which might have been the last cry of a lost soul. The ghastly scream is still ringing in my ears. Grief, unutterable grief, seemed to be expressed in it, and a great longing, and yet through it all there was an occasional wild note of exultation. It shrilled out from close beside me, and yet as I glared into the darkness I could discern nothing. I waited some little time, but without hearing any repetition of the sound, so I came below, more shaken than I have ever been in my life before. As I came down the companion I met Mr. Milne coming up to relieve the watch. "Weel, Doctor," he said, "maybe that's auld wives' clavers tae? Did ye no hear it skirling? Maybe that's a supersteetion? What d'ye think o't noo?" I was obliged to apologise to the honest fellow, and acknowledge that I was as puzzled by it as he was. Perhaps to-morrow things may look different. At present I dare hardly write all that I think. Reading it again in days to come, when I have shaken off all these associations, I should despise myself for having been so weak.

September 18th.—Passed a restless and uneasy night, still haunted by that strange sound. The captain does not look as if he had had much repose either, for his face is haggard and his eyes bloodshot. I have not told him of my adventure of last night, nor shall I. He is already restless and excited, standing up, sitting down, and apparently utterly unable to keep still.

A fine lead appeared in the pack this morning, as I had expected, and we were able to cast off our ice-anchor, and steam about twelve miles in a west-sou'-westerly direction. We were then brought to a halt by a great floe as massive as any which we have left behind us. It bars our progress completely, so we can do nothing but anchor again and wait until it breaks up, which it will probably do within twenty-four hours, if the wind holds. Several bladder-nosed seals were seen swimming in the water, and one was shot, an immense creature more than eleven feet long. They are fierce, pugnacious animals, and are said to be more than a match for a bear. Fortunately they are slow and clumsy in their movements, so that there is little danger in attacking them upon the ice.

The captain evidently does not think we have seen the last of our troubles, though why he should take a gloomy view of the situation is more than I can fathom, since everyone else on board considers that we have had a miraculous escape, and are sure now to reach the open sea.

"I suppose you think it's all right now, Doctor?" he said, as we sat together after dinner.

"I hope so," I answered.

"We mustn't be too sure—and yet no doubt you are

right. We'll all be in the arms of our own true loves before long, lad, won't we? But we mustn't be too sure—we mustn't be too sure."

He sat silent a little, swinging his leg thoughtfully backwards and forwards. "Look here," he continued; "it's a dangerous place this, even at its best—a treacherous, dangerous place. I have known men cut off very suddenly in a land like this. A slip would do it sometimes—a single slip, and down you go through a crack, and only a bubble on the green water to show where it was that you sank. It's a queer thing," he continued with a nervous laugh, "but all the years I've been in this country I never once thought of making a will—not that I have anything to leave in particular, but still when a man is exposed to danger he should have everything arranged and ready—don't you think so?"

"Certainly," I answered, wondering what on earth he was driving at.

"He feels better for knowing it's all settled," he went on. "Now if anything should ever befall me, I hope that you will look after things for me. There is very little in the cabin, but such as it is I should like it to be sold, and the money divided in the same proportion as the oil-money among the crew. The chronometer I wish you to keep yourself as some slight remembrance of our voyage. Of course all this is a mere precaution, but I thought I would take the opportunity of speaking to you about it. I suppose I might rely upon you if there were any necessity?"

"Most assuredly," I answered; "and since you are taking this step, I may as well——"

"You! you!" he interrupted. "*You're* all right. What the devil is the matter with *you*? There, I didn't mean to be peppery, but I don't like to hear a young fellow, that has hardly began life, speculating about death. Go up on deck and get some fresh air into your lungs instead of talking nonsense in the cabin, and encouraging me to do the same."

The more I think of this conversation of ours the less do I like it. Why should the man be settling his affairs at the very time when we seem to be emerging from all danger? There must be some method in his madness. Can it be that he contemplates suicide? I remember that upon one occasion he spoke in a deeply reverent manner of the heinousness of the crime of self-destruction. I shall keep my eye upon him, however, and though I cannot obtrude upon the privacy of his cabin, I shall at least make a point of remaining on deck as long as he stays up.

Mr. Milne pooh-poohs my fears, and says it is only the "skipper's little way." He himself takes a very rosy view of the situation. According to him we shall be out of the ice by the day after to-morrow, pass Jan Meyen two days after that, and sight Shetland in little more than a week. I hope he may not be too sanguine. His opinion may be fairly balanced against the gloomy precautions of the captain, for he is an old and experienced seaman, and weighs his words well before uttering them.

* * * * *

The long-impending catastrophe has come at last. I hardly know what to write about it. The captain is gone. He may come back to us again alive, but I fear me—I fear me. It is now seven o'clock of the morning of the 19th of September. I have spent the whole night traversing the great ice-floe in front of us with a party of seamen in the hope of coming upon some trace of him, but in vain. I shall try to give some account of the circumstances which attended upon his disappearance. Should anyone ever chance to read the words which I put down, I trust they will remember that I do not write from conjecture or from hearsay, but that I, a sane and educated man, am describing accurately what actually occurred before my very eyes. My inferences are my own, but I shall be answerable for the facts.

The captain remained in excellent spirits after the

conversation which I have recorded. He appeared to be nervous and impatient, however, frequently changing his position, and moving his limbs in an aimless choreic way which is characteristic of him at times. In a quarter of an hour he went upon deck seven times, only to descend after a few hurried paces. I followed him each time, for there was something about his face which confirmed my resolution of not letting him out of my sight. He seemed to observe the effect which his movements had produced, for he endeavoured by an overdone hilarity, laughing boisterously at the very smallest of jokes, to quiet my apprehensions.

After supper he went on to the poop once more, and I with him. The night was dark and very still, save for the melancholy soughing of the wind among the spars. A thick cloud was coming up from the northwest, and the ragged tentacles which it threw out in front of it were drifting across the face of the moon, which only shone now and again through a rift in the wrack. The captain paced rapidly backwards and forwards, and then seeing me still dogging him, he came across and hinted that he thought I should be better below—which, I need hardly say, had the effect of strengthening my resolution to remain on deck.

I think he forgot about my presence after this, for he stood silently leaning over the taffrail and peering out across the great desert of snow, part of which lay in shadow, while part glittered mistily in the moonlight. Several times I could see by his movements that he was referring to his watch, and once he muttered a short sentence, of which I could only catch the one word "ready." I confess to having felt an eerie feeling creeping over me as I watched the loom of his tall figure through the darkness, and noted how completely he fulfilled the idea of a man who is keeping a tryst. A tryst with whom? Some vague perception began to dawn upon me as I pieced one fact with another, but I was utterly unprepared for the sequel.

By the sudden intensity of his attitude I felt that he saw something. I crept up behind him. He was staring with an eager questioning gaze at what seemed to be a wreath of mist, blown swiftly in a line with the ship. It was a dim nebulous body, devoid of shape, sometimes more, sometimes less apparent, as the light fell on it. The moon was dimmed in its brilliancy at the moment by a canopy of thinnest cloud, like the coating of an anemone.

"Coming, lass, coming," cried the skipper, in a voice of unfathomable tenderness and compassion, like one who soothes a beloved one by some favour long looked for, and as pleasant to bestow as to receive.

What followed happened in an instant. I had no power to interfere. He gave one spring to the top of the bulwarks, and another which took him on to the ice, almost to the feet of the pale misty figure. He held out his hands as if to clasp it, and so ran into the darkness with outstretched arms and loving words. I still stood rigid and motionless, straining my eyes after his retreating form, until his voice died away in the distance. I never thought to see him again, but at that moment the moon shone out brilliantly through a chink in the cloudy heaven, and illuminated the great field of ice. Then I saw his dark figure already a very long way off, running with prodigious speed across the frozen plain. That was the last glimpse which we caught of him—perhaps the last we ever shall. A party was organized to follow him, and I accompanied them, but the men's hearts were not in the work, and nothing was found. Another will be formed within a few hours. I can hardly believe I have not been dreaming, or suffering from some hideous nightmare, as I write these things down.

7.30 P.M.—Just returned dead beat and utterly tired out from a second unsuccessful search for the captain. The floe is of enormous extent, for though we have traversed at least twenty miles of its surface, there has been no sign of its coming to an end. The frost has been so severe of late that the overlying snow is frozen as hard as granite, otherwise we might have had the footsteps to guide us. The crew are anxious that we should cast off and steam round the floe and so to the southward, for the ice has opened up during the night, and the sea is visible upon the horizon. They argue that Captain Craigie is certainly dead, and that we are all risking our lives to no purpose by remaining when we have an opportunity of escape. Mr. Milne and I have had the greatest difficulty in persuading them to wait until to-morrow night, and have been compelled to promise that we will not under any circumstances delay our departure longer than that. We propose therefore to take a few hours' sleep, and then to start upon a final search.

September 20th, evening.—I crossed the ice this morning with a party of men exploring the southern part of the floe, while Mr. Milne went off in a northerly direction. We pushed on for ten or twelve miles without seeing a trace of any living thing except a single bird, which fluttered a great way over our heads, and which by its flight I should judge to have been a falcon. The southern extremity of the ice-field tapered away into a long narrow spit which projected out into the sea. When we came to the base of this promontory, the men halted, but I begged them to continue to the extreme end of it, that we might have the satisfaction of knowing that no possible chance had been neglected.

We had hardly gone a hundred yards before M'Donald of Peterhead cried out that he saw something in front of us, and began to run. We all got a glimpse of it and ran too. At first it was only a vague darkness against the white ice, but as we raced along together it took the shape of a man, and eventually of the man of whom we were in search. He was lying face downwards upon a frozen bank. Many little crystals of ice and feathers of snow had drifted on to him as he lay, and sparkled upon his dark seaman's jacket. As we came up some wandering puff of wind caught these tiny flakes in its vortex, and they whirled up into the air, partially descended again, and then, caught once more in the current, sped rapidly away in the direction of the sea. To my eyes it seemed but a snow-drift, but many of my companions averred that it started up in the shape of a woman, stooped over the corpse and kissed it, and then hurried away across the floe. I have learned never to ridicule any man's opinion, however strange it may seem. Sure it is that Captain Nicholas Craigie had met with no painful end, for there was a bright smile upon his blue pinched features, and his hands were still outstretched as though grasping at the strange visitor which had summoned him away into the dim world that lies beyond the grave.

We buried him the same afternoon with the ship's ensign around him, and a thirty-two pound shot at his feet. I read the burial service, while the rough sailors wept like children, for there were many who owed much to his kind heart, and who showed now the affection which his strange ways had repelled during his lifetime. He went off the grating with a dull, sullen splash, and as I looked into the green water I saw him go down, down, down until he was but a little flickering patch of white hanging upon the outskirts of eternal darkness. Then even that faded away, and he was gone. There he shall lie, with his secret and his sorrows and his mystery all still buried in his breast, until that great day when the sea shall give up its dead, and Nicholas Craigie come out from among the ice with the smile upon his face, and his stiffened arms outstretched in greeting. I pray that his lot may be a happier one in that life than it has been in this.

I shall not continue my journal. Our road to home lies plain and clear before us, and the great ice-field will soon be but a remembrance of the past. It will be some time before I get over the shock produced by recent events. When I began this record of our voyage

I little thought of how I should be compelled to finish it. I am writing these final words in the lonely cabin, still starting at times and fancying I hear the quick nervous step of the dead man upon the deck above me. I entered his cabin to-night, as was my duty, to make a list of his effects in order that they might be entered in the official log. All was as it had been upon my previous visit, save that the picture which I have described as having hung at the end of his bed had been cut out of its frame, as with a knife, and was gone. With this last link in a strange chain of evidence I close my diary of the voyage of the *Polestar*.

[NOTE by Dr. John M'Alister Ray, senior.—I have read over the strange events connected with the death of the captain of the *Polestar*, as narrated in the journal of my son. That everything occurred exactly as he describes it I have the fullest confidence, and, indeed, the most positive certainty, for I know him to be a strong-nerved and unimaginative man, with the strictest regard for veracity. Still, the story is, on the face of it, so vague and so improbable, that I was long opposed to its publication. Within the last few days, however, I have had independent testimony upon the subject which throws a new light upon it. I had run down to Edinburgh to attend a meeting of the British Medical Association, when I chanced to come across Dr. P——, an old college chum of mine, now practising at Saltash, in Devonshire. Upon my telling him of this experience of my son's, he declared to me that he was familiar with the man, and proceeded, to my no small surprise, to give me a description of him, which tallied remarkably well with that given in the journal, except that he depicted him as a younger man. According to his account, he had been engaged to a young lady of singular beauty residing upon the Cornish coast. During his absence at sea his betrothed had died under circumstances of peculiar horror.]

21. *The Fiend of the Cooperage*

IT was no easy matter to bring the *Gamecock* up to the island, for the river had swept down so much silt that the banks extended for many miles out into the Atlantic. The coast was hardly to be seen when the first white curl of the breakers warned us of our danger, and from there onwards we made our way very carefully under mainsail and jib, keeping the broken water well to the left, as is indicated on the chart. More than once her bottom touched the sand (we were drawing something under six feet at the time), but we had always way enough and luck enough to carry us through. Finally, the water shoaled, very rapidly, but they had sent a canoe from the factory, and the Krooboy pilot brought us within two hundred yards of the island. Here we dropped our anchor, for the gestures of the negro indicated that we could not hope to get any farther. The blue of the sea had changed to the brown of the river, and, even under the shelter of the island, the current was singing and swirling round our bows. The stream appeared to be in spate, for it was over the roots of the palm trees, and everywhere upon its muddy greasy surface we could see logs of wood and debris of all sorts which had been carried down by the flood.

When I had assured myself that we swung securely at our moorings, I thought it best to begin watering at once, for the place looked as if it reeked with fever. The heavy river, the muddy, shining banks, the bright poisonous green of the jungle, the moist steam in the air, they were all so many danger signals to one who could read them. I sent the long-boat off, therefore, with two large hogsheads, which should be sufficient to last us until we made St. Paul de Loanda. For my own part I took the dinghy and rowed for the island, for I could see the Union Jack fluttering above the palms to mark the position of Armitage and Wilson's trading station.

When I had cleared the grove, I could see the place, a long, low, whitewashed building, with a deep verandah in front, and an immense pile of palm-oil barrels heaped upon either flank of it. A row of surf boats and canoes lay along the beach, and a single small jetty projected into the river. Two men in white suits with red cummerbunds round their waists were waiting upon the end of it to receive me. One was a large portly fellow with a greyish beard. The other was slender and tall, with a pale pinched face, which was half-concealed by a great mushroom-shaped hat.

"Very glad to see you," said the latter, cordially. "I am Walker, the agent of Armitage and Wilson. Let me introduce Doctor Severall of the same company. It is not often we see a private yacht in these parts."

"She's the *Gamecock*," I explained. "I'm owner and captain—Meldrum is the name."

"Exploring?" he asked.

"I'm a lepidopterist—a butterfly-catcher. I've been doing the west coast from Senegal downwards."

"Good sport?" asked the Doctor, turning a slow yellow-shot eye upon me.

"I have forty cases full. We came in here to water, and also to see what you have in my line."

These introductions and explanations had filled up the time whilst my two Krooboys were making the dinghy fast. Then I walked down the jetty with one of my new acquaintances upon either side, each plying me with questions, for they had seen no white man for months.

"What do we do?" said the Doctor, when I had begun asking questions in my turn. "Our business keeps us pretty busy, and in our leisure time we talk politics."

"Yes, by the special mercy of Providence Severall is a rank Radical, and I am a good stiff Unionist, and we talk Home Rule for two solid hours every evening."

"And drink quinine cocktails," said the Doctor. "We're both pretty well salted now, but our normal temperature was about 103 last year. I shouldn't, as an impartial adviser, recommend you to stay here very long unless you are collecting bacilli as well as butterflies. The mouth of the Ogowai River will never develop into a health resort."

There is nothing finer than the way in which these outlying pickets of civilization distil a grim humour out of their desolate situation, and turn not only a bold, but a laughing face upon the chances which their lives may bring. Everywhere from Sierra Leone downwards I had found the same reeking swamps, the same isolated fever-racked communities, and the same bad jokes. There is something approaching to the divine in that power of man to rise above his conditions and to use his mind for the purpose of mocking at the miseries of his body.

"Dinner will be ready in about half an hour, Captain Meldrum," said the Doctor. "Walker has gone in to see about it; he's the housekeeper this week. Meanwhile, if you like, we'll stroll round and I'll show you the sights of the island."

The sun had already sunk beneath the line of palm trees, and the great arch of the heaven above our head was like the inside of a huge shell, shimmering with dainty pinks and delicate iridescence. No one who has not lived in a land where the weight and heat of a napkin become intolerable upon the knees can imagine the blessed relief which the coolness of evening brings along with it. In this sweeter and purer air the Doctor and I walked round the little island, he pointing out the stores, and explaining the routine of his work.

"There's a certain romance about the place," said he, in answer to some remark of mine about the dullness of their lives. "We are living here just upon the edge of the great unknown. Up there," he continued, pointing to the north-east, "Du Chaillu penetrated, and found the home of the gorilla. That is the Gaboon country—the land of the great apes. In this direction," pointing to the south-east, "no one has been very far. The land which is drained by this river is practically unknown to Europeans. Every log which is carried past us by the current has come from an undiscovered country. I've often wished that I was a better botanist when I have seen the singular orchids and curious-looking plants which have been cast up on the eastern end of the island."

The place which the Doctor indicated was a sloping brown beach, freely littered with the flotsam of the stream. At each end was a curved point, like a little natural breakwater, so that a small shallow bay was left between. This was full of floating vegetation, with a single huge splintered tree lying stranded in the middle of it, the current rippling against its high black side.

"These are all from up country," said the Doctor. "They get caught in our little bay, and then when some extra freshet comes they are washed out again and carried out to sea."

"What is the tree?" I asked.

"Oh, some kind of teak, I should imagine, but pretty rotten by the look of it. We get all sorts of big hard-wood trees floating past here, to say nothing of the palms. Just come in here, will you?"

He led the way into a long building with an immense quantity of barrel staves and iron hoops littered about in it.

"This is our cooperage," said he. "We have the staves sent out in bundles, and we put them together ourselves. Now, you don't see anything particularly sinister about this building, do you?"

I looked round at the high corrugated iron roof, the white wooden walls, and the earthen floor. In one corner lay a mattress and a blanket.

"I see nothing very alarming," said I.

"And yet there's something out of the common, too," he remarked. "You see that bed? Well, I intend to sleep there to-night. I don't want to buck, but I think it's a bit of a test for nerve."

"Why?"

"Oh, there have been some funny goings on. You were talking about the monotony of our lives, but I assure you that they are sometimes quite as exciting as we wish them to be. You'd better come back to the house now, for after sundown we begin to get the fever-fog up from the marshes. There, you can see it coming across the river."

I looked and saw long tentacles of white vapour writhing out from among the thick green underwood and crawling at us over the broad swirling surface of the brown river. At the same time the air turned suddenly dank and cold.

"There's the dinner gong," said the Doctor. "If this matter interests you I'll tell you about it afterwards."

It did interest me very much, for there was something earnest and subdued in his manner as he stood in the empty cooperage, which appealed very forcibly to my imagination. He was a big, bluff, hearty man, this Doctor, and yet I had detected a curious expression in his eyes as he glanced about him—an expression which I would not describe as one of fear, but rather that of a man who is alert and on his guard.

"By the way," said I, as we returned to the house, "you have shown me the huts of a good many of your native assistants, but I have not seen any of the natives themselves."

"They sleep in the hulk over yonder," the Doctor answered, pointing over to one of the banks.

"Indeed. I should not have thought in that case they would need the huts."

"Oh, they used the huts until quite recently. We've put them on the hulk until they recover their confidence a little. They were all half mad with fright, so we let them go, and nobody sleeps on the island except Walker and myself."

"What frightened them?" I asked.

"Well, that brings us back to the same story. I suppose Walker has no objection to your hearing all about it. I don't know why we should make any secret about it, though it is certainly a pretty bad business."

He made no further allusion to it during the excellent

dinner which had been prepared in my honour. It appeared that no sooner had the little white topsail of the *Gamecock* shown round Cape Lopez than these kind fellows had begun to prepare their famous pepper-pot —which is the pungent stew peculiar to the West Coast —and to boil their yams and sweet potatoes. We sat down to as good a native dinner as one could wish, served by a smart Sierra Leone waiting boy. I was just remarking to myself that he at least had not shared in the general flight when, having laid the dessert and wine upon the table, he raised his hand to his turban.

"Anyting else I do, Massa Walker?" he asked.

"No, I think that is all right, Moussa," my host answered. "I am not feeling very well to-night, though, and I should much prefer if you would stay on the island."

I saw a struggle between his fears and his duty upon the swarthy face of the African. His skin had turned of that livid purplish tint which stands for pallor in a negro, and his eyes looked furtively about him.

"No, no, Massa Walker," he cried, at last, "you better come to the hulk with me, sah. Look after you much better in the hulk, sah!"

"That won't do, Moussa. White men don't run away from the posts where they are placed."

Again I saw the passionate struggle in the negro's face, and again his fears prevailed.

"No use, Massa Walker, sah!" he cried. "S'elp me, I can't do it. If it was yesterday or if it was to-morrow, but this is the third night, sah, an' it's more than I can face."

Walker shrugged his shoulders.

"Off with you then!" said he. "When the mail-boat comes you can get back to Sierra Leone, for I'll have no servant who deserts me when I need him most. I suppose this is all mystery to you, or has the Doctor told you, Captain Meldrum?"

"I showed Captain Meldrum the cooperage, but I did

not tell him anything," said Doctor Severall. "You're looking bad, Walker," he added, glancing at his companion. "You have a strong touch coming on you."

"Yes, I've had the shivers all day, and now my head is like a cannon-ball. I took ten grains of quinine, and my ears are singing like a kettle. But I want to sleep with you in the cooperage to-night."

"No, no, my dear chap. I won't hear of such a thing. You must get to bed at once, and I am sure Meldrum will excuse you. I shall sleep in the cooperage, and I promise you that I'll be round with your medicine before breakfast."

It was evident that Walker had been struck by one of those sudden and violent attacks of remittent fever which are the curse of the West Coast. His sallow cheeks were flushed and his eyes shining with fever, and suddenly as he sat there he began to croon out a song in the high-pitched voice of delirium.

"Come, come, we must get you to bed, old chap," said the Doctor, and with my aid he led his friend into his bedroom. There we undressed him and presently, after taking a strong sedative, he settled down into a deep slumber.

"He's right for the night," said the Doctor, as we sat down and filled our glasses once more. "Sometimes it is my turn and sometimes his, but, fortunately, we have never been down together. I should have been sorry to be out of it to-night, for I have a little mystery to unravel. I told you that I intended to sleep in the cooperage."

"Yes, you said so."

"When I said sleep I meant watch, for there will be no sleep for me. We've had such a scare here that no native will stay after sundown, and I mean to find out to-night what the cause of it all may be. It has always been the custom for a native watchman to sleep in the cooperage, to prevent the barrel hoops being stolen. Well, six days ago the fellow who slept there disappeared, and we have never seen a trace of him since. It was certainly singular, for no canoe had been taken, and these waters are too full of crocodiles for any man to swim to shore. What became of the fellow, or how he could have left the island is a complete mystery. Walker and I were merely surprised, but the blacks were badly scared and queer Voodoo tales began to get about amongst them. But the real stampede broke out three nights ago, when the new watchman in the cooperage also disappeared."

"What became of him?" I asked.

"Well, we not only don't know, but we can't even give a guess which would fit the facts. The niggers swear there is a fiend in the cooperage who claims a man every third night. They wouldn't stay in the island—nothing could persuade them. Even Moussa, who is a faithful boy enough, would, as you have seen, leave his master in a fever rather than remain for the night. If we are to continue to run this place we must reassure our niggers, and I don't know any better way of doing it than by putting in a night there myself. This is the third night, you see, so I suppose the thing is due, whatever it may be."

"Have you no clue?" I asked. "Was there no mark of violence, no blood-stain, no footprints, nothing to give a hint as to what kind of danger you may have to meet?"

"Absolutely nothing. The man was gone and that was all. Last time it was old Ali, who has been wharf-tender here since the place was started. He was always as steady as a rock, and nothing but foul play would take him from his work."

"Well," said I, "I really don't think that this is a one-man job. Your friend is full of laudanum, and come what might he can be of no assistance to you. You must let me stay and put in a night with you at the cooperage."

"Well, now, that's very good of you, Meldrum,"

said he heartily, shaking my hand across the table. " It's not a thing that I should have ventured to propose, for it is asking a good deal of a casual visitor, but if you really mean it——"

" Certainly I mean it. If you will excuse me a moment, I will hail the *Gamecock* and let them know that they need not expect me."

As we came back from the other end of the little jetty we were both struck by the appearance of the night. A huge blue-black pile of clouds had built itself up upon the landward side, and the wind came from it in little hot pants, which beat upon our faces like the draught from a blast furnace. Under the jetty the river was swirling and hissing, tossing little white spurts of spray over the planking.

" Confound it ! " said Doctor Severall. " We are likely to have a flood on the top of all our troubles. That rise in the river means heavy rain up-country, and when it once begins you never know how far it will go. We've had the island nearly covered before now. Well, we'll just go and see that Walker is comfortable, and then if you like we'll settle down in our quarters."

The sick man was sunk in a profound slumber, and we left him with some crushed limes in a glass beside him in case he should awake with the thirst of fever upon him. Then we made our way through the unnatural gloom thrown by that menacing cloud. The river had risen so high that the little bay which I have described at the end of the island had become almost obliterated through the submerging of its flanking peninsula. The great raft of driftwood, with the huge black tree in the middle, was swaying up and down in the swollen current.

" That's one good thing a flood will do for us," said the Doctor. " It carries away all the vegetable stuff which is brought down on to the east end of the island. It came down with the freshet the other day, and here it will stay until a flood sweeps it out into the main stream. Well, here's our room, and here are some books and here is my tobacco pouch, and we must try and put in the night as best we may."

By the light of our single lantern the great lonely room looked very gaunt and dreary. Save for the piles of staves and heaps of hoops there was absolutely nothing in it, with the exception of the mattress for the Doctor, which had been laid in the corner. We made a couple of seats and a table out of the staves, and settled down together for a long vigil. Severall had brought a revolver for me and was himself armed with a double-barrelled shot-gun. We loaded our weapons and laid them cocked within reach of our hands. The little circle of light and the black shadows arching over us were so melancholy that he went off to the house, and returned with two candles. One side of the cooperage was pierced, however, by several open windows, and it was only by screening our lights behind staves that we could prevent them from being extinguished.

The Doctor, who appeared to be a man of iron nerves, had settled down to a book, but I observed that every now and then he laid it upon his knee, and took an earnest look all round him. For my part, although I tried once or twice to read, I found it impossible to concentrate my thoughts upon the book. They would would always wander back to this great empty silent room, and to the sinister mystery which overshadowed it. I racked my brains for some possible theory which would explain the disappearance of these two men. There was the black fact that they were gone, and not the least tittle of evidence as to why or whither. And here we were waiting in the same place—waiting without an idea as to what we were waiting for. I was right in saying that it was not a one-man job. It was trying enough as it was, but no force upon earth would have kept me there without a comrade.

What an endless, tedious night it was! Outside we

heard the lapping and gurgling of the great river, and the soughing of the rising wind. Within, save for our breathing, the turning of the Doctor's pages, and the high, shrill ping of an occasional mosquito, there was a heavy silence. Once my heart sprang into my mouth as Severall's book suddenly fell to the ground and he sprang to his feet with his eyes on one of the windows.

"Did you see anything, Meldrum?"

"No, did you?"

"Well, I had a vague sense of movement outside that window." He caught up his gun and approached it. "No, there's nothing to be seen, and yet I could have sworn that something passed slowly across it."

"A palm leaf, perhaps," said I, for the wind was growing stronger every instant.

"Very likely," said he, and settled down to his book again, but his eyes were for ever darting little suspicious glances up at the window. I watched it also, but all was quiet outside.

And then suddenly our thoughts were turned into a new direction by the bursting of the storm. A blinding flash was followed by a clap which shook the building. Again and again came the vivid white glare with thunder at the same instant, like the flash and roar of a monstrous piece of artillery. And then down came the tropical rain, crashing and rattling on the corrugated iron roofing of the cooperage. The big hollow room boomed like a drum. From the darkness arose a strange mixture of noises, a gurgling, splashing, tinkling, bubbling, washing, dripping—every liquid sound that nature can produce from the thrashing and swishing of the rain to the deep steady boom of the river. Hour after hour the uproar grew louder and more sustained.

"My word," said Severall, "we are going to have the father of all the floods this time. Well, here's the dawn coming at last and that is a blessing. We've about exploded the third night superstition, anyhow."

A grey light was stealing through the room, and there

was the day upon us in an instant. The rain had eased off, but the coffee-coloured river was roaring past like a waterfall. Its power made me fear for the anchor of the *Gamecock*.

" I must get aboard," said I. " If she drags she'll never be able to beat up the river again."

" The island is as good as a breakwater," the Doctor answered. " I can give you a cup of coffee if you will come up to the house."

I was chilled and miserable, so the suggestion was a welcome one. We left the ill-omened cooperage with its mystery still unsolved, and we splashed our way up to the house.

" There's the spirit lamp," said Severall. " If you would just put a light to it, I will see how Walker feels this morning."

He left me, but was back in an instant with a dreadful face.

" He's gone ! " he cried hoarsely.

The words sent a thrill of horror through me. I stood with the lamp in my hand, glaring at him.

" Yes, he's gone ! " he repeated. " Come and look ! "

I followed him without a word, and the first thing that I saw as I entered the bedroom was Walker himself lying huddled on his bed in the grey flannel sleeping suit in which I had helped to dress him on the night before.

" Not dead, surely ! " I gasped.

The Doctor was terribly agitated. His hands were shaking like leaves in the wind.

" He's been dead some hours."

" Was it fever ? "

" Fever ! Look at his foot ! "

I glanced down and a cry of horror burst from my lips. One foot was not merely dislocated, but was turned completely round in a most grotesque contortion.

" Good God ! " I cried. " What can have done this ? "

Severall had laid his hand upon the dead man's chest.

" Feel here," he whispered.

I placed my hand at the same spot. There was no resistance. The body was absolutely soft and limp. It was like pressing a sawdust doll.

" The breast-bone is gone," said Severall in the same awed whisper. " He's broken to bits. Thank God that he had the laudanum. You can see by his face that he died in his sleep."

" But who can have done this ? "

" I've had about as much as I can stand," said the Doctor, wiping his forehead. " I don't know that I'm a greater coward than my neighbours, but this gets beyond me. If you're going out to the *Gamecock*——"

" Come on ! " said I, and off we started. If we did not run it was because each of us wished to keep up the last shadow of his self-respect before the other. It was dangerous in a light canoe on that swollen river, but we never paused to give the matter a thought. He bailing and I paddling we kept her above water, and gained the deck of the yacht. There, with two hundred yards of water between us and this cursed island we felt that we were our own men once more.

" We'll go back in an hour or so," said he. " But we need have a little time to steady ourselves. I wouldn't have had the niggers see me as I was just now for a year's salary."

" I've told the steward to prepare breakfast. Then we shall go back," said I. " But in God's name, Doctor Severall, what do you make of it all ? "

" It beats me—beats me clean. I've heard of Voodoo devilry, and I've laughed at it with the others. But that poor old Walker, a decent, God-fearing, nineteenth-century, Primrose-League Englishman should go under like this without a whole bone in his body—it's given me a shake, I won't deny it. But look there, Meldrum, is that hand of yours mad or drunk, or what is it ? "

Old Patterson, the oldest man of my crew, and as steady as the Pyramids, had been stationed in the bows with a boat-hook to fend off the drifting logs which came sweeping down with the current. Now he stood with crooked knees, glaring out in front of him, and one forefinger stabbing furiously at the air.

"Look at it!" he yelled. "Look at it!"

And at the same instant we saw it.

A huge black tree trunk was coming down the river, its broad glistening back just lapped by the water. And in front of it—about three feet in front—arching upwards like the figure-head of a ship, there hung a dreadful face, swaying slowly from side to side. It was flattened, malignant, as large as a small beer-barrel, of a faded fungoid colour, but the neck which supported it was mottled with a dull yellow and black. As it flew past the *Gamecock* in the swirl of the waters I saw two immense coils roll up out of some great hollow in the tree, and the villainous head rose suddenly to the height of eight or ten feet, looking with dull, skin-covered eyes at the yacht. An instant later the tree had shot past us and was plunging with its horrible passenger towards the Atlantic.

"What was it?" I cried.

"It is our fiend of the cooperage," said Doctor Severall, and he had become in an instant the same bluff, self-confident man that he had been before. "Yes, that is the devil who has been haunting our island. It is the great python of the Gaboon."

I thought of the stories which I had heard all down the coast of the monstrous constrictors of the interior, of their periodical appetite, and of the murderous effects of their deadly squeeze. Then it all took shape in my mind. There had been a freshet the week before. It had brought down this huge hollow tree with its hideous occupant. Who knows from what far distant tropical forest it may have come! It had been stranded on the little east bay of the island. The cooperage had been the nearest house. Twice with the return of its appetite it had carried off the watchman. Last night it had doubtless come again, when Severall had thought he saw something move at the window, but our lights had driven it away. It had writhed onwards and had slain poor Walker in his sleep.

"Why did it not carry him off?" I asked.

"The thunder and lightning must have scared the brute away. There's your steward, Meldrum. The sooner we have breakfast and get back to the island the better, or some of those niggers might think that we had been frightened."

22. *Jelland's Voyage*

"WELL," said our Anglo-Jap as we all drew up our chairs round the smoking-room fire, "it's an old tale out yonder, and may have spilt over into print for all I know. I don't want to turn this club-room into a chestnut stall, but it is a long way to the Yellow Sea, and it is just as likely that none of you have ever heard of the yawl *Matilda*, and of what happened to Henry Jelland and Willy McEvoy aboard of her.

"The middle of the 'sixties was a stirring time out in Japan. That was just after the Simonosaki bombardment, and before the Daimio affair. There was a Tory party and there was a Liberal party among the natives, and the question that they were wrangling over was whether the throats of the foreigners should be cut or not. I tell you all, politics have been tame to me since then. If you lived in a treaty port, you were bound to wake up and take an interest in them. And to make it better, the outsider had no way of knowing how the game was going. If the opposition won it would not be a newspaper paragraph that would tell him of it, but a good old Tory in a suit of chain mail, with a sword in each hand, would drop in and let him know all about it in a single upper cut.

"Of course it makes men reckless when they are living on the edge of a volcano like that. Just at first they are very jumpy, and then there comes a time when they learn to enjoy life while they have it. I tell you there's nothing makes life so beautiful as when the shadow of death begins to fall across it. Time is too precious to be dawdled away then, and a man lives every minute of it. That was the way with us in Yokohama. There were many European places of business which had to go on running, and the men who worked them made the place lively for seven nights in the week.

"One of the heads of the European colony was Randolph Moore, the big export merchant. His offices were in Yokohama, but he spent a good deal of his time at his house up in Jeddo, which had only just been opened to the trade. In his absence he used to leave his affairs in the hands of his head clerk, Jelland, whom he knew to be a man of great energy and resolution. But energy and resolution are two-edged things, you know, and when they are used against you you don't appreciate them so much.

"It was gambling that set Jelland wrong. He was a little dark-eyed fellow with black curly hair—more than three-quarters Celt, I should imagine. Every night in the week you would see him in the same place, on the left-hand side of the croupier at Matheson's *rouge et noir* table. For a long time he won, and lived in better style than his employer. And then came a turn of luck, and he began to lose so that at the end of a single week his partner and he were stone broke, without a dollar to their names.

"This partner was a clerk in the employ of the same firm—a tall, straw-haired young Englishman called McEvoy. He was a good boy enough at the start, but he was clay in the hands of Jelland, who fashioned him into a kind of weak model of himself. They were for ever on the prowl together, but it was Jelland who led and McEvoy who followed. Lynch and I and one or two others tried to show the youngster that he could come to no good along that line, and when we were talking to him we could win him round easily enough, but five minutes of Jelland would swing him back again. It may have been animal magnetism or what you like, but the little man could pull the big one along like a sixty-foot tug in front of a full-rigged ship. Even when they had lost all their money they would still take their places at the table and look on with shining eyes when anyone else was raking in the stamps.

"But one evening they could keep out of it no longer. Red had turned up sixteen times running, and it was more than Jelland could bear. He whispered to McEvoy, and then said a word to the croupier.

"'Certainly, Mr. Jelland; your cheque is as good as notes,' said he.

"Jelland scribbled a cheque and threw it on the black. The card was the king of hearts, and the croupier raked in the little bit of paper. Jelland grew angry, and McEvoy white. Another and a heavier cheque was written and thrown on the table. The card was the nine of diamonds. McEvoy leaned his head upon his hands and looked as if he would faint. 'By God!' growled Jelland, 'I won't be beat,' and he threw on a cheque that covered the other two. The card was the deuce of hearts. A few minutes later they were walking down the Bund, with the cool night-air playing upon their fevered faces.

"'Of course you know what this means,' said Jelland, lighting a cheroot; 'we'll have to transfer some of the office money to our current account. There's no occasion to make a fuss over it. Old Moore won't look over the books before Easter. If we have any luck, we can easily replace it before then.'

"'But if we have no luck?' faltered McEvoy.

"'Tut, man, we must take things as they come.

You stick to me, and I'll stick to you, and we'll pull through together. You shall sign the cheques to-morrow night, and we shall see if your luck is better than mine.'

"But if anything it was worse. When the pair rose from the table on the following evening, they had spent over £5,000 of their employer's money. But the resolute Jelland was as sanguine as ever.

"'We have a good nine weeks before us before the books will be examined,' said he. 'We must play the game out, and it will all come straight.'

"McEvoy returned to his rooms that night in an agony of shame and remorse. When he was with Jelland he borrowed strength from him; but alone he recognized the full danger of his position, and the vision of his old white-capped mother in England, who had been so proud when he had received his appointment, rose up before him to fill him with loathing and madness. He was still tossing upon his sleepless couch when his Japanese servant entered the bedroom. For an instant McEvoy thought that the long-expected outbreak had come, and plunged for his revolver. Then, with his heart in his mouth, he listened to the message which the servant had brought.

"Jelland was downstairs, and wanted to see him.

"What on earth could he want at that hour of night? McEvoy dressed hurriedly and rushed downstairs. His companion, with a set smile upon his lips, which was belied by the ghastly pallor of his face, was sitting in the dim light of a solitary candle, with a slip of paper in his hands.

"'Sorry to knock you up, Willy,' said he. 'No eavesdroppers, I suppose?'

"McEvoy shook his head. He could not trust himself to speak.

"'Well, then, our little game is played out. This note was waiting for me at home. It is from Moore, and says that he will be down on Monday morning for an examination of the books. It leaves us in a tight place.'

" 'Monday!' gasped McEvoy; 'to-day is Friday.'

" 'Saturday, my son, and 3 a.m. We have not much time to turn round in.'

" 'We are lost!' screamed McEvoy.

" 'We soon will be, if you make such an infernal row,' said Jelland harshly. 'Now do what I tell you, Willy, and we'll pull through yet.'

" 'I will do anything—anything.'

" 'That's better. Where's your whisky? It's a beastly time of the day to have to get your back stiff, but there must be no softness with us, or we are gone. First of all, I think there is something due to our relations, don't you?'

" McEvoy stared.

" 'We must stand or fall together, you know. Now I, for one, don't intend to set my foot inside a felon's dock under any circumstances. D'ye see? I'm ready to swear to that. Are you?'

" 'What d'you mean?' asked McEvoy, shrinking back.

" 'Why, man, we all have to die, and it's only the pressing of a trigger. I swear that I shall never be taken alive. Will you? If you don't, I leave you to your fate.'

" 'All right. I'll do whatever you think best.'

" 'You swear it?'

" 'Yes.'

" 'Well, mind, you must be as good as your word. Now we have two clear days to get off in. The yawl *Matilda* is on sale, and she has all her fixings and plenty of tinned stuff aboard. We'll buy the lot to-morrow morning, and whatever we want, and get away in her. But, first, we'll clear all that is left in the office. There are 5,000 sovereigns in the safe. After dark we'll get them aboard the yawl, and take our chance of reaching California. There's no use hesitating, my son, for we have no ghost of a look-in in any other direction. It's that or nothing.'

"'I'll do what you advise.'

"'All right; and mind you get a bright face on you to-morrow, for if Moore gets the tip and comes before Monday, then——' He tapped the side-pocket of his coat and looked across at his partner with eyes that were full of a sinister meaning.

"All went well with their plans next day. The *Matilda* was bought without difficulty; and, though she was a tiny craft for so long a voyage, had she been larger two men could not have hoped to manage her. She was stocked with water during the day, and after dark the two clerks brought down the money from the office and stowed it in the hold. Before midnight they had collected all their own possessions without exciting suspicion, and at two in the morning they left their moorings and stole quietly out from among the shipping. They were seen, of course, and were set down as keen yachtsmen who were on for a good long Sunday cruise; but there was no one who dreamed that that cruise would only end either on the American coast or at the bottom of the North Pacific Ocean. Straining and hauling, they got their mainsail up and set their foresail and jib. There was a slight breeze from the south-east, and the little craft went dipping along upon her way. Seven miles from land, however, the wind fell away and they lay becalmed, rising and falling on the long swell of a glassy sea. All Sunday they did not make a mile, and in the evening Yokohama still lay along the horizon.

"On Monday morning down came Randolph Moore from Jeddo, and made straight for the offices. He had had the tip from someone that his clerks had been spreading themselves a bit, and that had made him come down out of his usual routine; but when he reached his place and found the three juniors waiting in the street with their hands in their pockets he knew that the matter was serious.

"'What's this?' he asked. He was a man of action,

and a nasty chap to deal with when he had his topmasts lowered.

" 'We can't get in,' said the clerks.

" 'Where is Mr. Jelland ?'

" 'He has not come to-day.'

" 'And Mr. McEvoy ?'

" 'He has not come either.'

" Randolph Moore looked serious. 'We must have the door down,' said he.

" They don't build houses very solid in that land of earthquakes, and in a brace of shakes they were all in the office. Of course the thing told its own story. The safe was open, the money gone, and the clerks fled. Their employer lost no time in talk.

" 'Where were they seen last ?'

" 'On Saturday they bought the *Matilda* and started for a cruise.'

" Saturday ! The matter seemed hopeless if they had got two days' start. But there was still the shadow of a chance. He rushed to the beach and swept the ocean with his glasses.

" 'My God !' he cried. 'There's the *Matilda* out yonder. I know her by the rake of her mast. I have my hand upon the villains after all !'

" But there was a hitch even then. No boat had steam up, and the eager merchant had not patience to wait. Clouds were banking up along the haunch of the hills, and there was every sign of an approaching change of weather. A police boat was ready with ten armed men in her, and Randolph Moore himself took the tiller as she shot out in pursuit of the becalmed yawl.

" Jelland and McEvoy, waiting wearily for the breeze which never came, saw the dark speck which sprang out from the shadow of the land and grew larger with every swish of the oars. As she drew nearer, they could see also that she was packed with men, and the gleam of weapons told what manner of men they were. Jelland stood leaning against the tiller, and he looked at the threatening sky, the limp sails, and the approaching boat.

" 'It's a case with us, Willy,' said he. 'By the Lord, we are two most unlucky devils, for there's wind in that sky, and another hour would have brought it to us.'

" McEvoy groaned.

" 'There's no good softening over it, my lad,' said Jelland. 'It's the police boat right enough, and there's old Moore driving them to row like hell. It'll be a ten-dollar job for every man of them.'

" Willy McEvoy crouched against the side with his knees on the deck. 'My mother! my poor old mother!' he sobbed.

" 'She'll never hear that you have been in the dock anyway,' said Jelland. 'My people never did much for me, but I will do that much for them. It's no good, Mac. We can chuck our hands. God bless you, old man! Here's the pistol!'

" He cocked the revolver, and held the butt towards the youngster. But the other shrank away from it with little gasps and cries. Jelland glanced at the approaching boat. It was not more than a few hundred yards away.

" 'There's no time for nonsense,' said he. 'Damn it! man, what's the use of flinching? You swore it!'

" 'No, no, Jelland!'

" 'Well, anyhow, I swore that neither of us should be taken. Will you do it?'

" 'I can't! I can't!'

" 'Then I will for you.'

" The rowers in the boat saw him lean forwards, they heard two pistol shots, they saw him double himself across the tiller, and then, before the smoke had lifted, they found that they had something else to think of.

" For at that instant the storm broke—one of those short sudden squalls which are common in these seas. The *Matilda* heeled over, her sails bellied out, she plunged her lee-rail into a wave, and was off like a frightened deer. Jelland's body had jammed the helm, and she kept a course right before the wind, and fluttered away over the rising sea like a blown piece of paper. The rowers worked frantically, but the yawl still drew ahead, and in five minutes it had plunged into the storm-wrack never to be seen again by mortal eye. The boat put back, and reached Yokohama with the water washing half-way up to the thwarts.

"And that was how it came that the yawl *Matilda*, with a cargo of five thousand pounds and a crew of two dead young men, set sail across the Pacific Ocean. What the end of Jelland's voyage may have been no man knows. He may have foundered in that gale, or he may have been picked up by some canny merchant-man, who stuck to the bullion and kept his mouth shut, or he may still be cruising in that vast waste of waters, blown north to the Behring Sea, or south to the Malay Islands. It's better to leave it unfinished than to spoil a true story by inventing a tag to it."

23. *J. Habakuk Jephson's Statement*

IN the month of December in the year 1873, the British ship *Dei Gratia* steered into Gibraltar, having in tow the derelict brigantine *Marie Celeste*, which had been picked up in latitude 38° 40′, longitude 17° 15′ W. There were several circumstances in connection with the condition and appearance of this abandoned vessel which excited considerable comment at the time, and aroused a curiosity which has never been satisfied. What these circumstances were was summed up in an able article which appeared in the *Gibraltar Gazette*. The curious can find it in the issue for January 4, 1874, unless my memory deceives me. For the benefit of those, however, who may be unable to refer to the paper in question, I shall subjoin a few extracts which touch upon the leading features of the case.

"We have ourselves," says the anonymous writer in

the *Gazette*, "been over the derelict *Marie Celeste*, and have closely questioned the officers of the *Dei Gratia* on every point which might throw light on the affair. They are of opinion that she had been abandoned several days, or perhaps weeks, before being picked up. The official log, which was found in the cabin, states that the vessel sailed from Boston to Lisbon, starting upon October 16. It is, however, most imperfectly kept, and affords little information. There is no reference to rough weather, and, indeed, the state of the vessel's paint and rigging excludes the idea that she was abandoned for any such reason. She is perfectly watertight. No signs of a struggle or of violence are to be detected, and there is absolutely nothing to account for the disappearance of the crew. There are several indications that a lady was present on board, a sewing-machine being found in the cabin and some articles of female attire. These probably belonged to the captain's wife, who is mentioned in the log as having accompanied her husband. As an instance of the mildness of the weather, it may be remarked that a bobbin of silk was found standing upon the sewing-machine, though the least roll of the vessel would have precipitated it to the floor. The boats were intact and slung upon the davits; and the cargo, consisting of tallow and American clocks, was untouched. An old-fashioned sword of curious workmanship was discovered among some lumber in the forecastle, and this weapon is said to exhibit a longitudinal striation on the steel, as if it had been recently wiped. It has been placed in the hands of the police, and submitted to Dr. Monaghan, the analyst, for inspection. The result of his examination has not yet been published. We may remark, in conclusion, that Captain Dalton, of the *Dei Gratia*, an able and intelligent seaman, is of opinion that the *Marie Celeste* may have been abandoned a considerable distance from the spot at which she was picked up, since a powerful current runs up in that latitude from the African coast. He confesses his inability, however, to advance any hypothesis which can reconcile all the facts of the case. In the utter absence of a clue or grain of evidence, it is to be feared that the fate of the crew of the *Marie Celeste* will be added to those numerous mysteries of the deep which will never be solved until the great day when the sea shall give up its dead. If crime has been committed, as is much to be suspected, there is little hope of bringing the perpetrators to justice."

I shall supplement this extract from the *Gibraltar Gazette* by quoting a telegram from Boston, which went the round of the English papers, and represented the total amount of information which had been collected about the *Marie Celeste*. "She was," it said, "a brigantine of 170 tons burden, and belonged to White, Russell & White, wine importers, of this city. Captain J. W. Tibbs was an old servant of the firm, and was a man of known ability and tried probity. He was accompanied by his wife, aged thirty-one, and their youngest child, five years old. The crew consisted of seven hands, including two coloured seamen, and a boy. There were three passengers, one of whom was the well-known Brooklyn specialist on consumption, Dr. Habakuk Jephson, who was a distinguished advocate for Abolition in the early days of the movement, and whose pamphlet, entitled 'Where is thy Brother?' exercised a strong influence on public opinion before the war. The other passengers were Mr. J. Harton, a writer in the employ of the firm, and Mr. Septimius Goring, a half-caste gentleman, from New Orleans. All investigations have failed to throw any light upon the fate of these fourteen human beings. The loss of Dr. Jephson will be felt both in political and scientific circles."

I have here epitomised, for the benefit of the public, all that has been hitherto known concerning the *Marie Celeste* and her crew, for the past ten years have not in any way helped to elucidate the mystery. I have now taken up my pen with the intention of telling all that I know of the ill-fated voyage. I consider that it is a duty which I owe to society, for symptoms which I am familiar with in others lead me to believe that before many months my tongue and hand may be alike incapable of conveying information. Let me remark, as a preface to my narrative, that I am Joseph Habakuk Jephson, Doctor of Medicine of the University of Harvard, and ex-Consulting Physician of the Samaritan Hospital of Brooklyn.

Many will doubtless wonder why I have not proclaimed myself before, and why I have suffered so many conjectures and surmises to pass unchallenged. Could the ends of justice have been served in any way by my revealing the facts in my possession I should unhesitatingly have done so. It seemed to me, however, that there was no possibility of such a result; and when I attempted after the occurrence, to state my case to an English official, I was met with such offensive incredulity that I determined never again to expose myself to the chance of such an indignity. I can excuse the discourtesy of the Liverpool magistrate, however, when I reflect upon the treatment which I received at the hands of my own relatives, who, though they knew my unimpeachable character, listened to my statement with an indulgent smile as if humouring the delusion of a monomaniac. This slur upon my veracity led to a quarrel between myself and John Vanburger, the brother of my wife, and confirmed me in my resolution to let the matter sink into oblivion—a determination which I have only altered through my son's solicitations. In order to make my narrative intelligible, I must run lightly over one or two incidents in my former life which throw light upon subsequent events.

My father, William K. Jephson, was a preacher of the sect called Plymouth Brethren, and was one of the most respected citizens of Lowell. Like most of the other Puritans of New England, he was a determined opponent of slavery, and it was from his lips that I received those lessons which tinged every action of my life. While

I was studying medicine at Harvard University, I had already made a mark as an advanced Abolitionist; and when, after taking my degree, I bought a third share of the practice of Dr. Willis, of Brooklyn, I managed, in spite of my professional duties, to devote a considerable time to the cause which I had at heart, my pamphlet, "Where is thy Brother?" (Swarburgh, Lister & Co., 1859) attracting considerable attention.

When the war broke out I left Brooklyn and accompanied the 113th New York Regiment through the campaign. I was present at the second battle of Bull's Run and at the battle of Gettysburg. Finally, I was severely wounded at Antietam, and would probably have perished on the field had it not been for the kindness of a gentleman named Murray, who had me carried to his house and provided me with every comfort. Thanks to his charity, and to the nursing which I received from his black domestics, I was soon able to get about the plantation with the help of a stick. It was during this period of convalescence that an incident occurred which is closely connected with my story.

Among the most assiduous of the negresses who had watched my couch during my illness there was one old crone who appeared to exert considerable authority over the others. She was exceedingly attentive to me, and I gathered from the few words that passed between us that she had heard of me, and that she was grateful to me for championing her oppressed race.

One day as I was sitting alone in the verandah, basking in the sun, and debating whether I should rejoin Grant's army, I was surprised to see this old creature hobbling towards me. After looking cautiously around to see that we were alone, she fumbled in the front of her dress, and produced a small chamois leather bag which was hung round her neck by a white cord.

"Massa," she said, bending down and croaking the words into my ear, "me die soon. Me very old woman. Not stay long on Massa Murray's plantation."

"You may live a long time yet, Martha," I answered. "You know I am a doctor. If you feel ill let me know about it, and I will try to cure you."

"No wish to live—wish to die. I'm gwine to join the heavenly host." Here she relapsed into one of those half-heathenish rhapsodies in which negroes indulge. "But, massa, me have one thing must leave behind me when I go. No able to take it with me across the Jordan. That one thing very precious, more precious and more holy than all thing else in the world. Me, a poor old black woman, have this because my people, very great people, 'spose they was back in the old country. But you cannot understand this same as black folk could. My fader give it me, and his fader give it him, but now who shall I give it to? Poor Martha hab no child, no relation, nobody. All round I see black man very bad man. Black woman very stupid woman. Nobody worthy of the stone. And so I say, Here is Massa Jephson who write books and fight for coloured folk—he must be a good man, and he shall have it though he is white man, and nebber can know what it mean or where it came from." Here the old woman fumbled in the chamois leather bag and pulled out a flattish black stone with a hole through the middle of it. "Here, take it," she said, pressing it into my hand; "take it. No harm nebber come from anything good. Keep it safe—nebber lose it!" and with a warning gesture the old crone hobbled away in the same cautious way as she had come, looking from side to side to see if we had been observed.

I was more amused than impressed by the old woman's earnestness, and was only prevented from laughing during her oration by the fear of hurting her feelings. When she was gone I took a good look at the stone which she had given me. It was intensely black, of extreme hardness, and oval in shape—just such a flat stone as one would pick up on the seashore if one wished to throw a long way. It was about three inches long, and an inch and a half broad at the middle, but rounded off at the extremities. The most curious part about it was several well-marked ridges which ran in semicircles over its surface, and gave it exactly the appearance of a human ear. Altogether I was rather interested in my new possession and determined to submit it, as a geological specimen to my friend Professor Shroeder of the New York Institute upon the earliest opportunity. In the meantime I thrust it into my pocket, and rising from my chair started off for a short stroll in the shrubbery, dismissing the incident from my mind.

As my wound had nearly healed by this time, I took my leave of Mr. Murray shortly afterwards. The Union armies were everywhere victorious and converging on Richmond, so that my assistance seemed unnecessary, and I returned to Brooklyn. There I resumed my practice, and married the second daughter of Josiah Vanburger, the well-known wood engraver. In the course of a few years I built up a good connection and acquired considerable reputation in the treatment of pulmonary complaints. I still kept the old black stone in my pocket, and frequently told the story of the dramatic way in which I had become possessed of it. I also kept my resolution of showing it to Professor Shroeder, who was much interested both by the anecdote and the specimen. He pronounced it to be a piece of meteoric stone, and drew my attention to the fact that its resemblance to an ear was not accidental, but that it was most carefully worked into that shape. A dozen little anatomical points showed that the worker had been as accurate as he was skilful. "I should not wonder," said the Professor, "if it were broken off from some larger statue, though how such hard material could be so perfectly worked is more than I can understand. If there is a statue to correspond I should like to see it!" So I thought at the time, but I have changed my opinion since.

The next seven or eight years of my life were quiet and uneventful. Summer followed spring, and spring followed winter, without any variation in my duties. As the practice increased I admitted J. S. Jackson as partner, he to have one-fourth of the profits. The continued strain had told upon my constitution, however, and I became at last so unwell that my wife insisted upon my consulting Dr. Kavanagh Smith, who was my colleague at the Samaritan Hospital. That gentleman examined me, and pronounced the apex of my left lung to be in a state of consolidation, recommending me at the same time to go through a course of medical treatment and to take a long sea-voyage.

My own disposition, which is naturally restless, predisposed me strongly in favour of the latter piece of advice, and the matter was clinched by my meeting young Russell, of the firm of White, Russell & White, who offered me a passage in one of his father's ships, the *Marie Celeste*, which was just starting from Boston. "She is a snug little ship," he said, "and Tibbs, the captain, is an excellent fellow. There is nothing like a sailing ship for an invalid." I was very much of the same opinion myself, so I closed with the offer on the spot.

My original plan was that my wife should accompany me on my travels. She has always been a very poor sailor, however, and there were strong family reasons against her exposing herself to any risk at the time, so we determined that she should remain at home. I am not a religious or an effusive man; but oh, thank God for that! As to leaving my practice, I was easily reconciled to it, as Jackson, my partner, was a reliable and hard-working man.

I arrived in Boston on October 12, 1873, and proceeded immediately to the office of the firm in order to thank them for their courtesy. As I was sitting in the counting-house waiting until they should be at liberty to see me, the words *Marie Celeste* suddenly attracted my attention. I looked round and saw a very tall, gaunt man, who was leaning across the polished mahogany counter asking some questions of the clerk at the other side. His face was turned half towards me, and I could see that he had a strong dash of negro blood in him, being probably a quadroon or even nearer akin to the black. His curved aquiline nose and straight lank hair showed the white strain ; but the dark, restless eye, sensuous mouth, and gleaming teeth all told of his African origin. His complexion was of a sickly, unhealthy yellow, and as his face was deeply pitted with small-pox, the general impression was so unfavourable as to be almost revolting. When he spoke, however, it was in a soft, melodious voice, and in well-chosen words, and he was evidently a man of some education.

"I wished to ask a few questions about the *Marie Celeste*," he repeated, leaning across to the clerk. "She sails the day after to-morrow, does she not ?"

"Yes, sir," said the young clerk, awed into unusual politeness by the glimmer of a large diamond in the stranger's shirt front.

"Where is she bound for ?"

"Lisbon."

"How many of a crew ?"

"Seven, sir."

"Passengers ?"

"Yes, two. One of our young gentlemen, and a doctor from New York."

"No gentleman from the South ?" asked the stranger eagerly.

"No, none, sir."

"Is there room for another passenger ?"

"Accommodation, for three more," answered the clerk.

"I'll go," said the quadroon decisively ; "I'll go, I'll engage my passage at once. Put it down, will you—Mr. Septimius Goring, of New Orleans."

The clerk filled up a form and handed it over to the stranger, pointing to a blank space at the bottom. As Mr. Goring stooped over to sign it I was horrified to observe that the fingers of his right hand had been lopped off, and that he was holding the pen between his thumb and the palm. I have seen thousands slain in battle, and assisted at every conceivable surgical operation, but I cannot recall any sight which gave me such a thrill of disgust as that great brown sponge-like hand with the single member protruding from it. He used it skilfully enough, however, for, dashing off his signature, he nodded to the clerk and strolled out of the office just as Mr. White sent out word that he was ready to receive me.

I went down to the *Marie Celeste* that evening, and looked over my berth, which was extremely comfortable considering the small size of the vessel. Mr. Goring, whom I had seen in the morning, was to have the one next mine. Opposite was the captain's cabin and a small berth for Mr. John Harton, a gentleman who was going out in the interests of the firm. These little rooms were arranged on each side of the passage which led from the main-deck to the saloon. The latter was a comfortable room, the panelling tastefully done in oak and mahogany, with a rich Brussels carpet and luxurious settees. I was very much pleased with the accommodation, and also with Tibbs the captain, a bluff, sailor-like fellow, with a loud voice and hearty manner, who welcomed me to the ship with effusion, and insisted upon our splitting a bottle of wine in his cabin. He told me that he intended to take his wife and youngest child with him on the voyage, and that he hoped with good luck to make Lisbon in three weeks. We had a pleasant chat and parted the best of friends, he warning me to make the last of my preparations next morning, as he intended to make a start by the mid-day tide, having now shipped all his cargo. I went back to my hotel, where I found a letter from my wife awaiting me, and, after a refreshing night's sleep, returned to the boat in the morning. From this point I am able to quote from the journal which I kept in order to vary the monotony of the long sea-voyage. If it is somewhat bald in places

I can at least rely upon its accuracy in details, as it was written conscientiously from day to day.

October 16th.—Cast off our warps at half-past two and were towed out into the bay, where the tug left us, and with all sail set we bowled along at about nine knots an hour. I stood upon the poop watching the low land of America sinking gradually upon the horizon until the evening haze hid it from my sight. A single red light, however, continued to blaze balefully behind us, throwing a long track like a trail of blood upon the water, and it is still visible as I write, though reduced to a mere speck. The captain is in a bad humour, for two of his hands disappointed him at the last moment, and he was compelled to ship a couple of negroes who happened to be on the quay. The missing men were steady, reliable fellows, who had been with him several voyages, and their non-appearance puzzled as well as irritated him. Where a crew of seven men have to work a fair-sized ship the loss of two experienced seamen is a serious one, for though the negroes may take a spell at the wheel or swab the decks, they are of little or no use in rough weather. Our cook is also a black man, and Mr. Septimius Goring has a little darkie servant, so that we are rather a piebald community. The accountant, John Harton, promises to be an acquisition, for he is a cheery, amusing young fellow. Strange how little wealth has to do with happiness! He has all the world before him and is seeking his fortune in a far land, yet he is as transparently happy as a man can be. Goring is rich, if I am not mistaken, and so am I; but I know that I have a lung, and Goring has some deeper trouble still, to judge by his features. How poorly do we both contrast with the careless, penniless clerk!

October 17th.—Mrs. Tibbs appeared upon the deck for the first time this morning—a cheerful, energetic woman, with a dear little child just able to walk and prattle. Young Harton pounced on it at once, and carried it away to his cabin, where no doubt he will lay the seeds of future dyspepsia in the child's stomach. Thus medicine doth make cynics of us all! The weather is still all that could be desired, with a fine fresh breeze from the west-sou'-west. The vessel goes so steadily that you would hardly know that she was moving were it not for the creaking of the cordage, the bellying of the sails, and the long white furrow in our wake. Walked the quarter-deck all morning with the captain, and I think the keen fresh air has already done my breathing good, for the exercise did not fatigue me in any way. Tibbs is a remarkably intelligent man, and we had an interesting argument about Maury's observations on ocean currents, which we terminated by going down into his cabin to consult the original work. There we found Goring, rather to the captain's surprise, as it is not usual for passengers to enter that sanctum unless specially invited. He apologised for his intrusion, however, pleading his ignorance of the usages of ship life; and the good-natured sailor simply laughed at the incident, begging him to remain and favour us with his company. Goring pointed to the chronometers, the case of which he had opened, and remarked that he had been admiring them. He has evidently some practical knowledge of mathematical instruments, as he told at a glance which was the most trustworthy of the three, and also named their price within a few dollars. He had a discussion with the captain too upon the variation of the compass, and when we came back to the ocean currents he showed a thorough grasp of the subject. Altogether he rather improves upon acquaintance, and is a man of decided culture and refinement. His voice harmonises with his conversation, and both are the very antithesis of his face and figure.

The noonday observation shows that we have run two hundred and twenty miles. Towards evening the breeze freshened up, and the first mate ordered reefs to be taken in the topsails and top-gallant sails in expectation of a windy night. I observe that the barometer has fallen to twenty-nine. I trust our voyage will not be a rough one, as I am a poor sailor, and my health would probably derive more harm than good from a stormy trip, though I have the greatest confidence in the captain's seamanship and in the soundness of the vessel. Played cribbage with Mrs. Tibbs after supper, and Harton gave us a couple of tunes on the violin.

October 18th.—The gloomy prognostications of last night were not fulfilled, as the wind died away again and we are lying now in a long greasy swell, ruffled here, and there by a fleeting catspaw which is insufficient to fill the sails. The air is colder than it was yesterday, and I have put on one of the thick woollen jerseys which my wife knitted for me. Harton came into my cabin in the morning, and we had a cigar together. He says that he remembers having seen Goring in Cleveland, Ohio, in '69. He was, it appears, a mystery then as now, wandering about without any visible employment, and extremely reticent on his own affairs. The man interests me as a psychological study. At breakfast this morning I suddenly had that vague feeling of uneasiness which comes over some people when closely stared at, and, looking quickly up, I met his eyes bent upon me with an intensity which amounted to ferocity, though their expression instantly softened as he made some conventional remark upon the weather. Curiously enough, Harton says that he had a very similar experience yesterday upon deck. I observe that Goring frequently talks to the coloured seamen as he strolls about—a trait which I rather admire, as it is common to find half-breeds ignore their dark strain and treat their black kinsfolk with greater intolerance than a white man would do. His little page is devoted to him, apparently, which speaks well for his treatment of him. Altogether, the man is a curious mixture of incongruous qualities, and unless I am deceived in him will give me food for observation during the voyage.

The captain is grumbling about his chronometers,

which do not register exactly the same time. He says it is the first time that they have ever disagreed. We were unable to get a noonday observation on account of the haze. By dead reckoning, we have done about a hundred and seventy miles in the twenty-four hours. The dark seamen have proved, as the skipper prophesied, to be very inferior hands, but as they can both manage the wheel well they are kept steering, and so leave the more experienced men to work the ship. These details are trivial enough, but a small thing serves as food for gossip aboard ship. The appearance of a whale in the evening caused quite a flutter among us. From its sharp back and forked tail, I should pronounce it to have been a rorqual, or "finner," as they are called by the fishermen.

October 19th.—Wind was cold, so I prudently remained in my cabin all day, only creeping out for dinner. Lying in my bunk I can, without moving, reach my books, pipes, or anything else I may want, which is one advantage of a small apartment. My old wound began to ache a little to-day, probably from the cold. Read *Montaigne's Essays* and nursed myself. Harton came in in the afternoon with Doddy, the captain's child, and the skipper himself followed, so that I held quite a reception.

October 20th and 21st.—Still cold, with a continual drizzle of rain, and I have not been able to leave the cabin. This confinement makes me feel weak and depressed. Goring came in to see me, but his company did not tend to cheer me up much, as he hardly uttered a word, but contented himself with staring at me in a peculiar and rather irritating manner. He then got up and stole out of the cabin without saying anything. I am beginning to suspect that the man is a lunatic. I think I mentioned that his cabin is next to mine. The two are simply divided by a thin wooden partition which is cracked in many places, some of the cracks being so large that I can hardly avoid, as I lie in my bunk, observing his motions in the adjoining room. Without any wish to play the spy, I see him continually stooping over what appears to be a chart and working with a pencil and compasses. I have remarked the interest he displays in matters connected with navigation, but I am surprised that he should take the trouble to work out the course of the ship. However, it is a harmless amusement enough, and no doubt he verifies his results by those of the captain.

I wish the man did not run in my thoughts so much. I had a nightmare on the night of the 20th, in which I thought my bunk was a coffin, that I was laid out in it, and that Goring was endeavouring to nail up the lid, which I was frantically pushing away. Even when I woke up, I could hardly persuade myself that I was not in a coffin. As a medical man, I know that a nightmare is simply a vascular derangement of the cerebral hemispheres, and yet in my weak state I cannot shake off the morbid impression which it produces.

October 22nd.—A fine day, with hardly a cloud in the sky, and a fresh breeze from the sou'-west which wafts us gaily on our way. There has evidently been some heavy weather near us, as there is a tremendous swell on, and the ship lurches until the end of the fore-yard nearly touches the water. Had a refreshing walk up and down the quarter-deck, though I have hardly found my sea-legs yet. Several small birds—chaffinches, I think—perched in the rigging.

4.40 P.M.—While I was on deck this morning I heard a sudden explosion from the direction of my cabin, and, hurrying down, found that I had very nearly met with a serious accident. Goring was cleaning a revolver, it seems, in his cabin, when one of the barrels which he thought was unloaded went off. The ball passed through the side partition and imbedded itself in the bulwarks in the exact place where my head usually rests. I have been under fire too often to magnify trifles, but there is no doubt that if I had been in the bunk it must have killed me. Goring, poor fellow, did not know that I had gone on deck that day, and must therefore have felt terribly frightened. I never saw such emotion in a man's face as when, on rushing out of his cabin with the smoking pistol in his hand, he met me face to face as I came down from deck. Of course, he was profuse in his apologies, though I simply laughed at the incident.

11 P.M.—A misfortune has occurred so unexpected and so horrible that my little escape of the morning dwindles into insignificance. Mrs. Tibbs and her child have disappeared—utterly and entirely disappeared. I can hardly compose myself to write the sad details. About half-past eight Tibbs rushed into my cabin with a very white face and asked me if I had seen his wife. I answered that I had not. He then ran wildly into the saloon and began groping about for any trace of her, while I followed him, endeavouring vainly to persuade him that his fears were ridiculous. We hunted over the ship for an hour and a half without coming on any sign of the missing woman or child. Poor Tibbs lost his voice completely from calling her name. Even the sailors, who are generally stolid enough, were deeply affected by the sight of him as he roamed bareheaded and dishevelled about the deck, searching with feverish anxiety the most impossible places, and returning to them again and again with a piteous pertinacity. The last time she was seen was about seven o'clock, when she took Doddy on to the poop to give him a breath of fresh air before putting him to bed. There was no one there at the time except the black seaman at the wheel, who denies having seen her at all. The whole affair is wrapped in mystery. My own theory is that while Mrs. Tibbs was holding the child and standing near the bulwarks it gave a spring and fell overboard, and that in her convulsive attempt to catch or save it, she followed it. I cannot account for the double disappearance in any other way. It is quite feasible that such a tragedy should be enacted without the knowledge of the man at the wheel, since it was dark

at the time, and the peaked skylights of the saloon screen the greater part of the quarter-deck. Whatever the truth may be it is a terrible catastrophe, and has cast the darkest gloom upon our voyage. The mate has put the ship about, but of course there is not the slightest hope of picking them up. The captain is lying in a state of stupor in his cabin. I gave him a powerful dose of opium in his coffee that for a few hours at least his anguish may be deadened.

October 23rd.—Woke with a vague feeling of heaviness and misfortune, but it was not until a few moments' reflection that I was able to recall our loss of the night before. When I came on deck I saw the poor skipper standing gazing back at the waste of waters behind us which contains everything dear to him upon earth. I attempted to speak to him, but he turned brusquely away, and began pacing the deck with his head sunk upon his breast. Even now, when the truth is so clear, he cannot pass a boat or an unbent sail without peering under it. He looks ten years older than he did yesterday morning. Harton is terribly cut up, for he was fond of little Doddy, and Goring seems sorry too. At least he has shut himself up in his cabin all day, and when I got a casual glance at him his head was resting on his two hands as if in a melancholy reverie. I fear we are about as dismal a crew as ever sailed. How shocked my wife will be to hear of our disaster! The swell has gone down now, and we are doing about eight knots with all sail set and a nice little breeze. Hyson is practically in command of the ship, as Tibbs, though he does his best to bear up and keep a brave front, is incapable of applying himself to serious work.

October 24th.—Is the ship accursed? Was there ever a voyage which began so fairly and which changed so disastrously? Tibbs shot himself through the head during the night. I was awakened about three o'clock in the morning by an explosion, and immediately sprang out of bed and rushed into the captain's cabin to find out the cause, though with a terrible presentiment in my heart. Quickly as I went, Goring went more quickly still, for he was already in the cabin stooping over the dead body of the captain. It was a hideous sight, for the whole front of his face was blown in, and the little room was swimming in blood. The pistol was lying beside him on the floor, just as it had dropped from his hand. He had evidently put it to his mouth before pulling the trigger. Goring and I picked him reverently up and laid him on his bed. The crew had all clustered into his cabin, and the six white men were deeply grieved, for they were old hands who had sailed with him many years. There were dark looks and murmurs among them too, and one of them openly declared that the ship was haunted. Harton helped to lay the poor skipper out, and we did him up in canvas between us. At twelve o'clock the fore-yard was hauled aback, and we committed his body to the deep, Goring reading the Church of England burial service. The breeze has freshened up, and we have done ten knots all day and sometimes twelve. The sooner we reach Lisbon and get away from this accursed ship the better pleased shall I be. I feel as though we were in a floating coffin. Little wonder that the poor sailors are superstitious when I, an educated man, feel it so strongly.

October 25th.—Made a good run all day. Feel listless and depressed.

October 26th.—Goring, Harton, and I had a chat together on deck in the morning. Harton tried to draw Goring out as to his profession, and his object in going to Europe, but the quadroon parried all his questions and gave us no information. Indeed, he seemed to be slightly offended by Harton's pertinacity, and went down into his cabin. I wonder why we should both take such an interest in this man! I suppose it is his striking appearance, coupled with his apparent wealth, which piques our curiosity. Harton has a theory that he is really a detective, that he is after some criminal who has got away to Portugal, and that he chooses this peculiar way of travelling that he may arrive unnoticed and pounce upon his quarry unawares. I think the supposition is rather a far-fetched one, but Harton bases it upon a book which Goring left on deck, and which he picked up and glanced over. It was a sort of scrap-book, it seems, and contained a large number of newspaper cuttings. All these cuttings related to murders which had been committed at various times in the States during the last twenty years or so. The curious thing which Harton observed about them, however, was that they were invariably murders the authors of which had never been brought to justice. They varied in every detail, he says, as to the manner of execution and the social status of the victim, but they uniformly wound up with the same formula that the murderer was still at large, though, of course, the police had every reason to expect his speedy capture. Certainly the incident seems to support Harton's theory, though it may be a mere whim of Goring's, or, as I suggested to Harton, he may be collecting materials for a book which shall outvie De Quincy. In any case it is no business of ours.

October 27th, 28th.—Wind still fair, and we are making good progress. Strange how easily a human unit may drop out of its place and be forgotten! Tibbs is hardly ever mentioned now; Hyson has taken possession of his cabin, and all goes on as before. Were it not for Mrs. Tibbs's sewing-machine upon a side-table we might forget that the unfortunate family had ever existed. Another accident occurred on board to-day, though fortunately not a very serious one. One of our white hands had gone down the afterhold to fetch up a spare coil of rope, when one of the hatches which he had removed came crashing down on the top of him. He saved his life by springing out of the way, but one of his feet was terribly crushed, and he will be of little use for the remainder of the voyage. He attributes the accident to the carelessness of his negro companion, who had helped him to shift the hatches. The latter, however, puts it down to the roll of the ship. Whatever be the cause, it reduces our short-handed crew still further. This run of ill-luck seems to be depressing Harton, for he has lost his usual good spirits and joviality. Goring is the only one who preserves his cheerfulness. I see him still working at his chart in his own cabin. His nautical knowledge would be useful should anything happen to Hyson—which God forbid!

October 29th, 30th.—Still bowling along with a fresh breeze. All quiet and nothing of note to chronicle.

October 31st.—My weak lungs, combined with the exciting episodes of the voyage, have shaken my nervous system so much that the most trivial incident affects me. I can hardly believe that I am the same man who tied the external iliac artery, an operation requiring the nicest precision, under a heavy rifle fire at Antietam. I am as nervous as a child. I was lying half dozing last night about four bells in the middle watch trying in vain to drop into a refreshing sleep. There was no light inside my cabin, but a single ray of moonlight streamed in through the port-hole, throwing a silvery flickering circle upon the door. As I lay I kept my drowsy eyes upon this circle, and was conscious that it was gradually becoming less well-defined as my senses left me, when I was suddenly recalled to full wakefulness by the appearance of a small dark object in the very centre of the luminous disc. I lay quietly and breathlessly watching it. Gradually it grew larger and plainer, and then I perceived that it was a human hand which had been cautiously inserted through the chink of the half-closed door—a hand which, as I observed with a thrill of horror, was not provided with fingers. The door swung cautiously backwards, and Goring's head followed his hand. It appeared in the centre of the moonlight, and was framed as it were in a ghastly uncertain halo, against which his features showed out plainly. It seemed to me that I had never seen such an utterly fiendish and merciless expression upon a human face. His eyes were dilated and glaring, his lips drawn back so as to show his white fangs, and his straight black hair appeared to bristle over his low forehead like the hood of a cobra. The sudden and noiseless apparition had such an effect upon me that I sprang up in bed trembling in every limb, and held out my hand towards my revolver. I was heartily ashamed of my hastiness when he explained the object of his intrusion, as he immediately did in the most courteous language. He had been suffering from toothache, poor fellow! and had come in to beg some laudanum, knowing that I possessed a medicine chest. As to a sinister expression he is never a beauty, and what with my state of nervous tension and the effect of the shifting moonlight it was easy to conjure up something horrible. I gave him twenty drops. and he went off again, with many expressions of gratitude. I can hardly say how much this trivial incident affected me. I have felt unstrung all day.

A week's record of our voyage is here omitted, as nothing eventful occurred during the time, and my log consists merely of a few pages of unimportant gossip.

November 7th.—Harton and I sat on the poop all the morning, for the weather is becoming very warm as we come into southern latitudes. We reckon that we have done two-thirds of our voyage. How glad we shall be to see the green banks of the Tagus, and leave this unlucky ship for ever! I was endeavouring to amuse Harton to-day and to while away the time by telling him some of the experiences of my past life. Among others I related to him how I came into the possession of my black stone, and as a finale I rummaged in the side pocket of my old shooting coat and produced the identical object in question. He and I were bending over it together, I pointing out to him the curious ridges upon its surface, when we were conscious of a shadow falling between us and the sun, and looking round saw Goring standing behind us glaring over our shoulders at the stone. For some reason or other he appeared to be powerfully excited, though he was evidently trying to control himself and to conceal his emotion. He pointed once or twice at my relic with his stubby thumb before he could recover himself sufficiently to ask what it was and how I obtained it—a question put in such a brusque manner that I should have been offended had I not known the man to be an eccentric. I told him the story very much as I had told it to Harton. He listened with the deepest interest and then asked me if I had any idea what the stone was. I said I had not, beyond that it was meteoric. He asked me if I had ever tried its effect upon a negro. I said I had not. "Come," said he, "we'll see what our black friend at the wheel thinks of it." He took the stone in his hand and went across to the sailor, and the two examined it carefully. I could see the man gesticulating and nodding his head excitedly as if making some assertion, while his face betrayed the utmost astonishment, mixed, I think, with some reverence. Goring came across the deck to us presently, still holding the stone in his hand. "He says it is a worthless, useless thing," he said, "and fit only to be chucked overboard," with which he raised his hand and would most certainly have made an end of my relic, had the black sailor behind him not rushed forward and seized him by the wrist. Finding himself secured Goring dropped the stone and turned away with a very bad grace to avoid my angry remonstrances at his breach of faith. The black picked up the stone and handed it to me with a low bow and every sign of profound respect. The whole affair is inexplicable. I am rapidly coming to the conclusion that Goring is a maniac or something very near one. When I compare the effect produced by the stone upon the sailor, however, with the respect shown to Martha on the plantation, and the surprise of Goring on its first production, I cannot but come to the conclusion that I have really got hold of some powerful talisman which appeals to the whole dark race. I must not trust it in Goring's hands again.

November 8th, 9th.—What splendid weather we are having! Beyond one little blow, we have had nothing but fresh breezes the whole voyage. These two days we have made better runs than any hitherto. It is a pretty thing to watch the spray fly up from our prow as it cuts through the waves. The sun shines through it and breaks it up into a number of miniature rainbows —" sun-dogs," the sailors call them. I stood on the fo'c'sle-head for several hours to-day watching the effect, and surrounded by a halo of prismatic colours. The steersman has evidently told the other blacks about my wonderful stone, for I am treated by them all with the greatest respect. Talking about optical phenomena, we had a curious one yesterday evening which was pointed out to me by Hyson. This was the appearance of a triangular well-defined object high up in the heavens to the north of us. He explained that it was exactly like the Peak of Teneriffe as seen from a great distance —the peak was, however, at that moment at least five hundred miles to the south. It may have been a cloud, or it may have been one of those strange reflections of which one reads. The weather is very warm. The mate says that he never knew it so warm in these latitudes. Played chess with Harton in the evening.

November 10th.—It is getting warmer and warmer. Some land birds came and perched in the rigging to-day, though we are still a considerable way from our destination. The heat is so great that we are too lazy to do anything but lounge about the decks and smoke. Goring came over to me to-day and asked me some more questions about my stone; but I answered him rather shortly, for I have not quite forgiven him yet for the cool way in which he attempted to deprive me of it.

November 11th, 12th.—Still making good progress. I had no idea Portugal was ever as hot as this, but no doubt it is cooler on land. Hyson himself seemed surprised at it, and so do the men.

November 13th.—A most extraordinary event has happened, so extraordinary as to be almost inexplicable. Either Hyson has blundered wonderfully, or some magnetic influence has disturbed our instruments. Just about daybreak the watch on the fo'c'sle-head shouted out that he heard the sound of surf ahead, and Hyson thought he saw the loom of land. The ship was put about, and, though no lights were seen, none of us doubted that we had struck the Portuguese coast a little sooner than we had expected. What was our surprise to see the scene which was revealed to us at break of day! As far as we could look on either side was one long line of surf, great, green billows rolling in and breaking into a cloud of foam. But behind the surf what was there! Not the green banks nor the high cliffs of the shores of Portugal, but a great sandy waste which stretched away and away until it blended with the skyline. To right and left, look where you would, there was nothing but yellow sand, heaped in some places into fantastic mounds, some of them several hundred feet high, while in other parts were long stretches as level apparently as a billiard board. Harton and I, who had come on deck together, looked at each other in astonishment, and Harton burst out laughing. Hyson is exceedingly mortified at the occurrence, and protests that the instruments have been tampered with. There is no doubt that this is the mainland of Africa, and that it was really the Peak of Teneriffe which we saw some days ago upon the northern horizon. At the time when we saw the land birds we must have been passing some of the Canary Islands. If we continued on the same course, we are now to the north of Cape Blanco, near the unexplored country which skirts the great Sahara. All we can do is to rectify our instruments as far as possible and start afresh for our destination.

8.30 P.M.—Have been lying in a calm all day. The

coast is now about a mile and a half from us. Hyson has examined the instruments, but cannot find any reason for their extraordinary deviation.

This is the end of my private journal, and I must make the remainder of my statement from memory. There is little chance of my being mistaken about facts, which have seared themselves into my recollection. That very night the storm which had been brewing so long burst over us, and I came to learn whither all those little incidents were tending which I had recorded so aimlessly. Blind fool that I was not to have seen it sooner! I shall tell what occurred as precisely as I can.

I had gone into my cabin about half-past eleven, and was preparing to go to bed, when a tap came at my door. On opening it I saw Goring's little black page, who told me that his master would like to have a word with me on deck. I was rather surprised that he should want me at such a late hour, but I went up without hesitation. I had hardly put my foot on the quarter-deck before I was seized from behind, dragged down upon my back, and a handkerchief slipped round my mouth. I struggled as hard as I could, but a coil of rope was rapidly and firmly wound round me, and I found myself lashed to the davit of one of the boats, utterly powerless to do or say anything, while the point of a knife pressed to my throat warned me to cease my struggles. The night was so dark that I had been unable hitherto to recognize my assailants, but as my eyes became accustomed to the gloom, and the moon broke out through the clouds that obscured it, I made out that I was surrounded by the two negro sailors, the black cook, and my fellow-passenger, Goring. Another man was crouching on the deck at my feet, but he was in the shadow and I could not recognize him.

All this occurred so rapidly that a minute could hardly have elapsed from the time I mounted the companion until I found myself gagged and powerless. It was so sudden that I could scarce bring myself to realize it, or to comprehend what it all meant. I heard the gang round me speaking in short, fierce whispers to each other, and some instinct told me that my life was the question at issue. Goring spoke authoritatively and angrily—the others doggedly and all together, as if disputing his commands. Then they moved away in a body to the opposite side of the deck, where I could still hear them whispering, though they were concealed from my view by the saloon skylights.

All this time the voices of the watch on deck chatting and laughing at the other end of the ship were distinctly audible, and I could see them gathered in a group, little dreaming of the dark doings which were going on within thirty yards of them. Oh! That I could have given them one word of warning, even though I had lost my life in doing it! but it was impossible. The moon was shining fitfully through the scattered clouds, and I could see the silvery gleam of the surge, and beyond it the vast weird desert with its fantastic sand-hills. Glancing down, I saw that the man who had been crouching on the deck was still lying there, and as I gazed at him a flickering ray of moonlight fell full upon his upturned face. Great heaven! even now, when more than twelve years have elapsed, my hand trembles as I write that, in spite of distorted features and projecting eyes, I recognized the face of Harton, the cheery young clerk who had been my companion during the voyage. It needed no medical eye to see that he was quite dead, while the twisted handkerchief round the neck, and the gag in his mouth, showed the silent way in which the hell-hounds had done their work. The clue which explained every event of our voyage came upon me like a flash of light as I gazed on poor Harton's corpse. Much was dark and unexplained, but I felt a great dim perception of the truth.

I heard the striking of a match at the other side of the skylights, and then I saw the tall, gaunt figure of

Goring standing up on the bulwarks and holding in his hands what appeared to be a dark lantern. He lowered this for a moment over the side of the ship, and, to my inexpressible astonishment, I saw it answered instantaneously by a flash among the sand-hills on shore, which came and went so rapidly, that unless I had been following the direction of Goring's gaze, I should never have detected it. Again he lowered the lantern, and again it was answered from the shore. He then stepped down from the bulwarks, and in doing so slipped, making such a noise, that for a moment my heart bounded with the thought that the attention of the watch would be directed to his proceedings. It was a vain hope. The night was calm and the ship motionless, so that no idea of duty kept them vigilant. Hyson, who after the death of Tibbs was in command of both watches, had gone below to snatch a few hours' sleep, and the boatswain, who was left in charge, was standing with the other two men at the foot of the foremast. Powerless, speechless, with the cords cutting into my flesh and the murdered man at my feet, I awaited the next act in the tragedy.

The four ruffians were standing up now at the other side of the deck. The cook was armed with some sort of a cleaver, the others had knives, and Goring had a revolver. They were all leaning against the rail and looking out over the water as if watching for something. I saw one of them grasp another's arm and point as if at some object, and following the direction I made out the loom of a large moving mass making towards the ship. As it emerged from the gloom I saw that it was a great canoe crammed with men and propelled by at least a score of paddles. As it shot under our stern the watch caught sight of it also, and raising a cry hurried aft. They were too late, however. A swarm of gigantic negroes clambered over the quarter, and led by Goring swept down the deck in an irresistible torrent. All opposition was overpowered in a moment, the unarmed watch were knocked over and bound, and the sleepers dragged out of their bunks and secured in the same manner. Hyson made an attempt to defend the narrow passage leading to his cabin, and I heard a scuffle, and his voice shouting for assistance. There was none to assist, however, and he was brought on to the poop with the blood streaming from a deep cut in his forehead. He was gagged like the others, and a council was held upon our fate by the negroes. I saw our black seamen pointing towards me and making some statement, which was received with murmurs of astonishment and incredulity by the savages. One of them then came over to me, and plunging his hand into my pocket took out my black stone and held it up. He then handed it to a man who appeared to be a chief, who examined it as minutely as the light would permit, and muttering a few words passed it on to the warrior beside him, who also scrutinized it and passed it on until it had gone from hand to hand round the whole circle. The chief then said a few words to Goring in the native tongue, on which the quadroon addressed me in English. At this moment I seem to see the scene. The tall masts of the ship with the moonlight streaming down, silvering the yards and bringing the network of cordage into hard relief; the group of dusky warriors leaning on their spears; the dead man at my feet; the line of white-faced prisoners, and in front of me the loathsome half-breed, looking in his white linen and elegant clothes a strange contrast to his associates.

"You will bear me witness," he said in his softest accents, "that I am no party to sparing your life. If it rested with me you would die as these other men are about to do. I have no personal grudge against either you or them, but I have devoted my life to the destruction of the white race, and you are the first that has ever been in my power and has escaped me. You may thank that stone of yours for your life. These poor fellows reverence it, and indeed if it really be what they think it is they have cause. Should it prove when we get ashore that they are mistaken, and that its shape and material is a mere chance, nothing can save your life. In the meantime we wish to treat you well, so if there are any of your possessions which you would like to take with you, you are at liberty to get them." As he finished he gave a sign, and a couple of the negroes unbound me, though without removing the gag. I was led down into the cabin, where I put a few valuables into my pockets, together with a pocket-compass and my journal of the voyage. They then pushed me over the side into a small canoe, which was lying beside the large one, and my guards followed me, and shoving off began paddling for the shore. We had got about a hundred yards or so from the ship when our steersman held up his hand, and the paddlers paused for a moment and listened. Then on the silence of the night I heard a sort of dull, moaning sound, followed by a succession of splashes in the water. That is all I know of the fate of my poor shipmates. Almost immediately afterwards the large canoe followed us, and the deserted ship was left drifting about—a dreary spectre-like hulk. Nothing was taken from her by the savages. The whole fiendish transaction was carried through as decorously and temperately as though it were a religious rite.

The first grey of daylight was visible in the east as we passed through the surge and reached the shore. Leaving half a dozen men with the canoes, the rest of the negroes set off through the sand-hills, leading me with them, but treating me very gently and respectfully. It was difficult walking, as we sank over our ankles into the loose, shifting sand at every step, and I was nearlv dead beat by the time we reached the native village, or town rather, for it was a place of considerable dimensions. The houses were conical structures not unlike bee-hives, and were made of compressed seaweed cemented over with a rude form of mortar, there being neither stick nor stone upon the coast nor anywhere within many hundreds of miles. As we entered the town an enormous crowd of both sexes came swarming out to meet us, beating tom-toms and howling and screaming. On seeing me they redoubled their yells and assumed a threatening attitude, which was instantly quelled by a few words shouted by my escort. A buzz of wonder succeeded the war-cries and yells of the moment before, and the whole dense mass proceeded down the broad central street of the town, having my escort and myself in the centre.

My statement hitherto may seem so strange as to excite doubt in the minds of those who do not know me, but it was the fact which I am now about to relate which caused my own brother-in-law to insult me by disbelief. I can but relate the occurrence in the simplest words, and trust to chance and time to prove their truth. In the centre of this main street there was a large building, formed in the same primitive way as the others, but towering high above them; a stockade of beautifully polished ebony rails was planted all round it, the framework of the door was formed by two magnificent elephant's tusks sunk in the ground on each side and meeting at the top, and the aperture was closed by a screen of native cloth richly embroidered with gold. We made our way to this imposing-looking structure, but on reaching the opening in the stockade, the multitude stopped and squatted down upon their hams, while I was led through into the enclosure by a few of the chiefs and elders of the tribe, Goring accompanying us, and in fact directing the proceedings. On reaching the screen which closed the temple—for such it evidently was—my hat and my shoes were removed, and I was then led in, a venerable old negro leading the way carrying in his hand my stone, which had been taken from my pocket. The building was only lit up by a few long slits in the roof, through which the tropical sun poured, throwing broad golden bars upon the clay floor, alternating with intervals of darkness.

The interior was even larger than one would have imagined from the outside appearance. The walls were hung with native mats, shells, and other ornaments, but the remainder of the great space was quite empty, with the exception of a single object in the centre. This was the figure of a colossal negro, which I at first thought to be some real king or high priest of titanic size, but as I approached it I saw by the way in which the light was reflected from it that it was a statue admirably cut in jet-black stone. I was led up to this idol, for such it seemed to be, and looking at it closer I saw that though it was perfect in every other respect, one of its ears had been broken short off. The grey-haired negro who held my relic mounted upon a small stool, and stretching up his arm fitted Martha's black stone on to the jagged surface on the side of the statue's head. There could not be a doubt that the one had been broken off from the other. The parts dovetailed together so accurately that when the old man removed his hand the ear stuck in its place for a few seconds before dropping into his open palm. The group round me prostrated themselves upon the ground at the sight with a cry of reverence, while the crowd outside, to whom the result was communicated, set up a wild whooping and cheering.

In a moment I found myself converted from a prisoner into a demi-god. I was escorted back through the town in triumph, the people pressing forward to touch my clothing and to gather up the dust on which my foot had trod. One of the largest huts was put at my disposal, and a banquet of every native delicacy was served me. I still felt, however, that I was not a free man, as several spearmen were placed as a guard at the entrance of my hut. All day my mind was occupied with plans of escape, but none seemed in any way feasible. On the one side was the great arid desert stretching away to Timbuctoo, on the other was a sea untraversed by vessels. The more I pondered over the problem the more hopeless did it seem. I little dreamed how near I was to its solution.

Night had fallen, and the clamour of the negroes had died gradually away. I was stretched on the couch of skins which had been provided for me, and was still meditating over my future, when Goring walked stealthily into the hut. My first idea was that he had come to complete his murderous holocaust by making away with me, the last survivor, and I sprang up upon my feet, determined to defend myself to the last. He smiled when he saw the action, and motioned me down again while he seated himself upon the other end of the couch.

"What do you think of me?" was the astonishing question with which he commenced our conversation.

"Think of you!" I almost yelled. "I think you the vilest, most unnatural renegade that ever polluted the earth. If we were away from these black devils of yours I would strangle you with my hands!"

"Don't speak so loud," he said, without the slightest appearance of irritation. "I don't want our chat to be cut short. So you would strangle me, would you!" he went on, with an amused smile. "I suppose I am returning good for evil, for I have come to help you to escape."

"You!" I gasped incredulously.

"Yes, I," he continued. "Oh, there is no credit to me in the matter. I am quite consistent. There is no reason why I should not be perfectly candid with you. I wish to be king over these fellows—not a very high ambition, certainly, but you know what Cæsar said about being first in a village in Gaul. Well, this unlucky stone of yours has not only saved your life, but has turned all their heads so that they think you are come down from heaven, and my influence will be gone until you are out of the way. That is why I am going to help you to escape, since I cannot kill you"—this in the most natural and dulcet voice, as if the desire to do so were a matter of course.

"You would give the world to ask me a few questions,"

he went on, after a pause ; " but you are too proud to do it. Never mind, I'll tell you one or two things, because I want your fellow white men to know them when you go back—if you are lucky enough to get back. About that cursed stone of yours, for instance. These negroes, or at least so the legend goes, were Mahometans originally. While Mahomet himself was still alive, there was a schism among his followers, and the smaller party moved away from Arabia, and eventually crossed Africa. They took away with them, in their exile, a valuable relic of their old faith in the shape of a large piece of the black stone of Mecca. The stone was a meteoric one, as you may have heard, and in its fall upon the earth it broke into two pieces. One of these pieces is still at Mecca. The larger piece was carried away to Barbary, where a skilful worker modelled it into the fashion which you saw to-day. These men are the descendants of the original seceders from Mahomet, and they have brought their relic safely through all their wanderings until they settled in this strange place, where the desert protects them from their enemies."

"And the ear ? " I asked, almost involuntarily.

"Oh, that was the same story over again. Some of the tribe wandered away to the south a few hundred years ago, and one of them, wishing to have good luck for the enterprise, got into the temple at night and carried off one of the ears. There has been a tradition among the negroes ever since that the ear would come back some day. The fellow who carried it was caught by some slaver, no doubt, and that was how it got into America, and so into your hands—and you have had the honour of fulfilling the prophecy."

He paused for a few minutes, resting his head upon his hands, waiting apparently for me to speak. When he looked up again, the whole expression of his face had changed. His features were firm and set, and he changed the air of half-levity with which he had spoken before for one of sternness and almost ferocity.

"I wish you to carry a message back," he said, "to the white race, the great dominating race whom I hate and defy. Tell them that I have battened on their blood for twenty years, that I have slain them until even I became tired of what had once been a joy, that I did this unnoticed and unsuspected in the face of every precaution which their civilization could suggest. There is no satisfaction in revenge when your enemy does not know who has struck him. I am not sorry, therefore, to have you as a messenger. There is no need why I should tell you how this great hate became born in me. See this," and he held up his mutilated hand; "that was done by a white man's knife. My father was white, my mother was a slave. When he died she was sold again, and I, a child then, saw her lashed to death to break her of some of the little airs and graces which her late master had encouraged in her. My young wife, too, oh, my young wife!" a shudder ran through his whole frame. "No matter! I swore my oath, and I kept it. From Maine to Florida, and from Boston to San Francisco, you could track my steps by sudden deaths which baffled the police. I warred against the whole white race as they for centuries had warred against the black one. At last, as I tell you, I sickened of blood. Still, the sight of a white face was abhorrent to me, and I determined to find some bold free black people and to throw in my lot with them, to cultivate their latent powers and to form a nucleus for a great coloured nation. This idea possessed me, and I travelled over the world for two years seeking for what I desired. At last I almost despaired of finding it. There was no hope of regeneration in the slave-dealing Soudanese, the debased Fantee, or the Americanized negroes of Liberia. I was returning from my quest when chance brought me in contact with this magnificent tribe of dwellers in the desert, and I threw in my lot with them. Before doing so, however, my old instinct of revenge prompted me to make one last visit to the United States, and I returned from it in the *Marie Celeste*.

"As to the voyage itself, your intelligence will have told you by this time that, thanks to my manipulation, both compasses and chronometers were entirely untrustworthy. I alone worked out the course with correct instruments of my own, while the steering was done by my black friends under my guidance. I pushed Tibbs's wife overboard. What! You look surprised and shrink away. Surely you had guessed that by this time. I would have shot you that day through the partition, but unfortunately you were not there. I tried again afterwards, but you were awake. I shot Tibbs. I think the idea of suicide was carried out rather neatly. Of course when once we got on the coast the rest was simple. I had bargained that all on board should die; but that stone of yours upset my plans. I also bargained that there should be no plunder. No one can say we are pirates. We have acted from principle, not from any sordid motive."

I listened in amazement to the summary of his crimes which this strange man gave me, all in the quietest and most composed of voices, as though detailing incidents of every-day occurrence. I still seem to see him sitting like a hideous nightmare at the end of my couch, with the single rude lamp flickering over his cadaverous features.

"And now," he continued, "there is no difficulty about your escape. These stupid adopted children of mine will say that you have gone back to heaven from whence you came. The wind blows off the land. I have a boat all ready for you, well stored with provisions and water. I am anxious to be rid of you, so you may rely that nothing is neglected. Rise up and follow me."

I did what he commanded, and he led me through the door of the hut. The guards had either been withdrawn, or Goring had arranged matters with them. We passed unchallenged through the town and across the sandy plain. Once more I heard the roar of the sea, and saw the long white line of the surge. Two figures were standing upon the shore arranging the gear of a small boat. They were the two sailors who had been with us on the voyage.

"See him safely through the surf," said Goring. The two men sprang in and pushed off, pulling me in after them. With mainsail and jib we ran out from the land and passed safely over the bar. Then my two companions without a word of farewell sprang overboard, and I saw their heads like black dots on the white foam as they made their way back to the shore, while I scudded away into the blackness of the night. Looking back I caught my last glimpse of Goring. He was standing upon the summit of a sand-hill, and the rising moon behind him threw his gaunt angular figure into hard relief. He was waving his arms frantically to and fro; it may have been to encourage me on my way, but the gestures seemed to me at the time to be threatening ones, and I have often thought that it was more likely that his old savage instinct had returned when he realized that I was out of his power. Be that as it may, it was the last that I ever saw or ever shall see of Septimius Goring.

There is no need for me to dwell upon my solitary voyage. I steered as well as I could for the Canaries, but was picked up upon the fifth day by the British and African Steam Navigation Company's boat *Monrovia*. Let me take this opportunity of tendering my sincerest thanks to Captain Stornoway and his officers for the great kindness which they showed me from that time till they landed me in Liverpool, where I was enabled to take one of the Guion boats to New York.

From the day on which I found myself once more in the bosom of my family I have said little of what I have undergone. The subject is still an intensely painful one to me, and the little which I have dropped has been discredited. I now put the facts before the public as they occurred, careless how far they may be believed, and simply writing them down because my lung is growing weaker, and I feel the responsibility of holding my peace longer. I make no vague statement. Turn to your map of Africa. There above Cape Blanco, where the land trends away north and south from the westernmost point of the continent, there it is that Septimius Goring still reigns over his dark subjects, unless retribution has overtaken him ; and there, where the long green ridges run swiftly in to roar and hiss upon the hot yellow sand, it is there that Harton lies with Hyson and the other poor fellows who were done to death in the *Marie Celeste*.

24. *That Little Square Box*

"ALL aboard ?" said the captain.

"All aboard, sir !" said the mate.

"Then stand by to let her go."

It was nine o'clock on a Wednesday morning. The good ship *Spartan* was lying off Boston Quay with her cargo under hatches, her passengers shipped, and everything prepared for a start. The warning whistle had been sounded twice ; the final bell had been rung. Her bowsprit was turned towards England, and the hiss of escaping steam showed that all was ready for her run of three thousand miles. She strained at the warps that held her like a greyhound at its leash.

I have the misfortune to be a very nervous man. A sedentary literary life has helped to increase the morbid love of solitude which, even in my boyhood, was one of my distinguishing characteristics. As I stood upon the quarter-deck of the Transatlantic steamer, I bitterly cursed the necessity which drove me back to the land of my forefathers. The shouts of the sailors, the rattle of the cordage, the farewells of my fellow-passengers, and the cheers of the mob, each and all jarred upon my sensitive nature. I felt sad too. An indescribable feeling, as of some impending calamity, seemed to haunt me. The sea was calm, and the breeze light. There was nothing to disturb the equanimity of the most confirmed of landsmen, yet I felt as if I stood upon the verge of a great though indefinable danger. I have noticed that such presentiments occur often in men of my peculiar temperament, and that they are not uncommonly fulfilled. There is a theory that it arises from a species of second-sight, a subtle spiritual communication with the future. I well remember that Herr Raumer, the eminent spiritualist, remarked on one occasion that I was the most sensitive subject as regards supernatural phenomena that he had ever encountered in the whole of his wide experience. Be that as it may, I certainly felt far from happy as I threaded my way among the weeping, cheering groups which dotted the white decks of the good ship *Spartan*. Had I known the experience which awaited me in the course of the next twelve hours I should even then at the last moment have sprung upon the shore, and made my escape from the accursed vessel.

"Time's up!" said the captain, closing his chronometer with a snap, and replacing it in his pocket. "Time's up!" said the mate. There was a last wail from the whistle, a rush of friends and relatives upon the land. One warp was loosened, the gangway was being pushed away, when there was a shout from the bridge, and two men appeared, running rapidly down the quay. They were waving their hands and making frantic gestures, apparently with the intention of stopping the ship. "Look sharp!" shouted the crowd. "Hold hard!" cried the captain. "Ease her! stop her! Up with the gangway!" and the two men sprang aboard just as the second warp parted, and a convulsive throb of the engine shot us clear of the shore. There was a cheer from the deck, another from the quay, a mighty fluttering of handkerchiefs, and the great vessel ploughed its way out of the harbour, and steamed grandly away across the placid bay.

We were fairly started upon our fortnight's voyage. There was a general dive among the passengers in quest of berths and luggage, while a popping of corks in the saloon proved that more than one bereaved traveller was adopting artificial means for drowning the pangs of separation. I glanced round the deck and took a running inventory of my *compagnons de voyage*. They presented the usual types met with upon these occasions. There was no striking face among them. I speak as a connoisseur, for faces are a speciality of mine. I pounce upon a characteristic feature as a botanist does on a flower, and bear it away with me to analyse at my leisure, and classify and label it in my little anthropological museum. There was nothing worthy of me here. Twenty types of young America going to "Yurrup," a few respectable middle-aged couples as an antidote, a sprinkling of clergymen and professional men, young ladies, bagmen, British exclusives, and all the *olla podrida* of an ocean-going steamer. I turned away from them and gazed back at the receding shores of America, and, as a cloud of remembrances rose before me, my heart warmed towards the land of my adoption. A pile of portmanteaux and luggage chanced to be lying on one side of the deck, awaiting their turn to be taken below. With my usual love for solitude I walked behind these, and sitting on a coil of rope between them and the vessel's side, I indulged in a melancholy reverie.

I was aroused from this by a whisper behind me. "Here's a quiet place," said the voice. "Sit down, and we can talk it over in safety."

Glancing through a chink between two colossal chests, I saw that the passengers who had joined us at the last moment were standing at the other side of the pile. They had evidently failed to see me as I crouched in the shadow of the boxes. The one who had spoken was a tall and very thin man with a blue-black beard and a colourless face. His manner was nervous and excited. His companion was a short plethoric little fellow, with a brisk and resolute air. He had a cigar in his mouth, and a large ulster slung over his left arm. They both glanced round uneasily, as if to ascertain whether they were alone. "This is just the place," I heard the other say. They sat down on a bale of goods with their backs turned towards me, and I found myself, much against my will, playing the unpleasant part of eavesdropper to their conversation.

"Well, Muller," said the taller of the two, "we've got it aboard right enough."

"Yes," assented the man whom he had addressed as Muller, "it's safe aboard."

"It was rather a near go."

"It was that, Flannigan."

"It wouldn't have done to have missed the ship."

"No, it would have put our plans out."

"Ruined them entirely," said the little man, and puffed furiously at his cigar for some minutes.

"I've got it here," he said at last.

"Let me see it."

"Is no one looking?"

"No, they are nearly all below."

"We can't be too careful where so much is at stake," said Muller, as he uncoiled the ulster which hung over his arm, and disclosed a dark object which he laid upon the deck. One glance at it was enough to cause me to spring to my feet with an exclamation of horror. Luckily they were so engrossed in the matter on hand that neither of them observed me. Had they turned their heads they would infallibly have seen my pale face glaring at them over the pile of boxes.

From the first moment of their conversation a horrible misgiving had come over me. It seemed more than confirmed as I gazed at what lay before me. It was a little square box made of some dark wood, and ribbed with brass. I suppose it was about the size of a cubic foot. It reminded me of a pistol-case, only it was decidedly higher. There was an appendage to it, however, on which my eyes were riveted, and which suggested the pistol itself rather than its receptacle. This was a trigger-like arrangement upon the lid, to which a coil of string was attached. Beside this trigger there was a small square aperture through the wood. The tall man, Flannigan, as his companion called him, applied his eye to this; and peered in for several minutes with an expression of intense anxiety upon his face.

"It seems right enough," he said at last.

"I tried not to shake it," said his companion.

"Such delicate things need delicate treatment. Put in some of the needful, Muller."

The shorter man fumbled in his pocket for some time, and then produced a small paper packet. He opened this, and took out of it half a handful of whitish granules, which he poured down through the hole. A curious clicking noise followed from the inside of the box, and both men smiled in a satisfied way.

"Nothing much wrong there," said Flannigan.

"Right as a trivet," answered his companion.

"Look out! here's someone coming. Take it down to our berth. It wouldn't do to have anyone suspecting what our game is, or, worse still, have them fumbling with it, and letting it off by mistake."

"Well, it would come to the same, whoever let it off," said Muller.

"They'd be rather astonished if they pulled the trigger," said the taller, with a sinister laugh. "Ha, ha! fancy their faces! It's not a bad bit of workmanship, I flatter myself."

"No," said Muller. "I hear it is your own design, every bit of it, isn't it?"

"Yes, the spring and the sliding shutter are my own."

"We should take out a patent."

And the two men laughed again with a cold harsh

laugh, as they took up the little brass-bound package, and concealed it in Muller's voluminous overcoat.

"Come down, and we'll stow it in our berth," said, Flannigan. "We won't need it until to-night and it will be safe there."

His companion assented, and the two went arm-in-arm along the deck and disappeared down the hatchway, bearing the mysterious little box away with them. The last words I heard were a muttered injunction from Flannigan to carry it carefully, and avoid knocking it against the bulwarks.

How long I remained sitting on that coil of rope I shall never know. The horror of the conversation I had just overheard was aggravated by the first sinking qualms of sea-sickness. The long roll of the Atlantic was beginning to assert itself over both ship and passengers. I felt prostrated in mind and in body, and fell into a state of collapse, from which I was finally aroused by the hearty voice of our worthy quartermaster.

"Do you mind moving out of that, sir?" he said. "We want to get this lumber cleared off the deck."

His bluff manner and ruddy healthy face seemed to be a positive insult to me in my present condition. Had I been a courageous or a muscular man I could have struck him. As it was, I treated the honest sailor to a melodramatic scowl which seemed to cause him no small astonishment, and strode past him to the other side of the deck. Solitude was what I wanted—solitude in which I could brood over the frightful crime which was being hatched before my very eyes. One of the quarter-boats was hanging rather low down upon the davits. An idea struck me, and climbing on the bulwarks, I stepped into the empty boat and lay down in the bottom of it. Stretched on my back, with nothing but the blue sky above me, and an occasional view of the mizen as the vessel rolled, I was at least alone with my sickness and my thoughts.

I tried to recall the words which had been spoken

in the terrible dialogue I had overheard. Would they admit of any construction but the one which stared me in the face? My reason forced me to confess that they would not. I endeavoured to array the various facts which formed the chain of circumstantial evidence, and to find a flaw in it; but no, not a link was missing. There was the strange way in which our passengers had come aboard, enabling them to evade any examination of their luggage. The very name of "Flannigan" smacked of Fenianism, while "Muller" suggested nothing but socialism and murder. Then their mysterious manner; their remark that their plans would have been ruined had they missed the ship; their fear of being observed; last, but not least, the clenching evidence in the production of the little square box with the trigger, and their grim joke about the face of the man who should let it off by mistake—could these facts lead to any conclusion other than that they were the desperate emissaries of somebody, political or otherwise, who intended to sacrifice themselves, their fellow-passengers, and the ship, in one great holocaust? The whitish granules which I had seen one of them pour into the box formed no doubt a fuse or train for exploding it. I had myself heard a sound come from it which might have emanated from some delicate piece of machinery. But what did they mean by their allusion to to-night? Could it be that they contemplated putting their horrible design into execution on the very first evening of our voyage? The mere thought of it sent a cold shudder over me, and made me for a moment superior even to the agonies of sea-sickness.

I have remarked that I am a physical coward. I am a moral one also. It is seldom that the two defects are united to such a degree in the one character. I have known many men who were most sensitive to bodily danger, and yet were distinguished for the independence and strength of their minds. In my own case, however, I regret to say that my quiet and retiring habits had fostered a nervous dread of doing anything remarkable or making myself conspicuous, which exceeded, if possible, my fear of personal peril. An ordinary mortal placed under the circumstances in which I now found myself would have gone at once to the captain, confessed his fears, and put the matter into his hands. To me, however, constituted as I am, the idea was most repugnant. The thought of becoming the observed of all observers, cross-questioned by a stranger, and confronted with two desperate conspirators in the character of a denouncer, was hateful to me. Might it not by some remote possibility prove that I was mistaken ? What would be my feelings if there should turn out to be no grounds for my accusation ? No, I would procrastinate ; I would keep my eye on the two desperadoes and dog them at every turn. Anything was better than the possibility of being wrong.

Then it struck me that even at that moment some new phase of the conspiracy might be developing itself. The nervous excitement seemed to have driven away my incipient attack of sickness, for I was able to stand up and lower myself from the boat without experiencing any return of it. I staggered along the deck with the intention of descending into the cabin and finding how my acquaintances of the morning were occupying themselves. Just as I had my hand on the companion-rail, I was astonished by receiving a hearty slap on the back, which nearly shot me down the steps with more haste than dignity.

"Is that you, Hammond ?" said a voice which I seemed to recognize.

"God bless me," I said, as I turned round, "it can't be Dick Merton ! Why, how are you, old man ?"

This was an unexpected piece of luck in the midst of my perplexities. Dick was just the man I wanted ; kindly and shrewd in his nature, and prompt in his actions, I should have no difficulty in telling him my suspicions, and could rely upon his sound sense to point out the best course to pursue. Since I was a little lad in the second form at Harrow, Dick had been my adviser and protector. He saw at a glance that something had gone wrong with me.

"Hullo!" he said, in his kindly way, "what's put you about, Hammond? You look as white as a sheet. *Mal de mer*, eh?"

"No, not that altogether," said I. "Walk up and down with me, Dick; I want to speak to you. Give me your arm."

Supporting myself on Dick's stalwart frame, I tottered along by his side; but it was some time before I could muster resolution to speak.

"Have a cigar?" said he, breaking the silence.

"No, thanks," said I. "Dick, we shall be all corpses to-night."

"That's no reason against your having a cigar now," said Dick, in his cool way, but looking hard at me from under his shaggy eyebrows as he spoke. He evidently thought that my intellect was a little gone.

"No," I continued, "it's no laughing matter; and I speak in sober earnest, I assure you. I have discovered an infamous conspiracy, Dick, to destroy this ship and every soul that is in her"; and I then proceeded systematically, and in order, to lay before him the chain of evidence which I had collected. "There, Dick," I said, as I concluded, "what do you think of that and, above all, what am I to do?"

To my astonishment he burst into a hearty fit of laughter.

"I'd be frightened," he said, "if any fellow but you had told me as much. You always had a way, Hammond, of discovering mares' nests. I like to see the old traits breaking out again. Do you remember at school how you swore there was a ghost in the long room, and how it turned out to be your own reflection in the mirror? Why, man," he continued, "what object would anyone have in destroying this ship? We have no great political guns aboard. On the contrary, the majority of the passengers are Americans. Besides, in this sober nineteenth century, the most wholesale murderers stop at including themselves among their victims. Depend upon it, you have misunderstood them, and have mistaken a photographic camera, or something equally innocent, for an infernal machine."

"Nothing of the sort, sir," said I, rather touchily. "You will learn to your cost, I fear, that I have neither exaggerated nor misinterpreted a word. As to the box, I have certainly never before seen one like it. It contained delicate machinery; of that I am convinced, from the way in which the men handled it and spoke of it."

"You'd make out every packet of perishable goods to be a torpedo," said Dick, "if that is to be your only test."

"The man's name was Flannigan," I continued.

"I don't think that would go very far in a court of law," said Dick; "but come, I have finished my cigar. Suppose we go down together and split a bottle of claret. You can point out these two Orsinis to me if they are still in the cabin."

"All right," I answered; "I am determined not to lose sight of them all day. Don't look hard at them, though, for I don't want them to think that they are being watched."

"Trust me," said Dick; "I'll look as unconscious and guileless as a lamb"; and with that we passed down the companion and into the saloon.

A good many passengers were scattered about the great central table, some wrestling with refractory carpet-bags and rug-straps, some having their luncheon, and a few reading and otherwise amusing themselves. The objects of our quest were not there. We passed down the room and peered into every berth, but there was no sign of them. "Heavens!" thought I, "perhaps at this very moment they are beneath our feet, in the hold or engine-room, preparing their diabolical contrivance!"

It was better to know the worst than to remain in such suspense.

" Steward," said Dick, " are there any other gentlemen about ? "

" There's two in the smoking-room, sir," answered the steward.

The smoking-room was a little snuggery, luxuriously fitted up, and adjoining the pantry. We pushed the door open and entered. A sigh of relief escaped from my bosom. The very first object on which my eye rested was the cadaverous face of Flannigan, with its hard-set mouth and unwinking eye. His companion sat opposite to him. They were both drinking, and a pile of cards lay upon the table. They were engaged in playing as we entered. I nudged Dick to show him that we had found our quarry, and we sat down beside them with as unconcerned an air as possible. The two conspirators seemed to take little notice of our presence. I watched them both narrowly. The game at which they were playing was " Napoleon." Both were adepts at it, and I could not help admiring the consummate nerve of men who, with such a secret at their hearts, could devote their minds to the manipulation of a long suit or the finessing of a queen. Money changed hands rapidly ; but the run of luck seemed to be all against the taller of the two players. At last he threw down his cards on the table with an oath, and refused to go on.

" No, I'm hanged if I do," he said ; " I haven't had more than two of a suit for five hands."

" Never mind," said his comrade, as he gathered up his winnings ; " a few dollars one way or the other won't go very far after to-night's work."

I was astonished at the rascal's audacity, but took care to keep my eyes fixed abstractedly upon the ceiling, and drank my wine in as unconscious a manner as possible. I felt that Flannigan was looking towards me with his wolfish eyes to see if I had noticed the allusion. He whispered something to his companion which I failed to catch. It was a caution, I suppose, for the other answered rather angrily—

"Nonsense! Why shouldn't I say what I like? Over-caution is just what would ruin us."

"I believe you want it not to come off," said Flannigan.

"You believe nothing of the sort," said the other, speaking rapidly and loudly. "You know as well as I do that when I play for a stake I like to win it. But I won't have my words criticized and cut short by you or any other man. I have as much interest in our success as you have—more, I hope."

He was quite hot about it, and puffed furiously at his cigar for some minutes. The eyes of the other ruffian wandered alternately from Dick Merton to myself. I knew that I was in the presence of a desperate man, that a quiver of my lip might be the signal for him to plunge a weapon into my heart, but I betrayed more self-command than I should have given myself credit for under such trying circumstances. As to Dick, he was as immovable and apparently as unconscious as the Egyptian Sphinx.

There was silence for some time in the smoking-room, broken only by the crisp rattle of the cards, as the man Muller shuffled them up before replacing them in his pocket. He still seemed to be somewhat flushed and irritable. Throwing the end of his cigar into the spittoon, he glanced defiantly at his companion and turned towards me.

"Can you tell me, sir," he said, "when this ship will be heard of again?"

They were both looking at me; but though my face may have turned a trifle paler, my voice was as steady as ever as I answered—

"I presume, sir, that it will be heard of first when it enters Queenstown Harbour."

"Ha, ha!" laughed the angry little man, "I knew you would say that. Don't you kick me under the table, Flannigan, I won't stand it. I know what I am doing.

You are wrong, sir," he continued, turning to me, " utterly wrong."

" Some passing ship, perhaps," suggested Dick.

" No, nor that either."

" The weather is fine," I said ; " why should we not be heard of at our destination ? "

" I didn't say we shouldn't be heard of at our destination. Possibly we may not, and in any case that is not where we shall be heard of first."

" Where, then ? " asked Dick.

" That you shall never know. Suffice it that a rapid and mysterious agency will signal our whereabouts, and that before the day is out. Ha, ha ! " and he chuckled once again.

" Come on deck ! " growled his comrade ; " you have drunk too much of that confounded brandy and water. It has loosened your tongue. Come away ! " and taking him by the arm he half led him, half forced him out of the smoking-room, and we heard them stumbling up the companion together, and on to the deck.

" Well, what do you think now ? " I gasped, as I turned towards Dick. He was as imperturbable as ever.

" Think ! " he said ; " why, I think what his companion thinks, that we have been listening to the ravings of a half-drunken man. The fellow stunk of brandy."

" Nonsense, Dick ! you saw how the other tried to stop his tongue."

" Of course he did. He didn't want his friend to make a fool of himself before strangers. Maybe the short one is a lunatic, and the other his private keeper. It's quite possible."

" O, Dick, Dick," I cried, " how can you be so blind ! Don't you see that every word confirmed our previous suspicion ? "

" Humbug, man ! " said Dick ; " you're working yourself into a state of nervous excitement. Why, what the devil do *you* make of all that nonsense about a mysterious agent which would signal our whereabouts ? "

"I'll tell you what he meant, Dick," I said, bending forward and grasping my friend's arm. "He meant a sudden glare and a flash seen far out at sea by some lonely fisherman off the American coast. That's what he meant."

"I didn't think you were such a fool, Hammond," said Dick Merton testily. "If you try to fix a literal meaning on the twaddle that every drunken man talks, you will come to some queer conclusions. Let us follow their example, and go on deck. You need fresh air, I think. Depend upon it, your liver is out of order. A sea-voyage will do you a world of good."

"If ever I see the end of this one," I groaned, "I'll promise never to venture on another. They are laying the cloth, so it's hardly worth while my going up. I'll stay below and unpack my things."

"I hope dinner will find you in a more pleasant state of mind," said Dick; and he went out, leaving me to my thoughts until the clang of the great gong summoned us to the saloon.

My appetite, I need hardly say, had not been improved by the incidents which had occurred during the day. I sat down, however, mechanically at the table, and listened to the talk which was going on around me. There were nearly a hundred first-class passengers, and as the wine began to circulate, their voices combined with the clash of the dishes to form a perfect babel. I found myself seated between a very stout and nervous old lady and a prim little clergyman; and as neither made any advances I retired into my shell, and spent my time in observing the appearance of my fellow-voyagers. I could see Dick in the dim distance dividing his attentions between a jointless fowl in front of him and a self-possessed young lady at his side. Captain Dowie was doing the honours at my end, while the surgeon of the vessel was seated at the other. I was glad to notice that Flannigan was placed almost opposite to me. As long as I had him before my eyes I knew that, for the time at least, we were safe. He was sitting with what was meant to be a sociable smile on his grim face. It did not escape me that he drank largely of wine—so largely that even before the dessert appeared his voice had become decidedly husky. His friend Muller was seated a few places lower down. He ate little, and appeared to be nervous and restless.

"Now, ladies," said our genial captain, "I trust that you will consider yourselves at home aboard my vessel. I have no fears for the gentlemen. A bottle of champagne, steward. Here's to a fresh breeze and a quick passage! I trust our friends in America will hear of our safe arrival in eight days, or in nine at the very latest."

I looked up. Quick as was the glance which passed between Flannigan and his confederate, I was able to intercept it. There was an evil smile upon the former's thin lips.

The conversation rippled on. Politics, the sea, amusements, religion, each was in turn discussed. I remained a silent though an interested listener. It struck me that no harm could be done by introducing the subject which was ever in my mind. It could be managed in an offhand way, and would at least have the effect of turning the captain's thoughts in that direction. I could watch, too, what effect it would have upon the faces of the conspirators.

There was a sudden lull in the conversation. The ordinary subjects of interest appeared to be exhausted. The opportunity was a favourable one.

"May I ask, Captain," I said, bending forward and speaking very distinctly, "what you think of Fenian manifestos?"

The captain's ruddy face became a shade darker from honest indignation.

"They are poor cowardly things," he said, "as silly as they are wicked."

"The impotent threats of a set of anonymous scoundrels," said a pompous-looking old gentleman beside him.

"O Captain!" said the fat lady at my side, "you don't really think they would blow up a ship?"

"I have no doubt they would if they could. But I am very sure they shall never blow up mine."

"May I ask what precautions are taken against them?" asked an elderly man at the end of the table.

"All goods sent aboard the ship are strictly examined," said Captain Dowie.

"But suppose a man brought explosives aboard with him?" I suggested.

"They are too cowardly to risk their own lives in that way."

During this conversation Flannigan had not betrayed the slightest interest in what was going on. He raised his head now and looked at the captain.

"Don't you think you are rather underrating them?" he said. "Every secret society has produced desperate men—why shouldn't the Fenians have them too? Many men think it a privilege to die in the service of a cause which seems right in their eyes, though others may think it wrong."

"Indiscriminate murder cannot be right in anybody's eyes," said the little clergyman.

"The bombardment of Paris was nothing else," said Flannigan; "yet the whole civilized world agreed to look on with folded arms, and change the ugly word 'murder' into the more euphonious one of 'war.' It seemed right enough to German eyes; why shouldn't dynamite seem so to the Fenian?"

"At any rate their empty vapourings have led to nothing as yet," said the captain.

"Excuse me," returned Flannigan, "but is there not some room for doubt yet as to the fate of the *Dotterel*? I have met men in America who asserted from their own personal knowledge that there was a coal torpedo aboard that vessel."

"Then they lied," said the captain. "It was proved conclusively at the court-martial to have arisen from an explosion of coal-gas—but we had better change the subject, or we may cause the ladies to have a restless night; " and the conversation once more drifted back into its original channel.

During this little discussion Flannigan had argued his point with a gentlemanly deference and a quiet power for which I had not given him credit. I could not help admiring a man who, on the eve of a desperate enterprise, could courteously argue upon a point which must touch him so nearly. He had, as I have already mentioned, partaken of a considerable quantity of wine; but though there was a slight flush upon his pale cheek, his manner was as reserved as ever. He did not join in the conversation again, but seemed to be lost in thought.

A whirl of conflicting ideas was battling in my own mind. What was I to do? Should I stand up now and denounce them before both passengers and captain? Should I demand a few minutes' conversation with the latter in his own cabin, and reveal it all? For an instant I was half resolved to do it, but then the old constitutional timidity came back with redoubled force. After all there might be some mistake. Dick had heard the evidence and had refused to believe in it. I determined to let things go on their course. A strange, reckless feeling came over me. Why should I help men who were blind to their own danger? Surely it was the duty of the officers to protect us, not ours to give warning to them. I drank off a couple of glasses of wine, and staggered up on deck with the determination of keeping my secret locked in my own bosom.

It was a glorious evening. Even in my excited state of mind I could not help leaning against the bulwarks and enjoying the refreshing breeze. Away to the westward a solitary sail stood out as a dark speck against the great sheet of flame left by the setting sun. I shuddered as I looked at it. It was grand but appalling. A single star was twinkling faintly above our mainmast, but a thousand seemed to gleam in the water below with every stroke of our propeller. The only blot in the fair scene was the great trail of smoke which stretched away behind us like a black slash upon a crimson curtain. It was hard to believe that the great peace which hung over all Nature could be marred by a poor miserable mortal.

"After all," I thought, as I gazed into the blue depths beneath me, "if the worst comes to the worst, it is better to die here than to linger in agony upon a sick-bed on land." A man's life seems a very paltry thing amid the great forces of Nature. All my philosophy could not prevent my shuddering, however, when I turned my head and saw two shadowy figures at the other side of the deck, which I had no difficulty in recognizing. They seemed to be conversing earnestly, but I had no opportunity of overhearing what was said; so I contented myself with pacing up and down, and keeping a vigilant watch upon their movements.

It was a relief to me when Dick came on deck. Even an incredulous confidant is better than none at all.

"Well, old man," he said, giving me a facetious dig in the ribs, "we've not been blown up yet."

"No, not yet," said I; "but that's no proof that we are not going to be."

"Nonsense, man!" said Dick; "I can't conceive what has put this extraordinary idea into your head. I have been talking to one of your supposed assassins, and he seems a pleasant fellow enough; quite a sporting character, I should think, from the way he speaks."

"Dick," I said, "I am as certain that those men have an infernal machine, and that we are on the verge of eternity, as if I saw them putting the match to the fuse."

"Well, if you really think so," said Dick, half awed for the moment by the earnestness of my manner, "it is your duty to let the captain know of your suspicions."

"You are right," I said; "I will. My absurd timidity has prevented my doing so sooner. I believe our lives can only be saved by laying the whole matter before him."

"Well, go and do it now," said Dick; "but for goodness' sake don't mix me up in the matter."

"I'll speak to him when he comes off the bridge," I answered; "and in the meantime I don't mean to lose sight of them."

"Let me know of the result," said my companion; and with a nod he strolled away in search, I fancy, of his partner at the dinner-table.

Left to myself, I bethought me of my retreat of the morning, and climbing on the bulwark I mounted into the quarter-boat, and lay down there. In it I could reconsider my course of action, and by raising my head I was able at any time to get a view of my disagreeable neighbours.

An hour passed, and the captain was still on the bridge. He was talking to one of the passengers, a retired naval officer, and the two were deep in debate concerning some abstruse point in navigation. I could see the red tips of their cigars from where I lay. It was dark now, so dark that I could hardly make out the figures of Flannigan and his accomplice. They were still standing in the position which they had taken up after dinner. A few of the passengers were scattered about the deck, but many had gone below. A strange stillness seemed to pervade the air. The voices of the watch and the rattle of the wheel were the only sounds which broke the silence.

Another half-hour passed. The captain was still upon the bridge. It seemed as if he would never come down. My nerves were in a state of unnatural tension, so much so that the sound of two steps upon the deck made me start up in a quiver of excitement. I peered over the edge of the boat, and saw that our suspicious passengers had crossed from the other side, and were standing almost directly beneath me. The light of a binnacle fell full upon the ghastly face of the ruffian Flannigan. Even in that short glance I saw that Muller had the ulster, whose use I knew so well, slung loosely over his arm. I sank back with a groan. It seemed that my fatal procrastination had sacrificed two hundred innocent lives.

I had read of the fiendish vengeance which awaited a spy. I knew that men with their lives in their hands would stick at nothing. All I could do was to cower at the bottom of the boat and listen silently to their whispered talk below.

"This place will do," said a voice.

"Yes, the leeward side is best."

"I wonder if the trigger will act?"

"I am sure it will."

"We were to let it off at ten, were we not?"

"Yet, at ten sharp. We have eight minutes yet." There was a pause. Then the voice began again—

"They'll hear the drop of the trigger, won't they?"

"It doesn't matter. It will be too late for anyone to prevent its going off."

"That's true. There will be some excitement among those we have left behind, won't there?"

"Rather. How long do you reckon it will be before they hear of us?"

"The first news will get in at about midnight at earliest."

"That will be my doing."

"No, mine."

"Ha, ha! we'll settle that."

There was a pause here. Then I heard Muller's voice in a ghastly whisper, "There's only five minutes more."

How slowly the moments seemed to pass! I could count them by the throbbing of my heart.

"It'll make a sensation on land," said a voice.

"Yes, it will make a noise in the newspapers."

I raised my head and peered over the side of the boat. There seemed no hope, no help. Death stared me in the face, whether I did or did not give the alarm. The captain had at last left the bridge. The deck was deserted, save for those two dark figures crouching in the shadow of the boat.

Flannigan had a watch lying open in his hand.

" Three minutes more," he said. " Put it down upon the deck."

" No, put it here on the bulwarks."

It was the little square box. I knew by the sound that they had placed it near the davit, and almost exactly under my head.

I looked over again. Flannigan was pouring something out of a paper into his hand. It was white and granular—the same that I had seen him use in the morning. It was meant as a fuse, no doubt, for he shovelled it into the little box, and I heard the strange noise which had previously arrested my attention.

" A minute and a half more," he said. " Shall you or I pull the string ? "

" I will pull it," said Muller.

He was kneeling down and holding the end in his hand. Flannigan stood behind with his arms folded, and an air of grim resolution upon his face.

I could stand it no longer. My nervous system seemed to give way in a moment.

" Stop ! " I screamed, springing to my feet. " Stop, misguided and unprincipled men ! "

They both staggered backwards. I fancy they thought I was a spirit, with the moonlight streaming down upon my pale face.

I was brave enough now. I had gone too far to retreat.

" Cain was damned," I cried, " and he slew but one ; would you have the blood of two hundred upon your souls ? "

" He's mad ! " said Flannigan. " Time's up. Let it off, Muller."

I sprang down upon the deck.

" You shan't do it ! " I said.

" By what right do you prevent us ? "

" By every right, human and divine."

"It's no business of yours. Clear out of this."

"Never!" said I.

"Confound the fellow! There's too much at stake to stand on ceremony. I'll hold him, Muller, while you pull the trigger."

Next moment I was struggling in the herculean grasp of the Irishman. Resistance was useless; I was a child in his hands.

He pinned me up against the side of the vessel, and held me there.

"Now," he said, "look sharp. He can't prevent us."

I felt that I was standing on the verge of eternity. Half-strangled in the arms of the taller ruffian, I saw the other approach the fatal box. He stooped over it and seized the string. I breathed one prayer when I saw his grasp tighten upon it. Then came a sharp snap, a strange rasping noise. The trigger had fallen, the side of the box flew out, and let off—*two grey carrier pigeons!*

Little more need be said. It is not a subject on which I care to dwell. The whole thing is too utterly disgusting and absurd. Perhaps the best thing I can do is to retire gracefully from the scene, and let the sporting correspondent of the *New York Herald* fill my unworthy place. Here is an extract clipped from its columns shortly after our departure from America:

"*Pigeon-flying Extraordinary.*—A novel match has been brought off last week between the birds of John H. Flannigan, of Boston, and Jeremiah Muller, a well-known citizen of Lowell. Both men have devoted much time and attention to an improved breed of bird, and the challenge is an old-standing one. The pigeons were backed to a large amount, and there was considerable local interest in the result. The start was from the deck of the Transatlantic steamship *Spartan*, at ten o'clock on the evening of the day of starting, the vessel being then reckoned to be about a hundred miles from the land. The bird which reached home first was to be declared the winner. Considerable caution had, we believe, to be observed, as some captains have a prejudice against the bringing off of sporting events aboard their vessels. In spite of some little difficulty at the last moment, the trap was sprung almost exactly at ten o'clock. Muller's bird arrived in Lowell in an extreme state of exhaustion on the following morning, while Flannigan's has not been heard of. The backers of the latter have the satisfaction of knowing, however, that the whole affair has been characterized by extreme fairness. The pigeons were confined in a specially invented trap, which could only be opened by the spring. It was thus possible to feed them through an aperture in the top, but any tampering with their wings was quite out of the question. A few such matches would go far towards popularising pigeon-flying in America, and form an agreeable variety to the morbid exhibitions of human endurance which have assumed such proportions during the last few years."

TALES OF TERROR

25. *The Horror of the Heights*

(WHICH INCLUDES THE MANUSCRIPT KNOWN AS THE JOYCE-ARMSTRONG FRAGMENT)

THE idea that the extraordinary narrative which has been called the Joyce-Armstrong Fragment is an elaborate practical joke evolved by some unknown person, cursed by a perverted and sinister sense of humour, has now been abandoned by all who have examined the matter. The most *macabre* and imaginative of plotters would hesitate before linking his morbid fancies with the unquestioned and tragic facts which reinforce the statement. Though the assertions contained in it are amazing and even monstrous, it is none the less forcing itself upon the general intelligence that they are true, and that we must readjust our ideas to the new situation. This world of ours appears to be separated by a slight and precarious margin of safety from a most singular and unexpected danger. I will endeavour in this narrative, which reproduces the original document in its necessarily somewhat fragmentary form, to lay before the reader the whole of the facts up to date, prefacing my statement by saying that, if there be any who doubt the narrative of Joyce-Armstrong, there can be no question at all as to the facts concerning Lieutenant Myrtle, R.N., and Mr. Hay Connor, who undoubtedly met their end in the manner described.

The Joyce-Armstrong Fragment was found in the field which is called Lower Haycock, lying one mile to the westward of the village of Withyham, upon the Kent and Sussex border. It was on the fifteenth of September last that an agricultural labourer, James Flynn, in the employment of Mathew Dodd, farmer, of the Chauntry Farm, Withyham, perceived a briar pipe lying near the footpath which skirts the hedge in Lower Haycock. A few paces farther on he picked up a pair of broken binocular glasses. Finally, among some nettles in the ditch, he caught sight of a flat, canvas-backed book, which proved to be a note-book with detachable leaves, some of which had come loose and were fluttering along the base of the hedge. These he collected, but some, including the first, were never recovered, and leave a deplorable hiatus in this all-important statement. The note-book was taken by the labourer to his master, who in turn showed it to Dr. J. H. Atherton, of Hartfield. This gentleman at once recognized the need for an expert examination, and the manuscript was forwarded to the Aero Club in London, where it now lies.

The first two pages of the manuscript are missing. There is also one torn away at the end of the narrative, though none of these affect the general coherence of the story. It is conjectured that the missing opening is concerned with the record of Mr. Joyce-Armstrong's qualifications as an aeronaut, which can be gathered from other sources and are admitted to be unsurpassed among the air-pilots of England. For many years he has been looked upon as among the most daring and the most intellectual of flying men, a combination which has enabled him to both invent and test several new devices, including the common gyroscopic attachment which is known by his name. The main body of the manuscript is written neatly in ink, but the last few lines are in pencil and are so ragged as to be hardly legible—exactly, in fact, as they might be expected to appear if they were scribbled off hurriedly from the seat of a moving aeroplane. There are, it may be added, several stains, both on the last page and on the outside cover which have been pronounced by the Home Office experts to be blood—probably human and certainly mammalian. The fact that something closely resembling the organism of malaria was discovered in this blood, and that Joyce-Armstrong is known to have suffered from intermittent fever, is a remarkable example of the new weapons which modern science has placed in the hands of our detectives.

And now a word as to the personality of the author of this epoch-making statement. Joyce-Armstrong, according to the few friends who really knew something of the man, was a poet and a dreamer, as well as a mechanic and an inventor. He was a man of considerable wealth, much of which he had spent in the pursuit of his aeronautical hobby. He had four private aeroplanes in his hangars near Devizes, and is said to have made no fewer than one hundred and seventy ascents in the course of last year. He was a retiring man with dark moods, in which he would avoid the society of his fellows. Captain Dangerfield, who knew him better than anyone, says that there were times when his eccentricity threatened to develop into something more serious. His habit of carrying a shot-gun with him in his aeroplane was one manifestation of it.

Another was the morbid effect which the fall of Lieutenant Myrtle had upon his mind. Myrtle, who was attempting the height record, fell from an altitude of something over thirty thousand feet. Horrible to narrate, his head was entirely obliterated, though his body and limbs preserved their configuration. At every gathering of airmen, Joyce-Armstrong, according to Dangerfield, would ask, with an enigmatic smile: "And where, pray, is Myrtle's head?"

On another occasion after dinner, at the mess of the Flying School on Salisbury Plain, he started a debate as to what will be the most permanent danger which airmen will have to encounter. Having listened to successive opinions as to air-pockets, faulty construction, and overbanking, he ended by shrugging his shoulders and refusing to put forward his own views, though he gave the impression that they differed from any advanced by his companions.

It is worth remarking that after his own complete disappearance it was found that his private affairs were arranged with a precision which may show that he had a strong premonition of disaster. With these essential explanations I will now give the narrative exactly as it stands, beginning at page three of the blood-soaked notebook :—

" Nevertheless, when I dined at Rheims with Coselli and Gustav Raymond I found that neither of them was aware of any particular danger in the higher layers of the atmosphere. I did not actually say what was in my thoughts, but I got so near to it that if they had any corresponding idea they could not have failed to express it. But then they are two empty, vainglorious fellows with no thought beyond seeing their silly names in the newspaper. It is interesting to note that neither of them had ever been much beyond the twenty-thousand-foot level. Of course, men have been higher than this both in balloons and in the ascent of mountains. It must be well above that point that the aeroplane enters the danger zone—always presuming that my premonitions are correct.

" Aeroplaning has been with us now for more than twenty years, and one might well ask : Why should this peril be only revealing itself in our day ? The answer is obvious. In the old days of weak engines, when a hundred horse-power Gnome or Green was considered ample for every need, the flights were very restricted. Now that three hundred horse-power is the rule rather than the exception, visits to the upper layers have become easier and more common. Some of us can remember how, in our youth, Garros made a world-wide reputation by attaining nineteen thousand feet, and it was considered a remarkable achievement to fly over the Alps. Our standard now has been immeasurably raised, and there are twenty high flights for one in former years. Many of them have been undertaken with impunity. The thirty-thousand-foot level has been reached time after time with no discomfort beyond cold and asthma. What does this prove? A visitor might descend upon this planet a thousand times and never see a tiger. Yet tigers exist, and if he chanced to come down into a jungle he might be devoured. There are jungles of the upper air, and there are worse things than tigers which inhabit them. I believe in time they will map these jungles accurately out. Even at the present moment I could name two of them. One of them lies over the Pau-Biarritz district of France. Another is just over my head as I write here in my house in Wiltshire. I rather think there is a third in the Homburg-Wiesbaden district.

"It was the disappearance of the airmen that first set me thinking. Of course, everyone said that they had fallen into the sea, but that did not satisfy me at all. First, there was Verrier in France; his machine was found near Bayonne, but they never got his body. There was the case of Baxter also, who vanished, though his engine and some of the iron fixings were found in a wood in Leicestershire. In that case, Dr. Middleton, of Amesbury, who was watching the flight with a telescope, declares that just before the clouds obscured the view he saw the machine, which was at an enormous height, suddenly rise perpendicularly upwards in a succession of jerks in a manner that he would have thought to be impossible. That was the last seen of Baxter. There was a correspondence in the papers, but it never led to anything. There were several other similar cases, and then there was the death of Hay Connor. What a cackle there was about an unsolved mystery of the air, and what columns in the halfpenny papers, and yet how little was ever done to get to the bottom of the business! He came down in a tremendous vol-plané from an unknown height. He never got off his machine and died in his pilot's seat. Died of what? 'Heart disease,' said the doctors. Rubbish! Hay Connor's heart was as sound as mine is. What did Venables say? Venables was the only man who was at his side when he died. He said that he was shivering and looked like a man who had been badly scared. 'Died of fright,' said Venables, but could not imagine what he was frightened about. Only said one word to Venables, which sounded like 'Monstrous.' They could make nothing of that at the inquest. But I could make something of it. Monsters! That was the last word of poor Harry Hay Connor. And he *did* die of fright, just as Venables thought.

"And then there was Myrtle's head. Do you really believe—does anybody really believe—that a man's head could be driven clean into his body by the force of a fall? Well, perhaps it may be possible, but I, for one, have never believed that it was so with Myrtle. And the grease upon his clothes—'all slimy with grease,' said somebody at the inquest. Queer that nobody got thinking after that! I did—but, then, I had been thinking for a good long time. I've made three ascents—how Dangerfield used to chaff me about my shot-gun—but I've never been high enough. Now, with this new, light Paul Veroner machine and its one hundred and seventy-five Robur, I should easily touch the thirty thousand to-morrow. I'll have a shot at the record. Maybe I shall have a shot at something else as well. Of course, it's dangerous. If a fellow wants to avoid danger he had best keep out of flying altogether and subside finally into flannel slippers and a dressing-gown. But I'll visit the air-jungle to-morrow—and if there's anything there I shall know it. If I return, I'll find myself a bit of a celebrity. If I don't, this note-book may explain what I am trying to do, and how I lost my life in doing it. But no drivel about accidents or mysteries, if *you* please.

"I chose my Paul Veroner monoplane for the job. There's nothing like a monoplane when real work is to be done. Beaumont found that out in very early days. For one thing it doesn't mind damp, and the weather looks as if we should be in the clouds all the time. It's a bonny little model and answers my hand like a tender-mouthed horse. The engine is a ten-cylinder rotary Robur working up to one hundred and seventy-five. It has all the modern improvements—enclosed fuselage, high-curved landing skids, brakes, gyroscopic steadiers, and three speeds, worked by an alteration of the angle of the planes upon the Venetian-blind principle. I took a shot-gun with me and a dozen cartridges filled with buck-shot. You should have seen the face of Perkins, my old mechanic, when I directed him to put them in. I was dressed like an Arctic explorer, with two jerseys under my overalls, thick socks inside my padded boots, a storm-cap with flaps, and my talc goggles. It was stifling outside the hangars, but I was going for the summit of the Himalayas, and had to dress for the part. Perkins knew there was something on and implored me to take him with me. Perhaps I should if I were using the biplane, but a monoplane is a one-man show—if you want to get the last foot of lift out of it. Of course, I took an oxygen bag; the man who goes for the altitude record without one will either be frozen or smothered—or both.

"I had a good look at the planes, the rudder-bar, and the elevating lever before I got in. Everything was in order so far as I could see. Then I switched on my engine and found that she was running sweetly. When they let her go she rose almost at once upon the lowest speed. I circled my home field once or twice just to warm her up, and then, with a wave to Perkins and the others, I flattened out my planes and put her on her highest. She skimmed like a swallow down wind for eight or ten miles until I turned her nose up a little and she began to climb in a great spiral for the cloud-bank above me. It's all-important to rise slowly and adapt yourself to the pressure as you go.

"It was a close, warm day for an English September, and there was the hush and heaviness of impending rain.

Now and then there came sudden puffs of wind from the south-west—one of them so gusty and unexpected that it caught me napping and turned me half-round for an instant. I remember the time when gusts and whirls and air-pockets used to be things of danger—before we learned to put an overmastering power into our engines. Just as I reached the cloud-banks, with the altimeter marking three thousand, down came the rain. My word, how it poured! It drummed upon my wings and lashed against my face, blurring my glasses so that I could hardly see. I got down on to a low speed, for it was painful to travel against it. As I got higher it became hail, and I had to turn tail to it. One of my cylinders was out of action—a dirty plug, I should imagine, but still I was rising steadily with plenty of power. After a bit the trouble passed, whatever it was, and I heard the full, deep-throated purr—the ten singing as one. That's where the beauty of our modern silencers comes in. We can at last control our engines by ear. How they squeal and squeak and sob when they are in trouble! All those cries for help were wasted in the old days, when every sound was swallowed up by the monstrous racket of the machine. If only the early aviators could come back to see the beauty and perfection of the mechanism which have been bought at the cost of their lives!

"About nine-thirty I was nearing the clouds. Down below me, all blurred and shadowed with rain, lay the vast expense of Salisbury Plain. Half a dozen flying machines were doing hackwork at the thousand-foot level, looking like little black swallows against the green background. I dare say they were wondering what I was doing up in cloud-land. Suddenly a grey curtain drew across beneath me and the wet folds of vapours were swirling round my face. It was clammily cold and miserable. But I was above the hail-storm, and that was something gained. The cloud was as dark and thick as a London fog. In my anxiety to get clear, I cocked her nose up until the automatic alarm-bell rang, and I actually began to slide backwards. My sopped and dripping wings had made me heavier than I thought, but presently I was in lighter cloud, and soon had cleared the first layer. There was a second—opal-coloured and fleecy—at a great height above my head, a white, unbroken ceiling above, and a dark, unbroken floor below, with the monoplane labouring upwards upon a vast spiral between them. It is deadly lonely in these cloud-spaces. Once a great flight of some small water-birds went past me, flying very fast to the westwards. The quick whir of their wings and their musical cry were cheery to my ear. I fancy that they were teal, but I am a wretched zoologist. Now that we humans have become birds we must really learn to know our brethren by sight.

"The wind down beneath me whirled and swayed the broad cloud-plain. Once a great eddy formed in it, a whirlpool of vapour, and through it, as down a funnel, I caught sight of the distant world. A large white biplane was passing at a vast depth beneath me. I fancy it was the morning mail service betwixt Bristol and London. Then the drift swirled inwards again and the great solitude was unbroken.

"Just after ten I touched the lower edge of the upper cloud-stratum. It consisted of fine diaphanous vapour drifting swiftly from the westward. The wind had been steadily rising all this time and it was now blowing a sharp breeze—twenty-eight an hour by my gauge. Already it was very cold, though my altimeter only marked nine thousand. The engines were working beautifully, and we went droning steadily upwards. The cloud-bank was thicker than I had expected, but at last it thinned out into a golden mist before me, and then in an instant I had shot out from it, and there was an unclouded sky and a brilliant sun above my head—all blue and gold above, all shining silver below, one vast, glimmering plain as far as my eyes could reach. It was a quarter past ten o'clock, and the barograph needle pointed to twelve thousand eight hundred. Up I went and up, my ears concentrated upon the deep purring of my motor, my eyes busy always with the watch, the revolution indicator, the petrol lever, and the oil pump. No wonder aviators are said to be a fearless race. With so many things to think of there is no time to trouble about oneself. About this time I noted how unreliable is the compass when above a certain height from earth. At fifteen thousand feet mine was pointing east and a point south. The sun and the wind gave me my true bearings.

" I had hoped to reach an eternal stillness in these high altitudes, but with every thousand feet of ascent the gale grew stronger. My machine groaned and trembled in every joint and rivet as she faced it, and swept away like a sheet of paper when I banked her on the turn, skimming down wind at a greater pace, perhaps, than ever mortal man has moved. Yet I had always to turn again and tack up in the wind's eye, for it was not merely a height record that I was after. By all my calculations it was above little Wiltshire that my air-jungle lay, and all my labour might be lost if I struck the outer layers at some farther point.

" When I reached the nineteen-thousand-foot level, which was about midday, the wind was so severe that I looked with some anxiety to the stays of my wings, expecting momentarily to see them snap or slacken. I even cast loose the parachute behind me, and fastened its hook into the ring of my leathern belt, so as to be ready for the worst. Now was the time when a bit of scamped work by the mechanic is paid for by the life of the aeronaut. But she held together bravely. Every cord and strut was humming and vibrating like so many harp-strings, but it was glorious to see how, for all the beating and the buffeting, she was still the conqueror of Nature and the mistress of the sky. There is surely something divine in man himself that he should rise so superior to the limitations which Creation seemed to impose—rise, too, by such unselfish, heroic devotion as this air-conquest has shown. Talk of human degeneration! When has such a story as this been written in the annals of our race?

"These were the thoughts in my head as I climbed that monstrous, inclined plane with the wind sometimes beating in my face and sometimes whistling behind my ears, while the cloud-land beneath me fell away to such a distance that the folds and hummocks of silver had all smoothed out into one flat, shining plain. But suddenly I had a horrible and unprecedented experience. I have known before what it is to be in what our neighbours have called a *tourbillon*, but never on such a scale as this. That huge, sweeping river of wind of which I have spoken had, as it appears, whirlpools within it which were as monstrous as itself. Without a moment's warning I was dragged suddenly into the heart of one. I spun round for a minute or two with such velocity that I almost lost my senses, and then fell suddenly, left wing foremost, down the vacuum funnel in the centre. I dropped like a stone, and lost nearly a thousand feet. It was only my belt that kept me in my seat, and the shock and breathlessness left me hanging half-insensible over the side of the fuselage. But I am always capable of a supreme effort—it is my one great merit as an aviator. I was conscious that the descent was slower. The whirlpool was a cone rather than a funnel, and I had come to the apex. With a terrific wrench, throwing my weight all to one side, I levelled my planes and brought her head away from the wind. In an instant I had shot out of the eddies and was skimming down the sky. Then, shaken but victorious, I turned her nose up and began once more my steady grind on the upward spiral. I took a large sweep to avoid the danger-spot of the whirlpool, and soon I was safely above it. Just after one o'clock I was twenty-one thousand feet above the sea-level. To my great joy I had topped the gale, and with every hundred feet of ascent the air grew stiller. On the other hand, it was very cold, and I was conscious of that peculiar nausea which goes with rarefaction of the air. For the first time I unscrewed the mouth of my oxygen bag and took an occasional whiff of the glorious gas. I could feel it running like a cordial through my veins, and I was exhilarated almost to the point of drunkenness. I shouted and sang as I soared upwards into the cold, still outer world.

"It is very clear to me that the insensibility which came upon Glaisher, and in a lesser degree upon Coxwell, when, in 1862, they ascended in a balloon to the height of thirty thousand feet, was due to the extreme speed with which a perpendicular ascent is made. Doing it at an easy gradient and accustoming oneself to the lessened barometric pressure by slow degrees, there are no such dreadful symptoms. At the same great height I found that even without my oxygen inhaler I could breathe without undue distress. It was bitterly cold, however, and my thermometer was at zero, Fahrenheit. At one-thirty I was nearly seven miles above the surface of the earth, and still ascending steadily. I found, however, that the rarefied air was giving markedly less support to my planes, and that my angle of ascent had to be considerably lowered in consequence. It was already clear that even with my light weight and strong engine-power there was a point in front of me where I should be held. To make matters worse, one of my sparking-plugs was in trouble again and there was intermittent misfiring in the engine. My heart was heavy with the fear of failure.

"It was about that time that I had a most extraordinary experience. Something whizzed past me in a trail of smoke and exploded with a loud, hissing sound, sending forth a cloud of steam. For the instant I could not imagine what had happened. Then I remembered that the earth is for ever being bombarded by meteor stones, and would be hardly inhabitable were they not in nearly every case turned to vapour in the outer layers of the atmosphere. Here is a new danger for the high-altitude man, for two others passed me when I was nearing the forty-thousand-foot mark. I cannot doubt that at the edge of the earth's envelope the risk would be a very real one.

"My barograph needle marked forty-one thousand three hundred when I became aware that I could go no farther. Physically, the strain was not as yet greater than I could bear, but my machine had reached its limit. The attenuated air gave no firm support to the wings, and the least tilt developed into side-slip, while she seemed sluggish on her controls. Possibly, had the engine been at its best, another thousand feet might have been within our capacity, but it was still misfiring, and two out of the ten cylinders appeared to be out of action. If I had not already reached the zone for which I was searching then I should never see it upon this journey. But was it not possible that I had attained it? Soaring in circles like a monstrous hawk upon the forty-thousand-foot level I let the monoplane guide herself, and with my Mannheim glass I made a careful observation of my surroundings. The heavens were perfectly clear; there was no indication of those dangers which I had imagined.

"I have said that I was soaring in circles. It struck me suddenly that I would do well to take a wider sweep and open up a new air-tract. If the hunter entered an earth-jungle he would drive through it if he wished to find his game. My reasoning had led me to believe that the air-jungle which I had imagined lay somewhere over Wiltshire. This should be to the south and west of me. I took my bearings from the sun, for the compass was hopeless and no trace of earth was to be seen—nothing but the distant, silver cloud-plain. However, I got my direction as best I might and kept her head straight to the mark. I reckoned that my petrol supply would not last for more than another hour or so, but I could afford to use it to the last drop, since a single magnificent vol-plané could at any time take me to the earth.

"Suddenly I was aware of something new. The air

in front of me had lost its crystal clearness. It was full of long, ragged wisps of something which I can only compare to very fine cigarette-smoke. It hung about in wreaths and coils, turning and twisting slowly in the sunlight. As the monoplane shot through it, I was aware of a faint taste of oil upon my lips, and there was a greasy scum upon the woodwork of the machine. Some infinitely fine organic matter appeared to be suspended in the atmosphere. There was no life there. It was inchoate and diffuse, extending for many square acres and then fringing off into the void. No, it was not life. But might it not be the remains of life? Above all, might it not be the food of life, of monstrous life, even as the humble grease of the ocean is the food for the mighty whale? The thought was in my mind when my eyes looked upwards and I saw the most wonderful vision that ever man has seen. Can I hope to convey it to you even as I saw it myself last Thursday?

"Conceive a jelly-fish such as sails in our summer seas, bell-shaped and of enormous size—far larger, I should judge, than the dome of St. Paul's. It was of a light pink colour veined with a delicate green, but the whole huge fabric so tenuous that it was but a fairy outline against the dark blue sky. It pulsated with a delicate and regular rhythm. From it there depended two long, drooping, green tentacles, which swayed slowly backwards and forwards. This gorgeous vision passed gently with noiseless dignity over my head, as light and fragile as a soap-bubble, and drifted upon its stately way.

"I had half-turned my monoplane, that I might look after this beautiful creature, when, in a moment, I found myself amidst a perfect fleet of them, of all sizes, but none so large as the first. Some were quite small, but the majority about as big as an average balloon, and with much the same curvature at the top. There was in them a delicacy of texture and colouring which reminded me of the finest Venetian glass. Pale shades of pink and green were the prevailing tints, but all had a lovely iridescence where the sun shimmered through their dainty forms. Some hundreds of them drifted past me, a wonderful fairy squadron of strange, unknown argosies of the sky—creatures whose forms and substance were so attuned to these pure heights that one could not conceive anything so delicate within actual sight or sound of earth.

"But soon my attention was drawn to a new phenomenon—the serpents of the outer air. These were long, thin, fantastic coils of vapour-like material, which turned and twisted with great speed, flying round and round at such a pace that the eyes could hardly follow them. Some of these ghost-like creatures were twenty or thirty feet long, but it was difficult to tell their girth, for their outline was so hazy that it seemed to fade away into the air around them. These air-snakes were of a very light grey or smoke colour, with some darker lines within, which gave the impression of a definite organism. One of them whisked past my very face, and I was conscious of a cold, clammy contact, but their composition was so unsubstantial that I could not connect them with any thought of physical danger, any more than the beautiful bell-like creatures which had preceded them. There was no more solidity in their frames than in the floating spume from a broken wave.

"But a more terrible experience was in store for me. Floating downwards from a great height there came a purplish patch of vapour, small as I saw it first, but rapidly enlarging as it approached me, until it appeared to be hundreds of square feet in size. Though fashioned of some transparent, jelly-like substance, it was none the less of much more definite outline and solid consistence than anything which I had seen before. There were more traces, too, of a physical organization, especially two vast, shadowy, circular plates upon either side, which may have been eyes, and a perfectly solid white projection between them which was as curved and cruel as the beak of a vulture.

" The whole aspect of this monster was formidable and threatening, and it kept changing its colour from a very light mauve to a dark, angry purple so thick that it cast a shadow as it drifted between my monoplane and the sun. On the upper curve of its huge body there were three great projections which I can only describe as enormous bubbles, and I was convinced as I looked at them that they were charged with some extremely light gas which served to buoy up the misshapen and semi-solid mass in the rarefied air. The creature moved swiftly along, keeping pace easily with the monoplane, and for twenty miles or more it formed my horrible escort, hovering over me like a bird of prey which is waiting to pounce. Its method of progression—done so swiftly that it was not easy to follow—was to throw out a long, glutinous streamer in front of it, which in turn seemed to draw forward the rest of the writhing body. So elastic and gelatinous was it that never for two successive minutes was it the same shape, and yet each change made it more threatening and loathsome than the last.

" I knew that it meant mischief. Every purple flush of its hideous body told me so. The vague, goggling eyes which were turned always upon me were cold and merciless in their viscid hatred. I dipped the nose of my monoplane downwards to escape it. As I did so, as quick as a flash there shot out a long tentacle from this mass of floating blubber, and it fell as light and sinuous as a whip-lash across the front of my machine. There was a loud hiss as it lay for a moment across the hot engine, and it whisked itself into the air again, while the huge, flat body drew itself together as if in sudden pain. I dipped to a vol-piqué, but again a tentacle fell over the monoplane and was shorn off by the propeller as easily as it might have cut through a smoke wreath. A long, gliding, sticky, serpent-like coil came from behind and caught me round the waist, dragging me out of the fuselage. I tore at it, my fingers sinking into the smooth, glue-like surface, and for an instant I disengaged myself, but only to be caught round the boot by another coil, which gave me a jerk that tilted me almost on to my back.

"As I fell over I blazed off both barrels of my gun, though, indeed, it was like attacking an elephant with a pea-shooter to imagine that any human weapon could cripple that mighty bulk. And yet I aimed better than I knew, for, with a loud report, one of the great blisters upon the creature's back exploded with the puncture of the buck-shot. It was very clear that my conjecture was right, and that these vast, clear bladders were distended with some lifting gas, for in an instant the huge, cloud-like body turned sideways, writhing desperately to find its balance, while the white beak snapped and gaped in horrible fury. But already I had shot away on the steepest glide that I dared to attempt, my engine still full on, the flying propeller and the force of gravity shooting me downwards like an aerolite. Far behind me I saw a dull, purplish smudge growing swiftly smaller and merging into the blue sky behind it. I was safe out of the deadly jungle of the outer air.

"Once out of danger I throttled my engine, for nothing tears a machine to pieces quicker than running on full power from a height. It was a glorious, spiral volplané from nearly eight miles of altitude—first, to the level of the silver cloud-bank, then to that of the storm-cloud beneath it, and finally, in beating rain, to the surface of the earth. I saw the Bristol Channel beneath me as I broke from the clouds, but, having still some petrol in my tank, I got twenty miles inland before I found myself stranded in a field half a mile from the village of Ashcombe. There I got three tins of petrol from a passing motor-car, and at ten minutes past six that evening I alighted gently in my own home meadow at Devizes, after such a journey as no mortal upon earth has ever yet taken and lived to tell the tale. I have seen the beauty and I have seen the horror of the heights—and greater beauty or greater horror than that is not within the ken of man.

"And now it is my plan to go once again before I give my results to the world. My reason for this is that I must surely have something to show by way of proof before I lay such a tale before my fellow-men. It is true that others will soon follow and will confirm what I have said, and yet I should wish to carry conviction from the first. Those lovely iridescent bubbles of the air should not be hard to capture. They drift slowly upon their way, and the swift monoplane could intercept their leisurely course. It is likely enough that they would dissolve in the heavier layers of the atmosphere, and that some small heap of amorphous jelly might be all that I should bring to earth with me. And yet something there would surely be by which I could substantiate my story. Yes, I will go, even if I run a risk by doing so. These purple horrors would not seem to be numerous. It is probable that I shall not see one. If I do I shall dive at once. At the worst there is always the shotgun and my knowledge of . . ."

Here a page of the manuscript is unfortunately missing. On the next page is written, in large, straggling writing :—

"Forty-three thousand feet. I shall never see earth again. They are beneath me, three of them. God help me ; it is a dreadful death to die ! "

Such in its entirety is the Joyce-Armstrong Statement. Of the man nothing has since been seen. Pieces of his shattered monoplane have been picked up in the preserves of Mr. Budd-Lushington upon the borders of Kent and Sussex, within a few miles of the spot where the note-book was discovered. If the unfortunate aviator's theory is correct that this air-jungle, as he called it, existed only over the south-west of England, then it would seem that he had fled from it at the full speed of his monoplane, but had been overtaken and devoured by these horrible creatures at some spot in the outer atmosphere above the place where the grim relics were found. The picture of that monoplane skimming down the sky, with the nameless terrors flying as swiftly beneath it and cutting it off always from the earth while they gradually closed in upon their victim, is one upon which a man who valued his sanity would prefer not to dwell. There are many, as I am aware, who still jeer at the facts which I have here set down, but even they must admit that Joyce-Armstrong has disappeared, and I would commend to them his own words: "This note-book may explain what I am trying to do, and how I lost my life in doing it. But no drivel about accidents or mysteries, if *you* please."

26. *The Leather Funnel*

MY friend, Lionel Dacre, lived in the Avenue de Wagram, Paris. His house was that small one, with the iron railings and grass plot in front of it, on the left-hand side as you pass down from the Arc de Triomphe. I fancy that it had been there long before the avenue was constructed, for the grey tiles were stained with lichens, and the walls were mildewed and discoloured with age. It looked a small house from the street, five windows in front, if I remember right, but it deepened into a single long chamber at the back. It was here that Dacre had that singular library of occult literature, and the fantastic curiosities which served as a hobby for himself, and an amusement for his friends. A wealthy man of refined and eccentric tastes, he had spent much of his life and fortune in gathering together what was said to be a unique private collection of Talmudic, cabalistic, and magical works, many of them of great rarity and value. His tastes leaned toward the marvellous and the monstrous, and I have heard that his experiments in the direction of the unknown have passed all the bounds of civilization and of decorum. To his English friends he never alluded to such matters, and took the tone of the student and *virtuoso*; but a Frenchman whose tastes were of the same nature has assured me that the worst excesses of the black mass have been perpetrated in that large and lofty hall, which is lined with the shelves of his books, and the cases of his museum.

Dacre's appearance was enough to show that his deep interest in these psychic matters was intellectual rather than spiritual. There was no trace of asceticism upon his heavy face, but there was much mental force in his huge, dome-like skull, which curved upward from amongst his thinning locks, like a snow-peak above its fringe of fir trees. His knowledge was greater than his wisdom, and his powers were far superior to his character. The small bright eyes, buried deeply in his fleshy face, twinkled with intelligence and an unabated curiosity of life, but they were the eyes of a sensualist and an egotist. Enough of the man, for he is dead now, poor devil, dead at the very time that he had made sure that he had at last discovered the elixir of life. It is not with his complex character that I have to deal, but with the very strange and inexplicable incident which had its rise in my visit to him in the early spring of the year '82.

I had known Dacre in England, for my researches in the Assyrian Room of the British Museum had been conducted at the time when he was endeavouring to establish a mystic and esoteric meaning in the Babylonian tablets, and this community of interests had brought us together. Chance remarks had led to daily conversation, and that to something verging upon friendship. I had promised him that on my next visit to Paris I would call upon him. At the time when I was able to fulfil my compact I was living in a cottage at Fontainebleau, and as the evening trains were inconvenient, he asked me to spend the night in his house.

"I have only that one spare couch," said he, pointing

to a broad sofa in his large salon ; " I hope that you will manage to be comfortable there."

It was a singular bedroom, with its high walls of brown volumes, but there could be no more agreeable furniture to a bookworm like myself, and there is no scent so pleasant to my nostrils as that faint, subtle reek which comes from an ancient book. I assured him that I could desire no more charming chamber, and no more congenial surroundings.

" If the fittings are neither convenient nor conventional, they are at least costly," said he, looking round at his shelves. " I have expended nearly a quarter of a million of money upon these objects which surround you. Books, weapons, gems, carvings, tapestries, images —there is hardly a thing here which has not its history, and it is generally one worth telling."

He was seated as he spoke at one side of the open fireplace, and I at the other. His reading-table was on his right, and the strong lamp above it ringed it with a very vivid circle of golden light. A half-rolled palimpsest lay in the centre, and around it were many quaint articles of bric-à-brac. One of these was a large funnel, such as is used for filling wine casks. It appeared to be made of black wood, and to be rimmed with discoloured brass.

" That is a curious thing," I remarked. " What is the history of that ? "

" Ah ! " said he, " it is the very question which I have had occasion to ask myself. I would give a good deal to know. Take it in your hands and examine it."

I did so, and found that what I had imagined to be wood was in reality leather, though age had dried it into an extreme hardness. It was a large funnel, and might hold a quart when full. The brass rim encircled the wide end, but the narrow was also tipped with metal.

" What do you make of it ? " asked Dacre.

" I should imagine that it belonged to some vintner or maltster in the Middle Ages," said I. " I have seen in England leathern drinking flagons of the seventeenth century—' black jacks ' as they were called—which were of the same colour and hardness as this filler."

" I dare say the date would be about the same," said Dacre, " and, no doubt, also, it was used for filling a vessel with liquid. If my suspicions are correct, however, it was a queer vintner who used it, and a very singular cask which was filled. Do you observe nothing strange at the spout end of the funnel."

As I held it to the light I observed that at a spot some five inches above the brass tip the narrow neck of the leather funnel was all haggled and scored, as if someone had notched it round with a blunt knife. Only at that point was there any roughening of the dead black surface.

" Someone has tried to cut off the neck."

" Would you call it a cut ? "

" It is torn and lacerated. It must have taken some strength to leave these marks on such tough material, whatever the instrument may have been. But what do you think of it ? I can tell that you know more than you say."

Dacre smiled, and his little eyes twinkled with knowledge.

" Have you included the psychology of dreams among your learned studies ? " he asked.

" I did not even know that there was such a psychology."

" My dear sir, that shelf above the gem case is filled with volumes, from Albertus Magnus onward, which deal with no other subject. It is a science in itself."

" A science of charlatans."

" The charlatan is always the pioneer. From the astrologer came the astronomer, from the alchemist the chemist, from the mesmerist the experimental psychologist. The quack of yesterday is the professor of tomorrow. Even such subtle and elusive things as dreams will in time be reduced to system and order. When that time comes the researches of our friends on the bookshelf yonder will no longer be the amusement of the mystic, but the foundations of a science."

"Supposing that is so, what has the science of dreams to do with a large, black, brass-rimmed funnel?"

"I will tell you. You know that I have an agent who is always on the lookout for rarities and curiosities for my collection. Some days ago he heard of a dealer upon one of the Quais who had acquired some old rubbish found in a cupboard in an ancient house at the back of the Rue Mathurin, in the Quartier Latin. The dining-room of this old house is decorated with a coat of arms, chevrons, and bars rouge upon a field argent, which prove, upon inquiry, to be the shield of Nicholas de la Reynie, a high official of King Louis XIV. There can be no doubt that the other articles in the cupboard date back to the early days of that king. The inference is, therefore, that they were all the property of this Nicholas de la Reynie, who was, as I understand, the gentleman specially concerned with the maintenance and execution of the Draconic laws of that epoch."

"What then?"

"I would ask you now to take the funnel into your hands once more and to examine the upper brass rim. Can you make out any lettering upon it?"

There were certainly some scratches upon it, almost obliterated by time. The general effect was of several letters, the last of which bore some resemblance to a B.

"You make it a B?"

"Yes, I do."

"So do I. In fact, I have no doubt whatever that it is a B."

"But the nobleman you mentioned would have had R for his initial."

"Exactly! That's the beauty of it. He owned this curious object, and yet he had someone else's initials upon it. Why did he do this?"

"I can't imagine; can you?"

"Well, I might, perhaps, guess. Do you observe something drawn a little farther along the rim?"

"I should say it was a crown."

"It is undoubtedly a crown; but if you examine it in a good light, you will convince yourself that it is not an ordinary crown. It is a heraldic crown—a badge of rank, and it consists of an alternation of four pearls and strawberry leaves, the proper badge of a marquis. We may infer, therefore, that the person whose initials end in B was entitled to wear that coronet."

"Then this common leather filler belonged to a marquis?"

Dacre gave a peculiar smile.

"Or to some member of the family of a marquis," said he. "So much we have clearly gathered from this engraved rim."

"But what has all this to do with dreams?" I do not know whether it was from a look upon Dacre's face, or from some subtle suggestion in his manner, but a feeling of repulsion, of unreasoning horror, came upon me as I looked at the gnarled old lump of leather.

"I have more than once received important information through my dreams," said my companion in the didactic manner which he loved to affect. "I make it a rule now when I am in doubt upon any material point to place the article in question beside me as I sleep, and to hope for some enlightenment. The process does not appear to me to be very obscure, though it has not yet received the blessing of orthodox science. According to my theory, any object which has been intimately associated with any supreme paroxysm of human emotion, whether it be joy or pain, will retain a certain atmosphere or association which it is capable of communicating to a sensitive mind. By a sensitive mind I do not mean an abnormal one, but such a trained and educated mind as you or I possess."

"You mean, for example, that if I slept beside that old sword upon the wall, I might dream of some bloody incident in which that very sword took part?"

"An excellent example, for, as a matter of fact, that

sword was used in that fashion by me, and I saw in my sleep the death of its owner, who perished in a brisk skirmish, which I have been unable to identify, but which occurred at the time of the wars of the Frondists. If you think of it, some of our popular observances show that the fact has already been recognized by our ancestors, although we, in our wisdom, have classed it among superstitions."

"For example?"

"Well, the placing of the bride's cake beneath the pillow in order that the sleeper may have pleasant dreams. That is one of several instances which you will find set forth in a small *brochure* which I am myself writing upon the subject. But to come back to the point, I slept one night with this funnel beside me, and I had a dream which certainly throws a curious light upon its use and origin."

"What did you dream?"

"I dreamed——" He paused, and an intent look of interest came over his massive face. "By Jove, that's well thought of," said he. "This really will be an exceedingly interesting experiment. You are yourself a psychic subject—with nerves which respond readily to any impression."

"I have never tested myself in that direction."

"Then we shall test you to-night. Might I ask you as a very great favour, when you occupy that couch to-night, to sleep with this old funnel placed by the side of your pillow?"

The request seemed to me a grotesque one; but I have myself, in my complex nature, a hunger after all which is bizarre and fantastic. I had not the faintest belief in Dacre's theory, nor any hopes for success in such an experiment; yet it amused me that the experiment should be made. Dacre, with great gravity, drew a small stand to the head of my settee, and placed the funnel upon it. Then, after a short conversation, he wished me good night and left me.

* * * * *

I sat for some little time smoking by the smouldering fire, and turning over in my mind the curious incident which had occurred, and the strange experience which might lie before me. Sceptical as I was, there was something impressive in the assurance of Dacre's manner, and my extraordinary surroundings, the huge room with the strange and often sinister objects which were hung round it, struck solemnity into my soul. Finally I undressed, and turning out the lamp, I lay down. After long tossing I fell asleep. Let me try to describe as accurately as I can the scene which came to me in my dreams. It stands out now in my memory more clearly than anything which I have seen with my waking eyes.

There was a room which bore the appearance of a vault. Four spandrels from the corners ran up to join a sharp, cup-shaped roof. The architecture was rough, but very strong. It was evidently part of a great building.

Three men in black, with curious, top-heavy, black velvet hats, sat in a line upon a red-carpeted dais. Their faces were very solemn and sad. On the left stood two long-gowned men with portfolios in their hands, which seemed to be stuffed with papers. Upon the right, looking toward me, was a small woman with blonde hair and singular, light-blue eyes—the eyes of a child. She was past her first youth, but could not yet be called middle-aged. Her figure was inclined to stoutness and her bearing was proud and confident. Her face was pale, but serene. It was a curious face, comely and yet feline, with a subtle suggestion of cruelty about the straight, strong little mouth and chubby jaw. She was draped in some sort of loose, white gown. Beside her stood a thin, eager priest, who whispered in her ear, and continually raised a crucifix before her eyes. She turned her head and looked fixedly past the crucifix at the three men in black, who were, I felt, her judges.

As I gazed the three men stood up and said something, but I could distinguish no words, though I was aware that it was the central one who was speaking. They then swept out of the room, followed by the two men with the papers. At the same instant several rough-looking fellows in stout jerkins came bustling in and removed first the red carpet, and then the boards which formed the dais, so as to entirely clear the room. When this screen was removed I saw some singular articles of furniture behind it. One looked like a bed with wooden rollers at each end, and a winch handle to regulate its length. Another was a wooden horse. There were several other curious objects, and a number of swinging cords which played over pulleys. It was not unlike a modern gymnasium.

When the room had been cleared there appeared a new figure upon the scene. This was a tall, thin person clad in black, with a gaunt and austere face. The aspect of the man made me shudder. His clothes were all shining with grease and mottled with stains. He bore himself with a slow and impressive dignity, as if he took command of all things from the instant of his entrance. In spite of his rude appearance and sordid dress, it was now *his* business, *his* room, his to command. He carried a coil of light ropes over his left forearm. The lady looked him up and down with a searching glance, but her expression was unchanged. It was confident—even defiant. But it was very different with the priest. His face was ghastly white, and I saw the moisture glisten and run on his high, sloping forehead. He threw up his hands in prayer and he stooped continually to mutter frantic words in the lady's ear.

The man in black now advanced, and taking one of the cords from his left arm, he bound the woman's hands together. She held them meekly toward him as he did so. Then he took her arm with a rough grip and led her toward the wooden horse, which was little higher than her waist. On to this she was lifted and laid, with her back upon it, and her face to the ceiling, while the priest, quivering with horror, had rushed out of the room. The woman's lips were moving rapidly, and though I could hear nothing I knew that she was praying. Her feet hung down on either side of the horse, and I saw that the rough varlets in attendance had fastened cords to her ankles and secured the other ends to iron rings in the stone floor.

My heart sank within me as I saw these ominous preparations, and yet I was held by the fascination of horror, and I could not take my eyes from the strange spectacle. A man had entered the room with a bucket of water in either hand. Another followed with a third bucket. They were laid beside the wooden horse. The second man had a wooden dipper—a bowl with a straight handle—in his other hand. This he gave to the man in black. At the same moment one of the varlets approached with a dark object in his hand, which even in my dream filled me with a vague feeling of familiarity. It was a leathern filler. With horrible energy he thrust it—but I could stand no more. My hair stood on end with horror. I writhed, I struggled, I broke through the bonds of sleep, and I burst with a shriek into my own life, and found myself lying shivering with terror in the huge library, with the moonlight flooding through the window and throwing strange silver and black traceries upon the opposite wall. Oh, what a blessed relief to feel that I was back in the nineteenth century—back out of that mediæval vault into a world where men had human hearts within their bosoms. I sat up on my couch, trembling in every limb, my mind divided between thankfulness and horror. To think that such things were ever done—that they *could* be done without God striking the villains dead. Was it all a fantasy, or did it really stand for something which had happened in the black, cruel days of the world's history? I sank my throbbing head upon my shaking hands. And then, suddenly, my heart seemed to stand still in my bosom, and I could not even scream, so great was my terror. Something was advancing toward me through the darkness of the room.

It is a horror coming upon a horror which breaks a

man's spirit. I could not reason, I could not pray; I could only sit like a frozen image, and glare at the dark figure which was coming down the great room. And then it moved out into the white lane of moonlight, and I breathed once more. It was Dacre, and his face showed that he was as frightened as myself.

"Was that you? For God's sake what's the matter?" he asked in a husky voice.

"Oh, Dacre, I am glad to see you! I have been down into hell. It was dreadful."

"Then it was you who screamed?"

"I dare say it was."

"It rang through the house. The servants are all terrified." He struck a match and lit the lamp. "I think we may get the fire to burn up again," he added, throwing some logs upon the embers. "Good God, my dear chap, how white you are! You look as if you had seen a ghost."

"So I have—several ghosts."

"The leather funnel has acted, then?"

"I wouldn't sleep near the infernal thing again for all the money you could offer me."

Dacre chuckled.

"I expected that you would have a lively night of it," said he. "You took it out of me in return, for that scream of yours wasn't a very pleasant sound at two in the morning. I suppose from what you say that you have seen the whole dreadful business."

"What dreadful business?"

"The torture of the water—the 'Extraordinary Question,' as it was called in the genial days of 'Le Roi Soleil.' Did you stand it out to the end?"

"No, thank God, I awoke before it really began."

"Ah! it is just as well for you. I held out till the third bucket. Well, it is an old story, and they are all in their graves now anyhow, so what does it matter how they got there? I suppose that you have no idea what it was that you have seen?"

"The torture of some criminal. She must have been a terrible malefactor indeed if her crimes are in proportion to her penalty."

"Well, we have that small consolation," said Dacre, wrapping his dressing-gown round him and crouching closer to the fire. "They *were* in proportion to her penalty. That is to say, if I am correct in the lady's identity."

"How could you possibly know her identity?"

For answer Dacre took down an old vellum-covered volume from the shelf.

"Just listen to this," said he; "it is in the French of the seventeenth century, but I will give a rough translation as I go. You will judge for yourself whether I have solved the riddle or not."

"'The prisoner was brought before the Grand Chambers and Tournelles of Parliament, sitting as a court of justice, charged with the murder of Master Dreux d'Aubray, her father, and of her two brothers, MM. d'Aubray, one being civil lieutenant, and the other a counsellor of Parliament. In person it seemed hard to believe that she had really done such wicked deeds, for she was of a mild appearance, and of short stature, with a fair skin and blue eyes. Yet the Court, having found her guilty, condemned her to the ordinary and to the extraordinary question in order that she might be forced to name her accomplices, after which she should be carried in a cart to the Place de Grève, there to have her head cut off, her body being afterwards burned and her ashes scattered to the winds.'

The date of this entry is July 16, 1676."

"It is interesting," said I, "but not convincing. How do you prove the two women to be the same?"

"I am coming to that. The narrative goes on to tell of the woman's behaviour when questioned. 'When the executioner approached her she recognized him by the cords which he held in his hands, and she at once held out her own hands to him, looking at him from head to foot without uttering a word.' How's that?"

"Yes, it was so."

"'She gazed without wincing upon the wooden horse and rings which had twisted so many limbs and caused so many shrieks of agony. When her eyes fell upon the three pails of water, which were all ready for her, she said with a smile, "All that water must have been brought here for the purpose of drowning me, Monsieur. You have no idea, I trust, of making a person of my small stature swallow it all."' Shall I read the details of the torture?"

"No, for Heaven's sake, don't."

"Here is a sentence which must surely show you that what is here recorded is the very scene which you have gazed upon to-night: 'The good Abbé Pirot, unable to contemplate the agonies which were suffered by his penitent, had hurried from the room.' Does that convince you?"

"It does entirely. There can be no question that it is indeed the same event. But who, then, is this lady whose appearance was so attractive and whose end was so horrible?"

For answer Dacre came across to me, and placed the small lamp upon the table which stood by my bed. Lifting up the ill-omened filler, he turned the brass rim so that the light fell full upon it. Seen in this way the engraving seemed clearer than on the night before.

"We have already agreed that this is the badge of a marquis or of a marquise," said he. "We have also settled that the last letter is B."

"It is undoubtedly so."

"I now suggest to you that the other letters from left to right are, M, M, a small d, A, a small d, and then the final B."

"Yes, I am sure that you are right. I can make out the two small d's quite plainly."

"What I have read to you to-night," said Dacre, "is the official record of the trial of Marie Madeleine d'Aubray, Marquise de Brinvilliers, one of the most famous poisoners and murderers of all time."

I sat in silence, overwhelmed at the extraordinary nature of the incident, and at the completeness of the proof with which Dacre had exposed its real meaning. In a vague way I remembered some details of the woman's career, her unbridled debauchery, the cold-blooded and protracted torture of her sick father, the murder of her brothers for motives of petty gain. I recollected also that the bravery of her end had done something to atone for the horror of her life, and that all Paris had sympathised with her last moments, and blessed her as a martyr within a few days of the time when they had cursed her as a murderess. One objection, and one only, occurred to my mind.

"How came her initials and her badge of rank upon the filler? Surely they did not carry their mediæval homage to the nobility to the point of decorating instruments of torture with their titles?"

"I was puzzled with the same point," said Dacre, "but it admits of a simple explanation. The case excited extraordinary interest at the time, and nothing could be more natural than that La Reynie, the head of the police, should retain this filler as a grim souvenir. It was not often that a marchioness of France underwent the extraordinary question. That he should engrave her initials upon it for the information of others was surely a very ordinary proceeding upon his part."

"And this?" I asked, pointing to the marks upon the leathern neck.

"She was a cruel tigress," said Dacre, as he turned away. "I think it is evident that like other tigresses her teeth were both strong and sharp."

27. *The New Catacomb*

"LOOK here, Burger," said Kennedy, "I do wish that you would confide in me."

The two famous students of Roman remains sat together in Kennedy's comfortable room overlooking the Corso. The night was cold, and they had both pulled up their chairs to the unsatisfactory Italian stove which threw out a zone of stuffiness rather than of warmth. Outside under the bright winter stars lay the modern Rome, the long, double chain of the electric lamps, the brilliantly lighted cafés, the rushing carriages, and the dense throng upon the footpaths. But inside, in the sumptuous chamber of the rich young English archæologist, there was only old Rome to be seen. Cracked and timeworn friezes hung upon the walls, grey old busts of senators and soldiers with their fighting heads and their hard, cruel faces peered out from the corners. On the centre table, amidst a litter of inscriptions, fragments, and ornaments, there stood the famous reconstruction by Kennedy of the Baths of Caracalla, which excited such interest and admiration when it was exhibited in Berlin. Amphoræ hung from the ceiling, and a litter of curiosities strewed the rich red Turkey carpet. And of them all there was not one which was not of the most unimpeachable authenticity, and of the utmost rarity and value; for Kennedy, though little more than thirty, had a European reputation in this particular branch of research, and was, moreover, provided with that long purse which either proves to be a fatal handicap to the student's energies, or, if his mind is still true to its purpose, gives him an enormous advantage in the race for fame. Kennedy had often been seduced by whim and pleasure from his studies, but his mind was an incisive one, capable of long and concentrated efforts which ended in sharp reactions of sensuous languor. His handsome face, with its high, white forehead, its aggressive nose, and its somewhat loose and sensual mouth, was a fair index of the compromise between strength and weakness in his nature.

Of a very different type was his companion, Julius Burger. He came of a curious blend, a German father and an Italian mother, with the robust qualities of the North mingling strangely with the softer graces of the South. Blue Teutonic eyes lightened his sun-browned face, and above them rose a square, massive forehead, with a fringe of close yellow curls lying round it. His strong, firm jaw was clean-shaven, and his companion had frequently remarked how much it suggested those old Roman busts which peered out from the shadows in the corners of his chamber. Under its bluff German strength there lay always a suggestion of Italian subtlety, but the smile was so honest, and the eyes so frank, that one understood that this was only an indication of his ancestry, with no actual bearing upon his character. In age and in reputation, he was on the same level as his English companion, but his life and his work had both been far more arduous. Twelve years before, he had come as a poor student to Rome, and had lived ever since upon some small endowment for research which had been awarded to him by the University of Bonn. Painfully, slowly, and doggedly, with extraordinary tenacity and single-mindedness, he had climbed from rung to rung of the ladder of fame, until now he was a member of the Berlin Academy, and there was every reason to believe that he would shortly be promoted to the Chair of the greatest of German Universities. But the singleness of purpose which had brought him to the same high level as the rich and brilliant Englishman, had caused him in everything outside their work to stand infinitely below him. He had never found a pause in his studies in which to cultivate the social graces. It was only when he spoke of his own subject that his face was filled with life and soul. At other times he was silent and embarrassed, too conscious of his own limitations in larger subjects, and impatient of that small talk which is the conventional refuge of those who have no thoughts to express.

And yet for some years there had been an acquaintanceship which appeared to be slowly ripening into a friendship between these two very different rivals. The base and origin of this lay in the fact that in their own studies each was the only one of the younger men who had knowledge and enthusiasm enough to properly appreciate the other. Their common interests and pursuits had brought them together, and each had been attracted by the other's knowledge. And then gradually something had been added to this. Kennedy had been amused by the frankness and simplicity of his rival, while Burger in turn had been fascinated by the brilliancy and vivacity which had made Kennedy such a favourite in Roman society. I say "had," because just at the moment the young Englishman was somewhat under a cloud. A love-affair, the details of which had never quite come out, had indicated a heartlessness and callousness upon his part which shocked many of his friends. But in the bachelor circles of students and artists in which he preferred to move there is no very rigid code of honour in such matters, and though a head might be shaken or a pair of shoulders shrugged over the flight of two and the return of one, the general sentiment was probably one of curiosity and perhaps of envy rather than of reprobation.

"Look here, Burger," said Kennedy, looking hard at the placid face of his companion, "I do wish that you would confide in me."

As he spoke he waved his hand in the direction of a rug which lay upon the floor. On the rug stood a long, shallow fruit-basket of the light wicker-work which is used in the Campagna, and this was heaped with a litter of objects, inscribed tiles, broken inscriptions, cracked mosaics, torn papyri, rusty metal ornaments, which to the uninitiated might have seemed to have come straight from a dustman's bin, but which a specialist would have speedily recognized as unique of their kind. The pile of odds and ends in the flat wicker-work basket supplied exactly one of those missing links of social development which are of such interest to the student. It was the German who had brought them in, and the Englishman's eyes were hungry as he looked at them.

"I won't interfere with your treasure-trove, but I should very much like to hear about it," he continued, while Burger very deliberately lit a cigar. "It is evidently a discovery of the first importance. These inscriptions will make a sensation throughout Europe."

"For every one here there are a million there!" said the German. "There are so many that a dozen savants might spend a lifetime over them, and build up a reputation as solid as the Castle of St. Angelo."

Kennedy sat thinking with his fine forehead wrinkled and his fingers playing with his long, fair moustache.

"You have given yourself away, Burger!" said he at last. "Your words can only apply to one thing. You have discovered a new catacomb."

"I had no doubt that you had already come to that conclusion from an examination of these objects."

"Well, they certainly appeared to indicate it, but your last remarks make it certain. There is no place except a catacomb which could contain so vast a store of relics as you describe."

"Quite so. There is no mystery about that. I *have* discovered a new catacomb."

"Where?"

"Ah, that is my secret, my dear Kennedy. Suffice it that it is so situated that there is not one chance in a million of anyone else coming upon it. Its date is different from that of any known catacomb, and it has been reserved for the burial of the highest Christians, so that the remains and the relics are quite different from anything which has ever been seen before. If I was not aware of your knowledge and of your energy, my friend,

I would not hesitate, under the pledge of secrecy, to tell you everything about it. But as it is I think that I must certainly prepare my own report of the matter before I expose myself to such formidable competition."

Kennedy loved his subject with a love which was almost a mania—a love which held him true to it, amidst all the distractions which come to a wealthy and dissipated young man. He had ambition, but his ambition was secondary to his mere abstract joy and interest in everything which concerned the old life and history of the city. He yearned to see this new underworld which his companion had discovered.

"Look here, Burger," said he, earnestly, "I assure you that you can trust me most implicitly in the matter. Nothing would induce me to put pen to paper about anything which I see until I have your express permission. I quite understand your feeling and I think it is most natural, but you have really nothing whatever to fear from me. On the other hand, if you don't tell me I shall make a systematic search, and I shall most certainly discover it. In that case, of course, I should make what use I liked of it, since I should be under no obligation to you."

Burger smiled thoughtfully over his cigar.

"I have noticed, friend Kennedy," said he, "that when I want information over any point you are not always so ready to supply it."

"When did you ever ask me anything that I did not tell you? You remember, for example, my giving you the material for your paper about the temple of the Vestals."

"Ah, well, that was not a matter of much importance. If I were to question you upon some intimate thing would you give me an answer, I wonder! This new catacomb is a very intimate thing to me, and I should certainly expect some sign of confidence in return."

"What you are driving at I cannot imagine," said the Englishman, "but if you mean that you will answer my question about the catacomb if I answer any question which you may put to me I can assure you that I will certainly do so."

"Well, then," said Burger, leaning luxuriously back in his settee, and puffing a blue tree of cigar-smoke into the air, "tell me all about your relations with Miss Mary Saunderson."

Kennedy sprang up in his chair and glared angrily at his impassive companion.

"What the devil do you mean?" he cried. "What sort of a question is this? You may mean it as a joke, but you never made a worse one."

"No, I don't mean it as a joke," said Burger, simply. "I am really rather interested in the details of the matter. I don't know much about the world and women and social life and that sort of thing, and such an incident has the fascination of the unknown for me. I know you, and I knew her by sight—I had even spoken to her once or twice. I should very much like to hear from your own lips exactly what it was which occurred between you."

"I won't tell you a word."

"That's all right. It was only my whim to see if you would give up a secret as easily as you expected me to give up my secret of the new catacomb. You wouldn't, and I didn't expect you to. But why should you expect otherwise of me? There's Saint John's clock striking ten. It is quite time that I was going home."

"No; wait a bit, Burger," said Kennedy; "this is really a ridiculous caprice of yours to wish to know about an old love-affair which has burned out months ago. You know we look upon a man who kisses and tells as the greatest coward and villain possible."

"Certainly," said the German, gathering up his basket of curiosities, "when he tells anything about a girl which is previously unknown he must be so. But in this case, as you must be aware, it was a public matter which was the common talk of Rome, so that you are not really doing Miss Mary Saunderson any injury by discussing her case with me. But still, I respect your scruples, and so good night!"

"Wait a bit, Burger," said Kennedy, laying his hand upon the other's arm; "I am very keen upon this catacomb business, and I can't let it drop quite so easily. Would you mind asking me something else in return—something not quite so eccentric this time?"

"No, no; you have refused, and there is an end of it," said Burger, with his basket on his arm. "No doubt you are quite right not to answer, and no doubt I am quite right also—and so again, my dear Kennedy, good night!"

The Englishman watched Burger cross the room, and he had his hand on the handle of the door before his host sprang up with the air of a man who is making the best of that which cannot be helped.

"Hold on, old fellow," said he; "I think you are behaving in a most ridiculous fashion; but still, if this is your condition, I suppose that I must submit to it. I hate saying anything about a girl, but, as you say, it is all over Rome, and I don't suppose I can tell you anything which you do not know already. What was it you wanted to know?"

The German came back to the stove, and, laying down his basket, he sank into his chair once more.

"May I have another cigar?" said he. "Thank you very much! I never smoke when I work, but I enjoy a chat much more when I am under the influence of tobacco. Now, as regards this young lady, with whom you had this little adventure. What in the world has become of her?"

"She is at home with her own people."

"Oh, really—in England?"

"Yes."

"What part of England—London?"

"No, Twickenham."

"You must excuse my curiosity, my dear Kennedy, and you must put it down to my ignorance of the world.

No doubt it is quite a simple thing to persuade a young lady to go off with you for three weeks or so, and then to hand her over to her own family at—what did you call the place ?"

"Twickenham."

"Quite so—at Twickenham. But it is something so entirely outside my own experience that I cannot even imagine how you set about it. For example, if you had loved this girl your love could hardly disappear in three weeks, so I presume that you could not have loved her at all. But if you did not love her why should you make this great scandal which has damaged you and ruined her ?"

Kennedy looked moodily into the red eye of the stove. "That's a logical way of looking at it, certainly," said he. "Love is a big word, and it represents a good many different shades of feeling. I liked her, and—well, you say you've seen her—you know how charming she could look. But still I am willing to admit, looking back, that I could never have really loved her."

"Then, my dear Kennedy, why did you do it ?"

"The adventure of the thing had a great deal to do with it."

"What ! You are so fond of adventures !"

"Where would the variety of life be without them ? It was for an adventure that I first began to pay my attentions to her. I've chased a good deal of game in my time, but there's no chase like that of a pretty woman. There was the piquant difficulty of it also, for, as she was the companion of Lady Emily Rood, it was almost impossible to see her alone. On the top of all the other obstacles which attracted me, I learned from her own lips very early in the proceedings that she was engaged."

"Mein Gott ! To whom ?"

"She mentioned no names."

"I do not think that anyone knows that. So that made the adventure more alluring, did it ?"

"Well, it did certainly give a spice to it. Don't you think so?"

"I tell you that I am very ignorant about these things."

"My dear fellow, you can remember that the apple you stole from your neighbour's tree was always sweeter than that which fell from your own. And then I found that she cared for me."

"What—at once?"

"Oh, no, it took about three months of sapping and mining. But at last I won her over. She understood that my judicial separation from my wife made it impossible for me to do the right thing by her—but she came all the same, and we had a delightful time, as long as it lasted."

"But how about the other man?"

Kennedy shrugged his shoulders.

"I suppose it is the survival of the fittest," said he. "If he had been the better man she would not have deserted him. Let's drop the subject, for I have had enough of it!"

"Only one other thing. How did you get rid of her in three weeks?"

"Well, we had both cooled down a bit, you understand. She absolutely refused, under any circumstances, to come back to face the people she had known in Rome. Now, of course, Rome is necessary to me, and I was already pining to be back at my work—so there was one obvious cause of separation. Then, again, her old father turned up at the hotel in London, and there was a scene, and the whole thing became so unpleasant that really—though I missed her dreadfully at first—I was very glad to slip out of it. Now, I rely upon you not to repeat anything of what I have said."

"My dear Kennedy, I should not dream of repeating it. But all that you say interests me very much, for it gives me an insight into your way of looking at things, which is entirely different from mine, for I have seen so little of life. And now you want to know about my new catacomb. There's no use my trying to describe it, for you would never find it by that. There is only one thing, and that is for me to take you there."

"That would be splendid."

"When would you like to come?"

"The sooner the better. I am all impatience to see it."

"Well, it is a beautiful night—though a trifle cold. Suppose we start in an hour. We must be very careful to keep the matter to ourselves. If anyone saw us hunting in couples they would suspect that there was something going on."

"We can't be too cautious," said Kennedy. "Is it far?"

"Some miles."

"Not too far to walk?"

"Oh, no, we could walk there easily."

"We had better do so, then. A cabman's suspicions would be aroused if he dropped us both at some lonely spot in the dead of the night."

"Quite so. I think it would be best for us to meet at the Gate of the Appian Way at midnight. I must go back to my lodgings for the matches and candles and things."

"All right, Burger! I think it is very kind of you to let me into this secret, and I promise you that I will write nothing about it until you have published your report. Good-bye for the present! You will find me at the Gate at twelve."

The cold, clear air was filled with the musical chimes from that city of clocks as Burger, wrapped in an Italian overcoat, with a lantern hanging from his hand, walked up to the rendezvous. Kennedy stepped out of the shadow to meet him.

"You are ardent in work as well as in love!" said the German, laughing.

"Yes; I have been waiting here for nearly half an hour."

"I hope you left no clue as to where we were going."

"Not such a fool! By Jove, I am chilled to the bone! Come on, Burger, let us warm ourselves by a spurt of hard walking."

Their footsteps sounded loud and crisp upon the rough stone paving of the disappointing road which is all that is left of the most famous highway of the world. A peasant or two going home from the wine-shop, and a few carts of country produce coming up to Rome, were the only things which they met. They swung along, with the huge tombs looming up through the darkness upon each side of them, until they had come as far as the Catacombs of St. Calixtus, and saw against a rising moon the great circular bastion of Cecilia Metella in front of them. Then Burger stopped with his hand to his side.

"Your legs are longer than mine, and you are more accustomed to walking," said he, laughing. "I think that the place where we turn off is somewhere here. Yes, this is it, round the corner of the trattoria. Now, it is a very narrow path, so perhaps I had better go in front and you can follow."

He had lit his lantern, and by its light they were enabled to follow a narrow and devious track which wound across the marshes of the Campagna. The great Aqueduct of old Rome lay like a monstrous caterpillar across the moon-lit landscape, and their road led them under one of its huge arches, and past the circle of crumbling bricks which marks the old arena. At last Burger stopped at a solitary wooden cow-house, and he drew a key from his pocket.

"Surely your catacomb is not inside a house!" cried Kennedy.

"The entrance to it is. That is just the safeguard which we have against anyone else discovering it."

"Does the proprietor know of it?"

"Not he. He had found one or two objects which made me almost certain that his house was built on the entrance to such a place. So I rented it from him, and did my excavations for myself. Come in, and shut the door behind you."

It was a long, empty building, with the mangers of the cows along one wall. Burger put his lantern down on the ground, and shaded its light in all directions save one by draping his overcoat round it.

"It might excite remark if anyone saw a light in this lonely place," said he. "Just help me to move this boarding."

The flooring was loose in the corner, and plank by plank the two savants raised it and leaned it against the wall. Below there was a square aperture and a stair of old stone steps which led away down into the bowels of the earth.

"Be careful!" cried Burger, as Kennedy, in his impatience, hurried down them. "It is a perfect rabbits'-warren below, and if you were once to lose your way there the chances would be a hundred to one against your ever coming out again. Wait until I bring the light."

"How do you find your own way if it is so complicated?"

"I had some very narrow escapes at first, but I have gradually learned to go about. There is a certain system to it, but it is one which a lost man, if he were in the dark, could not possibly find out. Even now I always spin out a ball of string behind me when I am going far into the catacomb. You can see for yourself that it is difficult, but every one of these passages divides and subdivides a dozen times before you go a hundred yards."

They had descended some twenty feet from the level of the byre, and they were standing now in a square chamber cut out of the soft tufa. The lantern cast a flickering light, bright below and dim above, over the cracked brown walls. In every direction were the black openings of passages which radiated from this common centre.

"I want you to follow me closely, my friend," said

Burger. " Do not loiter to look at anything upon the way, for the place to which I will take you contains all that you can see, and more. It will save time for us to go there direct."

He led the way down one of the corridors, and the Englishman followed closely at his heels. Every now and then the passage bifurcated, but Burger was evidently following some secret marks of his own, for he neither stopped nor hesitated. Everywhere along the walls, packed like the berths upon an emigrant ship, lay the Christians of old Rome. The yellow light flickered over the shrivelled features of the mummies, and gleamed upon rounded skulls and long, white armbones crossed over fleshless chests. And everywhere as he passed Kennedy looked with wistful eyes upon inscriptions, funeral vessels, pictures, vestments, utensils, all lying as pious hands had placed them so many centuries ago. It was apparent to him, even in those hurried, passing glances, that this was the earliest and finest of the catacombs, containing such a storehouse of Roman remains as had never before come at one time under the observation of the student.

" What would happen if the light went out ? " he asked, as they hurried onwards.

" I have a spare candle and a box of matches in my pocket. By the way, Kennedy, have you any matches ? "

" No ; you had better give me some."

" Oh, that is all right. There is no chance of our separating."

" How far are we going ? It seems to me that we have walked at least a quarter of a mile."

" More than that, I think. There is really no limit to the tombs—at least, I have never been able to find any. This is a very difficult place, so I think that I will use our ball of string."

He fastened one end of it to a projecting stone and he carried the coil in the breast of his coat, paying it out as he advanced. Kennedy saw that it was no unnecessary precaution, for the passages had become more complex and tortuous than ever, with a perfect network of intersecting corridors. But these all ended in one large circular hall with a square pedestal of tufa topped with a slab of marble at one end of it.

"By Jove!" cried Kennedy in an ecstasy, as Burger swung his lantern over the marble. "It is a Christian altar—probably the first one in existence. Here is the little consecration cross cut upon the corner of it. No doubt this circular space was used as a church."

"Precisely," said Burger. "If I had more time I should like to show you all the bodies which are buried in these niches upon the walls, for they are the early popes and bishops of the Church, with their mitres, their croziers, and full canonicals. Go over to that one and look at it!"

Kennedy went across, and stared at the ghastly head which lay loosely on the shredded and mouldering mitre.

"This is most interesting," said he, and his voice seemed to boom against the concave vault. "As far as my experience goes, it is unique. Bring the lantern over, Burger, for I want to see them all."

But the German had strolled away, and was standing in the middle of a yellow circle of light at the other side of the hall.

"Do you know how many wrong turnings there are between this and the stairs?" he asked. "There are over two thousand. No doubt it was one of the means of protection which the Christians adopted. The odds are two thousand to one against a man getting out, even if he had a light; but if he were in the dark it would, of course, be far more difficult."

"So I should think."

"And the darkness is something dreadful. I tried it once for an experiment. Let us try it again!" He stooped to the lantern, and in an instant it was as if an invisible hand was squeezed tightly over each of Kennedy's eyes. Never had he known what such darkness was. It seemed to press upon him and to smother him. It was a solid obstacle against which the body shrank from advancing. He put his hands out to push it back from him.

"That will do, Burger," said he, "let's have the light again."

But his companion began to laugh, and in that circular room the sound seemed to come from every side at once.

"You seem uneasy, friend Kennedy," said he.

"Go on, man, light the candle!" said Kennedy impatiently.

"It's very strange, Kennedy, but I could not in the least tell by the sound in which direction you stand. Could you tell where I am?"

"No; you seem to be on every side of me."

"If it were not for this string which I hold in my hand I should not have a notion which way to go."

"I dare say not. Strike a light, man, and have an end of this nonsense."

"Well, Kennedy, there are two things which I understand that you are very fond of. The one is an adventure, and the other is an obstacle to surmount. The adventure must be the finding of your way out of this catacomb. The obstacle will be the darkness and the two thousand wrong turns which make the way a little difficult to find. But you need not hurry, for you have plenty of time, and when you halt for a rest now and then, I should like you just to think of Miss Mary Saunderson, and whether you treated her quite fairly."

"You devil, what do you mean?" roared Kennedy. He was running about in little circles and clasping at the solid blackness with both hands.

"Good-bye," said the mocking voice, and it was already at some distance. "I really do not think, Kennedy, even by your own showing that you did the right thing by that girl. There was only one little thing which you appeared not to know, and I can supply it. Miss Saunderson was engaged to a poor ungainly devil of a student, and his name was Julius Burger."

There was a rustle somewhere, the vague sound of a foot striking a stone, and then there fell silence upon that old Christian church—a stagnant, heavy silence which closed round Kennedy and shut him in like water round a drowning man.

* * * * *

Some two months afterwards the following paragraph made the round of the European Press :—

"One of the most interesting discoveries of recent years is that of the new catacomb in Rome, which lies some distance to the east of the well-known vaults of St. Calixtus. The finding of this important burial-place, which is exceeding rich in most interesting early Christian remains, is due to the energy and sagacity of Dr. Julius Burger, the young German specialist, who is rapidly taking the first place as an authority upon ancient Rome. Although the first to publish his discovery, it appears that a less fortunate adventurer had anticipated Dr. Burger. Some months ago Mr. Kennedy, the well-known English student, disappeared suddenly from his rooms in the Corso, and it was conjectured that his association with a recent scandal had driven him to leave Rome. It appears now that he had in reality fallen a victim to that fervid love of archæology which had raised him to a distinguished place among living scholars. His body was discovered in the heart of the new catacomb, and it was evident from the condition of his feet and boots that he had tramped for days through the tortuous corridors which make these subterranean tombs so dangerous to explorers. The deceased gentleman had, with inexplicable rashness, made his way into this labyrinth without, as far as can be discovered, taking with him either candles or matches, so that his sad fate was the natural result of his own temerity. What makes the matter more painful is that Dr. Julius Burger was an intimate friend of the deceased. His joy at the extraordinary find which he has been so fortunate as to make has been greatly marred by the terrible fate of his comrade and fellow-worker."

28. *The Case of Lady Sannox*

THE relations between Douglas Stone and the notorious Lady Sannox were very well known both among the fashionable circles of which she was a brilliant member, and the scientific bodies which numbered him among their most illustrious *confrères*. There was naturally, therefore, a very widespread interest when it was announced one morning that the lady had absolutely and for ever taken the veil, and that the world would see her no more. When, at the very tail of this rumour, there came the assurance that the celebrated operating surgeon, the man of steel nerves, had been found in the morning by his valet, seated on one side of his bed, smiling pleasantly upon the universe, with both legs jammed into one side of his breeches and his great brain about as valuable as a cap full of porridge, the matter was strong enough to give quite a little thrill of interest to folk who had never hoped that their jaded nerves were capable of such a sensation.

Douglas Stone in his prime was one of the most remarkable men in England. Indeed, he could hardly be said to have ever reached his prime, for he was but nine-and-thirty at the time of this little incident. Those who knew him best were aware that famous as he was as a surgeon, he might have succeeded with even greater rapidity in any of a dozen lines of life. He could have cut his way to fame as a soldier, struggled to it as an explorer, bullied for it in the courts, or built it out of stone and iron as an engineer. He was born to be great, for he could plan what another man dare not do, and he could do what another man dare not plan. In surgery none could follow him. His nerve, his judgment, his intuition, were things apart. Again and again his knife cut away death, but grazed the very springs of life in doing it, until his assistants were as white as the patient. His energy, his audacity, his full-blooded self-confidence —does not the memory of them still linger to the south of Marylebone Road and the north of Oxford Street?

His vices were as magnificent as his virtues, and infinitely more picturesque. Large as was his income, and it was the third largest of all professional men in London, it was far beneath the luxury of his living. Deep in his complex nature lay a rich vein of sensualism, at the sport of which he placed all the prizes of his life. The eye, the ear, the touch, the palate, all were his masters. The bouquet of old vintages, the scent of rare exotics, the curves and tints of the daintiest potteries of Europe, it was to these that the quick-running stream of gold was transformed. And then there came his sudden mad passion for Lady Sannox, when a single interview with two challenging glances and a whispered word set him ablaze. She was the loveliest woman in London and the only one to him. He was one of the handsomest men in London, but not the only one to her. She had a liking for new experiences, and was gracious to most men who wooed her. It may have been cause or it may have been effect that Lord Sannox looked fifty, though he was but six-and-thirty.

He was a quiet, silent, neutral-tinted man, this lord, with thin lips and heavy eyelids, much given to gardening, and full of home-like habits. He had at one time been fond of acting, had even rented a theatre in London, and on its boards had first seen Miss Marion Dawson, to whom he had offered his hand, his title, and the third of a county. Since his marriage this early hobby had become distasteful to him. Even in private theatricals it was no longer possible to persuade him to exercise the talent which he had often shown that he possessed. He was happier with a spud and a watering-can among his orchids and chrysanthemums.

It was quite an interesting problem whether he was absolutely devoid of sense, or miserably wanting in spirit. Did he know his lady's ways and condone them, or was he a mere blind, doting fool? It was a point to be discussed over the teacups in snug little drawing-rooms, or with the aid of a cigar in the bow windows of clubs. Bitter and plain were the comments among men upon his conduct. There was but one who had a good word to say for him, and he was the most silent member in the smoking-room. He had seen him break in a horse at the University, and it seemed to have left an impression upon his mind.

But when Douglas Stone became the favourite all doubts as to Lord Sannox's knowledge or ignorance were set for ever at rest. There was no subterfuge about Stone. In his high-handed, impetuous fashion, he set all caution and discretion at defiance. The scandal became notorious. A learned body intimated that his name had been struck from the list of its vice-presidents. Two friends implored him to consider his professional credit. He cursed them all three, and spent forty guineas on a bangle to take with him to the lady. He was at her house every evening, and she drove in his carriage in the afternoons. There was not an attempt on either side to conceal their relations; but there came at last a little incident to interrupt them.

It was a dismal winter's night, very cold and gusty, with the wind whooping in the chimneys and blustering against the window-panes. A thin spatter of rain tinkled on the glass with each fresh sough of the gale, drowning for the instant the dull gurgle and drip from the eaves. Douglas Stone had finished his dinner, and sat by his fire in the study, a glass of rich port upon the malachite table at his elbow. As he raised it to his lips, he held it up against the lamplight, and watched with the eye of a connoisseur the tiny scales of beeswing which floated in its rich ruby depths. The fire, as it spurted up, threw fitful lights upon his bold, clear-cut face, with its widely-opened grey eyes, its thick and yet firm lips, and the deep, square jaw, which had something Roman in its strength and its animalism. He smiled from time to time as he nestled back in his luxurious chair. Indeed, he had a right to feel well pleased, for, against the advice of six colleagues, he had performed an operation that day of which only two cases were on record, and the result had been brilliant beyond all expectation. No other man in London would have had the daring to plan, or the skill to execute, such a heroic measure.

But he had promised Lady Sannox to see her that evening and it was already half-past eight. His hand was outstretched to the bell to order the carriage when he heard the dull thud of the knocker. An instant later there was the shuffling of feet in the hall, and the sharp closing of a door.

"A patient to see you, sir, in the consulting room," said the butler.

"About himself?"

"No, sir; I think he wants you to go out."

"It is too late," cried Douglas Stone peevishly. "I won't go."

"This is his card, sir."

The butler presented it upon the gold salver which had been given to his master by the wife of a Prime Minister.

"'Hamil Ali, Smyrna.' Hum! The fellow is a Turk, I suppose."

"Yes, sir. He seems as if he came from abroad, sir. And he's in a terrible way."

"Tut, tut! I have an engagement. I must go somewhere else. But I'll see him. Show him in here, Pim."

A few moments later the butler swung open the door and ushered in a small and decrepit man, who walked with a bent back and with the forward push of the face and blink of the eyes which goes with extreme short sight. His face was swarthy, and his hair and beard of the deepest black. In one hand he held a turban of white muslin striped with red, in the other a small chamois leather bag.

"Good evening," said Douglas Stone, when the butler had closed the door. "You speak English, I presume?"

"Yes, sir. I am from Asia Minor, but I speak English when I speak slow."

"You wanted me to go out, I understand?"

"Yes, sir. I wanted very much that you should see my wife."

"I could come in the morning, but I have an engagement which prevents me from seeing your wife to-night."

The Turk's answer was a singular one. He pulled the string which closed the mouth of the chamois leather bag, and poured a flood of gold on to the table.

"There are one hundred pounds there," said he, "and I promise you that it will not take you an hour. I have a cab ready at the door."

Douglas Stone glanced at his watch. An hour would not make it too late to visit Lady Sannox. He had been there later. And the fee was an extraordinarily high one. He had been pressed by his creditors lately, and he could not afford to let such a chance pass. He would go.

"What is the case?" he asked.

"Oh, it is so sad a one! So sad a one! You have not, perhaps, heard of the daggers of the Almohades?"

"Never."

"Ah, they are Eastern daggers of a great age and of a singular shape, with the hilt like what you call a stirrup. I am a curiosity dealer, you understand, and that is why I have come to England from Smyrna, but next week I go back once more. Many things I brought with me, and I have a few things left, but among them, to my sorrow, is one of these daggers."

"You will remember that I have an appointment, sir," said the surgeon, with some irritation; "pray confine yourself to the necessary details."

"You will see that it is necessary. To-day my wife fell down in a faint in the room in which I keep my wares, and she cut her lower lip upon this cursed dagger of Almohades."

"I see," said Douglas Stone, rising. "And you wish me to dress the wound?"

"No, no, it is worse than that."

"What then?"

"These daggers are poisoned."

"Poisoned!"

"Yes, and there is no man, East or West, who can tell now what is the poison or what the cure. But all that is known I know, for my father was in this trade before me, and we have had much to do with these poisoned weapons."

"What are the symptoms?"

"Deep sleep, and death in thirty hours."

"And you say there is no cure. Why then should you pay me this considerable fee?"

"No drug can cure, but the knife may."

"And how?"

"The poison is slow of absorption. It remains for hours in the wound."

"Washing, then, might cleanse it?"

"No more than in a snake bite. It is too subtle and too deadly."

"Excision of the wound, then?"

"That is it. If it be on the finger, take the finger off. So said my father always. But think of where this wound is, and that it is my wife. It is dreadful!"

But familiarity with such grim matters may take the finer edge from a man's sympathy. To Douglas Stone this was already an interesting case, and he brushed aside as irrelevant the feeble objections of the husband.

"It appears to be that or nothing," said he brusquely. "It is better to lose a lip than a life."

"Ah, yes, I know that you are right. Well, well, it

is kismet, and it must be faced. I have the cab, and you will come with me and do this thing."

Douglas Stone took his case of bistouries from a drawer, and placed it with a roll of bandage and a compress of lint in his pocket. He must waste no more time if he were to see Lady Sannox.

"I am ready," said he, pulling on his overcoat. "Will you take a glass of wine before you go out into this cold air?"

His visitor shrank away, with a protesting hand upraised

"You forget that I am a Mussulman, and a true follower of the Prophet," said he. "But tell me what is the bottle of green glass which you have placed in your pocket?"

"It is chloroform."

"Ah, that also is forbidden to us. It is a spirit, and we make no use of such things."

"What! You would allow your wife to go through an operation without an anæsthetic?"

"Ah! she will feel nothing, poor soul. The deep sleep has already come on, which is the first working of the poison. And then I have given her of our Smyrna opium. Come, sir, for already an hour has passed."

As they stepped out into the darkness, a sheet of rain was driven in upon their faces, and the hall lamp, which dangled from the arm of a marble Caryatid, went out with a fluff. Pim, the butler, pushed the heavy door to, straining hard with his shoulder against the wind, while the two men groped their way towards the yellow glare which showed where the cab was waiting. An instant later they were rattling upon their journey.

"Is it far?" asked Douglas Stone.

"Oh, no. We have a very little quiet place off the Euston Road."

The surgeon pressed the spring of his repeater and listened to the little tings which told him the hour. It was a quarter past nine. He calculated the distances, and the short time which it would take him to perform so trivial an operation. He ought to reach Lady Sannox by ten o'clock. Through the fogged windows he saw the blurred gas lamps dancing past, with occasionally the broader glare of a shop front. The rain was pelting and rattling upon the leathern top of the carriage, and the wheels swashed as they rolled through puddle and mud. Opposite to him the white headgear of his companion gleamed faintly through the obscurity. The surgeon felt in his pockets and arranged his needles, his ligatures and his safety-pins, that no time might be wasted when they arrived. He chafed with impatience and drummed his foot upon the floor.

But the cab slowed down at last and pulled up. In an instant Douglas Stone was out, and the Smyrna merchant's toe was at his very heel.

"You can wait," said he to the driver.

It was a mean-looking house in a narrow and sordid street. The surgeon, who knew his London well, cast a swift glance into the shadows, but there was nothing distinctive—no shop, no movement, nothing but a double line of dull, flat-faced houses, a double stretch of wet flagstones which gleamed in the lamplight, and a double rush of water in the gutters which swirled and gurgled towards the sewer gratings. The door which faced them was blotched and discoloured, and a faint light in the fan pane above it served to show the dust and the grime which covered it. Above, in one of the bedroom windows, there was a dull yellow glimmer. The merchant knocked loudly, and, as he turned his dark face towards the light, Douglas Stone could see that it was contracted with anxiety. A bolt was drawn, and an elderly woman with a taper stood in the doorway, shielding the thin flame with her gnarled hand.

"Is all well?" gasped the merchant.

"She is as you left her, sir."

"She has not spoken?"

"No, she is in a deep sleep."

The merchant closed the door, and Douglas Stone walked down the narrow passage, glancing about him in some surprise as he did so. There was no oil-cloth, no mat, no hat-rack. Deep grey dust and heavy festoons of cobwebs met his eyes everywhere. Following the old woman up the winding stair, his firm footfall echoed harshly through the silent house. There was no carpet.

The bedroom was on the second landing. Douglas Stone followed the old nurse into it, with the merchant at his heels. Here, at least, there was furniture and to spare. The floor was littered and the corners piled with Turkish cabinets, inlaid tables, coats of chain mail, strange pipes, and grotesque weapons. A single small lamp stood upon a bracket on the wall. Douglas Stone took it down, and picking his way among the lumber, walked over to a couch in the corner, on which lay a woman dressed in the Turkish fashion, with yashmak and veil. The lower part of the face was exposed, and the surgeon saw a jagged cut which zigzagged along the border of the under lip.

"You will forgive the yashmak," said the Turk. "You know our views about woman in the East."

But the surgeon was not thinking about the yashmak. This was no longer a woman to him. It was a case. He stooped and examined the wound carefully.

"There are no signs of irritation," said he. "We might delay the operation until local symptoms develop."

The husband wrung his hands in uncontrollable agitation.

"Oh! sir, sir," he cried. "Do not trifle. You do not know. It is deadly. I know, and I give you my assurance that an operation is absolutely necessary. Only the knife can save her."

"And yet I am inclined to wait," said Douglas Stone.

"That is enough," the Turk cried, angrily. "Every minute is of importance, and I cannot stand here and see my wife allowed to sink. It only remains for me to give you my thanks for having come, and to call in some other surgeon before it is too late."

Douglas Stone hesitated. To refund that hundred pounds was no pleasant matter. But of course if he left the case he must return the money. And if the Turk were right and the woman died, his position before a coroner might be an embarrassing one.

"You have had personal experience of this poison?" he asked.

"I have."

"And you assure me that an operation is needful."

"I swear it by all that I hold sacred."

"The disfigurement will be frightful."

"I can understand that the mouth will not be a pretty one to kiss."

Douglas Stone turned fiercely upon the man. The speech was a brutal one. But the Turk has his own fashion of talk and of thought, and there was no time for wrangling. Douglas Stone drew a bistoury from his case, opened it and felt the keen straight edge with his forefinger. Then he held the lamp closer to the bed. Two dark eyes were gazing up at him through the slit in the yashmak. They were all iris, and the pupil was hardly to be seen.

"You have given her a very heavy dose of opium."

"Yes, she has had a good dose."

He glanced again at the dark eyes which looked straight at his own. They were dull and lustreless, but, even as he gazed, a little shifting sparkle came into them, and the lips quivered.

"She is not absolutely unconscious," said he.

"Would it not be well to use the knife while it will be painless?"

The same thought had crossed the surgeon's mind. He grasped the wounded lip with his forceps, and with two swift cuts he took out a broad V-shaped piece. The woman sprang up on the couch with a dreadful gurgling scream. Her covering was torn from her face. It was a face that he knew. In spite of that protruding upper lip and that slobber of blood, it was a face that he knew. She kept on putting her hand up to the gap and screaming. Douglas Stone sat down at the foot of the couch with his knife and his forceps. The room was whirling round, and he had felt something go like a ripping seam behind his ear. A bystander would have said that his face was the more ghastly of the two. As in a dream, or as if he had been looking at something at the play, he was conscious that the Turk's hair and beard lay upon the table, and that Lord Sannox was leaning against the wall with his hand to his side, laughing silently. The screams had died away now, and the dreadful head had dropped back again upon the pillow, but Douglas Stone still sat motionless, and Lord Sannox still chuckled quietly to himself.

"It was really very necessary for Marion, this operation," said he, "not physically, but morally, you know, morally."

Douglas Stone stooped forwards and began to play with the fringe of the coverlet. His knife tinkled down upon the ground, but he still held the forceps and something more.

"I had long intended to make a little example," said Lord Sannox, suavely. "Your note of Wednesday miscarried, and I have it here in my pocket-book. I took some pains in carrying out my idea. The wound, by the way, was from nothing more dangerous than my signet ring."

He glanced keenly at his silent companion, and cocked the small revolver which he held in his coat pocket. But Douglas Stone was still picking at the coverlet.

"You see you have kept your appointment after all," said Lord Sannox.

And at that Douglas Stone began to laugh. He laughed long and loudly. But Lord Sannox did not laugh now. Something like fear sharpened and hardened his features. He walked from the room, and he walked on tiptoe. The old woman was waiting outside.

" Attend to your mistress when she awakes," said Lord Sannox.

Then he went down to the street. The cab was at the door, and the driver raised his hand to his hat.

" John," said Lord Sannox, " you will take the doctor home first. He will want leading downstairs, I think. Tell his butler that he has been taken ill at a case."

" Very good, sir."

" Then you can take Lady Sannox home."

" And how about yourself, sir ? "

" Oh, my address for the next few months will be Hotel di Roma, Venice. Just see that the letters are sent on. And tell Stevens to exhibit all the purple chrysanthemums next Monday, and to wire me the result."

29. *The Terror of Blue John Gap*

THE following narrative was found among the papers of Dr. James Hardcastle, who died of phthisis on February 4, 1908, at 36, Upper Coventry Flats, South Kensington. Those who knew him best, while refusing to express an opinion upon this particular statement, are unanimous in asserting that he was a man of a sober and scientific turn of mind, absolutely devoid of imagination, and most unlikely to invent any abnormal series of events. The paper was contained in an envelope, which was docketed, " A Short Account of the Circumstances which occurred near Miss Allerton's Farm in North-West Derbyshire in the Spring of Last Year." The envelope was sealed, and on the other side was written in pencil—

" DEAR SEATON,—

" It may interest, and perhaps pain you, to know that the incredulity with which you met my story has prevented me from ever opening my mouth upon the subject again. I leave this record after my death, and perhaps strangers may be found to have more confidence in me than my friend."

Inquiry has failed to elicit who this Seaton may have been. I may add that the visit of the deceased to Allerton's Farm, and the general nature of the alarm there, apart from his particular explanation, have been absolutely established. With this foreword I append his account exactly as he left it. It is in the form of a diary, some entries in which have been expanded, while a few have been erased.

April 17.—Already I feel the benefit of this wonderful upland air. The farm of the Allertons lies fourteen hundred and twenty feet above sea-level, so it may well be a bracing climate. Beyond the usual morning cough I have very little discomfort, and, what with the fresh milk and the home-grown mutton, I have every chance of putting on weight. I think Saunderson will be pleased.

The two Miss Allertons are charmingly quaint and kind, two dear little hard-working old maids, who are ready to lavish all the heart which might have gone out to husband and to children upon an invalid stranger. Truly, the old maid is a most useful person, one of the reserve forces of the community. They talk of the superfluous woman, but what would the poor superfluous man do without her kindly presence? By the way, in their simplicity they very quickly let out the reason why Saunderson recommended their farm. The Professor rose from the ranks himself, and I believe that in his youth he was not above scaring crows in these very fields.

It is a most lonely spot, and the walks are picturesque in the extreme. The farm consists of grazing land lying at the bottom of an irregular valley. On each side are the fantastic limestone hills, formed of rock so soft that you can break it away with your hands. All this country is hollow. Could you strike it with some gigantic hammer it would boom like a drum, or possibly cave in altogether and expose some huge subterranean sea. A great sea there must surely be, for on all sides the streams run into the mountain itself, never to reappear. There are gaps everywhere amid the rocks, and when you pass through them you find yourself in great caverns, which wind down into the bowels of the earth. I have a small bicycle lamp, and it is a perpetual joy to me to carry it into these weird solitudes, and to see the wonderful silver and black effects when I throw its light upon the stalactites which drape the lofty roofs. Shut off the lamp, and you are in the blackest darkness. Turn it on, and it is a scene from the Arabian Nights.

But there is one of these strange openings in the earth which has a special interest, for it is the handiwork, not of nature, but of man. I had never heard of Blue John when I came to these parts. It is the name given to a peculiar mineral of a beautiful purple shade, which is only found at one or two places in the world. It is so rare that an ordinary vase of Blue John would be valued at a great price. The Romans, with that extraordinary instinct of theirs, discovered that it was to be found in this valley, and sank a horizontal shaft deep into the mountain side. The opening of their mine has been called Blue John Gap, a clean-cut arch in the rock, the mouth all overgrown with bushes. It is a goodly passage which the Roman miners have cut, and it intersects some of the great water-worn caves, so that if you enter Blue John Gap you would do well to mark your steps and to have a good store of candles, or you may never make your way back to the daylight again. I have not yet gone deeply into it, but this very day I stood at the mouth of the arched tunnel, and peering down into the black recesses beyond, I vowed that when my health returned I would devote some holiday to exploring those mysterious depths and finding out for myself how far the Roman had penetrated into the Derbyshire hills.

Strange how superstitious these countrymen are! I should have thought better of young Armitage, for he is a man of some education and character, and a very fine fellow for his station in life. I was standing at the Blue John Gap when he came across the field to me.

"Well, doctor," said he, "you're not afraid, anyhow."

"Afraid!" I answered. "Afraid of what?"

"Of it," said he, with a jerk of his thumb towards the black vault, "of the Terror that lives in the Blue John Cave."

How absurdly easy it is for a legend to arise in a lonely countryside! I examined him as to the reasons for his weird belief. It seems that from time to time sheep have been missing from the fields, carried bodily away, according to Armitage. That they could have wandered away of their own accord and disappeared among the mountains was an explanation to which he would not listen. On one occasion a pool of blood had been found, and some tufts of wool. That also, I pointed out, could be explained in a perfectly natural way. Further, the nights upon which sheep disappeared were invariably very dark, cloudy nights with no moon. This I met with the obvious retort that those were the nights which a commonplace sheep-stealer would naturally choose for his work. On one occasion a gap had been made in a wall, and some of the stones scattered for a considerable distance. Human agency again, in my opinion. Finally, Armitage clinched all his arguments by telling me that he had actually heard the Creature—indeed, that anyone could hear it who remained long enough at the Gap. It was a distant roaring of an immense volume. I could not but smile at this, knowing, as I do, the strange reverberations which come out of an underground water system running amid the chasms of a limestone formation. My incredulity annoyed Armitage so that he turned and left me with some abruptness.

And now comes the queer point about the whole business. I was still standing near the mouth of the cave turning over in my mind the various statements of Armitage, and reflecting how readily they could be explained away, when suddenly, from the depth of the tunnel beside me, there issued a most extraordinary sound. How shall I describe it? First of all, it seemed to be a great distance away, far down in the bowels of the earth. Secondly, in spite of this suggestion of distance, it was very loud. Lastly, it was not a boom, nor a crash, such as one would associate with falling water or tumbling rock, but it was a high whine, tremulous and vibrating, almost like the whinnying of a horse. It was certainly a most remarkable experience, and one which for a moment, I must admit, gave a new significance to Armitage's words. I waited by the Blue John Gap for half an hour or more, but there was no return of the sound, so at last I wandered back to the farmhouse, rather mystified by what had occurred. Decidedly I shall explore that cavern when my strength is restored. Of course, Armitage's explanation is too absurd for discussion, and yet that sound was certainly very strange. It still rings in my ears as I write.

April 20.—In the last three days I have made several expeditions to the Blue John Gap, and have even penetrated some short distance, but my bicycle lantern is so small and weak that I dare not trust myself very far. I shall do the thing more systematically. I have heard no sound at all, and could almost believe that I had been the victim of some hallucination suggested, perhaps, by Armitage's conversation. Of course, the whole idea is absurd, and yet I must confess that those bushes at the entrance of the cave do present an appearance as if some heavy creature had forced its way through them. I begin to be keenly interested. I have said nothing to the Miss Allertons, for they are quite superstitious enough already, but I have bought some candles, and mean to investigate for myself.

I observed this morning that among the numerous tufts of sheep's wool which lay among the bushes near the cavern there was one which was smeared with blood. Of course, my reason tells me that if sheep wander into such rocky places they are likely to injure themselves, and yet somehow that splash of crimson gave me a sudden shock, and for a moment I found myself shrinking back in horror from the old Roman arch. A fetid breath seemed to ooze from the black depths into which I peered. Could it indeed be possible that some nameless thing, some dreadful presence, was lurking down yonder? I should have been incapable of such feelings in the days of my strength, but one grows more nervous and fanciful when one's health is shaken.

For the moment I weakened in my resolution, and was ready to leave the secret of the old mine, if one exists, for ever unsolved. But to-night my interest has returned and my nerves grown more steady. Tomorrow I trust that I shall have gone more deeply into this matter.

April 22.—Let me try and set down as accurately as I can my extraordinary experience of yesterday. I started in the afternoon, and made my way to the Blue John Gap. I confess that my misgivings returned as I gazed into its depths, and I wished that I had brought a companion to share my exploration. Finally, with a return of resolution, I lit my candle, pushed my way through the briars, and descended into the rocky shaft.

It went down at an acute angle for some fifty feet, the floor being covered with broken stone. Thence there extended a long, straight passage cut in the solid rock. I am no geologist, but the lining of this corridor was certainly of some harder material than limestone, for there were points where I could actually see the tool-marks which the old miners had left in their excavation, as fresh as if they had been done yesterday. Down this strange, old-world corridor I stumbled, my feeble flame throwing a dim circle of light around me, which made the shadows beyond the more threatening and obscure. Finally, I came to a spot where the Roman tunnel opened into a water-worn cavern—a huge hall, hung with long white icicles of lime deposit. From this central chamber I could dimly perceive that a number of passages worn by the subterranean streams wound away into the depths of the earth. I was standing there wondering whether I had better return, or whether I dare venture farther into this dangerous labyrinth, when my eyes fell upon something at my feet which strongly arrested my attention.

The greater part of the floor of the cavern was covered with boulders of rock or with hard incrustations of lime, but at this particular point there had been a drip from the distant roof, which had left a patch of soft mud. In the very centre of this there was a huge mark—an ill-defined blotch, deep, broad and irregular, as if a great boulder had fallen upon it. No loose stone lay near, however, nor was there anything to account for the impression. It was far too large to be caused by any possible animal, and besides, there was only the one, and the patch of mud was of such a size that no reasonable stride could have covered it. As I rose from the examination of that singular mark and then looked round into the black shadows which hemmed me in, I must confess that I felt for a moment a most unpleasant sinking of my heart, and that, do what I could, the candle trembled in my outstretched hand.

I soon recovered my nerve, however, when I reflected how absurd it was to associate so huge and shapeless a mark with the track of any known animal. Even an elephant could not have produced it. I determined, therefore, that I would not be scared by vague and senseless fears from carrying out my exploration. Before proceeding, I took good note of a curious rock formation in the wall by which I could recognise the entrance of the Roman tunnel. The precaution was very necessary, for the great cave, so far as I could see it, was intersected by passages. Having made sure of my position, and reassured myself by examining my spare candles and my matches, I advanced slowly over the rocky and uneven surface of the cavern.

And now I come to the point where I met with such sudden and desperate disaster. A stream, some twenty feet broad, ran across my path, and I walked for some little distance along the bank to find a spot where I could cross dry-shod. Finally, I came to a place where a single flat boulder lay near the centre, which I could reach in a stride. As it chanced, however, the rock had been cut away and made top-heavy by the rush of the stream, so that it tilted over as I landed on it and shot me into the ice-cold water. My candle went out, and I found myself floundering about in utter and absolute darkness.

I staggered to my feet again, more amused than alarmed by my adventure. The candle had fallen from my hand, and was lost in the stream, but I had two others in my pocket, so that it was of no importance. I got one of them ready, and drew out my box of matches to light it. Only then did I realize my position. The box had been soaked in my fall into the river. It was impossible to strike the matches.

A cold hand seemed to close round my heart as I realized my position. The darkness was opaque and horrible It was so utter that one put one's hand up to one's face as if to press off something solid. I stood still, and by an effort I steadied myself. I tried to reconstruct in my mind a map of the floor of the cavern as I had last seen it. Alas! the bearings which had impressed themselves upon my mind were high on the wall, and not to be found by touch. Still, I remembered in a general way how the sides were situated, and I hoped that by groping my way along them I should at last come to the opening of the Roman tunnel. Moving very slowly, and continually striking against the rocks, I set out on this desperate quest.

But I very soon realized how impossible it was. In that black, velvety darkness one lost all one's bearings in an instant. Before I had made a dozen paces, I was utterly bewildered as to my whereabouts. The rippling of the stream, which was the one sound audible, showed me where it lay, but the moment that I left its bank I was utterly lost. The idea of finding my way back in absolute darkness through that limestone labyrinth was clearly an impossible one.

I sat down upon a boulder and reflected upon my unfortunate plight. I had not told anyone that I proposed to come to the Blue John mine, and it was unlikely that a search party would come after me. Therefore I must trust to my own resources to get clear of the danger. There was only one hope, and that was that the matches might dry. When I fell into the river, only half of me had got thoroughly wet. My left shoulder had remained above the water. I took the box of matches, therefore, and put it into my left armpit. The moist air of the cavern might possibly be counteracted by the heat of my body, but even so, I knew that I could not hope to get a light for many hours. Meanwhile there was nothing for it but to wait.

By good luck I had slipped several biscuits into my pocket before I left the farm-house. These I now devoured, and washed them down with a draught from that wretched stream which had been the cause of all my misfortunes. Then I felt about for a comfortable seat among the rocks, and, having discovered a place where I could get a support for my back, I stretched out my legs and settled myself down to wait. I was wretchedly damp and cold, but I tried to cheer myself with the reflection that modern science prescribed open windows and walks in all weather for my disease. Gradually, lulled by the monotonous gurgle of the stream, and by the absolute darkness, I sank into an uneasy slumber.

How long this lasted I cannot say. It may have been

for an hour, it may have been for several. Suddenly I sat up on my rock couch, with every nerve thrilling and every sense acutely on the alert. Beyond all doubt I had heard a sound—some sound very distinct from the gurgling of the waters. It had passed, but the reverberation of it still lingered in my ear. Was it a search party? They would most certainly have shouted, and vague as this sound was which had wakened me, it was very distinct from the human voice. I sat palpitating and hardly daring to breathe. There it was again! And again! Now it had become continuous. It was a tread—yes, surely it was the tread of some living creature. But what a tread it was! It gave one the impression of enormous weight carried upon sponge-like feet, which gave forth a muffled but ear-filling sound. The darkness was as complete as ever, but the tread was regular and decisive. And it was coming beyond all question in my direction.

My skin grew cold, and my hair stood on end as I listened to that steady and ponderous footfall. There was some creature there, and surely by the speed of its advance, it was one which could see in the dark. I crouched low on my rock and tried to blend myself into it. The steps grew nearer still, then stopped, and presently I was aware of a loud lapping and gurgling. The creature was drinking at the stream. Then again there was silence, broken by a succession of long sniffs and snorts of tremendous volume and energy. Had it caught the scent of me? My own nostrils were filled by a low fetid odour, mephitic and abominable. Then I heard the steps again. They were on my side of the stream now. The stones rattled within a few yards of where I lay. Hardly daring to breathe, I crouched upon my rock. Then the steps drew away. I heard the splash as it returned across the river, and the sound died away into the distance in the direction from which it had come.

For a long time I lay upon the rock, too much horrified

to move. I thought of the sound which I had heard coming from the depths of the cave, of Armitage's fears, of the strange impression in the mud, and now came this final and absolute proof that there was indeed some inconceivable monster, something utterly unearthly and dreadful, which lurked in the hollow of the mountain. Of its nature or form I could frame no conception, save that it was both light-footed and gigantic. The combat between my reason, which told me that such things could not be, and my senses, which told me that they were, raged within me as I lay. Finally, I was almost ready to persuade myself that this experience had been part of some evil dream, and that my abnormal condition might have conjured up an hallucination. But there remained one final experience which removed the last possibility of doubt from my mind.

I had taken my matches from my armpit and felt them. They seemed perfectly hard and dry. Stooping down into a crevice of the rocks, I tried one of them. To my delight it took fire at once. I lit the candle, and, with a terrified backward glance into the obscure depths of the cavern, I hurried in the direction of the Roman passage. As I did so I passed the patch of mud on which I had seen the huge imprint. Now I stood astonished before it, for there were three similar imprints upon its surface, enormous in size, irregular in outline, of a depth which indicated the ponderous weight which had left them. Then a great terror surged over me. Stooping and shading my candle with my hand, I ran in a frenzy of fear to the rocky archway, hastened up it, and never stopped until, with weary feet and panting lungs, I rushed up the final slope of stones, broke through the tangle of briars, and flung myself exhausted upon the soft grass under the peaceful light of the stars. It was three in the morning when I reached the farm-house, and to-day I am all unstrung and quivering after my terrific adventure. As yet I have told no one. I must move warily in the matter. What would the poor lonely women, or the uneducated yokels here think of it if I were to tell them my experience? Let me go to someone who can understand and advise.

April 25.—I was laid up in bed for two days after my incredible adventure in the cavern. I use the adjective with a very definite meaning, for I have had an experience since which has shocked me almost as much as the other. I have said that I was looking round for someone who could advise me. There is a Dr. Mark Johnson who practises some few miles away, to whom I had a note of recommendation from Professor Saunderson. To him I drove, when I was strong enough to get about, and I recounted to him my whole strange experience. He listened intently, and then carefully examined me, paying special attention to my reflexes and to the pupils of my eyes. When he had finished, he refused to discuss my adventure, saying that it was entirely beyond him, but he gave me the card of a Mr. Picton at Castleton, with the advice that I should instantly go to him and tell him the story exactly as I had done to himself. He was, according to my adviser, the very man who was pre-eminently suited to help me. I went on to the station, therefore, and made my way to the little town, which is some ten miles away. Mr. Picton appeared to be a man of importance, as his brass plate was displayed upon the door of a considerable building on the outskirts of the town. I was about to ring his bell, when some misgiving came into my mind, and, crossing to a neighbouring shop, I asked the man behind the counter if he could tell me anything of Mr. Picton. "Why," said he, "he is the best mad doctor in Derbyshire, and yonder is his asylum." You can imagine that it was not long before I had shaken the dust of Castleton from my feet and returned to the farm, cursing all unimaginative pedants who cannot conceive that there may be things in creation which have never yet chanced to come across their mole's vision. After all, now that I am cooler, I can afford to admit that I have been no more sympathetic to Armitage than Dr. Johnson has been to me.

April 27.—When I was a student I had the reputation of being a man of courage and enterprise. I remember that when there was a ghost-hunt at Coltbridge it was I who sat up in the haunted house. Is it advancing years (after all, I am only thirty-five), or is it this physical malady which has caused degeneration ? Certainly my heart quails when I think of that horrible cavern in the hill, and the certainty that it has some monstrous occupant. What shall I do ? There is not an hour in the day that I do not debate the question. If I say nothing, then the mystery remains unsolved. If I do say anything, then I have the alternative of mad alarm over the whole countryside, or of absolute incredulity which may end in consigning me to an asylum. On the whole, I think that my best course is to wait, and to prepare for some expedition which shall be more deliberate and better thought out than the last. As a first step I have been to Castleton and obtained a few essentials—a large acetylene lantern for one thing, and a good double-barrelled sporting rifle for another. The latter I have hired, but I have bought a dozen heavy game cartridges, which would bring down a rhinoceros. Now I am ready for my troglodyte friend. Give me better health and a little spate of energy, and I shall try conclusions with him yet. But who and what is he ? Ah ! there is the question which stands between me and my sleep. How many theories do I form, only to discard each in turn ! It is all so utterly unthinkable. And yet the cry, the footmark, the tread in the cavern—no reasoning can get past these. I think of the old-world legends of dragons and of other monsters, Were they, perhaps, not such fairy-tales as we have thought ? Can it be that there is some fact which underlies them, and am I, of all mortals, the one who is chosen to expose it ?

May 3.—For several days I have been laid up by the vagaries of an English spring, and during those days there have been developments, the true and sinister meaning of which no one can appreciate save myself. I may say that we have had cloudy and moonless nights of late, which according to my information were the seasons upon which sheep disappeared. Well, sheep *have* disappeared. Two of Miss Allerton's, one of old Pearson's of the Cat Walk, and one of Mrs. Moulton's. Four in all during three nights. No trace is left of them at all, and the countryside is buzzing with rumours of gipsies and of sheep-stealers.

But there is something more serious than that. Young Armitage has disappeared also. He left his moorland cottage early on Wednesday night and has never been heard of since. He was an unattached man, so there is less sensation than would otherwise be the case. The popular explanation is that he owes money, and has found a situation in some other part of the country, whence he will presently write for his belongings. But I have grave misgivings. Is it not much more likely that the recent tragedy of the sheep has caused him to take some steps which may have ended in his own destruction? He may, for example, have lain in wait for the creature and been carried off by it into the recesses of the mountains. What an inconceivable fate for a civilized Englishman of the twentieth century! And yet I feel that it is possible and even probable. But in that case, how far am I answerable both for his death and for any other mishap which may occur? Surely with the knowledge I already possess it must be my duty to see that something is done, or if necessary to do it myself. It must be the latter, for this morning I went down to the local police-station and told my story. The inspector entered it all in a large book and bowed me out with commendable gravity, but I heard a burst of laughter before I had got down his garden path. No doubt he was recounting my adventure to his family.

June 10.—I am writing this, propped up in bed, six

weeks after my last entry in this journal. I have gone through a terrible shock both to mind and body, arising from such an experience as has seldom befallen a human being before. But I have attained my end. The danger from the Terror which dwells in the Blue John Gap has passed never to return. Thus much at least I, a broken invalid, have done for the common good. Let me now recount what occurred as clearly as I may.

The night of Friday, May 3, was dark and cloudy—the very night for the monster to walk. About eleven o'clock I went from the farm-house with my lantern and my rifle, having first left a note upon the table of my bedroom in which I said that, if I were missing, search should be made for me in the direction of the Gap. I made my way to the mouth of the Roman shaft, and, having perched myself among the rocks close to the opening, I shut off my lantern and waited patiently with my loaded rifle ready to my hand.

It was a melancholy vigil. All down the winding valley I could see the scattered lights of the farm-houses, and the church clock of Chapel-le-Dale tolling the hours came faintly to my ears. These tokens of my fellow-men served only to make my own position seem the more lonely, and to call for a greater effort to overcome the terror which tempted me continually to get back to the farm, and abandon for ever this dangerous quest. And yet there lies deep in every man a rooted self-respect which makes it hard for him to turn back from that which he has once undertaken. This feeling of personal pride was my salvation now, and it was that alone which held me fast when every instinct of my nature was dragging me away. I am glad now that I had the strength. In spite of all that it has cost me, my manhood is at least above reproach.

Twelve o'clock struck in the distant church, then one, then two. It was the darkest hour of the night. The clouds were drifting low, and there was not a star in the sky. An owl was hooting somewhere among the rocks, but no other sound, save the gentle sough of the wind, came to my ears. And then suddenly I heard it! From far away down the tunnel came those muffled steps, so soft and yet so ponderous. I heard also the rattle of stones as they gave way under that giant tread. They drew nearer. They were close upon me. I heard the crashing of the bushes round the entrance, and then dimly through the darkness I was conscious of the loom of some enormous shape, some monstrous inchoate creature, passing swiftly and very silently out from the tunnel. I was paralysed with fear and amazement. Long as I had waited, now that it had actually come I was unprepared for the shock. I lay motionless and breathless, whilst the great dark mass whisked by me and was swallowed up in the night.

But now I nerved myself for its return. No sound came from the sleeping countryside to tell of the horror which was loose. In no way could I judge how far off it was, what it was doing, or when it might be back. But not a second time should my nerve fail me, not a second time should it pass unchallenged. I swore it between my clenched teeth as I laid my cocked rifle across the rock.

And yet it nearly happened. There was no warning of approach now as the creature passed over the grass. Suddenly, like a dark, drifting shadow, the huge bulk loomed up once more before me, making for the entrance of the cave. Again came that paralysis of volition which held my crooked forefinger impotent upon the trigger. But with a desperate effort I shook it off. Even as the brushwood rustled, and the monstrous beast blended with the shadow of the Gap, I fired at the retreating form. In the blaze of the gun I caught a glimpse of a great shaggy mass, something with rough and bristling hair of a withered grey colour, fading away to white in its lower parts, the huge body supported upon short, thick, curving legs. I had just that glance, and then I heard the rattle of the stones as the creature tore down into its burrow. In an instant, with a triumphant revulsion of feeling, I had cast my fears to the wind, and uncovering my powerful lantern, with my rifle in my hand, I sprang down from my rock and rushed after the monster down the old Roman shaft.

My splendid lamp cast a brilliant flood of vivid light in front of me, very different from the yellow glimmer which had aided me down the same passage only twelve days before. As I ran, I saw the great beast lurching along before me, its huge bulk filling up the whole space from wall to wall. Its hair looked like coarse faded oakum, and hung down in long, dense masses which swayed as it moved. It was like an enormous unclipped sheep in its fleece, but in size it was far larger than the largest elephant, and its breadth seemed to be nearly as great as its height. It fills me with amazement now to think that I should have dared to follow such a horror into the bowels of the earth, but when one's blood is up, and when one's quarry seems to be flying, the old primeval hunting-spirit awakes and prudence is cast to the wind. Rifle in hand, I ran at the top of my speed upon the trail of the monster.

I had seen that the creature was swift. Now I was to find out to my cost that it was also very cunning. I had imagined that it was in panic flight, and that I had only to pursue it. The idea that it might turn upon me never entered my excited brain. I have already explained that the passage down which I was racing opened into a great central cave. Into this I rushed, fearful lest I should lose all trace of the beast. But he had turned upon his own traces, and in a moment we were face to face.

That picture, seen in the brilliant white light of the lantern, is etched for ever upon my brain. He had reared up on his hind legs as a bear would do, and stood above me, enormous, menacing—such a creature as no nightmare had ever brought to my imagination. I have said that he reared like a bear, and there was something bear-like—if one could conceive a bear which was tenfold the bulk of any bear seen upon earth—in his whole pose and attitude, in his great crooked forelegs with their ivory-white claws, in his rugged skin, and in his red, gaping mouth, fringed with monstrous fangs. Only in one point did he differ from the bear, or from any other creature which walks the earth, and even at that supreme moment a shudder of horror passed over me as I observed that the eyes which glistened in the glow of my lantern were huge, projecting bulbs, white and sightless. For a moment his great paws swung over my head. The next he fell forward upon me, I and my broken lantern crashed to the earth, and I remember no more.

When I came to myself I was back in the farm-house of the Allertons. Two days had passed since my terrible adventure in the Blue John Gap. It seems that I had lain all night in the cave insensible from concussion of the brain, with my left arm and two ribs badly fractured. In the morning my note had been found, a search party of a dozen farmers assembled, and I had been tracked down and carried back to my bedroom, where I had lain in high delirium ever since. There was, it seems, no sign of the creature, and no bloodstain which would show that my bullet had found him as he passed. Save for my own plight and the marks upon the mud, there was nothing to prove that what I said was true.

Six weeks have now elapsed, and I am able to sit out once more in the sunshine. Just opposite me is the steep hillside, grey with shaly rock, and yonder on its flank is the dark cleft which marks the opening of the Blue John Gap. But it is no longer a source of terror. Never again through that ill-omened tunnel shall any strange shape flit out into the world of men. The educated and the scientific, the Dr. Johnsons and the like, may smile at my narrative, but the poorer folk of the countryside had never a doubt as to its truth. On the day after my recovering consciousness they assembled in their hundreds round the Blue John Gap. As the *Castleton Courier* said:

"It was useless for our correspondent, or for any of the adventurous gentlemen who had come from Matlock, Buxton, and other parts, to offer to descend, to explore the cave to the end, and to finally test the extraordinary narrative of Dr. James Hardcastle. The country people had taken the matter into their own hands, and from an early hour of the morning they had worked hard in stopping up the entrance of the tunnel. There is a sharp slope where the shaft begins, and great boulders, rolled along by many willing hands, were thrust down it until the Gap was absolutely sealed. So ends the episode which has caused such excitement throughout the country. Local opinion is fiercely divided upon the subject. On the one hand are those who point to Dr. Hardcastle's impaired health, and to the possibility of cerebral lesions of tubercular origin giving rise to strange hallucinations. Some *idée fixe*, according to these gentlemen, caused the doctor to wander down the tunnel, and a fall among the rocks was sufficient to account for his injuries. On the other hand, a legend of a strange creature in the Gap has existed for some months back, and the farmers look upon Dr. Hardcastle's narrative and his personal injuries as a final corroboration. So the matter stands, and so the matter will continue to stand, for no definite solution seems to us to be now possible. It transcends human wit to give any scientific explanation which could cover the alleged facts."

Perhaps before the *Courier* published these words they would have been wise to send their representative to me. I have thought the matter out, as no one else has occasion to do, and it is possible that I might have removed some of the more obvious difficulties of the narrative and brought it one degree nearer to scientific acceptance. Let me then write down the only explanation which seems to me to elucidate what I know to my cost to have been a series of facts. My theory may seem to be wildly improbable, but at least no one can venture to say that it is impossible.

My view is—and it was formed, as is shown by my diary, before my personal adventure—that in this part of England there is a vast subterranean lake or sea, which is fed by the great number of streams which pass down through the limestone. Where there is a large collection of water there must also be some evaporation, mists or rain, and a possibility of vegetation. This in turn suggests that there may be animal life, arising, as the vegetable life would also do, from those seeds and types which had been introduced at an early period of the world's history, when communication with the outer air was more easy. This place had then developed a fauna and flora of its own, including such monsters as the one which I had seen, which may well have been the old cave-bear, enormously enlarged and modified by its new environment. For countless æons the internal and the external creation had kept apart, growing steadily away from each other. Then there had come some rift in the depths of the mountain which had enabled one creature to wander up and, by means of the Roman tunnel, to reach the open air. Like all subterranean life, it had lost the power of sight, but this had no doubt been compensated for by nature in other directions. Certainly it had some means of finding its way about, and of hunting down the sheep upon the hillside. As to its choice of dark nights, it is part of my theory that light was painful to those great white eyeballs, and that it was only a pitch-black world which it could tolerate. Perhaps, indeed, it was the glare of my lantern which saved my life at that awful moment when we were face to face. So I read the riddle. I leave these facts behind me, and if you can explain them, do so ; or if you choose to doubt them, do so. Neither your belief nor your incredulity can alter them, nor affect one whose task is nearly over.

So ended the strange narrative of Dr. James Hard castle.

30. *The Brazilian Cat*

IT is hard luck on a young fellow to have expensive tastes, great expectations, aristocratic connections, but no actual money in his pocket, and no profession by which he may earn any. The fact was that my father, a good, sanguine, easy-going man, had such confidence in the wealth and benevolence of his bachelor elder brother, Lord Southerton, that he took it for granted that I, his only son, would never be called upon to earn a living for myself. He imagined that if there were not a vacancy for me on the great Southerton Estates, at least there would be found some post in that diplomatic service which still remains the special preserve of our privileged classes. He died too early to realize how false his calculations had been. Neither my uncle nor the State took the slightest notice of me, or showed any interest in my career. An occasional brace of pheasants, or basket of hares, was all that ever reached me to remind me that I was heir to Otwell House and one of the richest estates in the country. In the meantime, I found myself a bachelor and man about town, living in a suite of apartments in Grosvenor Mansions, with no occupation save that of pigeon-shooting and polo-playing at Hurlingham. Month by month I realized that it was more and more difficult to get the brokers to renew my bills, or to cash any further post-obits upon an unentailed property. Ruin lay right across my path, and every day I saw it clearer, nearer, and more absolutely unavoidable.

What made me feel my own poverty the more was that, apart from the great wealth of Lord Southerton, all my other relations were fairly well-to-do. The nearest of these was Everard King, my father's nephew and my own first cousin, who had spent an adventurous life in Brazil, and had now returned to this country to settle down on his fortune. We never knew how he made his money, but he appeared to have plenty of it, for he bought the estate of Greylands, near Clipton-on-the-Marsh, in Suffolk. For the first year of his residence in England he took no more notice of me than my miserly uncle; but at last one summer morning, to my very great relief and joy, I received a letter asking me to come down that very day and spend a short visit at Greylands Court. I was expecting a rather long visit to Bankruptcy Court at the time, and this interruption seemed almost providential. If I could only get on terms with this unknown relative of mine, I might pull through yet. For the family credit he could not let me go entirely to the wall. I ordered my valet to pack my valise, and I set off the same evening for Clipton-on-the-Marsh.

After changing at Ipswich, a little local train deposited me at a small, deserted station lying amidst a rolling grassy country, with a sluggish and winding river curving in and out amidst the valleys, between high, silted banks, which showed that we were within reach of the tide. No carriage was awaiting me (I found afterwards that my telegram had been delayed), so I hired a dog-cart at the local inn. The driver, an excellent fellow, was full of my relative's praises, and I learned from him that Mr. Everard King was already a name to conjure with in that part of the country. He had entertained the school-children, he had thrown his grounds open to visitors, he had subscribed to charities—in short, his benevolence had been so universal that my driver could only account for it on the supposition that he had Parliamentary ambitions.

My attention was drawn away from my driver's panegyric by the appearance of a very beautiful bird which settled on a telegraph-post beside the road. At first I thought that it was a jay, but it was larger, with a brighter plumage. The driver accounted for its presence at once by saying that it belonged to the very man whom we were about to visit. It seems that the acclimatization of foreign creatures was one of his hobbies, and that he had brought with him from Brazil a number of birds and beasts which he was endeavouring to rear in England. When once we had passed the gates of Greylands Park we had ample evidence of this taste of his. Some small spotted deer, a curious wild pig known, I believe, as a peccary, a gorgeously feathered oriole, some sort of armadillo, and a singular lumbering intoed beast like a very fat badger, were among the creatures which I observed as we drove along the winding avenue.

Mr. Everard King, my unknown cousin, was standing in person upon the steps of his house, for he had seen us in the distance, and guessed that it was I. His appearance was very homely and benevolent, short and stout, forty-five years old, perhaps, with a round, good-humoured face, burned brown with the tropical sun, and shot with a thousand wrinkles. He wore white linen clothes, in true planter style, with a cigar between his lips, and a large Panama hat upon the back of his head. It was such a figure as one associates with a verandahed bungalow, and it looked curiously out of place in front of this broad, stone English mansion, with its solid wings and its Palladio pillars before the doorway.

"My dear!" he cried, glancing over his shoulder; "my dear, here is our guest! Welcome, welcome to Greylands! I am delighted to make your acquaintance, Cousin Marshall, and I take it as a great compliment that you should honour this sleepy little country place with your presence."

Nothing could be more hearty than his manner, and he set me at my ease in an instant. But it needed all his cordiality to atone for the frigidity and even rudeness of his wife, a tall, haggard woman, who came forward at his summons. She was, I believe, of Brazilian extraction, though she spoke excellent English, and I excused her manners on the score of her ignorance of our customs. She did not attempt to conceal, however, either then or afterwards, that I was no very welcome visitor at Greylands Court. Her actual words were, as a rule, courteous, but she was the possessor of a pair of particularly expressive dark eyes, and I read in them very clearly from the first that she heartily wished me back in London once more.

However, my debts were too pressing and my designs upon my wealthy relative were too vital for me to allow them to be upset by the ill-temper of his wife, so I disregarded her coldness and reciprocated the extreme cordiality of his welcome. No pains had been spared by him to make me comfortable. My room was a charming one. He implored me to tell him anything which could add to my happiness. It was on the tip of my tongue to inform him that a blank cheque would materially help towards that end, but I felt that it might be premature in the present state of our acquaintance. The dinner was excellent, and as we sat together afterwards over his Havanas and coffee, which latter he told me was specially prepared upon his own plantation, it seemed to me that all my driver's eulogies were justified, and that I had never met a more large-hearted and hospitable man.

But, in spite of his cheery good nature, he was a man with a strong will and a fiery temper of his own. Of this I had an example upon the following morning. The curious aversion which Mrs. Everard King had conceived towards me was so strong, that her manner at breakfast was almost offensive. But her meaning became unmistakable when her husband had quitted the room.

"The best train in the day is at twelve fifteen," said she.

"But I was not thinking of going to-day," I answered, frankly—perhaps even defiantly, for I was determined not to be driven out by this woman.

"Oh, if it rests with you——" said she, and stopped with a most insolent expression in her eyes.

" I am sure," I answered, " that Mr. Everard King would tell me if I were outstaying my welcome."

" What's this ? What's this ? " said a voice, and there he was in the room. He had overheard my last words, and a glance at our faces had told him the rest. In an instant his chubby, cheery face set into an expression of absolute ferocity.

" Might I trouble you to walk outside, Marshall," said he ? (I may mention that my own name is Marshall King.)

He closed the door behind me, and then, for an instant, I heard him talking in a low voice of concentrated passion to his wife. This gross breach of hospitality had evidently hit upon his tenderest point. I am no eavesdropper, so I walked out on to the lawn. Presently I heard a hurried step behind me, and there was the lady, her face pale with excitement, and her eyes red with tears.

" My husband has asked me to apologize to you, Mr. Marshall King," said she, standing with downcast eyes before me.

" Please do not say another word, Mrs. King."

Her dark eyes suddenly blazed out at me.

" You fool ! " she hissed, with frantic vehemence, and turning on her heel swept back to the house.

The insult was so outrageous, so insufferable, that I could only stand staring after her in bewilderment. I was still there when my host joined me. He was his cheery, chubby self once more.

" I hope that my wife has apologized for her foolish remarks," said he.

" Oh, yes—yes, certainly ! "

He put his hand through my arm and walked with me up and down the lawn.

" You must not take it seriously," said he. " It would grieve me inexpressibly if you curtailed your visit by one hour. The fact is—there is no reason why there should be any concealment between relatives—that my poor dear wife is incredibly jealous. She hates that anyone—male or female—should for an instant come between us. Her ideal is a desert island and an eternal *tête-à-tête*. That gives you the clue to her actions, which are, I confess, upon this particular point, not very far removed from mania. Tell me that you will think no more of it."

"No, no; certainly not."

"Then light this cigar and come round with me and see my little menagerie."

The whole afternoon was occupied by this inspection, which included all the birds, beasts, and even reptiles which he had imported. Some were free, some in cages, a few actually in the house. He spoke with enthusiasm of his successes and his failures, his births and his deaths, and he would cry out in his delight, like a schoolboy, when, as we walked, some gaudy bird would flutter up from the grass, or some curious beast slink into the cover. Finally he led me down a corridor which extended from one wing of the house. At the end of this there was a heavy door with a sliding shutter in it, and beside it there projected from the wall an iron handle attached to a wheel and a drum. A line of stout bars extended across the passage.

"I am about to show you the jewel of my collection," said he. "There is only one other specimen in Europe, now that the Rotterdam cub is dead. It is a Brazilian cat."

"But how does that differ from any other cat?"

"You will soon see that," said he, laughing. "Will you kindly draw that shutter and look through?"

I did so, and found that I was gazing into a large, empty room, with stone flags, and small, barred windows upon the farther wall. In the centre of this room, lying in the middle of a golden patch of sunlight, there was stretched a huge creature, as large as a tiger, but as black and sleek as ebony. It was simply a very enormous and very well-kept black cat, and it cuddled up and basked in that yellow pool of light exactly as a cat would do. It was so graceful, so sinewy, and so gently and smoothly diabolical, that I could not take my eyes from the opening.

"Isn't he splendid?" said my host, enthusiastically.

"Glorious! I never saw such a noble creature."

"Some people call it a black puma, but really it is not a puma at all. That fellow is nearly eleven feet from tail to tip. Four years ago he was a little ball of black fluff, with two yellow eyes staring out of it. He was sold me as a new-born cub up in the wild country at the head-waters of the Rio Negro. They speared his mother to death after she had killed a dozen of them."

"They are ferocious, then?"

"The most absolutely treacherous and bloodthirsty creatures upon earth. You talk about a Brazilian cat to an up-country Indian, and see him get the jumps. They prefer humans to game. This fellow has never tasted living blood yet, but when he does he will be a terror. At present he won't stand anyone but me in his den. Even Baldwin, the groom, dare not go near him. As to me, I am his mother and father in one."

As he spoke he suddenly, to my astonishment, opened the door and slipped in, closing it instantly behind him. At the sound of his voice the huge, lithe creature rose, yawned and rubbed its round, black head affectionately against his side, while he patted and fondled it.

"Now, Tommy, into your cage!" said he.

The monstrous cat walked over to one side of the room and coiled itself up under a grating. Everard King came out, and taking the iron handle which I have mentioned, he began to turn it. As he did so the line of bars in the corridor began to pass through a slot in the wall and closed up the front of this grating, so as to make an effective cage. When it was in position he opened the door once more and invited me into the room, which was heavy with the pungent, musty smell peculiar to the great carnivora.

"That's how we work it," said he. "We give him the run of the room for exercise, and then at night we put him in his cage. You can let him out by turning the handle from the passage, or you can, as you have seen, coop him up in the same way. No, no, you should not do that!"

I had put my hand between the bars to pat the glossy, heaving flank. He pulled it back, with a serious face.

"I assure you that he is not safe. Don't imagine that because I can take liberties with him anyone else can. He is very exclusive in his friends—aren't you, Tommy? Ah, he hears his lunch coming to him! Don't you, boy?"

A step sounded in the stone-flagged passage, and the creature had sprung to his feet, and was pacing up and down the narrow cage, his yellow eyes gleaming, and his scarlet tongue rippling and quivering over the white line of his jagged teeth. A groom entered with a coarse joint upon a tray, and thrust it through the bars to him. He pounced lightly upon it, carried it off to the corner, and there, holding it between his paws, tore and wrenched at it, raising his bloody muzzle every now and then to look at us. It was a malignant and yet fascinating sight.

"You can't wonder that I am fond of him, can you?" said my host, as we left the room, "especially when you consider that I have had the rearing of him. It was no joke bringing him over from the centre of South America; but here he is safe and sound—and, as I have said, far the most perfect specimen in Europe. The people at the Zoo are dying to have him, but I really can't part with him. Now, I think that I have inflicted my hobby upon you long enough, so we cannot do better than follow Tommy's example, and go to our lunch."

My South American relative was so engrossed by his grounds and their curious occupants, that I hardly gave him credit at first for having any interests outside them. That he had some, and pressing ones, was soon borne in upon me by the number of telegrams which he received.

They arrived at all hours, and were always opened by him with the utmost eagerness and anxiety upon his face. Sometimes I imagined that it must be the Turf, and sometimes the Stock Exchange, but certainly he had some very urgent business going forwards which was not transacted upon the Downs of Suffolk. During the six days of my visit he had never fewer than three or four telegrams a day, and sometimes as many as seven or eight.

I had occupied these six days so well, that by the end of them I had succeeded in getting upon the most cordial terms with my cousin. Every night we had sat up late in the billiard-room, he telling me the most extraordinary stories of his adventures in America—stories so desperate and reckless, that I could hardly associate them with the brown little, chubby man before me. In return, I ventured upon some of my own reminiscences of London life, which interested him so much, that he vowed he would come up to Grosvenor Mansions and stay with me. He was anxious to see the faster side of city life, and certainly, though I say it, he could not have chosen a more competent guide. It was not until the last day of my visit that I ventured to approach that which was on my mind. I told him frankly about my pecuniary difficulties and my impending ruin, and I asked his advice—though I hoped for something more solid. He listened attentively, puffing hard at his cigar.

"But surely," said he, "you are the heir of our relative, Lord Southerton?"

"I have every reason to believe so, but he would never make me any allowance."

"No, no, I have heard of his miserly ways. My poor Marshall, your position has been a very hard one. By the way, have you heard any news of Lord Southerton's health lately?"

"He has always been in a critical condition ever since my childhood."

"Exactly—a creaking hinge, if ever there was one. Your inheritance may be a long way off. Dear me, how awkwardly situated you are!"

"I had some hopes, sir, that you, knowing all the facts, might be inclined to advance——"

"Don't say another word, my dear boy," he cried, with the utmost cordiality; "we shall talk it over to-night, and I give you my word that whatever is in my power shall be done."

I was not sorry that my visit was drawing to a close, for it is unpleasant to feel that there is one person in the house who eagerly desires your departure. Mrs. King's sallow face and forbidding eyes had become more and more hateful to me. She was no longer actively rude—her fear of her husband prevented her—but she pushed her insane jealousy to the extent of ignoring me, never addressing me, and in every way making my stay at Greylands as uncomfortable as she could. So offensive was her manner during that last day, that I should certainly have left had it not been for that interview with my host in the evening which would, I hoped, retrieve my broken fortunes.

It was very late when it occurred, for my relative, who had been receiving even more telegrams than usual during the day, went off to his study after dinner, and only emerged when the household had retired to bed. I heard him go round locking the doors, as his custom was of a night, and finally he joined me in the billiard-room. His stout figure was wrapped in a dressing-gown, and he wore a pair of red Turkish slippers without any heels. Settling down into an arm-chair, he brewed himself a glass of grog, in which I could not help noticing that the whisky considerably predominated over the water.

"My word!" said he, "what a night!"

It was, indeed. The wind was howling and screaming round the house, and the latticed windows rattled and shook as if they were coming in. The glow of the yellow lamps and the flavour of our cigars seemed the brighter and more fragrant for the contrast.

"Now, my boy," said my host, "we have the house and the night to ourselves. Let me have an idea of how your affairs stand, and I will see what can be done to set them in order. I wish to hear every detail."

Thus encouraged, I entered into a long exposition, in which all my tradesmen and creditors from my landlord to my valet, figured in turn. I had notes in my pocket-book, and I marshalled my facts, and gave, I flatter myself, a very business-like statement of my own unbusinesslike ways and lamentable position. I was depressed, however, to notice that my companion's eyes were vacant and his attention elsewhere. When he did occasionally throw out a remark it was so entirely perfunctory and pointless, that I was sure he had not in the least followed my remarks. Every now and then he roused himself and put on some show of interest, asking me to repeat or to explain more fully, but it was always to sink once more into the same brown study. At last he rose and threw the end of his cigar into the grate.

"I'll tell you what, my boy," said he. "I never had a head for figures, so you will excuse me. You must jot it all down upon paper, and let me have a note of the amount. I'll understand it when I see it in black and white."

The proposal was encouraging. I promised to do so.

"And now it's time we were in bed. By Jove, there's one o'clock striking in the hall."

The tingling of the chiming clock broke through the deep roar of the gale. The wind was sweeping past with the rush of a great river.

"I must see my cat before I go to bed," said my host. "A high wind excites him. Will you come?"

"Certainly," said I.

"Then tread softly and don't speak, for everyone is asleep."

We passed quietly down the lamp-lit Persian-rugged hall, and through the door at the farther end. All was dark in the stone corridor, but a stable lantern hung on a hook, and my host took it down and lit it. There was no grating visible in the passage, so I knew that the beast was in its cage.

"Come in!" said my relative, and opened the door.

A deep growling as we entered showed that the storm had really excited the creature. In the flickering light of the lantern, we saw it, a huge black mass coiled in the corner of its den and throwing a squat, uncouth shadow upon the whitewashed wall. Its tail switched angrily among the straw.

"Poor Tommy is not in the best of tempers," said Everard King, holding up the lantern and looking in at him. "What a black devil he looks, doesn't he? I must give him a little supper to put him in a better humour. Would you mind holding the lantern for a moment?"

I took it from his hand and he stepped to the door.

"His larder is just outside here," said he. "You will excuse me for an instant, won't you?" He passed out, and the door shut with a sharp metallic click behind him.

That hard crisp sound made my heart stand still. A sudden wave of terror passed over me. A vague perception of some monstrous treachery turned me cold. I sprang to the door, but there was no handle upon the inner side.

"Here!" I cried. "Let me out!"

"All right! Don't make a row!" said my host from the passage. "You've got the light all right."

"Yes, but I don't care about being locked in alone like this."

"Don't you?" I heard his hearty, chuckling laugh. "You won't be alone long."

"Let me out, sir!" I repeated angrily. "I tell you I don't allow practical jokes of this sort."

"Practical is the word," said he, with another hateful chuckle. And then suddenly I heard, amidst the roar of the storm, the creak and whine of the winch-handle turning, and the rattle of the grating as it passed through the slot. Great God, he was letting loose the Brazilian cat!

In the light of the lantern I saw the bars sliding slowly before me. Already there was an opening a foot wide at the farther end. With a scream I seized the last bar with my hands and pulled with the strength of a madman I *was* a madman with rage and horror. For a minute or more I held the thing motionless. I knew that he was straining with all his force upon the handle, and that the leverage was sure to overcome me. I gave inch by inch, my feet sliding along the stones, and all the time I begged and prayed this inhuman monster to save me from this horrible death. I conjured him by his kinship. I reminded him that I was his guest; I begged to know what harm I had ever done him. His only answers were the tugs and jerks upon the handle, each of which, in spite of all my struggles, pulled another bar through the opening. Clinging and clutching, I was dragged across the whole front of the cage, until at last, with aching wrists and lacerated fingers, I gave up the hopeless struggle. The grating clanged back as I released it, and an instant later I heard the shuffle of the Turkish slippers in the passage, and the slam of the distant door. Then everything was silent.

The creature had never moved during this time. He lay still in the corner, and his tail had ceased switching. This apparition of a man adhering to his bars and dragged screaming across him had apparently filled him with amazement. I saw his great eyes staring steadily at me. I had dropped the lantern when I seized the bars, but it still burned upon the floor, and I made a movement to grasp it, with some idea that its light might protect me. But the instant I moved, the beast gave a deep and menacing growl. I stopped and stood still, quivering with fear in every limb. The cat (if one may call so fearful a creature by so homely a name) was not more than ten feet from me. The eyes glimmered like two disks of phosphorus in the darkness. They appalled and yet fascinated me. I could not take my own eyes from them. Nature plays strange tricks with us at such moments of intensity, and those glimmering lights waxed and waned with a steady rise and fall. Sometimes they seemed to be tiny points of extreme brilliancy—little electric sparks in the black obscurity—then they would widen and widen until all that corner of the room was filled with their shifting and sinister light. And then suddenly they went out altogether.

The beast had closed its eyes. I do not know whether there may be any truth in the old idea of the dominance of the human gaze, or whether the huge cat was simply drowsy, but the fact remains that, far from showing any symptom of attacking me, it simply rested its sleek, black head upon its huge forepaws and seemed to sleep. I stood, fearing to move lest I should rouse it into malignant life once more. But at least I was able to think clearly now that the baleful eyes were off me. Here I was shut up for the night with the ferocious beast. My own instincts, to say nothing of the words of the plausible villain who laid this trap for me, warned me that the animal was as savage as its master. How could I stave it off until morning? The door was hopeless, and so were the narrow, barred windows. There was no shelter anywhere in the bare, stone-flagged room. To cry for assistance was absurd. I knew that this den was an outhouse, and that the corridor which connected it with the house was at least a hundred feet long. Besides, with that gale thundering outside, my cries were not likely to be heard. I had only my own courage and my own wits to trust to.

And then, with a fresh wave of horror, my eyes fell upon the lantern. The candle had burned low, and was already beginning to gutter. In ten minutes it would be out. I had only ten minutes then in which to do something, for I felt that if I were once left in the dark with that fearful beast I should be incapable of action. The very thought of it paralysed me. I cast my despairing eyes round this chamber of death, and they rested upon one spot which seemed to promise I will not say safety, but less immediate and imminent danger than the open floor.

I have said that the cage had a top as well as a front, and this top was left standing when the front was wound through the slot in the wall. It consisted of bars at a few inches' interval, with stout wire netting between, and it rested upon a strong stanchion at each end. It stood now as a great barred canopy over the crouching figure in the corner. The space between this iron shelf and the roof may have been from two to three feet. If I could only get up there, squeezed in between bars and ceiling, I should have only one vulnerable side. I should be safe from below, from behind, and from each side. Only on the open face of it could I be attacked. There, it is true, I had no protection whatever; but, at least, I should be out of the brute's path when he began to pace about his den. He would have to come out of his way to reach me. It was now or never, for if once the light were out it would be impossible. With a gulp in my throat I sprang up, seized the iron edge of the top, and swung myself panting on to it. I writhed in face downwards, and found myself looking straight into the terrible eyes and yawning jaws of the cat. Its fetid breath came up into my face like the steam from some foul pot.

It appeared, however, to be rather curious than angry. With a sleek ripple of its long, black back it rose, stretched itself, and then rearing itself on its hind legs, with one forepaw against the wall, it raised the other, and drew its claws across the wire meshes beneath me. One sharp, white hook tore through my trousers—for I may mention that I was still in evening dress—and dug a furrow in my knee. It was not meant as an attack, but rather as an experiment, for upon my giving a sharp cry of pain he dropped down again, and springing lightly into the room, he began walking swiftly round it, looking up every now and again in my direction. For my part I shuffled backwards until I lay with my back against the wall, screwing myself into the smallest space possible. The farther I got the more difficult it was for him to attack me.

He seemed more excited now that he had begun to move about, and he ran swiftly and noiselessly round and round the den, passing continually underneath the iron couch upon which I lay. It was wonderful to see so great a bulk passing like a shadow, with hardly the softest thudding of velvety pads. The candle was burning low—so low that I could hardly see the creature. And then, with a last flare and splutter it went out altogether. I was alone with the cat in the dark!

It helps one to face a danger when one knows that one has done all that possibly can be done. There is nothing for it then but to quietly await the result. In this case, there was no chance of safety anywhere except the precise spot where I was. I stretched myself out, therefore, and lay silently, almost breathlessly, hoping that the beast might forget my presence if I did nothing to remind him. I reckoned that it must already be two o'clock. At four it would be full dawn. I had not more than two hours to wait for daylight.

Outside, the storm was still raging, and the rain lashed continually against the little windows. Inside, the poisonous and fetid air was overpowering. I could neither hear nor see the cat. I tried to think about other things—but only one had power enough to draw my mind from my terrible position. That was the contemplation of my cousin's villainy, his unparalleled hypocrisy, his malignant hatred of me. Beneath that cheerful face there lurked the spirit of a mediæval assassin. And as I thought of it I saw more clearly how cunningly the thing had been arranged. He had apparently gone to bed with the others. No doubt he had his witnesses to prove it. Then, unknown to them, he had slipped down, had lured me into this den and abandoned me. His story would be so simple. He had left me to finish my cigar in the billiard-room. I had gone down on my own account to have a last look at the cat. I had entered the room without observing that the cage was opened, and I had been caught. How could such a crime be brought home to him? Suspicion, perhaps—but proof, never!

How slowly those dreadful two hours went by! Once I heard a low, rasping sound, which I took to be the creature licking its own fur. Several times those greenish eyes gleamed at me through the darkness, but never in a fixed stare, and my hopes grew stronger that my presence had been forgotten or ignored. At last the least faint glimmer of light came through the windows—I first dimly saw them as two grey squares upon the black wall, then grey turned to white, and I could see my terrible companion once more. And he, alas, could see me!

It was evident to me at once that he was in a much more dangerous and aggressive mood than when I had seen him last. The cold of the morning had irritated him, and he was hungry as well. With a continual growl he paced swiftly up and down the side of the room which was farthest from my refuge, his whiskers bristling angrily, and his tail switching and lashing. As he turned at the corners his savage eyes always looked upwards at me with a dreadful menace. I knew then that he meant to kill me. Yet I found myself even at that moment admiring the sinuous grace of the devilish thing, its long, undulating, rippling movements, the gloss of its beautiful flanks, the vivid, palpitating scarlet of the glistening tongue which hung from the jet-black muzzle. And all the time that deep, threatening growl was rising and rising in an unbroken crescendo. I knew that the crisis was at hand.

It was a miserable hour to meet such a death—so

cold, so comfortless, shivering in my light dress clothes upon this gridiron of torment upon which I was stretched. I tried to brace myself to it, to raise my soul above it, and at the same time, with the lucidity which comes to a perfectly desperate man, I cast round for some possible means of escape. One thing was clear to me. If that front of the cage was only back in its position once more, I could find a sure refuge behind it. Could I possibly pull it back? I hardly dared to move for fear of bringing the creature upon me. Slowly, very slowly, I put my hand forward until it grasped the edge of the front, the final bar which protruded through the wall. To my surprise it came quite easily to my jerk. Of course the difficulty of drawing it out arose from the fact that I was clinging to it. I pulled again, and three inches of it came through. It ran apparently on wheels. I pulled again . . . and then the cat sprang!

It was so quick, so sudden, that I never saw it happen. I simply heard the savage snarl, and in an instant afterwards the blazing yellow eyes, the flattened black head with its red tongue and flashing teeth, were within reach of me. The impact of the creature shook the bars upon which I lay, until I thought (as far as I could think of anything at such a moment) that they were coming down. The cat swayed there for an instant, the head and front paws quite close to me, the hind paws clawing to find a grip upon the edge of the grating. I heard the claws rasping as they clung to the wire-netting, and the breath of the beast made me sick. But its bound had been miscalculated. It could not retain its position. Slowly, grinning with rage, and scratching madly at the bars, it swung backwards and dropped heavily upon the floor. With a growl it instantly faced round to me and crouched for another spring.

I knew that the next few moments would decide my fate. The creature had learned by experience. It would not miscalculate again. I must act promptly, fearlessly, if I were to have a chance for life. In an instant I had formed my plan. Pulling off my dress-coat, I threw it down over the head of the beast. At the same moment I dropped over the edge, seized the end of the front grating, and pulled it frantically out of the wall.

It came more easily than I could have expected. I rushed across the room, bearing it with me ; but, as I rushed, the accident of my position put me upon the outer side. Had it been the other way, I might have come off scathless. As it was, there was a moment's pause as I stopped it and tried to pass in through the opening which I had left. That moment was enough to give time to the creature to toss off the coat with which I had blinded him and to spring upon me. I hurled myself through the gap and pulled the rails to behind me, but he seized my leg before I could entirely withdraw it. One stroke of that huge paw tore off my calf as a shaving of wood curls off before a plane. The next moment, bleeding and fainting, I was lying among the foul straw with a line of friendly bars between me and the creature which ramped so frantically against them.

Too wounded to move, and too faint to be conscious of fear, I could only lie, more dead than alive, and watch it. It pressed its broad, black chest against the bars and angled for me with its crooked paws as I have seen a kitten do before a mouse-trap. It ripped my clothes, but, stretch as it would, it could not quite reach me. I have heard of the curious numbing effect produced by wounds from the great carnivora, and now I was destined to experience it, for I had lost all sense of personality, and was as interested in the cat's failure or success as if it were some game which I was watching. And then gradually my mind drifted away into strange vague dreams, always with that black face and red tongue coming back into them, and so I lost myself in the nirvana of delirium, the blessed relief of those who are too sorely tried.

Tracing the course of events afterwards, I conclude that I must have been insensible for about two hours. What roused me to consciousness once more was that sharp metallic click which had been the precursor of my terrible experience. It was the shooting back of the spring lock. Then, before my senses were clear enough to entirely apprehend what they saw, I was aware of the round, benevolent face of my cousin peering in through the open door. What he saw evidently amazed him. There was the cat crouching on the floor. I was stretched upon my back in my shirt-sleeves within the cage, my trousers torn to ribbons and a great pool of blood all round me. I can see his amazed face now, with the morning sunlight upon it. He peered at me, and peered again. Then he closed the door behind him, and advanced to the cage to see if I were really dead.

I cannot undertake to say what happened. I was not in a fit state to witness or to chronicle such events. I can only say that I was suddenly conscious that his face was away from me—that he was looking towards the animal.

"Good old Tommy!" he cried. "Good old Tommy!"

Then he came near the bars, with his back still towards me.

"Down, you stupid beast!" he roared. "Down, sir! Don't you know your master?"

Suddenly even in my bemuddled brain a remembrance came of those words of his when he had said that the taste of blood would turn the cat into a fiend. My blood had done it, but he was to pay the price.

"Get away!" he screamed. "Get away, you devil! Baldwin! Baldwin! Oh, my God!"

And then I heard him fall, and rise, and fall again, with a sound like the ripping of sacking. His screams grew fainter until they were lost in the worrying snarl. And then, after I thought that he was dead, I saw, as in a nightmare, a blinded, tattered, blood-soaked figure running wildly round the room—and that was the last glimpse which I had of him before I fainted once again.

I was many months in my recovery—in fact, I cannot say that I have ever recovered, for to the end of my days I shall carry a stick as a sign of my night with the Brazilian cat. Baldwin, the groom, and the other servants could not tell what had occurred, when, drawn by the death-cries of their master, they found me behind the bars, and his remains—or what they afterwards discovered to be his remains—in the clutch of the creature which he had reared. They stalled him off with hot irons, and afterwards shot him through the loophole of the door before they could finally extricate me. I was carried to my bedroom, and there, under the roof of my would-be murderer, I remained between life and death for several weeks. They had sent for a surgeon from Clipton and a nurse from London, and in a month I was able to be carried to the station, and so conveyed back once more to Grosvenor Mansions.

I have one remembrance of that illness, which might have been part of the ever-changing panorama conjured up by a delirious brain were it not so definitely fixed in my memory. One night, when the nurse was absent, the door of my chamber opened, and a tall woman in blackest mourning slipped into the room. She came across to me, and as she bent her sallow face I saw by the faint gleam of the night-light that it was the Brazilian woman whom my cousin had married. She stared intently into my face, and her expression was more kindly than I had ever seen it.

"Are you conscious?" she asked.

I feebly nodded—for I was still very weak.

"Well, then, I only wished to say to you that you have yourself to blame. Did I not do all I could for you? From the beginning I tried to drive you from the house. By every means, short of betraying my husband, I tried to save you from him. I knew that he had a reason for bringing you here. I knew that he would never let you get away again. No one knew him as I knew him, who had suffered from him so often. I did not dare to tell you all this. He would have killed me. But I did my best for you. As things have turned out, you have been the best friend that I have ever had. You have set me free, and I fancied that nothing but death would do that. I am sorry if you are hurt, but I cannot reproach myself. I told you that you were a fool—and a fool you have been." She crept out of the room, the bitter, singular woman, and I was never destined to see her again. With what remained from her husband's property she went back to her native land, and I have heard that she afterwards took the veil at Pernambuco.

It was not until I had been back in London for some time that the doctors pronounced me to be well enough to do business. It was not a very welcome permission to me, for I feared that it would be the signal for an inrush of creditors; but it was Summers, my lawyer, who first took advantage of it.

"I am very glad to see that your lordship is so much better," said he. "I have been waiting a long time to offer my congratulations."

"What do you mean, Summers? This is no time for joking."

"I mean what I say," he answered. "You have been Lord Southerton for the last six weeks, but we feared that it would retard your recovery if you were to learn it."

Lord Southerton! One of the richest peers in England! I could not believe my ears. And then suddenly I thought of the time which had elapsed, and how it coincided with my injuries.

"Then Lord Southerton must have died about the same time that I was hurt?"

"His death occurred upon that very day." Summers looked hard at me as I spoke, and I am convinced—for he was a very shrewd fellow—that he had guessed the true state of the case. He paused for a moment as if awaiting a confidence from me, but I could not see what was to be gained by exposing such a family scandal.

"Yes, a very curious coincidence," he continued, with the same knowing look. "Of course, you are aware that your cousin Everard King was the next heir to the estates. Now, if it had been you instead of him who had been torn to pieces by this tiger, or whatever it was, then of course he would have been Lord Southerton at the present moment."

"No doubt," said I.

"And he took such an interest in it," said Summers. "I happen to know that the late Lord Southerton's valet was in his pay, and that he used to have telegrams from him every few hours to tell him how he was getting on. That would be about the time when you were down there. Was it not strange that he should wish to be so well informed, since he knew that he was not the direct heir?"

"Very strange," said I. "And now, Summers, if you will bring me my bills and a new cheque-book, we will begin to get things into order."

TALES OF MYSTERY

31. *The Lost Special*

THE confession of Herbert de Lernac, now lying under sentence of death at Marseilles, has thrown a light upon one of the most inexplicable crimes of the century—an incident which is, I believe, absolutely unprecedented in the criminal annals of any country. Although there is a reluctance to discuss the matter in official circles, and little information has been given to the Press, there are still indications that the statement of this arch-criminal is corroborated by the facts, and that we have at last found a solution for a most astounding business. As the matter is eight years old, and as its importance was somewhat obscured by a political crisis which was engaging the public attention at the time, it may be as well to state the facts as far as we have been able to ascertain them. They are collated from the Liverpool papers of that date, from the proceedings at the inquest upon John Slater, the engine-driver, and from the records of the London and West Coast Railway Company, which have been courteously put at my disposal. Briefly, they are as follows:

On the 3rd of June, 1890, a gentleman, who gave his name as Monsieur Louis Caratal, desired an interview with Mr. James Bland, the superintendent of the London and West Coast Central Station in Liverpool. He was a small man, middle-aged and dark, with a stoop which was so marked that it suggested some deformity of the spine. He was accompanied by a friend, a man of imposing physique, whose deferential manner and constant attention showed that his position was one of dependence. This friend or companion, whose name did not transpire, was certainly a foreigner, and probably from his swarthy complexion, either a Spaniard or a South American. One peculiarity was observed in him. He carried in his left hand a small black, leather dispatch-box, and it was noticed by a sharp-eyed clerk in the Central office that this box was fastened to his wrist by a strap. No importance was attached to the fact at the time, but subsequent events endowed it with some significance. Monsieur Caratal was shown up to Mr. Bland's office, while his companion remained outside.

Monsieur Caratal's business was quickly dispatched. He had arrived that afternoon from Central America. Affairs of the utmost importance demanded that he should be in Paris without the loss of an unnecessary hour. He had missed the London express. A special must be provided. Money was of no importance. Time was everything. If the company would speed him on his way, they might make their own terms.

Mr. Bland struck the electric bell, summoned Mr. Potter Hood, the traffic manager, and had the matter arranged in five minutes. The train would start in three-quarters of an hour. It would take that time to insure that the line should be clear. The powerful engine called Rochdale (No. 247 on the company's register) was attached to two carriages, with a guard's van behind. The first carriage was solely for the purpose of decreasing the inconvenience arising from the oscillation. The second was divided, as usual, into four compartments, a first-class, a first-class smoking, a second-class, and a second-class smoking. The first compartment, which was nearest to the engine, was the one allotted to the travellers. The other three were empty. The guard of the special train was James McPherson, who had been some years in the service of the company. The stoker, William Smith, was a new hand.

Monsieur Caratal, upon leaving the superintendent's

office, rejoined his companion, and both of them manifested extreme impatience to be off. Having paid the money asked, which amounted to fifty pounds five shillings, at the usual special rate of five shillings a mile, they demanded to be shown the carriage, and at once took their seats in it, although they were assured that the better part of an hour must elapse before the line could be cleared. In the meantime a singular coincidence had occurred in the office which Monsieur Caratal had just quitted.

A request for a special is not a very uncommon circumstance in a rich commercial centre, but that two should be required upon the same afternoon was most unusual. It so happened, however, that Mr. Bland had hardly dismissed the first traveller before a second entered with a similar request. This was a Mr. Horace Moore, a gentlemanly man of military appearance, who alleged that the sudden serious illness of his wife in London made it absolutely imperative that he should not lose an instant in starting upon the journey. His distress and anxiety were so evident that Mr. Bland did all that was possible to meet his wishes. A second special was out of the question, as the ordinary local service was already somewhat deranged by the first. There was the alternative, however, that Mr. Moore should share the expense of Monsieur Caratal's train, and should travel in the other empty first-class compartment, if Monsieur Caratal objected to having him in the one which he occupied. It was difficult to see any objection to such an arrangement, and yet Monsieur Caratal, upon the suggestion being made to him by Mr. Potter Hood, absolutely refused to consider it for an instant. The train was his, he said, and he would insist upon the exclusive use of it. All argument failed to overcome his ungracious objections, and finally the plan had to be abandoned. Mr. Horace Moore left the station in great distress, after learning that his only course was to take the ordinary slow train which leaves

Liverpool at six o'clock. At four thirty-one exactly by the station clock the special train, containing the crippled Monsieur Caratal and his gigantic companion, steamed out of the Liverpool station. The line was at that time clear, and there should have been no stoppage before Manchester.

The trains of the London and West Coast Railway run over the lines of another company as far as this town, which should have been reached by the special rather before six o'clock. At a quarter after six considerable surprise and some consternation were caused amongst the officials at Liverpool by the receipt of a telegram from Manchester to say that it had not yet arrived. An inquiry directed to St. Helens, which is a third of the way between the two cities, elicited the following reply—

"To James Bland, Superintendent, Central L. & W. C., Liverpool.—Special passed here at 4.52, well up to time.—Dowser, St. Helens."

This telegram was received at six forty. At six fifty a second message was received from Manchester—

"No sign of special as advised by you."

And then ten minutes later a third, more bewildering—

"Presume some mistake as to proposed running of special. Local train from St. Helens timed to follow it has just arrived and has seen nothing of it. Kindly wire advices.—Manchester."

The matter was assuming a most amazing aspect, although in some respects the last telegram was a relief to the authorities at Liverpool. If an accident had occurred to the special, it seemed hardly possible that the local train could have passed down the same line without observing it. And yet, what was the alternative? Where could the train be? Had it possibly been side-tracked for some reason in order to allow the slower train to go past? Such an explanation was possible if some small repair had to be effected. A telegram was dispatched to each of the stations between St. Helens and Manchester, and the superintendent and traffic manager waited in the utmost suspense at the instrument for the series of replies which would enable them to say for certain what had become of the missing train. The answers came back in the order of questions, which was the order of the stations beginning at the St. Helens end—

"Special passed here five o'clock.—Collins Green."

"Special passed here six past five.—Earlestown."

"Special passed here 5.10.—Newton."

"Special passed here 5.20.—Kenyon Junction."

"No special train has passed here.—Barton Moss."

The two officials stared at each other in amazement.

"This is unique in my thirty years of experience," said Mr. Bland.

"Absolutely unprecedented and inexplicable, sir. The special has gone wrong between Kenyon Junction and Barton Moss."

"And yet there is no siding, so far as my memory serves me, between the two stations. The special must have run off the metals."

"But how could the four-fifty parliamentary pass over the same line without observing it?"

"There's no alternative, Mr. Hood. It *must* be so. Possibly the local train may have observed something which may throw some light upon the matter. We will wire to Manchester for more information, and to Kenyon Junction with instructions that the line be examined instantly as far as Barton Moss."

The answer from Manchester came within a few minutes.

"No news of missing special. Driver and guard of slow train positive no accident between Kenyon Junction and Barton Moss. Line quite clear, and no sign of anything unusual.—Manchester."

"That driver and guard will have to go," said Mr. Bland, grimly. "There has been a wreck and they have missed it. The special has obviously run off the metals without disturbing the line—how it could have done so passes my comprehension—but so it must be, and we shall have a wire from Kenyon or Barton Moss presently to say that they have found her at the bottom of an embankment."

But Mr. Bland's prophecy was not destined to be fulfilled. Half an hour passed, and then there arrived the following message from the station-master of Kenyon Junction—

"There are no traces of the missing special. It is quite certain that she passed here, and that she did not arrive at Barton Moss. We have detached engine from goods train, and I have myself ridden down the line, but all is clear, and there is no sign of any accident."

Mr. Bland tore his hair in his perplexity.

"This is rank lunacy, Hood!" he cried. "Does a train vanish into thin air in England in broad daylight? The thing is preposterous. An engine, a tender, two carriages, a van, five human beings—and all lost on a straight line of railway! Unless we get something positive within the next hour I'll take Inspector Collins, and go down myself."

And then at last something positive did occur. It took the shape of another telegram from Kenyon Junction.

"Regret to report that the dead body of John Slater, driver of the special train, has just been found among the gorse bushes at a point two and a quarter miles from the Junction. Had fallen from his engine, pitched down the embankment, and rolled among bushes. Injuries to his head, from the fall, appear to be cause of death. Ground has now been carefully examined, and there is no trace of the missing train."

The country was, as has already been stated, in the throes of a political crisis, and the attention of the public was further distracted by the important and sensational developments in Paris, where a huge scandal threatened to destroy the Government and to wreck the reputations of many of the leading men in France. The papers were full of these events, and the singular disappearance of the special train attracted less attention than would have been the case in more peaceful times. The grotesque nature of the event helped to detract from its importance, for the papers were disinclined to believe the facts as reported to them. More than one of the London journals treated the matter as an ingenious hoax, until the coroner's inquest upon the unfortunate driver (an inquest which elicited nothing of importance) convinced them of the tragedy of the incident.

Mr. Bland, accompanied by Inspector Collins, the senior detective officer in the service of the company, went down to Kenyon Junction the same evening, and their research lasted throughout the following day, but was attended with purely negative results. Not only was no trace found of the missing train, but no conjecture could be put forward which could possibly explain the facts. At the same time, Inspector Collins's official report (which lies before me as I write) served to show that the possibilities were more numerous than might have been expected.

" In the stretch of railway between these two points," said he, " the country is dotted with ironworks and collieries. Of these, some are being worked and some have been abandoned. There are no fewer than twelve which have small gauge lines which run trolly-cars down to the main line. These can, of course, be disregarded. Besides these, however, there are seven which have, or have had, proper lines running down and connecting with points to the main line, so as to convey their produce from the mouth of the mine to the great centres of distribution. In every case these lines are only a few miles in length. Out of the seven, four belong to collieries which are worked out, or at least to shafts which are no longer used. These are the Redgauntlet, Hero, Slough of Despond, and Heartsease mines, the latter having ten years ago been one of the principal mines in Lancashire. These four side lines may be eliminated from our inquiry, for, to prevent possible accidents, the rails nearest to the main line have been taken up, and there is no longer any connection. There remain three other side lines leading—

(*a*) To the Carnstock Iron Works;
(*b*) To the Big Ben Colliery;
(*c*) To the Perseverance Colliery.

"Of these the Big Ben line is not more than a quarter of a mile long, and ends at a dead wall of coal waiting removal from the mouth of the mine. Nothing had been seen or heard there of any special. The Carnstock Iron Works line was blocked all day upon the 3rd of June by sixteen truckloads of hematite. It is a single line, and nothing could have passed. As to the Perseverance line, it is a large double line, which does a considerable traffic, for the output of the mine is very large. On the 3rd of June this traffic proceeded as usual; hundreds of men including a gang of railway platelayers, were working along the two miles and a quarter which constitute the total length of the line, and it is inconceivable that an unexpected train could have come down there without attracting universal attention. It may be remarked in conclusion that this branch line is nearer to St. Helens than the point at which the engine-driver was discovered, so that we have every reason to believe that the train was past that point before misfortune overtook her.

"As to John Slater, there is no clue to be gathered from his appearance or injuries. We can only say that, so far as we can see, he met his end by falling off his engine, though why he fell, or what became of the engine after his fall, is a question upon which I do not feel qualified to offer an opinion." In conclusion, the inspector offered his resignation to the Board, being much nettled by an accusation of incompetence in the London papers.

A month elapsed, during which both the police and

the company prosecuted their inquiries without the slightest success. A reward was offered and a pardon promised in case of crime, but they were both unclaimed. Every day the public opened their papers with the conviction that so grotesque a mystery would at last be solved, but week after week passed by, and a solution remained as far off as ever. In broad daylight, upon a June afternoon in the most thickly inhabited portion of England, a train with its occupants had disappeared as completely as if some master of subtle chemistry had volatilised it into gas. Indeed, among the various conjectures which were put forward in the public press, there were some which seriously asserted that supernatural, or, at least, preternatural, agencies had been at work, and that the deformed Monsieur Caratal was probably a person who was better known under a less polite name. Others fixed upon his swarthy companion as being the author of the mischief, but what it was exactly which he had done could never be clearly formulated in words.

Amongst the many suggestions put forward by various newspapers or private individuals, there were one or two which were feasible enough to attract the attention of the public. One which appeared in *The Times*, over the signature of an amateur reasoner of some celebrity at that date, attempted to deal with the matter in a critical and semi-scientific manner. An extract must suffice, although the curious can see the whole letter in the issue of the 3rd of July.

"It is one of the elementary principles of practical reasoning," he remarked, "that when the impossible has been eliminated the residuum, *however improbable*, must contain the truth. It is certain that the train left Kenyon Junction. It is certain that it did not reach Barton Moss. It is in the highest degree unlikely, but still possible, that it may have taken one of the seven available side lines. It is obviously impossible for a train to run where there are no rails, and, therefore, we may reduce our improbables to the three open lines, namely the Carnstock Iron Works, the Big Ben, and the Perseverance. Is there a secret society of colliers, an English *Camorra*, which is capable of destroying both train and passengers? It is improbable, but it is not impossible. I confess that I am unable to suggest any other solution. I should certainly advise the company to direct all their energies towards the observation of those three lines, and of the workmen at the end of them. A careful supervision of the pawnbrokers' shops of the district might possibly bring some suggestive facts to light."

The suggestion coming from a recognized authority upon such matters created considerable interest, and a fierce opposition from those who considered such a statement to be a preposterous libel upon an honest and deserving set of men. The only answer to this criticism was a challenge to the objectors to lay any more feasible explanations before the public. In reply to this two others were forthcoming (*Times*, July 7th and 9th). The first suggested that the train might have run off the metals and be lying submerged in the Lancashire and Staffordshire Canal, which runs parallel to the railway for some hundreds of yards. This suggestion was thrown out of court by the published depth of the canal, which was entirely insufficient to conceal so large an object. The second correspondent wrote calling attention to the bag which appeared to be the sole luggage which the travellers had brought with them, and suggesting that some novel explosive of immense and pulverising power might have been concealed in it. The obvious absurdity, however, of supposing that the whole train might be blown to dust while the metals remained uninjured reduced any such explanation to a farce. The investigation had drifted into this hopeless position when a new and most unexpected incident occurred.

This was nothing less than the receipt by Mrs. McPherson of a letter from her husband, James Mc-

Pherson, who had been the guard of the missing train. The letter, which was dated July 5th, 1890, was posted from New York and came to hand upon July 14th. Some doubts were expressed as to its genuine character, but Mrs. McPherson was positive as to the writing, and the fact that it contained a remittance of a hundred dollars in five-dollar notes was enough in itself to discount the idea of a hoax. No address was given in the letter, which ran in this way:

"My dear Wife,—

"I have been thinking a great deal, and I find it very hard to give you up. The same with Lizzie. I try to fight against it, but it will always come back to me. I send you some money which will change into twenty English pounds. This should be enough to bring both Lizzie and you across the Atlantic, and you will find the Hamburg boats which stop at Southampton very good boats, and cheaper than Liverpool. If you could come here and stop at the Johnston House I would try and send you word how to meet, but things are very difficult with me at present, and I am not very happy, finding it hard to give you both up. So no more at present, from your loving husband,

"James McPherson."

For a time it was confidently anticipated that this letter would lead to the clearing up of the whole matter, the more so as it was ascertained that a passenger who bore a close resemblance to the missing guard had travelled from Southampton under the name of Summers in the Hamburg and New York liner *Vistula*, which started upon the 7th of June. Mrs. McPherson and her sister Lizzie Dolton went across to New York as directed and stayed for three weeks at the Johnston House, without hearing anything from the missing man. It is probable that some injudicious comments in the Press may have warned him that the police were using them as a bait. However, this may be, it is certain that he neither wrote nor came, and the women were eventually compelled to return to Liverpool.

And so the matter stood, and has continued to stand up to the present year of 1898. Incredible as it may seem, nothing has transpired during these eight years which has shed the least light upon the extraordinary disappearance of the special train which contained Monsieur Caratal and his companion. Careful inquiries into the antecedents of the two travellers have only established the fact that Monsieur Caratal was well known as a financier and political agent in Central America, and that during his voyage to Europe he had betrayed extraordinary anxiety to reach Paris. His companion, whose name was entered upon the passenger lists as Eduardo Gomez, was a man whose record was a violent one, and whose reputation was that of a bravo and a bully. There was evidence to show, however, that he was honestly devoted to the interests of Monsieur Caratal, and that the latter, being a man of puny physique, employed the other as a guard and protector. It may be added that no information came from Paris as to what the objects of Monsieur Caratal's hurried journey may have been. This comprises all the facts of the case up to the publication in the Marseilles papers of the recent confession of Herbert de Lernac, now under sentence of death for the murder of a merchant named Bonvalot. This statement may be literally translated as follows:

"It is not out of mere pride or boasting that I give this information, for, if that were my object, I could tell a dozen actions of mine which are quite as splendid; but I do it in order that certain gentlemen in Paris may understand that I, who am able here to tell about the fate of Monsieur Caratal, can also tell in whose interest and at whose request the deed was done, unless the reprieve which I am awaiting comes to me very quickly.

Take warning, messieurs, before it is too late! You know Herbert de Lernac, and you are aware that his deeds are as ready as his words. Hasten then, or you are lost!

"At present I shall mention no names—if you only heard the names, what would you not think!—but I shall merely tell you how cleverly I did it. I was true to my employers then, and no doubt they will be true to me now. I hope so, and until I am convinced that they have betrayed me, these names, which would convulse Europe, shall not be divulged. But on that day . . . well, I say no more!

"In a word, then, there was a famous trial in Paris, in the year 1890, in connection with a monstrous scandal in politics and finance. How monstrous that scandal was can never be known save by such confidential agents as myself. The honour and careers of many of the chief men in France were at stake. You have seen a group of ninepins standing, all so rigid, and prim, and unbending. Then there comes the ball from far away and pop, pop, pop—there are your ninepins on the floor. Well, imagine some of the greatest men in France as these ninepins and then this Monsieur Caratal was the ball which could be seen coming from far away. If he arrived, then it was pop, pop, pop for all of them. It was determined that he should not arrive.

"I do not accuse them all of being conscious of what was to happen. There were, as I have said, great financial as well as political interests at stake, and a syndicate was formed to manage the business. Some subscribed to the syndicate who hardly understood what were its objects. But others understood very well, and they can rely upon it that I have not forgotten their names. They had ample warning that Monsieur Caratal was coming long before he left South America, and they knew that the evidence which he held would certainly mean ruin to all of them. The syndicate had the command of an unlimited amount of money—absolutely unlimited, you understand. They looked round for an agent who was capable of wielding this gigantic power. The man chosen must be inventive, resolute, adaptive —a man in a million. They chose Herbert de Lernac, and I admit that they were right.

"My duties were to choose my subordinates, to use freely the power which money gives, and to make certain that Monsieur Caratal should never arrive in Paris. With characteristic energy I set about my commission within an hour of receiving my instructions, and the steps which I took were the very best for the purpose which could possibly be devised.

"A man whom I could trust was dispatched instantly to South America to travel home with Monsieur Caratal. Had he arrived in time the ship would never have reached Liverpool; but alas! it had already started before my agent could reach it. I fitted out a small armed brig to intercept it, but again I was unfortunate. Like all great organizers I was, however, prepared for failure, and had a series of alternatives prepared, one or the other of which must succeed. You must not underrate the difficulties of my undertaking, or imagine that a mere commonplace assassination would meet the case. We must destroy not only Monsieur Caratal, but Monsieur Caratal's documents, and Monsieur Caratal's companions also, if we had reason to believe that he had communicated his secrets to them. And you must remember that they were on the alert, and keenly suspicious of any such attempt. It was a task which was in every way worthy of me, for I am always most masterful where another would be appalled.

"I was all ready for Monsieur Caratal's reception in Liverpool, and I was the more eager because I had reason to believe that he had made arrangements by which he would have a considerable guard from the moment that he arrived in London. Anything which was to be done must be done between the moment of his setting foot upon the Liverpool quay and that of his arrival at the London and West Coast terminus in London. We prepared six plans, each more elaborate than the last; which plan would be used would depend upon his own movements. Do what he would, we were ready for him. If he had stayed in Liverpool, we were ready. If he took an ordinary train, an express, or a special, all was ready. Everything had been foreseen and provided for.

"You may imagine that I could not do all this myself. What could I know of the English railway lines? But money can procure willing agents all the world over, and I soon had one of the acutest brains in England to assist me. I will mention no names, but it would be unjust to claim all the credit for myself. My English ally was worthy of such an alliance. He knew the London and West Coast line thoroughly, and he had the command of a band of workers who were trustworthy and intelligent. The idea was his, and my own judgment was only required in the details. We bought over several officials, amongst whom the most important was James McPherson, whom we had ascertained to be the guard most likely to be employed upon a special train. Smith, the stoker, was also in our employ. John Slater, the engine-driver, had been approached, but had been found to be obstinate and dangerous, so we desisted. We had no certainty that Monsieur Caratal would take a special, but we thought it very probable, for it was of the utmost importance to him that he should reach Paris without delay. It was for this contingency, therefore, that we made special preparations—preparations which were complete down to the last detail long before his steamer had sighted the shores of England. You will be amused to learn that there was one of my agents in the pilot-boat which brought that steamer to its moorings.

"The moment that Caratal arrived in Liverpool we knew that he suspected danger and was on his guard. He had brought with him as an escort a dangerous fellow, named Gomez, a man who carried weapons, and was prepared to use them. This fellow carried Caratal's confidential papers for him, and was ready to protect either them or his master. The probability was that Caratal had taken him into his counsels, and that to remove Caratal without removing Gomez would be a mere waste of energy. It was necessary that they should be involved in a common fate, and our plans to that end were much facilitated by their request for a special train. On that special train you will understand that two out of the three servants of the company were really in our employ, at a price which would make them independent for a lifetime. I do not go so far as to say that the English are more honest than any other nation, but I have found them more expensive to buy.

"I have already spoken of my English agent—who is a man with a considerable future before him, unless some complaint of the throat carries him off before his time. He had charge of all arrangements at Liverpool, whilst I was stationed at the inn at Kenyon, where I awaited a cipher signal to act. When the special was arranged for, my agent instantly telegraphed to me and warned me how soon I should have everything ready. He himself under the name of Horace Moore applied immediately for a special also, in the hope that he would be sent down with Monsieur Caratal, which might under certain circumstances have been helpful to us. If, for example, our great *coup* had failed, it would then have become the duty of my agent to have shot them both and destroyed their papers. Caratal was on his guard, however, and refused to admit any other traveller. My agent then left the station, returned by another entrance, entered the guard's van on the side farthest from the platform, and travelled down with McPherson the guard.

"In the meantime you will be interested to know what my movements were. Everything had been prepared for days before, and only the finishing touches were needed. The side line which we had chosen had once joined the main line, but it had been disconnected. We had only to replace a few rails to connect it once more. These rails had been laid down as far as could be done without danger of attracting attention, and now it was merely a case of completing a juncture with the line, and arranging the points as they had been before. The sleepers had never been removed, and the rails, fish-plates and rivets were all ready, for we had taken them from a siding on the abandoned portion of the line. With my small but competent band of workers, we had everything ready long before the special arrived. When it did arrive, it ran off upon the small side line so easily that the jolting of the points appears to have been entirely unnoticed by the two travellers.

"Our plan had been that Smith, the stoker, should chloroform John Slater, the driver, so that he should vanish with the others. In this respect, and in this respect only, our plans miscarried—I except the criminal folly of McPherson in writing home to his wife. Our stoker did his business so clumsily that Slater in his struggles fell off the engine, and though fortune was with us so far that he broke his neck in the fall, still he remained as a blot upon that which would otherwise have been one of those complete masterpieces which are only to be contemplated in silent admiration. The criminal expert will find in John Slater the one flaw in all our admirable combinations. A man who has had as many triumphs as I can afford to be frank, and I therefore lay my finger upon John Slater, and I proclaim him to be a flaw.

"But now I have got our special train upon the small line two kilometres, or rather more than one mile, in length, which leads, or rather used to lead, to the abandoned Heartsease mine, once one of the largest coal mines in England. You will ask how it is that no one saw the train upon this unused line. I answer that along its entire length it runs through a deep cutting, and that, unless someone had been on the edge of that cutting, he could not have seen it. There *was* someone on the edge of that cutting. I was there. And now I will tell you what I saw.

"My assistant had remained at the points in order that he might superintend the switching off of the train. He had four armed men with him, so that if the train ran off the line—we thought it probable, because the points were very rusty—we might still have resources to fall back upon. Having once seen it safely on the side line, he handed over the responsibility to me. I was waiting at a point which overlooks the mouth of the mine, and I was also armed, as were my two companions. Come what might, you see, I was always ready.

"The moment that the train was fairly on the side line, Smith, the stoker, slowed-down the engine, and then, having turned it on to the fullest speed again, he and McPherson, with my English lieutenant, sprang off before it was too late. It may be that it was this slowing-down which first attracted the attention of the travellers, but the train was running at full speed again before their heads appeared at the open window. It makes me smile to think how bewildered they must have been. Picture to yourself your own feelings if, on looking out of your luxurious carriage, you suddenly perceived that the lines upon which you ran were rusted and corroded, red and yellow with disuse and decay! What a catch must have come in their breath as in a second it flashed upon them that it was not Manchester but Death which was waiting for them at the end of that sinister line. But the train was running with frantic speed, rolling and rocking over the rotten line, while the wheels made a frightful screaming sound upon the rusted surface. I was close to them, and could see their faces. Caratal was praying, I think—there was something like a rosary dangling out of his hand. The other roared like a bull who smells the blood of the slaughter-house. He saw us standing on the bank, and he beckoned to us like a madman.

Then he tore at his wrist and threw his dispatch-box out of the window in our direction. Of course, his meaning was obvious. Here was the evidence, and they would promise to be silent if their lives were spared. It would have been very agreeable if we could have done so, but business is business. Besides, the train was now as much beyond our control as theirs.

"He ceased howling when the train rattled round the curve and they saw the black mouth of the mine yawning before them. We had removed the boards which had covered it, and we had cleared the square entrance. The rails had formerly run very close to the shaft for the convenience of loading the coal, and we had only to add two or three lengths of rail in order to lead to the very brink of the shaft. In fact, as the lengths would not quite fit, our line projected about three feet over the edge. We saw the two heads at the window: Caratal below, Gomez above; but they had both been struck silent by what they saw. And yet they could not withdraw their heads. The sight seemed to have paralysed them.

"I had wondered how the train running at a great speed would take the pit into which I had guided it, and I was much interested in watching it. One of my colleagues thought that it would actually jump it, and indeed it was not very far from doing so. Fortunately, however, it fell short, and the buffers of the engine struck the other lip of the shaft with a tremendous crash. The funnel flew off into the air. The tender, carriages, and van were all smashed up into one jumble, which, with the remains of the engine, choked for a minute or so the mouth of the pit. Then something gave way in the middle, and the whole mass of green iron, smoking coals, brass fittings, wheels, wood-work, and cushions all crumbled together and crashed down into the mine. We heard the rattle, rattle, rattle, as the debris struck against the walls, and then, quite a long time afterwards, there came a deep roar as the remains of the train struck the bottom. The boiler may have burst, for a sharp crash came after the roar, and then a dense cloud of steam and smoke swirled up out of the black depths, falling in a spray as thick as rain all round us. Then the vapour shredded off into thin wisps, which floated away in the summer sunshine, and all was quiet again in the Heartsease mine.

"And now, having carried out our plans so successfully, it only remained to leave no trace behind us. Our little band of workers at the other end had already ripped up the rails and disconnected the side line, replacing everything as it had been before. We were equally busy at the mine. The funnel and other fragments were thrown in, the shaft was planked over as it used to be, and the lines which led to it were torn up and taken away. Then, without flurry, but without delay, we all made our way out of the country, most of us to Paris, my English colleague to Manchester, and McPherson to Southampton, whence he emigrated to America. Let the English papers of that date tell how thoroughly we had done our work, and how completely we had thrown the cleverest of their detectives off our track.

"You will remember that Gomez threw his bag of papers out of the window, and I need not say that I secured that bag and brought them to my employers. It may interest my employers now, however, to learn that out of that bag I took one or two little papers as a souvenir of the occasion. I have no wish to publish these papers ; but, still, it is every man for himself in this world, and what else can I do if my friends will not come to my aid when I want them ? Messieurs, you may believe that Herbert de Lernac is quite as formidable when he is against you as when he is with you, and that he is not a man to go to the guillotine until he has seen that every one of you is *en route* for New Caledonia. For your own sake, if not for mine, make haste, Monsieur de ——, and General ——, and Baron —— (you can fill up the blanks for yourselves as you read this). I promise you that in the next edition there will be no blanks to fill.

"P.S.—As I look over my statement there is only one omission which I can see. It concerns the unfortunate man McPherson, who was foolish enough to write to his wife and to make an appointment with her in New York. It can be imagined that when interests like ours were at stake, we could not leave them to the chance of whether a man in that class of life would or would not give away his secrets to a woman. Having once broken his oath by writing to his wife, we could not trust him any more. We took steps therefore to insure that he should not see his wife. I have sometimes thought that it would be a kindness to write to her and to assure her that there is no impediment to her marrying again."

32. *The Beetle-Hunter*

A CURIOUS experience? said the Doctor. Yes, my friends, I have had one very curious experience. I never expect to have another, for it is against all doctrines of chances that two such events would befall any one man in a single lifetime. You may believe me or not, but the thing happened exactly as I tell it.

I had just become a medical man, but I had not started in practice, and I lived in rooms in Gower Street. The street has been renumbered since then, but it was in the only house which has a bow-window, upon the left-hand side as you go down from the Metropolitan Station. A widow named Murchison kept the house at that time, and she had three medical students and one engineer as lodgers. I occupied the top room, which was the cheapest, but cheap as it was it was more than I could afford. My small resources were dwindling away, and every week it became more necessary that I should find something to do. Yet I was very unwilling to go into general practice, for my tastes were all in the direction of science, and especially of zoology, towards which I had always a strong leaning. I had almost given the fight up and resigned myself to being a medical drudge for life, when the turning-point of my struggles came in a very extraordinary way.

One morning I had picked up the *Standard* and was glancing over its contents. There was a complete absence of news, and I was about to toss the paper down again, when my eyes were caught by an advertisement at the head of the personal column. It was worded in this way:

"Wanted for one or more days the services of a medical man. It is essential that he should be a man of strong physique, of steady nerves, and of a resolute nature. Must be an entomologist—coleopterist preferred. Apply, in person, at 77B, Brook Street. Application must be made before twelve o'clock to-day."

Now, I have already said that I was devoted to zoology. Of all branches of zoology, the study of insects was the most attractive to me, and of all insects beetles were the species with which I was most familiar. Butterfly collectors are numerous, but beetles are far more varied, and more accessible in these islands than are butterflies. It was this fact which had attracted my attention to them, and I had myself made a collection which numbered some hundred varieties. As to the other requisites of the advertisement, I knew that my nerves could be depended upon, and I had won the weight-throwing competition at the inter-hospital sports. Clearly, I was the very man for the vacancy. Within five minutes of my having read the advertisement I was in a cab and on my way to Brook Street.

As I drove, I kept turning the matter over in my head and trying to make a guess as to what sort of employment it could be which needed such curious qualifications. A strong physique, a resolute nature, a medical training, and a knowledge of beetles—what connection could there be between these various requisites? And then there was the disheartening fact that the situation was not a permanent one, but terminable from day to day, according to the terms of the advertisement. The more I pondered over it the more unintelligible did it become; but at the end of my meditations I always came back to the ground fact that, come what might, I had nothing to lose, that I was completely at the end of my resources, and that I was ready for any adventure, however desperate, which would put a few honest sovereigns into my pocket. The man fears to fail who has to pay for his failure, but there was no penalty which Fortune could exact from me. I was like the gambler with empty pockets, who is still allowed to try his luck with the others.

No. 77B, Brook Street, was one of those dingy and yet imposing houses, dun-coloured and flat-faced, with the intensely respectable and solid air which marks the Georgian builder. As I alighted from the cab, a young man came out of the door and walked swiftly down the street. In passing me, I noticed that he cast an inquisitive and somewhat malevolent glance at me, and I took the incident as a good omen, for his appearance was that of a rejected candidate, and if he resented my application it meant that the vacancy was not yet filled up. Full of hope, I ascended the broad steps and rapped with the heavy knocker.

A footman in powder and livery opened the door. Clearly I was in touch with people of wealth and fashion.

"Yes, sir?" said the footman.

"I came in answer to——"

"Quite so, sir," said the footman. "Lord Linchmere will see you at once in the library."

Lord Linchmere! I had vaguely heard the name, but could not for the instant recall anything about him. Following the footman, I was shown into a large, book-lined room in which there was seated behind a writing-desk a small man with a pleasant, clean-shaven, mobile face, and long hair shot with grey, brushed back from his forehead. He looked me up and down with a very shrewd, penetrating glance, holding the card which the footman had given him in his right hand. Then he smiled pleasantly, and I felt that externally at any rate I possessed the qualifications which he desired.

"You have come in answer to my advertisement, Dr. Hamilton?" he asked.

"Yes, sir."

"Do you fulfil the conditions which are there laid down?"

"I believe that I do."

"You are a powerful man, or so I should judge from your appearance."

"I think that I am fairly strong."

"And resolute?"

"I believe so."

"Have you ever known what it was to be exposed to imminent danger?"

"No, I don't know that I ever have."

"But you think you would be prompt and cool at such a time?"

"I hope so."

"Well, I believe that you would. I have the more confidence in you because you do not pretend to be certain as to what you would do in a position that was new to you. My impression is that, so far as personal qualities go, you are the very man of whom I am in search. That being settled, we may pass on to the next point."

"Which is?"

"To talk to me about beetles."

I looked across to see if he was joking, but, on the contrary, he was leaning eagerly forward across his desk, and there was an expression of something like anxiety in his eyes.

"I am afraid that you do not know about beetles," he cried.

"On the contrary, sir, it is the one scientific subject about which I feel that I really do know something."

"I am overjoyed to hear it. Please talk to me about beetles."

I talked. I do not profess to have said anything original upon the subject, but I gave a short sketch of the characteristics of the beetle, and ran over the more common species, with some allusions to the specimens in my own little collection and to the article upon "Burying Beetles" which I had contributed to the *Journal of Entomological Science.*

"What! not a collector?" cried Lord Linchmere. "You don't mean that you are yourself a collector?" His eyes danced with pleasure at the thought.

"You are certainly the very man in London for my purpose. I thought that among five millions of people there must be such a man, but the difficulty is to lay one's hands upon him. I have been extraordinarily fortunate in finding you."

He rang a gong upon the table, and the footman entered.

"Ask Lady Rossiter to have the goodness to step this way," said his lordship, and a few moments later the lady was ushered into the room. She was a small, middle-aged woman, very like Lord Linchmere in appearance, with the same quick, alert features and grey-black hair. The expression of anxiety, however, which I had observed upon his face was very much more marked upon hers. Some great grief seemed to have cast its shadow over her features. As Lord Linchmere presented me she turned her face full upon me, and I was shocked to observe a half-healed scar extending for two inches over her right eyebrow. It was partly concealed by plaster, but none the less I could see that it had been a serious wound and not long inflicted.

"Dr. Hamilton is the very man for our purpose, Evelyn," said Lord Linchmere. "He is actually a collector of beetles, and he has written articles upon the subject."

"Really!" said Lady Rossiter. "Then you must have heard of my husband. Everyone who knows anything about beetles must have heard of Sir Thomas Rossiter."

For the first time a thin little ray of light began to break into the obscure business. Here, at last, was a connection between these people and beetles. Sir Thomas Rossiter—he was the greatest authority upon the subject in the world. He had made it his life-long study, and had written a most exhaustive work upon it. I hastened to assure her that I had read and appreciated it.

"Have you met my husband?" she asked.

"No, I have not."

"But you shall," said Lord Linchmere, with decision.

The lady was standing beside the desk, and she put her hand upon his shoulder. It was obvious to me as I saw their faces together that they were brother and sister.

"Are you really prepared for this, Charles? It is noble of you, but you fill me with fears." Her voice quavered with apprehension, and he appeared to me to be equally moved, though he was making strong efforts to conceal his agitation.

"Yes, yes, dear; it is all settled, it is all decided; in fact, there is no other possible way, that I can see."

"There is one obvious way."

"No, no, Evelyn, I shall never abandon you—never. It will come right—depend upon it; it will come right, and surely it looks like the interference of Providence that so perfect an instrument should be put into our hands."

My position was embarrassing, for I felt that for the instant they had forgotten my presence. But Lord Linchmere came back suddenly to me and to my engagement.

"The business for which I want you, Dr. Hamilton,

is that you should put yourself absolutely at my disposal. I wish you to come for a short journey with me, to remain always at my side, and to promise to do without question whatever I may ask you, however unreasonable it may appear to you to be."

"That is a good deal to ask," said I.

"Unfortunately I cannot put it more plainly, for I do not myself know what turn matters may take. You may be sure, however, that you will not be asked to do anything which your conscience does not approve; and I promise you that, when all is over, you will be proud to have been concerned in so good a work."

"If it ends happily," said the lady.

"Exactly; if it ends happily," his lordship repeated.

"And terms?" I asked.

"Twenty pounds a day."

I was amazed at the sum, and must have showed my surprise upon my features.

"It is a rare combination of qualities, as must have struck you when you first read the advertisement," said Lord Linchmere; "such varied gifts may well command a high return, and I do not conceal from you that your duties might be arduous or even dangerous. Besides, it is possible that one or two days may bring the matter to an end."

"Please God!" sighed his sister.

"So now, Dr. Hamilton, may I rely upon your aid?"

"Most undoubtedly," said I. "You have only to tell me what my duties are."

"Your first duty will be to return to your home. You will pack up whatever you may need for a short visit to the country. We start together from Paddington Station at 3.40 this afternoon."

"Do we go far?"

"As far as Pangbourne. Meet me at the bookstall at 3.30. I shall have the tickets. Good-bye, Dr. Hamilton! And, by the way, there are two things which I should be very glad if you would bring with you, in case you have them. One is your case for collecting beetles, and the other is a stick, and the thicker and heavier the better."

You may imagine that I had plenty to think of from the time that I left Brook Street until I set out to meet Lord Linchmere at Paddington. The whole fantastic business kept arranging and rearranging itself in kaleidoscopic forms inside my brain, until I had thought out a dozen explanations, each of them more grotesquely improbable than the last. And yet I felt that the truth must be something grotesquely improbable also. At last I gave up all attempts at finding a solution, and contented myself with exactly carrying out the instructions which I had received. With a hand valise, specimen-case, and a loaded cane, I was waiting at the Paddington bookstall when Lord Linchmere arrived. He was an even smaller man than I had thought—frail and peaky, with a manner which was more nervous than it had been in the morning. He wore a long, thick travelling ulster, and I observed that he carried a heavy blackthorn cudgel in his hand.

"I have the tickets," said he, leading the way up the platform. "This is our train. I have engaged a carriage, for I am particularly anxious to impress one or two things upon you while we travel down."

And yet all that he had to impress upon me might have been said in a sentence, for it was that I was to remember that I was there as a protection to himself, and that I was not on any consideration to leave him for an instant. This he repeated again and again as our journey drew to a close, with an insistence which showed that his nerves were thoroughly shaken.

"Yes," he said at last, in answer to my looks rather than to my words, "I *am* nervous, Dr. Hamilton. I have always been a timid man, and my timidity depends upon my frail physical health. But my soul is firm, and I can bring myself up to face a danger which a less-nervous man might shrink from. What I am doing now is done from no compulsion, but entirely from a sense of duty, and yet it is, beyond doubt, a desperate risk. If things should go wrong, I will have some claims to the title of martyr."

This eternal reading of riddles was too much for me. I felt that I must put a term to it.

"I think it would be very much better, sir, if you were to trust me entirely," said I. "It is impossible for me to act effectively, when I do not know what are the objects which we have in view, or even where we are going."

"Oh, as to where we are going, there need be no mystery about that," said he; "we are going to Delamere Court, the residence of Sir Thomas Rossiter, with whose work you are so conversant. As to the exact object of our visit, I do not know that at this stage of the proceedings anything would be gained, Dr. Hamilton, by taking you into my complete confidence. I may tell you that we are acting—I say 'we,' because my sister, Lady Rossiter, takes the same view as myself—with the one object of preventing anything in the nature of a family scandal. That being so, you can understand that I am loth to give any explanations which are not absolutely necessary. It would be a different matter, Dr. Hamilton, if I were asking your advice. As matters stand, it is only your active help which I need, and I will indicate to you from time to time how you can best give it."

There was nothing more to be said, and a poor man can put up with a good deal for twenty pounds a day, but I felt none the less that Lord Linchmere was acting rather scurvily towards me. He wished to convert me into a passive tool, like the blackthorn in his hand. With his sensitive disposition I could imagine, however, that scandal would be abhorrent to him, and I realized that he would not take me into his confidence until no other course was open to him. I must trust to my own eyes and ears to solve the mystery, but I had every confidence that I should not trust to them in vain.

Delamere Court lies a good five miles from Pangbourne Station, and we drove for that distance in an open fly. Lord Linchmere sat in deep thought during the time, and he never opened his mouth until we were close to our destination. When he did speak it was to give me a piece of information which surprised me.

"Perhaps you are not aware," said he, "that I am a medical man like yourself?"

"No, sir, I did not know it."

"Yes, I qualified in my younger days, when there were several lives between me and the peerage. I have not had occasion to practise, but I have found it a useful education, all the same. I never regretted the years which I devoted to medical study. These are the gates of Delamere Court."

We had come to two high pillars crowned with heraldic monsters which flanked the opening of a winding avenue. Over the laurel bushes and rhododendrons I could see a long, many-gabled mansion, girdled with ivy, and toned to the warm, cheery, mellow glow of old brick-work. My eyes were still fixed in admiration upon this delightful house when my companion plucked nervously at my sleeve.

"Here's Sir Thomas," he whispered. "Please talk beetle all you can."

A tall, thin figure, curiously angular and bony, had emerged through a gap in the hedge of laurels. In his hand he held a spud, and he wore gauntleted gardener's gloves. A broad-brimmed, grey hat cast his face into shadow, but it struck me as exceedingly austere, with an ill-nourished beard and harsh, irregular features. The fly pulled up and Lord Linchmere sprang out.

"My dear Thomas, how are you?" said he, heartily.

But the heartiness was by no means reciprocal. The owner of the grounds glared at me over his brother-in-law's shoulder, and I caught broken scraps of sentences

—" well-known wishes . . . hatred of strangers . . . unjustifiable intrusion . . . perfectly inexcusable." Then there was a muttered explanation, and the two of them came over together to the side of the fly.

" Let me present you to Sir Thomas Rossiter, Dr. Hamilton," said Lord Linchmere. " You will find that you have a strong community of tastes."

I bowed. Sir Thomas stood very stiffly, looking at me severely from under the broad brim of his hat.

" Lord Linchmere tells me that you know something about beetles," said he. " What do you know about beetles ? "

" I know what I have learned from your work upon the coleoptera, Sir Thomas," I answered.

" Give me the names of the better-known species of the British scarabæi," said he.

I had not expected an examination, but fortunately I was ready for one. My answers seemed to please him, for his stern features relaxed.

" You appear to have read my book with some profit, sir," said he. " It is a rare thing for me to meet anyone who takes an intelligent interest in such matters. People can find time for such trivialities as sport or society, and yet the beetles are overlooked. I can assure you that the greater part of the idiots in this part of the country are unaware that I have ever written a book at all—I, the first man who ever described the true function of the elytra. I am glad to see you, sir, and I have no doubt that I can show you some specimens which will interest you." He stepped into the fly and drove up with us to the house, expounding to me as we went some recent researches which he had made into the anatomy of the lady-bird.

I have said that Sir Thomas Rossiter wore a large hat drawn down over his brows. As he entered the hall he uncovered himself, and I was at once aware of a singular characteristic which the hat had concealed. His forehead, which was naturally high, and higher still on account of receding hair, was in a continual state of movement. Some nervous weakness kept the muscles in a constant spasm, which sometimes produced a mere twitching and sometimes a curious rotary movement unlike anything which I had ever seen before. It was strikingly visible as he turned towards us after entering the study, and seemed the more singular from the contrast with the hard, steady, grey eyes which looked out from underneath those palpitating brows.

"I am sorry," said he, "that Lady Rossiter is not here to help me to welcome you. By the way, Charles, did Evelyn say anything about the date of her return?"

"She wished to stay in town for a few more days," said Lord Linchmere. "You know how ladies' social duties accumulate if they have been for some time in the country. My sister has many old friends in London at present."

"Well, she is her own mistress, and I should not wish to alter her plans, but I shall be glad when I see her again. It is very lonely here without her company."

"I was afraid that you might find it so, and that was partly why I ran down. My young friend, Dr. Hamilton, is so much interested in the subject which you have made your own, that I thought you would not mind his accompanying me."

"I lead a retired life, Dr. Hamilton, and my aversion to strangers grows upon me," said our host. "I have sometimes thought that my nerves are not so good as they were. My travels in search of beetles in my younger days took me into many malarious and unhealthy places. But a brother coleopterist like yourself is always a welcome guest, and I shall be delighted if you will look over my collection, which I think that I may without exaggeration describe as the best in Europe."

And so no doubt it was. He had a huge, oaken cabinet arranged in shallow drawers, and here, neatly ticketed and classified, were beetles from every corner of the earth, black, brown, blue, green, and mottled. Every now and then as he swept his hand over the lines and lines of impaled insects he would catch up some rare specimen, and, handling it with as much delicacy and reverence as if it were a precious relic, he would hold forth upon its peculiarities and the circumstances under which it came into his possession. It was evidently an unusual thing for him to meet with a sympathetic listener, and he talked and talked until the spring evening had deepened into night, and the gong announced that it was time to dress for dinner. All the time Lord Linchmere said nothing, but he stood at his brother-in-law's elbow, and I caught him continually shooting curious, little, questioning glances into his face. And his own features expressed some strong emotion, apprehension, sympathy, expectation: I seemed to read them all. I was sure that Lord Linchmere was fearing something and awaiting something, but what that something might be I could not imagine.

The evening passed quietly but pleasantly, and I should have been entirely at my ease if it had not been for that continual sense of tension upon the part of Lord Linchmere. As to our host, I found that he improved upon acquaintance. He spoke constantly with affection of his absent wife, and also of his little son, who had recently been sent to school. The house, he said, was not the same without them. If it were not for his scientific studies, he did not know how he could get through the days. After dinner we smoked for some time in the billiard-room, and finally went early to bed.

And then it was that, for the first time, the suspicion that Lord Linchmere was a lunatic crossed my mind. He followed me into my bedroom, when our host had retired.

"Doctor," said he, speaking in a low, hurried voice, "you must come with me. You must spend the night in my bedroom."

"What do you mean?"

"I prefer not to explain. But this is part of your

duties. My room is close by, and you can return to your own before the servant calls you in the morning."

"But why?" I asked.

"Because I am nervous of being alone," said he. "That's the reason, since you must have a reason."

It seemed rank lunacy, but the argument of those twenty pounds would overcome many objections. I followed him to his room.

"Well," said I, "there's only room for one in that bed."

"Only one shall occupy it," said he.

"And the other?"

"Must remain on watch."

"Why?" said I. "One would think you expected to be attacked."

"Perhaps I do."

"In that case, why not lock your door?"

"Perhaps I *want* to be attacked."

It looked more and more like lunacy. However, there was nothing for it but to submit. I shrugged my shoulders and sat down in the arm-chair beside the empty fireplace.

"I am to remain on watch, then?" said I, ruefully.

"We will divide the night. If you will watch until two, I will watch the remainder."

"Very good."

"Call me at two o'clock, then."

"I will do so."

"Keep your ears open, and if you hear any sounds wake me instantly—instantly, you hear?"

"You can rely upon it." I tried to look as solemn as he did.

"And for God's sake don't go to sleep," said he, and so, taking off only his coat, he threw the coverlet over him and settled down for the night.

It was a melancholy vigil, and made more so by my own sense of its folly. Supposing that by any chance Lord Linchmere had cause to suspect that he was subject to danger in the house of Sir Thomas Rossiter, why on earth could he not lock his door and so protect himself? His own answer that he might wish to be attacked was absurd. Why should he possibly wish to be attacked? And who would wish to attack him? Clearly, Lord Linchmere was suffering from some singular delusion, and the result was that on an imbecile pretext I was to be deprived of my night's rest. Still, however absurd, I was determined to carry out his injunctions to the letter as long as I was in his employment. I sat, therefore, beside the empty fireplace, and listened to a sonorous chiming clock somewhere down the passage, which gurgled and struck every quarter of an hour. It was an endless vigil. Save for that single clock, an absolute silence reigned throughout the great house. A small lamp stood on the table at my elbow, throwing a circle of light round my chair, but leaving the corners of the room draped in shadow. On the bed Lord Linchmere was breathing peacefully. I envied him his quiet sleep, and again and again my own eyelids drooped, but every time my sense of duty came to my help, and I sat up, rubbing my eyes and pinching myself with a determination to see my irrational watch to an end.

And I did so. From down the passage came the chimes of two o'clock, and I laid my hand upon the shoulder of the sleeper. Instantly he was sitting up, with an expression of the keenest interest upon his face.

"You have heard something?"

"No, sir. It is two o'clock."

"Very good. I will watch. You can go to sleep."

I lay down under the coverlet as he had done and was soon unconscious. My last recollection was of that circle of lamplight, and of the small, hunched-up figure and strained, anxious face of Lord Linchmere in the centre of it.

How long I slept I do not know; but I was suddenly aroused by a sharp tug at my sleeve. The room was in darkness, but a hot smell of oil told me that the lamp had only that instant been extinguished.

"Quick! Quick!" said Lord Linchmere's voice in my ear.

I sprang out of bed, he still dragging at my arm.

"Over here!" he whispered, and pulled me into a corner of the room. "Hush! Listen!"

In the silence of the night I could distinctly hear that someone was coming down the corridor. It was a stealthy step, faint and intermittent, as of a man who paused cautiously after every stride. Sometimes for half a minute there was no sound, and then came the shuffle and creak which told of a fresh advance. My companion was trembling with excitement. His hand, which still held my sleeve, twitched like a branch in the wind.

"What is it?" I whispered.

"It's he!"

"Sir Thomas?"

"Yes."

"What does he want?"

"Hush! Do nothing until I tell you."

I was conscious now that someone was trying the door. There was the faintest little rattle from the handle, and then I dimly saw a thin slit of subdued light. There was a lamp burning somewhere far down the passage, and it just sufficed to make the outside visible from the darkness of our room. The greyish slit grew broader and broader, very gradually, very gently, and then outlined against it I saw the dark figure of a man. He was squat and crouching, with the silhouette of a bulky and misshapen dwarf. Slowly the door swung open with this ominous shape framed in the centre of it. And then, in an instant, the crouching figure shot up, there was a tiger spring across the room and thud, thud, thud, came three tremendous blows from some heavy object upon the bed.

I was so paralysed with amazement that I stood

motionless and staring until I was aroused by a yell for help from my companion. The open door shed enough light for me to see the outline of things, and there was little Lord Linchmere with his arms round the neck of his brother-in-law, holding bravely on to him like a game bull-terrier with its teeth into a gaunt deerhound. The tall, bony man dashed himself about, writhing round and round to get a grip upon his assailant ; but the other, clutching on from behind, still kept his hold, though his shrill, frightened cries showed how unequal he felt the contest to be. I sprang to the rescue, and the two of us managed to throw Sir Thomas to the ground, though he made his teeth meet in my shoulder. With all my youth and weight and strength, it was a desperate struggle before we could master his frenzied struggles ; but at last we secured his arms with the waist-cord of the dressing-gown which he was wearing. I was holding his legs while Lord Linchmere was endeavouring to relight the lamp, when there came the pattering of many feet in the passage, and the butler and two footmen, who had been alarmed by the cries, rushed into the room. With their aid we had no further difficulty in securing our prisoner, who lay foaming and glaring upon the ground. One glance at his face was enough to prove that he was a dangerous maniac, while the short, heavy hammer which lay beside the bed showed how murderous had been his intentions.

"Do not use any violence ! " said Lord Linchmere, as we raised the struggling man to his feet. "He will have a period of stupor after this excitement. I believe that it is coming on already." As he spoke the convulsions became less violent, and the madman's head fell forward upon his breast, as if he were overcome by sleep. We led him down the passage and stretched him upon his own bed, where he lay unconscious, breathing heavily.

"Two of you will watch him," said Lord Linchmere. "And now, Dr. Hamilton, if you will return with me to my room, I will give you the explanation which my horror of scandal has perhaps caused me to delay too long. Come what may, you will never have cause to regret your share in this night's work.

"The case may be made clear in a very few words," he continued, when we were alone. "My poor brother-in-law is one of the best fellows upon earth, a loving husband and an estimable father, but he comes from a stock which is deeply tainted with insanity. He has more than once had homicidal outbreaks, which are the more painful because his inclination is always to attack the very person to whom he is most attached. His son was sent away to school to avoid this danger, and then came an attempt upon my sister, his wife, from which she escaped with injuries that you may have observed when you met her in London. You understand that he knows nothing of the matter when he is in his sound senses, and would ridicule the suggestion that he could under any circumstances injure those whom he loves so dearly. It is often, as you know, a characteristic of such maladies that it is absolutely impossible to convince the man who suffers from them of their existence.

"Our great object was, of course, to get him under restraint before he could stain his hands with blood, but the matter was full of difficulty. He is a recluse in his habits, and would not see any medical man. Besides, it was necessary for our purpose that the medical man should convince himself of his insanity; and he is sane as you or I, save on these very rare occasions. But, fortunately, before he has these attacks he always shows certain premonitory symptoms, which are providential danger-signals, warning us to be upon our guard. The chief of these is that nervous contortion of the forehead which you must have observed. This is a phenomenon which always appears from three to four days before his attacks of frenzy. The moment it showed itself his wife came into town on some pretext, and took refuge in my house in Brook Street.

"It remained for me to convince a medical man of Sir Thomas's insanity, without which it was impossible to put him where he could do no harm. The first problem was how to get a medical man into his house. I bethought me of his interest in beetles, and his love for anyone who shared his tastes. I advertised, therefore, and was fortunate enough to find in you the very man I wanted. A stout companion was necessary, for I knew that the lunacy could only be proved by a murderous assault, and I had every reason to believe that that assault would be made upon myself, since he had the warmest regard for me in his moments of sanity. I think your intelligence will supply all the rest. I did not know that the attack would come by night, but I thought it very probable, for the crises of such cases usually do occur in the early hours of the morning. I am a very nervous man myself, but I saw no other way in which I could remove this terrible danger from my sister's life. I need not ask you whether you are willing to sign the lunacy papers."

"Undoubtedly. But *two* signatures are necessary."

"You forget that I am myself a holder of a medical degree. I have the papers on a side-table here, so if you will be good enough to sign them now, we can have the patient removed in the morning."

So that was my visit to Sir Thomas Rossiter, the famous beetle-hunter, and that was also my first step upon the ladder of success, for Lady Rossiter and Lord Linchmere have proved to be staunch friends, and they have never forgotten my association with them in the time of their need. Sir Thomas is out and said to be cured, but I still think that if I spent another night at Delamere Court, I should be inclined to lock my door upon the inside.

33. *The Man with the Watches*

THERE are many who will still bear in mind the singular circumstances which, under the heading of the Rugby Mystery, filled many columns of the daily Press in the spring of the year 1892. Coming as it did at a period of exceptional dullness, it attracted perhaps rather more attention than it deserved, but it offered to the public that mixture of the whimsical and the tragic which is most stimulating to the popular imagination. Interest drooped, however, when, after weeks of fruitless investigation, it was found that no final explanation of the facts was forthcoming, and the tragedy seemed from that time to the present to have finally taken its place in the dark catalogue of inexplicable and unexpiated crimes. A recent communication (the authenticity of which appears to be above question) has, however, thrown some new and clear light upon the matter. Before laying it before the public it would be as well, perhaps, that I should refresh their memories as to the singular facts upon which this commentary is founded. These facts were briefly as follows:

At five o'clock on the evening of the 18th of March in the year already mentioned a train left Euston Station for Manchester. It was a rainy, squally day, which grew wilder as it progressed, so it was by no means the weather in which anyone would travel who was not driven to do so by necessity. The train, however, is a favourite one among Manchester business men who are returning from town, for it does the journey in four hours and twenty minutes, with only three stoppages upon the way. In spite of the inclement evening it was, therefore, fairly well filled upon the occasion of which I speak. The guard of the train was a tried servant of the company—a man who had worked for twenty-two years without blemish or complaint. His name was John Palmer.

The station clock was upon the stroke of five, and the guard was about to give the customary signal to the engine-driver when he observed two belated passengers hurrying down the platform. The one was an exceptionally tall man, dressed in a long, black overcoat with astrakhan collar and cuffs. I have already said that the evening was an inclement one, and the tall traveller had the high, warm collar turned up to protect his throat against the bitter March wind. He appeared, as far as the guard could judge by so hurried an inspection, to be a man between fifty and sixty years of age, who had retained a good deal of the vigour and activity of his youth. In one hand he carried a brown leather Gladstone bag. His companion was a lady, tall and erect, walking with a vigorous step which outpaced the gentleman beside her. She wore a long, fawn-coloured dust-cloak, a black, close-fitting toque, and a dark veil which concealed the greater part of her face. The two might very well have passed as father and daughter. They walked swiftly down the line of carriages, glancing in at the windows, until the guard, John Palmer, overtook them.

"Now, then, sir, look sharp, the train is going," said he.

"First-class," the man answered.

The guard turned the handle of the nearest door. In the carriage which he had opened, there sat a small man with a cigar in his mouth. His appearance seems to have impressed itself upon the guard's memory, for he was prepared, afterwards, to describe or to identify him. He was a man of thirty-four or thirty-five years of age, dressed in some grey material, sharp-nosed, alert, with a ruddy, weather-beaten face, and a small, closely cropped, black beard. He glanced up as the door was opened. The tall man paused with his foot upon the step.

"This is a smoking compartment. The lady dislikes smoke," said he, looking round at the guard.

"All right! Here you are, sir!" said John Palmer

He slammed the door of the smoking carriage, opened that of the next one, which was empty, and thrust the two travellers in. At the same moment he sounded his whistle and the wheels of the train began to move. The man with the cigar was at the window of his carriage, and said something to the guard as he rolled past him, but the words were lost in the bustle of the departure. Palmer stepped into the guard's van, as it came up to him, and thought no more of the incident.

Twelve minutes after its departure the train reached Willesden Junction, where it stopped for a very short interval. An examination of the tickets has made it certain that no one either joined or left it at this time, and no passenger was seen to alight upon the platform. At 5.14 the journey to Manchester was resumed, and Rugby was reached at 6.50, the express being five minutes late.

At Rugby the attention of the station officials was drawn to the fact that the door of one of the first-class carriages was open. An examination of that compartment, and of its neighbour, disclosed a remarkable state of affairs.

The smoking carriage in which the short, red-faced man with the black beard had been seen was now empty. Save for a half-smoked cigar, there was no trace whatever of its recent occupant. The door of this carriage was fastened. In the next compartment, to which attention had been originally drawn, there was no sign either of the gentleman with the astrakhan collar or of the young lady who accompanied him. All three passengers had disappeared. On the other hand, there was found upon the floor of this carriage—the one in which the tall traveller and the lady had been—a young man fashionably dressed and of elegant appearance. He lay with his knees drawn up, and his head resting against the farther door, an elbow upon either seat. A bullet had penetrated his heart and his death must have been instantaneous. No one had seen such a man enter the train, and no railway ticket was found in his pocket, neither were there any markings upon his linen, nor papers nor personal property which might help to identify him. Who he was, whence he had come, and how he had met his end were each as great a mystery as what had occurred to the three people who had started an hour and a half before from Willesden in those two compartments.

I have said that there was no personal property which might help to identify him, but it is true that there was one peculiarity about this unknown young man which was much commented upon at the time. In his pockets were found no fewer than six valuable gold watches, three in the various pockets of his waistcoat, one in his ticket-pocket, one in his breast-pocket, and one small one set in a leather strap and fastened round his left wrist. The obvious explanation that the man was a pickpocket, and that this was his plunder, was discounted by the fact that all six were of American make and of a type which is rare in England. Three of them bore the mark of the Rochester Watchmaking Company ; one was by Mason, of Elmira ; one was unmarked ; and the small one, which was highly jewelled and ornamented, was from Tiffany, of New York. The other contents of his pocket consisted of an ivory knife with a cork-screw by Rodgers, of Sheffield ; a small, circular mirror, one inch in diameter ; a re-admission slip to the Lyceum Theatre ; a silver box full of vesta matches, and a brown leather cigar-case containing two cheroots—also two pounds fourteen shillings in money. It was clear, then, that whatever motives may have led to his death, robbery was not among them. As already mentioned, there were no markings upon the man's linen, which appeared to be new, and no tailor's name upon his coat. In appearance he was young, short, smooth-cheeked, and delicately featured. One of his front teeth was conspicuously stopped with gold.

On the discovery of the tragedy an examination was

instantly made of the tickets of all passengers, and the number of the passengers themselves was counted. It was found that only three tickets were unaccounted for, corresponding to the three travellers who were missing. The express was then allowed to proceed, but a new guard was sent with it, and John Palmer was detained as a witness at Rugby. The carriage which included the two compartments in question was uncoupled and side-tracked. Then, on the arrival of Inspector Vane, of Scotland Yard, and of Mr. Henderson, a detective in the service of the railway company, an exhaustive inquiry was made into all the circumstances.

That crime had been committed was certain. The bullet, which appeared to have come from a small pistol or revolver, had been fired from some little distance, as there was no scorching of the clothes. No weapon was found in the compartment (which finally disposed of the theory of suicide), nor was there any sign of the brown leather bag which the guard had seen in the hand of the tall gentleman. A lady's parasol was found upon the rack, but no other trace was to be seen of the travellers in either of the sections. Apart from the crime, the question of how or why three passengers (one of them a lady) could get out of the train, and one other get in during the unbroken run between Willesden and Rugby, was one which excited the utmost curiosity among the general public, and gave rise to much speculation in the London Press.

John Palmer, the guard, was able at the inquest to give some evidence which threw a little light upon the matter. There was a spot between Tring and Cheddington, according to his statement, where, on account of some repairs to the line, the train had for a few minutes slowed down to a pace not exceeding eight or ten miles an hour. At that place it might be possible for a man, or even for an exceptionally active woman, to have left the train without serious injury. It was true that a gang of platelayers was there, and that they had seen nothing, but it was their custom to stand in the middle between the metals, and the open carriage door was upon the far side, so that it was conceivable that someone might have alighted unseen, as the darkness would by that time be drawing in. A steep embankment would instantly screen anyone who sprang out from the observation of the navvies.

The guard also deposed that there was a good deal of movement upon the platform at Willesden Junction, and that though it was certain that no one had either joined or left the train there, it was still quite possible that some of the passengers might have changed unseen from one compartment to another. It was by no means uncommon for a gentleman to finish his cigar in a smoking carriage and then to change to a clearer atmosphere. Supposing that the man with the black beard had done so at Willesden (and the half-smoked cigar upon the floor seemed to favour the supposition), he would naturally go into the nearest section, which would bring him into the company of the two other actors in this drama. Thus the first stage of the affair might be surmised without any great breach of probability. But what the second stage had been, or how the final one had been arrived at, neither the guard nor the experienced detective officers could suggest.

A careful examination of the line between Willesden and Rugby resulted in one discovery which might or might not have a bearing upon the tragedy. Near Tring, at the very place where the train slowed down, there was found at the bottom of the embankment a small pocket Testament, very shabby and worn. It was printed by the Bible Society of London, and bore an inscription: "From John to Alice. Jan. 13th, 1856," upon the fly-leaf. Underneath was written: "James, July 4th, 1859," and beneath that again: "Edward. Nov. 1st, 1869," all the entries being in the same handwriting. This was the only clue, if it could be called a clue, which the police obtained, and the coroner's verdict of "Murder by a person or persons unknown" was the unsatisfactory ending of a singular case. Advertisement, rewards, and inquiries proved equally fruitless, and nothing could be found which was solid enough to form the basis for a profitable investigation.

It would be a mistake, however, to suppose that no theories were formed to account for the facts. On the contrary, the Press, both in England and in America, teemed with suggestions and suppositions, most of which were obviously absurd. The fact that the watches were of American make, and some peculiarities in connection with the gold stopping of his front tooth, appeared to indicate that the deceased was a citizen of the United States, though his linen, clothes and boots were undoubtedly of British manufacture. It was surmised, by some, that he was concealed under the seat, and that, being discovered, he was for some reason, possibly because he had overheard their guilty secrets, put to death by his fellow-passengers. When coupled with generalities as to the ferocity and cunning of anarchical and other secret societies, this theory sounded as plausible as any.

The fact that he should be without a ticket would be consistent with the idea of concealment, and it was well known that women played a prominent part in the Nihilistic propaganda. On the other hand, it was clear, from the guard's statement, that the man must have been hidden there *before* the others arrived, and how unlikely the coincidence that conspirators should stray exactly into the very compartment in which a spy was already concealed! Besides, this explanation ignored the man in the smoking carriage, and gave no reason at all for his simultaneous disappearance. The police had little difficulty in showing that such a theory would not cover the facts, but they were unprepared in the absence of evidence to advance any alternative explanation.

There was a letter in the *Daily Gazette*, over the signature of a well-known criminal investigator, which gave rise to considerable discussion at the time. He had formed a hypothesis which had at least ingenuity to recommend it, and I cannot do better than append it in his own words.

"Whatever may be the truth," said he, "it must depend upon some bizarre and rare combination of events, so we need have no hesitation in postulating such events in our explanation. In the absence of data we must abandon the analytic or scientific method of investigation, and must approach it in the synthetic fashion. In a word, instead of taking known events and deducing from them what has occurred, we must build up a fanciful explanation if it will only be consistent with known events. We can then test this explanation by any fresh facts which may arise. If they all fit into their places, the probability is that we are upon the right track, and with each fresh fact this probability increases in a geometrical progression until the evidence becomes final and convincing.

"Now, there is one most remarkable and suggestive fact which has not met with the attention which it deserves. There is a local train running through Harrow and King's Langley, which is timed in such a way that the express must have overtaken it at or about the period when it eased down its speed to eight miles an hour on account of the repairs of the line. The two trains would at that time be travelling in the same direction at a similar rate of speed and upon parallel lines. It is within every one's experience how, under such circumstances, the occupant of each carriage can see very plainly the passengers in the other carriages opposite to him. The lamps of the express had been lit at Willesden, so that each compartment was brightly illuminated, and most visible to an observer from outside.

"Now, the sequence of events as I reconstruct them would be after this fashion. This young man with the abnormal number of watches was alone in the carriage of the slow train. His ticket, with his papers and gloves and other things, was, we will suppose, on the seat beside him. He was probably an American, and also probably a man of weak intellect. The excessive wearing of jewellery is an early symptom in some forms of mania.

" As he sat watching the carriages of the express which were (on account of the state of the line) going at the same pace as himself, he suddenly saw some people in it whom he knew. We will suppose for the sake of our theory that these people were a woman whom he loved and a man whom he hated—and who in return hated him. The young man was excitable and impulsive. He opened the door of his carriage, stepped from the footboard of the local train to the footboard of the express, opened the other door, and made his way into the presence of these two people. The feat (on the supposition that the trains were going at the same pace) is by no means so perilous as it might appear.

" Having now got our young man, without his ticket, into the carriage in which the elder man and the young woman are travelling, it is not difficult to imagine that a violent scene ensued. It is possible that the pair were also Americans, which is the more probable as the man carried a weapon—an unusual thing in England. If our supposition of incipient mania is correct, the young man is likely to have assaulted the other. As the upshot of the quarrel the elder man shot the intruder, and then made his escape from the carriage, taking the young lady with him. We will suppose that all this happened very rapidly, and that the train was still going at so slow a pace that it was not difficult for them to leave it. A woman might leave a train going at eight miles an hour. As a matter of fact, we know that this woman *did* do so.

" And now we have to fit in the man in the smoking carriage. Presuming that we have, up to this point, reconstructed the tragedy correctly, we shall find nothing in this other man to cause us to reconsider our conclusions. According to my theory, this man saw the young fellow cross from one train to the other, saw him open the door, heard the pistol-shot, saw the two fugitives spring out on to the line, realised that murder had been done, and sprang out himself in pursuit. Why he has never been heard of since—whether he met his own death in the pursuit, or whether, as is more likely, he was made to realise that it was not a case for his interference—is a detail which we have at present no means of explaining. I acknowledge that there are some difficulties in the way. At first sight, it might seem improbable that at such a moment a murderer would burden himself in his flight with a brown leather bag. My answer is that he was well aware that if the bag were found his identity would be established. It was absolutely necessary for him to take it with him. My theory stands or falls upon one point, and I call upon the railway company to make strict inquiry as to whether a ticket was found unclaimed in the local train through Harrow and King's Langley upon the 18th of March. If such a ticket were found my case is proved. If not, my theory may still be the correct one, for it is conceivable either that he travelled without a ticket or that his ticket was lost."

To this elaborate and plausible hypothesis the answer of the police and of the company was, first, that no such ticket was found; secondly, that the slow train would never run parallel to the express; and, thirdly, that the local train had been stationary in King's Langley Station when the express, going at fifty miles an hour, had flashed past it. So perished the only satisfying explanation, and five years have elapsed without supplying a new one. Now, at last, there comes a statement which covers all the facts, and which must be regarded as authentic. It took the shape of a letter dated from New York, and addressed to the same criminal investigator whose theory I have quoted. It is given here *in extenso*, with the exception of the two opening paragraphs, which are personal in their nature:—

"You'll excuse me if I'm not very free with names.

There's less reason now than there was five years ago when mother was still living. But for all that, I had rather cover up our tracks all I can. But I owe you an explanation, for if your idea of it was wrong, it was a mighty ingenious one all the same. I'll have to go back a little so as you may understand all about it.

"My people came from Bucks, England, and emigrated to the States in the early fifties. They settled in Rochester, in the State of New York, where my father ran a large dry goods store. There were only two sons: myself, James, and my brother, Edward. I was ten years older than my brother, and after my father died I sort of took the place of a father to him, as an elder brother would. He was a bright, spirited boy, and just one of the most beautiful creatures that ever lived. But there was always a soft spot in him, and it was like mould in cheese, for it spread and spread, and nothing that you could do would stop it. Mother saw it just as clearly as I did, but she went on spoiling him all the same, for he had such a way with him that you could refuse him nothing. I did all I could to hold him in, and he hated me for my pains.

"At last he fairly got his head, and nothing that we could do would stop him. He got off into New York, and went rapidly from bad to worse. At first he was only fast, and then he was criminal; and then, at the end of a year or two, he was one of the most notorious young crooks in the city. He had formed a friendship with Sparrow MacCoy, who was at the head of his profession as a bunco-steerer, green goodsman and general rascal. They took to card-sharping, and frequented some of the best hotels in New York. My brother was an excellent actor (he might have made an honest name for himself if he had chosen), and he would take the parts of a young Englishman of title, of a simple lad from the West, or of a college undergraduate, whichever suited Sparrow MacCoy's purpose. And then one day he dressed himself as a girl, and he carried it off so well, and made himself such a valuable decoy, that it was their favourite game afterwards. They had made it right with Tammany and with the police, so it seemed as if nothing could ever stop them, for those were in the days before the Lexow Commission, and if you only had a pull, you could do pretty nearly everything you wanted.

"And nothing would have stopped them if they had only stuck to cards and New York, but they must needs come up Rochester way, and forge a name upon a cheque. It was my brother that did it, though everyone knew that it was under the influence of Sparrow MacCoy. I bought up that cheque, and a pretty sum it cost me. Then I went to my brother, laid it before him on the table, and swore to him that I would prosecute if he did not clear out of the country. At first he simply laughed. I could not prosecute, he said, without breaking our mother's heart, and he knew that I would not do that. I made him understand, however, that our mother's heart was being broken in any case, and that I had set firm on the point that I would rather see him in Rochester gaol than in a New York hotel. So at last he gave in, and he made me a solemn promise that he would see Sparrow MacCoy no more, that he would go to Europe, and that he would turn his hand to any honest trade that I helped him to get. I took him down right away to an old family friend, Joe Willson, who is an exporter of American watches and clocks, and I got him to give Edward an agency in London, with a small salary and a 15 per cent. commission on all business. His manner and appearance were so good that he won the old man over at once, and within a week he was sent off to London with a case full of samples.

"It seemed to me that this business of the cheque had really given my brother a fright, and that there was some chance of his settling down into an honest line of life. My mother had spoken with him, and what she said had touched him, for she had always been the best of mothers to him and he had been the great sorrow of her life. But I knew that this man Sparrow MacCoy had a great influence over Edward and my chance of keeping the lad straight lay in breaking the connection between them. I had a friend in the New York detective force, and through him I kept a watch upon MacCoy. When, within a fortnight of my brother's sailing, I heard that MacCoy had taken a berth in the *Etruria*, I was as certain as if he had told me that he was going over to England for the purpose of coaxing Edward back again into the ways that he had left. In an instant I had resolved to go also, and to pit my influence against MacCoy's. I knew it was a losing fight, but I thought, and my mother thought, that it was my duty. We passed the last night together in prayer for my success, and she gave me her own Testament that my father had given her on the day of their marriage in the Old Country, so that I might always wear it next my heart.

"I was a fellow-traveller, on the steamship, with Sparrow MacCoy, and at least I had the satisfaction of spoiling his little game for the voyage. The very first night I went into the smoking-room, and found him at the head of a card-table, with half a dozen young fellows who were carrying their full purses and their empty skulls over to Europe. He was settling down for his harvest, and a rich one it would have been. But I soon changed all that.

"'Gentlemen,' said I, 'are you aware whom you are playing with?'

"'What's that to you? You mind your own business!' said he, with an oath.

"'Who is it, anyway?' asked one of the dudes.

"'He's Sparrow MacCoy, the most notorious card-sharper in the States.'

"Up he jumped with a bottle in his hand, but he remembered that he was under the flag of the effete Old Country, where law and order run, and Tammany has no pull. Gaol and the gallows wait for violence and murder, and there's no slipping out by the back door on board an ocean liner.

"'Prove your words, you——!' said he.

"'I will!' said I. 'If you will turn up your right shirt-sleeve to the shoulder, I will either prove my words or I will eat them.'

"He turned white and said not a word. You see, I knew something of his ways, and I was aware that part of the mechanism which he and all such sharpers use consists of an elastic down the arm with a clip just above the wrist. It is by means of this clip that they withdraw from their hands the cards which they do not want, while they substitute other cards from another hiding-place. I reckoned on it being there, and it was. He cursed me, slunk out of the saloon, and was hardly seen again during the voyage. For once, at any rate, I got level with Mister Sparrow MacCoy.

"But he soon had his revenge upon me, for when it came to influencing my brother he outweighed me every time. Edward had kept himself straight in London for the first few weeks, and had done some business with his American watches, until this villain came across his path once more. I did my best, but the best was little enough. The next thing I heard there had been a scandal at one of the Northumberland Avenue hotels: a traveller had been fleeced of a large sum by two confederate card-sharpers, and the matter was in the hands of Scotland Yard. The first I learned of it was in the evening paper, and I was at once certain that my brother and MacCoy were back at their old games. I hurried at once to Edward's lodgings. They told me that he and a tall gentleman (whom I recognized as MacCoy) had gone off together, and that he had left the lodgings and taken his things with him. The landlady had heard them give several directions to the cabman, ending with Euston Station, and she had accidentally overheard the tall gentleman saying something about Manchester. She believed that that was their destination.

"A glance at the time-table showed me that the most likely train was at five, though there was another at 4.35 which they might have caught. I had only time to get the later one, but found no sign of them either at the depôt or in the train. They must have gone on by the earlier one, so I determined to follow them to Manchester and search for them in the hotels there. One last appeal to my brother by all that he owed to my mother might even now be the salvation of him. My nerves were overstrung, and I lit a cigar to steady them. At that moment, just as the train was moving off, the door of my compartment was flung open, and there were MacCoy and my brother on the platform.

"They were both disguised, and with good reason, for they knew that the London police were after them. MacCoy had a great astrakhan collar drawn up, so that only his eyes and nose were showing. My brother was dressed like a woman, with a black veil half down his face, but of course it did not deceive me for an instant, nor would it have done so even if I had not known that he had often used such a dress before. I started up, and as I did so MacCoy recognised me. He said something, the conductor slammed the door, and they were shown into the next compartment. I tried to stop the train so as to follow them, but the wheels were already moving, and it was too late.

"When we stopped at Willesden, I instantly changed my carriage. It appears that I was not seen to do so, which is not surprising, as the station was crowded with people. MacCoy, of course, was expecting me, and he had spent the time between Euston and Willesden in saying all he could to harden my brother's heart and set him against me. That is what I fancy, for I had never found him so impossible to soften or to move. I tried this way and I tried that; I pictured his future in an English gaol; I described the sorrow of his mother when I came back with the news; I said everything to touch his heart, but all to no purpose. He sat there with a fixed sneer upon his handsome face, while every now and then Sparrow MacCoy would throw in a taunt at me, or some word of encouragement to hold my brother to his resolutions.

" 'Why don't you run a Sunday-school ?' he would say to me, and then, in the same breath : 'He thinks you have no will of your own. He thinks you are just the baby brother and that he can lead you where he likes. He's only just finding out that you are a man as well as he.'

" It was those words of his which set me talking bitterly. We had left Willesden, you understand, for all this took some time. My temper got the better of me, and for the first time in my life I let my brother see the rough side of me. Perhaps it would have been better had I done so earlier and more often.

" 'A man !' said I. 'Well, I'm glad to have your friend's assurance of it, for no one would suspect it to see you like a boarding-school missy. I don't suppose in all this country there is a more contemptible-looking creature than you are as you sit there with that Dolly pinafore upon you.' He coloured up at that, for he was a vain man, and he winced from ridicule.

" 'It's only a dust-cloak,' said he, and he slipped it off. 'One has to throw the coppers off one's scent, and I had no other way to do it.' He took his toque off with the veil attached, and he put both it and the cloak into his brown bag. 'Anyway, I don't need to wear it until the conductor comes round,' said he.

" 'Nor then, either,' said I, and taking the bag I slung it with all my force out of the window. 'Now,' said I, 'you'll never make a Mary Jane of yourself while I can help it. If nothing but that disguise stands between you and a gaol, then to gaol you shall go.'

" That was the way to manage him. I felt my advantage at once. His supple nature was one which yielded to roughness far more readily than to entreaty. He flushed with shame, and his eyes filled with tears. But

MacCoy saw my advantage also, and was determined that I should not pursue it.

" 'He's my pard, and you shall not bully him,' he cried.

" 'He's my brother, and you shall not ruin him,' said I. 'I believe a spell of prison is the very best way of keeping you apart, and you shall have it, or it will be no fault of mine.'

" 'Oh, you would squeal, would you ?' he cried, and in an instant he whipped out his revolver. I sprang for his hand, but saw that I was too late, and jumped aside. At the same instant he fired, and the bullet which would have struck me passed through the heart of my unfortunate brother.

"He dropped without a groan upon the floor of the compartment, and MacCoy and I, equally horrified, knelt at each side of him, trying to bring back some signs of life. MacCoy still held the loaded revolver in his hand, but his anger against me and my resentment towards him had both for the moment been swallowed up in this sudden tragedy. It was he who first realized the situation. The train was for some reason going very slowly at the moment, and he saw his opportunity for escape. In an instant he had the door open, but I was as quick as he, and jumping upon him the two of us fell off the footboard and rolled in each other's arms down a steep embankment. At the bottom I struck my head against a stone, and I remembered nothing more. When I came to myself I was lying among some low bushes, not far from the railroad track, and somebody was bathing my head with a wet handkerchief. It was Sparrow MacCoy.

" 'I guess I couldn't leave you,' said he. 'I didn't want to have the blood of two of you on my hands in one day. You loved your brother, I've no doubt ; but you didn't love him a cent more than I loved him, though you'll say that I took a queer way to show it. Anyhow, it seems a mighty empty world now that he is gone, and I don't care a continental whether you give me over to the hangman or not.'

"He had turned his ankle in the fall, and there we sat, he with his useless foot, and I with my throbbing head, and we talked and talked until gradually my bitterness began to soften and to turn into something like sympathy. What was the use of revenging his death upon a man who was as much stricken by that death as I was? And then, as my wits gradually returned, I began to realize also that I could do nothing against MacCoy which would not recoil upon my mother and myself. How could we convict him without a full account of my brother's career being made public—the very thing which of all others we wished to avoid? It was really as much our interest as his to cover the matter up, and from being an avenger of crime I found myself changed to a conspirator against Justice. The place in which we found ourselves was one of those pheasant preserves which are so common in the Old Country, and as we groped our way through it I found myself consulting the slayer of my brother as to how far it would be possible to hush it up.

"I soon realised from what he said that unless there were some papers of which we knew nothing in my brother's pockets, there was really no possible means by which the police could identify him or learn how he had got there. His ticket was in MacCoy's pocket, and so was the ticket for some baggage which they had left at the depôt. Like most Americans, he had found it cheaper and easier to buy an outfit in London than to bring one from New York, so that all his linen and clothes were new and unmarked. The bag, containing the dust-cloak, which I had thrown out of the window, may have fallen among some bramble patch where it is still concealed, or may have been carried off by some tramp, or may have come into the possession of the police, who kept the incident to themselves. Anyhow, I have seen nothing about it in the London papers. As to the watches, they were a selection from those which had been intrusted to him for business purposes. It may have been for the same business purposes that he was taking them to Manchester, but—well, it's too late to enter into that.

"I don't blame the police for being at fault. I don't see how it could have been otherwise. There was just one little clue that they might have followed up, but it was a small one. I mean that small, circular mirror which was found in my brother's pocket. It isn't a very common thing for a young man to carry about with him, is it? But a gambler might have told you what such a mirror may mean to a card-sharper. If you sit back a little from the table, and lay the mirror, face upwards, upon your lap, you can see, as you deal, every card that you give to your adversary. It is not hard to say whether you see a man or raise him when you know his cards as well as your own. It was as much a part of a sharper's outfit as the elastic clip upon Sparrow MacCoy's arm. Taking that, in connection with the recent frauds at the hotels, the police might have got hold of one end of the string.

"I don't think there is much more for me to explain. We got to a village called Amersham that night in the character of two gentlemen upon a walking tour, and afterwards we made our way quietly to London, whence MacCoy went on to Cairo and I returned to New York. My mother died six months afterwards, and I am glad to say that to the day of her death she never knew what happened. She was always under the delusion that Edward was earning an honest living in London, and I never had the heart to tell her the truth. He never wrote; but, then, he never did write at any time, so that made no difference. His name was the last upon her lips.

"There's just one other thing that I have to ask you, sir, and I should take it as a kind return for all this explanation, if you could do it for me. You remember that Testament that was picked up. I always carried it in my inside pocket, and it must have come out in my fall. I value it very highly, for it was the family book with my birth and my brother's marked by my father in the beginning of it. I wish you would apply at the proper place and have it sent to me. It can be of no possible value to anyone else. If you address it to X, Bassano's Library, Broadway, New York, it is sure to come to hand."

34. *The Japanned Box*

IT *was* a curious thing, said the private tutor; one of those grotesque and whimsical incidents which occur to one as one goes through life. I lost the best situation which I am ever likely to have through it. But I am glad that I went to Thorpe Place, for I gained—well, as I tell you the story you will learn what I gained.

I don't know whether you are familiar with that part of the Midlands which is drained by the Avon. It is the most English part of England. Shakespeare, the flower of the whole race, was born right in the middle of it. It is a land of rolling pastures, rising in higher folds to the westward, until they swell into the Malvern Hills. There are no towns, but numerous villages, each with its grey Norman church. You have left the brick of the southern and eastern counties behind you, and everything is stone—stone for the walls, and lichened slabs of stone for the roofs. It is all grim and solid and massive, as befits the heart of a great nation.

It was in the middle of this country, not very far from Evesham, that Sir John Bollamore lived in the old ancestral home of Thorpe Place, and thither it was that I came to teach his two little sons. Sir John was a widower—his wife had died three years before—and he had been left with these two lads aged eight and ten, and one dear little girl of seven. Miss Witherton, who is now my wife, was governess to this little girl. I was tutor to the two boys. Could there be a more obvious prelude to an engagement? She governs me now, and I tutor two little boys of our own. But, there—I have already revealed what it was which I gained in Thorpe Place!

It was a very, very old house, incredibly old—pre-Norman, some of it—and the Bollamores claimed to have lived in that situation since long before the Conquest. It struck a chill to my heart when first I came there, those enormously thick grey walls, the rude crumbling stones, the smell as from a sick animal which exhaled from the rotting plaster of the aged building. But the modern wing was bright and the garden was well kept. No house could be dismal which had a pretty girl inside it and such a show of roses in front.

Apart from a very complete staff of servants there were only four of us in the household. These were Miss Witherton, who was at that time four-and-twenty and as pretty—well, as pretty as Mrs. Colmore is now—myself, Frank Colmore, aged thirty, Mrs. Stevens, the housekeeper, a dry, silent woman, and Mr. Richards, a tall military-looking man, who acted as steward to the Bollamore estates. We four always had our meals together, but Sir John had his usually alone in the library. Sometimes he joined us at dinner, but on the whole we were just as glad when he did not.

For he was a very formidable person. Imagine a man six feet three inches in height, majestically built, with a high-nosed, aristocratic face, brindled hair, shaggy eyebrows, a small, pointed Mephistophelian beard, and lines upon his brow and round his eyes as deep as if they had been carved with a penknife. He had grey eyes, weary, hopeless-looking eyes, proud and yet pathetic, eyes which claimed your pity and yet dared you to show it. His back was rounded with study, but otherwise he was as fine a looking man of his age—five-and-fifty perhaps—as any woman would wish to look upon.

But his presence was not a cheerful one. He was always courteous, always refined, but singularly silent and retiring. I have never lived so long with any man and known so little of him. If he were indoors he spent his time either in his own small study in the Eastern Tower, or in the library in the modern wing. So regular was his routine that one could always say at any hour exactly where he would be. Twice in the day he would visit his study, once after breakfast, and once about ten at night. You might set your watch by the slam of the heavy door. For the rest of the day he would be in his library—save that for an hour or two in the afternoon he would take a walk or a ride, which was solitary like the rest of his existence. He loved his children, and was keenly interested in the progress of their studies, but they were a little awed by the silent, shaggy-browed figure, and they avoided him as much as they could. Indeed, we all did that.

It was some time before I came to know anything about the circumstances of Sir John Bollamore's life, for Mrs. Stevens, the housekeeper, and Mr. Richards, the land-steward, were too loyal to talk easily of their employer's affairs. As to the governess, she knew no more than I did, and our common interest was one of the causes which drew us together. At last, however, an incident occurred which led to a closer acquaintance with Mr. Richards and a fuller knowledge of the life of the man whom I served.

The immediate cause of this was no less than the falling of Master Percy, the youngest of my pupils, into the mill-race, with imminent danger both to his life and to mine, since I had to risk myself in order to save him. Dripping and exhausted—for I was far more spent than the child—I was making for my room when Sir John, who had heard the hubbub, opened the door of his little study and asked me what was the matter. I told him of the accident, but assured him that his child was in no danger, while he listened with a rugged, immobile face, which expressed in its intense eyes and tightened lips all the emotion which he tried to conceal.

"One moment! Step in here! Let me have the details!" said he, turning back through the open door.

And so I found myself within that little sanctum, inside which, as I afterwards learned, no other foot had for three years been set save that of the old servant who cleaned it out. It was a round room, conforming to the shape of the tower in which it was situated, with a low ceiling, a single narrow, ivy-wreathed window, and the simplest of furniture. An old carpet, a single chair, a deal table, and a small shelf of books made up the whole contents. On the table stood a full-length photograph of a woman—I took no particular notice of the features, but I remember that a certain gracious gentleness was the prevailing impression. Beside it were a large black japanned box and one or two bundles of letters or papers fastened together with elastic bands.

Our interview was a short one, for Sir John Bollamore perceived that I was soaked, and that I should change without delay. The incident led, however, to an instructive talk with Richards, the agent, who had never penetrated into the chamber which chance had opened to me. That very afternoon he came to me, all curiosity, and walked up and down the garden path with me, while my two charges played tennis upon the lawn beside us.

"You hardly realize the exception which has been made in your favour," said he. "That room has been kept such a mystery, and Sir John's visits to it have been so regular and consistent, that an almost superstitious feeling has arisen about it in the household. I assure you that if I were to repeat to you the tales which are flying about, tales of mysterious visitors there, and of voices overheard by the servants, you might suspect that Sir John had relapsed into his old ways."

"Why do you say relapsed?" I asked.

He looked at me in surprise.

"Is it possible," said he, "that Sir John Bollamore's previous history is unknown to you?"

"Absolutely."

"You astound me. I thought that every man in England knew something of his antecedents. I should not mention the matter if it were not that you are now one of ourselves, and that the facts might come to your ears in some harsher form if I were silent upon them. I always took it for granted that you knew that you were in the service of 'Devil' Bollamore."

"But why 'Devil'?" I asked.

"Ah, you are young and the world moves fast, but twenty years ago the name of 'Devil' Bollamore was one of the best known in London. He was the leader of the fastest set, bruiser, driver, gambler, drunkard—a survival of the old type, and as bad as the worst of them."

I stared at him in amazement.

"What!" I cried, "that quiet, studious, sad-faced man?"

"The greatest rip and debauchee in England! All between ourselves, Colmore. But you understand now what I mean when I say that a woman's voice in his room might even now give rise to suspicions."

"But what can have changed him so?"

"Little Beryl Clare, when she took the risk of becoming his wife. That was the turning point. He had got so far that his own fast set had thrown him over. There is a world of difference, you know, between a man who drinks and a drunkard. They all drink, but they taboo a drunkard. He had become a slave to it—hopeless and helpless. Then she stepped in, saw the possibilities of a fine man in the wreck, took her chance in marrying him, though she might have had the pick of a dozen, and, by devoting her life to it, brought him back to manhood and decency. You have observed that no liquor is ever kept in the house. There never has been any since her foot crossed its threshold. A drop of it would be like blood to a tiger even now."

"Then her influence still holds him?"

"That is the wonder of it. When she died three years ago, we all expected and feared that he would fall back into his old ways. She feared it herself, and the thought gave a terror to death, for she was like a guardian angel to that man, and lived only for the one purpose. By the way, did you see a black japanned box in his room?"

"Yes."

"I fancy it contains her letters. If ever he has occasion to be away, if only for a single night, he invariably takes his black japanned box with him. Well, well, Colmore, perhaps I have told you rather more than I should, but I shall expect you to reciprocate if anything of interest should come to your knowledge." I could see that the worthy man was consumed with curiosity and just a little piqued that I, the newcomer, should have been the first to penetrate into the untrodden chamber. But the fact raised me in his esteem, and from that time onwards I found myself upon more confidential terms with him.

And now the silent and majestic figure of my employer became an object of greater interest to me. I began to understand that strangely human look in his eyes, those deep lines upon his careworn face. He was a man who was fighting a ceaseless battle, holding at arm's length, from morning till night, a horrible adversary, who was for ever trying to close with him—an adversary which would destroy him body and soul could it but fix its claws once more upon him. As I watched the grim, round-backed figure pacing the corridor or walking in the garden, this imminent danger seemed to take bodily shape, and I could almost fancy that I saw this most loathsome and dangerous of all the fiends crouching closely in his very shadow, like a half-cowed beast which slinks beside its keeper, ready at any unguarded moment to spring at his throat. And the dead woman, the woman who had spent her life in warding off this danger, took shape also to my imagination, and I saw her as a shadowy but beautiful presence which intervened for ever with arms uplifted to screen the man whom she loved.

In some subtle way he divined the sympathy which I had for him, and he showed in his own silent fashion that he appreciated it. He even invited me once to share his afternoon walk, and although no word passed between us on this occasion, it was a mark of confidence which he had never shown to anyone before. He asked me also to index his library (it was one of the best private libraries in England), and I spent many hours in the evening in his presence, if not in his society, he reading at his desk and I sitting in a recess by the window reducing to order the chaos which existed among his books. In spite of these close relations I was never again asked to enter the chamber in the turret.

And then came my revulsion of feeling. A single incident changed all my sympathy to loathing, and made me realise that my employer still remained all that he had ever been, with the additional vice of hypocrisy. What happened was as follows.

One evening Miss Witherton had gone down to Broadway, the neighbouring village, to sing at a concert for some charity, and I, according to my promise, had walked over to escort her back. The drive sweeps round under the eastern turret, and I observed as I passed that the light was lit in the circular room. It was a summer evening, and the window, which was a little higher than our heads, was open. We were, as it happened, engrossed in our own conversation at the moment, and we had paused upon the lawn which skirts the old turret, when suddenly something broke in upon our talk and turned our thoughts away from our own affairs.

It was a voice—the voice undoubtedly of a woman.

It was low—so low that it was only in that still night air that we could have heard it, but, hushed as it was, there was no mistaking its feminine timbre. It spoke hurriedly, gaspingly for a few sentences, and then was silent—a piteous, breathless, imploring sort of voice. Miss Witherton and I stood for an instant staring at each other. Then we walked quickly in the direction of the hall-door.

"It came through the window," I said.

"We must not play the part of eavesdroppers," she answered. "We must forget that we have ever heard it."

There was an absence of surprise in her manner which suggested a new idea to me.

"You have heard it before," I cried.

"I could not help it. My own room is higher up on the same turret. It has happened frequently."

"Who can the woman be?"

"I have no idea. I had rather not discuss it."

Her voice was enough to show me what she thought. But granting that our employer led a double and dubious life, who could she be, this mysterious woman who kept him company in the old tower? I knew from my own inspection how bleak and bare a room it was. She certainly did not live there. But in that case where did she come from? It could not be anyone of the household. They were all under the vigilant eyes of Mrs. Stevens. The visitor must come from without. But how?

And then suddenly I remembered how ancient this building was, and how probable that some mediæval passage existed in it. There is hardly an old castle without one. The mysterious room was the basement of the turret, so that if there were anything of the sort it would open through the floor. There were numerous cottages in the immediate vicinity. The other end of the secret passage might lie among some tangle of bramble in the neighbouring copse. I said nothing to anyone, but I felt that the secret of my employer lay within my power.

And the more convinced I was of this the more I marvelled at the manner in which he concealed his true nature. Often as I watched his austere figure, I asked myself if it were indeed possible that such a man should be living this double life, and I tried to persuade myself that my suspicions might after all prove to be ill-founded. But there was the female voice, there was the secret nightly rendezvous in the turret-chamber—how could such facts admit of an innocent interpretation? I conceived a horror of the man. I was filled with loathing at his deep, consistent hypocrisy.

Only once during all those months did I ever see him without that sad but impassive mask which he usually presented towards his fellow-man. For an instant I caught a glimpse of those volcanic fires which he had damped down so long. The occasion was an unworthy one, for the object of his wrath was none other than the aged charwoman whom I have already mentioned as being the one person who was allowed within his mysterious chamber. I was passing the corridor which led to the turret—for my own room lay in that direction—when I heard a sudden, startled scream, and merged in it the husky, growling note of a man who is inarticulate with passion. It was the snarl of a furious wild beast. Then I heard his voice thrilling with anger. "You would dare!" he cried. "You would dare to disobey my directions!" An instant later the charwoman passed me, flying down the passage, white-faced and tremulous, while the terrible voice thundered behind her. "Go to Mrs. Stevens for your money! Never set foot in Thorpe Place again!" Consumed with curiosity, I could not help following the woman, and found her round the corner leaning against the wall and palpitating like a frightened rabbit.

"What is the matter, Mrs. Brown?" I asked.

"It's master!" she gasped. "Oh, 'ow 'e frightened

me! If you had seen 'is eyes, Mr. Colmore, sir. I thought 'e would 'ave been the death of me."

"But what had you done?"

"Done, sir! Nothing. At least nothing to make so much of. Just laid my 'and on that black box of 'is—'adn't even opened it, when in 'e came and you 'eard the way 'e went on. I've lost my place, and glad I am of it, for I would never trust myself within reach of 'im again."

So it was the japanned box which was the cause of this outburst—the box from which he would never permit himself to be separated. What was the connection, or was there any connection between this and the secret visits of the lady whose voice I had overheard? Sir John Bollamore's wrath was enduring as well as fiery, for from that day Mrs. Brown, the charwoman, vanished from our ken, and Thorpe Place knew her no more.

And now I wish to tell you the singular chance which solved all these strange questions and put my employer's secret in my possession. The story may leave you with some lingering doubt as to whether my curiosity did not get the better of my honour, and whether I did not condescend to play the spy. If you choose to think so I cannot help it, but can only assure you that, improbable as it may appear, the matter came about exactly as I describe it.

The first stage in this *dénouement* was that the small room in the turret became uninhabitable. This occurred through the fall of the worm-eaten oaken beam which supported the ceiling. Rotten with age, it snapped in the middle one morning, and brought down a quantity of plaster with it. Fortunately Sir John was not in the room at the time. His precious box was rescued from amongst the debris and brought into the library, where, henceforward, it was locked within his bureau. Sir John took no steps to repair the damage, and I never had an opportunity of searching for that secret passage, the existence of which I had surmised. As to the lady, I had thought that this would have brought her visits to an end, had I not one evening heard Mr. Richards asking Mrs. Stevens who the woman was whom he had overheard talking to Sir John in the library. I could not catch her reply, but I saw from her manner that it was not the first time that she had had to answer or avoid the same question.

"You've heard the voice, Colmore?" said the agent.

I confessed that I had.

"And what do *you* think of it?"

I shrugged my shoulders, and remarked that it was no business of mine.

"Come, come, you are just as curious as any of us. Is it a woman or not?"

"It is certainly a woman."

"Which room did you hear it from?"

"From the turret-room, before the ceiling fell."

"But I heard it from the library only last night. I passed the doors as I was going to bed, and I heard something wailing and praying just as plainly as I hear you. It may be a woman——"

"Why, what else *could* it be?"

He looked at me hard.

"There are more things in heaven and earth," said he. "If it is a woman, how does she get there?"

"I don't know."

"No, nor I. But if it is the other thing—but there, for a practical business man at the end of the nineteenth century this is rather a ridiculous line of conversation." He turned away, but I saw that he felt even more than he had said. To all the old ghost stories of Thorpe Place a new one was being added before our very eyes. It may by this time have taken its permanent place, for though an explanation came to me, it never reached the others.

And my explanation came in this way. I had suffered a sleepless night from neuralgia, and about midday I had taken a heavy dose of chlorodyne to alleviate the pain. At that time I was finishing the indexing of Sir John Bollamore's library, and it was my custom to work there from five till seven. On this particular day I struggled against the double effect of my bad night and the narcotic. I have already mentioned that there was a recess in the library, and in this it was my habit to work. I settled down steadily to my task, but my weariness overcame me and, falling back upon the settee, I dropped into a heavy sleep.

How long I slept I do not know, but it was quite dark when I awoke. Confused by the chlorodyne which I had taken, I lay motionless in a semi-conscious state. The great room with its high walls covered with books loomed darkly all round me. A dim radiance from the moonlight came through the farther window, and against this lighter background I saw that Sir John Bollamore was sitting at his study table. His well-set head and clearly cut profile were sharply outlined against the glimmering square behind him. He bent as I watched him, and I heard the sharp turning of a key and the rasping of metal upon metal. As if in a dream I was vaguely conscious that this was the japanned box which stood in front of him, and that he had drawn something out of it, something squat and uncouth, which now lay before him upon the table. I never realized—it never occurred to my bemuddled and torpid brain that I was intruding upon his privacy, that he imagined himself to be alone in the room. And then, just as it rushed upon my horrified perceptions, and I had half risen to announce my presence, I heard a strange, crisp, metallic clicking, and then the voice.

Yes, it was a woman's voice; there could not be a doubt of it. But a voice so charged with entreaty and with yearning love, that it will ring for ever in my ears. It came with a curious far-away tinkle, but every word was clear, though faint—very faint, for they were the last words of a dying woman.

"I am not really gone, John," said the thin, gasping

voice. " I am here at your very elbow, and shall be until we meet once more. I die happy to think that morning and night you will hear my voice. Oh, John, be strong, be strong, until we meet again."

I say that I had risen in order to announce my presence, but I could not do so while the voice was sounding. I could only remain half lying, half sitting, paralysed, astounded, listening to those yearning distant musical words. And he—he was so absorbed that even if I had spoken he might not have heard me. But with the silence of the voice came my half articulated apologies and explanations. He sprang across the room, switched on the electric light, and in its white glare I saw him, his eyes gleaming with anger, his face twisted with passion, as the hapless charwoman may have seen him weeks before.

" Mr. Colmore ! " he cried. " You here ! What is the meaning of this, sir ? "

With halting words I explained it all, my neuralgia, the narcotic, my luckless sleep and singular awakening. As he listened the glow of anger faded from his face, and the sad, impassive mask closed once more over his features.

" My secret is yours, Mr. Colmore," said he. " I havc only myself to blame for relaxing my precautions. Half confidences are worse than no confidences, and so you may know all since you know so much. The story may go where you will when I have passed away, but until then I rely upon your sense of honour that no human soul shall hear it from your lips. I am proud still—God help me !—or, at least, I am proud enough to resent that pity which this story would draw upon me. I have smiled at envy, and disregarded hatred, but pity is more than I can tolerate.

"You have heard the source from which the voice comes—that voice which has, as I understand, excited so much curiosity in my household. I am aware of the rumours to which it has given rise. These speculations, whether scandalous or superstitious, are such as I can disregard and forgive. What I should never forgive would be a disloyal spying and eavesdropping in order to satisfy an illicit curiosity. But of that, Mr. Colmore, I acquit you.

"When I was a young man, sir, many years younger than you are now, I was launched upon town without a friend or adviser, and with a purse which brought only too many false friends and false advisers to my side. I drank deeply of the wine of life—if there is a man living who has drunk more deeply he is not a man whom I envy. My purse suffered, my character suffered, my constitution suffered, stimulants became a necessity to me, I was a creature from whom my memory recoils. And it was at that time, the time of my blackest degradation, that God sent into my life the gentlest, sweetest spirit that ever descended as a ministering angel from above. She loved me, broken as I was, loved me, and spent her life in making a man once more of that which had degraded itself to the level of the beasts.

"But a fell disease struck her, and she withered away before my eyes. In the hour of her agony it was never of herself, of her own sufferings and her own death that she thought. It was all of me. The one pang which her fate brought to her was the fear that when her influence was removed I should revert to that which I had been. It was in vain that I made oath to her that no drop of wine would ever cross my lips. She knew only too well the hold that the devil had upon me—she who had striven so to loosen it—and it haunted her night and day the thought that my soul might again be within his grip.

"It was from some friend's gossip of the sick room that she heard of this invention—this phonograph—and with the quick insight of a loving woman she saw how she might use it for her ends. She sent me to London to procure the best which money could buy. With her dying breath she gasped into it the words which have held me straight ever since. Lonely and broken, what else have I in all the world to uphold me? But it is enough. Please God, I shall face her without shame when He is pleased to reunite us! That is my secret, Mr. Colmore, and whilst I live I leave it in your keeping."

35. *The Black Doctor*

BISHOP'S CROSSING is a small village lying ten miles in a south-westerly direction from Liverpool. Here in the early seventies there settled a doctor named Aloysius Lana. Nothing was known locally either of his antecedents or of the reasons which had prompted him to come to this Lancashire hamlet. Two facts only were certain about him; the one that he had gained his medical qualification with some distinction at Glasgow; the other that he came undoubtedly of a tropical race, and was so dark that he might almost have had a strain of the Indian in his composition. His predominant features were, however, European, and he possessed a stately courtesy and carriage which suggested a Spanish extraction. A swarthy skin, raven-black hair, and dark, sparkling eyes under a pair of heavily-tufted brows made a strange contrast to the flaxen or chestnut rustics of England, and the newcomer was soon known as "The Black Doctor of Bishop's Crossing." At first it was a term of ridicule and reproach; as the years went on it became a title of honour which was familiar to the whole country-side, and extended far beyond the narrow confines of the village.

For the newcomer proved himself to be a capable surgeon and an accomplished physician. The practice of that district had been in the hands of Edward Rowe, the son of Sir William Rowe, the Liverpool consultant, but he had not inherited the talents of his father, and Dr. Lana, with his advantages of presence and of manner, soon beat him out of the field. Dr. Lana's social success was as rapid as his professional. A remarkable surgical cure in the case of the Hon. James Lowry, the second son of Lord Belton, was the means of introducing him to county society, where he became a favourite through the charm of his conversation and the elegance of his manners. An absence of antecedents and of relatives is sometimes an aid rather than an impediment to social advancement, and the distinguished individuality of the handsome doctor was its own recommendation.

His patients had one fault—and one fault only—to find with him. He appeared to be a confirmed bachelor. This was the more remarkable since the house which he occupied was a large one, and it was known that his success in practice had enabled him to save considerable sums. At first the local matchmakers were continually coupling his name with one or other of the eligible ladies, but as years passed and Dr. Lana remained unmarried, it came to be generally understood that for some reason he must remain a bachelor. Some even went so far as to assert that he was already married, and that it was in order to escape the consequence of an early misalliance that he had buried himself at Bishop's Crossing. And, then, just as the matchmakers had finally given him up in despair, his engagement was suddenly announced to Miss Frances Morton, of Leigh Hall.

Miss Morton was a young lady who was well known upon the country-side, her father, James Haldane Morton, having been the Squire of Bishop's Crossing. Both her parents were, however, dead, and she lived with her only brother, Arthur Morton, who had inherited the family estate. In person Miss Morton was tall and stately, and she was famous for her quick, impetuous nature and for her strength of character. She met Dr. Lana at a garden-party, and a friendship, which quickly ripened into love, sprang up between them. Nothing could exceed their devotion to each other. There was some discrepancy in age, he being thirty-seven, and she twenty-four; but, save in that one respect, there was no possible objection to be found with the match. The engagement was in February, and it was arranged that the marriage should take place in August.

Upon the 3rd of June Dr. Lana received a letter from abroad. In a small village the postmaster is also in a position to be the gossip-master, and Mr. Bankley, of Bishop's Crossing, had many of the secrets of his neighbours in his possession. Of this particular letter he remarked only that it was in a curious envelope, that it was in a man's handwriting, that the postscript was Buenos Ayres, and the stamp of the Argentine Republic. It was the first letter which he had ever known Dr. Lana to have from abroad, and this was the reason why his attention was particularly called to it before he handed it to the local postman. It was delivered by the evening delivery of that date.

Next morning—that is, upon the 4th of June—Dr. Lana called upon Miss Morton, and a long interview followed, from which he was observed to return in a state of great agitation. Miss Morton remained in her room all that day, and her maid found her several times in tears. In the course of a week it was an open secret to the whole village that the engagement was at an end, that Dr. Lana had behaved shamefully to the young lady, and that Arthur Morton, her brother, was talking of horse-whipping him. In what particular respect the doctor had behaved badly was unknown—some surmised one thing and some another; but it was observed, and taken as the obvious sign of a guilty conscience, that he would go for miles round rather than pass the windows of Leigh Hall, and that he gave up attending morning service upon Sundays where he might have met the young lady. There was an advertisement also in the *Lancet* as to the sale of a practice which mentioned no names, but which was thought by some to refer to Bishop's Crossing, and to mean that Dr. Lana was thinking of abandoning the scene of his success. Such was the position of affairs when, upon the evening of Monday,

June 21st, there came a fresh development which changed what had been a mere village scandal into a tragedy which arrested the attention of the whole nation. Some detail is necessary to cause the facts of that evening to present their full significance.

The sole occupants of the doctor's house were his housekeeper, an elderly and most respectable woman, named Martha Woods, and a young servant—Mary Pilling. The coachman and the surgery-boy slept out. It was the custom of the doctor to sit at night in his study, which was next the surgery in the wing of the house which was farthest from the servants' quarters. This side of the house had a door of its own for the convenience of patients, so that it was possible for the doctor to admit and receive a visitor there without the knowledge of anyone. As a matter of fact, when patients came late it was quite usual for him to let them in and out by the surgery entrance, for the maid and the housekeeper were in the habit of retiring early.

On this particular night Martha Woods went into the doctor's study at half-past nine, and found him writing at his desk. She bade him good night, sent the maid to bed, and then occupied herself until a quarter to eleven in household matters. It was striking eleven upon the hall clock when she went to her own room. She had been there about a quarter of an hour or twenty minutes when she heard a cry or call, which appeared to come from within the house. She waited some time, but it was not repeated. Much alarmed, for the sound was loud and urgent, she put on a dressing-gown, and ran at the top of her speed to the doctor's study.

"Who's there?" cried a voice, as she tapped at the door.

"I am here, sir—Mrs. Woods."

"I beg that you will leave me in peace. Go back to your room this instant!" cried the voice, which was, to the best of her belief, that of her master. The tone was so harsh and so unlike her master's usual manner, that she was surprised and hurt.

"I thought I heard you calling, sir," she explained, but no answer was given to her. Mrs. Woods looked at the clock as she returned to her room, and it was then half-past eleven.

At some period between eleven and twelve (she could not be positive as to the exact hour) a patient called upon the doctor and was unable to get any reply from him. This late visitor was Mrs. Madding, the wife of the village grocer, who was dangerously ill of typhoid fever. Dr. Lana had asked her to look in the last thing and let him know how her husband was progressing. She observed that the light was burning in the study, but having knocked several times at the surgery door without response, she concluded that the doctor had been called out, and so returned home.

There is a short, winding drive with a lamp at the end of it leading down from the house to the road. As Mrs. Madding emerged from the gate a man was coming along the footpath. Thinking that it might be Dr. Lana returning from some professional visit, she waited for him, and was surprised to see that it was Mr. Arthur Morton, the young squire. In the light of the lamp she observed that his manner was excited, and that he carried in his hand a heavy hunting-crop. He was turning in at the gate when she addressed him.

"The doctor is not in, sir," said she.

"How do you know that?" he asked, harshly.

"I have been to the surgery door, sir."

"I see a light," said the young squire, looking up the drive. "That is in his study, is it not?"

"Yes, sir; but I am sure that he is out."

"Well, he must come in again," said young Morton, and passed through the gate while Mrs. Madding went upon her homeward way.

At three o'clock that morning her husband suffered a sharp relapse, and she was so alarmed by his symptoms that she determined to call the doctor without delay. As she passed through the gate she was surprised to see someone lurking among the laurel bushes. It was certainly a man, and to the best of her belief Mr. Arthur Morton. Preoccupied with her own troubles, she gave no particular attention to the incident, but hurried on upon her errand.

When she reached the house she perceived to her surprise that the light was still burning in the study. She therefore tapped at the surgery door. There was no answer. She repeated the knocking several times without effect. It appeared to her to be unlikely that the doctor would either go to bed or go out leaving so brilliant a light behind him, and it struck Mrs. Madding that it was possible that he might have dropped asleep in his chair. She tapped at the study window, therefore, but without result. Then, finding that there was an opening between the curtain and the woodwork, she looked through.

The small room was brilliantly lighted from a large lamp on the central table, which was littered with the doctor's books and instruments. No one was visible, nor did she see anything unusual, except that in the farther shadow thrown by the table a dingy white glove was lying upon the carpet. And then suddenly, as her eyes became more accustomed to the light, a boot emerged from the other end of the shadow, and she realized, with a thrill of horror, that what she had taken to be a glove was the hand of a man, who was prostrate upon the floor. Understanding that something terrible had occurred, she rang at the front door, roused Mrs. Woods, the housekeeper, and the two women made their way into the study, having first dispatched the maidservant to the police-station.

At the side of the table, away from the window, Dr. Lana was discovered stretched upon his back and quite dead. It was evident that he had been subjected to violence, for one of his eyes was blackened and there were marks of bruises about his face and neck. A slight thickening and swelling of his features appeared to suggest that the cause of his death had been strangulation. He was dressed in his usual professional clothes, but wore cloth slippers, the soles of which were perfectly clean. The carpet was marked all over, especially on the side of the door, with traces of dirty boots, which were presumably left by the murderer. It was evident that someone had entered by the surgery door, had killed the doctor, and had then made his escape unseen. That the assailant was a man was certain, from the size of the footprints and from the nature of the injuries. But beyond that point the police found it very difficult to go.

There were no signs of robbery, and the doctor's gold watch was safe in his pocket. He kept a heavy cash-box in the room, and this was discovered to be locked but empty. Mrs. Woods had an impression that a large sum was usually kept there, but the doctor had paid a heavy corn bill in cash only that very day, and it was conjectured that it was to this and not to a robber that the emptiness of the box was due. One thing in the room was missing—but that one thing was suggestive. The portrait of Miss Morton, which had always stood upon the side-table, had been taken from its frame, and carried off. Mrs. Woods had observed it there when she waited upon her employer that evening, and now it was gone. On the other hand, there was picked up from the floor a green eye-patch, which the housekeeper could not remember to have seen before. Such a patch might, however, be in the possession of a doctor, and there was nothing to indicate that it was in any way connected with the crime.

Suspicion could only turn in one direction, and Arthur Morton, the young squire, was immediately arrested. The evidence against him was circumstantial, but damning. He was devoted to his sister, and it was shown that since the rupture between her and Dr. Lana he had been heard again and again to express himself in the most vindictive terms towards her former lover. He had, as stated, been seen somewhere about eleven o'clock entering the doctor's drive with a hunting-crop in his hand. He had then, according to the theory of the police, broken in upon the doctor, whose exclamation of fear or of anger had been loud enough to attract the attention of Mrs. Woods. When Mrs. Woods descended, Dr. Lana had made up his mind to talk it over with his visitor, and had, therefore, sent his housekeeper back to her room. This conversation had lasted a long time, had become more and more fiery, and had ended by a personal struggle, in which the doctor lost his life. The fact, revealed by a *post-mortem*, that his heart was much diseased—an ailment quite unsuspected during his life—would make it possible that death might in his case ensue from injuries which would not be fatal to a healthy man. Arthur Morton had then removed his sister's photograph, and had made his way homeward, stepping aside into the laurel bushes to avoid Mrs. Madding at the gate. This was the theory of the prosecution, and the case which they presented was a formidable one.

On the other hand, there were some strong points for the defence. Morton was high-spirited and impetuous, like his sister, but he was respected and liked by everyone, and his frank and honest nature seemed to be incapable of such a crime. His own explanation was that he was anxious to have a conversation with Dr. Lana about some urgent family matters (from first to last he refused even to mention the name of his sister). He did not attempt to deny that this conversation would probably have been of an unpleasant nature. He had heard from a patient that the doctor was out, and he therefore waited until about three in the morning for his return, but as he had seen nothing of him up to that hour, he had given it up and had returned home. As to his death, he knew no more about it than the constable who arrested him. He had formerly been an intimate friend of the deceased man; but circumstances, which he would prefer not to mention, had brought about a change in his sentiments.

There were several facts which supported his innocence. It was certain that Dr. Lana was alive and in his study at half-past eleven o'clock. Mrs. Woods was prepared to swear that it was at that hour that she had heard his voice. The friends of the prisoner contended that it was probable that at that time Dr. Lana was not alone. The sound which had originally attracted the attention of the housekeeper, and her master's unusual impatience that she should leave him in peace, seemed to point to that. If this were so, then it appeared to be probable that he had met his end between the moment when the housekeeper heard his voice and the time when Mrs. Madding made her first call and found it impossible to attract his attention. But if this were the time of his death, then it was certain that Mr. Arthur Morton could not be guilty, as it was *after* this that she had met the young squire at the gate.

If this hypothesis were correct, and someone was with Dr. Lana before Mrs. Madding met Mr. Arthur Morton, then who was this someone, and what motives had he for wishing evil to the doctor? It was universally admitted that if the friends of the accused could throw light upon this, they would have gone a long way towards establishing his innocence. But in the meanwhile it was open to the public to say—as they did say—that there was no proof that anyone had been there at all except the young squire; while, on the other hand, there was ample proof that his motives in going were of a sinister kind. When Mrs. Madding called, the doctor might have retired to his room, or he might, as she thought at the time, have gone out and returned afterwards to find Mr. Arthur Morton waiting for him. Some of the supporters of the accused laid stress upon the fact that the photograph of his sister Frances, which had been removed from the doctor's room, had not been found in her brother's possession. This argument, however, did not count for much, as he had ample time before his arrest to burn it or to destroy it. As to the only positive evidence in the case—the muddy footmarks upon the floor—they were so blurred by the softness of the carpet that it was impossible to make any trustworthy deduction from them. The most that could be said was that their appearance was not inconsistent with the theory that they were made by the accused, and it was further shown that his boots were very muddy upon that night. There had been a heavy shower in the afternoon, and all boots were probably in the same condition.

Such is a bald statement of the singular and romantic series of events which centred public attention upon this Lancashire tragedy. The unknown origin of the doctor, his curious and distinguished personality, the position of the man who was accused of the murder, and the love affair which had preceded the crime, all combined to make the affair one of those dramas which absorb the whole interest of a nation. Throughout the three kingdoms men discussed the case of the Black Doctor of Bishop's Crossing, and many were the theories put forward to explain the facts; but it may safely be said that among them all there was not one which prepared the minds of the public for the extraordinary sequel, which caused so much excitement upon the first day of the trial, and came to a climax upon the second. The long files of the *Lancaster Weekly* with their report of the case lie before me as I write, but I must content myself with a synopsis of the case up to the point when, upon the evening of the first day, the evidence of Miss Frances Morton threw a singular light upon the case.

Mr. Porlock Carr, the counsel for the prosecution, had marshalled his facts with his usual skill, and as the day wore on, it became more and more evident how difficult was the task which Mr. Humphrey, who had been retained for the defence, had before him. Several witnesses were put up to swear to the intemperate expressions which the young squire had been heard to utter about the doctor, and the fiery manner in which he resented the alleged ill-treatment of his sister. Mrs. Madding repeated her evidence as to the visit which had been paid late at night by the prisoner to the deceased, and it was shown by another witness that the prisoner was aware that the doctor was in the habit of sitting up alone in this isolated wing of the house, and that he had chosen this very late hour to call because he knew that his victim would then be at his mercy. A servant at the squire's house was compelled to admit that he had heard his master return about three that morning, which corroborated Mrs. Madding's statement that she had seen him among the laurel bushes near the gate upon the occasion of her second visit. The muddy boots and an alleged similarity in the footprints were duly dwelt upon, and it was felt when the case for the prosecution had been presented that, however circumstantial it might be, it was none the less so complete and so convincing, that the fate of the prisoner was sealed, unless something quite unexpected should be disclosed by the defence. It was three o'clock when the prosecution closed. At half-past four, when the court rose, a new and unlooked for development had occurred. I extract the incident, or part of it, from the journal which I have already mentioned, omitting the preliminary observations of the counsel.

Considerable sensation was caused in the crowded court when the first witness called for the defence proved to be Miss Frances Morton, the sister of the prisoner. Our readers will remember that the young lady had been engaged to Dr. Lana, and that it was his anger over the sudden termination of this engagement which was thought to have driven her brother to the perpetration of this crime. Miss Morton had not, however, been directly implicated in the case in any way, either at the inquest or at the police-court proceedings, and her appearance as the leading witness for the defence came as a surprise upon the public.

Miss Frances Morton, who was a tall and handsome brunette, gave her evidence in a low but clear voice, though it was evident throughout that she was suffering from extreme emotion. She alluded to her engagement to the doctor, touched briefly upon its termination, which was due, she said, to personal matters connected with his family, and surprised the court by asserting that she had always considered her brother's resentment to be unreasonable and intemperate. In answer to a direct question from her counsel, she replied that she did not feel that she had any grievance whatever against Dr. Lana, and that in her opinion he had acted in a perfectly honourable manner. Her brother, on an insufficient knowledge of the facts, had taken another view, and she was compelled to acknowledge that, in spite of her entreaties, he had uttered threats of personal violence against the doctor, and had, upon the evening of the tragedy, announced his intention of "having it out with him." She had done her best to bring him to a more reasonable frame of mind, but he was very headstrong where his emotions or prejudices were concerned.

Up to this point the young lady's evidence had appeared to make against the prisoner rather than in his favour. The questions of her counsel, however, soon put a very different light upon the matter, and disclosed an unexpected line of defence.

Mr. Humphrey : Do you believe your brother to be guilty of this crime ?

The Judge : I cannot permit that question, Mr. Humphrey. We are here to decide upon questions of fact—not of belief.

Mr. Humphrey : Do you know that your brother is not guilty of the death of Doctor Lana ?

Miss Morton : Yes.

Mr. Humphrey : How do you know it ?

Miss Morton : Because Dr. Lana is not dead.

There followed a prolonged sensation in court, which interrupted the examination of the witness.

Mr. Humphrey : And how do you know, Miss Morton, that Dr. Lana is not dead ?

Miss Morton : Because I have received a letter from him since the date of his supposed death.

Mr. Humphrey : Have you this letter ?

Miss Morton : Yes, but I should prefer not to show it.

Mr. Humphrey : Have you the envelope ?

Miss Morton : Yes, it is here.

Mr. Humphrey : What is the post-mark ?

Miss Morton : Liverpool.

Mr. Humphrey : And the date ?

Miss Morton : June the 22nd.

Mr. Humphrey : That being the day after his alleged death. Are you prepared to swear to this handwriting, Miss Morton ?

Miss Morton : Certainly.

Mr. Humphrey : I am prepared to call six other witnesses, my lord, to testify that this letter is in the writing of Doctor Lana.

The Judge : Then you must call them to-morrow.

Mr. Porlock Carr (counsel for the prosecution) : In the meantime, my lord, we claim possession of this document, so that we may obtain expert evidence as to how far it is an imitation of the handwriting of the gentleman whom we still confidently assert to be deceased. I need not point out that the theory so unexpectedly sprung upon us may prove to be a very obvious device adopted by the friends of the prisoner in order to divert this inquiry. I would draw attention to the fact that the young lady must, according to her own account, have possessed this letter during the proceedings at the inquest and at the police-court. She desires us to believe that she permitted these to proceed, although she held in her pocket evidence which would at any moment have brought them to an end.

Mr. Humphrey : Can you explain this, Miss Morton ?

Miss Morton : Dr. Lana desired his secret to be preserved.

Mr. Porlock Carr: Then why have you made this public?

Miss Morton: To save my brother.

A murmur of sympathy broke out in court, which was instantly suppressed by the Judge.

The Judge: Admitting this line of defence, it lies with you, Mr. Humphrey, to throw a light upon who this man is whose body has been recognised by so many friends and patients of Dr. Lana as being that of the doctor himself.

A Juryman: Has anyone up to now expressed any doubt about the matter?

Mr. Porlock Carr: Not to my knowledge.

Mr. Humphrey: We hope to make the matter clear.

The Judge: Then the court adjourns until to-morrow.

This new development of the case excited the utmost interest among the general public. Press comment was prevented by the fact that the trial was still undecided, but the question was everywhere argued as to how far there could be truth in Miss Morton's declaration, and how far it might be a daring ruse for the purpose of saving her brother. The obvious dilemma in which the missing doctor stood was that if by any extraordinary chance he was not dead, then he must be held responsible for the death of this unknown man, who resembled him so exactly, and who was found in his study. This letter which Miss Morton refused to produce was possibly a confession of guilt, and she might find herself in the terrible position of only being able to save her brother from the gallows by the sacrifice of her former lover. The court next morning was crammed to overflowing, and a murmur of excitement passed over it when Mr. Humphrey was observed to enter in a state of emotion, which even his trained nerves could not conceal, and to confer with the opposing counsel. A few hurried words—words which left a look of amazement upon Mr. Porlock Carr's face—passed between them, and then the counsel for the defence, addressing the Judge, announced that, with the consent of the prosecution, the young lady who had given evidence upon the sitting before would not be recalled.

The Judge: But you appear, Mr. Humphrey, to have left matters in a very unsatisfactory state.

Mr. Humphrey: Perhaps, my lord, my next witness may help to clear them up.

The Judge: Then call your next witness.

Mr. Humphrey: I call Dr. Aloysius Lana.

The learned counsel has made many telling remarks in his day, but he has certainly never produced such a sensation with so short a sentence. The court was simply stunned with amazement as the very man whose fate had been the subject of so much contention appeared bodily before them in the witness-box. Those among the spectators who had known him at Bishop's Crossing saw him now, gaunt and thin, with deep lines of care upon his face. But in spite of his melancholy bearing and despondent expression, there were few who could say that they had ever seen a man of more distinguished presence. Bowing to the judge, he asked if he might be allowed to make a statement, and having been duly informed that whatever he said might be used against him, he bowed once more, and proceeded :—

"My wish," said he, "is to hold nothing back, but to tell with perfect frankness all that occurred upon the night of the 21st of June. Had I known that the innocent had suffered, and that so much trouble had been brought upon those whom I love best in the world, I should have come forward long ago; but there were reasons which prevented these things from coming to my ears. It was my desire that an unhappy man should vanish from the world which had known him, but I had not foreseen that others would be affected by my actions. Let me to the best of my ability repair the evil which I have done.

"To anyone who is acquainted with the history of the Argentine Republic the name of Lana is well known. My father, who came of the best blood of old Spain, filled all the highest offices of the State, and would have been President but for his death in the riots of San Juan. A brilliant career might have been open to my twin brother Ernest and myself had it not been for financial losses which made it necessary that we should earn our own living. I apologise, sir, if these details appear to be irrelevant, but they are a necessary introduction to that which is to follow.

"I had, as I have said, a twin brother named Ernest, whose resemblance to me was so great that even when we were together people could see no difference between us. Down to the smallest detail we were exactly the same. As we grew older this likeness became less marked because our expression was not the same, but with our features in repose the points of difference were very slight.

"It does not become me to say too much of one who is dead, the more so as he is my only brother, but I leave his character to those who knew him best. I will only say—for I *have* to say it—that in my early manhood I conceived a horror of him, and that I had good reason for the aversion which filled me. My own reputation suffered from his actions, for our close resemblance caused me to be credited with many of them. Eventually, in a peculiarly disgraceful business, he contrived to throw the whole odium upon me in such a way that I was forced to leave the Argentine for ever, and to seek a career in Europe. The freedom from his hated presence more than compensated me for the loss of my native land. I had enough money to defray my medical studies at Glasgow, and I finally settled in practice at Bishop's Crossing, in the firm conviction that in that remote Lancashire hamlet I should never hear of him again.

"For years my hopes were fulfilled, and then at last

he discovered me. Some Liverpool man who visited Buenos Ayres put him upon my track. He had lost all his money, and he thought that he would come over and share mine. Knowing my horror of him, he rightly thought that I would be willing to buy him off. I received a letter from him saying that he was coming. It was at a crisis in my own affairs, and his arrival might conceivably bring trouble, and even disgrace, upon some whom I was especially bound to shield from anything of the kind. I took steps to insure that any evil which might come should fall on me only, and that "—here he turned and looked at the prisoner—" was the cause of conduct upon my part which has been too harshly judged. My only motive was to screen those who were dear to me from any possible connection with scandal or disgrace. That scandal and disgrace would come with my brother was only to say that what had been would be again.

" My brother arrived himself one night not very long after my receipt of the letter. I was sitting in my study after the servants had gone to bed, when I heard a footstep upon the gravel outside, and an instant later I saw his face looking in at me through the window. He was a clean-shaven man like myself, and the resemblance between us was still so great that, for an instant, I thought it was my own reflection in the glass. He had a dark patch over his eye, but our features were absolutely the same. Then he smiled in a sardonic way which had been a trick of his from his boyhood, and I knew that he was the same brother who had driven me from my native land, and brought disgrace upon what had been an honourable name. I went to the door and I admitted him. That would be about ten o'clock that night.

" When he came into the glare of the lamp, I saw at once that he had fallen upon very evil days. He had walked from Liverpool, and he was tired and ill. I was quite shocked by the expression upon his face. My medical knowledge told me that there was some serious internal malady. He had been drinking also, and his face was bruised as the result of a scuffle which he had had with some sailors. It was to cover his injured eye that he wore this patch, which he removed when he entered the room. He was himself dressed in a pea-jacket and flannel shirt, and his feet were bursting through his boots. But his poverty had only made him more savagely vindictive towards me. His hatred rose to the height of a mania. I had been rolling in money in England, according to his account, while he had been starving in South America. I cannot describe to you the threats which he uttered or the insults which he poured upon me. My impression is, that hardships and debauchery had unhinged his reason. He paced about the room like a wild beast, demanding drink, demanding money, and all in the foulest language. I am a hot-tempered man, but I thank God that I am able to say that I remained master of myself, and that I never raised a hand against him. My coolness only irritated him the more. He raved, he cursed, he shook his fists in my face, and then suddenly a horrible spasm passed over his features, he clapped his hand to his side, and with a loud cry he fell in a heap at my feet. I raised him up and stretched him upon the sofa, but no answer came to my exclamations, and the hand which I held in mine was cold and clammy. His diseased heart had broken down. His own violence had killed him.

"For a long time I sat as if I were in some dreadful dream, staring at the body of my brother. I was aroused by the knocking of Mrs. Woods, who had been disturbed by that dying cry. I sent her away to bed. Shortly afterwards a patient tapped at the surgery door, but as I took no notice, he or she went off again. Slowly and gradually as I sat there a plan was forming itself in my head in the curious automatic way in which plans do form. When I rose from my chair my future movements were finally decided upon without my having been conscious of any process of thought. It was an instinct which irresistibly inclined me towards one course.

"Ever since that change in my affairs to which I have alluded, Bishop's Crossing had become hateful to me. My plans of life had been ruined, and I had met with hasty judgments and unkind treatment where I had expected sympathy. It is true that any danger of scandal from my brother had passed away with his life; but still, I was sore about the past, and felt that things could never be as they had been. It may be that I was unduly sensitive, and that I had not made sufficient allowance for others, but my feelings were as I describe. Any chance of getting away from Bishop's Crossing and of everyone in it would be most welcome to me. And here was such a chance as I could never have dared to hope for, a chance which would enable me to make a clean break with the past.

"There was this dead man lying upon the sofa, so like me that save for some little thickness and coarseness of the features there was no difference at all. No one had seen him come and no one would miss him. We were both clean-shaven, and his hair was about the same length as my own. If I changed clothes with him, then Dr. Aloysius Lana would be found lying dead in his study, and there would be an end of an unfortunate fellow, and of a blighted career. There was plenty of ready money in the room, and this I could carry away with me to help me to start once more in some other land. In my brother's clothes I could walk by night unobserved as far as Liverpool, and in that great seaport I would soon find some means of leaving the country. After my lost hopes, the humblest existence where I was unknown was far preferable, in my estimation, to a practice, however successful, in Bishop's Crossing, where at any moment I might come face to face with those whom I should wish, if it were possible, to forget. I determined to effect the change.

"And I did so. I will not go into particulars, for

the recollection is as painful as the experience; but in an hour my brother lay, dressed down to the smallest detail in my clothes, while I slunk out by the surgery door, and taking the back path which led across some fields, I started off to make the best of my way to Liverpool, where I arrived the same night. My bag of money and a certain portrait were all I carried out of the house, and I left behind me in my hurry the shade which my brother had been wearing over his eye. Everything else of his I took with me.

"I give you my word, sir, that never for one instant did the idea occur to me that people might think that I had been murdered, nor did I imagine that anyone might be caused serious danger through this stratagem by which I endeavoured to gain a fresh start in the world. On the contrary, it was the thought of relieving others from the burden of my presence which was always uppermost in my mind. A sailing vessel was leaving Liverpool that very day for Corunna, and in this I took my passage, thinking that the voyage would give me time to recover my balance, and to consider the future. But before I left my resolution softened. I bethought me that there was one person in the world to whom I would not cause an hour of sadness. She would mourn me in her heart, however harsh and unsympathetic her relatives might be. She understood and appreciated the motives upon which I had acted, and if the rest of her family condemned me, she, at least, would not forget. And so I sent her a note under the seal of secrecy to save her from a baseless grief. If under the pressure of events she broke that seal, she has my entire sympathy and forgiveness.

"It was only last night that I returned to England, and during all this time I have heard nothing of the sensation which my supposed death had caused, nor of the accusation that Mr. Arthur Morton had been concerned in it. It was in a late evening paper that I read an account of the proceedings of yesterday, and I have come this morning as fast as an express train could bring me to testify to the truth."

Such was the remarkable statement of Dr. Aloysius Lana which brought the trial to a sudden termination. A subsequent investigation corroborated it to the extent of finding out the vessel in which his brother Ernest Lana had come over from South America. The ship's doctor was able to testify that he had complained of a weak heart during the voyage, and that his symptoms were consistent with such a death as was described.

As to Dr. Aloysius Lana, he returned to the village from which he had made so dramatic a disappearance, and a complete reconciliation was effected between him and the young squire, the latter having acknowledged that he had entirely misunderstood the other's motives in withdrawing from his engagement. That another reconciliation followed may be judged from a notice extracted from a prominent column in the *Morning Post*:

> "A marriage was solemnised upon September 19th, by the Rev. Stephen Johnson, at the parish church of Bishop's Crossing, between Aloysius Xavier Lana, son of Don Alfredo Lana, formerly Foreign Minister of the Argentine Republic, and Frances Morton, only daughter of the late James Morton, J.P., of Leigh Hall, Bishop's Crossing, Lancashire."

36. *The Jew's Breastplate*

MY particular friend, Ward Mortimer, was one of the best men of his day at everything connected with Oriental archæology. He had written largely upon the subject, he had lived two years in a tomb at Thebes, while he excavated in the Valley of the Kings, and finally he had created a considerable sensation by his exhumation of the alleged mummy of Cleopatra in the inner room of the Temple of Horus, at Philæ. With such a record at the age of thirty-one, it was felt that a considerable career lay before him, and no one was surprised when he was elected to the curatorship of the Belmore Street Museum, which carries with it the lectureship at the Oriental College, and an income which has sunk with the fall in land, but which still remains at that ideal sum which is large enough to encourage an investigator, but not so large as to enervate him.

There was only one reason which made Ward Mortimer's position a little difficult at the Belmore Street Museum, and that was the extreme eminence of the man whom he had to succeed. Professor Andreas was a profound scholar and a man of European reputation. His lectures were frequented by students from every part of the world, and his admirable management of the collection intrusted to his care was a commonplace in all learned societies. There was, therefore, considerable surprise when, at the age of fifty-five, he suddenly resigned his position and retired from those duties which had been both his livelihood and his pleasure. He and his daughter left the comfortable suite of rooms which had formed his official residence in connection with the museum, and my friend, Mortimer, who was a bachelor, took up his quarters there.

On hearing of Mortimer's appointment Professor Andreas had written him a very kindly and flattering congratulatory letter. I was actually present at their first meeting, and I went with Mortimer round the museum when the Professor showed us the admirable collection which he had cherished so long. The Professor's beautiful daughter and a young man, Captain Wilson, who was, as I understood, soon to be her husband, accompanied us in our inspection. There were fifteen rooms, but the Babylonian, the Syrian, and the central hall, which contained the Jewish and Egyptian collection, were the finest of all. Professor Andreas was a quiet, dry, elderly man, with a clean-shaven face and an impassive manner, but his dark eyes sparkled and his features quickened into enthusiastic life as he pointed out to us the rarity and the beauty of some of his specimens. His hand lingered so fondly over them, that one could read his pride in them and the grief in his heart now that they were passing from his care into that of another.

He had shown us in turn his mummies, his papyri, his rare scarabs, his inscriptions, his Jewish relics, and his duplication of the famous seven-branched candlestick of the Temple, which was brought to Rome by Titus, and which is supposed by some to be lying at this instant in the bed of the Tiber. Then he approached a case which stood in the very centre of the hall, and he looked down through the glass with reverence in his attitude and manner.

"This is no novelty to an expert like yourself, Mr. Mortimer," said he; "but I daresay that your friend, Mr. Jackson, will be interested to see it."

Leaning over the case I saw an object, some five inches square, which consisted of twelve precious stones in a framework of gold, with golden hooks at two of the corners. The stones were all varying in sort and colour, but they were of the same size. Their shapes, arrangement, and gradation of tint made me think of a box of water-colour paints. Each stone had some hieroglyphic scratched upon its surface.

"You have heard, Mr. Jackson, of the urim and thummim?"

I had heard the term, but my idea of its meaning was exceedingly vague.

"The urim and thummim was a name given to the jewelled plate which lay upon the breast of the high priest of the Jews. They had a very special feeling of reverence for it—something of the feeling which an ancient Roman might have for the Sibylline books in the Capitol. There are, as you see, twelve magnificent stones, inscribed with mystical characters. Counting from the left-hand top corner, the stones are carnelian, peridot, emerald, ruby, lapis lazuli, onyx, sapphire, agate, amethyst, topaz, beryl, and jasper."

I was amazed at the variety and beauty of the stones.

"Has the breastplate any particular history?" I asked.

"It is of great age and of immense value," said Professor Andreas. "Without being able to make an absolute assertion, we have many reasons to think that it is possible that it may be the original urim and thummim of Solomon's Temple. There is certainly nothing so fine in any collection in Europe. My friend, Captain Wilson, here, is a practical authority upon precious stones, and he would tell you how pure these are."

Captain Wilson, a man with a dark, hard, incisive face, was standing beside his *fiancée* at the other side of the case.

"Yes," said he, curtly, "I have never seen finer stones."

"And the gold-work is also worthy of attention. The ancients excelled in——"—he was apparently about to indicate the setting of the stones, when Captain Wilson interrupted him.

"You will see a finer example of their gold-work in this candlestick," said he, turning to another table, and we all joined him in his admiration of its embossed stem and delicately ornamented branches. Altogether it was an interesting and a novel experience to have objects of such rarity explained by so great an expert; and when, finally, Professor Andreas finished our inspection by formally handing over the precious collection to the care of my friend, I could not help pitying him and envying his successor whose life was to pass in so pleasant a duty. Within a week, Ward Mortimer was duly installed in his new set of rooms, and had become the autocrat of the Belmore Street Museum.

About a fortnight afterwards my friend gave a small dinner to half a dozen bachelor friends to celebrate his promotion. When his guests were departing he pulled my sleeve and signalled to me that he wished me to remain.

"You have only a few hundred yards to go," said

he—I was living in chambers in the Albany. " You may as well stay and have a quiet cigar with me. I very much want your advice."

I relapsed into an arm-chair and lit one of his excellent Matronas. When he had returned from seeing the last of his guests out, he drew a letter from his dress-jacket and sat down opposite to me.

" This is an anonymous letter which I received this morning," said he. " I want to read it to you and to have your advice."

" You are very welcome to it for what it is worth."

" This is how the note runs : ' Sir,—I should strongly advise you to keep a very careful watch over the many valuable things which are committed to your charge. I do not think that the present system of a single watchman is sufficient. Be upon your guard, or an irreparable misfortune may occur.' "

" Is that all ? "

" Yes, that is all."

" Well," said I, " it is at least obvious that it was written by one of the limited number of people who are aware that you have only one watchman at night."

Ward Mortimer handed me the note, with a curious smile. " Have you an eye for handwriting ? " said he. " Now, look at this ! " He put another letter in front of me. " Look at the *c* in ' congratulate ' and the *c* in ' committed.' Look at the capital *I*. Look at the trick of putting in a dash instead of a stop ! "

" They are undoubtedly from the same hand—with some attempt at disguise in the case of this first one."

" The second," said Ward Mortimer, " is the letter of congratulation which was written to me by Professor Andreas upon my obtaining my appointment."

I stared at him in amazement. Then I turned over the letter in my hand, and there, sure enough, was " Martin Andreas " signed upon the other side. There could be no doubt, in the mind of anyone who had the slightest knowledge of the science of graphology, that the Professor had written an anonymous letter, warning his successor against thieves. It was inexplicable, but it was certain.

"Why should he do it?" I asked.

"Precisely what I should wish to ask you. If he had any such misgivings, why could he not come and tell me direct?"

"Will you speak to him about it?"

"There again I am in doubt. He might choose to deny that he wrote it."

"At any rate," said I, "this warning is meant in a friendly spirit, and I should certainly act upon it. Are the present precautions enough to insure you against robbery?"

"I should have thought so. The public are only admitted from ten till five, and there is a guardian to every two rooms. He stands at the door between them, and so commands them both."

"But at night?"

"When the public are gone, we at once put up the great iron shutters, which are absolutely burglar-proof. The watchman is a capable fellow. He sits in the lodge, but he walks round every three hours. We keep one electric light burning in each room all night."

"It is difficult to suggest anything more—short of keeping your day watchers all night."

"We could not afford that."

"At least, I should communicate with the police, and have a special constable put on outside in Belmore Street," said I. "As to the letter, if the writer wishes to be anonymous, I think he has a right to remain so. We must trust to the future to show some reason for the curious course which he has adopted."

So we dismissed the subject, but all that night after my return to my chambers I was puzzling my brain as to what possible motive Professor Andreas could have for writing an anonymous warning letter to his successor —for that the writing was his was as certain to me as if I had seen him actually doing it. He foresaw some danger to the collection. Was it because he foresaw it that he abandoned his charge of it? But if so, why should he hesitate to warn Mortimer in his own name? I puzzled and puzzled until at last I fell into a troubled sleep, which carried me beyond my usual hour of rising.

I was aroused in a singular and effective method, for about nine o'clock my friend Mortimer rushed into my room with an expression of consternation upon his face. He was usually one of the most tidy men of my acquaintance, but now his collar was undone at one end, his tie was flying, and his hat at the back of his head. I read his whole story in his frantic eyes.

"The museum has been robbed!" I cried, springing up in bed.

"I fear so! Those jewels! The jewels of the urim and thummim!" he gasped, for he was out of breath with running. "I'm going on to the police-station. Come to the museum as soon as you can, Jackson! Good-bye!" He rushed distractedly out of the room, and I heard him clatter down the stairs.

I was not long in following his directions, but I found when I arrived that he had already returned with a police inspector, and another elderly gentleman, who proved to be Mr. Purvis, one of the partners of Morson and Company, the well-known diamond merchants. As an expert in stones he was always prepared to advise the police. They were grouped round the case in which the breastplate of the Jewish priest had been exposed. The plate had been taken out and laid upon the glass top of the case, and the three heads were bent over it.

"It is obvious that it has been tampered with," said Mortimer. "It caught my eye the moment that I passed through the room this morning. I examined it yesterday evening, so that it is certain that this has happened during the night."

It was, as he had said, obvious that someone had been

at work upon it. The settings of the uppermost row of four stones—the carnelian, peridot, emerald, and ruby—were rough and jagged as if someone had scraped all round them. The stones were in their places, but the beautiful gold-work which we had admired only a few days before had been very clumsily pulled about.

"It looks to me," said the police inspector, "as if someone had been trying to take out the stones."

"My fear is," said Mortimer, "that he not only tried, but succeeded. I believe these four stones to be skilful imitations which have been put in the place of the originals."

The same suspicion had evidently been in the mind of the expert, for he had been carefully examining the four stones with the aid of a lens. He now submitted them to several tests, and finally turned cheerfully to Mortimer.

"I congratulate you, sir," said he, heartily. "I will pledge my reputation that all four of these stones are genuine, and of a most unusual degree of purity."

The colour began to come back to my poor friend's frightened face, and he drew a long breath of relief.

"Thank God!" he cried. "Then what in the world did the thief want?"

"Probably he meant to take the stones, but was interrupted."

"In that case one would expect him to take them out one at a time, but the setting of each of these has been loosened, and yet the stones are all here."

"It is certainly most extraordinary," said the inspector. "I never remember a case like it. Let us see the watchman."

The commissionaire was called—a soldierly, honest-faced man, who seemed as concerned as Ward Mortimer at the incident.

"No, sir, I never heard a sound," he answered, in reply to the questions of the inspector. "I made my rounds four times, as usual, but I saw nothing suspicious.

I've been in my position ten years, but nothing of the kind has ever occurred before."

"No thief could have come through the windows?"

"Impossible, sir."

"Or passed you at the door?"

"No, sir; I never left my post except when I walked my rounds."

"What other openings are there in the museum?"

"There is the door into Mr. Ward Mortimer's private rooms."

"That is locked at night," my friend explained, "and in order to reach it anyone from the street would have to open the outside door as well."

"Your servants?"

"Their quarters are entirely separate."

"Well, well," said the inspector, "this is certainly very obscure. However, there has been no harm done, according to Mr. Purvis."

"I will swear that those stones are genuine."

"So that the case appears to be merely one of malicious damage. But none the less, I should be very glad to go carefully round the premises, and to see if we can find any trace to show us who your visitor may have been."

His investigation, which lasted all the morning, was careful and intelligent, but it led in the end to nothing. He pointed out to us that there were two possible entrances to the museum which we had not considered. The one was from the cellars by a trap-door opening in the passage. The other through a skylight from the lumber-room, overlooking that very chamber to which the intruder had penetrated. As neither the cellar nor the lumber-room could be entered unless the thief was already within the locked doors, the matter was not of any practical importance, and the dust of cellar and attic assured us that no one had used either one or the other. Finally, we ended as we began, without the slightest clue as to how, why, or by whom the setting of these four jewels had been tampered with.

There remained one course for Mortimer to take, and he took it. Leaving the police to continue their fruitless researches, he asked me to accompany him that afternoon in a visit to Professor Andreas. He took with him the two letters, and it was his intention to openly tax his predecessor with having written the anonymous warning, and to ask him to explain the fact that he should have anticipated so exactly that which had actually occurred. The Professor was living in a small villa in Upper Norwood, but we were informed by the servant that he was away from home. Seeing our disappointment, she asked us if we should like to see Miss Andreas, and showed us into the modest drawing-room.

I have mentioned incidentally that the Professor's daughter was a very beautiful girl. She was a blonde, tall and graceful, with a skin of that delicate tint which the French call "mat," the colour of old ivory, or of the lighter petals of the sulphur rose. I was shocked, however, as she entered the room to see how much she had changed in the last fortnight. Her young face was haggard and her bright eyes heavy with trouble.

"Father has gone to Scotland," she said. "He seems to be tired, and has had a good deal to worry him. He only left us yesterday."

"You look a little tired yourself, Miss Andreas," said my friend.

"I have been so anxious about father."

"Can you give me his Scotch address?"

"Yes, he is with his brother, the Rev. David Andreas, 1, Arran Villas, Ardrossan."

Ward Mortimer made a note of the address, and we left without saying anything as to the object of our visit. We found ourselves in Belmore Street in the evening in exactly the same position in which we had been in the morning. Our only clue was the Professor's letter, and my friend had made up his mind to start for Ardrossan next day, and to get to the bottom of the anonymous letter, when a new development came to alter our plans.

Very early on the following morning I was aroused from my sleep by a tap upon my bedroom door. It was a messenger with a note from Mortimer.

" Do come round," it said ; " the matter is becoming more and more extraordinary."

When I obeyed his summons I found him pacing excitedly up and down the central room, while the old soldier who guarded the premises stood with military stiffness in a corner.

" My dear Jackson," he cried, " I am so delighted that you have come, for this is a most inexplicable business."

" What has happened, then ? "

He waved his hand towards the case which contained the breastplate.

" Look at it," said he.

I did so, and could not restrain a cry of surprise. The setting of the middle row of precious stones had been profaned in the same manner as the upper ones. Of the twelve jewels eight had been now tampered with in this singular fashion. The setting of the lower four was neat and smooth. The others jagged and irregular.

" Have the stones been altered ? " I asked.

" No, I am certain that these upper four are the same which the expert pronounced to be genuine, for I observed yesterday that little discoloration on the edge of the emerald. Since they have not extracted the upper stones, there is no reason to think the lower have been transposed. You say that you heard nothing, Simpson ? "

" No, sir," the commissionaire answered. " But when I made my round after daylight I had a special look at these stones, and I saw at once that someone had been meddling with them. Then I called you, sir, and told you. I was backwards and forwards all the night, and I never saw a soul or heard a sound."

" Come up and have some breakfast with me," said Mortimer, and he took me into his own chambers.— " Now, what *do* you think of this, Jackson ? " he asked.

" It is the most objectless, futile, idiotic business that ever I heard of. It can only be the work of a monomaniac."

" Can you put forward any theory ? "

A curious idea came into my head. " This object is a Jewish relic of great antiquity and sanctity," said I. " How about the anti-Semitic movement ? Could one conceive that a fanatic of that way of thinking might desecrate——"

" No, no, no ! " cried Mortimer. " That will never do ! Such a man might push his lunacy to the length of destroying a Jewish relic, but why on earth should he nibble round every stone so carefully that he can only do four stones in a night ? We must have a better solution than that, and we must find it for ourselves, for I do not think that our inspector is likely to help us. First of all, what do you think of Simpson, the porter ? "

" Have you any reason to suspect him ? "

" Only that he is the one person on the premises."

" But why should he indulge in such wanton destruction ? Nothing has been taken away. He has no motive."

" Mania ? "

" No, I will swear to his sanity."

" Have you any other theory ? "

" Well, yourself, for example. You are not a somnambulist, by any chance ? "

" Nothing of the sort, I assure you."

" Then I give it up."

" But I don't—and I have a plan by which we will make it all clear."

" To visit Professor Andreas ? "

" No, we shall find our solution nearer than Scotland. I will tell you what we shall do. You know that skylight which overlooks the central hall ? We will leave the electric lights in the hall, and we will keep watch in the lumber-room, you and I, and solve the mystery for ourselves. If our mysterious visitor is doing four stones at a time, he has four still to do, and there is every reason to think that he will return to-night and complete the job."

"Excellent!" I cried.

"We will keep our own secret, and say nothing either to the police or to Simpson. Will you join me?"

"With the utmost pleasure," said I; and so it was agreed.

It was ten o'clock that night when I returned to the Belmore Street Museum. Mortimer was, as I could see, in a state of suppressed nervous excitement, but it was still too early to begin our vigil, so we remained for an hour or so in his chambers, discussing all the possibilities of the singular business which we had met to solve. At last the roaring stream of hansom cabs and the rush of hurrying feet became lower and more intermittent as the pleasure-seekers passed on their way to their stations or their homes. It was nearly twelve when Mortimer led the way to the lumber-room which overlooked the central hall of the museum.

He had visited it during the day, and had spread some sacking so that we could lie at our ease, and look straight down into the museum. The skylight was of unfrosted glass, but was so covered with dust that it would be impossible for anyone looking up from below to detect that he was overlooked. We cleared a small piece at each corner, which gave us a complete view of the room beneath us. In the cold white light of the electric lamps everything stood out hard and clear, and I could see the smallest detail of the contents of the various cases.

Such a vigil is an excellent lesson, since one has no choice but to look hard at those objects which we usually pass with such half-hearted interest. Through my little peep-hole I employed the hours in studying every specimen, from the huge mummy-case which leaned against the wall to those very jewels which had brought us there, gleaming and sparkling in their glass case immediately beneath us. There was much precious gold-work and many valuable stones scattered through the numerous cases, but those wonderful twelve which made up the urim and thummim glowed and burned with a radiance which far eclipsed the others. I studied in turn the tomb-pictures of Sicara, the friezes from Karnak, the statues of Memphis, and the inscriptions of Thebes, but my eyes would always come back to that wonderful Jewish relic, and my mind to the singular mystery which surrounded it. I was lost in the thought of it when my companion suddenly drew his breath sharply in, and seized my arm in a convulsive grip. At the same instant I saw what it was which had excited him.

I have said that against the wall—on the right-hand side of the doorway (the right-hand side as we looked at it, but the left as one entered)—there stood a large mummy-case. To our unutterable amazement it was slowly opening. Gradually, gradually the lid was swinging back, and the black slit which marked the opening was becoming wider and wider. So gently and carefully was it done that the movement was almost imperceptible. Then, as we breathlessly watched it, a white thin hand appeared at the opening, pushing back the painted lid, then another hand, and finally a face—a face which was familiar to us both, that of Professor Andreas. Stealthily he slunk out of the mummy-case, like a fox stealing from its burrow, his head turning incessantly to left and to right, stepping, then pausing, then stepping again, the very image of craft and of caution. Once some sound in the street struck him motionless, and he stood listening, with his ear turned, ready to dart back to the shelter behind him. Then he crept onwards again upon tiptoe, very, very softly and slowly, until he had reached the case in the centre of the room. There he took a bunch of keys from his pocket, unlocked the case, took out the Jewish breastplate, and, laying it upon the glass in front of him, began to work upon it with some sort of small, glistening tool. He was so directly underneath us that his bent head covered his work, but we could guess from the movement of his hand that he was engaged in finishing the strange disfigurement which he had begun.

I could realize from the heavy breathing of my companion, and the twitchings of the hand which still clutched my wrist, the furious indignation which filled his heart as he saw this vandalism in the quarter of all others where he could least have expected it. He, the very man who a fortnight before had reverently bent over this unique relic, and who had impressed its antiquity and its sanctity upon us, was now engaged in this outrageous profanation. It was impossible, unthinkable —and yet there, in the white glare of the electric light beneath us, was that dark figure with the bent grey head, and the twitching elbow. What inhuman hypocrisy, what hateful depth of malice against his successor must underlie these sinister nocturnal labours. It was painful to think of and dreadful to watch. Even I, who had none of the acute feelings of a virtuoso, could not bear to look on and see this deliberate mutilation of so ancient a relic. It was a relief to me when my companion tugged at my sleeve as a signal that I was to follow him as he softly crept out of the room. It was not until we were within his own quarters that he opened his lips, and then I saw by his agitated face how deep was his consternation.

"The abominable Goth!" he cried. "Could you have believed it?"

"It is amazing."

"He is a villain or a lunatic—one or the other. We shall very soon see which. Come with me, Jackson, and we shall get to the bottom of this black business."

A door opened out of the passage which was the private entrance from his rooms into the museum. This he opened softly with his key, having first kicked off his shoes, an example which I followed. We crept together through room after room, until the large hall lay before us, with that-dark figure still stooping and working at the central case. With an advance as cautious as his own we closed in upon him, but softly as we went we could not take him entirely unawares. We were still a dozen yards from him when he looked round with a start, and uttering a husky cry of terror, ran frantically down the museum.

"Simpson! Simpson!" roared Mortimer, and far away down the vista of electric lighted doors we saw the stiff figure of the old soldier suddenly appear. Professor Andreas saw him also, and stopped running, with a gesture of despair. At the same instant we each laid a hand upon his shoulder.

"Yes, yes, gentlemen," he panted, "I will come with you. To your room, Mr. Ward Mortimer, if you please! I feel that I owe you an explanation."

My companion's indignation was so great that I could see that he dared not trust himself to reply. We walked on each side of the old Professor, the astonished commissionaire bringing up the rear. When we reached the violated case, Mortimer stopped and examined the breastplate. Already one of the stones of the lower row had had its setting turned back in the same manner as the others. My friend held it up and glanced furiously at his prisoner.

"How could you!" he cried. "How could you!"

"It is horrible—horrible!" said the Professor. "I don't wonder at your feelings. Take me to your room."

"But this shall not be left exposed!" cried Mortimer. He picked the breastplate up and carried it tenderly in his hand, while I walked beside the Professor, like a policeman with a malefactor. We passed into Mortimer's chambers, leaving the amazed old soldier to understand matters as best he could. The Professor sat down in Mortimer's arm-chair, and turned so ghastly a colour that for the instant all our resentment was changed to concern. A stiff glass of brandy brought the life back to him once more.

"There, I am better now!" said he. "These last few days have been too much for me. I am convinced that I could not stand it any longer. It is a nightmare—a horrible nightmare—that I should be arrested as a burglar in what has been for so long my own museum. And yet I cannot blame you. You could not have done otherwise. My hope always was that I should get it all over before I was detected. This would have been my last night's work."

"How did you get in?" asked Mortimer.

"By taking a very great liberty with your private door. But the object justified it. The object justified everything. You will not be angry when you know everything—at least, you will not be angry with me. I had a key to your side door and also to the museum door. I did not give them up when I left. And so you see it was not difficult for me to let myself into the museum. I used to come in early before the crowd had cleared from the street. Then I hid myself in the mummy-case, and took refuge there whenever Simpson came round. I could always hear him coming. I used to leave in the same way as I came."

"You ran a risk."

"I had to."

"But why? What on earth was your object—*you* to do a thing like that!" Mortimer pointed reproachfully at the plate which lay before him on the table.

"I could devise no other means. I thought and thought, but there was no alternative except a hideous public scandal, and a private sorrow which would have clouded our lives. I acted for the best, incredible as it may seem to you, and I only ask your attention to enable me to prove it."

"I will hear what you have to say before I take any further steps," said Mortimer, grimly.

"I am determined to hold back nothing, and to take

you both completely into my confidence. I will leave it to your own generosity how far you will use the facts with which I supply you."

" We have the essential facts already."

" And yet you understand nothing. Let me go back to what passed a few weeks ago, and I will make it all clear to you. Believe me that what I say is the absolute and exact truth.

" You have met the person who calls himself Captain Wilson. I say ' calls himself ' because I have reason now to believe that it is not his correct name. It would take me too long if I were to describe all the means by which he obtained an introduction to me and ingratiated himself into my friendship and the affection of my daughter. He brought letters from foreign colleagues which compelled me to show him some attention. And then, by his own attainments, which are considerable, he succeeded in making himself a very welcome visitor at my rooms. When I learned that my daughter's affections had been gained by him, I may have thought it premature, but I certainly was not surprised, for he had a charm of manner and of conversation which would have made him conspicuous in any society.

" He was much interested in Oriental antiquities, and his knowledge of the subject justified his interest. Often when he spent the evening with us he would ask permission to go down into the museum and have an opportunity of privately inspecting the various specimens. You can imagine that I, as an enthusiast, was in sympathy with such a request, and that I felt no surprise at the constancy of his visits. After his actual engagement to Elise, there was hardly an evening which he did not pass with us, and an hour or two were generally devoted to the museum. He had the free run of the place, and when I have been away for the evening I had no objection to his doing whatever he wished here. This state of things was only terminated by the fact of my resignation of my official duties and my retirement to

Norwood, where I hoped to have the leisure to write a considerable work which I had planned.

"It was immediately after this—within a week or so—that I first realized the true nature and character of the man whom I had so imprudently introduced into my family. The discovery came to me through letters from my friends abroad, which showed me that his introductions to me had been forgeries. Aghast at the revelation, I asked myself what motive this man could originally have had in practising this elaborate deception upon me. I was too poor a man for any fortune-hunter to have marked me down. Why, then, had he come? I remembered that some of the most precious gems in Europe had been under my charge, and I remembered also the ingenious excuses by which this man had made himself familiar with the cases in which they were kept. He was a rascal who was planning some gigantic robbery. How could I, without striking my own daughter, who was infatuated about him, prevent him from carrying out any plan which he might have formed? My device was a clumsy one, and yet I could think of nothing more effective. If I had written a letter under my own name, you would naturally have turned to me for details which I did not wish to give. I resorted to an anonymous letter, begging you to be upon your guard.

"I may tell you that my change from Belmore Street to Norwood had not affected the visits of this man, who had, I believe, a real and overpowering affection for my daughter. As to her, I could not have believed that any woman could be so completely under the influence of a man as she was. His stronger nature seemed to entirely dominate her. I had not realized how far this was the case, or the extent of the confidence which existed between them, until that very evening when his true character for the first time was made clear to me. I had given orders that when he called he should be shown into my study instead of to the drawing-room. There I told him bluntly that I knew all about him, that I had taken steps to defeat his designs, and that neither I nor my daughter desired ever to see him again. I added that I thanked God that I had found him out before he had time to harm those precious objects which it had been the work of my life-time to protect.

" He was certainly a man of iron nerve. He took my remarks without a sign either of surprise or of defiance, but listened gravely and attentively until I had finished. Then he walked across the room without a word and struck the bell.

" ' Ask Miss Andreas to be so kind as to step this way,' said he to the servant.

" My daughter entered, and the man closed the door behind her. Then he took her hand in his.

" ' Elise,' said he, ' your father has just discovered that I am a villain. He knows now what you knew before.'

" She stood in silence, listening.

" ' He says that we are to part for ever,' said he.

" She did not withdraw her hand.

" ' Will you be true to me, or will you remove the last good influence which is ever likely to come into my life ? '

" ' John,' she cried, passionately, ' I will never abandon you ! Never, never, not if the whole world were against you.'

" In vain I argued and pleaded with her. It was absolutely useless. Her whole life was bound up in this man before me. My daughter, gentlemen, is all that I have left to love, and it filled me with agony when I saw how powerless I was to save her from her ruin. My helplessness seemed to touch this man who was the cause of my trouble.

" ' It may not be as bad as you think, sir,' said he, in his quiet, inflexible way. ' I love Elise with a love which is strong enough to rescue even one who has such a record as I have. It was but yesterday that I promised her that never again in my whole life would I do a thing of which she should be ashamed. I have made up my mind to it, and never yet did I make up my mind to a thing which I did not do.'

"He spoke with an air which carried conviction with it. As he concluded he put his hand into his pocket and he drew out a small cardboard box.

"'I am about to give you a proof of my determination,' said he. 'This, Elise, shall be the first-fruits of your redeeming influence over me. You are right, sir, in thinking that I had designs upon the jewels in your possession. Such ventures have had a charm for me, which depended as much upon the risk run as upon the value of the prize. Those famous and antique stones of the Jewish priest were a challenge to my daring and my ingenuity. I determined to get them.'

"'I guessed as much.'

"'There was only one thing that you did not guess.'

"'And what is that?'

"'That I got them. They are in this box.'

"He opened the box, and tilted out the contents upon the corner of my desk. My hair rose and my flesh grew cold as I looked. There were twelve magnificent square stones engraved with mystical characters. There could be no doubt that they were the jewels of the urim and thummim.

"'Good God!' I cried. 'How have you escaped discovery?'

"'By the substitution of twelve others, made especially to my order, in which the originals are so carefully imitated that I defy the eye to detect the difference.'

"'Then the present stones are false?' I cried.

"'They have been for some weeks.'

"We all stood in silence, my daughter white with emotion, but still holding this man by the hand.

"'You see what I am capable of, Elise,' said he.

"'I see that you are capable of repentance and restitution,' she answered.

" ' Yes, thanks to your influence! I leave the stones in your hands, sir. Do what you like about it. But remember that whatever you do against me, is done against the future husband of your only daughter. You will hear from me soon again, Elise. It is the last time that I will ever cause pain to your tender heart,' and with these words he left both the room and the house.

" My position was a dreadful one. Here I was with these precious relics in my possession, and how could I return them without a scandal and an exposure? I knew the depth of my daughter's nature too well to suppose that I would ever be able to detach her from this man now that she had entirely given him her heart. I was not even sure how far it was right to detach her if she had such an ameliorating influence over him. How could I expose him without injuring her—and how far was I justified in exposing him when he had voluntarily put himself into my power? I thought and thought until at last I formed a resolution which may seem to you to be a foolish one, and yet, if I had to do it again, I believe it would be the best course open to me.

" My idea was to return the stones without anyone being the wiser. With my keys I could get into the museum at any time, and I was confident that I could avoid Simpson, whose hours and methods were familiar to me. I determined to take no one into my confidence —not even my daughter—whom I told that I was about to visit my brother in Scotland. I wanted a free hand for a few nights, without inquiry as to my comings and goings. To this end I took a room in Harding Street that very night, with an intimation that I was a Pressman, and that I should keep very late hours.

" That night I made my way into the museum, and I replaced four of the stones. It was hard work, and took me all night. When Simpson came round I always heard his footsteps, and concealed myself in the mummy-case. I had some knowledge of gold-work, but was far less skilful than the thief had been. He had replaced the setting so exactly that I defy anyone to see the difference. My work was rude and clumsy. However, I hoped that the plate might not be carefully examined, or the roughness of the setting observed, until my task was done. Next night I replaced four more stones. And to-night I should have finished my task had it not been for the unfortunate circumstance which has caused me to reveal so much which I should have wished to keep concealed. I appeal to you, gentlemen, to your sense of honour and of compassion, whether what I have told you should go any farther or not. My own happiness, my daughter's future, the hopes of this man's regeneration, all depend upon your decision."

"Which is," said my friend, "that all is well that ends well and that the whole matter ends here and at once. To-morrow the loose settings shall be tightened by an expert goldsmith, and so passes the greatest danger to which, since the destruction of the Temple, the urim and thummim has been exposed. Here is my hand, Professor Andreas, and I can only hope that under such difficult circumstances I should have carried myself as unselfishly and as well."

Just one footnote to this narrative. Within a month Elise Andreas was married to a man whose name, had I the indiscretion to mention it, would appeal to my readers as one who is now widely and deservedly honoured. But if the truth were known that honour is due not to him, but to the gentle girl who plucked him back when he had gone so far down that dark road along which few return.

37. *The Nightmare Room*

THE sitting-room of the Masons was a very singular apartment. At one end it was furnished with considerable luxury. The deep sofas, the low, luxurious chairs, the voluptuous statuettes, and the rich curtains hanging from deep and ornamental screens of metal-work made a fitting frame for the lovely woman who was the mistress of the establishment. Mason, a young but wealthy man of affairs, had clearly spared no pains and no expense to meet every want and every whim of his beautiful wife. It was natural that he should do so, for she had given up much for his sake. The most famous dancer in France, the heroine of a dozen extraordinary romances, she had resigned her life of glittering pleasure in order to share the fate of the young American, whose austere ways differed so widely from her own. In all that wealth could buy he tried to make amends for what she had lost. Some might perhaps have thought it in better taste had he not proclaimed this fact—had he not even allowed it to be printed—but save for some personal peculiarities of the sort, his conduct was that of a husband who has never for an instant ceased to be a lover. Even the presence of spectators would not prevent the public exhibition of his overpowering affection.

But the room was singular. At first it seemed familiar, and yet a longer acquaintance made one realise its sinister peculiarities. It was silent—very silent. No footfall could be heard upon those rich carpets and heavy rugs. A struggle—even the fall of a body—would make no sound. It was strangely colourless also, in a light which seemed always subdued. Nor was it all furnished in equal taste. One would have said that when the young banker had lavished thousands upon this boudoir, this inner jewel-case for his precious possession, he had failed to count the cost and had suddenly been arrested by a threat to his own solvency. It was luxurious where it looked out upon the busy street below. At the farther side it was bare, spartan, and reflected rather the taste of a most ascetic man than of a pleasure-loving woman. Perhaps that was why she only came there for a few hours, sometimes two, sometimes four, in the day, but while she was there she lived intensely, and within this nightmare room Lucille Mason was a very different and a more dangerous woman than elsewhere.

Dangerous—that was the word. Who could doubt it who saw her delicate figure stretched upon the great bearskin which draped the sofa. She was leaning upon her right elbow, her delicate but determined chin resting upon her hand, while her eyes, large and languishing, adorable but inexorable, stared out in front of her with a fixed intensity which had in it something vaguely terrible. It was a lovely face—a child's face, and yet Nature had placed there some subtle mark, some indefinable expression, which told that a devil lurked within. It had been noticed that dogs shrank from her, and that children screamed and ran from her caresses. There are instincts which are deeper than reason.

Upon this particular afternoon something had greatly moved her. A letter was in her hand, which she read and re-read with a tightening of those delicate little eyebrows and a grim setting of those delicious lips. Suddenly she started, and a shadow of fear softened the feline menace of her features. She raised herself upon her arm, and her eyes were fixed eagerly upon the door. She was listening intently—listening for something which she dreaded. For a moment a smile of relief played over her expressive face. Then with a look of horror she stuffed her letter into her dress. She had hardly done so before the door opened, and a young man came briskly into the room. It was Archie Mason, her husband—the man whom she had loved, the man for whom she had sacrificed her European fame, the man whom now she regarded as the one obstacle to a new and wonderful experience.

The American was a man about thirty, clean-shaven, athletic, dressed to perfection in a closely-cut suit, which outlined his perfect figure. He stood at the door with his arms folded, looking intently at his wife, with a face which might have been a handsome, sun-tinted mask save for those vivid eyes. She still leaned upon her elbow, but her eyes were fixed on his. There was something terrible in the silent exchange. Each interrogated the other, and each conveyed the thought that the answer to their question was vital. He might have been asking, "What have you done?" She in her turn seemed to be saying, "What do you know?" Finally, he walked forward, sat down upon the bearskin beside her, and taking her delicate ear gently between his fingers, turned her face towards his.

"Lucille," he said, "are you poisoning me?"

She sprang back from his touch with horror in her face and protests upon her lips. Too moved to speak, her surprise and her anger showed themselves rather in her darting hands and her convulsed features. She tried to rise, but his grasp tightened upon her wrist. Again he asked a question, but this time it had deepened in its terrible significance.

"Lucille, why are you poisoning me?"

"You are mad, Archie! Mad!" she gasped.

His answer froze her blood. With pale parted lips and blanched cheeks she could only stare at him in helpless silence, whilst he drew a small bottle from his pocket and held it before her eyes.

"It is from your jewel-case!" he cried.

Twice she tried to speak and failed. At last the words came slowly one by one from her contorted lips:—

"At least I never used it."

Again his hand sought his pocket. From it he drew a sheet of paper, which he unfolded and held before her.

"It is the certificate of Dr. Angus. It shows the presence of twelve grains of antimony. I have also the evidence of Du Val, the chemist who sold it."

Her face was terrible to look at. There was nothing to say. She could only lie with that fixed hopeless stare like some fierce creature in a fatal trap.

"Well?" he asked.

There was no answer save a movement of desperation and appeal.

"Why?" he said. "I want to know why." As he spoke his eye caught the edge of the letter which she had thrust into her bosom. In an instant he had snatched it. With a cry of despair she tried to regain it, but he held her off with one hand while his eyes raced over it.

"Campbell!" he gasped. "It was Campbell!"

She had found her courage again. There was nothing more to conceal. Her face set hard and firm. Her eyes were deadly as daggers.

"Yes," she said, "it is Campbell."

"My God! Campbell of all men!"

He rose and walked swiftly about the room. Campbell, the grandest man that he had ever known, a man whose whole life had been one long record of self-denial, of courage, of every quality which marks the chosen man. And yet, he, too, had fallen a victim to this siren, and had been dragged down to such a level that he had betrayed, in intention if not in actual deed, the man whose hand he shook in friendship. It was incredible—and yet here was the passionate, pleading letter imploring his wife to fly and share the fate of a penniless man. Every word of the letter showed that Campbell had at least no thought of Mason's death, which would have removed all difficulties. That devilish solution was the outcome of the deep and wicked brain which brooded within that perfect habitation.

Mason was a man in a million, a philosopher, a thinker, with a broad and tender sympathy for others. For an instant his soul had been submerged in his bitterness. He could for that brief period have slain both his wife and Campbell, and gone to his own death with the serene mind of a man who has done his plain duty. But already, as he paced the room, milder thoughts had begun to prevail. How could he blame Campbell? He knew the absolute witchery of this woman. It was not only her wonderful physical beauty. She had a unique power of seeming to take an interest in a man, in writhing into his inmost conscience, in penetrating those parts of his nature which were too sacred for the world, and in seeming to stimulate him towards ambition and even towards virtue. It was just there that the deadly cleverness of her net was shown. He remembered how it had been in his own case. She was free then—or so he thought—and he had been able to marry her. But suppose she had not been free. Suppose she had been married. And suppose she had taken possession of his soul in the same way. Would he have stopped there? Would he have been able to draw off with his unfulfilled longings? He was bound to admit that with all his New England strength he could not have done so. Why, then, should he feel so bitter with his unfortunate friend who was in the same position? It was pity and sympathy which filled his mind as he thought of Campbell.

And she? There she lay upon the sofa, a poor broken butterfly, her dreams dispersed, her plot detected, her future dark and perilous. Even for her, poisoner as she was, his heart relented. He knew something of her history. He knew her as a spoiled child from birth, untamed, unchecked, sweeping everything easily before her from her cleverness, her beauty, and her charm. She had never known an obstacle. And now one had risen across her path, and she had madly and wickedly tried to remove it. But if she had wished to remove it, was not that in itself a sign that he had been found wanting—that he was not the man who could bring her peace of mind and contentment of heart? He was too stern and self-contained for that sunny volatile nature. He was of the North, and she of the South, drawn strongly together for a time by the law of opposites, but impossible for permanent union. He should have seen to this—he should have understood it. It was on him, with his superior brain, that the responsibility for the situation lay. His heart softened towards her as it would to a little child which was in helpless trouble. For a time he had paced the room in silence, his lips compressed, his hands clenched till his nails had marked his palms. Now with a sudden movement he sat beside her and took her cold and inert hand in his. One thought beat in his brain. "Is it chivalry, or is it weakness?" The question sounded in his ears, it framed itself before his eyes, he could almost fancy that it materialised itself and that he saw it in letters which all the world could read.

It had been a hard struggle, but he had conquered.

"You shall choose between us, dear," he said. "If really you are sure—*sure*, you understand—that Campbell could make you happy as a husband, I will not be the obstacle."

"A divorce!" she gasped.

His hand closed upon the bottle of poison. "You can call it that," said he.

A new strange light shone in her eyes as she looked at him. This was a man who had been unknown to her. The hard, practical American had vanished. In his place she seemed to have a glimpse of a hero, and a saint, a man who could rise to an inhuman height of unselfish virtue. Both her hands were round that which held the fatal phial.

"Archie," she cried, "you could forgive me even that!"

He smiled at her. "You are only a little wayward kiddie after all."

Her arms were outstretched to him when there was a tap at the door, and the maid entered in the strange silent fashion in which all things moved in that nightmare room. There was a card on the tray. She glanced at it.

"Captain Campbell! I will not see him."

Mason sprang to his feet.

"On the contrary, he is most welcome. Show him up this instant."

A few minutes later a tall, sun-burned young soldier

had been ushered into the room. He came forward with a smile upon his pleasant features, but as the door closed behind him, and the faces before him resumed their natural expressions, he paused irresolutely and glanced from one to the other.

"Well?" he asked.

Mason stepped forward and laid his hand upon his shoulder.

"I bear no ill-will," he said.

"Ill-will?"

"Yes, I know all. But I might have done the same myself had the position been reversed."

Campbell stepped back and looked a question at the lady. She nodded and shrugged her graceful shoulders. Mason smiled.

"You need not fear that it is a trap for a confession. We have had a frank talk upon the matter. See, Jack, you were always a sportsman. Here's a bottle. Never mind how it came here. If one or other of us drink it, it would clear the situation." His manner was wild, almost delirious. "Lucille, which shall it be?"

There had been a strange force at work in the nightmare room. A third man was there, though not one of the three who had stood in the crisis of their life's drama had time or thought for him. How long he had been there—how much he had heard—none could say. In the corner farthest from the little group he lay crouched against the wall, a sinister snake-like figure, silent and scarcely moving save for a nervous twitching of his clenched right hand. He was concealed from view by a square case and by a dark cloth drawn cunningly above it, so as to screen his features. Intent, watching eagerly every new phase of the drama, the moment had almost come for his intervention. But the three thought little of that. Absorbed in the interplay of their own emotions they had lost sight of a force stronger than themselves—a force which might at any moment dominate the scene.

"Are you game, Jack?" asked Mason.

The soldier nodded.

"No !—for God's sake, no !" cried the woman.

Mason had uncorked the bottle, and turning to the side table he drew out a pack of cards. Cards and bottle stood together.

"We can't put the responsibility on her," he said. "Come, Jack, the best of three."

The soldier approached the table. He fingered the fatal cards. The woman, leaning upon her hand, bent her face forward and stared with fascinated eyes.

Then and only then the bolt fell.

The stranger had risen, pale and grave.

All three were suddenly aware of his presence. They faced him with eager inquiry in their eyes. He looked at them coldly, sadly, with something of the master in his bearing.

"How is it ?" they asked, all together.

"Rotten !" he answered. "Rotten ! We'll take the whole reel once more to-morrow."

TALES OF TWILIGHT AND THE UNSEEN

38. *The Brown Hand*

EVERYONE knows that Sir Dominick Holden, the famous Indian surgeon, made me his heir, and that his death changed me in an hour from a hard-working and impecunious medical man to a well-to-do landed proprietor. Many know also that there were at least five people between the inheritance and me, and that Sir Dominick's selection appeared to be altogether arbitrary and whimsical. I can assure them, however, that they are quite mistaken, and that, although I only knew Sir Dominick in the closing years of his life, there were, none the less, very real reasons why he should show his goodwill towards me. As a matter of fact, though I say it myself, no man ever did more for another than I did for my Indian uncle. I cannot expect the story to be believed, but it is so singular that I should feel that it was a breach of duty if I did not put it upon record—so here it is, and your belief or incredulity is your own affair.

Sir Dominick Holden, C.B., K.C.S.I., and I don't know what besides, was the most distinguished Indian surgeon of his day. In the Army originally, he afterwards settled down into civil practice in Bombay, and visited, as a consultant, every part of India. His name is best remembered in connection with the Oriental Hospital which he founded and supported. The time came, however, when his iron constitution began to show signs of the long strain to which he had subjected it, and his brother practitioners (who were not, perhaps, entirely disinterested upon the point) were unanimous in recommending him to return to England. He held on so long as he could, but at last he developed nervous symptoms of a very pronounced character, and so came back, a broken man, to his native county of Wiltshire. He bought a considerable estate with an ancient manor-house upon the edge of Salisbury Plain, and devoted his old age to the study of Comparative Pathology, which had been his learned hobby all his life, and in which he was a foremost authority.

We of the family were, as may be imagined, much excited by the news of the return of this rich and childless uncle to England. On his part, although by no means exuberant in his hospitality, he showed some sense of his duty to his relations, and each of us in turn had an invitation to visit him. From the accounts of my cousins it appeared to be a melancholy business, and it was with mixed feelings that I at last received my own summons to appear at Rodenhurst. My wife was so carefully excluded in the invitation that my first impulse was to refuse it, but the interests of the children had to be considered, and so, with her consent, I set out one October afternoon upon my visit to Wiltshire, with little thought of what that visit was to entail.

My uncle's estate was situated where the arable land of the plains begins to swell upwards into the rounded chalk hills which are characteristic of the county. As I drove from Dinton Station in the waning light of that autumn day, I was impressed by the weird nature of the scenery. The few scattered cottages of the peasants were so dwarfed by the huge evidences of prehistoric life, that the present appeared to be a dream and the past to be the obtrusive and masterful reality. The road wound through the valleys, formed by a succession of grassy hills, and the summit of each was cut and carved into the most elaborate fortifications, some circular, and some square, but all on a scale which has defied the winds and the rains of many centuries. Some call them Roman and some British, but their true origin and the reasons for this particular tract of country being so interlaced with entrenchments have never been finally made clear. Here and there on the long, smooth, olive-coloured slopes there rose small, rounded barrows or tumuli. Beneath them lie the cremated ashes of the race which cut so deeply into the hills, but their graves tell us nothing save that a jar full of dust represents the man who once laboured under the sun.

It was through this weird country that I approached my uncle's residence of Rodenhurst, and the house was, as I found, in due keeping with its surroundings. Two broken and weather-stained pillars, each surmounted by a mutilated heraldic emblem, flanked the entrance to a neglected drive. A cold wind whistled through the elms which lined it, and the air was full of the drifting leaves. At the far end, under the gloomy arch of trees, a single yellow lamp burned steadily. In the dim half-light of the coming night I saw a long, low building stretching out two irregular wings, with deep eaves, a sloping gambrel roof, and walls which were criss-crossed with timber balks in the fashion of the Tudors. The cheery light of a fire flickered in the broad, latticed window to the left of the low-porched door, and this, as it proved, marked the study of my uncle, for it was thither that I was led by his butler in order to make my host's acquaintance.

He was cowering over his fire, for the moist chill of an English autumn had set him shivering. His lamp was unlit, and I only saw the red glow of the embers beating upon a huge, craggy face, with a Red Indian nose and cheek, and deep furrows and seams from eye to chin, the sinister marks of hidden volcanic fires. He sprang up at my entrance with something of an old-world courtesy and welcomed me warmly to Rodenhurst. At the same time I was conscious, as the lamp was carried in, that it was a very critical pair of light-blue eyes which looked out at me from under shaggy eyebrows, like scouts beneath a bush, and that this outlandish uncle of mine was carefully reading off my character with all the ease of a practised observer and an experienced man of the world.

For my part I looked at him, and looked again, for I had never seen a man whose appearance was more fitted to hold one's attention. His figure was the framework of a giant, but he had fallen away until his coat dangled straight down in a shocking fashion from a pair of broad and bony shoulders. All his limbs were huge and yet emaciated, and I could not take my gaze from his knobby wrists, and long, gnarled hands. But his eyes —those peering, light-blue eyes—they were the most arrestive of any of his peculiarities. It was not their colour alone, nor was it the ambush of hair in which they lurked ; but it was the expression which I read in them. For the appearance and bearing of the man were masterful, and one expected a certain corresponding arrogance in his eyes, but instead of that I read the look which tells of a spirit cowed and crushed, the furtive, expectant look of the dog whose master has taken the whip from the rack. I formed my own medical diagnosis upon one glance at those critical and yet appealing eyes. I believed that he was stricken with some mortal ailment, that he knew himself to be exposed to sudden death, and that he lived in terror of it. Such was my judgment —a false one, as the event showed ; but I mention it that it may help you to realize the look which I read in his eyes..

My uncle's welcome was, as I have said, a courteous one, and in an hour or so I found myself seated between him and his wife at a comfortable dinner, with curious, pungent delicacies upon the table, and a stealthy, quick-eyed Oriental waiter behind his chair. The old couple had come round to that tragic imitation of the dawn of life when husband and wife, having lost or scattered all those who were their intimates, find themselves face to face and alone once more, their work done, and the end nearing fast. Those who have reached that stage in sweetness and love, who can change their winter into a gentle, Indian summer, have come as victors through the ordeal of life. Lady Holden was a small, alert woman with a kindly eye, and her expression as she glanced at him was a certificate of character to her husband. And yet, though I read a mutual love in their glances, I read also mutual horror, and recognized in her face some reflection of that stealthy fear which I had detected in his. Their talk was sometimes merry and sometimes sad, but there was a forced note in their merriment and a naturalness in their sadness which told me that a heavy heart beat upon either side of me.

We were sitting over our first glass of wine, and the servants had left the room, when the conversation took a turn which produced a remarkable effect upon my host and hostess. I cannot recall what it was which started the topic of the supernatural, but it ended in my showing them that the abnormal in psychical experiences was a subject to which I had, like many neurologists, devoted a great deal of attention. I concluded by narrating my experiences when, as a member of the Psychical Research Society, I had formed one of a committee of three who spent the night in a haunted house. Our adventures were neither exciting nor convincing, but, such as it was, the story appeared to interest my auditors in a remarkable degree. They listened with an eager silence, and I caught a look of intelligence between them which I could not understand. Lady Holden immediately afterwards rose and left the room.

Sir Dominick pushed the cigar-box over to me, and we smoked for some little time in silence. That huge, bony hand of his was twitching as he raised it with his cheroot to his lips, and I felt that the man's nerves were vibrating like fiddle-strings. My instincts told me that he was on the verge of some intimate confidence, and I feared to speak lest I should interrupt it. At last he turned towards me with a spasmodic gesture like a man who throws his last scruple to the winds.

"From the little that I have seen of you it appears to me, Dr. Hardacre," said he, "that you are the very man I have wanted to meet."

"I am delighted to hear it, sir."

"Your head seems to be cool and steady. You will acquit me of any desire to flatter you, for the circumstances are too serious to permit of insincerities. You have some special knowledge upon these subjects, and you evidently view them from that philosophical standpoint which robs them of all vulgar terror. I presume that the sight of an apparition would not seriously discompose you?"

"I think not, sir."

"Would even interest you, perhaps?"

"Most intensely."

"As a psychical observer, you would probably investigate it in as impersonal a fashion as an astronomer investigates a wandering comet?"

"Precisely."

He gave a heavy sigh.

"Believe me, Dr. Hardacre, there was a time when I could have spoken as you do now. My nerve was a byword in India. Even the Mutiny never shook it for an instant. And yet you see what I am reduced to—the most timorous man, perhaps, in all this county of Wiltshire. Do not speak too bravely upon this subject, or you may find yourself subjected to as long-drawn a test as I am—a test which can only end in the madhouse or the grave."

I waited patiently until he should see fit to go farther in his confidence. His preamble had, I need not say, filled me with interest and expectation.

"For some years, Dr. Hardacre," he continued, "my life and that of my wife have been made miserable by a cause which is so grotesque that it borders upon the ludicrous. And yet familiarity has never made it more easy to bear—on the contrary, as time passes my nerves become more worn and shattered by the constant attrition.

If you have no physical fears, Dr. Hardacre, I should very much value your opinion upon this phenomenon which troubles us so."

"For what it is worth my opinion is entirely at your service. May I ask the nature of the phenomenon?"

"I think that your experiences will have a higher evidential value if you are not told in advance what you may expect to encounter. You are yourself aware of the quibbles of unconscious cerebration and subjective impressions with which a scientific sceptic may throw a doubt upon your statement. It would be as well to guard against them in advance."

"What shall I do, then?"

"I will tell you. Would you mind following me this way?" He led me out of the dining-room and down a long passage until we came to a terminal door. Inside there was a large, bare room fitted as a laboratory, with numerous scientific instruments and bottles. A shelf ran along one side, upon which there stood a long line of glass jars containing pathological and anatomical specimens.

"You see that I still dabble in some of my old studies," said Sir Dominick. "These jars are the remains of what was once a most excellent collection, but unfortunately I lost the greater part of them when my house was burned down in Bombay in '92. It was a most unfortunate affair for me—in more ways than one. I had examples of many rare conditions, and my splenic collection was probably unique. These are the survivors."

I glanced over them, and saw that they really were of a very great value and rarity from a pathological point of view: bloated organs, gaping cysts, distorted bones, odious parasites—a singular exhibition of the products of India.

"There is, as you see, a small settee here," said my host. "It was far from our intention to offer a guest so meagre an accommodation, but since affairs have taken this turn, it would be a great kindness upon your part if you would consent to spend the night in this apartment. I beg that you will not hesitate to let me know if the idea should be at all repugnant to you."

"On the contrary," I said, "it is most acceptable."

"My own room is the second on the left, so that if you should feel that you are in need of company a call would always bring me to your side."

"I trust that I shall not be compelled to disturb you."

"It is unlikely that I shall be asleep. I do not sleep much. Do not hesitate to summon me."

And so with this agreement we joined Lady Holden in the drawing-room and talked of lighter things.

It was no affectation upon my part to say that the prospect of my night's adventure was an agreeable one. I have no pretence to greater physical courage than my neighbours, but familiarity with a subject robs it of those vague and undefined terrors which are the most appalling to the imaginative mind. The human brain is capable of only one strong emotion at a time, and if it be filled with curiosity or scientific enthusiasm, there is no room for fear. It is true that I had my uncle's assurance that he had himself originally taken this point of view, but I reflected that the break-down of his nervous system might be due to his forty years in India as much as to any psychical experiences which had befallen him. I at least was sound in nerve and brain, and it was with something of the pleasurable thrill of anticipation with which the sportsman takes his position beside the haunt of his game that I shut the laboratory door behind me, and partially undressing, lay down upon the rug-covered settee.

It was not an ideal atmosphere for a bed-room. The air was heavy with many chemical odours, that of methylated spirit predominating. Nor were the decorations of my chamber very sedative. The odious line of glass jars with their relics of disease and suffering stretched in front of my very eyes. There was no blind to the window, and a three-quarter moon streamed its white light into the room, tracing a silver square with filigree lattices upon the opposite wall. When I had extinguished my candle this one bright patch in the midst of the general gloom had certainly an eerie and discomposing aspect. A rigid and absolute silence reigned throughout the old house, so that the low swish of the branches in the garden came softly and smoothly to my ears. It may have been the hypnotic lullaby of this gentle susurrus, or it may have been the result of my tiring day, but after many dozings and many efforts to regain my clearness of perception, I fell at last into a deep and dreamless sleep.

I was awakened by some sound in the room, and I instantly raised myself upon my elbow on the couch. Some hours had passed, for the square patch upon the wall had slid downwards and sideways until it lay obliquely at the end of my bed. The rest of the room was in deep shadow. At first I could see nothing, presently, as my eyes became accustomed to the faint light, I was aware, with a thrill which all my scientific absorption could not entirely prevent, that something was moving slowly along the line of the wail. A gentle, shuffling sound, as of soft slippers, came to my ears, and I dimly discerned a human figure walking stealthily from the direction of the door. As it emerged into the patch of moonlight I saw very clearly what it was and how it was employed. It was a man, short and squat, dressed in some sort of dark-grey gown, which hung straight from his shoulders to his feet. The moon shone upon the side of his face, and I saw that it was chocolate-brown in colour, with a ball of black hair like a woman's at the back of his head. He walked slowly, and his eyes were cast upwards towards the line of bottles which contained those gruesome remnants of humanity. He seemed to examine each jar with attention, and then to pass on to the next. When he had come to the end of the line, immediately opposite my bed, he stopped, faced me, threw up his hands with a gesture of despair, and vanished from my sight.

I have said that he threw up his hands, but I should have said his arms, for as he assumed that attitude of despair I observed a singular peculiarity about his appearance. He had only one hand! As the sleeves drooped down from the upflung arms I saw the left plainly, but the right ended in a knobby and unsightly stump. In every other way his appearance was so natural, and I had both seen and heard him so clearly, that I could easily have believed that he was an Indian servant of Sir Dominick's who had come into my room in search of something. It was only his sudden disappearance which suggested anything more sinister to me. As it was I sprang from my couch, lit a candle, and examined the whole room carefully. There were no signs of my visitor, and I was forced to conclude that there had really been something outside the normal laws of Nature in his appearance. I lay awake for the remainder of the night, but nothing else occurred to disturb me.

I am an early riser, but my uncle was an even earlier one, for I found him pacing up and down the lawn at the side of the house. He ran towards me in his eagerness when he saw me come out from the door.

"Well, well!" he cried. "Did you see him?"

"An Indian with one hand?"

"Precisely."

"Yes, I saw him"—and I told him all that occurred. When I had finished, he led the way into his study.

"We have a little time before breakfast," said he. "It will suffice to give you an explanation of this extraordinary affair—so far as I can explain that which is essentially inexplicable. In the first place, when I tell you that for four years I have never passed one single night, either in Bombay, aboard ship, or here in England without my sleep being broken by this fellow, you will understand why it is that I am a wreck of my former self. His programme is always the same. He appears by my bedside, shakes me roughly by the shoulder, passes from my room into the laboratory, walks slowly along the line of my bottles, and then vanishes. For more than a thousand times he has gone through the same routine."

"What does he want?"

"He wants his hand."

"His hand?"

"Yes, it came about in this way. I was summoned to Peshawur for a consultation some ten years ago, and while there I was asked to look at the hand of a native who was passing through with an Afghan caravan. The fellow came from some mountain tribe living away at the back of beyond somewhere on the other side of Kaffiristan. He talked a bastard Pushtoo, and it was all I could do to understand him. He was suffering from a soft sarcomatous swelling of one of the metacarpal joints, and I made him realize that it was only by losing his hand that he could hope to save his life. After much persuasion he consented to the operation, and he asked me, when it was over, what fee I demanded. The poor fellow was almost a beggar, so that the idea of a fee was absurd, but I answered in jest that my fee should be his hand, and that I proposed to add it to my pathological collection.

"To my surprise he demurred very much to the suggestion, and he explained that according to his religion it was an all-important matter that the body should be reunited after death, and so make a perfect dwelling for the spirit. The belief is, of course, an old one, and the mummies of the Egyptians arose from an analogous superstition. I answered him that his hand was already off, and asked him how he intended to preserve it. He replied that he would pickle it in salt and carry it about with him. I suggested that it might be safer in my keeping than his, and that I had better means than salt for preserving it. On realizing that I really intended to carefully keep it, his opposition vanished instantly. 'But remember, sahib,' said he, 'I shall want it back when I am dead.' I laughed at the remark, and so the matter ended. I returned to my practice, and he no doubt in the course of time was able to continue his journey to Afghanistan.

"Well, as I told you last night, I had a bad fire in my house at Bombay. Half of it was burned down, and, among other things, my pathological collection was largely destroyed. What you see are the poor remains of it. The hand of the hillman went with the rest, but I gave the matter no particular thought at the time. That was six years ago.

"Four years ago—two years after the fire—I was awakened one night by a furious tugging at my sleeve. I sat up under the impression that my favourite mastiff was trying to arouse me. Instead of this, I saw my Indian patient of long ago, dressed in the long, grey gown which was the badge of his people. He was holding up his stump and looking reproachfully at me. He then went over to my bottles, which at that time I kept in my room, and he examined them carefully, after which he gave a gesture of anger and vanished. I realized that he had just died, and that he had come to claim my promise that I should keep his limb in safety for him.

"Well, there you have it all, Dr. Hardacre. Every night at the same hour for four years this performance has been repeated. It is a simple thing in itself, but it has worn me out like water dropping on a stone. It has brought a vile insomnia with it, for I cannot sleep now for the expectation of his coming. It has poisoned my old age and that of my wife, who has been the sharer in this great trouble. But there is the breakfast gong, and she will be waiting impatiently to know how it fared with you last night. We are both much indebted to you for your gallantry, for it takes something from the weight of our misfortune when we share it, even for a single night, with a friend, and it reassures us to our sanity, which we are sometimes driven to question."

This was the curious narrative which Sir Dominick

confided to me—a story which to many would have appeared to be a grotesque impossibility, but which, after my experience of the night before, and my previous knowledge of such things, I was prepared to accept as an absolute fact. I thought deeply over the matter, and brought the whole range of my reading and experience to bear upon it. After breakfast, I surprised my host and hostess by announcing that I was returning to London by the next train.

"My dear doctor," cried Sir Dominick in great distress, "you make me feel that I have been guilty of a gross breach of hospitality in intruding this unfortunate matter upon you. I should have borne my own burden."

"It is, indeed, that matter which is taking me to London," I answered; "but you are mistaken, I assure you, if you think that my experience of last night was an unpleasant one to me. On the contrary, I am about to ask your permission to return in the evening and spend one more night in your laboratory. I am very eager to see this visitor once again."

My uncle was exceedingly anxious to know what I was about to do, but my fears of raising false hopes prevented me from telling him. I was back in my own consulting-room a little after luncheon, and was confirming my memory of a passage in a recent book upon occultism which had arrested my attention when I read it.

"In the case of earth-bound spirits," said my authority, "some one dominant idea obsessing them at the hour of death is sufficient to hold them in this material world. They are the amphibia of this life and of the next, capable of passing from one to the other as the turtle passes from land to water. The causes which may bind a soul so strongly to a life which its body has abandoned are any violent emotion. Avarice, revenge, anxiety, love and pity have all been known to have this effect. As a rule it springs from some unfulfilled wish, and when the wish has been fulfilled the material bond relaxes. There are many cases upon record which show the singular persistence of these visitors, and also their disappearance when their wishes have been fulfilled, or in some cases when a reasonable compromise has been effected."

"*A reasonable compromise effected*"—those were the words which I had brooded over all the morning, and which I now verified in the original. No actual atonement could be made here—but a reasonable compromise! I made my way as fast as a train could take me to the Shadwell Seamen's Hospital, where my old friend Jack Hewett was house-surgeon. Without explaining the situation I made him understand what it was that I wanted.

"A brown man's hand!" said he, in amazement. "What in the world do you want that for?"

"Never mind. I'll tell you some day. I know that your wards are full of Indians."

"I should think so. But a hand——" He thought a little and then struck a bell.

"Travers," said he to a student-dresser, "what became of the hands of the Lascar which we took off yesterday? I mean the fellow from the East India Dock who got caught in the steam winch."

"They are in the *post-mortem* room, sir."

"Just pack one of them in antiseptics and give it to Dr. Hardacre."

And so I found myself back at Rodenhurst before dinner with this curious outcome of my day in town. I still said nothing to Sir Dominick, but I slept that night in the laboratory, and I placed the Lascar's hand in one of the glass jars at the end of my couch.

So interested was I in the result of my experiment that sleep was out of the question. I sat with a shaded lamp beside me and waited patiently for my visitor. This time I saw him clearly from the first. He appeared beside the door, nebulous for an instant, and then hardening into as distinct an outline as any living man. The slippers beneath his grey gown were red and heelless, which accounted for the low, shuffling sound which he made as he walked. As on the previous night he passed slowly along the line of bottles until he paused before that which contained the hand. He reached up to it, his whole figure quivering with expectation, took it down, examined it eagerly, and then, with a face which was convulsed with fury and disappointment, he hurled it down on the floor. There was a crash which resounded through the house, and when I looked up the mutilated Indian had disappeared. A moment later my door flew open and Sir Dominick rushed in.

"You are not hurt?" he cried.

"No—but deeply disappointed."

He looked in astonishment at the splinters of glass, and the brown hand lying upon the floor.

"Good God!" he cried. "What is this?"

I told him my idea and its wretched sequel. He listened intently, but shook his head.

"It was well thought of," said he, "but I fear that there is no such easy end to my sufferings. But one thing I now insist upon. It is that you shall never again upon any pretext occupy this room. My fears that something might have happened to you—when I heard that crash—have been the most acute of all the agonies which I have undergone. I will not expose myself to a repetition of it."

He allowed me, however, to spend the remainder of that night where I was, and I lay there worrying over the problem and lamenting my own failure. With the first light of morning there was the Lascar's hand still lying upon the floor to remind me of my fiasco. I lay looking at it—and as I lay suddenly an idea flew like a bullet through my head and brought me quivering with excitement out of my couch. I raised the grim relic from where it had fallen. Yes, it was indeed so. The hand was the *left* hand of the Lascar.

By the first train I was on my way to town, and hurried at once to the Seamen's Hospital. I remembered that both hands of the Lascar had been amputated, but I was terrified lest the precious organ which I was in search of might have been already consumed in the crematory. My suspense was soon ended. It had still been preserved in the *post-mortem* room. And so I returned to Rodenhurst in the evening with my mission accomplished and the material for a fresh experiment.

But Sir Dominick Holden would not hear of my occupying the laboratory again. To all my entreaties he turned a deaf ear. It offended his sense of hospitality, and he could no longer permit it. I left the hand, therefore, as I had done its fellow the night before, and I occupied a comfortable bedroom in another portion of the house, some distance from the scene of my adventures.

But in spite of that my sleep was not destined to be uninterrupted. In the dead of night my host burst into my room, a lamp in his hand. His huge, gaunt figure was enveloped in a loose dressing-gown, and his whole appearance might certainly have seemed more formidable to a weak-nerved man than that of the Indian of the night before. But it was not his entrance so much as his expression which amazed me. He had turned suddenly younger by twenty years at the least. His eyes were shining, his features radiant, and he waved one hand in triumph over his head. I sat up astounded, staring sleepily at this extraordinary visitor. But his words soon drove the sleep from my eyes.

"We have done it! We have succeeded!" he shouted. "My dear Hardacre, how can I ever in this world repay you?"

"You don't mean to say that it is all right?"

"Indeed I do. I was sure that you would not mind being awakened to hear such blessed news."

"Mind! I should think not indeed. But is it really certain?"

"I have no doubt whatever upon the point. I owe you such a debt, my dear nephew, as I have never owed a man before, and never expected to. What can I possibly do for you that is commensurate? Providence must have sent you to my rescue. You have saved both my reason and my life, for another six months of this must have seen me either in a cell or a coffin. And my wife—it was wearing her out before my eyes. Never could I have believed that any human being could have lifted this burden off me." He seized my hand and wrung it in his bony grip.

"It was only an experiment—a forlorn hope—but I am delighted from my heart that it has succeeded. But how do you know that it is all right? Have you seen something?"

He seated himself at the foot of my bed.

"I have seen enough," said he. "It satisfies me that I shall be troubled no more. What has passed is easily told. You know that at a certain hour this creature always comes to me. To-night he arrived at the usual time, and aroused me with even more violence than is his custom. I can only surmise that his disappointment of last night increased the bitterness of his anger against me. He looked angrily at me, and then went on his usual round. But in a few minutes I saw him, for the first time since this persecution began, return to my chamber. He was smiling. I saw the gleam of his white teeth through the dim light. He stood facing me at the end of my bed, and three times he made the low, Eastern salaam which is their solemn leave-taking. And the third time that he bowed he raised his arms over his head, and I saw his *two* hands outstretched in the air. So he vanished, and, as I believe, for ever."

So that is the curious experience which won me the affection and the gratitude of my celebrated uncle, the famous Indian surgeon. His anticipations were realised, and never again was he disturbed by the visits of the restless hillman in search of his lost member. Sir Dominick and Lady Holden spent a very happy old age, unclouded, so far as I know, by any trouble, and they finally died during the great influenza epidemic within a few weeks of each other. In his lifetime he always turned to me for advice in everything which concerned that English life of which he knew so little; and I aided him also in the purchase and development of his estates. It was no great surprise to me, therefore, that I found myself eventually promoted over the heads of five exasperated cousins, and changed in a single day from a hard-working country doctor into the head of an important Wiltshire family. I, at least, have reason to bless the memory of the man with the brown hand, and the day when I was fortunate enough to relieve Rodenhurst of his unwelcome presence.

39. *The Usher of Lea House School*

MR. LUMSDEN, the senior partner of Lumsden and Westmacott, the well-known scholastic and clerical agents, was a small, dapper man, with a sharp, abrupt manner, a critical eye, and an incisive way of speaking.

"Your name, sir?" said he, sitting, pen in hand, with his long, red-lined folio in front of him.

"Harold Weld."

"Oxford or Cambridge?"

"Cambridge."

"Honours?"

"No, sir."

"Athlete?"

"Nothing remarkable, I am afraid."

"Not a Blue?"

"Oh no."

Mr. Lumsden shook his head despondently and shrugged his shoulders in a way which sent my hopes down to zero. "There is a very keen competition for masterships, Mr. Weld," said he. "The vacancies are few and the applicants innumerable. A first-class athlete, oar, or cricketer, or a man who has passed very high in his examinations, can usually find a vacancy—I might say always in the case of the cricketer. But the average man—if you will excuse the description, Mr. Weld—has a very great difficulty, almost an insurmountable difficulty. We have already more than a hundred such names upon our lists, and if you think it worth while our adding yours, I dare say that in the course of some years we may possibly be able to find you some opening which——"

He paused on account of a knock at the door. It was a clerk with a note. Mr. Lumsden broke the seal and read it.

"Why, Mr. Weld," said he, "this is really rather an interesting coincidence. I understand you to say that Latin and English are your subjects, and that you would prefer for a time to accept a place in an elementary establishment, where you would have time for private study?"

"Quite so."

"This note contains a request from an old client of ours, Dr. Phelps McCarthy, of Willow Lea House Academy, West Hampstead, that I should at once send him a young man who should be qualified to teach Latin and English to a small class of boys under fourteen years of age. His vacancy appears to be the very one which you are looking for. The terms are not munificent—sixty pounds, board, lodging, and washing—but the work is not onerous, and you would have the evenings to yourself."

"That would do," I cried, with all the eagerness of the man who sees work at last after weary months of seeking.

"I don't know that it is quite fair to these gentlemen whose names have been so long upon our list," said Mr. Lumsden, glancing down at his open ledger. "But the coincidence is so striking that I feel we must really give you the refusal of it."

"Then I accept it, sir, and I am much obliged to you."

"There is one small provision in Dr. McCarthy's better. He stipulates that the applicant must be a man with an imperturbably good temper."

"I am the very man," said I, with conviction.

"Well," said Mr. Lumsden, with some hesitation, "I hope that your temper is really as good as you say, for I rather fancy that you may need it."

"I presume that every elementary schoolmaster does."

"Yes, sir, but it is only fair to you to warn you that there may be some especially trying circumstances in this particular situation. Dr. Phelps McCarthy does not make such a condition without some very good and pressing reason."

There was a certain solemnity in his speech which struck a chill in the delight with which I had welcomed this providential vacancy.

"May I ask the nature of these circumstances?" I asked.

"We endeavour to hold the balance equally between our clients, and to be perfectly frank with all of them. If I knew of objections to you I should certainly communicate them to Dr. McCarthy, and so I have no hesitation in doing as much for you. I find," he continued, glancing over the pages of his ledger, "that within the last twelve months we have supplied no fewer than seven Latin masters to Willow Lea House Academy, four of them having left so abruptly as to forfeit their month's salary, and none of them having stayed more than eight weeks."

"And the other masters? Have they stayed?"

"There is only one other residential master, and he appears to be unchanged. You can understand, Mr. Weld," continued the agent, closing both the ledger and the interview, "that such rapid changes are not desirable from a master's point of view, whatever may be said for them by an agent working on commission. I have no idea why these gentlemen have resigned their situations so early. I can only give you the facts, and advise you to see Dr. McCarthy at once and to form your own conclusions."

Great is the power of the man who has nothing to lose, and it was therefore with perfect serenity, but with a good deal of curiosity, that I rang, early that afternoon, the heavy, wrought-iron bell of the Willow Lea House Academy. The building was a massive pile, square and ugly, standing in its own extensive grounds, with a broad carriage-sweep curving up to it from the road. It stood high, and commanded a view on the one side of the grey roofs and bristling spires of Northern London, and on the other of the well-wooded and beautiful country which fringes the great city. The door was opened by a boy in buttons, and I was shown into a well-appointed study, where the principal of the academy presently joined me.

The warnings and insinuations of the agent had prepared me to meet a choleric and overbearing person—one whose manner was an insupportable provocation to those who worked under him. Anything further from the reality cannot be imagined. He was a frail, gentle creature, clean-shaven and round-shouldered, with a bearing which was so courteous that it became almost deprecating. His bushy hair was thickly shot with grey, and his age I should imagine to verge upon sixty. His voice was low and suave, and he walked with a certain mincing delicacy of manner. His whole appearance was that of a kindly scholar, who was more at home among his books than in the practical affairs of the world.

"I am sure that we shall be very happy to have your assistance, Mr. Weld," said he, after a few professional questions. "Mr. Percival Manners left me yesterday, and I should be glad if you could take over his duties to-morrow."

"May I ask if that is Mr. Percival Manners of Selwyn?" I asked.

"Precisely. Did you know him?"

"Yes; he is a friend of mine."

" An excellent teacher, but a little hasty in his disposition. It was his only fault. Now, in your case, Mr. Weld, is your own temper under good control ? Supposing, for argument's sake, that I were to so far forget myself as to be rude to you, or to speak roughly, or to jar your feelings in any way, could you rely upon yourself to control your emotions ? "

I smiled at the idea of this courteous, little, mincing creature ruffling my nerves.

" I think that I could answer for it, sir," said I.

" Quarrels are very painful to me," said he. " I wish everyone to live in harmony under my roof. I will not deny Mr. Percival Manners had provocation, but I wish to find a man who can raise himself above provocation, and sacrifice his own feelings for the sake of peace and concord."

" I will do my best, sir."

" You cannot say more, Mr. Weld. In that case I shall expect you to-night, if you can get your things ready so soon."

I not only succeeded in getting my things ready, but I found time to call at the Benedict Club in Piccadilly, where I knew that I should find Manners if he were still in town. There he was, sure enough, in the smoking-room, and I questioned him, over a cigarette, as to his reasons for throwing up his recent situation.

" You don't tell me that you are going to Dr. Phelps McCarthy's Academy ? " he cried, staring at me in surprise. " My dear chap, it's no use. You can't possibly remain there."

" But I saw him, and he seemed the most courtly, inoffensive fellow. I never met a man with more gentle manners."

" He ! oh, he's all right. There's no vice in him. Have you seen Theophilus St. James ? "

" I have never heard the name. Who is he ? "

" Your colleague. The other master."

" No, I have not seen him."

"*He's* the terror. If you can stand him, you have either the spirit of a perfect Christian or else you have no spirit at all. A more perfect bounder never bounded."

"But why does McCarthy stand it?"

My friend looked at me significantly through his cigarette smoke, and shrugged his shoulders.

"You will form your own conclusions about that. Mine were formed very soon, and I never found occasion to alter them."

"It would help me very much if you would tell me them."

"When you see a man in his own house allowing his business to be ruined, his comfort destroyed, and his authority defied by another man in a subordinate position, and calmly submitting to it without so much as a word of protest, what conclusion do you come to?"

"That the one has a hold over the other."

Percival Manners nodded his head.

"There you are! You've hit it first barrel. It seems to me that there's no other explanation which will cover the facts. At some period in his life the little Doctor has gone astray. *Humanum est errare.* I have even done it myself. But this was something serious, and the other man got a hold of it and has never let go. That's the truth. Blackmail is at the bottom of it. But he had no hold over me, and there was no reason why *I* should stand his insolence, so I came away—and I very much expect to see you do the same."

For some time he talked over the matter, but he always came to the same conclusion—that I should not retain my new situation very long.

It was with no very pleasant feelings after this preparation that I found myself face to face with the very man of whom I had received so evil an account. Dr. McCarthy introduced us to each other in his study on the evening of that same day immediately after my arrival at the school.

"This is your new colleague, Mr. St. James," said

he, in his genial, courteous fashion. "I trust that you will mutually agree, and that I shall find nothing but good feeling and sympathy beneath this roof."

I shared the good Doctor's hope, but my expectations of it were not increased by the appearance of my *confrère*. He was a young, bull-necked fellow about thirty years of age, dark-eyed and black-haired, with an exceedingly vigorous physique. I have never seen a more strongly built man, though he tended to run to fat in a way which showed that he was in the worst of training. His face was coarse, swollen, and brutal, with a pair of small, black eyes deeply sunken in his head. His heavy jowl, his projecting ears, and his thick, bandy legs all went to make up a personality which was as formidable as it was repellent.

"I hear you've never been out before," said he, in a rude, brusque fashion. "Well, it's a poor life: hard work and starvation pay, as you'll find out for yourself."

"But it has some compensations," said the principal. "Surely you will allow that, Mr. St. James?"

"Has it? I never could find them. What do you call compensations?"

"Even to be in the continual presence of youth is a privilege. It has the effect of keeping youth in one's own soul, for one reflects something of their high spirits and their keen enjoyment of life."

"Little beasts!" cried my colleague.

"Come, come, Mr. St. James, you are too hard upon them."

"I hate the sight of them! If I could put them and their blessed copybooks and lexicons and slates into one bonfire I'd do it to-night."

"This is Mr. St. James's way of talking," said the principal, smiling nervously as he glanced at me. "You must not take him too seriously. Now, Mr. Weld, you know where your room is, and no doubt you have your own little arrangements to make. The sooner you make them the sooner you will feel yourself at home."

It seemed to me that he was only too anxious to remove me at once from the influence of this extraordinary colleague, and I was glad to go, for the conversation had become embarrassing.

And so began an epoch which always seems to me as I look back to it to be the most singular in all my experience. The school was in many ways an excellent one. Dr. Phelps McCarthy was an ideal principal. His methods were modern and rational. The management was all that could be desired. And yet in the middle of this well-ordered machine there intruded the incongruous and impossible Mr. St. James, throwing everything into confusion. His duties were to teach English and mathematics, and how he acquitted himself of them I do not know, as our classes were held in separate rooms. I can answer for it, however, that the boys feared him and loathed him, and I know that they had good reason to do so, for frequently my own teaching was interrupted by his bellowings of anger, and even by the sound of his blows. Dr. McCarthy spent most of his time in his class, but it was, I suspect, to watch over the master rather than the boys, and to try to moderate his ferocious temper when it threatened to become dangerous.

It was in his bearing to the head master, however, that my colleague's conduct was most outrageous. The first conversation which I have recorded proved to be typical of their intercourse. He domineered over him openly and brutally. I have heard him contradict him roughly before the whole school. At no time would he show him any mark of respect, and my temper often rose within me when I saw the quiet acquiescence of the old Doctor, and his patient tolerance of this monstrous treatment. And yet the sight of it surrounded the principal also with a certain vague horror in my mind, for, supposing my friend's theory to be correct—and I could devise no better one—how black must have been the story which could be held over his head by this man and, by fear of its publicity, force him to undergo such humiliations. This quiet, gentle Doctor might be a profound hypocrite, a criminal, a forger possibly, or a poisoner. Only such a secret as this could account for the complete power which the young man held over him. Why else should he admit so hateful a presence into his house and so harmful an influence into his school? Why should he submit to degradations which could not be witnessed, far less endured, without indignation?

And yet, if it were so, I was forced to confess that my principal carried it off with extraordinary duplicity. Never by word or sign did he show that the young man's presence was distasteful to him. I have seen him look pained, it is true, after some peculiarly outrageous exhibition, but he gave me the impression that it was always on account of the scholars or of me, never on account of himself. He spoke to and of St. James in an indulgent fashion, smiling gently at what made my blood boil within me. In his way of looking at him and addressing him, one could see no trace of resentment, but rather a sort of timid and deprecating good will. His company he certainly courted, and they spent many hours together in the study and the garden.

As to my own relations with Theophilus St. James, I made up my mind from the beginning that I should keep my temper with him, and to that resolution I steadfastly adhered. If Dr. McCarthy chose to permit this disrespect, and to condone these outrages, it was his affair and not mine. It was evident that his one wish was that there should be peace between us, and I felt that I could help him best by respecting this desire. My easiest way to do so was to avoid my colleague, and this I did to the best of my ability. When we were thrown together I was quiet, polite and reserved. He, on his part, showed me no ill will, but met me rather with a coarse joviality, and a rough familiarity which he meant to be ingratiating. He was insistent in his attempts to get me into his room at night, for the purpose of playing euchre and of drinking.

"Old McCarthy doesn't mind," said he. "Don't you be afraid of him. We'll do what we like, and I'll answer for it that he won't object." Once only I went, and when I left, after a dull and gross evening, my host was stretched dead drunk upon the sofa. After that I gave the excuse of a course of study, and spent my spare hours alone in my own room.

One point upon which I was anxious to gain information was as to how long these proceedings had been going on. When did St. James assert his hold over Dr. McCarthy? From neither of them could I learn how long my colleague had been in his present situation. One or two leading questions upon my part were eluded or ignored in a manner so marked that it was easy to see that they were both of them as eager to conceal the point as I was to know it. But at last, one evening, I had the chance of a chat with Mrs. Carter, the matron—for the Doctor was a widower—and from her I got the information which I wanted. It needed no questioning to get at her knowledge, for she was so full of indignation that she shook with passion as she spoke of it, and raised her hands into the air in the earnestness of her denunciation, as she described the grievances which she had against my colleague.

"It was three years ago, Mr. Weld, that he first darkened this doorstep," she cried. "Three bitter years they have been to me. The school had fifty boys then. Now it has twenty-two. That's what he has done for us in three years. In another three there won't be one. And the Doctor, that angel of patience, you see how he treats him, though he is not fit to lace his boots for him. If it wasn't for the Doctor, you may be sure that I wouldn't stay for an hour under the same roof with such a man, and so I told him to his own face, Mr. Weld. If the Doctor would only pack him about his business—but I know that I am saying more than I should!" She stopped herself with an effort, and spoke no more upon the subject. She had remembered that I was almost a stranger in the school, and she feared that she had been indiscreet.

There were one or two very singular points about my colleague. The chief one was that he rarely took any exercise. There was a playing-field within the college grounds, and that was his farthest point. If the boys went out, it was I or Dr. McCarthy who accompanied them. St. James gave as a reason for this that he had injured his knee some years before, and that walking was painful to him. For my own part I put it down to pure laziness upon his part, for he was of an obese, heavy temperament. Twice, however, I saw him from my window stealing out of the grounds late at night, and the second time I watched him return in the grey of the morning and slink in through an open window. These furtive excursions were never alluded to, but they exposed the hollowness of his story about his knee, and they increased the dislike and distrust which I had of the man. His nature seemed to be vicious to the core.

Another point, small but suggestive, was that he hardly ever during the months that I was at Willow Lea House received any letters, and on those few occasions they were obviously tradesmen's bills. I am an early riser, and used every morning to pick my own correspondence out of the bundle upon the hall table. I could judge, therefore, how few were ever there for Mr. Theophilus St. James. There seemed to me to be something peculiarly ominous in this. What sort of a man could he be who during thirty years of life had never made a single friend, high or low, who cared to continue to keep in touch with him? And yet the sinister fact remained that the head master not only tolerated, but was even intimate with him. More than once on entering a room I had found them talking confidentially together, and they would walk arm in arm in deep conversation up and down the garden paths. So curious did I become to know what the tie was which bound them, that I found it gradually push out my other interests and become the main purpose of my life. In school and out of school, at meals and at play, I was perpetually engaged in watching Dr. Phelps McCarthy and Mr. Theophilus St. James, and in endeavouring to solve the mystery which surrounded them.

But, unfortunately, my curiosity was a little too open. I had not the art to conceal the suspicions which I felt about the relations which existed between these two men and the nature of the hold which the one appeared to have over the other. It may have been my manner of watching them, it may have been some indiscreet question, but it is certain that I showed too clearly what I felt. One night I was conscious that the eyes of Theophilus St. James were fixed upon me in a surly and menacing stare. I had a foreboding of evil, and I was not surprised when Dr. McCarthy called me, next morning, into his study.

"I am very sorry, Mr. Weld," said he, "but I am afraid that I shall be compelled to dispense with your services."

"Perhaps you would give me some reason for dismissing me," I answered, for I was conscious of having done my duties to the best of my power, and knew well that only one reason could be given.

"I have no fault to find with you," said he, and the colour came to his cheeks.

"You send me away at the suggestion of my colleague."

His eyes turned away from mine.

"We will not discuss the question, Mr. Weld. It is impossible for me to discuss it. In justice to you, I will give you the strongest recommendation for your next situation. I can say no more. I hope that you will continue your duties here until you have found a place elsewhere."

My whole soul rose against the injustice of it, and yet I had no appeal and no redress. I could only bow and leave the room, with a bitter sense of ill-usage at my heart.

My first instinct was to pack my boxes and leave the house. But the head master had given me permission to remain until I had found another situation. I was sure that St. James desired me to go, and that was a strong reason why I should stay. If my presence annoyed him, I should give him as much of it as I could. I had begun to hate him and to long to have my revenge upon him. If he had a hold over our principal, might not I in turn obtain one over him ? It was a sign of weakness that he should be so afraid of my curiosity. He would not resent it so much if he had not something to fear from it. I entered my name once more upon the books of the agents, but meanwhile I continued to fulfil my duties at Willow Lea House, and so it came about that I was present at the *dénouement* of this singular situation.

During that week—for it was only a week before the crisis came—I was in the habit of going down each evening, after the work of the day was done, to inquire about my new arrangements. One night, it was a cold and windy evening in March, I had just stepped out from the hall door when a strange sight met my eyes. A man was crouching before one of the windows of the house. His knees were bent and his eyes were fixed upon the small line of light between the curtain and the sash. The window threw a square of brightness in front of it, and in the middle of this the dark shadow of this ominous visitor showed clear and hard. It was but for an instant that I saw him, for he glanced up and was off in a moment through the shrubbery. I could hear the patter of his feet as he ran down the road, until it died away in the distance.

It was evidently my duty to turn back and to tell Dr. McCarthy what I had seen. I found him in his study. I had expected him to be disturbed at such an incident, but I was not prepared for the state of panic into which he fell. He leaned back in his chair, white and gasping, like one who has received a mortal blow.

"Which window, Mr. Weld?" he asked, wiping his forehead. "Which window was it?"

"The next to the dining-room—Mr. St. James's window."

"Dear me! Dear me! This is, indeed, unfortunate! A man looking through Mr. St. James's window!" He wrung his hands like a man who is at his wits' end what to do.

"I shall be passing the police-station, sir. Would you wish me to mention the matter?"

"No, no," he cried, suddenly, mastering his extreme agitation; "I have no doubt that it was some poor tramp who intended to beg. I attach no importance to the incident—none at all. Don't let me detain you, Mr. Weld, if you wish to go out."

I left him sitting in his study with reassuring words upon his lips, but with horror upon his face. My heart was heavy for my little employer as I started off once more for town. As I looked back from the gate at the square of light which marked the window of my colleague, I suddenly saw the black outline of Dr. McCarthy's figure passing against the lamp. He had hastened from his study, then, to tell St. James what he had heard. What was the meaning of it all, this atmosphere of mystery, this inexplicable terror, these confidences between two such dissimilar men? I thought and thought as I walked, but do what I would I could not hit upon any adequate conclusion. I little knew how near I was to the solution of the problem.

It was very late—nearly twelve o'clock—when I returned, and the lights were all out save one in the Doctor's study. The black, gloomy house loomed before me as I walked up the drive, its sombre bulk broken only by the one glimmering point of brightness. I let myself in with my latch-key, and was about to enter my own room when my attention was arrested by a short, sharp cry like that of a man in pain. I stood and listened, my hand upon the handle of my door.

All was silent in the house save for a distant murmur of voices which came, I knew, from the Doctor's room. I stole quietly down the corridor in that direction. The sound resolved itself now into two voices, the rough, bullying tones of St. James and the lower tone of the Doctor, the one apparently insisting and the other arguing and pleading. Four thin lines of light in the blackness showed me the door of the Doctor's room, and step by step I drew nearer to it in the darkness. St. James's voice within rose louder and louder, and his words now came plainly to my ear.

"I'll have every pound of it. If you won't give it me I'll take it. Do you hear?"

Dr. McCarthy's reply was inaudible, but the angry voice broke in again.

"Leave you destitute! I leave you this little goldmine of a school, and that's enough for one old man, is it not? How am I to set up in Australia without money? Answer me that!"

Again the Doctor said something in a soothing voice, but his answer only roused his companion to a higher pitch of fury.

"Done for me! What have you ever done for me except what you couldn't help doing? It was for your good name, not for my safety, that you cared. But enough cackle! I must get on my way before morning. Will you open your safe or will you not?"

"Oh, James, how can you use me so?" cried a wailing voice, and then there came a sudden little scream of pain. At the sound of that helpless appeal from brutal violence I lost for once that temper upon which I had prided myself. Every bit of manhood in me cried out against any further neutrality. With my walking-cane in my hand I rushed into the study. As I did so I was conscious that the hall-door bell was violently ringing.

"You villain!" I cried, "let him go!"

The two men were standing in front of a small safe, which stood against one wall of the Doctor's room.

St. James held the old man by the wrist, and he had twisted his arm round in order to force him to produce the key. My little head master, white but resolute, was struggling furiously in the grip of the burly athlete. The bully glared over his shoulder at me with a mixture of fury and terror upon his brutal features. Then, realizing that I was alone, he dropped his victim and made for me with a horrible curse.

"You infernal spy!" he cried. "I'll do for you anyhow before I leave."

I am not a very strong man, and I realised that I was helpless if once at close quarters. Twice I cut at him with my stick, but he rushed in at me with a murderous growl, and seized me by the throat with both his muscular hands. I fell backwards and he on the top of me, with a grip which was squeezing the life from me. I was conscious of his malignant, yellow-tinged eyes within a few inches of my own, and then, with a beating of pulses in my head and a singing in my ears, my senses slipped away from me. But even in that supreme moment I was aware that the door-bell was still violently ringing.

When I came to myself, I was lying upon the sofa in Dr. McCarthy's study, and the Doctor himself was seated beside me. He appeared to be watching me intently and anxiously, for as I opened my eyes and looked about me he gave a great cry of relief. "Thank God!" he cried. "Thank God!"

"Where is he?" I asked, looking round the room. As I did so, I became aware that the furniture was scattered in every direction, and that there were traces of an even more violent struggle than that in which I had been engaged.

The Doctor sank his face between his hands.

"They have him," he groaned. "After these years of trial they have him again. But how thankful I am that he has not for a second time stained his hands in blood."

As the Doctor spoke I became aware that a man in the

braided jacket of an inspector of police was standing in the doorway.

"Yes, sir," he remarked, "you have had a pretty narrow escape. If we had not got in when we did, you would not be here to tell the tale. I don't know that I ever saw anyone much nearer to the undertaker."

I sat up with my hands to my throbbing head.

"Dr. McCarthy," said I, "this is all a mystery to me. I should be glad if you could explain to me who this man is, and why you have tolerated him so long in your house."

"I owe you an explanation, Mr. Weld—and the more so since you have, in so chivalrous a fashion, almost sacrificed your life in my defence. There is no reason now for secrecy. In a word, Mr. Weld, this unhappy man's real name is James McCarthy, and he is my only son."

"Your son?"

"Alas, yes. What sin have I ever committed that I should have such a punishment? He has made my whole life a misery from the first years of his boyhood. Violent, headstrong, selfish, unprincipled, he has always been the same. At eighteen he was a criminal. At twenty, in a paroxysm of passion, he took the life of a boon companion and was tried for murder. He only just escaped the gallows, and he was condemned to penal servitude. Three years ago he succeeded in escaping, and managed, in face of a thousand obstacles, to reach my house in London. My wife's heart had been broken by his condemnation, and as he had succeeded in getting a suit of ordinary clothes, there was no one here to recognize him. For months he lay concealed in the attics until the first search of the police should be over. Then I gave him employment here, as you have seen, though by his rough and overbearing manners he made my own life miserable, and that of his fellow-masters unbearable. You have been with us for four months, Mr. Weld, but no other master endured him so long. I apologise now for all you have had to submit to, but I ask you what else could I do? For his dead mother's sake I could not let harm come to him as long as it was in my power to fend it off. Only under my roof could he find a refuge —the only spot in all the world—and how could I keep him here without its exciting remark unless I gave him some occupation? I made him English master, therefore, and in that capacity I have protected him here for three years. You have no doubt observed that he never, during the daytime, went beyond the college grounds. You now understand the reason. But when to-night you came to me with your report of a man who was looking through his window, I understood that his retreat was at last discovered. I besought him to fly at once, but he had been drinking, the unhappy fellow, and my words fell upon deaf ears. When at last he made up his mind to go he wished to take from me, in his flight, every shilling which I possessed. It was your entrance which saved me from him, while the police in turn arrived only just in time to rescue you. I have made myself amenable to the law by harbouring an escaped prisoner, and remain here in the custody of the inspector, but a prison has no terrors for me after what I have endured in this house during the last three years."

"It seems to me, Doctor," said the inspector, "that, if you have broken the law, you have had quite enough punishment already."

"God knows I have!" cried Dr. McCarthy, and sank his haggard face upon his hands.

40. *B. 24*

I TOLD my story when I was taken, and no one would listen to me. Then I told it again at the trial—the whole thing absolutely as it happened, without so much as a word added. I set it all out truly, so help me God, all that Lady Mannering said and did, and then all that I had said and done, just as it occurred. And what did I get for it? "The prisoner put forward a rambling and inconsequential statement, incredible in its details, and unsupported by any shred of corroborative evidence." That was what one of the London papers said, and others let it pass as if I had made no defence at all. And yet, with my own eyes I saw Lord Mannering murdered, and I am as guiltless of it as any man on the jury that tried me.

Now, sir, you are there to receive the petitions of prisoners. It all lies with you. All I ask is that you read it—just read it—and then that you make an inquiry or two about the private character of this "lady" Mannering, if she still keeps the name that she had three years ago, when to my sorrow and ruin I came to meet her. You could use a private inquiry agent or a good lawyer, and you would soon learn enough to show you that my story is the true one. Think of the glory it would be to you to have all the papers saying that there would have been a shocking miscarriage of justice if it had not been for your perseverance and intelligence! That must be your reward, since I am a poor man and can offer you nothing. But if you don't do it, may you never lie easy in your bed again! May no night pass that you are not haunted by the thought of the man who rots in gaol because you have not done the duty which you are paid to do! But you will do it, sir, I know. Just make one or two inquiries, and you will soon find which way the wind blows. Remember, also, that the only person who profited by the crime was herself, since it changed her from an unhappy wife to a rich young widow. There's the end of the string in your hand, and you only have to follow it up and see where it leads to.

Mind you, sir, I make no complaint as far as the burglary goes. I don't whine about what I have deserved, and so far I have had no more than I have deserved. Burglary it was, right enough, and my three years have gone to pay for it. It was shown at the trial that I had had a hand in the Merton Cross business, and did a year for that, so my story had the less attention on that account. A man with a previous conviction never gets a really fair trial. I own to the burglary, but when it comes to the murder which brought me a lifer—any judge but Sir James might have given me the gallows—then I tell you that I had nothing to do with it, and that I am an innocent man. And now I'll take that night, the 13th of September, 1894, and I'll give you just exactly what occurred, and may God's hand strike me down if I go one inch over the truth.

I had been at Bristol in the summer looking for work, and then I had a notion that I might get something at Portsmouth, for I was trained as a skilled mechanic, so I came tramping my way across the south of England, and doing odd jobs as I went. I was trying all I knew to keep off the cross, for I had done a year in Exeter Gaol, and I had had enough of visiting Queen Victoria. But it's cruel hard to get work when once the black mark is against your name, and it was all I could do to keep soul and body together. At last, after ten days of wood-cutting and stone-breaking on starvation pay, I found myself near Salisbury with a couple of shillings in my pocket, and my boots and my patience clean wore out. There's an ale-house called "The Willing Mind," which stands on the road between Blandford and Salisbury, and it was there, that night, I engaged a bed. I was sitting alone in the tap-room just about closing time when the inn-keeper—Allen his name was—came beside me and began yarning about the neighbours. He was a man that liked to talk and to have someone to listen to his talk, so I sat there smoking and drinking a mug of ale which he had stood me; and I took no great interest in what he said until he began to talk (as the devil would have it) about the riches of Mannering Hall.

"Meaning the large house on the right before I came to the village?" said I. "The one that stands in its own park?"

"Exactly," said he—and I am giving all our talk so

that you may know that I am telling you the truth and hiding nothing. " The long, white house with the pillars," said he. " At the side of the Blandford Road."

Now I had looked at it as I passed, and it had crossed my mind, as such thoughts will, that it was a very easy house to get into with that great row of grand windows and glass doors. I had put the thought away from me, and now here was this landlord bringing it back with his talk about the riches within. I said nothing, but I listened, and as luck would have it, he would always come back to this one subject.

" He was a miser young, so you can think what he is now in his age," said he. " Well, he's had some good out of his money."

" What good can he have had if he does not spend it ? " said I.

" Well, it bought him the prettiest wife in England, and that was some good that he got out of it. She thought she would have the spending of it, but she knows the difference now."

" Who was she then ? " I asked, just for the sake of something to say.

" She was nobody at all until the old Lord made her his Lady," said he. " She came from up London way, and some said that she had been on the stage there, but nobody knew. The old Lord was away for a year, and when he came home he brought a young wife back with him, and there she has been ever since. Stephens, the butler, did tell me once that she was the light of the house when fust she came, but what with her husband's mean and aggravatin' way, and what with her loneliness—for he hates to see a visitor within his doors ; and what with his bitter words—for he has a tongue like a hornet's sting—her life all went out of her, and she became a white, silent creature, moping about the country lanes. Some say that she loved another man, and that it was just the riches of the old Lord which tempted her to be false to her lover, and that now she is eating her heart out because she has lost the one without being any nearer to the other, for she might be the poorest woman in the parish for all the money that she has the handling of."

Well, sir, you can imagine that it did not interest me very much to hear about the quarrels between a Lord and a Lady. What did it matter to me if she hated the sound of his voice, or if he put every indignity upon her in the hope of breaking her spirit, and spoke to her as he would never have dared to speak to one of his servants? The landlord told me of these things, and of many more like them, but they passed out of my mind, for they were no concern of mine. But what I did want to hear was the form in which Lord Mannering kept his riches. Title-deeds and stock certificates are but paper, and more danger than profit to the man who takes them. But metal and stones are worth a risk. And then, as if he were answering my very thoughts, the landlord told me of Lord Mannering's great collection of gold medals, that it was the most valuable in the world, and that it was reckoned that if they were put into a sack the strongest man in the parish would not be able to raise them. Then his wife called him, and he and I went to our beds.

I am not arguing to make out a case for myself, but I beg you, sir, to bear all the facts in your mind, and to ask yourself whether a man could be more sorely tempted than I was. I make bold to say that there are few who could have held out against it. There I lay on my bed that night, a desperate man without hope or work, and with my last shilling in my pocket. I had tried to be honest, and honest folk had turned their backs upon me. They taunted me for theft; and yet they pushed me towards it. I was caught in the stream and could not get out. And then it was such a chance: the great house all lined with windows, the golden medals which could so easily be melted down. It was like putting a loaf before a starving man and expecting him not to eat it. I fought against it for a time, but it was no use. At last I sat up on the side of my bed, and I swore that that night I should either be a rich man and able to give up crime for ever, or that the irons should be on my wrists once more. Then I slipped on my clothes, and, having put a shilling on the table—for the landlord had treated me well, and I did not wish to cheat him—I passed out through the window into the garden of the inn.

There was a high wall round this garden, and I had a job to get over it, but once on the other side it was all plain sailing. I did not meet a soul upon the road, and the iron gate of the avenue was open. No one was moving at the lodge. The moon was shining, and I could see the great house glimmering white through an archway of trees. I walked up it for a quarter of a mile or so, until I was at the edge of the drive, where it ended in a broad, gravelled space before the main door. There I stood in the shadow and looked at the long building, with a full moon shining in every window and silvering the high, stone front. I crouched there for some time, and I wondered where I should find the easiest entrance. The corner window of the side seemed to be the one which was least overlooked, and a screen of ivy hung heavily over it. My best chance was evidently there. I worked my way under the trees to the back of the house, and then crept along in the black shadow of the building. A dog barked and rattled his chain, but I stood waiting until he was quiet, and then I stole on once more until I came to the window which I had chosen.

It is astonishing how careless they are in the country, in places far removed from large towns, where the thought of burglars never enters their heads. I call it setting temptation in a poor man's way when he puts his hand, meaning no harm, upon a door, and finds it swing open before him. In this case it was not so bad as that, but the window was merely fastened with the ordinary catch, which I opened with a push from the blade of my knife. I pulled up the window as quickly as possible, then I thrust the knife through the slit in the shutter and prized it open. They were folding shutters, and I shoved them before me and walked into the room.

"Good evening, sir! You are very welcome!" said a voice.

I've had some starts in my life, but never one to come up to that one. There, in the opening of the shutters, within reach of my arm, was standing a woman with a small coil of wax taper burning in her hand. She was tall and straight and slender, with a beautiful, white face that might have been cut out of clear marble, but her hair and eyes were as black as night. She was dressed in some sort of white dressing-gown which flowed down to her feet, and what with this robe and what with her face, it seemed as if a spirit from above was standing in front of me. My knees knocked together, and I held on to the shutter with one hand to give me support. I should have turned and run away if I had had the strength, but I could only just stand and stare at her.

She soon brought me back to myself once more.

"Don't be frightened!" said she, and they were strange words for the mistress of a house to have to use to a burglar. "I saw you out of my bedroom window when you were hiding under those trees, so I slipped downstairs, and then I heard you at the window. I should have opened it for you if you had waited, but you managed it yourself just as I came up."

I still held in my hand the long clasp-knife with which I had opened the shutter. I was unshaven and grimed from a week on the roads. Altogether, there are few people who would have cared to face me alone at one in the morning; but this woman, if I had been her lover meeting her by appointment, could not have looked upon me with a more welcoming eye. She laid her hand upon my sleeve and drew me into the room.

"What's the meaning of this, ma'am? Don't get trying any little games upon me," said I, in my roughest way—and I can put it on rough when I like. "It'll be the worse for you if you play me any trick," I added, showing her my knife.

"I will play you no trick," said she. "On the contrary, I am your friend, and I wish to help you."

"Excuse me, ma'am, but I find it hard to believe that," said I. "Why should you wish to help me?"

"I have my own reasons," said she; and then suddenly with those black eyes blazing out of her white face: "It's because I hate him, hate him, hate him! Now you understand."

I remembered what the landlord had told me, and I did understand. I looked at her Ladyship's face, and I knew that I could trust her. She wanted to revenge herself upon her husband. She wanted to hit him where it would hurt him most—upon the pocket. She hated him so that she would even lower her pride to take such a man as me into her confidence if she could gain her end by doing so. I've hated some folk in my time, but I don't think I ever understood what hate was until I saw that woman's face in the light of the taper.

"You'll trust me now?" said she, with another coaxing touch upon my sleeve.

"Yes, your Ladyship."

"You know me, then?"

"I can guess who you are."

"I dare say my wrongs are the talk of the county. But what does he care for that? He only cares for one thing in the whole world, and that you can take from him this night. Have you a bag?"

"No, your Ladyship."

"Shut the shutter behind you. Then no one can see the light. You are quite safe. The servants all sleep in the other wing. I can show you where all the most valuable things are. You cannot carry them all, so we must pick the best."

The room in which I found myself was long and low, with many rugs and skins scattered about on a polished wood floor. Small cases stood here and there, and the walls were decorated with spears and swords and paddles, and other things which find their way into museums. There were some queer clothes, too, which had been brought from savage countries, and the lady took down a large leather sack-bag from among them.

"This sleeping-sack will do," said she. "Now come with me and I will show you where the medals are."

It was like a dream to me to think that this tall, white woman was the lady of the house, and that she was lending me a hand to rob her own home. I could have burst out laughing at the thought of it, and yet there was something in that pale face of hers which stopped my laughter and turned me cold and serious. She swept on in front of me like a spirit, with the green taper in her hand, and I walked behind with my sack until we came to a door at the end of this museum. It was locked, but the key was in it, and she led me through.

The room beyond was a small one, hung all round with curtains which had pictures on them. It was the hunting of a deer that was painted on it, as I remember, and in the flicker of that light you'd have sworn that the dogs and the horses were streaming round the walls. The only other thing in the room was a row of cases made of walnut, with brass ornaments. They had glass tops, and beneath this glass I saw the long lines of those gold medals, some of them as big as a plate and half an inch thick, all resting upon red velvet and glowing and gleaming in the darkness. My fingers were just itching to be at them, and I slipped my knife under the lock of one of the cases to wrench it open.

"Wait a moment," said she, laying her hand upon my arm. "You might do better than this."

"I am very well satisfied, ma'am," said I, "and much obliged to your Ladyship for kind assistance."

"You can do better," she repeated. "Would not golden sovereigns be worth more to you than these things?"

"Why, yes," said I. "That's best of all."

"Well," said she. "He sleeps just above our head. It is but one short staircase. There is a tin box with money enough to fill this bag under his bed."

"How can I get it without waking him?"

"What matter if he does wake?" She looked very hard at me as she spoke. "You could keep him from calling out."

"No, no, ma'am, I'll have none of that."

"Just as you like," said she. "I thought that you were a stout-hearted sort of man by your appearance, but I see that I made a mistake. If you are afraid to run the risk of one old man, then of course you cannot have the gold which is under his bed. You are the best judge of your own business, but I should think that you would do better at some other trade."

"I'll not have murder on my conscience."

"You could overpower him without harming him. I never said anything about murder. The money lies under the bed. But if you are faint-hearted, it is better that you should not attempt it."

She worked upon me so, partly with her scorn and partly with this money that she held before my eyes, that I believe I should have yielded and taken my chances upstairs, had it not been that I saw her eyes following the struggle within me in such a crafty, malignant fashion, that it was evident she was bent upon making me the tool of her revenge, and that she would leave me no choice but to do the old man an injury or to be captured by him. She felt suddenly that she was giving herself away, and she changed her face to a kindly, friendly smile, but it was too late, for I had had my warning.

"I will not go upstairs," said I. "I have all I want here."

She looked her contempt at me, and there never was a face which could look it plainer.

"Very good. You can take these medals. I should be glad if you would begin at this end. I suppose they will all be the same value when melted down, but these are the ones which are the rarest, and, therefore, the most precious to him. It is not necessary to break the locks. If you press that brass knob you will find that there is a secret spring. So! Take that small one first—it is the very apple of his eye."

She had opened one of the cases, and the beautiful things all lay exposed before me. I had my hand upon the one which she had pointed out, when suddenly a change came over her face, and she held up one finger as a warning. "Hist!" she whispered. "What is that?"

Far away in the silence of the house we heard a low, dragging, shuffling sound, and the distant tread of feet. She closed and fastened the case in an instant.

"It's my husband!" she whispered. "All right. Don't be alarmed. I'll arrange it. Here! Quick, behind the tapestry!"

She pushed me behind the painted curtains upon the wall, my empty leather bag still in my hand. Then she took her taper and walked quickly into the room from which we had come. From where I stood I could see her through the open door.

"Is that you, Robert?" she cried.

The light of a candle shone through the door of the museum, and the shuffling steps came nearer and nearer. Then I saw a face in the doorway, a great, heavy face, all lines and creases, with a huge, curving nose, and a pair of gold glasses fixed across it. He had to throw his head back to see through the glasses, and that great nose thrust out in front of him like the beak of some sort of fowl. He was a big man, very tall and burly, so that in his loose dressing-gown his figure seemed to fill up the whole doorway. He had a pile of grey, curling hair all round his head, but his face was clean-shaven. His mouth was thin and small and prim, hidden away under his long, masterful nose. He stood there, holding the candle in front of him, and looking at his wife with a queer, malicious gleam in his eyes. It only needed that one look to tell me that he was as fond of her as she was of him.

"How's this?" he asked. "Some new tantrum? What do you mean by wandering about the house? Why don't you go to bed?"

"I could not sleep," she answered. She spoke languidly and wearily. If she was an actress once, she had not forgotten her calling.

"Might I suggest," said he, in the same mocking kind of voice, "that a good conscience is an excellent aid to sleep?"

"That cannot be true," she answered, "for you sleep very well."

"I have only one thing in my life to be ashamed of," said he, and his hair bristled up with anger until he looked like an old cockatoo. "You know best what that is. It is a mistake which has brought its own punishment with it."

"To me as well as to you. Remember that!"

"You have very little to whine about. It was I who stooped and you who rose."

"Rose!"

"Yes, rose. I suppose you do not deny that it is a promotion to exchange the music-hall for Mannering Hall. Fool that I was ever to take you out of your true sphere!"

"If you think so, why do you not separate?"

"Because private misery is better than public humiliation. Because it is easier to suffer for a mistake than to own to it. Because also I like to keep you in my sight, and to know that you cannot go back to him."

"You villain! You cowardly villain!"

"Yes, yes, my lady. I know your secret ambition, but it shall never be while I live, and if it happens after my death I will at least take care that you go to him as a beggar. You and dear Edward will never have the satisfaction of squandering my savings, and you may make up your mind to that, my lady. Why are those shutters and the window open?"

"I found the night very close."

"It is not safe. How do you know that some tramp may not be outside? Are you aware that my collection of medals is worth more than any similar collection in the world? You have left the door open also. What is there to prevent anyone from rifling the cases?"

"I was here."

"I know you were. I heard you moving about in the medal room, and that was why I came down. What were you doing?"

"Looking at the medals. What else should I be doing?"

"This curiosity is something new." He looked suspiciously at her and moved on towards the inner room, she walking beside him.

It was at this moment that I saw something which startled. I had laid my clasp-knife open upon the top of one of the cases, and there it lay in full view. She saw it before he did, and with a woman's cunning she held her taper out so that the light of it came between Lord Mannering's eyes and the knife. Then she took it with her left hand and held it against her gown out of his sight. He looked about from case to case—I could have put my hand at one time upon his long nose—but there was nothing to show that the medals had been tampered with, and so, still snarling and grumbling, he shuffled off into the other room once more.

And now I have to speak of what I heard rather than of what I saw, but I swear to you, as I shall stand some day before my Maker, that what I say is the truth.

When they passed into the outer room I saw him lay his candle upon the corner of one of the tables, and he sat himself down, but in such a position that he was just out of my sight. She moved behind him, as I could tell from the fact that the light of her taper threw his long, lumpy shadow upon the floor in front of him. Then he began talking about this man whom he called Edward, and every word that he said was like a blistering drop of vitriol. He spoke low, so that I could not hear it all, but from what I heard I should guess that she would as soon have been lashed with a whip. At first she said some hot words in reply, but then she was silent, and he went on and on in that cold, mocking voice of his, nagging and insulting and tormenting, until I wondered that she could bear to stand there in silence and listen to it. Then suddenly I heard him say in a sharp voice, "Come from behind me! Leave go of my collar! What! would you dare to strike me?" There was a sound like a blow, just a soft sort of thud, and then I heard him cry out, "My God, it's blood!" He shuffled with his feet as if he was getting up, and then I heard another blow, and he cried out, "Oh, you she-devil!" and was quiet, except for a dripping and splashing upon the floor.

I ran out from behind my curtain at that, and rushed into the other room, shaking all over with the horror of it. The old man had slipped down in the chair, and his dressing-gown had rucked up until he looked as if he had a monstrous hump to his back. His head, with the gold glasses still fixed on his nose, was lolling over upon one side, and his little mouth was open just like a dead fish. I could not see where the blood was coming from, but I could still hear it drumming upon the floor. She stood behind him with the candle shining full upon her face. Her lips were pressed together and her eyes shining, and a touch of colour had come into each of her cheeks. It just wanted that to make her the most beautiful woman I had ever seen in my life.

"You've done it now!" said I.

"Yes," said she, in her quiet way, "I've done it now."

"What are you going to do?" I asked. "They'll have you for murder as sure as fate."

"Never fear about me. I have nothing to live for, and it does not matter. Give me a hand to set him straight in the chair. It is horrible to see him like this!"

I did so, though it turned me cold all over to touch him. Some of his blood came on my hand and sickened me.

"Now," said she, "you may as well have the medals as anyone else. Take them and go."

"I don't want them. I only want to get away. I was never mixed up with a business like this before."

"Nonsense!" said she. "You came for the medals, and here they are at your mercy. Why should you not have them? There is no one to prevent you."

I held the bag still in my hand. She opened the case, and between us we threw a hundred or so of the medals into it. They were all from the one case, but I could not bring myself to wait for any more. Then I made for the window, for the very air of this house seemed to poison me after what I had seen and heard. As I looked back, I saw her standing there, tall and graceful, with the light in her hand, just as I had seen her first. She waved good-bye, and I waved back at her and sprang out into the gravel drive.

I thank God that I can lay my hand upon my heart and say that I have never done a murder, but perhaps it would be different if I had been able to read that woman's mind and thoughts. There might have been two bodies in the room instead of one if I could have seen behind that last smile of hers. But I thought of nothing but of getting safely away, and it never entered my head how she might be fixing the rope round my neck. I had not taken five steps out from the window skirting down the shadow of the house in the way that I had come, when I heard a scream that might have raised the parish, and then another and another.

"Murder!" she cried. "Murder! Murder! Help!" and her voice rang out in the quiet of the night-time and sounded over the whole country-side. It went through my head, that dreadful cry. In an instant lights began to move and windows to fly up, not only in the house behind me, but at the lodge and in the stables in front. Like a frightened rabbit I bolted down the drive, but I heard the clang of the gate being shut before I could reach it. Then I hid my bag of medals under some dry fagots, and I tried to get away across the park, but someone saw me in the moonlight, and presently I had half a dozen of them with dogs upon my heels. I crouched down among the brambles, but those dogs were too many for me, and I was glad enough when the men came up and prevented me from being torn into pieces. They seized me, and dragged me back to the room from which I had come.

"Is this the man, your Ladyship?" asked the oldest of them—the same whom I found out afterwards to be the butler.

She had been bending over the body, with her handkerchief to her eyes, and now she turned upon me with the face of a fury. Oh, what an actress that woman was!

"Yes, yes, it is the very man," she cried. "Oh, you villain, you cruel villain, to treat an old man so!"

There was a man there who seemed to be a village constable. He laid his hand upon my shoulder.

"What do you say to that?" said he.

"It was she who did it," I cried, pointing at the woman, whose eyes never flinched before mine.

"Come! come! Try another!" said the constable, and one of the men-servants struck at me with his fist.

"I tell you that I saw her do it. She stabbed him twice with a knife. She first helped me to rob him, and then she murdered him."

The footman tried to strike me again, but she held up her hand.

"Do not hurt him," said she. "I think that his punishment may safely be left to the law."

"I'll see to that, your Ladyship," said the constable. "Your Ladyship actually saw the crime committed, did you not?"

"Yes, yes, I saw it with my own eyes. It was horrible. We heard the noise and we came down. My poor husband was in front. The man had one of the cases open, and was filling a black leather bag which he held in his hand. He rushed past us, and my husband seized him. There was a struggle, and he stabbed him twice. There you can see the blood upon his hands. If I am not mistaken, his knife is still in Lord Mannering's body."

"Look at the blood upon her hands!" I cried.

"She has been holding up his Lordship's head, you lying rascal," said the butler.

"And here's the very sack her Ladyship spoke of," said the constable, as a groom came in with the one which I had dropped in my flight. "And here are the medals inside it. That's good enough for me. We will keep him safe here to-night, and to-morrow the inspector and I can take him into Salisbury."

"Poor creature," said the woman. "For my own part, I forgive him any injury which he has done me. Who knows what temptation may have driven him to crime? His conscience and the law will give him punishment enough without any reproach of mine rendering it more bitter."

I could not answer—I tell you, sir, I could not answer, so taken aback was I by the assurance of the woman. And so, seeming by my silence to agree to all that she had said, I was dragged away by the butler and the constable into the cellar, in which they locked me for the night.

There, sir, I have told you the whole story of the events which led up to the murder of Lord Mannering by his wife upon the night of September the 14th, in the year 1894. Perhaps you will put my statement on one side as the constable did at Mannering Towers, or the judge afterwards at the county assizes. Or perhaps you will see that there is the ring of truth in what I say, and you will follow it up, and so make your name for ever as a man who does not grudge personal trouble where justice is to be done. I have only you to look to, sir, and if you will clear my name of this false accusation, then I will worship you as one man never yet worshipped another. But if you fail me, then I give you my solemn promise that I will rope myself up, this day month, to the bar of my window, and from that time on I will come to plague you in your dreams if ever yet one man was able to come back and to haunt another. What I ask you to do is very simple. Make inquiries about this woman, watch her, learn her past history, find out what use she is making of the money which has come to her, and whether there is not a man Edward as I have stated. If from all this you learn anything which shows you her real character, or which seems to you to corroborate the story which I have told you, then I am sure that I can rely upon your goodness of heart to come to the rescue of an innocent man.

41. *The Great Keinplatz Experiment*

OF all the sciences which have puzzled the sons of men, none had such an attraction for the learned Professor von Baumgarten as those which relate to psychology and the ill-defined relations between mind and matter. A celebrated anatomist, a profound chemist, and one of the first physiologists in Europe, it was a relief for him to turn from these subjects and to bring his varied knowledge to bear upon the study of the soul and the mysterious relationship of spirits. At first, when as a young man he began to dip into the secrets of mesmerism, his mind seemed to be wandering in a strange land where all was chaos and darkness, save that here and there some great unexplainable and disconnected fact loomed out in front of him. As the years passed, however, and as the worthy Professor's stock of knowledge increased, for knowledge begets knowledge as money bears interest, much which had seemed strange and unaccountable began to take another shape in his eyes. New trains of reasoning became familiar to him, and he perceived connecting links where all had been incomprehensible and startling. By experiments which extended over twenty years, he obtained a basis of facts upon which it was his ambition to build up a new, exact science which should embrace mesmerism, spiritualism, and all cognate subjects. In this he was much helped by his intimate knowledge of the more intricate parts of animal physiology which treat of nerve currents and the working of the brain; for Alexis von Baumgarten was Regius Professor of Physiology at the University of Keinplatz, and had all the resources of the laboratory to aid him in his profound researches.

Professor von Baumgarten was tall and thin, with a hatchet face and steel-grey eyes, which were singularly bright and penetrating. Much thought had furrowed his forehead and contracted his heavy eyebrows, so that he appeared to wear a perpetual frown, which often misled people as to his character, for though austere he was tender-hearted. He was popular among the students, who would gather round him after his lectures and listen eagerly to his strange theories. Often he would call for volunteers from amongst them in order to conduct some experiment, so that eventually there was hardly a lad in the class who had not, at one time or another, been thrown into a mesmeric trance by his Professor.

Of all these young devotees of science there was none who equalled in enthusiasm Fritz von Hartmann. It had often seemed strange to his fellow-students that wild, reckless Fritz, as dashing a young fellow as ever hailed from the Rhinelands, should devote the time and trouble which he did in reading up abstruse works and in assisting the Professor in his strange experiments. The fact was, however, that Fritz was a knowing and long-headed fellow. Months before he had lost his heart to young Elise, the blue-eyed, yellow-haired daughter of the lecturer. Although he had succeeded in learning from her lips that she was not indifferent to his suit, he had never dared to announce himself to her family as a formal suitor. Hence he would have found it a difficult matter to see his young lady had he not adopted the expedient of making himself useful to the Professor. By this means he frequently was asked to the old man's house, where he willingly submitted to be experimented upon in any way as long as there was a chance of his receiving one bright glance from the eyes of Elise or one touch of her little hand.

Young Fritz von Hartmann was a handsome lad enough. There were broad acres, too, which would descend to him when his father died. To many he would have seemed an eligible suitor ; but Madame frowned upon his presence in the house, and lectured the Professor at times on his allowing such a wolf to prowl around their lamb. To tell the truth, Fritz had an evil name in Keinplatz. Never was there a riot or a duel, or any other mischief afoot, but the young Rhinelander figured as a ringleader in it. No one used more free and violent language, no one drank more, no one played cards more habitually, no one was more idle, save in the one solitary subject. No wonder, then, that the good Frau Professorin gathered her Fräulein under her wing, and resented the attentions of such a *mauvais sujet*. As to the worthy lecturer, he was too much engrossed by his strange studies to form an opinion upon the subject one way or the other.

For many years there was one question which had continually obtruded itself upon his thoughts. All his experiments and his theories turned upon a single point. A hundred times a day the Professor asked himself whether it was possible for the human spirit to exist apart from the body for a time and then to return to it once again. When the possibility first suggested itself to him his scientific mind had revolted from it. It clashed too violently with preconceived ideas and the prejudices of his early training. Gradually, however, as he proceeded farther and farther along the pathway of original research, his mind shook off its old fetters and became ready to face any conclusion which could reconcile the facts. There were many things which made him believe that it was possible for mind to exist apart from matter. At last it occurred to him that by a daring and original experiment the question might be definitely decided.

"It is evident," he remarked in his celebrated article upon invisible entities, which appeared in the *Keinplatz wochenliche Medicalschrift* about this time, and which surprised the whole scientific world—"it is evident that under certain conditions the soul or mind does separate itself from the body. In the case of a mesmerised person, the body lies in a cataleptic condition, but the spirit has left it. Perhaps you reply that the soul is there, but in a dormant condition. I answer that this is not so, otherwise how can one account for the condition of clairvoyance, which has fallen into disrepute through the knavery of certain scoundrels, but which can easily be shown to be an undoubted fact. I have been able myself, with a sensitive subject, to obtain an accurate description of what was going on in another room or another house. How can such knowledge be accounted for on any hypothesis save that the soul of the subject has left the body and is wandering through space? For a moment it is recalled by the voice of the operator and says what it has seen, and then wings its way once more through the air. Since the spirit is by its very nature invisible, we cannot see these comings and goings, but we see their effect in the body of the subject, now rigid and inert, now struggling to narrate impressions which could never have come to it by natural means. There is only one way which I can see by which the fact can be demonstrated. Although we in the flesh are unable to see these spirits, yet our own spirits, could we separate them from the body, would be conscious of the presence of others. It is my intention, therefore, shortly to mesmerise one of my pupils. I shall then mesmerise myself in a manner which has become easy to me. After that, if my theory holds good, my spirit will have no difficulty in meeting and communing with the spirit of my pupil, both being separated from the body. I hope to be able to communicate the result of this interesting experiment in an early number of the *Keinplatz wochenliche Medical-schrift.*"

When the good Professor finally fulfilled his promise, and published an account of what occurred, the narrative was so extraordinary that it was received with general incredulity. The tone of some of the papers was so offensive in their comments upon the matter that the angry savant declared that he would never open his mouth again or refer to the subject in any way—a promise which he has faithfully kept. This narrative has been compiled, however, from the most authentic sources, and the events cited in it may be relied upon as substantially correct.

It happened, then, that shortly after the time when Professor von Baumgarten conceived the idea of the above-mentioned experiment, he was walking thoughtfully homewards after a long day in the laboratory, when he met a crowd of roistering students who had just streamed out from a beer-house. At the head of them, half-intoxicated and very noisy, was young Fritz von Hartmann. The Professor would have passed them, but his pupil ran across and intercepted him.

"Heh! my worthy master," he said, taking the old man by the sleeve, and leading him down the road with him. "There is something that I have to say to you, and it is easier for me to say it now, when the good beer is humming in my head, than at another time."

"What is it, then, Fritz?" the physiologist asked, looking at him in mild surprise.

"I hear, mein herr, that you are about to do some wondrous experiment in which you hope to take a man's soul out of his body, and then to put it back again. Is it not so?"

"It is true, Fritz."

"And have you considered, my dear sir, that you may have some difficulty in finding someone on whom to try this? Potztausend! Suppose that the soul went out and would not come back. That would be a bad business. Who is to take the risk?"

"But Fritz," the Professor cried, very much startled by this view of the matter, "I had relied upon your assistance in the attempt. Surely you will not desert me. Consider the honour and glory."

"Consider the fiddlesticks!" the student cried angrily. "Am I to be paid always thus? Did I not stand two hours upon a glass insulator while you poured electricity into my body? Have you not stimulated my phrenic nerves, besides ruining my digestion with a galvanic current round my stomach? Four-and-thirty times you have mesmerised me, and what have I got from all this? Nothing. And now you wish to take my soul out, as you would take the works from a watch. It is more than flesh and blood can stand."

"Dear, dear!" the Professor cried in great distress. "That is very true, Fritz. I never thought of it before. If you can but suggest how I can compensate you, you will find me ready and willing."

"Then listen," said Fritz solemnly. "If you will pledge your word that after this experiment I may have the hand of your daughter, then I am willing to assist you; but if not, I shall have nothing to do with it. These are my only terms."

"And what would my daughter say to this?" the Professor exclaimed, after a pause of astonishment.

"Elise would welcome it," the young man replied. "We have loved each other long."

"Then she shall be yours," the physiologist said with decision, "for you are a good-hearted young man, and one of the best neurotic subjects that I have ever known—that is when you are not under the influence of alcohol. My experiment is to be performed upon the fourth of next month. You will attend at the physiological laboratory at twelve o'clock. It will be a great occasion, Fritz. Von Gruben is coming from Jena, and Hinterstein from Basle. The chief men of science of all South Germany will be there."

"I shall be punctual," the student said briefly; and so the two parted. The Professor plodded homeward, thinking of the great coming event, while the young man staggered along after his noisy companions, with his mind full of the blue-eyed Elise, and of the bargain which he had concluded with her father.

The Professor did not exaggerate when he spoke of the widespread interest excited by his novel psychological experiment. Long before the hour had arrived the room was filled by a galaxy of talent. Besides the celebrities whom he had mentioned, there had come from London the great Professor Lurcher, who had just established his reputation by a remarkable treatise upon cerebral centres. Several great lights of the Spiritualistic body had also come a long distance to be present, as had a Swedenborgian minister, who considered that the proceedings might throw some light upon the doctrines of the Rosy Cross.

There was considerable applause from this eminent assembly upon the appearance of Professor von Baumgarten and his subject upon the platform. The lecturer, in a few well-chosen words, explained what his views were, and how he proposed to test them. "I hold," he said, "that when a person is under the influence of mesmerism, his spirit is for the time released from his body, and I challenge anyone to put forward any other hypothesis which will account for the fact of clairvoyance. I therefore hope that upon mesmerising my young friend here, and then putting myself into a trance, our spirits may be able to commune together, though our bodies lie still and inert. After a time nature will resume her sway, our spirits will return into our respective bodies, and all will be as before. With your kind permission, we shall now proceed to attempt the experiment."

The applause was renewed at this speech, and the audience settled down in expectant silence. With a few rapid passes the Professor mesmerised the young man, who sank back in his chair, pale and rigid. He then took a bright globe of glass from his pocket, and by concentrating his gaze upon it and making a strong mental effort, he succeeded in throwing himself into the same condition. It was a strange and impressive sight to see the old man and the young sitting together in the same cataleptic condition. Whither, then, had their souls fled? That was the question which presented itself to each and every one of the spectators.

Five minutes passed, and then ten, and then fifteen, and then fifteen more, while the Professor and his pupil sat stiff and stark upon the platform. During that time not a sound was heard from the assembled savants, but every eye was bent upon the two pale faces, in search of the first signs of returning consciousness. Nearly an hour had elapsed before the patient watchers were rewarded. A faint flush came back to the cheeks of Professor von Baumgarten. The soul was coming back once more to its earthly tenement. Suddenly he stretched out his long, thin arms, as one awaking from sleep, and rubbing his eyes, stood up from his chair and gazed about him as though he hardly realised where he was. "Tausend Teufel!" he exclaimed, rapping out a tremendous South German oath, to the great astonishment of his audience and to the disgust of the Swedenborgian. "Where the Henker am I then, and what in thunder has occurred? Oh yes, I remember now. One of these nonsensical mesmeric experiments. There is no result this time, for I remember nothing at all since I became unconscious; so you have had all your long journeys for nothing, my learned friends, and a very good joke, too"; at which the Regius Professor of Physiology burst into a roar of laughter and slapped his thigh in a highly indecorous fashion. The audience were so enraged at this unseemly behaviour on the part of their host, that there might have been a considerable disturbance, had it not been for the judicious interference of young Fritz von Hartmann, who had now recovered from his lethargy. Stepping to the front of the platform, the young man apologised for the conduct of his companion.

"I am sorry to say," he said, "that he is a harum-scarum sort of fellow, although he appeared so grave at the commencement of this experiment. He is still suffering from mesmeric reaction, and is hardly accountable for his words. As to the experiment itself, I do not consider it to be a failure. It is very possible that our spirits may have been communing in space during this hour; but, unfortunately, our gross bodily memory is distinct from our spirit, and we cannot recall what has occurred. My energies shall now be devoted to devising some means by which spirits may be able to recollect what occurs to them in their free state, and I trust that when I have worked this out, I may have the pleasure of meeting you all once again in this hall, and demonstrating to you the result." This address, coming from so young a student, caused considerable astonishment among the audience, and some were inclined to be offended, thinking that he assumed rather too much importance. The majority, however, looked upon him as a young man of great promise, and many comparisons were made as they left the hall between his dignified conduct and the levity of his professor, who during the above remarks was laughing heartily in a corner, by no means abashed at the failure of the experiment.

Now although all these learned men were filing out of the lecture-room under the impression that they had seen nothing of note, as a matter of fact one of the most wonderful things in the whole history of the world had just occurred before their very eyes. Professor von Baumgarten had been so far correct in his theory that both his spirit and that of his pupil had been, for a time, absent from the body. But here a strange and unforeseen complication had occurred. In their return the spirit of Fritz von Hartmann had entered into the body of Alexis von Baumgarten, and that of Alexis von Baumgarten had taken up its abode in the frame of Fritz von Hartmann. Hence the slang and scurrility which issued from the lips of the serious Professor, and hence also the weighty words and grave statements which fell from the careless student. It was an unprecedented event, yet no one knew of it, least of all those whom it concerned.

The body of the Professor, feeling conscious suddenly of a great dryness about the back of the throat, sallied out into the street, still chuckling to himself over the result of the experiment, for the soul of Fritz within was reckless at the thought of the bride whom he had won so easily. His first impulse was to go up to the house and see her, but on second thoughts he came to the conclusion that it would be best to stay away until Madame Baumgarten should be informed by her husband of the agreement which had been made. He therefore made his way down to the Grüner Mann, which was one of the favourite trysting-places of the wilder students, and ran, boisterously waving his cane in the air, into the little parlour, where sat Spiegel and Müller and half a dozen other boon companions.

"Ha, ha! my boys," he shouted. "I knew I should find you here. Drink up, every one of you, and call for what you like, for I'm going to stand treat to-day."

Had the green man who is depicted upon the signpost of that well-known inn suddenly marched into the room and called for a bottle of wine, the students could not have been more amazed than they were by this unexpected entry of their revered professor. They were so astonished that for a minute or two they glared at him in utter bewilderment without being able to make any reply to his hearty invitation.

"Donner und Blitzen!" shouted the Professor angrily. "What the deuce is the matter with you, then? You sit there like a set of stuck pigs staring at me. What is it then?"

"It is the unexpected honour," stammered Spiegel, who was in the chair.

"Honour—rubbish!" said the Professor testily. "Do you think that just because I happen to have been exhibiting mesmerism to a parcel of old fossils, I am therefore too proud to associate with dear old friends like you? Come out of that chair, Spiegel, my boy, for I shall preside now. Beer, or wine, or schnapps, my lads—call for what you like, and put it all down to me."

Never was there such an afternoon in the Grüner Mann. The foaming flagons of lager and the green-necked bottles of Rhenish circulated merrily. By degrees the students lost their shyness in the presence of their Professor. As for him, he shouted, he sang, he roared, he balanced a long tobacco-pipe upon his nose, and offered to run a hundred yards against any member of the company. The Kellner and the barmaid whispered to each other outside the door their astonishment at such proceedings on the part of a Regius Professor of the ancient university of Keinplatz. They had still more to whisper about afterwards, for the learned man cracked the Kellner's crown, and kissed the barmaid behind the kitchen door.

"Gentlemen," said the Professor, standing up, albeit somewhat totteringly, at the end of the table, and balancing his high, old-fashioned wine glass in his bony hand, "I must now explain to you what is the cause of this festivity."

"Hear! hear!" roared the students, hammering their beer glasses against the table; "a speech, a speech!—silence for a speech!"

"The fact is, my friends," said the Professor, beaming through his spectacles, "I hope very soon to be married."

"Married!" cried a student, bolder than the others. "Is Madame dead, then?"

"Madame who?"

"Why, Madame von Baumgarten, of course."

"Ha, ha!" laughed the Professor; "I can see, then, that you know all about my former difficulties. No, she is not dead, but I have reason to believe that she will not oppose my marriage."

"That is very accommodating of her," remarked one of the company.

"In fact," said the Professor, "I hope that she will now be induced to aid me in getting a wife. She and I never took to each other very much; but now I hope all that may be ended, and when I marry she will come and stay with me."

"What a happy family!" exclaimed some wag.

"Yes, indeed; and I hope you will come to my wedding, all of you. I won't mention names, but here is to my little bride!" and the Professor waved his glass in the air.

"Here's to his little bride!" roared the roisterers, with shouts of laughter. "Here's her health. Sie soll leben—Hoch!" And so the fun waxed still more fast and furious, while each young fellow followed the Professor's example, and drank a toast to the girl of his heart.

While all this festivity had been going on at the Grüner Mann, a very different scene had been enacted elsewhere. Young Fritz von Hartmann, with a solemn face and a reserved manner, had, after the experiment, consulted and adjusted some mathematical instruments; after which, with a few peremptory words to the janitor, he had walked out into the street and wended his way slowly in the direction of the house of the Professor. As he walked he saw Von Althaus, the professor of anatomy, in front of him, and, quickening his pace, he overtook him.

"I say, Von Althaus," he exclaimed, tapping him on the sleeve, "you were asking me for some information the other day concerning the middle coat of the cerebral arteries. Now I find——"

"Donnerwetter!" shouted Von Althaus, who was a peppery old fellow. "What the deuce do you mean by your impertinence! I'll have you up before the Academical Senate for this, sir"; with which threat he turned on his heel and hurried away. Von Hartmann was much surprised at this reception. "It's on account of this failure of my experiment," he said to himself, and continued moodily on his way.

Fresh surprises were in store for him, however. He was hurrying along when he was overtaken by two students. These youths, instead of raising their caps or showing any other sign of respect, gave a wild whoop of delight the instant that they saw him, and rushing at him seized him by each arm and commenced dragging him along with them.

"Gott in Himmel!" roared Von Hartmann. "What is the meaning of this unparalleled insult? Where are you taking me?"

"To crack a bottle of wine with us," said the two students. "Come along! That is an invitation which you have never refused."

"I never heard of such insolence in my life!" cried Von Hartmann. "Let go my arms! I shall certainly have you rusticated for this. Let me go, I say!" and he kicked furiously at his captors.

"Oh, if you choose to turn ill-tempered, you may go where you like," the students said, releasing him. "We can do very well without you."

"I know you. I'll pay you out" said Von Hartmann furiously, and continued in the direction which he imagined to be his own home, much incensed at the two episodes which had occurred to him on the way.

Now, Madame von Baumgarten, who was looking out of the window and wondering why her husband was late for dinner, was considerably astonished to see the young student come stalking down the road. As already remarked, she had a great antipathy to him, and if ever he ventured into the house it was on sufferance, and under the protection of the Professor. Still more astonished was she, therefore, when she beheld him undo the wicket-gate and stride up the garden path with the air of one who is master of the situation. She could hardly believe her eyes, and hastened to the door with all her maternal instincts up in arms. From the upper windows the fair Elise had also observed this daring move upon the part of her lover, and her heart beat quick with mingled pride and consternation.

" Good day, sir," Madame Baumgarten remarked to the intruder, as she stood in gloomy majesty in the open doorway.

" A very fine day indeed, Martha," returned the other. " Now, don't stand there like a statue of Juno, but bustle about and get the dinner ready, for I am wellnigh starved."

" Martha ! Dinner ! " ejaculated the lady, falling back in astonishment.

" Yes, dinner, Martha, dinner ! " howled Von Hartmann, who was becoming irritable. " Is there anything wonderful in that request when a man has been out all day ? I'll wait in the dining-room. Anything will do. Schinken, and sausage, and prunes—any little thing that happens to be about. There you are, standing staring again. Woman, will you or will you not stir your legs ? "

This last address, delivered with a perfect shriek of rage, had the effect of sending good Madame Baumgarten flying along the passage and through the kitchen, where she locked herself up in the scullery and went into violent hysterics. In the meantime Von Hartmann strode into the room and threw himself down upon the sofa in the worst of tempers.

" Elise ! " he shouted. " Confound the girl ! Elise ! "

Thus roughly summoned, the young lady came timidly downstairs and into the presence of her lover. " Dearest ! " she cried, throwing her arms round him, " I know this is all done for my sake ! It is a *ruse* in order to see me."

Von Hartmann's indignation at this fresh attack upon him was so great that he became speechless for a minute from rage, and could only glare and shake his fists, while he struggled in her embrace. When he at last regained his utterance, he indulged in such a bellow of passion that the young lady dropped back, petrified with fear, into an arm-chair.

"Never have I passed such a day in my life," Von Hartmann cried, stamping upon the floor. "My experiment has failed. Von Althaus has insulted me. Two students have dragged me along the public road. My wife nearly faints when I ask her for dinner, and my daughter flies at me and hugs me like a grizzly bear."

"You are ill, dear," the young lady cried. "Your mind is wandering. You have not even kissed me once."

"No, and I don't intend to either," Von Hartmann said with decision. "You ought to be ashamed of yourself. Why don't you go and fetch my slippers, and help your mother to dish the dinner?"

"And is it for this," Elise cried, burying her face in her handkerchief—"is it for this that I have loved you passionately for upwards of ten months? Is it for this that I have braved my mother's wrath? Oh, you have broken my heart; I am sure you have!" and she sobbed hysterically.

"I can't stand much more of this," roared Von Hartmann furiously. "What the deuce does the girl mean? What did I do ten months ago which inspired you with such a particular affection for me? If you are really so very fond, you would do better to run away down and find the Schinken and some bread, instead of talking all this nonsense."

"Oh, my darling!" cried the unhappy maiden, throwing herself into the arms of what she imagined to be her lover, "you do but joke in order to frighten your little Elise."

Now it chanced that at the moment of this unexpected embrace Von Hartmann was still leaning back against the end of the sofa, which, like much German furniture, was in a somewhat rickety condition. It also chanced that beneath this end of the sofa there stood a tank full of water in which the physiologist was conducting certain experiments upon the ova of fish, and which he kept in his drawing-room in order to ensure an equable temperature. The additional weight of the maiden combined with the impetus with which she hurled herself upon him, caused the precarious piece of furniture to give way, and the body of the unfortunate student was hurled backwards into the tank, in which his head and shoulders were firmly wedged, while his lower extremities flapped helplessly about in the air. This was the last straw. Extricating himself with some difficulty from his unpleasant position, Von Hartmann gave an inarticulate yell of fury, and dashing out of the room, in spite of the entreaties of Elise, he seized his hat and rushed off into the town, all dripping and dishevelled, with the intention of seeking in some inn the food and comfort which he could not find at home.

As the spirit of Von Baumgarten encased in the body of Von Hartmann strode down the winding pathway which led down to the little town, brooding angrily over his many wrongs, he became aware that an elderly man was approaching him who appeared to be in an advanced state of intoxication. Von Hartmann waited by the side of the road and watched this individual, who came stumbling along, reeling from one side of the road to the other, and singing a student song in a very husky and drunken voice. At first his interest was merely excited by the fact of seeing a man of so venerable an appearance in such a disgraceful condition, but as he approached nearer, he became convinced that he knew the other well, though he could not recall when or where he had met him. This impression became so strong with him, that when the stranger came abreast of him he stepped in front of him and took a good look at his features.

" Well, sonny," said the drunken man, surveying Von Hartmann and swaying about in front of him, " where the Henker have I seen you before? I know you as well as I know myself. Who the deuce are you?"

"I am Professor von Baumgarten," said the student. "May I ask who you are? I am strangely familiar with your features."

"You should never tell lies, young man," said the other. "You're certainly not the Professor, for he is an ugly, snuffy old chap, and you are a big, broad-shouldered young fellow. As to myself, I am Fritz von Hartmann at your service."

"That you certainly are not," exclaimed the body of Von Hartmann. "You might very well be his father. But hullo, sir, are you aware that you are wearing my studs and my watch-chain?"

"Donnerwetter!" hiccoughed the other. "If those are not the trousers for which my tailor is about to sue me, may I never taste beer again."

Now as Von Hartmann, overwhelmed by the many strange things which had occurred to him that day, passed his hand over his forehead and cast his eyes downwards, he chanced to catch the reflection of his own face in a pool which the rain had left upon the road. To his utter astonishment he perceived that his face was that of a youth, that his dress was that of a fashionable young student, and that in every way he was the antithesis of the grave and scholarly figure in which his mind was wont to dwell. In an instant his active brain ran over the series of events which had occurred and sprang to the conclusion. He fairly reeled under the blow.

"Himmel!" he cried, "I see it all. Our souls are in the wrong bodies. I am you and you are I. My theory is proved—but at what an expense! Is the most scholarly mind in Europe to go about with this frivolous exterior? Oh, the labours of a lifetime are ruined!" and he smote his breast in his despair.

"I say," remarked the real Von Hartmann from the body of the Professor, "I quite see the force of your remarks, but don't go knocking my body about like that.

You received it in excellent condition, but I perceive that you have wet it and bruised it, and spilled snuff over my ruffled shirt-front."

"It matters little," the other said moodily. "Such as we are so must we stay. My theory is triumphantly proved, but the cost is terrible."

"If I thought so," said the spirit of the student, "it would be hard indeed. What could I do with these stiff old limbs, and how could I woo Elise and persuade her that I was not her father? No, thank Heaven, in spite of the beer which has upset me more than ever it could upset my real self, I can see a way out of it."

"How?" gasped the Professor.

"Why, by repeating the experiment. Liberate our souls once more, and the chances are that they will find their way back into their respective bodies."

No drowning man could clutch more eagerly at a straw than did Von Baumgarten's spirit at this suggestion. In feverish haste he dragged his own frame to the side of the road and threw it into a mesmeric trance; he then extracted the crystal ball from the pocket, and managed to bring himself into the same condition.

Some students and peasants who chanced to pass during the next hour were much astonished to see the worthy Professor of Physiology and his favourite student both sitting upon a very muddy bank and both completely insensible. Before the hour was up quite a crowd had assembled, and they were discussing the advisability of sending for an ambulance to convey the pair to hospital, when the learned savant opened his eyes and gazed vacantly around him. For an instant he seemed to forget how he had come there, but next moment he astonished his audience by waving his skinny arms above his head and crying out in a voice of rapture, "Gott sei gedanket! I am myself again. I feel I am!" Nor was the amazement lessened when the student, springing to his feet, burst into the same cry, and the two performed a sort of *pas de joie* in the middle of the road.

For some time after that people had some suspicion of the sanity of both the actors in this strange episode. When the Professor published his experiences in the *Medicalschrift* as he had promised, he was met by an intimation, even from his colleagues, that he would do well to have his mind cared for, and that another such publication would certainly consign him to a madhouse. The student also found by experience that it was wisest to be silent about the matter.

When the worthy lecturer returned home that night he did not receive the cordial welcome which he might have looked for after his strange adventures. On the contrary, he was roundly upbraided by both his female relatives for smelling of drink and tobacco, and also for being absent while a young scapegrace invaded the house and insulted its occupants. It was long before the domestic atmosphere of the lecturer's house resumed its normal quiet, and longer still before the genial face of Von Hartmann was seen beneath its roof. Perseverance, however, conquers every obstacle, and the student eventually succeeded in pacifying the enraged ladies and in establishing himself upon the old footing. He has now no longer any cause to fear the enmity of Madame, for he is Hauptmann von Hartmann of the Emperor's own Uhlans, and his loving wife Elise had already presented him with two little Uhlans as a visible sign and token of her affection.

42. *Cyprian Overbeck Wells*

A LITERARY MOSAIC

FROM my boyhood I have had an intense and overwhelming conviction that my real vocation lay in the direction of literature. I have, however, had a most unaccountable difficulty in getting any responsible person to share my views. It is true that private friends have sometimes, after listening to my effusions, gone the length of remarking, "Really, Smith, that's not half bad!" or, "You take my advice, old boy, and send that to some magazine!" but I have never on these occasions had the moral courage to inform my adviser that the article in question had been sent to well-nigh every publisher in London, and had come back again with a rapidity and precision which spoke well for the efficiency of our postal arrangements.

Had my manuscripts been paper boomerangs they could not have returned with greater accuracy to their unhappy despatcher. Oh, the vileness and utter degradation of the moment when the stale little cylinder of closely written pages, which seemed so fresh and full of promise a few days ago, is handed in by a remorseless postman! And what moral depravity shines through the editor's ridiculous plea of "want of space!" But the subject is a painful one, and a digression from the plain statement of facts which I originally contemplated.

From the age of seventeen to that of three-and-twenty I was a literary volcano in a constant state of eruption. Poems and tales, articles and reviews, nothing came amiss to my pen. From the great sea-serpent to the nebular hypothesis, I was ready to write on anything or everything, and I can safely say that I seldom handled a subject without throwing new lights upon it. Poetry and romance, however, had always the greatest attractions for me. How I have wept over the pathos of my heroines, and laughed at the comicalities of my buffoons! Alas! I could find no one to join me in my appreciation, and solitary admiration for one's self, however genuine, becomes satiating after a time. My father remonstrated with me too on the score of expense and loss of time, so that I was finally compelled to relinquish my dreams of literary independence and to become a clerk in a wholesale mercantile firm connected with the West African trade.

Even when condemned to the prosaic duties which fell to my lot in the office, I continued faithful to my first love. I have introduced pieces of word-painting into the most commonplace business letters which have, I am told, considerably astonished the recipients. My refined sarcasm has made defaulting creditors writhe and wince. Occasionally, like the great Silas Wegg, I would drop into poetry, and so raise the whole tone of the correspondence. Thus what could be more elegant than my rendering of the firm's instructions to the captain of one of their vessels. It ran in this way:—

> "From England, Captain, you must steer a
> Course directly to Madeira,
> Land the casks of salted beef,
> Then away to Teneriffe.
> Pray be careful, cool, and wary
> With the merchants of Canary.
> When you leave them make the most
> Of the trade-winds to the coast.
> Down it you shall sail as far
> As the land of Calabar,
> And from there you'll onward go
> To Bonny and Fernando Po"——

and so on for four pages. The captain, instead of treasuring up this little gem, called at the office next day, and demanded with quite unnecessary warmth what the thing meant, and I was compelled to translate it all back into prose. On this, as on other similar occasions, my employer took me severely to task—for he was, you see, a man entirely devoid of all pretensions to literary taste!

All this, however, is a mere preamble, and leads up to the fact that after ten years or so of drudgery I inherited a legacy which, though small, was sufficient to satisfy my simple wants. Finding myself independent, I rented a quiet house removed from the uproar and bustle of London, and there I settled down with the intention of producing some great work which should single me out from the family of the Smiths, and render my name immortal. To this end I laid in several quires of foolscap, a box of quill pens, and a sixpenny bottle of ink, and having given my housekeeper injunctions to deny me to all visitors, I proceeded to look round for a suitable subject.

I was looking round for some weeks. At the end of that time I found that I had by constant nibbling devoured a large number of the quills, and had spread the ink out to such advantage, what with blots, spills, and abortive commencements, that there appeared to be some everywhere except in the bottle. As to the story itself, however, the facility of my youth had deserted me completely, and my mind remained a complete blank ; nor could I, do what I would, excite my sterile imagination to conjure up a single incident or character.

In this strait I determined to devote my leisure to running rapidly through the works of the leading English novelists, from Daniel Defoe to the present day, in the hope of stimulating my latent ideas and of getting a good grasp of the general tendency of literature. For some time past I had avoided opening any work of fiction because one of the greatest faults of my youth had been that I invariably and unconsciously mimicked the style of the last author whom I had happened to read. Now, however, I made up my mind to seek safety in a multitude, and by consulting *all* the English classics to avoid the danger of imitating any one too closely. I had just accomplished the task of reading through the majority of the standard novels at the time when my narrative commences.

It was, then, about twenty minutes to ten on the night of the fourth of June, eighteen hundred and eighty-six, that, after disposing of a pint of beer and a Welsh rarebit for my supper, I seated myself in my arm-chair, cocked my feet upon a stool, and lit my pipe, as was my custom. Both my pulse and my temperature were, as far as I know, normal at the time. I would give the state of the barometer, but that unlucky instrument had experienced an unprecedented fall of forty-two inches—from a nail to the ground—and was not in a reliable condition. We live in a scientific age, and I flatter myself that I move with the times.

Whilst in that comfortable lethargic condition which accompanies both digestion and poisoning by nicotine, I suddenly became aware of the extraordinary fact that my little drawing-room had elongated into a great *salon*, and that my humble table had increased in proportion. Round this colossal mahogany were seated a great number of people who were talking earnestly together, and the surface in front of them was strewn with books and pamphlets. I could not help observing that these persons were dressed in a most extraordinary mixture of costumes, for those at the end nearest to me wore peruke wigs, swords, and all the fashions of two centuries back; those about the centre had tight knee-breeches, high cravats, and heavy bunches of seals; while among those at the far side the majority were dressed in the most modern style, and among them I saw, to my surprise, several eminent men of letters whom I had the honour of knowing. There were two or three women in the company. I should have risen to my feet to greet these unexpected guests, but all power of motion appeared to have deserted me, and I could only lie still and listen to their conversation, which I soon perceived to be all about myself.

"Egad!" exclaimed a rough, weather-beaten man, who was smoking a long churchwarden pipe at my end of the table, "my heart softens for him. Why, gossips, we've been in the same straits ourselves. Gadzooks, never did mother feel more concern for her eldest born than I when Rory Random went out to make his own way in the world."

"Right, Tobias, right!" cried another man, seated at my very elbow. "By my troth, I lost more flesh over poor Robin on his island, than had I the sweating sickness twice told. The tale was well-nigh done when in swaggers my Lord of Rochester—a merry gallant, and one whose word in matters literary might make or mar. 'How now, Defoe,' quoth he, 'hast a tale on hand?' 'Even so, your lordship,' I returned. 'A right merry one, I trust,' quoth he. 'Discourse unto me concerning thy heroine, a comely lass, Dan, or I mistake.' 'Nay,' I replied, 'there is no heroine in the matter.' 'Split not your phrases,' quoth he; 'thou weighest every word like a scald attorney. Speak to me of thy principal female character, be she heroine or no.' 'My lord,' I answered, 'there is no female character.' 'Then out upon thyself and thy book too!' he cried. 'Thou hadst best burn it!'—and so out in great dudgeon, whilst I fell to mourning over my poor romance, which was thus, as it were, sentenced to death before its birth. Yet there are a thousand now who have heard of Robin and his man Friday, to one who has heard of my Lord of Rochester."

"Very true, Defoe," said a genial-looking man in a red waistcoat, who was sitting at the modern end of the table. "But all this won't help our good friend Smith in making a start at his story, which, I believe, was the reason why we assembled."

"The Dickens it is!" stammered a little man beside him, and everybody laughed, especially the genial man, who cried out, "Charley Lamb, Charley Lamb, you'll never alter. You would make a pun if you were hanged for it."

"That would be a case of haltering," returned the other, on which everybody laughed again.

By this time I had begun to dimly realize in my confused brain the enormous honour which had been done me. The greatest masters of fiction in every age of English letters had apparently made a rendezvous beneath my roof, in order to assist me in my difficulties. There were many faces at the table whom I was unable to identify; but when I looked hard at others I often found them to be very familiar to me, whether from paintings or from mere description. Thus between the first two speakers, who had betrayed themselves as Defoe and Smollett, there sat a dark, saturnine, corpulent old man, with harsh prominent features, who I was sure could be none other than the famous author of Gulliver. There were several others of whom I was not so sure, sitting at the other side of the table, but I conjecture that both Fielding and Richardson were among them, and I could swear to the lantern-jaws and cadaverous visage of Lawrence Sterne. Higher up I could see among the crowd the high forehead of Sir Walter Scott, the masculine features of George Eliott, and the flattened nose of Thackeray; while amongst the living I recognised James Payn, Walter Besant, the lady known as "Ouida," Robert Louis Stevenson, and several of lesser note. Never before, probably, had such an assemblage of choice spirits gathered under one roof.

"Well," said Sir Walter Scott, speaking with a very pronounced accent, "ye ken the auld proverb, sirs, 'Ower mony cooks,' or as the Border minstrel sang—

> 'Black Johnstone wi' his troopers ten
> Might mak' the heart turn cauld,
> But Johnstone when he's a' alane
> Is waur ten thoosand fauld.'

The Johnstones were one of the Redesdale families, second cousins of the Armstrongs, and connected by marriage to——"

"Perhaps, Sir Walter," interrupted Thackeray, "you would take the responsibility off our hands by yourself dictating the commencement of a story to this young literary aspirant."

"Na, na!" cried Sir Walter; "I'll do my share, but there's Chairlie over there as full o' wut as a Radical's full o' treason. He's the laddie to give a cheery opening to it."

Dickens was shaking his head, and apparently about to refuse the honour, when a voice from among the moderns—I could not see who it was for the crowd—said:

"Suppose we begin at the end of the table and work round, anyone contributing a little as the fancy seizes him?"

"Agreed! agreed!" cried the whole company; and every eye was turned on Defoe, who seemed very uneasy, and filled his pipe from a great tobacco-box in front of him.

"Nay, gossips," he said, "there are others more worthy——"

But he was interrupted by loud cries of "No! no!" from the whole table; and Smollett shouted out, "Stand to it, Dan—stand to it! You and I and the Dean here will make three short tacks just to fetch her out of harbour, and then she may drift where she pleases." Thus encouraged, Defoe cleared his throat, and began in this way, talking between the puffs of his pipe:—

"My father was a well-to-do yeoman of Cheshire, named Cyprian Overbeck, but, marrying about the year 1617, he assumed the name of his wife's family, which was Wells; and thus I, their eldest son, was named Cyprian Overbeck Wells. The farm was a very fertile one, and contained some of the best grazing land in those parts, so that my father was enabled to lay by money to the extent of a thousand crowns, which he laid out in an adventure to the Indies with such surprising success that in less than three years it had increased fourfold. Thus encouraged, he bought a part share of the trader, and, fitting her out once more with such commodities as were most in demand (viz. old muskets, hangars and axes, besides glasses, needles, and the like), he placed me on board as supercargo to look after his interests, and dispatched us upon our voyage.

"We had a fair wind as far as Cape de Verde, and there, getting into the north-west trade-winds, made good progress down the African coast. Beyond sighting a Barbary rover once, whereat our mariners were in sad distress, counting themselves already as little better than slaves, we had good luck until we had come within a hundred leagues of the Cape of Good Hope, when the wind veered round to the southward and blew exceeding hard, while the sea rose to such a height that the end of the mainyard dipped into the water, and I heard the master say that though he had been at sea for five-and-thirty years he had never seen the like of it, and that he had little expectation of riding through it. On this I fell to wringing my hands and bewailing myself, until the mast going by the board with a crash, I thought that the ship had struck, and swooned with terror, falling into the scuppers and lying like one dead, which was the saving of me, as will appear in the sequel. For the mariners, giving up all hope of saving the ship, and being in momentary expectation that she would founder, pushed off in the long-boat, whereby I fear that they met the fate which they hoped to avoid, since I have never from that day heard anything of them. For my own part, on recovering from the swoon into which I had fallen, I found that, by the mercy of Providence, the sea had gone down, and that I was alone in the vessel. At which last discovery I was so terror-struck that I could but stand wringing my hands and bewailing my sad fate, until at last taking heart, I fell to comparing my lot with that of my unhappy camerados, on which I became more cheerful, and descending to the cabin, made a meal off such dainties as were in the captain's locker."

Having got so far, Defoe remarked that he thought he had given them a fair start, and handed over the story to Dean Swift, who, after premising that he feared he would find himself as much at sea as Master Cyprian Overbeck Wells, continued in this way :—

" For two days I drifted about in great distress, fearing that there should be a return of the gale, and keeping an eager look-out for my late companions. Upon the third day, towards evening, I observed to my extreme surprise that the ship was under the influence of a very powerful current, which ran to the north-east with such violence that she was carried, now bows on, now stern on, and occasionally drifting sideways like a crab, at a rate which I cannot compute at less than twelve or fifteen knots an hour. For several weeks I was borne away in this manner, until one morning, to my inexpressible joy, I sighted an island upon the starboard quarter. The current would, however, have carried me past it had I not made shift, though single-handed, to set the flying-jib so as to turn her bows, and then clapping on the sprit-sail, studding-sail, and fore-sail, I clewed up the halliards upon the port side, and put the wheel down hard a-star-board, the wind being at the time north-east-half-east."

At the description of this nautical manœuvre I observed that Smollett grinned, and a gentleman who was sitting higher up the table in the uniform of the Royal Navy, and who I guessed to be Captain Marryat, became very uneasy and fidgeted in his seat.

" By this means I got clear of the current and was able to steer within a quarter of a mile of the beach, which indeed I might have approached still nearer by making another tack, but being an excellent swimmer, I deemed it best to leave the vessel, which was almost waterlogged, and to make the best of my way to the shore.

" I had had my doubts hitherto as to whether this new-found country was inhabited or no, but as I approached nearer to it, being on the summit of a great wave, I perceived a number of figures on the beach, engaged apparently in watching me and my vessel. My joy, however, was considerably lessened when on reaching the land I found that the figures consisted of a vast concourse of animals of various sorts who were standing about in groups, and who hurried down to the water's edge to meet me. I had scarce put my foot upon the sand before I was surrounded by an eager crowd of deer, dogs, wild boars, buffaloes, and other creatures, none of whom showed the least fear either of me or of each other, but, on the contrary, were animated by a common feeling of curiosity, as well as, it would appear, by some degree of disgust."

" A second edition," whispered Lawrence Sterne to his neighbour ; " Gulliver served up cold."

"Did you speak, sir ?" asked the Dean very sternly, having evidently overheard the remark.

"My words were not addressed to you, sir," answered Sterne, looking rather frightened.

"They were none the less insolent," roared the Dean. "Your reverence would fain make a Sentimental Journey of the narrative, I doubt not, and find pathos in a dead donkey—though, faith, no man can blame thee for mourning over thy own kith and kin."

"Better that than to wallow in all the filth of Yahoo-land," returned Sterne warmly, and a quarrel would certainly have ensued but for the interposition of the remainder of the company. As it was, the Dean refused indignantly to have any further hand in the story, and Sterne also stood out of it, remarking with a sneer that he was loth to fit a good blade on to a poor handle. Under these circumstances some further unpleasantness might have occurred had not Smollett rapidly taken up the narrative, continuing it in the third person instead of the first :—

"Our hero, being considerably alarmed at this strange reception, lost little time in plunging into the sea again and regaining his vessel, being convinced that the worst which might befall him from the elements would be as nothing compared to the dangers of this mysterious island. It was as well that he took this course, for before nightfall his ship was overhauled and he himself picked up by a British man-of-war, the *Lightning* (74), then returning from the West Indies, where it had formed part of the fleet under the command of Admiral Benbow. Young Wells, being a likely lad enough, well-spoken and high-spirited, was at once entered on the books as officer's servant, in which capacity he both gained great popularity on account of the freedom of his manners, and found an opportunity for indulging in those practical pleasantries for which he had all his life been famous.

"Among the quartermasters of the *Lightning* there was one named Jedediah Anchorstock, whose appearance was so remarkable that it quickly attracted the attention of our hero. He was a man of about fifty, dark with exposure to the weather, and so tall that as he came along the 'tween decks he had to bend himself nearly double. The most striking peculiarity of this individual was, however, that in his boyhood some evil-minded person had tattooed eyes all over his countenance with such marvellous skill that it was difficult at a short distance to pick out his real ones among so many counterfeits. On this strange personage Master Cyprian determined to exercise his talents for mischief, the more so as he learned that he was extremely superstitious, and also that he had left behind him in Portsmouth a strong-minded spouse of whom he stood in mortal terror. With this object he secured one of the sheep which were kept on board for the officer's table, and pouring a can of rumbo down its throat, reduced it to a state of utter intoxication. He then conveyed it to Anchorstock's berth, and with the assistance of some other imps, as mischievous as himself, dressed it up in a high nightcap and gown, and covered it over with the bedclothes.

"When the quartermaster came down from his watch our hero met him at the door of his berth with an agitated face. 'Mr. Anchorstock,' said he, 'can it be that your wife is on board?' 'Wife!' roared the astonished sailor. 'Ye white-faced swab, what d'ye mean?' 'If she's not here in the ship it must be her ghost,' said Cyprian, shaking his head gloomily. 'In the ship! How in thunder could she get into the ship? Why, master, I believe as how you're weak in the upper works, d'ye see? to as much as think o' such a thing. My Poll is moored head and starn, behind the point at Portsmouth, more'n two thousand mile away.' 'Upon my word,' said our hero, very earnestly, 'I saw a female look out of your cabin not five minutes ago.' 'Ay, ay, Mr. Anchorstock,' joined in several of the conspirators. 'We all saw her—a spanking-looking craft with a dead-light mounted on one side.' 'Sure enough,' said Anchorstock, staggered by this accumulation of evidence, 'my Polly's starboard eye was doused for ever by long Sue Williams of the Hard. But if so be as she be there I must see her, be she ghost or quick'; with which the honest sailor, in much perturbation and trembling in every limb, began to shuffle forward into the cabin, holding the light well in front of him. It chanced, however, that the unhappy sheep, which was quietly engaged in sleeping off the effects of its unusual potations, was awakened by the noise of his approach, and finding herself in such an unusual position, sprang out of bed and rushed furiously for the door, bleating wildly, and rolling about like a brig in a tornado, partly from intoxication and partly from the nightdress which impeded her movements. As Anchorstock saw this extraordinary apparition bearing down upon him, he uttered a yell and fell flat upon his face, convinced that he had to do with a supernatural visitor, the more so as the confederates heightened the effect by a chorus of most ghastly groans and cries. The joke had nearly gone beyond what was originally intended, for the quartermaster lay as one dead, and it was only with the greatest difficulty that he could be brought to his senses. To the end of the voyage he stoutly asserted that he had seen the distant Mrs. Anchorstock, remarking with many oaths that though he was too woundily scared to take much note of the features, there was no mistaking the strong smell of rum which was characteristic of his better half.

" It chanced shortly after this to be the king's birthday, an event which was signalised aboard the *Lightning* by the death of the commander under singular circumstances. This officer, who was a real fair-weather Jack, hardly knowing the ship's keel from her ensign, had obtained his position through parliamentary interest, and used it with such tyranny and cruelty that he was universally execrated. So unpopular was he that when a plot was entered into by the whole crew to punish his misdeeds with death, he had not a single friend among six hundred souls to warn him of his danger. It was the custom on board the king's ships that upon his birthday the entire ship's company should be drawn up upon deck, and that at a signal they should discharge their muskets into the air in honour of his Majesty. On this occasion word had been secretly passed round for every man to slip a slug into his firelock, instead of the blank cartridge provided. On the boatswain blowing his whistle the men mustered upon deck and formed line, whilst the captain, standing well in front of them, delivered a few words to them. 'When I give the word,' he concluded, 'you shall discharge your pieces, and by thunder, if any man is a second before or a second after his fellows I shall trice him up to the weather rigging!' With these words he roared 'Fire!' on which every man levelled his musket straight at his head and pulled the trigger. So accurate was the aim and so short the distance, that more than five hundred bullets struck him simultaneously, blowing away his head and a large portion of his body. There were so many concerned in this matter, and it was so hopeless to trace it to any individual, that the officers were unable to punish anyone for the affair—the more readily as the captain's haughty ways and heartless conduct had made him quite as hateful to them as to the men whom he commanded.

"By his pleasantries and the natural charm of his manners our hero so far won the good wishes of the ship's company that they parted with infinite regret upon their arrival in England. Filial duty, however, urged him to return home and report himself to his father, with which object he posted from Portsmouth to London, intending to proceed thence to Shropshire. As it chanced, however, one of the horses sprained his off foreleg while passing through Chichester, and as no change could be obtained, Cyprian found himself compelled to put up at the Crown and Bull for the night.

"Ods bodikins!" continued Smollett, laughing, "I never could pass a comfortable hostel without stopping and so, with your permission, I'll e'en stop here, and whoever wills may lead friend Cyprian to his further adventures. Do you, Sir Walter, give us a touch of the Wizard of the North."

With these words Smollett produced a pipe, and filling it at Defoe's tobacco-pot, waited patiently for the continuation of the story.

"If I must, I must," remarked the illustrious Scotchman, taking a pinch of snuff; "but I must beg leave to put Mr. Wells back a few hundred years, for of all things I love the true mediæval smack. To proceed then:—

"Our hero being anxious to continue his journey, and learning that it would be some time before any conveyance would be ready, determined to push on alone mounted on his gallant grey steed. Travelling was particularly dangerous at that time, for besides the usual perils which beset wayfarers, the southern parts of England were in a lawless and disturbed state which bordered on insurrection. The young man, however, having loosened his sword in his sheath, so as to be ready for every eventuality, galloped cheerily upon his way, guiding himself to the best of his ability by the light of the rising moon.

"He had not gone far before he realised that the cautions which had been impressed upon him by the landlord, and which he had been inclined to look upon as self-interested advice, were only too well justified. At a spot where the road was particularly rough, and ran across some marshland, he perceived a short distance from him a dark shadow, which his practised eye detected at once as a body of crouching men. Reining up his horse within a few yards of the ambuscade, he wrapped his cloak round his bridle-arm and summoned the party to stand forth.

"'What ho, my masters!' he cried. 'Are beds so scarce, then, that ye must hamper the high road of the king with your bodies? Now, by St. Ursula of Alpuxerra, there be those who might think that birds who fly o' nights were after higher game than the moorhen or the woodcock!'

"'Blades and targets, comrades!' exclaimed a tall powerful man, springing into the centre of the road with several companions, and standing in front of the frightened horse. 'Who is this swashbuckler who summons his Majesty's lieges from their repose? A very soldado, o' truth. Hark ye, sir, or my lord, or thy grace, or whatsoever title your honour's honour may be pleased to approve, thou must curb thy tongue play, or by the seven witches of Gambleside thou may find thyself in but a sorry plight.'

"'I prythee, then, that thou wilt expound to me who and what ye are,' quoth our hero, 'and whether your purpose be such as an honest man may approve of. As to your threats, they turn from my mind as your caitiffly weapons would shiver upon my hauberk from Milan.'

"'Nay, Allen,' interrupted one of the party, addressing him who seemed to be their leader; 'this is a lad of mettle, and such a one as our honest Jack longs for. But we lure not hawks with empty hands. Look ye, sir, there is game afoot which it may need such bold hunters as thyself to follow. Come with us and take a firkin of canary, and we will find better work for that glaive of thine than getting its owner into broil and bloodshed; for, by my troth! Milan or no Milan, if my curtel axe do but ring against that morion of thine it will be an ill day for thy father's son.'

"For a moment our hero hesitated as to whether it would best become his knightly traditions to hurl himself against his enemies, or whether it might not be better to obey their requests. Prudence, mingled with a large share of curiosity, eventually carried the day, and dismounting from his horse, he intimated that he was ready to follow his captors.

"'Spoken like a man!' cried he whom they addressed as Allen. 'Jack Cade will be right glad of such a recruit. Blood and carrion! but thou hast the thews of a young ox; and I swear, by the haft of my sword, that it might have gone ill with some of us hadst thou not listened to reason!'

"'Nay, not so, good Allen—not so,' squeaked a very small man, who had remained in the background while there was any prospect of a fray, but who now came pushing to the front. 'Hadst thou been alone it might indeed have been so, perchance, but an expert swordsman can disarm at pleasure such a one as this young knight. Well I remember in the Palatinate how I clove to the chine even such another—the Baron von Slogstaff. He struck at me, look ye, so; but I, with buckler and blade, did, as one might say, deflect it; and then, countering in carte, I returned in tierce, and so—St. Agnes save us! who comes here?'

"The apparition which frightened the loquacious little man was sufficiently strange to cause a qualm even in the bosom of the knight. Through the darkness there loomed a figure which appeared to be of gigantic size, and a hoarse voice, issuing apparently some distance above the heads of the party, broke roughly on the silence of the night.

"'Now out upon thee, Thomas Allen, and foul be thy fate if thou hast abandoned thy post without good and sufficient cause. By St. Anselm of the Holy Grove, thou hadst best have never been born than rouse my spleen this night. Wherefore is it that you and your men are trailing over the moor like a flock of geese when Michaelmas is near?'

"'Good captain,' said Allen, doffing his bonnet, an example followed by others of the band, 'we have captured a goodly youth who was pricking it along the London road. Methought that some word of thanks were meet reward for such service, rather than taunt or threat.'

"'Nay, take it not to heart, bold Allen,' exclaimed their leader, who was none other than the great Jack Cade himself. 'Thou knowest of old that my temper is somewhat choleric, and my tongue not greased with that unguent which oils the mouths of the lip-serving lords of the land. And you,' he continued, turning suddenly upon our hero, 'are you ready to join the great cause which will make England what it was when the learned Alfred reigned in the land? Zounds, man, speak out, and pick not your phrases.'

"'I am ready to do aught which may become a knight and a gentleman,' said the soldier stoutly.

"'Taxes shall be swept away!' cried Cade excitedly —'the impost and the anpost—the tithe and the hundred-tax. The poor man's salt-box and flour-bin shall be as free as the nobleman's cellar. Ha! wnat sayest thou?'

"'It is but just,' said our hero.

"'Ay, but they give us such justice as the falcon gives the leveret!' roared the orator. 'Down with them, I say—down with every man of them! Noble and judge, priest and king, down with them all!'

"'Nay,' said Sir Overbeck Wells, drawing himself up to his full heigh t, and laying his hand upon the hilt of his sword, 'there I cannot follow thee, but must rather defy thee as traitor and fainéant, seeing that thou art no true man, but one who would usurp the rights of our master the king. whom may the Virgin protect!'

"At these bold words, and the defiance which they conveyed, the rebels seemed for a moment utterly bewildered; but, encouraged by the hoarse shout of their leader they brandished their weapons and prepared to fall upon the knight, who placed himself in a posture for defence and awaited their attack.

"There now!" cried Sir Walter, rubbing his hands and chuckling, "I've put the chiel in a pretty warm corner, and we'll see which of you moderns can take him oot o't. Ne'er a word more will ye get frae me to help him one way or the other."

"You try your hand, James," cried several voices, and the author in question had got so far as to make an allusion to a solitary horseman who was approaching, when he was interrupted by a tall gentleman a little farther down with a slight stutter and a very nervous manner.

"Excuse me," he said, "but I fancy that I may be able to do something here. Some of my humble productions have been said to excel Sir Walter at his best, and I was undoubtedly stronger all round. I could picture modern society as well as ancient; and as to my plays, why Shakespeare never came near *The Lady of Lyons* for popularity. There is this little thing——" (Here he rummaged among a great pile of papers in front of him). "Ah! that's a report of mine, when I was in India! Here it is. No, this is one of my speeches in the House, and this is my criticism on Tennyson. Didn't I warm him up? I can't find what I wanted, but of course you have read them all—*Rienzi*, and *Harold*, and *The Last of the Barons*. Every schoolboy knows them by heart, as poor Macaulay would have said. Allow me to give you a sample:—

"In spite of the gallant knight's valiant resistance the combat was too unequal to be sustained. His sword was broken by a slash from a brown bill, and he was borne to the ground. He expected immediate death, but such did not seem to be the intention of the ruffians who had captured him. He was placed upon the back of his own charger and borne, bound hand and foot, over the trackless moor, in the fastnesses of which the rebels secreted themselves.

"In the depths of these wilds there stood a stone building which had once been a farmhouse, but having been for some reason abandoned had fallen into ruin, and had now become the headquarters of Cade and his men. A large cow-house near the farm had been utilised as sleeping quarters, and some rough attempts had been made to shield the principal room of the main building from the weather by stopping up the gaping apertures in the walls. In this apartment was spread out a rough meal for the returning rebels, and our hero was thrown, still bound, into an empty outhouse, there to await his fate."

Sir Walter had been listening with the greatest impatience to Bulwer Lytton's narrative, but when it had reached this point he broke in impatiently.

" We want a touch of your own style, man," he said. "The animal-magnetico-electro-hysterical-biological-mysterious sort of story is all your own, but at present you are just a poor copy of myself, and nothing more."

There was a murmur of assent from the company, and Defoe remarked, " Truly, Master Lytton, there is a plaguey resemblance in the style, which may indeed be but a chance, and yet methinks it is sufficiently marked to warrant such words as our friend hath used."

" Perhaps you will think that this is an imitation also," said Lytton bitterly, and leaning back in his chair with a morose countenance, he continued the narrative in this way :—

" Our unfortunate hero had hardly stretched himself upon the straw with which his dungeon was littered, when a secret door opened in the wall and a venerable old man swept majestically into the apartment. The prisoner gazed upon him with astonishment not unmixed with awe, for on his broad brow was printed the seal of much knowledge—such knowledge as it is not granted to a son of man to know. He was clad in a long white robe, crossed and chequered with mystic devices in the Arabic character, while a high scarlet tiara marked with the square and circle enhanced his venerable appearance. ' My son,' he said, turning his piercing and yet dreamy gaze upon Sir Overbeck, ' all things lead to nothing, and nothing is the foundation of all things. Cosmos is impenetrable. Why then should we exist ? '

" Astounded at this weighty query, and at the philosophic demeanour of his visitor, our hero made shift to bid him welcome and to demand his name and quality. As the old man answered him his voice rose and fell in musical cadences, like the sighing of the east wind, while an ethereal and aromatic vapour pervaded the apartment.

" 'I am the eternal non-ego,' he answered. 'I am the concentrated negative—the everlasting essence of nothing. You see in me that which existed before the beginning of matter many years before the commencement of time. I am the algebraic *x* which represents the infinite divisibility of a finite particle.'

" Sir Overbeck felt a shudder as though an ice-cold hand had been placed upon his brow. 'What is your message?' he whispered, falling prostrate before his mysterious visitor.

" 'To tell you that the eternities beget chaos, and that the immensities are at the mercy of the divine ananke. Infinitude crouches before a personality. The mercurial essence is the prime mover in spirituality, and the thinker is powerless before the pulsating inanity. The cosmical procession is terminated only by the unknowable and unpronounceable'——

" May I ask, Mr. Smollett, what you find to laugh at?"

" Gadzooks, master," cried Smollett, who had been sniggering for some time back. " It seems to me that there is little danger of anyone venturing to dispute that style with you."

" It's all your own," murmured Sir Walter.

" And very pretty, too," quoth Lawrence Sterne, with a malignant grin. " Pray, sir, what language do you call it?"

Lytton was so enraged at these remarks, and at the favour with which they appeared to be received, that he endeavoured to stutter out some reply, and then, losing control of himself completely, picked up all his loose papers and strode out of the room, dropping pamphlets and speeches at every step. This incident amused the company so much that they laughed for several minutes without cessation. Gradually the sound of their laughter sounded more and more harshly in my ears, the lights on the table grew dim and the company more misty, until they and their symposium vanished away altogether. I was sitting before the embers of what had been a roaring fire, but was now little more than a heap of grey ashes, and the merry laughter of the august company had changed to the recriminations of my wife, who was shaking me violently by the shoulder and exhorting me to choose some more seasonable spot for my slumbers. So ended the wondrous adventures of Master Cyprian Overbeck Wells, but I still live in the hopes that in some future dream the great masters may themselves finish that which they have begun.

43. *Playing with Fire*

I CANNOT pretend to say what occurred on the 14th of April last at No. 17, Badderly Gardens. Put down in black and white, my surmise might seem too crude, too grotesque, for serious consideration. And yet that something did occur, and that it was of a nature which will leave its mark upon every one of us for the rest of our lives, is as certain as the unanimous testimony of five witnesses can make it. I will not enter into any argument or speculation. I will only give a plain statement, which will be submitted to John Moir, Harvey Deacon, and Mrs. Delamere, and withheld from publication unless they are prepared to corroborate every detail. I cannot obtain the sanction of Paul Le Duc, for he appears to have left the country.

It was John Moir (the well-known senior partner of Moir, Moir, and Sanderson) who had originally turned our attention to occult subjects. He had, like many very hard and practical men of business, a mystic side to his nature, which had led him to the examination, and eventually to the acceptance, of those elusive phenomena which are grouped together with much that is foolish, and much that is fraudulent, under the common heading of spiritualism. His researches, which had begun with an open mind, ended unhappily in dogma, and he became as positive and fanatical as any other bigot. He represented in our little group the body of men who have turned these singular phenomena into a new religion.

Mrs. Delamere, our medium, was his sister, the wife of Delamere, the rising sculptor. Our experience had shown us that to work on these subjects without a medium was as futile as for an astronomer to make observations without a telescope. On the other hand, the introduction of a paid medium was hateful to all of us. Was it not obvious that he or she would feel bound to return some result for money received, and that the temptation to fraud would be an overpowering one? No phenomena could be relied upon which were produced at a guinea an hour. But, fortunately, Moir had discovered that his sister was mediumistic—in other words, that she was a battery of that animal magnetic force which is the only form of energy which is subtle enough to be acted upon from the spiritual plane as well as from our own material one. Of course, when I say this, I do not mean to beg the question; but I am simply indicating the theories upon which we were ourselves, rightly or wrongly, explaining what we saw. The lady came, not altogether with the approval of her husband, and though she never gave indications of any very great psychic force, we were able, at least, to obtain those usual phenomena of message-tilting which are at the same time so puerile and so inexplicable. Every Sunday evening we met in Harvey Deacon's studio at Badderly Gardens, the next house to the corner of Merton Park Road.

Harvey Deacon's imaginative work in art would prepare anyone to find that he was an ardent lover of everything which was *outré* and sensational. A certain picturesqueness in the study of the occult had been the quality which had originally attracted him to it, but his attention was speedily arrested by some of those phenomena to which I have referred, and he was coming rapidly to the conclusion that what he had looked upon as an amusing romance and an after-dinner entertainment was really a very formidable reality. He is a man with a remarkably clear and logical brain—a true descendant of his ancestor, the well-known Scotch professor—and he represented in our small circle the critical element, the man who has no prejudices, is prepared to follow facts as far as he can see them, and refuses to theorise in advance of his data. His caution annoyed Moir as much as the latter's robust faith amused Deacon, but each in his own way was equally keen upon the matter.

And I? What am I to say that I represented? I was not the devotee. I was not the scientific critic. Perhaps the best that I can claim for myself is that I was the dilettante man about town, anxious to be in the swim of every fresh movement, thankful for any new sensation which would take me out of myself and open up fresh possibilities of existence. I am not an enthusiast myself, but I like the company of those who are. Moir's talk, which made me feel as if we had a private pass-key through the door of death, filled me with a vague contentment. The soothing atmosphere of the séance with the darkened lights was delightful to me. In a word, the thing amused me, and so I was there.

It was, as I have said, upon the 14th of April last that the very singular event which I am about to put upon record took place. I was the first of the men to arrive at the studio, but Mrs. Delamere was already there, having had afternoon tea with Mrs. Harvey Deacon. The two ladies and Deacon himself were standing in front of an unfinished picture of his upon the easel. I am not an expert in art, and I have never professed to understand what Harvey Deacon meant by his pictures; but I could see in this instance that it was all very clever and imaginative, fairies and animals and allegorical figures of all sorts. The ladies were loud in their praises, and indeed the colour effect was a remarkable one.

"What do you think of it, Markham?" he asked.

"Well, it's above me," said I. "These beasts—what are they?"

"Mythical monsters, imaginary creatures, heraldic emblems—a sort of weird, bizarre procession of them."

"With a white horse in front!"

"It's not a horse," said he, rather testily—which was surprising, for he was a very good-humoured fellow as a rule, and hardly ever took himself seriously.

"What is it, then?"

"Can't you see the horn in front? It's a unicorn. I told you they were heraldic beasts. Can't you recognize one?"

"Very sorry, Deacon," said I, for he really seemed to be annoyed.

He laughed at his own irritation.

"Excuse me, Markham!" said he; "the fact is that I have had an awful job over the beast. All day I have been painting him in and painting him out, and trying to imagine what a real live, ramping unicorn would look like. At last I got him, as I hoped; so when you failed to recognise it, it took me on the raw."

"Why, of course it's a unicorn," said I, for he was evidently depressed at my obtuseness. "I can see the horn quite plainly, but I never saw a unicorn except beside the Royal Arms, and so I never thought of the creature. And these others are griffins and cockatrices, and dragons of sorts?"

"Yes, I had no difficulty with them. It was the unicorn which bothered me. However, there's an end of it until to-morrow." He turned the picture round upon the easel, and we all chatted about other subjects.

Moir was late that evening, and when he did arrive he brought with him, rather to our surprise, a small, stout Frenchman, whom he introduced as Monsieur Paul Le Duc. I say to our surprise, for we held a theory that any intrusion into our spiritual circle deranged the conditions, and introduced an element of suspicion. We knew that we could trust each other, but all our results were vitiated by the presence of an outsider. However, Moir soon reconciled us to the innovation. Monsieur Paul Le Duc was a famous student of occultism, a seer, a medium, and a mystic. He was travelling in England with a letter of introduction to Moir from the President of the Parisian brothers of the Rosy Cross. What more natural than that he should bring him to our little séance, or that we should feel honoured by his presence?

He was, as I have said, a small, stout man, undistinguished in appearance, with a broad, smooth, clean-shaven face, remarkable only for a pair of large, brown, velvety eyes, staring vaguely out in front of him. He was well dressed, with the manners of a gentleman, and his curious little turns of English speech set the ladies smiling. Mrs. Deacon had a prejudice against our researches and left the room, upon which we lowered the lights, as was our custom, and drew up our chairs to the square mahogany table which stood in the centre of the studio. The light was subdued, but sufficient to allow us to see each other quite plainly. I remember that I could even observe the curious, podgy little square-topped hands which the Frenchman laid upon the table.

"What a fun!" said he. "It is many years since I have sat in this fashion, and it is to me amusing. Madame is medium. Does madame make the trance?"

"Well, hardly that," said Mrs. Delamere. "But I am always conscious of extreme sleepiness."

"It is the first stage. Then you encourage it, and there comes the trance. When the trance comes, then out jumps your little spirit and in jumps another little spirit, and so you have direct talking or writing. You leave your machine to be worked by another. *Hein?* But what have unicorns to do with it?"

Harvey Deacon started in his chair. The Frenchman was moving his head slowly round and staring into the shadows which draped the walls.

"What a fun!" said he. "Always unicorns. Who has been thinking so hard upon a subject so bizarre?"

"This is wonderful!" cried Deacon. "I have been trying to paint one all day. But how could you know it?"

"You have been thinking of them in this room."

"Certainly."

"But thoughts are things, my friend. When you imagine a thing you make a thing. You did not know it, *hein?* But I can see your unicorns because it is not only with my eye that I can see."

"Do you mean to say that I create a thing which has never existed by merely thinking of it?"

"But certainly. It is the fact which lies under all other facts. That is why an evil thought is also a danger."

"They are, I suppose, upon the astral plane?" said Moir.

"Ah, well, these are but words, my friends. They are there—somewhere—everywhere—I cannot tell myself. I see them. I could touch them."

"You could not make *us* see them."

"It is to materialise them. Hold! It is an experiment. But the power is wanting. Let us see what power we have, and then arrange what we shall do. May I place you as I wish?"

"You evidently know a great deal more about it than we do," said Harvey Deacon; "I wish that you would take complete control."

"It may be that the conditions are not good. But we will try what we can do. Madame will sit where she is, I next, and this gentleman beside me. Meester Moir will sit next to madame, because it is well to have blacks and blondes in turn. So! And now with your permission I will turn the lights all out."

"What is the advantage of the dark?" I asked.

"Because the force with which we deal is a vibration of ether and so also is light. We have the wires all for ourselves now—*hein?* You will not be frightened in the darkness, madame? What a fun is such a séance!"

At first the darkness appeared to be absolutely pitchy, but in a few minutes our eyes became so far accustomed to it that we could just make out each other's presence—very dimly and vaguely, it is true. I could see nothing else in the room—only the black loom of the motionless figures. We were all taking the matter much more seriously than we had ever done before.

"You will place your hands in front. It is hopeless that we touch, since we are so few round so large a table. You will compose yourself, madame, and if sleep should come to you you will not fight against it. And now we sit in silence and we expect—*hein ?*"

So we sat in silence and expected, staring out into the blackness in front of us. A clock ticked in the passage. A dog barked intermittently far away. Once or twice a cab rattled past in the street, and the gleam of its lamps through the chink in the curtains was a cheerful break in that gloomy vigil. I felt those physical symptoms with which previous séances had made me familiar—the coldness of the feet, the tingling in the hands, the glow of the palms, the feeling of a cold wind upon the back. Strange little shooting pains came in my forearms, especially as it seemed to me in my left one, which was nearest to our visitor—due no doubt to disturbance of the vascular system, but worthy of some attention all the same. At the same time I was conscious of a strained feeling of expectancy which was almost painful. From the rigid, absolute silence of my companions I gathered that their nerves were as tense as my own.

And then suddenly a sound came out of the darkness—a low, sibilant sound, the quick, thin breathing of a woman. Quicker and thinner yet it came, as between clenched teeth, to end in a loud gasp with a dull rustle of cloth.

"What's that ? Is all right ?" someone asked in the darkness.

"Yes, all is right," said the Frenchman. "It is madame. She is in her trance. Now, gentlemen, if you will wait quiet you will see something, I think, which will interest you much."

Still the ticking in the hall. Still the breathing, deeper and fuller now, from the medium. Still the occasional flash, more welcome than ever, of the passing lights of the hansoms. What a gap we were bridging, the half-raised veil of the eternal on the one side and the cabs of London on the other. The table was throbbing with a mighty pulse. It swayed steadily, rhythmically, with an easy swooping, scooping motion under our fingers. Sharp little raps and cracks came from its substance, file-firing, volley-firing, the sounds of a fagot burning briskly on a frosty night.

"There is much power," said the Frenchman. "See it on the table!"

I had thought it was some delusion of my own, but all could see it now. There was a greenish-yellow phosphorescent light—or I should say a luminous vapour rather than a light—which lay over the surface of the table. It rolled and wreathed and undulated in dim glimmering folds, turning and swirling like clouds of smoke. I could see the white, square-ended hands of the French medium in this baleful light.

"What a fun!" he cried. "It is splendid!"

"Shall we call the alphabet?" asked Moir.

"But no—for we can do much better," said our visitor. "It is but a clumsy thing to tilt the table for every letter of the alphabet, and with such a medium as madame we should do better than that."

"Yes, you will do better," said a voice.

"Who was that? Who spoke? Was that you, Markham?"

"No, I did not speak."

"It was madame who spoke."

"But it was not her voice."

"Is that you, Mrs. Delamere?"

"It is not the medium, but it is the power which uses the organs of the medium," said the strange, deep voice.

"Where is Mrs. Delamere? It will not hurt her, I trust."

"The medium is happy in another plane of existence. She has taken my place, as I have taken hers."

"Who are you?"

"It cannot matter to you who I am. I am one who has lived as you are living, and who has died as you will die."

We heard the creak and grate of a cab pulling up next door. There was an argument about the fare, and the cabman grumbled hoarsely down the street. The green-yellow cloud still swirled faintly over the table, dull elsewhere, but glowing into a dim luminosity in the direction of the medium. It seemed to be piling itself up in front of her. A sense of fear and cold struck into my heart. It seemed to me that lightly and flippantly we had approached the most real and august of sacraments, that communion with the dead of which the fathers of the Church had spoken.

"Don't you think we are going too far? Should we not break up this séance?" I cried.

But the others were all earnest to see the end of it. They laughed at my scruples.

"All the powers are made for use," said Harvey Deacon. "If we *can* do this, we *should* do this. Every new departure of knowledge has been called unlawful in its inception. It is right and proper that we should inquire into the nature of death."

"It is right and proper," said the voice.

"There, what more could you ask?" cried Moir, who was much excited. "Let us have a test. Will you give us a test that you are really there?"

"What test do you demand?"

"Well, now—I have some coins in my pocket. Will you tell me how many?"

"We come back in the hope of teaching and of elevating, and not to guess childish riddles."

"Ha, ha, Meester Moir, you catch it that time," cried

the Frenchman. " But surely this is very good sense what the Control is saying."

" It is a religion, not a game," said the cold, hard voice.

" Exactly—the very view I take of it," cried Moir. " I am sure I am very sorry if I have asked a foolish question. You will not tell me who you are ? "

" What does it matter ? "

" Have you been a spirit long ? "

" Yes."

" How long ? "

" We cannot reckon time as you do. Our conditions are different."

" Are you happy ? "

" Yes."

" You would not wish to come back to life ? "

" No—certainly not."

" Are you busy ? "

" We could not be happy if we were not busy."

" What do you do ? "

" I have said that the conditions are entirely different."

" Can you give us no idea of your work ? "

" We labour for our own improvement and for the advancement of others."

" Do you like coming here to-night ? "

" I am glad to come if I can do any good by coming."

" Then to do good is your object ? "

" It is the object of all life on every plane."

" You see, Markham, that should answer your scruples."

It did, for my doubts had passed and only interest remained.

" Have you pain in your life ? " I asked.

" No ; pain is a thing of the body."

" Have you mental pain ? "

" Yes ; one may always be sad or anxious."

" Do you meet the friends whom you have known on earth ? "

"Some of them."

"Why only some of them?"

"Only those who are sympathetic."

"Do husbands meet wives?"

"Those who have truly loved."

"And the others?"

"They are nothing to each other."

"There must be a spiritual connection?"

"Of course."

"Is what we are doing right?"

"If done in the right spirit."

"What is the wrong spirit?"

"Curiosity and levity."

"May harm come of that?"

"Very serious harm."

"What sort of harm?"

"You may call up forces over which you have no control."

"Evil forces?"

"Undeveloped forces."

"You say they are dangerous. Dangerous to body or mind?"

"Sometimes to both."

There was a pause, and the blackness seemed to grow blacker still, while the yellow-green fog swirled and smoked upon the table.

"Any questions you would like to ask, Moir?" said Harvey Deacon.

"Only this—do you pray in your world?"

"One should pray in every world."

"Why?"

"Because it is the acknowledgment of forces outside ourselves."

"What religion do you hold over there?"

"We differ exactly as you do."

"You have no certain knowledge?"

"We have only faith."

"These questions of religion," said the Frenchman,

" they are of interest to you serious English people, but they are not so much fun. It seems to me that with this power here we might be able to have some great experience—*hein?* Something of which we could talk."

" But nothing could be more interesting than this," said Moir.

" Well, if you think so, that is very well," the Frenchman answered, peevishly. " For my part, it seems to me that I have heard all this before, and that to-night I should weesh to try some experiment with all this force which is given to us. But if you have other questions, then ask them, and when you are finish we can try something more."

But the spell was broken. We asked and asked, but the medium sat silent in her chair. Only her deep, regular breathing showed that she was there. The mist still swirled upon the table.

" You have disturbed the harmony. She will not answer."

" But we have learned already all that she can tell—*hein?* For my part I wish to see something that I have never seen before."

" What then ? "

" You will let me try ? "

" What would you do ? "

" I have said to you that thoughts are things. Now I wish to *prove* it to you, and to show you that which is only a thought. Yes, yes, I can do it and you will see. Now I ask you only to sit still and say nothing, and keep ever your hands quiet upon the table."

The room was blacker and more silent than ever. The same feeling of apprehension which had lain heavily upon me at the beginning of the séance was back at my heart once more. The roots of my hair were tingling.

" It is working ! It is working ! " cried the Frenchman, and there was a crack in his voice as he spoke which told me that he also was strung to his tightest.

The luminous fog drifted slowly off the table, and

wavered and flickered across the room. There in the farther and darkest corner it gathered and glowed, hardening down into a shining core—a strange, shifty, luminous, and yet non-illuminating patch of radiance, bright itself, but throwing no rays into the darkness. It had changed from a greenish-yellow to a dusky sullen red. Then round this centre there coiled a dark, smoky substance, thickening, hardening, growing denser and blacker. And then the light went out, smothered in that which had grown round it.

"It has gone."

"Hush—there's something in the room."

We heard it in the corner where the light had been, something which breathed deeply and fidgeted in the darkness.

"What is it? Le Duc, what have you done?"

"It is all right. No harm will come." The Frenchman's voice was treble with agitation.

"Good heavens, Moir, there's a large animal in the room. Here it is, close by my chair! Go away! Go away!"

It was Harvey Deacon's voice, and then came the sound of a blow upon some hard object. And then . . . And then . . . how can I tell you what happened then?

Some huge thing hurtled against us in the darkness, rearing, stamping, smashing, springing, snorting. The table was splintered. We were scattered in every direction. It clattered and scrambled amongst us, rushing with horrible energy from one corner of the room to another. We were all screaming with fear, grovelling upon our hands and knees to get away from it. Something trod upon my left hand, and I felt the bones splinter under the weight.

"A light! A light!" someone yelled.

"Moir, you have matches, matches!"

"No, I have none. Deacon, where are the matches? For God's sake, the matches!"

"I can't find them. Here, you Frenchman, stop it!"

" It is beyond me. Oh, *mon Dieu*, I cannot stop it. The door ! Where is the door ? "

My hand, by good luck, lit upon the handle as I groped about in the darkness. The hard-breathing, snorting, rushing creature tore past me and butted with a fearful crash against the oaken partition. The instant that it had passed I turned the handle, and next moment we were all outside, and the door shut behind us. From within came a horrible crashing and rending and stamping.

" What is it ? In Heaven's name, what is it ? "

" A horse. I saw it when the door opened. But Mrs. Delamere——? "

" We must fetch her out. Come on, Markham ; the longer we wait the less we shall like it."

He flung open the door and we rushed in. She was there on the ground amidst the splinters of her chair. We seized her and dragged her swiftly out, and as we gained the door I looked over my shoulder into the darkness. There were two strange eyes glowing at us, a rattle of hoofs, and I had just time to slam the door when there came a crash upon it which split it from top to bottom.

" It's coming through ! It's coming ! "

" Run, run for your lives ! " cried the Frenchman.

Another crash, and something shot through the riven door. It was a long white spike, gleaming in the lamplight. For a moment it shone before us, and then with a snap it disappeared again.

" Quick ! Quick ! This way ! " Harvey Deacon shouted. " Carry her in ! Here ! Quick ! "

We had taken refuge in the dining-room, and shut the heavy oak door. We laid the senseless woman upon the sofa, and as we did so, Moir, the hard man of business, drooped and fainted across the hearthrug. Harvey Deacon was as white as a corpse, jerking and twitching like an epileptic. With a crash we heard the studio door fly to pieces, and the snorting and stamping were in the passage, up and down, up and down, shaking the house with their fury. The Frenchman had sunk his face on his hands, and sobbed like a frightened child.

"What shall we do?" I shook him roughly by the shoulder. "Is a gun any use?"

"No, no. The power will pass. Then it will end."

"You might have killed us all—you unspeakable fool—with your infernal experiments."

"I did not know. How could I tell that it would be frightened? It is mad with terror. It was his fault. He struck it."

Harvey Deacon sprang up. "Good heavens!" he cried.

A terrible scream sounded through the house.

"It's my wife! Here, I'm going out. If it's the Evil One himself I am going out!"

He had thrown open the door and rushed out into the passage. At the end of it, at the foot of the stairs, Mrs. Deacon was lying senseless, struck down by the sight which she had seen. But there was nothing else.

With eyes of horror we looked about us, but all was perfectly quiet and still. I approached the black square of the studio door, expecting with every slow step that some atrocious shape would hurl itself out of it. But nothing came, and all was silent inside the room. Peeping and peering, our hearts in our mouths, we came to the very threshold, and stared into the darkness. There was still no sound, but in one direction there was also no darkness. A luminous, glowing cloud, with an incandescent centre, hovered in the corner of the room. Slowly it dimmed and faded, growing thinner and fainter, until at last the same dense, velvety blackness filled the whole studio. And with the last flickering gleam of that baleful light the Frenchman broke into a shout of joy.

"What a fun!" he cried. "No one is hurt, and only the door broken, and the ladies frightened. But, my friends, we have done what has never been done before."

"And as far as I can help," said Harvey Deacon, "it will certainly never be done again."

And that was what befell on the 14th of April last at No. 17 Badderly Gardens. I began by saying that it would seem too grotesque to dogmatise as to what it was which actually did occur; but I give my impressions, *our* impressions (since they are corroborated by Harvey Deacon and John Moir), for what they are worth. You may, if it pleases you, imagine that we were the victims of an elaborate and extraordinary hoax. Or you may think with us that we underwent a very real and a very terrible experience. Or perhaps you may know more than we do of such occult matters, and can inform us of some similar occurrence. In this latter case a letter to William Markham, 146M, The Albany, would help to throw a light upon that which is very dark to us.

44. *The Ring of Thoth*

MR. JOHN VANSITTART SMITH, F.R.S., of 147A Gower Street, was a man whose energy of purpose and clearness of thought might have placed him in the very first rank of scientific observers. He was the victim, however, of a universal ambition which prompted him to aim at distinction in many subjects rather than pre-eminence in one. In his early days he had shown an aptitude for zoology and for botany which caused his friends to look upon him as a second Darwin, but when a professorship was almost within his reach he had suddenly discontinued his studies and turned his whole attention to chemistry. Here his researches upon the spectra of the metals had won him his fellowship in the Royal Society; but again he played the coquette with his subject, and after a year's absence from the laboratory he joined the Oriental Society, and delivered a paper on the Hieroglyphic and Demotic inscriptions of El Kab, thus giving a crowning example both of the versatility and of the inconstancy of his talents.

The most fickle of wooers, however, is apt to be caught at last, and so it was with John Vansittart Smith. The more he burrowed his way into Egyptology the more impressed he became by the vast field which it opened to the inquirer, and by the extreme importance of a subject which promised to throw a light upon the first germs of human civilisation and the origin of the greater part of our arts and sciences. So struck was Mr. Smith that he straightway married an Egyptological young lady who had written upon the sixth dynasty, and having thus secured a sound base of operations he set himself to collect materials for a work which should unite the research of Lepsius and the ingenuity of Champollion. The preparation of this *magnum opus* entailed many hurried visits to the magnificent Egyptian collections of the Louvre, upon the last of which, no longer ago than the middle of last October, he became involved in a most strange and noteworthy adventure.

The trains had been slow and the Channel had been rough, so that the student arrived in Paris in a somewhat befogged and feverish condition. On reaching the Hôtel de France, in the Rue Laffitte, he had thrown himself upon a sofa for a couple of hours, but finding that he was unable to sleep, he determined, in spite of his fatigue, to make his way to the Louvre, settle the point which he had come to decide, and take the evening train back to Dieppe. Having come to his conclusion, he donned his greatcoat, for it was a raw rainy day, and made his way across the Boulevard des Italiens and down the Avenue de l'Opéra. Once in the Louvre he was on familiar ground, and he speedily made his way to the collection of papyri which it was his intention to consult.

The warmest admirers of John Vansittart Smith could hardly claim for him that he was a handsome man. His high-beaked nose and prominent chin had something of the same acute and incisive character which distinguished his intellect. He held his head in a birdlike fashion, and birdlike, too, was the pecking motion with which, in conversation, he threw out his objections and retorts. As he stood, with the high collar of his greatcoat raised to his ears, he might have seen from the reflection in the glass-case before him that his appearance was a singular one. Yet it came upon him as a sudden jar when an English voice behind him exclaimed in very audible tones, " What a queer-looking mortal ! "

The student had a large amount of petty vanity in his composition which manifested itself by an ostentatious and overdone disregard of all personal considerations. He straightened his lips and looked rigidly at the roll of papyrus, while his heart filled with bitterness against the whole race of travelling Britons.

" Yes," said another voice, " he really is an extraordinary fellow."

" Do you know," said the first speaker, " one could almost believe that by the continual contemplation of mummies the chap has become half a mummy himself ? "

" He has certainly an Egyptian cast of countenance," said the other.

John Vansittart Smith spun round upon his heel with the intention of shaming his countrymen by a corrosive remark or two. To his surprise and relief, the two young fellows who had been conversing had their shoulders turned towards him, and were gazing at one of the Louvre attendants who was polishing some brass-work at the other side of the room.

" Carter will be waiting for us at the Palais Royal," said one tourist to the other, glancing at his watch, and they clattered away, leaving the student to his labours.

" I wonder what these chatterers call an Egyptian cast of countenance," thought John Vansittart Smith, and he moved his position slightly in order to catch a glimpse of the man's face. He started as his eyes fell upon it. It was indeed the very face with which his studies had made him familiar. The regular statuesque features, broad brow, well-rounded chin, and dusky complexion were the exact counterpart of the innumerable statues, mummy-cases, and pictures which adorned the walls of the apartment. The thing was beyond all coincidence. The man must be an Egyptian. The national angularity of the shoulders and narrowness of the hips were alone sufficient to identify him.

John Vansittart Smith shuffled towards the attendant with some intention of addressing him. He was not light of touch in conversation, and found it difficult to strike the happy mean between the brusqueness of the superior and the geniality of the equal. As he came nearer, the man presented his side face to him, but kept his gaze still bent upon his work. Vansittart Smith, fixing his eyes upon the fellow's skin, was conscious of a sudden impression that there was something inhuman and preternatural about its appearance. Over the temple and cheek-bone it was as glazed and as shiny as varnished parchment. There was no suggestion of pores. One could not fancy a drop of moisture upon that arid surface. From brow to chin, however, it was cross-hatched by a million delicate wrinkles, which shot and interlaced as though Nature in some Maori mood had tried how wild and intricate a pattern she could devise.

"Où est la collection de Memphis?" asked the student, with the awkward air of a man who is devising a question merely for the purpose of opening a conversation.

"C'est là," replied the man brusquely, nodding his head at the other side of the room.

"Vous êtes un Egyptien, n'est-ce pas?" asked the Englishman.

The attendant looked up and turned his strange dark eyes upon his questioner. They were vitreous, with a misty dry shininess, such as Smith had never seen in a human head before. As he gazed into them he saw some strong emotion gather in their depths, which rose and deepened until it broke into a look of something akin both to horror and to hatred.

"Non, monsieur; je suis français." The man turned

abruptly and bent low over his polishing. The student gazed at him for a moment in astonishment, and then turning to a chair in a retired corner behind one of the doors he proceeded to make notes of his researches among the papyri. His thoughts, however, refused to return into their natural groove. They would run upon the enigmatical attendant with the sphinx-like face and the parchment skin.

"Where have I seen such eyes?" said Vansittart Smith to himself. "There is something saurian about them, something reptilian. There's the membrana nictitans of the snakes," he mused, bethinking himself of his zoological studies. "It gives a shiny effect. But there was something more here. There was a sense of power, of wisdom—so I read them—and of weariness, utter weariness, and ineffable despair. It may be all imagination, but I never had so strong an impression. By Jove, I must have another look at them!" He rose and paced round the Egyptian rooms, but the man who had excited his curiosity had disappeared.

The student sat down again in his quiet corner, and continued to work at his notes. He had gained the information which he required from the papyri, and it only remained to write it down while it was still fresh in his memory. For a time his pencil travelled rapidly over the paper, but soon the lines became less level, the words more blurred, and finally the pencil tinkled down upon the floor, and the head of the student dropped heavily forward upon his chest. Tired out by his journey, he slept so soundly in his lonely post behind the door that neither the clanking civil guard, nor the footsteps of sightseers, nor even the loud hoarse bell which gives the signal for closing, were sufficient to arouse him.

Twilight deepened into darkness, the bustle from the Rue de Rivoli waxed and then waned, distant Notre Dame clanged out the hour of midnight, and still the dark and lonely figure sat silently in the shadow. It was not until close upon one in the morning that, with a sudden gasp and an intaking of the breath, Vansittart Smith returned to consciousness. For a moment it flashed upon him that he had dropped asleep in his study-chair at home. The moon was shining fitfully through the unshuttered window, however, and as his eye ran along the lines of mummies and the endless array of polished cases, he remembered clearly where he was and how he came there. The student was not a nervous man. He possessed that love of a novel situation which is peculiar to his race. Stretching out his cramped limbs, he looked at his watch, and burst into a chuckle as he observed the hour. The episode would make an admirable anecdote to be introduced into his next paper as a relief to the graver and heavier speculations. He was a little cold, but wide awake and much refreshed. It was no wonder that the guardians had overlooked him, for the door threw its heavy black shadow right across him.

The complete silence was impressive. Neither outside nor inside was there a creak or a murmur. He was alone with the dead men of a dead civilisation. What though the outer city reeked of the garish nineteenth century! In all this chamber there was scarce an article, from the shrivelled ear of wheat to the pigment-box of the painter, which had not held its own against four thousand years. Here was the flotsam and jetsam washed up by the great ocean of time from that far-off empire. From stately Thebes, from lordly Luxor, from the great temples of Heliopolis, from a hundred rifled tombs, these relics had been brought. The student glanced round at the long-silent figures who flickered vaguely up through the gloom, at the busy toilers who were now so restful, and he fell into a reverent and thoughtful mood. An unwonted sense of his own youth and insignificance came over him. Leaning back in his chair, he gazed dreamily down the long vista of rooms, all silvery with the moonshine, which extend through the whole wing of the widespread building. His eyes fell upon the yellow glare of a distant lamp.

John Vansittart Smith sat up on his chair with his nerves all on edge. The light was advancing slowly towards him, pausing from time to time, and then coming jerkily onwards. The bearer moved noiselessly. In the utter silence there was no suspicion of the pat of a footfall. An idea of robbers entered the Englishman's head. He snuggled up farther into the corner. The light was two rooms off. Now it was in the next chamber, and still there was no sound. With something approaching to a thrill of fear the student observed a face, floating in the air as it were, behind the flare of the lamp. The figure was wrapped in shadow, but the light fell full upon the strange, eager face. There was no mistaking the metallic, glistening eyes and the cadaverous skin. It was the attendant with whom he had conversed.

Vansittart Smith's first impulse was to come forward and address him. A few words of explanation would set the matter clear, and lead doubtless to his being conducted to some side-door from which he might make his way to his hotel. As the man entered the chamber, however, there was something so stealthy in his movements, and so furtive in his expression, that the Englishman altered his intention. This was clearly no ordinary official walking the rounds. The fellow wore felt-soled slippers, stepped with a rising chest, and glanced quickly from left to right, while his hurried, gasping breathing thrilled the flame of his lamp. Vansittart Smith crouched silently back into the corner and watched him keenly, convinced that his errand was one of secret and probably sinister import.

There was no hesitation in the other's movements. He stepped lightly and swiftly across to one of the great cases, and, drawing a key from his pocket, he unlocked it. From the upper shelf he pulled down a mummy, which he bore away with him, and laid it with much care and solicitude upon the ground. By it he placed his lamp, and then squatting down beside it in Eastern fashion he began with long, quivering fingers to undo the cerecloths and bandages which girt it round. As the crackling rolls of linen peeled off one after the other, a strong aromatic odour filled the chamber, and fragments of scented wood and of spices pattered down upon the marble floor.

It was clear to John Vansittart Smith that this mummy had never been unswathed before. The operation interested him keenly. He thrilled all over with curiosity, and his bird-like head protruded farther and farther from behind the door. When, however, the last roll had been removed from the four-thousand-year-old head, it was all that he could do to stifle an outcry of amazement. First, a cascade of long, black, glossy tresses poured over the workman's hands and arms. A second turn of the bandage revealed a low, white forehead, with a pair of delicately arched eyebrows. A third uncovered a pair of bright, deeply fringed eyes, and a straight, well-cut nose, while a fourth and last showed a sweet, full, sensitive mouth, and a beautifully curved chin. The whole face was one of extraordinary loveliness, save for the one blemish that in the centre of the forehead there was a single irregular, coffee-coloured splotch. It was a triumph of the embalmer's art. Vansittart Smith's eyes grew larger and larger as he gazed upon it, and he chirruped in his throat with satisfaction.

Its effect upon the Egyptologist was as nothing, however, compared with that which it produced upon the strange attendant. He threw his hands up into the air, burst into a harsh clatter of words, and then, hurling himself down upon the ground beside the mummy, he threw his arms round her, and kissed her repeatedly upon the lips and brow. "Ma petite!" he groaned in French. "Ma pauvre petite!" His voice broke with emotion, and his innumerable wrinkles quivered and writhed, but the student observed in the lamp-light that his shining eyes were still dry and tearless as two beads of steel. For some minutes he lay, with a twitching face, crooning and moaning over the beautiful head. Then he broke into a sudden smile, said some words in an unknown tongue, and sprang to his feet with the vigorous air of one who has braced himself for an effort.

In the centre of the room there was a large, circular case which contained, as the student had frequently remarked, a magnificent collection of early Egyptian rings and precious stones. To this the attendant strode, and, unlocking it, threw it open. On the ledge at the side he placed his lamp, and beside it a small, earthenware jar which he had drawn from his pocket. He then took a handful of rings from the case, and with a most serious and anxious face he proceeded to smear each in turn with some liquid substance from the earthen pot, holding them to the light as he did so. He was clearly disappointed with the first lot, for he threw them petulantly back into the case and drew out some more. One of these, a massive ring with a large crystal set in it, he seized and eagerly tested with the contents of the jar. Instantly he uttered a cry of joy, and threw out his arms in a wild gesture which upset the pot and set the liquid streaming across the floor to the very feet of the Englishman. The attendant drew a red handkerchief from his bosom, and, mopping up the mess, he followed it into the corner, where in a moment he found himself face to face with his observer.

"Excuse me," said John Vansittart Smith, with all imaginable politeness; "I have been unfortunate enough to fall asleep behind this door."

"And you have been watching me?" the other asked in English, with a most venomous look on his corpse-like face.

The student was a man of veracity. "I confess," said he, "that I have noticed your movements, and that they have aroused my curiosity and interest in the highest degree."

The man drew a long, flamboyant-bladed knife from his bosom. "You have had a very narrow escape," he said; "had I seen you ten minutes ago, I should have driven this through your heart. As it is, if you touch me or interfere with me in any way you are a dead man."

"I have no wish to interfere with you," the student answered. "My presence here is entirely accidental. All I ask is that you will have the extreme kindness to show me out through some side-door." He spoke with great suavity, for the man was still pressing the tip of his dagger against the palm of his left hand, as though to assure himself of its sharpness, while his face preserved its malignant expression.

"If I thought——" said he. "But no, perhaps it is as well. What is your name?"

The Englishman gave it.

"Vansittart Smith," the other repeated. "Are you the same Vansittart Smith who gave a paper in London upon El Kab? I saw a report of it. Your knowledge of the subject is contemptible."

"Sir!" cried the Egyptologist.

"Yet it is superior to that of many who make even greater pretensions. The whole keystone of our old life in Egypt was not the inscriptions or monuments of which you make so much, but was our hermetic philosophy and mystic knowledge of which you say little or nothing."

"Our old life!" repeated the scholar, wide-eyed; and then suddenly, "Good God, look at the mummy's face!"

The strange man turned and flashed his light upon the dead woman, uttering a long, doleful cry as he did so. The action of the air had already undone all the art of the embalmer. The skin had fallen away, the eyes had sunk inwards, the discoloured lips had writhed away from the yellow teeth, and the brown mark upon the forehead alone showed that it was indeed the same face which had shown such youth and beauty a few short minutes before.

The man flapped his hands together in grief and horror.

Then mastering himself by a strong effort he turned his hard eyes once more upon the Englishman.

"It does not matter," he said, in a shaking voice. "It does not really matter. I came here to-night with the fixed determination to do something. It is now done. All else is as nothing. I have found my quest. The old curse is broken. I can rejoin her. What matter about her inanimate shell so long as her spirit is awaiting me at the other side of the veil!"

"These are wild words," said Vansittart Smith. He was becoming more and more convinced that he had to do with a madman.

"Time presses, and I must go," continued the other. "The moment is at hand for which I have waited this weary time. But I must show you out first. Come with me."

Taking up the lamp, he turned from the disordered chamber, and led the student swiftly through the long series of the Egyptian, Assyrian, and Persian apartments. At the end of the latter he pushed open a small door let into the wall and descended a winding, stone stair. The Englishman felt the cold, fresh air of the night upon his brow. There was a door opposite him which appeared to communicate with the street. To the right of this another door stood ajar, throwing a spurt of yellow light across the passage. "Come in here!" said the attendant shortly.

Vansittart Smith hesitated. He had hoped that he had come to the end of his adventure. Yet his curiosity was strong within him. He could not leave the matter unsolved, so he followed his strange companion into the lighted chamber.

It was a small room, such as is devoted to a *concierge*. A wood fire sparkled in the grate. At one side stood a truckle bed, and at the other a coarse, wooden chair, with a round table in the centre, which bore the remains of a meal. As the visitor's eye glanced round he could not but remark with an ever-recurring thrill that all the small details of the room were of the most quaint design and antique workmanship. The candlesticks, the vases upon the chimney-piece, the fire-irons, the ornaments upon the walls, were all such as he had been wont to associate with the remote past. The gnarled, heavy-eyed man sat himself down upon the edge of the bed, and motioned his guest into the chair.

"There may be design in this," he said, still speaking excellent English. "It may be decreed that I should leave some account behind as a warning to all rash mortals who would set their wits up against workings of Nature. I leave it with you. Make such use as you will of it. I speak to you now with my feet upon the threshold of the other world.

"I am, as you surmised, an Egyptian—not one of the down-trodden race of slaves who now inhabit the Delta of the Nile, but a survivor of that fiercer and harder people who tamed the Hebrew, drove the Ethiopian back into the southern deserts, and built those mighty works which have been the envy and the wonder of all after generations. It was in the reign of Tuthmosis, sixteen hundred years before the birth of Christ, that I first saw the light. You shrink away from me. Wait, and you will see that I am more to be pitied than to be feared.

"My name was Sosra. My father had been the chief priest of Osiris in the great temple of Abaris, which stood in those days upon the Bubastic branch of the Nile. I was brought up in the temple and was trained in all those mystic arts which are spoken of in your own Bible. I was an apt pupil. Before I was sixteen I had learned all which the wisest priest could teach me. From that time on I studied Nature's secrets for myself, and shared my knowledge with no man.

"Of all the questions which attracted me there were none over which I laboured so long as over those which concern themselves with the nature of life. I probed deeply into the vital principle. The aim of medicine had been to drive away disease when it appeared. It seemed to me that a method might be devised which should so fortify the body as to prevent weakness or death from ever taking hold of it. It is useless that I should recount my researches. You would scarce comprehend them if I did. They were carried out partly upon animals, partly upon slaves, and partly on myself. Suffice it that their result was to furnish me with a substance which, when injected into the blood, would endow the body with strength to resist the effects of time, of violence, or of disease. It would not indeed confer immortality, but its potency would endure for many thousands of years. I used it upon a cat, and afterwards drugged the creature with the most deadly poisons. That cat is alive in Lower Egypt at the present moment. There was nothing of mystery or magic in the matter. It was simply a chemical discovery, which may well be made again.

"Love of life runs high in the young. It seemed to me that I had broken away from all human care now that I had abolished pain and driven death to such a distance. With a light heart I poured the accursed stuff into my veins. Then I looked round for someone whom I could benefit. There was a young priest of Thoth, Parmes by name, who had won my goodwill by his earnest nature and his devotion to his studies. To him I whispered my secret, and at his request I injected him with my elixir. I should now, I reflected, never be without a companion of the same age as myself.

"After this grand discovery I relaxed my studies to some extent, but Parmes continued his with redoubled energy. Every day I could see him working with his flasks and his distiller in the Temple of Thoth, but he said little to me as to the result of his labours. For my own part, I used to walk through the city and look around me with exultation as I reflected that all this was destined to pass away, and that only I should remain. The people would bow to me as they passed me, for the fame of my knowledge had gone abroad.

"There was war at this time, and the Great King had sent down his soldiers to the eastern boundary to drive away the Hyksos. A Governor, too, was sent to Abaris, that he might hold it for the King. I had heard much of the beauty of the daughter of this Governor, but one day as I walked out with Parmes we met her, borne upon the shoulders of her slaves. I was struck with love as with lightning. My heart went out from me. I could have thrown myself beneath the feet of her bearers. This was my woman. Life without her was impossible. I swore by the head of Horus that she should be mine. I swore it to the Priest of Thoth. He turned away from me with a brow which was as black as midnight.

"There is no need to tell you of our wooing. She came to love me even as I loved her. I learned that Parmes had seen her before I did, and had shown her that he, too, loved her, but I could smile at his passion, for I knew that her heart was mine. The white plague had come upon the city and many were stricken, but I laid my hands upon the sick and nursed them without fear or scathe. She marvelled at my daring. Then I told her my secret, and begged her that she would let me use my art upon her.

"'Your flower shall then be unwithered, Atma,' I said. 'Other things may pass away, but you and I, and our great love for each other, shall outlive the tomb of King Chefru.'

"But she was full of timid, maidenly objections. 'Was it right?' she asked, 'was it not a thwarting of the will of the gods? If the great Osiris had wished that our years should be so long, would he not himself have brought it about?'

"With fond and loving words I overcame her doubts, and yet she hesitated. It was a great question, she said. She would think it over for this one night. In the morning I should know of her resolution. Surely one night was not too much to ask. She wished to pray to Isis for help in her decision.

"With a sinking heart and a sad foreboding of evil I left her with her tirewomen. In the morning, when the early sacrifice was over, I hurried to her house. A frightened slave met me upon the steps. Her mistress was ill, she said, very ill. In a frenzy I broke my way through the attendants, and rushed through hall and corridor to my Atma's chamber. She lay upon her couch, her head high upon the pillow, with a pallid face and a glazed eye. On her forehead there blazed a single angry, purple patch. I knew that hell-mark of old. It was the scar of the white plague, the sign-manual of death.

"Why should I speak of that terrible time? For months I was mad, fevered, delirious, and yet I could not die. Never did an Arab thirst after the sweet wells as I longed after death. Could poison or steel have shortened the thread of my existence, I should soon have rejoined my love in the land with the narrow portal. I tried, but it was of no avail. The accursed influence was too strong upon me. One night as I lay upon my couch, weak and weary, Parmes, the priest of Thoth, came to my chamber. He stood in the circle of the lamp-light, and he looked down upon me with eyes which were bright with a mad joy.

"'Why did you let the maiden die?' he asked; 'why did you not strengthen her as you strengthened me?'

"'I was too late,' I answered. 'But I had forgot. You also loved her. You are my fellow in misfortune. Is it not terrible to think of the centuries which must pass ere we look upon her again? Fools, fools, that we were to take death to be our enemy!'

"'You may say that,' he cried with a wild laugh; 'the words come well from your lips. For me they have no meaning.'

"'What mean you?' I cried, raising myself upon my elbow. 'Surely, friend, this grief has turned your brain.' His face was aflame with joy, and he writhed and shook like one who hath a devil.

"'Do you know whither I go?' he asked.

"'Nay,' I answered, 'I cannot tell.'

"'I go to her,' said he. 'She lies embalmed in the farther tomb by the double palm-tree beyond the city wall.'

"'Why do you go there?' I asked.

"'To die!' he shrieked, 'to die! I am not bound by earthen fetters.'

"'But the elixir is in your blood,' I cried.

"'I can defy it,' said he; 'I have found a stronger principle which will destroy it. It is working in my veins at this moment, and in an hour I shall be a dead man. I shall join her, and you shall remain behind.'

"As I looked upon him I could see that he spoke words of truth. The light in his eye told me that he was indeed beyond the power of the elixir.

"'You will teach me!' I cried.

"'Never!' he answered.

"'I implore you, by the wisdom of Thoth, by the majesty of Anubis!'

"'It is useless,' he said coldly.

"'Then I will find it out,' I cried.

"'You cannot,' he answered; 'it came to me by chance. There is one ingredient which you can never get. Save that which is in the ring of Thoth, none will ever more be made.'

"'In the ring of Thoth!' I repeated, 'where then is the ring of Thoth?'

"'That also you shall never know,' he answered. 'You won her love. Who has won in the end? I leave you to your sordid earth life. My chains are broken. I must go!' He turned upon his heel and fled from the chamber. In the morning came the news that the Priest of Thoth was dead.

"My days after that were spent in study. I must find this subtle poison which was strong enough to undo the elixir. From early dawn to midnight I bent over the test-tube and the furnace. Above all, I collected the papyri and the chemical flasks of the Priest of Thoth. Alas! they taught me little. Here and there some hint or stray expression would raise hope in my bosom, but no good ever came of it. Still, month after month, I struggled on. When my heart grew faint I would make my way to the tomb by the palm-trees. There, standing by the dead casket from which the jewel had been rifled, I would feel her sweet presence, and would whisper to her that I would rejoin her if mortal wit could solve the riddle.

"Parmes had said that his discovery was connected with the ring of Thoth. I had some remembrance of the trinket. It was a large and weighty circlet, made, not of gold, but of a rarer and heavier metal brought from the mines of Mount Harbal. Platinum, you call it. The ring had, I remembered, a hollow crystal set in it, in which some few drops of liquid might be stored. Now, the secret of Parmes could not have to do with the metal alone, for there were many rings of that metal in the Temple. Was it not more likely that he had stored his precious poison within the cavity of the crystal? I had scarce come to this conclusion before, in hunting through his papers, I came upon one which told me that it was indeed so, and that there was still some of the liquid unused.

"But how to find the ring? It was not upon him when he was stripped for the embalmer. Of that I made sure. Neither was it among his private effects. In vain I searched every room that he had entered, every box and vase and chattel that he had owned. I sifted the very sand of the desert in the places where he had been wont to walk; but, do what I would, I could come upon no traces of the ring of Thoth. Yet it may be that my labours would have overcome all obstacles had it not been for a new and unlooked-for misfortune.

"A great war had been waged against the Hyksos, and the Captains of the Great King had been cut off in the desert, with all their bowmen and horsemen. The shepherd tribes were upon us like the locusts in a dry year. From the wilderness of Shur to the great, bitter lake there was blood by day and fire by night. Abaris was the bulwark of Egypt, but we could not keep the savages back. The city fell. The Governor and the soldiers were put to the sword, and I, with many more, was led away into captivity.

"For years and years I tended cattle in the great plains by the Euphrates. My master died, and his son grew old, but I was still as far from death as ever. At last I escaped upon a swift camel, and made my way back to Egypt. The Hyksos had settled in the land which they had conquered, and their own King ruled over the country. Abaris had been torn down, the city had been burned, and of the great Temple there was nothing left save an unsightly mound. Everywhere the tombs had been rifled and the monuments destroyed. Of my Atma's grave no sign was left. It was buried in the sands of the desert, and the palm-trees which marked the spot had long disappeared. The papers of Parmes and the remains of the Temple of Thoth were either destroyed or scattered far and wide over the deserts of Syria. All search after them was vain.

"From that time I gave up all hope of ever finding the ring or discovering the subtle drug. I set myself to live as patiently as might be until the effect of the elixir should wear away. How can you understand how terrible a thing time is, you who have experience only of the narrow course which lies between the cradle and the grave! I know it to my cost, I who have floated down the whole stream of history. I was old when Ilium fell. I was very old when Herodotus came to Memphis. I was bowed down with years when the new gospel came upon earth. Yet you see me much as other men are, with the cursed elixir still sweetening my blood, and guarding me against that which I would court. Now, at last, at last I have come to the end of it!

"I have travelled in all lands and I have dwelt with

all nations. Every tongue is the same to me. I learned them all to help pass the weary time. I need not tell you how slowly they drifted by, the long dawn of modern civilization, the dreary middle years, the dark times of barbarism. They are all behind me now. I have never looked with the eyes of love upon another woman. Atma knows that I have been constant to her.

"It was my custom to read all that the scholars had to say upon Ancient Egypt. I have been in many positions, sometimes affluent, sometimes poor, but I have always found enough to enable me to buy the journals which deal with such matters. Some nine months ago I was in San Francisco, when I read an account of some discoveries made in the neighbourhood of Abaris. My heart leapt into my mouth as I read it. It said that the excavator had busied himself in exploring some tombs recently unearthed. In one there had been found an unopened mummy with an inscription upon the outer case setting forth that it contained the body of the daughter of the Governor of the city in the days of Tuthmosis. It added that on removing the outer case there had been exposed a large platinum ring set with a crystal, which had been laid upon the breast of the embalmed woman. This, then, was where Parmes had hid the ring of Thoth. He might well say that it was safe, for no Egyptian would ever stain his soul by moving even the outer case of a buried friend.

"That very night I set off from San Francisco, and in a few weeks I found myself once more at Abaris, if a few sand-heaps and crumbling walls may retain the name of the great city. I hurried to the Frenchmen who were digging there and asked them for the ring. They replied that both the ring and the mummy had been sent to the Boulak Museum at Cairo. To Boulak I went, but only to be told that Mariette Bey had claimed them and had shipped them to the Louvre. I followed them, and there, at last, in the Egyptian chamber, I came, after close upon four thousand years, upon the remains of my Atma, and upon the ring for which I had sought so long.

"But how was I to lay hands upon them? How was I to have them for my very own? It chanced that the office of attendant was vacant. I went to the Director. I convinced him that I knew much about Egypt. In my eagerness I said too much. He remarked that a Professor's chair would suit me better than a seat in the conciergerie. I knew more, he said, than he did. It was only by blundering, and letting him think that he had over-estimated my knowledge, that I prevailed upon him to let me move the few effects which I have retained into this chamber. It is my first and my last night here.

"Such is my story, Mr. Vansittart Smith. I need not say more to a man of your perception. By a strange chance you have this night looked upon the face of the woman whom I loved in those far-off days. There were many rings with crystals in the case, and I had to test for the platinum to be sure of the one which I wanted. A glance at the crystal has shown me that the liquid is indeed within it, and that I shall at last be able to shake off that accursed health which has been worse to me than the foulest disease. I have nothing more to say to you. I have unburdened myself. You may tell my story or you may withhold it at your pleasure. The choice rests with you. I owe you some amends, for you have had a narrow escape of your life this night. I was a desperate man, and not to be baulked in my purpose. Had I seen you before the thing was done, I might have put it beyond your power to oppose me or to raise an alarm. This is the door. It leads into the Rue de Rivoli. Good night."

The Englishman glanced back. For a moment the lean figure of Sosra the Egyptian stood framed in the narrow doorway. The next the door had slammed, and the heavy rasping of a bolt broke on the silent night.

It was on the second day after his return to London

that Mr. John Vansittart Smith saw the following concise narrative in the Paris correspondence of *The Times* :—

"*Curious Occurrence in the Louvre.*—Yesterday morning a strange discovery was made in the principal Eastern chamber. The *ouvriers* who are employed to clean out the rooms in the morning found one of the attendants lying dead upon the floor with his arms round one of the mummies. So close was his embrace that it was only with the utmost difficulty that they were separated. One of the cases containing valuable rings had been opened and rifled. The authorities are of opinion that the man was bearing away the mummy with some idea of selling it to a private collector, but that he was struck down in the very act by long-standing disease of the heart. It is said that he was a man of uncertain age and eccentric habits, without any living relations to mourn over his dramatic and untimely end."

45. *The Los Amigos Fiasco*

I USED to be the leading practitioner of Los Amigos. Of course, every one has heard of the great electrical generating gear there. The town is widespread, and there are dozens of little townlets and villages all around, which receive their supply from the same centre, so that the works are on a very large scale. The Los Amigos folk say that they are the largest upon earth, but then we claim that for everything in Los Amigos except the gaol and the death-rate. Those are said to be the smallest.

Now, with so fine an electrical supply, it seemed to be a sinful waste of hemp that the Los Amigos criminals should perish in the old-fashioned manner. And then came the news of the electrocutions in the East, and how the results had not after all been so instantaneous as had been hoped. The Western engineers raised their eyebrows when they read of the puny shocks by which these men had perished, and they vowed in Los Amigos that when an irreclaimable came their way he should be dealt handsomely by, and have the run of all the big dynamos.

There should be no reserve, said the engineers, but he should have all that they had got. And what the result of that would be none could predict, save that it must be absolutely blasting and deadly. Never before had a man been so charged with electricity as they would charge him. He was to be smitten by the essence of ten thunderbolts. Some prophesied combustion, and some disintegration and disappearance. They were waiting eagerly to settle the question by actual demonstration, and it was just at that moment that Duncan Warner came that way.

Warner had been wanted by the law, and by nobody else, for many years. Desperado, murderer, train robber and road agent, he was a man beyond the pale of human pity. He had deserved a dozen deaths, and the Los Amigos folk grudged him so gaudy a one as that. He seemed to feel himself to be unworthy of it, for he made two frenzied attempts at escape. He was a powerful, muscular man, with a lion head, tangled black locks, and a sweeping beard which covered his broad chest. When he was tried, there was no finer head in all the crowded court. It's no new thing to find the best face looking from the dock. But his good looks could not balance his bad deeds. His advocate did all he knew, but the cards lay against him, and Duncan Warner was handed over to the mercy of the big Los Amigos dynamos.

I was there at the committee meeting when the matter was discussed. The town council had chosen four experts to look after the arrangements. Three of them were admirable. There was Joseph M'Connor, the very man who had designed the dynamos, and there was Joshua Westmacott, the chairman of the Los Amigos Electrical Supply Company, Limited. Then there was myself as the chief medical man, and lastly an old German of the name of Peter Stulpnagel. The Germans were a strong body at Los Amigos, and they all voted for their man. That was how he got on the committee.

It was said that he had been a wonderful electrician at home, and he was eternally working with wires and insulators and Leyden jars; but, as he never seemed to get any further, or to have any results worth publishing, he came at last to be regarded as a harmless crank, who had made science his hobby. We three practical men smiled when we heard that he had been elected as our colleague, and at the meeting we fixed it all up very nicely among ourselves without much thought of the old fellow who sat with his ears scooped forward in his hands, for he was a trifle hard of hearing, taking no more part in the proceedings than the gentlemen of the press who scribbled their notes on the back benches.

We did not take long to settle it all. In New York a strength of some two thousand volts had been used, and death had not been instantaneous. Evidently their shock had been too weak. Los Amigos should not fall into that error. The charge should be six times greater, and therefore, of course, it would be six times more effective. Nothing could possibly be more logical. The whole concentrated force of the great dynamos should be employed on Duncan Warner.

So we three settled it, and had already risen to break up the meeting, when our silent companion opened his mouth for the first time.

"Gentlemen," said he, "you appear to me to show an extraordinary ignorance upon the subject of electricity. You have not mastered the first principles of its actions upon a human being."

The committee was about to break into an angry reply to this brusque comment, but the chairman of the Electrical Company tapped his forehead to claim its indulgence for the crankiness of the speaker.

"Pray tell us, sir," said he, with an ironical smile, "what is there in our conclusions with which you find fault?"

"With your assumption that a large dose of electricity will merely increase the effect of a small dose. Do you not think it possible that it might have an entirely different result? Do you know anything, by actual experiment, of the effect of such powerful shocks?"

"We know it by analogy," said the chairman pompously. "All drugs increase their effect when they increase their dose; for example—for example——"

"Whisky," said Joseph M'Connor.

"Quite so. Whisky. You see it there."

Peter Stulpnagel smiled and shook his head.

"Your argument is not very good," said he. "When I used to take whisky, I used to find that one glass would excite me, but that six would send me to sleep, which is just the opposite. Now, suppose that electricity were to act in just the opposite way also, what then?"

We three practical men burst out laughing. We had known that our colleague was queer, but we never had thought that he would be as queer as this.

"What then?" repeated Peter Stulpnagel.

"We'll take our chances," said the chairman.

"Pray consider," said Peter, "that workmen who have touched the wires, and who have received shocks of only a few hundred volts, have died instantly. The fact is well known. And yet when a much greater force was used upon a criminal at New York, the man struggled for some little time. Do you not clearly see that the smaller dose is the more deadly?"

"I think, gentlemen, that this discussion has been carried on quite long enough," said the chairman, rising again. "The point, I take it, has already been decided by the majority of the committee, and Duncan Warner shall be electrocuted on Tuesday by the full strength of the Los Amigos dynamos. Is it not so?"

"I agree," said Joseph M'Connor.

"I agree," said I.

"And I protest," said Peter Stulpnagel.

"Then the motion is carried, and your protest will be duly entered in the minutes," said the chairman, and so the sitting was dissolved.

The attendance at the electrocution was a very small one. We four members of the committee were, of course, present with the executioner, who was to act under their orders. The others were the United States Marshal, the governor of the gaol, the chaplain, and three members of the press. The room was a small, brick chamber, forming an out-house to the Central Electrical station. It had been used as a laundry, and had an oven and copper at one side, but no other furniture save a single chair for the condemned man. A metal plate for his feet was placed in front of it, to which ran a thick, insulated wire. Above, another wire depended from the ceiling, which could be connected with a small, metallic rod projecting from a cap which was to be placed upon his head. When this connection was established Duncan Warner's hour was come.

There was a solemn hush as we waited for the coming of the prisoner. The practical engineers looked a little pale, and fidgeted nervously with the wires. Even the hardened Marshal was ill at ease, for a mere hanging was one thing, and this blasting of flesh and blood a very different one. As to the pressmen, their faces were whiter than the sheets which lay before them. The only man who appeared to feel none of the influence of these preparations was the little German crank, who strolled from one to the other with a smile on his lips and mischief in his eyes. More than once he even went so far as to burst into a shout of laughter, until the chaplain sternly rebuked him for his ill-timed levity.

"How can you so far forget yourself, Mr. Stulpnagel," said he, "as to jest in the presence of death?"

But the German was quite unabashed.

"If I were in the presence of death I should not jest," said he, "but since I am not I may do what I choose."

This flippant reply was about to draw another and a sterner reproof from the chaplain, when the door was swung open and two warders entered leading Duncan

Warner between them. He glanced round him with a set face, stepped resolutely forward, and seated himself upon the chair.

"Touch her off!" said he.

It was barbarous to keep him in suspense. The chaplain murmured a few words in his ear, the attendant placed the cap upon his head, and then, while we all held our breath, the wire and the metal were brought in contact.

"Great Scott!" shouted Duncan Warner.

He had bounded in his chair as the frightful shock crashed through his system. But he was not dead. On the contrary, his eyes gleamed far more brightly than they had done before. There was only one change, but it was a singular one. The black had passed from his hair and beard as the shadow passes from a landscape. They were both as white as snow. And yet there was no other sign of decay. His skin was smooth and plump and lustrous as a child's.

The Marshal looked at the committee with a reproachful eye.

"There seems to be some hitch here, gentlemen," said he.

We three practical men looked at each other.

Peter Stulpnagel smiled pensively.

"I think that another one should do it," said I.

Again the connection was made, and again Duncan Warner sprang in his chair and shouted, but, indeed, were it not that he still remained in the chair none of us would have recognised him. His hair and his beard had shredded off in an instant, and the room looked like a barber's shop on a Saturday night. There he sat, his eyes still shining, his skin radiant with the glow of perfect health, but with a scalp as bald as a Dutch cheese, and a chin without so much as a trace of down. He began to revolve one of his arms, slowly and doubtfully at first, but with more confidence as he went on.

"That jint," said he, "has puzzled half the doctors

on the Pacific Slope. It's as good as new, and as limber as a hickory twig."

"You are feeling pretty well?" asked the old German.

"Never better in my life," said Duncan Warner cheerily.

The situation was a painful one. The Marshal glared at the committee. Peter Stulpnagel grinned and rubbed his hands. The engineers scratched their heads. The bald-headed prisoner revolved his arm and looked pleased.

"I think that one more shock——" began the chairman.

"No, sir," said the Marshal; "we've had foolery enough for one morning. We are here for an execution, and an execution we'll have."

"What do you propose?"

"There's a hook handy upon the ceiling. Fetch a rope, and we'll soon set this matter straight."

There was another awkward delay while the warders departed for the cord. Peter Stulpnagel bent over Duncan Warner, and whispered something in his ear. The desperado stared in surprise.

"You don't say?" he asked.

The German nodded.

"What! No ways?"

Peter shook his head, and the two began to laugh as though they shared some huge joke between them.

The rope was brought, and the Marshal himself slipped the noose over the criminal's neck. Then the two warders, the assistant and he swung their victim into the air. For half an hour he hung—a dreadful sight—from the ceiling. Then in solemn silence they lowered him down, and one of the warders went out to order the shell to be brought round. But as he touched ground again what was our amazement when Duncan Warner put his hands up to his neck, loosened the noose, and took a long, deep breath.

"Paul Jefferson's sale is goin' well," he remarked

" I could see the crowd from up yonder," and he nodded at the hook in the ceiling.

" Up with him again ! " shouted the Marshal, " we'll get the life out of him somehow."

In an instant the victim was up at the hook once more. They kept him there for an hour, but when he came down he was perfectly garrulous.

" Old man Plunket goes too much to the Arcady Saloon," said he. " Three times he's been there in an hour ; and him with a family. Old man Plunket would do well to swear off."

It was monstrous and incredible, but there it was. There was no getting round it. The man was there talking when he ought to have been dead. We all sat staring in amazement, but United States Marshal Carpenter was not a man to be euchred so easily. He motioned the others to one side, so that the prisoner was left standing alone.

" Duncan Warner," said he slowly, " you are here to play your part, and I am here to play mine. Your game is to live if you can, and my game is to carry out the sentence of the law. You've beat us on electricity. I'll give you one there. And you've beat us on hanging, for you seem to thrive on it. But it's my turn to beat you now, for my duty has to be done."

He pulled a six-shooter from his coat as he spoke, and fired all the shots through the body of the prisoner. The room was so filled with smoke that we could see nothing, but when it cleared the prisoner was still standing there, looking down in disgust at the front of his coat.

" Coats must be cheap where you come from," said he. " Thirty dollars it cost me, and look at it now. The six holes in front are bad enough, but four of the balls have passed out, and a pretty fine state the back must be in."

The Marshal's revolver fell from his hand, and he dropped his arms to his sides, a beaten man.

"Maybe some of you gentlemen can tell me what this means," said he, looking helplessly at the committee.

Peter Stulpnagel took a step forward.

"I'll tell you all about it," said he.

"You seem to be the only person who knows anything."

"I *am* the only person who knows anything. I should have warned these gentlemen; but, as they would not listen to me, I have allowed them to learn by experience. What you have done with your electricity is that you have increased the man's vitality until he can defy death for centuries."

"Centuries!"

"Yes, it will take the wear of hundreds of years to exhaust the enormous nervous energy with which you have drenched him. Electricity is life, and you have charged him with it to the utmost. Perhaps in fifty years you might execute him, but I am not sanguine about it."

"Great Scott! What shall I do with him?" cried the unhappy Marshal.

Peter Stulpnagel shrugged his shoulders.

"It seems to me that it does not much matter what you do with him now," said he.

"Maybe we could drain the electricity out of him again. Suppose we hang him up by the heels?"

"No, no, it's out of the question."

"Well, well, he shall do no more mischief in Los Amigos, anyhow," said the Marshal, with decision. "He shall go into the new gaol. The prison will wear him out."

"On the contrary," said Peter Stulpnagel, "I think that it is much more probable that he will wear out the prison."

It was rather a fiasco, and for years we didn't talk more about it than we could help, but it's no secret now, and I thought you might like to jot down the facts in your case-book.

46. *How it Happened*

SHE was a writing medium. This is what she wrote :—

I can remember some things upon that evening most distinctly, and others are like some vague, broken dreams. That is what makes it so difficult to tell a connected story. I have no idea now what it was that had taken me to London and brought me back so late. It just merges into all my other visits to London. But from the time that I got out at the little country station everything is extraordinarily clear. I can live it again—every instant of it.

I remember so well walking down the platform and looking at the illuminated clock at the end which told me that it was half-past eleven. I remember also my wondering whether I could get home before midnight. Then I remember the big motor, with its glaring headlights and glitter of polished brass, waiting for me outside. It was my new thirty-horse-power Robur, which had only been delivered that day. I remember also asking Perkins, my chauffeur, how she had gone, and his saying that he thought she was excellent.

" I'll try her myself," said I, and I climbed into the driver's seat.

" The gears are not the same," said he. " Perhaps, sir, I had better drive."

" No ; I should like to try her," said I.

And so we started on the five-mile drive for home.

My old car had the gears as they used always to be in notches on a bar. In this car you passed the gear-lever through a gate to get on the higher ones. It was not difficult to master, and soon I thought that I understood it. It was foolish, no doubt, to begin to learn a new system in the dark, but one often does foolish things.

and one has not always to pay the full price for them. I got along very well until I came to Claystall Hill. It is one of the worst hills in England, a mile and a half long and one in six in places, with three fairly sharp curves. My park gate stands at the very foot of it upon the main London road.

We were just over the brow of this hill, where the grade is steepest, when the trouble began. I had been on the top speed, and wanted to get her on the free; but she stuck between gears, and I had to get her back on the top again. By this time she was going at a great rate, so I clapped on both brakes, and one after the other they gave way. I didn't mind so much when I felt my footbrake snap, but when I put all my weight on my side-brake, and the lever clanged to its full limit without a catch, it brought a cold sweat out of me. By this time we were fairly tearing down the slope. The lights were brilliant, and I brought her round the first curve all right. Then we did the second one, though it was a close shave for the ditch. There was a mile of straight then with the third curve beneath it, and after that the gate of the park. If I could shoot into that harbour all would be well, for the slope up to the house would bring her to a stand.

Perkins behaved splendidly. I should like that to be known. He was perfectly cool and alert. I had thought at the very beginning of taking the bank, and he read my intention.

"I wouldn't do it, sir," said he. "At this pace it must go over and we should have it on the top of us."

Of course he was right. He got to the electric switch and had it off, so we were in the free; but we were still running at a fearful pace. He laid his hands on the wheel.

"I'll keep her steady," said he, "if you care to jump and chance it. We can never get round that curve. Better jump, sir."

"No," said I; "I'll stick it out. You can jump if you like."

"I'll stick it with you, sir," said he.

If it had been the old car I should have jammed the gear-lever into the reverse, and seen what would happen. I expect she would have stripped her gears or smashed up somehow, but it would have been a chance. As it was, I was helpless. Perkins tried to climb across, but you couldn't do it going at that pace. The wheels were whirring like a high wind and the big body creaking and groaning with the strain. But the lights were brilliant, and one could steer to an inch. I remember thinking what an awful and yet majestic sight we should appear to anyone who met us. It was a narrow road, and we were just a great, roaring, golden death to anyone who came in our path.

We got round the corner with one wheel three feet high upon the bank. I thought we were surely over, but after staggering for a moment she righted and darted onwards. That was the third corner and the last one. There was only the park gate now. It was facing us, but, as luck would have it, not facing us directly. It was about twenty yards to the left up the main road into which we ran. Perhaps I could have done it, but I expect that the steering-gear had been jarred when we ran on the bank. The wheel did not turn easily. We shot out of the lane. I saw the open gate on the left. I whirled round my wheel with all the strength of my wrists. Perkins and I threw our bodies across, and then the next instant, going at fifty miles an hour, my right wheel struck full on the right-hand pillar of my own gate. I heard the crash. I was conscious of flying through the air, and then—and then——!

When I became aware of my own existence once more I was among some brushwood in the shadow of the oaks upon the lodge side of the drive. A man was standing beside me. I imagined at first that it was Perkins, but when I looked again I saw that it was Stanley, a man whom I had known at college some years before, and for whom I had a really genuine affection. There was always something peculiarly sympathetic to me in Stanley's personality; and I was proud to think that I had some similar influence upon him. At the present moment I was surprised to see him, but I was like a man in a dream, giddy and shaken and quite prepared to take things as I found them without questioning them.

"What a smash!" I said. "Good Lord, what an awful smash!"

He nodded his head, and even in the gloom I could see that he was smiling the gentle, wistful smile which I connected with him.

I was quite unable to move. Indeed, I had not any desire to try to move. But my senses were exceedingly alert. I saw the wreck of the motor lit up by the moving lanterns. I saw the little group of people and heard the hushed voices. There were the lodge-keeper and his wife, and one or two more. They were taking no notice of me, but were very busy round the car. Then suddenly I heard a cry of pain.

"The weight is on him. Lift it easy," cried a voice.

"It's only my leg!" said another one, which I recognised as Perkins's. "Where's master?" he cried.

"Here I am," I answered, but they did not seem to hear me. They were all bending over something which lay in front of the car.

Stanley laid his hand upon my shoulder, and his touch was inexpressibly soothing. I felt light and happy, in spite of all.

"No pain, of course?" said he.

"None," said I.

"There never is," said he.

And then suddenly a wave of amazement passed over me. Stanley! Stanley! Why, Stanley had surely died of enteric at Bloemfontein in the Boer War!

"Stanley!" I cried, and the words seemed to choke my throat—"Stanley, you are dead."

He looked at me with the same old gentle, wistful smile.

"So are you," he answered.

47. *Lot No. 249*

OF the dealings of Edward Bellingham with William Monkhouse Lee, and of the cause of the great terror of Abercrombie Smith, it may be that no absolute and final judgment will ever be delivered. It is true that we have the full and clear narrative of Smith himself, and such corroboration as he could look for from Thomas Styles the servant, from the Reverend Plumptree Peterson, Fellow of Old's, and from such other people as chanced to gain some passing glance at this or that incident in a singular chain of events. Yet, in the main, the story must rest upon Smith alone, and the most will think that it is more likely that one brain, however outwardly sane, has some subtle warp in its texture, some strange flaw in its workings, than that the path of Nature has been overstepped in open day in so famed a centre of learning and light as the University of Oxford. Yet when we think how narrow and how devious this path of Nature is, how dimly we can trace it, for all our lamps of science, and how from the darkness which girds it round great and terrible possibilities loom ever shadowly upwards, it is a bold and confident man who will put a limit to the strange by-paths into which the human spirit may wander.

In a certain wing of what we will call Old College in Oxford there is a corner turret of an exceeding great age. The heavy arch which spans the open door has bent downwards in the centre under the weight of its years, and the grey, lichen-blotched blocks of stone are bound and knitted together with withes and strands of ivy, as though the old mother had set herself to brace them up against wind and weather. From the door a stone stair curves upward spirally, passing two landings, and terminating in a third one, its steps all shapeless and hollowed by the tread of so many generations of the seekers after knowledge. Life has flowed like water down this winding stair, and, waterlike, has left these smooth-worn grooves behind it. From the long-gowned, pedantic scholars of Plantagenet days down to the young bloods of a later age, how full and strong had been that tide of young, English life. And what was left now of all those hopes, those strivings, those fiery energies, save here and there in some old-world churchyard a few scratches upon a stone, and perchance a handful of dust in a mouldering coffin? Yet here were the silent stair and the grey, old wall, with bend and saltire and many another heraldic device still to be read upon its surface, like grotesque shadows thrown back from the days that had passed.

In the month of May, in the year 1884, three young men occupied the sets of rooms which opened on to the separate landings of the old stair. Each set consisted simply of a sitting-room and of a bedroom, while the two corresponding rooms upon the ground-floor were used, the one as a coal-cellar, and the other as the living-room of the servant, or scout, Thomas Styles, whose duty it was to wait upon the three men above him. To right and to left was a line of lecture-rooms and of offices, so that the dwellers in the old turret enjoyed a certain seclusion, which made the chambers popular among the more studious undergraduates. Such were the three who occupied them now—Abercrombie Smith above, Edward Bellingham beneath him, and William Monkhouse Lee upon the lowest storey.

It was ten o'clock on a bright, spring night, and Abercrombie Smith lay back in his arm-chair, his feet upon the fender, and his briar-root pipe between his lips. In a similar chair, and equally at his ease, there lounged on the other side of the fireplace his old school friend Jephro

Hastie. Both men were in flannels, for they had spent their evening upon the river, but apart from their dress no one could look at their hard-cut, alert faces without seeing that they were open-air men—men whose minds and tastes turned naturally to all that was manly and robust. Hastie, indeed, was stroke of his college boat, and Smith was an even better oar, but a coming examination had already cast its shadow over him and held him to his work, save for the few hours a week which health demanded. A litter of medical books upon the table, with scattered bones, models, and anatomical plates, pointed to the extent as well as the nature of his studies, while a couple of single-sticks and a set of boxing-gloves above the mantelpiece hinted at the means by which, with Hastie's help, he might take his exercise in its most compressed and least-distant form. They knew each other very well—so well that they could sit now in that soothing silence which is the very highest development of companionship.

"Have some whisky," said Abercrombie Smith at last between two cloudbursts. "Scotch in the jug and Irish in the bottle."

"No, thanks. I'm in for the sculls. I don't liquor when I'm training. How about you?"

"I'm reading hard. I think it best to leave it alone."

Hastie nodded, and they relapsed into a contented silence.

"By the way, Smith," asked Hastie, presently, "have you made the acquaintance of either of the fellows on your stair yet?"

"Just a nod when we pass. Nothing more."

"Hum! I should be inclined to let it stand at that. I know something of them both. Not much, but as much as I want. I don't think I should take them to my bosom if I were you. Not that there's much amiss with Monkhouse Lee."

"Meaning the thin one?"

"Precisely. He is a gentlemanly little fellow. I don't

think there is any vice in him. But then you can't know him without knowing Bellingham."

"Meaning the fat one?"

"Yes, the fat one. And he's a man whom I, for one, would rather not know."

Abercrombie Smith raised his eyebrows and glanced across at his companion.

"What's up, then?" he asked. "Drink? Cards? Cad? You used not to be censorious."

"Ah! you evidently don't know the man, or you wouldn't ask. There's something damnable about him—something reptilian. My gorge always rises at him. I should put him down as a man with secret vices—an evil liver. He's no fool, though. They say that he is one of the best men in his line that they have ever had in the college."

"Medicine or classics?"

"Eastern languages. He's a demon at them. Chillingworth met him somewhere above the second cataract last long, and he told me that he just prattled to the Arabs as if he had been born and nursed and weaned among them. He talked Coptic to the Copts, and Hebrew to the Jews, and Arabic to the Bedouins, and they were all ready to kiss the hem of his frock-coat. There are some old hermit Johnnies up in those parts who sit on rocks and scowl and spit at the casual stranger. Well, when they saw this chap Bellingham, before he had said five words they just lay down on their bellies and wriggled. Chillingworth said that he never saw anything like it. Bellingham seemed to take it as his right, too, and strutted about among them and talked down to them like a Dutch uncle. Pretty good for an undergrad. of Old's, wasn't it?"

"Why do you say you can't know Lee without knowing Bellingham?"

"Because Bellingham is engaged to his sister Eveline. Such a bright little girl, Smith! I know the whole family well. It's disgusting to see that brute with her.

A toad and a dove, that's what they always remind me of."

Abercrombie Smith grinned and knocked his ashes out against the side of the grate.

"You show every card in your hand, old chap," said he. "What a prejudiced, green-eyed, evil-thinking old man it is! You have really nothing against the fellow except that."

"Well, I've known her ever since she was as long as that cherry-wood pipe, and I don't like to see her taking risks. And it is a risk. He looks beastly. And he has a beastly temper, a venomous temper. You remember his row with Long Norton?"

"No; you always forget that I am a freshman."

"Ah, it was last winter. Of course. Well, you know the towpath along by the river. There were several fellows going along it, Bellingham in front, when they came on an old market-woman coming the other way. It had been raining—you know what those fields are like when it has rained—and the path ran between the river and a great puddle that was nearly as broad. Well, what does this swine do but keep the path, and push the old girl into the mud, where she and her marketings came to terrible grief. It was a blackguard thing to do, and Long Norton, who is as gentle a fellow as ever stepped, told him what he thought of it. One word led to another, and it ended in Norton laying his stick across the fellow's shoulders. There was the deuce of a fuss about it, and it's a treat to see the way in which Bellingham looks at Norton when they meet now. By Jove, Smith, it's nearly eleven o'clock!"

"No hurry. Light your pipe again."

"Not I. I'm supposed to be in training. Here I've been sitting gossiping when I ought to have been safely tucked up. I'll borrow your skull, if you can share it. Williams has had mine for a month. I'll take the little bones of your ear, too, if you are sure you won't need them. Thanks very much. Never mind a bag, I can carry them very well under my arm. Good night, my son, and take my tip as to your neighbour."

When Hastie, bearing his anatomical plunder, had clattered off down the winding stair, Abercrombie Smith hurled his pipe into the wastepaper basket, and drawing his chair nearer to the lamp, plunged into a formidable, green-covered volume, adorned with great, coloured maps of that strange, internal kingdom of which we are the hapless and helpless monarchs. Though a freshman at Oxford, the student was not so in medicine, for he had worked for four years at Glasgow and at Berlin, and this coming examination would place him finally as a member of his profession. With his firm mouth, broad forehead, and clear-cut, somewhat hard-featured face, he was a man who, if he had no brilliant talent, was yet so dogged, so patient, and so strong that he might in the end overtop a more showy genius. A man who can hold his own among Scotchmen and North Germans is not a man to be easily set back. Smith had left a name at Glasgow and at Berlin, and he was bent now upon doing as much at Oxford, if hard work and devotion could accomplish it.

He had sat reading for about an hour, and the hands of the noisy carriage clock upon the side-table were rapidly closing together upon the twelve, when a sudden sound fell upon the student's ear—a sharp, rather shrill sound, like the hissing intake of a man's breath who gasps under some strong emotion. Smith laid down his book and slanted his ear to listen. There was no one on either side or above him, so that the interruption came certainly from the neighbour beneath—the same neighbour of whom Hastie had given so unsavoury an account. Smith knew him only as a flabby, pale-faced man of silent and studious habits, a man whose lamp threw a golden bar from the old turret even after he had extinguished his own. This community in lateness had formed a certain silent bond between them. It was soothing to Smith when the hours stole on towards dawning to feel that there was another so close who set as small a value upon his sleep as he did. Even now, as his thoughts turned towards him, Smith's feelings were kindly. Hastie was a good fellow, but he was rough, strong-fibred, with no imagination or sympathy. He could not tolerate departures from what he looked upon as the model type of manliness. If a man could not be measured by a public-school standard, then he was beyond the pale with Hastie. Like so many who are themselves robust, he was apt to confuse the constitution with the character, to ascribe to want of principle what was really a want of circulation. Smith, with his stronger mind, knew his friend's habit, and made allowance for it now as his thoughts turned towards the man beneath him.

There was no return of the singular sound, and Smith was about to turn to his work once more, when suddenly there broke out in the silence of the night a hoarse cry, a positive scream—the call of a man who is moved and shaken beyond all control. Smith sprang out of his chair and dropped his book. He was a man of fairly firm fibre, but there was something in this sudden, uncontrollable shriek of horror which chilled his blood and pringled in his skin. Coming in such a place and at such an hour, it brought a thousand fantastic possibilities into his head. Should he rush down, or was it better to wait? He had all the national hatred of making a scene, and he knew so little of his neighbour that he would not lightly intrude upon his affairs. For a moment he stood in doubt and even as he balanced the matter there was a quick rattle of footsteps upon the stairs, and young Monkhouse Lee, half-dressed and as white as ashes, burst into his room.

"Come down!" he gasped. "Bellingham's ill."

Abercrombie Smith followed him closely downstairs into the sitting-room which was beneath his own, and intent as he was upon the matter in hand, he could not but take an amazed glance around him as he crossed the threshold. It was such a chamber as he had never seen before—a museum rather than a study. Walls and ceiling were thickly covered with a thousand strange relics from Egypt and the East. Tall, angular figures bearing burdens or weapons stalked in an uncouth frieze round the apartments. Above were bull-headed, stork-headed, cat-headed, owl-headed statues, with viper-crowned, almond-eyed monarchs, and strange, beetle-like deities cut out of the blue Egyptian lapis lazuli. Horus and Isis and Osiris peeped down from every niche and shelf, while across the ceiling a true son of Old Nile, a great, hanging-jawed crocodile, was slung in a double noose.

In the centre of this singular chamber was a large, square table, littered with papers, bottles, and the dried leaves of some graceful, palm-like plant. These varied objects had all been heaped together in order to make room for a mummy case, which had been conveyed from the wall, as was evident from the gap there, and laid across the front of the table. The mummy itself, a horrid, black, withered thing, like a charred head on a gnarled bush, was lying half out of the case, with its claw-like hand and bony forearm resting upon the table. Propped up against the sarcophagus was an old, yellow scroll of papyrus, and in front of it, in a wooden armchair, sat the owner of the room, his head thrown back, his widely opened eyes directed in a horrified stare to the crocodile above him, and his blue, thick lips puffing loudly with every expiration.

"My God! he's dying!" cried Monkhouse Lee, distractedly.

He was a slim, handsome young fellow, olive-skinned and dark-eyed, of a Spanish rather than of an English type, with a Celtic intensity of manner which contrasted with the Saxon phlegm of Abercrombie Smith.

"Only a faint, I think," said the medical student. "Just give me a hand with him. You take his feet. Now on to the sofa. Can you kick all those little wooden devils off? What a litter it is! Now he will be all rignt if we undo his collar and give him some water. What has he been up to at all?"

"I don't know. I heard him cry out. I ran up. I know him pretty well, you know. It is very good of you to come down."

"His heart is going like a pair of castanets," said Smith, laying his hand on the breast of the unconscious man. "He seems to me to be frightened all to pieces. Chuck the water over him! What a face he has got on him!"

It was indeed a strange and most repellent face, for colour and outline were equally unnatural. It was white, not with the ordinary pallor of fear, but with an absolutely bloodless white, like the under side of a sole. He was very fat, but gave the impression of having at some time been considerably fatter, for his skin hung loosely in creases and folds, and was shot with a meshwork of wrinkles. Short, stubbly brown hair bristled up from his scalp, with a pair of thick, wrinkled ears protruding at the sides. His light-grey eyes were still open, the pupils dilated and the balls projecting in a fixed and horrid stare. It seemed to Smith as he looked down upon him that he had never seen Nature's danger signals flying so plainly upon a man's countenance, and his thoughts turned more seriously to the warning which Hastie had given him an hour before.

"What the deuce can have frightened him so?" he asked.

"It's the mummy."

"The mummy? How, then?"

"I don't know. It's beastly and morbid. I wish he would drop it. It's the second fright he has given me. It was the same last winter. I found him just like this, with that horrid thing in front of him."

"What does he want with the mummy, then?"

"Oh, he's a crank, you know. It's his hobby. He knows more about these things than any man in England. But I wish he wouldn't! Ah, he's beginning to come to."

A faint tinge of colour had begun to steal back into Bellingham's ghastly cheeks, and his eyelids shivered like a sail after a calm. He clasped and unclasped his hands, drew a long, thin breath between his teeth, and suddenly jerking up his head, threw a glance of recognition around him. As his eyes fell upon the mummy, he sprang off the sofa, seized the roll of papyrus, thrust it into a drawer, turned the key, and then staggered back on to the sofa.

"What's up?" he asked. "What do you chaps want?"

"You've been shrieking out and making no end of a fuss," said Monkhouse Lee. "If our neighbour here from above hadn't come down, I'm sure I don't know what I should have done with you."

"Ah, it's Abercrombie Smith," said Bellingham, glancing up at him. "How very good of you to come in! What a fool I am! Oh, my God, what a fool I am!"

He sank his head on to his hands, and burst into peal after peal of hysterical laughter.

"Look here! Drop it!" cried Smith, shaking him roughly by the shoulder.

"Your nerves are all in a jangle. You must drop these little midnight games with mummies, or you'll be going off your chump. You're all on wires now."

"I wonder," said Bellingham, "whether you would be as cool as I am if you had seen——"

"What then?"

"Oh, nothing. I meant that I wonder if you could sit up at night with a mummy without trying your nerves. I have no doubt that you are quite right. I dare say that I have been taking it out of myself too much lately. But I am all right now. Please don't go, though. Just wait for a few minutes until I am quite myself."

"The room is very close," remarked Lee, throwing open the window and letting in the cool night air.

"It's balsamic resin," said Bellingham. He lifted

up one of the dried palmate leaves from the table and frizzled it over the chimney of the lamp. It broke away into heavy smoke wreaths, and a pungent, biting odour filled the chamber. " It's the sacred plant—the plant of the priests," he remarked. " Do you know anything of Eastern languages, Smith ? "

" Nothing at all. Not a word."

The answer seemed to lift a weight from the Egyptologist's mind.

" By the way," he continued, " how long was it from the time that you ran down, until I came to my senses ? "

" Not long. Some four or five minutes."

" I thought it could not be very long," said he, drawing a long breath. " But what a strange thing unconsciousness is ! There is no measurement to it. I could not tell from my own sensations if it were seconds or weeks. Now that gentleman on the table was packed up in the days of the eleventh dynasty, some forty centuries ago, and yet if he could find his tongue, he would tell us that this lapse of time has been but a closing of the eyes and a reopening of them. He is a singularly fine mummy, Smith."

Smith stepped over to the table and looked down with a professional eye at the black and twisted form in front of him. The features, though horribly discoloured, were perfect, and two little nut-like eyes still lurked in the depths of the black, hollow sockets. The blotched skin was drawn tightly from bone to bone, and a tangled wrap of black, coarse hair fell over the ears. Two thin teeth, like those of a rat, overlay the shrivelled lower lip. In its crouching position, with bent joints and craned head, there was a suggestion of energy about the horrid thing which made Smith's gorge rise. The gaunt ribs, with their parchment-like covering, were exposed, and the sunken, leaden-hued abdomen, with the long slit where the embalmer had left his mark ; but the lower limbs were wrapped round with coarse, yellow bandages. A number of little clove-like pieces of myrrh and of cassia were sprinkled over the body, and lay scattered on the inside of the case.

"I don't know his name," said Bellingham, passing his hand over the shrivelled head. "You see the outer sarcophagus with the inscriptions is missing. Lot 249 is all the title he has now. You see it printed on his case. That was his number in the auction at which I picked him up."

"He has been a very pretty sort of fellow in his day," remarked Abercrombie Smith.

"He has been a giant. His mummy is six feet seven in length, and that would be a giant over there, for they were never a very robust race. Feel these great, knotted bones, too. He would be a nasty fellow to tackle."

"Perhaps these very hands helped to build the stones into the pyramids," suggested Monkhouse Lee, looking down with disgust in his eyes at the crooked, unclean talons.

"No fear. This fellow has been pickled in natron, and looked after in the most approved style. They did not serve hodsmen in that fashion. Salt or bitumen was enough for them. It has been calculated that this sort of thing cost about seven hundred and thirty pounds in our money. Our friend was a noble at the least. What do you make of that small inscription near his feet, Smith?"

"I told you that I know no Eastern tongue."

"Ah, so you did. It is the name of the embalmer, I take it. A very conscientious worker he must have been. I wonder how many modern works will survive four thousand years?"

He kept on speaking lightly and rapidly, but it was evident to Abercrombie Smith that he was still palpitating with fear. His hands shook, his lower lip trembled, and look where he would, his eye always came sliding round to his gruesome companion. Through all his fear, however, there was a suspicion of triumph in his tone and manner. His eyes shone, and his footstep, as he paced the room, was brisk and jaunty. He gave the impression of a man who has gone through an ordeal, the marks of which he still bears upon him, but which has helped him to his end.

"You're not going yet?" he cried, as Smith rose from the sofa.

At the prospect of solitude, his fears seemed to crowd back upon him, and he stretched out a hand to detain him.

"Yes, I must go. I have my work to do. You are all right now. I think that with your nervous system you should take up some less morbid study."

"Oh, I am not nervous as a rule; and I have unwrapped mummies before."

"You fainted last time," observed Monkhouse Lee.

"Ah, yes, so I did. Well, I must have a nerve tonic or a course of electricity. You are not going, Lee?"

"I'll do whatever you wish, Ned."

"Then I'll come down with you and have a shake-down on your sofa. Good night, Smith. I am so sorry to have disturbed you with my foolishness."

They shook hands, and as the medical student stumbled up the spiral and irregular stair he heard a key turn in a door, and the steps of his two new acquaintances as they descended to the lower floor.

In this strange way began the acquaintance between Edward Bellingham and Abercrombie Smith, an acquaintance which the latter, at least, had no desire to push further. Bellingham, however, appeared to have taken a fancy to his rough-spoken neighbour, and made his advances in such a way that he could hardly be repulsed without absolute brutality. Twice he called to thank Smith for his assistance, and many times afterwards he looked in with books, papers and such other civilities as two bachelor neighbours can offer each other. He was, as Smith soon found, a man of wide reading, with catholic tastes and an extraordinary memory. His manner, too, was so pleasing and suave that one came, after a time, to overlook his repellent appearance. For a jaded and wearied man he was no unpleasant companion, and Smith found himself, after a time, looking forward to his visits, and even returning them.

Clever as he undoubtedly was, however, the medical student seemed to detect a dash of insanity in the man. He broke out at times into a high, inflated style of talk which was in contrast with the simplicity of his life.

" It is a wonderful thing," he cried, " to feel that one can command powers of good and of evil—a ministering angel or a demon of vengeance." And again, of Monkhouse Lee, he said,—" Lee is a good fellow, an honest fellow, but he is without strength or ambition. He would not make a fit partner for a man with a great enterprise. He would not make a fit partner for me."

At such hints and innuendoes stolid Smith, puffing solemnly at his pipe, would simply raise his eyebrows and shake his head, with little interjections of medical wisdom as to earlier hours and fresher air.

One habit Bellingham had developed of late which Smith knew to be a frequent herald of a weakening mind. He appeared to be for ever talking to himself. At late hours of the night, when there could be no visitor with him, Smith could still hear his voice beneath him in a low, muffled monologue, sunk almost to a whisper, and yet very audible in the silence. This solitary babbling annoyed and distracted the student, so that he spoke more than once to his neighbour about it. Bellingham, however, flushed up at the charge, and denied curtly that he had uttered a sound ; indeed, he showed more annoyance over the matter than the occasion seemed to demand.

Had Abercrombie Smith had any doubt as to his own ears he had not to go far to find corroboration. Tom Styles, the little wrinkled man-servant who had attended to the wants of the lodgers in the turret for a longer time than any man's memory could carry him, was sorely put to it over the same matter.

"If you please, sir," said he, as he tidied down the top chamber one morning, "do you think Mr. Bellingham is all right, sir?"

"All right, Styles?"

"Yes, sir. Right in his head, sir."

"Why should he not be, then?"

"Well, I don't know, sir. His habits has changed of late. He's not the same man he used to be, though I make free to say that he was never quite one of my gentlemen, like Mr. Hastie or yourself, sir. He's took to talkin' to himself something awful. I wonder it don't disturb you. I don't know what to make of him, sir."

"I don't know what business it is of yours, Styles."

"Well, I takes an interest, Mr. Smith. It may be forward of me, but I can't help it. I feel sometimes as if I was mother and father to my young gentlemen. It all falls on me when things go wrong and the relations come. But Mr. Bellingham, sir. I want to know what it is that walks about his room sometimes when he's out and when the door's locked on the outside."

"Eh? you're talking nonsense, Styles."

"Maybe so, sir; but I heard it more'n once with my own ears."

"Rubbish, Styles."

"Very good, sir. You'll ring the bell if you want me."

Abercrombie Smith gave little heed to the gossip of the old man-servant, but a small incident occurred a few days later which left an unpleasant effect upon his mind, and brought the words of Styles forcibly to his memory.

Bellingham had come up to see him late one night, and was entertaining him with an interesting account of the rock tombs of Beni Hassan in Upper Egypt, when Smith, whose hearing was remarkably acute, distinctly heard the sound of a door opening on the landing below.

"There's some fellow gone in or out of your room," he remarked.

Bellingham sprang up and stood helpless for a moment, with the expression of a man who is half-incredulous and half-afraid.

"I surely locked it. I am almost positive that I locked it," he stammered. "No one could have opened it."

"Why, I hear someone coming up the steps now," said Smith.

Bellingham rushed out through the door, slammed it loudly behind him, and hurried down the stairs. About half-way down Smith heard him stop, and thought he caught the sound of whispering. A moment later the door beneath him shut, a key creaked in a lock, and Bellingham, with beads of moisture upon his pale face, ascended the stairs once more, and re-entered the room.

"It's all right," he said, throwing himself down in a chair. "It was that fool of a dog. He had pushed the door open. I don't know how I came to forget to lock it."

"I didn't know you kept a dog," said Smith, looking very thoughtfully at the disturbed face of his companion.

"Yes, I haven't had him long. I must get rid of him. He's a great nuisance."

"He must be, if you find it so hard to shut him up. I should have thought that shutting the door would have been enough, without locking it."

"I want to prevent old Styles from letting him out. He's of some value, you know, and it would be awkward to lose him."

"I am a bit of a dog-fancier myself," said Smith, still gazing hard at his companion from the corner of his eyes. "Perhaps you'll let me have a look at it."

"Certainly. But I am afraid it cannot be to-night; I have an appointment. Is that clock right? Then I am a quarter of an hour late already. You'll excuse me, I am sure."

He picked up his cap and hurried from the room. In spite of his appointment, Smith heard him re-enter his own chamber and lock his door upon the inside.

This interview left a disagreeable impression upon the medical student's mind. Bellingham had lied to him, and lied so clumsily that it looked as if he had desperate reasons for concealing the truth. Smith knew that his neighbour had no dog. He knew, also, that the step which he had heard upon the stairs was not the step of an animal. But if it were not, then what could it be? There was old Style's statement about the something which used to pace the room at times when the owner was absent. Could it be a woman? Smith rather inclined to the view. If so, it would mean disgrace and expulsion to Bellingham if it were discovered by the authorities, so that his anxiety and falsehoods might be accounted for. And yet it was inconceivable that an undergraduate could keep a woman in his rooms without being instantly detected. Be the explanation what it might, there was something ugly about it, and Smith determined, as he turned to his books, to discourage all further attempts at intimacy on the part of his soft-spoken and ill-favoured neighbour.

But his work was destined to interruption that night. He had hardly caught up the broken threads when a firm, heavy footfall came three steps at a time from below, and Hastie, in blazer and flannels, burst into the room.

"Still at it!" said he, plumping down into his wonted arm-chair. "What a chap you are to stew! I believe an earthquake might come and knock Oxford into a cocked hat, and you would sit perfectly placid with your books among the ruins. However, I won't bore you long. Three whiffs of baccy, and I am off."

"What's the news, then?" asked Smith, cramming a plug of bird's-eye into his briar with his forefinger.

"Nothing very much. Wilson made 70 for the freshmen against the eleven. They say that they will play him instead of Buddicomb, for Buddicomb is clean off colour. He used to be able to bowl a little, but it's nothing but half-volleys and long hops now."

"Medium right," suggested Smith, with the intense

gravity which comes upon a 'varsity man when he speaks of athletics.

"Inclining to fast, with a work from leg. Comes with the arm about three inches or so. He used to be nasty on a wet wicket. Oh, by the way, have you heard about Long Norton?"

"What's that?"

"He's been attacked."

"Attacked?"

"Yes, just as he was turning out of the High Street, and within a hundred yards of the gate of Old's."

"But who——"

"Ah, that's the rub! If you said 'what,' you would be more grammatical. Norton swears that it was not human, and, indeed, from the scratches on his throat, I should be inclined to agree with him."

"What, then? Have we come down to spooks?"

Abercrombie Smith puffed his scientific contempt.

"Well, no; I don't think that is quite the idea, either. I am inclined to think that if any showman has lost a great ape lately, and the brute is in these parts, a jury would find a true bill against it. Norton passes that way every night, you know, about the same hour. There's a tree that hangs low over the path—the big elm from Rainy's garden. Norton thinks the thing dropped on him out of the tree. Anyhow, he was nearly strangled by two arms, which, he says, were as strong and as thin as steel bands. He saw nothing; only those beastly arms that tightened and tightened on him. He yelled his head nearly off, and a couple of chaps came running, and the thing went over the wall like a cat. He never got a fair sight of it the whole time. It gave Norton a shake up, I can tell you. I tell him it has been as good as a change at the seaside for him."

"A garrotter, most likely," said Smith.

"Very possibly. Norton says not; but we don't mind what he says. The garrotter had long nails, and was pretty smart at swinging himself over walls. By the way, your beautiful neighbour would be pleased if he heard about it. He had a grudge against Norton, and he's not a man, from what I know of him, to forget his little debts. But hallo, old chap, what have you got in your noddle ?"

"Nothing," Smith answered curtly.

He had started in his chair, and the look had flashed over his face which comes upon a man who is struck suddenly by some unpleasant idea.

"You looked as if something I had said had taken you on the raw. By the way, you have made the acquaintance of Master B. since I looked in last, have you not ? Young Monkhouse Lee told me something to that effect."

"Yes ; I know him slightly. He has been up here once or twice."

"Well, you're big enough and ugly enough to take care of yourself. He's not what I should call exactly a healthy sort of Johnny, though, no doubt, he's very clever, and all that. But you'll soon find out for yourself. Lee is all right ; he's a very decent little fellow. Well, so long, old chap ! I row Mullins for the Vice-Chancellor's pot on Wednesday week, so mind you come down, in case I don't see you before."

Bovine Smith laid down his pipe and turned stolidly to his books once more. But with all the will in the world, he found it very hard to keep his mind upon his work. It would slip away to brood upon the man beneath him, and upon the little mystery which hung round his chambers. Then his thoughts turned to this singular attack of which Hastie had spoken, and to the grudge which Bellingham was said to owe the object of it. The two ideas would persist in rising together in his mind, as though there were some close and intimate connection between them. And yet the suspicion was so dim and vague that it could not be put down in words.

"Confound the chap !" cried Smith, as he shied his book on pathology across the room. "He has spoiled my night's reading, and that's reason enough, if there were no other, why I should steer clear of him in the future."

For ten days the medical student confined himself so closely to his studies that he neither saw nor heard anything of either of the men beneath him. At the hours when Bellingham had been accustomed to visit him, he took care to sport his oak, and though he more than once heard a knocking at his outer door, he resolutely refused to answer it. One afternoon, however, he was descending the stairs when, just as he was passing it, Bellingham's door flew open, and young Monkhouse Lee came out with his eyes sparkling and a dark flush of anger upon his olive cheeks. Close at his heels followed Bellingham, his fat, unhealthy face all quivering with malignant passion.

"You fool!" he hissed. "You'll be sorry."

"Very likely," cried the other. "Mind what I say. It's off! I won't hear of it!"

"You've promised, anyhow."

"Oh, I'll keep that! I won't speak. But I'd rather little Eva was in her grave. Once for all, it's off. She'll do what I say. We don't want to see you again."

So much Smith could not avoid hearing, but he hurried on, for he had no wish to be involved in their dispute. There had been a serious breach between them, that was clear enough, and Lee was going to cause the engagement with his sister to be broken off. Smith thought of Hastie's comparison of the toad and the dove, and was glad to think that the matter was at an end. Bellingham's face when he was in a passion was not pleasant to look upon. He was not a man to whom an innocent girl could be trusted for life. As he walked, Smith wondered languidly what could have caused the quarrel, and what the promise might be which Bellingham had been so anxious that Monkhouse Lee should keep.

It was the day of the sculling match between Hastie and Mullins, and a stream of men were making their way down to the banks of the Isis. A May sun was shining brightly, and the yellow path was barred with the black shadows of the tall elm-trees. On either side the grey colleges lay back from the road, the hoary old mothers of minds looking out from their high, mullioned windows at the tide of young life which swept so merrily past them. Black-clad tutors, prim officials, pale, reading men, brown-faced, straw-hatted young athletes in white sweaters or many-coloured blazers, all were hurrying towards the blue, winding river which curves through the Oxford meadows.

Abercrombie Smith, with the intuition of an old oarsman, chose his position at the point where he knew that the struggle, if there were a struggle, would come. Far off he heard the hum which announced the start, the gathering roar of the approach, the thunder of running feet, and the shouts of the men in the boats beneath him. A spray of half-clad, deep-breathing runners shot past him, and craning over their shoulders, he saw Hastie pulling a steady thirty-six, while his opponent, with a jerky forty, was a good boat's length behind him. Smith gave a cheer for his friend, and pulling out his watch, was starting off again for his chambers, when he felt a touch upon his shoulder, and found that young Monkhouse Lee was beside him.

"I saw you there," he said, in a timid, deprecating way. "I wanted to speak to you, if you could spare me a half-hour. This cottage is mine. I share it with Harrington of King's. Come in and have a cup of tea."

"I must be back presently," said Smith. "I am hard on the grind at present. But I'll come in for a few minutes with pleasure. I wouldn't have come out only Hastie is a friend of mine."

"So he is of mine. Hasn't he a beautiful style? Mullins wasn't in it. But come into the cottage. It's a little den of a place, but it is pleasant to work in during the summer months."

It was a small, square, white building, with green doors and shutters, and a rustic trellis-work porch, standing back some fifty yards from the river's bank. Inside, the main room was roughly fitted up as a study—deal table, unpainted shelves with books, and a few cheap oleographs upon the wall. A kettle sang upon a spirit-stove, and there were tea things upon a tray on the table.

"Try that chair and have a cigarette," said Lee. "Let me pour you out a cup of tea. It's so good of you to come in, for I know that your time is a good deal taken up. I wanted to say to you that, if I were you, I should change my rooms at once."

"Eh?"

Smith sat staring with a lighted match in one hand and his unlit cigarette in the other.

"Yes; it must seem very extraordinary, and the worst of it is that I cannot give my reasons, for I am under a solemn promise—a very solemn promise. But I may go so far as to say that I don't think Bellingham is a very safe man to live near. I intend to camp out here as much as I can for a time."

"Not safe! What do you mean?"

"Ah, that's what I mustn't say. But do take my advice and move your rooms. We had a grand row to-day. You must have heard us, for you came down the stairs."

"I saw that you had fallen out."

"He's a horrible chap, Smith. That is the only word for him. I have had doubts about him ever since that night when he fainted—you remember, when you came down. I taxed him to-day, and he told me things that made my hair rise, and wanted me to stand in with him. I'm not straight-laced, but I am a clergyman's son, you know, and I think there are some things which are quite beyond the pale. I only thank God that I found him out before it was too late, for he was to have married into my family."

"This is all very fine, Lee," said Abercrombie Smith curtly. "But either you are saying a great deal too much or a great deal too little."

" I give you a warning."

" If there is real reason for warning, no promise can bind you. If I see a rascal about to blow a place up with dynamite no pledge will stand in my way of preventing him."

" Ah, but I cannot prevent him, and I can do nothing but warn you."

" Without saying what you warn me against."

" Against Bellingham."

" But that is childish. Why should I fear him, or any man ? "

" I can't tell you. I can only entreat you to change your rooms. You are in danger where you are. I don't even say that Bellingham would wish to injure you. But it might happen, for he is a dangerous neighbour just now."

" Perhaps I know more than you think," said Smith, looking keenly at the young man's boyish, earnest face. " Suppose I tell you that someone else shares Bellingham's rooms."

Monkhouse Lee sprang from his chair in uncontrollable excitement.

" You know, then ?" he gasped.

" A woman."

Lee dropped back again with a groan.

" My lips are sealed," he said. " I must not speak."

" Well, anyhow," said Smith, rising, " it is not likely that I should allow myself to be frightened out of rooms which suit me very nicely. It would be a little too feeble for me to move out all my goods and chattels because you say that Bellingham might in some unexplained way do me an injury. I think that I'll just take my chance, and stay where I am, and as I see that it's nearly five o'clock, I must ask you to excuse me."

He bade the young student adieu in a few curt words, and made his way homeward through the sweet spring evening, feeling half-ruffled, half-amused, as any other strong, unimaginative man might who has been menaced by a vague and shadowy danger.

There was one little indulgence which Abercrombie Smith always allowed himself, however closely his work might press upon him. Twice a week, on the Tuesday and the Friday, it was his invariable custom to walk over to Farlingford, the residence of Doctor Plumptree Peterson, situated about a mile and a half out of Oxford. Peterson had been a close friend of Smith's elder brother, Francis, and as he was a bachelor, fairly well-to-do, with a good cellar and a better library, his house was a pleasant goal for a man who was in need of a brisk walk. Twice a week, then, the medical student would swing out there along the dark country roads and spend a pleasant hour in Peterson's comfortable study, discussing, over a glass of old port, the gossip of the 'varsity or the latest developments of medicine or of surgery.

On the day which followed his interview with Monkhouse Lee, Smith shut up his books at a quarter past eight, the hour when he usually started for his friend's house. As he was leaving his room, however, his eyes chanced to fall upon one of the books which Bellingham had lent him, and his conscience pricked him for not having returned it. However repellent the man might be, he should not be treated with discourtesy. Taking the book, he walked downstairs and knocked at his neighbour's door. There was no answer ; but on turning the handle he found that it was unlocked. Pleased at the thought of avoiding an interview, he stepped inside, and placed the book with his card upon the table.

The lamp was turned half down, but Smith could see the details of the room plainly enough. It was all much as he had seen it before—the frieze, the animal-headed gods, the hanging crocodile, and the table littered over with papers and dried leaves. The mummy case stood upright against the wall, but the mummy itself was missing. There was no sign of any second occupant of the room, and he felt as he withdrew that he had probably done Bellingham an injustice. Had he a guilty secret to preserve, he would hardly leave his door open so that all the world might enter.

The spiral stair was as black as pitch, and Smith was slowly making his way down its irregular steps, when he was suddenly conscious that something had passed him in the darkness. There was a faint sound, a whiff of air, a light brushing past his elbow, but so slight that he could scarcely be certain of it. He stopped and listened, but the wind was rustling among the ivy outside, and he could hear nothing else.

"Is that you, Styles?" he shouted.

There was no answer, and all was still behind him. It must have been a sudden gust of air, for there were crannies and cracks in the old turret. And yet he could almost have sworn that he heard a footfall by his very side. He had emerged into the quadrangle, still turning the matter over in his head, when a man came running swiftly across the smooth-cropped lawn.

"Is that you, Smith?"

"Hullo, Hastie!"

"For God's sake come at once! Young Lee is drowned! Here's Harrington of King's with the news. The doctor is out. You'll do, but come along at once. There may be life in him."

"Have you brandy?"

"No."

"I'll bring some. There's a flask on my table."

Smith bounded up the stairs, taking three at a time, seized the flask, and was rushing down with it, when, as he passed Bellingham's room, his eyes fell upon something which left him gasping and staring upon the landing.

The door, which he had closed behind him, was now open, and right in front of him, with the lamp-light shining upon it, was the mummy case. Three minutes ago it had been empty. He could swear to that. Now it framed the lank body of its horrible occupant, who stood, grim and stark, with his black, shrivelled face towards the door. The form was lifeless and inert, but it seemed to Smith as he gazed that there still lingered a lurid spark of vitality, some faint sign of consciousness in the little eyes which lurked in the depths of the hollow sockets. So astounded and shaken was he that he had forgotten his errand, and was still staring at the lean, sunken figure when the voice of his friend below recalled him to himself.

"Come on, Smith!" he shouted. "It's life and death, you know. Hurry up! Now, then," he added, as the medical student reappeared, "let us do a sprint. It is well under a mile, and we should do it in five minutes. A human life is better worth running for than a pot."

Neck and neck they dashed through the darkness, and did not pull up until panting and spent, they had reached the little cottage by the river. Young Lee, limp and dripping like a broken water-plant, was stretched upon the sofa, the green scum of the river upon his black hair, and a fringe of white foam upon his leaden-hued lips. Beside him knelt his fellow-student, Harrington, endeavouring to chafe some warmth back into his rigid limbs.

"I think there's life in him," said Smith, with his hand to the lad's side. "Put your watch glass to his lips. Yes, there's dimming on it. You take one arm, Hastie. Now work it as I do, and we'll soon pull him round."

For ten minutes they worked in silence, inflating and depressing the chest of the unconscious man. At the end of that time a shiver ran through his body, his lips trembled, and he opened his eyes. The three students burst out into an irrepressible cheer.

"Wake up, old chap. You've frightened us quite enough."

"Have some brandy. Take a sip from the flask."

"He's all right now," said his companion Harrington. "Heavens, what a fright I got! I was reading here, and he had gone out for a stroll as far as the river, when I heard a scream and a splash. Out I ran, and by the time I could find him and fish him out, all life seemed to have gone. Then Simpson couldn't get a doctor, for he has a game-leg, and I had to run, and I don't know what I'd have done without you fellows. That's right, old chap. Sit up."

Monkhouse Lee had raised himself on his hands, and looked wildly about him.

"What's up?" he asked. "I've been in the water. Ah, yes; I remember."

A look of fear came into his eyes, and he sank his face into his hands.

"How did you fall in?"

"I didn't fall in."

"How then?"

"I was thrown in. I was standing by the bank, and something from behind picked me up like a feather and hurled me in. I heard nothing, and I saw nothing. But I know what it was, for all that."

"And so do I," whispered Smith.

Lee looked up with a quick glance of surprise.

"You've learned, then?" he said. "You remember the advice I gave you?"

"Yes, and I begin to think that I shall take it."

"I don't know what the deuce you fellows are talking about," said Hastie, "but I think, if I were you, Harrington, I should get Lee to bed at once. It will be time enough to discuss the why and the wherefore when he is a little stronger. I think, Smith, you and I can leave him alone now. I am walking back to college; if you are coming in that direction, we can have a chat."

But it was little chat that they had upon their homeward path. Smith's mind was too full of the incidents of the evening, the absence of the mummy from his neighbour's rooms, the step that passed him on the stair, the reappearance—the extraordinary, inexplicable reappearance of the grisly thing—and then this attack upon Lee, corresponding so closely to the previous outrage upon another man against whom Bellingham bore a grudge. All this settled in his thoughts, together with the many little incidents which had previously turned him against his neighbour, and the singular circumstances under which he was first called in to him. What had been a dim suspicion, a vague, fantastic conjecture, had suddenly taken form, and stood out in his mind as a grim fact, a thing not to be denied. And yet, how monstrous it was! how unheard of! how entirely beyond all bounds of human experience. An impartial judge, or even the friend who walked by his side, would simply tell him that his eyes had deceived him, that the mummy had been there all the time, that young Lee had tumbled into the river as any other man tumbles into a river, and the blue pill was the best thing for a disordered liver. He felt that he would have said as much if the positions had been reversed. And yet he could swear that Bellingham was a murderer at heart, and that he wielded a weapon such as no man had ever used in all the grim history of crime.

Hastie had branched off to his rooms with a few crisp and emphatic comments upon his friend's unsociability, and Abercrombie Smith crossed the quadrangle to his corner turret with a strong feeling of repulsion for his chambers and their associations. He would take Lee's advice, and move his quarters as soon as possible, for how could a man study when his ear was ever straining for every murmur or footstep in the room below? He observed, as he crossed over the lawn, that the light was still shining in Bellingham's window, and as he passed up the staircase the door opened, and the man himself looked out at him. With his fat, evil face he was like some bloated spider fresh from the weaving of his poisonous web.

"Good evening," said he. "Won't you come in?"

"No," cried Smith fiercely.

"No? You are as busy as ever? I wanted to ask you about Lee. I was sorry to hear that there was a rumour that something was amiss with him."

His features were grave, but there was the gleam of a hidden laugh in his eyes as he spoke. Smith saw it, and he could have knocked him down for it.

"You'll be sorrier still to hear that Monkhouse Lee is doing very well, and is out of all danger," he answered. "Your hellish tricks have not come off this time. Oh, you needn't try to brazen it out. I know all about it."

Bellingham took a step back from the angry student, and half-closed the door as if to protect himself.

"You are mad," he said. "What do you mean? Do you assert that I had anything to do with Lee's accident?"

"Yes," thundered Smith. "You and that bag of bones behind you; you worked it between you. I tell you what it is, Master B., they have given up burning folk like you, but we still keep a hangman, and, by George! if any man in this college meets his death while you are here, I'll have you up, and if you don't swing for it, it won't be my fault. You'll find that your filthy Egyptian tricks won't answer in England."

"You're a raving lunatic," said Bellingham.

"All right. You just remember what I say, for you'll find that I'll be better than my word."

The door slammed, and Smith went fuming up to his chamber, where he locked the door upon the inside, and spent half the night in smoking his old briar and brooding over the strange events of the evening.

Next morning Abercrombie Smith heard nothing of his neighbour, but Harrington called upon him in the afternoon to say that Lee was almost himself again. All day Smith stuck fast to his work, but in the evening he determined to pay the visit to his friend Doctor Peterson upon which he had started the night before. A good walk and a friendly chat would be welcome to his jangled nerves.

Bellingham's door was shut as he passed, but glancing back when he was some distance from the turret, he saw his neighbour's head at the window outlined against the lamp-light, his face pressed apparently against the glass as he gazed out into the darkness. It was a blessing to be away from all contact with him, if but for a few hours, and Smith stepped out briskly, and breathed the soft spring air into his lungs. The half-moon lay in the west between two Gothic pinnacles, and threw upon the silvered street a dark tracery from the stone-work above. There was a brisk breeze, and light, fleecy clouds drifted swiftly across the sky. Old's was on the very border of the town, and in five minutes Smith found himself beyond the houses and between the hedges of a May-scented, Oxfordshire lane.

It was a lonely and little-frequented road which led to his friend's house. Early as it was, Smith did not meet a single soul upon his way. He walked briskly along until he came to the avenue gate, which opened into the long, gravel drive leading up to Farlingford. In front of him he could see the cosy, red light of the windows glimmering through the foliage. He stood with his hand upon the iron latch of the swinging gate, and he glanced back at the road along which he had come. Something was coming swiftly down it.

It moved in the shadow of the hedge, silently and furtively, a dark, crouching figure, dimly visible against the black background. Even as he gazed back at it, it had lessened its distance by twenty paces, and was fast closing upon him. Out of the darkness he had a glimpse of a scraggy neck, and of two eyes that will ever haunt him in his dreams. He turned, and with a cry of terror he ran for his life up the avenue. There were the red lights, the signals of safety, almost within a stone's-throw of him. He was a famous runner, but never had he run as he ran that night.

The heavy gate had swung into place behind him but he heard it dash open again before his pursuer. As he rushed madly and wildly through the night, he could hear a swift, dry patter behind him, and could see, as he threw back a glance, that this horror was bounding like a tiger at his heels, with blazing eyes and one stringy arm out-thrown. Thank God, the door was ajar. He could see the thin bar of light which shot from the lamp in the hall. Nearer yet sounded the clatter from behind. He heard a hoarse gurgling at his very shoulder. With a shriek he flung himself against the door, slammed and bolted it behind him, and sank half-fainting on to the hall chair.

" My goodness, Smith, what's the matter ? " asked Peterson, appearing at the door of his study.

" Give me some brandy."

Peterson disappeared, and came rushing out again with a glass and a decanter.

" You need it," he said, as his visitor drank off what he poured out for him. " Why, man, you are as white as a cheese."

Smith laid down his glass, rose up, and took a deep breath.

" I am my own man again now," said he. " I was never so unmanned before. But, with your leave, Peterson, I will sleep here to-night, for I don't think I could face that road again except by daylight. It's weak, I know, but I can't help it."

Peterson looked at his visitor with a very questioning eye.

" Of course you shall sleep here if you wish. I'll tell Mrs. Burney to make up the spare bed. Where are you off to now ? "

" Come up with me to the window that overlooks the door. I want you to see what I have seen."

They went up to the window of the upper hall whence they could look down upon the approach to the house. The drive and the fields on either side lay quiet and still, bathed in the peaceful moonlight.

" Well, really, Smith," remarked Peterson, " it is well that I know you to be an abstemious man. What in the world can have frightened you ? "

" I'll tell you presently. But where can it have gone ?

Ah, now, look, look! See the curve of the road just beyond your gate."

"Yes, I see; you needn't pinch my arm off. I saw someone pass. I should say a man, rather thin, apparently, and tall, very tall. But what of him? And what of yourself? You are still shaking like an aspen leaf."

"I have been within hand-grip of the devil, that's all. But come down to your study, and I shall tell you the whole story."

He did so. Under the cheery lamp-light with a glass of wine on the table beside him, and the portly form and florid face of his friend in front, he narrated, in their order, all the events, great and small, which had formed so singular a chain, from the night on which he had found Bellingham fainting in front of the mummy case until this horrid experience of an hour ago.

"There now," he said as he concluded, "that's the whole, black business. It is monstrous and incredible, but it is true."

Doctor Plumptree Peterson sat for some time in silence with a very puzzled expression upon his face.

"I never heard of such a thing in my life, never!" he said at last. "You have told me the facts. Now tell me your inferences."

"You can draw your own."

"But I should like to hear yours. You have thought over the matter, and I have not."

"Well, it must be a little vague in detail, but the main points seem to me to be clear enough. This fellow Bellingham, in his Eastern studies, has got hold of some infernal secret by which a mummy—or possibly only this particular mummy—can be temporarily brought to life. He was trying this disgusting business on the night when he fainted. No doubt the sight of the creature moving had shaken his nerve, even though he had expected it. You remember that almost the first words he said were to call out upon himself as a fool. Well, he got more hardened afterwards, and carried the matter through without fainting. The vitality which he could put into it was evidently only a passing thing, for I have seen it continually in its case as dead as this table. He has some elaborate process, I fancy, by which he brings the thing to pass. Having done it, he naturally bethought him that he might use the creature as an agent. It has intelligence and it has strength. For some purpose he took Lee into his confidence ; but Lee, like a decent Christian, would have nothing to do with such a business. Then they had a row, and Lee vowed that he would tell his sister of Bellingham's true character. Bellingham's game was to prevent him, and he nearly managed it, by setting this creature of his on his track. He had already tried its powers upon another man—Norton—towards whom he had a grudge. It is the merest chance that he has not two murders upon his soul. Then, when I taxed him with the matter, he had the strongest reasons for wishing to get me out of the way before I could convey my knowledge to anyone else. He got his chance when I went out, for he knew my habits and where I was bound for. I have had a narrow shave, Peterson, and it is mere luck you didn't find me on your doorstep in the morning. I'm not a nervous man as a rule, and I never thought to have the fear of death put upon me as it was to-night."

"My dear boy, you take the matter too seriously," said his companion. "Your nerves are out of order with your work, and you make too much of it. How could such a thing as this stride about the streets of Oxford, even at night, without being seen ?"

"It has been seen. There is quite a scare in the town about an escaped ape, as they imagine the creature to be. It is the talk of the place."

"Well, it's a striking chain of events. And yet, my dear fellow, you must allow that each incident in itself is capable of a more natural explanation."

"What ! even my adventure of to-night ?"

"Certainly. You come out with your nerves all

unstrung, and your head full of this theory of yours. Some gaunt, half-famished tramp steals after you, and seeing you run, is emboldened to pursue you. Your fears and imagination do the rest."

"It won't do, Peterson; it won't do."

"And again, in the instance of your finding the mummy case empty, and then a few moments later with an occupant, you know that it was lamp-light, that the lamp was half turned down, and that you had no special reason to look hard at the case. It is quite possible that you may have overlooked the creature in the first instance."

"No, no; it is out of the question."

"And then Lee may have fallen into the river, and Norton been garrotted. It is certainly a formidable indictment that you have against Bellingham; but if you were to place it before a police magistrate, he would simply laugh in your face."

"I know he would. That is why I mean to take the matter into my own hands."

"Eh?"

"Yes; I feel that a public duty rests upon me, and, besides, I must do it for my own safety, unless I choose to allow myself to be hunted by this beast out of the college, and that would be a little too feeble. I have quite made up my mind what I shall do. And first of all, may I use your paper and pens for an hour?"

"Most certainly. You will find all that you want upon that side-table."

Abercrombie Smith sat down before a sheet of foolscap, and for an hour, and then for a second hour his pen travelled swiftly over it. Page after page was finished and tossed aside while his friend leaned back in his arm-chair, looking across at him with patient curiosity. At last, with an exclamation of satisfaction, Smith sprang to his feet, gathered his papers up into order, and laid the last one upon Peterson's desk.

"Kindly sign this as a witness," he said.

"A witness? Of what?"

" Of my signature, and of the date. The date is the most important. Why, Peterson, my life might hang upon it."

" My dear Smith, you are talking wildly. Let me beg you to go to bed."

" On the contrary, I never spoke so deliberately in my life. And I will promise to go to bed the moment you have signed it."

" But what is it ? "

" It is a statement of all that I have been telling you to-night. I wish you to witness it."

" Certainly," said Peterson, signing his name under that of his companion. " There you are ! But what is the idea ? "

" You will kindly retain it, and produce it in case I am arrested."

" Arrested ? For what ? "

" For murder. It is quite on the cards. I wish to be ready for every event. There is only one course open to me, and I am determined to take it."

" For Heaven's sake, don't do anything rash ! "

" Believe me, it would be far more rash to adopt any other course. I hope that we won't need to bother you, but it will ease my mind to know that you have this statement of my motives. And now I am ready to take your advice and to go to roost, for I want to be at my best in the morning."

Abercrombie Smith was not an entirely pleasant man to have as an enemy. Slow and easy-tempered, he was formidable when driven to action. He brought to every purpose in life the same deliberate resoluteness which had distinguished him as a scientific student. He had laid his studies aside for a day, but he intended that the day should not be wasted. Not a word did he say to his host as to his plans, but by nine o'clock he was well on his way to Oxford.

In the High Street he stopped at Clifford's, the gunmaker's, and bought a heavy revolver, with a box of central-fire cartridges. Six of them he slipped into the chambers, and half-cocking the weapon, placed it in the pocket of his coat. He then made his way to Hastie's rooms, where the big oarsman was lounging over his breakfast, with the *Sporting Times* propped up against the coffee-pot.

"Hullo! What's up?" he asked. "Have some coffee?"

"No, thank you. I want you to come with me, Hastie, and do what I ask you."

"Certainly, my boy."

"And bring a heavy stick with you."

"Hullo!" Hastie stared. "Here's a hunting crop that would fell an ox."

"One other thing. You have a box of amputating knives. Give me the longest of them."

"There you are. You seem to be fairly on the war trail. Anything else?"

"No; that will do." Smith placed the knife inside his coat, and led the way to the quadrangle. "We are neither of us chickens, Hastie," said he. "I think I can do this job alone, but I take you as a precaution. I am going to have a little talk with Bellingham. If I have only him to deal with, I won't, of course, need you. If I shout, however, up you come, and lam out with your whip as hard as you can lick. Do you understand?"

"All right. I'll come if I hear you bellow."

"Stay here, then. I may be a little time, but don't budge until I come down."

"I'm a fixture."

Smith ascended the stairs, opened Bellingham's door and stepped in. Bellingham was seated behind his table, writing. Beside him, among his litter of strange possessions, towered the mummy case, with its sale number 249 still stuck upon its front, and its hideous occupant stiff and stark within it. Smith looked very deliberately round him, closed the door, and then, stepping across to the fireplace, struck a match and set the fire alight. Bellingham sat staring, with amazement and rage upon his bloated face.

"Well, really now, you make yourself at home," he gasped.

Smith sat himself deliberately down, placing his watch upon the table, drew out his pistol, cocked it, and laid it in his lap. Then he took the long amputating knife from his bosom, and threw it down in front of Bellingham.

"Now, then," said he, "just get to work and cut up that mummy."

"Oh, is that it?" said Bellingham with a sneer.

"Yes, that is it. They tell me that the law can't touch you. But I have a law that will set matters straight. If in five minutes you have not set to work, I swear by the God who made me that I will put a bullet through your brain!"

"You would murder me?"

Bellingham had half-risen, and his face was the colour of putty.

"Yes."

"And for what?"

"To stop your mischief. One minute has gone."

"But what have I done?"

"I know and you know."

"This is mere bullying."

"Two minutes are gone."

"But you must give reasons. You are a madman—a dangerous madman. Why should I destroy my own property? It is a valuable mummy."

"You must cut it up, and you must burn it."

"I will do no such thing."

"Four minutes are gone."

Smith took up the pistol and he looked towards Bellingham with an inexorable face. As the second-hand stole round, he raised his hand, and the finger twitched upon the trigger.

"There! there! I'll do it!" screamed Bellingham.

In frantic haste he caught up the knife and hacked at the figure of the mummy, ever glancing round to see the eye and the weapon of his terrible visitor bent upon him. The creature crackled and snapped under every stab of the keen blade. A thick, yellow dust rose up from it. Spices and dried essences rained down upon the floor. Suddenly, with a rending crack, its backbone snapped asunder, and it fell, a brown heap of sprawling limbs, upon the floor.

"Now into the fire!" said Smith.

The flames leaped and roared as the dried and tinder-like debris was piled upon it. The little room was like the stoke-hole of a steamer and the sweat ran down the faces of the two men; but still the one stooped and worked, while the other sat watching him with a set face. A thick, fat smoke oozed out from the fire, and a heavy smell of burned resin and singed hair filled the air. In a quarter of an hour a few charred and brittle sticks were all that was left of Lot No. 249.

"Perhaps that will satisfy you," snarled Bellingham, with hate and fear in his little grey eyes as he glanced back at his tormentor.

"No; I must make a clean sweep of all your materials. We must have no more devil's tricks. In with all these leaves! They may have something to do with it."

"And what now?" asked Bellingham, when the leaves also had been added to the blaze.

"Now the roll of papyrus which you had on the table that night. It is in that drawer, I think."

"No, no," shouted Bellingham. "Don't burn that! Why, man, you don't know what you do. It is unique; it contains wisdom which is nowhere else to be found."

"Out with it!"

"But look here, Smith, you can't really mean it. I'll share the knowledge with you. I'll teach you all that is in it. Or, stay, let me only copy it before you burn it!"

Smith stepped forward and turned the key in the drawer. Taking out the yellow, curled roll of paper, he threw it into the fire, and pressed it down with his heel. Bellingham screamed, and grabbed at it ; but Smith pushed him back and stood over it until it was reduced to a formless, grey ash.

" Now, Master B.," said he, " I think I have pretty well drawn your teeth. You'll hear from me again, if you return to your old tricks. And now good morning, for I must go back to my studies."

And such is the narrative of Abercrombie Smith as to the singular events which occurred in Old College, Oxford, in the spring of '84. As Bellingham left the university immediately afterwards, and was last heard of in the Soudan, there is no one who can contradict his statement. But the wisdom of men is small, and the ways of Nature are strange, and who shall put a bound to the dark things which may be found by those who seek for them ?

48. " *De Profundis* "

SO long as the oceans are the ligaments which bind together the great, broadcast British Empire, so long will there be a dash of romance in our minds. For the soul is swayed by the waters, as the waters are by the moon, and when the great highways of an empire are along such roads as these, so full of strange sights and sounds, with danger ever running like a hedge on either side of the course, it is a dull mind indeed which does not bear away with it some trace of such a passage. And now, Britain lies far beyond herself, for the three-mile limit of every seaboard is her frontier, which has been won by hammer and loom and pick rather than by arts of war. For it is written in history that neither king nor army can bar the path to the man who, having two-pence in his strong box, and knowing well where he can turn it to threepence, sets his mind to that one end. And as the frontier has broadened, the mind of Britain has broadened, too, spreading out until all men can see that the ways of the island are continental, even as those of the Continent are insular.

But for this a price must be paid, and the price is a grievous one. As the beast of old must have one young, human life as a tribute every year, so to our Empire we throw from day to day the pick and flower of our youth. The engine is world-wide and strong, but the only fuel that will drive it is the lives of British men. Thus it is that in the grey, old cathedrals as we look round upon the brasses on the walls, we see strange names, such names as they who reared those walls had never heard, for it is in Peshawur, and Umballah, and Korti, and Fort Pearson that the youngsters die, leaving only a precedent and a brass behind them. But if every man had his obelisk, even where he lay, then no frontier line need be drawn, for a cordon of British graves would ever show how high the Anglo-Celtic tide had lapped.

This, then, as well as the waters which join us to the world, has done something to tinge us with romance. For when so many have their loved ones over the seas, walking amid hillmen's bullets, or swamp malaria, where death is sudden and distance great, then mind communes with mind, and strange stories arise of dream, presentiment, or vision, where the mother sees her dying son, and is past the first bitterness of her grief ere the message comes which should have broken the news. The learned have of late looked into the matter and have even labelled it with a name ; but what can we know more of it save that a poor, stricken soul, when hard-pressed and driven, can shoot across the earth some ten-thousand-mile-distant picture of its trouble to the mind which is most akin to it. Far be it from me to say that there lies no such power within us, for of all things which the brain will grasp the last will be itself ; but yet it is well to be very cautious over such matters, for once at least I have known that which was within the laws of Nature seem to be far upon the further side of them.

John Vansittart was the younger partner of the firm of Hudson and Vansittart, coffee exporters of the Island of Ceylon, three-quarters Dutchman by descent, but wholly English in his sympathies. For years I had been his agent in London, and when in '72 he came over to England for a three months' holiday, he turned to me for the introductions which would enable him to see something of town and country life. Armed with seven letters he left my offices, and for many weeks scrappy notes from different parts of the country let me know that he had found favour in the eyes of my friends. Then came word of his engagement to Emily Lawson, of a cadet branch of the Hereford Lawsons, and at the very tail of the first flying rumour the news of his absolute marriage, for the wooing of a wanderer must be short, and the days were already crowding on towards the date when he must be upon his homeward journey. They were to return together to Colombo in one of the firm's own thousand-ton, barque-rigged sailing ships, and this was to be their princely honeymoon, at once a necessity and a delight.

Those were the royal days of coffee-planting in Ceylon, before a single season and a rotting fungus drove a whole community through years of despair to one of the greatest commercial victories which pluck and ingenuity ever won. Not often is it that men have the heart when their one great industry is withered to rear up, in a few years, another as rich to take its place, and the tea-fields of Ceylon are as true a monument to courage as is the lion at Waterloo. But in '72 there was no cloud yet above the skyline, and the hopes of the planters were as high and as bright as the hill-sides on which they reared their crops. Vansittart came down to London with his young and beautiful wife. I was introduced, dined with them, and it was finally arranged that I, since business called me also to Ceylon, should be a fellow-passenger with them on the

Eastern Star, which was timed to sail on the following Monday.

It was on the Sunday evening that I saw him again. He was shown up into my rooms about nine o'clock at night, with the air of a man who is bothered and out of sorts. His hand, as I shook it, was hot and dry.

"I wish, Atkinson," said he, "that you could give me a little lime-juice and water. I have a beastly thirst upon me, and the more I take the more I seem to want."

I rang and ordered a caraffe and glasses. "You are flushed," said I. "You don't look the thing."

"No, I'm clean off colour. Got a touch of rheumatism in my back, and don't seem to taste my food. It is this vile London that is choking me. I'm not used to breathing air which has been used up by four million lungs all sucking away on every side of you." He flapped his crooked hands before his face, like a man who really struggles for his breath.

"A touch of the sea will soon set you right."

"Yes, I'm of one mind with you there. That's the thing for me. I want no other doctor. If I don't get to sea to-morrow I'll have an illness. There are no two ways about it." He drank off a tumbler of lime-juice, and clapped his two hands with his knuckles doubled up into the small of his back.

"That seems to ease me," said he, looking at me with a filmy eye. "Now I want your help, Atkinson, for I am rather awkwardly placed."

"As how?"

"This way. My wife's mother got ill and wired for her. I couldn't go—you know best yourself how tied I have been—so she had to go alone. Now I've had another wire to say that she can't come to-morrow, but that she will pick up the ship at Falmouth on Wednesday. We put in there, you know, though I count it hard, Atkinson, that a man should be asked to believe in a mystery, and cursed if he can't do it. Cursed, mind you, no less." He leaned forward and began to draw a catchy breath like a man who is poised on the very edge of a sob.

Then first it came into my mind that I had heard much of the hard-drinking life of the island, and that from brandy came these wild words and fevered hands. The flushed cheek and the glazing eye were those of one whose drink is strong upon him. Sad it was to see so noble a young man in the grip of that most bestial of all the devils.

" You should lie down," I said, with some severity.

He screwed up his eyes like a man who is striving to wake himself, and looked up with an air of surprise.

" So I shall presently," said he, quite rationally. " I felt quite swimmy just now, but I am my own man again now. Let me see, what was I talking about ? Oh ah, of course, about the wife. She joins the ship at Falmouth. Now I want to go round by water. I believe my health depends upon it. I just want a little clean, first-lung air to set me on my feet again. I ask you, like a good fellow, to go to Falmouth by rail, so that in case we should be late you may be there to look after the wife. Put up at the Royal Hotel, and I will wire her that you are there. Her sister will bring her down, so that it will be all plain sailing."

" I'll do it with pleasure," said I. " In fact, I would rather go by rail, for we shall have enough and to spare of the sea before we reach Colombo. I believe, too, that you badly need a change. Now, I should go and turn in, if I were you."

" Yes, I will. I sleep aboard to-night. You know," he continued, as the film settled down again over his eyes, " I've not slept well the last few nights. I've been troubled with theolololog—that is to say, theolological—hang it," with a desperate effort, " with the doubts of theologicians. Wondering why the Almighty made us, you know, and why He made our heads swimmy, and fixed little pains into the small of our backs. Maybe I'll do better to-night." He rose and steadied himself with an effort against the corner of the chair back.

"Look here, Vansittart," said I gravely, stepping up to him, and laying my hand upon his sleeve, "I can give you a shakedown here. You are not fit to go out. You are all over the place. You've been mixing your drinks."

"Drinks!" He stared at me stupidly.

"You used to carry your liquor better than this."

"I give you my word, Atkinson, that I have not had a drain for two days. It's not drink. I don't know what it is. I suppose you think this is drink." He took up my hand in his burning grasp, and passed it over his own forehead.

"Great Lord!" said I.

His skin felt like a thin sheet of velvet beneath which lies a close-packed layer of small shot. It was smooth to the touch at any one place, but to a finger passed along it, rough as a nutmeg-grater.

"It's all right," said he, smiling at my startled face. "I've had the prickly heat nearly as bad."

"But this is never prickly heat."

"No, it's London. It's breathing bad air. But to-morrow it'll be all right. There's a surgeon aboard, so I shall be in safe hands. I must be off now."

"Not you," said I, pushing him back into a chair. "This is past a joke. You don't move from here until a doctor sees you. Just stay where you are."

I caught up my hat, and rushing round to the house of a neighbouring physician, I brought him back with me. The room was empty and Vansittart gone. I rang the bell. The servant said that the gentleman had ordered a cab the instant that I had left, and had gone off in it. He had told the cabman to drive to the docks.

"Did the gentleman seem ill?" I asked.

"Ill!" The man smiled. "No, sir, he was singin' his 'ardest all the time."

The information was not as reassuring as my servant seemed to think, but I reflected that he was going straight back to the *Eastern Star*, and that there was a doctor aboard of her, so that there was nothing which I could do in the matter. None the less, when I thought of his thirst, his burning hands, his heavy eye, his tripping speech, and lastly, of that leprous forehead, I carried with me to bed an unpleasant memory of my visitor and his visit.

At eleven o'clock next day I was at the docks, but the *Eastern Star* had already moved down the river, and was nearly at Gravesend. To Gravesend I went by train, but only to see her topmasts far off, with a plume of smoke from a tug in front of her. I would hear no more of my friend until I rejoined him at Falmouth. When I got back to my offices, a telegram was awaiting me from Mrs. Vansittart, asking me to meet her; and next evening found us both at the Royal Hotel, Falmouth, where we were to wait for the *Eastern Star*. Ten days passed, and there came no news of her.

They were ten days which I am not likely to forget. On the very day that the *Eastern Star* had cleared from the Thames, a furious, easterly gale had sprung up, and blew on from day to day for the greater part of a week without the sign of a lull. Such a screaming, raving, long-drawn storm has never been known on the southern coast. From our hotel windows the sea view was all banked in haze, with a little rain-swept half-circle under our very eyes, churned and lashed into one tossing stretch of foam. So heavy was the wind upon the waves that little sea could rise, for the crest of each billow was torn shrieking from it, and lashed broadcast over the bay. Clouds, wind, sea, all were rushing to the west, and there, looking down at this mad jumble of elements, I waited on day after day, my sole companion a white, silent woman, with terror in her eyes, her forehead pressed ever against the window, her gaze from early morning to the fall of night fixed upon that wall of grey haze through which the loom of a vessel might come. She said nothing, but that face of hers was one long wail of fear.

On the fifth day I took counsel with an old seaman. I should have preferred to have done so alone, but she saw me speak with him, and was at our side in an instant, with parted lips and a prayer in her eyes.

"Seven days out from London," said he, "and five in the gale. Well, the Channel's swept clear by this wind. There's three things for it. She may have popped into port on the French side. That's like enough."

"No, no; he knew we were here. He would have telegraphed."

"Ah, yes, so he would. Well, then, he might have run for it, and if he did that he won't be very far from Madeira by now. That'll be it, marm, you may depend."

"Or else? You said there was a third chance."

"Did I, marm. No, only two, I think. I don't think I said anything of a third. Your ship's out there, depend upon it, away out in the Atlantic, and you'll hear of it time enough, for the weather is breaking. Now don't you fret, marm, and wait quiet and you'll find a real blue Cornish sky to-morrow."

The old seaman was right in his surmise, for the next day broke calm and bright, with only a low, dwindling cloud in the west to mark the last trailing wreaths of the storm-wrack. But still there came no word from the sea, and no sign of the ship. Three more weary days had passed, the weariest that I have ever spent, when there came a seafaring man to the hotel with a letter. I gave a shout of joy. It was from the captain of the *Eastern Star*. As I read the first lines of it I whisked my hand over it, but she laid her own upon it and drew it away. "I have seen it," said she, in a cold, quiet voice. "I may as well see the rest, too."

"DEAR SIR," said the letter,

"Mr. Vansittart is down with the small-pox, and we are blown so far on our course that we don't know what to do, he being off his head and unfit to tell us. By dead reckoning we are but three hundred miles from Funchal, so I take it that it is best that we should push on there, get Mr. V. into hospital, and wait in the Bay until you come. There's a sailing-ship due from Falmouth to Funchal in a few days' time, as I understand. This goes by the brig *Marian* of Falmouth, and five pounds is due to the master,

" Yours respectfully,
" JNO. HINES."

She was a wonderful woman that, only a chit of a girl fresh from school, but as quiet and strong as a man. She said nothing—only pressed her lips together tight, and put on her bonnet.

" You are going out ? " I asked.

" Yes."

" Can I be of use ? "

" No ; I am going to the doctor's."

" To the doctor's ? "

" Yes. To learn how to nurse a small-pox case."

She was busy at that all the evening, and next morning we were off with a fine ten-knot breeze in the barque *Rose of Sharon* for Madeira. For five days we made good time, and were no great way from the island ; but on the sixth there fell a calm, and we lay without motion on a sea of oil, heaving slowly, but making not a foot of way.

At ten o'clock that night Emily Vansittart and I stood leaning on the starboard railing of the poop, with a full moon shining at our backs, and casting a black shadow of the barque, and of our own two heads, upon the shining water. From the shadow a broadening path of moonshine stretched away to the lonely skyline, flickering and shimmering in the gentle heave of the swell. We were talking with bent heads, chatting of the calm, of the chances of wind, of the look of the sky, when there came a sudden plop, like a rising salmon, and there, in the clear light, John Vansittart sprang out of the water and looked up at us.

I never saw anything clearer in my life than I saw that man. The moon shone full upon him, and he was but three oars' length away. His face was more puffed than when I had seen him last, mottled here and there with dark scabs, his mouth and eyes open as one who is struck with some overpowering surprise. He had some white stuff streaming from his shoulders, and one hand was raised to his ear, the other crooked across his breast. I saw him leap from the water into the air, and in the dead calm the waves of his coming lapped up against the sides of the vessel. Then his figure sank back into the water again, and I heard a rending, crackling sound like a bundle of brushwood snapping in the fire on a frosty night. There were no signs of him when I looked again, but a swift swirl and eddy on the still sea still marked the spot where he had been. How long I stood there, tingling to my finger-tips, holding up an unconscious woman with one hand, clutching at the rail of the vessel with the other, was more than I could afterwards tell. I had been noted as a man of slow and unresponsive emotions, but this time at least I was shaken to the core. Once and twice I struck my foot upon the deck to be certain that I was indeed the master of my own senses, and that this was not some mad prank of an unruly brain. As I stood, still marvelling, the woman shivered, opened her eyes, gasped, and then standing erect with her hands upon the rail, looked out over the moonlit sea with a face which had aged ten years in a summer night.

"You saw his vision?" she murmured.

"I saw something."

"It was he! It was John! He is dead!"

I muttered some lame words of doubt.

"Doubtless he died at this hour," she whispered. "In hospital at Madeira. I have read of such things. His thoughts were with me. His vision came to me. Oh, my John, my dear, dear, lost John!"

She broke out suddenly into a storm of weeping, and I led her down into her cabin, where I left her with her sorrow. That night a brisk breeze blew up from the east, and in the evening of the next day we passed the two islets of Los Desertos, and dropped anchor at sundown in the Bay of Funchal. The *Eastern Star* lay no great distance from us, with the quarantine flag flying from her main, and her Jack half-way up her peak.

"You see," said Mrs. Vansittart quickly. She was dry-eyed now, for she had known how it would be.

That night we received permission from the authorities to move on board the *Eastern Star*. The captain, Hines, was waiting upon deck with confusion and grief contending upon his bluff face as he sought for words with which to break this heavy tidings, but she took the story from his lips.

"I know that my husband is dead," she said. "He died yesterday night, about ten o'clock, in hospital at Madeira, did he not?"

The seaman stared aghast. "No, marm, he died eight days ago at sea, and we had to bury him out there, for we lay in a belt of calm, and could not say when we might make the land."

Well, those are the main facts about the death of John Vansittart, and his appearance to his wife somewhere about lat. 35 N. and long. 15 W. A clearer case of a wraith has seldom been made out, and since then it has been told as such, and put into print as such, and endorsed by a learned society as such, and so floated off with many others to support the recent theory of telepathy. For myself, I hold telepathy to be proved, but I would snatch this one case from amid the evidence, and say that I do not think that it was the wraith of John Vansittart, but John Vansittart himself whom we saw that night leaping into the moonlight out of the depths of the Atlantic. It has ever been my belief that some strange chance—one of those chances which seem so improbable and yet so constantly occur—had becalmed us over the very spot where the man had been buried a week before. For the rest, the surgeon tells me that the leaden weight was not too firmly fixed, and that seven days bring about changes which fetch a body to the surface. Coming from the depth to which the weight would have sunk it, he explains that it might well attain such a velocity as to carry it clear of the water. Such is my own explanation of the matter, and if you ask me what then became of the body, I must recall to you that snapping, crackling sound, with the swirl in the water. The shark is a surface feeder and is plentiful in those parts.

49. *The Lift*

FLIGHT-COMMANDER STANGATE should have been happy. He had come safely through the war without a hurt, and with a good name in the most heroic of services. He had only just turned thirty, and a great career seemed to lie ahead of him. Above all, beautiful Mary MacLean was walking by his side, and he had her promise that she was there for life. What could a young man ask for more? And yet there was a heavy load upon his heart.

He could not explain it himself, and endeavoured to reason himself out of it. There was the blue sky above him, the blue sea in front, the beautiful gardens with their throngs of happy pleasure-seekers around. Above all, there was that sweet face turned upon his with questioning concern. Why could he not raise himself to so joyful an environment? He made effort after effort, but they were not convincing enough to deceive the quick instinct of a loving woman.

"What is it, Tom?" she asked anxiously. "I can see that something is clouding you. Do tell me if I can help you in any way."

He laughed in shamefaced fashion.

"It is such a sin to spoil our little outing," he said. "I could kick myself round these gardens when I think of it. Don't worry, my darling, for I know the cloud will roll off. I suppose I am a creature of nerves, though I should have got past that by now. The Flying Service is supposed either to break you or to warrant you for life."

"It is nothing definite, then?"

"No, it is nothing definite. That's the worst of it. You could fight it more easily if it was. It's just a dead, heavy depression here in my chest and across my forehead. But do forgive me, dear girl! What a brute I am to shadow you like this."

"But I love to share even the smallest trouble."

"Well, it's gone—vamosed—vanished. We will talk about it no more."

She gave him a swift, penetrating glance.

"No, no, Tom; your brow shows, as well as feels. Tell me, dear, have you often felt like this? You really look very ill. Sit here, dear, in the shade and tell me of it."

They sat together in the shadow of the great, latticed Tower which reared itself six hundred feet high beside them.

"I have an absurd faculty," said he; "I don't know that I have ever mentioned it to anyone before. But when imminent danger is threatening me I get these strange forebodings. Of course it is absurd to-day in these peaceful surroundings. It only shows how queerly these things work. But it is the first time that it has deceived me."

"When had you it before?"

"When I was a lad it seized me one morning. I was nearly drowned that afternoon. I had it when the burglar came to Morton Hall and I got a bullet through my coat. Then twice in the war when I was overmatched and escaped by a miracle, I had this strange feeling before ever I climbed into my machine. Then it lifts quite suddenly, like a mist in the sunshine. Why, it is lifting now. Look at me! Can't you see that it is so?"

She could indeed. He had turned in a minute from a haggard man to a laughing boy. She found herself laughing in sympathy. A rush of high spirits and energy had swept away his strange foreboding and filled his whole soul with the vivid, dancing joy of youth.

"Thank goodness!" he cried. "I think it is your dear eyes that have done it. I could not stand that wistful look in them. What a silly, foolish nightmare it all has been! There's an end for ever in my belief in presentiments. Now, dear girl, we have just time for one good turn before luncheon. After that the gardens get so crowded that it is hopeless to do anything. Shall we have a side-show, or the great wheel, or the flying boat, or what?"

"What about the Tower?" she asked, glancing upwards. "Surely that glorious air and the view from the top would drive the last wisps of cloud out of your mind."

He looked at his watch.

"Well, it's past twelve, but I suppose we could do it all in an hour. But it doesn't seem to be working. What about it, conductor?"

The man shook his head and pointed to a little knot of people who were assembled at the entrance.

"They've all been waiting, sir. It's hung up, but the gear is being overhauled, and I expect the signal every minute. If you join the others I promise it won't be long."

They had hardly reached the group when the steel face of the lift rolled aside—a sign that there was hope in the future. The motley crowd drifted through the opening and waited expectantly upon the wooden platform. They were not numerous, for the gardens are not crowded until the afternoon, but they were fair samples of the kindly, good-humoured north-country folk who take their annual holiday at Northam. Their faces were all upturned now, and they were watching with keen interest a man who was descending the steel framework. It seemed a dangerous, precarious business, but he came as swiftly as an ordinary mortal upon a staircase.

"My word!" said the conductor, glancing up. "Jim has got a move on this morning."

"Who is he?" asked Commander Stangate.

"That's Jim Barnes, sir, the best workman that ever went on a scaffold. He fair lives up there. Every bolt and rivet are under his care. He's a wonder, is Jim."

"But don't argue religion with him," said one of the group.

The attendant laughed.

"Ah, you know him, then," said he. "No, don't argue religion with him."

"Why not?" asked the officer.

"Well, he takes it very hard, he does. He's the shining light of his sect."

"It ain't hard to be that," said the knowing one. "I've heard there are only six folk in the fold. He's one of those who picture heaven as the exact size of their own back street conventicle and everyone else left outside it."

"Better not tell him so while he's got that hammer in his hand," said the conductor, in a hurried whisper. "Hallo, Jim, how goes it this morning?"

The man slid swiftly down the last thirty feet, and then balanced himself on a cross-bar while he looked at the little group in the lift. As he stood there, clad in a leather suit, with his pliers and other tools dangling from his brown belt, he was a figure to please the eye of an artist. The man was very tall and gaunt, with great, straggling limbs and every appearance of giant strength. His face was a remarkable one, noble and yet sinister, with dark eyes and hair, a prominent, hooked nose, and a beard which flowed over his chest. He steadied himself with one knotted hand, while the other held a steel hammer dangling by his knee.

"It's all ready aloft," said he. "I'll go up with you if I may." He sprang down from his perch and joined the others in the lift.

"I suppose you are always watching it," said the young lady.

"That is what I am engaged for, miss. From morning

to night, and often from night to morning, I am up here. There are times when I feel as if I were not a man at all, but a fowl of the air. They fly round me, the creatures, as I lie out on the girders, and they cry to me until I find myself crying back to the poor, soulless things."

"It's a great charge," said the Commander, glancing up at the wonderful tracery of steel outlined against the deep blue sky.

"Aye, sir, and there is not a nut nor a screw that is not in my keeping. Here's my hammer to ring them true and my spanner to wrench them tight. As the Lord over the earth, so am I—even I—over the Tower, with power of life and power of death, aye of death and of life."

The hydraulic machinery had begun to work and the lift very slowly ascended. As it mounted, the glorious panorama of the coast and bay gradually unfolded itself. So engrossing was the view that the passengers hardly noticed it when the platform stopped abruptly between stages at the five hundred foot level. Barnes, the workman, muttered that something must be amiss, and springing like a cat across the gap which separated them from the trellis-work of metal he clambered out of sight. The motley little party, suspended in mid-air, lost something of their British shyness under such unwonted conditions and began to compare notes with each other. One couple, who addressed each other as Dolly and Billy, announced to the company that they were the particular stars of the Hippodrome bill, and kept their neighbours tittering with their rather obvious wit. A buxom mother, her precocious son, and two married couples upon holiday formed an appreciative audience.

"You'd like to be a sailor, would you?" said Billy the comedian, in answer to some remark of the boy. "Look 'ere, my nipper, you'll end up as a blooming corpse if you ain't careful. See 'im standin' at the edge. At this hour of the morning I can't bear to watch it."

"What's the hour got to do with it?" asked a stout commercial traveller.

" My nerves are worth nothin' before midday. Why, lookin' down there, and seein' those folk like dots, puts me all in a twitter. My family is all alike in the mornin'."

" I expect," said Dolly, a high-coloured young woman, " that they're all alike the evening before."

There was a general laugh, which was led by the comedian.

" You got it across that time, Dolly. It's K.O. for Battling Billy—still senseless when last heard of. If my family is laughed at I'll leave the room."

" It's about time we did," said the commercial traveller, who was a red-faced, choleric person. " It's a disgrace the way they hold us up. I'll write to the company."

" Where's the bell-push ? " said Billy. " I'm goin' to ring."

" What for—the waiter ? " asked the lady.

" For the conductor, the chauffeur, whoever it is that drives the old bus up and down. Have they run out of petrol, or broke the mainspring, or what ? "

" We have a fine view, anyhow," said the Commander.

" Well, I've had that," remarked Billy. " I'm done with it, and I'm for getting on."

" I'm getting nervous," cried the stout mother. " I do hope there is nothing wrong with the lift."

" I say, hold on to the slack of my coat, Dolly. I'm going to look over and chance it. Oh, Lord, it makes me sick and giddy ! There's a horse down under, and it ain't bigger than a mouse. I don't see anyone lookin' after us. Where's old Isaiah the prophet who came up with us ? "

" He shinned out of it mighty quick when he thought trouble was coming."

" Look here," said Dolly, looking very perturbed, " this is a nice thing, I don't think. Here we are five hundred foot up, and stuck for the day as like as not. I'm due for the *matinée* at the Hippodrome. I'm sorry for the company if they don't get me down in time for that. I'm billed all over the town for a new song."

"A new one! What's that, Dolly?"

"A real pot o' ginger, I tell you. It's called 'On the Road to Ascot.' I've got a hat four foot across to sing it in."

"Come on, Dolly, let's have a rehearsal while we wait."

"No, no; the young lady here wouldn't understand."

"I'd be very glad to hear it," cried Mary MacLean. "Please don't let me prevent you."

"The words were written to the hat. I couldn't sing the verses without the hat. But there's a nailin' good chorus to it:

"'If you want a little mascot
When you're on the way to Ascot,
Try the lady with the cartwheel hat.'"

She had a tuneful voice and a sense of rhythm which set everyone nodding. "Try it now all together," she cried; and the strange little haphazard company sang it with all their lungs.

"I say," said Billy, "that ought to wake somebody up. What? Let's try a shout all together."

It was a fine effort, but there was no response. It was clear that the management down below was quite ignorant or impotent. No sound came back to them.

The passengers became alarmed. The commercial traveller was rather less rubicund. Billy still tried to joke, but his efforts were not well received. The officer in his blue uniform at once took his place as rightful leader in a crisis. They all looked to him and appealed to him.

"What would you advise, sir? You don't think there's any danger of it coming down, do you?"

"Not the least. But it's awkward to be stuck here all the same. I think I could jump across on to that girder. Then perhaps I could see what is wrong."

"No, no, Tom; for goodness' sake, don't leave us!"

"Some people have a nerve," said Billy. "Fancy jumping across a five-hundred-foot drop!"

"I dare say the gentleman did worse things in the war."

"Well, I wouldn't do it myself—not if they starred me in the bills. It's all very well for old Isaiah. It's his job, and I wouldn't do him out of it."

Three sides of the lift were shut in with wooden partitions, pierced with windows for the view. The fourth side, facing the sea, was clear. Stangate leaned over as far as he could and looked upwards. As he did so there came from above him a peculiar, sonorous, metallic twang, as if a mighty harp-string had been struck. Some distance up—a hundred feet, perhaps—he could see a long, brown, corded arm, which was working furiously among the wire cordage above. The form was beyond his view, but he was fascinated by this bare, sinewy arm which tugged and pulled and sagged and stabbed.

"It's all right," he said, and a general sigh of relief broke from his strange comrades at his words. "There is someone above us setting things right."

"It's old Isaiah," said Billy, stretching his neck round the corner. "I can't see him, but it's his arm for a dollar. What's he got in his hand? Looks like a screwdriver or something. No, by George, it's a file."

As he spoke there came another sonorous twang from above. There was a troubled frown upon the officer's brow.

"I say, dash it all, that's the very sound our steel hawser made when it parted, strand by strand, at Dixmude. What the deuce is the fellow about? Heh, there! what are you trying to do?"

The man had ceased his work and was now slowly descending the iron trellis.

"All right, he's coming," said Stangate to his startled companions. "It's all right, Mary. Don't be frightened, any of you. It's absurd to suppose he would really weaken the cord that holds us."

A pair of high boots appeared from above. Then came the leathern breeches, the belt with its dangling tools, the muscular form, and, finally, the fierce, swarthy, eagle face of the workman. His coat was off and his shirt open showing the hairy chest. As he appeared there came another sharp, snapping vibration from above. The man made his way down in leisurely fashion, and then, balancing himself upon the cross-girder and leaning against the side-piece, he stood with folded arms, looking from under his heavy black brows at the huddled passengers upon the platform.

"Hallo!" said Stangate. "What's the matter?"

The man stood impassive and silent, with something indescribably menacing in his fixed, unwinking stare.

The flying officer grew angry.

"Hallo! Are you deaf?" he cried. "How long do you mean to have us stuck here?"

The man stood silent. There was something devilish in his appearance.

"I'll complain of you, my lad," said Billy, in a quivering voice. "This won't stop here, I can promise you."

"Look here!" cried the officer. "We have ladies here and you are alarming them. Why are we stuck here? Has the machinery gone wrong?"

"You are here," said the man, "because I have put a wedge against the hawser above you."

"You fouled the line! How dared you do such a thing! What right have you to frighten the women and put us all to this inconvenience? Take that wedge out this instant, or it will be the worse for you."

The man was silent.

"Do you hear what I say? Why the devil don't you answer? Is this a joke or what? We've had about enough of it, I tell you."

Mary MacLean had gripped her lover by the arm in an agony of sudden panic.

"Oh, Tom!" she cried. "Look at his eyes—look at his horrible eyes! The man is a maniac."

The workman stirred suddenly into sinister life. His dark face broke into writhing lines of passion, and his fierce eyes glowed like embers, while he shook one long arm in the air.

"Behold," he cried, "those who are mad to the children of this world are in very truth the Lord's anointed and the dwellers in the inner temple. Lo, I am one who is prepared to testify even to the uttermost, for of a verity the day has now come when the humble will be exalted and the wicked will be cut off in their sins!"

"Mother! Mother!" cried the little boy, in terror.

"There, there! It's all right, Jack," said the buxom woman, and then, in a burst of womanly wrath, "What d'you want to make the child cry for? You're a pretty man, you are!"

"Better he should cry now than in the outer darkness. Let him seek safety while there is yet time."

The officer measured the gap with a practised eye. It was a good eight feet across, and the fellow could push him over before he could steady himself. It would be a desperate thing to attempt. He tried soothing words once more.

"See here, my lad, you've carried this joke too far. Why should you wish to injure us? Just shin up and get that wedge out, and we will agree to say no more about it."

Another rending snap came from above.

"By George, the hawser is going!" cried Stangate. "Here! Stand aside! I'm coming over to see to it."

The workman had plucked the hammer from his belt, and waved it furiously in the air.

"Stand back, young man! Stand back! Or come—if you would hasten your end."

"Tom, Tom, for God's sake, don't spring! Help! Help!"

The passengers all joined in the cry for aid. The man smiled malignly as he watched them.

"There is no one to help. They could not come if they would. You would be wiser to turn to your own souls that ye be not cast to the burning. Lo, strand by strand the cable snaps which holds you. There is yet another, and with each that goes there is more strain upon the rest. Five minutes of time, and all eternity beyond."

A moan of fear rose from the prisoners in the lift. Stangate felt a cold sweat upon his brow as he passed his arm round the shrinking girl. If this vindictive devil could only be coaxed away for an instant he would spring across and take his chance in a hand-to-hand fight.

"Look here, my friend! We give you best!" he cried. "We can do nothing. Go up and cut the cable if you wish. Go on—do it now, and get it over!"

"That you may come across unharmed. Having set my hand to the work, I will not draw back from it."

Fury seized the young officer.

"You devil!" he cried. "What do you stand there grinning for? I'll give you something to grin about. Give me a stick, one of you."

The man waved his hammer.

"Come, then! Come to judgment!" he howled.

"He'll murder you, Tom! Oh, for God's sake, don't! If we must die, let us die together."

"I wouldn't try it, sir," cried Billy. "He'll strike you down before you get a footing. Hold up, Dolly, my dear! Faintin' won't 'elp us. You speak to him, miss. Maybe he'll listen to you."

"Why should you wish to hurt us?" said Mary. "What have we ever done to you? Surely you will be sorry afterwards if we are injured. Now do be kind and reasonable and help us to get back to the ground."

For a moment there may have been some softening in the man's fierce eyes as he looked at the sweet face which was upturned to him. Then his features set once more into their grim lines of malice.

"My hand is set to the work, woman. It is not for the servant to look back from his task."

"But why should this be your task?"

"Because there is a voice within me which tells me

so. In the night-time I have heard it, and in the daytime, too, when I have lain out alone upon the girders and seen the wicked dotting the streets beneath me, each busy on his own evil intent. 'John Barnes, John Barnes,' said the voice. 'You are here that you may give a sign to a sinful generation—such a sign as shall show them that the Lord liveth and that there is a judgment upon sin.' Who am I that I should disobey the voice of the Lord?"

"The voice of the devil," said Stangate. "What is the sin of this lady, or of these others, that you should seek their lives?"

"You are as the others, neither better nor worse. All day they pass me, load by load, with foolish cries and empty songs and vain babble of voices. Their thoughts are set upon the things of the flesh. Too long have I stood aside and watched and refused to testify. But now the day of wrath is come and the sacrifice is ready. Think not that a woman's tongue can turn me from my task."

"It is useless!" Mary cried. "Useless! I read death in his eyes."

Another cord had snapped.

"Repent! Repent!" cried the madman. "One more, and it is over!"

Commander Stangate felt as if it were all some extraordinary dream—some monstrous nightmare. Could it be possible that he, after all his escapes of death in warfare, was now, in the heart of peaceful England, at the mercy of a homicidal lunatic, and that his dear girl, the one being whom he would shield from the very shadow of danger, was helpless before this horrible man? All his energy and manhood rose up in him for one last effort.

"Here, we won't be killed like sheep in the shambles!" he cried, throwing himself against the wooden wall of the lift and kicking with all his force. "Come on, boys! Kick it! Beat it! It's only match-boarding, and it is giving. Smash it down! Well done! Once more all together! There she goes! Now for the side! Out with it! Splendid!"

First the back and then the side of the little compartment had been knocked out, and the splinters dropped down into the abyss. Barnes danced upon his girder, his hammer in the air.

"Strive not!" he shrieked. "It avails not. The day is surely come."

"It's not two feet from the side-girder," cried the officer. "Get across! Quick! Quick! All of you. I'll hold this devil off!" He had seized a stout stick from the commercial traveller and faced the madman, daring him to spring across.

"Your turn now, my friend!" he hissed. "Come on, hammer and all! I'm ready for you."

Above him he heard another snap, and the frail platform began to rock. Glancing over his shoulder, he saw that his companions were all safe upon the side-girder. A strange line of terrified castaways they appeared as they clung in an ungainly row to the trellis-work of steel. But their feet were on the iron support. With two quick steps and a spring he was at their side. At the same instant the murderer, hammer in hand, jumped the gap. They had one vision of him there—a vision which will haunt their dreams—the convulsed face, the blazing eyes, the wind-tossed, raven locks. For a moment he balanced himself upon the swaying platform. The next, with a rending crash, he and it were gone. There was a long silence and then, far down, the thud and clatter of a mighty fall.

With white faces, the forlorn group clung to the cold steel bars and gazed down into the terrible abyss. It was the Commander who broke the silence.

"They'll send for us now. It's all safe," he cried, wiping his brow. "But, by Jove, it was a close call!"

TALES OF ADVENTURE

50. *The Début of Bimbashi Joyce*

IT was in the days when the tide of Mahdism, which had swept in such a flood from the great Lakes and Darfur to the confines of Egypt, had at last come to its full, and even begun, as some hoped, to show signs of a turn. At its outset it had been terrible. It had engulfed Hicks's army, swept over Gordon and Khartoum, rolled behind the British forces as they retired down the river, and finally cast up a spray of raiding parties as far north as Assouan. Then it found other channels to east and to west, to Central Africa and to Abyssinia, and retired a little on the side of Egypt. For ten years there ensued a lull, during which the frontier garrisons looked out upon those distant, blue hills of Dongola. Behind the violet mists which draped them, lay a land of blood and horror. From time to time some adventurer went south towards those haze-girt mountains, tempted by stories of gum and ivory, but none ever returned. Once a mutilated Egyptian and once a Greek woman, mad with thirst and fear, made their way to the lines. They were the only exports of that country of darkness. Sometimes the sunset would turn those distant mists into a bank of crimson, and the dark mountains would rise from that sinister reek like islands in a sea of blood. It seemed a grim symbol in the southern heaven when seen from the fort-capped hills by Wady Halfa.

Ten years of lust in Khartoum, ten years of silent work in Cairo, and then all was ready, and it was time for civilisation to take a trip south once more, travelling, as her wont is, in an armoured train. Everything was ready, down to the last pack-saddle of the last camel, and yet no one suspected it, for an unconstitutional Government has its advantages. A great administrator had argued, and managed, and cajoled ; a great soldier had organised and planned, and made piastres do the work of pounds. And then one night these two master spirits met and clasped hands, and the soldier vanished away upon some business of his own. And just at that very time Bimbashi Hilary Joyce, seconded from the Royal Mallow Fusiliers, and temporarily attached to the Ninth Soudanese, made his first appearance in Cairo.

Napoleon had said, and Hilary Joyce had noted, that great reputations are only to be made in the East. Here he was in the East with four tin cases of baggage, a Wilkinson sword, a Bond's slug-throwing pistol, and a copy of *Green's Introduction to the Study of Arabic*. With such a start, and the blood of youth running hot in his veins, everything seemed easy. He was a little frightened of the General, he had heard stories of his sternness to young officers, but with tact and suavity he hoped for the best. So, leaving his effects at Shepheard's Hotel, he reported himself at headquarters.

It was not the General, but the head of the Intelligence Department who received him, the Chief being still absent upon that business which had called him. Hilary Joyce found himself in the presence of a short, thick-set officer, with a gentle voice and a placid expression which covered a remarkably acute and energetic spirit. With that quiet smile and guileless manner he had undercut and outwitted the most cunning of Orientals. He stood, a cigarette between his fingers, looking at the new-comer.

"I heard that you had come. Sorry the Chief isn't here to see you. Gone up to the frontier, you know."

"My regiment is at Wady Halfa. I suppose, sir, that I should report myself there at once?"

"No; I was to give you your orders." He led the way to a map upon the wall, and pointed with the end of his cigarette. "You see this place. It's the Oasis of Kurkur—a little quiet, I am afraid, but excellent air. You are to get out there as quick as possible. You'll find a company of the Ninth, and half a squadron of cavalry. You will be in command."

Hilary Joyce looked at the name, printed at the intersection of two black lines, without another dot upon the map for several inches round it.

"A village, sir?"

"No, a well. Not very good water, I'm afraid, but you soon get accustomed to natron. It's an important post, as being at the junction of two caravan routes. All routes are closed now, of course, but still you never know who *might* come along them."

"We are there, I presume, to prevent raiding?"

"Well, between you and me, there's really nothing to raid. You are there to intercept messengers. They must call at the wells. Of course you have only just come out, but you probably understand already enough about the conditions of this country to know that there is a great deal of disaffection about, and that the Khalifa is likely to try and keep in touch with his adherents. Then, again, Senoussi lives up that way"—he waved his cigarette to the westward—"the Khalifa might send a message to him along that route. Anyhow, your duty is to arrest everyone coming along, and get some account of him before you let him go. You don't talk Arabic, I suppose?"

"I am learning, sir."

"Well, well, you'll have time enough for study there. And you'll have a native officer, Ali something or other, who speaks English, and can interpret for you. Well, good-bye—I'll tell the Chief that you reported yourself. Get on to your post now as quickly as you can."

Railway to Baliani, the post-boat to Assouan, and then two days on a camel in the Libyan Desert, with an

Ababdeh guide, and three baggage-camels to tie one down to their own exasperating pace. However, even two and a half miles an hour mount up in time, and at last, on the third evening, from the blackened slag-heap of a hill which is called the Jebel Kurkur, Hilary Joyce looked down upon a distant clump of palms, and thought that this cool patch of green in the midst of the merciless blacks and yellows was the fairest colour effect that he had ever seen. An hour later he had ridden into the little camp, the guard had turned out to salute him, his native subordinate had greeted him in excellent English, and he had fairly entered into his own.

It was not an exhilarating place for a lengthy residence. There was one large, bowl-shaped, grassy depression sloping down to the three pits of brown and brackish water. There was the grove of palm-trees also, beautiful to look upon, but exasperating in view of the fact that Nature has provided her least-shady trees on the very spot where shade is needed most. A single wide-spread acacia did something to restore the balance. Here Hilary Joyce slumbered in the heat, and in the cool he inspected his square-shouldered, spindle-shanked Soudanese, with their cheery, black faces and their funny little pork-pie forage caps. Joyce was a martinet at drill, and the blacks loved being drilled, so the Bimbashi was soon popular among them. But one day was exactly like another. The weather, the view, the employment, the food—everything was the same. At the end of three weeks he felt that he had been there for interminable years. And then at last there came something to break the monotony.

One evening, as the sun was sinking, Hilary Joyce rode slowly down the old caravan road. It had a fascination for him, this narrow track, winding among the boulders and curving up the nullahs, for he remembered how in the map it had gone on and on, stretching away into the unknown heart of Africa. The countless pads of innumerable camels through many centuries had beaten it smooth, so that now, unused and deserted, it still wound away, the strangest of roads, a foot broad, and perhaps two thousand miles in length. Joyce wondered as he rode how long it was since any traveller had journeyed up it from the south, and then he raised his eyes, and there was a man coming along the path.

For an instant Joyce thought that it might be one of his own men, but a second glance assured him that this could not be so. The stranger was dressed in the flowing robes of an Arab, and not in the close-fitting khaki of a soldier. He was very tall, and a high turban made him seem gigantic. He strode swiftly along, with head erect, and the bearing of a man who knows no fear.

Who could he be, this formidable giant coming out of the unknown? The precursor possibly of a horde of savage spearmen. And where could he have walked from? The nearest well was a long hundred miles down the track. At any rate the frontier post of Kurkur could not afford to receive casual visitors. Hilary Joyce whisked round his horse, galloped into camp, and gave the alarm. Then, with twenty horsemen at his back, he rode out again to reconnoitre.

The man was still coming on in spite of these hostile preparations. For an instant he had hesitated when first he saw the cavalry, but escape was out of the question, and he advanced with the air of one who makes the best of a bad job. He made no resistance, and said nothing when the hands of two troopers clutched at his shoulders, but walked quietly between their horses into camp. Shortly afterwards the patrols came in again. There were no signs of any Dervishes. The man was alone. A splendid trotting camel had been found lying dead a little way down the track. The mystery of the stranger's arrival was explained. But why, and whence, and whither?—these were questions for which a zealous officer must find an answer.

Hilary Joyce was disappointed that there were no

Dervishes. It would have been a great start for him in the Egyptian army had he fought a little action on his own account. But even as it was, he had a rare chance of impressing the authorities. He would love to show his capacity to the head of the Intelligence, and even more to that grim Chief who never forgot what was smart, or forgave what was slack. The prisoner's dress and bearing showed that he was of importance. Mean men do not ride pure-bred trotting camels. Joyce sponged his head with cold water, drank a cup of strong coffee, put on an imposing official tarboosh instead of his sun-helmet, and formed himself into a court of inquiry and judgment under the acacia tree.

He would have liked his people to have seen him now, with his two black orderlies in waiting, and his Egyptian native officer at his side. He sat behind a camp-table, and the prisoner, strongly guarded, was led up to him. The man was a handsome fellow, with bold, grey eyes and a long, black beard.

"Why!" cried Joyce, "the rascal is making faces at me."

A curious contraction had passed over the man's features, but so swiftly that it might have been a nervous twitch. He was now a model of Oriental gravity.

"Ask him who he is, and what he wants?"

The native officer did so, but the stranger made no reply, save that the same sharp spasm passed once more over his face.

"Well, I'm blessed!" cried Hilary Joyce. "Of all the impudent scoundrels! He keeps on winking at me. Who are you, you rascal? Give an account of yourself! D'ye hear?"

But the tall Arab was as impervious to English as to Arabic. The Egyptian tried again and again. The prisoner looked at Joyce with his inscrutable eyes, and occasionally twitched his face at him, but never opened his mouth. The Bimbashi scratched his head in bewilderment.

"Look here, Mahomet Ali, we've got to get some sense out of this fellow. You say there are no papers on him?"

"No, sir; we found no papers."

"No clue of any kind?"

"He has come far, sir. A trotting camel does not die easily. He has come from Dongola, at least."

"Well, we must get him to talk."

"It is possible that he is deaf and dumb."

"Not he. I never saw a man look more all there in my life."

"You might send him across to Assouan."

"And give someone else the credit! No, thank you. This is my bird. But how are we going to get him to find his tongue?"

The Egyptian's dark eyes skirted the encampment and rested on the cook's fire.

"Perhaps," said he, "if the Bimbashi thought fit ——" He looked at the prisoner and then at the burning wood.

"No, no, it wouldn't do. No, by Jove, that's going too far."

"A very little might do it."

"No, no. It's all very well here, but it would sound just awful if ever it got as far as Fleet Street. But, I say," he whispered, "we might frighten him a bit. There's no harm in that."

"No, sir."

"Tell them to undo the man's galabeeah. Order them to put a horseshoe in the fire and make it red-hot."

The prisoner watched the proceedings with an air which had more of amusement than of uneasiness. He never winced as the black sergeant approached with the glowing shoe held upon two bayonets.

"Will you speak now?" asked the Bimbashi savagely.

The prisoner smiled gently and stroked his beard.

"Oh, chuck the infernal thing away!" cried Joyce

jumping up in a passion. "There's no use trying to bluff the fellow. He knows we won't do it. But I *can* and I *will* flog him, and you tell him from me that if he hasn't found his tongue by to-morrow morning, I'll take the skin off his back as sure as my name's Joyce. Have you said all that?"

"Yes, sir."

"Well, you can sleep upon it, you beauty, and a good night's rest may it give you!"

He adjourned the Court, and the prisoner, as imperturbable as ever, was led away by the guard to his supper of rice and water.

Hilary Joyce was a kind-hearted man, and his own sleep was considerably disturbed by the prospect of the punishment which he must inflict next day. He had hopes that the mere sight of the koorbash and the thongs might prevail over his prisoner's obstinacy. And then, again, he thought how shocking it would be if the man proved to be really dumb after all. The possibility shook him so that he had almost determined by daybreak that he would send the stranger on unhurt to Assouan. And yet what a tame conclusion it would be to the incident! He lay upon his angareeb still debating it when the question suddenly and effectively settled itself. Ali Mahomet rushed into his tent.

"Sir," he cried, "the prisoner is gone!"

"Gone!"

"Yes, sir, and your own best riding camel as well. There is a slit cut in the tent, and he got away unseen in the early morning."

The Bimbashi acted with all energy. Cavalry rode along every track; scouts examined the soft sand of the wadys for signs of the fugitive, but no trace was discovered. The man had utterly disappeared. With a heavy heart Hilary Joyce wrote an official report of the matter and forwarded it to Assouan. Five days later there came a curt order from the Chief that he should report himself there. He feared the worst from the stern soldier, who spared others as little as he spared himself.

And his worst forebodings were realised. Travel-stained and weary, he reported himself one night at the General's quarters. Behind a table piled with papers and strewn with maps the famous soldier and his Chief of Intelligence were deep in plans and figures. Their greeting was a cold one.

"I understand, Captain Joyce," said the General, "that you have allowed a very important prisoner to slip through your fingers."

"I am sorry, sir."

"No doubt. But that will not mend matters. Did you ascertain anything about him before you lost him?"

"No, sir."

"How was that?"

"I could get nothing out of him, sir."

"Did you try?"

"Yes, sir; I did what I could."

"What did you do?"

"Well, sir, I threatened to use physical force."

"What did he say?"

"He said nothing."

"What was he like?"

"A tall man, sir. Rather a desperate character, I should think."

"Any way by which we could identify him?"

"A long black beard, sir. Grey eyes. And a nervous way of twitching his face."

"Well, Captain Joyce," said the General, in his stern, inflexible voice, "I cannot congratulate you upon your first exploit in the Egyptian army. You are aware that every English officer in this force is a picked man. I have the whole British army from which to draw. It is necessary, therefore, that I should insist upon the very highest efficiency. It would be unfair upon the others to pass over any obvious want of zeal or intelligence. You are seconded from the Royal Mallows, I understand ?"

"Yes, sir."

"I have no doubt that your Colonel will be glad to see you fulfilling your regimental duties again."

Hilary Joyce's heart was too heavy for words. He was silent.

"I will let you know my final decision to-morrow morning."

Joyce saluted and turned upon his heel.

"You can sleep upon that, you beauty, and a good night's rest may it give you !"

Joyce turned in bewilderment. Where had those words been used before ? Who was it who had used them ?

The General was standing erect. Both he and the Chief of the Intelligence were laughing. Joyce stared at the tall figure, the erect bearing, the inscrutable grey eyes.

"Good Lord !" he gasped.

"Well, well, Captain Joyce, we are quits !" said the General, holding out his hand. "You gave me a bad ten minutes with that infernal, red-hot horseshoe of yours. I've done as much for you. I don't think we can spare you for the Royal Mallows just yet awhile."

"But, sir ; but——!"

"The fewer questions the better, perhaps. But of course it must seem rather amazing. I had a little private business with the Kabbabish. It must be done in person. I did it, and came to your post in my return. I kept on winking at you as a sign that I wanted a word with you alone."

"Yes, yes. I begin to understand."

"I couldn't give it away before all those blacks, or where should I have been the next time I used my false beard and Arab dress ? You put me in a very awkward position. But at last I had a word alone with your Egyptian officer, who managed my escape all right."

"He! Mahomet Ali!"

"I ordered him to say nothing. I had a score to settle with you. But we dine at eight, Captain Joyce. We live plainly here, but I think I can do you a little better than you did me at Kurkur."

51. *The Surgeon of Gaster Fell*

I—HOW THE WOMAN CAME TO KIRKBY-MALHOUSE

BLEAK and wind-swept is the little town of Kirkby-Malhouse, harsh and forbidding are the fells upon which it stands. It stretches in a single line of grey-stone, slate-roofed houses, dotted down the furze-clad slope of the rolling moor.

In this lonely and secluded village, I, James Upperton, found myself in the summer of '85. Little as the hamlet had to offer, it contained that for which I yearned above all things—seclusion and freedom from all which might distract my mind from the high and weighty subjects which engaged it. But the inquisitiveness of my landlady made my lodgings undesirable and I determined to seek new quarters.

As it chanced, I had in one of my rambles come upon an isolated dwelling in the very heart of these lonely moors, which I at once determined should be my own. It was a two-roomed cottage, which had once belonged to some shepherd, but had long been deserted, and was crumbling rapidly to ruin. In the winter floods, the Gaster Beck, which runs down Gaster Fell, where the little dwelling stood, had overswept its banks and torn away a part of the wall. The roof was in ill case, and the scattered slates lay thick amongst the grass. Yet the main shell of the house stood firm and true; and it was no great task for me to have all that was amiss set right.

The two rooms I laid out in a widely different manner

—my own tastes are of a Spartan turn, and the outer chamber was so planned as to accord with them. An oil-stove by Rippingille of Birmingham furnished me with the means of cooking; while two great bags, the one of flour, and the other of potatoes, made me independent of all supplies from without. In diet I had long been a Pythagorean, so that the scraggy, long-limbed sheep which browsed upon the wiry grass by the Gaster Beck had little to fear from their new companion. A nine-gallon cask of oil served me as a sideboard; while a square table, a deal chair and a truckle-bed completed the list of my domestic fittings. At the head of my couch hung two unpainted shelves—the lower for my dishes and cooking utensils, the upper for the few portraits which took me back to the little that was pleasant in the long, wearisome toiling for wealth and for pleasure which had marked the life I had left behind.

If this dwelling-room of mine were plain even to squalor, its poverty was more than atoned for by the luxury of the chamber which was destined to serve me as my study. I had ever held that it was best for my mind to be surrounded by such objects as would be in harmony with the studies which occupied it, and that the loftiest and most ethereal conditions of thought are only possible amid surroundings which please the eye and gratify the senses. The room which I had set apart for my mystic studies was set forth in a style as gloomy and majestic as the thoughts and aspirations with which it was to harmonise. Both walls and ceilings were covered with a paper of the richest and glossiest black, on which was traced a lurid and arabesque pattern of dead gold. A black velvet curtain covered the single diamond-paned window; while a thick, yielding carpet of the same material prevented the sound of my own footfalls, as I paced backward and forward, from breaking the current of my thought. Along the cornices ran gold rods, from which depended six pictures, all of the sombre and imaginative caste, which chimed best with my fancy.

And yet it was destined that ere ever I reached this quiet harbour I should learn that I was still one of humankind, and that it is an ill thing to strive to break the bond which binds us to our fellows. It was but two nights before the date I had fixed upon for my change of dwelling, when I was conscious of a bustle in the house beneath, with the bearing of heavy burdens up the creaking stair, and the harsh voice of my landlady, loud in welcome and protestations of joy. From time to time, amid the whirl of words, I could hear a gentle and softly modulated voice, which struck pleasantly upon my ear after the long weeks during which I had listened only to the rude dialect of the dalesmen. For an hour I could hear the dialogue beneath—the high voice and the low, with clatter of cup and clink of spoon, until at last a light, quick step passed my study door, and I knew that my new fellow-lodger had sought her room.

On the morning after this incident I was up betimes, as is my wont; but I was surprised, on glancing from my window, to see that our new inmate was earlier still. She was walking down the narrow pathway, which zigzags over the fell—a tall woman, slender, her head sunk upon her breast, her arms filled with a bristle of wild flowers, which she had gathered in her morning rambles. The white and pink of her dress, and the touch of deep red ribbon in her broad, drooping hat, formed a pleasant dash of colour against the dun-tinted landscape. She was some distance off when I first set eyes upon her, yet I knew that this wandering woman could be none other than our arrival of last night, for there was a grace and refinement in her bearing which marked her from the dwellers of the fells. Even as I watched she passed swiftly and lightly down the pathway, and turning through the wicket gate, at the farther end of our cottage garden, she seated herself upon the green bank which faced my window, and strewing her flowers in front of her, set herself to arrange them.

As she sat there, with the rising sun at her back, and the glow of the morning spreading like an aureole around her stately and well-poised head, I could see that she was a woman of extraordinary personal beauty. Her face was Spanish rather than English in its type —oval, olive, with black, sparkling eyes, and a sweetly sensitive mouth. From under the broad straw hat two thick coils of blue-black hair curved down on either side of her graceful, queenly neck. I was surprised, as I watched her, to see that her shoes and skirt bore witness to a journey rather than to a mere morning ramble. Her light dress was stained, wet and bedraggled; while her boots were thick with the yellow soil of the fells. Her face, too, wore a weary expression, and her young beauty seemed to be clouded over by the shadow of inward trouble. Even as I watched her, she burst suddenly into wild weeping, and throwing down her bundle of flowers, ran swiftly into the house.

Distrait as I was and weary of the ways of the world, I was conscious of a sudden pang of sympathy and grief as I looked upon the spasm of despair which seemed to convulse this strange and beautiful woman. I bent to my books, and yet my thoughts would ever turn to her proud, clear-cut face, her weather-stained dress, her drooping head, and the sorrow which lay in each line and feature of her pensive face.

Mrs. Adams, my landlady, was wont to carry up my frugal breakfast; yet it was very rarely that I allowed her to break the current of my thoughts, or to draw my mind by her idle chatter from weightier things. This morning, however, for once, she found me in a listening mood, and with little prompting, proceeded to pour into my ears all that she knew of our beautiful visitor.

"Miss Eva Cameron be her name, sir," she said: "but who she be, or where she came fra, I know little more than yoursel'. Maybe it was the same reason that brought her to Kirkby-Malhouse as fetched you there yoursel', sir."

"Possibly," said I, ignoring the covert question; "but I should hardly have thought that Kirkby-Malhouse was a place which offered any great attractions to a young lady."

"Heh, sir!" she cried, "there's the wonder of it. The leddy has just come fra France; and how her folk come to learn of me is just a wonder. A week ago, up comes a man to my door—a fine man, sir, and a gentleman, as one could see with half an eye. 'You are Mrs. Adams,' says he. 'I engage your rooms for Miss Cameron,' says he. 'She will be here in a week,' says he; and then off without a word of terms. Last night there comes the young leddy hersel'—soft-spoken and downcast, with a touch of the French in her speech. But my sakes, sir! I must away and mak' her some tea, for she'll feel lonesome-like, poor lamb, when she wakes under a strange roof."

II—HOW I WENT FORTH TO GASTER FELL

I was still engaged upon my breakfast when I heard the clatter of dishes and the landlady's footfall as she passed toward her new lodger's room. An instant afterward she had rushed down the passage and burst in upon me with uplifted hand and startled eyes. "Lord 'a mercy, sir!" she cried, "and asking your pardon for troubling you, but I'm feared o' the young leddy, sir; she is not in her room."

"Why, there she is," said I, standing up and glancing through the casement. "She has gone back for the flowers she left upon the bank."

"Oh, sir, see her boots and her dress!" cried the landlady wildly. "I wish her mother was here, sir—I do. Where she has been is more than I ken, but her bed has not been lain on this night."

"She has felt restless, doubtless, and went for a walk, though the hour was certainly a strange one."

Mrs. Adams pursed her lip and shook her head. But then as she stood at the casement, the girl beneath looked smilingly up at her and beckoned to her with a merry gesture to open the window.

"Have you my tea there?" she asked in a rich, clear voice, with a touch of the mincing French accent.

"It is in your room, miss."

"Look at my boots, Mrs. Adams!" she cried, thrusting them out from under her skirt. "These fells of yours are dreadful places—*effroyable*—one inch, two inch; never have I seen such mud! My dress, too—*voilà!*"

"Eh, miss, but you are in a pickle," cried the landlady, as she gazed down at the bedraggled gown. "But you must be main weary and heavy for sleep."

"No, no," she answered laughingly, "I care not for sleep. What is sleep? it is a little death—*voilà tout.* But for me to walk, to run, to breathe the air—that is to live. I was not tired, and so all night I have explored these fells of Yorkshire."

"Lord 'a mercy, miss, and where did you go?" asked Mrs. Adams.

She waved her hand round in a sweeping gesture which included the whole western horizon. "There," she cried. "O comme elles sont tristes et sauvages, ces collines! But I have flowers here. You will give me water, will you not? They will wither else." She gathered her treasures in her lap, and a moment later we heard her light, springy footfall upon the stair.

So she had been out all night, this strange woman. What motive could have taken her from her snug room on to the bleak, wind-swept hills? Could it be merely the restlessness, the love of adventure of a young girl? Or was there, possibly, some deeper meaning in this nocturnal journey?

Deep as were the mysteries which my studies had taught me to solve, here was a human problem which for the moment at least was beyond my comprehension. I had walked out on the moor in the forenoon, and on my return, as I topped the brow that overlooks the little town, I saw my fellow-lodger some little distance off amongst the gorse. She had raised a light easel in front of her, and, with papered board laid across it, was preparing to paint the magnificent landscape of rock and moor which stretched away in front of her. As I watched her I saw that she was looking anxiously to right and left. Close by me a pool of water had formed in a hollow. Dipping the cup of my pocket-flask into it, I carried it across to her.

"Miss Cameron, I believe," said I. "I am your fellow-lodger. Upperton is my name. We must introduce ourselves in these wilds if we are not to be for ever strangers."

"Oh, then, you live also with Mrs. Adams!" she cried. "I had thought that there were none but peasants in this strange place."

"I am a visitor, like yourself," I answered. "I am a student, and have come for quiet and repose, which my studies demand."

"Quiet, indeed!" said she, glancing round at the vast circle of silent moors, with the one tiny line of grey cottages which sloped down beneath us.

"And yet not quiet enough," I answered, laughing, "for I have been forced to move farther into the fells for the absolute peace which I require."

"Have you, then, built a house upon the fells?" she asked, arching her eyebrows.

"I have, and hope, within a few days, to occupy it."

"Ah, but that is *triste*," she cried. "And where is it, then, this house which you have built?"

"It is over yonder," I answered. "See that stream which lies like a silver band upon the distant moor? It is the Gaster Beck, and it runs through Gaster Fell."

She started, and turned upon me her great, dark, questioning eyes with a look in which surprise, incredulity, and something akin to horror seemed to be struggling for mastery.

"And you will live on the Gaster Fell?" she cried.

"So I have planned. But what do you know of Gaster Fell, Miss Cameron?" I asked. "I had thought that you were a stranger in these parts."

"Indeed, I have never been here before," she answered. "But I have heard my brother talk of these Yorkshire moors; and, if I mistake not, I have heard him name this very one as the wildest and most savage of them all."

"Very likely," said I carelessly. "It is indeed a dreary place."

"Then why live there?" she cried eagerly. "Consider the loneliness, the barrenness, the want of all comfort and of all aid, should aid be needed."

"Aid! What aid should be needed on Gaster Fell?"

She looked down and shrugged her shoulders. "Sickness may come in all places," said she. "If I were a man I do not think I would live alone on Gaster Fell."

"I have braved worse dangers than that," said I, laughing; "but I fear that your picture will be spoiled, for the clouds are banking up, and already I feel a few raindrops."

Indeed, it was high time we were on our way to shelter, for even as I spoke there came the sudden, steady swish of the shower. Laughing merrily, my companion threw her light shawl over her head, and, seizing picture and easel, ran with the lithe grace of a young fawn down the furze-clad slope, while I followed after with camp-stool and paint-box.

* * * * *

It was the eve of my departure from Kirkby-Malhouse that we sat upon the green bank in the garden, she with dark, dreamy eyes looking sadly out over the sombre fells; while I, with a book upon my knee, glanced covertly at her lovely profile and marvelled to myself how twenty years of life could have stamped so sad and wistful an expression upon it.

"You have read much," I remarked at last. "Women have opportunities now such as their mothers never knew. Have you ever thought of going further—or seeking a course of college or even a learned profession ? "

She smiled wearily at the thought.

" I have no aim, no ambition," she said. " My future is black—confused—a chaos. My life is like to one of these paths upon the fells. You have seen them, Monsieur Upperton. They are smooth and straight and clear where they begin ; but soon they wind to left and wind to right, and so mid rocks and crags until they lose themselves in some quagmire. At Brussels my path was straight ; but now, *mon Dieu!* who is there can tell me where it leads ? "

" It might take no prophet to do that, Miss Cameron," quoth I, with the fatherly manner which twoscore years may show toward one. " If I may read your life, I would venture to say that you were destined to fulfil the lot of women—to make some good man happy, and to shed around, in some wider circle, the pleasure which your society has given me since first I knew you."

" I will never marry," said she, with a sharp decision, which surprised and somewhat amused me.

" Not marry—and why ? "

A strange look passed over her sensitive features, and she plucked nervously at the grass on the bank beside her.

" I dare not," said she in a voice that quivered with emotion.

" Dare not ? "

" It is not for me. I have other things to do. That path of which I spoke is one which I must tread alone."

" But this is morbid," said I. " Why should your lot, Miss Cameron, be separated from that of my own sisters, or the thousand other young ladies whom every season brings out into the world ? But perhaps it is that you have a fear and distrust of mankind. Marriage brings a risk as well as a happiness."

" The risk would be with the man who married

me," she cried. And then in an instant, as though she had said too much, she sprang to her feet and drew her mantle round her. "The night air is chill, Mr. Upperton," said she, and so swept swiftly away, leaving me to muse over the strange words which had fallen from her lips.

Clearly, it was time that I should go. I set my teeth and vowed that another day should not have passed before I should have snapped this newly formed tie and sought the lonely retreat which awaited me upon the moors. Breakfast was hardly over in the morning before a peasant dragged up to the door the rude hand-cart which was to convey my few personal belongings to my new dwelling. My fellow-lodger had kept her room; and, steeled as my mind was against her influence, I was yet conscious of a little throb of disappointment that she should allow me to depart without a word of farewell. My hand-cart with its load of books had already started, and I, having shaken hands with Mrs. Adams, was about to follow it, when there was a quick scurry of feet on the stair, and there she was beside me all panting with her own haste.

"Then you go—you really go?" said she.

"My studies call me."

"And to Gaster Fell?" she asked.

"Yes; to the cottage which I have built there."

"And you will live alone there?"

"With my hundred companions who lie in that cart."

"Ah, books!" she cried, with a pretty shrug of her graceful shoulders. "But you will make me a promise?"

"What is it?" I asked, in surprise.

"It is a small thing. You will not refuse me?"

"You have but to ask it."

She bent forward her beautiful face with an expression of the most intense earnestness. "You will bolt your door at night?" said she; and was gone ere I could say a word in answer to her extraordinary request.

It was a strange thing for me to find myself at last

duly installed in my lonely dwelling. For me, now, the horizon was bounded by the barren circle of wiry, unprofitable grass, patched over with furze bushes and scarred by the profusion of Nature's gaunt and granite ribs. A duller, wearier waste I have never seen; but its dullness was its very charm.

And yet the very first night which I spent at Gaster Fell there came a strange incident to lead my thoughts back once more to the world which I had left behind me.

It had been a sullen and sultry evening, with great, livid cloud-banks mustering in the west. As the night wore on, the air within my little cabin became closer and more oppressive. A weight seemed to rest upon my brow and my chest. From far away the low rumble of thunder came moaning over the moor. Unable to sleep, I dressed, and standing at my cottage door, looked on the black solitude which surrounded me.

Taking the narrow sheep path which ran by this stream, I strolled along it for some hundred yards, and had turned to retrace my steps, when the moon was finally buried beneath an ink-black cloud, and the darkness deepened so suddenly that I could see neither the path at my feet, the stream upon my right, nor the rocks upon my left. I was standing groping about in the thick gloom, when there came a crash of thunder with a flash of lightning which lighted up the whole, vast fell, so that every bush and rock stood out clear and hard in the vivid light. It was but for an instant, and yet that momentary view struck a thrill of fear and astonishment through me, for in my very path, not twenty yards before me, there stood a woman, the livid light beating upon her face and showing up every detail of her dress and features.

There was no mistaking those dark eyes, that tall, graceful figure. It was she—Eva Cameron, the woman whom I thought I had for ever left. For an instant I stood petrified, marvelling whether this could indeed be she, or whether it was some figment conjured up by my excited brain. Then I ran swiftly forward in the direction where I had seen her, calling loudly upon her, but without reply. Again I called, and again no answer came back, save the melancholy wail of the owl. A second flash illuminated the landscape, and the moon burst out from behind its cloud. But I could not, though I climbed upon a knoll which overlooked the whole moor, see any sign of this strange, midnight wanderer. For an hour or more I traversed the fell, and at last found myself back at my little cabin, still uncertain as to whether it had been a woman or a shadow upon which I gazed.

III—OF THE GREY COTTAGE IN THE GLEN

It was either on the fourth or the fifth day after I had taken possession of my cottage that I was astonished to hear footsteps upon the grass outside, quickly followed by a crack, as from a stick upon the door. The explosion of an infernal machine would hardly have surprised or discomfited me more. I had hoped to have shaken off all intrusion for ever, yet here was somebody beating at my door with as little ceremony as if it had been a village ale-house. Hot with anger, I flung down my book and withdrew the bolt just as my visitor had raised his stick to renew his rough application for admittance. He was a tall, powerful man, tawny-bearded and deep-chested, clad in a loose-fitting suit of tweed, cut for comfort rather than elegance. As he stood in the shimmering sunlight, I took in every feature of his face. The large, fleshy nose ; the steady, blue eyes, with their thick thatch of overhanging brows ; the broad forehead, all knitted and lined with furrows, which were strangely at variance with his youthful bearing. In spite of his weather-stained felt hat, and the coloured handkerchief slung round his muscular, brown neck, I could see at a glance he was a man of breeding and education. I had been prepared for some wandering shepherd or uncouth tramp, but this apparition fairly disconcerted me.

"You look astonished," said he, with a smile. "Did you think, then, that you were the only man in the world with a taste for solitude? You see that there are other hermits in the wilderness besides yourself."

"Do you mean to say that you live here?" I asked in no conciliatory voice.

"Up yonder," he answered, tossing his head backward. "I thought as we were neighbours, Mr. Upperton, that I could not do less than look in and see if I could assist you in any way."

"Thank you," I said coldly, standing with my hand upon the latch of the door. "I am a man of simple tastes, and you can do nothing for me. You have the advantage of me in knowing my name."

He appeared to be chilled by my ungracious manner. "I learned it from the masons who were at work here," he said. "As for me, I am a surgeon, the surgeon of Gaster Fell. That is the name I have gone by in these parts, and it serves as well as another."

"Not much room for practice here?" I observed.

"Not a soul except yourself for miles on either side."

"You appear to have had need of some assistance yourself," I remarked, glancing at a broad, white splash, as from the recent action of some powerful acid, upon his sunburnt cheek.

"That is nothing," he answered, curtly, turning his face half round to hide the mark. "I must get back, for I have a companion who is waiting for me. If I can ever do anything for you, pray let me know. You have only to follow the beck upward for a mile or so to find my place. Have you a bolt on the inside of your door?"

"Yes," I answered, rather startled at this question.

"Keep it bolted, then," he said. "The fell is a strange place. You never know who may be about. It is as well to be on the safe side. Good-bye." He raised his hat, turned on his heel and lounged away along the bank of the little stream.

I was still standing with my hand upon the latch, gazing after my unexpected visitor, when I became aware of yet another dweller in the wilderness. Some distance along the path which the stranger was taking there lay a great, grey boulder, and leaning against this was a small, wizened man, who stood erect as the other approached, and advanced to meet him. The two talked for a minute or more, the taller man nodding his head frequently in my direction, as though describing what had passed between us. Then they walked on together, and disappeared in a dip of the fell. Presently I saw them ascending once more some rising ground farther on. My acquaintance had thrown his arm round his elderly friend, either from affection or from a desire to aid him up the steep incline. The square, burly figure and its shrivelled, meagre companion stood out against the skyline, and turning their faces, they looked back at me. At the sight, I slammed the door, lest they should be encouraged to return. But when I peeped from the window some minutes afterward, I perceived that they were gone.

All day I bent over the Egyptian papyrus upon which I was engaged; but neither the subtle reasonings of the ancient philosopher of Memphis, nor the mystic meaning which lay in his pages, could raise my mind from the things of earth. Evening was drawing in before I threw my work aside in despair. My heart was bitter against this man for his intrusion. Standing by the beck which purled past the door of my cabin, I cooled my heated brow, and thought the matter over. Clearly it was the small mystery hanging over these neighbours of mine which had caused my mind to run so persistently on them. That cleared up, they would no longer cause an obstacle to my studies. What was to hinder me, then, from walking in the direction of their dwelling, and observing for myself, without permitting them to suspect my presence, what manner of men they might be? Doubtless, their mode of life would be found to admit of some simple and prosaic explanation. In any case, the evening was fine, and a walk would be bracing for mind and body. Lighting my pipe, I set off over the moors in the direction which they had taken.

About half-way down a wild glen there stood a small clump of gnarled and stunted oak trees. From behind these, a thin, dark column of smoke rose into the still evening air. Clearly this marked the position of my neighbour's house. Trending away to the left, I was able to gain the shelter of a line of rocks, and so reach a spot from which I could command a view of the building without exposing myself to any risk of being observed. It was a small, slate-covered cottage, hardly larger than the boulders among which it lay. Like my own cabin, it showed signs of having been constructed for the use of some shepherd; but, unlike mine, no pains had been taken by the tenants to improve and enlarge it. Two little peeping windows, a cracked and weather-beaten door, and a discoloured barrel for catching the rain-water, were the only external objects from which I might draw deductions as to the dwellers within. Yet even in these there was food for thought, for as I drew nearer, still concealing myself behind the ridge, I saw that thick bars of iron covered the windows, while the old door was slashed and plated with the same metal. These strange precautions, together with the wild surroundings and unbroken solitude, gave an indescribably ill omen and fearsome character to the solitary building. Thrusting my pipe into my pocket, I crawled upon my hands and knees through the gorse and ferns until I was within a hundred yards of my neighbour's door. There, finding that I could not approach nearer without fear of detection, I crouched down, and set myself to watch.

I had hardly settled into my hiding-place, when the

door of the cottage swung open, and the man who had introduced himself to me as the surgeon of Gaster Fell came out, bareheaded, with a spade in his hands. In front of the door there was a small, cultivated patch containing potatoes, peas and other forms of green stuff, and here he proceeded to busy himself, trimming, weeding and arranging, singing the while in a powerful though not very musical voice. He was all engrossed in his work, with his back to the cottage, when there emerged from the half-open door the same attenuated creature whom I had seen in the morning. I could perceive now that he was a man of sixty, wrinkled, bent, and feeble, with sparse, grizzled hair, and long, colourless face. With a cringing, sidelong gait, he shuffled toward his companion, who was unconscious of his approach until he was close upon him. His light footfall or his breathing may have finally given notice of his proximity, for the worker sprang round and faced him. Each made a quick step toward the other, as though in greeting, and then—even now I feel the horror of the instant—the tall man rushed upon and knocked his companion to the earth, then whipping up his body, ran with great speed over the intervening ground and disappeared with his burden into the house.

Case-hardened as I was by my varied life, the suddenness and violence of the thing made me shudder. The man's age, his feeble frame, his humble and deprecating manner, all cried shame against the deed. So hot was my anger, that I was on the point of striding up to the cabin, unarmed as I was, when the sound of voices from within showed me that the victim had recovered. The sun had sunk beneath the horizon, and all was grey, save a red feather in the cap of Pennigent. Secure in the failing light, I approached near and strained my ears to catch what was passing. I could hear the high, querulous voice of the elder man and the deep, rough monotone of his assailant, mixed with a strange metallic jangling and clanking. Presently the surgeon came out, locked the door behind him and stamped up and down in the twilight, pulling at his hair and brandishing his arms, like a man demented. Then he set off, walking rapidly up the valley, and I soon lost sight of him among the rocks.

When his footsteps had died away in the distance, I drew nearer to the cottage. The prisoner within was still pouring forth a stream of words, and moaning from time to time like a man in pain. These words resolved themselves, as I approached, into prayers—shrill, voluble prayers, pattered forth with the intense earnestness of one who sees impending and imminent danger. There was to me something inexpressibly awesome in this gush of solemn entreaty from the lonely sufferer, meant for no human ear, and jarring upon the silence of the night. I was still pondering whether I should mix myself in the affair or not, when I heard in the distance the sound of the surgeon's returning footfall. At that I drew myself up quickly by the iron bars and glanced in through the diamond-paned window. The interior of the cottage was lighted up by a lurid glow, coming from what I afterward discovered to be a chemical furnace. By its rich light I could distinguish a great litter of retorts, test tubes and condensers, which sparkled over the table, and threw strange, grotesque shadows on the wall. On the farther side of the room was a wooden framework resembling a hen-coop, and in this, still absorbed in prayer, knelt the man whose voice I heard. The red glow beating upon his upturned face made it stand out from the shadow like a painting from Rembrandt, showing up every wrinkle upon the parchment-like skin. I had but time for a fleeting glance; then, dropping from the window, I made off through the rocks and the heather, nor slackened my pace until I found myself back in my cabin once more. There I threw myself upon my couch, more disturbed and shaken than I had ever thought to feel again.

Such doubts as I might have had as to whether I

had indeed seen my former fellow-lodger upon the night of the thunderstorm were resolved the next morning. Strolling along down the path which led to the fell, I saw in one spot where the ground was soft the impressions of a foot—the small, dainty foot of a well-booted woman. That tiny heel and high instep could have belonged to none other than my companion of Kirkby-Malhouse. I followed her trail for some distance, till it still pointed, so far as I could discern it, to the lonely and ill-omened cottage. What power could there be to draw this tender girl, through wind and rain and darkness, across the fearsome moors to that strange rendezvous ?

I have said that a little beck flowed down the valley and past my very door. A week or so after the doings which I have described, I was seated by my window when I perceived something white drifting slowly down the stream. My first thought was that it was a drowning sheep ; but picking up my stick, I strolled to the bank and hooked it ashore. On examination it proved to be a large sheet, torn and tattered, with the initials J. C. in the corner. What gave it its sinister significance, however, was that from hem to hem it was all dabbled and discoloured.

Shutting the door of my cabin, I set off up the glen in the direction of the surgeon's cabin. I had not gone far before I perceived the very man himself. He was walking rapidly along the hillside, beating the furze bushes with a cudgel and bellowing like a madman. Indeed, at the sight of him, the doubts as to his sanity which had risen in my mind were strengthened and confirmed.

As he approached I noticed that his left arm was suspended in a sling. On perceiving me he stood irresolute, as though uncertain whether to come over to me or not. I had no desire for an interview with him, however, so I hurried past him, on which he continued on his way, still shouting and striking about with his club.

When he had disappeared over the fells, I made my way down to his cottage, determined to find some clue to what had occurred. I was surprised, on reaching it, to find the iron-plated door flung wide open. The ground immediately outside it was marked with the signs of a struggle. The chemical apparatus within and the furniture were all dashed about and shattered. Most suggestive of all, the sinister wooden cage was stained with blood-marks and its unfortunate occupant had disappeared. My heart was heavy for the little man, for I was assured I should never see him in this world more.

There was nothing in the cabin to throw any light upon the identity of my neighbours. The room was stuffed with chemical instruments. In one corner a small book-case contained a choice selection of works of science. In another was a pile of geological specimens collected from the limestone.

I caught no glimpse of the surgeon upon my homeward journey; but when I reached my cottage I was astonished and indignant to find that somebody had entered it in my absence. Boxes had been pulled out from under the bed, the curtains disarranged, the chairs drawn out from the wall. Even my study had not been safe from this rough intruder, for the prints of a heavy boot were plainly visible on the ebony-black carpet.

IV—OF THE MAN WHO CAME IN THE NIGHT

The night set in gusty and tempestuous, and the moon was all girt with ragged clouds. The wind blew in melancholy gusts, sobbing and sighing over the moor, and setting all the gorse bushes a-groaning. From time to time a little sputter of rain pattered up against the window-pane. I sat until near midnight, glancing over the fragment on immortality by Iamblichus, the Alexandrian platonist, of whom the Emperor Julian said that he was posterior to Plato in time but not in genius. At last, shutting up my book, I opened my door and took a last look at the dreary fell and still more dreary sky. As I protruded my head, a swoop of wind caught me and sent the red ashes of my pipe sparkling and dancing through the darkness. At the same moment the moon shone brilliantly out from between two clouds and I saw, sitting on the hillside, not two hundred yards from my door, the man who called himself the surgeon of Gaster Fell. He was squatted among the heather, his elbows upon his knees, and his chin resting upon his hands, as motionless as a stone, with his gaze fixed steadily upon the door of my dwelling.

At the sight of this ill-omened sentinel, a chill of horror and of fear shot through me, for his gloomy and mysterious associations had cast a glamour round the man, and the hour and place were in keeping with his sinister presence. In a moment, however, a manly glow of resentment and self-confidence drove this petty emotion from my mind, and I strode fearlessly in his direction. He rose as I approached and faced me, with the moon shining on his grave, bearded face and glittering on his eyeballs. "What is the meaning of this?" I cried, as I came upon him. "What right have you to play the spy on me?"

I could see the flush of anger rise on his face. "Your stay in the country has made you forget your manners," he said. "The moor is free to all."

"You will say next that my house is free to all," I said, hotly. "You have had the impertinence to ransack it in my absence this afternoon."

He started, and his features showed the most intense excitement. "I swear to you that I had no hand in it!" he cried. "I have never set foot in your house in my life. Oh, sir, sir, if you will but believe me, there is a danger hanging over you, and you would do well to be careful."

"I have had enough of you," I said. "I saw that cowardly blow you struck when you thought no human eye rested upon you. I have been to your cottage, too, and know all that it has to tell. If there is a law in England, you shall hang for what you have done. As to me, I am an old soldier, sir, and I am armed. I shall not fasten my door. But if you or any other villain attempt to cross my threshold it shall be at your own risk." With these words, I swung round upon my heel and strode into my cabin.

For two days the wind freshened and increased, with constant squalls of rain until on the third night the most furious storm was raging which I can ever recollect in England. I felt that it was positively useless to go to bed, nor could I concentrate my mind sufficiently to read a book. I turned my lamp half down to moderate the glare, and leaning back in my chair, I gave myself up to reverie. I must have lost all perception of time, for I have no recollection how long I sat there on the borderland betwixt thought and slumber. At last, about 3 or possibly 4 o'clock, I came to myself with a start—not only came to myself, but with every sense and nerve upon the strain. Looking round my chamber in the dim light, I could not see anything to justify my sudden trepidation. The homely room, the rain-blurred window and the rude wooden door were all as they had been. I had begun to persuade myself that some half-formed dream had sent that vague thrill through my nerves, when in a moment I became conscious of what it was. It was a sound—the sound of a human step outside my solitary cottage.

Amid the thunder and the rain and the wind I could hear it—a dull, stealthy footfall, now on the grass, now on the stones—occasionally stopping entirely, then resumed, and ever drawing nearer. I sat breathlessly, listening to the eerie sound. It had stopped now at my very door, and was replaced by a panting and gasping, as of one who has travelled fast and far.

By the flickering light of the expiring lamp I could see that the latch of my door was twitching, as though a gentle pressure was exerted on it from without. Slowly,

slowly, it rose, until it was free of the catch, and then there was a pause of a quarter minute or more, while I still sat silent with dilated eyes and drawn sabre. Then, very slowly, the door began to revolve upon its hinges, and the keen air of the night came whistling through the slit. Very cautiously it was pushed open, so that never a sound came from the rusty hinges. As the aperture enlarged, I became aware of a dark, shadowy figure upon my threshold, and of a pale face that looked in at me. The features were human, but the eyes were not. They seemed to burn through the darkness with a greenish brilliancy of their own; and in their baleful, shifty glare I was conscious of the very spirit of murder. Springing from my chair, I had raised my naked sword, when, with a wild shouting, a second figure dashed up to my door. At its approach my shadowy visitant uttered a shrill cry, and fled away across the fells, yelping like a beaten hound.

Tingling with my recent fear, I stood at my door, peering through the night with the discordant cry of the fugitives still ringing in my ears. At that moment a vivid flash of lightning illuminated the whole landscape and made it as clear as day. By its light I saw far away upon the hillside two dark figures pursuing each other with extreme rapidity across the fells. Even at that distance the contrast between them forbid all doubt as to their identity. The first was the small, elderly man, whom I had supposed to be dead; the second was my neighbour, the surgeon. For an instant they stood out clear and hard in the unearthly light; in the next, the darkness had closed over them, and they were gone. As I turned to re-enter my chamber, my foot rattled against something on my threshold. Stooping, I found it was a straight knife, fashioned entirely of lead, and so soft and brittle that it was a strange choice for a weapon. To render it more harmless, the top had been cut square off. The edge, however, had been assiduously sharpened against a stone, as was evident from the markings upon it, so that it was still a dangerous implement in the grasp of a determined man.

And what was the meaning of it all? you ask. Many a drama which I have come across in my wandering life, some as strange and as striking as this one, has lacked the ultimate explanation which you demand. Fate is a grand weaver of tales; but she ends them, as a rule, in defiance of all artistic laws, and with an unbecoming want of regard for literary propriety. As it happens, however, I have a letter before me as I write which I may add without comment, and which will clear all that may remain dark.

" KIRKBY LUNATIC ASYLUM,
" *September 4th*, 1885.

" SIR,—I am deeply conscious that some apology and explanation is due to you for the very startling and, in your eyes, mysterious events which have recently occurred, and which have so seriously interfered with the retired existence which you desire to lead. I should have called upon you on the morning after the recapture of my father, but my knowledge of your dislike to visitors and also of—you will excuse my saying it—your very violent temper, led me to think that it was better to communicate with you by letter.

" My poor father was a hard-working general practitioner in Birmingham, where his name is still remembered and respected. About ten years ago he began to show signs of mental aberration, which we were inclined to put down to overwork and the effects of a sunstroke. Feeling my own incompetence to pronounce upon a case of such importance, I at once sought the highest advice in Birmingham and London. Among others we consulted the eminent alienist, Mr. Fraser Brown, who pronounced my father's case to be intermittent in its nature, but dangerous during the paroxysms. ' It may take a homicidal, or it may take a religious turn,' he said; ' or it may prove to be a mixture of both.

For months he may be as well as you or me, and then in a moment he may break out. You will incur a great responsibility if you leave him without supervision.'

"I need say no more, sir. You will understand the terrible task which has fallen upon my poor sister and me in endeavouring to save my father from the asylum which in his sane moments filled him with horror. I can only regret that your peace has been disturbed by our misfortunes, and I offer you in my sister's name and my own our apologies.

"Yours truly,
"J. CAMERON."

52. *Borrowed Scenes*

"It cannot be done. People really would not stand it. I know because I have tried."—*Extract from an unpublished paper upon George Borrow and his writings.*

YES, I tried and my experience may interest other people. You must imagine, then, that I am soaked in George Borrow, especially in his *Lavengro* and his *Romany Rye*, that I have modelled both my thoughts, my speech and my style very carefully upon those of the master, and that finally I set forth one summer day actually to lead the life of which I had read. Behold me, then, upon the country road which leads from the railway-station to the Sussex village of Swinehurst.

As I walked, I entertained myself by recollections of the founders of Sussex, of Cerdic that mighty sea-rover, and of Ella his son, said by the bard to be taller by the length of a spear-head than the tallest of his fellows. I mentioned the matter twice to peasants whom I met upon the road. One, a tallish man with a freckled face, sidled past me and ran swiftly towards the station. The other, a smaller and older man, stood entranced while I recited to him that passage of the Saxon Chronicle which begins, "Then came Leija with longships forty-four, and the fyrd went out against him." I was pointing out to him that the Chronicle had been written partly by the monks of Saint Albans and afterwards by those of Peterborough, but the fellow sprang suddenly over a gate and disappeared.

The village of Swinehurst is a straggling line of half-timbered houses of the early English pattern. One of these houses stood, as I observed, somewhat taller than the rest, and seeing by its appearance and by the sign which hung before it that it was the village inn, I approached it, for indeed I had not broken my fast since I had left London. A stoutish man, five foot eight perhaps in height, with black coat and trousers of a greyish shade, stood outside, and to him I talked in the fashion of the master.

"Why a rose and why a crown?" I asked as I pointed upwards.

He looked at me in a strange manner. The man's whole appearance was strange. "Why not?" he answered, and shrank a little backwards.

"The sign of a king," said I.

"Surely," said he. "What else should we understand from a crown?"

"And which king?" I asked.

"You will excuse me," said he, and tried to pass.

"Which king?" I repeated.

"How should I know?" he asked.

"You should know by the rose," said I, "which is the symbol of that Tudor-ap-Tudor, who, coming from the mountains of Wales, yet seated his posterity upon the English throne. Tudor," I continued, getting between the stranger and the door of the inn, through which he appeared to be desirous of passing, "was of the same blood as Owen Glendower, the famous chieftain, who is by no means to be confused with Owen Gwynedd, the father of Madoc of the Sea, of whom the bard made the famous cnylyn, which runs in the Welsh as follows:—"

I was about to repeat the famous stanza of Dafydd-ap-Gwilyn when the man, who had looked very fixedly and strangely at me as I spoke, pushed past me and entered the inn. "Truly," said I aloud, "it is surely Swinehurst to which I have come, since the same means the grove of the hogs." So saying I followed the fellow into the bar parlour, where I perceived him seated in a corner with a large chair in front of him. Four persons of various degrees were drinking beer at a central table, whilst a small man of active build, in a black, shiny suit, which seemed to have seen much service, stood before the empty fireplace. Him I took to be the landlord, and I asked him what I should have for my dinner.

He smiled, and said that he could not tell.

"But surely, my friend," said I, "you can tell me what is ready?"

"Even that I cannot do," he answered; "but I doubt not that the landlord can inform us." On this he rang the bell, and a fellow answered, to whom I put the same question.

"What would you have?" he asked.

I thought of the master, and I ordered a cold leg of pork to be washed down with tea and beer.

"Did you say tea *and* beer?" asked the landlord.

"I did."

"For twenty-five years have I been in business," said the landlord, "and never before have I been asked for tea and beer."

"The gentleman is joking," said the man with the shining coat.

"Or else——" said the elderly man in the corner.

"Or what, sir?" I asked.

"Nothing," said he—"nothing." There was something very strange in this man in the corner—him to whom I had spoken of Dafydd-ap-Gwilyn.

"Then you are joking," said the landlord.

I asked him if he had read the works of my master, George Borrow. He said that he had not. I told him that in those five volumes he would not, from cover to cover, find one trace of any sort of a joke. He would also find that my master drank tea and beer together. Now it happens that about tea I have read nothing either in the sagas or in the bardic cnylynions, but, whilst the landlord had departed to prepare my meal, I recited to the company those Icelandic stanzas which praise the beer of Gunnar, the long-haired son of Harold the Bear. Then, lest the language should be unknown to some of them, I recited my own translation, ending with the line—

> " If the beer be small, then let the mug be large."

I then asked the company whether they went to church or to chapel. The question surprised them, and especially the strange man in the corner, upon whom I now fixed my eye. I had read his secret, and as I looked at him he tried to shrink behind the clock-case.

" The church or the chapel ? " I asked him.

" The church," he gasped.

" *Which* church ? " I asked.

He shrank farther behind the clock. " I have never been so questioned," he cried.

I showed him that I knew his secret. " Rome was not built in a day," said I.

" He ! He ! " he cried. Then, as I turned away, he put his head from behind the clock-case and tapped his forehead with his fore-finger. So also did the man with the shiny coat, who stood before the empty fireplace.

Having eaten the cold leg of pork—where is there a better dish, save only boiled mutton with capers ?—and having drunk both the tea and the beer, I told the company that such a meal had been called " to box Harry " by the master, who had observed it to be in great favour with commercial gentlemen out of Liverpool. With this information and a stanza or two from Lopez de Vega I left the Inn of the Rose and Crown behind me, having first paid my reckoning. At the door the landlord asked me for my name and address.

"And why?" I asked.

"Lest there should be inquiry for you," said the landlord.

"But why should they inquire for me?"

"Ah, who knows?" said the landlord, musing. And so I left him at the door of the Inn of the Rose and Crown whence came, I observed, a great tumult of laughter. "Assuredly," thought I, "Rome was not built in a day."

Having walked down the main street of Swinehurst, which, as I have observed, consists of half-timbered buildings in the ancient style, I came out upon the country road, and proceeded to look for those wayside adventures, which are, according to the master, as thick as blackberries for those who seek them upon an English highway. I had already received some boxing lessons before leaving London, so it seemed to me that if I should chance to meet some traveller whose size and age seemed such as to encourage the venture, I would ask him to strip off his coat and settle any differences which we could find in the old English fashion. I waited, therefore, by a stile for anyone who should chance to pass, and it was while I stood there that the screaming horror came upon me, even as it came upon the master in the dingle. I gripped the bar of the stile, which was of good British oak. Oh, who can tell the terrors of the screaming horror! That was what I thought as I grasped the oaken bar of the stile. Was it the beer—or was it the tea? Or was it that the landlord was right and that other, the man with the black, shiny coat, he who had answered the sign of the strange man in the corner? But the master drank tea with beer. Yes, but the master also had the screaming horror. All this I thought as I grasped the bar of British oak, which was the top of the stile. For half an hour the horror was upon me. Then it passed, and I was left feeling very weak and still grasping the oaken bar.

I had not moved from the stile, where I had been seized by the screaming horror, when I heard the sound of steps behind me, and turning round I perceived that a pathway led across the field upon the farther side of the stile. A woman was coming towards me along this pathway, and it was evident to me that she was one of those gipsy Rias, of whom the master has said so much. Looking beyond her, I could see the smoke of a fire from a small dingle, which showed where her tribe were camping. The woman herself was of a moderate height, neither tall nor short, with a face which was much sunburned and freckled. I must confess that she was not beautiful, but I do not think that anyone, save the master, has found very beautiful women walking about upon the high-roads of England. Such as she was I must make the best of her, and well I knew how to address her, for many times had I admired the mixture of politeness and audacity which should be used in such a case. Therefore, when the woman had come to the stile, I held out my hand and helped her over.

"What says the Spanish poet Calderon?" said I. "I doubt not that you have read the couplet which has been thus Englished:

'Oh, maiden, may I humbly pray
That I may help you on your way.'"

The woman blushed, but said nothing.

"Where," I asked, "are the Romany chals and the Romany chis?"

She turned her head away and was silent.

"Though I am a gorgio," said I, "I know something of the Romany lil," and to prove it I sang the stanza—

"Coliko, coliko saulo wer
Apopli to the farming ker
Will wel and mang him mullo,
Will wel and mang his truppo."

The girl laughed, but said nothing. It appeared to me from her appearance that she might be one of those who make a living at telling fortunes or " dukkering," as the master calls it, at racecourses and other gatherings of the sort.

" Do you dukker ? " I asked.

She slapped me on the arm. " Well, you *are* a pot of ginger ! " said she.

I was pleased at the slap, for it put me in mind of the peerless Belle. " You can use Long Melford," said I, an expression which, with the master, meant fighting.

" Get along with your sauce ! " said she, and struck me again.

" You are a very fine young woman," said I, " and remind me of Grunelda, the daughter of Hjalmar, who stole the golden bowl from the King of the Islands."

She seemed annoyed at this. " You keep a civil tongue, young man," said she.

" I meant no harm, Belle. I was but comparing you to one of whom the saga says her eyes were like the shine of sun upon icebergs."

This seemed to please her, for she smiled. " My name ain't Belle," she said at last.

" What is your name ? "

" Henrietta."

" The name of a queen," I said aloud.

" Go on," said the girl.

" Of Charles's queen," said I, " of whom Waller the poet (for the English also have their poets, though in this respect far inferior to the Basques)—of whom, I say, Waller the poet said :

> 'That she was Queen was the Creator's act,
> Belated man could but endorse the fact.' "

" I say ! " cried the girl. " How you do go on ! "

" So now," said I, " since I have shown you that you are a queen you will surely give me a choomer " —this being a kiss in Romany talk.

" I'll give you one on the ear-hole," she cried.

"Then I will wrestle with you," said I. "If you should chance to put me down, I will do penance by teaching you the Armenian alphabet—the very word alphabet, as you will perceive, shows us that our letters came from Greece. If, on the other hand, I should chance to put you down, you will give me a choomer."

I had got so far, and she was climbing the stile with some pretence of getting away from me, when there came a van along the road, belonging, as I discovered, to a baker in Swinehurst. The horse, which was of a brown colour, was such as is bred in the New Forest, being somewhat under fifteen hands and of a hairy, ill-kempt variety. As I know less than the master about horses, I will say no more of this horse, save to repeat that its colour was brown—nor indeed had the horse or the horse's colour anything to do with my narrative. I might add, however, that it could either be taken as a small horse or as a large pony, being somewhat tall for the one, but undersized for the other. I have now said enough about this horse, which has nothing to do with my story, and I will turn my attention to the driver.

This was a man with a broad, florid face and brown side-whiskers. He was of a stout build and had rounded shoulders, with a small mole of a reddish colour over his left eyebrow. His jacket was of velveteen, and he had large, iron-shod boots, which were perched upon the splashboard in front of him. He pulled up the van as he came up to the stile near which I was standing with the maiden who had come from the dingle, and in a civil fashion he asked me if I could oblige him with a light for his pipe. Then, as I drew a matchbox from my pocket, he threw his reins over the splashboard, and removing his large, iron-shod boots he descended on to the road. He was a burly man, but inclined to fat and scant of breath. It seemed to me that it was a chance for one of those wayside boxing adventures which were so common in the olden times. It was my intention that I should fight the man, and that the maiden from the dingle standing by me should tell me when to use my right or my left, as the case might be, picking me up also in case I should be so unfortunate as to be knocked down by the man with the iron-shod boots and the small mole of a reddish colour over his left eyebrow.

"Do you use Long Melford?" I asked.

He looked at me in some surprise, and said that any mixture was good enough for him.

"By Long Melford," said I, "I do not mean, as you seem to think, some form of tobacco, but I mean that art and science of boxing which was held in such high esteem by our ancestors, that some famous professors of it, such as the great Gully, have been elected to the highest offices of the State. There were men of the highest character amongst the bruisers of England, of whom I would particularly mention Tom of Hereford, better known as Tom Spring, though his father's name, as I have been given to understand, was Winter. This, however, has nothing to do with the matter in hand, which is that you must fight me."

The man with the florid face seemed very much surprised at my words, so that I cannot think that adventures of this sort were as common as I had been led by the master to expect.

"Fight!" said he. "What about?"

"It is a good old English custom," said I, "by which we may determine which is the better man."

"I've nothing against you," said he.

"Nor I against you," I answered. "So that we will fight for love, which was an expression much used in olden days. It is narrated by Harold Sygvynson that among the Danes it was usual to do so even with battle-axes, as is told in his second set of runes. Therefore you will take off your coat and fight." As I spoke, I stripped off my own.

The man's face was less florid than before. "I'm not going to fight," said he.

"Indeed you are," I answered, "and this young woman will doubtless do you the service to hold your coat."

"You're clean balmy," said Henrietta.

"Besides," said I, "if you will not fight me for love, perhaps you will fight me for this," and I held out a sovereign. "Will you hold his coat?" I said to Henrietta.

"I'll hold the thick 'un," said she.

"No, you don't," said the man, and put the sovereign into the pocket of his trousers, which were of a corduroy material. "Now," said he, "what am I to do to earn this?"

"Fight," said I.

"How do you do it?" he asked.

"Put up your hands," I answered.

He put them up as I had said, and stood there in a sheepish manner with no idea of anything further. It seemed to me that if I could make him angry he would do better, so I knocked off his hat, which was black and hard, of the kind which is called billy-cock.

"Heh, guv'nor!" he cried, "what are you up to?"

"That was to make you angry," said I.

"Well, I am angry," said he.

"Then here is your hat," said I, "and afterwards we shall fight."

I turned as I spoke to pick up his hat, which had rolled behind where I was standing. As I stooped to reach it, I received such a blow that I could neither rise erect nor yet sit down. This blow which I received as I stooped for his billy-cock hat was not from his fist, but from his iron-shod boot, the same which I had observed upon the splashboard. Being unable either to rise erect or yet to sit down, I leaned upon the oaken bar of the stile and groaned loudly on account of the pain of the blow which I had received. Even the screaming horror had given me less pain than this blow from the iron-shod boot. When at last I was able to stand erect, I found that the florid-faced man had driven away with his cart, which could no longer be seen. The maiden from the dingle was standing at the other side of the stile, and a ragged man was running across the field from the direction of the fire.

"Why did you not warn me, Henrietta ?" I asked.

"I hadn't time," said she. "Why were you such a chump as to turn your back on him like that ?"

The ragged man had reached us, where I stood talking to Henrietta by the stile. I will not try to write his conversation as he said it, because I have observed that the master never condescends to dialect, but prefers by a word introduced here and there to show the fashion of a man's speech. I will only say that the man from the dingle spoke as did the Anglo-Saxons who were wont, as is clearly shown by the venerable Bede, to call their leaders 'Enjist and 'Orsa, two words which in their proper meaning signify a horse and a mare.

"What did he hit you for ?" asked the man from the dingle. He was exceedingly ragged, with a powerful frame, a lean brown face, and an oaken cudgel in his hand. His voice was very hoarse and rough, as is the case with those who live in the open air. "The bloke hit you," said he. "What did the bloke hit you for ?"

"He asked him to," said Henrietta.

"Asked him to—asked him what ?"

"Why, he asked him to hit him. Gave him a thick 'un to do it."

The ragged man seemed surprised. "See here, gov'nor," said he. "If you're collectin', I could let you have one half-price."

"He took me unawares," said I.

"What else would the bloke do when you bashed his hat ?" said the maiden from the dingle.

By this time I was able to straighten myself up by the aid of the oaken bar which formed the top of the stile. Having quoted a few lines of the Chinese poet Lo-tun-an to the effect that, however hard a knock might be, it might always conceivably be harder, I looked about for my coat, but could by no means find it.

" Henrietta," I said, " what have you done with my coat ? "

" Look here, gov'nor," said the man from the dingle, " not so much Henrietta, if it's the same to you. This woman's my wife. Who are you to call her Henrietta ? "

I assured the man from the dingle that I had meant no disrespect to his wife. " I had thought she was a mort," said I ; " but the ria of a Romany chal is always sacred to me."

" Clean balmy," said the woman.

" Some other day," said I, " I may visit you in your camp in the dingle and read you the master's book about the Romanys."

" What's Romanys ? " asked the man.

Myself. Romanys are gipsies.

The Man. We ain't gipsies.

Myself. What are you then ?

The Man. We are hoppers.

Myself (to Henrietta). Then how did you understand all I have said to you about gipsies ?

Henrietta. I didn't.

I again asked for my coat, but it was clear now that before offering to fight the florid-faced man with the mole over his left eyebrow I must have hung my coat upon the splashboard of his van. I therefore recited a verse from Ferideddin-Atar, the Persian poet, which signifies that it is more important to preserve your skin than your clothes, and bidding farewell to the man from the dingle and his wife I returned into the old English village of Swinehurst, where I was able to buy a second-hand coat, which enabled me to make my way to the station, where I should start for London. I could not but remark with some surprise that I was followed to the station by many of the villagers, together with the man with the shiny coat, and that other, the strange man, he who had slunk behind the clock-case. From time to time I turned and approached them, hoping to fall into conversation with them; but as I did so they would break and hasten down the road. Only the village constable came on, and he walked by my side and listened while I told him the history of Hunyadi Janos and the events which occurred during the wars between that hero, known also as Corvinus or the crow-like, and Mahommed the second, he who captured Constantinople, better known as Byzantium, before the Christian epoch. Together with the constable I entered the station, and seating myself in a carriage I took paper from my pocket and I began to write upon the paper all that had occurred to me, in order that I might show that it was not easy in these days to follow the example of the master. As I wrote, I heard the constable talk to the station-master, a stout, middle-sized man with a red neck-tie, and tell him of my own adventures in the old English village of Swinehurst.

"He is a gentleman too," said the constable, "and I doubt not that he lives in a big house in London town."

"A very big house if every man had his rights," said the station-master, and waving his hand he signalled that the train should proceed.

53. *The Man from Archangel*

ON the fourth day of March, in the year 1867, I being at that time in my five-and-twentieth year, I wrote down the following words in my note-book—the result of much mental perturbation and conflict:

"The solar system, amidst a countless number of other systems as large as itself, rolls ever silently through space in the direction of the constellation of Hercules. The great spheres of which it is composed spin and spin through the eternal void ceaselessly and noiselessly. Of these one of the smallest and most insignificant is that conglomeration of solid and of liquid particles which we have named the earth. It whirls onwards now as it has done before my birth, and will do after my death—a revolving mystery, coming none know whence, and going none know whither. Upon the outer crust of this moving mass crawl many mites, of whom I, John M'Vittie, am one, helpless, impotent, being dragged aimlessly through space. Yet such is the state of things amongst us that the little energy and glimmering of reason which I possess is entirely taken up with the labours which are necessary in order to procure certain metallic discs, wherewith I may purchase the chemical elements necessary to build up my ever-wasting tissues, and keep a roof over me to shelter me from the inclemency of the weather. I thus have no thought to expend upon the vital questions which surround me on every side. Yet, miserable entity as I am, I can still at times feel some degree of happiness, and am even—save the mark!—puffed up occasionally with a sense of my own importance."

These words, as I have said, I wrote down in my note-book, and they reflected accurately the thoughts which I found rooted far down in my soul, ever present and unaffected by the passing emotions of the hour. At last, however, came a time when my uncle, M'Vittie of Glencairn, died—the same who was at one time chairman of committees of the House of Commons. He divided his great wealth among his many nephews, and I found myself with sufficient to provide amply for my wants during the remainder of my life, and became at the same time the owner of a bleak tract of land upon the coast of Caithness, which I think the old man must have bestowed upon me in derision, for it was sandy and valueless, and he had ever a grim sense of humour. Up to this time I had been an attorney in a midland town in England. Now I saw that I could put my thoughts into effect, and, leaving all petty and sordid aims, could elevate my mind by the study of the secrets of nature. My departure from my English home was somewhat accelerated by the fact that I had nearly slain a man in a quarrel, for my temper was fiery, and I was apt to forget my own strength when enraged. There was no legal action taken in the matter, but the papers yelped at me, and folk looked askance when I met them. It ended by my cursing them and their vile, smoke-polluted town, and hurrying to my northern possession, where I might at last find peace and an opportunity for solitary study and contemplation. I borrowed from my capital before I went, and so was able to take with me a choice collection of the most modern philosophical instruments and books, together with chemicals and such other things as I might need in my retirement.

The land which I had inherited was a narrow strip, consisting mostly of sand, and extending for rather over two miles round the coast of Mansie Bay, in Caithness. Upon this strip there had been a rambling, greystone building—when erected or wherefore none could tell me—and this I had repaired, so that it made a dwelling quite good enough for one of my simple tastes. One room was my laboratory, another my sitting-room, and in a third, just under the sloping roof, I slung the hammock in which I always slept. There were three other rooms, but I left them vacant, except one which was given over to the old crone who kept house for me. Save the Youngs and the M'Leods, who were fisherfolk living round at the other side of Fergus Ness, there were no other people for many miles in each direction. In front of the house was the great bay, behind it were two long barren hills, capped by other loftier ones beyond. There was a glen between the hills, and when the wind was from the land it used to sweep down this with a melancholy sough and whisper among the branches of the fir-trees beneath my attic window.

I dislike my fellow-mortals. Justice compels me to add that they appear for the most part to dislike me. I hate their little crawling ways, their conventionalities, their deceits, their narrow rights and wrongs. They take offence at my brusque outspokenness, my disregard for their social laws, my impatience of all constraint. Among my books and my drugs in my lonely den at

Mansie I could let the great drove of the human race pass onwards with their politics and inventions and tittle-tattle, and I remained behind stagnant and happy. Not stagnant either, for I was working in my own little groove, and making progress. I have reason to believe that Dalton's atomic theory is founded upon error, and I know that mercury is not an element.

During the day I was busy with my distillations and analyses. Often I forgot my meals, and when old Madge summoned me to my tea I found my dinner lying untouched upon the table. At night I read Bacon, Descartes, Spinoza, Kant—all those who have pried into what is unknowable. They are all fruitless and empty, barren of result, but prodigal of polysyllables, reminding me of men who, while digging for gold, have turned up many worms, and then exhibit them exultantly as being what they sought. At times a restless spirit would come upon me, and I would walk thirty and forty miles without rest or breaking fast. On these occasions, when I used to stalk through the country villages, gaunt, unshaven, and dishevelled, the mothers would rush into the road and drag their children indoors, and the rustics would swarm out of their pot-houses to gaze at me. I believe that I was known far and wide as the "mad laird o' Mansie." It was rarely, however, that I made these raids into the country, for I usually took my exercise upon my own beach, where I soothed my spirit with strong black tobacco, and made the ocean my friend and my confidant.

What companion is there like the great restless, throbbing sea? What human mood is there which it does not match and sympathize with? There are none so gay but that they may feel gayer when they listen to its merry turmoil, and see the long green surges racing in, with the glint of the sunbeams in their sparkling crests. But when the grey waves toss their heads in anger, and the wind screams above them, goading them on to madder and more tumultuous efforts, then the darkest-minded of men feels that there is a melancholy principle in Nature which is as gloomy as his own thoughts. When it was calm in the Bay of Mansie the surface would be as clear and bright as a sheet of silver, broken only at one spot some little way from the shore, where a long black line projected out of the water looking like the jagged back of some sleeping monster. This was the top of the dangerous ridge of rocks known to the fishermen as the " ragged reef o' Mansie." When the wind blew from the east the waves would break upon it like thunder, and the spray would be tossed far over my house and up to the hills behind. The bay itself was a bold and noble one, but too much exposed to the northern and eastern gales, and too much dreaded for its reef, to be much used by mariners. There was something of romance about this lonely spot. I have lain in my boat upon a calm day, and peering over the edge I have seen far down the flickering, ghostly forms of great fish—fish, as it seemed to me, such as naturalist never knew, and which my imagination transformed into the genii of that desolate bay. Once, as I stood by the brink of the waters upon a quiet night, a great cry, as of a woman in hopeless grief, rose from the bosom of the deep, and swelled out upon the still air, now sinking and now rising, for a space of thirty seconds. This I heard with my own ears.

In this strange spot, with the eternal hills behind me and the eternal sea in front, I worked and brooded for more than two years unpestered by my fellow men. By degrees I had trained my old servant into habits of silence, so that she now rarely opened her lips, though I doubt not that when twice a year she visited her relations in Wick, her tongue during those few days made up for its enforced rest. I had come almost to forget that I was a member of the human family, and to live entirely with the dead whose books I pored over, when a sudden incident occurred which threw all my thoughts into a new channel.

Three rough days in June had been succeeded by one calm and peaceful one. There was not a breath of air that evening. The sun sank down in the west behind a line of purple clouds, and the smooth surface of the bay was gashed with scarlet streaks. Along the beach the pools left by the tide showed up like gouts of blood against the yellow sand, as if some wounded giant had toilfully passed that way, and had left these red traces of his grievous hurt behind him. As the darkness closed in, certain ragged clouds which had lain low on the eastern horizon coalesced and formed a great irregular cumulus. The glass was still low, and I knew that there was mischief brewing. About nine o'clock a dull moaning sound came up from the sea, as from a creature who, much harassed, learns that the hour of suffering has come round again. At ten a sharp breeze sprang up from the eastward. At eleven it had increased to a gale, and by midnight the most furious storm was raging which I ever remember upon that weather-beaten coast.

As I went to bed the shingle and seaweed were pattering up against my attic window, and the wind was screaming as though every gust were a lost soul. By that time the sounds of the tempest had become a lullaby to me. I knew that the grey walls of the old house would buffet it out, and for what occurred in the world outside I had small concern. Old Madge was usually as callous to such things as I was myself. It was a surprise to me when, about three in the morning, I was awoke by the sound of a great knocking at my door and excited cries in the wheezy voice of my housekeeper. I sprang out of my hammock, and roughly demanded of her what was the matter.

"Eh, maister, maister!" she screamed in her hateful dialect. "Come doun, mun; come doun! There's a muckle ship gaun ashore on the reef, and the puir folks are a' yammerin' and ca'in' for help—and I doobt they'll a' be drooned. Oh, Maister M'Vittie, come doun!"

"Hold your tongue, you hag!" I shouted back in a passion. "What is it to you whether they are drowned or not? Get back to your bed and leave me alone." I turned in again and drew the blankets over me. "Those men out there," I said to myself, "have already gone through half the horrors of death. If they be saved they will but have to go through the same once more in the space of a few brief years. It is best therefore that they should pass away now, since they have suffered that anticipation which is more than the pain of dissolution." With this thought in my mind I endeavoured to compose myself to sleep once more, for that philosophy which had taught me to consider death as a small and trivial incident in man's eternal and everchanging career, had also broken me of much curiosity concerning worldly matters. On this occasion I found, however, that the old leaven still fermented strongly in my soul. I tossed from side to side for some minutes endeavouring to beat down the impulses of the moment by the rules of conduct which I had framed during months of thought. Then I heard a dull roar amid the wild shriek of the gale, and I knew that it was the sound of a signal-gun. Driven by an uncontrollable impulse, I rose, dressed, and having lit my pipe, walked out on to the beach.

It was pitch dark when I came outside, and the wind blew with such violence that I had to put my shoulder against it and push my way along the shingle. My face pringled and smarted with the sting of the gravel which was blown against it, and the red ashes of my pipe streamed away behind me, dancing fantastically through the darkness. I went down to where the great waves were thundering in, and shading my eyes with my hands to keep off the salt spray, I peered out to sea. I could distinguish nothing, and yet it seemed to me that shouts and great inarticulate cries were borne to me by the blasts. Suddenly as I gazed I made out the glint of a light, and then the whole bay and the beach were lit up in a moment by a vivid blue glare. They were burning a coloured signal-light on board of the vessel. There she lay on her beam ends right in the centre of the jagged reef, hurled over to such an angle that I could see all the planking of her deck. She was a large two-masted schooner, of foreign rig, and lay perhaps a hundred and eighty or two hundred yards from the shore. Every spar and rope and writhing piece of cordage showed up hard and clear under the livid light which sputtered and flickered from the highest portion of the forecastle. Beyond the doomed ship out of the great darkness came the long rolling lines of black waves, never ending, never tiring, with a petulant tuft of foam here and there upon their crests. Each as it reached the broad circle of unnatural light appeared to gather strength and volume, and to hurry on more impetuously until, with a roar and a jarring crash, it sprang upon its victim. Clinging to the weather shrouds I could distinctly see some ten or twelve frightened seamen, who, when their light revealed my presence, turned their white faces towards me and waved their hands imploringly. I felt my gorge rise against these poor cowering worms. Why should they presume to shirk the narrow pathway along which all that is great and noble among mankind has travelled? There was one there who interested me more than they. He was a tall man, who stood apart from the others, balancing himself upon the swaying wreck as though he disdained to cling to rope or bulwark. His hands were clasped behind his back and his head was sunk upon his breast, but even in that despondent attitude there was a litheness and decision in his pose and in every motion which marked him as a man little likely to yield to despair. Indeed, I could see by his occasional rapid glances up and down and all around him that he was weighing every chance of safety, but though he often gazed across the raging surf to where he could see my dark figure upon the beach, his self-respect or some other reason forbade him from imploring my help in any way. He stood, dark, silent, and inscrutable, looking down on the black sea, and waiting for whatever fortune Fate might send him.

It seemed to me that that problem would very soon be settled. As I looked, an enormous billow, topping all the others, and coming after them, like a driver following a flock, swept over the vessel. Her foremast snapped short off, and the men who clung to the shrouds were brushed away like a swarm of flies. With a rending, riving sound the ship began to split in two, where the sharp back of the Mansie reef was sawing into her keel. The solitary man upon the forecastle ran rapidly across the deck and seized hold of a white bundle which I had already observed but failed to make out. As he lifted it up the light fell upon it, and I saw that the object was a woman, with a spar lashed across her body and under her arms in such a way that her head should always rise above water. He bore her tenderly to the side and seemed to speak for a minute or so to her, as though explaining the impossibility of remaining upon the ship. Her answer was a singular one. I saw her deliberately raise her hand and strike him across the face with it. He appeared to be silenced for a moment or so by this, but he addressed her again, directing her, as far as I could gather from his motions, how she should behave when in the water. She shrank away from him, but he caught her in his arms. He stooped over her for a moment and seemed to press his lips against her forehead. Then a great wave came welling up against the side of the breaking vessel, and leaning over he placed her upon the summit of it as gently as a child might be committed to its cradle. I saw her white dress flickering among the foam on the crest of the dark billow, and then the light sank gradually lower, and the riven ship and its lonely occupant were hidden from my eyes.

As I watched those things my manhood overcame my philosophy, and I felt a frantic impulse to be up and doing. I threw my cynicism to one side as a garment which I might don again at leisure, and I rushed wildly to my boat and my sculls. She was a leaky tub, but what then? Was I, who had cast many a wistful, doubtful glance at my opium bottle, to begin now to weigh chances and to cavil at danger? I dragged her down to the sea with the strength of a maniac and sprang in. For a moment or two it was a question whether she could live among the boiling surge, but a dozen frantic strokes took me through it, half full of water but still afloat. I was out on the unbroken waves now, at one time climbing, climbing up the broad black breast of one, then sinking down, down on the other side, until looking up I could see the gleam of the foam all around me against the dark heavens. Far behind me I could hear the wild wailings of old Madge, who, seeing me start, thought no doubt that my madness had come to a climax. As I rowed I peered over my shoulder, until at last on the belly of a great wave which was sweeping towards me I distinguished the vague white outline of the woman. Stooping over, I seized her as she swept by me, and with an effort lifted her, all sodden with water, into the boat. There was no need to row back, for the next billow carried us in and threw us upon the beach. I dragged the boat out of danger, and then lifting up the woman I carried her to the house, followed by my housekeeper, loud with congratulation and praise.

Now that I had done this thing a reaction set in upon me. I felt that my burden lived, for I heard the faint beat of her heart as I pressed my ear against her side in carrying her. Knowing this, I threw her down beside the fire which Madge had lit, with as little sympathy as though she had been a bundle of fagots. I never glanced at her to see if she were fair or no. For many years I had cared little for the face of a woman. As I lay in my hammock upstairs, however, I heard the old woman as she chafed the warmth back into her, crooning a chorus of, " Eh, the puir lassie ! Eh, the bonnie lassie ! " from which I gathered that this piece of jetsam was both young and comely.

The morning after the gale was peaceful and sunny. As I walked along the long sweep of sand I could hear the panting of the sea. It was heaving and swirling about the reef, but along the shore it rippled in gently enough. There was no sign of the schooner, nor was there any wreckage upon the beach, which did not surprise me, as I knew there was a great undertow in those waters. A couple of broad-winged gulls were hovering and skimming over the scene of the shipwreck, as though many strange things were visible to them beneath the waves. At times I could hear their raucous voices as they spoke to one another of what they saw.

When I came back from my walk the woman was waiting at the door for me. I began to wish when I saw her that I had never saved her, for here was an end of my privacy. She was very young—at the most nineteen, with a pale somewhat refined face, yellow hair, merry blue eyes, and shining teeth. Her beauty was of an ethereal type. She looked so white and light and fragile that she might have been the spirit of that storm-foam from out of which I plucked her. She had wreathed some of Madge's garments round her in a way which was quaint and not unbecoming. As I strode heavily up the pathway, she put out her hands with a pretty child-like gesture, and ran down towards me, meaning, as I surmise, to thank me for having saved her, but I put her aside with a wave of my hand and passed her. At this she seemed somewhat hurt, and the tears sprang into her eyes, but she followed me into the sitting-room and watched me wistfully. " What country do you come from ? " I asked her suddenly.

She smiled when I spoke, but shook her head.

" Français ? " I asked. " Deutsch ? " " Espagnol ? " —each time she shook her head, and then she rippled off into a long statement in some tongue of which I could not understand one word.

After breakfast was over, however, I got a clue to her nationality. Passing along the beach once more, I saw that in a cleft of the ridge a piece of wood had been jammed. I rowed out to it in my boat, and brought it ashore. It was part of the sternpost of a boat, and on it, or rather on the piece of wood attached to it, was the word "Archangel," painted in strange, quaint lettering. "So," I thought, as I paddled slowly back, "this pale damsel is a Russian. A fit subject for the White Czar and a proper dweller on the shores of the White Sea!" It seemed to me strange that one of her apparent refinement should perform so long a journey in so frail a craft. When I came back into the house, I pronounced the word "Archangel" several times in different intonations, but she did not appear to recognise it.

I shut myself up in the laboratory all the morning, continuing a research which I was making upon the nature of the allotropic forms of carbon and of sulphur. When I came out at mid-day for some food she was sitting by the table with a needle and thread, mending some rents in her clothes, which were now dry. I resented her continued presence, but I could not turn her out on the beach to shift for herself. Presently she presented a new phase of her character. Pointing to herself and then to the scene of the shipwreck, she held up one finger, by which I understood her to be asking whether she was the only one saved. I nodded my head to indicate that she was. On this she sprang out of her chair with a cry of great joy, and holding the garment which she was mending over her head, and swaying it from side to side with the motion of her body, she danced as lightly as a feather all round the room, and then out through the open door into the sunshine. As she whirled round she sang in a plaintive shrill voice some uncouth barbarous chant, expressive of exultation.

I called out to her, "Come in, you young fiend, come in and be silent!" but she went on with her dance. Then she suddenly ran towards me, and catching my hand before I could pluck it away, she kissed it. While we were at dinner she spied one of my pencils, and taking it up she wrote the two words "Sophie Ramusine" upon a piece of paper, and then pointed to herself as a sign that that was her name. She handed the pencil to me, evidently expecting that I would be equally communicative, but I put it in my pocket as a sign that I wished to hold no intercourse with her.

Every moment of my life now I regretted the unguarded precipitancy with which I had saved this woman. What was it to me whether she had lived or died? I was no young, hot-headed youth to do such things. It was bad enough to be compelled to have Madge in the house, but she was old and ugly, and could be ignored. This one was young and lively, and so fashioned as to divert attention from graver things. Where could I send her, and what could I do with her? If I sent information to Wick it would mean that officials and others would come to me and pry, and peep, and chatter—a hateful thought. It was better to endure her presence than that.

I soon found that there were fresh troubles in store for me. There is no place safe from the swarming, restless race of which I am a member. In the evening, when the sun was dipping down behind the hills, casting them into dark shadow, but gilding the sands and casting a great glory over the sea, I went, as is my custom, for a stroll along the beach. Sometimes on these occasions I took my book with me. I did so on this night, and stretching myself upon a sand-dune I composed myself to read. As I lay there I suddenly became aware of a shadow which interposed itself between the sun and myself. Looking round, I saw to my great surprise a very tall, powerful man, who was standing a few yards off, and who, instead of looking at me, was ignoring my existence completely, and was gazing over my head with a stern set face at the bay and the black line of the Mansie reef. His complexion was dark, with black hair, and short, curling beard, a hawk-like nose, and golden earrings in his ears—the general effect being wild and somewhat noble. He wore a faded velveteen jacket, a red-flannel shirt, and high sea boots, coming half-way up his thighs. I recognised him at a glance as being the same man who had been left on the wreck the night before.

"Hullo!" I said, in an aggrieved voice. "You got ashore all right, then?"

"Yes," he answered, in good English. "It was no doing of mine. The waves threw me up. I wish to God I had been allowed to drown!" There was a slight foreign lisp in his accent which was rather pleasing. "Two good fishermen, who live round yonder point, pulled me out and cared for me; yet I could not honestly thank them for it."

"Ho! ho!" thought I, "here is a man of my own kidney. Why do you wish to be drowned?" I asked.

"Because," he cried, throwing out his long arms with a passionate, despairing gesture, "there—there in that blue smiling bay, lies my soul, my treasure—everything that I loved and lived for."

"Well, well," I said. "People are ruined every day, but there's no use making a fuss about it. Let me inform you that this ground on which you walk is my ground, and that the sooner you take yourself off it the better pleased I shall be. One of you is quite trouble enough."

"One of us?" he gasped.

"Yes—if you could take her off with you I should be still more grateful."

He gazed at me for a moment as if hardly able to realise what I said, and then with a wild cry he ran away from me with prodigious speed and raced along the sands towards my house. Never before or since have I seen a human being run so fast. I followed as rapidly as I could, furious at this threatened invasion, but long before I reached the house he had disappeared through the open door. I heard a great scream from the inside, and as I came nearer the sound of a man's bass voice speaking rapidly and loudly. When I looked in the girl, Sophie Ramusine, was crouching in a corner, cowering away, with fear and loathing expressed on her averted face and in every line of her shrinking form. The other, with his dark eyes flashing, and his outstretched hands quivering with emotion, was pouring forth a torrent of passionate pleading words. He made a step forward to her as I entered, but she writhed still farther away, and uttered a sharp cry like that of a rabbit when the weasel has him by the throat.

"Here!" I said, pulling him back from her. "This is a pretty to-do! What do you mean? Do you think this is a wayside inn or place of public accommodation?"

"Oh, sir," he said, "excuse me. This woman is my wife, and I feared that she was drowned. You have brought me back to life."

"Who are you?" I asked roughly.

"I am a man from Archangel," he said simply; "a Russian man."

"What is your name?"

"Ourganeff."

"Ourganeff!—and hers is Sophie Ramusine. She is no wife of yours. She has no ring."

"We are man and wife in the sight of Heaven," he said solemnly, looking upwards. "We are bound by higher laws than those of earth." As he spoke the girl slipped behind me and caught me by the other hand, pressing it as though beseeching my protection. "Give me up my wife, sir," he went on. "Let me take her away from here."

"Look here, you—whatever your name is," I said sternly; "I don't want this wench here. I wish I had never seen her. If she died it would be no grief to me. But as to handing her over to you, when it is clear she fears and hates you, I won't do it. So now just clear your great body out of this, and leave me to my books. I hope I may never look upon your face again."

"You won't give her up to me?" he said hoarsely.

"I'll see you damned first!" I answered.

"Suppose I take her," he cried, his dark face growing darker.

All my tigerish blood flashed up in a moment. I picked up a billet of wood from beside the fireplace. "Go," I said, in a low voice; "go quick, or I may do you an injury." He looked at me irresolutely for a moment, and then he left the house. He came back again in a moment, however, and stood in the doorway looking in at us.

"Have a heed what you do," he said. "The woman is mine, and I shall have her. When it comes to blows, a Russian is as good a man as a Scotchman."

"We shall see that," I cried, springing forward, but he was already gone, and I could see his tall form moving away through the gathering darkness.

For a month or more after this things went smoothly with us. I never spoke to the Russian girl, nor did she ever address me. Sometimes when I was at work in my laboratory she would slip inside the door and sit silently there watching me with her great eyes. At first this intrusion annoyed me, but by degrees, finding that she made no attempt to distract my attention, I suffered her to remain. Encouraged by this concession, she gradually came to move the stool on which she sat nearer and nearer to my table, until after gaining a little every day during some weeks, she at last worked her way right up to me, and used to perch herself beside me whenever I worked. In this position she used, still without ever obtruding her presence in any way, to make herself very useful by holding my pens, test-tubes, or bottles and handing me whatever I wanted, with never-failing sagacity. By ignoring the fact of her being a human being, and looking upon her as a useful automatic machine I accustomed myself to her presence so far as to miss her on the few occasions when she was not at her post. I have a habit of talking aloud to myself at times when I work, so as to fix my results better in my mind. The girl must have had a surprising memory for sounds, for she could always repeat the words which I let fall in this way, without, of course, understanding in the least what they meant. I have often been amused at hearing her discharge a volley of chemical equations and algebraic symbols at old Madge, and then burst into a ringing laugh when the crone would shake her head, under the impression, no doubt, that she was being addressed in Russian.

She never went more than a few yards from the house, and indeed never put her foot over the threshold without looking carefully out of each window in order to be sure that there was nobody about. By this I knew that she suspected that her fellow-countryman was still in the neighbourhood, and feared that he might attempt to carry her off. She did something else which was significant. I had an old revolver with some cartridges, which had been thrown away among the rubbish. She found this one day, and at once proceeded to clean it and oil it. She hung it up near the door, with the cartridges in a little bag beside it, and whenever I went for a walk, she would take it down and insist upon my carrying it with me. In my absence she would always bolt the door. Apart from her apprehensions she seemed fairly happy, busying herself in helping Madge when she was not attending upon me. She was wonderfully nimble-fingered and natty in all domestic duties.

It was not long before I discovered that her suspicions were well founded, and that this man from Archangel was still lurking in the vicinity. Being restless one night I rose and peered out of the window. The weather was somewhat cloudy, and I could barely make out the line of the sea, and the loom of my boat upon the beach. As I gazed, however, and my eyes became accustomed to the obscurity, I became aware that there was some other dark blur upon the sands, and that in front of my very door, where certainly there had been nothing of the sort the preceding night. As I stood at my diamond-paned lattice, still peering and peeping to make out what this might be, a great bank of clouds rolled slowly away from the face of the moon, and a flood of cold, clear light was poured down upon the silent bay and the long sweep of its desolate shores. Then I saw what this was which haunted my doorstep. It was he, the Russian. He squattered there like a gigantic toad, with his legs doubled under him in strange Mongolian fashion, and his eyes fixed apparently upon the window of the room in which the young girl and the housekeeper slept. The light fell upon his upturned face, and I saw once more the hawk-like grace of his countenance, with the single deeply-indented line of care upon his brow, and the protruding beard which marks the passionate nature. My first impulse was to shoot him as a trespasser, but, as I gazed, my resentment changed into pity and contempt. "Poor fool," I said to myself, "is it then possible that you, whom I have seen looking open-eyed at present death, should have your whole thoughts and ambition centred upon this wretched slip of a girl—a girl, too, who flies from you and hates you? Most women would love you—were it but for that dark face and great handsome body of yours—and yet you must needs hanker after the one in a thousand who will have no traffic with you." As I returned to my bed I chuckled much to myself over this thought. I knew that my bars were strong and my bolts thick. It mattered little to me whether this strange man spent his night at my door or a hundred leagues off, so long as he was gone by the morning. As I expected, when I rose and went out there was no sign of him, nor had he left any trace of his midnight vigil.

It was not long, however, before I saw him again. I had been out for a row one morning, for my head was aching, partly from prolonged stooping, and partly from the effects of a noxious drug which I had inhaled the night before. I pulled along the coast some miles, and then, feeling thirsty, I landed at a place where I knew that a fresh-water stream trickled down into the sea. This rivulet passed through my land, but the mouth of it, where I found myself that day, was beyond my boundary line. I felt somewhat taken aback when rising from the stream at which I had slaked my thirst I found myself face to face with the Russian. I was as much a trespasser now as he was, and I could see at a glance that he knew it.

"I wish to speak a few words to you," he said gravely.

"Hurry up, then!" I answered, glancing at my watch. "I have no time to listen to chatter."

"Chatter!" he repeated angrily. "Ah, but there. You Scotch people are strange men. Your face is hard and your words rough, but so are those of the good fishermen with whom I stay, yet I find that beneath it all there lie kind honest natures. No doubt you are kind and good, too, in spite of your roughness."

"In the name of the devil," I said, "say your say, and go your way. I am weary of the sight of you."

"Can I not soften you in any way?" he cried. "Ah, see—see here"—he produced a small Grecian cross from inside his velvet jacket. "Look at this. Our religions may differ in form, but at least we have some common thoughts and feelings when we see this emblem."

"I am not so sure of that," I answered.

He looked at me thoughtfully.

"You are a very strange man," he said at last. "I cannot understand you. You still stand between me and Sophie. It is a dangerous position to take, sir. Oh, believe me, before it is too late. If you did but know what I have done to gain that woman—how I have risked my body, how I have lost my soul! You are a small obstacle to some which I have surmounted—you, whom a rip with a knife, or a blow from a stone, would put out of my way for ever. But God preserve me from that," he cried wildly. "I am deep—too deep—already. Anything rather than that."

"You would do better to go back to your country," I said, "than to skulk about these sand-hills and disturb my leisure. When I have proof that you have gone away I shall hand this woman over to the protection of the Russian Consul at Edinburgh. Until then, I shall guard her myself, and not you, nor any Muscovite that ever breathed, shall take her from me."

"And what is your object in keeping me from Sophie?" he asked. "Do you imagine that I would injure her? Why, man, I would give my life freely to save her from the slightest harm. Why do you do this thing?"

"I do it because it is my good pleasure to act so," I answered. "I give no man reasons for my conduct."

"Look here!" he cried, suddenly blazing into fury, and advancing towards me with his shaggy mane bristling and his brown hands clenched. "If I thought you had one dishonest thought towards this girl—if for a moment I had reason to believe that you had any base motive for detaining her—as sure as there is a God in Heaven I should drag the heart out of your bosom with my hands." The very idea seemed to have put the man in a frenzy, for his face was all distorted and his hands opened and shut convulsively. I thought that he was about to spring at my throat.

"Stand off," I said, putting my hand on my pistol. "If you lay a finger on me I shall kill you."

He put his hand into his pocket, and for a moment I thought he was about to produce a weapon too, but instead of that he whipped out a cigarette and lit it, breathing the smoke rapidly into his lungs. No doubt he had found by experience that this was the most effectual way of curbing his passions.

"I told you," he said in a quieter voice, "that my name is Ourganeff—Alexis Ourganeff. I am a Finn by birth, but I have spent my life in every part of the world. I was one who could never be still, nor settle down to a quiet existence. After I came to own my own ship there is hardly a port from Archangel to Australia which I have not entered. I was rough and wild and free, but there was one at home, sir, who was prim and white-handed and soft-tongued, skilful in little fancies and conceits which women love. This youth by his wiles and tricks stole from me the love of the girl whom I had ever marked as my own, and who up to that time had seemed in some sort inclined to return my passion. I had been on a voyage to Hammerfest for ivory, and coming back unexpectedly I learned that my pride and treasure was to be married to this soft-skinned boy, and that the party had actually gone to the church, In such moments, sir, something gives way in my head, and I hardly know what I do. I landed with a boat's crew—all men who had sailed with me for years, and who were as true as steel. We went up to the church. They were standing, she and he, before the priest, but the thing had not been done. I dashed between them and caught her round the waist. My men beat back the frightened bridegroom and the lookers on. We bore her down to the boat and aboard our vessel, and then getting up anchor we sailed away across the White Sea until the spires of Archangel sank down behind the horizon. She had my cabin, my room, every comfort. I slept among the men in the forecastle. I hoped that in time her aversion to me would wear away, and that she would consent to marry me in England or in France. For days and days we sailed. We saw the North Cape die away behind us, and we skirted the grey Norwegian coast, but still, in spite of every attention, she would not forgive me for tearing her from that pale-faced lover of hers. Then came this cursed storm which shattered both my ship and my hopes, and has deprived me even of the sight of the woman for whom I have risked so much. Perhaps she may learn to love me yet. You, sir," he said wistfully, "look like one who has seen much of the world. Do you not think that she may come to forget this man and to love me ? "

" I am tired of your story," I said, turning away. " For my part, I think you are a great fool. If you imagine that this love of yours will pass away you had best amuse yourself as best you can until it does. If, on the other hand, it is a fixed thing, you cannot do better than cut your throat, for that is the shortest way out of it. I have no more time to waste on the matter." With this I hurried away and walked down to the boat. I never looked round, but I heard the dull sound of his feet upon the sands as he followed me.

" I have told you the beginning of my story," he said, " and you shall know the end some day. You would do well to let the girl go."

I never answered him, but pushed the boat off. When I had rowed some distance out I looked back and saw his tall figure upon the yellow sand as he stood gazing thoughtfully after me. When I looked again some minutes later he had disappeared.

For a long time after this my life was as regular and as monotonous as it had been before the shipwreck. At times I hoped that the man from Archangel had gone away altogether, but certain footsteps which I saw upon the sand, and more particularly a little pile of cigarette ash which I found one day behind a hillock from which a view of the house might be obtained, warned me that, though invisible, he was still in the vicinity. My relations with the Russian girl remained the same as before. Old Madge had been somewhat jealous of her presence at first, and seemed to fear that what little authority she had would be taken away from her. By degrees, however, as she came to realise my utter indifference, she became reconciled to the situation, and, as I have said before, profited by it, as our visitor performed much of the domestic work.

And now I am coming near the end of this narrative of mine, which I have written a great deal more for my own amusement than for that of anyone else. The termination of the strange episode in which these two Russians had played a part was as wild and as sudden as the commencement. The events of one single night freed me from all my troubles, and left me once more alone with my books and my studies, as I had been before their intrusion. Let me endeavour to describe how this came about.

I had had a long day of heavy and wearying work, so that in the evening I determined upon taking a long walk. When I emerged from the house my attention was attracted by the appearance of the sea. It lay like a sheet of glass, so that never a ripple disturbed its surface. Yet the air was filled with that indescribable moaning sound which I have alluded to before—a sound as though the spirits of all those who lay beneath those treacherous waters were sending a sad warning of coming troubles to their brethren in the flesh. The fishermen's wives along that coast know the eerie sound, and look anxiously across the waters for the brown sails making for the land. When I heard it I stepped back into the house and looked at the glass. It was down below 29°. Then I knew that a wild night was coming upon us.

Underneath the hills where I walked that evening it was dull and chill, but their summits were rosy-red, and the sea was brightened by the sinking sun. There were no clouds of importance in the sky, yet the dull groaning of the sea grew louder and stronger. I saw, far to the eastward, a brig beating up for Wick, with a reef in her topsails. It was evident that her captain had read the signs of nature as I had done. Behind her a long, lurid haze lay low upon the water, concealing the horizon. "I had better push on," I thought to myself, "or the wind may rise before I can get back."

I suppose I must have been at least half a mile from the house when I suddenly stopped and listened breathlessly. My ears were so accustomed to the noises of nature, the sighing of the breeze and the sob of the waves, that any other sound made itself heard at a great distance. I waited, listening with all my ears. Yes, there it was again—a long-drawn, shrill cry of despair, ringing over the sands and echoed back from the hills behind me—a piteous appeal for aid. It came from the direction of my house. I turned and ran back homewards at the top of my speed, ploughing through the sand, racing over the shingle. In my mind there was a great dim perception of what had occurred.

About a quarter of a mile from the house there is a high sand-hill, from which the whole country round is visible. When I reached the top of this I paused for a moment. There was the old grey building—there the boat. Everything seemed to be as I had left it. Even as I gazed, however, the shrill scream was repeated, louder than before, and the next moment a tall figure emerged from my door, the figure of the Russian sailor. Over his shoulder was the white form of the young girl, and even in his haste he seemed to bear her tenderly and with gentle reverence. I could hear her wild cries and see her desperate struggles to break away from him. Behind the couple came my old housekeeper, staunch and true, as the aged dog, who can no longer bite, still snarls with toothless gums at the intruder. She staggered feebly along at the heels of the ravisher, waving her long, thin arms, and hurling, no doubt, volleys of Scotch curses and imprecations at his head. I saw at a glance that he was making for the boat. A sudden hope sprang up in my soul that I might be in time to intercept him. I ran for the beach at the top of my speed. As I ran I slipped a cartridge into my revolver. This I determined should be the last of these invasions.

I was too late. By the time I reached the water's edge he was a hundred yards away, making the boat spring with every stroke of his powerful arms. I uttered a wild cry of impotent anger, and stamped up and down the sands like a maniac. He turned and saw me. Rising from his seat he made me a graceful bow, and waved his hand to me. It was not a triumphant or a derisive gesture. Even my furious and distempered mind recognised it as being a solemn and courteous leave-taking. Then he settled down to his oars once more, and the little skiff shot away out over the bay. The sun had gone down now, leaving a single dull, red streak upon the water, which stretched away until it blended with the purple haze on the horizon. Gradually the skiff grew smaller and smaller as it sped across this lurid band, until the shades of night gathered round it and it became a mere blur upon the lonely sea. Then this vague loom died away also and darkness settled over it—a darkness which should never be raised.

And why did I pace the solitary shore, hot and wrathful as a wolf whose whelp has been torn from it? Was it that I loved this Muscovite girl? No—a thousand times no. I am not one who, for the sake of a white skin or a blue eye, would belie my own life, and change the whole tenor of my thoughts and existence. My heart was untouched. But my pride—ah, there I had been cruelly wounded. To think that I had been unable to afford protection to the helpless one who craved it of me, and who relied on me! It was that which made my heart sick and sent the blood buzzing through my ears.

That night a great wind rose up from the sea, and the wild waves shrieked upon the shore as though they would tear it back with them into the ocean. The turmoil and the uproar were congenial to my vexed spirit. All night I wandered up and down, wet with spray and rain, watching the gleam of the white breakers and listening to the outcry of the storm. My heart was bitter against the Russian. I joined my feeble pipe to the screaming of the gale. "If he would but come back again!" I cried, with clenched hands; "if he would but come back!"

He came back. When the grey light of morning

spread over the eastern sky, and lit up the great waste of yellow, tossing waters, with the brown clouds drifting swiftly over them, then I saw him once again. A few hundred yards off along the sand there lay a long dark object, cast up by the fury of the waves. It was my boat, much shattered and splintered. A little farther on, a vague, shapeless something was washing to and fro in the shallow water, all mixed with shingle and with seaweed. I saw at a glance that it was the Russian, face downwards and dead. I rushed into the water and dragged him up on to the beach. It was only when I turned him over that I discovered that she was beneath him, his dead arms encircling her, his mangled body still intervening between her and the fury of the storm. It seemed that the fierce German Sea might beat the life from him, but with all its strength it was unable to tear this one-idea'd man from the woman whom he loved. There were signs which led me to believe that during that awful night the woman's fickle mind had come at last to learn the worth of the true heart and strong arm which struggled for her and guarded her so tenderly. Why else should her little head be nestling so lovingly on his broad breast, while her yellow hair entwined itself with his flowing beard? Why too should there be that bright smile of ineffable happiness and triumph, which death itself had not had power to banish from his dusky face? I fancy that death had been brighter to him than life had ever been.

Madge and I buried them there on the shores of the desolate northern sea. They lie in one grave deep down beneath the yellow sand. Strange things may happen in the world around them. Empires may rise and may fall, dynasties may perish, great wars may come and go, but, heedless of it all, those two shall embrace each other for ever and aye, in their lonely shrine by the side of the sounding ocean. I sometimes have thought that their spirits flit like shadowy sea-mews over the wild waters of the bay. No cross or symbol marks their resting-place, but old Madge puts wild flowers upon it at times, and when I pass on my daily walk and see the fresh blossoms scattered over the sand, I think of the strange couple who came from afar, and broke for a little space the dull tenor of my sombre life.

54. *The Great Brown-Pericord Motor*

IT was a cold, foggy, dreary evening in May. Along the Strand blurred patches of light marked the position of the lamps. The flaring shop windows flickered vaguely with steamy brightness through the thick and heavy atmosphere.

The high lines of houses which led down to the Embankment were all dark and deserted, or illuminated only by the glimmering lamp of the caretaker. At one point, however, there shone out from three windows upon the second floor a rich flood of light, which broke the sombre monotony of the terrace. Passers-by glanced up curiously, and drew each other's attention to the ruddy glare, for it marked the chambers of Francis Pericord, the inventor and electrical engineer. Long into the watches of the night the gleam of his lamps bore witness to the untiring energy and restless industry which was rapidly carrying him to the first rank in his profession.

Within the chamber sat two men. The one was Pericord himself—hawk-faced and angular, with the black hair and brisk bearing which spoke of his Celtic origin. The other—thick, sturdy, and blue-eyed, was Jeremy Brown, the well-known mechanician. They had been partners in many an invention, in which the creative genius of the one had been aided by the practical abilities of the other. It was a question among their friends as to which was the better man.

It was no chance visit which had brought Brown into

Pericord's workshop at so late an hour. Business was to be done—business which was to decide the failure or success of months of work, and which might affect their whole careers. Between them lay a long brown table, stained and corroded by strong acids, and littered with giant carboys, Faure's accumulators, voltaic piles, coils of wire, and great blocks of non-conducting porcelain. In the midst of all this lumber there stood a singular whizzing, whirring machine, upon which the eyes of both partners were riveted.

A small square metal receptacle was connected by numerous wires to a broad steel girdle, furnished on either side with two powerful projecting joints. The girdle was motionless, but the joints with the short arms attached to them flashed round every few seconds, with a pause between each rhythmic turn. The power which moved them came evidently from the metal box. A subtle odour of ozone was in the air.

"How about the flanges, Brown?" asked the inventor.

"They were too large to bring. They are seven foot by three. There is power enough there to work them, however. I will answer for that."

"Aluminium with an alloy of copper?"

"Yes."

"See how beautifully it works." Pericord stretched out a thin, nervous hand, and pressed a button upon the machine. The joints revolved more slowly, and came presently to a dead stop. Again he touched a spring and the arms shivered and woke up again into their crisp metallic life. "The experimenter need not exert his muscular powers," he remarked. "He has only to be passive, and use his intelligence."

"Thanks to my motor," said Brown.

"*Our* motor," the other broke in sharply.

"Oh, of course," said his colleague impatiently. "The motor which you thought of, and which I reduced to practice—call it what you like."

"I call it the Brown-Pericord Motor," cried the

inventor, with an angry flash of his dark eyes. "You worked out the details, but the abstract thought is mine, and mine alone."

"An abstract thought won't turn an engine," said Brown doggedly.

"That was why I took you into partnership," the other retorted, drumming nervously with his fingers upon the table. "I invent, you build. It is a fair division of labour."

Brown pursed up his lips, as though by no means satisfied upon the point. Seeing, however, that further argument was useless, he turned his attention to the machine, which was shivering and rocking with each swing of its arms, as though a very little more would send it skimming from the table.

"Is it not splendid?" cried Pericord.

"It is satisfactory," said the more phlegmatic Anglo-Saxon.

"There's immortality in it!"

"There's money in it!"

"Our names will go down with Montgolfier's."

"With Rothschild's, I hope."

"No, no, Brown; you take too material a view," cried the inventor, raising his gleaming eyes from the machine to his companion. "Our fortunes are a mere detail. Money is a thing which every heavy-witted plutocrat in the country shares with us. My hopes rise to something higher than that. Our true reward will come in the gratitude and goodwill of the human race."

Brown shrugged his shoulders. "You may have my share of that," he said. "I am a practical man. We must test our invention."

"Where can we do it?"

"That is what I wanted to speak about. It must be absolutely secret. If we had private grounds of our own it would be an easy matter, but there is no privacy in London."

"We must take it into the country."

"I have a suggestion to offer," said Brown. "My brother has a place in Sussex on the high land near Beachy Head. There is, I remember, a large and lofty barn near the house. Will is in Scotland, but the key is always at my disposal. Why not take the machine down to-morrow and test it in the barn?"

"Nothing could be better."

"There is a train to Eastbourne at one."

"I shall be at the station."

"Bring the gear with you, and I will bring the flanges," said the mechanician, rising. "To-morrow will prove whether we have been following a shadow, or whether fortune is at our feet. One o'clock at Victoria." He walked swiftly down the stair and was quickly reabsorbed into the flood of comfortless clammy humanity which ebbed and flowed along the Strand.

* * * * *

The morning was bright and spring-like. A pale blue sky arched over London, with a few gauzy white clouds drifting lazily across it. At eleven o'clock Brown might have been seen entering the Patent Office with a great roll of parchment, diagrams, and plans under his arm. At twelve he emerged again smiling, and, opening his pocket book, he packed away very carefully a small slip of official blue paper. At five minutes to one his cab rolled into Victoria Station. Two giant canvas-covered parcels, like enormous kites, were handed down by the cabman from the top, and consigned to the care of a guard. On the platform Pericord was pacing up and down, with long, eager step and swinging arms, a tinge of pink upon his sunken and sallow cheeks.

"All right?" he asked.

Brown pointed in answer to his baggage.

"I have the motor and the girdle already packed away in the guard's van. Be careful, guard, for it is delicate machinery of great value. So! Now we can start with an easy conscience."

At Eastbourne the precious motor was carried to a

four-wheeler, and the great flanges hoisted on the top. A long drive took them to the house where the keys were kept, whence they set off across the barren Downs. The building which was their destination was a commonplace whitewashed structure, with straggling stables and out-houses, standing in a grassy hollow which sloped down from the edge of the chalk cliffs. It was a cheerless house even when in use, but now with its smokeless chimneys and shuttered windows it looked doubly dreary. The owner had planted a grove of young larches and firs around it but the sweeping spray had blighted them, and they hung their withered heads in melancholy groups. It was a gloomy and forbidding spot.

But the inventors were in no mood to be moved by such trifles. The lonelier the place, the more fitted for their purpose. With the help of the cabman they carried their packages down the footpath, and laid them in the darkened dining-room. The sun was setting as the distant murmur of wheels told them that they were finally alone.

Pericord had thrown open the shutters and the mellow evening light streamed in through the discoloured windows. Brown drew a knife from his pocket and cut the pack-thread with which the canvas was secured. As the brown covering fell away it disclosed two great yellow metal fans. These he leaned carefully against the wall. The girdle, the connecting-bands, and the motor were then in turn unpacked. It was dark before all was set out in order. A lamp was lit, and by its light the two men continued to tighten screws, clinch rivets, and make the last preparations for their experiment.

"That finishes it," said Brown at last, stepping back and surveying the machine.

Pericord said nothing, but his face glowed with pride and expectation.

"We must have something to eat," Brown remarked, laying out some provisions which he had brought with him.

"Afterwards."

"No, now," said the stolid mechanician. "I am half starved." He pulled up to the table and made a hearty meal, while his Celtic companion strode impatiently up and down, with twitching fingers and restless eyes.

"Now then," said Brown, facing round, and brushing the crumbs from his lap, "who is to put it on?"

"I shall," cried his companion eagerly. "What we do to-night is likely to be historic."

"But there is some danger," suggested Brown. "We cannot quite tell how it may act."

"That is nothing," said Pericord, with a wave of his hand.

"But there is no use our going out of our way to incur danger."

"What then? One of us must do it."

"Not at all. The motor would act equally well if attached to any inanimate object."

"That is true," said Pericord thoughtfully.

"There are bricks by the barn. I have a sack here. Why should not a bagful of them take our place?"

"It is a good idea. I see no objection."

"Come on then," and the two sallied out, bearing with them the various sections of their machine. The moon was shining cold and clear, though an occasional ragged cloud drifted across her face. All was still and silent upon the Downs. They stood and listened before they entered the barn, but not a sound came to their ears, save the dull murmur of the sea and the distant barking of a dog. Pericord journeyed backwards and forwards with all that they might need, while Brown filled a long narrow sack with bricks.

When all was ready, the door of the barn was closed, and the lamp balanced upon an empty packing-case. The bag of bricks was laid upon two trestles, and the broad steel girdle was buckled round it. Then the great flanges, the wires, and the metal box containing the motor were in turn attached to the girdle. Last of all a flat steel rudder, shaped like a fish's tail, was secured to the bottom of the sack.

"We must make it travel in a small circle," said Pericord, glancing round at the bare high walls.

"Tie the rudder down at one side," suggested Brown. "Now it is ready. Press the connection and off she goes!"

Pericord leaned forward, his long sallow face quivering with excitement. His white nervous hands darted here and there among the wires. Brown stood impassive with critical eyes. There was a sharp burr from the machine. The huge yellow wings gave a convulsive flap. Then another. Then a third, slower and stronger, with a fuller sweep. Then a fourth which filled the barn with a blast of driven air. At the fifth the bag of bricks began to dance upon the trestles. At the sixth it sprang into the air, and would have fallen to the ground, but the seventh came to save it, and fluttered it forward through the air. Slowly rising, it flapped heavily round in a circle, like some great clumsy bird, filling the barn with its buzzing and whirring. In the uncertain yellow light of the single lamp it was strange to see the loom of the ungainly thing, flapping off into the shadows, and then circling back into the narrow zone of light.

The two men stood for a while in silence. Then Pericord threw his long arms up into the air.

"It acts!" he cried. "The Brown-Pericord Motor acts!" He danced about like a madman in his delight. Brown's eyes twinkled, and he began to whistle.

"See how smoothly it goes, Brown!" cried the inventor. "And the rudder—how well it acts! We must register it to-morrow."

His comrade's face darkened and set. "It *is* registered," he said, with a forced laugh.

"Registered?" said Pericord. "Registered?" He repeated the word first in a whisper, and then in a kind of scream. "Who has dared to register my invention?"

"I did it this morning. There is nothing to be excited about. It is all right."

"You registered the motor! Under whose name?"

"Under my own," said Brown sullenly. "I consider that I have the best right to it."

"And my name does not appear?"

"No, but——"

"You villain!" screamed Pericord. "You thief and villain! You would steal my work! You would filch my credit! I will have that patent back if I have to tear your throat out!" A sombre fire burned in his black eyes, and his hands writhed themselves together with passion. Brown was no coward, but he shrank back as the other advanced upon him.

"Keep your hands off!" he said, drawing a knife from his pocket. "I will defend myself if you attack me."

"You threaten me?" cried Pericord, whose face was livid with anger. "You are a bully as well as a cheat. Will you give up the patent?"

"No, I will not."

"Brown, I say, give it up!"

"I will not. I did the work."

Pericord sprang madly forward with blazing eyes and clutching fingers. His companion writhed out of his grasp, but was dashed against the packing-case, over which he fell. The lamp was extinguished, and the whole barn plunged into darkness. A single ray of moonlight shining through a narrow chink flickered over the great waving fans as they came and went.

"Will you give up the patent, Brown?"

There was no answer.

"Will you give it up?"

Again no answer. Not a sound save the humming and creaking overhead. A cold pang of fear and doubt struck through Pericord's heart. He felt aimlessly about in the dark and his fingers closed upon a hand. It was cold and unresponsive. With all his anger turned to icy horror he struck a match, set the lamp up, and lit it.

Brown lay huddled up on the other side of the packing-case. Pericord seized him in his arms, and with convulsive strength lifted him across. Then the mystery of his silence was explained. He had fallen with his right arm doubled up under him, and his own weight had driven the knife deeply into his body. He had died without a groan. The tragedy had been sudden, horrible, and complete.

Pericord sat silently on the edge of the case, staring blankly down, and shivering like one with the ague, while the great Brown-Pericord Motor boomed and hurtled above him. How long he sat there can never be known. It might have been minutes or it might have been hours. A thousand mad schemes flashed through his dazed brain. It was true that he had been only the indirect cause. But who would believe that? He glanced down at his blood-spattered clothing. Everything was against him. It would be better to fly than to give himself up, relying upon his innocence. No one in London knew where they were. If he could dispose of the body he might have a few days clear before any suspicion would be aroused.

Suddenly a loud crash recalled him to himself. The flying sack had gradually risen with each successive circle until it had struck again the rafters. The blow displaced the connecting-gear, and the machine fell heavily to the ground. Pericord undid the girdle. The motor was uninjured. A sudden, strange thought flashed upon him as he looked at it. The machine had become hateful to him. He might dispose both of it and the body in a way that would baffle all human search.

He threw open the barn door, and carried his companion out into the moonlight. There was a hillock outside, and on the summit of this he laid him reverently down. Then he brought from the barn the motor, the girdle and the flanges. With trembling fingers he fastened the broad steel belt round the dead man's waist. Then he screwed the wings into the sockets. Beneath he slung the motor-box, fastened the wires, and switched on the connection. For a minute or two the huge yellow fans flapped and flickered. Then the body began to move in little jumps down the side of the hillock, gathering a gradual momentum, until at last it heaved up into the air and soared heavily off in the moonlight. He had not used the rudder, but had turned the head for the south. Gradually the weird thing rose higher, and sped faster, until it had passed over the line of cliff, and was sweeping over the silent sea. Pericord watched it with a white drawn face, until it looked like a black bird with golden wings half shrouded in the mist which lay over the waters.

* * * * *

In the New York State Lunatic Asylum there is a wild-eyed man whose name and birthplace are alike unknown. His reason has been unseated by some sudden shock, the doctors say, though of what nature they are unable to determine. "It is the most delicate machine which is most readily put out of gear," they remark, and point, in proof of their axiom, to the complicated electric engines, and remarkable aeronautic machines which the patient is fond of devising in his more lucid moments.

55. *The Sealed Room*

A SOLICITOR of an active habit and athletic tastes who is compelled by his hopes of business to remain within the four walls of his office from ten till five must take what exercise he can in the evenings. Hence it was that I was in the habit of indulging in very long nocturnal excursions, in which I sought the heights of Hampstead and Highgate in order to cleanse my system from the impure air of Abchurch

Lane. It was in the course of one of these aimless rambles that I first met Felix Stanniford, and so led up to what has been the most extraordinary adventure of my lifetime.

One evening—it was in April or early May of the year 1894—I made my way to the extreme northern fringe of London, and was walking down one of those fine avenues of high brick villas which the huge city is for ever pushing farther and farther out into the country. It was a fine, clear spring night, the moon was shining out of an unclouded sky, and I, having already left many miles behind me, was inclined to walk slowly and look about me. In this contemplative mood, my attention was arrested by one of the houses which I was passing.

It was a very large building, standing in its own grounds, a little back from the road. It was modern in appearance, and yet it was far less so than its neighbours, all of which were crudely and painfully new. Their symmetrical line was broken by the gap caused by the laurel-studded lawn, with the great, dark, gloomy house looming at the back of it. Evidently it had been the country retreat of some wealthy merchant, built perhaps when the nearest street was a mile off, and now gradually overtaken and surrounded by the red brick tentacles of the London octopus. The next stage, I reflected, would be its digestion and absorption, so that the cheap builder might rear a dozen eighty-pound-a-year villas upon the garden frontage. And then, as all this passed vaguely through my mind, an incident occurred which brought my thoughts into quite another channel.

A four-wheeled cab, that opprobrium of London, was coming jolting and creaking in one direction, while in the other there was a yellow glare from the lamp of a cyclist. They were the only moving objects in the whole long, moonlit road, and yet they crashed into each other with that malignant accuracy which brings two ocean liners together in the broad waste of the Atlantic. It was the cyclist's fault. He tried to cross in front of the cab, miscalculated his distance, and was knocked sprawling by the horse's shoulder. He rose, snarling; the cabman swore back at him, and then, realizing that his number had not yet been taken, lashed his horse and lumbered off. The cyclist caught at the handles of his prostrate machine, and then suddenly sat down with a groan. "Oh, Lord!" he said.

I ran across the road to his side. "Any harm done?" I asked.

"It's my ankle," said he. "Only a twist, I think; but it's pretty painful. Just give me your hand, will you?"

He lay in the yellow circle of the cycle lamp, and I noted as I helped him to his feet that he was a gentlemanly young fellow, with a slight dark moustache and large, brown eyes, sensitive and nervous in appearance, with indications of weak health upon his sunken cheeks. Work or worry had left its traces upon his thin, yellow face. He stood up when I pulled his hand, but he held one foot in the air, and he groaned as he moved it.

"I can't put it to the ground," said he.

"Where do you live?"

"Here!" he nodded his head towards the big, dark house in the garden. "I was cutting across to the gate when that confounded cab ran into me. Could you help me so far?"

It was easily done. I put his cycle inside the gate, and then I supported him down the drive, and up the steps to the hall door. There was not a light anywhere, and the place was as black and silent as if no one had ever lived in it.

"That will do. Thank you very much," said he, fumbling with his key in the lock.

"No, you must allow me to see you safe."

He made some feeble, petulant protest, and then realised that he could really do nothing without me. The door had opened into a pitch-dark hall. He lurched forward, with my hand still on his arm.

"This door to the right," said he, feeling about in the darkness.

I opened the door, and at the same moment he managed to strike a light. There was a lamp upon the table, and we lit it between us. "Now, I'm all right. You can leave me now! Good-bye!" said he, and with the words he sat down in the arm-chair and fainted dead away.

It was a queer position for me. The fellow looked so ghastly, that really I was not sure that he was not dead. Presently his lips quivered and his breast heaved, but his eyes were two white slits and his colour was horrible. The responsibility was more than I could stand. I pulled at the bell-rope, and heard the bell ringing furiously far away. But no one came in response. The bell tinkled away into silence, which no murmur or movement came to break. I waited, and rang again, with the same result. There must be someone about. This young gentleman could not live all alone in that huge house. His people ought to know of his condition. If they would not answer the bell, I must hunt them out myself. I seized the lamp and rushed from the room.

What I saw outside amazed me. The hall was empty. The stairs were bare, and yellow with dust. There were three doors opening into spacious rooms, and each was uncarpeted and undraped, save for the grey webs which drooped from the cornice, and rosettes of lichen which had formed upon the walls. My feet reverberated in those empty and silent chambers. Then I wandered on down the passage, with the idea that the kitchens, at least, might be tenanted. Some caretaker might lurk in some secluded room. No, they were all equally desolate. Despairing of finding any help, I ran down another corridor, and came on something which surprised me more than ever.

The passage ended in a large, brown door, and the

door had a seal of red wax the size of a five-shilling piece over the key-hole. This seal gave me the impression of having been there for a long time, for it was dusty and discoloured. I was still staring at it, and wondering what that door might conceal, when I heard a voice calling behind me, and, running back, found my young man sitting up in his chair and very much astonished at finding himself in darkness.

"Why on earth did you take the lamp away?" he asked.

"I was looking for assistance."

"You might look for some time," said he. "I am alone in the house."

"Awkward if you get an illness."

"It was foolish of me to faint. I inherit a weak heart from my mother, and pain or emotion has that effect upon me. It will carry me off some day, as it did her. You're not a doctor, are you?"

"No, a lawyer. Frank Alder is my name."

"Mine is Felix Stanniford. Funny that I should meet a lawyer, for my friend, Mr. Perceval, was saying that we should need one soon."

"Very happy, I am sure."

"Well, that will depend upon him, you know. Did you say that you had run with that lamp all over the ground floor?"

"Yes."

"*All* over it?" he asked, with emphasis, and he looked at me very hard.

"I think so. I kept on hoping that I should find someone."

"Did you enter *all* the rooms?" he asked, with the same intent gaze.

"Well, all that I could enter."

"Oh, then you *did* notice it!" said he, and he shrugged his shoulders with the air of a man who makes the best of a bad job.

"Notice what?"

"Why, the door with the seal on it."

"Yes, I did."

"Weren't you curious to know what was in it?"

"Well, it did strike me as unusual."

"Do you think you could go on living alone in this house, year after year, just longing all the time to know what is at the other side of that door, and yet not looking?"

"Do you mean to say," I cried, "that you don't know yourself?"

"No more than you do."

"Then why don't you look?"

"I mustn't," said he.

He spoke in a constrained way, and I saw that I had blundered on to some delicate ground. I don't know that I am more inquisitive than my neighbours, but there certainly was something in the situation which appealed very strongly to my curiosity. However, my last excuse for remaining in the house was gone now that my companion had recovered his senses. I rose to go.

"Are you in a hurry?" he asked.

"No; I have nothing to do."

"Well, I should be very glad if you would stay with me a little. The fact is that I live a very retired and secluded life here. I don't suppose there is a man in London who leads such a life as I do. It is quite unusual for me to have anyone to talk with."

I looked round at the little room, scantily furnished, with a sofa-bed at one side. Then I thought of the great, bare house, and the sinister door with the discoloured red seal upon it. There was something queer and grotesque in the situation, which made me long to know a little more. Perhaps I should, if I waited. I told him that I should be very happy.

"You will find the spirits and a siphon upon the side-table. You must forgive me if I cannot act as host, but I can't get across the room. Those are cigars in the tray there. I'll take one myself, I think. And so you are a solicitor, Mr. Alder ? "

" Yes."

" And I am nothing. I am that most helpless of living creatures, the son of a millionaire. I was brought up with the expectation of great wealth ; and here I am, a poor man, without any profession at all. And then, on the top of it all, I am left with this great mansion on my hands, which I cannot possibly keep up. Isn't it an absurd situation ? For me to use this as my dwelling is like a coster drawing his barrow with a thoroughbred. A donkey would be more useful to him, and a cottage to me."

" But why not sell the house ? " I asked.

" I mustn't."

" Let it, then ? "

" No, I mustn't do that either."

I looked puzzled, and my companion smiled.

" I'll tell you how it is, if it won't bore you," said he.

" On the contrary, I should be exceedingly interested."

" I think, after your kind attention to me, I cannot do less than relieve any curiosity that you may feel. You must know that my father was Stanislaus Stanniford, the banker."

Stanniford, the banker ! I remembered the name at once. His flight from the country some seven years before had been one of the scandals and sensations of the time.

" I see that you remember," said my companion. " My poor father left the country to avoid numerous friends, whose savings he had invested in an unsuccessful speculation. He was a nervous, sensitive man, and the responsibility quite upset his reason. He had committed no legal offence. It was purely a matter of sentiment. He would not even face his own family, and he died among strangers without ever letting us know where he was."

"He died!" said I.

"We could not prove his death, but we know that it must be so, because the speculations came right again, and so there was no reason why he should not look any man in the face. He would have returned if he were alive. But he must have died in the last two years."

"Why in the last two years?"

"Because we heard from him two years ago."

"Did he not tell you then where he was living?"

"The letter came from Paris, but no address was given. It was when my poor mother died. He wrote to me then, with some instructions and some advice, and I have never heard from him since."

"Had you heard before?"

"Oh, yes, we had heard before, and that's where our mystery of the sealed door, upon which you stumbled to-night, has its origin. Pass me that desk, if you please. Here I have my father's letters, and you are the first man except Mr. Perceval who has seen them."

"Who is Mr. Perceval, may I ask?"

"He was my father's confidential clerk, and he has continued to be the friend and adviser of my mother and then of myself. I don't know what we should have done without Perceval. He saw the letters, but no one else. This is the first one, which came on the very day when my father fled, seven years ago. Read it to yourself."

This is the letter which I read:

"My Ever Dearest Wife,—

"Since Sir William told me how weak your heart is, and how harmful any shock might be, I have never talked about my business affairs to you. The time has come when at all risks I can no longer refrain from telling you that things have been going badly with me. This will cause me to leave you for a little time, but it is with the absolute assurance that we shall see each other very soon. On this you can thoroughly rely. Our parting is only for a very short time, my own darling, so don't let it fret you, and above all don't let it impair your health, for that is what I want above all things to avoid.

"Now, I have a request to make, and I implore you by all that binds us together to fulfil it exactly as I tell you. There are some things which I do not wish to be seen by anyone in my dark room—the room which I use for photographic purposes at the end of the garden passage. To prevent any painful thoughts, I may assure you once for all, dear, that it is nothing of which I need be ashamed. But still I do not wish you or Felix to enter that room. It is locked, and I implore you when you receive this to at once place a seal over the lock, and leave it so. Do not sell or let the house, for in either case my secret will be discovered. As long as you or Felix are in the house, I know that you will comply with my wishes. When Felix is twenty-one he may enter the room—not before.

"And now, good-bye, my own best of wives. During our short separation you can consult Mr. Perceval on any matters which may arise. He has my complete confidence. I hate to leave Felix and you—even for a time—but there is really no choice.

"Ever and always your loving husband,

"STANISLAUS STANNIFORD.

"*June 4th*, 1887."

"These are very private family matters for me to inflict upon you," said my companion apologetically. "You must look upon it as done in your professional capacity. I have wanted to speak about it for years."

"I am honoured by your confidence," I answered, "and exceedingly interested by the facts."

"My father was a man who was noted for his almost morbid love of truth. He was always pedantically accurate. When he said, therefore, that he hoped to see my mother very soon, and when he said that he had nothing to be ashamed of in that dark room, you may rely upon it that he meant it."

"Then what can it be?" I ejaculated.

"Neither my mother nor I could imagine. We carried out his wishes to the letter, and placed the seal upon the door; there it has been ever since. My mother lived for five years after my father's disappearance, although at the time all the doctors said that she could not survive long. Her heart was terribly diseased. During the first few months she had two letters from my father. Both had the Paris post-mark, but no address. They were short and to the same effect: that they would soon be reunited, and that she should not fret. Then there was a silence, which lasted until her death; and then came a letter to me of so private a nature that I cannot show it to you, begging me never to think evil of him, giving me much good advice, and saying that the sealing of the room was of less importance now than during the lifetime of my mother, but that the opening might still cause pain to others, and that, therefore, he thought it best that it should be postponed until my twenty-first year, for the lapse of time would make things easier. In the meantime, he committed the care of the room to me; so now you can understand how it is that, although I am a very poor man, I can neither let nor sell this great house."

"You could mortgage it."

"My father had already done so."

"It is a most singular state of affairs."

"My mother and I were gradually compelled to sell the furniture and to dismiss the servants, until now, as you see, I am living unattended in a single room. But I have only two more months."

"What do you mean?"

"Why, that in two months I come of age. The first thing that I do will be to open that door; the second, to get rid of the house."

"Why should your father have continued to stay

away when these investments had recovered themselves?"

"He must be dead."

"You say that he had not committed any legal offence when he fled the country?"

"None."

"Why should he not take your mother with him?"

"I do not know."

"Why should he conceal his address?"

"I do not know."

"Why should he allow your mother to die and be buried without coming back?"

"I do not know."

"My dear sir," said I, "if I may speak with the frankness of a professional adviser, I should say that it is very clear that your father had the strongest reasons for keeping out of the country, and that, if nothing has been proved against him, he at least thought that something might be, and refused to put himself within the power of the law. Surely that must be obvious, for in what other possible way can the facts be explained?"

My companion did not take my suggestion in good part.

"You had not the advantage of knowing my father, Mr. Alder," he said coldly. "I was only a boy when he left us, but I shall always look upon him as my ideal man. His only fault was that he was too sensitive and too unselfish. That anyone should lose money through him would cut him to the heart. His sense of honour was most acute, any theory of his disappearance which conflicts with that is a mistaken one."

It pleased me to hear the lad speak out so roundly, and yet I knew that the facts were against him, and that he was incapable of taking an unprejudiced view of the situation.

"I only speak as an outsider," said I. "And now I must leave you, for I have a long walk before me. Your story has interested me so much that I should be glad if you could let me know the sequel."

"Leave me your card," said he; and so, having bade him "good night," I left him.

I heard nothing more of the matter for some time, and had almost feared that it would prove to be one of those fleeting experiences which drift away from our direct observation and end only in a hope or a suspicion. One afternoon, however, a card bearing the name of Mr. J. H. Perceval was brought up to my office in Abchurch Lane, and its bearer, a small dry, bright-eyed fellow of fifty, was ushered in by the clerk.

"I believe, sir," said he, "that my name has been mentioned to you by my young friend, Mr. Felix Stanniford?"

"Of course," I answered, "I remember."

"He spoke to you, I understand, about the circumstances in connection with the disappearance of my former employer, Mr. Stanislaus Stanniford, and the existence of a sealed room in his former residence."

"He did."

"And you expressed an interest in the matter."

"It interested me extremely."

"You are aware that we hold Mr. Stanniford's permission to open the door on the twenty-first birthday of his son?"

"I remember."

"The twenty-first birthday is to-day."

"Have you opened it?" I asked eagerly.

"Not yet, sir," said he gravely. "I have reason to believe that it would be well to have witnesses present when that door is opened. You are a lawyer, and you are acquainted with the facts. Will you be present on the occasion?"

"Most certainly."

"You are employed during the day, and so am I. Shall we meet at nine o'clock at the house?"

"I will come with pleasure."

"Then you will find us waiting for you. Good-bye, for the present." He bowed solemnly, and took his leave.

I kept my appointment that evening, with a brain which was weary with fruitless attempts to think out some plausible explanation of the mystery which we were about to solve. Mr. Perceval and my young acquaintance were waiting for me in the little room. I was not surprised to see the young man looking pale and nervous, but I was rather astonished to find the dry little City man in a state of intense, though partially suppressed, excitement. His cheeks were flushed, his hands twitching, and he could not stand still for an instant.

Stanniford greeted me warmly, and thanked me many times for having come. "And now, Perceval," said he to his companion, "I suppose there is no obstacle to our putting the thing through without delay? I shall be glad to get it over."

The banker's clerk took up the lamp and led the way. But he paused in the passage outside the door, and his hand was shaking, so that the light flickered up and down the high, bare walls.

"Mr. Stanniford," said he, in a cracking voice, "I hope you will prepare yourself in case any shock should be awaiting you when that seal is removed and the door is opened."

"What could there be, Perceval? You are trying to frighten me."

"No, Mr. Stanniford; but I should wish you to be ready . . . to be braced up . . . not to allow yourself. . . ." He had to lick his dry lips between every jerky sentence, and I suddenly realised, as clearly as if he had told me, that he knew what was behind that closed door, and that it *was* something terrible. "Here are the keys, Mr. Stanniford, but remember my warning!"

He had a bunch of assorted keys in his hand, and the young man snatched them from him. Then he thrust a knife under the discoloured seal and jerked it off. The lamp was rattling and shaking in Perceval's hands, so I took it from him and held it near the keyhole, while Stanniford tried key after key. At last one turned in the lock, the door flew open, he took one step into the room, and then, with a horrible cry, the young man fell senseless at our feet.

If I had not given heed to the clerk's warning, and braced myself for a shock, I should certainly have dropped the lamp. The room, windowless and bare, was fitted up as a photographic laboratory, with a tap and sink at the side of it. A shelf of bottles and measures stood at one side, and a peculiar, heavy smell, partly chemical, partly animal, filled the air. A single table and chair were in front of us, and at this, with his back turned towards us, a man was seated in the act of writing. His outline and attitude were as natural as life; but as the light fell upon him, it made my hair rise to see that the nape of his neck was black and wrinkled, and no thicker than my wrist. Dust lay upon him—thick, yellow dust—upon his hair, his shoulders, his shrivelled, lemon-coloured hands. His head had fallen forward upon his breast. His pen still rested upon a discoloured sheet of paper.

"My poor master! My poor, poor master!" cried the clerk, and the tears were running down his cheeks.

"What!" I cried, "Mr. Stanislaus Stanniford!"

"Here he has sat for seven years. Oh, why would he do it? I begged him, I implored him, I went on my knees to him, but he would have his way. You see the key on the table. He had locked the door upon the inside. And he has written something. We must take it."

"Yes, yes, take it, and for God's sake, let us get out of this," I cried; "the air is poisonous. Come, Stanniford, come!" Taking an arm each, we half led and half carried the terrified man back to his own room.

"It was my father!" he cried, as he recovered his consciousness. "He is sitting there dead in his chair. You knew it, Perceval! This was what you meant when you warned me."

"Yes, I knew it, Mr. Stanniford. I have acted for the best all along, but my position has been a terribly difficult one. For seven years I have known that your father was dead in that room."

"You knew it, and never told us!"

"Don't be harsh with me, Mr. Stanniford, sir! Make allowance for a man who has had a hard part to play."

"My head is swimming round. I cannot grasp it!" He staggered up, and helped himself from the brandy bottle. "These letters to my mother and to myself—were they forgeries?"

"No, sir; your father wrote them and addressed them, and left them in my keeping to be posted. I have followed his instructions to the very letter in all things. He was my master, and I have obeyed him."

The brandy had steadied the young man's shaken nerves. "Tell me about it. I can stand it now," said he.

"Well, Mr. Stanniford, you know that at one time there came a period of great trouble upon your father, and he thought that many poor people were about to lose their savings through his fault. He was a man who was so tender-hearted that he could not bear the thought. It worried him and tormented him, until he determined to end his life. Oh, Mr. Stanniford, if you knew how I have prayed him and wrestled with him over it, you would never blame me! And he in turn prayed me as no man has ever prayed me before. He had made up his mind, and he would do it in any case, he said; but it rested with me whether his death should be happy and easy or whether it should be most miserable. I read in his eyes that he meant what he said. And at last I yielded to his prayers, and I consented to do his will.

"What was troubling him was this. He had been told by the first doctor in London that his wife's heart would fail at the slightest shock. He had a horror of accelerating her end, and yet his own existence had become unendurable to him. How could he end himself without injuring her?

"You know now the course that he took. He wrote the letter which she received. There was nothing in it which was not literally true. When he spoke of seeing her again so soon, he was referring to her own approaching death, which he had been assured could not be delayed more than a very few months. So convinced was he of this, that he only left two letters to be forwarded at intervals after his death. She lived five years, and I had no letters to send.

"He left another letter with me to be sent to you, sir, upon the occasion of the death of your mother. I posted all these in Paris to sustain the idea of his being abroad. It was his wish that I should say nothing, and I have said nothing. I have been a faithful servant. Seven years after his death, he thought no doubt that the shock to the feelings of his surviving friends would be lessened. He was always considerate for others."

There was a silence for some time. It was broken by young Stanniford.

"I cannot blame you, Perceval. You have spared my mother a shock, which would certainly have broken her heart. What is that paper?"

"It is what your father was writing, sir. Shall I read it to you?"

"Do so."

"'I have taken the poison, and I feel it working in my veins. It is strange, but not painful. When these words are read I shall, if my wishes have been faithfully carried out, have been dead many years. Surely no one who has lost money through me will still bear me animosity. And you, Felix, you will forgive me this family scandal. May God find rest for a sorely wearied spirit!'"

"Amen!" we cried, all three.

TALES OF MEDICAL LIFE

56. *A Physiologist's Wife*

PROFESSOR AINSLIE GREY had not come down to breakfast at the usual hour. The presentation chiming-clock which stood between the terra-cotta busts of Claude Bernard and of John Hunter upon the dining-room mantelpiece had rung out the half-hour and the three-quarters. Now its golden hand was verging upon the nine, and yet there were no signs of the master of the house.

It was an unprecedented occurrence. During the twelve years that she had kept house for him, his younger sister had never known him a second behind his time. She sat now in front of the high silver coffee-pot, uncertain whether to order the gong to be resounded or to wait on in silence. Either course might be a mistake. Her brother was not a man who permitted mistakes.

Miss Ainslie Grey was rather above the middle height, thin, with peering, puckered eyes, and the rounded shoulders which mark the bookish woman. Her face was long and spare, flecked with colour above the cheekbones, with a reasonable, thoughtful forehead, and a dash of absolute obstinacy in her thin lips and prominent chin. Snow-white cuffs and collar, with a plain dark dress, cut with almost Quaker-like simplicity, bespoke the primness of her taste. An ebony cross hung over her flattened chest. She sat very upright in her chair, listening with raised eyebrows, and swinging her eyeglasses backwards and forwards with a nervous gesture which was peculiar to her.

Suddenly she gave a sharp, satisfied jerk of the head,

and began to pour out the coffee. From outside there came the dull thudding sound of heavy feet upon thick carpet. The door swung open, and the Professor entered with a quick, nervous step. He nodded to his sister, and seating himself at the other side of the table, began to open the small pile of letters which lay beside his plate.

Professor Ainslie Grey was at that time forty-three years of age—nearly twelve years older than his sister. His career had been a brilliant one. At Edinburgh, at Cambridge, and at Vienna he had laid the foundations of his great reputation, both in physiology and in zoology.

His pamphlet, " On the Mesoblastic Origin of Excito-motor Nerve Roots," had won him his fellowship of the Royal Society ; and his researches, " Upon the Nature of Bathybius, with some Remarks upon Lithococci," had been translated into at least three European languages. He had been referred to by one of the greatest living authorities as being the very type and embodiment of all that was best in modern science. No wonder, then, that when the commercial city of Birchespool decided to create a medical school, they were only too glad to confer the chair of physiology upon Mr. Ainslie Grey. They valued him the more from the conviction that their class was only one step in his upward journey, and that the first vacancy would remove him to some more illustrious seat of learning.

In person he was not unlike his sister. The same eyes, the same contour, the same intellectual forehead. His lips, however, were firmer, and his long, thin lower jaw was sharper and more decided. He ran his finger and thumb down it from time to time, as he glanced over his letters.

" Those maids are very noisy," he remarked, as a clack of tongues sounded in the distance.

" It is Sarah," said his sister ; " I shall speak about it."

She had handed over his coffee-cup and was sipping

at her own, glancing furtively through her narrowed lids at the austere face of her brother.

"The first great advance of the human race," said the Professor, "was when, by the development of their left frontal convolutions, they attained the power of speech. Their second advance was when they learned to control that power. Woman has not yet attained the second stage."

He half closed his eyes as he spoke, and thrust his chin forward, but as he ceased he had a trick of suddenly opening both eyes very wide and staring sternly at his interlocutor.

"I am not garrulous, John," said his sister.

"No, Ada; in many respects you approach the superior or male type."

The Professor bowed over his egg with the manner of one who utters a courtly compliment; but the lady pouted, and gave an impatient little shrug of her shoulders.

"You were late this morning, John," she remarked, after a pause.

"Yes, Ada; I slept badly. Some little cerebral congestion, no doubt due to overstimulation of the centres of thought. I have been a little disturbed in my mind."

His sister stared across at him in astonishment. The Professor's mental processes had hitherto been as regular as his habits. Twelve years' continual intercourse had taught her that he lived in a serene and rarefied atmosphere of scientific calm, high above the petty emotions which affect humbler minds.

"You are surprised, Ada," he remarked. "Well, I cannot wonder at it. I should have been surprised myself if I had been told that I was so sensitive to vascular influences. For, after all, all disturbances are vascular if you probe them deep enough. I am thinking of getting married."

"Not Mrs. O'James?" cried Ada Grey, laying down her egg-spoon.

"My dear, you have the feminine quality of receptivity very remarkably developed. Mrs. O'James is the lady in question."

"But you know so little of her. The Esdailes themselves know so little. She is really only an acquaintance, although she is staying at The Lindens. Would it not be wise to speak to Mrs. Esdaile first, John?"

"I do not think, Ada, that Mrs. Esdaile is at all likely to say anything which would materially affect my course of action. I have given the matter due consideration. The scientific mind is slow at arriving at conclusions, but having once formed them, it is not prone to change. Matrimony is the natural condition of the human race. I have, as you know, been so engaged in academical and other work, that I have had no time to devote to merely personal questions. It is different now, and I see no valid reason why I should forgo this opportunity of seeking a suitable helpmate."

"And you are engaged?"

"Hardly that, Ada. I ventured yesterday to indicate to the lady that I was prepared to submit to the common lot of humanity. I shall wait upon her after my morning lecture, and learn how far my proposals meet with her acquiescence. But you frown, Ada!"

His sister started, and made an effort to conceal her expression of annoyance. She even stammered out some few words of congratulation, but a vacant look had come into her brother's eyes, and he was evidently not listening to her.

"I am sure, John," she said, "that I wish you the happiness which you deserve. If I hesitated at all, it is because I know how much is at stake, and because the thing is so sudden, so unexpected." Her thin, white hand stole up to the black cross upon her bosom. "These are moments when we need guidance, John. If I could persuade you to turn to spiritual——"

The Professor waved the suggestion away with a deprecating hand.

"It is useless to reopen that question," he said. "We cannot argue upon it. You assume more than I can grant. I am forced to dispute your premises. We have no common basis."

His sister sighed.

"You have no faith," she said.

"I have faith in those great evolutionary forces which are leading the human race to some unknown but elevated goal."

"You believe in nothing."

"On the contrary, my dear Ada, I believe in the differentiation of protoplasm."

She shook her head sadly. It was the one subject upon which she ventured to dispute her brother's infallibility.

"This is rather beside the question," remarked the Professor, folding up his napkin. "If I am not mistaken, there is some possibility of another matrimonial event occurring in the family. Eh, Ada? What!"

His small eyes glittered with sly facetiousness as he shot a twinkle at his sister. She sat very stiff, and traced patterns upon the cloth with the sugar-tongs.

"Dr. James M'Murdo O'Brien——" said the Professor sonorously.

"Don't, John, don't!" cried Miss Ainslie Grey.

"Dr. James M'Murdo O'Brien," continued her brother inexorably, "is a man who has already made his mark upon the science of the day. He is my first and my most distinguished pupil. I assure you, Ada, that his 'Remarks upon the Bile-Pigments, with special reference to Urobilin,' is likely to live as a classic. It is not too much to say that he has revolutionised our view about urobilin."

He paused, but his sister sat silent, with bent head and flushed cheeks. The little ebony cross rose and fell with her hurried breathings.

"Dr. James M'Murdo O'Brien has, as you know, the offer of the physiological chair at Melbourne. He has been in Australia five years, and has a brilliant future before him. To-day he leaves us for Edinburgh, and in two months' time he goes out to take over his new duties. You know his feeling towards you. It rests with you as to whether he goes out alone. Speaking for myself, I cannot imagine any higher mission for a woman of culture than to go through life in the company of a man who is capable of such a research as that which Dr. James M'Murdo O'Brien has brought to a successful conclusion."

"He has not spoken to me," murmured the lady.

"Ah, there are signs which are more subtle than speech," said her brother, wagging his head. "You are pale. Your vasomotor system is excited. Your arterioles have contracted. Let me entreat you to compose yourself. I think I hear the carriage. I fancy that you may have a visitor this morning, Ada. You will excuse me now."

With a quick glance at the clock he strode off into the hall, and within a few minutes he was rattling in his quiet, well-appointed brougham through the brick-lined streets of Birchespool.

His lecture over, Professor Ainslie Grey paid a visit to his laboratory, where he adjusted several scientific instruments, made a note as to the progress of three separate infusions of bacteria, cut half a dozen sections with a microtome, and finally resolved the difficulties of seven different gentlemen, who were pursuing researches in as many separate lines of inquiry. Having thus conscientiously and methodically completed the routine of his duties, he returned to his carriage and ordered the coachman to drive him to The Lindens. His face as he drove was cold and impassive, but he drew his fingers from time to time down his prominent chin with a jerky, twitchy movement.

The Lindens was an old-fashioned, ivy-clad house which had once been in the country, but was now caught in the long, red-brick feelers of the growing city. It still stood back from the road in the privacy of its own grounds. A winding path, lined with laurel bushes, led to the arched and porticoed entrance. To the right was a lawn, and at the far side, under the shadow of a hawthorn, a lady sat in a garden-chair with a book in her hands. At the click of the gate she started, and the Professor, catching sight of her, turned away from the door, and strode in her direction.

"What! won't you go in and see Mrs. Esdaile?" she asked, sweeping out from under the shadow of the hawthorn.

She was a small woman, strongly feminine, from the rich coils of her light-coloured hair to the dainty garden-slipper which peeped from under her cream-tinted dress. One tiny, well-gloved hand was outstretched in greeting, while the other pressed a thick, green-covered volume against her side. Her decision and quick, tactful manner bespoke the mature woman of the world; but her upraised face had preserved a girlish and even infantile expression of innocence in its large, fearless grey eyes, and sensitive, humorous mouth. Mrs. O'James was a widow, and she was two-and-thirty years of age; but neither fact could have been deduced from her appearance.

"You will surely go in and see Mrs. Esdaile," she repeated, glancing up at him with eyes which had in them something between a challenge and a caress.

"I did not come to see Mrs. Esdaile," he answered, with no relaxation of his cold and grave manner; "I came to see you."

"I am sure I should be highly honoured," she said, with just the slightest little touch of brogue in her accent. "What are the students to do without their Professor?"

"I have already completed my academic duties. Take my arm, and we shall walk in the sunshine. Surely we cannot wonder that Eastern people should have made a deity of the sun. It is the great, beneficent force of Nature—man's ally against cold, sterility, and all that is abhorrent to him. What were you reading?"

" Hale's *Matter and Life.*"

The Professor raised his thick eyebrows.

" Hale ! " he said, and then again in a kind of whisper, " Hale ! "

" You differ from him ? " she asked.

" It is not I who differ from him. I am only a monad —a thing of no moment. The whole tendency of the highest plane of modern thought differs from him. He defends the indefensible. He is an excellent observer, but a feeble reasoner. I should not recommend you to found your conclusions upon 'Hale.' "

" I must read *Nature's Chronicle* to counteract his pernicious influence," said Mrs. O'James, with a soft, cooing laugh.

Nature's Chronicle was one of the many books in which Professor Ainslie Grey had enforced the negative doctrines of scientific agnosticism.

" It is a faulty work," said he ; " I cannot recommend it. I would rather refer you to the standard writings of some of my older and more eloquent colleagues."

There was a pause in their talk as they paced up and down on the green, velvet-like lawn in the genial sunshine.

" Have you thought at all," he asked at last, " of the matter upon which I spoke to you last night ? "

She said nothing, but walked by his side with her eyes averted and her face aslant.

" I would not hurry you unduly," he continued. " I know that it is a matter which can scarcely be decided off-hand. In my own case, it cost me some thought before I ventured to make the suggestion. I am not an emotional man, but I am conscious in your presence of the great evolutionary instinct which makes either sex the complement of the other."

" You believe in love, then ? " she asked, with a twinkling, upward glance.

" I am forced to."

" And yet you can deny the soul ? "

"How far these questions are psychic and how far material is still *sub judice*," said the Professor, with an air of toleration. "Protoplasm may prove to be the physical basis of love as well as of life."

"How inflexible you are!" she exclaimed; "you would draw love down to the level of physics."

"Or draw physics up to the level of love."

"Come, that is much better," she cried, with her sympathetic laugh. "That is really very pretty, and puts science in quite a delightful light."

Her eyes sparkled, and she tossed her chin with a pretty, wilful air of a woman who is mistress of the situation.

"I have reason to believe," said the Professor, "that my position here will prove to be only a stepping-stone to some wider scene of scientific activity. Yet, even here, my chair brings me in some fifteen hundred pounds a year, which is supplemented by a few hundreds from my books. I should therefore be in a position to provide you with those comforts to which you are accustomed. So much for my pecuniary position. As to my constitution, it has always been sound. I have never suffered from any illness in my life, save fleeting attacks of cephalalgia, the result of too prolonged a stimulation of the centres of cerebration. My father and mother had no sign of any morbid diathesis, but I will not conceal from you that my grandfather was afflicted with podagra."

Mrs. O'James looked startled.

"Is that very serious?" she asked.

"It is gout," said the Professor.

"Oh, is that all? It sounded much worse than that."

"It is a grave taint, but I trust that I shall not be a victim to atavism. I have laid these facts before you because they are factors which cannot be overlooked in forming your decision. May I ask now whether you see your way to accepting my proposal?"

He paused in his walk, and looked earnestly and expectantly down at her.

A struggle was evidently going on in her mind. Her eyes were cast down, her little slipper tapped the lawn, and her fingers played nervously with her chatelaine. Suddenly, with a sharp, quick gesture which had in it something of *abandon* and recklessness, she held out her hand to her companion.

"I accept," she said.

They were standing under the shadow of the hawthorn. He stooped gravely down, and kissed her glove-covered fingers.

"I trust that you may never have cause to regret your decision," he said.

"I trust that *you* never may," she cried, with a heaving breast.

There were tears in her eyes, and her lips twitched with some strong emotion.

"Come into the sunshine again," said he. "It is the great restorative. Your nerves are shaken. Some little congestion of the medulla and pons. It is always instructive to reduce psychic or emotional conditions to their physical equivalents. You feel that your anchor is still firm in a bottom of ascertained fact."

"But it is so dreadfully unromantic," said Mrs. O'James, with her old twinkle.

"Romance is the offspring of imagination and of ignorance. Where science throws her calm, clear light there is happily no room for romance."

"But is not love romance?" she asked.

"Not at all. Love has been taken away from the poets, and has been brought within the domain of true science. It may prove to be one of the great cosmic elementary forces. When the atom of hydrogen draws the atom of chlorine towards it to form the perfected molecule of hydrochloric acid, the force which it exerts may be intrinsically similar to that which draws me to you. Attraction and repulsion appear to be the primary forces. This is attraction."

"And here is repulsion," said Mrs. O'James, as a

stout, florid lady came sweeping across the lawn in their direction. " So glad you have come out, Mrs. Esdaile! Here is Professor Grey."

" How do you do, Professor ? " said the lady, with some little pomposity of manner. " You were very wise to stay out here on so lovely a day. Is it not heavenly ? "

" It is certainly very fine weather," the Professor answered.

" Listen to the wind sighing in the trees ! " cried Mrs. Esdaile, holding up one finger. " It is Nature's lullaby. Could you not imagine it, Professor Grey, to be the whisperings of angels ? "

" The idea had not occurred to me, madam."

" Ah, Professor, I have always the same complaint against you. A want of *rapport* with the deeper meanings of Nature. Shall I say a want of imagination ? You do not feel an emotional thrill at the singing of that thrush ? "

" I confess that I am not conscious of one, Mrs. Esdaile."

" Or at the delicate tint of that background of leaves ? See the rich greens ! "

" Chlorophyll," murmured the Professor.

" Science is so hopelessly prosaic. It dissects and labels, and loses sight of the great things in its attention to the little ones. You have a poor opinion of woman's intellect, Professor Grey. I think that I have heard you say so."

" It is a question of avoirdupois," said the Professor, closing his eyes and shrugging his shoulders. " The female cerebrum averages two ounces less in weight than the male. No doubt there are exceptions. Nature is always elastic."

" But the heaviest thing is not always the strongest," said Mrs. O'James, laughing. " Isn't there a law of compensation in science ? May we not hope to make up in quality what we lack in quantity ? "

" I think not," remarked the Professor gravely. " But

there is your luncheon-gong. No, thank you, Mrs. Esdaile, I cannot stay. My carriage is waiting. Good-bye. Good-bye, Mrs. O'James."

He raised his hat and stalked slowly away among the laurel bushes.

"He has no taste," said Mrs. Esdaile—"no eye for beauty."

"On the contrary," Mrs. O'James answered, with a saucy little jerk of the chin. "He has just asked me to be his wife."

As Professor Ainslie Grey ascended the steps of his house, the hall-door opened and a dapper gentleman stepped briskly out. He was somewhat sallow in the face, with dark, beady eyes, and a short, black beard with an aggressive bristle. Thought and work had left their traces upon his face, but he moved with the brisk activity of a man who had not yet bade good-bye to his youth.

"I'm in luck's way," he cried. "I wanted to see you."

"Then come back into the library," said the Professor; "you must stay and have lunch with us."

The two men entered the hall, and the Professor led the way into his private sanctum. He motioned his companion into an arm-chair.

"I trust that you have been successful, O'Brien," said he. "I should be loath to exercise any undue pressure upon my sister Ada; but I have given her to understand that there is no one whom I should prefer for a brother-in-law to my most brilliant scholar, the author of 'Some Remarks upon the Bile-Pigments, with special reference to Urobilin.'"

"You are very kind, Professor Grey—you have always been very kind," said the other. "I approached Miss Grey upon the subject; she did not say No."

"She said Yes, then?"

"No; she proposed to leave the matter open until

my return from Edinburgh. I go to-day, as you know, and I hope to commence my research to-morrow."

"On the comparative anatomy of the vermiform appendix, by James M'Murdo O'Brien," said the Professor sonorously. "It is a glorious subject—a subject which lies at the very root of evolutionary philosophy."

"Ah, she is the dearest girl," cried O'Brien, with a sudden little spurt of Celtic enthusiasm—"she is the soul of truth and of honour."

"The vermiform appendix——" began the Professor.

"She is an angel from heaven," interrupted the other. "I fear that it is my advocacy of scientific freedom in religious thought which stands in my way with her."

"You must not truckle upon that point. You must be true to your convictions; let there be no compromise there."

"My reason is true to agnosticism, and yet I am conscious of a void—a vacuum. I had feelings at the old church at home between the scent of the incense and the roll of the organ, such as I have never experienced in the laboratory or the lecture-room."

"Sensuous—purely sensuous," said the Professor, rubbing his chin. "Vague hereditary tendencies stirred into life by the stimulation of the nasal and auditory nerves."

"Maybe so, maybe so," the younger man answered thoughtfully. "But this was not what I wished to speak to you about. Before I enter your family, your sister and you have a claim to know all that I can tell you about my career. Of my worldly prospects I have already spoken to you. There is only one point which I have omitted to mention. I am a widower."

The Professor raised his eyebrows.

"This is news indeed," said he.

"I married shortly after my arrival in Australia. Miss Thurston was her name. I met her in society. It was a most unhappy match."

Some painful emotion possessed him. His quick,

expressive features quivered, and his white hands tightened upon the arms of the chair. The Professor turned away towards the window.

"You are the best judge," he remarked; "but I should not think that it was necessary to go into details."

"You have a right to know everything—you and Miss Grey. It is not a matter on which I can well speak to her direct. Poor Jinny was the best of women, but she was open to flattery, and liable to be misled by designing persons. She was untrue to me, Grey. It is a hard thing to say of the dead, but she was untrue to me. She fled back to Auckland with a man whom she had known before her marriage. The brig which carried them foundered, and not a soul was saved."

"This is very painful, O'Brien," said the Professor, with a deprecatory motion of his hand. "I cannot see, however, how it affects your relation to my sister."

"I have eased my conscience," said O'Brien, rising from his chair; "I have told you all that there is to tell. I should not like the story to reach you through any lips but my own."

"You are right, O'Brien. Your action has been most honourable and considerate. But you are not to blame in the matter, save that perhaps you showed a little precipitancy in choosing a life-partner without due care and inquiry."

O'Brien drew his hand across his eyes.

"Poor girl!" he cried. "God help me, I love her still! But I must go."

"You will lunch with us?"

"No, Professor; I have my packing still to do. I have already bade Miss Grey adieu. In two months I shall see you again."

"You will probably find me a married man."

"Married!"

"Yes, I have been thinking of it."

"My dear Professor, let me congratulate you with all my heart. I had no idea. Who is the lady?"

"Mrs. O'James is her name—a widow of the same nationality as yourself. But to return to matters of importance, I should be very happy to see the proofs of your paper upon the vermiform appendix. I may be able to furnish you with material for a footnote or two."

"Your assistance will be invaluable to me," said O'Brien, with enthusiasm, and the two men parted in the hall. The Professor walked back into the dining-room, where his sister was already seated at the luncheon-table.

"I shall be married at the registrar's," he remarked; "I should strongly recommend you to do the same."

Professor Ainslie Grey was as good as his word. A fortnight's cessation of his classes gave him an opportunity which was too good to let pass. Mrs. O'James was an orphan, without relations and almost without friends in the country. There was no obstacle in the way of a speedy wedding. They were married, accordingly, in the quietest manner possible, and went off to Cambridge together, where the Professor and his charming wife were present at several academic observances, and varied the routine of their honeymoon by incursions into biological laboratories and medical libraries. Scientific friends were loud in their congratulations, not only upon Mrs. Grey's beauty, but upon the unusual quickness and intelligence she displayed in discussing physiological questions. The professor was himself astonished at the accuracy of her information. "You have a remarkable range of knowledge for a woman, Jeannette," he remarked upon more than one occasion. He was even prepared to admit that her cerebrum might be of the normal weight.

One foggy, drizzling morning they returned to Birchespool, for the next day would reopen the session, and Professor Ainslie Grey prided himself upon having never once in his life failed to appear in his lecture-room at the very stroke of the hour. Miss Ada Grey welcomed them with a constrained cordiality and handed over the keys of office to the new mistress. Mrs. Grey pressed her warmly to remain, but she explained that she had already accepted an invitation which would engage her for some months. The same evening she departed for the south of England.

A couple of days later the maid carried a card, just after breakfast, into the library where the Professor sat revising his morning lecture. It announced the re-arrival of Dr. James M'Murdo O'Brien. Their meeting was effusively genial on the part of the younger man, and coldly precise on that of his former teacher.

"You see there have been changes," said the Professor.

"So I heard. Miss Grey told me in her letters, and I read the notice in the *British Medical Journal*. So it's really married you are. How quickly and quietly you have managed it all!"

"I am constitutionally averse to anything in the nature of show or ceremony. My wife is a sensible woman—I may even go the length of saying that, for a woman, she is abnormally sensible. She quite agreed with me in the course which I have adopted."

"And your research on Vallisneria?"

"This matrimonial incident has interrupted it, but I have resumed my classes, and we shall soon be quite in harness again."

"I must see Miss Grey before I leave England. We have corresponded, and I think that all will be well. She must come out with me. I don't think I could go without her."

The Professor shook his head.

"Your nature is not so weak as you pretend," he said. "Questions of this sort are, after all, quite subordinate to the great duties of life."

O'Brien smiled.

"You would have me take out my Celtic soul and put in a Saxon one," he said. "Either my brain is too small or my heart is too big. But when may I call and pay my respects to Mrs. Grey? Will she be at home this afternoon?"

"She is at home now. Come into the morning-room. She will be glad to make your acquaintance."

They walked across the linoleum-paved hall. The Professor opened the door of the room, and walked in, followed by his friend. Mrs. Grey was sitting in a basket-chair by the window, light and fairy-like in a loose-flowing, pink morning-gown. Seeing a visitor, she rose and swept towards them. The Professor heard a dull thud behind him. O'Brien had fallen back into a chair, with his hand pressed tight to his side.

"Jinny!" he gasped—"Jinny!"

Mrs. Grey stopped dead in her advance, and stared at him with a face from which every expression had been struck out, save one of astonishment and horror. Then with a sharp intaking of the breath she reeled, and would have fallen had the Professor not thrown his long, nervous arm round her.

"Try this sofa," said he.

She sank back among the cushions with the same white, cold, dead look upon her face. The Professor stood with his back to the empty fireplace and glanced from the one to the other.

"So, O'Brien," he said at last, "you have already made the acquaintance of my wife!"

"Your wife," cried his friend hoarsely. "She is no wife of yours. God help me, she is *my* wife."

The Professor stood rigidly upon the hearth-rug. His long, thin fingers were intertwined, and his head had sunk a little forward. His two companions had eyes only for each other.

"Jinny!" said he.

"James!"

"How could you leave me so, Jinny? How could you have the heart to do it? I thought you were dead. I mourned for your death—ay, and you have made me mourn for you living. You have withered my life."

She made no answer, but lay back among the cushions with her eyes still fixed upon him.

"Why do you not speak?"

"Because you are right, James. I have treated you cruelly—shamefully. But it is not as bad as you think."

"You fled with De Horta."

"No, I did not. At the last moment my better nature prevailed. He went alone. But I was ashamed to come back after what I had written to you. I could not face you. I took passage alone to England under a new name, and here I have lived ever since. It seemed to me that I was beginning life again. I knew that you thought I was drowned. Who could have dreamed that Fate would throw us together again! When the Professor asked me——"

She stopped and gave a gasp for breath.

"You are faint," said the Professor—"keep the head low; it aids the cerebral circulation." He flattened down the cushion. "I am sorry to leave you, O'Brien; but I have my class duties to look to. Possibly I may find you here when I return."

With a grim and rigid face he strode out of the room. Not one of the three hundred students who listened to his lecture saw any change in his manner and appearance, or could have guessed that the austere gentleman in front of them had found out at last how hard it is to rise above one's humanity. The lecture over, he performed his routine duties in the laboratory, and then drove back to his own house. He did not enter by the front door, but passed through the garden to the folding glass casement which led out of the morning-room. As he approached he heard his wife's voice and O'Brien's in loud and animated talk. He paused among the rose-bushes, uncertain whether to interrupt them or no. Nothing was further from his nature than to play the eavesdropper; but as he stood, still hesitating, words fell upon his ear which struck him rigid and motionless.

"You are still my wife, Jinny," said O'Brien; "I

forgive you from the bottom of my heart. I love you, and I have never ceased to love you, though you had forgotten me."

"No, James, my heart was always in Melbourne. I have always been yours. I thought that it was better for you that I should seem to be dead."

"You must choose between us now, Jinny. If you determine to remain here, I shall not open my lips. There shall be no scandal. If, on the other hand, you come with me, it's little I care about the world's opinion. Perhaps I am as much to blame as you are. I thought too much of my work and too little of my wife."

The Professor heard the cooing, caressing laugh which he knew so well.

"I shall go with you, James," she said.

"And the Professor——?"

"The poor Professor! But he will not mind much, James; he has no heart."

"We must tell him our resolution."

"There is no need," said Professor Ainslie Grey, stepping in through the open casement. "I have overheard the latter part of your conversation. I hesitated to interrupt you before you came to a conclusion."

O'Brien stretched out his hand and took that of the woman. They stood together with the sunshine on their faces. The Professor paused at the casement with his hands behind his back and his long, black shadow fell between them.

"You have come to a wise decision," said he. "Go back to Australia together, and let what has passed be blotted out of your lives."

"But you—you——" stammered O'Brien.

The Professor waved his hand.

"Never trouble about me," he said.

The woman gave a gasping cry.

"What can I do or say?" she wailed. "How could I have foreseen this? I thought my old life was dead. But it has come back again, with all its hopes and its desires. What can I say to you, Ainslie? I have brought shame and disgrace upon a worthy man. I have blasted your life. How you must hate and loathe me! I wish to God that I had never been born!"

"I neither hate nor loathe you, Jeannette," said the Professor quietly. "You are wrong in regretting your birth, for you have a worthy mission before you in aiding the life-work of a man who has shown himself capable of the highest order of scientific research. I cannot with justice blame you personally for what has occurred. How far the individual monad is to be held responsible for hereditary and engrained tendencies, is a question upon which science has not yet said her last word."

He stood with his finger-tips touching, and his body inclined as one who is gravely expounding a difficult and impersonal subject. O'Brien had stepped forward to say something, but the other's attitude and manner froze the words upon his lips. Condolence or sympathy would be an impertinence to one who could so easily merge his private griefs in broad questions of abstract philosophy.

"It is needless to prolong the situation," the Professor continued, in the same measured tones. "My brougham stands at the door. I beg that you will use it as your own. Perhaps it would be as well that you should leave the town without unnecessary delay. Your things, Jeannette, shall be forwarded."

O'Brien hesitated with a hanging head.

"I hardly dare offer you my hand," he said.

"On the contrary. I think that of the three of us you come best out of the affair. You have nothing to be ashamed of."

"Your sister——"

"I shall see that the matter is put to her in its true light. Good-bye! Let me have a copy of your recent research. Good-bye, Jeannette!"

"Good-bye!"

Their hands met, and for one short moment their

eyes also. It was only a glance, but for the first and last time the woman's intuition cast a light for itself into the dark places of a strong man's soul. She gave a little gasp, and her other hand rested for an instant, as white and as light as thistle-down, upon his shoulder.

"James, James!" she cried. "Don't you see that he is stricken to the heart?"

He turned her quietly away from him.

"I am not an emotional man," he said. "I have my duties—my research on Vallisneria. The brougham is there. Your cloak is in the hall. Tell John where you wish to be driven. He will bring you anything you need. Now go."

His last two words were so sudden, so volcanic, in such contrast to his measured voice and mask-like face, that they swept the two away from him. He closed the door behind them and paced slowly up and down the room. Then he passed into the library and looked out over the wire blind. The carriage was rolling away. He caught a last glimpse of the woman who had been his wife. He saw the feminine droop of her head, and the curve of her beautiful throat.

Under some foolish, aimless impulse, he took a few quick steps towards the door. Then he turned, and, throwing himself into his study chair, he plunged back into his work.

There was little scandal about this singular, domestic incident. The Professor had few personal friends, and seldom went into society. His marriage had been so quiet that most of his colleagues had never ceased to regard him as a bachelor. Mrs. Esdaile and a few others might talk, but their field for gossip was limited, for they could only guess vaguely at the cause of this sudden separation.

The Professor was as punctual as ever at his classes, and as zealous in directing the laboratory work of those who studied under him. His own private researches were pushed on with feverish energy. It was no uncommon thing for his servants, when they came down of a morning, to hear the shrill scratchings of his tireless pen, or to meet him on the staircase as he ascended, grey and silent, to his room. In vain his friends assured him that such a life must undermine his health. He lengthened his hours until day and night were one long, ceaseless task.

Gradually under this discipline a change came over his appearance. His features, always inclined to gauntness, became even sharper and more pronounced. There were deep lines about his temples and across his brow. His cheek was sunken and his complexion bloodless. His knees gave under him when he walked; and once when passing out of his lecture-room he fell and had to be assisted to his carriage.

This was just before the end of the session; and soon after the holidays commenced, the professors who still remained in Birchespool were shocked to hear that their brother of the chair of physiology had sunk so low that no hopes could be entertained of his recovery. Two eminent physicians had consulted over his case without being able to give a name to the affection from which he suffered. A steadily decreasing vitality appeared to be the only symptom—a bodily weakness which left the mind unclouded. He was much interested himself in his own case, and made notes of his subjective sensations as an aid to diagnosis. Of his approaching end he spoke in his usual unemotional and somewhat pedantic fashion. "It is the assertion," he said, "of the liberty of the individual cell as opposed to the cell-commune. It is the dissolution of a co-operative society. The process is one of great interest."

And so one grey morning his co-operative society dissolved. Very quietly and softly he sank into his eternal sleep. His two physicians felt some slight embarrassment when called upon to fill in his certificate.

"It is difficult to give it a name," said one.

" Very," said the other.

" If he were not such an unemotional man, I should have said that he had died from some sudden nervous shock—from, in fact, what the vulgar would call a broken heart."

" I don't think poor Grey was that sort of a man at all."

" Let us call it cardiac, anyhow," said the other physician.

So they did so.

57. *Behind the Times*

MY first interview with Dr. James Winter was under dramatic circumstances. It occurred at two in the morning in the bedroom of an old country house. I kicked him twice on the white waistcoat and knocked off his gold spectacles, while he, with the aid of a female accomplice, stifled my angry cries in a flannel petticoat and thrust me into a warm bath. I am told that one of my parents, who happened to be present, remarked in a whisper that there was nothing the matter with my lungs. I cannot recall how Dr. Winter looked at the time, for I had other things to think of, but his description of my own appearance is far from flattering. A fluffy head, a body like a trussed goose, very bandy legs, and feet with the soles turned inwards—those are the main items which he can remember.

From this time onwards the epochs of my life were the periodical assaults which Dr. Winter made upon me. He vaccinated me, he cut me for an abscess, he blistered me for mumps. It was a world of peace, and he the one dark cloud that threatened. But at last there came a time of real illness—a time when I lay for months together inside my wicker-work basket bed, and then it was that I learned that that hard face could relax, that those country-made, creaking boots could steal very gently to a bedside, and that that rough voice could thin into a whisper when it spoke to a sick child.

And now the child is himself a medical man, and yet Dr. Winter is the same as ever. I can see no change since first I can remember him, save that perhaps the brindled hair is a trifle whiter, and the huge shoulders a little more bowed. He is a very tall man, though he loses a couple of inches from his stoop. That big back of his has curved itself over sick-beds until it has set in that shape. His face is of a walnut brown, and tells of long winter drives over bleak country roads with the wind and the rain in his teeth. It looks smooth at a little distance, but as you approach him you see that it is shot with innumerable fine wrinkles, like a last year's apple. They are hardly to be seen when he is in repose, but when he laughs his face breaks like a starred glass, and you realise then that, though he looks old, he must be older than he looks.

How old that is I could never discover. I have often tried to find out, and have struck his stream as high up as George the Fourth and even of the Regency, but without ever getting quite to the source. His mind must have been open to impressions very early, but it must also have closed early, for the politics of the day have little interest for him, while he is fiercely excited about questions which are entirely prehistoric. He shakes his head when he speaks of the first Reform Bill and expresses grave doubts as to its wisdom, and I have heard him, when he was warmed by a glass of wine, say bitter things about Robert Peel and his abandoning of the Corn Laws. The death of that statesman brought the history of England to a definite close, and Dr. Winter refers to everything which had happened since then as to an insignificant anti-climax.

But it was only when I had myself become a medical man that I was able to appreciate how entirely he is a survival of a past generation. He had learned his medicine under that obsolete and forgotten system by which a youth was apprenticed to a surgeon, in the days when the study of anatomy was often approached through a violated grave. His views upon his own profession are even more reactionary than his politics. Fifty years have brought him little and deprived him of less. Vaccination was well within the teaching of his youth, though I think he has a secret preference for inoculation. Bleeding he would practise freely but for public opinion. Chloroform he regards as a dangerous innovation, and he always clicks with his tongue when it is mentioned. He has even been known to say vain things about Laennec, and to refer to the stethoscope as " a new-fangled French toy." He carries one in his hat out of deference to the expectations of his patients; but he is very hard of hearing, so that it makes little difference whether he uses it or not.

He always reads, as a duty, his weekly medical paper, so that he has a general idea as to the advance of modern science. He persists in looking upon it, however, as a huge and rather ludicrous experiment. The germ theory of disease set him chuckling for a long time, and his favourite joke in the sick-room was to say, " Shut the door, or the germs will be getting in." As to the Darwinian theory, it struck him as being the crowning joke of the century. " The children in the nursery and the ancestors in the stable," he would cry, and laugh the tears out of his eyes.

He is so very much behind the day that occasionally, as things move round in their usual circle, he finds himself, to his own bewilderment, in the front of the fashion. Dietetic treatment, for example, had been much in vogue in his youth, and he has more practical knowledge of it than anyone whom I have met. Massage, too, was familiar to him when it was new to our generation. He had been trained also at a time when instruments were in a rudimentary state and when men learned to trust more to their own fingers. He has a model surgical hand, muscular in the palm, tapering in the fingers, "with an eye at the end of each." I shall not easily forget how Dr. Patterson and I cut Sir John Sirwell, the County Member, and were unable to find the stone. It was a horrible moment. Both our careers were at stake. And then it was that Dr. Winter, whom we had asked out of courtesy to be present, introduced into the wound a finger which seemed to our excited senses to be about nine inches long, and hooked out the stone at the end of it.

"It's always well to bring one in your waistcoat pocket," said he with a chuckle, "but I suppose you youngsters are above all that."

We made him President of our Branch of the British Medical Association, but he resigned after the first meeting. "The young men are too much for me," he said. "I don't understand what they are talking about." Yet his patients do very well. He has the healing touch—that magnetic thing which defies explanation or analysis, but which is a very evident fact none the less. His mere presence leaves the patient with more hopefulness and vitality. The sight of disease affects him as dust does a careful housewife. It makes him angry and impatient. "Tut, tut, this will never do!" he cries, as he takes over a new case. He would shoo death out of the room as though he were an intrusive hen. But when the intruder refuses to be dislodged, when the blood moves more slowly and the eyes grow dimmer, then it is that Dr. Winter is of more avail than all the drugs in his surgery. Dying folk cling to his hand as if the presence of his bulk and vigour gives them more courage to face the change; and that kindly, wind-beaten face has been the last earthly impression which many a sufferer has carried into the unknown.

When Dr. Patterson and I, both of us young, energetic, and up-to-date, settled in the district, we were most cordially received by the old doctor, who would have been only too happy to be relieved of some of his patients. The patients themselves, however, followed their own inclinations, which is a reprehensible way that patients have, so that we remained neglected with our modern instruments and our latest alkaloids, while he was serving out senna and calomel to all the country-side. We both of us loved the old fellow, but at the same time, in the privacy of our own intimate conversations, we could not help commenting upon this deplorable lack of judgment.

" It is all very well for the poorer people," said Patterson, " but after all the educated classes have a right to expect that their medical man will know the difference between a mitral murmur and a bronchitic rale. It's the judicial frame of mind, not the sympathetic, which is the essential one."

I thoroughly agreed with Patterson in what he said. It happened, however, that very shortly afterwards the epidemic of influenza broke out, and we were all worked to death. One morning I met Patterson on my round, and found him looking rather pale and fagged out. He made the same remark about me. I was in fact feeling far from well, and I lay upon the sofa all afternoon with a splitting headache and pains in every joint. As evening closed in I could no longer disguise the fact that the scourge was upon me, and I felt that I should have medical advice without delay. It was of Patterson naturally that I thought, but somehow the idea of him had suddenly become repugnant to me. I thought of his cold, critical attitude, of his endless questions, of his tests and his tappings. I wanted something more soothing—something more genial.

" Mrs. Hudson," said I to my housekeeper, " would you kindly run along to old Dr. Winter and tell him that I should be obliged to him if he would step round."

She was back with an answer presently.

" Dr. Winter will come round in an hour or so, sir, but he has just been called in to attend Dr. Patterson."

58. *His First Operation*

IT was the first day of a winter session, and the third year's man was walking with the first year's man. Twelve o'clock was just booming out from the Tron Church.

"Let me see," said the third year's man, "you have never seen an operation ?"

"Never."

"Then this way, please. This is Rutherford's historic bar. A glass of sherry, please, for this gentleman. You are rather sensitive, are you not ?"

"My nerves are not very strong, I am afraid."

"Hum ! Another glass of sherry for this gentleman. We are going to an operation now, you know."

The novice squared his shoulders and made a gallant attempt to look unconcerned.

"Nothing very bad—eh ?"

"Well, yes—pretty bad."

"An—an amputation ?"

"No, it's a bigger affair than that."

"I think—I think they must be expecting me at home."

"There's no sense in funking. If you don't go to-day you must to-morrow. Better get it over at once. Feel pretty fit ?"

"Oh, yes, all right."

The smile was not a success.

"One more glass of sherry, then. Now come on or we shall be late. I want you to be well in front."

"Surely that is not necessary."

"Oh, it is far better. What a drove of students ! There are plenty of new men among them. You can tell them easily enough, can't you ? If they were going down to be operated upon themselves they could not look whiter."

"I don't think I should look as white."

"Well, I was just the same myself. But the feeling soon wears off. You see a fellow with a face like plaster, and before the week is out he is eating his lunch in the dissecting rooms. I'll tell you all about the case when we get to the theatre."

The students were pouring down the sloping street which led to the infirmary—each with his little sheaf of note-books in his hand. There were pale, frightened lads, fresh from the High Schools, and callous old chronics, whose generation had passed on and left them. They swept in an unbroken, tumultuous stream from the University gate to the hospital. The figures and gait of the men were young, but there was little youth in most of their faces. Some looked as if they ate too little—a few as if they drank too much. Tall and short, tweed coated and black, round-shouldered, bespectacled and slim, they crowded with clatter of feet and rattle of sticks through the hospital gate. Now and again they thickened into two lines as the carriage of a surgeon of the staff rolled over the cobblestones between.

"There's going to be a crowd at Archer's," whispered the senior man with suppressed excitement. "It is grand to see him at work. I've seen him jab all round the aorta until it made me jumpy to watch him. This way, and mind the whitewash."

They passed under an archway and down a long, stone-flagged corridor with drab-coloured doors on either side, each marked with a number. Some of them were ajar, and the novice glanced into them with tingling nerves. He was reassured to catch a glimpse of cheery fires, lines of white-counterpaned beds and a profusion of coloured texts upon the wall. The corridor opened upon a small hall with a fringe of poorly clad people seated all round upon benches. A young man with a pair of scissors stuck, like a flower, in his button-hole, and a note-book in his hand, was passing from one to the other, whispering and writing.

"Anything good?" asked the third year's man.

"You should have been here yesterday," said the out-patient clerk, glancing up. "We had a regular field day. A popliteal aneurism, a Colles' fracture, a spina bifida, a tropical abscess, and an elephantiasis. How's that for a single haul?"

"I'm sorry I missed it. But they'll come again, I suppose. What's up with the old gentleman?"

A broken workman was sitting in the shadow, rocking himself slowly to and fro and groaning. A woman beside him was trying to console him, patting his shoulder with a hand which was spotted over with curious little white blisters.

"It's a fine carbuncle," said the clerk, with the air of a connoisseur who describes his orchids to one who can appreciate them. "It's on his back, and the passage is draughty, so we must not look at it, must we, daddy? Pemphigus," he added carelessly, pointing to the woman's disfigured hands. "Would you care to stop and take out a metacarpal?"

"No, thank you, we are due at Archer's. Come on"; and they rejoined the throng, which was hurrying to the theatre of the famous surgeon.

The tiers of horse-shoe benches, rising from the floor to the ceiling, were already packed, and the novice as he entered saw vague, curving lines of faces in front of him, and heard the deep buzz of a hundred voices and sounds of laughter from somewhere up above him. His companion spied an opening on the second bench, and they both squeezed into it.

"This is grand," the senior man whispered; "you'll have a rare view of it all."

Only a single row of heads intervened between them and the operating table. It was of unpainted deal, plain, strong and scrupulously clean. A sheet of brown waterproofing covered half of it, and beneath stood a large tin tray full of sawdust. On the farther side, in front of the window, there was a board which was strewed with glittering instruments, forceps, tenacula, saws, cannulas, and trocars. A line of knives, with long, thin, delicate blades, lay at one side. Two young men lounged in front of this ; one threading needles, the other doing something to a brass coffee-pot-like thing which hissed out puffs of steam.

"That's Peterson," whispered the senior. "The big, bald man in the front row. He's the skin-grafting man, you know. And that's Anthony Browne, who took a larynx out successfully last winter. And there's Murphy the pathologist, and Stoddart the eye man. You'll come to know them all soon."

"Who are the two men at the table ?"

"Nobody—dressers. One has charge of the instruments and the other of the puffing Billy. It's Lister's antiseptic spray, you know, and Archer's one of the carbolic acid men. Hayes is the leader of the cleanliness-and-cold-water school, and they all hate each other like poison."

A flutter of interest passed through the closely packed benches as a woman in petticoat and bodice was led in by two nurses. A red, woollen shawl was draped over her head and round her neck. The face which looked out from it was that of a woman in the prime of her years, but drawn with suffering and of a peculiar bees-wax tint. Her head drooped as she walked, and one of the nurses, with her arm round her waist, was whispering consolation in her ear. She gave a quick side glance at the instrument table as she passed, but the nurses turned her away from it.

"What ails her ?" asked the novice.

"Cancer of the parotid. It's the devil of a case, extends right away back behind the carotids. There's hardly a man but Archer would dare to follow it. Ah, here he is himself."

As he spoke, a small, brisk, iron-grey man came striding into the room, rubbing his hands together as he walked. He had a clean-shaven face of the Naval officer type, with large, bright eyes, and a firm, straight mouth. Behind him came his big house surgeon with his gleaming pince-nez and a trail of dressers, who grouped themselves into the corners of the room.

"Gentlemen," cried the surgeon in a voice as hard and brisk as his manner. "We have here an interesting case of tumour of the parotid, originally cartilaginous but now assuming malignant characteristics, and therefore requiring excision. On to the table, nurse! Thank you! Chloroform, clerk! Thank you! You can take the shawl off, nurse."

The woman lay back upon the waterproofed pillow and her murderous tumour lay revealed. In itself it was a pretty thing, ivory white with a mesh of blue veins, and curving gently from jaw to chest. But the lean, yellow face, and the stringy throat were in horrible contrast with the plumpness and sleekness of this monstrous growth. The surgeon placed a hand on each side of it and pressed it slowly backwards and forwards.

"Adherent at one place, gentlemen," he cried. "The growth involves the carotids and jugulars, and passes behind the ramus of the jaw, whither we must be prepared to follow it. It is impossible to say how deep our dissection may carry us. Carbolic tray, thank you! Dressings of carbolic gauze, if you please! Push the chloroform, Mr. Johnson. Have the small saw ready in case it is necessary to remove the jaw."

The patient was moaning gently under the towel which had been placed over her face. She tried to raise her arms and to draw up her knees, but two dressers restrained her. The heavy air was full of the penetrating smells of carbolic acid and of chloroform. A muffled cry came from under the towel and then a snatch of a song, sung in a high, quavering, monotonous voice.

"He says, says he,
If you fly with me
You'll be mistress of the ice-cream van;
You'll be mistress of the——"

It mumbled off into a drone and stopped. The surgeon came across, still rubbing his hands, and spoke to an elderly man in front of the novice.

"Narrow squeak for the Government," he said.

"Oh, ten is enough."

"They won't have ten long. They'd do better to resign before they are driven to it."

"Oh, I should fight it out."

"What's the use. They can't get past the committee, even if they get a vote in the House. I was talking to——"

"Patient's ready, sir," said the dresser.

"Talking to M'Donald—but I'll tell you about it presently." He walked back to the patient, who was breathing in long, heavy gasps. "I propose," said he, passing his hand over the tumour in an almost caressing fashion, "to make a free incision over the posterior border and to take another forward at right angles to the lower end of it. Might I trouble you for a medium knife, Mr. Johnson?"

The novice, with eyes which were dilating with horror, saw the surgeon pick up the long, gleaming knife, dip it into a tin basin and balance it in his fingers as an artist might his brush. Then he saw him pinch up the skin above the tumour with his left hand. At the sight, his nerves, which had already been tried once or twice that day, gave way utterly. His head swam round and he felt that in another instant he might faint. He dared not look at the patient. He dug his thumbs into his ears lest some scream should come to haunt him, and he fixed his eyes rigidly upon the wooden ledge in front of him. One glance, one cry, would, he knew, break down the shred of self-possession which he still retained. He tried to think of cricket, of green fields and rippling water, of his sisters at home —of anything rather than of what was going on so near him.

And yet, somehow, even with his ears stopped up,

sounds seemed to penetrate to him and to carry their own tale. He heard, or thought that he heard, the long hissing of the carbolic engine. Then he was conscious of some movement among the dressers. Were there groans, too, breaking in upon him, and some other sound, some fluid sound, which was more dreadfully suggestive still? His mind would keep building up every step of the operation, and fancy made it more ghastly than fact could have been. His nerves tingled and quivered. Minute by minute the giddiness grew more marked, the numb, sickly feeling at his heart more distressing. And then suddenly, with a groan, his head pitching forward and his brow cracking sharply upon the narrow, wooden shelf in front of him, he lay in a dead faint.

When he came to himself he was lying in the empty theatre with his collar and shirt undone. The third year's man was dabbing a wet sponge over his face, and a couple of grinning dressers were looking on.

"All right," cried the novice, sitting up and rubbing his eyes; "I'm sorry to have made an ass of myself."

"Well, so I should think," said his companion. "What on earth did you faint about?"

"I couldn't help it. It was that operation."

"What operation?"

"Why, that cancer."

There was a pause, and then the three students burst out laughing.

"Why, you juggins," cried the senior man, "there never was an operation at all. They found the patient didn't stand the chloroform well, and so the whole thing was off. Archer has been giving us one of his racy lectures, and you fainted just in the middle of his favourite story."

59. *The Third Generation*

SCUDAMORE LANE, sloping down riverwards from just behind the Monument, lies, at night, in the shadow of two black and monstrous walls which loom high above the glimmer of the scattered gas-lamps. The footpaths are narrow, and the causeway is paved with rounded cobblestones so that the endless drays roar along it like so many breaking waves. A few old-fashioned houses lie scattered among the business premises, and in one of these—half-way down on the left-hand side—Dr. Horace Selby conducts his large practice. It is a singular street for so big a man, but a specialist who has a European reputation can afford to live where he likes. In his particular branch, too, patients do not always consider seclusion to be a disadvantage.

It was only ten o'clock. The dull roar of the traffic which converged all day upon London Bridge had died away now to a mere confused murmur. It was raining heavily, and the gas shone dimly through the streaked and dripping glass, throwing little yellow circles upon the glistening cobblestones. The air was full of the sounds of rain, the thin swish of its fall, the heavier drip from the eaves, and the swirl and gurgle down the two steep gutters and through the sewer grating. There was only one figure in the whole length of Scudamore Lane. It was that of a man, and it stood outside the door of Dr. Horace Selby.

He had just rung and was waiting for an answer. The fanlight beat full upon the gleaming shoulders of his waterproof and upon his upturned features. It was a wan, sensitive, clear-cut face, with some subtle, nameless peculiarity in its expression—something of the startled horse in the white-rimmed eye, something, too, of the helpless child in the drawn cheek and the weakening of the lower lip. The man-servant knew the stranger as a patient at a bare glance at those frightened eyes. Such a look had been seen at that door before.

"Is the doctor in?"

The man hesitated.

"He has had a few friends to dinner, sir. He does not like to be disturbed outside his usual hours, sir."

"Tell him that I *must* see him. Tell him that it is of the very first importance. Here is my card." He fumbled with his trembling fingers in trying to draw one from the case. "Sir Francis Norton is the name. Tell him that Sir Francis Norton of Deane Park must see him at once."

"Yes, sir." The butler closed his fingers upon the card and the half-sovereign which accompanied it. "Better hang your coat up here in the hall. It is very wet. Now, if you will wait here in the consulting-room I have no doubt that I shall be able to send the doctor in to you."

It was a large and lofty room in which the young baronet found himself. The carpet was so soft and thick that his feet made no sound as he walked across it. The two gas-jets were turned only half-way up, and the dim light with the faint, aromatic smell which filled the air had a vaguely religious suggestion. He sat down in a shining, leather arm-chair by the smouldering fire and looked gloomily about him. Two sides of the room were taken up with books, fat and sombre, with broad, gold lettering upon their backs. Beside him was the high, old-fashioned mantelpiece of white marble, the top of it strewed with cotton wadding and bandages, graduated measures and little bottles. There was one with a broad neck, just above him, containing bluestone, and another narrower one with what looked like the ruins of a broken pipe-stem, and "Caustic" outside upon a red label. Thermometers, hypodermic syringes, bistouries and spatulas were scattered thickly about, both on the mantelpiece and on the central table on either side of the sloping desk. On the same table to the right stood copies of the five books which Dr. Horace Selby had written upon the subject with which his name is peculiarly associated, while on the left, on the top of a red medical directory, lay a huge glass model of a human eye, the size of a turnip, which opened down the centre to expose the lens and double chamber within.

Sir Francis Norton had never been remarkable for his powers of observation, and yet he found himself watching these trifles with the keenest attention. Even the corrosion of the cork of an acid bottle caught his eye and he wondered that the doctor did not use glass stoppers. Tiny scratches where the light glinted off the table, little stains upon the leather of the desk, chemical formulæ scribbled upon the labels of some of the phials—nothing was too slight to arrest his attention. And his sense of hearing was equally alert. The heavy ticking of the solemn, black clock above the fireplace struck quite painfully upon his ears. Yet, in spite of it, and in spite also of the thick, old-fashioned wooden partition walls, he could hear the voices of men talking in the next room and could even catch scraps of their conversation. "Second hand was bound to take it." "Why, you drew the last of them yourself." "How could I play the queen when I knew the ace was against me?" The phrases came in little spurts, falling back into the dull murmur of conversation. And then suddenly he heard a creaking of a door, and a step in the hall, and knew with a tingling mixture of impatience and horror that the crisis of his life was at hand.

Dr. Horace Selby was a large, portly man, with an imposing presence. His nose and chin were bold and pronounced, yet his features were puffy—a combination which would blend more freely with the wig and cravat of the early Georges, than with the close-cropped hair and black frockcoat of the end of the nineteenth century. He was clean shaven, for his mouth was too good to cover, large, flexible and sensitive, with a kindly human softening at either corner, which, with his brown, sympathetic eyes, had drawn out many a shame-struck sinner's secret. Two masterful, little, bushy, side whiskers bristled out from under his ears, spindling away upwards to merge in the thick curves of his brindled hair. To his patients there was something reassuring in the mere bulk and dignity of the man. A high and easy bearing in medicine, as in war, bears with it a hint of victories in the past, and a promise of others to come. Dr. Horace Selby's face was a consolation, and so, too, were the large, white, soothing hands, one of which he held out to his visitor.

"I am sorry to have kept you waiting. It is a conflict of duties, you perceive. A host to his guests and an adviser to his patient. But now I am entirely at your disposal, Sir Francis. But, dear me, you are very cold."

"Yes, I am cold."

"And you are trembling all over. Tut, tut, this will never do. This miserable night has chilled you. Perhaps some little stimulant——"

"No, thank you. I would really rather not. And it is not the night which has chilled me. I am frightened, doctor."

The doctor half turned in his chair and patted the arch of the young man's knee as he might the neck of a restless horse.

"What, then?" he asked, looking over his shoulder at the pale face with the startled eyes.

Twice the young man parted his lips. Then he stooped with a sudden gesture and turning up the right leg of his trousers he pulled down his sock and thrust forward his shin. The doctor made a clicking noise with his tongue as he glanced at it.

"Both legs?"

" No, only one."

" Suddenly ? "

" This morning."

" Hum ! " The doctor pouted his lips, and drew his finger and thumb down the line of his chin. " Can you account for it ? " he said briskly.

" No."

A trace of sternness came into the large, brown eyes. " I need not point out to you that unless the most absolute frankness——"

The patient sprang from his chair.

" So help me God, doctor," he cried, " I have nothing in my life with which to reproach myself. Do you think that I would be such a fool as to come here and tell you lies ? Once for all, I have nothing to regret."

He was a pitiful, half-tragic and half-grotesque figure as he stood with one trouser leg rolled to his knee, and that ever-present horror still lurking in his eyes. A burst of merriment came from the card-players in the next room and the two looked at each other in silence.

" Sit down ! " said the doctor abruptly. " Your assurance is quite sufficient." He stooped and ran his finger down the line of the young man's shin, raising it at one point. " Hum ! Serpiginous ! " he murmured, shaking his head ; " any other symptoms ? "

" My eyes have been a little weak."

" Let me see your teeth ! " He glanced at them, and again made the gentle clicking sound of sympathy and disapprobation.

" Now the eye ! " He lit a lamp at the patient's elbow, and holding a small, crystal lens to concentrate the light, he threw it obliquely upon the patient's eye. As he did so a glow of pleasure came over his large, expressive face, a flush of such enthusiasm as the botanist feels when he packs the rare plant into his tin knapsack, or the astronomer when the long-sought comet first swims into the field of his telescope

"This is very typical—very typical indeed," he murmured, turning to his desk and jotting down a few memoranda upon a sheet of paper. "Curiously enough I am writing a monograph upon the subject. It is singular that you should have been able to furnish so well-marked a case."

He had so forgotten the patient in his symptom that he had assumed an almost congratulatory air towards its possessor. He reverted to human sympathy again as his patient asked for particulars.

"My dear sir, there is no occasion for us to go into strictly professional details together," said he soothingly. "If, for example, I were to say that you have interstitial keratitis, how would you be the wiser? There are indications of a strumous diathesis. In broad terms I may say that you have a constitutional and hereditary taint."

The young baronet sank back in his chair and his chin fell forward upon his chest. The doctor sprang to a side-table and poured out a half glass of liqueur brandy which he held to his patient's lips. A little fleck of colour came into his cheeks as he drank it down.

"Perhaps I spoke a little abruptly," said the doctor. "But you must have known the nature of your complaint, why otherwise should you have come to me?"

"God help me, I suspected it—but only to-day when my leg grew bad. My father had a leg like this."

"It was from him, then?"

"No, from my grandfather. You have heard of Sir Rupert Norton, the great Corinthian?"

The doctor was a man of wide reading with a retentive memory. The name brought back to him instantly the remembrance of the sinister reputation of its owner—a notorious buck of the thirties, who had gambled and duelled and steeped himself in drink and debauchery until even the vile set with whom he consorted had shrunk away from him in horror, and left him to a sinister old age with the barmaid wife whom in some drunken frolic he had espoused. As he looked at the young man still leaning back in the leather chair, there seemed for the instant to flicker up behind him some vague presentiment of that foul old dandy with his dangling seals, many-wreathed scarf, and dark, satyric face. What was he now? An armful of bones in a mouldy box? But his deeds—they were living and rotting the blood in the veins of an innocent man.

"I see that you have heard of him," said the young baronet. "He died horribly, I have been told, but not more horribly than he had lived. My father was his only son. He was a studious man, fond of books and canaries and the country. But his innocent life did not save him."

"His symptoms were cutaneous, I understand."

"He wore gloves in the house. That was the first thing I can remember. And then it was his throat, and then his legs. He used to ask me so often about my own health, and I thought him so fussy, for how could I tell what the meaning of it was? He was always watching me—always with a sidelong eye fixed upon me. Now at last I know what he was watching for."

"Had you brothers or sisters?"

"None, thank God!"

"Well, well, it is a sad case, and very typical of many which come in my way. You are no lonely sufferer, Sir Francis. There are many thousands who bear the same cross as you do."

"But where's the justice of it, doctor?" cried the young man, springing from the chair and pacing up and down the consulting-room. "If I were heir to my grandfather's sins as well as to their results I could understand it, but I am of my father's type; I love all that is gentle and beautiful, music and poetry and art. The coarse and animal is abhorrent to me. Ask any of my friends and they would tell you that. And now that this vile, loathsome thing—Ach, I am polluted to the marrow, soaked in abomination! And why? Haven't I a right to ask why? Did I do it? Was it my fault? Could I help being born? And look at me now, blighted and blasted, just as life was at its sweetest! Talk about the sins of the father! How about the sins of the Creator!"

He shook his two clenched hands in the air, the poor, impotent atom with his pin-point of brain caught in the whirl of the infinite.

The doctor rose and placing his hands upon his shoulders he pressed him back into his chair again.

"There, there, my dear lad," said he. "You must not excite yourself! You are trembling all over. Your nerves cannot stand it. We must take these great questions upon trust. What are we after all? Half-evolved creatures in a transition stage; nearer, perhaps, to the medusa on the one side than to perfected humanity on the other. With half a complete brain we can't expect to understand the whole of a complete fact, can we, now? It is all very dim and dark, no doubt, but I think Pope's famous couplet sums the whole matter up, and from my heart, after fifty years of varied experience, I can say that——"

But the young baronet gave a cry of impatience and disgust.

"Words, words, words! You can sit comfortably there in your chair and say them—and think them, too, no doubt. You've had your life. But I've never had mine. You've healthy blood in your veins. Mine is putrid. And yet I am as innocent as you. What would words do for you if you were in this chair and I in that? Ah, it's such a mockery and a make-belief. Don't think me rude, though, doctor. I don't mean to be that. I only say that it is impossible for you or any man to realise it. But I've a question to ask you, doctor. It's one on which my whole life must depend."

He writhed his fingers together in an agony of apprehension.

"Speak out, my dear sir. I have every sympathy with you."

"Do you think—do you think the poison has spent itself on me? Do you think if I had children that they would suffer?"

"I can only give one answer to that. 'The third and fourth generation,' says the trite old text. You may in time eliminate it from your system, but many years must pass before you can think of marriage."

"I am to be married on Tuesday," whispered the patient.

It was Dr. Horace Selby's turn to be thrilled with horror. There were not many situations which would yield such a sensation to his well-seasoned nerves. He sat in silence while the babble of the card-table broke in again upon them. "We had a double ruff if you had returned a heart." "I was bound to clear the trumps." They were hot and angry about it.

"How could you?" cried the doctor severely. "It was criminal."

"You forget that I have only learned how I stand to-day." He put his two hands to his temples and pressed them convulsively. "You are a man of the world, Doctor Selby. You have seen or heard of such things before. Give me some advice. I'm in your hands. It is all very sudden and horrible, and I don't think I am strong enough to bear it."

The doctor's heavy brows thickened into two straight lines and he bit his nails in perplexity.

"The marriage must not take place."

"Then what am I to do?"

"At all costs it must not take place."

"And I must give her up?"

"There can be no question about that!"

The young man took out a pocket-book and drew from it a small photograph, holding it out towards the doctor. The firm face softened as he looked at it.

"It is very hard on you, no doubt. I can appreciate

it more now that I have seen that. But there is no alternative at all. You must give up all thought of it."

"But this is madness, doctor—madness, I tell you. No, I won't raise my voice! I forgot myself! But realise it, man! I am to be married on Tuesday—this coming Tuesday, you know. And all the world knows it. How can I put such a public affront upon her? It would be monstrous."

"None the less it must be done. My dear sir, there is no way out of it."

"You would have me simply write brutally and break the engagement at this last moment without a reason? I tell you I couldn't do it."

"I had a patient once who found himself in a somewhat similar situation some years ago," said the doctor thoughtfully. "His device was a singular one. He deliberately committed a penal offence and so compelled the young lady's people to withdraw their consent to the marriage."

The young baronet shook his head.

"My personal honour is as yet unstained," said he. "I have little else left, but that at least I will preserve."

"Well, well, it's a nice dilemma and the choice lies with you."

"Have you no other suggestion?"

"You don't happen to have property in Australia?"

"None."

"But you have capital?"

"Yes."

"Then you could buy some—to-morrow morning, for example. A thousand mining shares would do. Then you might write to say that urgent business affairs have compelled you to start at an hour's notice to inspect your property. That would give you six months at any rate."

"Well, that would be possible—yes, certainly it would be possible. But think of her position—the house full of wedding presents—guests coming from a distance. It is awful. And you say there is no alternative."

The doctor shrugged his shoulders.

"Well, then, I might write it now, and start to-morrow—eh? Perhaps you would let me use your desk. Thank you! I am so sorry to keep you from your guests so long. But I won't be a moment now." He wrote an abrupt note of a few lines. Then, with a sudden impulse, he tore it to shreds and flung it into the fireplace. "No, I can't sit down and tell her a lie, doctor," said he rising. "We must find some other way out of this. I will think it over, and let you know my decision. You must allow me to double your fee as I have taken such an unconscionable time. Now, good-bye, and thank you a thousand times for your sympathy and advice."

"Why, dear me, you haven't even got your prescription yet. This is the mixture, and I should recommend one of these powders every morning and the chemist will put all directions upon the ointment box. You are placed in a cruel situation, but I trust that these may be but passing clouds. When may I hope to hear from you again?"

"To-morrow morning."

"Very good. How the rain is splashing in the street. You have your waterproof there. You will need it. Good-bye, then, until to-morrow."

He opened the door. A gust of cold, damp air swept into the hall. And yet the doctor stood for a minute or more watching the lonely figure which passed slowly through the yellow splotches of the gas-lamps and into the broad bars of darkness between. It was but his own shadow which trailed up the wall as he passed the lights, and yet it looked to the doctor's eye as though some huge and sombre figure walked by a manikin's side, and led him silently up the lonely street.

Doctor Horace Selby heard again of his patient next morning and rather earlier than he had expected. A paragraph in the *Daily News* caused him to push away his breakfast untasted, and turned him sick and faint while he read it. "A Deplorable Accident" it was headed, and it ran in this way :—

"A fatal accident of a peculiarly painful character is reported from King William Street. About eleven o'clock last night a young man was observed, while endeavouring to get out of the way of a hansom, to slip and fall under the wheels of a heavy two-horse dray. On being picked up, his injuries were found to be of a most shocking character, and he expired while being conveyed to the hospital. An examination of his pocket-book and card-case shows beyond any question that the deceased is none other than Sir Francis Norton of Deane Park, who has only within the last year come into the baronetcy. The accident is made the more deplorable as the deceased, who was only just of age, was on the eve of being married to a young lady belonging to one of the oldest families in the south. With his wealth and his talents the ball of fortune was at his feet, and his many friends will be deeply grieved to know that his promising career has been cut short in so sudden and tragic a fashion."

60. *The Curse of Eve*

ROBERT JOHNSON was an essentially commonplace man, with no feature to distinguish him from a million others. He was pale of face, ordinary in looks, neutral in opinions, thirty years of age, and a married man. By trade he was a gentleman's outfitter in the New North Road, and the competition of business squeezed out of him the little character that was left. In his hope of conciliating customers he had become cringing and pliable, until working ever in the same routine from day to day he seemed to have sunk into a soulless machine rather than a man. No great question had ever stirred him. At the end of this snug century, self-contained in his own narrow circle, it seemed impossible that any of the mighty, primitive passions of mankind could ever reach him.

Yet birth, and lust, and illness, and death are changeless things, and when one of these harsh facts springs out upon a man at some sudden turn of the path of life, it dashes off for the moment his mask if civilisation and gives a glimpse of the stranger and stronger face below.

Johnson's wife was a quiet little woman, with brown hair and gentle ways. His affection for her was the one positive trait in his character. Together they would lay out the shop window every Monday morning, the spotless shirts in their green cardboard boxes below, the neckties above hung in rows over the brass rails, the cheap studs glistening from the white cards at either side, while in the background were the rows of cloth caps and the bank of boxes in which the more valuable hats were screened from the sunlight. She kept the books and sent out the bills. No one but she knew the joys and sorrows which crept into his small life. She had shared his exultation when the gentleman who was going to India had bought ten dozen shirts and an incredible number of collars, and she had been stricken as he when, after the goods had gone, the bill was returned from the hotel address with the intimation that no such person had lodged there. For five years they had worked, building up the business, thrown together all the more closely because their marriage had been a childless one. Now, however, there were signs that a change was at hand, and that speedily. She was unable to come downstairs, and her mother, Mrs. Peyton, came over from Camberwell to nurse her and to welcome her grandchild.

Little qualms of anxiety came over Johnson as his wife's time approached. However, after all, it was a natural process. Other men's wives went through it unharmed, and why should not his? He was himself one of a family of fourteen, and yet his mother was alive and hearty. It was quite the exception for anything to go wrong. And yet, in spite of his reasonings, the remembrance of his wife's condition was always like a sombre background to all his other thoughts.

Doctor Miles of Bridport Place, the best man in the neighbourhood, was retained five months in advance, and, as time stole on, many little packets of absurdly small, white garments with frill work and ribbons began to arrive among the big consignments of male necessities. And then one evening, as Johnson was ticketing the scarves in the shop, he heard a bustle upstairs, and Mrs. Peyton came running down to say that Lucy was bad and that she thought the doctor ought to be there without delay.

It was not Robert Johnson's nature to hurry. He was prim and staid and liked to do things in an orderly fashion. It was a quarter of a mile from the corner of the New North Road where his shop stood to the doctor's house in Bridport Place. There were no cabs in sight, so he set off upon foot, leaving the lad to mind the shop. At Bridport Place he was told that the doctor had just gone to Harman Street to attend a man in a fit. Johnson started off for Harman Street, losing a little of his primness as he became more anxious. Two full cabs but no empty ones passed him on the way. At Harman Street he learned that the doctor had gone on to a case of measles, fortunately he had left the address—69 Dunstan Road, at the other side of the Regent's Canal. Johnson's primness had vanished now as he thought of the women waiting at home, and he began to run as hard as he could down the Kingsland Road. Some way along he sprang into a cab which stood by the curb and drove to Dunstan Road. The doctor had just left, and Robert Johnson felt inclined to sit down upon the steps in despair.

Fortunately he had not sent the cab away, and he was soon back at Bridport Place. Doctor Miles had not returned yet, but they were expecting him every instant. Johnson waited, drumming his fingers on his knees, in a high, dim-lit room, the air of which was charged with a faint, sickly smell of ether. The furniture was massive, and the books in the shelves were sombre and a squat, black clock ticked mournfully on the mantelpiece. It told him that it was half-past seven, and that he had been gone an hour and a quarter. Whatever would the women think of him! Every time that a distant door slammed he sprang from his chair in a quiver of eagerness. His ears strained to catch the deep notes of the doctor's voice. And then, suddenly, with a gush of joy he heard a quick step outside, and the sharp click of the key in the lock. In an instant he was out in the hall, before the doctor's foot was over the threshold.

"If you please, doctor, I've come for you," he cried; "the wife was taken bad at six o'clock."

He hardly knew what he expected the doctor to do. Something very energetic, certainly—to seize some drugs, perhaps, and rush excitedly with him through the gas-lit streets. Instead of that Doctor Miles threw his umbrella into the rack, jerked off his hat with a somewhat peevish gesture, and pushed Johnson back into the room.

"Let's see! You *did* engage me, didn't you?" he asked in no very cordial voice.

"Oh yes, doctor, last November. Johnson, the outfitter, you know, in the New North Road."

"Yes, yes. It's a bit overdue," said the doctor, glancing at a list of names in a note-book with a very shiny cover. "Well, how is she?"

"I don't——"

"Ah, of course, it's your first. You'll know more about it next time."

"Mrs. Peyton said it was time you were there, sir."

"My dear sir, there can be no very pressing hurry in a first case. We shall have an all-night affair, I fancy, You can't get an engine to go without coals, Mr. Johnson. and I have had nothing but a light lunch."

"We could have something cooked for you—something hot and a cup of tea."

"Thank you, but I fancy my dinner is actually on the table. I can do no good in the earlier stages. Go home and say that I am coming, and I will be round immediately afterwards."

A sort of horror filled Robert Johnson as he gazed at this man who could think about his dinner at such a moment. He had not imagination enough to realise that the experience which seemed so appallingly important to him, was the merest everyday matter of business to the medical man who could not have lived for a year had he not, amid the rush of work, remembered what was due to his own health. To Johnson he seemed little better than a monster. His thoughts were bitter as he sped back to his shop.

"You've taken your time," said his mother-in-law reproachfully, looking down the stairs as he entered.

"I couldn't help it!" he gasped. "Is it over?"

"Over! She's got to be worse, poor dear, before she can be better. Where's Doctor Miles?"

"He's coming after he's had dinner."

The old woman was about to make some reply, when, from the half-opened door behind, a high, whinnying voice cried out for her. She ran back and closed the door, while Johnson, sick at heart, turned into the shop. There he sent the lad home and busied himself frantically in putting up shutters and turning out boxes. When all was closed and finished he seated himself in the parlour behind the shop. But he could not sit still. He rose incessantly to walk a few paces and then fall back into a chair once more. Suddenly the clatter of china fell upon his ear, and he saw the maid pass the door with a cup on a tray and a smoking teapot.

"Who is that for, Jane?" he asked.

"For the mistress, Mr. Johnson. She says she would fancy it."

There was immeasurable consolation to him in that homely cup of tea. It wasn't so very bad after all if his wife could think of such things. So light-hearted was he that he asked for a cup also. He had just finished it when the doctor arrived, with a small, black-leather bag in his hand.

"Well, how is she?" he asked genially.

"Oh, she's very much better," said Johnson, with enthusiasm.

"Dear me, that's bad!" said the doctor. "Perhaps it will do if I look in on my morning round?"

"No, no," cried Johnson, clutching at his thick frieze overcoat. "We are so glad that you have come. And, doctor, please come down soon and let me know what you think about it."

The doctor passed upstairs, his firm, heavy steps resounding through the house. Johnson could hear his boots creaking as he walked about the floor above him, and the sound was a consolation to him. It was crisp and decided, the tread of a man who had plenty of self-confidence. Presently, still straining his ears to catch what was going on, he heard the scraping of a chair as it was drawn along the floor, and a moment later he heard the door fly open, and someone came rushing downstairs. Johnson sprang up with his hair bristling, thinking that some dreadful thing had occurred, but it was only his mother-in-law, incoherent with excitement and searching for scissors and some tape. She vanished again and Jane passed up the stairs with a pile of newly aired linen. Then, after an interval of silence, Johnson heard the heavy, creaking tread and the doctor came down into the parlour.

"That's better," said he, pausing with his hand upon the door. "You look pale, Mr. Johnson."

"Oh no, sir, not at all," he answered deprecatingly, mopping his brow with his handkerchief.

"There is no immediate cause for alarm," said Doctor Miles. "The case is not all that we could wish it. Still we will hope for the best."

"Is there danger, sir?" gasped Johnson.

"Well, there is always danger, of course. It is not

altogether a favourable case, but still it might be much worse. I have given her a draught. I saw as I passed that they have been doing a little building opposite to you. It's an improving quarter. The rents go higher and higher. You have a lease of your own little place, eh ?"

"Yes, sir, yes !" cried Johnson, whose ears were straining for every sound from above, and who felt, none the less, that it was very soothing that the doctor should be able to chat so easily at such a time. "That's to say no, sir, I am a yearly tenant."

"Ah, I should get a lease if I were you. There's Marshall, the watchmaker, down the street, I attended his wife twice and saw him through the typhoid when they took up the drains in Prince Street. I assure you his landlord sprung his rent nearly forty a year and he had to pay or clear out."

"Did his wife get through it, doctor ?"

"Oh yes, she did very well. Hullo ! Hullo !"

He slanted his ear to the ceiling with a questioning face, and then darted swiftly from the room.

It was March and the evenings were chill, so Jane had lit the fire, but the wind drove the smoke downwards and the air was full of its acrid taint. Johnson felt chilled to the bone, though rather by his apprehensions than by the weather. He crouched over the fire with his thin, white hands held out to the blaze. At ten o'clock Jane brought in the joint of cold meat and laid his place for supper, but he could not bring himself to touch it. He drank a glass of the beer, however, and felt the better for it. The tension of his nerves seemed to have reacted upon his hearing, and he was able to follow the most trivial things in the room above. Once, when the beer was still heartening him, he nerved himself to creep on tiptoe up the stair and to listen to what was going on. The bedroom door was half an inch open, and through the slit he could catch a glimpse of the clean-shaven face of the doctor, looking wearier and more anxious than before. Then he rushed downstairs like a lunatic, and running to the door he tried to distract his thoughts by watching what was going on in the street. The shops were all shut, and some rollicking, boon companions came shouting along from the public-house. He stayed at the door until the stragglers had thinned down, and then came back to his seat by the fire. In his dim brain he was asking himself questions which had never intruded themselves before. Where was the justice of it? What had his sweet, innocent little wife done that she should be used so? Why was Nature so cruel! He was frightened at his own thoughts, and yet wondered that they had never occurred to him before.

As the early morning drew in, Johnson, sick at heart and shivering in every limb, sat with his great-coat huddled round him, staring at the grey ashes and waiting hopelessly for some relief. His face was white and clammy, and his nerves had been numbed into a half-conscious state by the long monotony of misery. But suddenly all his feelings leapt into keen life again as he heard the bedroom door open and the doctor's steps upon the stair. Robert Johnson was precise and unemotional in everyday life, but he almost shrieked now as he rushed forward to know if it were over.

One glance at the stern, drawn face which met him showed that it was no pleasant news which had sent the doctor downstairs. His appearance had altered as much as Johnson's during the last few hours. His hair was on end, his face flushed, his forehead dotted with beads of perspiration. There was a peculiar fierceness in his eye, and about the lines of his mouth, a fighting look as befitted a man who for hours on end had been striving with the hungriest of foes for the most precious of prizes. But there was a sadness, too, as though his grim opponent had been overmastering him. He sat down and leaned his head upon his hand like a man who is fagged out.

"I thought it my duty to see you, Mr. Johnson, and to tell you that it is a very nasty case. Your wife's heart is not strong, and she has some symptoms which I do not like. What I wanted to say is that if you would like to have a second opinion I shall be very glad to meet anyone whom you might suggest."

Johnson was so dazed by his want of sleep and the evil news that he could hardly grasp the doctor's meaning. The other, seeing him hesitate, thought that he was considering the expense.

"Smith or Hawley would come for two guineas," said he. "But I think Pritchard of the City Road is the best man."

"Oh yes, bring the best man," cried Johnson.

"Pritchard would want three guineas. He is a senior man, you see."

"I'd give him all I have if he would pull her through. Shall I run for him?"

"Yes. Go to my house first and ask for the green baize bag. The assistant will give it to you. Tell him I want the A.C.E. mixture. Her heart is too weak for chloroform. Then go for Pritchard and bring him back with you."

It was heavenly for Johnson to have something to do and to feel that he was of some use to his wife. He ran swiftly to Bridport Place, his footfalls clattering through the silent streets, and the big, dark policemen turning their yellow funnels of light on him as he passed. Two tugs at the night-bell brought down a sleepy, half-clad assistant, who handed him a stoppered glass bottle and a cloth bag which contained something which clinked when you moved it. Johnson thrust the bottle into his pocket, seized the green bag, and pressing his hat firmly down ran as hard as he could set foot to ground until he was in the City Road and saw the name of Pritchard engraved in white upon a red ground. He bounded in triumph up the three steps which led to the door, and as he did so there was a crash behind him. His precious bottle was in fragments upon the pavement.

For a moment he felt as if it were his wife's body that was lying there. But the run had freshened his wits and he saw that the mischief might be repaired. He pulled vigorously at the night-bell.

"Well, what's the matter?" asked a gruff voice at his elbow. He started back and looked up at the windows, but there was no sign of life. He was approaching the bell again with the intention of pulling it, when a perfect roar burst from the wall.

"I can't stand shivering here all night," cried the voice. "Say who you are and what you want or I shut the tube."

Then for the first time Johnson saw that the end of a speaking-tube hung out of the wall just above the bell. He shouted up it—

"I want you to come with me to meet Doctor Miles at a confinement at once."

"How far?" shrieked the irascible voice.

"The New North Road, Hoxton."

"My consultation fee is three guineas, payable at the time."

"All right," shouted Johnson. "You are to bring a bottle of A.C.E. mixture with you."

"All right! Wait a bit!"

Five minutes later an elderly, hard-faced man with grizzled hair flung open the door. As he emerged a voice from somewhere in the shadows cried—

"Mind you take your cravat, John," and he impatiently growled something over his shoulder in reply.

The consultant was a man who had been hardened by a life of ceaseless labour, and who had been driven, as so many others have been, by the needs of his own increasing family to set the commercial before the philanthropic side of his profession. Yet beneath his rough crust he was a man with a kindly heart.

"We don't want to break a record," said he, pulling

up and panting after attempting to keep up with Johnson for five minutes. "I would go quicker if I could, my dear sir, and I quite sympathise with your anxiety, but really I can't manage it."

So Johnson, on fire with impatience, had to slow down until they reached the New North Road, when he ran ahead and had the door open for the doctor when he came. He heard the two meet outside the bedroom, and caught scraps of their conversation. "Sorry to knock you up—nasty case—decent people." Then it sank into a mumble and the door closed behind them.

Johnson sat up in his chair now, listening keenly, for he knew that a crisis must be at hand. He heard the two doctors moving about, and was able to distinguish the step of Pritchard, which had a drag in it, from the clean, crisp sound of the other's footfall. There was silence for a few minutes and then a curious, drunken, mumbling, sing-song voice came quavering up, very unlike anything which he had heard hitherto. At the same time a sweetish, insidious scent, imperceptible perhaps to any nerves less strained than his, crept down the stairs and penetrated into the room. The voice dwindled into a mere drone and finally sank away into silence, and Johnson gave a long sigh of relief, for he knew that the drug had done its work and that, come what might, there should be no more pain for the sufferer.

But soon the silence became even more trying to him than the cries had been. He had no clue now as to what was going on, and his mind swarmed with horrible possibilities. He rose and went to the bottom of the stairs again. He heard the clink of metal against metal, and the subdued murmur of the doctors' voices. Then he heard Mrs. Peyton say something, in a tone as of fear or expostulation, and again the doctors murmured together. For twenty minutes he stood there leaning against the wall, listening to the occasional rumbles of talk without being able to catch a word of it. And then of a sudden there rose out of the silence the strangest little piping cry, and Mrs. Peyton screamed out in her delight and the man ran into the parlour and flung himself down upon the horse-hair sofa, drumming his heels on it in his ecstasy.

But often the great cat Fate lets us go, only to clutch us again in a fiercer grip. As minute after minute passed and still no sound came from above save those thin, glutinous cries, Johnson cooled from his frenzy of joy, and lay breathless with his ears straining. They were moving slowly about. They were talking in subdued tones. Still minute after minute passing, and no word from the voice for which he listened. His nerves were dulled by his night of trouble, and he waited in limp wretchedness upon his sofa. There he still sat when the doctors came down to him—a bedraggled, miserable figure with his face grimy and his hair unkempt from his long vigil. He rose as they entered, bracing himself against the mantelpiece.

"Is she dead?" he asked.

"Doing well," answered the doctor.

And at the words that little conventional spirit which had never known until that night the capacity for fierce agony which lay within it, learned for the second time that there were springs of joy also which it had never tapped before. His impulse was to fall upon his knees, but he was shy before the doctors.

"Can I go up?"

"In a few minutes."

"I'm sure, doctor, I'm very—I'm very——" he grew inarticulate. "Here are your three guineas, Doctor Pritchard. I wish they were three hundred."

"So do I," said the senior man, and they laughed as they shook hands.

Johnson opened the shop door for them and heard their talk as they stood for an instant outside.

"Looked nasty at one time."

"Very glad to have your help."

"Delighted, I'm sure. Won't you step round and have a cup of coffee?"

"No, thanks. I'm expecting another case."

The firm step and the dragging one passed away to the right and the left. Johnson turned from the door still with that turmoil of joy in his heart. He seemed to be making a new start in life. He felt that he was a stronger and a deeper man. Perhaps all this suffering had an object then. It might prove to be a blessing both to his wife and to him. The very thought was one which he would have been incapable of conceiving twelve hours before. He was full of new emotions. If there had been a harrowing, there had been a planting, too.

"Can I come up?" he cried, and then, without waiting for an answer, he took the steps three at a time.

Mrs. Peyton was standing by a soapy bath with a bundle in her hands. From under the curve of a brown shawl there looked out at him the strangest little red face with crumpled features, moist, loose lips, and eyelids which quivered like a rabbit's nostrils. The weak neck had let the head topple over, and it rested upon the shoulder.

"Kiss it, Robert!" cried the grandmother. "Kiss your son!"

But he felt a resentment to the little, red, blinking creature. He could not forgive it yet for that long night of misery. He caught sight of a white face in the bed and he ran towards it with such love and pity as his speech could find no words for.

"Thank God it is over! Lucy dear, it was dreadful!"

"But I'm so happy now. I never was so happy in my life."

Her eyes were fixed upon the brown bundle.

"You mustn't talk," said Mrs. Peyton.

"But don't leave me," whispered his wife.

So he sat in silence with his hand in hers. The lamp was burning dim and the first cold light of dawn was breaking through the window. The night had been long and dark, but the day was the sweeter and the purer in consequence. London was waking up. The roar began to rise from the street. Lives had come and lives had gone, but the great machine was still working out its dim and tragic destiny.

61. *A Medical Document*

MEDICAL men are, as a class, very much too busy to take stock of singular situations or dramatic events. Thus it happens that the ablest chronicler of their experiences in our literature was a lawyer. A life spent in watching over deathbeds—or over birth-beds which are infinitely more trying—takes something from a man's sense of proportion, as constant strong waters might corrupt his palate. The overstimulated nerve ceases to respond. Ask the surgeon for his best experiences and he may reply that he has seen little that is remarkable, or break away into the technical. But catch him some night when the fire has spurted up and his pipe is reeking, with a few of his brother practitioners for company and an artful question or allusion to set him going. Then you will get some raw, green facts new plucked from the tree of life.

It is after one of the quarterly dinners of the Midland Branch of the British Medical Association. Twenty coffee cups, a dozen liqueur glasses, and a solid bank of blue smoke which swirls slowly along the high, gilded, ceiling gives a hint of a successful gathering. But the members have shredded off to their homes. The line of heavy, bulge-pocketed overcoats and of stethoscope-bearing top hats is gone from the hotel corridor. Round the fire in the sitting-room three medicos are still lingering, however, all smoking and arguing, while a fourth, who is a mere layman and young at that, sits back at the table. Under cover of an open journal he is writing furiously with a stylographic pen, asking a question in an innocent voice from time to time and so flickering up the conversation whenever it shows a tendency to wane.

The three men are all of that staid middle age which begins early and lasts late in the profession. They are none of them famous, yet each is of good repute, and a fair type of his particular branch. The portly man with the authoritative manner and the white, vitriol splash upon his cheek is Charley Manson, chief of the Wormley Asylum, and author of the brilliant monograph, "Obscure Nervous Lesions in the Unmarried." He always wears his collar high like that, since the half-successful attempt of a student of Revelations to cut his throat with a splinter of glass. The second, with the ruddy face and the merry brown eyes, is a general practitioner, a man of vast experience, who, with his three assistants and his five horses, takes twenty-five hundred a year in half-crown visits and shilling consultations out of the poorest quarter of a great city. That cheery face of Theodore Foster is seen at the side of a hundred sick-beds a day, and if he has one-third more names on his visiting list than in his cash-book he always promises himself that he will get level some day when a millionaire with a chronic complaint—the ideal combination—shall seek his services. The third, sitting on the right with his dress-shoes shining on the top of the fender, is Hargrave, the rising surgeon. His face has none of the broad humanity of Theodore Foster's, the eye is stern and critical, the mouth straight and severe, but there is strength and decision in every line of it, and it is nerve rather than sympathy which the patient demands when he is bad enough to come to Hargrave's door. He calls himself a jawman, "a mere jawman," as he modestly puts it, but in point of fact he is too young and too poor to confine himself to a speciality, and there is nothing surgical which Hargrave has not the skill and the audacity to do.

"Before, after, and during," murmurs the general practitioner in answer to some interpolation of the outsider's. "I assure you, Manson, one sees all sorts of evanescent forms of madness."

"Ah, puerperal!" throws in the other, knocking the curved, grey ash from his cigar. "But you had some case in your mind, Foster."

"Well, there was one only last week which was new to me. I had been engaged by some people of the name of Silcoe, When the trouble came round I went myself, for they would not hear of an assistant. The husband, who was a policeman, was sitting at the head of the bed on the farther side. 'This won't do,' said I. 'Oh yes, doctor, it must do,' said she. 'It's quite irregular, and he must go,' said I. 'It's that or nothing,' said she. 'I won't open my mouth or stir a finger the whole night,' said he. So it ended by my allowing him to remain, and there he sat for eight hours on end. She was very good over the matter, but every now and again *he* would fetch a hollow groan, and I noticed that he held his right hand just under the sheet all the time, where I had no doubt that it was clasped by her left. When it was all happily over, I looked at him and his face was the colour of this cigar ash, and his head had dropped on to the edge of the pillow. Of course I thought he had fainted with emotion, and I was just telling myself what I thought of myself for having been such a fool as to let him stay there, when suddenly I saw that the sheet over his hand was all soaked with blood; I whisked it down, and there was the fellow's wrist half cut through. The woman had one bracelet of a policeman's handcuff over her left wrist and the other round his right one. When she had been in pain she had twisted with all her strength and the iron had fairly eaten into the bone of the man's arm. 'Aye, doctor,' said she, when she saw I had noticed it. 'He's got to take his share as well as me. Turn and turn,' said she."

"Don't you find it a very wearing branch of the profession?" asks Foster after a pause.

"My dear fellow, it was the fear of it that drove me into lunacy work."

"Aye, and it has driven men into asylums who never found their way on to the medical staff. I was a very shy fellow myself as a student, and I know what it means."

"No joke that in general practice," says the alienist.

"Well, you hear men talk about it as though it were, but I tell you it's much nearer tragedy. Take some poor, raw, young fellow who has just put up his plate in a strange town. He has found it a trial all his life, perhaps, to talk to a woman about lawn tennis and church services. When a young man *is* shy he is shyer than any girl. Then down comes an anxious mother and consults him upon the most intimate family matters. 'I shall never go to that doctor again,' says she afterwards. 'His manner is so stiff and unsympathetic.' Unsympathetic! Why, the poor lad was struck dumb and paralysed. I have known general practitioners who were so shy that they could not bring themselves to ask the way in the street. Fancy what sensitive men like that must endure before they get broken into medical practice. And then they know that nothing is so catching as shyness, and that if they do not keep a face of stone, their patient will be covered with confusion. And so they keep their face of stone, and earn the reputation perhaps of having a heart to correspond. I suppose nothing would shake *your* nerve, Manson."

"Well, when a man lives year in year out among a thousand lunatics, with a fair sprinkling of homicidals among them, one's nerves either get set or shattered. Mine are all right so far."

"I was frightened once," says the surgeon. "It was when I was doing dispensary work. One night I had a call from some very poor people, and gathered from the few words they said that their child was ill.

When I entered the room I saw a small cradle in the corner. Raising the lamp I walked over and putting back the curtains I looked down at the baby. I tell you it was sheer Providence that I didn't drop that lamp and set the whole place alight. The head on the pillow turned, and I saw a face looking up at me which seemed to me to have more malignancy and wickedness than ever I had dreamed of in a nightmare. It was the flush of red over the cheek-bones, and the brooding eyes full of loathing of me, and of everything else, that impressed me. I'll never forget my start as, instead of the chubby face of an infant, my eyes fell upon this creature. I took the mother into the next room. 'What is it?' I asked. 'A girl of sixteen,' said she, and then throwing up her arms, 'Oh, pray God she may be taken!' The poor thing, though she spent her life in this little cradle, had great, long, thin limbs which she curled up under her. I lost sight of the case and don't know what became of it, but I'll never forget the look in her eyes."

"That's creepy," says Doctor Foster. "But I think one of my experiences would run it close. Shortly after I put up my plate I had a visit from a little hunch-backed woman, who wished me to come and attend to her sister in her trouble. When I reached the house, which was a very poor one, I found two other little hunch-backed women, exactly like the first, waiting for me in the sitting-room. Not one of them said a word, but my companion took the lamp and walked upstairs with her two sisters behind her, and me bringing up the rear. I can see those three queer shadows cast by the lamp upon the wall as clearly as I can see that tobacco pouch. In the room above was the fourth sister, a remarkably beautiful girl in evident need of my assistance. There was no wedding ring upon her finger. The three deformed sisters seated themselves round the room, like so many graven images, and all night not one of them opened her mouth. I'm not romancing, Hargrave; this is absolute fact. In the early morning a fearful thunderstorm broke out, one of the most violent I have ever known. The little garret burned blue with the lightning, and the thunder roared and rattled as if it were on the very roof of the house. It wasn't much of a lamp I had, and it was a queer thing when a spurt of lightning came to see those three twisted figures sitting round the walls, or to have the voice of my patient drowned by the booming of the thunder. By Jove, I don't mind telling you that there was a time when I nearly bolted from the room. All came right in the end, but I never heard the true story of the unfortunate beauty and her three crippled sisters."

"That's the worst of these medical stories," sighs the outsider. "They never seem to have an end."

"When a man is up to his neck in practice, my boy, he has no time to gratify his private curiosity. Things shoot across him and he gets a glimpse of them, only to recall them, perhaps, at some quiet moment like this. But I've always felt, Manson, that your line had as much of the terrible in it as any other."

"More," groans the alienist. "A disease of the body is bad enough, but this seems to be a disease of the soul. Is it not a shocking thing—a thing to drive a reasoning man into absolute Materialism—to think that you may have a fine, noble fellow with every divine instinct and that some little vascular change, the dropping, we will say, of a minute spicule of bone from the inner table of his skull on to the surface of his brain may have the effect of changing him to a filthy and pitiable creature with every low and debasing tendency? What a satire an asylum is upon the majesty of man, and no less upon the ethereal nature of the soul."

"Faith and hope," murmurs the general practitioner.

"I have no faith, not much hope, and all the charity I can afford," says the surgeon. "When theology squares itself with the facts of life I'll read it up."

"You were talking about cases," says the outsider, jerking the ink down into his stylographic pen.

"Well, take a common complaint which kills many thousands every year, like G.P., for instance."

"What's G.P.?"

"General practitioner," suggests the surgeon with a grin.

"The British public will have to know what G.P. is," says the alienist gravely. "It's increasing by leaps and bounds, and it has the distinction of being absolutely incurable. General paralysis is its full title, and I tell you it promises to be a perfect scourge. Here's a fairly typical case now which I saw last Monday week. A young farmer, a splendid fellow, surprised his friends by taking a very rosy view of things at a time when the whole country-side was grumbling. He was going to give up wheat, give up arable land, too, if it didn't pay, plant two thousand acres of rhododendrons and get a monopoly of the supply for Covent Garden—there was no end to his schemes, all sane enough but just a bit inflated. I called at the farm, not to see him, but on an altogether different matter. Something about the man's way of talking struck me and I watched him narrowly. His lip had a trick of quivering, his words slurred themselves together, and so did his handwriting when he had occasion to draw up a small agreement. A closer inspection showed me that one of his pupils was ever so little larger than the other. As I left the house his wife came after me. 'Isn't it splendid to see Job looking so well, doctor?' said she; 'he's that full of energy he can hardly keep himself quiet.' I did not say anything, for I had not the heart, but I knew that the fellow was as much condemned to death as though he were lying in the cell at Newgate. It was a characteristic case of incipient G.P."

"Good heavens!" cries the outsider. "My own lips tremble. I often slur my words. I believe I've got it myself."

Three little chuckles come from the front of the fire.

"There's the danger of a little medical knowledge to the layman."

"A great authority has said that every first year's student is suffering, in silent agony, from four diseases," remarks the surgeon. "One is heart disease, of course; another is cancer of the parotid. I forget the two other."

"Where does the parotid come in?"

"Oh, it's the last wisdom tooth coming through!"

"And what would be the end of that young farmer?" asks the outsider.

"Paresis of all the muscles, ending in fits, coma and death. It may be a few months, it may be a year or two. He was a very strong young man and would take some killing."

"By the way," says the alienist, "did I ever tell you about the first certificate I ever signed? I stood as near ruin then as a man could go."

"What was it, then?"

"I was in practice at the time. One morning a Mrs. Cooper called upon me and informed me that her husband had shown signs of delusions lately. They took the form of imagining that he had been in the army and had distinguished himself very much. As a matter of fact he was a lawyer and had never been out of England. Mrs. Cooper was of opinion that if I were to call it might alarm him, so it was agreed between us that she should send him up in the evening on some pretext to my consulting-room, which would give me the opportunity of having a chat with him and, if I were convinced of his insanity, of signing his certificate. Another doctor had already signed, so that it only needed my concurrence to have him placed under treatment. Well, Mr. Cooper arrived in the evening about half an hour before I had expected him, and consulted me as to some malarious symptoms from which he said that he suffered. According to his account he had just returned from the Abyssinian Campaign, and had been one of the first of the British forces to enter Magdala. No delusion could possibly be more marked, for he would talk of little else, so I filled in the papers without the slightest hesitation. When his wife arrived, after he had left, I put some questions to her to complete the form. 'What is his age ? ' I asked. 'Fifty,' said she. 'Fifty ! ' I cried. 'Why, the man I examined could not have been more than thirty ! ' And so it came out that the real Mr. Cooper had never called upon me at all, but that by one of those coincidences which take a man's breath away another Cooper, who really was a very distinguished young officer of artillery, had come in to consult me. My pen was wet to sign the paper when I discovered it," says Dr. Manson, mopping his forehead.

"We were talking about nerve just now," observes the surgeon. "Just after my qualifying I served in the Navy for a time, as I think you know. I was on the flag-ship on the West African Station, and I remember a singular example of nerve which came to my notice at that time. One of our small gunboats had gone up the Calabar river, and while there the surgeon died of coast fever. On the same day a man's leg was broken by a spar falling upon it, and it became quite obvious that it must be taken off above the knee if his life was to be saved. The young lieutenant who was in charge of the craft searched among the dead doctor's effects and laid his hands upon some chloroform, a hip-joint knife, and a volume of Grey's *Anatomy*. He had the man laid by the steward upon the cabin table, and with a picture of a cross section of the thigh in front of him he began to take off the limb. Every now and then, referring to the diagram, he would say : 'Stand by with the lashings, steward. There's blood on the chart about here.' Then he would jab with his knife until he cut the artery, and he and his assistant would tie it up before they went any further. In this way they gradually whittled the leg off, and upon my word they made a very excellent job of it. The man is hopping about the Portsmouth Hard at this day.

" It's no joke when the doctor of one of these isolated gunboats himself falls ill," continues the surgeon after a pause. " You might think it easy for him to prescribe for himself, but this fever knocks you down like a club, and you haven't strength left to brush a mosquito off your face. I had a touch of it at Lagos, and I know what I am telling you. But there was a chum of mine who really had a curious experience. The whole crew gave him up, and, as they had never had a funeral aboard the ship, they began rehearsing the forms so as to be ready. They thought that he was unconscious, but he swears he could hear every word that passed. 'Corpse comin' up the 'atchway!' cried the cockney sergeant of Marines. 'Present harms!' He was so amused, and so indignant, too, that he just made up his mind that he wouldn't be carried through that hatchway, and he wasn't, either."

" There's no need for fiction in medicine," remarks Foster, " for the facts will always beat anything you can fancy. But it has seemed to me sometimes that a curious paper might be read at some of these meetings about the uses of medicine in popular fiction."

" How?"

" Well, of what the folk die of, and what diseases are made most use of in novels. Some are worn to pieces, and others, which are equally common in real life, are never mentioned. Typhoid is fairly frequent, but scarlet fever is unknown. Heart disease is common, but then heart disease, as we know it, is usually the sequel of some foregoing disease, of which we never hear anything in the romance. Then there is the mysterious malady called brain fever, which always attacks the heroine after a crisis, but which is unknown under that name to the text-books. People when they are overexcited in novels fall down in a fit. In a fairly large experience I have never known anyone to do so in real life. The small complaints simply don't exist. Nobody ever gets shingles or quinsy, or mumps in a novel. All the diseases, too, belong to the upper part of the body. The novelist never strikes below the belt."

"I'll tell you what, Foster," says the alienist, "there is a side of life which is too medical for the general public and too romantic for the professional journals, but which contains some of the richest human materials that a man could study. It's not a pleasant side, I am afraid, but if it is good enough for Providence to create, it is good enough for us to try and understand. It would deal with strange outbursts of savagery and vice in the lives of the best men, curious momentary weaknesses in the record of the sweetest women, known but to one or two, and inconceivable to the world around. It would deal, too, with the singular phenomena of waxing and of waning manhood, and would throw a light upon those actions which have cut short many an honoured career and sent a man to a prison when he should have been hurried to a consulting-room. Of all evils that may come upon the sons of men, God shield us principally from that one!"

"I had a case some little time ago which was out of the ordinary," says the surgeon. "There's a famous beauty in London Society—I mention no names—who used to be remarkable a few seasons ago for the very low dresses which she would wear. She had the whitest of skins, and most beautiful of shoulders, so it was no wonder. Then gradually the frilling at her neck lapped upwards and upwards, until last year she astonished every one by wearing quite a high collar at a time when it was completely out of fashion. Well, one day this very woman was shown into my consulting-room. When the footman was gone she suddenly tore off the upper part of her dress. 'For God's sake do something for me!' she cried. Then I saw what the trouble was. A rodent ulcer was eating its way upwards, coiling on in its serpiginous fashion until the end of it was flush with her collar. The red streak of its trail was lost below the line of her bust. Year by year it had ascended and she had heightened her dress to hide it, until now it was about to invade her face. She had been too proud to confess her trouble, even to a medical man."

"And did you stop it?"

"Well, with zinc chloride I did what I could. But it may break out again. She was one of those beautiful white-and-pink creatures who are rotten with struma. You may patch, but you can't mend."

"Dear! dear! dear!" cries the general practitioner, with that kindly softening of the eyes which had endeared him to so many thousands. "I suppose we mustn't think ourselves wiser than Providence, but there are times when one feels that something is wrong in the scheme of things. I've seen some sad things in my life. Did I ever tell you that case where Nature divorced a most loving couple? He was a fine young fellow, an athlete and a gentleman, but he overdid athletics. You know how the force that controls us gives us a little tweak to remind us when we get off the beaten track. It may be a pinch on the great toe if we drink too much and work too little. Or it may be a tug on our nerves if we dissipate energy too much. With the athlete, of course, it's the heart or the lungs. He had bad phthisis and was sent to Davos. Well, as luck would have it, she developed rheumatic fever, which left her heart very much affected. Now, do you see the dreadful dilemma in which those poor people found themselves? When he came below 4,000 feet or so, his symptoms became terrible. She could come up about 2,500, and then her heart reached its limit. They had several interviews half-way down the valley, which left them nearly dead, and at last, the doctors had to absolutely forbid it. And so for four years they lived within three miles of each other and never met. Every morning he would go to a place which overlooked the chalet in which she lived and would wave a great white cloth and she answer from below. They could see each other quite plainly with their field-glasses, and they might have been in different planets for all their chance of meeting."

"And one at last died," says the outsider.

"No, sir. I'm sorry not to be able to clinch the story, but the man recovered and is now a successful stockbroker in Drapers Gardens. The woman, too, is the mother of a considerable family. But what are you doing there?"

"Only taking a note or two of your talk."

The three medical men laugh as they walk towards their overcoats.

"Why, we've done nothing but talk shop," says the general practitioner. "What possible interest can the public take in that?"

62. *The Surgeon Talks*

"MEN die of the diseases which they have studied most," remarked the surgeon, snipping off the end of a cigar with all his professional neatness and finish. "It's as if the morbid condition was an evil creature which, when it found itself closely hunted, flew at the throat of its pursuer. If you worry the microbes too much they may worry you. I've seen cases of it, and not necessarily in microbic diseases either. There was, of course, the well-known instance of Liston and the aneurism; and a dozen others that I could mention. You couldn't have a clearer case than that of poor old Walker of St. Christopher's. Not heard of it? Well, of course, it was a little before your time, but I wonder that it should have been forgotten. You youngsters are so busy in keeping up to the day that you lose a good deal that is interesting of yesterday.

"Walker was one of the best men in Europe on nervous disease. You must have read his little book on sclerosis of the posterior columns. It's as interesting as a novel, and epoch-making in its way. He worked like a horse, did Walker—huge consulting practice—hours a day in the clinical wards—constant original investigations. And then he enjoyed himself also. '*De mortuis*,' of course, but still it's an open secret among all who knew him. If he died at forty-five, he crammed eighty years into it. The marvel was that he could have held on so long at the pace at which he was going. But he took it beautifully when it came.

"I was his clinical assistant at the time. Walker was lecturing on locomotor ataxia to a wardful of youngsters. He was explaining that one of the early signs of the complaint was that the patient could not put his heels together with his eyes shut without staggering. As he spoke, he suited the action to the word. I don't suppose the boys noticed anything. I did, and so did he, though he finished his lecture without a sign.

"When it was over he came into my room and lit a cigarette.

"'Just run over my reflexes, Smith,' said he.

"There was hardly a trace of them left. I tapped away at his knee-tendon and might as well have tried to get a jerk out of that sofa-cushion. He stood with his eyes shut again, and he swayed like a bush in the wind.

"'So,' said he, 'it was not intercostal neuralgia after all.'

"Then I knew that he had had the lightning pains, and that the case was complete. There was nothing to say, so I sat looking at him while he puffed and puffed at the cigarette. Here he was, a man in the prime of life, one of the handsomest men in London, with money, fame, social success, everything at his feet, and now, without a moment's warning, he was told that inevitable death lay before him, a death accompanied by more refined and lingering tortures than if he were bound upon a Red Indian stake. He sat in the middle of the blue cigarette cloud with his eyes cast down, and the slightest little tightening of his lips. Then he rose with a motion of his arms, as one who throws off old thoughts and enters upon a new course.

"'Better put this thing straight at once,' said he. 'I must make some fresh arrangements. May I use your paper and envelopes?'

"He settled himself at my desk and he wrote half a dozen letters. It is not a breach of confidence to say that they were not addressed to his professional brothers. Walker was a single man, which means that he was not restricted to a single woman. When he had finished, he walked out of that little room of mine, leaving every hope and ambition of his life behind him. And he might have had another year of ignorance and peace if it had not been for the chance illustration in his lecture.

"It took five years to kill him, and he stood it well. If he had ever been a little irregular he atoned for it in that long martyrdom. He kept an admirable record of his own symptoms, and worked out the eye changes more fully than has ever been done. When the ptosis got very bad he would hold his eyelid up with one hand while he wrote. Then, when he could not co-ordinate his muscles to write, he dictated to his nurse. So died, in the odour of science, James Walker, æt. 45.

"Poor old Walker was very fond of experimental surgery, and he broke ground in several directions. Between ourselves, there may have been some more ground-breaking afterwards, but he did his best for his cases. You know M'Namara, don't you? He always wears his hair long. He lets it be understood that it comes from his artistic strain, but it is really to conceal the loss of one of his ears. Walker cut the other one off, but you must not tell Mac I said so.

"It was like this. Walker had a fad about the portio dura—the motor to the face, you know—and he thought paralysis of it came from a disturbance of the blood supply. Something else which counterbalanced that disturbance might, he thought, set it right again. We had a very obstinate case of Bell's paralysis in the wards, and had tried it with every conceivable thing, blistering, tonics, nerve-stretching, galvanism, needles, but all without result. Walker got it into his head that removal of the ear would increase the blood supply to the part, and he very soon gained the consent of the patient to the operation.

"Well, we did it at night. Walker, of course, felt that it was something of an experiment, and did not wish too much talk about it unless it proved successful. There were half a dozen of us there, M'Namara and I among the rest. The room was a small one, and in the centre was the narrow table, with a mackintosh over the pillow, and a blanket which extended almost to the floor on either side. Two candles, on a side-table near the pillow, supplied all the light. In came the patient, with one side of his face as smooth as a baby's, and the other all in a quiver with fright. He lay down, and the chloroform towel was placed over his face, while Walker threaded his needles in the candle-light. The chloroformist stood at the head of the table, and M'Namara was stationed at the side to control the patient. The rest of us stood by to assist.

"Well, the man was about half over when he fell into one of those convulsive flurries which come with the semi-unconscious stage. He kicked and plunged and struck out with both hands. Over with a crash went the little table which held the candles, and in an instant we were left in total darkness. You can think what a rush and a scurry there was, one to pick up the table, one to find the matches, and some to restrain the patient, who was still dashing himself about. He was held down by two dressers, the chloroform was pushed, and by the time the candles were relit, his incoherent, half-smothered shoutings had changed to a stertorous snore. His head was turned on the pillow and the towel was still kept over his face while the operation was carried through. Then the towel was withdrawn, and you can conceive our amazement when we looked upon the face of M'Namara.

"How did it happen? Why, simply enough. As the candles went over, the chloroformist had stopped for an instant and had tried to catch them. The patient, just as the light went out, had rolled off and under the table. Poor M'Namara, clinging frantically to him, had been dragged across it, and the chloroformist, feeling him there, had naturally clapped the towel across his mouth and nose. The others had secured him, and the more he roared and kicked the more they drenched him with chloroform. Walker was very nice about it, and made the most handsome apologies. He offered to do a plastic on the spot, and make as good an ear as he could, but M'Namara had had enough of it. As to the patient, we found him sleeping placidly under the table, with the ends of the blanket screening him on both sides. Walker sent M'Namara round his ear next day in a jar of methylated spirit, but Mac's wife was very angry about it, and it led to a good deal of ill-feeling.

"Some people say that the more one has to do with human nature, and the closer one is brought in contact with it, the less one thinks of it. I don't believe that those who know most would uphold that view. My own experience is dead against it. I was brought up in the miserable-mortal-clay school of theology, and yet here I am, after thirty years of intimate acquaintance with humanity, filled with respect for it. The evil lied commonly upon the surface. The deeper strata are good. A hundred times I have seen folk condemned to death as suddenly as poor Walker was. Sometimes it was to blindness or to mutilations which are worse than death. Men and women, they almost all took it beautifully, and some with such lovely unselfishness, and with such complete absorption in the thought of how their fate would affect others, that the man about town, or the frivolously-dressed woman had seemed to change into an angel before my eyes. I have seen deathbeds, too, of all ages and of all creeds and want of creeds. I never saw any of them shrink, save only one poor, imaginative young fellow, who had spent his blameless life in the strictest of sects. Of course, an exhausted frame is incapable of fear, as anyone can vouch who is told, in the midst of his sea-sickness, that the ship is going to the bottom. That is why I rate courage in the face of mutilation to be higher than courage when a wasting illness is fining away into death.

"Now, I'll take a case which I had in my own practice last Wednesday. A lady came in to consult me—the wife of a well-known sporting baronet. The husband had come with her, but remained, at her request, in the waiting-room. I need not go into details, but it proved to be a peculiarly malignant case of cancer. 'I knew it,' said she. 'How long have I to live?' 'I fear that it may exhaust your strength in a few months,' I answered. 'Poor old Jack!' said she. 'I'll tell him that it is not dangerous.' 'Why should you deceive him?' I asked. 'Well, he's very uneasy about it, and he is quaking now in the waiting-room. He has two old friends to dinner to-night, and I haven't the heart to spoil his evening. To-morrow will be time enough for him to learn the truth.' Out she walked, the brave little woman, and a moment later her husband, with his big, red face shining with joy came plunging into my room to shake me by the hand. No, I respected her wish and I did not undeceive him. I dare bet that evening was one of the brightest, and the next morning the darkest, of his life.

"It's wonderful how bravely and cheerily a woman can face a crushing blow. It is different with men. A man can stand it without complaining, but it knocks him dazed and silly all the same. But the woman does not lose her wits any more than she does her courage. Now, I had a case only a few weeks ago which would show you what I mean. A gentleman consulted me about his wife, a very beautiful woman. She had a small tubercular nodule upon her upper arm, according to him. He was sure that it was of no importance, but he wanted to know whether Devonshire or the Riviera would be the better for her. I examined her and found a frightful sarcoma of the bone, hardly showing upon the surface, but involving the shoulder-blade and clavicle as well as the humerus. A more malignant case I have never seen. I sent her out of the room and I told him the truth. What did he do? Why, he walked slowly round that room with his hands behind his back, looking with the greatest interest at the pictures. I can see him now, putting up his gold *pince-nez* and staring at them with perfectly vacant eyes, which told me that he saw neither them nor the wall behind them. 'Amputation of the arm?' he asked at last. 'And of the collar-bone and shoulder-blade,' said I. 'Quite so. The collar-bone and shoulder-blade,' he repeated, still staring about him with those lifeless eyes. It settled him. I don't believe he'll ever be the same man again. But the woman took it as bravely and brightly as could be, and she has done very well since. The mischief was so great that the arm snapped as we drew it from the night-dress. No, I don't think that there will be any return, and I have every hope of her recovery.

"The first patient is a thing which one remembers all one's life. Mine was commonplace, and the details are of no interest. I had a curious visitor, however, during the first few months after my plate went up. It was an elderly woman, richly dressed, with a wicker-work picnic basket in her hand. This she opened with the tears streaming down her face, and out there waddled the fattest, ugliest and mangiest little pug-dog that I have ever seen. 'I wish you to put him painlessly out of the world, doctor,' she cried. 'Quick, quick, or my resolution may give way.' She flung herself down, with hysterical sobs, upon the sofa. The less experienced a doctor is, the higher are his notions of professional dignity, as I need not remind you, my young friend, so I was about to refuse the commission with indignation, when I bethought me that, quite apart from medicine, we were gentleman and lady, and that she had asked me to do something for her which was evidently of the greatest possible importance in her eyes. I led off the poor little doggie, therefore, and with the help of a saucerful of milk and a few drops of prussic acid his exit was as speedy and painless as could be desired. 'Is it over?' she cried as I entered. It was really tragic to see how all the love which should have gone to husband and children had, in default of them, been centred upon this uncouth little animal. She left, quite broken down, in her carriage, and it was only after her departure that I saw an envelope sealed with a large red seal, and lying upon the blotting pad of my desk. Outside, in pencil, was written :—'I have no doubt that you would willingly have done this without a fee, but I insist upon your acceptance of the enclosed.' I opened it with some vague notions of an eccentric millionaire and a fifty-pound note, but all I found was a postal order for four and sixpence. The whole incident struck me as so whimsical that I laughed until I was tired. You'll find there's so much tragedy in a doctor's life, my boy, that he would not be able to stand it if it were not for the strain of comedy which comes every now and then to leaven it.

"And a doctor has very much to be thankful for also. Don't you ever forget it. It is such a pleasure to do a little good that a man should pay for the privilege instead of being paid for it. Still, of course, he has his home to keep up and his wife and children to support. But his patients are his friends—or they should be so. He goes from house to house, and his step and his voice are loved and welcomed in each. What could a man ask for more than that? And besides, he is forced to be a good man. It is impossible for him to be anything else. How can a man spend his whole life in seeing suffering bravely borne and yet remain a hard or a vicious man? It is a noble, generous, kindly profession, and you youngsters have got to see that it remains so."

63. *The Doctors of Hoyland*

DOCTOR JAMES RIPLEY was always looked upon as an exceedingly lucky dog by all of the profession who knew him. His father had preceded him in a practice in the village of Hoyland, in the north of Hampshire, and all was ready for him on the very first day that the law allowed him to put his name at the foot of a prescription. In a few years the old gentleman retired, and settled on the South Coast, leaving his son in undisputed possession of the whole country-side. Save for Doctor Horton, near Basingstoke, the young surgeon had a clear run of six miles in every direction, and took his fifteen hundred pounds a year, though, as is usual in country practices, the stable swallowed up most of what the consulting-room earned.

Doctor James Ripley was two-and-thirty years of age, reserved, learned, unmarried, with set, rather stern features, and a thinning of the dark hair upon the top of his head, which was worth quite a hundred a year to him. He was particularly happy in his management of ladies. He had caught the tone of bland sternness and decisive suavity which dominates without offending. Ladies, however, were not equally happy in their management of him. Professionally, he was always at their service. Socially, he was a drop of quicksilver. In vain the country mammas spread out their simple lures in front of him. Dances and picnics were not to his taste, and he preferred during his scanty leisure to shut himself up in his study, and to bury himself in Virchow's *Archives* and the professional journals.

Study was a passion with him, and he would have none of the rust which often gathers round a country practitioner. It was his ambition to keep his knowledge as fresh and bright as at the moment when he had stepped out of the examination hall. He prided himself on being able at a moment's notice to rattle off the seven ramifications of some obscure artery, or to give the exact percentage of any physiological compound. After a long day's work he would sit up half the night performing iridectomies and extractions upon the sheep's eyes sent in by the village butcher, to the horror of his housekeeper, who had to remove the debris next morning. His love for his work was the one fanaticism which found a place in his dry, precise nature.

It was the more to his credit that he should keep up to date in his knowledge, since he had no competition to force him to exertion. In the seven years during which he had practised in Hoyland three rivals had pitted themselves against him, two in the village itself and one in the neighbouring hamlet of Lower Hoyland. Of these one had sickened and wasted, being, as it was said, himself the only patient whom he had treated during his eighteen months of ruralising. A second had bought a fourth share of a Basingstoke practice, and had departed honourably, while a third had vanished one September night, leaving a gutted house and an unpaid drug bill behind him. Since then the district had become a monopoly, and no one had dared to measure himself against the established fame of the Hoyland doctor.

It was, then, with a feeling of some surprise and considerable curiosity that on driving through Lower Hoyland one morning he perceived that the new house at the end of the village was occupied, and that a virgin brass plate glistened upon the swinging gate which faced the high road. He pulled up his fifty-guinea chestnut mare and took a good look at it. "Verrinder Smith, M.D.," was printed across it in very neat, small lettering. The last man had had letters half a foot long, with a lamp like a fire-station. Doctor James Ripley noted the difference, and deduced from it that the new-comer might possibly prove a more formidable opponent. He was convinced of it that evening when he came to consult the current medical directory. By it he learned that Doctor Verrinder Smith was the holder of superb degrees, that he had studied with distinction at Edinburgh, Paris, Berlin, and Vienna, and finally that he had been awarded a gold medal and the Lee Hopkins scholarship for original research, in recognition of an exhaustive inquiry into the functions of the anterior spinal nerve roots. Doctor Ripley passed his fingers through his thin hair in bewilderment as he read his rival's record. What on earth could so brilliant a man mean by putting up his plate in a little Hampshire hamlet.

But Doctor Ripley furnished himself with an explanation to the riddle. No doubt Dr. Verrinder Smith had simply come down there in order to pursue some scientific research in peace and quiet. The plate was up as an address rather than as an invitation to patients. Of course, that must be the true explanation. In that case the presence of this brilliant neighbour would be a splendid thing for his own studies. He had often longed for some kindred mind, some steel on which he might strike his flint. Chance had brought it to him, and he rejoiced exceedingly.

And this joy it was which led him to take a step which was quite at variance with his usual habits. It is the custom for a new-comer among medical men to call first upon the older, and the etiquette upon the subject is strict. Doctor Ripley was pedantically exact on such points, and yet he deliberately drove over next day and called upon Doctor Verrinder Smith. Such a waiving of ceremony was, he felt, a gracious act upon his part, and a fit prelude to the intimate relations which he hoped to establish with his neighbour.

The house was neat and well appointed, and Doctor Ripley was shown by a smart maid into a dapper little consulting-room. As he passed in he noticed two or three parasols and a lady's sun-bonnet hanging in the hall. It was a pity that his colleague should be a married man. It would put them upon a different footing, and interfere with those long evenings of high scientific talk which he had pictured to himself. On the other hand, there was much in the consulting-room to please him. Elaborate instruments, seen more often in hospitals than in the houses of private practitioners, were scattered about. A sphygmograph stood upon the table and a gasometer-like engine, which was new to Doctor Ripley, in the corner. A book-case full of ponderous volumes in French and German, paper-covered for the most part, and varying in tint from the shell to the yolk of a duck's egg, caught his wandering eyes, and he was deeply absorbed in their titles when the door opened suddenly behind him. Turning round, he found himself facing a little woman, whose plain, palish face was remarkable only for a pair of shrewd, humorous eyes of a blue which had two shades too much green in it. She held a *pince-nez* in her left hand, and the doctor's card in her right.

"How do you do, Doctor Ripley?" said she.

"How do you do, madam?" returned the visitor. "Your husband is perhaps out?"

"I am not married," said she simply.

"Oh, I beg your pardon! I meant the doctor—Dr. Verrinder Smith."

"I am Doctor Verrinder Smith."

Doctor Ripley was so surprised that he dropped his hat and forgot to pick it up again.

"What!" he gasped, "the Lee Hopkins prizeman! You!"

He had never seen a woman doctor before, and his whole conservative soul rose up in revolt at the idea. He could not recall any Biblical injunction that the man should remain ever the doctor and the woman the nurse, and yet he felt as if a blasphemy had been committed. His face betrayed his feelings only too clearly.

"I am sorry to disappoint you," said the lady drily.

"You certainly have surprised me," he answered, picking up his hat.

"You are not among our champions, then?"

"I cannot say that the movement has my approval."

"And why?"

"I should much prefer not to discuss it."

"But I am sure you will answer a lady's question."

"Ladies are in danger of losing their privileges when they usurp the place of the other sex. They cannot claim both."

"Why should a woman not earn her bread by her brains?"

Doctor Ripley felt irritated by the quiet manner in which the lady cross-questioned him.

"I should much prefer not to be led into a discussion, Miss Smith."

"Doctor Smith," she interrupted.

"Well, Doctor Smith! But if you insist upon an answer, I must say that I do not think medicine a suitable profession for women and that I have a personal objection to masculine ladies."

It was an exceedingly rude speech, and he was ashamed of it the instant after he had made it. The lady, however, simply raised her eyebrows and smiled.

"It seems to me that you are begging the question," said she. "Of course, if it makes women masculine that *would* be a considerable deterioration."

It was a neat little counter, and Doctor Ripley, like a pinked fencer, bowed his acknowledgment.

"I must go," said he.

"I am sorry that we cannot come to some more friendly conclusion since we are to be neighbours," she remarked.

He bowed again, and took a step towards the door.

"It was a singular coincidence," she continued, "that at the instant that you called I was reading your paper on 'Locomotor Ataxia,' in the *Lancet*."

"Indeed," said he drily.

"I thought it was a very able monograph."

"You are very good."

"But the views which you attribute to Professor Pitres, of Bordeaux, have been repudiated by him."

"I have his pamphlet of 1890," said Doctor Ripley angrily.

"Here is his pamphlet of 1891." She picked it from among a litter of periodicals. "If you have time to glance your eye down this passage——"

Doctor Ripley took it from her and shot rapidly through the paragraph which she indicated. There was no denying that it completely knocked the bottom out of his own article. He threw it down, and with another frigid bow he made for the door. As he took the reins from the groom he glanced round and saw that the lady was standing at her window, and it seemed to him that she was laughing heartily.

All day the memory of this interview haunted him. He felt that he had come very badly out of it. She had showed herself to be his superior on his own pet subject. She had been courteous while he had been rude, self-possessed when he had been angry. And then, above all, there was her presence, her monstrous intrusion to rankle in his mind. A woman doctor had been an abstract thing before, repugnant but distant. Now she was there in actual practice, with a brass plate up just like his own, competing for the same patients. Not that he feared competition, but he objected to this lowering of his ideal of womanhood. She could not be more than thirty, and had a bright, mobile face, too. He thought of her humorous eyes, and of her strong, well-turned chin. It revolted him the more to recall the details of her education. A man, of course, could come through such an ordeal with all his purity, but it was nothing short of shameless in a woman.

But it was not long before he learned that even her competition was a thing to be feared. The novelty of her presence had brought a few curious invalids into her consulting-rooms, and, once there, they had been so impressed by the firmness of her manner and by the singular, new-fashioned instruments with which she tapped, and peered, and sounded, that it formed the core of their conversation for weeks afterwards. And soon there were tangible proofs of her powers upon the country-side. Farmer Eyton, whose callous ulcer had been quietly spreading over his shin for years back under a gentle régime of zinc ointment, was painted round with blistering fluid, and found, after three blasphemous nights, that his sore was stimulated into healing. Mrs. Crowder, who had always regarded the birthmark upon her second daughter Eliza as a sign of the indignation of the Creator at a third helping of raspberry tart which she had partaken of during a critical period, learned that, with the help of two galvanic needles, the mischief was not irreparable. In a month Doctor Verrinder Smith was known, and in two she was famous.

Occasionally, Doctor Ripley met her as he drove upon his rounds. She had started a high dog-cart, taking the reins herself, with a little tiger behind. When they met he invariably raised his hat with punctilious politeness, but the grim severity of his face showed how formal was the courtesy. In fact, his dislike was rapidly deepening into absolute detestation. "The unsexed woman," was the description of her which he permitted himself to give to those of his patients who still remained staunch. But, indeed, they were a rapidly-decreasing body, and every day his pride was galled by the news of some fresh defection. The lady had somehow impressed the country-folk with almost superstitious belief in her power, and from far and near they flocked to her consulting-room.

But what galled him most of all was, when she did something which he had pronounced to be impracticable. For all his knowledge he lacked nerve as an operator, and usually sent his worst cases up to London. The lady, however, had no weakness of the sort, and took everything that came in her way. It was agony to him to hear that she was about to straighten little Alec Turner's club-foot, and right at the fringe of the rumour came a note from his mother, the rector's wife, asking him if he would be so good as to act as chloroformist. It would be inhumanity to refuse, as there was no other who could take the place, but it was gall and wormwood to his sensitive nature. Yet, in spite of his vexation, he could not but admire the dexterity with which the thing was done. She handled the little wax-like foot so gently, and held the tiny tenotomy knife as an artist holds his pencil. One straight insertion, one snick of a tendon, and it was all over without a stain upon the white towel which lay beneath. He had never seen anything more masterly, and he had the honesty to say so, though her skill increased his dislike of her. The operation spread her fame still further at his expense, and self-preservation was added to his other grounds for detesting her. And this very detestation it was which brought matters to a curious climax.

One winter's night, just as he was rising from his lonely dinner, a groom came riding down from Squire Faircastle's, the richest man in the district, to say that his daughter had scalded her hand, and that medical help was needed on the instant. The coachman had ridden for the lady doctor, for it mattered nothing to the Squire who came as long as it were speedily. Doctor Ripley rushed from his surgery with the determination that she should not effect an entrance into this stronghold of his if hard driving on his part could prevent it. He did not even wait to light his lamps, but sprang into his gig and flew off as fast as hoof could rattle. He lived rather nearer to the Squire's than she did, and was convinced that he could get there well before her.

And so he would but for that whimsical element of chance, which will for ever muddle up the affairs of this world and dumbfound the prophets. Whether it came from the want of his lights, or from his mind being full of the thoughts of his rival, he allowed too little by half a foot in taking the sharp turn upon the Basingstoke road.

The empty trap and the frightened horse clattered away into the darkness, while the Squire's groom crawled out of the ditch into which he had been shot. He struck a match, looked down at his groaning companion, and then, after the fashion of rough, strong men when they see what they have not seen before, he was very sick.

The doctor raised himself a little on his elbow in the glint of the match. He caught a glimpse of something white and sharp bristling through his trouser-leg half-way down the shin.

"Compound!" he groaned. "A three months' job," and fainted.

When he came to himself the groom was gone, for he had scudded off to the Squire's house for help, but a small page was holding a gig-lamp in front of his injured leg, and a woman, with an open case of polished instruments gleaming in the yellow light, was deftly slitting up his trouser with a crooked pair of scissors.

"It's all right, doctor," said she soothingly. "I am so sorry about it. You can have Doctor Horton to-morrow, but I am sure you will allow me to help you to-night. I could hardly believe my eyes when I saw you by the roadside."

"The groom has gone for help," groaned the sufferer.

"When it comes we can move you into the gig. A little more light, John! So! Ah, dear, dear, we shall have laceration unless we reduce this before we move you. Allow me to give you a whiff of chloroform, and I have no doubt that I can secure it sufficiently to——"

Doctor Ripley never heard the end of that sentence. He tried to raise a hand and to murmur something in protest, but a sweet smell was in his nostrils, and a sense of rich peace and lethargy stole over his jangled nerves. Down he sank, through clear, cool water, ever down and down into the green shadows beneath, gently, without effort, while the pleasant chiming of a great belfry rose and fell in his ears. Then he rose again, up and up, and ever up, with a terrible tightness about his temples, until at last he shot out of those green shadows and was in the light once more. Two bright, shining, golden spots gleamed before his dazed eyes. He blinked and blinked before he could give a name to them. They were only the two brass balls at the end posts of his bed, and he was lying in his own little room, with a head like a cannon ball, and a leg like an iron bar. Turning his eyes, he saw the calm face of Doctor Verrinder Smith looking down at him.

"Ah, at last!" said she. "I kept you under all the way home, for I knew how painful the jolting would be. It is in good position now with a strong side splint. I have ordered a morphia draught for you. Shall I tell your groom to ride for Doctor Horton in the morning?"

"I should prefer that you should continue the case," said Doctor Ripley feebly, and then, with a half-hysterical laugh—"You have all the rest of the parish as patients, you know, so you may as well make the thing complete by having me also."

It was not a very gracious speech, but it was a look of pity and not of anger which shone in her eyes as she turned away from his bedside.

Doctor Ripley had a brother, William, who was assistant surgeon at a London hospital, and who was down in Hampshire within a few hours of his hearing of the accident. He raised his brows when he heard the details.

"What! You are pestered with one of those!" he cried.

"I don't know what I should have done without her."

"I've no doubt she's an excellent nurse."

"She knows her work as well as you or I."

"Speak for yourself, James," said the London man with a sniff. "But apart from that, you know that the principle of the thing is all wrong."

"You think there is nothing to be said on the other side?"

"Good heavens! do you?"

"Well, I don't know. It struck me during the night that we may have been a little narrow in our views."

"Nonsense, James. It's all very fine for women to win prizes in the lecture-room, but you know as well as I do that they are no use in an emergency. Now I warrant that this woman was all nerves when she was setting your leg. That reminds me that I had better just take a look at it and see that it is all right."

"I would rather that you did not undo it," said the patient. "I have her assurance that it is all right."

Brother William was deeply shocked.

"Of course, if a woman's assurance is of more value than the opinion of the assistant surgeon of a London hospital, there is nothing more to be said," he remarked.

"I should prefer that you did not touch it," said the patient firmly, and Doctor William went back to London that evening in a huff.

The lady, who had heard of his coming, was much surprised on learning his departure.

"We had a difference upon a point of professional etiquette," said Doctor James, and it was all the explanation he would vouchsafe.

For two long months Doctor Ripley was brought in contact with his rival every day, and he learned many things which he had not known before. She was a charming companion, as well as a most assiduous doctor. Her short presence during the long, weary day was like a flower in a sand waste. What interested him was precisely what interested her, and she could meet him at every point upon equal terms. And yet under all her learning and her firmness ran a sweet, womanly nature, peeping out in her talk, shining in her greenish eyes, showing itself in a thousand subtle ways which the dullest of men could read. And he, though a bit of a prig and a pedant, was by no means dull, and had honesty enough to confess when he was in the wrong.

"I don't know how to apologise to you," he said in his shamefaced fashion one day, when he had progressed so far as to be able to sit in an arm-chair with his leg upon another one; "I feel that I have been quite in the wrong."

"Why, then?"

"Over this woman question. I used to think that a woman must inevitably lose something of her charm if she took up such studies."

"Oh, you don't think they are necessarily unsexed, then?" she cried, with a mischievous smile.

"Please don't recall my idiotic expression."

"I feel so pleased that I should have helped in changing your views. I think that it is the most sincere compliment that I have ever had paid me."

"At any rate, it is the truth," said he, and was happy all night at the remembrance of the flush of pleasure which made her pale face look quite comely for the instant.

For, indeed, he was already far past the stage when he would acknowledge her as the equal of any other woman. Already he could not disguise from himself that she had become the one woman. Her dainty skill, her gentle touch, her sweet presence, the community of their tastes, had all united to hopelessly upset his previous opinions. It was a dark day for him now when his convalescence allowed her to miss a visit, and darker still that other one which he saw approaching when all occasion for her visits would be at an end. It came round at last, however, and he felt that his whole life's fortune would hang upon the issue of that final interview. He was a direct man by nature, so he laid his hand upon hers as it felt for his pulse, and he asked her if she would be his wife.

"What, and unite the practices?" said she.

He started in pain and anger.

" Surely you do not attribute any such base motive to me ! " he cried. " I love you as unselfishly as ever a woman was loved."

" No, I was wrong. It was a foolish speech," said she, moving her chair a little back, and tapping her stethoscope upon her knee. " Forget that I ever said it. I am so sorry to cause you any disappointment, and I appreciate most highly the honour which you do me, but what you ask is quite impossible."

With another woman he might have urged the point, but his instincts told him that it was quite useless with this one. Her tone of voice was conclusive. He said nothing, but leaned back in his chair a stricken man.

" I am so sorry," she said again. " If I had known what was passing in your mind I should have told you earlier that I intend to devote my life entirely to science. There are many women with a capacity for marriage, but few with a taste for biology. I will remain true to my own line, then. I came down here while waiting for an opening in the Paris Physiological Laboratory. I have just heard that there is a vacancy for me there, and so you will be troubled no more by my intrusion upon your practice. I have done you an injustice just as you did me one. I thought you narrow and pedantic, with no good quality. I have learned during your illness to appreciate you better, and the recollection of our friendship will always be a very pleasant one to me."

And so it came about that in a very few weeks there was only one doctor in Hoyland. But folks noticed that the one had aged many years in a few months, that a weary sadness lurked always in the depths of his blue eyes, and that he was less concerned than ever with the eligible young ladies whom chance, or their careful country mammas, placed in his way.

64. *Crabbe's Practice*

I WONDER how many men remember Tom Waterhouse Crabbe, student of medicine in this city. He was a man whom it was not easy to forget if you had once come across him. Geniuses are more commonly read about than seen, but one could not speak five minutes with Crabbe without recognising that he had inherited some touch of that subtle, indefinable essence. There was a bold originality in his thought, and a convincing earnestness in his mode of expressing it, which pointed to something higher than mere cleverness. He studied spasmodically and irregularly, yet he was one of the first men—certainly the most independent thinker—of his year. Poor Crabbe—there was something delightfully original even in his mistakes. I can remember how he laboriously explained to his examiner that the Spanish fly *grew* in Spain. And how he gave five drops of Sabin oil credit for producing that state which it is usually believed to rectify.

Crabbe was not at all the type of man whom we usually associate with the word "genius." He was not pale nor thin, neither was his hair of abnormal growth. On the contrary he was a powerfully built, square-shouldered fellow, full of vitality, with a voice like a bull and a laugh that could be heard across the Meadows. A muscular Christian too, and one of the best Rugby forwards in Edinburgh.

I remember my first meeting with Crabbe. It gave me a respect both for his cool reasoning powers and for his courage. It was at one of the Bulgarian Atrocity meetings held in Edinburgh in '78. The hall was densely packed and the ventilation defective, so that I was not sorry to find that owing to my lateness I was unable to get any place, and had to stand in the doorway. Leaning against the wall there I could both enjoy the cool air and hear the invectives which speaker after speaker was hurling at the Conservative ministry. The audience seemed enthusiastically unanimous. A burst of cheering hailed every argument and sarcasm. There was not one dissentient voice. The speaker paused to moisten his lips, and there was a silence over the hall. Then a clear voice rose from the middle of it: "All very fine, but what did Gladstone——" There was a howl of execration and yells of "Turn him out!" But the voice was still audible. "What did Gladstone do in '63?" it demanded. "Turn him out. Show him out of the window! Put him out!" There was a perfect hurricane of threats and abuse. Men sprang upon the benches shaking their sticks and peering over each other's shoulders to get a glimpse of the daring Conservative. "What did Gladstone do in '63?" roared the voice; "I insist upon being answered." There was another howl of execration, a great swaying of the crowd, and an eddy in the middle of it. Then the mass of people parted and a man was borne out kicking and striking, and after a desperate resistance was precipitated down the stairs.

As the meeting became somewhat monotonous after this little divertisement, I went down into the street to cool myself. There was my inquisitive friend leaning up against a lamp-post with his coat torn to shreds and a pipe in his mouth. Recognising him by his cut as being a medical student, I took advantage of the freemasonry which exists between members of that profession.

"Excuse me," I said, "you are a medical, aren't you?"

"Yes," he said; "Thomas Crabbe, a 'Varsity man."

"My name is Barton," I said. "Pardon my curiosity, but would you mind telling me what Gladstone *did* do in '63?"

"My dear chap," said Crabbe, taking my arm and marching up the street with me, "I haven't the remotest idea in the world. You see, I was confoundedly hot and I wanted a smoke, and there seemed no chance of getting out, for I was jammed up right in the middle of the hall, so I thought I'd just make them carry me out; and I did—not a bad idea, was it? If you have nothing better to do, come up to my digs and have some supper."

"Certainly," said I; and that was the foundation of my friendship with Thomas Crabbe.

Crabbe took his degree a year before I did, and went down to a large port in England with the intention of setting up there. A brilliant career seemed to lie before him, for besides his deep knowledge of medicine, acquired in the most practical school in the world, he had that indescribable manner which gains a patient's confidence at once. It is curious how seldom the two are united. That charming doctor, my dear madam, who pulled young Charley through the measles so nicely, and had such a pleasant manner and such a clever face, was a noted duffer at college and the laughing-stock of his year. While poor little Doctor Grinder whom you snubbed so, and who seemed so nervous and didn't know where to put his hands, he won a gold medal for original research and was as good a man as his professors. After all, it is generally the outside case, not the inside works, which is noticed in this world.

Crabbe went down with his young degree, and a still younger wife, to settle in this town, which we will call Brisport. I was acting as assistant to a medical man in Manchester, and heard little from my former friend, save that he had set up in considerable style, and was making a bid for a high-class practice at once. I read one most deep and erudite paper in a medical journal, entitled "Curious Development of a Discopherous Bone in the Stomach of a Duck," which emanated from his pen, but beyond this and some remarks on the embryology of fishes he seemed strangely quiet.

One day to my surprise I received a telegram from

Mrs. Crabbe begging me to run down to Brisport and see her husband, as he was far from well. Having obtained leave of absence from my principal, I started by the next train, seriously anxious about my friend. Mrs. Crabbe met me at the station. She told me Tom was getting very much broken down by continued anxiety; the expenses of keeping up his establishment were heavy, and patients were few and far between. He wished my advice and knowledge of practical work to guide him in this crisis.

I certainly found Crabbe altered very much for the worse. He looked gaunt and cadaverous, and much of his old reckless joyousness had left him, though he brightened up wonderfully on seeing an old friend.

After dinner the three of us held a solemn council of war, in which he laid before me all his difficulties. "What in the world am I to do, Barton?" he said. "If I could make myself known it would be all right, but no one seems to look at my door-plate, and the place is overstocked with doctors. I believe they think I am a D.D. I wouldn't mind if these other fellows were good men, but they are not. They are all antiquated old fogies at least half a century behind the day. Now there is old Markham, who lives in that brick house over there and does most of the practice in the town. I'll swear he doesn't know the difference between locomotor ataxia and a hypodermic syringe, but he is known, so they flock into his surgery in a manner which is simply repulsive. And Davidson down the road, he is only an L.S.A. Talked about epispastic paralysis at the Society the other night—confused it with liquor epispasticus, you know. Yet that fellow makes a pound to my shilling."

"Get your name known and write," said I.

"But what on earth am I to write about?" asked Crabbe. "If a man has no cases, how in the world is he to describe them? Help yourself and pass the bottle."

"Couldn't you invent a case just to raise the wind?"

"Not a bad idea," said Crabbe thoughtfully. "By the way, did you see my 'Discopherous Bone in a Duck's Stomach'?"

"Yes; it seemed rather good."

"Good, I believe you! Why, man, it was a domino which the old duck had managed to gorge itself with. It was a perfect godsend. Then I wrote about embryology of fishes because I knew nothing about it and reasoned that ninety-nine men in a hundred would be in the same boat. But as to inventing whole cases, it seems rather daring, does it not?"

"A desperate disease needs desperate remedies," said I. "You remember old Hobson at college. He writes once a year to the British Medical and asks if any correspondent can tell him how much it costs to keep a horse in the country. And then he signs himself in the Medical Register as 'The contributor of several unostentatious queries and remarks to scientific papers!'"

It was quite a treat to hear Crabbe laugh with his old student guffaw. "Well, old man," he said, "we'll talk it over to-morrow. We mustn't be selfish and forget that you are a visitor here. Come along out, and see the beauties (save the mark!) of Brisport." So saying he donned a funereal coat, a pair of spectacles, and a hat with a desponding brim, and we spent the remainder of the evening roaming about and discussing mind and matter.

We had another council of war next day. It was a Sunday, and as we sat in the window, smoking our pipes and watching the crowded street, we brooded over many plans for gaining notoriety.

"I've done Bob Sawyer's dodge," said Tom despondingly. "I never go to church without rushing out in the middle of the sermon, but no one knows who I am, so it is no good. I had a nice slide in front of the door last winter for three weeks, and used to give it a polish up after dusk every night. But there was only one man ever fell on it, and he actually limped right across the road to Markham's surgery. Wasn't that hard lines?"

"Very hard indeed," said I.

"Something might be done with orange peel," continued Tom, "but it looks so awfully bad to have the whole pavement yellow with peel in front of a doctor's house."

"It certainly does," I agreed.

"There was one fellow came in with a cut head one night," said Tom, "and I sewed him up, but he had forgotten his purse. He came back in a week to have the stitches taken out, but without the money. That man is going about to this day, Jack, with half a yard of my catgut in him—and in him it'll stay until I see the coin."

"Couldn't we get up some incident," said I, "which would bring your name really prominently before the public?"

"My dear fellow, that's exactly what I want. If I could get my name into the *Brisport Chronicle* it would be worth five hundred a year to me. There's a family connection, you know, and people only want to realise that I am here. But how am I to do it unless by brawling in the street or by increasing my family? Now, there was the excitement about the discopherous bone. If Huxley or some of these fellows had taken the matter up it might have been the making of me. But they took it all in with a disgusting complacency as if it was the most usual thing in the world and dominoes were the normal food of ducks. I'll tell you what I'll do," he continued, moodily eyeing his fowls. "I'll puncture the floors of their fourth ventricles and present them to Markham. You know that makes them ravenous, and they'd eat him out of house and home in time. Eh, Jack?"

"Look here, Thomas," said I, "you want your name in the papers—is that it?"

"That's about the state of the case."

"Well, by Jove, you shall have it."

"Eh? Why? How?"

"There's a pretty considerable crowd of people outside, isn't there, Tom?" I continued. "They are coming out of church, aren't they? If there was an accident now it would make some noise."

"I say, you're not going to let rip among them with a shot gun, are you, in order to found a practice for me?"

"No, not exactly. But how would this read in to-morrow's *Chronicle*?—'Painful occurrence in George Street.—As the congregation were leaving George Street Cathedral after the morning service, they were horrified to see a handsome, fashionably dressed gentleman stagger and fall senseless upon the pavement. He was taken up and carried writhing in terrible convulsions into the surgery of the well-known practitioner, Doctor Crabbe, who had been promptly upon the spot. We are happy to state that the fit rapidly passed off, and that, owing to the skilful attention which he received, the gentleman, who is a distinguished visitor in our city, was able to regain his hotel and is now rapidly becoming convalescent.' How would that do, eh?"

"Splendid, Jack—splendid!"

"Well, my boy, I'm your fashionably dressed stranger, and I promise you they won't carry me into Markham's."

"My dear fellow, you are a treasure—you won't mind my bleeding you?"

"Bleeding me, confound you! Yes, I do very much mind."

"Just opening a little vein," pleaded Tom.

"Not a capillary," said I. "Now, look here; I'll throw up the whole business unless you give me your word to behave yourself. I don't draw the line at brandy."

"Very well, brandy be it," grumbled Tom.

"Well, I'm off," said I. "I'll go into the fit against your garden gate."

"All right, old man."

"By the way, what sort of a fit would you like? I could give you either an epileptic or an apoplectic easily, but perhaps you'd like something more ornate—a catalepsy or a trade spasm, maybe—with miner's nystagmus or something of that kind?"

"Wait a bit till I think," said Tom, and he sat puffing at his pipe for five minutes. "Sit down again, Jack," he continued. "I think we could do something better than this. You see, a fit isn't a very deadly thing, and if I did bring you through one there would be no credit in it. If we are going to work this thing, we may as well work it well. We can only do it once. It wouldn't do for the same fashionably dressed stranger to be turning up a second time. People would begin to smell a rat."

"So they would," said I; "but hang it, you can't expect me to tumble off the cathedral spire, in order that you may hold an inquest on my remains! You may command me in anything reasonable, however. What shall it be?"

Tom seemed lost in thought. "Can you swim?" he said presently.

"Fairly well."

"You could keep yourself afloat for five minutes?"

"Yes, I could do that."

"You're not afraid of water?"

"I'm not much afraid of anything."

"Then come out," said Tom, "and we'll go over the ground."

I couldn't get one word out of him as to his intentions, so I trotted along beside him, wondering what in the wide world he was going to do. Our first stoppage was at a small dock which is crossed by a swinging iron bridge. He hailed an amphibious man with top-boots. "Do you keep rowing-boats and let them out?" he asked.

"Yes, sir," said the man.

"Then, good day," and to the boatman's profound and audible disgust we set off at once in the other direction.

Our next stoppage was at the Jolly Mariner's Arms. Did they keep beds? Yes, they kept beds. We then proceeded to the chemist's. Did he keep a galvanic battery? Once again the answer was in the affirmative, and with a satisfied smile Tom Crabbe headed for home once more, leaving some very angry people behind him.

That evening, over a bowl of punch, he revealed his plan—and the council of three revised it, modified it, and ended by adopting it, with the immediate result that I at once changed my quarters to the Brisport Hotel.

I was wakened next day by the sun streaming in at my bedroom window. It was a glorious morning. I sprang out of bed and looked at my watch. It was nearly nine o'clock. "Only an hour," I muttered, "and nearly a mile to walk," and proceeded to dress with all the haste I could. "Well," I soliloquised as I sharpened my razor, "if old Tom Crabbe doesn't get his name in the papers to-day, it isn't my fault. I wonder if any friend would do as much for me!" I finished my toilet, swallowed a cup of coffee and sallied out.

Brisport seemed unusually lively this morning. The streets were crowded with people. I wormed my way down Waterloo Street, through the old Square and past Crabbe's house. The cathedral bells were chiming ten o'clock as I reached the above-mentioned little dock with the iron swinging bridge. A man was standing on the bridge leaning over the balustrades. There was no mistaking the heart-broken hat rim and the spectacles of Thomas Waterhouse Crabbe, M.B.

I passed him without sign of recognition, dawdled a little on the quay, and then sauntered down to the boathouse. Our friend of yesterday was standing at the door with a short pipe in his mouth.

"Could I have a boat for an hour?" I asked.

He beamed all over. "One minute, sir," he said, "an' I'll get the sculls. Would you want me to row you, sir?"

"Yes, you'd better," I replied.

He bustled about, and in a short time managed to launch a leaky-looking old tub, into which he stepped, while I squatted down in the sheets.

"Take me round the docks," I said. "I want to have a look at the shipping."

"Aye, aye, sir," said he, and away we went, and paddled about the docks for the best part of an hour. At the end of that time we turned back and pulled up to the little quay from which we had started. It was past eleven now and the place was crowded with people. Half Brisport seemed to have concentrated round the iron bridge. The melancholy hat was still visible.

"Shall I pull in, sir?" asked the boatman.

"Give me the sculls," said I. "I want a bit of exercise—let us change places," and I stood up.

"Take care, sir!" yelled the boatman as I gave a stagger. "Look out!" and he made a frantic grab at me, but too late, for with a melodramatic scream I reeled and fell over into the Brisport dock.

I hardly realised what it was I was going to do until I had done it. It was not a pleasant feeling to have the thick, clammy water closing over one's head. I struck the bottom with my feet, and shot up again to the surface. The air seemed alive with shouts. "Heave a rope!" "Where's a boat-hook!" "Catch him!" "There he is!" The boatman managed to hit me a smart blow on the head with something, an oar, I fancy, and I went down again, but not before I had got my lungs well filled with air. I came up again and my top-booted friend seized me by the hair of my head as if he would tear my scalp off. "Don't struggle!" he yelled, "and I'll save you yet." But I shook him off, and took another plunge. There was no resisting him next time, however, for he got a boat-hook into my collar, and though I kept my head under water as long as possible I was ignominiously hauled to land.

There I lay on the hard stones of the quay, feeling very much inclined to laugh, but looking, no doubt, very blue and ghastly. "He's gone, poor chap!" said someone. "Send for a doctor." "Run, run to Markham." "Quite dead." "Turn him upside down." "Feel his pulse." "Slap him on the back."

"Stop," said a solemn voice—"stop! Can I be of any assistance? I am a medical man. What has occurred?"

"A man drowned," cried a score of voices. "Stand back, make a ring—room for the doctor!"

"My name is Doctor Crabbe. Dear me, poor young gentleman! Drop his hand," he roared at a man who was making for my pulse. "I tell you in such a state the least pressure or impediment to the arterial circulation might prove fatal."

To save my life I couldn't help giving a very audible, inward chuckle at Tom's presence of mind. There was a murmur of surprise among the crowd. Tom solemnly took off his hat. "The death rattle!" he whispered. "The young soul has flown—yet perchance science may yet recall it. Bear him up to the tavern."

A shutter was brought, I was solemnly hoisted on to the top of it, and the melancholy cortège passed along the quay, the corpse being really the most cheerful member of the company.

We got to the Mariner's Arms and I was stripped and laid in the best bed. The news of the accident seemed to have spread, for there was a surging crowd in the street, and the staircase was thronged with people. Tom would only admit about a dozen of the more influential of the townspeople into the room, but issued bulletins out of the window every five minutes to the crowd below.

"Quite dead," I heard him roar. "Respiration has

ceased—no pulsation—but we still persevere, it is our duty."

"Shall I bring brandy?" said the landlady.

"Yes, and towels, and a hip bath and a basin—but the brandy first."

This sentiment met with the hearty approbation of the corpse.

"Why, he's drinking it," said the landlady, as she applied the glass to my lips.

"Merely an instance of a reflex, automatic action," said Tom. "My good woman, any corpse will drink brandy if you only apply it to the glossopharyngeal tract. Stand aside and we will proceed to try Marshall Hall's method of resuscitation."

The citizens stood round in a solemn ring, while Tom stripped off his coat and, climbing on the bed, proceeded to roll me about in a manner which seemed to dislocate every bone in my body.

"Hang it, man, stop!" I growled, but he only paused to make a dart for the window and yell out "No sign of life," and then fell upon me with greater energy than ever. "We will now try Sylvestre's method," he said, when the perspiration was fairly boiling out of him; and with that he seized me again, and performed a series of evolutions even more excruciating than the first. "It is hopeless!" he said at last, stopping and covering my head reverently with the bedclothes. "Send for the coroner! He has gone to a better land. Here is my card," he continued to an inspector of police who had arrived. "Doctor Crabbe of George Street. You will see that the matter is accurately reported. Poor young man!" And Tom drew his handkerchief across his eyes and walked towards the door, while a groan of sympathy rose from the crowd outside.

He had his hand upon the handle when a thought seemed to strike him, and he turned back. "There is yet a possible hope," he said, "we have not tried the magical effects of electricity—that subtle power, next of kin to nervous force. Is there a chemist's near?"

"Yes, doctor, there's Mr. McLagan just round the corner."

"Then run! run! A human life trembles in the balance—get his strongest battery, quick!" And away went half the crowd racing down the street and tumbling over each other in the effort to be first at Mr. McLagan's. They came back very red and hot, and one of them bore a shining, brown mahogany box in his arms which contained the instrument in question.

"Now, gentlemen," said Tom, "I believe I may say that I am the first practitioner in Great Britain who has applied electricity to this use. In my student days I have seen the learned Rokilansky of Vienna employ it in some such way. I apply the negative pole over the solar plexus, while the positive I place on the inner side of the patella. I have seen it produce surprising effects; it may again in this case."

It certainly did. Whether it was an accident or whether Tom's innate reckless devilry got the better of him I cannot say. He himself always swore that it was an accident, but at any rate he sent the strongest current of a most powerful battery rattling and crashing through my system. I gave one ear-splitting yell and landed with a single bound into the middle of the room. I was charged with electricity like a Leyden jar. My very hair bristled with it.

"You confounded idiot!" I shouted, shaking my fist in Tom's face. "Isn't it enough to dislocate every bone in my body with your ridiculous resuscitations without ruining my constitution with this thing?" and I gave a vicious kick at the mahogany box. Never was there such a stampede! The inspector of police and the correspondent of the *Chronicle* sprang down the staircase, followed by the twelve respectable citizens. The landlady crawled under the bed. A lodger who was nursing her baby while she conversed with a neighbour in the street below let the child drop upon her friend's head. In fact Tom might have founded the nucleus of a practice there and then. As it was, his usual presence of mind carried him through. "A miracle!" he yelled from the window. "A miracle! Our friend has been brought back to us; send for a cab." And then *sotto voce*, "For goodness' sake, Jack, behave like a Christian and crawl into bed again. Remember the landlady is in the room and don't go prancing about in your shirt."

"Hang the landlady," said I, "I feel like a lightning conductor—you've ruined me!"

"Poor fellow," cried Tom, once more addressing the crowd, "he is alive, but his intellect is irretrievably affected. He thinks he is a lightning conductor. Make way for the cab. That's right! Now help me to lead him in. He is out of all danger now. He can dress at his hotel. If any of you have any information to give which may throw light upon this case my address is 81 George Street. Remember, Doctor Crabbe, 81 George Street. Good day, kind friends, good-bye!" And with that he bundled me into the cab to prevent my making any further disclosures, and drove off amid the enthusiastic cheers of the admiring crowd.

I could not stay in Brisport long enough to see the effects of my *coup d'état*. Tom gave us a champagne supper that night, and the fun was fast and furious, but in the midst of it a telegram from my principal was handed in ordering me to return to Manchester by the next train. I waited long enough to get an early copy of the *Brisport Chronicle*, and beguiled the tedious journey by perusing the glowing account of my mishap. A column and a half was devoted to Dr. Crabbe and the extraordinary effects of electricity upon a drowned man. It ultimately got into some of the London papers, and was gravely commented upon in the *Lancet*.

As to the pecuniary success of our little experiment I can only judge from the following letter from Tom Crabbe, which I transcribe exactly as I received it:

"WHAT HO! MY RESUSCITATED CORPSE,

"You want to know how all goes in Brisport, I suppose. Well, I'll tell you. I'm cutting Markham and Davidson out completely, my boy. The day after our little joke I got a bruised leg (that baby), a cut head (the woman the baby fell upon), an erysipelas, and a bronchitis. Next day a fine, rich cancer of Markham's threw him up and came over to me. Also a pneumonia and a man who swallowed a sixpence. I've never had a day since without half a dozen new names on the list, and I'm going to start a trap this week. Just let me know when you are going to set up, and I'll manage to run down, old man, and give you a start in business, if I have to stand on my head in the water-butt. Good-bye. Love from the Missus.

"Ever yours,

"THOMAS WATERHOUSE CRABBE,

"M.B. Edin.

"81 George Street,
Brisport."

TALES OF LONG AGO

MONTIJO, the Roman [illegible] of his palatial [illegible] looked with perp[illegible] which he had just [illegible] messenger who had brou[illegible] black eyes were [illegible] a darker [illegible] was looking [illegible] so full was his mind of this sudden and most [illegible] order. To him it seemed as if the solid earth [illegible] beneath his feet. His life and the work of [illegible] had [illegible]

"Very good," he said [illegible]

[illegible]

[illegible] the General [illegible]

[illegible] waiting, your [illegible]

[illegible] show him in [illegible]

[illegible] minutes later [illegible] military [illegible] was a large bearded man [illegible] with the [illegible] bronzed and seamed [illegible] were shadowed [illegible] eyes [illegible]

"I [illegible] your excellency [illegible] you have [illegible]"

65. *The Last of the Legions*

PONTUS, the Roman viceroy, sat in the atrium of his palatial villa by the Thames, and he looked with perplexity at the scroll of papyrus which he had just unrolled. Before him stood the messenger who had brought it, a swarthy little Italian, whose black eyes were glazed with want of sleep, and his olive features darker still from dust and sweat. The viceroy was looking fixedly at him, yet he saw him not, so full was his mind of this sudden and most unexpected order. To him it seemed as if the solid earth had given way beneath his feet. His life and the work of his life had come to irremediable ruin.

"Very good," he said at last in a hard, dry voice, "you can go."

The man saluted and staggered out of the hall. A yellow-haired British major-domo came forward for orders.

"Is the General there?"

"He is waiting, your excellency."

"Then show him in, and leave us together."

A few minutes later Licinius Crassus, the head of the British military establishment, had joined his chief. He was a large bearded man in a white civilian toga, hemmed with the Patrician purple. His rough, bold features, burned and seamed and lined with the long African wars, were shadowed with anxiety as he looked with questioning eyes at the drawn, haggard face of the viceroy.

"I fear, your excellency, that you have had bad news from Rome."

"The worst, Crassus. It is all over with Britain. It is a question whether even Gaul will be held."

"Saint Albus save us! Are the orders precise?"

"Here they are, with the Emperor's own seal."

"But why? I had heard a rumour, but it had seemed too incredible."

"So had I only last week, and had the fellow scourged for having spread it. But here it is as clear as words can make it: 'Bring every man of the Legions by forced marches to the help of the Empire. Leave not a cohort in Britain.' These are my orders."

"But the cause?"

"They will let the limbs wither so that the heart be stronger. The old German hive is about to swarm once more. There are fresh crowds of Barbarians from Dacia and Scythia. Every sword is needed to hold the Alpine passes. They cannot let three legions lie idle in Britain."

The soldier shrugged his shoulders.

"When the legions go no Roman would feel that his life was safe here. For all that we have done, it is none the less the truth that it is no country of ours, and that we hold it as we won it, by the sword."

"Yes, every man, woman, and child of Latin blood must come with us to Gaul. The galleys are already waiting at Portus Dubris. Get the orders out, Crassus, at once. As the Valerian legion falls back from the Wall of Hadrian it can take the northern colonists with it. The Jovians can bring in the people from the west, and the Batavians can escort the easterns if they will muster at Camboricum. You will see to it." He sank his face for a moment in his hands. "It is a fearsome thing," said he, "to tear up the roots of so goodly a tree."

"To make more space for such a crop of weeds," said the soldier bitterly. "My God, what will be the end of these poor Britons! From ocean to ocean there is not a tribe which will not be at the throat of its neighbour when the last Roman Lictor has turned his back. With these hot-headed Silures it is hard enough now to keep the swords in their sheaths."

"The kennel might fight as they choose among themselves until the best hound won," said the Roman Governor. "At least the victor would keep the arts and the religion which we have brought them, and Britain would be one land. No, it is the bear from the north and the wolves from oversea, the painted savage from beyond the walls and the Saxon pirate from over the water, who will succeed to our rule. Where we saved, they will slay; where we built, they will burn; where we planted, they will ravage. But the die is cast, Crassus. You will carry out the orders."

"I will send out the messengers within an hour. This very morning there has come news that the Barbarians are through the old gap in the wall, and their outriders as far south as Vinovia."

The Governor shrugged his shoulders.

"These things concern us no longer," said he. Then a bitter smile broke upon his aquiline, clean-shaven face. "Whom think you that I see in audience this morning?"

"Nay, I know not."

"Caradoc and Regnus, and Celticus the Icenian, who, like so many of the richer Britons, have been educated at Rome, and who would lay before me their plans as to the ruling of this country."

"And what is their plan?"

"That they themselves should do it."

The Roman soldier laughed. "Well, they will have their will," said he, as he saluted and turned upon his heel. "Farewell, your excellency. There are hard days coming for you and for me."

An hour later the British deputation was ushered into the presence of the Governor. They were good, steadfast men, men who with a whole heart, and at some risk to themselves, had taken up their country's cause, so far as they could see it. At the same time they well knew that under the mild and beneficent rule of Rome it was only when they passed from words to deeds that their backs or their necks would be in danger. They stood now, earnest and a little abashed, before the throne of the viceroy. Celticus was a swarthy, black-bearded little Iberian. Caradoc and Regnus were tall, middle-aged men of the fair flaxen British type. All three were dressed in the draped, yellow toga after the Latin fashion, instead of in the bracae and tunic which distinguished their more insular fellow-countrymen.

"Well?" asked the Governor.

"We are here," said Celticus boldly, "as the spokesmen of a great number of our fellow-countrymen, for the purpose of sending our petition through you to the Emperor and to the Roman Senate, that we may urge upon them the policy of allowing us to govern this country after our own ancient fashion." He paused, as if awaiting some outburst as an answer to his own temerity; but the Governor merely nodded his head as a sign that he should proceed. "We had laws of our own before ever Cæsar set foot in Britain, which have served their purpose since first our forefathers came from the land of Ham. We are not a child among the nations, but our history goes back in our own traditions further even than that of Rome, and we are galled by this yoke which you have laid upon us."

"Are not our laws just?" asked the Governor.

"The code of Cæsar is just, but it is always the code of Cæsar. Our own laws were made for our own uses and our own circumstances, and we would fain have them again."

"You speak Roman as if you had been bred in the Forum; you wear a Roman toga; your hair is filleted in Roman fashion—are not these the gifts of Rome?"

"We would take all the learning and all the arts that Rome or Greece could give, but we would still be Britain, and ruled by Britons."

The viceroy smiled. " By the rood of Saint Helena," said he, " had you spoken thus to some of my heathen ancestors, there would have been an end to your politics. That you have dared to stand before my face and say as much is a proof for ever of the gentleness of our rule. But I would reason with you for a moment upon this your request. You know weil that this land has never been one kingdom, but was always under many chiefs and many tribes, who have made war upon each other. Would you in very truth have it so again ? "

" Those were in the evil pagan days, the days of the Druid and the oak-grove, your excellency. But now we are held together by a gospel of peace."

The viceroy shook his head. " If all the world were of the same way of thinking, then it would be easier," said he. " It may be that this blessed doctrine of peace will be little help to you when you are face to face with strong men who still worship the god of war. What would you do against the Picts of the north ? "

" Your excellency knows that many of the bravest legionaries are of British blood. These are our defence."

" But discipline, man, the power to command, the knowledge of war, the strength to act—it is in these things that you would fail. Too long have you leaned upon the crutch."

" The times may be hard, but when we have gone through them, Britain will be herself again."

" Nay, she will be under a different and a harsher master," said the Roman. " Already the pirates swarm upon the eastern coast. Were it not for our Roman Count of the Saxon shore they would land to-morrow. I see the day when Britain may, indeed, be one ; but that will be because you and your fellows are either dead or are driven into the mountains of the west. All goes into the melting-pot, and if a better Albion should come forth from it, it will be after ages of strife, and neither you nor your people will have part or lot in it."

Regnus, the tall young Celt, smiled. " With the

help of God and our own right arms we should hope for a better end," said he. "Give us but the chance, and we will bear the brunt."

"You are as men that are lost," said the viceroy sadly. "I see this broad land, with its gardens and orchards, its fair villas and its walled towns, its bridges and its roads, all the work of Rome. Surely it will pass even as a dream, and these three hundred years of settled order will leave no trace behind. For learn that it will indeed be as you wish, and that this very day the orders have come to me that the legions are to go."

The three Britons looked at each other in amazement. Their first impulse was towards a wild exultation, but reflection and doubt followed close upon its heels.

"This is indeed wondrous news," said Celticus. "This is a day of days to the motherland. When do the legions go, your excellency, and what troops will remain behind for our protection?"

"The legions go at once," said the viceroy. "You will doubtless rejoice to hear that within a month there will be no Roman soldier in the island, nor, indeed, a Roman of any sort, age, or sex, if I can take them with me."

The faces of the Britons were shadowed, and Caradoc, a grave and thoughtful man, spoke for the first time.

"But this is over sudden, your excellency," said he. "There is much truth in what you have said about the pirates. From my villa near the fort of Anderida I saw eighty of their galleys only last week, and I know well that they would be on us like ravens on a dying ox. For many years to come it would not be possible for us to hold them off."

The viceroy shrugged his shoulders. "It is your affair now," said he. "Rome must look to herself."

The last traces of joy had passed from the faces of the Britons. Suddenly the future had started up clearly before them, and they quailed at the prospect.

"There is a rumour in the market-place," said Celticus, "that the northern Barbarians are through the gap in the wall. Who is to stop their progress?"

"You and your fellows," said the Roman.

Clearer still grew the future, and there was terror in the eyes of the spokesmen as they faced it.

"But your excellency, if the legions should go at once, we should have the wild Scots at York, and the Northmen in the Thames within the month. We can build ourselves up under your shield, and in a few years it would be easier for us; but not now, your excellency, not now."

"Tut, man; for years you have been clamouring in our ears and raising the people. Now you have got what you asked. What more would you have? Within the month you will be as free as were your ancestors before Cæsar set foot upon your shore."

"For God's sake, your excellency, put our words out of your head. The matter had not been well considered. We will send to Rome. We will ride post-haste ourselves. We will fall at the Emperor's feet. We will kneel before the Senate and beg that the legions remain."

The Roman proconsul rose from his chair and motioned that the audience was at an end.

"You will do what you please," said he. "I and my men are for Italy."

And even as he said, so was it, for before the spring had ripened into summer, the troops were clanking down the via Aurelia on their way to the Ligurian passes, whilst every road in Gaul was dotted with the carts and the waggons which bore the Brito-Roman refugees on their weary journey to their distant country. But ere another summer had passed Celticus was dead, for he was flayed alive by the pirates and his skin nailed upon the door of a church near Caistor. Regnus, too, was dead, for he was tied to a tree and shot with arrows when the painted men came to the sacking of Isca. Caradoc only was alive, but he was a slave to Elda the red Caledonian and his wife was mistress to Mordred the wild chief of the western Cymri. From the ruined wall in the north to Vectis in the south blood and ruin and ashes covered the fair land of Britain. And after many days it came out fairer than ever, but, even as the Roman had said, neither the Britons nor any men of their blood came into the heritage of that which had been their own.

66. *The Last Galley*

"Mutato nomine, de te, Britannia, fabula narratur."

IT was a spring morning, one hundred and forty-six years before the coming of Christ. The North African coast, with its broad hem of golden sand, its green belt of feathery palm-trees, and its background of barren, red-scarped hills, shimmered like a dream country in the opal light. Save for a narrow edge of snow-white surf, the Mediterranean lay blue and serene as far as the eye could reach. In all its vast expanse there was no break but for a single galley, which was slowly making its way from the direction of Sicily and heading for the distant harbour of Carthage.

Seen from afar it was a stately and beautiful vessel, deep red in colour, double-banked with scarlet oars, its broad, flapping sail stained with Tyrian purple, its bulwarks gleaming with brass work. A brazen, three-pronged ram projected in front, and a high, golden figure of Baal, the God of the Phœnicians, children of Canaan, shone upon the after-deck. From the single high mast above the huge sail streamed the tiger-striped flag of Carthage. So, like some stately, scarlet bird, with golden beak and wings of purple, she swam upon the face of the waters—a thing of might and of beauty as seen from the distant shore.

But approach and look at her now! What are these dark streaks which foul her white decks and dapple her brazen shields? Why do the long, red oars move out of time, irregular, convulsive? Why are some missing from the staring portholes, some snapped with jagged, yellow edges, some trailing inert against the side? Why are two prongs of the brazen ram twisted and broken? See, even the high image of Baal is battered and disfigured! By every sign this ship has passed through some grievous trial, some day of terror, which has left its heavy marks upon her.

And now stand upon the deck itself, and see more closely the men who man her! There are two decks forward and aft, while in the open waist are the double banks of seats, above and below, where the rowers, two to an oar, tug and bend at their endless task. Down the centre is a narrow platform, along which pace a line of warders, lash in hand, who cut cruelly at the slave who pauses, be it only for an instant to sweep the sweat from his dripping brow. But these slaves—look at them! Some are captured Romans, some Sicilians, many black Libyans, but all are in the last exhaustion, their weary eyelids drooped over their eyes, their lips thick with black crusts, and pink with bloody froth, their arms and backs moving mechanically to the hoarse chant of the overseer. Their bodies of all tints from ivory to jet, are stripped to the waist, and every glistening back shows the angry stripes of the warders. But it is not from these that the blood comes which reddens the seats and tints the salt water washing beneath their manacled feet. Great gaping wounds, the marks of sword slash and spear stab, show crimson upon their naked chests and shoulders, while many lie huddled and senseless athwart the benches, careless for ever of the whips which still hiss above them. Now we can understand those empty portholes and those trailing oars.

Nor were the crew in better case than their slaves.

The decks were littered with wounded and dying men. It was but a remnant who still remained upon their feet. The most lay exhausted upon the fore-deck, while a few of the more zealous were mending their shattered armour, restringing their bows, or cleaning the deck from the marks of combat. Upon a raised platform at the base of the mast stood the sailing-master who conned the ship, his eyes fixed upon the distant point of Megara which screened the eastern side of the Bay of Carthage. On the after-deck were gathered a number of officers, silent and brooding, glancing from time to time at two of their own class who stood apart deep in conversation. The one, tall, dark, and wiry, with pure, Semitic features, and the limbs of a giant, was Magro, the famous Carthaginian captain, whose name was still a terror on every shore, from Gaul to the Euxine. The other, a white-bearded, swarthy man, with indomitable courage and energy stamped upon every eager line of his keen, aquiline face, was Gisco the politician, a man of the highest Punic blood, a Suffete of the purple robe, and the leader of that party in the state which had watched and striven amid the selfishness and slothfulness of his fellow-countrymen to rouse the public spirit and waken the public conscience to the ever-increasing danger from Rome. As they talked, the two men glanced continually, with earnest, anxious faces, towards the northern skyline.

"It is certain," said the older man, with gloom in his voice and bearing, "none have escaped save ourselves."

"I did not leave the press of the battle whilst I saw one ship which I could succour," Magro answered. "As it was, we came away, as you saw, like a wolf which has a hound hanging on to either haunch. The Roman dogs can show the wolf-bites which prove it. Had any other galley won clear, they would surely be with us by now, since they have no place of safety save Carthage."

The younger warrior glanced keenly ahead to the

distant point which marked his native city. Already the low, leafy hill could be seen, dotted with the white villas of the wealthy Phœnician merchants. Above them, a gleaming dot against the pale blue morning sky, shone the brazen roof of the citadel of Byrsa, which capped the sloping town.

"Already they can see us from the watch-towers," he remarked. "Even from afar they may know the galley of Black Magro. But which of all of them will guess that we alone remain of all that goodly fleet which sailed out with blare of trumpet and roll of drum but one short month ago?"

The patrician smiled bitterly. "If it were not for our great ancestors and for our beloved country, the Queen of the Waters," said he, "I could find it in my heart to be glad at this destruction which has come upon this vain and feeble generation. You have spent your life upon the seas, Magro. You do not know how it has been with us on the land. But I have seen this canker grow upon us which now leads us to our death. I and others have gone down into the market-place to plead with the people, and been pelted with mud for our pains. Many a time have I pointed to Rome, and said, 'Behold these people, who bear arms themselves, each man for his own duty and pride. How can you who hide behind mercenaries hope to stand against them?'—a hundred times I have said it."

"And had they no answer?" asked the Rover.

"Rome was far off and they could not see it, so to them it was nothing," the old man answered. "Some thought of trade, and some of votes, and some of profits from the State, but none would see that the State itself, the mother of all things, was sinking to her end. So might the bees debate who should have wax or honey when the torch was blazing which would bring to ashes the hive and all therein. 'Are we not rulers of the sea?' 'Was not Hannibal a great man?' Such were their cries, living ever in the past and blind to the future.

Before that sun sets there will be tearing of hair and rending of garments ; but what will that now avail us ? "

" It is some sad comfort," said Magro, " to know that what Rome holds she cannot keep."

" Why say you that ? When we go down, she is supreme in all the world."

" For a time, and only for a time," Magro answered gravely. " Yet you will smile, perchance, when I tell you how it is that I know it. There was a wise woman who lived in that part of the Tin Islands which juts forth into the sea, and from her lips I have heard many things, but not one which has not come aright. Of the fall of our own country, and even of this battle, from which we now return, she told me clearly. There is much strange lore amongst these savage peoples in the west of the land of Tin."

" What said she of Rome ? "

" That she also would fall, even as we, weakened by her riches and her factions."

Gisco rubbed his hands. " That at least makes our own fall less bitter," said he. " But since we have fallen, and Rome will fall, who in turn may hope to be Queen of the Waters ? "

" That also I asked her," said Magro, " and gave her my Tyrian belt with the golden buckle as a guerdon for her answer. But, indeed, it was too high payment for the tale she told, which must be false if all else she said was true. She would have it that in coming days it was her own land, this fog-girt isle where painted savages can scarce row a wicker coracle from point to point, which shall at last take the trident which Carthage and Rome have dropped."

The smile which flickered upon the old patrician's keen features died away suddenly, and his fingers closed upon his companion's wrist. The other had set rigid, his head advanced, his hawk eyes upon the northern skyline. Its straight, blue horizon was broken by two low, black dots.

"Galleys!" whispered Gisco.

The whole crew had seen them. They clustered along the starboard bulwarks, pointing and chattering. For a moment the gloom of defeat was lifted, and a buzz of joy ran from group to group at the thought that they were not alone—that someone had escaped the great carnage as well as themselves.

"By the spirit of Baal," said Black Magro, "I could not have believed that any could have fought clear from such a welter. Could it be young Hamilcar in the *Africa*, or is it Beneva in the blue Syrian ship? We three, with others, may form a squadron and make head against them yet. If we hold our course, they will join us ere we round the harbour mole."

Slowly the injured galley toiled on her way, and more swiftly the two new-comers swept down from the north. Only a few miles off lay the green point and the white houses which flanked the great African city. Already, upon the headland, could be seen a dark group of waiting townsmen. Gisco and Magro were still watching with puckered gaze the approaching galleys, when the brown Libyan boatswain, with flashing teeth and gleaming eyes, rushed upon the poop, his long, thin arm stabbing to the north.

"Romans!" he cried. "Romans!"

A hush had fallen over the great vessel. Only the wash of the water and the measured rattle and beat of the oars broke in upon the silence.

"By the horns of God's altar, I believe the fellow is right!" cried old Gisco. "See how they swoop upon us like falcons. They are full-manned and full-oared."

"Plain wood, unpainted," said Magro. "See how it gleams yellow where the sun strikes it."

"And yonder thing beneath the mast. Is it not the cursed bridge they use for boarding?"

"So they grudge us even one," said Magro with a bitter laugh. "Not even one galley shall return to the old sea-mother. Well, for my part, I would as soon have it so. I am of a mind to stop the oars and await them."

"It is a man's thought," answered old Gisco; "but the city will need us in the days to come. What shall it profit us to make the Roman victory complete? Nay, Magro, let the slaves row as they never rowed before, not for our own safety, but for the profit of the State."

So the great red ship laboured and lurched onwards, like a weary, panting stag which seeks shelter from his pursuers, while ever swifter and ever nearer sped the two lean, fierce galleys from the north. Already the morning sun shone upon the lines of low Roman helmets above the bulwarks, and glistened on the silver wave where each sharp prow shot through the still, blue water. Every moment the ships drew nearer, and the long, thin scream of the Roman trumpets grew louder upon the ear.

Upon the high bluff of Megara there stood a great concourse of the people of Carthage who had hurried forth from the city upon the news that the galleys were in sight. They stood now, rich and poor, effete and plebeian, white Phœnician and dark Kabyle, gazing with breathless interest at the spectacle before them. Some hundreds of feet beneath them the Punic galley had drawn so close that with their naked eyes they could see those stains of battle which told their dismal tale. The Romans, too, were heading in such a way that it was before their very faces that their ship was about to be cut off; and yet of all this multitude not one could raise a hand in its defence. Some wept in impotent grief, some cursed with flashing eyes and knotted fists, some on their knees held up appealing hands to Baal; but neither prayer, tears nor curses could undo the past nor mend the present. That broken, crawling galley meant that their fleet was gone. Those two fierce, darting ships meant that the hands of Rome were already at their throat. Behind them would come others and others, the innumerable trained hosts of the great Republic, long mistress of the land, now dominant also upon the waters. In a month, two months, three at the most, their armies would be there, and what could all the untrained multitudes of Carthage do to stop them ?

" Nay ! " cried one, more hopeful than the rest, " at least we are brave men with arms in our hands."

" Fool ! " said another, " is it not such talk which has brought us to our ruin ? What is the brave man untrained to the brave man trained ? When you stand before the sweep and rush of a Roman legion you may learn the difference."

" Then let us train ! "

" Too late ! A full year is needful to turn a man to a soldier. Where will you—where will your city be within the year ? Nay, there is but one chance for us. If we give up our commerce and our colonies, if we strip ourselves of all that made us great, then perchance the Roman conqueror may hold his hand."

And already the last sea-fight of Carthage was coming swiftly to an end before them. Under their very eyes the two Roman galleys had shot in, one on either side of the vessel of Black Magro. They had grappled with him, and he, desperate in his despair, had cast the crooked flukes of his anchors over their gunwales, and bound them to him in an iron grip, whilst with hammer and crowbar he burst great holes in his own sheathing. The last Punic galley should never be rowed into Ostia, a sight for the holiday-makers of Rome. She would lie in her own waters. And the fierce, dark soul of her rover captain glowed as he thought that not alone should she sink into the depths of the mother sea.

Too late did the Romans understand the man with whom they had to deal. Their boarders who had flooded the Punic decks, felt the planking sink and sway beneath them. They rushed to gain their own vessels ; but they, too, were being drawn downwards, held in the dying grip of the great red galley. Over they went and ever over. Now the deck of Magro's ship is flush with the water, and the Romans', drawn towards it by the iron bonds which hold them, are tilted downwards, one bulwark upon the waves, one reared high in the air. Madly they strain to cast off the death-grip of the galley. She is under the surface now, and ever swifter, with the greater weight, the Roman ships heel after her. There is a rending crash. The wooden side is torn out of one, and mutilated, dismembered, she rights herself, and lies a helpless thing upon the water. But a last, yellow gleam in the blue water shows where her consort has been dragged to her end in the iron death-grapple of her foeman. The tiger-striped flag of Carthage has sunk beneath the swirling surface, never more to be seen upon the face of the sea.

For in that year a great cloud hung for seventeen days over the African coast, a deep black cloud which was the dark shroud of the burning city. And when the seventeen days were over, Roman ploughs were driven from end to end of the charred ashes, and salt was scattered there as a sign that Carthage should be no more. And far off a huddle of naked, starving folk stood upon the distant mountains, and looked down upon the desolate plain which had once been the fairest and richest upon earth. And they understood too late that it is the law of heaven that the world is given to the hardy and to the self-denying, whilst he who would escape the duties of manhood will soon be stripped of the pride, the wealth, and the power, which are the prizes which manhood brings.

67. *Through the Veil*

HE was a great shock-headed, freckle-faced Borderer, the lineal descendant of a cattle-thieving clan in Liddesdale. In spite of his ancestry he was as solid and sober a citizen as one would wish to see, a town councillor of Melrose, an elder of the Church, and the chairman of the local branch of the Young Men's Christian Association. Brown was his name—and you saw it printed up as " Brown and Handiside " over the great grocery stores in the High Street. His wife, Maggie Brown, was an Armstrong before her marriage, and came from an old farming stock in the wilds of Teviothead. She was small, swarthy, and dark-eyed, with a strangely nervous temperament for a Scotch woman. No greater contrast could be found than the big, tawny man and the dark little woman, but both were of the soil as far back as any memory could extend.

One day—it was the first anniversary of their wedding—they had driven over together to see the excavations of the Roman Fort at Newstead. It was not a particularly picturesque spot. From the northern bank of the Tweed, just where the river forms a loop, there extends a gentle slope of arable land. Across it run the trenches of the excavators, with here and there an exposure of old stonework to show the foundations of the ancient walls. It had been a huge place, for the camp was fifty acres in extent, and the fort fifteen. However, it was all made easy for them since Mr. Brown knew the farmer to whom the land belonged. Under his guidance they spent a long summer evening inspecting the trenches, the pits, the ramparts and all the strange variety of objects which were waiting to be transported to the Edinburgh Museum of Antiquities. The buckle of a woman's belt had been dug up that very day, and the farmer was discoursing upon it when his eyes fell upon Mrs. Brown's face.

" Your good leddy's tired," said he. " Maybe you'd best rest a wee before we gang further."

Brown looked at his wife. She was certainly very pale, and her dark eyes were bright and wild.

" What is it, Maggie ? I've wearied you. I'm thinkin' it's time we went back."

"No, no, John, let us go on. It's wonderful! It's like a dreamland place. It all seems so close and so near to me. How long were the Romans here, Mr. Cunningham?"

"A fair time, mam. If you saw the kitchen midden-pits you would guess it took a long time to fill them."

"And why did they leave?"

"Well, mam, by all accounts they left because they had to. The folk round could thole them no longer, so they just up and burned the fort aboot their lugs. You can see the fire marks on the stanes."

The woman gave a quick little shudder. "A wild night—a fearsome night," said she. "The sky must have been red that night—and these grey stones, they may have been red also."

"Aye, I think they were red," said her husband. "It's a queer thing, Maggie, and it may be your words that have done it; but I seem to see that business aboot as clear as ever I saw anything in my life. The light shone on the water."

"Aye, the light shone on the water. And the smoke gripped you by the throat. And all the savages were yelling."

The old farmer began to laugh. "The leddy will be writin' a story aboot the old fort," said he. "I've shown many a one ower it, but I never heard it put so clear afore. Some folk have the gift."

They had strolled along the edge of the foss, and a pit yawned upon the right of them.

"That pit was fourteen foot deep," said the farmer. "What d'ye think we dug oot from the bottom o't? Weel, it was just the skeleton of a man wi' a spear by his side. I'm thinkin' he was grippin' it when he died. Now, how cam' a man wi' a spear doon a hole fourteen foot deep. He wasna' buried there, for they aye burned their dead. What make ye o' that, mam?"

"He sprang doon to get clear of the savages," said the woman.

"Weel, it's likely enough, and a' the professors from Edinburgh couldna gie a better reason. I wish you were aye here, mam, to answer a' oor deeficulties sae readily. Now, here's the altar that we foond last week. There's an inscreeption. They tell me it's Latin, and it means that the men o' this fort give thanks to God for their safety."

They examined the old worn stone. There was a large, deeply cut "VV" upon the top of it.

"What does 'VV' stand for?" asked Brown.

"Naebody kens," the guide answered.

"*Valeria Victrix*," said the lady softly. Her face was paler than ever, her eyes far away, as one who peers down the dim aisles of over-arching centuries.

"What's that?" asked her husband sharply.

She started as one who wakes from sleep. "What were we talking about?" she asked.

"About this 'VV' upon the stone."

"No doubt it was just the name of the Legion which put the altar up."

"Aye, but you gave some special name."

"Did I? How absurd! How should I ken what the name was?"

"You said something—'*Victrix*,' I think."

"I suppose I was guessing. It gives me the queerest feeling, this place, as if I were not myself, but someone else."

"Aye, it's an uncanny place," said her husband, looking round with an expression almost of fear in his bold grey eyes. "I feel it mysel'. I think we'll just be wishin' you good evenin', Mr. Cunningham, and get back to Melrose before the dark sets in."

Neither of them could shake off the strange impression which had been left upon them by their visit to the excavations. It was as if some miasma had risen from those damp trenches and passed into their blood. All the evening they were silent and thoughtful, but such remarks as they did make showed that the same subject was in the mind of each. Brown had a restless night, in which he dreamed a strange, connected dream, so vivid that he woke sweating and shivering like a frightened horse. He tried to convey it all to his wife as they sat together at breakfast in the morning.

"It was the clearest thing, Maggie," said he. "Nothing that has ever come to me in my waking life has been more clear than that. I feel as if these hands were sticky with blood."

"Tell me of it—tell me slow," said she.

"When it began, I was oot on a braeside. I was laying flat on the ground. It was rough, and there were clumps of heather. All round me was just darkness, but I could hear the rustle and the breathin' of men. There seemed a great multitude on every side of me, but I could see no one. There was a low chink of steel sometimes, and then a number of voices would whisper, 'Hush!' I had a ragged club in my hand, and it had spikes o' iron near the end of it. My heart was beatin' quickly, and I felt that a moment of great danger and excitement was at hand. Once I dropped my club, and again from all round me the voices in the darkness cried, 'Hush!' I put oot my hand, and it touched the foot of another man lying in front of me. There was someone at my very elbow on either side. But they said nothin'.

"Then we all began to move. The whole braeside seemed to be crawlin' downwards. There was a river at the bottom and a high-arched wooden bridge. Beyond the bridge were many lights—torches on a wall. The creepin' men all flowed towards the bridge. There had been no sound of any kind, just a velvet stillness. And then there was a cry in the darkness, the cry of a man who had been stabbed suddenly to the hairt. That one cry swelled out for a moment, and then the roar of a thoosand furious voices. I was runnin'. Everyone was runnin'. A bright red light shone out, and the river was a scarlet streak. I could see my companions now. They were more like devils than men, wild figures clad in skins, with their hair and beards streamin'. They were all mad with rage, jumpin' as they ran, their mouths open, their arms wavin', the red light beatin' on their faces. I ran, too, and yelled out curses like the rest. Then I heard a great cracklin' of wood, and I knew that the palisades were doon. There was a loud whistlin' in my ears, and I was aware that arrows were flying past me. I got to the bottom of a dyke, and I saw a hand stretched doon from above. I took it, and was dragged to the top. We looked doon, and there were silver men beneath us holdin' up their spears. Some of our folk sprang on to the spears. Then we others followed, and we killed the soldiers before they could draw the spears oot again. They shouted loud in some foreign tongue, but no mercy was shown them. We went ower them like a wave, and trampled them doon into the mud, for they were few, and there was no end to our numbers.

"I found myself among buildings, and one of them was on fire. I saw the flames spoutin' through the roof. I ran on, and then I was alone among the buildings. Someone ran across in front o' me. It was a woman. I caught her by the arm, and I took her chin and turned her face so as the light of the fire would strike it. Whom think you that it was, Maggie?"

His wife moistened her dry lips. "It was I," she said.

He looked at her in surprise. "That's a good guess," said he. "Yes, it was just you. Not merely like you, you understand. It was you—you yourself. I saw the same soul in your frightened eyes. You looked white and bonnie and wonderful in the firelight. I had just one thought in my head—to get you awa' with me; to keep you all to mysel' in my own home somewhere beyond the hills. You clawed at my face with your nails. I heaved you over my shoulder, and

I tried to find a way oot of the light of the burning hoose and back into the darkness.

"Then came the thing that I mind best of all. You're ill, Maggie. Shall I stop? My God! you have the very look on your face that you had last night in my dream. You screamed. He came runnin' in the firelight. His head was bare; his hair was black and curled; he had a naked sword in his hand, short and broad, little more than a dagger. He stabbed at me, but he tripped and fell. I held you with one hand, and with the other——"

His wife had sprung to her feet with writhing features.

"Marcus!" she cried. "My beautiful Marcus! Oh, you brute! you brute! you brute!" There was a clatter of tea-cups as she fell forward senseless upon the table.

They never talk about that strange, isolated incident in their married life. For an instant the curtain of the past had swung aside, and some strange glimpse of a forgotten life had come to them. But it closed down, never to open again. They live their narrow round—he in his shop, she in her household—and yet new and wider horizons have vaguely formed themselves around them since that summer evening by the crumbling Roman fort.

68. *The Coming of the Huns*

IN the middle of the fourth century the state of the Christian religion was a scandal and a disgrace. Patient, humble, and long-suffering in adversity, it had become positive, aggressive, and unreasonable with success. Paganism was not yet dead, but it was rapidly sinking, finding its most faithful supporters among the conservative aristocrats of the best families on the one hand, and among those benighted villagers on the other who gave their name to the expiring creed. Between these two extremes the great majority of reasonable men had turned from the conception of many gods to that of one, and had rejected for ever the beliefs of their forefathers. But with the vices of polytheism, they had also abandoned its virtues, among which toleration and religious good humour had been conspicuous. The strenuous earnestness of the Christians had compelled them to examine and define every point of their own theology ; but as they had no central authority by which such definitions could be checked, it was not long before a hundred heresies had put forward their rival views, while the same earnestness of conviction led the stronger bands of schismatics to endeavour, for conscience' sake, to force their views upon the weaker, and thus to cover the Eastern world with confusion and strife.

Alexandria, Antioch, and Constantinople were centres of theological warfare. The whole north of Africa, too, was rent by the strife of the Donatists, who upheld their particular schism by iron flails and the war-cry of "Praise to the Lord!" But minor local controversies sank to nothing when compared with the huge argument of the Catholic and the Arian, which rent every village in twain, and divided every household from the cottage to the palace. The rival doctrines of the Homoousian and of the Homoiousian, containing metaphysical differences so attenuated that they could hardly be stated, turned bishop against bishop and congregation against congregation. The ink of the theologians and the blood of the fanatics were spilled in floods on either side, and gentle followers of Christ were horrified to find that their faith was responsible for such a state of riot and bloodshed as had never yet disgraced the religious history of the world. Many of the more earnest among them, shocked and scandalised, slipped away to the Libyan Desert, or to the solitude of Pontus, there to await in self-denial and prayer that second coming which was supposed to be at hand. Even in the deserts they could not escape the echo of the distant strife, and the hermits themselves scowled fiercely from their dens at passing travellers who might be contaminated by the doctrines of Athanasius or of Arius.

Such a hermit was Simon Melas, of whom I write. A Trinitarian and a Catholic, he was shocked by the excesses of the persecution of the Arians, which could be only matched by the similar outrages with which these same Arians in the day of their power avenged their treatment on their brother Christians. Weary of the whole strife, and convinced that the end of the world was indeed at hand, he left his home in Constantinople and travelled as far as the Gothic settlements in Dacia beyond the Danube, in search of some spot where he might be free from the never-ending disputes. Still journeying to the north and east, he crossed the river which we now call the Dniester, and there, finding a rocky hill rising from an immense plain, he formed a cell near its summit, and settled himself down to end his life in self-denial and meditation. There were fish in the stream, the country teemed with game, and there was an abundance of wild fruits, so that his spiritual exercises were not unduly interrupted by the search of sustenance for his mortal frame.

In this distant retreat he expected to find absolute solitude, but the hope was in vain. Within a week of his arrival, in an hour of worldly curiosity, he explored the edges of the high, rocky hill upon which he lived. Making his way up to a cleft, which was hung with olives and myrtles, he came upon a cave in the opening of which sat an aged man, white-bearded, white-haired, and infirm—a hermit like himself. So long had this stranger been alone that he had almost forgotten the use of his tongue; but at last, words coming more freely, he was able to convey the information that his name was Paul of Nicopolis, that he was a Greek citizen, and that he also had come out into the desert for the saving of his soul, and to escape from the contamination of heresy.

"Little I thought, brother Simon," said he, "that I should ever find anyone else who had come so far upon the same holy errand. In all these years, and they are so many that I have lost count of them, I have never seen a man, save indeed one or two wandering shepherds far out upon yonder plain."

From where they sat, the huge steppe, covered with waving grass and gleaming with a vivid green in the sun, stretched away as level and as unbroken as the sea, to the eastern horizon. Simon Melas stared across it with curiosity.

"Tell me, brother Paul," said he, "you who have lived here so long—what lies at the farther side of that plain?"

The old man shook his head. "There is no farther side to the plain," said he. "It is the earth's boundary, and stretches away to eternity. For all these years I have sat beside it, but never once have I seen anything come across it. It is manifest that if there had been a farther side there would certainly at some time have come some traveller from that direction. Over the great river yonder is the Roman post of Tyras; but that is a long day's journey from here, and they have never disturbed my meditations."

"On what do you meditate, brother Paul?"

"At first I meditated on many sacred mysteries; but now, for twenty years, I have brooded continually on the nature of the Logos. What is your view upon that vital matter, brother Simon?"

"Surely," said the younger man, "there can be no question as to that. The Logos is assuredly but a name used by St. John to signify the Diety."

The old hermit gave a hoarse cry of fury, and his brown, withered face was convulsed with anger. Seizing the huge cudgel which he kept to beat off the wolves, he shook it murderously at his companion.

"Out with you! Out of my cell!" he cried. "Have I lived here so long to have it polluted by a vile Trinitarian

—a follower of the rascal Athanasius? Wretched idolater, learn once for all, that the Logos is in truth an emanation from the Diety, and in no sense equal or co-eternal with Him! Out with you, I say, or I will dash out your brains with my staff!"

It was useless to reason with the furious Arian, and Simon withdrew in sadness and wonder, that at this extreme verge of the known earth the spirit of religious strife should still break upon the peaceful solitude of the wilderness. With hanging head and heavy heart he made his way down the valley, and climbed up once more to his own cell, which lay at the crown of the hill, with the intention of never again exchanging visits with his Arian neighbour.

Here, for a year, dwelt Simon Melas, leading a life of solitude and prayer. Three was no reason why anyone should ever come to this outermost point of human habitation. Once a young Roman officer—Caius Crassus—rode out a day's journey from Tyras, and climbed the hill to have speech with the anchorite. He was of an equestrian family, and still held his belief in the old dispensation. He looked with interest and surprise, but also with some disgust, at the ascetic arrangements of that humble abode.

"Whom do you please by living in such a fashion?" he asked.

"We show that our spirit is superior to our flesh," Simon answered. "If we fare badly in this world, we believe that we shall reap an advantage in the world to come."

The centurion shrugged his shoulders. "There are philosophers among our people, Stoics and others, who have the same idea. When I was in the Herulian Cohort of the Fourth Legion we were quartered in Rome itself, and I saw much of the Christians, but I could never learn anything from them which I had not heard from my own father, whom you, in your arrogance, would call a Pagan. It is true that we talk of numerous gods; but for many years we have not taken them very seriously. Our thoughts upon virtue and duty and a noble life are the same as your own."

Simon Melas shook his head.

"If you have not the holy books," said he, "then what guide have you to direct your steps?"

"If you will read our philosophers, and above all the divine Plato, you will find that there are other guides who may take you to the same end. Have you by chance read the book which was written by our Emperor Marcus Aurelius? Do you not discover there every virtue which man could have, although he knew nothing of your creed? Have you considered, also, the words and actions of our late Emperor Julian, with whom I served my first campaign when he went out against the Persians? Where could you find a more perfect man than he?"

"Such talk is unprofitable, and I will have no more of it," said Simon sternly. "Take heed while there is time, and embrace the true faith; for the end of the world is at hand, and when it comes there will be no mercy for those who have shut their eyes to the light." So saying, he turned back once more to his praying-stool and to his crucifix, while the young Roman walked in deep thought down the hill, and mounting his horse, rode off to his distant post. Simon watched him until his brazen helmet was but a bead of light on the western edge of the great plain; for this was the first human face that he had seen in all this long year, and there were times when his heart yearned for the voices and the faces of his kind.

So another year passed, and save for the change of weather and the slow change of the seasons, one day was as another. Every morning when Simon opened his eyes, he saw the same grey line ripening into red in the farthest east, until the bright rim pushed itself above that far-off horizon across which no living creature had ever been known to come. Slowly the sun swept across the huge arch of the heavens, and as the shadows shifted from the black rocks which jutted upward from above his cell, so did the hermit regulate his terms of prayer and meditation. There was nothing on earth to draw his eye, or to distract his mind, for the grassy plain below was as void from month to month as the heaven above. So the long hours passed, until the red rim slipped down on the farther side, and the day ended in the same pearl-grey shimmer with which it had begun. Once two ravens circled for some days round the lonely hill, and once a white fish-eagle came from the Dniester and screamed above the hermit's head. Sometimes red dots were seen on the green plain where the antelopes grazed, and often a wolf howled in the darkness from the base of the rocks. Such was the uneventful life of Simon Melas the anchorite, until there came the day of wrath.

It was in the late spring of the year 375 that Simon came out from his cell, his gourd in his hand, to draw water from the spring. Darkness had closed in, the sun had set, but one last glimmer of rosy light rested upon a rocky peak, which jutted forth from the hill, on the farther side from the hermit's dwelling. As Simon came forth from under his ledge, the gourd dropped from his hand, and he stood gazing in amazement.

On the opposite peak a man was standing, his outline black in the fading light. He was a strange, almost a deformed figure, short-statured, round-backed, with a large head, no neck, and a long rod jutting out from between his shoulders. He stood with his face advanced, and his body bent, peering very intently over the plain to the westward. In a moment he was gone, and the lonely, black peak showed up hard and naked against the faint eastern glimmer. Then the night closed down, and all was black once more.

Simon Melas stood long in bewilderment, wondering who this stranger could be. He had heard, as had every Christian, of those evil spirits which were wont to haunt the hermits in the Thebaid and on the skirts of the Ethiopian waste. The strange shape of this solitary creature, its dark outline and prowling, intent attitude, suggestive rather of a fierce, rapacious beast than of a man, all helped him to believe that he had at last encountered one of those wanderers from the pit, of whose existence, in those days of robust faith, he had no more doubt than of his own. Much of the night he spent in prayer, his eyes glancing continually at the low arch of his cell door, with its curtain of deep purple wrought with stars. At any instant some crouching monster, some horned abomination, might peer in upon him, and he clung with frenzied appeal to his crucifix, as his human weakness quailed at the thought. But at last his fatigue overcame his fears, and falling upon his couch of dried grass, he slept until the bright daylight brought him to his senses.

It was later than was his wont, and the sun was far above the horizon. As he came forth from his cell, he looked across at the peak of rock, but it stood there bare and silent. Already it seemed to him that that strange, dark figure which had startled him so was some dream, some vision of the twilight. His gourd lay where it had fallen, and he picked it up with the intention of going to the spring. But suddenly he was aware of something new. The whole air was throbbing with sound. From all sides it came, rumbling, indefinite, an inarticulate mutter, low, but thick and strong, rising, falling, reverberating among the rocks, dying away into vague whispers, but always there. He looked round at the blue, cloudless sky in bewilderment. Then he scrambled up the rocky pinnacle above him, and sheltering himself in its shadow, he stared out over the plain. In his wildest dream he had never imagined such a sight.

The whole vast expanse was covered with horsemen, hundreds and thousands and tens of thousands, all riding slowly and in silence, out of the unknown east. It was the multitudinous beat of their horses' hoofs which caused that low throbbing in his ears. Some were so close to him as he looked down upon them that he could see clearly their thin, wiry horses, and the strange, humped figures of their swarthy riders, sitting forward on the withers, shapeless bundles, their short legs hanging stirrupless, their bodies balanced as firmly as though they were part of the beast. In those nearest he could see the bow and the quiver, the long spear and the short sword, with the coiled lasso behind the rider, which told that this was no helpless horde of wanderers, but a formidable army upon the march. His eyes passed on from them and swept farther and farther, but still to the very horizon, which quivered with movement, there was no end to this monstrous cavalry. Already the vanguard was far past the island of rock upon which he dwelt, and he could now understand that in front of this vanguard were single scouts who guided the course of the army and that it was one of these whom he had seen the evening before.

All day, held spellbound by this wonderful sight, the hermit crouched in the shadow of the rocks, and all day the sea of horsemen rolled onward over the plain beneath. Simon had seen the swarming quays of Alexandria, he had watched the mob which blocked the hippodrome of Constantinople, yet never had he imagined such a multitude as now defiled beneath his eyes, coming from that eastern skyline which had been the end of his world. Sometimes the dense streams of horsemen were broken by droves of brood-mares and foals, driven along by mounted guards; sometimes there were herds of cattle; sometimes there were lines of waggons with skin canopies above them; but then once more, after every break, came the horsemen, the horsemen, the hundreds and the thousands and the tens of thousands, slowly, ceaselessly, silently drifting from the east to the west. The long day passed, the light waned, and the shadows fell, but still the great broad stream was flowing by.

But the night brought a new and ever-stranger sight. Simon had marked bundles of faggots upon the backs of many of the led horses, and now he saw their use. All over the great plain, red pin-points gleamed through the darkness, which grew and brightened into flickering columns of flame. So far as he could see both to east and west the fires extended, until they were but points of light in the farthest distance. White stars shone in the vast heavens above, red ones in the great plain below. And from every side rose the low, confused murmur of voices, with the lowing of oxen and the neighing of horses.

Simon had been a soldier and a man of affairs before ever he forsook the world, and the meaning of all that he had seen was clear to him. History told him how the Roman world had ever been assailed by fresh swarms of Barbarians, coming from the outer darkness, and that the eastern Empire had already, in its fifty years of existence since Constantine had moved the capital of the world to the shores of the Bosphorus, been tormented in the same way. Gepidæ and Heruli, Ostrogoths and Sarmatians, he was familiar with them all. What the advanced sentinel of Europe had seen from this lonely outlying hill, was a fresh swarm breaking in upon the Empire, distinguished only from the others by its enormous, incredible size and by the strange aspect of the warriors who composed it. He alone of all civilised men knew of the approach of this dreadful shadow, sweeping like a heavy storm-cloud from the unknown depths of the east. He thought of the little Roman posts along the Dniester, of the ruined Dacian wall of Trajan behind them, and then of the scattered, defenceless villages which lay with no thought of danger over all the open country which stretched down to the Danube. Could he but give them the alarm! Was it not, perhaps, for that very end that God had guided him to the wilderness?

Then suddenly he remembered his Arian neighbour,

who dwelt in the cave beneath him. Once or twice during the last year he had caught a glimpse of his tall, bent figure hobbling round to examine the traps which he laid for quails and partridges. On one occasion they had met at the brook; but the old theologian waved him away as if he were a leper. What did he think now of this strange happening? Surely their differences might be forgotten at such a moment. He stole down the side of the hill, and made his way to his fellow-hermit's cave.

But there was a terrible silence as he approached it. His heart sank at that deadly stillness in the little valley. No glimmer of light came from the cleft in the rocks. He entered and called, but no answer came back. Then, with flint, steel, and the dry grass which he used for tinder, he struck a spark, and blew it into a blaze. The old hermit, his white hair dabbled with crimson, lay sprawling across the floor. The broken crucifix, with which his head had been beaten in, lay in splinters across him. Simon had dropped on his knees beside him, straightening his contorted limbs, and muttering the office for the dead, when the thud of a horse's hoofs was heard ascending the little valley which led to the hermit's cell. The dry grass had burned down, and Simon crouched trembling in the darkness, pattering prayers to the Virgin that his strength might be upheld.

It may have been that the new-comer had seen the gleam of the light, or it may have been that he had heard from his comrades of the old man whom they had murdered, and that his curiosity had led him to the spot. He stopped his horse outside the cave, and Simon, lurking in the shadows within, had a fair view of him in the moonlight. He slipped from his saddle, fastened the bridle to a root, and then stood peering through the opening of the cell. He was a very short, thick man, with a dark face, which was gashed with three cuts upon either side. His small eyes were sunk deep in his head, showing like black holes in the heavy, flat, hairless face. His legs were short and very bandy, so that he waddled uncouthly as he walked.

Simon crouched in the darkest angle, and he gripped in his hand that same knotted cudgel which the dead theologian had once raised against him. As that hideous, stooping head advanced into the darkness of the cell, he brought the staff down upon it with all the strength of his right arm, and then, as the stricken savage fell forward upon his face, he struck madly again and again, until the shapeless figure lay limp and still. One roof covered the first slain of Europe and of Asia.

Simon's veins were throbbing and quivering with the unwonted joy of action. All the energy stored up in those years of repose came in a flood at this moment of need. Standing in the darkness of the cell, he saw, as in a map of fire, the outlines of the great Barbaric host, the line of the river, the position of the settlements, the means by which they might be warned. Silently he waited in the shadow until the moon had sunk. Then he flung himself upon the dead man's horse, guided it down the gorge, and set forth at a gallop across the plain.

There were fires on every side of him, but he kept clear of the rings of light. Round each he could see, as he passed, the circle of sleeping warriors, with the long lines of picketed horses. Mile after mile and league after league stretched that huge encampment. And then, at last, he had reached the open plain which led to the river, and the fires of the invaders were but a dull smoulder against the black eastern sky. Ever faster and faster he sped across the steppe, like a single fluttered leaf which whirls before the storm. Even as the dawn whitened the sky behind him, it gleamed also upon the broad river in front, and he flogged his weary horse through the shallows, until he plunged into its full, yellow tide.

So it was that, as the young Roman centurion—Caius

Crassus—made his morning round in the fort of Tyras he saw a single horseman, who rode towards him from the river. Weary and spent, drenched with water and caked with dirt and sweat, both horse and man were at the last stage of their endurance. With amazement the Roman watched their progress, and recognized in the ragged, swaying figure, with flying hair and staring eyes, the hermit of the eastern desert. He ran to meet him, and caught him in his arms as he reeled from the saddle.

"What is it, then?" he asked. "What is your news?"

But the hermit could only point at the rising sun. "To arms!" he croaked. "To arms! The day of wrath is come!" And as he looked, the Roman saw —far across the river—a great dark shadow, which moved slowly over the distant plain.

69. *The Contest*

IN the year of our Lord 66, the Emperor Nero, being at that time in the twenty-ninth year of his life and the thirteenth of his reign, set sail for Greece with the strangest company and the most singular design that any monarch has ever entertained. With ten galleys he went forth from Puteoli, carrying with him great stores of painted scenery and theatrical properties, together with a number of knights and senators, whom he feared to leave behind him at Rome, and who were all marked for death in the course of his wanderings. In his train he took Natus, his singing coach; Cluvius, a man with a monstrous voice, who should bawl out his titles; and a thousand trained youths who had learned to applaud in unison whenever their master sang or played in public. So deftly had they been taught that each had his own rôle to play. Some did no more than give forth a low, deep hum of speechless appreciation. Some clapped with enthusiasm. Some, rising from approbation into absolute frenzy, shrieked, stamped and beat sticks upon the benches. Some—and they were the most effective—had learned from an Alexandrian a long, droning musical note which they all uttered together, so that it boomed over the assembly. With the aid of these mercenary admirers, Nero had every hope, in spite of his indifferent voice and clumsy execution, to return to Rome, bearing with him the chaplets for song offered for free competition by the Greek cities. As his great gilded galley with two tiers of oars passed down the Mediterranean, the Emperor sat in his cabin all day, his teacher by his side, rehearsing from morning to night those compositions which he had selected, whilst every few hours a Nubian slave massaged the Imperial throat with oil and balsam, that it might be ready for the great ordeal which lay before it in the land of poetry and song. His food, his drink, and his exercise were prescribed for him as for an athlete who trains for a contest, and the twanging of his lyre, with the strident notes of his voice, resounded continually from the Imperial quarters.

Now it chanced that there lived in those days a Grecian goatherd named Policles, who tended and partly owned a great flock which grazed upon the long flanks of the hills near Herœa, which is five miles north of the river Alpheus, and no great distance from the famous Olympia. This person was noted over all the country-side as a man of strange gifts and singular character. He was a poet who had twice been crowned for his verses, and he was a musician to whom the use and sound of an instrument were so natural that one would more easily meet him without his staff than his harp. Even in his lonely vigils on the winter hills he would bear it always slung over his shoulder, and would pass the long hours by its aid, so that it had come to be part of his very self. He was beautiful also, swarthy and eager, with a head like Adonis, and in strength there was no one who could compete with him But all was ruined by his disposition, which was so masterful that he would brook no opposition nor contradiction. For this reason he was continually at enmity with all his neighbours, and in his fits of temper he would spend months at a time in his stone hut among the mountains, hearing nothing from the world, and living only for his music and his goats.

One spring morning, in the year of 67, Policles, with the aid of his boy Dorus, had driven his goats over to a new pasturage which overlooked from afar the town of Olympia. Gazing down upon it from the mountain, the shepherd was surprised to see that a portion of the famous amphitheatre had been roofed in, as though some performance was being enacted. Living far from the world and from all news, Policles could not imagine what was afoot, for he was well aware that the Grecian games were not due for two years to come. Surely some poetic or musical contest must be proceeding of which he had heard nothing. If so, there would, perhaps, be some chance of his gaining the votes of the judges; and in any case he loved to hear the compositions and admire the execution of the great minstrels who assembled on such an occasion. Calling to Dorus, therefore, he left the goats to his charge, and strode swiftly away, his harp upon his back, to see what was going forward in the town.

When Policles came into the suburbs, he found them deserted; but he was still more surprised when he reached the main street to see no single human being in the place. He hastened his steps, therefore, and as he approached the theatre he was conscious of a low, sustained hum which announced the concourse of a huge assembly. Never in all his dreams had he imagined any musical competition upon so vast a scale as this. There were some soldiers clustering outside the door; but Policles pushed his way swiftly through them, and found himself upon the outskirts of the multitude who filled the great space formed by roofing over a portion of the national stadium. Looking around him, Policles saw a great number of his neighbours, whom he knew by sight, tightly packed upon the benches, all with their eyes fixed upon the stage. He also observed that there were soldiers round the walls, and that a considerable part of the hall was filled by a body of youths of foreign aspect, with white gowns and long hair. All this he perceived; but what it meant he could not imagine. He bent over to a neighbour to ask him, but a soldier prodded him at once with the butt end of his spear, and commanded him fiercely to hold his peace. The man whom he had addressed, thinking that Policles had demanded a seat, pressed closer to his neighbour, and so the shepherd found himself sitting at the end of the bench which was nearest to the door. Thence he concentrated himself upon the stage, on which Metas, a well-known minstrel from Corinth and an old friend of Policles, was singing and playing without much encouragement from the audience. To Policles it seemed that Metas was having less than his due, so he applauded loudly, but he was surprised to observe that the soldiers frowned at him, and that all his neighbours regarded him with some surprise. Being a man of strong and obstinate character, he was the more inclined to persevere in his clapping when he perceived that the general sentiment was against him.

But what followed filled the shepherd poet with absolute amazement. When Metas of Corinth had made his bow and withdrawn to half-hearted and perfunctory applause, there appeared upon the stage amid the wildest enthusiasm upon the part of the audience, a most extraordinary figure. He was a short, fat man, neither old nor young, with a bull neck and a round, heavy face, which hung in creases in front like the dewlap of an ox. He was absurdly clad in a short, blue tunic, braced at the waist with a golden belt. His neck and part of his chest were exposed, and his short, fat legs were bare from the buskins below to the middle of his thighs, which was as far as his tunic extended. In his hair were two golden wings, and the same upon his heels, after the fashion of the god Mercury. Behind him walked a negro bearing a harp, and beside him a richly dressed officer who bore rolls of music. This strange creature took the harp from the hands of the attendant, and advanced to the front of the stage, whence he bowed and smiled to the cheering audience. "This is some foppish singer from Athens," thought Policles to himself, but at the same time he understood that only a great master of song could receive such a reception from a Greek audience. This was evidently some wonderful performer whose reputation had preceded him. Policles settled hown, therefore, and prepared to give his soul up to the music.

The blue-clad player struck several chords upon his lyre, and then burst suddenly out into the "Ode of Niobe." Policles sat straight up on his bench and gazed at the stage in amazement. The tune demanded a rapid transition from a low note to a high, and had been purposely chosen for this reason. The low note was a grunting, a rumble, the deep, discordant growling of an ill-conditioned dog. Then suddenly the singer threw up his face, straightened his tubby figure, rose upon his tiptoes, and with wagging head and scarlet cheeks emitted such a howl as the same dog might have given had his growl been checked by a kick from his master. All the while the lyre twanged and thrummed, sometimes in front of and sometimes behind the voice of the singer. But what amazed Policles most of all was the effect of this performance upon the audience. Every Greek was a trained critic, and as unsparing in his hisses as he was lavish in his applause. Many a singer far better than this absurd fop had been driven amid execration and abuse from the platform. But now, as the man stopped and wiped the abundant sweat from his fat face, the whole assembly burst into a delirium of appreciation. The shepherd held his hands to his bursting head, and felt that his reason must be leaving him. It was surely a dreadful musical nightmare, and he would wake soon and laugh at the remembrance. But no; the figures were real, the faces were those of his neighbours, the cheers which resounded in his ears were indeed from an audience which filled the theatre of Olympia. The whole chorus was in full blast, the hummers humming, the shouters bellowing, the tappers hard at work upon the benches, while every now and then came a musical cyclone of "Incomparable! Divine!" from the trained phalanx who intoned their applause, their united voices sweeping over the tumult as the drone of the wind dominates the roar of the sea. It was madness—insufferable madness! If this were allowed to pass, there was an end of all musical justice in Greece. Policles' conscience would not permit him to be still. Standing upon his bench with waving hands and upraised voice, he protested with all the strength of his lungs against the mad judgment of the audience.

At first, amid the tumult, his action was hardly noticed. His voice was drowned in the universal roar which broke out afresh at each bow and smirk from the fatuous musician. But gradually the folk round Policles ceased clapping, and stared at him in astonishment. The silence grew in ever widening circles, until the whole great assembly sat mute, staring at this wild and magnificent creature who was storming at them from his perch near the door.

"Fools!" he cried. "What are you clapping at? What are you cheering? Is this what you call music? Is this cat-calling to earn an Olympian prize? The fellow has not a note in his voice. You are either deaf or mad, and I for one cry shame upon you for your folly."

Soldiers ran to pull him down, and the whole audience was in confusion, some of the bolder cheering the sentiments of the shepherd, and others crying that he should be cast out of the building. Meanwhile the successful singer, having handed his lyre to his negro attendant, was inquiring from those around him on the stage as to the cause of the uproar. Finally a herald with an enormously powerful voice stepped forward to the front, and proclaimed that if the foolish person at the back of the hall, who appeared to differ from the opinion of the rest of the audience, would come forward upon the platform, he might, if he dared, exhibit his own powers, and see if he could outdo the admirable and wonderful exhibition which they had just had the privilege of hearing.

Policles sprang readily to his feet at the challenge, and the great company making way for him to pass, he found himself a minute later standing in his unkempt garb, with his frayed and weather-beaten harp in his hand, before the expectant crowd. He stood for a moment tightening a string here and slackening another there until his chords rang true. Then, amid a murmur of laughter and jeers from the Roman benches immediately before him, he began to sing.

He had prepared no composition, but he had trained himself to improvise, singing out of his heart for the joy of the music. He told of the land of Elis, beloved of Jupiter, in which they were gathered that day, of the great bare mountain slopes, of the swift shadows of the clouds, of the winding, blue river, of the keen air of the uplands, of the chill of the evenings, and the beauties of earth and sky. It was all simple and childlike, but it went to the hearts of the Olympians, for it spoke of the land which they knew and loved. Yet when he at last dropped his hand, few of them dared to applaud, and their feeble voices were drowned by a storm of hisses and groans from his opponents. He shrank back in horror from so unusual a reception, and in an instant his blue-clad rival was in his place. If he had sung badly before, his performance now was inconceivable. His screams, his grunts, his discords, and harsh, jarring cacophanies were an outrage to the very name of music.

And yet every time that he paused for breath or to wipe his streaming forehead a fresh thunder of applause came rolling back from the audience. Policles sank his face in his hands and prayed that he might not be insane. Then, when the dreadful performance ceased, and the uproar of admiration showed that the crown was certainly awarded to this impostor, a horror of the audience, a hatred of this race of fools, and a craving for the peace and silence of the pastures mastered every feeling in his mind. He dashed through the mass of people waiting at the wings, and emerged in the open air. His old rival and friend Metas of Corinth was waiting there with an anxious face.

"Quick, Policles, quick!" he cried. "My pony is tethered behind yonder grove. A grey he is, with red trappings. Get you gone as hard as hoof will bear you, for if you are taken you will have no easy death."

"No easy death! What mean you, Metas? Who is the fellow?"

"Great Jupiter! did you not know? Where have you lived? It is Nero the Emperor! Never would he pardon what you have said about his voice. Quick, man, quick, or the guards will be at your heels!"

An hour later the shepherd was well on his way to his mountain home, and about the same time the Emperor, having received the Chaplet of Olympia for the incomparable excellence of his performance, was making inquiries with a frowning brow as to who the insolent person might be who had dared to utter such contemptuous criticisms.

"Bring him to me here this instant," said he, "and let Marcus with his knife and branding-iron be in attendance."

"If it please you, great Cæsar," said Arsenius Platus, the officer of attendance, "the man cannot be found, and there are some very strange rumours flying about."

"Rumours!" cried the angry Nero. "What do

you mean, Arsenius? I tell you that the fellow was an ignorant upstart with the bearing of a boor and the voice of a peacock. I tell you also that there are a good many who are as guilty as he among the people, for I heard them with my own ears raise cheers for him when he had sung his ridiculous ode. I have half a mind to burn their town about their ears, so that they may remember my visit."

"It is not to be wondered at if he won their votes, Cæsar," said the soldier, "for from what I hear it would have been no disgrace had you, even you, been conquered in this contest."

"I conquered! You are mad, Arsenius. What do you mean?"

"None know him, great Cæsar! He came from the mountains, and he disappeared into the mountains. You marked the wildness and strange beauty of his face. It is whispered that for once the great god Pan has condescended to measure himself against a mortal."

The cloud cleared from Nero's brow. "Of course, Arsenius! You are right! No man would have dared to brave me so. What a story for Rome! Let the messenger leave this very night, Arsenius, to tell them how their Emperor has upheld their honour in Olympia this day."

70. *The First Cargo*

"Ex ovo omnia"

WHEN you left Britain with your legion, my dear Crassus, I promised that I would write to you from time to time when a messenger chanced to be going to Rome, and keep you informed as to anything of interest which might occur in this country. Personally, I am very glad that I remained behind when the troops and so many of our citizens left, for though the living is rough and the climate is infernal, still by dint of the three voyages which I have made for amber to the Baltic, and the excellent prices which I obtained for it here, I shall soon be in a position to retire, and to spend my old age under my own fig tree, or even perhaps to buy a small villa at Baiæ or Posuoli, where I could get a good sun-bath after the continued fogs of this accursed island. I picture myself on a little farm, and I read the Georgics as a preparation; but when I hear the rain falling and the wind howling, Italy seems very far away.

In my previous letter I let you know how things were going in this country. The poor folk, who had given up all soldiering during the centuries that we guarded them, are now perfectly helpless before these Picts and Scots, tattooed Barbarians from the north, who overrun the whole country and do exactly what they please. So long as they kept to the north, the people in the south, who are the most numerous, and also the most civilised of the Britons, took no heed of them; but now the rascals have come as far as London, and the lazy folk in these parts have had to wake up. Vortigern, the king, is useless for anything but drink or women, so he sent across to the Baltic to get over some of the North Germans, in the hope that they would come and help him. It is bad enough to have a bear in your house, but it does not seem to me to mend matters if you call in a pack of ferocious wolves as well. However, nothing better could be devised, so an invitation was sent and very promptly accepted. And it is here that your humble friend appears upon the scene. In the course of my amber trading I had learned the Saxon speech, and so I was sent down in all haste to the Kentish shore that I might be there when our new allies came. I arrived there on the very day when their first vessel appeared, and it is of my adventures that I wish to tell you. It is perfectly clear to me that the landing of these warlike Germans in England will prove to be an event of historical importance, and so your inquisitive mind will not feel wearied if I treat the matter in some detail.

It was, then, upon the day of Mercury, immediately following the Feast of Our Blessed Lord's Ascension, that I found myself upon the south bank of the river Thames, at the point where it opens into a wide estuary. There is an island there named Thanet, which was the spot chosen for the landfall of our visitors. Sure enough, I had no sooner ridden up than there was a great red ship, the first, as it seems, of three, coming in under full sail. The white horse, which is the ensign of these rovers, was hanging from her topmast, and she appeared to be crowded with men. The sun was shining brightly, and the great scarlet ship, with snow-white sails and a line of gleaming shields slung over her side, made as fair a picture on that blue expanse as one would wish to see.

I pushed off at once in a boat, because it had been arranged that none of the Saxons should land until the king had come down to speak with their leaders. Presently I was under the ship, which had a gilded dragon in the bows, and a tier of oars along either side. As I looked up, there was a row of helmeted heads looking down at me, and among them I saw, to my great surprise and pleasure, that of Eric the Swart, with whom I do business at Venta every year. He greeted me heartily when I reached the deck, and became at once my guide, friend, and counsellor. This helped me greatly with these Barbarians, for it is their nature that they are very cold and aloof unless one of their own number can vouch for you, after which they are very hearty and hospitable. Try as they will, they find it hard, however, to avoid a certain suggestion of condescension, and in the baser sort, of contempt, when they are dealing with a foreigner.

It was a great stroke of luck meeting Eric, for he was able to give me some idea of how things stood before I was shown into the presence of Kenna, the leader of this particular ship. The crew, as I learned from him, was entirely made up of three tribes or families—those of Kenna, of Lanc, and of Hasta. Each of these tribes gets its name by putting the letters " ing " after the name of the chief, so that the people on board would describe themselves as Kennings, Lancings, and Hastings. I observed in the Baltic that the villages were named after the family who lived in them, each keeping to itself, so that I have no doubt that if these fellows get a footing on shore, we shall see settlements with names like these rising up among the British towns.

The greater part of the men were sturdy fellows with red, yellow or brown hair, mostly the latter. To my surprise, I saw several women among them. Eric, in answer to my question, explained that they always take their women with them so far as they can, and that instead of finding them an encumbrance as our Roman dames would be, they look upon them as helpmates and advisers. Of course, I remembered afterwards that our excellent and accurate Tacitus has remarked upon this characteristic of the Germans. All laws in the tribes are decided by votes, and a vote has not yet been given to the women, but many are in favour of it, and it is thought that woman and man may soon have the same power in the State, though many of the women themselves are opposed to such an innovation. I observed to Eric that it was fortunate there were several women on board, as they could keep each other company ; but he answered that the wives of chiefs had no desire to know the wives of the inferior officers, and that both of them combined against the more common women, so that any companionship was out of the question. He pointed as he spoke to Editha, the wife of Kenna, a red-faced, elderly woman, who walked among the others, her chin in the air, taking no more notice than if they did not exist.

Whilst I was talking to my friend Eric a sudden altercation broke out upon the deck, and a great number of the men paused in their work, and flocked towards the spot with faces which showed that they were deeply interested in the matter. Eric and I pushed our way among the others, for I was very anxious to see as much as I could of the ways and manners of these Barbarians. A quarrel had broken out about a child, a little blue-eyed fellow with curly, yellow hair, who appeared to be greatly amused by the hubbub of which he was the cause. On one side of him stood a white-bearded old man, of very majestic aspect, who signified by his gestures that he claimed the lad for himself, while on the other was a thin, earnest, anxious person, who strongly objected to the boy being taken from him. Eric whispered in my ear that the old man was the tribal high priest, who was the official sacrificer to their great god, Woden, whilst the other was a man who took somewhat different views, not upon Woden, but upon the means by which he should be worshipped. The majority of the crew were on the side of the old priest; but a certain number, who liked greater liberty of worship, and to invent their own prayers instead of always repeating the official ones, followed the lead of the younger man. The difference was too deep and too old to be healed among the grown men, but each had a great desire to impress his view upon the children. This was the reason why these two were now so furious with each other, and the argument between them ran so high that several of their followers on either side had drawn the short saxes, or knives from which their name of Saxon is derived, when a burly, red-headed man pushed his way through the throng, and in a voice of thunder brought the controversy to an end.

"You priests, who argue about the things which no man can know, are more trouble aboard this ship than all the dangers of the sea," he cried. "Can you not be content with worshipping Woden, over which we are all agreed, and not make so much of those small points upon which we may differ? If there is all this fuss about the teaching of the children, then I shall forbid either of you to teach them, and they must be content with as much as they can learn from their mothers."

The two angry teachers walked away with discontented faces; and Kenna—for it was he who spoke—ordered that a whistle should be sounded, and that the crew should assemble. I was pleased with the free bearing of these people, for though this was their greatest chief, they showed none of the exaggerated respect which soldiers of a legion might show to the Prætor, but met him on a respectful equality, which showed how highly they rated their own manhood.

From our Roman standard, his remarks to his men would seem very wanting in eloquence, for there were no graces nor metaphors to be found in them, and yet they were short, strong and to the point. At any rate it was very clear that they were to the minds of his hearers. He began by reminding them that they had left their own country because the land was all taken up, and that there was no use returning there, since there was no place where they could dwell as free and independent men. This island of Britain was but sparsely inhabited, and there was a chance that every one of them would be able to found a home of his own.

"You, Whitta," he said, addressing some of them by name, "you will found a Whitting hame, and you, Bucka, we shall see you in a Bucking hame, where your children's and your children's children will bless you for the broad acres which your valour will have gained for them." There was no word of glory or of honour in his speech, but he said that he was aware that they would do their duty, on which they all struck their swords upon their shields so that the Britons on the beach could hear the clang. Then, his eyes falling upon me, he asked me whether I was the messenger from Vortigern, and on my answering, he bid me follow him into his cabin, where Lanc and Hasta, the other chiefs, were waiting for a council.

Picture me, then, my dear Crassus, in a very low-roofed cabin, with these three huge Barbarians seated round me. Each was clad in some sort of saffron tunic, with a chain-mail shirt over it, and a helmet with the horns of oxen on the sides, laid upon the table before him. Like most of the Saxon chiefs, their beards were shaved, but they wore their hair long and their huge, light-coloured moustaches drooped down on to their shoulders. They are gentle, slow, and somewhat heavy in their bearing, but I can well fancy that their fury is the more terrible when it does arise.

Their minds seem to be of a very practical and positive nature, for they at once began to ask me a series of questions upon the numbers of the Britons, the resources of the kingdom, the conditions of its trade and other such subjects. They then set to work arguing over the information which I had given, and became so absorbed in their own contention that I believe there were times when they forgot my presence. Everything, after due discussion, was decided between them by the vote, the one who found himself in the minority always submitting, though sometimes with very bad grace. Indeed, on one occasion Lanc, who usually differed from the others, threatened to refer the matter to the general vote of the whole crew. There was a constant conflict in the point of view; for whereas Kenna and Hasta were anxious to extend the Saxon power, and to make it greater in the eyes of the world, Lanc was of opinion that they should give less thought to conquest and more to the comfort and advancement of their followers. At the same time it seemed to me that really Lanc was the most combative of the three; so much so that, even in time of peace, he could not forgo this contest with his own brethren. Neither of the others seemed very fond of him, for they were each, as was easy to see, proud of their chieftainship, and anxious to use their authority, referring continually to those noble ancestors from whom it was derived; while Lanc, though he was equally well born, took the view of the common men upon every occasion, claiming that the interests of the many were superior to the privileges of the few. In a word, Crassus, if you could imagine a free-booting Gracchus on one side, and two piratical Patricians upon the other, you would understand the effect which my companions produced upon me.

There was one peculiarity which I observed in their conversation which soothed me very much. I am fond of these Britons, among whom I have spent so much of my life, and I wish them well. It was very pleasing, therefore, to notice that these men insisted upon it in their conversation that the whole object of their visit was the good of the Islanders. Any prospect of advantage to themselves was pushed into the background. I was not clear that these professions could be made to agree with the speech in which Kenna had promised a hundred hides of land to every man on the ship; but on my making this remark, the three chiefs seemed very surprised and hurt by my suspicions, and explained very plausibly that, as the Britons needed them as a guard, they could not aid them better than by settling on the soil, and so being continually at hand in order to help them. In time, they said, they hoped to raise and train the natives to such a point that they would be able to look after themselves. Lanc spoke with some degree of eloquence upon the nobleness of the mission which they had undertaken, and the others clattered their cups of mead (a jar of that unpleasant drink was on the table) in token of their agreement.

I observed also how much interested, and how very earnest and intolerant these Barbarians were in the matter of religion. Of Christianity they knew nothing, so that although they were aware that the Britons were Christians, they had not a notion of what their creed really was. Yet without examination they started by taking it for granted that their own worship of Woden was absolutely right, and that therefore this other creed must be absolutely wrong. "This vile religion," "This sad superstition," and "This grievous error" were among the phrases which they used towards it. Instead of expressing pity for anyone who had been misinformed upon so serious a question, their feelings were those of anger, and they declared most earnestly that they would spare no pains to set the matter right, fingering the hilts of their long broadswords as they said so.

Well, my dear Crassus, you will have had enough of me and of my Saxons. I have given you a short sketch of these people and their ways. Since I began this letter, I have visited the two other ships which have come in, and as I find the same characteristics among the people on board them, I cannot doubt that they lie deeply in the race. For the rest, they are brave, hardy, and very pertinacious in all that they undertake; whereas the Britons, though a great deal more spirited, have not the same steadiness of purpose, their quicker imaginations suggesting always some other course, and their more fiery passions being succeeded by reaction. When I looked from the deck of the first Saxon ship, and saw the swaying, excited multitude of Britons on the beach, contrasting them with the intent, silent men who stood beside me, it seemed to me more than ever dangerous to call in such allies. So strongly did I feel it that I turned to Kenna, who was also looking towards the beach.

"You will own this island before you have finished," said I.

His eyes sparkled as he gazed. "Perhaps," he cried; and then suddenly correcting himself and thinking that he had said too much, he added—

"A temporary occupation—nothing more."

71. *An Iconoclast*

IT was daybreak of a March morning in the year of Christ 92. Outside the long Semita Alta was already thronged with people, with buyers and sellers, callers and strollers, for the Romans were so early-rising a people that many a Patrician preferred to see his clients at six in the morning. Such was the good republican tradition, still upheld by the more conservative; but with more modern habits of luxury, a night of pleasure and banqueting was no uncommon thing. Thus one, who had learned the new and yet adhered to the old, might find his hours overlap, and without so much as a pretence of sleep come straight from his night of debauch into his day of business, turning with heavy wits and an aching head to that round of formal duties which consumed the life of a Roman gentleman.

So it was with Emilius Flaccus that March morning. He and his fellow-senator, Caius Balbus, had passed the night in one of those gloomy drinking bouts to which the Emperor Domitian summoned his chosen friends at the high palace on the Palatine. Now, having reached the portals of the house of Flaccus, they stood together under the pomegranate-fringed portico which fronted the peristyle and, confident in each other's tried discretion, made up by the freedom of their criticism for the long self-suppression of that melancholy feast.

"If he would but feed his guests," said Balbus, a little red-faced, choleric nobleman with yellow-shot, angry eyes. "What had we? Upon my life, I have forgotten. Plovers' eggs, a mess of fish, some bird or other, and then his eternal apples."

"Of which," said Flaccus, "he ate only the apples. Do him the justice to confess that he takes even less than he gives. At least they cannot say of him as of Vitellius, that his teeth beggared the empire."

"No, nor his thirst either, great as it is. That fiery Sabine wine of his could be had for a few sesterces the amphora. It is the common drink of the carters at every wine-house on the country roads. I longed for a glass of my own rich Falernian or the mellow Coan that was bottled in the year that Titus took Jerusalem. Is it even now too late? Could we not wash this rasping stuff from our palates?"

"Nay, better come in with me now and take a bitter draught ere you go upon your way. My Greek physician Stephanos has a rare prescription for a morning head. What! Your clients await you? Well, I will see you later at the Senate house."

The Patrician had entered his atrium, bright with rare flowers, and melodious with strange singing birds. At the jaws of the hall, true to his morning duties, stood Lebs, the little Nubian slave, with snow-white tunic and turban, a salver of glasses in one hand, whilst in the other he held a flask of thin, lemon-tinted liquid. The master of the house filled up a bitter aromatic bumper, and was about to drink it off, when his hand was arrested by a sudden perception that something was much amiss in his household. It was to be read all around him—in the frightened eyes of the black boy, in the agitated face of the keeper of the atrium, in the gloom and silence of the little knot of ordinarii, the procurator or major-domo at their head, who had assembled to greet their master. Stephanos the physician Cleios the Alexandrine reader, Promus the steward, each turned his head away to avoid his master's questioning gaze.

"What in the name of Pluto is the matter with you all?" cried the amazed senator, whose night of potations had left him in no mood for patience. "Why do you stand moping there? Stephanos, Vacculus, is anything amiss? Here, Promus, you are the head of my household. What is it, then? Why do you turn your eyes away from me?"

The burly steward, whose fat face was haggard and mottled with anxiety, laid his hand upon the sleeve of the domestic beside him.

"Sergius is responsible for the atrium, my lord. It is for him to tell you the terrible thing that has befallen in your absence."

"Nay, it was Datus who did it. Bring him in, and let him explain it himself," said Sergius in a sulky voice.

The patience of the Patrician was at an end. "Speak this instant, you rascal!" he shouted angrily. "Another minute, and I will have you dragged to the ergastulum, where, with your feet in the stocks and the gyves round your wrists, you may learn quicker obedience. Speak, I say, and without delay."

"It is the Venus," the man stammered; "the Greek Venus of Praxiteles."

The senator gave a cry of apprehension and rushed to the corner of the atrium, where a little shrine, curtained off by silken drapery, held the precious statue, the greatest art treasure of his collection—perhaps of the whole world. He tore the hangings aside and stood in speechless anger before the outraged goddess. The red, perfumed lamp which always burned before her had been spilled and broken; her altar fire had been quenched, her chaplet had been dashed aside. But worst of all—insufferable sacrilege!—her own beautiful nude body of glistening Pantelic marble, as white and fair as when the inspired Greek had hewed it out five hundred years before, had been most brutally mishandled. Three fingers of the gracious, outstretched hand had been struck off, and lay upon the pedestal beside her. Above her delicate breast a dark mark showed, where a blow had disfigured the marble. Emilius Flaccus, the most delicate and judicious connoisseur in Rome, stood gasping and croaking, his hand to his throat, as he gazed at his disfigured masterpiece. Then he turned upon his slaves, his fury in his convulsed face; but, to his amazement, they were not looking at him, but had all turned in attitudes of deep respect towards the opening of the peristyle. As he faced round and saw who had just entered his house, his own rage fell away from him in an instant, and his manner became as humble as that of his servants.

The new-comer was a man forty-three years of age, clean shaven, with a massive head, large, engorged eyes, a small, clear-cut nose, and the full bull neck which was the especial mark of his breed. He had entered through the peristyle with a swaggering, rolling gait, as one who walks upon his own ground, and now he stood, his hands upon his hips, looking round him at the bowing slaves, and finally at their master, with a half-humorous expression upon his flushed and brutal face.

"Why, Emilius," said he, "I had understood that your household was the best-ordered in Rome. What is amiss with you this morning?"

"Nothing could be amiss with us now that Cæsar has deigned to come under my roof," said the courtier. "This is indeed a most glad surprise which you have prepared for me."

"It was an afterthought," said Domitian. "When you and the others had left me, I was in no mood for sleep, and so it came into my mind that I would have a breath of morning air by coming down to you, and seeing this Grecian Venus of yours, about which you discoursed so eloquently between the cups. But, indeed, by your appearance and that of your servants, I should judge that my visit was an ill-timed one."

"Nay, dear master; say not so. But, indeed, it is truth that I was in trouble at the moment of your welcome entrance, and this trouble was, as the Fates have willed it, brought forth by that very statue in which you have been graciously pleased to show your interest. There it stands, and you can see for yourself how rudely it has been mishandled."

"By Pluto and all the nether gods, if it were mine

some of you should feed the lampreys," said the Emperor, looking round with his fierce eyes at the shrinking slaves. "You were always overmerciful, Emilius. It is the common talk that your catenæ are rusted for want of use. But surely this is beyond all bounds. Let me see how you handle the matter. Whom do you hold responsible ?"

"The slave Sergius is responsible, since it is his place to tend the atrium," said Flaccus. "Stand forward, Sergius. What have you to say ?"

The trembling slave advanced to his master. "If it please you, sir, the mischief has been done by Datus the Christian."

"Datus ! Who is he ?"

"The matulator, the scavenger, my lord. I did not know that he belonged to these horrible people, or I should not have admitted him. He came with his broom to brush out the litter of the birds. His eyes fell upon the Venus, and in an instant he had rushed upon her and struck her two blows with his wooden besom. Then we fell upon him and dragged him away. But alas ! alas ! it was too late, for already the wretch had dashed off the fingers of the goddess."

The Emperor smiled grimly, while the Patrician's thin face grew pale with anger.

"Where is the fellow ?" he asked.

"In the ergastulum, your honour, with the furca on his neck."

"Bring him hither and summon the household."

A few minutes later the whole back of the atrium was thronged by the motley crowd who ministered to the household needs of a great Roman nobleman. There was the arcarius, or account keeper, with his stylum behind his ear ; the sleek prægustator, who sampled all foods, so as to stand between his master and poison, and beside him his predecessor, now a half-witted idiot through the interception twenty years before of a datura draught from Canidia ; the cellarman, summoned from amongst his amphoræ ; the cook, with his basting-ladle in his hand ; the pompous nomenclator, who ushered the guests ; the cubicularius, who saw to their accommodation ; the silentiarius, who kept order in the house ; the structor, who set forth the tables ; the carptor, who carved the food ; the cinerarius, who lit the fires—these and many more, half-curious, half-terrified, came to the judging of Datus. Behind them a chattering, giggling swarm of Lalages, Marias, Cerusas, and Amaryllides, from the laundries and the spinning-rooms, stood upon their tiptoes, and extended their pretty, wondering faces over the shoulders of the men. Through this crowd came two stout varlets leading the culprit between them. He was a small, dark, rough-headed man, with an unkempt beard and wild eyes which shone brightly with strong inward emotion. His hands were bound behind him, and over his neck was the heavy wooden collar or furca which was placed upon refractory slaves. A smear of blood across his cheek showed that he had not come uninjured from the preceding scuffle.

" Are you Datus the scavenger ? " asked the Patrician.

The man drew himself up proudly. " Yes," said he, " I am Datus."

" Did you do this injury to my statue ? "

" Yes, I did."

There was an uncompromising boldness in the man's reply which compelled respect. The wrath of his master became tinged with interest.

" Why did you do this ? " he asked.

" Because it was my duty."

" Why, then, was it your duty to destroy your master's property ? "

" Because I am a Christian." His eyes blazed suddenly out of his dark face. " Because there is no God but the one eternal, and all else are sticks and stones. What has this naked harlot to do with Him to whom the great firmament is but a garment and the earth a footstool ? It was in His service that I have broken your statue."

Domitian looked with a smile at the Patrician. "You will make nothing of him," said he. "They speak even so when they stand before the lions in the arena. As to argument, not all the philosophers of Rome can break them down. Before my very face they refuse to sacrifice in my honour. Never were such impossible people to deal with. I should take a short way with him if I were you."

"What would Cæsar advise?"

"There are the games this afternoon. I am showing the new hunting-leopard which King Juba has sent from Numidia. This slave may give us some sport when he finds the hungry beast sniffing at his heels."

The Patrician considered for a moment. He had always been a father to his servants. It was hateful to him to think of any injury befalling them. Perhaps even now, if this strange fanatic would show his sorrow for what he had done, it might be possible to spare him. At least it was worth trying.

"Your offence deserves death," he said. "What reasons can you give why it should not befall you, since you have injured this statue, which is worth your own price a hundred times over?"

The slave looked steadfastly at his master. "I do not fear death," he said. "My sister Candida died in the arena, and I am ready to do the same. It is true that I have injured your statue, but I am able to find you something of far greater value in exchange. I will give you the truth and the gospel in exchange for your broken idol."

The Emperor laughed. "You will do nothing with him, Emilius," he said. "I know his breed of old. He is ready to die; he says so himself. Why save him, then?"

But the Patrician still hesitated. He would make a last effort.

"Throw off his bonds," he said to the guards. "Now take the furca off his neck. So! Now, Datus, I have released you to show you that I trust you. I have no wish to do you any hurt if you will but acknowledge your error, and so set a better example to my household here assembled."

"How, then, shall I acknowledge my error?" the slave asked.

"Bow your head before the goddess, and entreat her forgiveness for the violence you have done her. Then perhaps you may gain my pardon as well."

"Put me, then, before her," said the Christian.

Emilius Flaccus looked triumphantly at Domitian. By kindness and tact he was effecting that which the Emperor had failed to do by violence. Datus walked in front of the mutilated Venus. Then with a sudden spring he tore the baton out of the hand of one of his guardians, leaped upon the pedestal, and showered his blows upon the lovely marble woman. With a crack and a dull thud her right-arm dropped to the ground. Another fierce blow and the left had followed. Flaccus danced and screamed with horror, while his servants dragged the raving iconoclast from his impassive victim. Domitian's brutal laughter echoed through the hall.

"Well, friend, what think you now?" he cried. "Are you wiser than your Emperor? Can you indeed tame your Christian with kindness?"

Emilius Flaccus wiped the sweat from his brow. "He is yours, great Cæsar. Do with him as you will."

"Let him be at the gladiator's entrance of the circus an hour before the games begin," said the Emperor. "Now, Emilius, the night has been a merry one. My Ligurian galley waits by the river quay. Come, cool your head with a spin to Ostia ere the business of State calls you to the Senate."

72. *Giant Maximin*

I—THE COMING OF MAXIMIN

MANY are the strange vicissitudes of history. Greatness has often sunk to the dust, and has tempered itself to its new surrounding. Smallness has risen aloft, has flourished for a time, and then has sunk once more. Rich monarchs have become poor monks, brave conquerors have lost their manhood, eunuchs and women have overthrown armies and kingdoms. Surely there is no situation which the mind of man could invent which has not taken shape and been played out upon the world stage. But of all the strange careers and of all the wondrous happenings, stranger than Charles in his monastery, or Justin on his throne, there stands the case of Giant Maximin, what he attained, and how he attained it. Let me tell the sober facts of history, tinged only by that colouring to which the more austere historians could not condescend. It is a record as well as a story.

In the heart of Thrace some ten miles north of the Rhodope mountains, there is a valley which is named Harpessus, after the stream which runs down it. Through this valley lies the main road from the east to the west, and along the road, returning from an expedition against the Alani, there marched, upon the fifth day of the month of June in the year 210, a small but compact Roman army. It consisted of three legions —the Jovian, the Cappadocian, and the men of Hercules. Ten turmæ of Gallic cavalry led the van, whilst the rear was covered by a regiment of Batavian Horse Guards, the immediate attendants of the Emperor Septimus Severus, who had conducted the campaign in person. The peasants who lined the low hills which fringed the valley looked with indifference upon the long files of dusty, heavily burdened infantry, but they broke into murmurs of delight at the gold-faced cuirasses and high, brazen, horse-hair helmets of the guardsmen, applauding their stalwart figures, their martial bearing, and the stately black chargers which they rode. A soldier might know that it was the little weary men with their short swords, their heavy pikes over their shoulders, and their square shields slung upon their backs, who were the real terror of the enemies of the Empire, but to the eyes of the wondering Thracians it was this troop of glittering Apollos who bore Rome's victory upon their banners, and upheld the throne of the purple-togaed prince who rode before them.

Among the scattered groups of peasants who looked on from a respectful distance at this military pageant, there were two men who attracted much attention from those who stood immediately around them. The one was commonplace enough—a little grey-headed man, with uncouth dress and a frame which was bent and warped by a long life of arduous toil, goat-driving and wood-chopping, among the mountains. It was the appearance of his youthful companion which had drawn the amazed observation of the bystanders. In stature he was such a giant as is seen but once or twice in each generation of mankind. Eight feet and two inches was his measure from his sandalled sole to the topmost curls of his tangled hair. Yet for all his mighty stature there was nothing heavy or clumsy in the man. His huge shoulders bore no redundant flesh, and his figure was straight and hard and supple as a young pine tree. A frayed suit of brown leather clung close to his giant body, and a cloak of undressed sheep-skin was slung from his shoulder. His bold blue eyes, shock of yellow hair and fair skin showed that he was of Gothic or northern blood, and the amazed expression upon his broad, frank face as he stared at the passing troops told of a simple and uneventful life in some back valley of the Macedonian mountains.

"I fear your mother was right when she advised that we keep you at home," said the old man anxiously. "Tree-cutting and wood-carrying will seem but dull work after such a sight as this."

"When I see mother next it will be to put a golden torque round her neck," said the young giant. "And you, daddy; I will fill your leather pouch with gold pieces before I have done."

The old man looked at his son with startled eyes. "You would not leave us, Theckla! What could we do without you?"

"My place is down among yonder men," said the young man. "I was not born to drive goats and carry logs, but to sell this manhood of mine in the best market. There is my market in the Emperor's own Guard. Say nothing, daddy, for my mind is set, and if you weep now it will be to laugh hereafter. I will to great Rome with the soldiers."

The daily march of the heavily laden Roman legionary was fixed at twenty miles; but on this afternoon, though only half the distance had been accomplished, the silver trumpets blared out their welcome news that a camp was to be formed. As the men broke their ranks, the reason of their light march was announced by the decurions. It was the birthday of Geta, the younger son of the Emperor, and in his honour there would be games and a double ration of wine. But the iron discipline of the Roman army required that under all circumstances certain duties should be performed, and foremost among them that the camp should be made secure. Laying down their arms in the order of their ranks, the soldiers seized their spades and axes, and worked rapidly and joyously until sloping vallum and gaping fossa girdled them round, and gave them safe refuge against a night attack. Then in noisy, laughing, gesticulating crowds they gathered in their thousands round the grassy arena where the sports were to be held. A long, green hillside sloped down to a level plain, and on this gentle incline the army lay watching the strife of the chosen athletes who contended before them. They stretched themselves in the glare of the sunshine, their heavy tunics thrown off, and their naked limbs sprawling, wine-cups and baskets of fruit and cakes circling amongst them, enjoying rest and peace as only those can to whom it comes so rarely.

The five-mile race was over, and had been won as usual by Decurion Brennus, the crack long-distance champion of the Herculians. Amid the yells of the Jovians, Capellus of the corps had carried off both the long and the high jump. Big Brebix the Gaul had outthrown the long guardsman Serenus with the fifty pound stone. Now, as the sun sank towards the western ridge, and turned the Harpessus to a riband of gold, they had come to the final of the wrestling, where the pliant Greek, whose name is lost in the nickname of "Python," was tried out against the bull-necked Lictor of the military police, a hairy Hercules, whose heavy hand had in the way of duty oppressed many of the spectators.

As the two men, stripped save for their loincloths, approached the wrestling-ring, cheers and counter-cheers burst from their adherents, some favouring the Lictor for his Roman blood, some the Greek from their own private grudge. And then, of a sudden, the cheering died, heads were turned towards the slope away from the arena, men stood up and peered and pointed, until finally, in a strange hush, the whole great assembly had forgotten the athletes, and were watching a single man walking swiftly towards them down the green curve of the hill. This huge, solitary figure, with the oaken club in his hand, the shaggy fleece flapping from his great shoulders, and the setting sun gleaming upon a halo of golden hair, might have been the tutelary god of the fierce and barren mountains from which he had issued. Even the Emperor rose from his chair and gazed with open-eyed amazement at the extraordinary being who approached him.

The man, whom we already know as Theckla the Thracian, paid no heed to the attention which he had aroused, but strode onwards, stepping as lightly as a deer, until he reached the fringe of the soldiers. Amid their open ranks he picked his way, sprang over the ropes which guarded the arena, and advanced towards the Emperor, until a spear at his breast warned him that he must go no nearer. Then he sunk upon his right knee and called out some words in the Gothic speech.

"Great Jupiter! Whoever saw such a body of a man!" cried the Emperor. "What says he? What is amiss with the fellow? Whence comes he, and what is his name?"

An interpreter translated the Barbarian's answer. "He says, great Cæsar, that he is of good blood, and sprung by a Gothic father from a woman of the Alani. He says that his name is Theckla, and that he would fain carry a sword in Cæsar's service."

The Emperor smiled. "Some post could surely be found for such a man, were it but as janitor at the Palatine Palace," said he to one of the Prefects. "I would fain see him walk even as he is through the forum. He would turn the heads of half the women in Rome. Talk to him, Crassus. You know his speech."

The Roman officer turned to the giant. "Cæsar says that you are to come with him, and he will make you the servant at his door."

The Barbarian rose, and his fair cheeks flushed with resentment.

"I will serve Cæsar as a soldier," said he, "but I will be house-servant to no man—not even to him. If Cæsar would see what manner of man I am let him put one of his guardsmen up against me."

"By the shade of Milo this is a bold fellow!" cried

the Emperor. "How say you, Crassus? Shall he make good his words?"

"By your leave, Cæsar," said the blunt soldier, "good swordsmen are too rare in these days that we should let them slay each other for sport. Perhaps if the Barbarian would wrestle a fall——"

"Excellent!" cried the Emperor. "Here is the Python, and here Varus the Lictor, each stripped for the bout. Have a look at them, Barbarian, and see which you would choose. What does he say? He would take them both? Nay then he is either the king of wrestlers or the king of boasters, and we shall soon see which. Let him have his way, and he has himself to thank if he comes out with a broken neck."

There was some laughter when the peasant tossed his sheep-skin mantle to the ground and, without troubling to remove his leathern tunic, advanced towards the two wrestlers; but it became uproarious when with a quick spring he seized the Greek under one arm and the Roman under the other, holding them as in a vice. Then with a terrific effort he tore them both from the ground, carried them writhing and kicking round the arena, and finally walking up to the Emperor's throne, threw his two athletes down in front of him. Then, bowing to Cæsar, the huge Barbarian withdrew, and laid his great bulk down among the ranks of the applauding soldiers, whence he watched with stolid unconcern the conclusion of the sports.

It was still daylight, when the last event had been decided, and the soldiers returned to the camp. The Emperor Severus had ordered his horse, and in the company of Crassus, his favourite Prefect, rode down the winding pathway which skirts the Harpessus, chatting over the future dispersal of the army. They had ridden for some miles when Severus, glancing behind him, was surprised to see a huge figure which trotted lightly along at the very heels of his horse.

"Surely this is Mercury as well as Hercules that

we have found among the Thracian mountains," said he with a smile. "Let us see how soon our Syrian horses can out-distance him."

The two Romans broke into a gallop, and did not draw rein until a good mile had been covered at the full pace of their splendid chargers. Then they turned and looked back; but there, some distance off, still running with a lightness and a spring which spoke of iron muscles and inexhaustible endurance, came the great Barbarian. The Roman Emperor waited until the athlete had come up to them.

"Why do you follow me?" he asked.

"It is my hope, Cæsar, that I may always follow you." His flushed face as he spoke was almost level with that of the mounted Roman.

"By the god of war, I do not know where in all the world I could find such a servant!" cried the Emperor. "You shall be my own body-guard, the one nearest to me of all."

The giant fell upon his knee. "My life and strength are yours," he said. "I ask no more than to spend them for Cæsar."

Crassus had interpreted this short dialogue. He now turned to the Emperor.

"If he is indeed to be always at your call, Cæsar, it would be well to give the poor Barbarian some name which your lips can frame. Theckla is as uncouth and craggy a word as one of his native rocks."

The Emperor pondered for a moment. "If I am to have the naming of him," said he, "then surely I shall call him Maximus, for there is not such a giant upon earth."

"Hark you," said the Prefect. "The Emperor has deigned to give you a Roman name, since you have come into his service. Henceforth you are no longer Theckla, but you are Maximus. Can you say it after me?"

"Maximin," repeated the Barbarian, trying to catch the Roman word.

The Emperor laughed at the mincing accent. "Yes, yes, Maximin let it be. To all the world you are Maximin, the body-guard of Severus. When we have reached Rome, we will soon see that your dress shall correspond with your office. Meanwhile march with the guard until you have my further orders."

So it came about that as the Roman army resumed its march next day, and left behind it the fair Valley of the Harpessus, a huge recruit, clad in brown leather, with a rude sheep-skin floating from his shoulders, marched beside the Imperial troop. But far away in the wooden farmhouse of a distant Macedonian valley two old country folk wept salt tears, and prayed to the gods for the safety of their boy who had turned his face to Rome.

II—THE RISE OF GIANT MAXIMIN

Exactly twenty-five years had passed since the day that Theckla the huge, Thracian peasant, had turned into Maximin, the Roman guardsman. They had not been good years for Rome. Gone for ever were the great Imperial days of the Hadrians and the Trajans. Gone also the golden age of the two Antonines, when the highest were for once the most worthy and most wise. It had been an epoch of weak and cruel men. Severus, the swarthy African, a stark, grim man had died in far away York, after fighting all the winter with the Caledonian Highlanders—a race who have ever since worn the martial garb of the Romans. His son, known only by his slighting nickname of Caracalla, had reigned during six years of insane lust and cruelty, before the knife of an angry soldier avenged the dignity of the Roman name. The nonentity Macrinus had filled the dangerous throne for a single year before he also met a bloody end, and made room for the most grotesque of all monarchs, the unspeakable Heliogabalus with his foul mind and his painted face. He in turn was cut to pieces by the soldiers ; and Severus Alexander, a gentle youth, scarce seventeen years of age, had been thrust into his place. For thirteen years now he had ruled, striving with some success to put some virtue and stability into the rotting Empire, but raising many fierce enemies as he did so—enemies whom he had not the strength nor the wit to hold in check.

And Giant Maximin—what of him ? He had carried his eight feet of manhood through the lowlands of Scotland and the passes of the Grampians. He had seen Severus pass away, and had soldiered with his son. He had fought in Armenia, in Dacia, and in Germany. They had made him a centurion upon the field when with his hands he plucked out one by one the stockades of a northern village, and so cleared a path for the stormers. His strength had been the jest and the admiration of the soldiers. Legends about him had spread through the army, and were the common gossip round the camp fires—of his duel with the German axeman on the Island of the Rhine, and of the blow with his fist that broke the leg of a Scythian's horse. Gradually he had won his way upwards, until now, after quarter of a century's service, he was tribune of the fourth legion and superintendent of recruits for the whole army. The young soldier who had come under the glare of Maximin's eyes, or had been lifted up with one huge hand while he was cuffed by the other, had his first lesson from him in the discipline of the service.

It was nightfall in the camp of the fourth legion upon the Gallic shore of the Rhine. Across the moonlit water, amid the thick forests which stretched away to the dim horizon, lay the wild, untamed German tribes. Down on the river bank the light gleamed upon the helmets of the Roman sentinels who kept guard along the river. Far away a red point rose and fell in the darkness—a watch-fire of the enemy upon the farther shore.

Outside his tent, beside some smouldering logs, Giant Maximin was seated, a dozen of his officers around him. He had changed much since the day when we first met him in the Valley of the Harpessus. His huge frame was as erect as ever, and there was no sign of diminution of his strength. But he had aged none the less. The yellow tangle of hair was gone, worn down by the ever-pressing helmet. The fresh young face was drawn and hardened, with austere lines wrought by trouble and privation. The nose was more hawk-like, the eyes more cunning, the expression more cynical and more sinister. In his youth, a child would have run to his arms. Now it would shrink screaming from his gaze. That was what twenty-five years with the eagles had done for Theckla, the Thracian peasant.

He was listening now—for he was a man of few words—to the chatter of his centurions. One of them, Balbus the Sicilian, had been to the main camp at Mainz, only four miles away, and had seen the Emperor Alexander arrive that very day from Rome. The rest were eager at the news, for it was a time of unrest, and the rumour of great changes was in the air.

"How many had he with him?" asked Labienus, a black-browed veteran from the south of Gaul. "I'll wager a month's pay that he was not so trustful as to come alone among his faithful legions."

"He had no great force," replied Balbus. "Ten or twelve cohorts of the Prætorians and a handful of horse."

"Then indeed his head is in the lion's mouth," cried Sulpicius, a hot-headed youth from the African Pentapolis. "How was he received?"

"Coldly enough. There was scarce a shout as he came down the line."

"They are ripe for mischief," said Labienus. "And who can wonder, when it is we soldiers who uphold the Empire upon our spears, while the lazy citizens at Rome reap all of our sowing. Why cannot a soldier have what the soldier gains? So long as they throw us our denarius a day, they think that they have done with us."

"Aye," croaked a grumbling old greybeard. "Our limbs, our blood, our lives—what do they care so long as the Barbarians are held off, and they are left in peace to their feastings and their circus? Free bread, free wine, free games—everything for the loafer at Rome. For us the frontier guard and a soldier's fare."

Maximin gave a deep laugh. "Old Plancus talks like that," said he; "but we know that for all the world he would not change his steel plate for a citizen's gown. You've earned the kennel, old hound, if you wish it. Go and gnaw your bone and growl in peace."

"Nay, I am too old for change. I will follow the eagle till I die. And yet I had rather die in serving a soldier master than a long-gowned Syrian who comes of a stock where the women are men and the men are women."

There was a laugh from the circle of soldiers, for sedition and mutiny were rife in the camp, and even the old centurion's outbreak could not draw a protest. Maximin raised his great mastiff head and looked at Balbus.

"Was any name in the mouths of the soldiers?" he asked in a meaning voice.

There was a hush for the answer. The sigh of the wind among the pines and the low lapping of the river swelled out louder in the silence. Balbus looked hard at his commander.

"Two names were whispered from rank to rank," said he. "One was Ascenius Pollio, the General. The other was——"

The fiery Sulpicius sprang to his feet waving a glowing brand above his head.

"Maximinus!" he yelled, "Imperator Maximinus Augustus!"

Who could tell how it came about? No one had thought of it an hour before. And now it sprang in an instant to full accomplishment. The shout of the frenzied young African had scarcely rung through the darkness when from the tents, from the watch-fires, from the sentries, the answer came pealing back : " Ave Maximinus ! Ave Maximinus Augustus ! " From all sides men came rushing, half-clad, wild-eyed, their eyes staring, their mouths agape, flaming wisps of straw or flaring torches above their heads. The giant was caught up by scores of hands, and sat enthroned upon the bull necks of the legionaries. " To the camp ! " they yelled. " To the camp ! Hail ! Hail to the soldier Cæsar ! "

That same night Severus Alexander, the young Syrian Emperor, walked outside his Prætorian camp, accompanied by his friend Licinius Probus, the Captain of the Guard. They were talking gravely of the gloomy faces and seditious bearing of the soldiers. A great foreboding of evil weighed heavily upon the Emperor's heart, and it was reflected upon the stern, bearded face of his companion.

" I like it not," said he. " It is my counsel, Cæsar, that with the first light of morning we make our way south once more."

" But surely," the Emperor answered, " I could not for shame turn my back upon the danger. What have they against me ? How have I harmed them that they should forget their vows and rise upon me ? "

" They are like children who ask always for something new. You heard the murmur as you rode along the ranks. Nay, Cæsar, fly to-morrow, and your Prætorians will see that you are not pursued. There may be some loyal cohorts among the legions, and if we join forces——"

A distant shout broke in upon their conversation—a low, continued roar, like the swelling tumult of a sweeping wave. Far down the road upon which they stood there twinkled many moving lights, tossing and sinking as they rapidly advanced, whilst the hoarse, tumultuous bellowing broke into articulate words, the same tremendous words, a thousand-fold repeated. Licinius seized the Emperor by the wrist and dragged him under the cover of some bushes.

" Be still, Cæsar ! For your life be still ! " he whispered. " One word and we are lost ! "

Crouching in the darkness, they saw that wild procession pass, the rushing, screaming figures, the tossing arms, the bearded, distorted faces, now scarlet and now grey, as the brandished torches waxed or waned. They heard the rush of many feet, the clamour of hoarse voices, the clang of metal upon metal. And then suddenly, above them all, they saw a vision of a monstrous man, a huge bowed back, a savage face, grim hawk eyes, that looked out over the swaying shields. It was seen for an instant in a smoke-fringed circle of fire, and then it had swept on into the night.

" Who is he ? " stammered the Emperor, clutching at his guardsman's sleeve. " They call him Cæsar."

" It is surely Maximin, the Thracian peasant." In the darkness the Prætorian officer looked with strange eyes at his master.

" It is all over, Cæsar. Let us fly together to your tent."

But even as they went a second shout had broken forth tenfold louder than the first. If the one had been the roar of the oncoming wave, the other was the full turmoil of the tempest. Twenty thousand voices from the camp had broken into one wild shout which echoed through the night, until the distant Germans round their watch-fires listened in wonder and alarm.

" Ave ! " cried the voices. " Ave Maximinus Augustus ! "

High upon their bucklers stood the giant, and looked round him at the great floor of upturned faces below. His own savage soul was stirred by the clamour, but only his gleaming eyes spoke of the fire within. He waved his hand to the shouting soldiers as the huntsman waves to the leaping pack. They passed him up a coronet of oak leaves, and clashed their swords in homage as he placed it on his head. And then there came a swirl in the crowd before him, a little space was cleared, and there knelt an officer in the Prætorian garb, blood upon his face, blood upon his bared forearm, blood upon his naked sword. Licinius, too, had gone with the tide.

"Hail, Cæsar, hail!" he cried, as he bowed his head before the giant. "I come from Alexander. He will trouble you no more."

III—THE FALL OF MAXIMIN

For three years the soldier Emperor had been upon the throne. His palace had been his tent, and his people had been the legionaries. With them he was supreme; away from them he was nothing. He had gone with them from one frontier to the other. He had fought against Dacians, Sarmatians, and once again against the Germans. But Rome knew nothing of him, and all her turbulence rose against a master who cared so little for her or her opinion that he never deigned to set foot within her walls. There were cabals and conspiracies against the absent Cæsar. Then his heavy hand fell upon them, and they were cuffed, even as the young soldiers had been who passed under his discipline. He knew nothing, and cared as much for consuls, senates, and civil laws. His own will and the power of the sword were the only forces which he could understand. Of commerce and the arts he was as ignorant as when he left his Thracian home. The whole vast Empire was to him a huge machine for producing the money by which the legions were to be rewarded. Should he fail to get that money, his fellow-soldiers would bear him a grudge. To watch their interests they had raised him upon their shields that night. If city funds had to be plundered or temples desecrated, still the money must be got. Such was the point of view of Giant Maximin.

But there came resistance, and all the fierce energy of the man, all the hardness which had given him the leadership of hard men, sprang forth to quell it. From his youth he had lived amidst slaughter. Life and death were cheap things to him. He struck savagely at all who stood up to him, and when they hit back, he struck more savagely still. His giant shadow lay black across the Empire from Britain to Syria. A strange, subtle vindictiveness became also apparent in him. Omnipotence ripened every fault and swelled it into crime.

In the old days he had been rebuked for his roughness. Now a sullen, dangerous anger rose against those who had rebuked him. He sat by the hour with his craggy chin between his hands, and his elbows resting on his knees, while he recalled all the misadventures, all the vexations of his early youth, when Roman wits had shot their little satires upon his bulk and his ignorance. He could not write, but his son Verus placed the names upon his tablets, and they were sent to the Governor of Rome. Men who had long forgotten their offence were called suddenly to make most bloody reparation.

A rebellion broke out in Africa, but was quelled by his lieutenant. But the mere rumour of it set Rome in a turmoil. The Senate found something of its ancient spirit. So did the Italian people. They would not be for ever bullied by the legions. As Maximin approached from the frontier, with the sack of rebellious Rome in his mind, he was faced with every sign of a national resistance. The country-side was deserted, the farms abandoned, the fields cleared of crops and cattle. Before him lay the walled town of Aquileia. He flung himself fiercely upon it, but was met by as fierce a resistance. The walls could not be forced, and yet there was no food in the country round for his legions. The men were starving and dissatisfied. What did it matter to them who was Emperor? Maximin was no better than themselves. Why should they call down the curse of the whole Empire upon their heads by upholding him? He saw their sullen faces and their averted eyes, and he knew that the end had come.

That night he sat with his son Verus in his tent, and he spoke softly and gently as the youth had never heard him speak before. He had spoken thus in old days with Paullina, the boy's mother; but she had been dead these many years, and all that was soft and gentle in the big man had passed away with her. Now her spirit seemed very near him, and his own was tempered by its presence.

"I would have you go back to the Thracian mountains," he said. "I have tried both, boy, and I can tell you that there is no pleasure which power can bring which can equal the breath of the wind and the smell of the kine upon a summer morning. Against you they have no quarrel. Why should they mishandle you. Keep far from Rome and the Romans. Old Eudoxus has money, and to spare. He awaits you with two horses outside the camp. Make for the Valley of the Harpessus, lad. It was thence that your father came, and there you will find his kin. Buy and stock a homestead, and keep yourself far from the paths of greatness and of danger. God keep you, Verus, and send you safe to Thrace."

When his son had kissed his hand and had left him, the Emperor drew his robe around him and sat long in thought. In his slow brain he revolved the past—his early, peaceful days, his years with Severus, his memories of Britain, his long campaigns, his strivings and battlings, all leading to that mad night by the Rhine. His fellow-soldiers had loved him then. And now he had read death in their eyes. How had he failed them? Others he might have wronged, but they at least had no complaint against him. If he had his time again, he would think less of them and more of his people, he would try to win love instead of fear, he would live for peace and not for war. If he had his time again! But there were shuffling steps, furtive whispers, and the low rattle of arms outside his tent. A bearded face looked in at him, a swarthy African face that he knew well. He laughed, and baring his arm, he took his sword from the table beside him.

"It is you, Sulpicius," said he. "You have not come

to cry 'Ave Imperator Maximin!' as once by the camp fire. You are tired of me, and by the gods I am tired of you, and glad to be at the end of it. Come and have done with it, for I am minded to see how many of you I can take with me when I go."

They clustered at the door of the tent, peeping over each other's shoulders, and none wishing to be the first to close with that laughing, mocking giant. But something was pushed forward upon a spear point, and as he saw it, Maximin groaned and his sword sank to the earth.

"You might have spared the boy," he sobbed. "He would not have hurt you. Have done with it then, for I will gladly follow him."

So they closed upon him and cut and stabbed and thrust, until his knees gave way beneath him and he dropped upon the floor.

"The tyrant is dead!" they cried. "The tyrant is dead," and from all the camp beneath them and from the walls of the beleaguered city the joyous cry came echoing back, "He is dead, Maximin is dead!"

I sit in my study, and upon the table before me lies a denarius of Maximin, as fresh as when the triumvir of the Temple of Juno Moneta sent it from the mint. Around it are recorded his resounding titles—Imperator Maximinus, Pontifex Maximus, Tribunitia potestate, and the rest. In the centre is the impress of a great craggy head, a massive jaw, a rude fighting face, a contracted forehead. For all the pompous roll of titles it is a peasant's face, and I see him not as the Emperor of Rome, but as the great Thracian boor who strode down the hill-side on that far-distant summer day when first the eagles beckoned him to Rome.

73. *The Red Star*

THE house of Theodosius, the famous eastern merchant, was in the best part of Constantinople at the Sea Point which is near the church of Saint Demetrius. Here he would entertain in so princely a fashion that even the Emperor Maurice had been known to come privately from the neighbouring Bucoleon palace in order to join in the revelry. On the night in question, however, which was the fourth of November in the year of our Lord 630, his numerous guests had retired early, and there remained only two intimates, both of them successful merchants like himself, who sat with him over their wine on the marble verandah of his house whence on the one side they could see the lights of the shipping in the Sea of Marmora, and on the other the beacons which marked out the course of the Bosphorus. Immediately at their feet lay a narrow strait of water, with the low, dark loom of the Asiatic hills beyond. A thin haze hid the heavens, but away to the south a single great red star burned sullenly in the darkness.

The night was cool, the light was soothing, and the three men talked freely, letting their minds drift back into the earlier days when they had staked their capital, and often their lives, on the ventures which had built up their present fortunes. The host spoke of his long journeys in North Africa, the land of the Moors; how he had travelled, keeping the blue sea ever upon his right, until he had passed the ruins of Carthage, and so on and ever on until a great tidal ocean beat upon a yellow strand before him, while on the right he could see the high rock across the waves which marked the Pillars of Hercules. His talk was of dark-skinned, bearded men, of lions, and of monstrous serpents. Then Demetrius, the Cilician, an austere man of sixty, told how he also had built up his mighty wealth. He spoke of a journey over the Danube and through the country of the fierce Huns, until he and his friends had found themselves in the mighty forest of Germany, on the shores of the great river which is called the Elbe. His stories were of huge men, sluggish of mind, but murderous in their cups, of sudden midnight broils and nocturnal flights, of villages buried in dense woods, of bloody heathen sacrifices, and of the bears and wolves who haunted the forest paths. So the two elder men capped each other's stories and awoke each other's memories, while Manuel Ducas, the young merchant of gold and ostrich feathers, whose name was already known all over the Levant, sat in silence and listened to their talk. At last, however, they called upon him also for an anecdote, and leaning his cheek upon his elbow, with his eyes fixed upon the great red star which burned in the south, the younger man began to speak.

" It is the sight of that star which brings a story into my mind," said he. " I do not know its name. Old Lascaris the astronomer would tell me if I asked, but I have no desire to know. Yet at this time of the year I always look out for it, and I never fail to see it burning in the same place. But it seems to me that it is redder and larger than it was.

" It was some ten years ago that I made an expedition into Abyssinia, where I traded to such good effect that I set forth on my return with more than a hundred camel-loads of skins, ivory, gold, spices, and other African produce. I brought them to the sea-coast at Arsinoe, and carried them up the Arabian Gulf in five of the small boats of the country. Finally, I landed near Sava which is a starting-point for caravans, and, having assembled my camels and hired a guard of forty men from the wandering Arabs, I set forth for Macoraba. From this point, which is the sacred city of the idolaters of those parts, one can always join the large caravans which go north twice a year to Jerusalem and the sea-coast of Syria.

"Our route was a long and weary one. On our left hand was the Arabian Gulf, lying like a pool of molten metal under the glare of day, but changing to blood-red as the sun sank each evening behind the distant African coast. On our right was a monstrous desert which extends, so far as I know, across the whole of Arabia and away to the distant kingdom of the Persians. For many days we saw no sign of life save our own long, straggling line of laden camels with their tattered, swarthy guardians. In these deserts the soft sand deadens the footfall of the animals, so that their silent progress day after day through a scene which never changes, and which is itself noiseless, becomes at last like a strange dream. Often as I rode behind my caravan, and gazed at the grotesque figures which bore my wares in front of me, I found it hard to believe that it was indeed reality, and that it was I, I, Manuel Ducas, who lived near the Theodosian Gate of Constantinople, and shouted for the Green at the hippodrome every Sunday afternoon, who was there in so strange a land and with such singular comrades.

"Now and then, far out at sea, we caught sight of the white, triangular sails of the boats which these people use, but as they are all pirates, we were very glad to be safely upon shore. Once or twice, too, by the water's edge we saw dwarfish creatures—one could scarcely say if they were men or monkeys—who burrow for homes among the seaweed, drink the pools of brackish water, and eat what they can catch. These are the fish-eaters, the Ichthyophagi, of whom old Herodotus talks—surely the lowest of all the human race. Our Arabs shrank from them with horror, for it is well known that, should you die in the desert, these little people will settle on you like carrion crows, and leave not a bone unpicked. They gibbered and croaked and waved their skinny arms at us as we passed, knowing well that they could swim far out to sea if we attempted to pursue them ; for it is said that even the sharks turn with disgust from their foul bodies.

"We had travelled in this way for ten days, camping every evening at the vile wells which offered a small quantity of abominable water. It was our habit to rise very early and to travel very late, but to halt during the intolerable heat of the afternoon, when, for want of trees, we would crouch in the shadow of a sandhill, or, if that were wanting, behind our own camels and merchandise, in order to escape from the insufferable glare of the sun. On the seventh day we were near the point where one leaves the coast in order to strike inland to Macoraba. We had concluded our midday halt, and were just starting once more, the sun still being so hot that we could hardly bear it, when, looking up, I saw a remarkable sight. Standing on a hillock to our right there was a man about forty feet high, holding in his hand a spear which was the size of the mast of a large ship. You look surprised, my friends, and you can therefore imagine my feelings when I saw such a sight. But my reason soon told me that the object in front of me was really a wandering Arab, whose form had been enormously magnified by the strange distorting effects which the hot air of the desert is able to cause.

"However, the actual apparition caused more alarm to my companions than the imagined one had to me, for with a howl of dismay they shrank together into a frightened group, all pointing and gesticulating as they gazed at the distant figure. I then observed that the man was not alone, but that from all the sandhills a line of turbaned heads was gazing down upon us. The chief of the escort came running to me, and informed me of the cause of their terror, which was that they recognised, by some peculiarity in their headgear, that these men belonged to the tribe of the Dilwas, the most ferocious and unscrupulous of the Bedouin, who had evidently laid an ambuscade for us at this point with the intention of seizing our caravan. When I thought of all my efforts in Abyssinia, of the length of my journey and of the dangers and fatigues which I had endured, I could not bear to think of this total disaster coming upon me at the last instant and robbing me not only of my profits, but also of my original outlay. It was evident, however, that the robbers were too numerous for us to attempt to defend ourselves, and that we should be very fortunate if we escaped with our lives. Sitting upon a packet, therefore, I commended my soul to our Blessesd Saint Helena, while I watched with despairing eyes the stealthy and menacing approach of the Arab robbers.

" It may have been our own good fortune, or it may have been the handsome offering of beeswax candles—four to the pound—which I had mentally vowed to the Blessed Helena, but at that instant I heard a great outcry of joy from among my own followers. Standing upon the packet that I might have a better view, I was overjoyed to see a long caravan—five hundred camels at least—with a numerous armed guard, coming along the route from Macoraba. It is, I need not tell you, the custom of all caravans to combine their forces against the robbers of the desert, and with the aid of these newcomers we had become the stronger party. The marauders recognised it at once, for they vanished as if their native sands had swallowed them. Running up to the summit of a sandhill, I was just able to catch a glimpse of a dust-cloud whirling away across the yellow plain, with the long necks of their camels, the flutter of their loose garments, and the gleam of their spears breaking out from the heart of it. So vanished the marauders.

" Presently I found, however, that I had only exchanged one danger for another. At first I had hoped that this new caravan might belong to some Roman citizen, or at least to some Syrian Christian, but I found that it was entirely Arab. The trading Arabs who are settled in the numerous towns of Arabia are, of course, very much more peaceable than the Bedouin of the wilderness.

those sons of Ishmael of whom we read in Holy Writ. But the Arab blood is covetous and lawless, so that when I saw several hundred of them formed in a semicircle round our camels, looking with greedy eyes at my boxes of precious metals and my packets of ostrich feathers, I feared the worst.

"The leader of the new caravan was a man of dignified bearing and remarkable appearance. His age I would judge to be about forty. He had aquiline features, a noble black beard, and eyes so luminous, so searching and so intense that I cannot remember in all my wanderings to have seen any which could be compared with them. To my thanks and salutations he returned a formal bow, and stood stroking his beard and looking in silence at the wealth which had suddenly fallen into his power. A murmur from his followers showed the eagerness with which they awaited the order to fall upon the plunder, and a young ruffian, who seemed to be on intimate terms with the leader, came to his elbow and put the desires of his companions into words.

"'Surely, O Revered One,' said he, 'these people and their treasure have been delivered into our hands. When we return with it to the holy place, who of all the Koraish will fail to see the finger of God which has led us?'

"But the leader shook his head. 'Nay, Ali, it may not be,' he answered. 'This man is, as I judge, a citizen of Rome, and we may not treat him as though he were an idolater.'

"'But he is an unbeliever,' cried the youth, fingering a great knife which hung in his belt. 'Were I to be judge, he would lose not only his merchandise, but his life also, if he did not accept the faith.'

"The older man smiled and shook his head. 'Nay, Ali; you are too hot-headed,' said he, 'seeing that there are not as yet three hundred faithful in the world, our hands would indeed be full if we were to take the lives and property of all who are not with us. Forget not, dear lad, that charity and honesty are the very nose-ring and halter of the true faith.'

"'Among the faithful,' said the ferocious youth.

"'Nay, towards everyone. It is the law of Allah. And yet'—here his countenance darkened, and his eyes shone with a most sinister light—'the day may soon come when the hour of grace is past, and woe, then, to those who have not hearkened! Then shall the sword of Allah be drawn, and it shall not be sheathed until the harvest is reaped. First it shall strike the idolaters on the day when my own people and kinsmen, the unbelieving Koraish, shall be scattered, and the three hundred and sixty idols of the Caaba thrust out upon the dungheaps of the town. Then shall the Caaba be the home and temple of one God only who brooks no rival on earth or in heaven.'

"The man's followers had gathered round him, their spears in their hands, their ardent eyes fixed upon his face, and their dark features convulsed with such fanatic enthusiasm as showed the hold which he had upon their love and respect.

"'We shall be patient,' said he; 'but some time next year, the year after, the day may come when the great angel Gabriel shall bear me the message that the time of words has gone by, and that the hour of the sword has come. We are few and weak, but if it is His will, who can stand against us? Are you of Jewish faith, stranger?' he asked.

"I answered that I was not.

"'The better for you,' he answered, with the same furious anger in his swarthy face. 'First shall the idolaters fall, and then the Jews, in that they have not known those very prophets whom they had themselves foretold. Then last will come the turn of the Christians, who follow indeed a true Prophet, greater than Moses or Abraham, but who have sinned in that they have confounded a creature with the Creator. To each in turn—idolater, Jew, and Christian—the day of reckoning will come.'

"The ragamuffins behind him all shook their spears as he spoke. There was no doubt about their earnestness, but when I looked at their tattered dresses and simple arms, I could not help smiling to think of their ambitious threats, and to picture what their fate would be upon the day of battle before the battle-axes of our Imperial Guards, or the spears of the heavy cavalry of the Armenian Themes. However, I need not say that I was discreet enough to keep my thoughts to myself, as I had no desire to be the first martyr in this fresh attack upon our blessed faith.

"It was now evening, and it was decided that the two caravans should camp together—an arrangement which was the more welcome as we were by no means sure that we had seen the last of the marauders. I had invited the leader of the Arabs to have supper with me, and after a long exercise of prayer with his followers, he came to join me, but my attempt at hospitality was thrown away, for he would not touch the excellent wine which I had unpacked for him, nor would he eat any of my dainties, contenting himself with stale bread, dried dates, and water. After this meal we sat alone by the smouldering fire, the magnificent arch of the heavens above us of that deep, rich blue with those gleaming, clear-cut stars which can only be seen in that dry desert air. Our camp lay before us, and no sound reached our ears save the dull murmur of the voices of our companions and the occasional shrill cry of a jackal among the sandhills around us. Face to face I sat with this strange man, the glow of the fire beating upon his eager and imperious features and reflecting from his passionate eyes. It was the strangest vigil, and one which will never pass from my recollection. I have spoken with many wise and famous men upon my travels, but never with one who left the impression of this one.

"And yet much of his talk was unintelligible to me, though, as you are aware, I speak Arabian like an Arab. It rose and fell in the strangest way. Sometimes it was the babble of a child, sometimes the incoherent raving of a fanatic, sometimes the lofty dreams of a prophet and philosopher. There were times when his stories of demons, of miracles, of dreams, and of omens, were such as an old woman might tell to please the children of an evening. There were others when, as he talked with shining face of his converse with angels, of the intentions of the Creator, and the end of the universe, I felt as if I were in the company of someone more than mortal, someone who was indeed the direct messenger of the Most High.

"There were good reasons why he should treat me with such confidence. He saw in me a messenger to Constantinople and to the Roman Empire. Even as Saint Paul had brought Christianity to Europe, so he hoped that I might carry his doctrines to my native city. Alas! be the doctrines what they may, I fear that I am not the stuff of which Pauls are made. Yet he strove with all his heart during that long Arabian night to bring me over to his belief. He had with him a holy book, written, as he said, from the dictation of an angel, which he carried in tablets of bone in the nose-bag of a camel. Some chapters of this he read me; but though the precepts were usually good, the language seemed wild and fanciful. There were times when I could scarce keep my countenance as I listened to him. He planned out his future movements, and indeed, as he spoke, it was hard to remember that he was only the wandering leader of an Arab caravan, and not one of the great ones of the earth.

"'When God has given me sufficient power, which will be within a few years,' said he, 'I will unite all Arabia under my banner. Then I will spread my doctrine over Syria and Egypt. When this has been done, I will turn to Persia, and give them the choice of the true faith or the sword. Having taken Persia, it will be easy then to overrun Asia Minor, and so to make our way to Constantinople.'

"I bit my lip to keep from laughing. 'And how long will it be before your victorious troops have reached the Bosphorus?' I asked.

"'Such things are in the hands of God, whose servants we are,' said he. 'It may be that I shall myself have passed away before these things are accomplished, but before the days of our children are completed, all that I have now told you will come to pass. Look at that star,' he added, pointing to a beautiful clear planet above our heads. 'That is the symbol of Christ. See how serene and peaceful it shines, like His own teaching and the memory of His life. Now,' he added, turning his outstretched hand to a dusky red star upon the horizon—the very one on which we are gazing now—'that is my star, which tells of wrath, of war, of a scourge upon sinners. And yet both are indeed stars, and each does as Allah may ordain.'

"Well, that was the experience which was called to my mind by the sight of this star to-night. Red and angry, it still broods over the south, even as I saw it that night in the desert. Somewhere down yonder that man is working and striving. He may be stabbed by some brother fanatic or slain in a tribal skirmish. If so, that is the end. But if he lives, there was that in his eyes and in his presence which tells me that Mahomet the son of Abdallah—for that was his name—will testify in some noteworthy fashion to the faith that is in him."

74. *The Silver Mirror*

JAN. 3.—This affair of White and Wotherspoon's accounts proves to be a gigantic task. There are twenty thick ledgers to be examined and checked. Who would be a junior partner? However, it is the first big bit of business which has been left entirely in my hands. I must justify it. But it has to be finished so that the lawyers may have the result in time for the trial. Johnson said this morning that I should have to get the last figure out before the twentieth of the month. Good Lord! Well, have at it, and if human brain and nerve can stand the strain, I'll win out at the other side. It means office-work from ten to five, and then a second sitting from about eight to one in the morning. There's drama in an accountant's life. When I find myself in the still early hours, while all the world sleeps, hunting through column after column for those missing figures which will turn a respected alderman into a felon, I understand that it is not such a prosaic profession after all.

On Monday I came on the first trace of defalcation. No heavy game hunter ever got a finer thrill when first he caught sight of the trail of his quarry. But I look at the twenty ledgers and think of the jungle through which I have to follow him before I get my kill. Hard work—but rare sport, too, in a way! I saw the fat fellow once at a City dinner, his red face glowing above a white napkin. He looked at the little pale man at the end of the table. He would have been pale, too, if he could have seen the task that would be mine.

Jan. 6.—What perfect nonsense it is for doctors to prescribe rest when rest is out of the question! Asses! They might as well shout to a man who has a pack of wolves at his heels that what he wants is absolute quiet. My figures must be out by a certain date; unless they are so, I shall lose the chance of my lifetime, so how on earth am I to rest? I'll take a week or so after the trial.

Perhaps I was myself a fool to go to the doctor at all. But I get nervous and highly strung when I sit alone at my work at night. It's not a pain—only a sort of fullness of the head with an occasional mist over the eyes. I thought perhaps some bromide, or chloral, or something of the kind might do me good. But stop work? It's absurd to ask such a thing. It's like a long-distance race. You feel queer at first and your heart thumps and your lungs pant, but if you have only the pluck to keep on, you get your second wind. I'll stick to my work and wait for my second wind. If it never comes—all the same, I'll stick to my work. Two ledgers are done, and I am well on in the third. The rascal has covered his tracks well, but I pick them up for all that.

Jan. 9.—I had not meant to go to the doctor again. And yet I have had to. "Straining my nerves, risking a complete breakdown, even endangering my sanity." That's a nice sentence to have fired off at one. Well, I'll stand the strain and I'll take the risk, and so long as I can sit in my chair and move a pen I'll follow the old sinner's slot.

By the way, I may as well set down here the queer experience which drove me this second time to the doctor. I'll keep an exact record of my symptoms and sensations, because they are interesting in themselves —"a curious psycho-physiological study," says the doctor—and also because I am perfectly certain that when I am through with them they will all seem blurred and unreal, like some queer dream betwixt sleeping and waking. So now, while they are fresh, I will just make a note of them if only as a change of thought after the endless figures.

There's an old silver-framed mirror in my room. It was given me by a friend who had a taste for antiquities, and he, as I happen to know, picked it up at a sale and had no notion where it came from. It's a large thing—three feet across and two feet high—and it leans at the back of a side-table on my left as I write. The frame is flat, about three inches across, and very old; far too old for hall-marks or other methods of determining its age. The glass part projects, with a bevelled edge, and has the magnificent reflecting power which is only, as it seems to me, to be found in very old mirrors. There's a feeling of perspective when you look into it such as no modern glass can ever give.

The mirror is so situated that as I sit at the table I can usually see nothing in it but the reflection of the red window curtains. But a queer thing happened last night. I had been working for some hours, very much against the grain, with continual bouts of that mistiness of which I had complained. Again and again I had to stop and clear my eyes. Well, on one of these occasions I chanced to look at the mirror. It had the oddest appearance. The red curtains which should have been reflected in it were no longer there, but the glass seemed to be clouded and steamy, not on the surface, which glittered like steel, but deep down in the very grain of it. This opacity, when I stared hard at it, appeared to slowly rotate this way and that, until it was a thick, white cloud swirling in heavy wreaths. So real and solid was it, and so reasonable was I, that I remember turning, with the idea that the curtains were on fire. But everything was deadly still in the room—no sound save the ticking of the clock, no movement save the slow gyration of that strange woolly cloud deep in the heart of the old mirror.

Then, as I looked, the mist, or smoke, or cloud, or whatever one may call it, seemed to coalesce and solidify at two points quite close together, and I was aware, with a thrill of interest rather than of fear, that these were two eyes looking out into the room. A vague outline of a head I could see—a woman's by the hair, but this was very shadowy. Only the eyes were quite distinct; such eyes—dark, luminous, filled with some passionate emotion, fury or horror, I could not say which. Never have I seen eyes which were so full of intense, vivid life. They were not fixed upon me, but stared out into the room. Then as I sat erect, passed my hand over my brow, and made a strong conscious effort to pull myself together, the dim head faded into the general opacity, the mirror slowly cleared, and there were the red curtains once again.

A sceptic would say, no doubt, that I had dropped

asleep over my figures, and that my experience was a dream. As a matter of fact, I was never more vividly awake in my life. I was able to argue about it even as I looked at it, and to tell myself that it was a subjective impression—a chimera of the nerves—begotten by worry and insomnia. But why this particular shape? And who is the woman, and what is the dreadful emotion which I read in those wonderful brown eyes? They come between me and my work. For the first time I have done less than the daily tally which I had marked out. Perhaps that is why I have had no abnormal sensations to-night. To-morrow I must wake up, come what may.

Jan. 11.—All well, and good progress with my work. I wind the net, coil after coil, round that bulky body. But the last smile may remain with him if my own nerves break over it. The mirror would seem to be a sort of barometer which marks my brain pressure. Each night I have observed that it had clouded before I reached the end of my task.

Dr. Sinclair (who is, it seems, a bit of a psychologist) was so interested in my account that he came round this evening to have a look at the mirror. I had observed that something was scribbled in crabbed old characters upon the metal work at the back. He examined this with a lens, but could make nothing of it. "Sanc. X. Pal." was his final reading of it, but that did not bring us any further. He advised me to put it away into another room; but, after all, whatever I may see in it is, by his own account, only a symptom. It is in the cause that the danger lies. The twenty ledgers—not the silver mirror—should be packed away if I could only do it. I'm at the eighth now, so I progress.

Jan 13.—Perhaps it would have been wiser after all if I had packed away the mirror. I had an extraordinary experience with it last night. And yet I find it so interesting, so fascinating, that even now I will keep it in its place. What on earth is the meaning of it all?

I suppose it was about one in the morning, and I was closing my books preparatory to staggering off to bed, when I saw her there in front of me. The stage of mistiness and development must have passed unobserved, and there she was in all her beauty and passion and distress, as clear-cut as if she were really in the flesh before me. The figure was small, but very distinct—so much so that every feature, and every detail of dress, are stamped in my memory. She is seated on the extreme left of the mirror. A sort of shadowy figure crouches down beside her—I can dimly discern that it is a man—and then behind them is cloud, in which I see figures—figures which move. It is not a mere picture upon which I look. It is a scene in life, an actual episode. She crouches and quivers. The man beside her cowers down. The vague figures make abrupt movements and gestures. All my fears were swallowed up in my interest. It was maddening to see so much and not to see more.

But I can at least describe the woman to the smallest point. She is very beautiful and quite young—not more than five-and-twenty, I should judge. Her hair is of a very rich brown, with a warm chestnut shade fining into gold at the edges. A little flat-pointed cap comes to an angle in front and is made of lace edged with pearls. The forehead is high, too high perhaps for perfect beauty; but one would not have it otherwise, as it gives a touch of power and strength to what would otherwise be a softly feminine face. The brows are most delicately curved over heavy eyelids, and then come those wonderful eyes—so large, so dark, so full of overmastering emotion, of rage and horror, contending with a pride of self-control which holds her from sheer frenzy! The cheeks are pale, the lips white with agony, the chin and throat most exquisitely rounded. The figure sits and leans forward in the chair, straining and rigid, cataleptic with horror. The dress is black velvet, a jewel gleams like a flame in the breast, and a golden crucifix smoulders in the shadow of a fold. This is the lady whose image still lives in the old silver mirror. What dire deed could it be which has left its impress there, so that now, in another age, if the spirit of a man be but worn down to it, he may be conscious of its presence?

One other detail: On the left side of the skirt of the black dress was, as I thought at first, a shapeless bunch of white ribbon. Then, as I looked more intently or as the vision defined itself more clearly, I perceived what it was. It was the hand of a man, clenched and knotted in agony, which held on with a convulsive grasp to the fold of the dress. The rest of the crouching figure was a mere vague outline, but that strenuous hand shone clear on the dark background, with a sinister suggestion of tragedy in its frantic clutch. The man is frightened—horribly frightened. That I can clearly discern. What has terrified him so? Why does he grip the woman's dress? The answer lies amongst those moving figures in the background. They have brought danger both to him and to her. The interest of the thing fascinated me. I thought no more of its relation to my own nerves. I stared and stared as if in a theatre. But I could get no further. The mist thinned. There were tumultuous movements in which all the figures were vaguely concerned. Then the mirror was clear once more.

The doctor says I must drop work for a day, and I can afford to do so, for I have made good progress lately. It is quite evident that the visions depend entirely upon my own nervous state, for I sat in front of the mirror for an hour to-night, with no result whatever. My soothing day has chased them away. I wonder whether I shall ever penetrate what they all mean? I examined the mirror this evening under a good light, and besides the mysterious inscription "Sanc. X. Pal.," I was able to discern some signs of heraldic marks, very faintly visible upon the silver. They must be very ancient, as they are almost obliterated. So far as I could make out, they were three spear-heads, two above and one below. I will show them to the doctor when he calls to-morrow.

Jan. 14.—Feel perfectly well again, and I intend that nothing else shall stop me until my task is finished. The doctor was shown the marks on the mirror and agreed that they were armorial bearings. He is deeply interested in all that I have told him, and cross-questioned me closely on the details. It amuses me to notice how he is torn in two by conflicting desires—the one that his patient should lose his symptoms, the other that the medium—for so he regards me—should solve this mystery of the past. He advised continued rest, but did not oppose me too violently when I declared that such a thing was out of the question until the ten remaining ledgers have been checked.

Jan. 17.—For three nights I have had no experiences—my day of rest has borne fruit. Only a quarter of my task is left, but I must make a forced march, for the lawyers are clamouring for their material. I will give them enough and to spare. I have him fast on a hundred counts. When they realise what a slippery, cunning rascal he is, I should gain some credit from the case. False trading accounts, false balance-sheets, dividends drawn from capital, losses written down as profits, suppression of working expenses, manipulation of petty cash—it is a fine record!

Jan. 18.—Headaches, nervous twitches, mistiness, fullness of the temples—all the premonitions of trouble, and the trouble came sure enough. And yet my real sorrow is not so much that the vision should come as that it should cease before all is revealed.

But I saw more to-night. The crouching man was as visible as the lady whose gown he clutched. He is a little swarthy fellow, with a black, pointed beard. He has a loose gown of damask trimmed with fur. The prevailing tints of his dress are red. What a fright the fellow is in, to be sure! He cowers and shivers and glares back over his shoulder. There is a small knife in his other hand, but he is far too tremulous and cowed to use it. Dimly now I begin to see the figures in the background. Fierce faces, bearded and dark, shape themselves out of the mist. There is one terrible creature, a skeleton of a man, with hollow cheeks and eyes sunk in his head. He also has a knife in his hand. On the right of the woman stands a tall man, very young, with flaxen hair, his face sullen and dour. The beautiful woman looks up at him in appeal. So does the man on the ground. This youth seems to be the arbiter of their fate. The crouching man draws closer and hides himself in the woman's skirts. The tall youth bends and tries to drag her away from him. So much I saw last night before the mirror cleared. Shall I never know what it leads to and whence it comes? It is not a mere imagination, of that I am very sure. Somewhere, some time, this scene has been acted, and this old mirror has reflected it. But when—where?

Jan. 20.—My work draws to a close, and it is time. I feel a tenseness within my brain, a sense of intolerable strain, which warns me that something must give. I have worked myself to the limit. But to-night should be the last night. With a supreme effort I should finish the final ledger and complete the case before I rise from my chair. I will do it. I will.

Feb. 7.—I did. My God, what an experience! I hardly know if I am strong enough yet to set it down.

Let me explain in the first instance that I am writing this in Dr. Sinclair's private hospital some three weeks after the last entry in my diary. On the night of January 20 my nervous system finally gave way, and I remembered nothing afterwards until I found myself, three days ago, in the home of rest. And I can rest with a good conscience. My work was done before I went under. My figures are in the solicitors' hands. The hunt is over.

And now I must describe that last night. I had

sworn to finish my work, and so intently did I stick to it, though my head was bursting, that I would never look up until the last column had been added. And yet it was fine self-restraint, for all the time I knew that wonderful things were happening in the mirror. Every nerve in my body told me so. If I looked up there was an end of my work. So I did not look up till all was finished. Then, when at last with throbbing temples I threw down my pen and raised my eyes, what a sight was there!

The mirror in its silver frame was like a stage, brilliantly lit, in which a drama was in progress. There was no mist now. The oppression of my nerves had wrought this amazing clarity. Every feature, every movement, was as clear-cut as in life. To think that I, a tired accountant, the most prosaic of mankind, with the account-books of a swindling bankrupt before me, should be chosen of all the human race to look upon such a scene!

It was the same scene and the same figures, but the drama had advanced a stage. The tall young man was holding the woman in his arms. She strained away from him and looked up at him with loathing in her face. They had torn the crouching man away from his hold upon the skirt of her dress. A dozen of them were round him—savage men, bearded men. They hacked at him with knives. All seemed to strike him together. Their arms rose and fell. The blood did not flow from him—it squirted. His red dress was dabbled in it. He threw himself this way and that, purple upon crimson, like an over-ripe plum. Still they hacked, and still the jets shot from him. It was horrible—horrible! They dragged him kicking to the door. The woman looked over her shoulder at him and her mouth gaped. I heard nothing, but I knew that she was screaming. And then whether it was this nerve-racking vision before me, or whether, my task finished, all the overwork of the past weeks came in one crushing weight upon me, the room danced round me, the floor seemed to sink away beneath my feet, and I remembered no more. In the early morning my landlady found me stretched senseless before the silver mirror, but I knew nothing myself until three days ago I awoke in the deep peace of the doctor's nursing home.

Feb. 9.—Only to-day have I told Dr. Sinclair my full experience. He had not allowed me to speak of such matters before. He listened with an absorbed interest. " You don't identify this with any well-known scene in history ? " he asked, with suspicion in his eyes. I assured him that I knew nothing of history. " Have you no idea whence that mirror came and to whom it once belonged ? " he continued. " Have you ? " I asked, for he spoke with meaning. " It's incredible," said he, " and yet how else can one explain it ? The scenes which you described before suggested it, but now it has gone beyond all range of coincidence. I will bring you some notes in the evening."

Later.—He has just left me. Let me set down his words as closely as I can recall them. He began by laying several musty volumes upon my bed.

" These you can consult at your leisure," said he. " I have some notes here which you can confirm. There is not a doubt that what you have seen is the murder of Rizzio by the Scottish nobles in the presence of Mary, which occurred in March 1566. Your description of the woman is accurate. The high forehead and heavy eyelids combined with great beauty could hardly apply to two women. The tall young man was her husband, Darnley. Rizzio, says the chronicle, 'was dressed in a loose dressing-gown of furred damask, with hose of russet velvet.' With one hand he clutched Mary's gown, with the other he held a dagger. Your fierce, hollow-eyed man was Ruthven, who was new-risen from a bed of sickness. Every detail is exact."

" But why to me ? " I asked, in bewilderment. " Why of all the human race to me ? "

"Because you were in the fit mental state to receive the impression. Because you chanced to own the mirror which gave the impression."

"The mirror! You think, then, that it was Mary's mirror—that it stood in the room where the deed was done?"

"I am convinced that it was Mary's mirror. She had been Queen of France. Her personal property would be stamped with the Royal arms. What you took to be three spear-heads were really the lilies of France."

"And the inscription?"

"'Sanc. X. Pal.' You can expand it into Sanctæ Crucis Palatium. Someone has made a note upon the mirror as to whence it came. It was the Palace of the Holy Cross."

"Holyrood!" I cried.

"Exactly. Your mirror came from Holyrood. You have had one very singular experience, and have escaped. I trust that you will never put yourself into the way of having such another."

75. *The Home-Coming*

IN the spring of the year 528, a small brig used to run as a passenger boat between Chalcedon on the Asiatic shore and Constantinople. On the morning in question, which was that of the feast of Saint George, the vessel was crowded with excursionists who were bound for the great city in order to take part in the religious and festive celebrations which marked the festival of the Megalo-martyr, one of the most choice occasions in the whole vast hagiology of the Eastern Church. The day was fine and the breeze light, so that the passengers in their holiday mood were able to enjoy without a qualm the many objects of interest which marked the approach to the greatest and most beautiful capital in the world.

On the right, as they sped up the narrow strait, there stretched the Asiatic shore, sprinkled with white villages and with numerous villas peeping out from the woods which adorned it. In front of them, the Prince's Islands, rising as green as emeralds out of the deep sapphire blue of the Sea of Marmora, obscured for the moment the view of the capital. As the brig rounded these, the great city burst suddenly upon their sight, and a murmur of admiration and wonder rose from the crowded deck. Tier above tier it rose, white and glittering, a hundred brazen roofs and gilded statues gleaming in the sun, with high over all the magnificent shining cupola of Saint Sophia. Seen against a cloudless sky, it was the city of a dream—too delicate, too airily lovely for earth.

In the prow of the small vessel were two travellers of singular appearance. The one was a very beautiful boy, ten or twelve years of age, swarthy, clear-cut, with dark, curling hair and vivacious black eyes, full of intelligence and of the joy of living. The other was an elderly man, gaunt-faced and grey-bearded, whose stern features were lit up by a smile as he observed the excitement and interest with which his young companion viewed the beautiful distant city and the many vessels which thronged the narrow strait.

"See! see!" cried the lad. "Look at the great red ships which sail out from yonder harbour. Surely, your holiness, they are the greatest of all ships in the world."

The old man, who was the abbot of the Monastery of Saint Nicephorus in Antioch, laid his hand upon the boy's shoulder.

"Be wary, Leon, and speak less loudly, for until we have seen your mother we should keep ourselves secret. As to the red galleys they are indeed as large as any, for they are the Imperial ships of war, which come forth from the harbour of Theodosius. Round yonder green point is the Golden Horn, where the merchant ships are moored. But now, Leon, if you follow the line of buildings past the great church, you will see a long row of pillars fronting the sea. It marks the Palace of the Cæsars."

The boy looked at it with fixed attention. "And my mother is there," he whispered.

"Yes, Leon, your mother the Empress Theodora and her husband the great Justinian dwell in yonder palace."

The boy looked wistfully up into the old man's face. "Are you sure, Father Luke, that my mother will indeed be glad to see me?"

The abbot turned away his face to avoid those questioning eyes.

"We cannot tell, Leon. We can only try. If it should prove that there is no place for you, then there is always a welcome among the brethren of Saint Nicephorus."

"Why did you not tell my mother that we were coming, Father Luke? Why did you not wait until you had her command?"

"At a distance, Leon, it would be easy to refuse you. An Imperial messenger would have stopped us. But when she sees you, Leon—your eyes, so like her own, your face, which carries memories of one whom she loved—then, if there be a woman's heart within her bosom, she will take you into it. They say that the Emperor can refuse her nothing. They have no child of their own. There is a great future before you, Leon. When it comes, do not forget the poor brethren of Saint Nicephorus, who took you in when you had no friend in the world."

The old abbot spoke cheerily, but it was easy to see from his anxious countenance that the nearer he came to the capital the more doubtful did his errand appear. What had seemed easy and natural from the quiet cloisters of Antioch became dubious and dark now that the golden domes of Constantinople glittered so close at hand. Ten years before, a wretched woman, whose very name was an offence throughout the eastern world, where she was as infamous for her dishonour as famous for her beauty, had come to the monastery gate, and had persuaded the monks to take charge of her infant son, the child of her shame. There he had been ever since. But she, Theodora, the harlot, returning to the capital, had by the strangest turn of Fortune's wheel caught the fancy and finally the enduring love of Justinian the heir to the throne. Then on the death of his uncle Justin, the young man had become the greatest monarch upon the earth, and had raised Theodora to be not only his wife and Empress, but to be absolute ruler with powers equal to and independent of his own. And she, the polluted one, had risen to the dignity, had cut herself sternly away from all that related to her past life, and had shown signs already of being a great Queen, stronger and wiser than her husband, but fierce, vindictive, and unbending, a firm support to her friends, but a terror to her foes. This was the woman to whom the Abbot Luke of Antioch was bringing Leon, her forgotten son. If ever her mind strayed back to the days when, abandoned by her lover Ecebolus, the Governor of the African Pentapolis, she had made her way on foot through Asia Minor, and left her infant with the monks, it was only to persuade herself that the brethren cloistered far from the world would never identify Theodora the Empress with Theodora the dissolute wanderer, and that the fruits of her sin would be for ever concealed from her Imperial husband.

The little brig had now rounded the point of the Acropolis, and the long, blue stretch of the Golden Horn lay before it. The high wall of Theodosius lined the whole harbour, but a narrow verge of land had been left between it and the water's edge to serve as a quay. The vessel ran alongside near the Neorion Gate, and the passengers, after a short scrutiny from the group of helmeted guards who lounged beside it, were allowed to pass through into the great city.

The abbot, who had made several visits to Constantinople upon the business of his monastery, walked with the assured step of one who knows his ground; while the boy, alarmed and yet pleased by the rush of people, the roar and clatter of passing chariots, and the vista of magnificent buildings, held tightly to the loose gown of his guide, while staring eagerly about him in every direction. Passing through the steep and narrow streets which led up from the water, they emerged into the open space which surrounds the magnificent pile of Saint Sophia, the great church begun by Constantine, hallowed by Saint Chrysostom, and now the seat of the Patriarch, and the very centre of the Eastern Church. Only with many crossings and genuflections did the pious abbot succeed in passing the revered shrine of his religion, and hurried on to his difficult task.

Having passed Saint Sophia, the two travellers crossed the marble-paved Augusteum, and saw upon their right the gilded gates of the hippodrome through which a vast crowd of people was pressing, for though the morning had been devoted to the religious ceremony, the afternoon was given over to secular festivities. So great was the rush of the populace that the two strangers had some difficulty in disengaging themselves from the stream and reaching the huge arch of black marble which formed the outer gate of the palace. Within they were fiercely ordered to halt by a gold-crested and magnificent sentinel who laid his shining spear across their breasts until his superior officer should give them permission to pass. The abbot had been warned, however, that all obstacles would give way if he mentioned the name of Basil the eunuch, who acted as chamberlain of the palace and also as Parakimomen—a high office which meant that he slept at the door of the Imperial bed-chamber. The charm worked wonderfully, for at the mention of that potent name the Protosphathaire, or Head of the Palace Guards, who chanced to be upon the spot, immediately detached one of his soldiers with instructions to convoy the two strangers into the presence of the chamberlain.

Passing in succession a middle guard and an inner guard, the travellers came at last into the palace proper, and followed their majestic guide from chamber to chamber, each more wonderful than the last. Marbles and gold, velvet and silver, glittering mosaics, wonderful carvings, ivory screens, curtains of Armenian tissue and of Indian silk, damask from Arabia, and amber from the Baltic—all these things merged themselves in the minds of the two simple provincials, until their eyes ached and their senses reeled before the blaze and the glory of this, the most magnificent of the dwellings of man. Finally, a pair of curtains, crusted with gold, were parted, and their guide handed them over to a negro eunuch who stood within. A heavy, fat, brown-skinned man, with a large, flabby, hairless face, was pacing up and down the small apartment, and he turned upon them as they entered with an abominable and threatening smile. His loose lips and pendulous cheeks were those of a gross old woman, but above them there shone a pair of dark, malignant eyes, full of fierce intensity of observation and judgment.

"You have entered the palace by using my name," he said. "It is one of my boasts that any of the populace can approach me in this way. But it is not fortunate for those who take advantage of it without due cause." Again he smiled a smile which made the frightened boy cling tightly to the loose serge skirts of the abbot.

But the ecclesiastic was a man of courage. Undaunted by the sinister appearance of the great chamberlain, or by the threat which lay in his words, he laid his hand upon his young companion's shoulder and faced the eunuch with a confident smile.

"I have no doubt, your excellency," said he, "that the importance of my mission has given me the right to enter the palace. The only thing which troubles me is whether it may not be so important as to forbid me from broaching it to you, or indeed, to anybody save the Empress Theodora, since it is she only whom it concerns."

The eunuch's thick eyebrows bunched together over his vicious eyes.

"You must make good those words," he said. "If my gracious master—the ever-glorious Emperor Justinian—does not disdain to take me into his most intimate confidence in all things, it would be strange if there were any subject within your knowledge which I might not hear. You are, as I gather from your garb and bearing, the abbot of some Asiatic monastery?"

"You are right, your excellency, I am the Abbot of the Monastery of St. Nicephorus in Antioch. But I repeat that I am assured that what I have to say is for the ear of the Empress Theodora only."

The eunuch was evidently puzzled, and his curiosity aroused by the old man's persistence. He came nearer, his heavy face thrust forward, his flabby brown hands, like two sponges, resting upon the table of yellow jasper before him.

"Old man," said he, "there is no secret which concerns the Empress which may not be told to me. But if you refuse to speak, it is certain that you will never see her. Why should I admit you, unless I know your errand? How should I know that you are not a Manichean heretic with a poniard in your bosom, longing for the blood of the mother of the Church?"

The abbot hesitated no longer. "If there be a mistake in the matter, then on your head be it," said he. "Know then that this lad Leon is the son of Theodora the Empress, left by her in our monastery within a month of his birth ten years ago. This papyrus which I hand you will show you that what I say is beyond all question or doubt."

The eunuch Basil took the paper, but his eyes were fixed upon the boy, and his features showed a mixture of amazement at the news that he had received, and of cunning speculation as to .how he could turn it to profit.

"Indeed, he is the very image of the Empress," he muttered; and then, with sudden suspicion, "Is it not the chance of this likeness which has put the scheme into your head, old man?"

"There is but one way to answer that," said the abbot. "It is to ask the Empress herself whether what I say is not true, and to give her the glad tidings that her boy is alive and well."

The tone of confidence, together with the testimony of the papyrus, and the boy's beautiful face, removed the last shadow of doubt from the eunuch's mind. Here was a great fact; but what use could he make of it? Above all, what advantage could he draw from it? He stood with his fat chin in his hand, turning it over in his cunning brain.

"Old man," said he at last, "to how many have you told this secret?"

"To no one in the whole world," the other answered. "There is Deacon Bardas at the monastery and myself. No one else knows anything."

"You are sure of this?"

"Absolutely certain."

The eunuch had made up his mind. If he alone of all men in the palace knew of this event, he would have a powerful hold over his masterful mistress. He was certain that Justinian the Emperor knew nothing of this. It would be a shock to him. It might even alienate his affections from his wife. She might care to take precautions to prevent him from knowing. And if he, Basil the eunuch, was her confederate in those precautions, then how very close it must draw him to her. All this flashed through his mind as he stood, the papyrus in his hand, looking at the old man and the boy.

"Stay here," said he. "I will be with you again."

With a swift rustle of his silken robes he swept from the chamber.

A few minutes had elapsed when a curtain at the end of the room was pushed aside, and the eunuch, reappearing, held it back, doubling his unwieldy body into a profound obeisance as he did so. Through the gap came a small, alert woman, clad in golden tissue, with a loose outer mantle and shoes of the Imperial purple. That colour alone showed that she could be none other than the Empress; but the dignity of her carriage, the fierce authority of her magnificent dark eyes, and the perfect beauty of her haughty face, all proclaimed that it could only be that Theodora who, in spite of her lowly origin, was the most majestic as well as the most maturely lovely of all the women in her kingdom. Gone now were the buffoon tricks which the daughter of Acacius the bearward had learned in the amphitheatre; gone, too, was the light charm of the wanton, and what was left was the worthy mate of a great king, the measured dignity of one who was every inch an empress.

Disregarding the two men, Theodora walked up to the boy, placed her two white hands upon his shoulders, and looked with a long, questioning gaze, a gaze which began with hard suspicion and ended with tender recognition, into those large, lustrous eyes which were the very reflection of her own. At first the sensitive lad was chilled by the cold, intent question of the look; but as it softened, his own spirit responded, until suddenly with a cry of "Mother! Mother!" he cast himself into her arms, his hands locked round her neck, his face buried in her bosom. Carried away by the sudden natural outburst of emotion, her own arms tightened round the lad's figure, and she strained him for an instant to her heart. Then, the strength of the Empress gaining instant command over the temporary weakness of the mother, she pushed him back from her, and waved that they should leave her to herself. The slaves in attendance hurried the two visitors from the room. Basil the eunuch lingered, looking down at his mistress, who had thrown herself upon a damask couch, her lips white and her bosom heaving with the tumult of her emotion. She glanced up and met the chancellor's crafty gaze, her woman's instinct reading the threat that lurked within it.

"I am in your power," she said. "The Emperor must never know of this."

"I am your slave," said the eunuch, with his ambiguous smile. "I am an instrument in your hand. If it is your will that the Emperor should know nothing, then who is to tell him?"

"But the monk, the boy? What are we to do?"

"There is only one way for safety," said the eunuch.

She looked at him with horrified eyes. His spongy hands were pointing down to the floor. There was an underground world to this beautiful palace, a shadow that was ever close to the light, a region of dimly lit passages, of shadowed corners, of noiseless, tongueless slaves, of sudden sharp screams in the darkness. To this the eunuch was pointing.

A terrible struggle rent her breast. The beautiful boy was hers, flesh of her flesh, bone of her bone. She knew it beyond all question or doubt. It was her one child, and her whole heart went out to him. But Justinian! She knew the Emperor's strange limitations. Her career in the past was forgotten. He had swept it all aside by special Imperial decree published throughout the Empire, as if she were new-born through the power of his will, and her association with his person. But they were childless, and this sight of one which was not his own would cut him to the quick. He could dismiss her infamous past from his mind, but if it took the concrete shape of this beautiful child, then how could he wave it aside as if it had never been? All her instincts and intimate knowledge of the man told her that even her charm and her influence might fail under such circumstances to save her from ruin. Her divorce would be as easy to him as her elevation had been. She was balanced upon a giddy pinnacle, the highest in the world, and yet the higher the deeper the fall. Everything that earth could give was now at her feet. Was she to risk the losing of it all—for what? For a weakness which was unworthy of an Empress, for a foolish, new-born spasm of love, for that which had no existence within her in the morning? How could she be so foolish as to risk losing such a substance for such a shadow?

"Leave it to me," said the brown, watchful face above her.

"Must it be—death?"

"There is no real safety outside. But if your heart is too merciful, then by the loss of sight and speech——"

She saw in her mind the white-hot iron approaching those glorious eyes, and she shuddered at the thought.

"No, no! Better death than that!"

"Let it be death then. You are wise, great Empress, for there only is real safety and assurance of silence."

"And the monk?"

"Him also."

"But the Holy Synod! He is a tonsured priest. What would the Patriarch do?"

"Silence his babbling tongue. Then let them do what they will. How are we of the palace to know that this conspirator, taken with a dagger in his sleeve, is really what he says?"

Again she shuddered and shrank down among the cushions.

"Speak not of it, think not of it," said the eunuch. "Say only that you leave it in my hands. Nay, then, if you cannot say it, do but nod your head, and I take it as your signal."

In that moment there flashed before Theodora's mind a vision of all her enemies, of all those who envied her rise, of all whose hatred and contempt would rise into a clamour of delight could they see the daughter of the bearward hurled down again into that abyss from which she had been dragged. Her face hardened, her lips tightened, her little hands clenched in the agony of her thought.

"Do it!" she said.

In an instant, with a terrible smile, the messenger of death hurried from the room. She groaned aloud, and buried herself yet deeper amid the silken cushions, clutching them frantically with convulsed and twitching hands.

The eunuch wasted no time, for this deed, once done, he became—save for some insignificant monk in Asia Minor, whose fate would soon be sealed—the only sharer of Theodora's secret, and therefore the only person who could curb and bend that most imperious nature. Hurrying into the chamber where the visitors were waiting, he gave a sinister signal, only too well known in those iron days. In an instant the black mutes in attendance seized the old man and the boy, pushing them swiftly down a passage and into a meaner portion of the palace, where the heavy smell of luscious cooking proclaimed the neighbourhood of the kitchens. A side corridor led to a heavily barred iron door, and this in turn opened upon a steep flight of stone steps, feebly illuminated by the glimmer of wall lamps. At the head and foot stood a mute sentinel like an ebony statue, and below, along the dusky and forbidding passages from which the cells opened, a succession of niches in the wall were each occupied by a similar guardian. The unfortunate visitors were dragged brutally down a number of stone-flagged and dismal corridors until they descended another long stair which led so deeply into the earth that the damp feeling in the heavy air and the drip of water all round showed that they had come down to the level of the sea. Groans and cries, like those of sick animals, from the various grated doors which they passed showed how many there were who spent their whole lives in this humid and poisonous atmosphere

At the end of this lowest passage was a door which opened into a single large, vaulted room. It was devoid of furniture, but in the centre was a large and heavy wooden board clamped with iron. This lay upon a rude stone parapet, engraved with inscriptions beyond the wit of the eastern scholars, for this old well dated from a time before the Greeks founded Byzantium, when men of Chaldea and Phœnicia built with huge, unmortared blocks, far below the level of the town of Constantine. The door was closed, and the eunuch beckoned to the slaves that they should remove the slab which covered the well of death. The frightened boy screamed and clung to the abbot, who, ashy-pale and trembling, was pleading hard to melt the heart of the ferocious eunuch.

"Surely, surely, you would not slay the innocent boy!" he cried. "What has he done? Was it his fault that he came here? I alone—I and Deacon Bardas—are to blame. Punish us, if someone must indeed be punished. We are old. It is to-day or to-morrow with us. But he is so young and so beautiful, with all his life before him. Oh, sir! oh, your excellency, you would not have the heart to hurt him!"

He threw himself down and clutched at the eunuch's knees, while the boy sobbed piteously and cast horror-stricken eyes at the black slaves who were tearing the wooden slab from the ancient parapet beneath. The only answer which the chamberlain gave to the frantic pleadings of the abbot was to take a stone which lay on the coping of the well and toss it in. It could be heard clattering against the old, damp, mildewed walls, until it fell with a hollow boom into some far-distant subterranean pool. Then he again motioned with his hands and the black slaves threw themselves upon the boy and dragged him away from his guardian. So shrill was his clamour that no one heard the approach of the

Empress. With a swift rush she had entered the room, and her arms were round her son.

"It shall not be! It cannot be!" she cried. "No, no, my darling! my darling! they shall do you no hurt. I was mad to think of it—mad and wicked to dream of it. Oh, my sweet boy! to think that your mother might have had your blood upon her head!"

The eunuch's brows were gathered together at this failure of his plans, at this fresh example of feminine caprice.

"Why kill them, great lady, if it pains your gracious heart?" said he. "With a knife and a branding-iron they can be disarmed for ever."

She paid no attention to his words. "Kiss me, Leon!" she cried. "Just once let me feel my own child's soft lips rest upon mine. Now again! No, no more, or I shall weaken for what I have still to say and still to do. Old man, you are very near a natural grave, and I cannot think from your venerable aspect that words of falsehood would come readily to your lips. You have indeed kept my secret all these years, have you not?"

"I have in very truth, great Empress. I swear to you by Saint Nicephorus, patron of our house, that save old Deacon Bardas, there is none who knows."

"Then let your lips still be sealed. If you have kept faith in the past, I see no reason why you should be a babbler in the future. And you, Leon"—she bent her wonderful eyes with a strange mixture of sternness and of love upon the boy——"can I trust you? Will you keep a secret which could never help you, but would be the ruin and downfall of your mother?"

"Oh, mother, I would not hurt you! I swear that I will be silent."

"Then I trust you both. Such provision will be made for your monastery and for your own personal comforts as will make you bless the day you came to my palace. Now you may go. I wish never to see you again. If I did, you might find me in a softer mood, or in a harder, and the one would lead to my undoing, the other to yours. But if by whisper or rumour I have reason to think that you have failed me, then you and your monks and your monastery will have such an end as will be a lesson for ever to those who would break faith with their Empress."

"I will never speak," said the old abbot; "neither will Deacon Bardas; neither will Leon. For all three I can answer. But there are others—these slaves, the chancellor. We may be punished for another's fault."

"Not so," said the Empress, and her eyes were like flints. "These slaves are voiceless; nor have they any means to tell those secrets which they know. As to you, Basil——" She raised her white hand with the same deadly gesture which he had himself used so short a time before. The black slaves were on him like hounds on a stag.

"Oh, my gracious mistress, dear lady, what is this? What is this? You cannot mean it!" he screamed, in his high, cracked voice. "Oh, what have I done? Why should I die?"

"You have turned me against my own. You have goaded me to slay my own son. You have intended to use my secret against me. I read it in your eyes from the first. Cruel, murderous villain, taste the fate which you have yourself given to so many others. This is your doom. I have spoken."

The old man and the boy hurried in horror from the vault. As they glanced back they saw the erect, inflexible, shimmering, gold-clad figure of the Empress. Beyond they had a glimpse of the green-scummed lining of the well, and of the great red, open mouth of the eunuch, as he screamed and prayed while every tug of the straining slaves brought him one step nearer to the brink. With their hands over their ears they rushed away, but even so they heard that last woman-like shriek, and then the heavy plunge far down in the dark abysses of the earth.

76. *A Point of Contact*

A CURIOUS train of thought is started when one reflects upon those great figures who have trod the stage of this earth, and actually played their parts in the same act, without ever coming face to face, or even knowing of each other's existence. Baber, the Great Mogul, was, for example, overrunning India at the very moment when Hernando Cortez was overrunning Mexico, and yet the two could never have heard of each other. Or, to take a more supreme example, what could the Emperor Augustus Cæsar know of a certain Carpenter's shop wherein there worked a dreamy-eyed boy who was destined to change the whole face of the world? It may be, however, that sometimes these great contemporary forces did approach, touch, and separate—each unaware of the true meaning of the other. So it was in the instance which is now narrated.

It was evening in the port of Tyre, some eleven hundred years before the coming of Christ. The city held, at that time, about a quarter of a million of inhabitants, the majority of whom dwelt upon the mainland, where the buildings of the wealthy merchants, each in its own tree-girt garden, extended for seven miles along the coast. The great island, however, from which the town got its name, lay out some distance from the shore, and contained within its narrow borders the more famous of the temples and public buildings. Of these temples the chief was that of Melmoth, which covered with its long colonnades the greater part of that side of the island which looked down upon the Sidonian port, so called because only twenty miles away the older city of Sidon maintained a constant stream of traffic with its rising offshoot.

Inns were not yet in vogue, but the poorer traveller

found his quarters with hospitable citizens, while men of distinction were frequently housed in the annexe of the temples, where the servants of the priests attended to their wants. On that particular evening there stood in the portico of the temple of Melmoth two remarkable figures who were the centre of observation for a considerable fringe of Phœnician idlers. One of these men was clearly by his face and demeanour a great chieftain. His strongly marked features were those of a man who had led an adventurous life, and were suggestive of every virile quality from brave resolve to desperate execution. His broad, high brow and contemplative eyes showed that he was a man of wisdom as well as of valour. He was clad, as became a Greek nobleman of the period, with a pure white linen tunic, a gold-studded belt supporting a short sword, and a purple cloak. The lower legs were bare, and the feet covered by sandals of red leather, while a cap of white cloth was pushed back upon his brown curls, for the heat of the day was past and the evening breeze most welcome.

His companion was a short, thick-set man, bull-necked and swarthy, clad in some dusky cloth which gave him a sombre appearance relieved only by the vivid scarlet of his woollen cap. His manner towards his comrade was one of deference, and yet there was in it also something of that freshness and frankness which go with common dangers and a common interest.

"Be not impatient, sire," he was saying. "Give me two days, or three at the most, and we shall make as brave a show at the muster as any. But indeed, they would smile if they saw us crawl up to Tenedos with ten missing oars and the mainsail blown into rags."

The other frowned and stamped his foot with anger.

"We should have been there now had it not been for this cursed mischance," said he. "Aeolus played us a pretty trick when he sent such a blast out of a cloudless sky."

"Well, sire, two of the Cretan galleys foundered,

and Trophimes, the pilot, swears that one of the Argos ships was in trouble. Pray Zeus that it was not the galley of Menelaus. We shall not be the last at the muster."

"It is well that Troy stands a good ten miles from the sea, for if they came out at us with a fleet they might have us at a disadvantage. We had no choice but to come here and refit, yet I shall have no happy hour until I see the white foam from the lash of our oars once more. Go, Seleucas, and speed them all you may."

The officer bowed and departed, while the chieftain stood with his eyes fixed upon his great dismantled galley over which the riggers and carpenters were swarming. Farther out in the roadstead lay eleven other smaller galleys, waiting until their wounded flagship should be ready for them. The sun, as it shone upon them, gleamed upon hundreds of bronze helmets and breast-plates, telling of the war-like nature of the errand upon which they were engaged. Save for them the port was filled with bustling merchant ships taking in cargoes or disgorging them upon the quays. At the very feet of the Greek chieftain three broad barges were moored, and gangs of labourers with wooden shovels were heaving out the mussels brought from Dor, destined to supply the famous Tyrian dye-works which adorn the most noble of all garments. Beside them was a tin ship from Britain, and the square boxes of that precious metal, so needful for the making of bronze, were being passed from hand to hand to the waiting wagons. The Greek found himself smiling at the uncouth wonder of a Cornishman who had come with his tin, and who was now lost in amazement as he stared at the long colonnades of the Temple of Melmoth and the high front of the Shrine of Ashtaroth behind it. Even as he gazed some of his shipmates passed their hands through his arms and led him along the quay to a wine-shop, as being a building much more within his comprehension. The Greek, still smiling, was turning on his heels to return to the

Temple, when one of the clean-shaven priests of Baal came towards him.

"It is rumoured, sire," said he, "that you are on a very distant and dangerous venture. Indeed, it is well known from the talk of your soldiers what it is that you have on hand."

"It is true," said the Greek, "that we have a hard task before us. But it would have been harder to bide at home and to feel that the honour of a leader of the Argives had been soiled by this dog from Asia."

"I hear that all Greece has taken up the quarrel."

"Yes, there is not a chief from Thessaly to the Malea who has not called out his men, and there were twelve hundred galleys in the harbour of Aulis."

"It is a great host," said the priest. "But have ye any seers or prophets among ye who can tell what will come to pass?"

"Yes, we had one such, Calchas his name. He has said that for nine years we shall strive, and only on the tenth will the victory come."

"That is but cold comfort," said the priest. "It is, indeed, a great prize which can be worth ten years of a man's life."

"I would give," the Greek answered, "not ten years but all my life if I could but lay proud Ilium in ashes and carry back Helen to her palace on the hill of Argos."

"I pray Baal, whose priest I am, that you may have good fortune," said the Phœnician. "I have heard that these Trojans are stout soldiers, and that Hector, the son of Priam, is a mighty leader."

The Greek smiled proudly.

"They must be stout and well-led also," said he, "if they can stand the brunt against the long-haired Argives with such captains as Agamemnon, the son of Atreus from golden Mycenæ, or Achilles, son of Peleus, with his myrmidons. But these things are on the knees of the Fates. In the meantime, my friend, I would fain know who these strange people are who come down the street, for their chieftain has the air of one who is made for great deeds."

A tall man clad in a long, white robe, with a golden fillet through his flowing auburn hair, was striding down the street with the free, elastic gait of one who has lived an active life in the open. His face was ruddy and noble, with a short, crisp beard covering a strong, square jaw. In his clear blue eyes as he looked at the evening sky and the busy waters beneath him there was something of the exaltation of the poet, while a youth walking beside him and carrying a harp hinted at the graces of music. On the other side of him, however, a second squire bore a brazen shield and a heavy spear, so that his master might never be caught unawares by his enemies. In his train there came a tumultuous rabble of dark, hawk-like men, armed to the teeth, and peering about with covetous eyes at the signs of wealth which lay in profusion around them. They were swarthy as Arabs, and yet they were better clad and better armed than the wild children of the desert.

"They are but barbarians," said the priest. "He is a small king from the mountain parts opposite Philistia, and he comes here because he is building up the town of Jebus, which he means to be his chief city. It is only here that he can find the wood, and stone, and craftsmanship that he desires. The youth with the harp is his son. But I pray you, chief, if you would know what is before you at Troy, to come now into the outer hall of the Temple with me, for we have there a famous seer, the prophetess Alaga who is also the priestess of Ashtaroth. It may be that she can do for you what she has done for many others, and send you forth from Tyre in your hollow ships with a better heart than you came."

To the Greeks, who by oracles, omens, and auguries were for ever prying into the future, such a suggestion was always welcome. The Greek followed the priest to the inner sanctuary, where at the famous Pythoness

—a tall, fair woman of middle age, who sat at a stone table upon which was an abacus or tray filled with sand. She held a style of chalcedony, and with this she traced strange lines and curves upon the smooth surface, her chin leaning upon her other hand and her eyes cast down. As the chief and the priest approached her she did not look up, but she quickened the movements of her pencil, so that curve followed curve in quick succession. Then, still with downcast eyes, she spoke in a strange, high, sighing voice like wind amid the trees.

"Who, then, is this who comes to Alaga of Tyre, the handmaiden of great Ashtaroth? Behold I see an island to the west, and an old man who is the father, and the great chief, and his wife, and his son who now waits him at home, being too young for the wars. Is this not true?"

"Yes, maiden, you have said truth," the Greek answered.

"I have had many great ones before me, but none greater than you, for three thousand years from now people will still talk of your bravery and of your wisdom. They will remember also the faithful wife at home, and the name of the old man, your father, and of the boy, your son—all will be remembered when the very stones of noble Sidon and royal Tyre are no more."

"Nay, say not so, Alaga!" cried the priest.

"I speak not what I desire but what it is given to me to say. For ten years you will strive, and then you will win, and victory will bring rest to others, but only new troubles to you. Ah!" The prophetess suddenly started in violent surprise, and her hand made ever faster markings on the sand.

"What is it that ails you, Alaga?" asked the priest.

The woman had looked up with wild, inquiring eyes. Her gaze was neither for the priest nor for the chief, but shot past them to the farther door. Looking round the Greek was aware that two new figures had entered the room. They were the ruddy barbarian whom he had marked in the street, together with the youth who bore his harp.

"It is a marvel upon marvels that two such should enter my chamber on the same day," cried the priestess. "Have I not said that you were the greatest that ever came, and yet behold here is already one who is greater. For he and his son—even this youth whom I see before me—will also be in the minds of all men when lands beyond the Pillars of Hercules shall have taken the place of Phœnicia and of Greece. Hail to you, stranger, hail! Pass on to your work, for it awaits you, and it is great beyond words of mine." Rising from her stool the woman dropped her pencil upon the sand and passed swiftly from the room.

"It is over," said the priest. "Never have I heard her speak such words."

The Greek chief looked with interest at the barbarian. "You speak Greek?" he asked.

"Indifferently well," said the other. "Yet I should understand it seeing that I spent a long year at Ziklag in the land of the Philistines."

"It would seem," said the Greek, "that the gods have chosen us both to play a part in the world."

"Stranger," the barbarian answered, "there is but one God."

"Say you so? Well, it is a matter to be argued at some better time. But I would fain have your name and style and what is it you purpose to do, so that we may perchance hear of each other in years to come. For my part I am Odysseus, known also as Ulysses, the King of Ithaca, with the good Laertes as my father and young Telemachus as my son. For my work, it is the taking of Troy."

"And my work," said the barbarian, "is the building of Jebus, which now we call Jerusalem. Our ways lie separate, but it may come back to your memory that you have crossed the path of David, second King of the

Hebrews, together with his young son Solomon, who may follow him upon the throne of Israel."

So he turned and went forth into the darkened streets where his spearmen were awaiting him, while the Greek passed down to his boat that he might see what was still to be done ere he could set forth upon his voyage.